CRYPTONOMICON

CRYPTONOMICON

NEAL STEPHENSON

WILLIAM HEINEMANN : LONDON

First published in the United Kingdom in 1999 by William Heinemann

3 5 7 9 10 8 6 4 2

William Heinemann
The Random House Group Limited
20 Vauxhall Bridge Road, London SW1V 2SA

Random House Australia (Pty) Limited
20 Alfred Street, Milsons Point, Sydney,
New South Wales 2061, Australia

Random House New Zealand Limited
18 Poland Road, Glenfield
Auckland 10, New Zealand

Random House (Pty) Limited
Endulini, 5a Jubilee Road, Parktown 2193, South Africa

The Random House Group Limited Reg. No. 954009

www.randomhouse.co.uk

A CIP catalogue record for this book is available
from the British Library

Papers used by Random House are natural, recyclable products made from wood
grown in sustainable forests. The manufacturing processes conform to the
environmental regulations of the country of origin

Printed and bound in Great Britain by
Creative Print and Design (Wales), Ebbw Vale

ISBN 0 434 00883 4

To S. Town Stephenson,
who flew kites from battleships

ACKNOWLEDGMENTS

Bruce Schneier invented Solitaire, graciously consented to my use of it in this novel, and wrote the appendix. Ian Goldberg wrote the Perl script that appears on p. 480.

Except for the odd quotation, the rest of the book was, for better or worse, written by me. I am indebted to many other people, though. Accounting for one's debts in this way can easily lead all the way back to Adam and Eve, and so I've chosen to pick World War II as my gratitude cutoff date, and to divide everyone I'm grateful to into three general groups.

First: towering figures of the 1937–45 Titanomachia. Almost every family has its own small pantheon of war figures—such as my uncle Keith Wells, who served as a Marine on Florida and Guadalcanal Islands, and who may have been the first American Marine to hit a beach, in an offensive operation, during that war. But this novel is basically about the technically inclined people who were called upon to do incredibly peculiar things during the war years. Among all these great wartime hackers, some kind of special recognition must go to William Friedman, who sacrificed his health to break the Japanese machine cipher called Purple before the war even began.

But I have dedicated this novel to my late grandfather S. Town Stephenson. In doing so, I run the risk that people will make all kinds of false suppositions about resemblances between his family—which is to say, *my* family—and characters in this book. So, just for the record, let me state that I made all of this up—honest!—and that it is not a *roman à clef*; this book is merely a novel, and not a sneaky way of unloading deep dark familial secrets on unsuspecting readers.

Second: acquaintances of mine who (mostly unwittingly) exerted huge influences on the direction of this project. These include, in alphabetical order, Douglas Barnes, Geoff Bishop, George Dyson, Marc and Krist Geriene of Nova Marine Exploration, Jim Gibbons, Bob Grant, David Handley, Kevin Kelly, Bruce Sterling, and Walter Wriston—who ran around the Philippines with a crypto machine during the war, and survived to tell me yarns about prewar Shanghai banking fifty years later.

Third: people whose efforts made it possible, or at least much easier, for me to write this book. Sometimes their contributions were huge outpourings of love and support, as in the case of my wife, my children, and my children's grandparents. Others supported me through the deceptively simple procedure of doing their jobs steadfastly and well: my editor, Jennifer Hershey, and my agents, Liz Darhansoff and Tal Gregory. And many people made unwitting contributions to this book simply by having interesting conversations with me that they have probably long since forgotten: Wayne Barker, Christian Borgs, Jeremy Bornstein, Al Butler, Jennifer Chayes, Evelyn Corbett, Hugh Davis, Dune, John Gilmore, Ben and Zenaida Gonda, Mike Hawley, Eric Hughes, Cooper Moo, Dan Simon, and Linda Stone.

—Neal Town Stephenson

"There is a remarkably close parallel between the problems of the physicist and those of the cryptographer. The system on which a message is enciphered corresponds to the laws of the universe, the intercepted messages to the evidence available, the keys for a day or a message to important constants which have to be determined. The correspondence is very close, but the subject matter of cryptography is very easily dealt with by discrete machinery, physics not so easily."

—Alan Turing

This morning [Imelda Marcos] offered the latest in a series of explanations of the billions of dollars that she and her husband, who died in 1989, are believed to have stolen during his presidency.

"It so coincided that Marcos had money," she said. "After the Bretton Woods agreement he started buying gold from Fort Knox. Three thousand tons, then 4,000 tons. I have documents for these: 7,000 tons. Marcos was so smart. He had it all. It's funny; America didn't understand him."

—*The New York Times*, Monday, 4 March, 1996

Two tires fly. Two wail.
A bamboo grove, all chopped down
From it, warring songs.

✠ . . . IS THE BEST THAT CORPORAL BOBBY SHAFTOE CAN DO ON short notice—he's standing on the running board, gripping his Springfield with one hand and the rearview mirror with the other, so counting the syllables on his fingers is out of the question. Is "tires" one syllable or two? How about "wail?" The truck finally makes up its mind not to tip over, and thuds back onto four wheels. The wail—and the moment—are lost. Bobby can still hear the coolies singing, though, and now too there's the gunlike snicking of the truck's clutch linkage as Private Wiley downshifts. Could Wiley be losing his nerve? And, in the back, under the tarps, a ton and a half of file cabinets clanking, code books slaloming, fuel spanking the tanks of Station Alpha's electrical generator. The modern world's hell on haiku writers: "Electrical generator" is, what, eight syllables? You couldn't even fit that onto the *second* line!

"Are we allowed to run over people?" Private Wiley inquires, and then mashes the horn button before Bobby Shaftoe can answer. A Sikh policeman hurdles a night soil cart. Shaftoe's gut reaction is: *Sure, what're they going to do, declare war on us?* but as the highest-ranking man on this truck he's probably supposed to be using his head or something, so he doesn't blurt it out just yet. He takes stock of the situation:

Shanghai, 1645 hours, Friday, the 28th of November 1941. Bobby Shaftoe, and the other half-dozen Marines on his truck, are staring down the length of Kiukiang Road, onto which they've just made this careening high-speed turn. Cathedral's going by to the right, so that means they are, what? two blocks away from the Bund. A Yangtze River Patrol gunboat is tied up there, waiting for the stuff they've got in the back of this truck. The only real problem is that those particular two blocks are inhabited by about five million Chinese people.

Now these Chinese are sophisticated urbanites, not suntanned yokels who've never seen cars before—they'll get out of your way if you drive fast and honk your horn. And indeed many of them flee to one side of the street or the other, producing the illusion that the truck its moving faster than the forty-three miles an hour shown on its speedometer.

But the bamboo grove in Bobby Shaftoe's haiku has not been added just to put a little Oriental flavor into the poem and wow the folks back home in Oconomowoc. There is a *lot* of heavy bamboo in front of this truck, dozens of makeshift turnpikes blocking their path to the river, for the officers of the U.S. Navy's Asiatic Fleet, and of the Fourth Marines, who dreamed up this little operation forgot to take the Friday Afternoon factor into account. As Bobby Shaftoe could've explained to them, if only they'd bothered to ask a poor dumb jarhead, their route took them through the heart of the banking district. Here you've got the Hong Kong and Shanghai Bank of course, City Bank, Chase Manhattan, the Bank of America, and BBME and the Agricultural Bank of China and any number of crappy little provincial banks, and several of those banks have contracts with what's left of the Chinese Government to print currency. It must be a cutthroat business because they slash costs by printing it on old newspapers, and if you know how to read Chinese, you can see last year's news stories and polo scores peeking through the colored numbers and pictures that transform these pieces of paper into legal tender.

As every chicken-peddler and rickshaw operator in Shanghai knows, the money-printing contracts stipulate that all of the bills these banks print have to be backed by such-and-such an amount of silver; i.e., anyone should be able to walk into one of those banks at the end of Kiukiang Road and slap down a pile of bills and (provided that those bills were printed by that same bank) receive actual metallic silver in exchange.

Now if China weren't right in the middle of getting systematically drawn and quartered by the Empire of Nippon, it would probably send official bean counters around to keep tabs on how much silver was actually present in these banks' vaults, and it would all be quiet and orderly. But as it stands, the only thing keeping these banks honest is the other banks.

Here's how they do it: during the normal course of business, lots of paper money will pass over the counters of (say) Chase Manhattan Bank. They'll take it into a back room and sort it, throwing into money boxes (a couple of feet square and a yard deep, with ropes on the four corners) all of the bills that were printed by (say) Bank of America in one, all of the City Bank bills into another. Then, on Friday afternoon they will bring in coolies. Each coolie, or pair of coolies, will of course have his great big long bamboo pole with him—a coolie without his pole is like a China Marine without his nickel-plated bayonet—and will poke their pole through the ropes on the corners of the box. Then one coolie will get underneath each end of the pole, hoisting the box into the air. They have to move in unison or else the box begins flailing around and everything gets out of whack. So as they head towards their destination—whatever bank whose name is printed on the bills in their box—they sing to each other, and plant their feet on the pavement in time to the music. The pole's pretty long, so they are that far apart, and they have to sing loud to hear each other, and of course each pair of coolies in the street is singing their own particular song, trying to drown out all of the others so that they don't get out of step.

So ten minutes before closing time on Friday afternoon, the doors of many banks burst open and numerous pairs of coolies march in singing, like the curtain-raiser on a fucking Broadway musical, slam their huge boxes of tattered currency down, and demand silver in exchange. All of the banks do this to each other. Sometimes, they'll all do it on the same Friday, particularly at times like 28 November 1941, when even a grunt like Bobby Shaftoe can understand that it's better to be holding silver than piles of old cut-up newspaper. And that is why, once the normal pedestrians and food-cart operators and furious Sikh cops have scurried out of the way, and plastered themselves up against the clubs and shops and bordellos on Kiukiang Road, Bobby Shaftoe and the other Marines on the truck still cannot even *see* the gunboat that is their destination, because of this horizontal forest of mighty bamboo poles. They cannot even hear the honking of their own truck horn because of the wild throbbing pentatonic cacophony of coolies singing. This ain't just your *regular* Friday P.M. Shanghai bank-district money-rush. This is an ultimate settling of accounts before the whole Eastern Hemisphere catches fire. The millions of promises printed on those slips of bumwad will *all* be kept or broken in the next ten minutes; actual pieces of silver and gold will move, or they won't. It is some kind of fiduciary Judgment Day.

"Jesus Christ, I can't—" Private Wiley hollers.

"The captain said don't stop for any reason whatsofuckinever," Shaftoe reminds him. He's *not* telling Wiley to run over the coolies, he's reminding Wiley that if he refrains from running over them, they will have some explaining to do—which will be complicated by the fact that the captain's right behind them in a car stuffed with Tommy Gun-toting China Marines. And from the way the captain's been acting about this Station Alpha thing, it's pretty clear that he already has a few preliminary strap marks on his ass, courtesy of some admiral in Pearl Harbor or even (drumroll) Marine Barracks, Eight and Eye Streets Southeast, Washington, D.C.

Shaftoe and the other Marines have always known Station Alpha as a mysterious claque of pencil-necked swabbies who hung out on the roof of a building in the International Settlement in a shack of knot-pocked cargo pallet planks with antennas sticking out of it every which way. If you stood there long enough you could see some of those antennas moving, zeroing in on something out to sea. Shaftoe even wrote a haiku about it:

> Antenna searches
> Retriever's nose in the wind
> Ether's far secrets

This was only his second haiku *ever*—clearly *not* up to November 1941 standards—and he cringes to remember it.

But in no way did any of the Marines comprehend what a big deal Station Alpha was until today. Their job had turned out to involve wrapping a ton of equipment and several tons of paper in tarps and moving it out of doors. Then they spent Thursday tearing the shack apart, making it into a bonfire, and burning certain books and papers.

"Sheeeyit!" Private Wiley hollers. Only a few of the coolies have gotten out of the way, or even seen them. But then there is this fantastic boom from the river, like the sound of a mile-thick bamboo pole being snapped over God's knee. Half a second later there're no coolies in the street anymore—just a lot of boxes with unmanned bamboo poles teeter-tottering on them, bonging into the streets like wind-chimes. Above, a furry mushroom of grey smoke rises from the gunboat. Wiley shifts up to high gear and floors it. Shaftoe cringes against the truck's door and lowers his head, hoping that his campy Great War doughboy helmet will be good for something. Then money-boxes start to rupture and explode as the truck rams through them. Shaftoe peers up through a blizzard of notes and sees giant bamboo poles soaring and bounding and windmilling toward the waterfront.

> The leaves of Shanghai:
> Pale doorways in a steel sky.
> Winter has begun.

✠ LET'S SET THE EXISTENCE-OF-GOD ISSUE ASIDE FOR A LATER VOL-
ume, and just stipulate that in *some* way, self-replicating organisms
came into existence on this planet and immediately began trying
to get rid of each other, either by spamming their environments with
rough copies of themselves, or by more direct means which hardly need
to be belabored. Most of them failed, and their genetic legacy was erased
from the universe forever, but a few found some way to survive and to
propagate. After about three billion years of this sometimes zany, frequently tedious fugue of carnality and carnage, Godfrey Waterhouse IV
was born, in Murdo, South Dakota, to Blanche, the wife of a Congregational preacher named Bunyan Waterhouse. Like every other creature
on the face of the earth, Godfrey was, by birthright, a stupendous badass,
albeit in the somewhat narrow technical sense that he could trace his
ancestry back up a long line of slightly less highly evolved stupendous
badasses to that first self-replicating gizmo—which, given the number
and variety of its descendants, might justifiably be described as the most
stupendous badass of all time. Everyone and everything that wasn't a
stupendous badass was dead.

As nightmarishly lethal, memetically programmed death-machines
went, these were the nicest you could ever hope to meet. In the tradition
of his namesake (the Puritan writer John Bunyan, who spent much of
his life in jail, or trying to avoid it) the Rev. Waterhouse did not preach
in any one place for long. The church moved him from one small town
in the Dakotas to another every year or two. It is possible that Godfrey
found the lifestyle more than a little alienating, for, sometime during the
course of his studies at Fargo Congregational College, he bolted from
the fold and, to the enduring agony of his parents, fell into worldy
pursuits, and ended up, somehow, getting a Ph.D. in Classics from a
small private university in Ohio. Academics being no less nomadic than
Congregational preachers, he took work where he could find it. He
became a Professor of Greek and Latin at Bolger Christian College (en-
rollment 322) in West Point, Virginia, where the Mattaponi and Pamun-
key Rivers came together to form the estuarial James, and the loathsome
fumes of the big paper mill permeated every drawer, every closet, even
the interior pages of books. Godfrey's young bride, nee Alice Pritchard,
who had grown up following *her* itinerant-preacher father across the

vastnesses of eastern Montana—where air smelt of snow and sage—threw up for three months. Six months later she gave birth to Lawrence Pritchard Waterhouse.

The boy had a peculiar relationship with sound. When a fire engine passed, he was not troubled by the siren's howl or the bell's clang. But when a hornet got into the house and swung across the ceiling in a broad Lissajous, droning almost inaudibly, he cried in pain at the noise. And if he saw or smelled something that scared him, he would clap his hands over his ears.

One noise that troubled him not at all was the pipe organ in the chapel at Bolger Christian College. The chapel itself was nothing worth mentioning, but the organ had been endowed by the paper mill family and would have sufficed for a church four times the size. It nicely complemented the organist, a retired high school math teacher who felt that certain attributes of the Lord (violence and capriciousness in the Old Testament, majesty and triumph in the New) could be directly conveyed into the souls of the enpewed sinners through a kind of frontal sonic impregnation. That he ran the risk of blowing out the stained-glass windows was of no consequence since no one liked them anyway, and the paper mill fumes were gnawing at the interstitial lead. But after one little old lady too many staggered down the aisle after a service, reeling from tinnitus, and made a barbed comment to the minister about the exceedingly *dramatic* music, the organist was replaced.

Nevertheless, he continued to give lessons on the instrument. Students were not allowed to touch the organ until they were proficient at the piano, and when this was explained to Lawrence Pritchard Waterhouse, he taught himself, in three weeks, how to play a Bach fugue, and signed up for organ lessons. Since he was only five years old at the time, he was unable to reach both the manuals and the pedals, and had to play standing—or rather strolling, from pedal to pedal.

When Lawrence was twelve, the organ broke down. That paper mill family had not left any endowment for maintenance, so the math teacher decided to have a crack at it. He was in poor health and required a nimble assistant: Lawrence, who helped him open up the hood of the thing. For the first time in all those years, the boy saw what had been happening when he had been pressing those keys.

For each stop—each timbre, or type of sound, that the organ could make (viz. blockflöte, trumpet, piccolo)—there was a separate row of pipes, arranged in a line from long to short. Long pipes made low notes, short high. The tops of the pipes defined a graph: not a straight line but an upward-tending curve. The organist/math teacher sat down with a few loose pipes, a pencil, and paper, and helped Lawrence figure out why. When Lawrence understood, it was as if the math teacher had suddenly played the good part of Bach's Fantasia and Fugue in G Minor on a pipe organ the size of the Spiral Nebula in Andromeda—the part where Uncle Johann dissects the architecture of the Universe in one merciless descending ever-mutating chord, as if his foot is thrusting through skidding layers of garbage until it finally strikes bedrock. In particular, the final steps of the organist's explanation were like a falcon's dive through layer after layer of pretense and illusion, thrilling or sickening or confusing depending on what you were. The heavens were riven open. Lawrence glimpsed choirs of angels ranking off into geometrical infinity.

The pipes sprouted in parallel ranks from a broad flat box of compressed air. All of the pipes for a given note—but belonging to different stops—lined up with each other along one axis. All of the pipes for a given stop—but tuned at different pitches—lined up with each other along the other, perpendicular axis. Down there in the flat box of air, then, was a mechanism that got air to the right pipes at the right times. When a key or pedal was depressed, all of the pipes capable of sounding the corresponding note would speak, as long as their stops were pulled out.

Mechanically, all of this was handled in a fashion that was perfectly clear, simple, and logical. Lawrence had supposed that the machine must be at least as complicated as the most intricate fugue that could be played on it. Now he had learned that a machine, simple in its design, could produce results of infinite complexity.

Stops were rarely used alone. They tended to be piled on top of each other in combinations that were designed to take advantage of the available harmonics (more tasty mathematics here!). Certain combinations in particular were used over and over again. Lots of blockflötes, in varying lengths, for the quiet Offertory, for example. The organ included an ingenious mechanism called the preset, which enabled the organist to select a particular combination of stops—stops he himself had chosen—instantly. He would punch a button and several stops would bolt out from the console, driven by pneumatic pressure, and in that instant the organ would become a different instrument with entirely new timbres.

The next summer both Lawrence and Alice, his mother, were colonized by a distant cousin—a stupendous badass of a virus. Lawrence escaped from it with an almost imperceptible tendency to drag one of his feet. Alice wound up in an iron lung. Later, unable to cough effectively, she got pneumonia and died.

Lawrence's father Godfrey freely confessed that he was not equal to the burdens now laid on his shoulders. He resigned from his position at the small college in Virginia and moved, with his son, to a small house in Moorhead, Minnesota, next door to where Bunyan and Blanche had settled. Later he got a job teaching at a nearby normal school.

At this point, all of the responsible adults in Lawrence's life seemed to arrive at a tacit agreement that the best way to raise him—certainly the easiest—was to leave him alone. On the rare occasions when Lawrence requested adult intervention in his life, he was usually asking questions that no one could answer. At the age of sixteen, having found nothing in the local school system to challenge him, Lawrence Pritchard Waterhouse went off to college. He matriculated at Iowa State College, which among other things was the site of a Naval ROTC installation in which he was forcibly enrolled.

The Iowa State Naval ROTC had a band, and was delighted to hear that Lawrence had an interest in music. Since it was hard to drill on the deck of a dreadnought while playing a pipe organ, they issued him a glockenspiel and a couple of little dingers.

When not marching back and forth on the flood plain of the Skunk River making loud dinging noises, Lawrence was majoring in mechanical engineering. He ended up doing poorly in this area because he had fallen in with a Bulgarian professor named John Vincent Atanasoff and his graduate student, Clifford Berry, who were building a machine that was intended to automate the solution of some especially tedious differential equations.

The basic problem for Lawrence was that he was lazy. He had figured out that everything was much simpler if, like Superman with his X-ray vision, you just stared through the cosmetic distractions and saw the underlying mathematical skeleton. Once you found the math in a thing, you knew everything about it, and you could manipulate it to your heart's content with nothing more than a pencil and a napkin. He saw it in the curve of the silver bars on his glockenspiel, saw it in the catenary arch of a bridge and in the capacitor-studded drum of Atanasoff and Berry's computing machine. Actually pounding on the glockenspiel, riveting the bridge together, or trying to figure out why the computing machine wasn't working were not as interesting to him.

Consequently he got poor grades. From time to time, though, he would perform some stunt on the blackboard that would leave his professor weak in the knees and the other students baffled and hostile. Word got around.

At the same time, his grandmother Blanche was invoking her extensive Congregational connections, working the angles on Lawrence's behalf, totally unbeknownst to him. Her efforts culminated in triumph when

Lawrence was awarded an obscure scholarship, endowed by a St. Paul oat-processing heir, whose purpose was to send Midwestern Congregationalists to the Ivy League for one year, which (evidently) was deemed a long enough period of time to raise their IQs by a few crucial points but not long enough to debauch them. So Lawrence got to be a sophomore in Princeton.

Now Princeton was an august school and going there was a great honor, but no one got around to mentioning either of these facts to Lawrence, who had no way of knowing. This had bad and good consequences. He accepted the scholarship with a faintness of gratitude that infuriated the oat lord. On the other hand, he adjusted to Princeton easily because *it was just another place*. It reminded him of the nicer bits of Virginia, and there were some nice pipe organs in town, though he was not all that happy with his engineering homework of bridge-designing and sprocket-cutting problems. As always, these eventually came down to math, most of which he could handle easily. From time to time he would get stuck, though, which led him to the Fine Hall: the headquarters of the Math Department.

There was a motley assortment of fellows wandering around in Fine Hall, many sporting British or European accents. Administratively speaking, many of these fellows were not members of the Math Department at all, but a separate thing called IAS, which stood for Institute for Advanced something-or-other. But they were all in the same building and they all knew a thing or two about math, so the distinction didn't exist for Lawrence.

Quite a few of these men would pretend shyness when Lawrence sought their advice, but others were at least willing to hear him out. For example: he had come up with a way to solve a difficult sprocket tooth shape problem that, as normally solved by engineers, would require any number of perfectly reasonable but aesthetically displeasing approximations. Lawrence's solution would provide exact results. The only drawback was that it would require a quintillion slide-rule operators a quintillion years to solve. Lawrence was working on a radically different approach that, if it worked, would bring those figures down to a trillion and a trillion respectively. Unfortunately, Lawrence was unable to interest anyone at Fine Hall in anything as prosaic as gears, until all of a sudden he made friends with an energetic British fellow, whose name he promptly forgot, but who had been doing a lot of literal sprocket-making himself lately. This fellow was trying to build, of all things, a mechanical calculating machine—specifically a machine to calculate certain values of the Riemann Zeta Function

$$\zeta(s) = \sum_{n=1}^{\infty} \frac{1}{n^s} = 1 + \frac{1}{2^s} + \frac{1}{3^s} + \ldots$$

where s is a complex number.

Lawrence found this zeta function to be no more and no less interesting than any other math problem until his new friend assured him that it was frightfully important, and that some of the best mathematicians in the world had been gnawing on it for decades. The two of them ended up staying awake until three in the morning working out the solution to Lawrence's sprocket problem. Lawrence presented the results proudly to his engineering professor, who snidely rejected it, on grounds of practicality, and gave him a poor grade for his troubles.

Lawrence finally remembered, after several more contacts, that the name of the friendly Brit was Al something-or-other. Because Al was a passionate cyclist, he and Al went on quite a few bicycle rides through the countryside of the Garden State. As they rode around New Jersey, they talked about math, and particularly about machines for taking the dull part of math off their hands.

But Al had been thinking about this subject for longer than Lawrence, and had figured out that computing machines were much more than just labor-saving devices. He'd been working on a radically different sort of computing mechanism that would work out any arithmetic problem whatsoever, as long as you knew how to write the problem down. From a pure logic standpoint, he had already figured out everything there was to know about this (as yet hypothetical) machine, though he had yet to build one. Lawrence gathered that actually building machinery was looked on as undignified at Cambridge (England, that is, where this Al character was based) or for that matter at Fine Hall. Al was thrilled to have found, in Lawrence, someone who did not share this view.

Al delicately asked him, one day, if Lawrence would terribly mind calling him by his full and proper name, which was Alan and not Al. Lawrence apologized and said he would try very hard to keep it in mind.

One day a couple of weeks later, as the two of them sat by a running stream in the woods above the Delaware Water Gap, Alan made some kind of an outlandish proposal to Lawrence involving penises. It required a great deal of methodical explanation, which Alan delivered with lots of blushing and stuttering. He was ever so polite, and several times emphasized that he was acutely aware that not everyone in the world was interested in this sort of thing.

Lawrence decided that he was probably one of those people.

Alan seemed vastly impressed that Lawrence had paused to think about it *at all* and apologized for putting him out. They went directly back to a discussion of computing machines, and their friendship continued unchanged. But on their next bicycle ride—an overnight camping trip to the Pine Barrens—they were joined by a new fellow, a German named Rudy von something-or-other.

Alan and Rudy's relationship seemed closer, or at least more multilay-ered, than Alan and Lawrence's. Lawrence concluded that Alan's penis scheme must have finally found a taker.

It got Lawrence to thinking. From an evolution standpoint, what was the point of having people around who were not inclined to have off-spring? There must be some good, and fairly subtle, reason for it.

The only thing he could work out was that it was groups of people— societies—rather than individual creatures, who were now trying to out-reproduce and/or kill each other, and that, in a society, there was plenty of room for someone who didn't have kids as long as he was up to something useful.

Alan and Rudy and Lawrence rode south, anyway, looking for the Pine Barrens. After a while the towns became very far apart, and the horse farms gave way to a low stubble of feeble, spiny trees that appeared to extend all the way to Florida—blocking their view, but not the head-wind. "Where are the Pine Barrens I wonder?" Lawrence asked a couple of times. He even stopped at a gas station to ask someone that question. His companions began to make fun of him.

"Vere are ze Pine Barrens?" Rudy inquired, looking about quizzically.

"I should look for something rather barren-looking, with numerous pine trees," Alan mused.

There was no other traffic and so they had spread out across the road to pedal three abreast, with Alan in the middle.

"A forest, as Kafka would imagine it," Rudy muttered.

By this point Lawrence had figured out that they were, in fact, in the Pine Barrens. But he didn't know who Kafka was. "A mathematician?" he guessed.

"*Zat* is a scary sing to sink of," Rudy said.

"He is a writer," Alan said. "Lawrence, please don't be offended that I ask you this, but: do you recognize *any other people's names* at all? Other than family and close friends, I mean."

Lawrence must have looked baffled. "I'm trying to figure out whether it all comes from in here," Alan said, reaching out to rap his knuckles on the side of Lawrence's head, "or do you sometimes take in new ideas from other human beings?"

"When I was a little boy, I saw angels in a church in Virginia," Lawrence said, "but I think that they came from inside my head."

"Very well," Alan said.

But later Alan had another go at it. They had reached the fire lookout tower and it had been a thunderous disappointment: just an alienated staircase leading nowhere, and a small cleared area below that was glittery with shards of liquor bottles. They pitched their tent by the side of a pond that turned out to be full of rust-colored algae that stuck to the hairs on their bodies. Then there was nothing left to do but drink schnapps and talk about math.

Alan said, "Look, it's like this: Bertrand Russell and another chap named Whitehead wrote *Principia Mathematica* . . ."

"Now I know you're pulling my leg," Waterhouse said. "Even I know that Sir Isaac Newton wrote *that*."

"Newton wrote a *different* book, *also* called *Principia Mathematica,* which isn't *really* about mathematics at all; it's about what we would *today* call physics."

"Then why did he call it *Principia Mathematica?*"

"Because the distinction between mathematics and physics wasn't especially clear in Newton's day—"

"Or maybe even in zis day," Rudy said.

"—which is directly relevant to what I'm talking about," Alan continued. "I am talking about *Russell's P.M.,* in which he and Whitehead started absolutely from *scratch,* I mean from *nothing,* and built it all up— all mathematics—from a small number of first principles. And why I am telling you this, Lawrence, is that—Lawrence! Pay attention!"

"Hmmm?"

"Rudy—take this stick, here—that's right—and keep a close eye on Lawrence, and when he gets that foggy look on his face, poke him with it!"

"Zis is not an English school, you can't do zese kind of sing."

"I'm listening," Lawrence said.

"What came out of *P.M.,* which was terrifically radical, was the ability to say that all of math, really, can be expressed as a certain ordering of symbols."

"Leibniz said it a long time before zen!" protested Rudy.

"Er, Leibniz invented the notation we use for *calculus,* but—"

"I'm not talking about zat!"

"And he invented matrices, but—"

"I'm not talking about zat eezer!"

"And he did some work with binary arithmetic, but—"

"Zat is completely different!"

"Well, what the hell are you talking about, then, Rudy?"

"Leibniz invented ze basic alphabet—wrote down a set of symbols, for expressing statements about logic."

"Well, I wasn't aware that Herr Leibniz counted formal logic among his interests, but—"

"Of course! He wanted to do what Russell and Whitehead did, except not just with mathematics, but with everything in ze whole world!"

"Well from the fact that you are the only man on the planet, Rudy, who seems to know about this undertaking of Leibniz's, can we assume that he failed?"

"*You* can *assume* anything that *pleases your fancy*, Alan," Rudy responded, "but *I* am a mathematician and I do not assume *anything*."

Alan sighed woundedly, and gave Rudy a Significant Look which Waterhouse assumed meant that there would be trouble later. "If I may just make some headway, here," he said, "all I'm really trying to get you to agree on, is that mathematics can be expressed as a series of symbols," (he snatched the Lawrence-poking stick and began drawing things like + = 3) $\sqrt{-1}\pi$ in the dirt) "and frankly I could not care less whether they happen to be Leibniz's symbols, or Russell's, or the hexagrams of the I Ching. . . ."

"Leibniz was fascinated by the I Ching!" Rudy began.

"Shut up about Leibniz for a moment, Rudy, because look here: You—Rudy—and I are on a train, as it were, sitting in the dining car, having a nice conversation, and that train is being pulled along at a *terrific* clip by certain locomotives named *The Bertrand Russell* and *Riemann* and *Euler* and others. And our friend Lawrence is running alongside the train, trying to keep up with us—it's not that we're smarter than he is, necessarily, but that he's a *farmer* who didn't get a ticket. And I, Rudy, am simply reaching out through the open window here, trying to pull him onto the *fucking* train with us so that the three of us can have a nice little chat about mathematics without having to listen to him panting and gasping for breath the whole way."

"All right, Alan."

"Won't take a minute if you will just stop interrupting."

"But there is a locomotive too named Leibniz."

"Is it that you don't think I give enough credit to Germans? Because I am about to mention a fellow with an umlaut."

"Oh, would it be Herr Türing?" Rudy said slyly.

"Herr Türing comes later. I was actually thinking of Gödel."

"But he's not German! He's Austrian!"

"I'm afraid that it's all the same now, isn't it?"

"Ze Anschluss wasn't my idea, you don't have to look at me that way, I think Hitler is appalling."

"I've heard of Gödel," Waterhouse put in helpfully. "But could we back up just a sec?"

"Of course Lawrence."

"Why bother? Why did Russell do it? Was there something wrong with math? I mean, two plus two equals four, right?"

Alan picked up two bottlecaps and set them down on the ground. "Two. One-two. Plus—" He set down two more. "Another two. One-two. Equals four. One-two-three-four."

"What's so bad about that?" Lawrence said.

"But Lawrence—when you really *do math,* in an abstract way, you're not counting bottlecaps, are you?"

"I'm not counting *anything.*"

Rudy broke the following news: "Zat is a very modern position for you to take."

"It is?"

Alan said, "There was this implicit belief, for a long time, that math was a sort of physics of bottlecaps. That any mathematical operation you could do on paper, no matter how complicated, could be reduced—in theory, anyway—to messing about with actual physical counters, such as bottlecaps, in the real world."

"But you can't have two point one bottlecaps."

"All right, all right, say we use bottlecaps for integers, and for real numbers like two point one, we use physical measurements, like the length of this stick." Alan tossed the stick down next to the bottlecaps.

"Well what about pi, then? You can't have a stick that's exactly pi inches long."

"Pi is from geometry—ze same story," Rudy put in.

"Yes, it was believed that Euclid's geometry was really a kind of physics, that his lines and so on represented properties of the physical world. But—you know Einstein?"

"I'm not very good with names."

"That white-haired chap with the big mustache?"

"Oh, yeah," Lawrence said dimly, "I tried to ask him my sprocket question. He *claimed* he was late for an appointment or something."

"That fellow has come up with a general relativity theory, which is sort of a practical application, not of Euclid's, but of *Riemann's* geometry—"

"The same Riemann of your zeta function?"

"Same Riemann, different subject. Now let's not get sidetracked here Lawrence—"

"Riemann showed you could have many many different geometries that were not the geometry of Euclid but that still made sense internally," Rudy explained.

"All right, so back to *P.M.* then," Lawrence said.

"Yes! Russell and Whitehead. It's like this: when mathematicians began fooling around with things like the square root of negative one, and quaternions, then they were no longer dealing with things that you could translate into sticks and bottlecaps. And yet they were still getting sound results."

"Or at least internally consistent results," Rudy said.

"Okay. Meaning that math was more than a physics of bottlecaps."

"It appeared that way, Lawrence, but this raised the question of was mathematics really *true* or was it just a game played with symbols? In other words—are we discovering Truth, or just wanking?"

"It has to be true because if you do physics with it, it all works out! I've heard of that general relativity thing, and I know they did experiments and figured out it was true."

"Ze great majority of mathematics does not lend itself to experimental testing," Rudy said.

"The whole idea of this project is to sever the ties to physics," Alan said.

"And yet not to be vanking ourselves."

"That's what *P.M.* was trying to do?"

"Russell and Whitehead broke all mathematical concepts down into brutally simple things like sets. From there they got to integers, and so on."

"But how can you break something like pi down into a set?"

"You can't," Alan said, "but you can express it as a long string of digits. Three point one four one five nine, and so on."

"And digits are integers," Rudy said.

"But no fair! Pi *itself* is not an integer!"

"But you can *calculate the digits* of pi, one at a time, by using certain formulas. And you can write down the formulas like so!" Alan scratches this in the dirt:

$$\pi = 4 \sum_{n=0}^{\infty} \frac{(-1)^n}{2n+1}$$

"I have used the Leibniz series in order to placate our friend. See, Lawrence? It is a string of symbols."

"Okay. I see the string of symbols," Lawrence said reluctantly.

"Can we move on? Gödel said, just a few years ago, 'Say! If you buy into this business about mathematics being just strings of symbols, guess what?' And he pointed out that any string of symbols—such as this very formula, here—can be translated into integers."

"How?"

"Nothing fancy, Lawrence—it's just simple encryption. Arbitrary. The number '538' might be written down instead of this great ugly Σ, and so on."

"Seems pretty close to wanking, now."

"No, no. Because then Gödel sprang the trap! Formulas can act on numbers, right?"

"Sure. Like 2*x*."

"Yes. You can substitute any number for *x* and the formula 2*x* will double it. But if *another mathematical formula,* such as this one right here, for calculating pi, *can be encoded as a number,* then you can have another formula *act on it*. Formulas acting on formulas!"

"Is that all?"

"No. Then he showed, really through a very simple argument, that if formulas really can refer to themselves, it's possible to write one down saying 'this statement cannot be proved.' Which was tremendously startling to Hilbert and everyone else, who expected the opposite result."

"Have you mentioned this Hilbert guy before?"

"No, he is new to this discussion, Lawrence."

"Who is he?"

"A man who asks difficult questions. He asked a whole list of them once. Gödel answered one of them."

"And Türing answered another," Rudy said.

"Who's that?"

"It's me," Alan said. "But Rudy's joking. 'Turing' doesn't really have an umlaut in it."

"He's going to have an umlaut in him later tonight," Rudy said, looking at Alan in a way that, in retrospect, years later, Lawrence would understand to have been smoldering.

"Well, don't keep me in suspense. Which one of his questions did you answer?"

"The *Entscheidungsproblem,*" Rudy said.

"Meaning?"

Alan explained, "Hilbert wanted to know whether any given statement could, in principle, be found true or false."

"But after Gödel got finished, it changed," Rudy pointed out.

"That's true—after Gödel it became 'Can we determine whether any given statement is provable or non-provable?' In other words, is there some sort of mechanical process we could use to separate the provable statements from the nonprovable ones?"

" 'Mechanical process' is supposed to be a *metaphor,* Alan. . . ."

"Oh, stop it, Rudy! Lawrence and I are quite comfortable with machinery."

"I get it," Lawrence said.

"What do you mean, you get it?" Alan said.

"Your machine—not the zeta-function calculator, but the other one. The one we've been talking about building—"

"It is called Universal Turing Machine," Rudy said.

"The whole point of that gizmo is to separate provable from nonprovable statements, isn't it?"

"That's why I came up with the basic idea for it," Alan said. "So Hilbert's question has been answered. Now I just want to actually build one so that I can beat Rudy at chess."

"You haven't told poor Lawrence the answer yet!" Rudy protested.

"Lawrence can figure it out," Alan said. "It'll give him something to do."

Soon it became clear that Alan really meant: *It'll give him something to do while we're fucking.* Lawrence shoved a notebook into the waistband of his trousers and rode his bicycle a few hundred yards to the fire tower, then climbed up the stairs to the platform at the top and sat down, back to the setting sun, notebook propped up on his knees to catch the light.

He could not collect his thoughts, and then he was distracted by a false sunrise that lit up the clouds off to the northeast. He thought at first that some low clouds were bouncing fragments of the sunset back to him, but it was too concentrated and flickering for that. Then he thought it was lightning. But the color of the light was not blue enough. It fluctuated sharply, modulated by (one had to assume) great, startling events that were occulted by the horizon. As the sun went down on the opposite side of the world, the light on the New Jersey horizon focused to a steady, lambent core the color of a flashlight when you shine it through the palm of your hand under the bedsheets.

Lawrence climbed down the stairs and got on his bicycle and rode through the Pine Barrens. Before long he came to a road that led in the general direction of the light. Most of the time he could not see anything, not even the road, but after a couple of hours the glow bouncing off the low cloud layer lit up flat stones in the road, and turned the barrens' wandering rivulets into glowing crevices.

The road began to tend in the wrong direction and so Lawrence cut directly into the woods, because he was very close now, and the light in the sky was strong enough that he could see it through the sparse carpet of scrubby pines—black sticks that appeared to have been burned, though they hadn't. The ground had turned into sand, but it was damp and compacted, and his bicycle had fat tires that rode over it well. At one point he had to stop and throw the bike over a barbed-wire fence. Then he broke out of the sticks and onto a perfectly flat expanse of white sand, stitched down with tufts of beach grass, and just then he was dazzled by a low fence of quiet steady flames that ran across a part of the horizon about as wide as the harvest moon when it sinks into the sea. Its brightness made it difficult to see anything else—Lawrence kept riding into little ditches and creeks that meandered across the flats. He learned not to stare directly at the flames. Looking off to the sides was more interesting anyway: the table-land was marked at wide intervals by the largest buildings he had ever seen, cracker-box structures built by Pharaohs, and in the mile-wide plazas between them, gnomons of triangulated steel were planted in wide stances: the internal skeletons of pyramids. The largest of these pierced the center of a perfectly circular railway line a few hundred feet in diameter: two argent curves scored on the dull ground, interrupted in one place where the tower's shadow, a stopped sundial, told the time. He rode by a building smaller than the others, with oval tanks standing next to it. Steam murmured from valves on the tops of the tanks, but instead of rising into the air it dribbled down the sides and struck the ground and spread out, coating the seagrass with jackets of silver.

A thousand sailors in white were standing in a ring around the long flame. One of them held up his hand and waved Lawrence down. Lawrence came to a stop next to the sailor and planted one foot on the sand to steady himself. He and the sailor stared at each other for a moment and then Lawrence, who could not think of anything else, said, "I am in the Navy also." Then the sailor seemed to make up his mind about something. He saluted Lawrence through, and pointed him towards a small building off to the side of the fire.

The building looked only like a wall glowing in the firelight, but sometimes a barrage of magnesium blue light made its windowframes jump out of the darkness, a rectangular lightning-bolt that echoed many times across the night. Lawrence started pedaling again and rode past that building: a spiraling flock of alert fedoras, prodding at slim terse notebooks with stately Ticonderogas, crab-walking photogs turning their huge chrome daisies, crisp rows of people sleeping with blankets over their faces, a sweating man with Brilliantined hair chalking umlauted names on a blackboard. Finally coming around this building he smelled hot fuel oil, felt the heat of the flames on his face and saw beach-glass curled toward it and desiccated.

He stared down upon the world's globe, not the globe fleshed with continents and oceans but only its skeleton: a burst of meridians, curving backwards to cage an inner dome of orange flame. Against the light of the burning oil those longitudes were thin and crisp as a draftsman's ink-strokes. But coming closer he saw them resolve into clever works of rings and struts, hollow as a bird's bones. As they spread away from the pole they sooner or later began to wander, or split into bent parts, or just broke off and hung in the fire oscillating like dry stalks. The perfect geometry was also mottled, here and there, by webs of cable and harnesses of electrical wiring. Lawrence almost rode over a broken wine bottle and decided he should now walk, to spare his bicycle's tires, so he laid the bike down, the front wheel covering an aluminum vase that appeared to have been spun on a lathe, with a few charred roses hanging out of it. Some sailors had joined their hands to form a sort of throne, and were bearing along a human-shaped piece of charcoal dressed in a coverall of immaculate asbestos. As they walked the toes of their shoes caught in vast, ramified snarls of ropes and piano-wires, cables and wires, creative furtive movements in the grass and the sand dozens of yards every direction. Lawrence began planting his feet very thoughtfully one in front of the other, trying to measure the greatness of what he had come and seen. A rocket-shaped pod stuck askew from the sand, supporting an umbrella of bent-back propellers. The duralumin struts and cat-walks rambled on above him for miles. There was a suitcase spilled open, with a pair of women's shoes displayed as if in the window of a downtown store, and a menu that had been charred to an oval glow, and then some tousled wall-slabs, like a whole room that had dropped out of the sky—these were decorated, one with a giant map of the world, great circles arcing away from Berlin to pounce on cities near and far, and another with a photograph of a famous, fat German in a uniform, grinning on a flowered platform, the giant horizon of a new Zeppelin behind him.

After a while he stopped seeing new things. Then he got on his bicycle and rode back through the Pine Barrens. He got lost in the dark and so didn't find his way back to the fire tower until dawn. But he didn't mind being lost because while he rode around in the dark he thought about the Turing machine. Finally he came back to the shore of the pond where they had camped. The dawn-light shining on the saucer of calm reddish water made it look like a pool of blood. Alan Mathison Turing and Rudolf von Hacklheber were lying together like spoons on the shore, still smudged a little bit from their swim yesterday. Lawrence started a little fire and made some tea and they woke up eventually.

"Did you solve the problem?" Alan asked him.

"Well you can turn that Universal Turing Machine of yours into any machine by changing the presets—"

"Presets?"

"Sorry, Alan, I think of your U.T.M. as being kind of like a pipe organ."

"Oh."

"Once you've done that, anyway, you can do any calculation you please, if the tape is long enough. But gosh, Alan, making a tape that's long enough, and that you can write symbols on, and erase them, is going to be sort of tricky—Atanasoff's capacitor drum would only work up to a certain size—you'd have to—"

"This is a digression," Alan said gently.

"Yeah, okay, well—if you had a machine like that, then any given preset could be represented by a number—a string of symbols. And the tape that you would feed into it to start the calculation would contain another string of symbols. So it's Gödel's proof all over again—if any possible combination of machine and data can be represented by a string of numbers, then you can just arrange all of the possible strings of numbers into a big table, and then it turns into a Cantor diagonal type of argument, and the answer is that there must be some numbers that cannot be computed."

"And ze *Entscheidungsproblem?*" Rudy reminded him.

"Proving or disproving a formula—once you've encrypted the formula into numbers, that is—is just a calculation on that number. So it means that the answer to the question is, no! Some formulas cannot be proved or disproved by any mechanical process! So I guess there's some point in being human after all!"

Alan looked pleased until Lawrence said this last thing, and then his face collapsed. "Now there you go making unwarranted assumptions."

"Don't listen to him, Lawrence!" Rudy said. "He's going to tell you that our brains are Turing machines."

"Thank you, Rudy," Alan said patiently. "Lawrence, I submit that our brains are Turing machines."

"But you proved that there's a whole lot of formulas that a Turing machine can't process!"

"And you have proved it too, Lawrence."

"But don't you think that we can do some things that a Turing machine couldn't?"

"Gödel agrees with you, Lawrence," Rudy put in, "and so does Hardy."

"Give me one example," Alan said.

"Of a noncomputable function that a human can do, and a Turing machine can't?"

"Yes. And don't give me any sentimental nonsense about creativity. I believe that a Universal Turing Machine could show behaviors that we would construe as creative."

"Well, I don't know then . . . I'll try to keep my eye out for that kind of thing in the future."

But later, as they were riding back towards Princeton, he said, "What about dreams?"

"Like those angels in Virginia?"

"I guess so."

"Just noise in the neurons, Lawrence."

"Also I dreamed last night that a zeppelin was burning."

Soon, Alan got his Ph.D. and went back to England. He wrote Lawrence a couple of letters. The last of these stated, simply, that he would not be able to write Lawrence any more letters "of substance" and that Lawrence should not take it personally. Lawrence perceived right away that Alan's society had put him to work doing something useful—probably figuring out how to keep it from being eaten alive by certain of its neighbors. Lawrence wondered what use America would find for *him*.

He went back to Iowa State, considered changing his major to mathematics, but didn't. It was the consensus of all whom he consulted that mathematics, like pipe-organ restoration, was a fine thing, but that one needed some way to put bread on the table. He remained in engineering and did more and more poorly at it until the middle of his senior year, when the university suggested that he enter a useful line of work, such as roofing. He walked straight out of college into the waiting arms of the Navy.

They gave him an intelligence test. The first question on the math part had to do with boats on a river: Port Smith is 100 miles upstream of Port Jones. The river flows at 5 miles per hour. The boat goes through water at 10 miles per hour. How long does it take to go from Port Smith to Port Jones? How long to come back?

Lawrence immediately saw that it was a trick question. You would have to be some kind of idiot to make the facile assumption that the current would add or subtract 5 miles per hour to or from the speed of the boat. Clearly, 5 miles per hour was nothing more than the *average* speed. The current would be faster in the middle of the river and slower at the banks. More complicated variations could be expected at bends in the river. Basically it was a question of hydrodynamics, which could be tackled using certain well-known systems of differential equations. Lawrence dove into the problem, rapidly (or so he thought) covering both sides of ten sheets of paper with calculations. Along the way, he realized that one of his assumptions, in combination with the simplified Navier-Stokes equations, had led him into an exploration of a particularly interesting family of partial differential equations. Before he knew it, he had proved a new theorem. If that didn't prove his intelligence, what would?

Then the time bell rang and the papers were collected. Lawrence managed to hang onto his scratch paper. He took it back to his dorm, typed it up, and mailed it to one of the more approachable math professors at Princeton, who promptly arranged for it to be published in a Parisian mathematics journal.

Lawrence received two free, freshly printed copies of the journal a few months later, in San Diego, California, during mail call on board a large ship called the U.S.S. *Nevada*. The ship had a band, and the Navy had given Lawrence the job of playing the glockenspiel in it, because their testing procedures had proven that he was not intelligent enough to do anything else.

The sack of mail carrying Lawrence's contribution to the mathematical literature arrived just in the nick of time. Lawrence's ship, and quite a few of her sisters, had until then been based in California. But at just this moment, all of them were transferred to some place called Pearl Harbor, Hawaii, in order to show the Nips who was boss.

Lawrence had never really known what he wanted to do with his life, but he quickly decided that being glockenspiel player on a battleship in Hawaii during peacetime was a long way from the worst life you could possibly have. The harshest part of the job was sometimes having to sit or march in very warm conditions, and enduring occasional fluffed notes by other band members. He had abundant free time, which he spent working on a series of new theorems in the field of information theory. The field had been invented and pretty much encompassed by his friend Alan, but there was much detail work to be done. He and Alan and Rudy had sketched out a general plan of what needed to be proved or disproved. Lawrence tore through the list. He wondered what Alan and Rudy were up to in Britain and Germany, but he couldn't write to them and find out, so he kept his work to himself. When he wasn't playing the glockenspiel or working out theorems, there were bars and dances to go to. Waterhouse did some penis work of his own, got the clap, had it cured,* bought condoms. All of the sailors did this. They were like three-year olds who shove pencils in their ears, discover that it hurts, and stop doing it. Lawrence's first year went by almost instantly. Time just blazed by. Nowhere could be sunnier, more relaxing, than Hawaii.

---

*1940 being a good year to begin experimenting with venereal diseases in that the new injectable penicillin was just becoming available

✝⊳̶ "FILIPINOS ARE A WARM, GENTLE, CARING, GIVING PEOPLE," AVI says, "which is a good thing since so many of them carry concealed weapons."

Randy is in Tokyo's airport, ambling down a concourse with a slowness that is infuriating to his fellow travelers. They have all spent the last half-day strapped into bad chairs, stuffed into an aluminum tube aslosh with jet fuel. Over the safety-engineered nubs molded into the jetway floor, their rolling suitcases drone like fighter planes. They graze the backs of his knees as they bank around his husky columnar body. Randy is holding his new GSM phone to the side of his head. Supposedly it works anywhere in the world, except for the United States. This is his first chance to try it out.

"You sound clear as a bell," Avi says. "How was the flight over?"

"All right," Randy says. "They had one of those animated maps up on the video screen."

Avi sighs. "All the airlines have those now," he announces monotonically.

"The only feature between San Francisco and Tokyo was Midway Island."

"So?"

"It kind of hung there for hours. MIDWAY. Mute embarrassment all around."

Randy reaches the departure gate for Manila, and pauses to admire a five-foot-wide high-definition TV set bearing the logo of a major Nipponese consumer-electronics company. It is running a video in which a wacky cartoon professor and his adorable canine sidekick cheerfully tick off the three transmission routes of the AIDS virus.

"I have a fingerprint for you," Randy says.

"Shoot."

Randy stares at the palm of his hand, on which he has written a string of numbers and letters in ballpoint pen. "AF 10 06 E9 99 BA 11 07 64 C1 89 E3 40 8C 72 55."

"Got it," Avi says. "That's from Ordo, right?"

"Right. I e-mailed you the key from SFO."

"The apartment situation is still resolving," Avi says. "So I just reserved you a suite at the Manila Hotel."

"What do you mean, it's still resolving?"

"The Philippines is one of those post-Spanish countries with no clear boundaries between business and personal relationships," Avi says. "I don't think you can secure lodgings there without marrying into a family with a major street named after it."

Randy takes a seat in the departure area. Perky gate attendants in jaunty, improbable hats zero in on Filipinos with too many carry-ons, and subject them to a public ritual of filling out little tags and surrendering their possessions. The Filipinos roll their eyes and stare longingly out the windows. But most of the waiting passengers are Nipponese—some businessmen, mostly vacationers. They are watching an educational video about how to get mugged in foreign countries.

"Huh," Randy says, looking out the window, "got another 747 down to Manila."

"In Asia, no decent airline bothers to dick around anything smaller than a 747," Avi snaps. "If someone tries to pack you on board a 737 or god forbid an Airbus, run, don't walk, away from the boarding lounge, and call me on my Sky Pager and I'll send in a chopper to evacuate you."

Randy laughs.

Avi continues. "Now, listen. This hotel you're going to is very old, very grand, but it's in the middle of nowhere."

"Why would they build a grand hotel in the middle of nowhere?"

"It used to be a happening place—it's on the waterfront, right on the edge of Intramuros."

Randy's high-school Spanish is enough to translate that: Inside the Walls.

"But Intramuros was annihilated by the Nipponese in 1945," Avi continues. "Systematically. All of the business hotels and office buildings are in a new neighborhood called Makati, much closer to the airport."

"So you want to put our office in Intramuros."

"How'd you guess?" Avi says, sounding a little spooked. He prides himself on unpredictability.

"I'm not an intuitive guy generally," Randy says, "but I've been on a plane for thirteen hours and my brain has been turned inside out and hung up to dry."

Avi rattles off canned justifications: office space is much cheaper in Intramuros. Government ministries are closer. Makati, the gleaming new business district, is too isolated from the real Philippines. Randy pays no attention to it.

"You want to work out of Intramuros because it was systematically annihilated, and because you're obsessed with the Holocaust," Randy finally says, quietly and without rancor.

"Yeah. So?" Avi says.

Randy stares out the window of the Manila-bound 747, sipping on a fluorescent green Nipponese soft drink made from bee extracts (at least, it has pictures of bees on it) and munching on something that a flight attendant handed him called Japanese Snack. Sky and ocean are the same color, a shade of blue that makes his teeth freeze. The plane is so high that, whether he looks up or down, he sees foreshortened views of boiling cumulonimbus stacks. The clouds erupt from the hot Pacific as if immense warships were exploding all over the place. The speed and power of their growth is alarming, the forms they adopt as bizarre and varied as those of deep-sea organisms, and all of them, he supposes, are as dangerous to an airplane as punji stakes to a barefoot pedestrian. The red-orange meatball painted on the wingtip startles him when he notices it. He feels like he's been thrown into an old war film.

He turns on his laptop. Electronic mail from Avi, encrypted to a fare-thee-well, has been piling up in his in-box. It is a gradual accumulation of tiny files, thrown at him by Avi whenever a thought popped into his head over the last three days; it would be obvious, even if Randy didn't know it, that Avi owns a portable e-mail machine that talks to the Internet by radio. Randy fires up a piece of software that is technically called Novus Ordo Seclorum but that everyone calls Ordo for short. It is a fairly strained pun based on the fact that Ordo's job, as a piece of cryptographic software, is to put a message's bits in a New Order and that it will take Centuries for nosy governments to decrypt it. A scanned image of a Great Pyramid appears in the middle of his screen, and a single eye gradually materializes at its apex.

Ordo can handle this in one of two ways. The obvious way is to decrypt all of the messages and convert them into plaintext files on his hard disk, which he can then read any time he wants. The problem with this (if you are paranoid) is that anyone who gets his hands on Randy's hard disk can then read the files. For all he knows, the customs officials in Manila will decide to ransack his computer for child pornography. Or, fogged by jet lag, he'll leave his laptop in a taxi. So instead he puts Ordo into a streaming mode where it will decrypt the files just long enough for him to read them and then, when he closes the windows, expunge the plaintext from the computer's memory and from its hard drive.

The subject heading of Avi's first message is: "Guideline 1."

> We look for places where the math is right. Meaning what?
> Meaning that pop. is about to explode---we can predict
> that just by looking at age histogram---and per capita
> income is about to take off the way it did in Nippon, Tai-
> wan, Singapore. Multiply those two things together and
> you get the kind of exponential growth that should get us
> all into fuck-you money before we turn forty.

This is an allusion to a Randy/Avi conversation of two years ago wherein Avi actually calculated a specific numerical value for "fuck-you money." It was not a fixed constant, however, but rather a cell in a spreadsheet linked to any number of continually fluctuating economic indicators. Sometimes when Avi is working at his computer he will leave the spreadsheet running in a tiny window in the corner so that he can see the current value of "fuck-you money" at a glance.

The second message, sent a couple of hours later, is called "Guideline 2."

> Two: pick a tech where no one can compete with us. Right
> now, that=networking. We're kicking the crap out of ev-
> eryone else in the world when it comes to networking. It's
> not even funny.

The next day, Avi sent a message called, simply, "More." Perhaps he had lost track of the number of guidelines he'd issued so far.

> Another principle: this time we retain control of the cor-
> poration. That means that we keep at least fifty percent of
> the shares---which means little to no outside investment
> until we've built up some value.

"You don't have to convince me," Randy mumbles to himself, as he reads this.

> This shapes the kinds of businesses we can get into. For-
> get anything that requires a big initial investment.

Luzon is green-black jungle mountains gouged with rivers that would appear to be avalanches of silt. As the navy-blue ocean verges on its khaki beaches, the water takes on the shocking iridescent hue of a suburban swimming pool. Farther south, the mountains are swidden-scarred—the soil beneath is bright red and so these parts look like fresh lacerations. But most is covered with foliage that looks like the nubby green stuff that model railroaders put over their papiér-mâché hills, and in vast stretches of the mountains there are no signs whatsoever that human

beings have ever existed. Closer to Manila, some of the slopes are defor-
ested, sprinkled with structures, ribboned with power-line cuts. Rice
paddies line the basins. The towns are accretions of shanties, nucleated
around large cross-shaped churches with good roofs.

The view gets blurry as they belly down into the pall of sweaty smog
above the city. The plane begins to sweat like a giant glass of iced tea.
The water streams off in sheets, collects in crevices, whips off the flaps'
trailing edges.

Suddenly they are banking over Manila Bay, which is marked with
endless streaks of brilliant red—some kind of algal bloom. Oil tankers
trail long time-delayed rainbows that flourish in their wakes. Every cove
is jammed with long skinny boats with dual outriggers, looking like
brightly painted water skaters.

And then they are down on the runway at NAIA, Ninoy Aquino
International Airport. Guards and cops of various stripes are ambling
around with M-16s or pistol-handled pump shotguns, wearing burnooses
fashioned from handkerchiefs clamped to the head with American baseball caps. A man dressed in a radiant white uniform stands below the
ragged maw of the jetway holding his hands downwards with fluorescent
orange sticks in them, like Christ dispensing mercy on a world of sinners.
Sulfurous, fulminating tropical air begins to leak in through the jumbo's
air vents. Everything moistens and wilts.

He is in Manila. He takes his passport out of his shirt pocket. It says,
RANDALL LAWRENCE WATERHOUSE.

This is how Epiphyte Corporation came into existence:

"I am channeling the bad shit!" Avi said.

The number came through on Randy's pager while he was sitting
around a table in a grubhouse along the coast with his girlfriend's crowd.
A place where, every day, they laser-printed fresh menus on 100% recycled imitation parchment, where oscilloscope tracings of neon-colored
sauces scribbled across the plates, and the entrees were towering, architec-
tonic stacks of rare ingredients carved into gemlike prisms. Randy had
spent the entire meal trying to resist the temptation to invite one of
Charlene's friends (any one of them, it didn't matter) out on the sidewalk
for a fistfight.

He glanced at his pager expecting to see the number of the Three
Siblings Computer Center, which was where he worked (technically, still
does). The fell digits of Avi's phone number penetrated the core of his
being in the same way that 666 would a fundamentalist's.

Fifteen seconds later, Randy was out on the sidewalk, swiping his card through a pay phone like an assassin drawing a single-edged razor blade across the throat of a tubby politician.

"The power is coming down from On High," Avi continued. "Tonight, it happens to be coming through me—you poor bastard."

"What do you want me to do?" Randy asked, adopting a cold, almost hostile tone to mask sick excitement.

"Buy a ticket to Manila," Avi said.

"I have to talk it over with Charlene first," Randy said.

"You don't even believe that yourself," Avi said.

"Charlene and I have a long-standing relationsh—"

"It's been ten years. You haven't married her. Fill in the fucking blanks."

(Seventy-two hours later, he would be in Manila, looking at the One-Note Flute.)

"Everyone in Asia is wondering when the Philippines is finally going to get its shit together," Avi said, "it's the question of the nineties."

(The One-Note Flute is the first thing you see when you make it through passport control.)

"I flashed on this when I was standing in line at Passport Control at Ninoy Aquino International Airport," Avi said, compressing that entire name into a single, sharply articulated burst. "You know how they have different lanes?"

"I guess so," Randy said. A parallelpiped of seared tuna did a barrel roll in his gullet. He felt a perverse craving for a double ice-cream cone. He did not travel as much as Avi, and had only a vague idea of what he meant by *lanes*.

"You know. One lane for citizens. One for foreigners. Maybe one for diplomats."

(Now, standing there waiting to have his passport stamped, Randy can see it clearly. For once he doesn't mind the wait. He gets in a lane next to the OCW lane and studies them. They are Epiphyte Corp.'s market. Mostly young women, many of them fashionably dressed, but still with a kind of Catholic boarding-school demureness. Exhausted from long flights, tired of the wait, they slump, then suddenly straighten up and elevate their fine chins, as if an invisible nun were making her way up the line whacking their manicured knuckles with a ruler.)

But seventy-two hours ago he hadn't really understood what Avi meant by lanes, so he just said, "Yeah, I've seen the lane thing."

"At Manila, they have a whole lane just for returning OCWs!"

"OCWs?"

"Overseas Contract Workers. Filipinos working abroad—because the economy of the Philippines is so lame. As maids and nannies in Saudi.

Nurses and anesthesiologists in the States. Singers in Hong Kong, whores in Bangkok."

"Whores in Bangkok?" Randy had been there, at least, and his mind reeled at the concept of importing prostitutes to Thailand.

"The Filipino women are more beautiful," Avi said quietly, "and have a ferocity that makes them more interesting, to the innately masochistic business traveler, than all those grinning Thai bimbos." Both of them knew that this was complete bullshit; Avi was a family man and had no firsthand experience whereof he spoke. Randy didn't call him on it, though. As long as Avi retained this extemporaneous bullshitting ability there was a better than even chance of all of them making fuck-you money.

(Now that he's here, it is tempting to speculate as to which of the girls in the OCW lane are hustlers. But he can't see that going anywhere but wrong, so he squares his shoulders and marches toward the yellow line.

The government has set up glass display cases in the concourse leading from passport control to the security barrier. The cases contain artifacts demonstrating the glories of pre-Magellan Filipino culture. The first one of these contains the *pièce de résistance:* a rustic hand-carved musical instrument labeled with a long and unreadable name in Tagalog. Underneath that, in smaller letters, is the English translation: ONE-NOTE FLUTE.)

"See? The Philippines is innately hedged," Avi said. "You know how rare that is? When you find an innately hedged environment, Randy, you lunge into it like a rabid ferret going into a pipe full of raw meat."

A word about Avi: his father's people had just barely gotten out of Prague. As Central European Jews went, they were fairly typical. The only thing about them that was really anomalous was that they were still alive. But his mother's people were unbelievably peculiar New Mexican crypto-Jews who had been living on mesas, dodging Jesuits, shooting rattlesnakes and eating jimson weed for three hundred years; they looked like Indians and talked like cowboys. In his relations with other people, therefore, Avi dithered. Most of the time he was courtly and correct in a way that was deeply impressive to businesspeople—Nipponese ones especially—but there were these eruptions, from time to time, as if he'd been dipping into the loco weed. Randy had learned to deal with it, which is why Avi called him at times like this.

"Oh, calm down!" Randy said. He watched a tanned girl rollerblade past him, on her way up from the beach. "Innately hedged?"

"As long as the Philippines don't have their shit together, there'll be plenty of OCWs. They will want to communicate with their families—

the Filipinos are incredibly family-oriented. They make Jews look like a bunch of alienated loners."

"Okay. You know more about both groups than I do."

"They are sentimental and affectionate in a way that's very easy for us to sneer at."

"You don't have to be defensive," Randy said, "I'm not sneering at them."

"When you hear their song dedications on the radio, you'll sneer," Avi said. "But frankly, we could take some pointers from the Pinoys on this front."

"You are so close to being sanctimonious right now—"

"I apologize," Avi said, with absolute sincerity. Avi's wife had been pregnant almost continuously for the four years they'd been married. He was getting more religiously observant daily and couldn't make it through a conversation without mentioning the Holocaust. Randy was a bachelor who was just about to break up with the chick he'd been living with.

"I believe you, Avi," Randy said. "Is it a problem with you if I buy a business-class ticket?"

Avi didn't hear him, so Randy assumed that meant yes. "As long as that's the case, there will be a big market for Pinoy-grams."

"Pinoy-grams?"

"For god's sake, don't say it out loud! I'm filling out the trademark application as we speak," Avi said. Randy could hear a rattling sound in the background, computer keys impacting so rapidly it sounded like Avi was simply holding the keyboard between his pale, spindly hands and shaking it violently up and down. "But if the Filipinos do get their shit together, then we see explosive growth in telecoms, as in any other Arday."

"Arday?"

"R-D-A-E. Rapidly Developing Asian Economy. Either way, we win."

"I gather you want to do something with telecoms?"

"Bingo." In the background, a baby began to cough and cry. "Gotta go," Avi said, "Shlomo's asthma is spiking again. Take down this fingerprint."

"Fingerprint?"

"For my encryption key. For e-mail."

"Ordo?"

"Yeah."

Randy took out a ballpoint pen and, finding no paper in his pocket, poised it over the palm of his hand. "Shoot."

"67 81 A4 AE FF 40 25 9B 43 0E 29 8D 56 60 E3 2F." Then Avi hung up the phone.

Randy went back into the restaurant. On his way back, he asked the waiter to bring him a half-bottle of good red wine. Charlene heard him, and glowered. Randy was still thinking about innate ferocity, and did not see it in her face; only a schoolmarmishness common among all of her friends. My god! I have to get out of California, he realized.

SEAWEED

Woman holds baby
Eyes pale as a muzzle flash
Band chimes frozen tears

THE FOURTH MARINES ARE MARCHING DOWNHILL TO THE strains of John Philip Sousa, which ought to be second nature to a Marine. But the Fourth Marines have been in Shanghai (which ain't no halls of Montezuma nor shores of Tripoli) for too long, longer than Marines should ever stay in one place, and Bobby's already seen his sergeant, one Frick, throw up from opium withdrawal.

A Marine band is several Shanghai blocks ahead. Bobby's platoon can hear the thumpity-thump of the big drums and the piercing noises from piccolos and glockenspiels but he can't follow the tune. Corporal Shaftoe is effectively their leader, because Sergeant Frick is useless.

Shaftoe marches alongside the formation, supposedly to keep an eye on his men, but mostly he's just staring at Shanghai.

Shanghai stares back, and mostly gives them a standing ovation. Of course there is a type of young street rowdy who makes it a point of honor to let the Marines know he isn't scared of them, and they are jeering the Marines from a safe distance, and setting off strings of fire-crackers, which does nothing to steady anyone's nerves. The Europeans are applauding—a whole chorus line of Russian dancing girls from Del-monte's is showing thigh and blowing kisses. But most of the Chinese look pretty stonefaced, which—Bobby suspects—means they're scared shitless.

The worst thing is the women carrying half-white babies. A few of these women are rabid, hysterical, throwing themselves into formations of massed Marines, undeterred by rifle butts. But most of them are stoic: they stand with their light-eyed babies and glare, searching the ranks and files for the guilty party. They've all heard about what happened upriver in Nanjing when the Nips came there, and they know that when it's all over, the only trace that they and their babies ever existed may be a really bad memory in the mind of some American Marine.

It works for Shaftoe: he has hunted deer in Wisconsin and seen them limping across the snow, bleeding to death. He saw a man die in basic training at Parris Island. He has seen whole tangles of bodies in the Yangtze, downstream of where the Nipponese were prosecuting the China Incident, and he has seen refugees from places like Nanjing starve to death in the gutters of Shanghai. He has himself killed people who were trying to storm the riverboats it was his duty to protect. He thinks that he has never seen, and will never see, anything as terrible as those stone-faced Chinese women holding their white babies, not even blinking as the firecrackers explode all around them.

Until, that is, he looks into the faces of certain Marines who stare into that crowd and see their own faces looking back at them, pudgy with baby fat and streaked with tears. Some of them seem to think it's all a joke. But many of the Marines who march out of their empty barracks that morning sane and solid men, have, by the time they reach the gunboats waiting for them at the Bund, gone mad. They don't show it. But Shaftoe can see in their eyes that something has given way inside.

The very best men in the regiment are in a foul mood. The ones like Shaftoe, who didn't get involved with the Chinese women, are still leaving plenty behind: houses with maids and shoeshine boys and coolies, with women and opium for almost nothing. They don't know where they are being shipped off to, but it's safe to say that their twenty-one dollars a month won't go as far. They'll be in barracks and they'll have to learn to polish their own boots again. When the gangplanks are drawn in from the stone edge of the Bund, they are cut off from a whole world that they'll never see again, a world where they were kings. Now they are Marines again. It's okay with Shaftoe, who wants to be a Marine. But many of the men have become middle-aged here, and don't.

The guilty men duck belowdecks. Shaftoe remains on the deck of the gunboat, which casts off from the Bund, headed for the cruiser *Augusta,* which awaits in mid-channel.

The Bund is jammed with onlookers in a riot of differently colored clothing, so one patch of uniform drab catches his eye: a group of Nip soldiers who've come down to bid their Yank counterparts a sarcastic farewell. Shaftoe scans the group looking for someone tall and bulky, and picks him out easily. Goto Dengo's waving to him.

Shaftoe takes his helmet off and waves back. Then, on impulse, just for the hell of it, he winds up and flings the helmet directly at Goto

Dengo's head. The throw goes awry and Goto Dengo has to knock down about a dozen of his comrades in order to catch it. All of them seem to think that it is a high honor, as well as tremendously amusing, to be knocked down by Goto Dengo.

Twenty seconds later, a comet sails up out of the flesh cosmos of the Bund and bounces on the wooden deck of the gunboat—a hell of a throw. Goto Dengo is showing off his follow-through. The projectile is a rock with a white streamer wrapped around it. Shaftoe runs over and snatches it. The streamer is one of those thousand-stitch headbands (supposedly; he's taken a few off of unconscious Nips, but he's never bothered to count the stitches) that they tie around their heads as a good-luck charm; it has a meatball in the center and some Nip writing to either side. He unties it from around the rock. In so doing he realizes, suddenly, that it's not a rock after all; it is a hand grenade! But good old Goto Dengo was just joking—he didn't pull the pin. A nice souvenir for Bobby Shaftoe.

Shaftoe's first haiku (December 1940) was a quick and dirty adaptation of the Marine Creed:

> This is my rifle
> There are many like it but
> This rifle is mine.

He wrote it under the following circumstances: Shaftoe and the rest of Fourth Marines were stationed in Shanghai so that they could guard the International Settlement and work as muscle on the gunboats of the Yangtze River Patrol. His platoon had just come back from the Last Patrol: a thousand-mile reconnaissance-in-force all the way up past what was left of Nanjing, to Hankow, and back. Marines had been doing this ever since the Boxer Rebellion, through civil wars and everything else. But towards the end of 1940, what with the Nips* basically running all of northeast China now, the politicians back in D.C. had finally thrown in the towel and told the China Marines not to steam up the Yangtze any more.

Now, the Old Breed Marines like Frick claimed they could tell the difference between organized brigands; armed mobs of starving peasants; rogue Nationalists; Communist guerrillas; and the irregular forces in the

---

*As the Nipponese were invariably called by Marines, who never used a three-syllable word where a three-letter one would do.

pay of warlords. But to Bobby Shaftoe they were all just crazy, armed slopes who wanted a piece of the Yangtze River Patrol. The Last Patrol had been a wild trip. But it was over and they were back in Shanghai now, the safest place you could be in China, and about a hundred times more dangerous than the most dangerous place you could be in America. They had climbed off the gunboat six hours ago, gone to a bar, and not come out until just now, when they had decided it was high time they went to a whorehouse. On their way, they happened to pass this Nip restaurant.

Bobby Shaftoe had looked in the windows of the place before, and watched the man with the knife, trying to figure out what the hell he was doing. It looked a hell of a lot like he was cutting up uncooked fish and putting the raw meat on bullets of rice and handing it over to the Nips on the other side of the counter, who were wolfing it down.

It had to be some kind of optical illusion. The fish must have been precooked in the back room.

This had been nagging at Shaftoe for about a year. As he and the other horny drunk Marines went by the place, he slowed down to peer through the window, trying to gather more evidence. He could swear that some of that fish looked ruby red, which it wouldn't have been if it were cooked.

One of his buddies, Rhodes from Shreveport, noticed him looking. He dared Shaftoe to go in there and sit down at that bar. Then another private, Gowicki from Pittsburgh, double-dared him!

Shaftoe sucked his teeth and considered the matter. He had already made up his mind that he was going to do it. He was a sniper scout, and it was in his nature to do crazy shit like this; but it was also part of his training to scan the terrain carefully before venturing in.

The restaurant was three-quarters full, and everyone in the place was a uniformed member of the Nipponese military. At the bar where the man was cutting up the apparently raw fish, there was a marked concentration of officers; if you only had one grenade, that's where you'd throw it. Most of the place was filled with long tables where enlisted men sat, drinking noodle soup from steaming urns. Shaftoe paid particular attention to these, because they were the ones who were going to be beating the shit out of him in about sixty seconds. Some were there alone, with reading material. A cluster of them, back in one corner, were paying attention to one fellow who was apparently telling a joke or story.

The longer Shaftoe spent reconnoitering the place, the more convinced Rhodes and Gowicki became that he was actually going to do it. They became excited and called for the other Marines, who had gone ahead of them down the block, headed for that whorehouse.

Shaftoe saw the others coming back—his tactical reserve. "What the fuck," he said, and went into the restaurant. Behind him, he could hear the others shouting excitedly; they couldn't believe he was doing it. When Shaftoe stepped over the threshold of that Nip restaurant, he passed into the realm of legend.

All the Nips looked up at him when he came in the door. If they were surprised, they didn't show it. The chef behind the counter began to holler out some kind of ritual greeting, which faltered and trailed off as he got a look at what had just come in. The fellow in the back of the room—a husky, pink-cheeked Nip—continued telling his joke or story or whatever it was.

Shaftoe nodded to no one in particular, then stepped to the nearest empty chair at the bar and sat down.

Other Marines would have waited until the whole squad had assembled. Then they would have invaded the restaurant en masse, knocked over a few chairs, spilled some soup. But Shaftoe had seized the initiative before the others could do any such thing and gone in by himself, as a sniper scout was supposed to do. It was not just because he was a sniper scout, though. It was also because he was Bobby Shaftoe, and he was sincerely curious about this place, and if he could, he wanted to spend a few calm minutes in here and learn a few things about it before the fun started.

It helped, of course, that Shaftoe was a quiet and contemplative drunk, not a dangerous explosive drunk. He must have reeked of beer (those Krauts in Tsingtao cranked out a brew whose taste took him right back to Wisconsin, and he was homesick). But he wasn't hollering or knocking things over.

The chef was busy crafting one of his little morsels and pretended to ignore Shaftoe. The other men at the counter stared coldly at Shaftoe for a while, then turned their attentions back to their food. Shaftoe looked at the array of raw fish laid out on shaved ice behind the bar, then looked around the room. The guy back in the corner was talking in short bursts, reading from a notebook. He would speak maybe ten or twenty words, and then his little audience would turn to one another and grin, or grimace, or sometimes even make a patter of applause. He wasn't delivering his material like a dirty joke. He spoke precisely and expressively.

Fuck! He was reading poetry! Shaftoe had no idea what he was saying, but he could tell, by the sound of it, that it must be poetry. Didn't rhyme though. But the Nips did everything queerly.

He noticed that the chef was glaring at him. He cleared his throat, which was useless since he couldn't speak Nip. He looked at some of that ruby red fish behind the bar, pointed to it, held up two fingers.

Everyone was startled that the American had actually placed an order. The tension was broken, only a little. The chef went to work and produced two morsels, which he served up on a wooden pedestal.

Shaftoe had been trained to eat insects, and to bite the heads off chickens, so he figured he could handle this. He picked the morsels up in his fingers, just like the Nips were doing, and ate them. They were good. He ordered two more, of another variety. The guy in the corner kept reading poetry. Shaftoe ate his morsels and then ordered some more. For perhaps ten seconds, between the taste of the fish and the sound of the poetry, he actually felt comfortable here, and forgot that he was merely instigating a vicious racial brawl.

The third order looked different: laid over the top of the raw fish were thin translucent sheets of some kind of moist, glistening material. It looked sort of like butcher paper soaked in oil. Shaftoe gawked at it for a while, trying to identify it, but it looked like no foodstuff he knew of. He glanced left and right, hoping that one of the Nips had ordered the same stuff, so that he could watch and learn the right way to eat it. No luck.

Hell, they were officers. Maybe one of them spoke a little English. " 'Scuse me. What's this?" Shaftoe said, peeling up one corner of the eerie membrane.

The chef looked up at him nervously, then scanned the bar, polling the customers. Discussion ensued. Finally, a Nip officer at the end of the bar, a naval lieutenant, stood up and spoke to Bobby Shaftoe.

"Seaweed."

Shaftoe did not particularly like the lieutenant's tone of voice—hostile and sullen. This, combined with the look on his face, seemed to say, *You'll never understand it, you farmer, so why don't you just think of it as seaweed.*

Shaftoe folded his hands primly in his lap, regarded the seaweed for a few moments, and then looked up at the lieutenant, who was still gazing at him expressionlessly. "What *kind* of seaweed, sir?" he said.

Significant glances began flying around the restaurant, like semaphores before a naval engagement. The poetry reading seemed to have stopped, and a migration of enlisted men had begun from the back of the room. Meanwhile the lieutenant translated Shaftoe's inquiry to the others, who discussed it in some detail, as if it were a major policy initiative from Franklin Delano Roosevelt.

The lieutenant and the chef exchanged words. Then the lieutenant looked at Shaftoe again. "He say, you pay now." The chef held up one hand and rubbed his fingers and thumb together.

A year of working the Yangtze River Patrol had given Bobby Shaftoe nerves of titanium, and unlimited faith in his comrades, and so he resisted the impulse to turn his head and look out the window. He already knew exactly what he would see: Marines, shoulder to shoulder, ready to die for him. He scratched the new tattoo on his forearm: a dragon. His dirty fingernails, passing over the fresh scabs, made a rasping sound in the utterly silent restaurant.

"You didn't answer my question," Shaftoe said, pronouncing the words with a drunk's precision.

The lieutenant translated this into Nipponese. More discussion. But this time it was curt and decisive. Shaftoe could tell that they were about to bounce him. He squared his shoulders.

The Nips were good; they mounted an organized charge out the door, onto the sidewalk, and engaged the Marines, before anyone actually laid a hand on Shaftoe. This spoiling attack prevented the Marines from invading the restaurant proper, which would have disturbed the officers' meal and, with any luck, led to untold property damage. Shaftoe then felt himself being grabbed from behind by at least three people and hoisted into the air. He made eye contact with the lieutenant while this was happening, and shouted: "Are you bullshitting me about the seaweed?"

As brawls went, the only remarkable part of this one was the way he was carried out to the street before he could actually get started. Then it was like all the other street fights he'd been in with Nip soldiers in Shanghai. These all came down to American brawn (you didn't get picked for the Fourth Regiment unless you were an impressive-looking six-footer) versus that Nipponese chop-socky.

Shaftoe wasn't a boxer. He was a wrestler. This was to his advantage. The other Marines would put up their dukes and try to fight it out— Marquis of Queensberry style—no match for chop-socky. Shaftoe had no illusions about his boxing, so he would just put his head down and charge like a bull, take a few blows to the face on his way in, but usually get a solid hold on his opponent and slam him into the cobblestones. Usually that shook the Nip up enough that Shaftoe could get him in a full-nelson or a hammerlock and get him to cry uncle.

The guys who were carrying him out of the restaurant got jumped by Marines as soon as they were in the open. Shaftoe found himself going up against an opponent who was at least as tall as he was, which was unusual. This one had a solid build, too. Not like a sumo wrestler. More like a football player—a lineman, with a bit of a gut. He was a strong S.O.B. and Shaftoe knew right away that he was in for a real scrape. The guy had a different style of wrestling from the American, which (as Shaftoe learned the hard way) included some illegal maneuvers: partial strangulation and powerful, short punches to major nerve centers. The gulf between Shaftoe's mind and body, already wedged open by alcohol, was yanked open to a chasm by these techniques. He ended up lying on the sidewalk, helpless and paralyzed, staring up into the chubby face of his opponent. This was (he realized) the same guy who'd been sitting in the corner of the restaurant reading poetry. He was a good wrestler for a poet. Or maybe vice versa.

"It is *not seaweed*," said the big Nip. He had a look on his face like a naughty schoolkid getting away with something. "The English word is maybe *calabash?*" Then he turned and walked back into the restaurant.

So much for legend. What none of the other Marines knows is that this was not the last encounter between Bobby Shaftoe and Goto Dengo. The incident left Shaftoe with any number of nagging questions about subjects as diverse as seaweed, poetry, and chop-socky. He sought out Goto Dengo after that, which was not that hard—he just paid some Chinese boys to follow the conspicuous Nip around town and file daily reports. From this he learned that Goto Dengo and some of his comrades gathered every morning in a certain park to practice their chop-socky. After making sure that his will was in order and writing a last letter to his parents and siblings in Oconomowoc, Shaftoe went to that park one morning, reintroduced himself to the surprised Goto Dengo, and made arrangements to serve as human punching bag. They found his self-defense skills hilariously primitive but admired his resilience, and so, for the small cost of a few broken ribs and digits, Bobby Shaftoe got a preliminary course in the particular type of chop-socky favored by Goto Dengo, which is called judo. Over time, this even led to a few social engagements in bars, and restaurants, where Shaftoe learned to recognize four types of seaweed, three types of fish eggs, and several flavors of Nip poetry. Of course he had no idea what the fuck they were saying, but he could count syllables, which, as far as he could tell, is about all there is to Nip poetry appreciation.

Not that this—or any other knowledge of their culture—is going to do him any good now that it will soon be his job to kill them.

In return, Shaftoe taught Goto Dengo how not to throw like a girl. A lot of the Nips are good at baseball and so it was hilarious, even to them, to see their burly friend pushing ineffectually at a baseball. But it was Shaftoe who taught Goto Dengo to stand sideways, to rotate his shoulders, and to follow through. He's paid a lot of attention to the big Nip's throwing form during the last year, and maybe that's why the image of Goto Dengo planting his feet on the ashlars of the Bund, winding up, throwing the streamer-wrapped grenade, and following through almost daintily on one combat-booted foot stays in Shaftoe's mind all the way to Manila and beyond.

A couple of days into the voyage it becomes apparent that Sergeant Frick has forgotten how to shine his boots. Every night he puts them on the deck beside his bunk, like he's expecting a coolie to come around and shine them up during the night. Every morning he wakes up and finds them in a sorrier state than before. After a few days he starts to draw reprimands from On High, starts to get a lot of potato-peeling duty.

Now in and of itself this is forgivable. Frick started out his career chasing bandolier-draped desperadoes away from mail trains on the High Chaparral, for God's sake. In '27 he got shipped off to Shanghai on very short notice, and no doubt had to display some adaptability. Fine. And now he's on this miserable pre-Great War cruiser and it's a little hard on him. Fine. But he does not take all of this with the dignity that is demanded of Marines by Marines. He whines about it. He lets himself get humiliated. He gets angry. A lot of the other old China Marines see things his way.

One day Bobby Shaftoe is up on the deck of the destroyer tossing the old horsehide around with a couple of the other young Marines when he sees a few of these older guys accumulating into a sort of human booger on the afterdeck. He can tell by the looks on their faces and by their gestures that they are bellyaching.

Shaftoe hears a couple of the ship's crew talking to each other nearby. "What the hell is wrong with those Marines?" one of them says. The other one shakes his head sadly, like a doctor who has just seen a patient's eyeballs roll up into their sockets. "Those poor bastards have gone Asiatic," he says.

And then they turn and look at Shaftoe.

That evening, at mess, Bobby Shaftoe gulps his food down double-time, then stands up and approaches the table where those Old Breed Marines are sullenly gathered. "Begging your pardon, Sergeant!" he hollers. "Request permission to shine your boots, Sarge!"

Frick's mouth drops open, revealing a half-chewed plug of boiled beef. "Whud you say, Corporal?"

The mess has gone silent. "Respectfully request permission to shine your boots, Sarge!"

Frick is not the quickest guy in the world even when he's sober, and it's pretty obvious, just from looking at his pupils, that he and his comrades have brought some opium aboard. "Wull, uh, I guess so," he says. He looks around at his crew of gripers, who are a little confused and a little amused. He unlaces his boots. Bobby Shaftoe takes those disgraceful things away and returns a bit later with them resplendently shined. By this time, Frick has gotten high and mighty. "Wull, those boots look real good, Corporal Shaftoe," he says in a brassy voice. "Darned if you ain't as good a shoe-shiner as my coolie boy was."

At lights out, Frick and crew are short-sheeted. Various other, ruder practical jokes ensue during the nighttime. One of them gets jumped in his bunk and beaten by unspecified attackers. The brass call a surprise inspection the next morning and cuss them out. The "gone Asiatic" crew spend most of the next day gathered in a cluster, watching each other's backs.

Around midday, Frick finally gets it through his head that all of this was triggered by Shaftoe's gesture, and that Shaftoe knew, all along, what was going to happen. So he rushes Bobby Shaftoe up on the deck and tries to throw him over the rail.

Shaftoe's warned at the last minute by one of his compadres, and spins around just enough to throw off Frick's attack. Frick caroms off the rail, turns around, and tries to grab Shaftoe's nuts. Shaftoe pokes him in the eye, which straightens him right up. They back away from each other. The opening formalities having been finished; they put up their dukes.

Frick and Shaftoe box for a couple of rounds. A large crowd of Marines gathers. On most of their cards, Frick is winning the fight. Frick was always dim-witted, and is now crazy to boot, but he knows his way around a boxing ring, and he has forty pounds on Shaftoe.

Shaftoe puts up with it until Frick socks him pretty hard in the mouth and gives him a bloody lip.

"How far are we from Manila?" Shaftoe hollers. This question, as usual, leaves Sergeant Frick confused and bewildered, and straightens him up for a moment.

"Two days," answers one of the ship's officers.

"Well, goddamn," Bobby Shaftoe says. "How'm I gonna kiss my girl with this fat lip?"

Frick answers, "Just go out and find a cheaper one."

That's all he needs. Shaftoe puts his head down and charges in on Frick, hollering like a Nip. Before Frick can get his brain in gear, Bobby Shaftoe has him wrapped up in one of those chop-socky holds that Goto Dengo taught him in Shanghai. He works his way up Frick's body to a choke-hold and then clamps down until Sergeant Frick's lips turn the color of the inside of an oyster shell. Then he hangs Frick over the rail, holding him upside-down by the ankles, until Frick recovers enough to shout, "Uncle!"

A disciplinary proceeding is hastily called. Shaftoe is found guilty of being courteous (by shining Frick's boots) and defending the life of a Marine (himself) from a crazed attacker. The crazed attacker goes straight to the brig. Within a few hours, the noises Frick makes lets all of the Marines know what opium withdrawal feels like.

So Sergeant Frick does not get to see their entrance into Manila Bay. Shaftoe almost feels sorry for the poor bastard.

The island of Luzon lies to port all day long, a black hulk barely visible through the haze, with glimpses of palm trees and beaches down below. All of the Marines have been this way before and so they can pick out the Cordillera Central up north, and later the Zambales Mountains, which eventually plunge down to meet the sea near Subic Bay. Subic triggers a barrage of salty anecdotes. The ship does not put in there, but continues to swing southward around Bata'an, turning inland toward the entrance of Manila Bay. The ship reeks of shoe polish, talcum powder, and after-shave lotion; the Fourth Marines may have specialized in whoring and opium abuse, but they've always been known as the best-*looking* Marines in the Corps.

They pass by Corregidor. An island shaped like a bead of water on a waxed boot, it is gently rounded in the middle but steeply sloping into the water. It has a long, bony, dry tail that trails off at one end. The Marines know that the island is riddled with tunnels and bristling with terrible guns, but the only sign of these fortifications is the clusters of concrete barracks up in the hills, housing the men who serve the weapons. A tangle of antennas rises up above Topside. Their shapes are familiar to Shaftoe, because many of the same antennas rose above Station Alpha in Shanghai, and he had to take them apart and load them into the truck.

There is a giant limestone cliff descending nearly into the sea, and at the base of it is the entrance to the tunnel where all the spooks and radio men have their hideaway. Nearby is a dock, quite busy at the moment, with supplies being offloaded from civilian transports and stacked right there on the beach. This detail is noticed by all of the Marines as a positive sign of approaching war. *Augusta* drops anchor in the cove, and all of that tarp-wrapped radio stuff is unloaded into launches and taken to that dock, along with all of the odd pencil-necked Navy men who tended that gear in Shanghai.

The swell dies as they pass Corregidor and enter the bay. Greenish-brown algae floats in swirls and curlicues near the surface. Navy ships lay brown ropes of smoke across the still sea. Undisturbed by wind, these unfold into rugged shapes like translucent mountain ranges. They pass the big military base at Cavite—a sheet of land so low and flat that its boundary with the water would be invisible except for the picket line of palm trees. A few hangars and water towers rise from it, and low dark clusters of barracks farther inland. Manila is dead ahead of them, still veiled in haze. It is getting on toward evening.

Then the haze dissolves, the atmosphere suddenly becomes as limpid as a child's eyes, and for about an hour they can see to infinity. They are steaming into an arena of immense thunderheads with lightning corkscrewing down through them all around. Flat grey clouds like shards of broken slate peek out between anvils. Behind them are higher clouds vaulting halfway to the moon, glowing pink and salmon in the light of the setting sun. Behind that, more clouds nestled within banks of humidity like Christmas ornaments wrapped in tissue paper, expanses of blue sky, more thunderheads exchanging bolts of lightning twenty miles long. Skies nested within skies nested within skies.

It was cold up there in Shanghai, and it's gotten warmer every day since. Some days it's even been hot and muggy. But around the time Manila heaves into view, a warm breeze springs up over the deck and all of the Marines sigh, as if they have all ejaculated in unison.

> Manila's perfume
> Fanned by the coconut palms
> The thighs of Glory

Manila's spreading tile roofs have a mestizo shape about them, half-Spanish and half-Chinese. The city has a concave seawall with a flat promenade on the top. Strollers turn and wave to the Marines; some of them blow kisses. A wedding party is gushing down the steps of a church and across the boulevard to the seawall, where they are getting their pictures taken in the flattering peach-colored light of the sunset. The men are in their fancy, gauzy Filipino shirts, or in U.S. military uniforms. The women are in spectacular gowns and dresses. The Marines holler and whistle at them and the women turn towards them, hitching up their skirts slightly so that they won't trip, and wave enthusiastically. The Marines get woozy and practically fall overboard.

As their ship is easing into its dock, a crescent-shaped formation of flying fish erupts from the water. It moves away like a dune being blown across the desert. The fish are silver and leaf-shaped. Each one strikes the water with a metallic click, and the clicks merge into a crisp ripping noise. The crescent glides beneath a pier, flowing around its pilings, and disappears in the shadows underneath.

Manila, the Pearl of the Orient, early on a Sunday evening, the 7th of December, 1941. In Hawaii, on the other side of the Date Line, it is only just past midnight. Bobby Shaftoe and his comrades have a few hours of freedom. The city is modern, prosperous, English-speaking, and Christian, by far the wealthiest and most advanced city in Asia, practically like being back home in the States. For all its Catholicity, it has areas that seem to have been designed, from the foundation-stones upwards, to the specifications of horny sailors. You get to those parts of town by turning right once your feet are on dry land.

Bobby Shaftoe turns left, politely excuses himself past a legion of excited prostitutes, and sets his course on the looming walls of Intramuros. He stops only to buy a sheaf of roses from a vendor in the park, who is doing land-office business. The park and the walls above it are crowded with strolling lovers, the men mostly in uniforms and the women in demure but stunning dresses, twirling parasols on their shoulders.

A couple of fellows driving horse-drawn taxis want to do business with Bobby Shaftoe but he turns them down. A taxi will only get him there faster, and he is too nervous to get there fast. He walks through a gate in the wall and into the old Spanish city.

Intramuros is a maze of buff-colored stone walls rising abruptly from narrow streets. The first-floor windows along the sidewalks are guarded by black ironwork cages. The bars swell, swirl, and sprout finedly hammered leaves. The second stories hang out overhead, sporting gas lights that are just now being lit by servants with long, smoking poles. The sound of laughter and music drifts out of the windows above, and when he passes by the archways that open into the inner courtyards, he can smell flowers back in the gardens.

Damned if he can tell these places apart. He remembers the street name of Magallanes, because Glory told him once it was the same thing as "Magellan." And he remembers the view of the cathedral from the Pascuals' window. He wanders around a block a couple of times, certain that he is close. Then he hears an exaltation of girlish laughter coming from a second-story window, and moves toward it like a jellyfish sucked into an intake pipe. It all comes together. This is the place. The girls are all gossiping, in English, about one of their instructors. He does not hear Glory's voice but he thinks he hears her laughter.

"Glory!" he says. Then he says it louder. If they hear him, they pay him no mind. Finally he winds up and flings the bouquet of roses like a potato-masher grenade over the wooden railing, through a narrow gap between the mother-of-pearl shutters, and into the room.

Miraculous silence from within the room, and then gales of laughter. The nacre shutters part with slow, agonizing coyness. A girl of nineteen steps out onto the balcony. She is dressed in the uniform of a nursing student. It is as white as starlight shining on the North Pole. She has let her long black hair down to brush it, and it stirs languidly in the evening breeze. The last ruddy light of the sunset makes her face glow like a coal. She hides behind the bouquet for a moment, buries her nose in it, inhales deeply, peeking out at him over the blossoms with her black eyes. Then she lowers the bouquet gradually to reveal her high cheeks, her perfect little nose, the fantastic sculpture of her lips, and teeth, white but fetchingly crooked, barely visible. She is smiling.

"Jesus H. Christ," Bobby Shaftoe says, "your cheekbones are like a fucking snowplow."

She puts her finger to her lips. The gesture of anything touching Glory's lips puts an invisible spear through Shaftoe's chest. She eyes him for a while, establishing, in her own mind, that she has the boy's attention and that he is not going anywhere. Then she turns her back on him. The light grazes her buttocks, *showing* nothing but *suggesting* cleavage. She goes back inside and the shutter glides shut behind her.

Suddenly the room full of girls becomes quiet, except for occasional ripples of suppressed laughter. Shaftoe bites his tongue. They are screwing it all up. Mr. or Mrs. Pascual will notice their silence and become suspicious.

Ironwork clangs and a big gate swings open. The porter beckons him inside. Shaftoe follows the old fellow down the black, arched tunnel of the porte-cochere. The hard soles of his shiny black shoes skid on the cobblestones. A horse back in the stable whinnies at the smell of his aftershave. Sleepy American music, slow-dance stuff from the Armed Forces station, spills tinnily from a radio in the porter's nook.

Flowering vines grow up the stone walls of the courtyard. It is a tidy, quiet, enclosed world, almost like being indoors. The porter waves him in the direction of one of the stairways that lead up to the second floor. Glory calls it the entresuelo and says that it's really a floor between the floors, but it looks like a full-fledged, regular floor to Bobby Shaftoe. He mounts the steps and looks up to see Mr. Pascual standing there, a tiny bald man with glasses and a trim little mustache. He is wearing a short-sleeved shirt, American style, and khaki trousers, and slippers, and is holding a glass of San Miguel in one hand and a cigarette in the other. "Private Shaftoe! Welcome back," he says.

So. Glory has decided to play this one by the book. The Pascuals have been alerted. A few hours of socializing now stand between Bobby Shaftoe and his girl. But a Marine is never fazed by such setbacks.

"Begging your pardon, Mr. Pascual, but I am a corporal now."

Mr. Pascual puts his cigarette in his mouth and shakes Corporal

Shaftoe's hand. "Well, congratulations! I just saw your uncle Jack last week. I don't think he had any idea you were on your way back."

"It was a surprise to everyone, sir," Bobby Shaftoe says.

Now they are on a raised walkway that runs around the courtyard. Only livestock and servants live at ground level. Mr. Pascual leads them around to a door that takes them into the entresuelo. The walls here are rough stone, the ceilings are simple painted planks. They pass through a dark, somber office where Mr. Pascual's father and grandfather used to receive the managers of the family's haciendas and plantations. For a moment, Bobby Shaftoe gets his hopes up. This level has a few rooms that back in the old days were apartments for high-ranking servants, bachelor uncles, and spinster aunts. Now that the hacienda business ain't what it used to be, the Pascuals are renting them out to female students. Perhaps Mr. Pascual is leading him directly to Glory.

But this goes the way of all foolish, horny illusions as Shaftoe finds himself at the foot of a vast staircase of polished nara wood. He can see pressed-tin ceiling up there, chandeliers, and the imposing superstructure of Mrs. Pascual, contained within a mighty bodice that looks like something dreamed up by naval engineers. They ascend the stairs into the antesala, which according to Glory is strictly for casual, drop-in visitors but is fancier than any room Bobby Shaftoe has ever seen. There are big vases and pots all over the place, supposedly old, and supposedly from Japan and China. A fresh breeze runs through; he looks out a window and sees, neatly framed in it, the green dome of the cathedral with its Celtic cross on top, just as he remembered it. Mrs. Pascual holds out her hand and Shaftoe clasps it. "Mrs. Pascual," he says, "thank you for welcoming me into your home."

"Please sit down," she says, "we want to hear everything."

Shaftoe sits in a fancy chair next to the piano, adjust his trousers a bit so that they will not cramp his erect penis, checks his shave. It probably has a few good hours left. A wing of airplanes drones overhead. Mrs. Pascual is giving instructions to the maid in Tagalog. Shaftoe examines the crusted lacerations on his knuckles and wonders whether Mrs. Pascual has the slightest idea of what she would be in for if he really told her everything. Perhaps a little anecdote about hand-to-hand combat with Chinese river pirates on the banks of the Yangtze would break the ice. Through a door and down the hall, he can see a corner of the family chapel, all Gothic arches, a gilded altar, and in front of it an embroidered kneeler worn threadbare by the patellas of Mrs. Pascual.

Cigarettes are brought round, stacked in a large lacquer box like artillery shells in a crate. They drink tea and exchange small talk for what seems like about thirty-six hours. Mrs. Pascual wants to be reassured, over and over again, that everything is fine and that there will not be a war. Mr. Pascual obviously believes that war is just around the corner, and mostly broods. Business has been good lately. He and Jack Shaftoe, Bobby's uncle, have been shipping a lot of stuff between here and Singapore. But business will get a lot worse soon, he thinks.

Glory appears. She has changed out of her student's uniform and into a dress. Bobby Shaftoe nearly topples backward out of the window. Mrs. Pascual formally reintroduces them. Bobby Shaftoe kisses Glory's hand in what he thinks is more than likely a very gallant gesture. He's glad he did, because Glory is palming a tiny wadded-up note which ends up in his hand.

Glory takes a seat and is duly issued her own teacup. Another eternity of small talk. Mr. Pascual asks him for the eighty-seventh time whether he has touched base with Uncle Jack yet, and Shaftoe reiterates that he literally just stepped off the boat and will certainly see Uncle Jack tomorrow morning. He excuses himself to the bathroom, which is an old-fashioned two-holer mounted above deep shafts that must descend all the way to hell. He unwads and reads Glory's note, memorizes the instructions, tears it up and sprinkles it down the hole.

Mrs. Pascual allows the two young lovers a full half hour of "private" time together, meaning that the Pascuals leave the room and only come back every five minutes or so to check up on them. There is a painfully elaborate and lengthy good-bye ceremony which ends in Shaftoe returning to the street and Glory waving to him from her balcony.

Half an hour later, they are doing tongue judo in the back of a horse-drawn taxi galloping over the cobblestones toward the nightclubs of Malate. The extraction of Glory from the Pascual residence was a simple matter for a highly motivated China Marine and a squadron of saucy nursing students.

But Glory must be kissing him with her eyes open because all of a sudden she wriggles loose and says to the taxi driver, "Stop! Please stop, sir!"

"What is it?" Shaftoe says blurrily. He looks around and sees nothing but a great big old stone church looming up above them. This brings a preliminary stab of fear. But the church is dark, there's no Filipinas in long dresses, no Marines in dress uniforms, it can't be his wedding.

"I want to show you something," Glory says, and clambers down out of the taxi. Shaftoe has to pursue her into the place—the Church of San Augustin. He's gone by this pile many times but he never reckoned he would come inside—on a *date*.

She stands at the bottom of a huge staircase and says, "See?"

Shaftoe looks up into darkness, thinks there might be a stained-glass window or two up there, maybe a Laceration of Christ or an Impalement of the Blessed Thorax, but—

"Look *down*," Glory says, and taps one miniature foot against the first tread of the staircase. It is a single great big huge slab of granite.

"Looks like ten or twenty tons of rock there I'd estimate," he says authoritatively.

"It came from Mexico."

"Ah, go on!"

Glory smiles at him. "Carry me up the stairs." And in case Shaftoe's thinking of refusing, she sort of falls into him, and he has no choice but to catch her up in his arms. She traps his nape in the crook of her arm, the better to pull her face close to his, but what he remembers is how the silk of her sleeve feels against the freshly shaved skin of his neck. He begins the ascent. Glory doesn't weigh much, but after four steps he has broken a fine sweat. She is watching him, from four inches away, for signs of fatigue, and he feels himself blushing. Good thing that the whole staircase is lit up by about two candles. There's a lovely bust of a thorn-crowned Jesus with long parallel blood-drops running down his face, and on the right—

"These giant stones you are walking on were quarried in Mexico, centuries and centuries ago, before America was even a country. They were brought over in the bottoms of the Manila Galleons, as ballast." She pronounces it *bayast*.

"I'll be damned."

"When those galleons arrived, the stones were brought out of their bellies, one by one, and taken here to the Church of San Agustin, and piled up. Each stone on top of the last year's stone. Until finally after many, many years this staircase was finished."

After a while it seems to Shaftoe as though it's going to take at least that many years to reach the top of the damn thing. The summit is adorned with a life-sized Jesus carrying a cross that appears to be at least as heavy as one of those stair-treads. So who's he to complain? Then Glory says, "Now carry me down, so you will remember the story."

"You think I'm some horny jarhead who won't remember a story unless it's got a pretty girl in it?"

"Yes," Glory says, and laughs in his face. He carries her down to the bottom again. Then, before she goes off on some other tangent, he carries her straight out the door and into the taxi.

Bobby Shaftoe is not one to lose his cool in the heat of action, but the rest of the evening is a blurry fever dream to him. Only a few impressions penetrate the haze: alighting from the taxi in front of a waterfront hotel; all of the other boys gaping at Glory; Bobby Shaftoe

glaring at them, threatening to teach them some manners. Slow dancing
with Glory in the ballroom, Glory's silk-clad thigh gradually slipping
between his legs, her firm body pressing harder and harder against his.
Strolling along the seawall, hand in hand beneath the starlight. Noticing
that the tide is out. Exchanging a look. Carrying her down from the
seawall to the thin strip of rocky beach beneath it.

By the time he is actually fucking her, he has more or less lost consciousness, he is off in some fantastic, libidinal dream. He and Glory
fuck without the slightest hesitation, without any doubts, without any
troublesome thinking whatsoever. Their bodies have spontaneously
merged, like a pair of drops running together on a windowpane. If he
is thinking anything at all, it is that his entire life has culminated in this
moment. His upbringing in Oconomowoc, high school prom night, deer
hunting in the Upper Peninsula, Parris Island boot camp, all of the brawls
and struggles in China, his duel with Sergeant Frick, they are wood
behind the point of a spear.

Sirens are blowing somewhere. He startles back to awareness. Has he
been here all night long, holding Glory up against the seawall, her thighs
wrapped around his waist? That would not be possible. The tide hasn't
come in at all.

"What is it?" she says. Her hands are clasped around the back of his
neck. She lets go and runs them down his chest.

Still holding her up, his hands making a sling under her warm and
flawless ass, Shaftoe backs away from the seawall and turns around on
the beach, looking at the sky. He sees searchlights beginning to come
on. And it ain't no Hollywood premiere.

"It's war, baby," he says.

FORAYS

THE LOBBY OF THE MANILA HOTEL IS ABOUT THE SIZE OF A FOOT-
ball field. It smells like last year's perfume, rare tropical orchids,
and bug spray. There is a metal detector set up at the front door,
because the Prime Minister of Zimbabwe happens to be staying here for
a couple of days. Big Africans in good suits stand around the place in
clusters of two and three. Mini-throngs of Nipponese tourists, in their
Bermuda shorts, sandals and white socks, have lodged themselves in the
deep, thick, wide sofas and sit quietly, waiting for a prearranged signal.
Upper-class Filipino children brandish cylindrical potato chip canisters

like tribal chieftains carrying ceremonial maces. A dignified old bellman carrying a hand-pumped tank circulates around the defensive perimeter and silently sprays insecticide against the baseboard. Enter Randall Lawrence Waterhouse, in a turquoise polo shirt embroidered with the logo of one of the bankrupt high-tech companies that he and Avi have founded, and relaxed-fit blue jeans held up with suspenders, and bulky athletic shoes that once were white.

As soon as he got through the formalities at the airport, he perceived that the Philippines are, like Mexico, one of those countries where Shoes Matter. He approaches the registration counter quickly so that the ravishing young woman in the navy-blue uniform will not see his feet. A couple of bellhops are engaged in a pathetic, Sisyphean contest with his bag, which has roughly the dimensions and mass of a two-drawer filing cabinet. "You will not be able to find technical books there," Avi told him, "bring anything you might conceivably need."

Randy's suite is a bedroom and living room, both with fourteen-foot ceilings, and a corridor along one side containing several closets and various plumbing-related technologies. The entire thing is lined in some kind of tropical hardwood stained to a lovely glowing auburn, which would be dismal in the northern latitudes but, here, gives it a cozy and cool feeling. The two main rooms each have huge windows with tiny signs by the latch handles warning of tropical insects. Each room is defended from its windows by a multilayered system of interlocking barriers: incredibly massive wooden shutters that rumble back and forth on tracks, like freight trains maneuvering in a switching yard; a second layer of shutters consisting of two-inch squares of nacre held in a polished wooden grid, sliding on its own set of tracks; window sheers, and finally, heavy-gauge blackout curtains, each suspended from its own set of clanging industrial rails.

He orders up a large pot of coffee, which barely keeps him awake long enough to unpack. It is late afternoon. Purple clouds tumble out of the surrounding mountains with the palpable momentum of volcanic mudflows and turn half of the sky into a blank wall striped with vertical bolts of lightning; the walls of the hotel room flash with it as though paparazzi are working outside the window. Below, food vendors in Rizal Park run up and down the sidewalks to get out of the rain, which falls, as it has been doing for about half a millennium, on the sloping black walls of Intramuros. If those walls did not run in straight lines they could be mistaken for a natural freak of geology: ridges of bare, dark volcanic rock erupting from the grass like teeth from gums. The walls have dovetail-shaped notches that converge to old gun emplacements, providing interlocking fields of fire across a dry moat.

Living in the States, you never see anything older than about two and a half centuries, and you have to visit the eastern fringe of the country to see that. The business traveler's world of airports and taxicabs looks the same everywhere. Randy never really believes he's in a different country until he sees something like Intramuros, and then he has to stand there like an idiot for a long time, ruminating.

Right now, across the Pacific Ocean, in a small, tasteful Victorian town located a third of the way from San Francisco to Los Angeles, computers are seizing up, crucial files are disappearing, and e-mail is careening into intergalactic space, because Randy Waterhouse is not there to keep an eye on things. The town in question sports three small colleges: one founded by the State of California and two founded by Protestant denominations that are now actively reviled by the majority of their faculty. Taken together these colleges—the Three Siblings—comprise an academic center of middling importance. Their computer systems are linked into one. They exchange teachers and students. From time to time they host academic conferences. This part of California has beaches, mountains, redwood forests, vineyards, golf courses, and sprawling penal facilities all over the place. There are plenty of three- and four-star hotel rooms, and the Three Siblings, taken together, have enough auditoria and meeting rooms to host a conference of several thousand.

Avi's telephone call, some eighty hours ago, arrived in the middle of a major interdisciplinary conference called "The Intermediate Phase (1939–45) of the Global Hegemony Struggle of the Twentieth Century (Common Era)." This is a bit of a mouthful and so it has been given a pithy nickname: "War as Text."

People are coming from places like Amsterdam and Milan. The conference's organizing committee—which includes Randy's girlfriend, Charlene, who actually gives every indication of being his *ex*-girlfriend now—hired an artist in San Francisco to come up with a poster. He started with a black-and-white halftone photo of a haggard World War Two infantryman with a cigarette dangling from his lower lip. He worked this image over using a photocopier, blowing the halftone dots up into rough lumps, like rubber balls chewed by a dog, and wreaking any number of other distortions on it until it had an amazingly stark, striking, jagged appearance; the soldier's pale eyes turned an eerie white. Then he added a few elements in color: red lipstick, blue eyeshadow, and a trace of a red brassiere strap peeking out from the soldier's unbuttoned uniform shirt.

The poster won some kind of an award almost the moment it came out. This led to a press release, which in turn led to the poster's being enshrined by the news media as an Official Object of Controversy. An enterprising journalist managed to track down the soldier depicted in the original photograph—a decorated combat veteran and retired tool-and-die maker who, as it happened, was not merely alive but in excellent health, and, since the death of his wife from breast cancer, had spent his retirement roaming around the Deep South in his pickup truck, helping to rebuild black churches that had been torched by drunken yahoos.

The artist who had designed the poster then confessed that he had simply copied it from a book and had made no effort whatsoever to obtain permission—the entire concept of getting permission to use other people's work was faulty, since all art was derivative of other art. High-powered trial lawyers converged, like dive bombers, on the small town in Kentucky where the aggrieved veteran was up on the roof of a black church with a mouthful of nails, hammering down slabs of A/D exterior plywood and mumbling "no comment" to a horde of reporters down on the lawn. After a series of conferences in a room at the town's Holiday Inn, the veteran emerged, accompanied by one of the five most famous lawyers on the face of the planet, and announced that he was filing a civil suit against the Three Siblings that would, if it succeeded, turn them and their entire community into a flat, smoking abrasion in the earth's crust. He promised to split the proceeds between the black churches and various disabled veterans' and breast cancer research groups.

The organizing committee pulled the poster from circulation, which caused thousands of bootleg copies to go up on the World Wide Web and, in general, brought it to the attention of millions who never would have seen it otherwise. They also filed suit against the artist, whose net worth could be tallied up on the back of a ticket stub: he had assets of about a thousand dollars and debts (mostly student loans) amounting to sixty-five thousand.

All of this happened before the conference even began. Randy was aware of it only because Charlene had roped him into providing computer support for the conference, which meant setting up a Web site and e-mail access for the attendees. When all of this hit the news, e-mail began to flood in, and quickly jammed up all of the lines and filled up all of the disk capacity that Randy had spent the last month setting up.

Conferees began to arrive. A lot of them seemed to be sleeping in the house where Randy and Charlene had been living together for seven years. It was a big old Victorian house and there was plenty of room. They stumbled in from Heidelberg and Paris and Berkeley and Boston, then sat around Randy and Charlene's kitchen table drinking coffee and talking at great length about the Spectacle. Randy inferred that the Spectacle meant the poster furor, but as they went on and on about it, he sensed that they were using the word not in a conventional sense but as part of some academic jargon; that it carried a heavy load of shadings and connotations to them, none of which Randy would ever understand unless he became one of them.

To Charlene, and to all of the people attending War as Text, it was self-evident that the veteran who filed the lawsuit was the very worst kind of human being—just the sort they had gathered together to debunk, burn in effigy, and sweep into the ash-bin of posthistorical discourse. Randy had spent a lot of time around these people, and thought he'd gotten used to them, but during those days he had a headache all the time, from clenching his teeth, and he kept jumping to his feet in the middle of meals or conversations and going out for solitary walks. This was partly to keep himself from saying something undiplomatic, and partly as a childish but fruitless tactic to get the attention he craved from Charlene.

He knew the whole poster saga was going to be a disaster from early on. He kept warning Charlene and the others. They listened coolly, clinically, as if Randy were a test subject on the wrong side of a one-way mirror.

Randy forces himself to stay awake long enough for it to get dark. Then he lies in bed for a few hours trying to sleep. The container port is just north of the hotel, and all night long, Rizal Boulevard, along the base of the old Spanish wall, is jammed from one end to the other with container-carrying semis. The whole city is a cauldron of internal combustion. Manila seems to have more pistons and exhaust pipes than the rest of the world combined. Even at two in the morning the hotel's seemingly unshakable mass hums and rattles from the seismic energy pouring from all of those motors. The noise detonates car alarms down in the hotel's lot. The noise of one alarm triggers others, and so on. It is not the noise that keeps Randy awake so much as the insane stupidity of this chain reaction. It is an object lesson: the kind of nightmarish, snowballing technological fuck-up that keeps hackers awake at night even when they *can't* hear the results.

He paws open a Heineken from his minibar and stands in front of the window, looking. Many of the trucks are adorned with brilliant displays of multicolored lights—not quite as flashy as those of the few jeepneys that scurry and jostle among them. Seeing so many people awake and working puts sleep out of the question.

He is too jet-lagged to accomplish anything that requires actual thought—but there is one important job he can do, which requires no thinking whatsoever. He starts up his laptop again. Seeming to levitate in the center of his dark room, the screen is a perfect rectangle of light the color of diluted milk, of a Nordic dawn. This light originates in small fluorescent tubes imprisoned in the polycarbonate coffin of his computer's display. It can only escape through a pane of glass, facing Randy, which is entirely covered by small transistors arranged in a grid, which let photons through, or don't, or let through only those of a particular wavelength, cracking the pale light into colors. By turning those transistors on and off according to some systematic plan, meaning is conveyed to Randy Waterhouse. A good filmmaker could convey a whole story to Randy by seizing control of those transistors for a couple of hours.

Unfortunately, there are a lot more laptop computers floating around than there are filmmakers worth paying attention to. The transistors are almost never put into the hands of human beings. They are controlled, instead, by software. Randy used to be fascinated by software, but now he isn't. It's hard enough to find human beings who are interesting.

The pyramid and the eyeball appear. Randy spends so much time using Ordo now that he has his machine boot it up automatically.

Nowadays the laptop has only one function for Randy: he uses it to communicate with other people, through e-mail. When he communicates with Avi, he has to use Ordo, which is a tool for taking his ideas and converting them into streams of bits that are almost indistinguishable from white noise, so that they can be sent to Avi in privacy. In exchange, it receives noise from Avi and converts it into Avi's thoughts. At the moment, Epiphyte has no assets other than information—it is an idea, with some facts and data to back it up. This makes it eminently stealable. So encryption is definitely a good idea. The question is: how much paranoia is really appropriate?

Avi sent him encrypted e-mail:

> When you get to Manila I would like you to generate a 4096-bit key pair and keep it on a floppy disk that you carry on your person at all times. Do not keep it on your hard disk. Anyone could break into your hotel room while you're out and steal that key.

Now, Randy pulls down a menu and picks an item labeled: "New key. . . ."

A box pops up giving him several KEY LENGTH options: 768 bits, 1024, 1536, 2048, 3072, or Custom. Randy picks the latter option and then, wearily, types in 4096.

Even a 768-bit key requires vast resources to break. Add one bit, to make it 769 bits long, and it becomes twice as difficult. A 770-bit key is twice as difficult yet, and so on. By using 768-bit keys, Randy and Avi could keep their communications secret from nearly every entity in the world for at least the next several years. A 1024-bit key would be vastly, astronomically more difficult to break.

Some people go so far as to use keys 2048 or even 3072 bits in length. These will stop the very best codebreakers on the face of the earth for astronomical periods of time, barring the invention of otherworldly technologies such as quantum computers. Most encryption software— even stuff written by extremely security-conscious cryptography experts—can't even handle keys larger than that. But Avi insists on using Ordo, generally considered the best encryption software in the world, because it can handle keys of unlimited length—as long as you don't mind waiting for it to crunch all the numbers.

Randy begins typing. He is not bothering to look at the screen; he is staring out the window at the lights on the trucks and the jeepneys. He is only using one hand, just flailing away loosely at the keyboard.

Inside Randy's computer is a precise clock. Whenever he strikes a key, Ordo uses that clock to record the current time, down to microseconds. He hits a key at 03:05:56.935788 and he hits another one at 03:05:57.290664, or about .354876 seconds later. Another .372307 seconds later, he hits another one. Ordo keeps track of all of these intervals and discards the more significant digits (in this example the .35 and the .37) because these parts will tend to be similar from one event to the next.

Ordo wants randomness. It only wants the least significant digits—say, the 76 and the 07 at the very ends of these numbers. It wants a whole lot of random numbers, and it wants them to be very, very random. It is taking somewhat random numbers and feeding them through hash functions that make them even more random. It is running statistical routines on the results to make sure that they contain no hidden patterns. It has breathtakingly high standards for randomness, and it will not stop asking Randy to whack on the keyboard until those standards are met.

The longer the key you are trying to generate, the longer this takes. Randy is trying to generate one that is ridiculously long. He has pointed out to Avi, in an encrypted e-mail message, that if every particle of matter in the universe could be used to construct one single cosmic supercomputer, and this computer was put to work trying to break a 4096-bit encryption key, it would take longer than the lifespan of the universe.

"Using today's technology," Avi shot back, "that is true. But what about quantum computers? And what if new mathematical techniques are developed that can simplify the factoring of large composite numbers?"

"How long do you want these messages to remain secret?" Randy asked, in his last message before leaving San Francisco. "Five years? Ten years? Twenty-five years?"

After he got to the hotel this afternoon, Randy decrypted and read Avi's answer. It is still hanging in front of his eyes, like the afterimage of a strobe:

> I want them to remain secret for as long as men are capable
> of evil.

The computer finally beeps. Randy rests his tired hand. Ordo politely warns him that it may be busy for a while, and then goes to work. It is searching the cosmos of pure numbers, looking for two big primes that can be multiplied by each other to produce a number 4096 bits long.

If you want your secrets to remain secret past the end of your life expectancy, then, in order to choose a key length, you have to be a futurist. You have to anticipate how much faster computers will get during this time. You must also be a student of politics. Because if the entire world were to become a police state obsessed with recovering old secrets, then vast resources might be thrown at the problem of factoring large prime numbers.

So the length of the key that you use is, in and of itself, a code of sorts. A knowledgeable government eavesdropper, noting Randy's and Avi's use of a 4096-bit key, will conclude one of the following:

—Avi doesn't know what he's talking about. This can be ruled out with a bit of research into his past accomplishments. Or,

—Avi is clinically paranoid. This can also be ruled out with some research. Or,

—Avi is extremely optimistic about the future development of computer technology, or pessimistic about the political climate, or both. Or,

—Avi has a planning horizon that extends over a period of at least a century.

Randy paces around his room while his computer soars through number space. The shipping containers on the backs of those trucks bear exactly the same logos as the ones that used to fill the streets of South Seattle when a ship was unloading. To Randy this is oddly satisfying, as if, by making this crazy lunge across the Pacific, he has brought some kind of antipodal symmetry to his life. He has gone from the place where things are consumed to where they are produced, from a land where onanism has been enshrined at the highest levels of the society to one where cars have "NO to contraception!" stickers in their windows. It feels bizarrely right. He has not felt this way since Avi and he founded their first doomed business venture twelve years ago.

Randy grew up in a college town in eastern Washington State, graduated from the University of Washington in Seattle, and landed a Clerk Typist II job at the library there—specifically the Interlibrary Loan Department—where his job was to process incoming loan requests mailed in from smaller libraries all over the region and, conversely, to mail out requests to other libraries. If nine-year-old Randy Waterhouse had been able to look into the future and see himself in this career, he would have been delighted beyond measure: the primary tool of the Interlibrary Loan Department was the Staple Remover. Young Randy had seen one of these devices in the hands of his fourth-grade teacher and been enthralled by its cunning and deadly appearance, so like the jaws of some futuristic robot dragon. He had, in fact, gone out of his way to staple things incorrectly just so he could prevail on his teacher to unstaple them, giving him another glimpse of the blood-chilling mandibles in action. He had gone so far as to steal a staple remover from an untended desk at church and then incorporate it into an Erector-set robot hunter-killer device with which he terrorized much of the neighborhood; its pit-viper yawn separated many a cheap plastic toy from its parts and accessories before the theft was discovered and Randy made an example of before God and man. Now, in the Interlibrary Loan office, Randy had not just one but several staple removers in his desk drawer and was actually obligated to use them for an hour or two a day.

Since the UW library was well-endowed, its patrons didn't request books from other libraries unless they had been stolen from their own or were, in some way, peculiar. The ILL office (as Randy and his coworkers affectionately called it) had its regulars—people who had a whole lot of peculiar books on their wish lists. These people tended to be either tedious or scary or both. Randy always ended up dealing with the "both" subgroup, because Randy was the only Clerk Typist in the office who was not a lifer. It seemed clear that Randy, with his astronomy degree and his extensive knowledge of computers, would one day move on, whereas his coworkers did not harbor further ambitions. His larger sphere of interests, his somewhat broader concept of normalcy, was useful when certain patrons came into the office.

By the standards of many, Randy was himself a tedious, scary, obsessed character. He was not merely obsessed with science but also with fantasy role-playing games. The only way he could tolerate working at such a stupid job for a couple of years was that his off time was completely occupied with enacting fantasy scenarios of a depth and complexity that exercised all of the cranial circuitry that was so conspicuously going to waste in the ILL office. He was part of a group that would meet every Friday night and play until sometime on Sunday. The other stalwarts in the group were a computer science/music double major named Chester, and a history grad student named Avi.

When a new master's degree candidate named Andrew Loeb walked into the ILL office one day, with a certain glint in his eye, and produced a three-inch-thick stack of precisely typed request forms from his shitty old knapsack, he was recognized immediately as being of a particular type, and shunted in the direction of Randy Waterhouse. It was an instant meeting of minds, though Randy did not fully realize this until the books that Loeb had requested began to arrive on the trolley from the mail room.

Andy Loeb's project was to figure out the energy budgets of the local Indian tribes. A human body has to expend a certain amount of energy just to keep breathing and to maintain its body temperature. This figure goes up when it gets cold or when the body in question is doing work. The only way to obtain that energy is by eating food. Some foods have a higher energy content than others. For example, trout is highly nutritious but so low in fat and carbohydrates that you can starve to death eating it three times a day. Other foods might have lots of energy, but might require so much work to obtain and prepare that eating them would be a losing proposition, BTU-wise. Andy Loeb was trying to figure out what foods had historically been eaten by certain Northwest Indian tribes, how much energy they expended to get these foods and how much they obtained by eating them. He wanted to do this calculation for coastal Indians like the Salish (who had easy access to seafood) and for inland ones like the Cayuse (who didn't) as part of an extremely convoluted plan to prove some sort of point about the relative standards of living of these tribes and how this affected their cultural development (coastal tribes made lots of fantastically detailed art and inland ones occasionally scratched stick figures on rocks).

To Andrew Loeb it was an exercise in meta-historical scholarship. To Randy Waterhouse, it sounded like the beginnings of a pretty cool game. Strangle a muskrat and you get 136 Energy Points. Lose the muskrat and your core temp drops another degree.

Andy was nothing if not methodical and so he had simply looked up every book that had ever been written on such topics, and every book mentioned in those books' bibliographies, yea, even unto four or five generations; checked out all of them that were available locally; and ordered the rest from ILL. All of the latter passed across Randy's desk.

Randy read some and skimmed all. He got to learn about how much blubber the Arctic explorers had to eat in order to keep from starving to death. He perused detailed specifications for Army C-rations. After a while, he actually began sneaking into the photocopy room and making copies of key data.

In order to run a realistic fantasy role-playing game, you had to keep track of how much food the imaginary characters were getting and how much trouble was involved in getting it. Characters passing across the Gobi desert in November of the year 5000 B.C. would have to spend more time worrying about food than, say, ones who were traveling across central Illinois in 1950.

Randy was hardly the first game designer to notice this. There were a few incredibly stupid games in which you didn't have to think about food, but Randy and his friends disdained them. In all of the games that he participated in, or that he himself designed, you had to devote a realistic amount of effort to getting food for your character. But it was not easy to determine what was realistic. Like most designers, Randy got over the problem by slapping together a few rudimentary equations that he basically just pulled out of thin air. But in the books, articles, and dissertations that Andrew Loeb was borrowing through ILL, he found exactly the raw data that a mathematically inclined person would need to come up with a sophisticated rules system based on scientific fact.

Simulating all of the physical processes going on in each character's body was out of the question, especially in a game where you might be dealing with armies of a hundred thousand men. Even a crude simulation, tracking only a few variables and using simple equations, would involve a nightmarish amount of paperwork if you did it all by hand. But all of this was happening in the mid-1980s, when personal computers had become cheap and ubiquitous. A computer could automatically track a large database and tell you whether each character was well-fed or starving. There was no reason not to do it on a computer.

Unless, like Randy Waterhouse, you had such a shitty job that you couldn't afford a computer.

Of course, there's a way to dodge any problem. The university had lots of computers. If Randy could get an account on one of them, he could write his program there and run it for free.

Unfortunately, accounts were only available to students or faculty members, and Randy was neither.

Fortunately, he started dating a grad student named Charlene at just about this time.

How the hell did a generally keg-shaped guy, a hard scientist, working a dead-end Clerk Typist job, and spending all his spare time in the consummately nerdy pastime of fantasy role-playing games, end up in a relationship with a slender and not unattractive young liberal arts student who spent her spare time sea kayaking and going to foreign films? It must have been one of those opposites-attract kind of deals, a complementary relationship. They met, naturally, in the ILL office, where the highly intelligent but steady and soothing Randy helped the highly intelligent but scattered and flighty Charlene organize a messy heap of loan requests. He should have asked her out then and there, but he was shy. Second and third opportunities came along when the books she'd requested began to filter up from the mailroom, and finally he asked her out and they went to see a film together. Both of them turned out to be not just willing but eager, and possibly even desperate. Before they knew it, Randy had given Charlene a key to his apartment, and Charlene had given Randy the password to her free university computer account, and everything was just delightful.

The university computer system was better than no computer at all. But Randy was humiliated. Like every other high-powered academic computing network, this one was based on an industrial-strength operating system called UNIX, which had a learning curve like the Matterhorn, and lacked the cuddly and stylish features of the personal computers then coming into vogue. Randy had used it quite a bit as an undergraduate and knew his way around. Even so, learning how to write good code on the thing required a lot of time. His life had changed when Charlene had come along, and now it changed more: he dropped out of the fantasy role-playing game circuit altogether, stopped going to meetings of the Society for Creative Anachronism, and began to spend all of his free time either with Charlene or in front of a computer terminal. All in all, this was probably a change for the better. With Charlene, he did things he wouldn't have done otherwise, like getting exercise, or going to see live music. And at the computer, he was learning new skills, and he was creating something. It might be something completely useless, but at least he was creating.

He spent a lot of time talking to Andrew Loeb, who actually went out and did the stuff he was writing programs for; he'd disappear for a few days and come back all wobbly and haggard, with fish scales caught in his whiskers or dried animal blood under his fingernails. He'd ram down a couple of Big Macs, sleep for twenty-four hours, then meet Randy in a bar (Charlene wasn't comfortable with having him in the house) and talk learnedly of the difficulties of day-to-day life, aboriginal style. They argued about whether aborigines would eat the more disgusting parts of certain animals or throw them away. Andrew voted for yes. Randy disagreed—just because they were primitive didn't mean they couldn't have taste. Andrew accused him of being a romantic. Finally, to settle it, they went up into the mountains together, armed with nothing but knives and Andrew's collection of exquisitely crafted vermin snares. By the third night, Randy found himself seriously thinking about eating some insects. "Q.E.D.," Andrew said.

Anyway, Randy finished his software after a year and a half. It was a success; Chester and Avi liked it. Randy was moderately pleased at having built something so complicated that actually worked, but he had no illusions about its being good for anything. He was sort of embarrassed at having wasted so much time and mental energy on the project. But he knew that if he hadn't been writing code, he'd have spent the same amount of time playing games or going to Society for Creative Anachronism meetings in medieval drag, so it all zeroed out in the end. Spending the time in front of the computer was arguably better, because it had honed his programming skills, which had been pretty sharp to begin with. On the other hand, he'd done it all on the UNIX system, which was for scientists and engineers—not a savvy move in an age when all the money was in personal computers.

Chester and Randy had nicknamed Avi "Avid," because he really, really liked fantasy games. Avi had always claimed that he played them as a way of understanding what it was really like to live in ancient times, and he was a maniac about historical authenticity. That was okay; they all had half-assed excuses, and Avi's historical acumen frequently came in handy.

Not long after this, Avi graduated and disappeared, and popped up a few months later in Minneapolis, where he had gotten a job with a major publisher of fantasy role-playing games. He offered to buy Randy's game software for the astonishingly large sum of $1000 plus a small cut of future profits. Randy accepted the offer in its general outlines, asked Avi to send him a contract, then went out and found Andrew boiling some fish guts in a birchbark kettle atop a Weber grill on the roof of the apartment building where he lived. He wanted to give Andrew the good news, and to cut him in on the proceeds. What ensued was a really unpleasant conversation, standing up there in a pelting, spitting, wind-blown rain.

To begin with, Andrew took this deal far more seriously than Randy did. Randy saw it as a windfall, a lark. Andrew, who was the son of a lawyer, treated it as if it were a major corporate merger, and asked many tedious and niggling questions about the contract, which did not exist yet and which would probably cover a single piece of paper when it did. Randy didn't realize it at the time, but by asking so many questions for which Randy had no answers, Andrew was, in effect, arrogating to himself the role of Business Manager. He was implicitly forming a business partnership with Randy that did not, in fact, exist.

Furthermore, Andrew didn't have the first notion of how much time and effort Randy had put into writing the code. Or (as Randy was to realize later) maybe he did. In any case, Andrew assumed from the get-go that he would share a fifty-fifty split with Randy, which was wildly out of proportion to the work he'd actually done on the project. Basically, Andrew acted as if all of the work he'd ever done on the subject of aboriginal dining habits was a part of this undertaking, and that it entitled him to an equal split.

By the time Randy extricated himself from this conversation, his mind was reeling. He had gone in with one view of reality and been radically challenged by another one that was clearly preposterous; but after an hour of Andrew's browbeating he was beginning to doubt himself. After two or three sleepless nights, he decided to call the whole thing off. A paltry few hundred dollars wasn't worth all of this agony.

But Andrew (who was, by now, represented by an associate of his father's Santa Barbara law firm) vehemently objected. He and Randy had, according to his lawyer, jointly created something that had economic value, and a failure on Randy's part to sell it at market value amounted to taking money out of Andrew's pocket. It had become an unbelievable Kafkaesque nightmare, and Randy could only withdraw to a corner table at his favorite pub, drink pints of stout (frequently in the company of Chester) and watch this fantastic psychodrama unfold. He had, he now realized, blundered into some serious domestic weirdness involving Andrew's family. It turned out that Andrew's parents were divorced and, long ago, had fought savagely over custody of him, their only child. Mom had turned into a hippie and joined a religious cult in Oregon and taken Andrew with her. It was rumored that this cult engaged in sexual abuse of children. Dad had hired private dicks to kidnap Andrew back and then showered him with material possessions to demonstrate his superior love. There had followed an interminable legal battle in which Dad had hired some rather fringey psychotherapists to hypnotize Andrew and get him to dredge up repressed memories of unspeakable and improbable horrors.

This was just the executive summary of a weird life that Randy only learned about in bits and pieces as the years went on. Later, he was to decide that Andrew's life had been fractally weird. That is, you could take any small piece of it and examine it in detail and it, in and of itself, would turn out to be just as complicated and weird as the whole thing in its entirety.

Anyway Randy had blundered into this life and become enveloped in the weirdness. One of the young eager beavers in Andrew's dad's law firm decided, as a preemptive move, to obtain copies of all of Randy's computer files, which were still stored on the UW computer system. Needless to say, he went about it in a heavy-handed way, and when the university's legal department began to receive his sullen letters, it responded by informing both Andrew's lawyer, and Randy, that anyone who used the university's computer system to create a commercial product had to split the proceeds with the university. So now Randy was getting ominous letters from not one but two groups of deadly lawyers. Andrew then threatened to sue him for having made this blunder, which had halved the value of Andrew's share!

In the end, just to cut his losses and get out of it clean, Randy had to hire a lawyer of his own. The final cost to him was a hair more than five thousand dollars. The software was never sold to anyone, and indeed could not have been; it was so legally encumbered by that point that it would have been like trying to sell someone a rusty Volkswagen that had been dismantled and its parts hidden in attack dog kennels all over the world.

It was the only time in his life when he had ever thought about suicide. He did not think about it very hard, or very seriously, but he did think about it.

When it was all over, Avi sent him a handwritten letter saying, "I enjoyed doing business with you and look forward to continuing our relationship both as friends and, should opportunities arise, as creative partners."

INDIGO

LAWRENCE PRITCHARD WATERHOUSE AND THE REST OF THE band are up on the deck of the *Nevada* one morning, playing the national anthem and watching the Stars and Stripes ratchet up the mast, when they are startled to find themselves in the midst of one hundred and ninety airplanes of unfamiliar design. Some of them are down low, traveling horizontally, and others are up high, plunging nearly straight down. The latter are going so fast that they appear to be falling apart; little bits are dropping off of them. It is terrible to see— some training exercise gone miserably awry. But they pull out of their suicidal trajectories in plenty of time. The bits that have fallen off of them plunge smoothly and purposefully, not tumbling and fluttering as chunks of debris would. They are coming down all over the place. Perversely, they all seem to be headed for the berthed ships. It is incredibly dangerous—they might hit someone! Lawrence is outraged.

There is a short-lived phenomenon taking place in one of the ships down the line. Lawrence turns to look at it. This is the first real explosion he's ever seen and so it takes him a long time to recognize it as such. He can play the very hardest glockenspiel parts with his eyes closed, and *The Star Spangled Banner* is much easier to ding than to sing.

His scanning eyes fasten, not on the source of the explosion, but on a couple of airplanes that are headed right toward them, skimming just above the water. Each drops a long skinny egg and then their tailplanes visibly move and they angle upwards and pass overhead. The rising sun shines directly through the glass of their canopies. Lawrence is able to look into the eyes of the pilot of one of the planes. He notes that it appears to be some sort of Asian gentleman.

This is an incredibly realistic training exercise—even down to the point of using ethnically correct pilots, and detonating fake explosives on the ships. Lawrence heartily approves. Things have just been too lax around this place.

A tremendous shock comes up through the deck of the ship, making his feet and legs feel as if he had just jumped off a ten-foot precipice onto solid concrete. But he's just standing there flatfooted. It makes no sense at all.

The band have finished playing the national anthem and are looking about at the spectacle. Sirens and horns are speaking up all over the place, from the *Nevada,* from the *Arizona* in the next berth, from buildings onshore. Lawrence doesn't see any antiaircraft fire going up, doesn't see any familiar planes in the air. The explosions just keep coming. Lawrence wanders over to the rail and stares across a few yards of open water towards the *Arizona.*

Another one of those plunging airplanes drops a projectile that shoots straight down onto *Arizona*'s deck but then, strangely, vanishes. Lawrence blinks and sees that it has left a neat bomb-shaped hole in the deck, just like a panicky Warner Brothers cartoon character passing at high speed through a planar structure such as a wall or ceiling. Fire jets from that hole for about a microsecond before the whole deck bulges up, disintegrating, and turns into a burgeoning globe of fire and blackness. Waterhouse is vaguely aware of a lot of stuff coming at him really fast. It is so big that he feels more like he is falling into it. He freezes up. It goes by him, over him, and through him. A terrible noise pierces his skull, a chord randomly struck, discordant but not without some kind of deranged harmony. Musical qualities aside, it is so goddamned loud that it almost kills him. He claps his hands over his ears.

Still the noise is there, like red-hot knitting needles through the eardrums. Hell's Bells. He spins away from it, but it follows him. He has this big thick strap around his neck, sewn together at groin level where it supports a cup. Thrust into the cup is the central support of his glockenspiel, which stands in front of him like a lyre-shaped breastplate, huge fluffy tassels dangling gaily from the upper corners. Oddly, one of the tassels is burning. That isn't the only thing now wrong with the glockenspiel, but he can't quite make it out because his vision keeps getting obscured by something that must be wiped away every few moments. All he knows is that the glockenspiel has eaten a huge quantum of pure energy and been kicked up to some incredibly high state never before achieved by such an instrument; it is a burning, glowing, shrieking, ringing, radiating monster, a comet, an archangel, a tree of flaming magnesium, strapped to his body, standing on his groin. The energy is transmitted down its humming, buzzing central axis, through the cup, and into his genitals, which would be tumescing in other circumstances.

Lawrence spends some time wandering aimlessly around the deck. Eventually he has to help open a hatch for some men, and then he realizes that his hands are still clapped over his ears, and have been for a long time except for when he was wiping stuff out of his eyes. When he takes them off, the ringing has stopped, and he no longer hears airplanes. He was thinking that he wanted to go belowdecks, because the bad things are coming from the sky and he would like to get some big heavy permanent-seeming stuff between him and it, but a lot of sailors are taking the opposite view. He hears that they have been hit by one and maybe two of something that rhymes with "torpedoes," and that they are trying to raise steam. Officers and noncoms, black and red with smoke and blood, keep deputizing him for different, extremely urgent tasks that he doesn't quite understand, not least because he keeps putting his hands over his ears.

Probably half an hour goes by before he hits upon the idea of discarding his glockenspiel, which is, after all, just getting in the way. It was issued to him by the Navy with any number of stern warnings about the consequences of misusing it. Lawrence is conscientious about this kind of thing, dating back to when he was first given organ-playing privileges in West Point, Virginia. But at this point, for the first time in his life, as he stands there watching the *Arizona* burn and sink, he just says to himself: Well, to heck with it! He takes that glockenspiel out of its socket and has one last look at it, it is the last time in his life he will ever touch a glockenspiel. There is no point in saving it now anyway, he realizes; several of the bars have been bent. He flips it around and discovers that chunks of blackened, distorted metal have been impact-welded onto several of the bars. Really throwing caution to the winds now, he flings it overboard in the general direction of the *Arizona*, a military lyre of burnished steel that sings a thousand men to their resting places on the bottom of the harbor.

As it vanishes into a patch of burning oil, the second wave of attacking airplanes arrives. The Navy's antiaircraft guns finally open up and begin to rain shells down into the surrounding community and blow up occupied buildings. He can see human-shaped flames running around in the streets, pursued by people with blankets.

The rest of the day is spent, by Lawrence Pritchard Waterhouse and the rest of the Navy, grappling with the fact that many two-dimensional structures on this and other ships, which were put into place to prevent various fluids from commingling (e.g. fuel and air) have holes in them, and not only that but a lot of shit is on fire too and things are more than a little smoky. Certain objects that are supposed to (a) remain horizontal and (b) support heavy things have ceased to do either.

Nevada's engineering section manages to raise steam in a couple of boilers and the captain tries to get the ship out of the harbor. As soon as she gets underway, she comes under concerted attack, mostly by dive bombers who are eager to sink her in the channel and block the harbor altogether. Eventually, the captain runs her aground rather than see this happen. Unfortunately, what *Nevada* has in common with most other naval vessels is that she is not really engineered to work from a stationary position, and consequently she is hit three more times by dive bombers. So it is a pretty exciting morning overall. As a member of the band who does not even have his instrument any more, Lawrence's duties are quite poorly defined, and he spends more time than he should watching the airplanes and the explosions. He has gone back to his earlier train of thought regarding societies and their efforts to outdo each other. It is very clear to him, as wave after wave of Nipponese dive bombers hurl themselves, with calligraphic precision, at the ship he is standing on, and as the cream of his society's navy burns and explodes and sinks, putting up virtually no resistance, that his society is going to have to rethink a thing or two.

At some point he burns his hand on something. It is his right hand, which is preferable—he is left-handed. Also, he becomes more clearly aware that a portion of *Arizona* has tried to take his scalp off. These are minor injuries by Pearl Harbor standards and he does not stay long in the hospital. The doctor warns him that the skin on his hand might contract and limit his fingers' range of motion. As soon as he can withstand the pain, Lawrence begins to play Bach's *Art of Fugue* in his lap whenever he is not otherwise occupied. Most of those tunes start out simple; you can easily picture old Johann Sebastian sitting there on the bench on a cold morning in Leipzig, one or two blockflöte stops yanked out, left hand in his lap, a fat choirboy or two over in the corner heaving away on the bellows, faint gasping noises coming from all the leaks in the works, and Johann's right hand wandering aimlessly across the forbidding simplicity of the Great manual, stroking those cracked and yellowed elephant tusks, searching for some melody he hadn't already invented. That is good stuff for Lawrence right now, and so he makes his right hand go through the same motions as Johann's, even though it is a gauze-wrapped hand and he is using an upside-down dinner tray as a substitute for the keyboard, and he has to hum the music under his breath. When he really gets into it, his feet skid around and piston under the sheets, playing imaginary pedals, and his neighbors complain.

He is out of the hospital in a few days, just in time for him and the rest of *Nevada*'s band to begin their new, wartime assignment. This was evidently something of a poser for the Navy's manpower experts. These musicians were (from a killing-Nips point of view) completely useless to begin with. As of 7 December, they no longer have even a functioning ship and most of them have lost their clarinets.

Still, it isn't all about loading shells and pulling triggers. No large organization can kill Nips in any kind of systematic way without doing a nearly unbelievable amount of typing and filing. It is logical to suppose that men who can play the clarinet will not botch that kind of work any worse than anyone else. And so Waterhouse and his bandmates receive orders assigning them to what would appear to be one of the typing-and-filing branches of the Navy.

This is located in a building, not a ship. There are quite a few Navy people who sneer at the whole idea of working in a building, and Lawrence and some of the other recent recruits, eager to fit in, have gotten into the habit of copping the same attitude. But now that they have seen what happens to a ship when you detonate hundreds of pounds of high explosive on, in, and around it, Waterhouse and many others are reassessing their feelings about working in buildings. They report to their new post with high morale.

Their new commanding officer is not so cheerful, and his feelings appear to be shared by everyone in the entire section. The musicians are greeted without being welcomed and saluted without being honored. The people who have been working in this building—far from being overawed by their status as guys who not only worked on an actual ship until recently but *furthermore* have been very close to things that were exploding, burning, etc., and not as the result of routine lapses in judgment but because bad men deliberately made it happen—do not seem to feel that Lawrence and his bandmates *deserve* to be entrusted with this new work, whatever the hell it is.

Glumly, almost despairingly, the commanding officer and his subordinates get the musicians squared away. Even if they don't have enough desks to go around, each man can at least have a chair at a table or counter. Some ingenuity is displayed in finding places for all the new arrivals. It is clear that these people are trying their best at what they considered to be a hopeless task.

Then there is some talk about secrecy. A *great deal* of talk about it. They run through drills intended to test their ability to *throw things away* properly. This goes on for a *long* time and the longer it continues, without an explanation as to why, the more mysterious it becomes. The musicians, who were at first a little put out by their chilly reception, start to speculate amongst themselves as to what kind of an operation they have gotten themselves into now.

Finally, one morning, the musicians are assembled in a classroom in front of the cleanest chalkboard Waterhouse has ever seen. The last few days have imbued him with just enough paranoia that he suspects it is that clean for a reason—erasing chalkboards is not to be taken lightly during wartime.

They are seated in little chairs with desks attached to them, desks designed for right-handers. Lawrence puts his notepad in his lap, then rests his bandaged right hand on the desk and begins to play a ditty from *Art of Fugue,* grimacing and even grunting with pain as his burned skin stretches and slides over his knuckles.

Someone chucks him on the shoulder. He opens his eyes to see that he is the only person in the room sitting down; an officer is on the deck. He stands up and his weak leg nearly buckles. When he finally gets himself fully to his feet, he sees that the officer (if he even *is* an officer) is out of uniform. *Way* out of uniform. He's wearing a bathrobe and smoking a pipe. The bathrobe is extraordinarily worn, and not in the sense of, say, a hospital or hotel bathrobe that gets laundered frequently. This thing hasn't been laundered in a long time, but boy has it seen some *use*. The *elbows* are worn out and the bottom of the right sleeve is ashy grey and slippery with graphite from being dragged back and forth, tens of thousands of times, across sheets of paper dense with number-two pencil work. The terrycloth has a dandruffy appearance, but it has nothing to do with exfoliation of the scalp; these flakes are way too big, and too geometric: rectangles and circular dots of oaktag, punched out of cards and tape respectively. The pipe went out a long time ago and the officer (or whatever he is) is not even pretending to worry about getting it relit. It is there just to give him something to bite down on, which he does as vigorously as a civil war infantryman having a leg sawed off.

Some other fellow—one who actually bothered to shave, shower, and put on a uniform—introduces bathrobe man as Commander Shane-spelled-s-c-h-o-e-n, but Schoen is having none of it; he turns his back on them, exposing the back side of his bathrobe, which around the buttocks is worn transparent as a negligee. Reading from a notebook, he writes out the following in block letters:

$$19 \ 17 \ 17 \ 19 \ 14 \quad 20 \ 23 \ 18 \ 19 \ 8 \quad 12 \ 16 \ 19 \ 8 \ 3$$
$$21 \ 8 \ 25 \ 18 \ 14 \quad 18 \ 6 \ 3 \ 18 \ 8 \quad 15 \ 18 \ 22 \ 18 \ 11$$

Around the time that the fourth or fifth number is going up on the chalkboard, Waterhouse feels the hairs standing up on the back of his neck. By the time the third group of five numbers is written out, he has not failed to notice that none of them is larger than 26—that being the number of letters in the alphabet. His heart is pounding more wildly than it did when Nipponese bombs were tracing parabolic trajectories toward the deck of the grounded *Nevada*. He pulls a pencil out of his pocket. Finding no paper handy, he writes down the numbers from 1 to 26 on the surface of his little writing desk.

By the time the man in the bathrobe is done writing out the last group of numbers, Waterhouse is already well into his frequency count. He wraps it up as Bathrobe Man is saying something along the lines of "this might look like a meaningless sequence of numbers to you, but to a Nip naval officer it might look like something entirely different." Then the man laughs nervously, shakes his head sadly, squares his jaw resolutely, and runs through a litany of other emotion-laden expressions not a single one of which is appropriate here.

Waterhouse's frequency count is simply a tally of how frequently each number appears on the blackboard. It looks like this:

1		7	
2		8	| | | |
3	| |	9	
4		10	
5		11	|
6	|	12	|

13		20	|
14	| |	21	|
15	|	22	|
16	|	23	|
17	| |	24	
18	| | | | | |	25	|
19	| | | |	26	

The most interesting thing about this is that ten of the possible symbols (viz. 1, 2, 4, 5, 7, 9, 10, 13, 24, and 26) are not even used. Only sixteen different numbers appear in the message. Assuming each of those sixteen represents one and only one letter of the alphabet, this message has (Lawrence reckons in his head) 111136315345735680000 possible meanings. This is a funny number because it begins with four ones and ends with four zeroes; Lawrence snickers, wipes his nose, and gets on with it.

The most common number is 18. It probably represents the letter E. If he substitutes E into the message everywhere he sees an 18, then—

Well, to be honest, then he'll have to write out the whole message again, substituting Es for 18s, and it will take a long time, and it might be time wasted because he might have guessed wrong. On the other hand, if he just *restrains* his mind to *construe* 18s as Es—an operation that he thinks of as being loosely analogous to changing the presets on a pipe organ's console—then what he sees in his mind's eye when he looks at the blackboard is

$$19\ 17\ 17\ 19\ 14 \quad 20\ 23\ E\ 19\ 8 \quad 12\ 16\ 19\ 8\ 3$$
$$21\ 8\ 25\ E\ 14 \quad E\ 6\ 3\ E\ 8 \quad 15\ E\ 22\ E\ 11$$

which only has 10103301395066880000 possible meanings. This is a funny number too because of all those ones and zeroes—but it is an absolutely meaningless coincidence.

"The science of making secret codes is called cryptography," Commander Schoen says, "and the science of breaking them is cryptanalysis." Then he sighs, grapples visibly with some more widely divergent emotional states, and resignedly plods into the mandatory exercise of breaking these words down into their roots, which are either Latin or Greek (Lawrence isn't paying attention, doesn't care, only glimpses the stark word CRYPTO written in handsized capitals).

The opening sequence "19 17 17 19" is peculiar. 19, along with 8, is the second most common number in the list. 17 is only half as common. You can't have four vowels or four consonants in a row (unless the words are German) so either 17 is a vowel and 19 a consonant or the other way round. Since 19 appears more frequently (four times) in the message, it is more likely to be the vowel than 17 (which only appears twice). A is the most common vowel after E, so if he assumes that 19 is A, he gets

```
A 17 17  A 14     20 23  E  A  8     12 16  A  8  3
21  8 25  E 14      E  6  3  E  8     15  E 22  E 11
```

This narrows it down quite a bit, to a mere 841941782922240000 possible answers. He's already reduced the solution space by a couple of orders of magnitude!

Schoen has talked himself up into a disturbingly heavy sweat, now, and is almost bodily flinging himself into a historical overview of the science of CRYPTOLOGY, as the union of cryptography and cryptanalysis is called. There's some talk about an English fellow name of Wilkins, and book called *Cryptonomicon* that he wrote hundreds of years ago, but (perhaps because he doesn't rate the intelligence of his audience too highly) he goes very easy on the historical background, and jumps directly from Wilkins to Paul Revere's "one if by land, two if by sea" code. He even makes a mathematics in-joke about this being one of the earliest practical applications of binary notation. Lawrence dutifully brays and snorts, drawing an appalled look from the saxophonist seated in front of him.

Earlier in his talk, the Schoen mentioned that this message was (in what's obviously a fictional scenario ginned up to make this mathematical exercise more interesting to a bunch of musicians who are assumed not to give a shit about math) addressed to a Nip naval officer. Given that context, Lawrence cannot but guess that the first word of the message is ATTACK. This would mean that 17 represented T, 14 C, and 20 K. When he fills these in, he gets

```
A  T  T  T  A  C     K 23  E  A  8     12 16  A  8  3
21  8 25  E  C        E  6  3  E  8     15  E 22  E 11
```

and then the rest is so obvious he doesn't bother to write it out. He cannot restrain himself from jumping to his feet. He's so excited he forgets about the weak legs and topples over across a couple of his neighbors' desks, which makes a lot of noise.

"Do you have a problem, sailor?" says one of the officers in the corner, one who actually bothered to wear a uniform.

"Sir! The message is, 'Attack Pearl Harbor December Seven!' Sir!" Lawrence shouts, and then sits down. His whole body is quivering with excitement. Adrenalin has taken over his body and mind. He could strangle twenty sumo wrestlers on the spot.

Commander Schoen is completely impassive except that he blinks once, very slowly. He turns to one of his subordinates, who is standing against the wall with his hands clasped behind his back, and says, "Get this one a copy of the *Cryptonomicon*. And a desk—as close to the coffee machine as possible. And why don't you promote the son of a bitch as long as you're at it."

The part about the promotion turns out to be either military humor or further evidence of Commander Schoen's mental instability. Other than that small bit of drollery, the story of Waterhouse past this point, for the next ten months, is not much more complicated than the story of a bomb that has just been released from the belly of a plunging airplane. The barriers placed in his path (working his way through the *Cryptonomicon*, breaking the Nipponese Air Force Meteorological Code, breaking the Coral naval attache machine cipher, breaking Unnamed Nipponese Army Water Transport Code 3A, breaking the Greater East Asia Ministry Code) present about as much resistance as successive decks of a worm-eaten wooden frigate. Within a couple of months he is actually writing *new* chapters of the *Cryptonomicon*. People speak of it as though it were a book, but it's not. It is basically a compilation of all of the papers and notes that have drifted up in a particular corner of Commander Schoen's office over the roughly two-year period that he's been situated at Station Hypo, as this place is called.* It is everything that Commander Schoen knows about breaking codes, which amounts to everything that the United States of America knows. At any moment it could have been annihilated if a janitor had stepped into the room for a few minutes and tidied the place up. Understanding this, Commander Schoen's colleagues in the officers' ranks of Station Hypo have devised strenuous measures to prevent any type of tidying or hygienic operations, of any description, in the entire wing of the building that contains Commander Schoen's office. They know enough, in other words, to understand that the *Cryptonomicon* is terribly important, and they have the wit to take the measures necessary to keep it safe. Some of them actually consult it from time to time, and use its wisdom to break Nipponese messages, or even solve whole cryptosystems. But Waterhouse is the first guy to come along who is good enough to (at first) point out errors in what Schoen has written,

---

*"Hypo" is a military way of saying the letter H. Bright boy Waterhouse infers that there must be at least seven others: Alpha, Bravo, Charlie, etc.

and (soon) assemble the contents of the pile into something like an orderly work, and (eventually) add original material onto it.

At some point Schoen takes him downstairs and leads him to the end of a long windowless corridor to a slab of a door guarded by hulking Myrmidons and lets him see the second coolest thing they've got at Pearl Harbor, a roomful of machinery from the Electrical Till Corporation that they use mainly for doing frequency counts on Nip intercepts.

The most remarkable machine* at Station Hypo, however—and the first coolest thing in Pearl Harbor—is even deeper in the cloaca of the building. It is contained in something that might be likened to a bank vault if it weren't all wired up with explosives so that its contents can be vaporized in the event of a total Nip invasion.

This is the machine that Commander Schoen made, more than a year ago, for breaking the Nipponese cipher called Indigo. Apparently, as of the beginning of 1940, Schoen was a well-adjusted and mentally healthy young man into whose lap was dumped some great big long lists of numbers compiled from intercept stations around the Pacific (perhaps, Waterhouse thinks, Alpha, Bravo, etc.). These numbers were Nipponese messages that had been encrypted somehow—circumstantial evidence suggested that it had been done by some kind of machine. But absolutely nothing was known *about* the machine: whether it used gears or rotary switches or plugboards, or some combination thereof, or some other kind of mechanism that hadn't even been thought of by white people yet; how *many* such mechanisms it did or didn't use; specific details of *how* it used them. All that could be said was that these numbers, which seemed completely random, had been transmitted, perhaps even incorrectly. Other than that, Schoen had nothing—*nothing*—to work on.

As of the middle of 1941, then, this machine existed in this vault, here at Station Hypo. It existed because Schoen had built it. The machine perfectly decrypted every Indigo message that the intercept stations picked up, and was, therefore, necessarily an exact functional duplication of the Nipponese Indigo code machine, though neither Schoen nor any other American had ever laid eyes on one. Schoen had built the thing simply by looking at those great big long lists of essentially random numbers, and using some process of induction to figure it out. Somewhere along the line he had become totally debilitated psychologically, and begun to suffer nervous breakdowns at the rate of about one every week or two.

As of the actual outbreak of war with Nippon, Schoen is on disability, and taking lots of drugs. Waterhouse spends as much time with Schoen

---

*Assuming, provisionally, that Alan is wrong and that human brains are not machines.

as he is allowed to, because he's pretty sure that whatever happened inside of Schoen's head, between when the lists of apparently random numbers were dumped into his lap and when he finished building his machine, is an example of a noncomputable process.

Waterhouse's security clearance is upgraded about once a month, until it reaches the highest conceivable level (or so he thinks) which is Ultra/Magic. Ultra is what the Brits call the intelligence they get from having broken the German Enigma machine. Magic is what the Yanks call the intelligence they get from Indigo. In any case, Lawrence now gets to see the Ultra/Magic summaries, which are bound documents with dramatic, alternating red and black paragraphs printed on the front cover. Paragraph number three states:

NO ACTION IS TO BE TAKEN ON INFORMATION HEREIN REPORTED, REGARDLESS OF TEMPORARY ADVANTAGE, IF SUCH ACTION MIGHT HAVE THE EFFECT OF REVEALING THE EXISTENCE OF THE SOURCE TO THE ENEMY.

Seems clear enough, right? But Lawrence Pritchard Waterhouse is not so damn sure.

. . . IF SUCH ACTION MIGHT HAVE THE EFFECT OF REVEALING . . .

At about the same time, Waterhouse has made a realization about himself. He has found that he works best when he is not horny, which is to say in the day or so following ejaculation. So as a part of his duty to the United States he has begun to spend a lot of time in whorehouses. But he can't have that much actual sex on what is still a glockenspiel player's pay and so he limits himself to what are euphemistically called massages.

. . . ACTION . . . EFFECT . . . REVEALING . . .

The words stay with him like the clap. He lies on his back during these massages, arms crossed over his eyes, mumbling the words to himself. Something bothers him. He has learned that when something bothers him in this particular way it usually leads to his writing a new paper. But first he has to do a lot of hard mental pick-and-shovel work.

It all comes to him, explosively, during the Battle of Midway, while he and his comrades are spending twenty-four hours a day down among those ETC machines, decrypting Yamamoto's messages, telling Nimitz exactly where to find the Nip fleet.

What are the chances of Nimitz finding that fleet by accident? That's what Yamamoto must be asking himself.

It is all a question (oddly enough!) of information theory.

. . . ACTION . . .

What is an action? It might be anything. It might be something obvious like bombing a Nipponese military installation. Everyone would agree that this would constitute an action. But it might also be something like changing the course of an aircraft carrier by five degrees—or *not* doing so. Or having exactly the right package of forces off Midway to hammer the Nipponese invasion fleet. It could mean something much less dramatic, like canceling plans for an action. An action, in a certain sense, might even be the total absence of activity. Any of these might be rational responses, on the part of some commander, to INFORMATION HEREIN REPORTED. But any of them might be observable by the Nipponese—and hence any of them would impart information to the Nipponese. How good might those Nips be at abstracting information from a noisy channel? Do they have any Schoens?

. . . EFFECT . . .

So what if the Nips did observe it? What would the *effect* be exactly? And under what circumstances might the effect be REVEALING THE EXISTENCE OF THE SOURCE TO THE ENEMY?

If the action is one that could never have happened unless the Americans were breaking Indigo, then it will constitute proof, to the Nipponese, that the Americans have broken it. The existence of the source—the machine that Commander Schoen built—will be revealed.

Waterhouse trusts that no Americans will be that stupid. But what if it isn't that clear-cut? What if the action is one that would merely be *really improbable* unless the Americans were breaking the code? What if the Americans, in the long run, are just too damn lucky?

And how closely can you play that game? A pair of loaded dice that comes up sevens every time is detected in a few throws. A pair that comes up sevens only one percent more frequently than a straight pair is harder to detect—you have to throw the dice many more times in order for your opponent to prove anything.

If the Nips keep getting ambushed—if they keep finding their own ambushes spoiled—if their merchant ships happen to cross paths with American subs more often than pure probability would suggest—how long until they figure it out?

Waterhouse writes papers on the subject, keeps pestering people with them. Then, one day, Waterhouse receives a new set of orders.

The orders arrive encrypted into groups of five random-looking letters, printed out on the blue tissue paper that is used for top-secret cablegrams. The message has been encrypted in Washington using a one-time pad, which is a slow and awkward but, in theory, perfectly unbreakable cipher used for the most important messages. Waterhouse knows this because he is one of the only two persons in Pearl Harbor who has clearance to decrypt it. The other one is Commander Schoen, and he is under sedation today. The duty officer opens up the appropriate safe and gives him the one-time pad for the day, which is basically a piece of graph paper covered with numbers printed in groups of five. The numbers have been chosen by secretaries in a basement in Washington by shuffling cards or drawing chits out of a hat. They are pure noise. One copy of the pure noise is in Waterhouse's hands, and the other copy is used by the person who encrypted this message in Washington.

Waterhouse sits down and gets to work, subtracting noise from ciphertext to produce plaintext.

The first thing he sees is that this message's classification is not merely Top Secret, or even Ultra, but something entirely new: ULTRA MEGA.

The messages states that after thoroughly destroying this message, he—Lawrence Pritchard Waterhouse—is to proceed to London, England, by the fastest available means. All ships, trains, and airplanes, even submarines, will be made available to him. Though a member of the U.S. Navy, he is even to be provided with an extra uniform—an Army uniform—in case it simplifies matters for him.

The one thing he must never, ever do is place himself in a situation where he could be captured by the enemy. In this sense, the war is suddenly over for Lawrence Pritchard Waterhouse.

THE SPAWN OF ONAN

A NETWORK OF CHUNNEL-SIZED AIR DUCTS AS VAST AND UN-fathomable as the global Internet ramifies through the thick walls and ceilings of the hotel and makes dim, attenuated noises that suggest that hidden deep within that system are jet engine proving grounds, Iron Age smithys, wretched prisoners draped with clanging chains, and writhing clumps of snakes. Randy knows that the system is not a closed loop—that it is somewhere connected to the earth's atmosphere—because faint street smells drift in from outside. For all he knows, they may take an hour to work their way into his room. After he has been living there for a couple of weeks, the smells come to function as an olfactory alarm clock. He sleeps to the smell of diesel exhaust because the traffic conditions of Manila require that the container ships load and unload only at night. Manila sprawls along a warm and placid bay that is an infinite reservoir of mugginess, and because the atmosphere is as thick and opaque and hot as a glass of milk straight from the cow's udder, it begins to glow when the sun rises. At this, Manila's regiments and divisions of fighting cocks, imprisoned in makeshift hutches on every rooftop, balcony and yard, begin to crow. The people come awake and begin to burn coal. Coal smoke is the smell that wakes Randy up.

Randy Waterhouse is in merely decent physical condition. His doctor ritualistically tells him that he could lose twenty pounds, but it's not obvious where that twenty pounds would actually come from—he has no beer gut, no flagrant love handles. The offending pounds seem to be spread evenly over his keglike torso. Or so he tells himself every morning, standing in front of the billboard-sized mirror of his suite. Randy and Charlene's house in California contains practically no mirrors and he had lost track of what he looks like. Now he sees that he has become atavistically hairy, and his beard glints, because it is shot through with grey hairs.

Every day, he dares himself to shave that beard off. In the tropics, you want to have as much skin as possible exposed to the air, with sweat sheeting down it.

One evening when Avi and his family had been over for dinner, Randy had said, "I'm the beard, Avi's the suit," as a way of explaining their business relationship, and from that point Charlene had been off and running. Charlene has recently finished a scholarly article, deconstructing beards. In particular, she was aiming at beard culture in the Northern California high-tech community—Randy's crowd. Her paper began by demolishing, somehow, the assumption that beards were more "natural" or easier to maintain than clean-shavenness—she actually published statistics from Gillette's research department comparing the amount of time that bearded and beardless men spent in the bathroom each day, proving that the difference was not statistically significant. Randy had any number of objections to the way in which these statistics were gathered, but Charlene was having none of it. "It is counterintuitive," she said.

She was in a big hurry to move on to the meat of her argument. She went up to San Francisco and bought a few hundred dollars' worth of pornography at a boîte that catered to shaving fetishists. For a couple of weeks, Randy couldn't come home in the evening without finding Charlene sacked out in front of the TV with a bowl of popcorn and a Dictaphone, watching a video of a straight razor being drawn along wet, soapy flesh. She taped a few lengthy interviews with some actual shaving fetishists who described in great detail the feeling of nakedness and vulnerability shaving gave them, and how erotic that was, especially when freshly shaved areas were slapped or spanked. She worked up a detailed comparison of the iconography of shaving-fetishist porn and that of shaving-product commercials shown on national TV during football games, and proved that they were basically indistinguishable (you could actually buy videotapes of bootleg shaving-cream and razor ads in the same places that sold the out-and-out pornography).

She pulled down statistics on racial variation in beard growth. American Indians didn't grow beards, Asians hardly did, Africans were a special case because daily shaving gave them a painful skin condition. "The ability to grow heavy, full beards as a matter of choice appears to be a privilege accorded by nature solely to white males," she wrote.

Alarm bells, red lights, and screaming klaxons went off in Randy's mind when he happened across that phrase.

"But this assertion buys into a specious subsumption. 'Nature' is a socially constructed discourse, not an objective reality [many footnotes here]. That is doubly true in the case of the 'nature' that accords full beards to the specific minority population of northern European males. *Homo sapiens* evolved in climatic zones where facial hair was of little practical use. The development of an offshoot of the species characterized by densely bearded males is an adaptive response to cold climates. These climates did not 'naturally' invade the habitats of early humans—rather, the humans invaded geographical regions where such climates prevailed. This geographical transgression was strictly a sociocultural event and so all physical adaptations to it must be placed in the same category— including the development of dense facial hair."

Charlene published the results of a survey she had organized, in which a few hundred women were asked for their opinions. Essentially all of them said that they preferred clean-shaven men to those who were either stubbly or bearded. In short order, Charlene proved that having a beard was just one element of a syndrome strongly correlated to racist and sexist attitudes, and to the pattern of emotional unavailability so often bemoaned by the female partners of white males, especially ones who were technologically oriented.

"The boundary between Self and Environment is a social con[struct]. In Western cultures this boundary is supposed to be sharp and distinct. The beard is an outward symbol of that boundary, a distancing technique. To shave off the beard (or any body hair) is to symbolically annihilate the (essentially specious) boundary separating Self from Other . . ."

And so on. The paper was rapturously received by the peer reviewers and immediately accepted for publication in a major international journal. Charlene is presenting some related work at the War as Text conference: "Unshavenness as signifier in World War II Movies." On the strength of her beard work, three different Ivy League schools are fighting over who will get to hire her.

Randy does not want to move to the East Coast. Worse yet, he has a full beard, which makes him feel dreadfully incorrect whenever he ventures out with her. He proposed to Charlene that perhaps he should issue a press release stating that he shaves the rest of his body every day. She did not think it was very funny. He realized, when he was halfway over the Pacific Ocean, that all of her work was basically an elaborate prophecy of the doom of their relationship.

Now he is thinking of shaving his beard off. He might do his scalp and his upper body, while he's at it.

He is in the habit of doing a lot of vigorous walking. By the standards of the body nazis who infest California and Seattle, this is only a marginal improvement over (say) sitting in front of a television chain-smoking unfiltered cigarettes and eating suet from a tub. But he has stuck to his walking doggedly while his friends have taken up fitness fads and dropped them. It has become a point of pride with him, and he's not about to stop just because he is living in Manila.

But damn, it's hot. Hairlessness would be a good thing here.

Only two good things came out of Randy's ill-fated First Business Foray with the food-gathering software. First, it scared him away from trying to do any kind of business, at least until he had the foggiest idea of what he was getting into. Second, he developed a lasting friendship with Avi, his old gaming buddy, now in Minneapolis, who displayed integrity and a good sense of humor.

At the suggestion of his lawyer (who by that point was one of his major creditors), Randy declared personal bankruptcy and then moved to central California with Charlene. She had gotten her Ph.D. and landed a teaching-assistant job at one of the Three Siblings. Randy enrolled at another Sibling with the aim of getting his master's degree in astronomy. This made him a grad student, and grad students existed not to learn things but to relieve the tenured faculty members of tiresome burdens such as educating people and doing research.

Within a month of his arrival, Randy solved some trivial computer problems for one of the other grad students. A week later, the chairman of the astronomy department called him over and said, "So, you're the UNIX guru." At the time, Randy was still stupid enough to be flattered by this attention, when he should have recognized them as bone-chilling words.

Three years later, he left the Astronomy Department without a degree, and with nothing to show for his labors except six hundred dollars in his bank account and a staggeringly comprehensive knowledge of UNIX. Later, he was to calculate that, at the going rates for programmers, the department had extracted about a quarter of a million dollars' worth of work from him, in return for an outlay of less than twenty thousand. The only compensation was that his knowledge didn't seem so useless anymore. Astronomy had become a highly networked discipline, and you could now control a telescope on another continent, or in orbit, by typing commands into your keyboard, watching the images it produced on your monitor.

Randy was now superbly knowledgeable when it came to networks. Years ago, this would have been of limited usefulness. But this was the age of networked applications, the dawn of the World Wide Web, and the timing couldn't have been better.

In the meantime, Avi had moved to San Francisco and started a new company that was going to take role-playing games out of the nerd-ghetto and make them mainstream. Randy signed on as the head technologist. He tried to recruit Chester, but he'd already taken a job with a software company back up in Seattle. So they brought in a guy who had worked for a few video game companies, and later they brought in some other guys to do hardware and communications, and they raised enough seed money to build a playable prototype. Using that as their dog-and-pony show, they went down to Hollywood and found someone to back them to the tune of ten million dollars. They rented out some industrial space in Gilroy, filled it full of graphics workstations, hired a lot of sharp programmers and a few artists, and went to work.

Six months later, they were frequently mentioned as among Silicon Valley's rising stars, and Randy got a little photograph in *Time* magazine in an article about Siliwood—the growing collaboration between Silicon Valley and Hollywood. A year after that, the entire enterprise had crashed and burned.

This was an epic tale not worth telling. The conventional wisdom circa the early nineties had been that the technical wizards of Northern California would meet the creative minds of Southern California halfway and create a brilliant new collaboration. But this was rooted in a naive view of what Hollywood was all about. Hollywood was merely a specialized bank—a consortium of large financial entities that hired talent, almost always for a flat rate, ordered that talent to create a product, and then marketed that product to death, all over the world, in every conceivable medium. The goal was to find products that would keep on making money forever, long after the talent had been paid off and sent packing. *Casablanca,* for example, was still putting asses in seats decades after Bogart had been paid off and smoked himself into an early grave.

In the view of Hollywood, the techies of Silicon Valley were just a particularly naive form of talent. So when the technology reached a certain point—the point where it could be marketed to a certain large

Nipponese electronics company at a substantial profit—the backers of
Avi's company staged a lightning coup that had obviously been lovingly
planned. Randy and the others were given a choice: they could leave
the company now and hold on to some of their stock, which was still
worth a decent amount of money. Or they could stay—in which case
they would find themselves sabotaged from within by fifth columnists
who had been infiltrated into key positions. At the same time they would
be besieged from without by lawyers demanding their heads for the
things that were suddenly going wrong.

Some of the founders stayed on as court eunuchs. Most of them left
the company, and of that group, most sold their stock immediately because they could see it was going nowhere but down. The company was
gutted by the transfer of its technology to Japan, and the empty husk
eventually dried up and blew away.

Even today, bits and pieces of the technology keep popping up in the
oddest places, such as advertisements for new video game platforms. It
always gives Randy the creeps to see this. When it all started to go
wrong, the Nipponese tried to hire him directly, and he actually made
some money flying over there to work, for a week or a month at a
time, as a consultant. But they couldn't keep the technology running
with the programmers they had, and so it hasn't lived up to its potential.

Thus ended Randy's Second Business Foray. He came out of it with
a couple of hundred thousand dollars, most of which he plowed into the
Victorian house he shares with Charlene. He hadn't trusted himself with
that much liquid cash, and locking it up in the house gave him a feeling
of safety, like reaching home base in a frenzied game of full-contact tag.

He has spent the years since running the Three Siblings' computer
system. He hasn't made much money, but he hasn't had much stress
either.

Randy was forever telling people, without rancor, that they were full of
shit. That was the only way to get anything done in hacking. No one
took it personally.

Charlene's crowd most definitely *did* take it personally. It wasn't being
told that they were wrong that offended them, though—it was the underlying assumption that a person *could* be right or wrong about *anything*.
So on the Night in Question—the night of Avi's fateful call—Randy
had done what he usually did, which was to withdraw from the conversation. In the Tolkien, not the endocrinological or Snow White sense,
Randy is a Dwarf. Tolkien's Dwarves were stout, taciturn, vaguely magical characters who spent a lot of time in the dark hammering out beauti-

ful things, e.g. Rings of Power. Thinking of himself as a Dwarf who had hung up his war-ax for a while to go sojourning in the Shire, where he was surrounded by squabbling Hobbits (i.e., Charlene's friends), had actually done a lot for Randy's peace of mind over the years. He knew perfectly well that if he were stuck in academia these people, and the things they said, would seem momentous to him. But where he came from, nobody had been taking these people seriously for years. So he just withdrew from the conversation and drank his wine and looked out over the Pacific surf and tried not to do anything really obvious like shaking his head and rolling his eyes.

Then the topic of the Information Superhighway came up, and Randy could feel faces turning in his direction like searchlights, casting almost palpable warmth on his skin.

Dr. G. E. B. Kivistik had a few things to say about the Information Superhighway. He was a fiftyish Yale professor who had just flown in from someplace that had sounded really cool and impressive when he had gone out of his way to mention it several times. His name was Finnish, but he was British as only a non-British Anglophile could be. Ostensibly he was here to attend War as Text. Really he was there to recruit Charlene, and really *really* (Randy suspected) to fuck her. This was probably not true at all, but just a symptom of how wacked out Randy was getting by this point. Dr. G. E. B. Kivistik had been showing up on television pretty frequently. Dr. G. E. B. Kivistik had a couple of books out. Dr. G. E. B. Kivistik was, in short, parlaying his strongly contrarian view of the Information Superhighway into more air time than anyone who hadn't been accused of blowing up a day care center should get.

A Dwarf on sojourn in the Shire would probably go to a lot of dinner parties where pompous boring Hobbits would hold forth like this. This Dwarf would view the whole thing as entertainment. He would know that he could always go back out into the real world, so much vaster and more complex than these Hobbits imagined, and slay a few Trolls and remind himself of what really mattered.

That was what Randy always told himself, anyway. But on the Night in Question, it didn't work. Partly because Kivistik was too big and real to be a Hobbit—probably more influential in the real world than Randy would ever be. Partly because another faculty spouse at the table—a likable, harmless computerphile named Jon—decided to take issue with some of Kivistik's statements and was cheerfully shot down for his troubles. Blood was in the water.

Randy had ruined his relationship with Charlene by wanting to have kids. Kids raise issues. Charlene, like all of her friends, couldn't handle issues. Issues meant disagreement. Voicing disagreement was a form of conflict. Conflict, acted out openly and publicly, was a male mode of social interaction—the foundation for patriarchal society which brought with it the usual litany of dreadful things. Regardless, Randy decided to get patriarchal with Dr. G. E. B. Kivistik.

"How many slums will we bulldoze to build the Information Super-highway?" Kivistik said. This profundity was received with thoughtful nodding around the table.

Jon shifted in his chair as if Kivistik had just dropped an ice cube down his collar. "What does that mean?" he asked. Jon was smiling, trying not to be a conflict-oriented patriarchal hegemonist. Kivistik, in response, raised his eyebrows and looked around at everyone else, as if to say *Who invited this poor lightweight?* Jon tried to dig himself out from his tactical error, as Randy closed his eyes and tried not to wince visibly. Kivistik had spent more years sparring with really smart people over high table at Oxford than Jon had been alive. "You don't have to bulldoze anything. There's nothing there to bulldoze," Jon pleaded.

"Very well, let me put it this way," Kivistik said magnanimously—he was not above dumbing down his material for the likes of Jon. "How many on-ramps will connect the world's ghettos to the Information Superhighway?"

Oh, that's much clearer, everyone seemed to think. Point well taken, Geb! No one looked at Jon, that argumentative pariah. Jon looked help-lessly over at Randy, signaling for help.

Jon was a Hobbit who'd actually been out of the Shire recently, so he knew Randy was a dwarf. Now he was fucking up Randy's life by calling upon Randy to jump up on the table, throw off his homespun cloak, and whip out his two-handed ax.

The words came out of Randy's mouth before he had time to think better of it. "The Information Superhighway is just a fucking metaphor! Give me a break!" he said.

There was a silence as everyone around the table winced in unison. Dinner had now, officially, crashed and burned. All they could do now was grab their ankles, put their heads between their knees, and wait for the wreckage to slide to a halt.

"That doesn't tell me very much," Kivistik said. "Everything is a metaphor. The word 'fork' is a metaphor for this object." He held up a fork. "All discourse is built from metaphors."

"That's no excuse for using bad metaphors," Randy said.

"Bad? Bad? Who decides what is bad?" Kivistik said, doing his killer impression of a heavy-lidded, mouth-breathing undergraduate. There was scattered tittering from people who were desperate to break the tension.

Randy could see where it was going. Kivistik had gone for the usual academician's ace in the hole: everything is relative, it's all just differing perspectives. People had already begun to resume their little side conversations, thinking that the conflict was over, when Randy gave them all a start with: "Who decides what's bad? *I do.*"

Even Dr. G. E. B. Kivistik was flustered. He wasn't sure if Randy was joking. "Excuse me?"

Randy was in no great hurry to answer the question. He took the opportunity to sit back comfortably, stretch, and take a sip of his wine. He was feeling good. "It's like this," he said. "I've read your book. I've seen you on TV. I've heard you tonight. I personally typed up a list of your credentials when I was preparing press materials for this conference. So I know that you're not qualified to have an opinion about technical issues."

"Oh," Kivistik said in mock confusion, "I didn't realize one had to have qualifications."

"I think it's clear," Randy said, "that if you are ignorant of a particular subject, that your opinion is completely worthless. If I'm sick, I don't ask a plumber for advice. I go to a doctor. Likewise, if I have questions about the Internet, I will seek opinions from people who know about it."

"Funny how all of the technocrats seem to be in favor of the Internet," Kivistik said cheerily, milking a few more laughs from the crowd.

"You have just made a statement that is demonstrably not true," Randy said, pleasantly enough. "A number of Internet experts have written well-reasoned books that are sharply critical of it."

Kivistik was finally getting pissed off. All the levity was gone.

"So," Randy continued, "to get back to where we started, the Information Superhighway is a bad metaphor for the Internet, because I say it is. There might be a thousand people on the planet who are as conversant with the Internet as I am. I know most of these people. None of them takes that metaphor seriously. Q.E.D."

"Oh. I see," Kivistik said, a little hotly. He had seen an opening. "So we should rely on the technocrats to tell us what to think, and how to think, about this technology."

The expressions of the others seemed to say that this was a telling blow, righteously struck.

"I'm not sure what a technocrat is," Randy said. "Am I a technocrat? I'm just a guy who went down to the bookstore and bought a couple of textbooks on TCP/IP, which is the underlying protocol of the Internet, and read them. And then I signed on to a computer, which anyone can do nowadays, and I messed around with it for a few years, and now I know all about it. Does that make me a technocrat?"

"You belonged to the technocratic elite even before you picked up that book," Kivistik said. "The ability to wade through a technical text, and to understand it, is a privilege. It is a privilege conferred by an education that is available only to members of an elite class. That's what I mean by technocrat."

"I went to a public school," Randy said. "And then I went to a state university. From that point on, I was self-educated."

Charlene broke in. She had been giving Randy dirty looks ever since this started and he had been ignoring her. Now he was going to pay. "And your family?" Charlene asked frostily.

Randy took a deep breath, stifled the urge to sigh. "My father's an engineer. He teaches at a state college."

"And his father?"

"A mathematician."

Charlene raised her eyebrows. So did nearly everyone else at the table. Case closed.

"I strenuously object to being labeled and pigeonholed and stereotyped as a technocrat," Randy said, deliberately using oppressed-person's language, maybe in an attempt to turn their weapons against them but more likely (he thinks, lying in bed at three A.M. in the Manila Hotel) out of an uncontrollable urge to be a prick. Some of them, out of habit, looked at him soberly; etiquette dictated that you give all sympathy to the oppressed. Others gasped in outrage to hear these words coming from the lips of a known and convicted white male technocrat. "No one in my family has ever had much money or power," he said.

"I think that the point that Charlene's making is like this," said Tomas, one of their houseguests who had flown in from Prague with his wife Nina. He had now appointed himself conciliator. He paused long enough to exchange a warm look with Charlene. "Just by virtue of coming from a scientific family, you are a member of a privileged elite. You're not aware of it—but members of privileged elites are rarely aware of their privileges."

Randy finished the thought. "Until people like you come along to explain to us how stupid, to say nothing of morally bankrupt, we are."

"The false consciousness Tomas is speaking of is exactly what makes entrenched power elites so entrenched," Charlene said.

"Well, I don't feel very entrenched," Randy said. "I've worked my ass off to get where I've gotten."

"A lot of people work hard all their lives and get nowhere," someone said accusingly. Look out! The sniping had begun.

"Well, I'm sorry I haven't had the good grace to get nowhere," Randy said, now feeling just a bit surly for the first time, "but I have found that if you work hard, educate yourself, and keep your wits about you, you can find your way in this society."

"But that's straight out of some nineteenth-century Horatio Alger book," Tomas sputtered.

"So? Just because it's an old idea, doesn't mean it's wrong," Randy said.

A small strike force of waitpersons had been forming up around the fringes of the table, arms laden with dishes, making eye contact with each other as they tried to decide when it was okay to break up the fight and serve dinner. One of them rewarded Randy with a platter carrying a wigwam devised from slabs of nearly raw tuna. The pro-consensus, anti-confrontation elements then seized control of the conversation and broke it up into numerous small clusters of people all vigorously agreeing with one another. Jon cast a watery look at Randy, as if to say, was it good for you too? Charlene was ignoring him intensely; she was caught up in a consensus cluster with Tomas. Tomas's wife Nina kept trying to catch Randy's eye, but he studiously avoided this because he was afraid that she wanted to favor him with a smoldering come-hither look, and all Randy wanted to do right then was to go thither. Ten minutes later, his pager went off, and he looked down to see Avi's number on it.

BURN

THE AMERICAN BASE AT CAVITE, ALONG THE SHORE OF MANILA Bay, burns real good once the Nips have set it on fire. Bobby Shaftoe and the rest of the Fourth Marines get a good long look at it as they cruise by, sneaking out of Manila like thieves in the night. He has never felt more personally disgraced in his life, and the same thing goes for the other Marines. The Nips have already landed in Malaya and are headed for Singapore like a runaway train, they are besieging Guam and Wake and Hong Kong and God knows what else, and it should be obvious to anyone that they are going to hit the Philippines next. Seems like a regiment of hardened China Marines might actually come in handy around here.

But MacArthur seems to think he can defend Luzon all by himself, standing on the walls of Intramuros with his Colt .45. So they are shipping out. They have no idea where to. Most of them would rather hit the beaches of Nippon itself than stay here in Army territory.

The night the war began, Bobby Shaftoe had first gotten Glory back into the bosom of her family.

The Altamiras live in the neighborhood of Malate, a couple of miles south of Intramuros, and not too far from the place where Shaftoe has just had his half hour of Glory along the seawall. The city has gone mad, and it's impossible to get a car. Sailors, marines, and soldiers are spewing from bars, nightclubs, and ballrooms and commandeering taxis in groups of four and six—it's as crazy as Shanghai on Saturday night—like the war's already *here*. Shaftoe ends up carrying Glory halfway home, because her shoes aren't made for walking.

The family Altamira is vast enough to constitute an ethnic group unto itself, and all of them live in the same building—practically in the same room. Once or twice, Glory had begun to explain to Bobby Shaftoe how they are all related. Now there are many Shaftoes—mostly in Tennessee—but the Shaftoe family tree still fits on a cross-stitch sampler. The family Shaftoe is to the Altamira clan as a single, alienated sapling is to a jungle. Filipino families, in addition to being gigantic and Catholic, are massively crosslinked by godparent/godchild relationships, like lianas stretched from branch to branch and tree to tree. If asked, Glory is happy, even eager, to talk for six hours nonstop about how the Altamiras are related to one another, and that is just to give a general overview. Shaftoe's brain always shuts off after the first thirty seconds.

He gets her to the apartment, which is usually in a state of hysterical uproar even when the nation is not under military assault by the Empire of Nippon. Despite this, the appearance of Glory, shortly after the outbreak of war, borne in the arms of a United States Marine, is received by the Altamiras in much the same way as if Christ were to materialize in the center of their living room with the Virgin Mary slung over his back. All around him, middle-aged women are thudding down onto their knees, as if the place has just been mustard-gassed. But they are just doing it to shout hallelujah! Glory alights nimbly upon her high heels, tears exploring the exceptional geometry of her cheeks, and kisses everyone in the entire clan. All of the kids are wide awake, though it is three in the morning. Shaftoe happens to catch the eye of a squad of boys, aged maybe three to ten, all brandishing wooden rifles and swords. They are all staring at Bobby Shaftoe, replendent in his uniform, and they are perfectly thunderstruck; he could throw a baseball into the mouth of each one from across the room. In his peripheral vision, he sees a middle-aged woman who is related to Glory by some impossibly complex chain of relationships, and who already has one of Glory's lipstick marks on her cheek, vectoring toward him on a collision course, grimly determined to kiss him. He knows that he must get out of this place now or he will never leave it. So, ignoring the woman, and holding the gaze of those stunned boys, he rises to attention and snaps out a perfect salute.

The boys salute back, raggedly, but with fantastic bravado. Bobby Shaftoe turns on his heel and marches out of the room, moving like a bayonet thrust. He reckons that he will come back to Malate tomorrow, when things are calmer, and check up on Glory and the rest of the Altamiras.

He does not see her again.

He reports back to his ship, and is not granted any more shore leave. He does manage to have a conversation with Uncle Jack, who pulls up alongside in a small motorboat long enough for them to shout a few sentences back and forth. Uncle Jack is the last of the Manila Shaftoes, a branch of the family spawned by Nimrod Shaftoe of the Tennessee Volunteers. Nimrod took a bullet in his right arm somewhere around Quingua, courtesy of some rebellious Filipino riflemen. Recovering in a Manila hospital, old Nimrod, or "Lefty" as he was called by that point, decided that he liked the pluck of these Filipino men, in order to kill whom a whole new class of ridiculously powerful sidearm (the Colt .45) had had to be invented. Not only that, he liked the looks of their women. Promptly discharged from the service, he found that full disability pay would go a long way on the local economy. He set up an export business along the Pasig riverfront, married a half-Spanish woman, and sired a son (Jack) and two daughters. The daughters ended up in the States, back in the Tennessee mountains that have been the ancestral wellspring of all Shaftoes ever since they broke out of the indentured servitude racket back in the 1700s. Jack stayed in Manila and inherited Nimrod's business, but never married. By Manila standards he makes a decent amount of money. He has always been an odd combination of salty waterfront trader and perfumed dandy. He and Mr. Pascual have been in business together forever, which is how Bobby Shaftoe knows Mr. Pascual, and which is how he originally met Glory.

When Bobby Shaftoe repeats the latest rumors, Uncle Jack's face collapses. No one hereabouts is willing to face the fact that they are about to be besieged by Nips. His next words ought to be, "Shit then, I'm getting the hell out of here, I'll send you a postcard from Australia." But instead he says something like "I'll come by in a few days to check up on you."

Bobby Shaftoe bites his tongue and does not say what he's thinking, which is that he is a Marine, and he is on a ship, and this is a war, and Marines on ships in wars are not known for staying put. He just stands there and watches as Uncle Jack putt-putts away on his little boat, turning back every so often to wave at him with his fine Panama hat. The sailors around Bobby Shaftoe watch with amusement, and a bit of admiration. The waterfront is churning insanely as every piece of military gear that's not set in concrete gets thrown onto ships and sent to Bata'an or Corregidor, and Uncle Jack, standing upright in his boat, in his good cream-colored suit and Panama hat, weaves through the traffic with aplomb. Bobby Shaftoe watches him until he disappears around the bend into the Pasig River, knowing that he is probably the last member of his family who will ever see Uncle Jack alive.

Despite all of those premonitions, he's surprised when they ship out after only a few days of war, pulling out of their slip in the middle of the night without any of the traditional farewell ceremonies. Manila is supposedly lousy with Nip spies, and there's nothing the Nips would like better than to sink a transport ship stuffed with experienced Marines.

Manila disappears behind them into the darkness. The awareness that he hasn't seen Glory since that night is like a slow hot dentist's drill. He wonders how she's doing. Maybe, once the war settles down a little bit, and the battle lines firm up, he can figure out a way to get stationed in this part of the world. MacArthur's a tough old bastard who will put up a hell of a fight when the Nips come. And even if the Philippines fall, FDR won't let them remain in enemy hands for very long. With any luck, inside of six months, Bobby Shaftoe will be marching up Manila's Taft Avenue, in full dress uniform, behind a Marine Band, perhaps nursing a minor war wound or two. The parade will come to a section of the avenue that is lined, for a distance of about a mile, with Altamiras. About halfway along, the crowd will part, and Glory will run out and jump into his arms and smother him with kisses. He'll carry the girl straight up the steps of some nice little church where a priest in a white cassock is waiting with a big grin on his face—

That dream-image dissolves in a mushroom cloud of orange fire rising up from the American base at Cavite. The place has been burning all day, and another fuel dump has just gone up. He can feel the heat on his face from miles away. Bobby Shaftoe is on the deck of the ship, all bundled up in a life vest in case they get torpedoed. He takes advantage of the flaring light to look down a long line of other Marines in life vests, staring at the flame with stunned expressions on their tired, sweaty faces.

Manila is only half an hour behind them, but it might as well be a million miles away.

He remembers Nanking, and what the Nips did there. What happened to the women.

Once, long ago, there was a city named Manila. There was a girl there. Her face and name are best forgotten. Bobby Shaftoe starts forgetting just as fast as he can.

PEDESTRIAN

....

✝ RESPECT THE PEDESTRIAN, SAY THE STREET SIGNS OF METRO
Manila. As soon as Randy saw those he knew that he was in
trouble.

For the first couple of weeks he spent in Manila, his work consisted of walking. He walked all over the city carrying a handheld GPS receiver, taking down latitudes and longitudes. He encrypted the data in his hotel room and e-mailed it to Avi. It became part of Epiphyte's intellectual property. It became equity.

Now, they had secured some actual office space. Randy walks to it, doggedly. He knows that the first time he takes a taxi there, he'll never walk again.

RESPECT THE PEDESTRIAN, the signs say, but the drivers, the physical environment, local land use customs, and the very layout of the place conspire to treat the pedestrian with the contempt he so richly deserves. Randy would get more respect if he went to work on a pogo stick with a propeller beanie on his head. Every morning the bellhops ask him if he wants a taxi, and practically lose consciousness when he says no. Every morning the taxi drivers lined up in front of the hotel, leaning against their cars and smoking, shout "Taxi? Taxi?" to him. When he turns them down, they say witty things to each other in Tagalog and roar with laughter.

Just in case Randy hasn't gotten the message yet, a new red-and-white chopper swings in low over Rizal Park, turns around once or twice like a dog preparing to lie down, and settles in, not far from some palm trees, right in front of the hotel.

Randy has gotten into the habit of reaching Intramuros by cutting through Rizal Park. This is not a direct route. The direct route passes over a no-man's land, a vast, dangerous intersection lined with squatters' huts (it is dangerous because of the cars, not the squatters). If you go through the park, on the other hand, you only have to brush off a lot of whores. But Randy's gotten good at that. The whores cannot conceive of a man rich enough to stay at the Manila Hotel who voluntarily walks around the city every day, and they have given him up as a maniac. He has passed into the realm of irrational things that you must simply accept, and in the Philippines this is a nearly infinite domain.

Randy could never understand why everything smelled so bad until he came upon a large, crisp rectangular hole in the sidewalk, and stared down into a running flume of raw sewage. The sidewalks are nothing more than lids on the sewers. Access to the depths is provided by concrete slabs with rebar lifting loops protruding from them. Squatters fashion wire harnesses onto those loops so that they can pull them up and create instant public latrines. These slabs are frequently engraved with the initials, team name, or graffiti tag of the gentlemen who manufactured them, and their competence and attentiveness to detail vary, but their esprit de corps is fixed at a very high level.

There are only so many gates that lead into Intramuros. Randy must run a daily gauntlet of horse-drawn taxis, some of whom have nothing better to do than follow him down the street for a quarter of an hour muttering, "Sir? Sir? Taxi? Taxi?" One of them, in particular, is the most tenacious capitalist Randy has ever seen. Every time he draws alongside Randy, a rope of urine uncoils from his horse's belly and cracks into the pavement and hisses and foams. Tiny comets of pee strike Randy's pant legs. Randy always wears long pants no matter how hot it is.

Intramuros is a strangely quiet and lazy neighborhood. This is mostly because it was destroyed during the war, and hasn't been undestroyed yet. Much of it is open weed farms still, which is very odd in the middle of a vast, crowded metropolis.

Several miles south, towards the airport, amid nice suburban developments, is Makati. This would be the logical place to base Epiphyte Corp. It's got a couple of giant five-star luxury hotels on every block, and office towers that look clean and cool, and modern condos. But Avi, with his perverse real estate sense, has decided to forego all of that in favor of what he described on the phone as texture. "I do not like to buy or lease real estate when it is peaking," he said.

Understanding Avi's motives is like peeling an onion with a single chopstick. Randy knows there is much more to it: perhaps he's earning a favor, or repaying one, to a landlord. Perhaps he's been reading some management guru who counsels young entrepreneurs to get deeply involved in a country's culture. Not that Avi has ever been one for gurus. Randy's latest theory is that it all has to do with lines of sight—the latitudes and longitudes.

Sometimes Randy walks along the top of the Spanish wall. Around Calle Victoria, where MacArthur had his headquarters before the war, it is as wide as a four-lane street. Lovers nestle in the trapezoidal gunslits and put up umbrellas for privacy. Below him, to the left, is the moat, a good city block or two in width, mostly dry. Squatters have built shacks on it. In the parts that are still submerged, they dig for mud crabs or string improvised nets among the purple and magenta lotus blossoms.

To the right is Intramuros. A few buildings poke up out of a jumbled wilderness of strewn stone. Ancient Spanish cannon are sprinkled around the place, half-buried. The rubble fields have been colonized by tropical vegetation and squatters. Their clothesline poles and television antennas are all wrapped up in jungle creepers and makeshift electrical wiring. Utility poles jut into the air at odd angles, like widowmakers in a burned forest, some of them almost completely obscured by the glass bubbles of electrical meters. Every dozen yards or so, for no discernable reason, a pile of rubble smolders.

As he goes by the cathedral, children follow him, whining and begging piteously until he puts pesos in their hands. Then they beam and sometimes give him a bright "Thank you!" in perfect American-scented shopping-mall English. The beggars in Manila never seem to take their work very seriously, for even they have been infected by the cultural fungus of irony and always seem to be fighting back a grin, as if they can't believe they're doing anything so corny.

They do not understand that he is working. That's okay.

Ideas have always come to Randy faster than he could use them. He spent the first thirty years of his life pursuing whatever idea appealed to him at the moment, discarding it when a better one came along.

Now he is working for a company again, and has some kind of responsibility to use his time productively. Good ideas come to him as fast and thick as ever, but he has to keep his eye on the ball. If the idea is not relevant to Epiphyte, he has to jot it down and forget about it for now. If it is relevant, he has to restrain his urge to dive into it and consider: has anyone else come up with this idea before him? Is it possible to just go out and buy the technology? Can he delegate the work to a contract coder in the States?

He walks slowly, partly because otherwise he will suffer heatstroke and fall dead in the gutter. Worse yet, he may fall through an open hatch into a torrent of sewage, or brush against one of the squatters's electrical wires, which dangle from overhead like patient asps. The constant dangers of sudden electrocution from above or drowning in liquid shit below keep him looking up and down as well as side-to-side. Randy has never felt more trapped between a capricious and dangerous heaven and a hellish underworld. This place is as steeped in religion as India, but all of it is Catholic.

At the northern end of Intramuros is a little business district. It is sandwiched between Manila Cathedral and Fort Santiago, which the Spaniards constructed to command the outlet of the Pasig River. You can tell it's a business district because of the phone wires. As in other Rapidly Developing Asian Economies, it is difficult to tell whether these are pirate wires, or official ones that have been incredibly badly installed. They are a case study in why incrementalism is bad. The bundles are so thick in some places that Randy probably could not wrap both arms around them. Their weight and tension have begun to pull the phone poles over, especially at curves in the roads, where the wires go round a corner and exert a net sideways force on the pole.

All of these buildings are constructed in the least expensive way conceivable: concrete poured in place in wooden forms, over grids of hand-tied rebar. They are blocky, grey, and completely indistinguishable from one another. A couple of much taller buildings, twenty or thirty stories, loom over the district from a big intersection nearby, wind and birds circulating through their broken windows. They were badly shaken up in an earthquake during the 1980s and have not been put to rights yet.

He passes by a restaurant with a squat concrete blockhouse in front, its openings covered with blackened steel grates, rusty exhaust pipes sticking out the top to vent the diesel generator locked inside. NO BROWNOUT has been proudly stenciled all over it. Beyond that is a postwar office building, four stories high, with an especially thick sheaf of telephone wires running into it. The logo of a bank is bolted to the front of the building, down low. There is angle parking in front. The two spaces in front of the main entrance are blocked off with hand-painted signs: RESERVED FOR ARMORED CAR and RESERVED FOR BANK MANAGER. A couple of guards stand in front of the entrance clutching the fat wooden pistol grips of riot guns, weapons that have the hulking, cartoonish appearance of action-figure accessories. One of the guards remains behind a bulletproof podium with a sign on it: PLEASE DEPOSIT GUNS/FIREARMS TO THE GUARD.

Randy exchanges nods with the gunmen and goes into the building's lobby, which is just as hot as outside. Bypassing the bank, ignoring the unreliable elevators, he goes through a steel door that takes him into a narrow stairwell. Today, it is dark. The building's electrical system is a patchwork—several different systems coexisting in the same space, controlled by different panels, some on generators and some not. So blackouts begin and end in phases. Somewhere near the top of the stairwell, small birds chirp, competing with the sound of car alarms being set off outside.

Epiphyte Corp. rents the building's top floor, although he is the only person working there so far. He keys his way in. Thank god; the air-conditioning has been working. The money they paid for their own generator was worth it. He disables the alarm systems, goes to the fridge, and gets two one-liter bottles of water. His rule of thumb, after a walk, is to drink water until he begins to urinate again. Then he can consider other activities.

He is too sweaty to sit down. He must keep moving so that the cold dry air will flow around his body. He flicks globes of sweat out of his beard and does an orbit of the floor, looking out the windows, checking out the lines of sight. He pulls a ballistic nylon traveler's wallet out of his trousers and lets it dangle from his belt loop so that the skin underneath it can breathe. It contains his passport, a virgin credit card, ten crisp new hundred dollar bills, and a floppy disk with his 4096-bit encryption key on it.

Northwards he can survey the greens and ramparts of Fort Santiago, where phalanxes of Nipponese tourists toil, recording their fun with forensic determination. Beyond that is the Pasig River, choked with floating debris. Across the river is Quiapo, a built-up area: high-rise apartment and office buildings with corporate names emblazoned on their top storeys and satellite dishes on the roofs.

Unwilling to stop moving just yet, Randy strolls clockwise around the office. Intramuros is ringed with a belt of green, its former moat. He has just walked up its western verge. The eastern one is studded with heavy neoclassical buildings housing various government ministries. The Post and Telecommunications Authority sits on the Pasig's edge, at a vertex in the river from which three closely spaced bridges radiate into Quiapo. Beyond the large new structures above the river, Quiapo and the adjoining neighborhood of San Miguel are a patchwork of giant institutions: a train station, an old prison, many universities, and Malacanang Palace, which is farther up the Pasig.

Back on this side of the river, it is Intramuros in the foreground (cathedrals and churches surrounded by dormant land), government institutions, colleges, and universities in the middle ground, and, beyond that, a seemingly infinite sprawl of low-lying, smoky city. Miles to the south is the gleaming business city of Makati, built around a square where two big roads intersect at an acute angle, echoing the intersecting runways at NAIA, a bit farther south. An emerald city of big houses perched on big lawns spreads away from Makati: it is where the ambassadors and corporate presidents live. Continuing his clockwise stroll he can follow Roxas Boulevard coming toward him up the seawall, marked by a picket line of tall palm trees. Manila Bay is jammed with heavy shipping, big cargo ships filling the water like logs in a boom. The container port is just below him to the west: a grid of warehouses on reclaimed land that is about as flat, and as natural, as a sheet of particle board.

If he looks over the cranes and containers, due west across the bay, he can barely make out the mountainous silhouette of the Bata'an Peninsula, some forty miles distant. Following its black skyline southwards—tracing the route taken by the Nipponese in '42—he can almost resolve a lump lying off its southern tip. That would be the island of Corregidor. This is the first time he's ever been able to see it; the air is unusually clear today.

A fragment of historical trivia floats to the surface of his melted brain. The galleon from Acapulco. The signal fire on Corregidor.

He punches in Avi's GSM number. Avi, somewhere in the world, answers it. He sounds like he is in a taxi, in one of those countries where horn-honking is still an inalienable right. "What's on your mind, Randy?"

"Lines of sight," Randy says.

"Huh!" Avi blurts, as if a medicine ball has just slammed into his belly. "You figured it out."

GUADALCANAL

THE MARINE RAIDERS' BODIES ARE NO LONGER PRESSURIZED with blood and breath. The weight of their gear flattens them into the sand. The accelerating surf has already begun to shovel silt over them; comet trails of blood fade back into the ocean, red carpets for any sharks who may be browsing the coastline. Only one of them is a giant lizard, but all have the same general shape: fat in the middle and tailing off at the ends, streamlined by the waves.

A little convoy of Nip boats is moving down the slot, towing barges loaded with supplies packed into steel drums. Shaftoe and his platoon ought to be lobbing mortars at them right now. When the American planes show up and begin to kick the shit out of them, the Nips will throw the drums overboard and run away, and hope that some of them will wash ashore on Guadalcanal.

The war is over for Bobby Shaftoe, and hardly for the first or last time. He trudges among the platoon. Waves hit him in the knees, then spread into magic carpets of foam and vegetable matter that skim along the beach so that his footing appears to glide out from under him. He keeps twisting around for no reason and falling on his ass.

Finally he reaches the corpsman's corpse, and divests it of anything with a red cross on it. He turns his back on the Nip convoy and looks up a long glacis toward the tideline. It might as well be Mt. Everest as seen from a low base camp. Shaftoe decides to tackle the challenge on hands and knees. Every so often, a big wave spanks him on the ass, rushes up between his legs orgasmically and washes his face. It feels good and also keeps him from pitching forward and falling asleep below the high-tide mark.

The next couple of days are a handful of dirty, faded black-and-white snapshots, shuffled and dealt over and over again: the beach under water, positions of corpses marked by standing waves. The beach empty. The beach under water again. The beach strewn with black lumps, like a slice of Grandma Shaftoe's raisin bread. A morphine bottle half-buried in the sand. Small, dark people, mostly naked, moving along the beach at low tide and looting the corpses.

Hey, wait a sec! Shaftoe is on his feet somehow, clutching his Springfield. The jungle doesn't want to let go of him; creepers have actually grown over his limbs in the time he has lain there. As he emerges, dragging foliage behind him like a float in a ticker-tape parade, the sun floods over him like warm syrup of ipecac. He can see the ground headed his way. He spins as he falls—momentarily glimpsing a big man with a rifle—and then his face is pressed into the cool sand. The surf roars in his skull: a nice standing ovation from a studio audience of angels, who having all died themselves, know a good death when they see one.

Little hands roll him over onto his back. One of his eyes is frozen shut by sand. Peering through the other he sees a big fellow with a rifle slung over his shoulder standing over him. The fellow has a red beard, which makes it just a bit less probable that he is a Nipponese soldier. But what is he?

He prods like a doctor and prays like a priest—in Latin, even. Silver hair buzzed close to a tanned skull. Shaftoe scans the fellow's clothing for some kind of insignia. He's hoping to see a *Semper Fidelis* but instead he reads: *Societas Eruditorum* and *Ignoti et quasi occulti*.

"Ignoti et . . . what the fuck does that mean?" he asks.

"Hidden and unknown—more or less," says the man. He's got a weird accent, sort of Australian, sort of German. He checks out Shaftoe's insignia in turn. "What's a Marine Raider? Some kind of new outfit?"

"Like a Marine, only more so," Shaftoe says. Which might sound like bravado. Indeed it partly is. But this comment is as heavy laden with irony as Shaftoe's clothes are with sand, because at this particular moment in history, a Marine isn't just a tough s.o.b. He is a tough S.O.B. stuck out in the middle of nowhere (Guadalcanal) with no food or weapons (owing, as every Marine can tell you, to a sinister conspiracy between General MacArthur and the Nips) totally making everything up as he goes along, improvising weapons from found objects, addled, half the time, by disease and the drugs supplied to keep diseases at bay. And in every one of those senses, a Marine Raider is (as Shaftoe says) like a Marine, only more so.

"Are you some kind of commando or something?" Shaftoe asks, interrupting Red as he is mumbling.

"No. I live on the mountain."

"Oh, yeah? What do you do up there, Red?"

"I watch. And talk on the radio, in code." Then he goes back to mumbling.

"Who you talkin' to, Red?"

"Do you mean, just now in Latin, or on the radio in code?"

"Both I reckon."

"On the radio in code, I talk to the good guys."

"Who are the good guys?"

"Long story. If you live, maybe I'll introduce you to some of them," says Red.

"How about just now in Latin?"

"Talking to God," Red says. "Last rites, in case you *don't* live."

This makes him think of the others. He remembers why he made that insane decision to stand up in the first place. "Hey! Hey!" He tries to sit up, and finding that impossible, twists around. "Those bastards are looting the corpses!"

His eyes aren't focusing and he has to rub sand out of the one.

Actually, they are focusing just fine. What looked like steel drums strewn around the beach turn out to be—steel drums strewn around the beach. The natives are pawing them out of the sucking sand, digging with their hands like dogs, rolling them up the beach and into the jungle.

Shaftoe blacks out.

When he wakes up there's a row of crosses on the beach—sticks lashed together with vines, draped with jungle flowers. Red is pounding them in with the butt of his rifle. All the steel drums, and most of the natives, are gone. Shaftoe needs morphine. He says as much to Red.

"If you think you need it now," Red says, "just wait." He tosses his rifle to a native, strides up to Shaftoe, and heaves him up over his shoulders in a fireman's carry. Shaftoe screams. A couple of Zeroes fly overhead, as they stride into the jungle. "My name is Enoch Root," says Red, "but you can call me Brother."

GALLEON

ONE MORNING, RANDY WATERHOUSE RISES EARLY, TAKES A long hot shower, plants himself before the mirror of his Manila Hotel suite, and shaves his face bloody. He was thinking of farming this work out to a specialist: the barber in the hotel's lobby. But this is the first time Randy's face will be visible in ten years, and Randy wants to be the first person to see it. His heart actually thumps, partly out of primal brute fear of the knife, and partly from the sheer anticipation. It is like the scene in corny old movies where the bandages are finally taken off of the patient's face, and a mirror proffered.

The effect is, first of all, intense déjà vu, as if the last ten years of his life were but a dream, and he now has them to live over again.

Then he begins to notice subtle ways in which his face has been changing since it was last exposed to air and light. He is mildly astonished to find that these changes are not entirely bad. Randy has never thought of himself as especially good-looking, and has never especially cared. But the blood-spotted visage in the mirror is, arguably, better looking than the one that faded into the deepening shade of stubble a decade ago. It looks like a grownup's face.

It has been a week since he and Avi laid out the entire plan for the high officials of the PTA: the Post and Telecoms Authority. PTA is a generic term that telecom businessmen slap, like a yellow stickynote, onto whatever government department handles these matters in whatever country they happen to be visiting this week. In the Philippines, it is actually called something else.

Americans brought, or at least accompanied, the Philippines into the twentieth century and erected the apparatus of its central government. Intramuros, the dead heart of Manila, is surrounded by a loose ring of giant neoclassical buildings, very much after the fashion of the District of Columbia, housing various parts of that apparatus. The PTA is headquartered in one of those buildings, just south of the Pasig.

Randy and Avi get there early because Randy, accustomed to Manila traffic, insists that they budget a full hour to cover the one- or two-mile taxi ride from the hotel. But traffic is perversely light and they end up with a full twenty minutes to kill. They stroll around the side of the building and up onto the green levee. Avi draws a bead on the Epiphyte Corp. building, just to reassure himself that their line of sight is clear. Randy is already satisfied of this, and just stands there with arms crossed, looking at the river. It is choked, bank to bank, with floating debris: some plant material but mostly old mattresses, cushions, pieces of plastic litter, hunks of foam, and, most of all, plastic shopping bags in various bright colors. The river has the consistency of vomit.

Avi wrinkles his nose. "What's that?"

Randy sniffs the air and smells, among everything else, burnt plastic. He gestures downstream. "Squatter camp on the other side of Fort Santiago," he explains. "They sieve plastic out of the river and burn it for fuel."

"I was in Mexico a couple of weeks ago," Avi says. "They have plastic forests there!"

"What does that mean?"

"Downwind of the city, the trees sort of comb the plastic shopping bags out of the air. They get totally covered with them. The trees die because light and air can't get through to the leaves. But they remain standing, totally encased in fluttering, ragged plastic, all different colors."

Randy shrugs his blazer off, rolls up his sleeves; Avi does not seem to notice the heat. "So that's Fort Santiago," Avi says, and starts walking towards it.

"You've heard of it?" Randy asks, following him, and heaving a sigh. The air is so hot that when it comes out of your lungs it has actually cooled down by several degrees.

"It's mentioned in the video," Avi says, holding up a videotape cassette and wiggling it.

"Oh, yeah."

Soon they are standing before the fort's entrance, which is flanked by carvings of a pair of guards cut into the foamy volcanic tuff: halberd-brandishing Spaniards in blousy pants and conquistador helmets. They have been standing here for close to half a millennium, and a hundred thousand tropical thundershowers have streamed down their bodies and polished them smooth.

Avi is working on a much shorter time horizon—he has eyes only for the bullet craters that have disfigured these soldiers far worse than time and water. He puts his hands in them, like doubting Thomas. Then he steps back and begins to mutter in Hebrew. Two ponytailed German tourists stroll through the gate in rustic sandals.

"We have five minutes," Randy says.

"Okay, let's come back here later."

Charlene wasn't totally wrong. Blood seeps out of tiny, invisible painless cuts on Randy's face and neck for ten or fifteen minutes after he has shaved. Moments ago, that blood was accelerating through his ventricles, or seeping through the parts of his brain that make him a conscious entity. Now the same stuff is exposed to the air; he can reach up and wipe it off. The boundary between Randy and his environment has been annihilated.

He gets out a big tube of heavy waterproof sunblock and greases his face, neck, arms, and the small patch of scalp on the top of his head where the hair is getting thin. Then he pulls on khakis, boat shoes, and a loose cotton shirt, and a beltpack containing his GPS receiver and a couple of other essentials like a wad of toilet paper and a disposable camera. He drops his key off at the front desk, and the employees all do double-takes and grin. The bellhops seem particularly delighted by his makeover. Or perhaps it is just that he is wearing leather shoes for once: topsiders, which he's always thought of as the mark of effete preppies, but which are actually a reasonable thing for him to wear today. Bellhops make ready to haul the front door open, but instead, Randy cuts across the lobby towards the back of the hotel, skirts the swimming pool, and walks through a line of palm trees to a stone railing along the top of a seawall. Below him is the hotel's dock, which sicks out into a small cove that opens onto Manila Bay.

His ride isn't here yet, so he stands at the railing for a minute. One side of the cove is accessible from Rizal Park. A few gnarly Filipino squatter types are lazing on the benches, staring back at him. Down below the breakwater, a middle-aged man, wearing only boxer shorts, stands in knee-deep water with a pointed stick, staring with feline intensity into the lapping water. A black helicopter makes slow, banking circles against a sugar-white sky. It is a Vietnam-vintage Huey, a wappity-wap kind of chopper that also makes a fierce reptilian hissing noise as it slithers overhead.

A boat materializes from the steam rising off the bay, cuts its engines, and coasts into the cove, shoving a bow wave in front of it, like a wrinkle in a heavy rug. A tall, slender woman is poised on the prow like a living figurehead, holding a coil of heavy rope.

The big satellite dishes on the roof of the PTA's building are pointed almost straight up, like birdbaths, because Manila is so close to the equator. On its stone walls, spackle is coming loose from the bullet and shrapnel craters into which it was troweled after the war. Window air conditioners centered in the building's Roman arches drip water onto the limestone balusters below, gradually melting them away. The limestone is blackened with some kind of organic slime, and pitted by the root systems of little plants that have taken root in them—probably grown from seeds conveyed in the shit of the birds that congregate there to bathe and drink, the squatters of the aerial realm.

In a paneled conference room, a dozen people are waiting, equally divided between table-sitting big wheels and wall-crawling minions. As Randy and Avi enter a great flurry of hand-shaking and card-presenting ensues, though most of the introductions zoom through Randy's short-term memory like a supersonic fighter blowing past shoddy Third World air defense systems. He is left only with a stack of business cards. He deals them out on his patch of table like a senescent codger playing Klondike on his meal tray. Avi, of course, knows all of these people already—seems to be on a first-name basis with most of them, knows their children's names and ages, their hobbies, their blood types, chronic medical conditions, what books they are reading, whose parties they have been going to. All of them are evidently delighted by this, and all of them, thank god, completely ignore Randy.

Of the half-dozen important people in the room, three are middle-aged Filipino men. One of these is a high-ranking official in the PTA. The second is the president of an upstart telecommunications company called FiliTel, which is trying to compete against the traditional monopoly. The third is the vice president of a company called 24 Jam that runs about half of the convenience stores in the Philippines, as well as quite a few in Malaysia. Randy has trouble telling these men apart, but by watching them converse with Avi, and by using inductive logic, he is soon able to match business card with face.

The other three are easy: two Americans and one Nipponese, and one of the Americans is a woman. She is wearing lavender pumps color-coordinated with a neat little skirt suit, and matching nails. She looks as if she might have stepped straight off the set of an infomercial for fake fingernails or home permanents. Her card identifies her as Mary Ann Carson, and claims that she is a V.P. with AVCLA, Asia Venture Capital Los Angeles, which Randy knows dimly as a Los Angeles-based firm that invests in Rapidly Developing Asian Economies. The American man is blond and has a hard-jawed quasi-military look about him. He seems alert, disciplined, impassive, which Charlene's crowd would interpret as hostility born of repression born of profound underlying mental disorder. He represents the Subic Bay Free Port. The Nipponese man is the executive vice president of a subsidiary of a ridiculously colossal consumer-electronics company. He is about six feet tall. He has a small body and a large head shaped like an upside-down Bosc pear, thick hair edged with gray, and wire-rimmed glasses. He smiles frequently, and projects the serene confidence of a man who has memorized a two-thousand-page encyclopedia of business etiquette.

Avi wastes little time in starting the videotape, which at the moment, represents about seventy-five percent of Epiphyte Corp.'s assets. Avi had it produced by a hot multimedia startup in San Francisco, and the contract to produce it accounted for one hundred percent of the startup's revenue this year. "Pies crumble when you slice them too thin," Avi likes to say.

It starts with footage—pilfered from a forgotten made-for-TV movie—of a Spanish galleon making headway through heavy seas. Superimpose title: SOUTH CHINA SEA—A.D. 1699. The soundtrack has been beefed up and Dolbyized from its original monaural version. It is quite impressive.

("Half of the investors in AVCLA are into yachting," Avi explained.)

Cut to a shot (produced by the multimedia company, and seamlessly spliced in) of a mangy, exhausted lookout in a crow's nest, peering through a brass spyglass, hollering the Spanish equivalent of "Land ho!"

Cut to the galleon's captain, a rugged, bearded character, emerging from his cabin to stare with Keatsian wild surmise at the horizon. "Corregidor!" he exclaims.

Cut to a stone tower on the crown of a green tropical island, where a lookout is sighting the (digitally inserted) galleon on the horizon. The lookout cups his hands around his mouth and bellows, in Spanish, "It is the galleon! Light the signal fire!"

("The family of the guy who runs the PTA is really into local history," Avi said, "they run the Museum of the Philippines.")

With a lusty cheer, Spaniards (actually, Mexican-American actors) in conquistador helmets plunge firebrands into a huge pile of dry wood which evolves into a screaming pyramid of flame powerful enough to flash-roast an ox.

Cut to the battlements of Manila's Fort Santiago (foreground: carved styrofoam; background: digitally generated landscape), where another conquistador spies a light flaring up on the horizon. "Mira! El galleon!" he cries.

Cut to a series of shots of Manila townsfolk rushing to the seawall to adore the signal fire, including an Augustinian monk who clasps his rosary-strewn hands and bursts into clerical Latin on the spot ("the family that runs FiliTel endowed a chapel at Manila Cathedral") as well as a clean-cut family of Chinese merchants unloading bales of silk from a junk ("24 Jam, the convenience store chain, is run by Chinese mestizos").

A voiceover begins, deep and authoritative, English with a Filipino accent ("The actor is the brother of the godfather of the grandson of the man who runs the PTA"). Subtitles appear on the bottom of the screen in Tagalog ("the PTA people have a heavy political commitment to the native language").

"In the heyday of the Spanish Empire, the most important event of the year was the arrival of the galleon from Acapulco, laden with silver from the rich mines of America—silver to buy the silks and spices of Asia, silver that made the Philippines into the economic fountainhead of Asia. The approach of the galleon was heralded by a beacon of light from the island of Corregidor, at the entrance of Manila Bay."

Cut (finally!) from the beaming, greed-lit faces of the Manila townsfolk to a 3-D graphics rendering of Manila Bay, the Bata'an Peninsula, and the small islands off the tip of Bata'an, including Corregidor. The point of view swoops and zooms in on Corregidor where a hokily, badly rendered fire blazes up. A beam of yellow light, like a phaser blast in *Star Trek,* shoots across the bay. Our point of view follows it. It splashes against the walls of Fort Santiago.

"The signal fire was an ancient and simple technology. In the language of modern science, its light was a form of *electromagnetic radiation,* propagating in a straight line across Manila Bay, and carrying a single bit of information. But, in an age starved for information, that single bit meant everything to the people of Manila."

Cue that funky music. Cut to shots of teeming modern Manila. Shopping malls and luxury hotels in Makati. Electronics factories, schoolchildren sitting in front of computer screens. Satellite dishes. Ships unloading at the big free port of Subic Bay. Lots and lots of grinning and thumbs-up gestures.

"The Philippines of today is an emerging economic dynamo. As its economy grows, so does its hunger for information—not single bits, but hundreds of billions of them. But the technology for transmitting that information has not changed as much as you might imagine."

Back to the 3-D rendering of Manila Bay. This time, instead of a bonfire on Corregidor, there's a microwave horn up on a tower on the isle's summit, gunning electric-blue sine waves at the sprawl of Metro Manila.

"Electromagnetic radiation—in this case, microwave beams—propagating in straight lines, over line-of-sight routes, can transmit vast quantities of information quickly. Modern cryptographic technology makes the signal safe from would-be eavesdroppers."

Cut back to the galleon-and-lookout footage. "In the old days, Corregidor's position at the entrance of Manila Bay made it a natural lookout—a place where information about approaching ships could be gathered."

Cut to a shot of a barge in a cove somewhere, feeding thick tarry cable overboard, divers at work with queues of round orange buoys. "Today, Corregidor's geographical situation makes it an ideal place to land deep-sea fiberoptic cables. The information coming down these cables—from Taiwan, Hong Kong, Malaysia, Nippon, and the United States—can from there be transmitted directly into the heart of Manila. *At the speed of light!"*

More 3-D graphics. This time, it's a detailed rendering of the cityscape of Manila. Randy knows it by heart because he gathered the data for the damn thing by walking around town with his GPS receiver. The beam of bits from Corregidor comes straight in off the bay and scores a bullseye on the rooftop antenna of a nondescript four-story office building between Fort Santiago and the Manila Cathedral. It is Epiphyte's building, and the antenna is discreetly labeled with the name and logo of Epiphyte Corp. Other antennas then retransmit information to the PTA building and to other nearby sites: skyscrapers in Makati, government offices in Quezon City, and an Air Force base south of town.

Hotel staff throw a carpeted gangway across the gap between seawall and boat. As Randy is walking across it, the woman extends her hand to him. He reaches out to shake it. "Randy Waterhouse," he says.

She grabs his hand and pulls him on board—not so much greeting him as making sure he doesn't fall overboard. "Hi. Amy Shaftoe," she says. "Welcome to *Glory*."

"Pardon me?"

"*Glory*. The name of this junk is *Glory*," she says. She speaks forthrightly and with great clarity, as though communicating over a noisy two-way radio. "Actually, it's *Glory IV*," she continues. Her accent is largely Midwestern, with a trace of Southern twang, and a little bit of Filipino, too. If you saw her on the streets of some Midwestern town you might not notice the traces of Asian ancestry around her eyes. She has dark brown hair, sun-streaked, just long enough to form a secure ponytail, no longer.

"Scuse me a sec," she says, pokes her head into the pilot house, and speaks to the pilot in a mixture of Tagalog and English. The pilot nods, looks around, and begins to manipulate the controls. The hotel staff pull the gangway back. "Hey," Amy says quietly, and underhands a pack of Marlboros across the gap to each one of them. They snatch them out of the air, grin, and thank her. *Glory IV* begins to back away from the dock.

Amy spends the next few minutes walking around the deck, going through some kind of mental checklist. Randy counts four men in addition to Amy and the pilot—two Caucasians and two Filipinos. All of them are fiddling around with engines or diving gear in a way Randy recognizes, through many cultural and technological barriers, as debugging. Amy walks past Randy a couple of times, but avoids looking him in the eye. She's not a shy person. Her body language is eloquent enough: "I am aware that men are in the habit of looking at whatever women happen to be nearby, in the hopes of deriving enjoyment from their physical beauty, their hair, makeup, fragrance, and clothing. I will ignore this, politely and patiently, until you get over it." Amy is a long-limbed girl in paint-stained jeans, a sleeveless t-shirt, and high-tech sandals, and she lopes easily around the boat. Finally she approaches him, meeting his eyes for just a second and then glancing away as if bored.

"Thanks for giving me the ride," Randy says.

"It's nothing," she says.

"I feel embarrassed that I didn't tip the guys at the dock. Can I reimburse you?"

"You can reimburse me with information," she says without hesitation. Amy reaches up with one hand to rub the back of her neck. Her elbow pokes up in the air. He notices about a month's growth of hair in her armpit, then glimpses the corner of a tattoo poking out from under her shirt. "You're in the information business, right?" She watches his face, hoping that he'll take the cue and laugh, or at least grin. But he's too preoccupied to catch it. She glances away, now with a knowing, sardonic look on her face—you don't understand me, Randy, which is absolutely typical, and I'm fine with that. She reminds Randy of level-headed blue-collar lesbians he has known, drywall-hanging urban dykes with cats and cross-country ski racks.

She takes him into an air-conditioned cabin with a lot of windows and a coffee maker. It has fake wood-veneer paneling like a suburban basement, and framed exhibits on the walls—official documents like licenses and registrations, and enlarged black-and-white photographs of people and boats. It smells like coffee, soap, and oil. There is a boom box held down with bungee cords, and a shoebox with a couple of dozen CDs in it, mostly albums by American woman singer-songwriters of the offbeat, misunderstood, highly intelligent but intensely emotional school, getting rich selling music to consumers who understand what it's like not to be understood.* Amy pours two mugs of coffee and sets them down on the cabin's bolted-down table, then fishes in the tight pockets of her jeans, pulls out a waterproof nylon wallet, extracts two business cards, and shoots them across the table, one after the other, to

---

*An evident paradox, but nothing out of the ordinary—being out of America has just made this kind of thing more obvious to Randy.

Randy. She seems to enjoy doing this—a small, private smile comes onto her lips and then vanishes the moment Randy sees it. The cards bear the logo of Semper Marine Services and the name America Shaftoe.

"Your name's America?" Randy asks.

Amy looks out the window, bored, afraid he's going to make a big deal out of it. "Yeah," she says.

"Where'd you grow up?"

She seems to be fascinated by the view out the window: big cargo ships strewn around Manila Bay as far as the eye can see, ships hailing from Athens, Shanghai, Vladivostok, Cape Town, Monrovia. Randy infers that looking at big rusty boats is more interesting than talking to Randy.

"So, would you mind telling me what's going on?" she asks. She turns to face him, lifts the mug to her lips, and finally, looks him straight in the eye.

Randy's a little nonplussed. The question is basically impertinent coming from America Shaftoe. Her company, Semper Marine Services, is a contractor at the very lowest level of Avi's virtual corporation—only one of a dozen boats-and-divers outfits that they could have hired—so this is a bit like being interrogated by one's janitor or taxi driver.

But she's smart and unusual, and, precisely because of all her efforts not to be, she's cute. As an interesting female, and a fellow American, she is pulling rank, demanding to be accorded a higher status. Randy tries to be careful.

"Is there something bothering you?" he asks.

She looks away. She's afraid she's given him the wrong impression. "Not in particular," she says, "I'm just nosy. I like to hear stories. Divers always sit around and tell each other stories."

Randy sips his coffee. America continues, "In this business, you never know where your next job is going to come from. Some people have really weird reasons for wanting to get stuff done underwater, which I like to hear." She concludes, "It's fun!" which is clearly all the motivation she needs.

Randy views all of the above as a fairly professional bullshitting job. He decides to give Amy press-release material only. "All the Filipinos are in Manila. That's where the information needs to go. It is somewhat awkward, getting information to Manila, because it has mountains in back of it and Manila Bay in front. The bay is a nightmare place to run submarine cables—"

She's nodding. Of course she would know this already. Randy hits the fast-forward. "Corregidor's a pretty good place. From Corregidor you can shoot a line-of-sight microwave transmission across the bay to downtown Manila."

"So you are extending the North Luzon coastal festoon from Subic Bay down to Corregidor," she says.

"Uh—two things about what you just said," Randy says, and pauses for a moment to get the answer queued up in his output buffer. "One, you have to be careful about your pronouns—what do you mean when you say 'you'? I work for Epiphyte Corporation, which is designed from the ground up to work, not on its own, but as an element in a virtual corporation, kind of like—"

"I know what an epiphyte is," she says. "What's two?"

"Okay, good," Randy says, a little off balance. "Two is that the extension of the North Luzon Festoon is just the first of what we hope will be several linkups. We want to lay a lot of cable, eventually, into Corregidor."

Some kind of machinery behind Amy's eyes begins to hum. The message is clear enough. There will be work aplenty for Semper Marine, if they handle this first job well.

"In this case, the entity that's doing the work is a joint venture including us, FiliTel, 24 Jam, and a big Nipponese electronics company, among others."

"What does 24 Jam have to do with it? They're convenience stores."

"They're the retail outlet—the distribution system—for Epiphyte's product."

"And that is?"

"Pinoy-grams." Randy manages to suppress the urge to tell her that the name is trademarked.

"Pinoy-grams?"

"Here's how it works. You are an Overseas Contract Worker. Before you leave home for Saudi or Singapore or Seattle or wherever, you buy or rent a little gizmo from us. It's about the size of a paperback book and encases a thimble-sized video camera, a tiny screen, and a lot of memory chips. The components come from all over the place—they are shipped to the free port at Subic and assembled in a Nipponese plant there. So they cost next to nothing. Anyway, you take this gizmo overseas with you. Whenever you feel like communicating with the folks at home, you turn it on, aim the camera at yourself, and record a little video greeting card. It all goes onto the memory chips. It's highly compressed. Then you plug the gizmo into a phone line and let it work its magic."

"What's the magic? It sends the video down the phone line?"

"Right."

"Haven't people being messing around with video phones for a long time?"

"The difference here is our software. We don't try to send the video in real time—that's too expensive. We store the data at central servers, then take advantage of lulls, when traffic is low through the undersea cables, and shoot the data down those cables when time can be had cheap. Eventually the data winds up at Epiphyte's facility in Intramuros. From there we can use wireless technology to send the data to 24 Jam stores all over Metro Manila. The store just needs a little pie-plate dish on the roof, and a decoder and a regular VCR down behind the counter. The Pinoy-gram is recorded on a regular videotape. Then, when Mom comes in to buy eggs or Dad comes in to buy cigarettes, the storekeeper says, 'Hey, you got a Pinoy-gram today,' and hands them the videotape. They can take it home and get the latest news from their child overseas. When they're done, they bring the videotape back to 24 Jam for reuse."

About halfway through this, Amy understands the basic concept, looks out the window again and begins trying to work a fragment of breakfast out of her teeth with the tip of her tongue. She does it with her mouth tastefully closed, but it seems to occupy her thoughts more than the explanation of Pinoy-grams.

Randy is gripped by a crazy, unaccountable desire not to bore Amy. It's not that he is getting a crush on her, because he puts the odds at fifty-fifty that she's a lesbian, and he knows better. She is so frank, so guileless, that he feels he could confide anything in her, as an equal.

This is why he hates business. He wants to tell everyone everything. He wants to make friends with people.

"So, let me guess," she says, "you are the guy doing the software."

"Yeah," he admits, a little defensive, "but the software is the only interesting part of this whole project. All the rest is making license plates."

That wakes her up a little. "Making license plates?"

"It's an expression that my business partner and I use," Randy says. "With any job, there's some creative work that needs to be done—new technology to be developed or whatever. Everything else—ninety-nine percent of it—is making deals, raising capital, going to meetings, marketing and sales. We call that stuff making license plates."

She nods, looking out the window. Randy is on the verge of telling her that Pinoy-grams are nothing more than a way to create cash flow, so that they can move on to part two of the business plan. He is sure that this would elevate his stature beyond that of dull software boy. But Amy puffs sharply across the top of her coffee, like blowing out a candle, and says, "Okay. Thanks. I guess that was worth the three packs of cigarettes."

NIGHTMARE

✞ BOBBY SHAFTOE HAS BECOME A CONNOISSEUR OF NIGHTMARES. Like a fighter pilot ejecting from a burning plane, he has just been catapulted out of an old nightmare, and into a brand-new, even better one. It is creepy and understated; no giant lizards here.

It begins with heat on his face. When you take enough fuel to push a fifty-thousand-ton ship across the Pacific Ocean at twenty-five knots, and put it all in one tank and the Nips fly over and torch it all in a few seconds, while you stand close enough to see the triumphant grins on the pilots' faces, then you can feel the heat on your face in this way.

Bobby Shaftoe opens his eyes, expecting that, in so doing, he is raising the curtain on a corker of a nightmare, probably the final moments of *Torpedo Bombers at two o-clock!* (his all-time favorite) or the surprise beginning of *Strafed by Yellow Men XVII*.

But the sound track to this nightmare does not seem to be running. It is as quiet as an ambush. He is sitting up in a hospital bed surrounded by a firing squad of hot klieg lights that make it difficult to see anything else. Shaftoe blinks and focuses on an eddy of cigarette smoke hanging in the air, like spilled fuel oil in a tropical cove. It sure smells good.

A young man is sitting near his bed. All that Shaftoe can see of this man is an asymmetrical halo where the lights glance from the petroleum glaze on his pompadour. And the red coal of his cigarette. As he looks more carefully he can make out the silhouette of a military uniform. Not a Marine uniform. Lieutenant's bars gleam on his shoulders, light shining through double doors.

"Would you like another cigarette?" the lieutenant says. His voice is hoarse but weirdly gentle.

Shaftoe looks down at his own hand and sees the terminal half-inch of a Lucky Strike wedged between his fingers.

"Ask me a tough one," he manages to say. His own voice is deep and slurred, like a gramophone winding down.

The butt is swapped for a new one. Shaftoe raises it to his lips. There are bandages on that arm, and underneath them, he can feel grievous wounds trying to inflict pain. But something is blocking the signals.

Ah, the morphine. It can't be too bad of a nightmare if it comes with morphine, can it?

"You ready?" the voice says. God damn it, that voice is familiar.

"Sir, ask me a tough one, sir!" Shaftoe says.

"You already said that."

"Sir, if you ask a Marine if he wants another cigarette, or if he's ready, the answer is always the same, sir!"

"That's the spirit," the voice says. "Roll film."

A clicking noise starts up in the outer darkness beyond the klieg light firmament. "Rolling," says a voice.

Something big descends towards Shaftoe. He flattens himself into the bed, because it looks exactly like the sinister eggs laid in midair by Nip dive-bombers. But then it stops and just hovers there.

"Sound," says another voice.

Shaftoe looks harder and sees that it is not a bomb but a large bullet-shaped microphone on the end of a boom.

The lieutenant with the pompadour leans forward now, instinctively seeking the light, like a traveler on a cold winter's night.

It is that guy from the movies. What's-his-name. Oh, yeah!

Ronald Reagan has a stack of three-by-five cards in his lap. He skids up a new one: "What advice do you, as the youngest American fighting man ever to win both the Navy Cross and the Silver Star, have for any young Marines on their way to Guadalcanal?"

Shaftoe doesn't have to think very long. The memories are still as fresh as last night's eleventh nightmare: ten plucky Nips in *Suicide Charge!*

"Just kill the one with the sword first."

"Ah," Reagan says, raising his waxed and penciled eyebrows, and cocking his pompadour in Shaftoe's direction. "*Smarrrt*—you target them because they're the officers, right?"

"No, fuckhead!" Shaftoe yells. "You kill 'em because they've got fucking swords! You ever had anyone running at you waving a *fucking sword?*"

Reagan backs down. He's scared now, sweating off some of his makeup, even though a cool breeze is coming in off the bay and through the window.

Reagan wants to turn tail and head back down to Hollywood and nail a starlet fast. But he's stuck here in Oakland, interviewing the war hero. He flips through his stack of cards, rejects about twenty in a row. Shaftoe's in no hurry, he's going to be flat on his back in this hospital bed for approximately the rest of his life. He incinerates half of that cigarette with one long breath, holds it, blows out a smoke ring.

When they fought at night, the big guns on the warships made rings of incandescent gas. Not fat doughnuts but long skinny ones that twisted around like lariats. Shaftoe's body is saturated with morphine. His eyelids avalanche down over his eyes, blessing those orbs that are burning and swollen from the film lights and the smoke of the cigarettes. He and his platoon are racing an incoming tide, trying to get around a headland. They are Marine Raiders and they have been chasing a particular unit of Nips across Guadalcanal for two weeks, whittling them down. As long as they're in the neighborhood, they've been ordered to make their way to a certain point on the headland from which they ought to be able to lob mortar rounds against the incoming Tokyo Express. It is a somewhat harebrained and reckless tactic, but they don't call this Operation Shoestring for nothing; it is all wacky improvisation from the get-go. They are behind schedule because this paltry handful of Nips has been really tenacious, setting ambushes behind every fallen log, taking potshots at them every time they come around one of these headlands. . . .

Something clammy hits him on the forehead: it is the makeup artist taking a swipe at him. Shaftoe finds himself back in the nightmare within which the lizard nightmare was nested.

"Did I tell you about the lizard?" Shaftoe says.

"Several times," his interrogator says. "This'll just take another minute." Ronald Reagan squeezes a fresh three-by-five card between thumb and forefinger, fastening onto something a little less emotional: "What did you and your buddies do in the evenings, when the day's fighting was done?"

"Pile up dead Nips with a bulldozer," Shaftoe says, "and set fire to 'em. Then go down to the beach with a jar of hooch and watch our ships get torpedoed."

Reagan grimaces. "Cut!" he says, quietly but commanding. The clicking noise of the film camera stops.

"How'd I do?" Bobby Shaftoe says as they are squeegeeing the Maybelline off his face, and the men are packing up their equipment. The klieg lights have been turned off, clear northern California light streams in through the windows. The whole scene looks almost real, as if it weren't a nightmare at all.

"You did great," Lieutenant Reagan says, without looking him in the eye. "A real morale booster." He lights a cigarette. "You can go back to sleep now."

"Haw!" Shaftoe says. "I been asleep the whole time. Haven't I?"

He feels a lot better once he gets out of the hospital. They give him a couple of weeks of leave, and he goes straight to the Oakland station and hops the next train for Chicago. Fellow-passengers recognize him from his newspaper pictures, buy him drinks, pose with him for snapshots. He stares out the windows for hours, watching America go by, and sees that all of it is beautiful and clean. There might be wildness, there might be deep forest, there might even be grizzly bears and mountain lions, but it is cleanly sorted out, and the rules (don't mess with bear cubs, hang your food from a tree limb at night) are well-known, and published in the Boy Scout Manual. In those Pacific islands there is too much that is alive, and all of it is in a continual process of eating and being eaten by something else, and once you set foot in the place, you're buying into the deal. Just sitting in that train for a couple of days, his feet in clean white cotton socks, not being eaten alive by anything, goes a long way towards clearing his head up. Only once, or possibly two or three times, does he really feel the need to lock himself in the can and squirt morphine into his arm.

But when he closes his eyes, he finds himself on Guadalcanal, sloshing around that last headland, racing the incoming tide. The big waves are rolling in now, picking up the men and slamming them into rocks.

Finally they turn the corner and see the cove: just a tiny notch in the coast of Guadalcanal. A hundred yards of tidal mudflats backed up by a cliff. They will have to get across those mudflats and establish a foothold on the lower part of the cliff if they aren't going to be washed out to sea by the tide. . . .

The Shaftoes are Tennessee mountain people—miners, among other things. About the time Nimrod Shaftoe went to the Philippines, a couple of his brothers moved up to western Wisconsin to work in lead mines. One of them—Bobby's grandpa—became a foreman. Sometimes he would go to Oconomowoc to pay a visit to the owner of the mine, who had a summer house on one of the lakes. They would go out in a boat and fish for pike. Frequently the mine owner's neighbors—owners of banks and breweries—would come along. That is how the Shaftoes moved to Oconomowoc, and got out of mining, and became fishing and hunting guides. The family has been scrupulous about holding on to the ancestral twang, and to certain other traditions such as military service. One of his sisters and two of his brothers are still living there with Mom and Dad, and his two older brothers are in the Army. Bobby's not the first to have won a Silver Star, though he is the first to have won the Navy Cross.

Bobby goes and talks to Oconomowoc's Boy Scout troop. He gets to be grand marshal of the town parade. Other than that, he hardly budges from the house for two weeks. Sometimes he goes out into the yard and plays catch with his kid brothers. He helps Dad fix up a rotten dock. Guys and gals from his high school keep coming round to visit, and Bobby soon learns the trick that his father and his uncles and granduncles all knew, which is that you never talk about the specifics of what happened over there. No one wants to hear about how you dug half of your buddy's molars out of your leg with the point of a bayonet. All of these kids seem like idiots and lightweights to him now. The only person he can stand to be around is his great-grandfather Shaftoe, ninety-four years of age and sharp as a tack, who was there at Petersburg when Burnside blew a huge hole in the Confederate lines with buried explosives and sent his men rushing into the crater where they got slaughtered. He never talks about it, of course, just as Bobby Shaftoe never talks about the lizard.

Soon enough his time is up, and then he gets a grand sendoff at the Milwaukee train station, hugs Mom, hugs Sis, shakes hands with Dad and the brothers, hugs Mom again, and he's off.

Bobby Shaftoe knows nothing of his future. All he knows is that he has been promoted to sergeant, detached from his former unit (no great adjustment, since he is the only surviving member of his platoon) and reassigned to some unheard-of branch of the Corps in Washington, D.C.

D.C.'s a busy place, but last time Bobby Shaftoe checked the newspapers, there wasn't any combat going on there, and so it's obvious he's not going to get a combat job. He's done his bit anyway, killed many more than his share of Nips, won his medals, suffered from his wounds. As he lacks administrative training, he expects that his new assignment will be to travel around the country being a war hero, raising morale and suckering young men into joining the Corps.

He reports, as ordered, to Marine Barracks, Washington, D.C. It's the Corps's oldest post, a city block halfway between the Capitol and the Navy Yard, a green quadrangle where the Marine Band struts and the drill team drills. He half expects to see strategic reserves of spit and of polish stored in giant tanks nearby.

Two Marines are in the office: a major, who is his new, nominal commanding officer, and a colonel, who looks and acts like he was born here. It is shocking beyond description that two such personages would be there to greet a mere sergeant. Must be the Navy Cross that got their attention. But these Marines have Navy Crosses of their own—two or three apiece.

The major introduces the colonel in a way that doesn't really explain a damn thing to Shaftoe. The colonel says next to nothing; he's there to observe. The major spends a while fingering some typewritten documents.

"Says right here you are gung-ho."

"Sir, yes sir!"

"What the hell does that mean?"

"Sir, it is a Chinese word! There's a Communist there, name of Mao, and he's got an army. We tangled with 'em on more'n one occasion, sir. Gung-ho is their battle cry, it means 'all together' or something like that, so after we got done kicking the crap out of them, sir, we stole it from them, sir!"

"Are you saying you have gone Asiatic like those other China Marines, Shaftoe?"

"Sir! On the contrary, sir, as I think my record demonstrates, sir!"

"You really think that?" the major says incredulously. "We have an interesting report here on a film interview that you did with some soldier* named Lieutenant Reagan."

"Sir! This Marine apologizes for his disgraceful behavior during that interview, sir! This Marine let down himself and his fellow Marines, sir!"

"Aren't you going to give me an excuse? You were wounded. Shell-shocked. Drugged. Suffering from malaria."

"Sir! There is no excuse, sir!"

The major and the colonel nod approvingly at each other.

This "sir, yes sir" business, which would probably sound like horseshit to any civilian in his right mind, makes sense to Shaftoe and to the officers in a deep and important way. Like a lot of others, Shaftoe had trouble with military etiquette at first. He soaked up quite a bit of it growing up in a military family, but living the life was a different matter. Having now experienced all the phases of military existence except for the terminal ones (violent death, court-martial, retirement), he has come to understand the culture for what it is: a system of etiquette within which it becomes possible for groups of men to live together for years, travel to the ends of the earth, and do all kinds of incredibly weird shit without killing each other or completely losing their minds in the process. The extreme formality with which he addresses these officers carries an important subtext: your problem, sir, is deciding what you want me to do, and my problem, sir, is doing it. My gung-ho posture says that once you give the order I'm not going to bother you with any of the details—and *your* half of the bargain is you had better stay on your side of the line, sir, and not bother me with any of the chickenshit politics that you have to deal with for a living. The implied responsibility placed upon the officer's shoulders by the subordinate's unhesitating willingness to follow orders is a withering burden to any officer with half a brain, and Shaftoe has more than once seen seasoned noncoms reduce green lieutenants to quivering blobs simply by standing before them and agreeing, cheerfully, to carry out their orders.

---

*A deprecatory term for a fighting man not good enough to be in the Corps.

"This Lieutenant Reagan complained that you kept trying to tell him a story about a lizard," the major says.

"Sir! Yes, sir! A giant lizard, sir! An interesting story, sir!" Shaftoe says.

"I don't care," the major says. "The question is, was it an appropriate story to tell in that circumstance?"

"Sir! We were making our way around the coast of the island, trying to get between these Nips and a Tokyo Express landing site, sir! . . ." Shaftoe begins.

"Shut up!"

"Sir! Yes sir!"

There is a sweaty silence that is finally broken by the colonel. "We had the shrinks go over your statement, Sergeant Shaftoe."

"Sir! Yes, sir!"

"They are of the opinion that the whole giant lizard thing is a classic case of projection."

"Sir! Could you please tell me what the hell that is, sir!"

The colonel flushes, turns his back, peers through blinds at sparse traffic out on Eye Street. "Well, what they are saying is that there really was no giant lizard. That you killed that Jap* in hand-to-hand combat. And that your memory of the giant lizard is basically your id coming out."

"Id, sir!"

"That there is this id thing inside your brain and that it took over and got you fired up to kill that Jap bare-handed. Then your imagination dreamed up all this crap about the giant lizard afterwards, as a way of explaining it."

"Sir! So you are saying that the lizard was just a metaphor, sir!"

"Yes."

"Sir! Then I would respectfully like to know how that Nip got chewed in half, sir!"

The colonel screws up his face dismissively. "Well, by the time you were rescued by that coastwatcher, Sergeant, you had been in that cove for three days along with all of those dead bodies. And in that tropical heat with all those bugs and scavengers, there was no way to tell from looking at that Jap whether he had been chewed up by a giant lizard or run through a brush chipper, if you know what I mean."

"Sir! Yes I do, sir!"

The major goes back to the report. "This Reagan fellow says that you also repeatedly made disparaging comments about General MacArthur."

---

*Men with experience in Asia use the word "Nip." The Colonel's use of "Jap" suggests that his career has been spent in the Atlantic and/or Caribbean.

"Sir, yes sir! He is a son of a bitch who hates the Corps, sir! He is trying to get us all killed, sir!"

The major and the colonel look at each other. It is clear that they have, wordlessly, just arrived at some decision.

"Since you insist on reenlisting, the typical thing would be to have you go around the country showing off your medals and recruiting young men into the Corps. But this lizard story kind of rules that out."

"Sir! I do not understand, sir!"

"The Recruitment Office has reviewed your file. They have seen Reagan's report. They are nervous that you are going to be in West Bumfuck, Arkansas, riding in the Memorial Day parade in your shiny dress uniform, and suddenly you are going to start spouting all kinds of nonsense about lizards and scare everyone shitless and put a kink in the war effort."

"Sir! I respectfully—"

"Permission to speak denied," the major says. "I won't even get into your obsession with General MacArthur."

"Sir! The general is a murdering—"

"Shut up!"

"Sir! Yes, sir!"

"We have another job for you, Marine."

"Sir! Yes, sir!"

"You're going to be part of something very special."

"Sir! The Marine Raiders are already a very special part of a very special Corps, sir!"

"That's not what I mean. I mean that this assignment is . . . unusual." The major looks over at the colonel. He is not sure how to proceed.

The colonel puts his hand in his pocket, jingles coins, then reaches up and checks his shave.

"It is not exactly a Marine Corps assignment," he finally says. "You will be part of a special international detachment. An American Marine Raider platoon and a British Special Air Services squadron, operating together under one command. A bunch of tough hombres who've shown they can handle any assignment, under any conditions. Is that a fair description of you, Marine?"

"Sir! Yes, sir!"

"It is a very unusual setup," the colonel muses, "not the kind of thing that *military* men would ever dream up. Do you know what I'm saying, Shaftoe?"

"Sir, no sir! But I do detect a strong odor of politics in the room now, sir!"

The colonel gets a little twinkle in his eye, and glances out the window towards the Capitol dome. "These politicians can be real picky about how they get things done. Everything has to be just so. They don't like excuses. Do you follow me, Shaftoe?"

"Sir! Yes, sir!"

"The Corps had to fight to get this. They were going to make it an Army thing. We pulled a few strings with some former Naval persons in high places. Now the assignment is ours. Some would say, it is ours to screw up."

"Sir! The assignment will not be screwed up, sir!"

"The reason that son of a bitch MacArthur is killing Marines like flies down in the South Pacific is because sometimes we don't play the political game that well. If you and your new unit do not perform brilliantly, that situation will only worsen."

"Sir! You can rely on this Marine, sir!"

"Your commanding officer will be Lieutenant Ethridge. An Annapolis man. Not much combat experience, but knows how to move in the right circles. He can run interference for you at the political level. The responsibility for getting things done on the ground will be entirely yours, Sergeant Shaftoe."

"Sir! Yes, sir!"

"You'll be working closely with British Special Air Service. Very good men. But I want you and your men to outshine them."

"Sir! You can count on it, sir!"

"Well, get ready to ship out, then," the major says. "You're on your way to North Africa, Sergeant Shaftoe."

LONDINIUM

THE MASSIVE BRITISH COINAGE CLANKS IN HIS POCKET LIKE PEWter dinner plates. Lawrence Pritchard Waterhouse walks down a street wearing the uniform of a commander in the United States Navy. This must not be taken to imply that he is actually a commander, or indeed that he is even in the Navy, though he is. The United States part is, however, a safe bet, because every time he arrives at a curb, he either comes close to being run over by a shooting-brake or he falters in his stride; diverts his train of thought onto a siding, much to the disturbance of its passengers and crew; and throws some large part of his mental calculation circuitry into the job of trying to reflect his surroundings through a large mirror. They drive on the left side of the street here.

He knew about that before he came. He had seen pictures. And Alan had complained of it in Princeton, always nearly being run over as, lost in thought, he stepped off curbs looking the wrong way.

The curbs are sharp and perpendicular, not like the American smoothly molded sigmoid-cross-section curves. The transition between the sidewalk and the street is a crisp vertical. If you put a green lightbulb on Waterhouse's head and watched him from the side during the blackout, his trajectory would look just like a square wave traced out on the face of a single-beam oscilloscope: up, down, up, down. If he were doing this at home, the curbs would be evenly spaced, about twelve to the mile, because his home town is neatly laid out on a grid.

Here in London, the street pattern is irregular and so the transitions in the square wave come at random-seeming times, sometimes very close together, sometimes very far apart.

A scientist watching the wave would probably despair of finding any pattern; it would look like a random circuit, driven by noise, triggered perhaps by the arrival of cosmic rays from deep space, or the decay of radioactive isotopes.

But if he had depth and ingenuity, it would be a different matter.

Depth could be obtained by putting a green light bulb on the head of every person in London and then recording their tracings for a few nights. The result would be a thick pile of graph-paper tracings, each one as seemingly random as the others. The thicker the pile, the greater the depth.

Ingenuity is a completely different matter. There is no systematic way to get it. One person could look at the pile of square wave tracings and see nothing but noise. Another might find a source of fascination there, an irrational feeling impossible to explain to anyone who did not share it. Some deep part of the mind, adept at noticing patterns (or the existence of a pattern) would stir awake and frantically signal the dull quotidian parts of the brain to *keep looking* at the pile of graph paper. The signal is dim and not always heeded, but it would instruct the recipient to

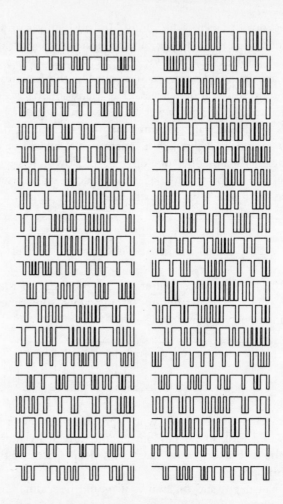

stand there for days if necessary, shuffling through the pile of graphs like an autist, spreading them out over a large floor, stacking them in piles according to some inscrutable system, pencilling numbers, and letters from dead alphabets, into the corners, cross-referencing them, finding patterns, cross-checking them against others.

One day this person would walk out of that room carrying a highly accurate street map of London, reconstructed from the information in all of those square wave plots.

Lawrence Pritchard Waterhouse is one of those people.

As a result, the authorities of his country, the United States of America, have made him swear a mickle oath of secrecy, and keep supplying him with new uniforms of various services and ranks, and now have sent him to London.

He steps off a curb, glancing reflexively to the left. A jingling sounds in his right ear, bicycle brakes trumpet. It is merely a Royal Marine (Waterhouse is beginning to recognize the uniforms) off on some errand; but he has reinforcements behind him in the form of a bus/coach painted olive drab and stenciled all over with inscrutable code numbers.

"Pardon me, sir!" the Royal Marine says brightly, and swerves around him, apparently reckoning that the coach can handle any mopping-up work. Waterhouse leaps forward, directly into the path of a black taxi coming the other way.

After making it across that particular street, though, he arrives at his Westminster destination without further life-threatening incidents, unless you count being a few minutes' airplane ride from a tightly organized horde of murderous Germans with the best weapons in the world. He has found himself in a part of town that seems almost like certain lightless, hemmed-in parts of Manhattan: narrow streets lined with buildings on the order of ten stories high. Occasional glimpses of ancient and mighty gothic piles at street-ends clue him in to the fact that he is nigh unto Greatness. As in Manhattan, the people walk fast, each with some clear purpose in mind.

The amended heels of the pedestrians' wartime shoes pop metallically. Each pedestrian has a fairly consistent stride length and clicks with nearly metronomic precision. A microphone in the sidewalk would provide an eavesdropper with a cacophony of clicks, seemingly random like the noise from a Geiger counter. But the right kind of person could abstract signal from noise and count the pedestrians, provide a male/female break-down and a leg-length histogram . . .

He has to stop this. He would like to concentrate on the matter at hand, but that is still a mystery.

A massive, blocky modern sculpture sits over the door of the St. James's Park tube station, doing twenty-four hour surveillance on the Broadway Buildings, which is actually just a single building. Like every other intelligence headquarters Waterhouse had seen, it is a great disappointment.

It is, after all, just a building—orange stone, ten or so stories, an unreasonably high mansard roof accounting for the top three, some smid-gens of classical ornament above the windows, which like all windows in London are divided into eight right triangles by strips of masking tape. Waterhouse finds that this look blends better with classical architecture than, say, gothic.

He has some grounding in physics and finds it implausible that, when a few hundred pounds of trinitrotoluene are set off in the neighborhood and the resulting shock wave propagates through a large pane of glass, the people on the other side of it will derive any benefit from an asterisk of paper tape. It is a superstitious gesture, like hexes on Pennsylvania Dutch farmhouses. The sight of it probably helps keep people's minds focused on the war.

Which doesn't seem to be working for Waterhouse. He makes his way carefully across the street, thinking very hard about the direction of the traffic, on the assumption that someone inside will be watching him. He goes inside, holding the door for a fearsomely brisk young woman in a quasimilitary outfit—who makes it clear that Waterhouse had better not expect to Get Anywhere just because he's holding the door for her— and then for a tired-looking septuagenarian gent with a white mustache.

The lobby is well guarded and there is some business with Water-house's credentials and his orders. Then he makes the obligatory mistake of going to the wrong floor because they are numbered differently here. This would be a lot funnier if this were not a military intelligence head-quarters in the thick of the greatest war in the history of the world.

When he does get to the right floor, though, it is a bit posher than the wrong one was. Of course, the underlying structure of everything in England is posh. There is no in-between with these people. You have to walk a mile to find a telephone booth, but when you find it, it is built as if the senseless dynamiting of pay phones had been a serious problem at some time in the past. And a British mailbox can presumably stop a German tank. None of them have cars, but when they do, they are three-ton hand-built beasts. The concept of stamping out a whole lot of cars is unthinkable—there are certain procedures that have to be followed, Mr. Ford, such as the hand-brazing of radiators, the traditional whittling of the tyres from solid blocks of cahoutchouc.

Meetings are all the same. Waterhouse is always the Guest; he has never actually hosted a meeting. The Guest arrives at an unfamiliar build-ing, sits in a waiting area declining offers of caffeinated beverages from a personable but chaste female, and is, in time, ushered to the Room, where the Main Guy and the Other Guys are awaiting him. There is a system of introductions which the Guest need not concern himself with because he is operating in a passive mode and need only respond to stimuli, shaking all hands that are offered, declining all further offers of caffeinated and (now) alcoholic beverages, sitting down when and where invited. In this case, the Main Guy and all but one of the Other Guys happen to be British, the selection of beverages is slightly different, the room, being British, is thrown together from blocks of stone like a Pharaoh's inner tomb, and the windows have the usual unconvincing strips of tape on them. The Predictable Humor Phase is much shorter than in America, the Chitchat Phase longer.

Waterhouse has forgotten all of their names. He always immediately forgets the names. Even if he remembered them, he would not know their significance, as he does not actually have the organization chart of the Foreign Ministry (which runs Intelligence) and the Military laid out in front of him. They keep saying "woe to hice!" but just as he actually begins to feel sorry for this Hice fellow, whoever he is, he figures out that this is how they pronounce "Waterhouse." Other than that, the one remark that actually penetrates his brain is when one of the Other Guys says something about the Prime Minister that implies considerable familiarity. And he's not even the Main Guy. The Main Guy is much older and more distinguished. So it seems to Waterhouse (though he has completely stopped listening to what all of these people are saying to him) that a good half of the people in the room have recently had conversations with Winston Churchill.

Then, suddenly, certain words come into the conversation. Waterhouse was not paying attention, but he is pretty sure that within the last ten seconds, the word Ultra was uttered. He blinks and sits up straighter.

The Main Guy looks bemused. The Other Guys look startled.

"Was something said, a few minutes ago, about the availability of coffee?" Waterhouse says.

"Miss Stanhope, coffee for Captain Woe To Hice," says the Main Guy into an electrical intercom. It is one of only half a dozen office intercoms in the British Empire. However, it is cast in a solid ingot from a hundred pounds of iron and fed by 420-volt cables as thick as Waterhouse's index finger. "And if you would be so good as to bring tea."

So, now Waterhouse knows the name of the Main Guy's secretary. That's a start. From that, with a bit of research he might be able to recover the memory of the Main Guy's name.

This seems to have thrown them back into the Chitchat Phase, and though American important guys would be fuming and frustrated, the Brits seem enormously relieved. Even more beverages are ordered from Miss Stanhope.

"Have you seen Dr. Shehrrrn recently?" the Main Guy inquires of Waterhouse. He has a touch of concern in his voice.

"Who?" Then Waterhouse realizes that the person in question is Commander Schoen, and that here in London the name is apt to be pronounced correctly, *Shehrrn* instead of *Shane*.

"Commander Waterhouse?" the Main Guy says, several minutes later. On the fly, Waterhouse has been trying to invent a new cryptosystem based upon alternative systems of pronouncing words and hasn't said anything in quite a while.

"Oh, yeah! Well, I stopped in briefly and paid my respects to Schoen before getting on the ship. Of course, when he's, uh, feeling under the weather, everyone's under strict orders not to talk cryptology with him."

"Of course."

"The problem is that when your whole relationship with the fellow is built around cryptology, you can't even really poke your head in the door without violating that order."

"Yes, it is most awkward."

"I guess he's doing okay." Waterhouse does not say this very convincingly and there is an appropriate silence around the table.

"When he was in better spirits, he wrote glowingly of your work on the *Cryptonomicon*," says one of the Other Guys, who has not spoken very much until now. Waterhouse pegs him as some kind of unspecified mover and shaker in the world of machine cryptology.

"He's a heck of a fella," Waterhouse says.

The Main Guy uses this as an opening. "Because of your work with Dr. Schoen's Indigo machine, you are, by definition, on the Magic list. Now that this country and yours have agreed—at least in principle—to cooperate in the field of cryptanalysis, this automatically puts you on the Ultra list."

"I understand, sir," Waterhouse says.

"Ultra and Magic are more symmetrical than not. In each case, a belligerent Power has developed a machine cypher which it considers to be perfectly unbreakable. In each case, an allied Power has in fact broken that cypher. In America, Dr. Schoen and his team broke Indigo and devised the Magic machine. Here, it was Dr. Knox's team that broke Enigma and devised the Bombe. The leading light here seems to have been Dr. Turing. The leading light with you chaps was Dr. Schoen, who is, as you said, under the weather. But he holds you up as comparable to Turing, Commander Waterhouse."

"That's pretty darn generous," Waterhouse says.

"But you studied with Turing at Princeton, did you not?"

"We were there at the same time, if that's what you mean. We rode bikes. His work was a lot more advanced."

"But Turing was pursuing graduate studies. You were merely an undergraduate."

"Sure. But even allowing for that, he's way smarter than me."

"You are too modest, Captain Waterhouse. How many undergraduates have published papers in international journals?"

"We just rode bikes," Waterhouse insists. "Einstein wouldn't give me the time of day."

"Dr. Turing has shown himself to be rather handy with information theory," says a prematurely haggard guy with long limp grey hair, whom

Waterhouse now pegs as some sort of Oxbridge don. "You must have discussed this with him."

The don turns to the others and says, donnishly, "Information Theory would inform a mechanical calculator in much the same way as, say, fluid dynamics would inform the hull of a ship." Then he turns back to Waterhouse and says, somewhat less formally: "Dr. Turing has continued to develop his work on the subject since he vanished, from your point of view, into the realm of the Classified. Of particular interest has been the subject of just how much information can be extracted from seemingly random data."

Suddenly all of the other people in the room are exchanging those amused looks again. "I gather from your reaction," says the Main Guy, "that this has been of continuing interest to you as well."

Waterhouse wonders what his reaction was. Did he grow fangs? Drool into his coffee?

"That's good," says the Main Guy before Waterhouse can answer, "because it is of the highest interest to us as well. You see, now that we are making efforts—and I must emphasize the preliminary and unsatisfactory level of these efforts to this point—to coordinate intelligence between America and Britain, we find ourselves in the oddest situation that has ever faced a pair of allies in a war. We know everything, Commander Waterhouse. We receive Hitler's personal communications to his theater commanders, frequently before the commanders do! This knowledge is obviously a powerful tool. But just as obviously, it cannot help us win the war unless we allow it to change our actions. That is, if, through Ultra, we become aware of a convoy sailing from Taranto to supply Rommel in North Africa, the knowledge does us no good unless we go out and sink that convoy."

"Clearly," Waterhouse says.

"Now, if ten convoys are sent out and all of them are sunk, even those under cover of clouds and darkness, the Germans will ask themselves how we knew where those convoys could be found. They will realize that we have penetrated the Enigma cypher, and change it, and then this tool will be lost to us. It is safe to say that Mr. Churchill will be displeased by such an outcome." The Main Guy looks at all of the others, who nod knowingly. Waterhouse gets the feeling that Mr. Churchill has been bearing down rather hard on this particular point.

"Let us recast this in information theory terms," says the don. "Information flows from Germany to us, through the Ultra system at Bletchley Park. That information comes to us as seemingly random Morse code transmissions on the wireless. But because we have very bright people who can discover order in what is seemingly random, we can extract information that is crucial to our endeavors. Now, the Germans have not broken our important cyphers. But they can observe our actions—the routing of our convoys in the North Atlantic, the deployment of our air forces. If the convoys always avoid the U-boats, if the air forces always go straight to the German convoys, then it is clear to the Germans—I'm speaking of a very bright sort of German here, a German of the professor type—that there is not randomness here. This German can find correlations. He can see that we know more than we should. In other words, there is a certain point at which information begins to flow from us back to the Germans."

"We need to know where that point is," says the Main Guy. "Exactly where it is. We need then to stay on the right side of it. To develop the appearance of randomness."

"Yes," Waterhouse says, "and it has to be a kind of randomness that would convince someone like Rudolf von Hacklheber."

"Exactly the fellow we had in mind," the don says. "Dr. von Hacklheber, as of last year."

"Oh!" Waterhouse says. "Rudy got his Ph.D.?" Since Rudy got called back into the embrace of the Thousand-Year Reich, Waterhouse has assumed the worst: imagining him out there in a greatcoat, sleeping in drifts and besieging Leningrad or something. But apparently the Nazis, with their sharp eye for talent (as long as it isn't Jewish talent) have given him a desk job.

Still, it's touch and go for a while after Waterhouse shows pleasure that Rudy's okay. One of the Other Guys, trying to break the ice, jokes that if someone had had the foresight to lock Rudy up in New Jersey for the duration, there would be no need for the new category of secret known as Ultra Mega. No one seems to think it's funny, so Waterhouse assumes it's true.

They show him the organizational chart for RAF Special Detachment No. 2701, which contains the names of all of the twenty-four people in the world who are on to Ultra Mega. The top is cluttered with names such as Winston Churchill and Franklin Delano Roosevelt. Then come some other names that seem oddly familiar to Waterhouse—perhaps the names of these very gents here in this room. Below them, one Chattan, a youngish RAF colonel who (Waterhouse is assured) accomplished some very fine things during the Battle of Britain.

In the next rank of the chart is the name Lawrence Pritchard Waterhouse. There are two other names: one is an RAF captain and the other is a captain in the United States Marine Corps. There is also a dotted line veering off to one side, leading to the name Dr. Alan Mathison

Turing. Taken as a whole, this chart may be the most irregular and bizarre ad-hocracy ever grafted onto a military organization.

In the bottom row of the chart are two groups of half a dozen names, clustered beneath the names of the RAF captain and the Marine captain respectively. These are the squads that represent the executive wing of the organization: as one of the guys at the Broadway Building puts it, "the men at the coal-face," and as the one American Guy translates it for him, "this is where the rubber meets the road."

"Do you have any questions?" the Main Guy asks.

"Did Alan choose the number?"

"You mean Dr. Turing?"

"Yes. Did he choose the number 2701?"

This level of detail is clearly several ranks beneath the station of the men in the Broadway Buildings. They look startled and almost offended, as if Waterhouse has suddenly asked them to take dictation.

"Possibly," says the Main Guy. "Why do you ask?"

"Because," Waterhouse says, "the number 2701 is the product of two primes, and those numbers, 37 and 73, when expressed in decimal notation, are, as you can plainly see, the reverse of each other."

All heads swivel toward the don, who looks put out. "We'd best change that," he says, "it is the sort of thing that Dr. von Hacklheber would notice." He stands up, withdraws a Mont Blanc fountain pen from his pocket, and amends the organizational chart so that it reads 2702 instead of 2701. As he is doing this, Waterhouse looks at the other men in the room and thinks that they look satisfied. Clearly, this is just the sort of parlor trick they have hired Waterhouse to perform.

CORREGIDOR

THERE IS NO FIXED BOUNDARY BETWEEN THE WATER OF MANILA Bay and the humid air above it, only a featureless blue-grey shroud hanging a couple of miles away. *Glory IV* maneuvers cautiously through an immense strewing of anchored cargo ships for about half an hour, then picks up speed and heads out into the center of the bay. The air thins a bit, allowing Randy a good view of Bata'an off to starboard: black mountains mostly veiled in haze and speckled by the mushroom-cap-shaped clouds of ascending thermals. For the most part, it has no beaches, just red cliffs plummeting the last few yards into the sea. But as they work their way out to the end of the peninsula, the land tails off more gently and supports a few pale green fields. At the very tip of Bata'an are a couple of stabbing limestone crags that Randy recognizes from Avi's video. But by this point he has eyes mostly for Corregidor itself, which lies a few miles off the end of the peninsula.

America Shaftoe, or Amy as she likes to be called, spends most of the voyage bustling around on the deck, engaging the Filipino and American divers in bursts of serious conversation, sometimes sitting cross-legged on the deck plates to go over papers or charts. She has donned a frayed straw cowboy hat to protect her head from solar radiation. Randy's in no hurry to expose himself. He ambles around the air-conditioned cabin, sipping his coffee and looking at the photographs on the walls.

He is naively expecting to see pictures of divers landing submarine cables on beaches. Semper Marine Services does a fair amount of cable work—and does it well, he checked their references before hiring them—but they apparently do not consider that kind of work interesting enough to photograph. Most of these pictures are of undersea salvage operations: divers, with enormous grins on their leathery faces, triumphantly holding up barnacle-encrusted vases, like hockey players brandishing the Stanley Cup.

From a distance, Corregidor is a lens of jungle bulging out of the water with a flat shelf extending off to one side. From the maps, he knows that it is really a sperm-shaped affair. What looks like a shelf from this angle is its tail, which snakes off to the east as if the sperm were trying to swim out of Manila Bay to impregnate Asia.

Amy storms past and throws the cabin door open. "Come to the bridge," she says, "you should see this."

Randy follows her. "Who's the guy in most of those pictures?" he asks.

"Scary, crew cut?"

"Yeah."

"That's my father," she says. "Doug."

"Would that be Douglas MacArthur Shaftoe?" Randy asks. He's seen the name on some of the documents that he's exchanged with Semper Marine.

"The same."

"The ex-SEAL?"

"Yeah. But he doesn't like to be referred to that way. It is *such* a cliche."

"Why does he seem familiar to me?"

Amy sighs. "He had his fifteen minutes of fame back in 1975."

"I'm having trouble remembering."

"You know Comstock?"

"Attorney General Paul Comstock? Hates crypto?"

"I'm talking about his father. Earl Comstock."

"Cold War policy guy—the brains behind the Vietnam War—right?"

"I've never heard him described that way, but yeah, we're talking about the same guy. You might remember that back in 1975, Earl Comstock fell, or was pushed, off a ski lift in Colorado, and broke his arms."

"Oh, yeah. It's sort of coming back to me."

"My pop—" Amy does a little head-fake towards one of the photographs "—happened to be seated right next to him at the time."

"By accident, or—"

"Total chance. Not planned."

"That's one way to look at it," Randy says, "but on the other hand, if Earl Comstock went skiing frequently, the probability was actually rather high that *sooner or later* he'd find himself sitting, fifty feet off the ground, next to a Vietnam combat veteran."

"Whatever. All I'm saying is—I don't want to talk about it, actually."

"Am I going to get to meet this character?" Randy asks, looking at the photograph.

Amy bites her lip and squints at the horizon. "Ninety percent of the time his presence is a sign that something really weird is going on." She opens the hatch to the bridge and holds it for him, pointing out the high step.

"The other ten percent?"

"He's bored, or on the outs with his girlfriend."

Glory's pilot is concentrating intensely and ignores them, which Randy takes to be a sign of professionalism. The bridge has many counters fashioned from doors or thick plywood, and all of the available space is covered with electronic gear: a fax, a smaller machine that spews out weather bulletins, three computers, a satellite phone, a few GSM phones socketed into their chargers, depth-sounding gear. Amy leads him over to a machine with a big screen that is showing what looks like a black-and-white photo of rugged terrain. "Sidescan sonar," she explains, "one of our best tools for this kind of work. Shows us what's on the bottom." She checks one of the computer screens for their current coordinates and then runs a quick calculation in her head. "Ernesto, change course five degrees to starboard please."

"Yes ma'am," Ernesto says, and makes it happen.

"What are you looking for?"

"This is a freebie—like the cigarettes at the hotel," Amy explains. "Just an extra added bonus for doing business with us. Sometimes we like to play tour guide. See? Check that out." She uses her pinkie to point out something that is just becoming visible on the screen. Randy hunches over and peers at it. It is clearly a manmade shape: a jumble of straight lines and right angles.

"Looks like a heap of debris," he says.

"It is now," Amy says, "but it used to be a good chunk of the Filipino treasury."

"What?"

"During the war," Amy says, "after Pearl Harbor, but before the Japanese took Manila, the government emptied out the treasury. They put all the gold and silver into crates and shipped it to Corregidor for safekeeping—supposedly."

"What do you mean, supposedly?"

She shrugs. "This is the Philippines," she says. "I have the feeling a lot of it ended up elsewhere. But a lot of the silver ended up there." She straightens up and nods out the window at Corregidor. "At the time they thought Corregidor was impregnable."

"When was this, roughly?"

"December '41 or January '42. Anyway, it became obvious that Corregidor was going to fall. A submarine came and took away the gold at the beginning of February. Then another sub came and took off guys they couldn't allow to be captured, like codebreakers. But they didn't have enough subs to carry away all the silver. MacArthur left in March. They started taking the silver out, in crates, in the middle of the night, and dropping it into the water."

"You're shitting me!"

"They could always come back later and try to recover it," Amy says. "Better to lose it all than let the Japanese take it, right?"

"I guess so."

"The Japanese recovered a lot of that silver—they captured a bunch of American divers on Bata'an and Corregidor, and made them go down, right down below where we are at this moment, and recover it. But those same divers managed to hide a lot of silver from their guards and get it to Filipinos, who smuggled it into Manila, where it became so common that it totally debased the Japanese occupation currency."

"So what are we seeing right now?"

"The remains of old crates that burst open when they hit the seafloor," Amy says.

"Was there any of that silver left when the war ended?"

"Oh, sure," Amy says breezily. "Most of it was dumped here, and those divers got it, but some was dumped in other areas. My dad recovered some of it as late as the 1970s."

"Wow. That doesn't make any sense!"

"Why not?"

"I can't believe that piles of silver just sat on the bottom of the ocean for thirty years, free for the taking."

"You don't know the Philippines very well," Amy says.

"I know that it's a poor country. Why didn't someone come out and get that silver?"

"Most of the treasure hunters in this part of the world are looking for much bigger game," Amy says, "or easier."

Randy's nonplussed. "A pile of silver on the bottom of the bay seems big and easy to me."

"It's not. Silver's not worth that much. A Sung Dynasty vase, cleaned up, can go for more than its weight in gold. Gold. And it's easier to find the vase—you just scan the seafloor, looking for something shaped like a junk. A sunken junk makes a distinctive image on sonar. Whereas an old crate, all busted up and covered with coral and barnacles, tends to look like a rock."

As they draw closer to Corregidor, Randy can see that the tail of the island is lumpy, with big stacks of rock protruding from it here and there. The color of the land fades gradually from dark jungle green to pale green and then a sere reddish-brown as the tail extends from the fat center of the island out to the end, and the soil becomes dryer. Randy's gaze is fixed on one of those rocky crags, which is surmounted by a new steel tower. Atop the tower is a microwave horn aimed east, toward Epiphyte's building in Intramuros.

"See those caves along the waterline?" Amy says. She seems to regret having mentioned sunken treasure in the first place, and now wants to get off the subject.

Randy tears himself away from admiring the microwave antenna, of which he is part owner, and looks in the direction Amy's pointing. The limestock flank of the island, which drops vertically the last few meters into the water, is riddled with holes.

"Yeah."

"Built by Americans to house beach defense guns. Enlarged by the Japanese as launch sites for suicide boats."

"Wow."

Randy notices a deep gargling noise, and looks over to see that a boat has fallen in alongside them. It is a canoe-shaped affair maybe forty feet long, with long outriggers on either side. A couple of ragged flags fly from a short mast, and bright laundry flaps gaily from various lines strung here and there. A big, naked diesel engine sits in the middle of the hull flailing the atmosphere with black smoke. Forward of that, several Filipinos, including women and children, are gathered in the shade of a bright blue tarpaulin, eating. Aft, a couple of men are fiddling with diving equipment. One of them is holding something up to his mouth: a microphone. A voice blares from *Glory*'s radio, speaking Tagalog. Ernesto stifles a laugh, picks up the mike, and answers briefly. Randy doesn't know what they are saying, but he suspects it is something like "Let's horse around later, our client is on the bridge right now."

"Business associates," Amy explains dryly. Her body language says that she wants to get away from Randy and back to work.

"Thanks for the tour," Randy says. "One question."

Amy raises her eyebrows, trying to look patient.

"How much of Semper Marine's revenue derives from treasure hunting?"

"This month? This year? The last ten years? Over the lifetime of the company?" Amy says.

"Whatever."

"That kind of income is sporadic," Amy says. "*Glory* was paid for, and then some, by pottery that we recovered from a junk. But some years we get all of our revenue from jobs like this one."

"In other words, boring jobs that suck?" Randy says. He just blurts it out. Normally he controls his tongue a little better. But shaving off his beard has blurred his ego boundaries, or something.

He's expecting her to laugh or at least wink a him, but she takes it very seriously. She has a pretty good poker face. "Think of it as making license plates," she says.

"So you guys are basically a bunch of treasure hunters," Randy says. "You just make license plates to stabilize your cash flow."

"Call us treasure hunters if you like," Amy says. "Why are you in business, Randy?" She turns around and stalks out of the place.

Randy's still watching her go when he hears Ernesto cursing under his breath, not so much angry as astonished. *Glory* is swinging around the tip of Corregidor's tail now and the entire southern side of the island is becoming visible for the first time. The last mile or so of the tail curves around to form a semicircular bay. Anchored in the center of this bay is a white ship that Randy identifies, at first, as a small ocean liner with rakish and wicked lines. Then he sees the name painted on its stern: RUI FALEIRO—SANTA MONICA, CALIFORNIA.

Randy goes and stands next to Ernesto and they stare at the white ship for a while. Randy has heard about it, and Ernesto, like everyone else in the Philippines, knows about it. But seeing it is another thing entirely. A helicopter sits on its afterdeck like a toy. A dagger-shaped muscle boat hangs from a davit, ready for use as a dinghy. A brown-skinned man in a gleaming white uniform can be seen polishing a brass rail.

"Rui Faleiro was Magellan's cosmographer," Randy says.

"Cosmographer?"

"The brains of the operation," Randy says, tapping his head.

"He came here with Magellan?" Ernesto asks.

In most of the world, Magellan is thought of as the first guy who went around the world. Here, everyone knows he only made it as far as Mactan Island, where he was killed by Filipinos.

"When Magellan set out on his ship, Faleiro stayed behind in Seville," Randy says. "He went crazy."

"You know a lot about Magallanes, eh?" Ernesto says.

"No," Randy says, "I know a lot about the Dentist."

"Don't talk to the Dentist. Ever. Not about anything. Not even tech stuff. Any technical question he asks you is just a stalking horse for some business tactic that is as far beyond your comprehension as Gödel's Proof would be to Daffy Duck."

Avi told Randy this spontaneously one evening, as they were tucking into dinner at a restaurant in downtown Makati. Avi refuses to discuss anything important within a mile of the Manila Hotel because he thinks every room, and every table, is under surveillance.

"Thanks for the vote of confidence," Randy said.

"Hey," Avi said, "I'm just trying to stake out my turf here—justify my existence in this project. I'll handle the business stuff."

"You're not being a little paranoid?"

"Listen. The Dentist has at least a billion dollars of his own, and another ten billion under management—half the fucking orthodontists in Southern California retired at age forty because he dectupled their IRAs in the space of two or three years. You don't achieve those kinds of results by being a nice guy."

"Maybe he just got lucky."

"He did get lucky. But that doesn't mean he's a nice guy. My point is that he put that money into investments that were extremely risky. He played Russian roulette with his investors' life savings, keeping them in the dark. I mean, this guy would invest in a Mindanao kidnapping ring if it gave a good rate of return."

"Does he understand that he was lucky, I wonder?"

"That's my question. I'm guessing no. I think he considers himself to be an instrument of Divine Providence, like Douglas MacArthur."

Rui Faleiro is the pride of Seattle's superyacht industry, which has been burgeoning, ever so discreetly, of late. Randy gleaned a few facts about it from a marketing brochure that was published before the Dentist actually bought the ship. So he knows that the helicopter and the speedboat came included in the purchase price, which has never been divulged. The vessel contains, among other things, ten tons of marble. The master bedroom suite contains full his and hers bathrooms lined with black marble and pink marble respectively, so that the Dentist and the Diva don't have to fight over sink space when they are primping for a big event in the yacht's grand ballroom.

"The Dentist?" Ernesto says.

"Kepler. Doctor Kepler," Randy says. "In the States, some people call him the Dentist." People in the high-tech industry.

Ernesto nods knowingly. "A man like that could have had any woman in the world," he says. "But he picked a Filipina."

"Yes," Randy says cautiously.

"In the States, do people know the story of Victoria Vigo?"

"I must tell you that she is not as famous in the States as she is here."

"Of course."

"But some of her songs were very popular. Many people know that she came from great poverty."

"Do people in the States know about Smoky Mountain? The garbage dump in Tondo, where children hunt for food?"

"Some of them do. It will be very famous when the movie about Victoria Vigo's life shows on television."

Ernesto nods, seemingly satisfied. Everyone here knows that a movie about the Diva's life is being made, starring herself. They generally don't know that it's a vanity project, financed by the Dentist, and that it will be aired only on cable television in the middle of the night.

But they probably know that it will leave out all the good parts.

"As far as the Dentist is concerned," Avi said, "our advantage is that, when it comes to the Philippines, he will be predictable. Tame. Even docile." He smiles cryptically.

"How so?"

"Victoria Vigo whored her way up out of Smoky Mountain, right?"

"Well, there seems to be a lot of nudging and winking to that effect, but I've never heard anyone come out and *say* it before," Randy said, glancing around nervously.

"Believe me, it's the only way she could have gotten out of there. Pimping arrangements were handled by the Bolobolos. This is a group from Northern Luzon that was brought into power along with Marcos. They run that part of town—police, organized crime, local politics, you name it. Consequently, they own her—they have photographs, videos from the days when she was an underage prostitute and porn film starlet."

Randy shook his head in disgust and amazement. "How the hell do you get this information?"

"Never mind. Believe me, in some circles it's as well known as the value of pi."

"Not my circles."

"Anyway, the point is that her interests are aligned with the Bolobolos and always will be. And the Dentist is always going to obediently do whatever his wife tells him to."

"Can you really assume that?" Randy said. "He's a tough guy. He probably has a lot more money and power than the Bolobolos. He can do whatever he wants."

"But he won't," Avi says, smiling that little smile again. "He'll do what his wife tells him to."

"How do you know that?"

"Look," Avi said, "Kepler is a major control freak—just like most powerful, rich men. Right?"

"Right."

"If you are that much of a control freak, what sexual preferences does that translate into?"

"I hope I'll never know. I suppose you would want to dominate a woman."

"Wrong!" Avi said. "Sex is more complicated than that, Randy. Sex is a place where people's repressed desires come out. People get most turned on when their innermost secrets are revealed—"

"Shit! Kepler's a masochist?"

"He is such a fucking masochist that he was famous for it. At least in the Southeast Asian sex industry. Pimps and Madams in Hong Kong, Bangkok, Shenzhen, Manila, they all had files on him—they knew exactly what he wanted. And that's how he met Victoria Vigo. He was in Manila, see, working on the FiliTel deal. Spent a lot of time here, staying in a hotel that's owned, and bugged, by the Bolobolos. They studied his mating habits like entomologists watching the reproductive habits of ants. They groomed Victoria Vigo—their ace, their bombshell, their sexual Terminator—to give Kepler exactly what Kepler wanted. Then they sent her into his life like a guided fucking missile and pow! true love."

"You'd think he would have been suspicious, or something. I'm surprised he'd get that involved with a whore."

"He didn't know she was a whore! That's the beauty of the plan! The Bolobolos set her up with a fake identity as a concierge at Kepler's hotel! A demure Catholic school girl! It starts with her getting him tickets to a play, and inside of a year, he's chained to his bed on that fucking mega-yacht of his with strap marks on his ass, and she's standing over him with a wedding ring on her finger the size of a headlamp, the hundred and thirty-eighth richest woman in the world."

"Hundred and twenty-fifth," Randy corrected him, "FiliTel stock has been on a bull run lately."

Randy spends the next days trying not to run into the Dentist. He stays at a small private inn up on the top of the island, eating continental breakfast every morning with an assortment of American and Nipponese war veterans who have come here with their wives to (Randy supposes) deal with emotional issues a millon times more profound than anything Randy's ever had to contend with. The *Rui Faleiro* is nothing if not conspicuous, and Randy can get a pretty good idea of whether the Dentist is aboard it by watching the movements of the helicopter and the speedboat.

When he thinks it's safe, he goes down to the beach below the micro-wave antenna and watches Amy's divers work on the cable installation. Some of them are working out in the surf zone, bolting sections of cast-iron pipe around the cable. Some are working a couple of miles offshore, coordinating with a barge that is injecting the cable directly into the muddy seafloor with a giant, cleaver-like appendage.

The shore end of the cable runs into a new reinforced-concrete building set back about a hundred meters from the high-tide level. It is basically just a big room filled with batteries, generators, air-conditioning units, and racks of electronic equipment. The software running on that equipment is Randy's responsibility, and so he spends most of his time in that building, staring into a computer screen and typing. From there, transmission lines run up the hill to the microwave tower.

The other end is being extended out towards a buoy that is bobbing in the South China Sea a few kilometers away. Attached to that buoy is the end of the North Luzon Coastal Festoon, a cable, owned by FiliTel, that runs up the coast of the island. If you follow it far enough you reach a building at the northern tip of the island, where a big cable from Taiwan comes in. Taiwan, in turn, is heavily webbed into the world submarine cable network; it is easy and cheap to get data into or out of Taiwan.

There is only one gap left in the private chain of transmission that Epiphyte and FiliTel are trying to establish from Taiwan to downtown Manila, and that gap gets narrower by the day, as the cable barge grinds its way towards the buoy.

When it finally gets there, *Rui Faleiro* weighs anchor and glides out to meet it. The helicopter and the speedboat, and a flotilla of hired boats, go into action ferrying dignitaries and media crews out from Manila. Avi shows up carrying two fresh tuxedos from a tailor shop in Shanghai ("All those famous Hong Kong tailors were refugees from Shanghai"). He and Randy tear off the tissue paper, put them on, and then ride in an un-air-conditioned jeepney down the hill to the dock, where *Glory* awaits them.

Two hours later, Randy gets to lay eyes on the Dentist and the Diva for the first time ever—in the grand ballroom of the *Rui Faleiro*. To Randy the party is like any other: he shakes hands with a few people, forgets their names, finds a place to sit down, and enjoys the wine and the food in blissful solitude.

The one thing that is special about this party is that two tar-covered cables, each about the thickness of a baseball bat, are running up onto the quarterdeck. If you go to the rail and look down you can see them disappear into the brine. The cable ends meet on a tabletop in the middle of the deck, where a technician, flown in from Hong Kong and duded up in a tuxedo, sits with a box of tools, working on the splice. He is also working on a big hangover, but that is fine with Randy since he knows that it's all fake—the cables are just scraps, their loose ends trailing in the water alongside the yacht. The real splice was performed yesterday and is already lying on the bottom of the sea with bits running through it.

There is another man on the quarterdeck, mostly staring at Bata'an and Corregidor but also keeping an eye on Randy. The moment Randy notices him, this man nods, as if checking something off a list in his head, stands up, walks over, and joins him. He is wearing a very ornate uniform, the U.S. Navy equivalent of black tie. He is mostly bald, and what hair he does have is battleship grey, and shorn to a length of perhaps five millimeters. As he walks toward Randy, several Filipinos watch him with obvious curiosity.

"Randy," he says. Medals clink together as he grips Randy's right hand and shakes it. He looks to be around fifty, but he has the skin of an eighty-year-old Bedouin. He has a lot of ribbons on his chest, and many of them are red and yellow, which are colors that Randy vaguely associates with Vietnam. Above his pocket is a little plastic nameplate reading, SHAFTOE. "Don't be deceived, Randy," says Douglas MacArthur Shaftoe, "I'm not on active duty. Retired eons ago. But I'm still entitled to wear this uniform. And it's a hell of a lot easier than going out and trying to find a tuxedo that fits me."

"Pleased to meet you."

"Pleasure's mine. Where'd you get yours, by the way?"

"My tuxedo?"

"Yeah."

"My partner had it made."

"Your business partner, or your sexual partner?"

"My business partner. At the moment, I am without a sexual partner."

Doug Shaftoe nods impassively. "It is telling that you have not obtained one in Manila. As our host did, for example."

Randy looks into the ballroom at Victoria Vigo, who, if she were any more radiant, would cause paint to peel from the walls and windowpanes to sag like caramel.

"I guess I'm just shy, or something," Randy says.

"Are you too shy to listen to a business proposition?"

"Not at all."

"My daughter asserts that you and our host might lay some more cables around here in coming years."

"In business, people rarely plan to do a thing only once," Randy says. "It messes up the spreadsheets."

"You are aware, by now, that the water in this area is shallow."

"Yeah."

"You know that cables cannot be laid in shallow water without extremely detailed, high-resolution sidescan sonar surveys."

"Yes."

"I would like to perform those surveys for you, Randy."

"I see."

"No, I don't think you do see. But I want you to see, and so I'm going to explain it."

"Okay," Randy says. "Should I bring my partner out?"

"The concept I am about to convey to you is very simple and does not require two first-rate minds in order to process it," Doug Shaftoe says.

"Okay. What is the concept?"

"The detailed survey will be just chock-full of new information about what is on the floor of the ocean in this part of the world. Some of that information might be valuable. More valuable than you imagine."

"Ah," Randy says. "You mean that it might be the kind of thing that your company knows how to capitalize on."

"That's right," says Doug Shaftoe. "Now, if you hire one of my competitors to perform your survey, and they stumble on this kind of information, they will not tell you about it. They will exploit it themselves. You will not know that they have found anything and you will not profit from it. But if you hire Semper Marine Services, I will tell you about whatever I find, and I will cut you and your company in on a share of any proceeds."

"Hmmmm," Randy says. He is trying to figure out how to do a poker face, but he knows that Shaftoe sees right through him.

"On one condition," Doug Shaftoe says.

"I suspected there might be a condition."

"Every hook that's worth a damn has a barb. This is the barb."

"What is it?" Randy asks.

"We keep it a secret from that son of a bitch," Doug Shaftoe says, jerking his thumb at Hubert Kepler. "Because if the Dentist finds out, then he and the Bolobolos will just split the entire thing up between them and we'll see nothing. There's even a chance we would end up dead."

"Well, the being dead part is something that we will certainly have to think about," Randy says, "but I will convey your proposal to my partner."

TUBE

WATERHOUSE AND A FEW DOZEN STRANGERS ARE STANDING AND sitting in an extraordinarily long, narrow room that rocks from side to side. The room is lined with windows but no light comes into them, only sound: a great deal of rumbling, rattling, and screeching. Everyone is pensive and silent, as if they were sitting in church waiting for the service to kick off.

Waterhouse is standing up gripping a ceiling-mounted protuberance that keeps him from being rocked right onto his can. For the last couple of minutes he has been staring at a nearby poster providing instructions on how to put on a gas mask. Waterhouse, like everyone else, is carrying one such device with him in a small dun canvas shoulder bag. Waterhouse's looks different from everyone else's because it is American and military. It has drawn a stare or two from the others.

On the poster is a lovely and stylish woman with white skin, and auburn hair which appears to have been chemically melted and reset into its current shape at a quality salon. She stands upright, her spine like a flagpole, chin in the air, elbows bent, hands ritualistically posed: fingers splayed, thumbs sticking straight up in the air just in front of her face. A sinister lump dangles between her hands, held in a cat's-cradle of khaki strapping. Her upthrust thumbs are the linchpins of this tidy web.

Waterhouse has been in London for a couple of days now and so he knows the next part of the story. He would know this pose anywhere. This woman is poised for the chin thrust. If gas ever falls on the capital, the gas rattles will sound and the tops of the massive mailboxes, which have all been treated with special paint, will turn black. Twenty million thumbs will point into the greenish, poison sky, ten million gas masks will dangle from them, ten million chins will thrust. He can just imagine the crisp luscious sound of this woman's soft white skin forcing itself into the confining black rubber.

Once the chin-thrust is complete, all is well. You have to get the straps neatly arranged atop your auburn permanent and get indoors, but the worst danger is past. The British gas masks have a squat round fitting on the front to allow exhalation, which looks exactly like the snout of a pig, and no woman would be caught dead in such a thing if the models in the gas mask posters were not such paragons of high-caste beauty.

Something catches his eye out in the darkness beyond the window. The train has reached one of those parts of the Underground where, dim gun-barrel-colored light sifts down, betraying the stygian secrets of the Tube. Everyone in the car blinks, glances, and draws breath. The World has rematerialized around them for a moment. Fragments of wall, encrusted trusses, bundles of cable, hang in space out there, revolving slowly, like astronomical bodies, as the train works its way past.

The cables catch Waterhouse's eye: neatly bracketed to the stone walls in parallel courses. They are like the creepers of some plutonic ivy that spreads through the darkness of the Tube when the maintenance men aren't paying attention, seeking a place to break out and up into the light.

When you walk along the street, up there in the Overground, you see the first tendrils making their way up the ancient walls of the buildings. Neoprene-jacketed vines that grow in straight lines up sheer stone and masonry and inject themselves through holes in windowframes, homing in particularly on offices. Sometimes they are sheathed in metal tubes. Sometimes the owners have painted them over. But all of them share a common root system that flourishes in the unused channels and crevices of the Underground, converging on giant switching stations in deep bomb-proof vaults.

The train invades a cathedral of dingy yellow light, and groans to a stop, hogging the aisle. Lurid icons of national paranoia glow in the niches and grottoes. An angelic chin-thrusting woman anchors one end of the moral continuum. At the opposite we have a succubus in a tight skirt, sprawled on a davenport in the midst of a party, smirking through her false eyelashes as she eavesdrops on the naive young servicemen gabbing away behind her.

Signs on the wall identify this as Euston in a tasteful sans-serif that screams official credibility. Waterhouse and most of the other people get off the train. After fifteen minutes or so of ricocheting around the station's precincts, asking directions and puzzling out timetables, Waterhouse finds himself sitting aboard an intercity train bound for Birmingham. Along the way, it is promised, it will stop at a place called Bletchley.

Part of the reason for the confusion is that there is another train about to leave from an adjacent siding, which goes straight to Bletchley, its final destination, with no stops in between. Everyone on that train, it seems, is a female in a quasimilitary uniform.

The RAF men with the Sten guns, standing watch by each door of that train, checking papers and passes, will not let him aboard. Waterhouse looks through the yellowing influence of the windows at the Bletchley girls in the train, facing each other in klatsches of four and five, getting their knitting out of their bags, turning balls of Scottish wool into balaclavas and mittens for convoy crews in the North Atlantic, writing letters to their brothers in the service and their mums and dads at home. The RAF gunmen remain by the doors until all of them are closed and the train has begun to move out of the station. As it builds speed, the rows and rows of girls, knitting and writing and chatting, blur together into something that probably looks a good deal like what sailors and soldiers the world over are commonly seeing in their dreams. Waterhouse will never be one of those soldiers, out on the front line, out in contact with the enemy. He has tasted the apple of forbidden knowledge. He is forbidden to go anywhere in the world where he might be captured by the enemy.

———

The train climbs up out of the night and into a red-brick arroyo, headed northwards out of the city. It is about three in the afternoon; that special BP train must have been carrying swing shift gals.

Waterhouse has the feeling he will not be working anything like a regular shift. His duffel bag—which was packed for him—is pregnant with sartorial possibilities: thick oiled-wool sweaters, tropical-weight Navy and Army uniforms, black ski mask, condoms.

The train slowly pulls free of the city and passes into a territory patched with small residential towns. Waterhouse feels heavy in his seat, and suspects a slight uphill tendency. They pass through a cleft that has been made across a low range of hills, like a kerf in the top of a log, and enter into a lovely territory of subtly swelling emerald green fields strewn randomly with small white capsules that he takes to be sheep.

Of course, their distribution is probably not random at all—it probably reflects local variations in soil chemistry producing grass that the sheep find more or less desirable. From aerial reconnaissance, the Germans could draw up a map of British soil chemistry based upon analysis of sheep distribution.

The fields are enclosed by old hedges, stone fences, or, especially in the uplands, long swaths of forest. After an hour or so, the forest comes right up along the left side of the train, covering a bank that rises up gently from the railway siding. The train's brakes come on gassily, and the train grumbles to a stop in a whistle-stop station. But the line has forked and ramified quite a bit, more than is warranted by the size of the station. Waterhouse stands, plants his feet squarely, squats down in a sumo wrestler's stance, and engages his duffel bag. Duffel appears to be winning as it seemingly pushes Waterhouse out the door of the train and onto the platform.

There is a stronger than usual smell of coal, and a good deal of noise coming from not far away. Waterhouse looks up the line and discovers a heavy industrial works unfurled across the many sidings. He stands and stares for a couple of minutes, as his train pulls away, headed for points north, and sees that they are in the business of repairing steam locomotives here at Bletchley Depot. Waterhouse likes trains.

But that is not why he got a free suit of clothes and a ticket to Bletchley, and so once again Waterhouse engages Duffel and gets it up the stairs to the enclosed bridge that flies over all of the parallel lines. Looking toward the station, he sees more Bletchley girls, WAAFs and WRENs, coming towards him; the day shift, finished with their work, which consists of the processing of ostensibly random letters and digits on a heavy-industrial scale. Not wanting to appear ridiculous in their sight, he finally gets Duffel maneuvered onto his back, gets his arms through the shoulder straps, and allows its weight to throw him forward across the bridge.

The WAAFs and WRENs are only moderately interested in the sight of a newly arriving American officer. Or perhaps they are only being demure. In any case, Waterhouse knows he is one of the few, but not the first. Duffel shoves him through the one-room station like a fat cop chivvying a hammerlocked drunk across the lobby of a two-star hotel. Waterhouse is ejected into a strip of open territory running along the north–south road. Directly across from him the woods rise up. Any notion that they might be woods of the inviting sort is quickly dissolved by a dense spray of gelid light glinting from the border of the wood as the low sun betrays that the place is saturated with sharpened metal. There is an orifice in the woods, spewing WAAFs and WRENs like the narrow outlet of a giant yellowjacket nest.

Waterhouse must either move forward or be pulled onto his back by Duffel and left squirming helplessly in the parking lot like a flipped beetle, so he staggers forward, across the street and onto the wide footpath into the woods. The Bletchley girls surround him. They have celebrated the end of their shift by applying lipstick. Wartime lipstick is necessarily cobbled together from whatever tailings and gristle were left over once all of the good stuff was used to coat propeller shafts. A florid and cloying scent is needed to conceal its unspeakable mineral and animal origins.

It is the smell of War.

Waterhouse has not even been given the full tour of BP yet, but he knows the gist of it. He knows that these demure girls, obediently shuffling reams of gibberish through their machines, shift after shift, day after day, have killed more men than Napoleon.

He makes slow and apologetic progress against the tide of the departing day shift. At one point he simply gives up, steps aside, body-slams Duffel into the ivy, lights up a cigarette, and waits for a burst of a hundred or so girls to go by him. Something pokes at his ankle: a wild raspberry cane, furious with thorns. It supports an uncannily small and tidy spiderweb whose geodesic strands gleam in a beam of low afternoon light. The spider in the center is an imperturbable British sort, perfectly unruffled by Waterhouse's clumsy Yank antics.

Waterhouse reaches out and catches a yellow-brown elm leaf that happens to fall through the air before him. He hunkers down, plants his cigarette in his mouth, and, using both hands for steadiness, draws the sawtooth rim of the elm leaf across one of the web's radial strands, which, he knows, will not have any sticky stuff on it. Like a fiddle bow on a string, the leaf sets up a fairly regular vibration in the web. The spider spins to face it, rotating instantly, like a character in a badly spliced movie. Waterhouse is so startled by the speed of the move that he starts back just a bit, then he draws the leaf across the web again. The spider tenses, feeling the vibrations.

Eventually it returns to its original position and carries on as before, ignoring Waterhouse completely.

Spiders can tell from the vibrations what sort of insect they have caught, and home in on it. There is a reason why the webs are radial, and the spider plants itself at the convergence of the radii. The strands are an extension of its nervous system. Information propagates down the gossamer and into the spider, where it is processed by some kind of internal Turing machine. Waterhouse has tried many different tricks, but he has never been able to spoof a spider. Not a good omen!

The rush hour seems to have ended during Waterhouse's science experiment. He engages Duffel once more. The struggle takes them another

hundred yards down the path, which finally empties out into a road just
at the point where it is barred by an iron gate slung between stupid
obelisks of red brick. The guards are, again, RAF men with Sten guns,
and right now they are examining the papers of a man in a canvas
greatcoat and goggles, who has just ridden up on an Army green motorcycle with panniers slung over the rear wheel. The panniers are not
especially full, but they have been carefully secured; they contain the
ammunition that the girls feed into the chattering teeth of their ravenous weapons.

The motorcyclist is waved through, and makes an immediate left turn
down a narrow lane. Attention falls upon Lawrence Pritchard Waterhouse, who after a suitable exchange of salutes, presents his credentials.

He has to choose among his several sets, which he doesn't manage to
hide from the guards. But the guards do not seem alarmed or even
curious about this, which sets them distinctly apart from most whom
Waterhouse has dealt with. Naturally, these men are not on the Ultra
Mega list, and so it would be a grave breach of security to tell them that
he was here on Ultra Mega business. They appear to have greeted many
other men who can't state their real business, however, and don't bat an
eyelash when Lawrence pretends to be one of the naval intelligence
liaisons in Hut 4 or Hut 8.

Hut 8 is where they decrypt naval Enigma transmissions. Hut 4 accepts
the decrypts from Hut 8 and analyzes them. If Waterhouse pretends to
be a Hut 4 man the disguise will not last for long, because those fellows
have to actually know something about the Navy. He perfectly fits the
profile of a Hut 8 man, who need not know anything except pure math.

One of the RAF men peruses his papers, then steps into a small
guardhouse and stirs the crank on a telephone. Waterhouse stands there
awkwardly, marveling at the weapons slung from the shoulders of the
RAF men. They are, as far as he can tell, nothing more than steel pipes
with a trigger mounted toward one end. A small window cut through
the pipe provides a view of a coil spring nested inside. A few handles
and fittings bolted on from place to place do not make the Sten gun
look any less like an ill-conceived high school metal shop project.

"Captain Waterhouse? You are to proceed to the Mansion," says the
guard who had spoken on the telephone. "You can't miss it."

Waterhouse walks for about fifty feet and finds that the Mansion is,
indeed, tragically unmissable. He stands and stares at it for a minute,
trying to fathom what the architect had been thinking. It is a busy piece
of work, with an excessive number of gables. He can only suppose that
the designer wanted to build what was really a large, single dwelling, but
sought to camouflage it as a line of at least half a dozen wildly mis-

matched urban row-houses inexplicably crammed together in the middle of six hundred acres of Buckinghamshire farmland.

The place has been well looked after, but as Waterhouse draws closer, he can see black lianas climbing up the brickwork. The root system that he glimpsed in the Underground has spread beneath forest and pasture even to this place and has begun to throw its neoprene creepers upwards. But this organism is not phototropic—it does not grow towards the light, always questing towards the sun. It is infotropic. And it has spread to this place for the same reason that infotropic humans like Lawrence Pritchard Waterhouse and Dr. Alan Mathison Turing have come here, because Bletchley Park has roughly the same situation in the info world as the sun does in the solar system. Armies, nations, prime ministers, presidents and geniuses fall around it, not in steady planetlike orbits but in the crazy careening ellipses and hyperbolae of comets and stray asteroids.

Dr. Rudolf von Hacklheber can't see Bletchley Park, because it is the second best kept secret in the world, after Ultra Mega. But from his office in Berlin, sifting through dispatches from the Beobachtung Dienst, he can glimpse fragments of those trajectories, and dream up hypotheses to explain why they are just so. If the only logical hypothesis is that the Allies have broken Enigma, then Detachment 2702 will have failed.

Lawrence displays further credentials and enters between a pair of weathered gryphons. The mansion is nicer once you can no longer see its exterior. Its faux-rowhouse design provides many opportunities for bay windows, providing sorely needed light. The hall is held up by gothic arches and pillars made of a conspicuously low grade of brown marble that looks like vitrified sewage.

The place is startlingly noisy; there is a rushing, clattering noise, like rabid applause, permeating walls and doors, carried on a draft of hot air with a stinging, oily scent. It is the peculiar scent of electric teletypes— or teleprinters, as the Brits call them. The noise and the heat suggests there must be dozens of them in one of the mansion's lower rooms.

Waterhouse climbs a paneled stairway to what the Brits call the first floor, and find it quieter and cooler. The high panjandrums of Bletchley have their offices here. If the organization is run true to bureaucratic form, Waterhouse will never see this place again once his initial interview is finished. He finds his way to the office of Colonel Chattan, who (Waterhouse's memory jogged by the sight of the name on the door) is the fellow at the top of the chart of Detachment 2702.

Chattan rises to shake his hand. He's strawberry blond, blue-eyed, and probably would be rosy-cheeked if he didn't have such a deep desert tan at the moment. He is wearing a dress uniform; British officers have their uniforms tailor-made, it is the only way to obtain them. Waterhouse is hardly a clothes horse, but he can see at a glance that Chattan's uniform was not thrown together by Mummy in a few evenings in front of a flickering coal grate. No, Chattan has himself an honest-to-god tailor somewhere. Yet, when he speaks Waterhouse's name, he does not say "woe to hice" like the Broadway Buildings crowd. The R comes through hard and crackling and the "house" part is elongated into something like "hoos." He has some kind of a wild-ass accent on him, this Chattan.

With Chattan is a smaller man in British fatigues—tight at the wrists and ankles, otherwise blousy, of thick khaki flannel that would be intolerably hot if these people couldn't rely on a steady ambient temperature, indoors and out, of about fifty-five degrees. The overall effect always reminds Waterhouse of Dr. Dentons. This fellow is introduced as Leftenant Robson, and he is the leader of one of 2702's two squads—the RAF one. He has a bristly mustache, trimmed very short, of silver and auburn whiskers. He is a cheerful sort, at least in the presence of higher ranks, and smiles frequently. His teeth splay out radially from the gumline so that each mandible has the appearance of a coffee can in which a small grenade has been detonated.

"This the fellow we've been waiting for," Chattan says to Robson. "The one we could've used in Algiers."

"Yes!" Robson says. "Welcome to Detachment 2701, Captain Waterhouse."

"2702," Waterhouse says.

Chattan and Robson look ever so mildly startled.

"We can't use 2701 because it is the product of two primes."

"I beg your pardon?" Robson says.

One thing Waterhouse likes about these Brits is that when they don't know what the hell you are talking about, they are at least open to the possibility that it might be their fault. Robson has the look of a man who has come up through the ranks. A Yank of that type would already be scornful and blustery.

"Which ones?" Chattan says. That is encouraging; he at least knows what a prime number is.

"73 and 37," Waterhouse says.

This makes a profound impression on Chattan. "Ah, yes, I see." He shakes his head. "I shall have to give the Prof a good chaffing about this."

Robson has cocked his head far to one side so that it is almost resting upon the thick woolly beret chucked into his epaulet. He is squinting, and has an aghast look about him. His hypothetical Yank counterpart would probably demand, at this point, a complete explanation of prime number theory, and when it was finished, denounce it as horseshit. But

Robson just lets it go by. "Am I to understand that we are changing the number of our Detachment?"

Waterhouse swallows. It seems clear from Robson's reaction that this is going to involve a great deal of busy-work for Robson and his men: weeks of painting and stenciling and of trying to propagate the new number throughout the military bureaucracy. It will be a miserable pain in the ass.

"2702 it is," Chattan says breezily. Unlike Waterhouse, he has no difficulty issuing difficult, unpopular commands.

"Right then, I must see to some things. Pleasure making your acquaintance, Captain Waterhouse."

"Pleasure's mine."

Robson shakes Waterhouse's hand again and excuses himself.

"We have a billet for you in one of the huts to the south of the canteen," Chattan says. "Bletchley Park is our nominal headquarters, but we anticipate that we will spend most of our time in those theaters where heaviest use is being made of Ultra."

"I take it you've been in North Africa," Waterhouse says.

"Yes." Chattan raises his eyebrows, or rather the ridges of skin where his eyebrows are presumably located; the hairs are colorless and transparent, like nylon monofilament line. "Just got out by the skin of our teeth there, I'm afraid."

"Had a close shave, did you?"

"Oh, I don't mean it that way," Chattan says. "I'm talking about the integrity of the Ultra secret. We are still not sure whether we have survived it. But the Prof has done some calculations suggesting that we may be out of the woods."

"The Prof is what you call Dr. Turing?"

"Yes. He recommended you personally, you know."

"When the orders came through, I speculated as much."

"Turing is presently engaged on at least two other fronts of the information war, and could not be part of our happy few."

"What happened in North Africa, Colonel Chattan?"

"It's still happening," Chattan says bemusedly. "Our Marine squad is still in-theater, widening the bell curve."

"Widening the bell curve?"

"Well, you know better than I do that random things typically have a bell-shaped distribution. Heights, for example. Come over to this window, Captain Waterhouse."

Waterhouse joins Chattan at a bay window, where there is a view across acres of what used to be gently undulating farmland. Looking beyond the wooded belt to the uplands miles away, he can see what

Bletchley Park probably used to look like: green fields dotted with clusters of small buildings.

But that is not what it looks like now. There is hardly a piece of land
within half a mile that has not been recently paved or built upon. Once
you get beyond the Mansion and its quaint little outbuildings, the park
consists of one-story brick structures, nothing more than long corridors
with multiple transepts: +++++++, and new +'s being added as fast as
the masons can slap bricks on mud (Waterhouse wonders, idly, whether
Rudy has seen aerial reconnaissance photos of this place, and deduced
from all of those +'s the mathematical nature of the enterprise). The
tortuous channels between buildings are narrow, and each is made twice
as narrow by an eight-foot-high blast wall running down the middle of it,
so that the Jerries will have to spend at least one bomb for each building.

"In that building there," Chattan says, pointing to a small building
not far away—a truly wretched-looking brick hovel—"are the Turing
Bombes. That's 'bombe' with an 'e' on the end. They are calculating
machines invented by your friend the Prof."

"Are they true universal Turing machines?" Waterhouse blurts. He is
in the grip of a stunning vision of what Bletchley Park might, in fact,
be: a secret kingdom in which Alan has somehow found the resources
needed to realize his great vision. A kingdom ruled not by men but by
information, where humble buildings made of + signs house Universal
Machines that can be configured to perform any computable operation.

"No," Chattan says, with a gentle, sad smile.

Waterhouse exhales for a long time. "Ah."

"Perhaps that will come next year, or the next."

"Perhaps."

"The bombes were adapted, by Turing and Welchman and others, from
a design dreamed up by Polish cryptanalysts. They consist of rotating drums
that test many possible Enigma keys with great speed. I'm sure the Prof will
explain it to you. But the point is that they have these vast pegboards in the
back, like telephone switchboards, and some of our girls have the job of
putting the right pegs into the right holes and wiring the things up every
day. Requires good eyesight, careful attention, and height."

"Height?"

"You'll notice that the girls who are assigned to that particular duty
are unusually tall. If the Germans were to somehow get their hands on
the personnel records for all of the people who work at Bletchley Park,
and graph their heights on a histogram, they would see a normal bell-
shaped curve, representing most of the workers, with an abnormal bump
on it—representing the unusual population of tall girls whom we have
brought in to work the plug boards."

"Yes, I see," Waterhouse says, "and someone like Rudy—Dr. von Hacklheber—would notice the anomaly, and wonder about it."

"Precisely," Chattan says. "And it would then be the job of Detachment 2702—the Ultra Mega Group—to plant false information that would throw your friend Rudy off the scent." Chattan turns away from the window, strolls over to his desk, and opens a large cigarette box, neatly stacked with fresh ammunition. He offers one to Waterhouse with a deft hand gesture, and Waterhouse accepts it, just to be social. As Chattan is giving him a light, he gazes through the flame into Waterhouse's eye and says, "I put it to you now. How would you go about concealing from your friend Rudy that we had a lot of tall girls here?"

"Assuming that he already had the personnel records?"

"Yes."

"Then it would be too late to conceal anything."

"Granted. Let us instead assume that he has some channel of information that is bringing him these records, a few at a time. This channel is still open and functioning. We cannot shut it down. Or perhaps we choose not to shut it down, because even the absence of this channel will tell Rudy something important."

"Well, there you go then," Waterhouse says. "We gin up some false personnel records and plant them in the channel."

There is a small chalkboard on the wall of Chattan's office. It is a palimpsest, not very well erased; the housekeeping detail here must have a standing order never to clean it, lest something important be lost. As Waterhouse approaches it, he can see older calculations layered atop each other, fading off into the blackness like transmissions of white light propagating into deep space.

He recognizes Alan's handwriting all over the place. It takes a physical effort not to stand there and try to reconstruct Alan's calculations from the ghosts lingering on the slate. He draws over them only with reluctance.

Waterhouse slashes an abscissa and an ordinate onto the board, then sweeps out a bell-shaped curve. On top of the curve, to the right of the peak, he adds a little bump.

"The tall girls," he explains. "The problem is this notch." He points

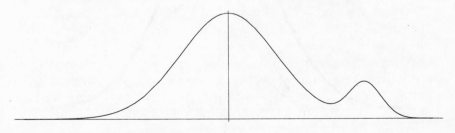

to the valley between the main peak and the bump. Then he draws a
new peak high and wide enough to cover both:

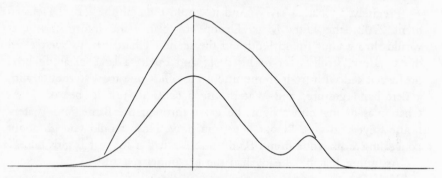

"We can do that by planting fake personnel records in Rudy's channel,
giving heights that are taller than the overall average, but shorter than
the bombe girls."

"But now you've dug yourself another hole," Chattan says. He is
leaning back in his officer's swivel chair, holding the cigarette in front
of his face, regarding Waterhouse through a motionless cloud of smoke.

Waterhouse says, "The new curve looks a little better because I filled
in that gap, but it's not really bell-shaped. It doesn't tail off right, out
here at the edges. Dr. von Hacklheber will notice that. He'll realize
that someone's been tampering with his channel. To prevent that from
happening I would have to plant more fake records, giving some unusually large and small values."

"Invent some fake girls who were exceptionally short or tall," Chattan says.

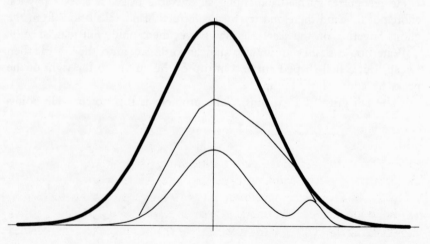

"Yes. That would make the curve tail off in the way that it should." Chattan continues to look at him expectantly.

Waterhouse says, "So, the addition of a small number of what would otherwise be bizarre anomalies makes it all look perfectly normal."

"As I said," Chattan says, "our squad is in North Africa—even as we speak—widening the bell curve. Making it all look perfectly normal."

MEAT

OKAY, SO PRIVATE FIRST CLASS GERALD HOTT, LATE OF CHIcago, Illinois, did not exactly shoot up through the ranks during his fifteen-year tenure in the United States Army. He did, however, carve a bitchin' loin roast. He was as deft with a boning knife as Bobby Shaftoe is with a bayonet. And who is to say that a military butcher, by conserving the limited resources of a steer's carcass and by scrupulously observing the mandated sanitary practices, might not save as many lives as a steely-eyed warrior? The military is not just about killing Nips, Krauts, and Dagoes. It is also about killing livestock—and eating them. Gerald Hott was a front-line warrior who kept his freezer locker as clean as an operating room and so it is only fitting that he has ended up there.

Bobby Shaftoe makes this little elegy up in his head as he is shivering in the sub-Arctic chill of a formerly French, and now U.S. Army, meat locker the size and temperature of Greenland, surrounded by the earthly remains of several herds of cattle and one butcher. He has attended more than a few military funerals during his brief time in the service, and has always been bowled over by the skill of the chaplains in coming up with moving elegies for the departed. He has heard rumors that when the military inducts 4-Fs who are discovered to have brains, it teaches them to type and assigns them to sit at desks and type these things out, day after day. Nice duty if you can get it.

The frozen carcasses dangle from meathooks in long rows. Bobby Shaftoe gets tenser and tenser as he works his way up and down the aisles, steeling himself for the bad thing he is about to see. It is almost preferable when your buddy's head suddenly explodes just as he is puffing his cigarette into life—buildup like this can drive you nuts.

Finally he rounds the end of a row and discovers a man slumbering on the floor, locked in embrace with a pork carcass, which he was apparently about to butcher at the time of his death. He has been there for about twelve hours now and his body temp is hovering around minus ten degrees Fahrenheit.

Bobby Shaftoe squares himself to face the body and draws a deep breath of frosty, meat-scented air. He clasps his cyanotic hands in front of his chest in a manner that is both prayerful and good for warming them up. "Dear Lord," he says out loud. His voice does not echo; the carcasses soak it up. "Forgive this marine for these, his duties, which he is about to perform, and while you are at it, by all means forgive this marine's superiors whom You in Your infinite wisdom have seen fit to bless him with, and forgive their superiors for getting the whole deal together."

He considers going on at some length but finally decides that this is no worse than bayonetting Nips and so let's get on with it. He goes to the locked bodies of PFC Gerald Hott and Frosty the Pig and tries to separate them without success. He squats by them and gives the former a good look. Hott is blond. His eyes are half-closed, and when Shaftoe shines a flashlight into the slit, he can see a glint of blue. Hott is a big man, easily two-twenty-five in fighting trim, easily two-fifty now. Life in a military kitchen does not make it easy for a fellow to keep his weight down, or (unfortunately for Hott) his cardiovascular system in any kind of dependable working order.

Hott and his uniform were both dry when the heart attack happened, so thank god the fabric is not frozen onto the skin. Shaftoe is able to cut most of it off with several long strokes of his exquisitely sharpened V-44 "Gung Ho" knife. But the V-44's machetelike nine-and-a-half-inch blade is completely inappropriate for close infighting—viz., the de-nuding of the armpits and groin—and he was told to be careful about inflicting scratches, so there he has to break out the USMC Marine Raider stiletto, whose slender double-edged seven-and-a-quarter-inch blade might have been designed for exactly this sort of procedure, though the fish-shaped handle, which is made of solid metal, begins freezing to the sweaty palm of Shaftoe's hand after a while.

Lieutenant Ethridge is hovering outside the locker's tomblike door. Shaftoe barges past him and heads straight for the building's exit, ignoring Ethridge's queries: "Shaftoe? How 'bout it?"

He does not stop until he is out of the shade of the building. The North African sunshine breaks over his body like a washtub of morphine. He closes his eyes and turns his face into it, holds his frozen hands up to cup the warmth and let it trickle down his forearms, drip from his elbows.

"How 'bout it?" Ethridge says again.

Shaftoe opens his eyes and looks around.

The harbor's a blue crescent with miles of sere jetties snaking around each other like diagrams of dance steps. One of them's covered with worn stumps of ancient bastions and next to it a French battleship lies half-sunk, still piping smoke and steam into the air. All around it, the ships of Operation Torch are unloading shit faster than you can believe. Cargo nets rise from the holds of the transports and splat onto the quays like giant loogies. Longshoremen haul, trucks carry, troops march, French girls smoke Yankee cigarettes, Algerians propose joint ventures.

Between those ships, and the Army's meat operation, up here on this rock, is what Bobby Shaftoe takes to be the City of Algiers. To his discriminating Wisconsinan eye it does not appear to have been *built* so much as swept up on the hillside by a tidal wave. A lot of acreage has been devoted to keeping the fucking sun off, so from above, it has a shuttered-up look about it—lots of red tile, decorated with flowers and Arabs. Looks like a few modern concrete structures (e.g. this meat locker) have been thrown up by the French in the wake of some kind of vigorous slum-clearing offensive. Still, there's a lot of slums left to be cleared—target number one being this human beehive or anthill just off to Shaftoe's left, the Casbah, they call it. Maybe it's a neighborhood. Maybe it's a single poorly organized building. Has to be seen to be believed. Arabs packed into the place like fraternity pledges into a telephone booth.

Shaftoe turns around and looks again at the meat locker, which is dangerously exposed to enemy air attack here, but no one gives a fuck because who cares if the Krauts blow up a bunch of meat?

Lieutenant Ethridge, almost as desperately sunburned as Bobby Shaftoe, squints.

"Blond," Shaftoe says.

"Okay."

"Blue-eyed."

"Good."

"Anteater—not mushroom."

"Huh?"

"He's not circumcised, sir!"

"Excellent! How 'bout the other thing?"

"One tattoo, sir!"

Shaftoe is enjoying the slow buildup of tension in Ethridge's voice: "Describe the tattoo, Sergeant!"

"Sir! It is a commonly seen military design, sir! Consisting of a heart with a female's name in it."

"What is that name, Sergeant?" Ethridge is on the verge of pissing his pants.

"Sir! The name inscribed on the tattoo is the following name: Griselda. Sir!"

"Aaaah!" Lieutenant Ethridge lets loose deep from the diaphragm. Veiled women turn and look. Over in that Casbah, starved-looking, shave-needing ragheads lean out of spindly towers yodeling out of key.

Ethridge shuts up and contents himself with clenching his fists until they go white. When he speaks again, his voice is hushed with emotion. "Battles have hinged on lesser strokes of luck than this one, Sergeant!"

"You're telling me!?" Shaftoe says. "When I was on Guadalcanal, sir, we got trapped in this little cove and pinned down—"

"I don't want to hear the lizard story, Sergeant!"

"Sir! Yes, sir!"

———————

Once when Bobby Shaftoe was still in Oconomowoc, he had to help his brother move a mattress up a stairway and learned new respect for the difficulty of manipulating heavy but floppy objects. Hott, may God have mercy on his soul, is a heavy S.O.B., and so it is excellent luck that he is frozen solid. After the Mediterranean sun has its way with him, he is sure enough going to be floppy. And then some.

All of Shaftoe's men are down in the detachment's staging area. This is a cave built into a sheer artificial cliff that rises from the Mediterranean, just above the docks. These caves go on for miles and there is a boulevard running over the top of them. But even the approaches to their particular cave have been covered with tents and tarps so that no one, not even Allied troops, can see what they are up to: namely, looking for any equipment with 2701 painted on it, painting over the last digit, and changing it to 2. The first operation is handled by men with green paint and the second by men with white or black paint.

Shaftoe picks one man from each color group so that the operation as a whole will not be disrupted. The sun is stunningly powerful here, but in that cavern, with a cool maritime breeze easing through, it's not really that bad. The sharp smell of petroleum distillates comes off all of those warm painted surfaces. To Bobby Shaftoe, it is a comforting smell, because you never paint stuff when you're in combat. But the smell also makes him a little tingly, because you frequently paint stuff just *before* you go into combat.

Shaftoe is about to brief his three handpicked Marines on what is to come when the private with black paint on his hands, Daniels, looks past him and smirks. "What's the lieutenant looking for now do you suppose, Sarge?" he says.

Shaftoe and Privates Nathan (green paint) and Branph (white) look over to see that Ethridge has gotten sidetracked. He is going through the wastebaskets again.

"We have all noticed that Lieutenant Ethridge seems to think it is his mission in life to go through wastebaskets," Sergeant Shaftoe says in a low, authoritative voice. "He is an Annapolis graduate."

Ethridge straightens up and, in the most accusatory way possible, holds up a fistful of pierced and perforated oaktag. "Sergeant! Would you identify this material?"

"Sir! It is general issue military stencils, Sir!"

"Sergeant! How many letters are there in the alphabet?"

"Twenty-six, sir!" responds Shaftoe crisply.

Privates Daniels, Nathan and Branph whistle coolly at each other—this Sergeant Shaftoe is sharp as a tack.

"Now, how many numerals?"

"Ten, sir!"

"And of the thirty-six letters and numerals, how many of them are represented by unused stencils in this wastebasket?"

"Thirty-five, sir! All except for the numeral 2, which is the only one we need to carry out your orders, sir!"

"Have you forgotten the second part of my order, Sergeant?"

"Sir, yes, sir!" No point in lying about it. Officers actually like it when you forget their orders because it reminds them of how much smarter they are than you. It makes them feel needed.

"The second part of my order was to take strict measures to leave behind no trace of the changeover!"

"Sir, yes, I do remember that now, sir!"

Lieutenant Ethridge, who was just a bit huffy first, has now calmed down quite a bit, which speaks well of him and is duly, silently noted by all of the men, who have known him for less than six hours. He is now speaking calmly and conversationally, like a friendly high school teacher. He is wearing the heavy-rimmed black military eyeglasses known in the trade as RPGs, or Rape Prevention Glasses. They are strapped to his head by a hunk of black elastic. They make him look like a mental retard. "If some enemy agent were to go through the contents of this wastebasket, as enemy agents have been known to do, what would he find?"

"Stencils, sir!"

"And if he were to count the numerals and letters, would he notice anything unusual?"

"Sir! All of them would be clean except for the numeral twos which would be missing or covered with paint, sir!"

Lieutenant Ethridge says nothing for a few minutes, allowing his message to sink in. In reality no one knows what the fuck he is talking about. The atmosphere becomes tinderlike until finally, Sergeant Shaftoe makes a desperate stab. He turns away from Ethridge and towards the men. "I want you Marines to get paint on all of those goddamn stencils!" he barks.

The Marines charge the wastebaskets as if they were Nip pillboxes, and Lieutenant Ethridge seems mollified. Bobby Shaftoe, having scored massive points, leads Privates Daniels, Nathan, and Branph out into the street before Lieutenant Ethridge figures out that he was just guessing. They head for the meat locker up on the ridge, double-time.

These Marines are all lethal combat veterans or else they never would have gotten into a mess this bad—trapped on a gratuitously dangerous continent (Africa) surrounded by the enemy (United States Army troops). Still, when they get into that locker and take their first gander at PFC Hott, a hush comes over them.

Private Branph clasps his hands, rubbing them together surreptitiously. "Dear Lord—"

"Shut up, Private!" Shaftoe says, "I already did that."

"Okay, Sarge."

"Go find a meat saw!" Shaftoe says to Private Nathan.

The privates all gasp.

"For the fucking pig!" Shaftoe clarifies. Then he turns to Private Daniels, who is carrying a featureless bundle, and says, "Open it up!"

The bundle (which was issued by Ethridge to Shaftoe) turns out to contain a black wetsuit. Nothing GI; some kind of European model. Shaftoe unfolds it and examines its various parts while Privates Nathan and Branph dismember Frosty the Pig with vigorous strokes of an enormous bucksaw.

They are all working away silently when a new voice interrupts. "Dear Lord," the voice begins, as they all look up to see a man standing nearby, hands clasped prayerfully. His words, sacramentally condensed into an outward and visible cloud of steam, veil his face. His uniform and rank are obscured by an Army blanket thrown over his shoulders. He'd look like a camel-riding Holy Land prophet if he were not clean-shaven and wearing Rape Prevention Glasses.

"Goddamn it!" Shaftoe says. "I already said a fucking prayer."

"But are we praying for Private Hott, or for ourselves?" the man says.

This is a poser. Everything becomes quiet as the meat saw stops moving. Shaftoe drops the wetsuit and stands up. Blanket Man's got very short grizzly hair, or maybe that's frost coalescing on his scalp. His ice-colored eyes meet Shaftoe's through the mile-thick lenses of his RPGs, as if he's really expecting an answer. Shaftoe takes a step closer and realizes that the man is wearing a clerical collar.

"You tell me, Rev," Shaftoe says.

Then he recognizes Blanket Man. He's about to let fly with a lusty *What in the fuck are you doing here,* but something makes him hold back. The chaplain's eyes make a sideways dart so small and so fast that only Shaftoe, who's practically rubbing noses with him, could possibly see it. The message being: *Shut up, Bobby, we'll talk later.*

"Private Hott is with God now—or wherever people go after they die," says Enoch "You can call me Brother" Root.

"What kind of an attitude is that!? Course he's with God. Jesus Christ! 'Wherever they go when they die.' What kind of a chaplain are you?"

"I guess I'm a Detachment 2702 kind of chaplain," the chaplain says. Lieutenant Enoch Root finally breaks eye contact with Shaftoe and turns his gaze to where the action is. "As you were, fellows," he says. "Looks like bacon tonight, huh?"

The men chuckle nervously and resume sawing.

Once they get the pig's carcass disentangled from Hott's, each of the Marines grabs a limb. They carry Hott out into the butcher shop, which has been temporarily evacuated for purposes of this operation, so that Hott's former comrades-in-shanks will not spread rumors.

Hasty evacuation of a butcher shop after one of its workers has been found dead on the floor could spawn a few rumors in and of itself. So the cover story du jour, freshly spun by Lieutenant Ethridge, is that Detachment 2702 is (contrary to all outward appearances) an elite, crack medical team concerned that Hott had been struck down by a rare new form of North African food poisoning. Maybe even something deliberately left behind by the French, who are, by accounts, a little irritable about having their battleship sunk. Anyway, the whole shop (the story goes) has to be shut down for the day and gone over with a nit comb. Hott's corpse will be cremated before being sent back to the family, just to make sure that the dreaded affliction does not spread into Chicago— the planetary abbatoir capital—where its incalculable consequences could alter the outcome of the war.

There is a GI coffin laid out on the floor, just to preserve the fiction. Shaftoe and his men ignore it completely and begin dressing the body, first in an appalling pair of swim trunks, then various components of the wetsuit.

"Hey!" Ethridge says. "I thought you were going to do the gloves last."

"Sir, we're doing them first, by your leave, sir!" Bobby Shaftoe says.

"On account of his fingers will thaw out first and once that happens we are screwed, sir!"

"Well, slap this on him first," Ethridge says, and hands over a wristwatch. Shaftoe hefts it and whistles. It's a beaut: a Swiss chronometer in solid uranium, its jewel-laden movement throbbing away like the heartbeat of a small mammal. He swings it on the end of its wristband, made in cunningly joined armor plates. It is heavy enough to stun a muskellunge.

"Nice," Shaftoe says, "but it doesn't tell time too good."

"In the time zone where we are going," Ethridge says, "it does."

The chastened Shaftoe sets about his work. Meanwhile, Lieutenants Ethridge and Root are making themselves useful. They carry the crudely sawed remains of Frosty the Pig into the butcher shop and throw them on a gigantic scale. They add up to some thirty kilograms, whatever the fuck *that* means. Enoch Root, showing an appetite for physical labor that is duly and silently noted by the men, hauls in another pig carcass, stiff as a Radio Flyer, and dumps it onto the scale, bringing the total up to seventy. Ethridge does the breaststroke through clouds of flies to gather up all the cuts of meat that were on the chopping blocks when the place was evacuated. He throws them on the scale and the needle swings up to near the one-hundred mark. From that point they are able to bring it up to one-thirty by ferrying hams and roasts in from the freezer one at a time. Enoch Root—who seems to be conversant with exotic systems of measurement—has made a calculation, and checked it twice, establishing that the weight of Gerald Hott, converted into kilograms, is one hundred and thirty.

All the meat goes into the coffin. Ethridge slams the lid shut, trapping some flies who have no idea what they are in for. Root goes around with a clawhammer, driving in sixteen-penny nails with sure, powerful, Carpenter-of-Nazareth-like strokes. Meanwhile, Ethridge has taken a GI manual out of his briefcase. Shaftoe is close enough to read the title, printed in block letters on its olive drab cover:

COFFIN SEALING PROCEDURES

PART III: TROPICAL ENVIRONMENTS

VOL. II: HIGH DISEASE RISK SITUATIONS (BUBONIC PLAGUE, ETC.)

The two lieutenants devote a good hour to following the instructions in that manual. The instructions are not that complicated, but Enoch Root keeps noticing syntactical ambiguities and wants to explore their ramifications. First this rattles Ethridge, then his emotions tend towards impatience and, finally, extreme pragmatism. To make the chaplain shut up, Ethridge confiscates the manual and starts Root on stenciling Hott's name on the coffin and pasting it up with red stickers printed with medical warnings so appalling that the topic headings alone induce faint nausea. By the time Root is finished, the only person who can legally open this coffin is General George C. Marshall himself, and even he would have to first get special permission from the Surgeon General and evacuate all living things within a hundred-mile radius.

"Chaplain talks kind of funny," says Private Nathan at one point, listening, slackjawed, to one of these Root/Ethridge debates.

"Yeah!" exclaims Private Branph, as if the accent took a really keen listener to notice. "What kind of an accent is that anyway?"

All eyes turn to Bobby Shaftoe, who pretends to listen for a bit and then says, "Well, fellas, I would guess that this Enoch Root is the off-spring of a long line of Dutch and possibly German missionaries in the South Sea Islands, interbred with Aussies. And furthermore, I would guess that—being as how he grew up in territories controlled by the British—that he carries a British passport and was drafted into their military when the war started and is now part of ANZAC."

"Haw!" roars Private Daniels, "if you got all of that right, I'll give you *five bucks.*"

"Deal," Shaftoe says.

Ethridge and Root finish sealing the coffin at about the same time Shaftoe and his Marines are wrestling the last bits of the wetsuit into place. It takes a shitload of talcum powder, but they get it done. Ethridge supplies them with the talcum powder, which is not GI talc; it is from somewhere in Europe. Some of the letters on the label have pairs of dots over them, which Shaftoe knows to be a characteristic of the German language.

A truck backs up to the loading dock, smelling the fresh paint (it is a Detachment 2702 truck). In go the sealed coffin and the now-vulcanized dead butcher.

"I'm going to stay behind and check the wastebaskets," Lieutenant Ethridge tells Shaftoe. "I'll meet you at the airfield in one hour."

Shaftoe imagines one hour in the back of a hot truck with this cargo. "You want me to keep him on ice, sir?" he asks.

Ethridge has to think about this one for a while. He sucks his teeth, checks his watch, hems and haws. But when he finally answers, he sounds definite. "Negative. It is imperative, for purposes of this mission, that we now get him into a thawed mode."

PFC General Hott and his meat-laden coffin occupy the center of the truck's bed. The Marines sit to the sides, arranged like pallbearers. Shaftoe finds himself staring across the carnage into the face of Enoch Root, which is wearing an expression of forced nonchalance.

Shaftoe knows he ought to wait, but he just can't stand it. "What are you *doing* here?" he finally says.

"The detachment is relocating," the Rev says. "Closer to the front."

"We just got off the fucking boat," Shaftoe says. "Of course we're going closer to the goddamn front—we can't go any *farther* unless we *swim*."

"As long as we're pulling up stakes," Root says coolly, "I'll be coming along for the ride."

"I don't mean that," Bobby Shaftoe says. "I mean, why should the detachment have a chaplain?"

"You know the military," Root says. "Every unit has to have one."

"It's bad luck."

"It's *bad luck* to have a chaplain? Why?"

"It means the waffle-butts are expecting a lot of funerals, is why."

"So you are taking the position that the only thing a cleric can do is to preside over funerals? Interesting."

"And weddings and baptisms," Shaftoe says. All of the other Marines chortle.

"Could it be you're feeling a little anxious about the unusual nature of Detachment 2702's first mission?" Root inquires, casting a significant glance at the late Hott, then staring directly into Shaftoe's eyes.

"Anxious? Listen, Rev, I done some things on Guadalcanal that make this look like Emily Fucking Post."

All of the other Marines think this is a great line, but Root is undeterred.

"Did you know why you were doing those things on Guadalcanal?"

"Sure! To stay alive."

"Do you know why you're doing this?"

"Fuck no."

"Doesn't that irritate you a little bit? Or are you too much of a stupid jarhead to care?"

"Well, you kind of backed me into a corner there, Rev," Shaftoe says. After a pause he goes on, "I'll admit to being a little curious."

"If there were someone in Detachment 2702 who could help answer your questions about *why,* would that be useful?"

"I guess so," Shaftoe grumbles. "It just seems weird to have a chaplain."

"Why does it seem weird?"

"Because of what kind of unit this is."

"What kind of unit *is* it?" Root asks. He asks it with a certain sadistic pleasure.

"We're not supposed to talk about it," Shaftoe says. "And anyway, we don't know."

Down the hill, immense zigzagging ramps descend pompously over rows of tiger-striped arches to the strand of ramifying railway lines that feed the port from the south. "It's like standing in the drain of a fucking pinball machine," says B. Shaftoe, looking up at the way they have just come, thinking about what might come rolling down out of the Casbah. They head south along those railway lines and come into a zone of ore dumps and coal heaps and smokestacks, clearly recognizable to Great Lakes Eagle Scout Shaftoe, but here operated through some kind of cross-cultured gear train about a million meshings deep. They pull up in front of the *Société Algérienne d'Éclairage et de Force,* a double-smokestacked behemoth with the biggest coal-pile of all. They're in the middle of nowhere, but it's obvious that they are expected. Here—as everywhere else that Detachment 2702 goes—a strange Rank Inflation Effect is taking place. The coffin is carried into the *SAEF* by two lieutenants, a captain, and a major, overseen by a colonel! There is not a single enlisted man in sight, and Bobby Shaftoe, a mere sergeant, worries about what sort of work they'll find for *him.* There is also a Paperwork Negation Effect going on here; whenever Shaftoe expects to be stalled by the usual half an hour's worth of red tape, an anxious officer runs up and waves his hands furiously and he is allowed to proceed.

An Arab, wearing what appears to be a red coffee can on his head, hauls an iron door open; flames lunge at him and he beats them back with a blackened iron stick. The pallbearers center the head of the coffin in the opening and then shove it through, like ramming a big shell home into a sixteen-inch gun, and the man with the can on his head clangs the door shut, a tassel on the top of his can whipping around crazily. Before he's even got it latched he's yodeling just like those guys up in the Casbah. The officers all stand around agreeing with each other and signing their names on clipboards.

So with a dearth of complications that can only strike combat veteran Bobby Shaftoe as eerie, the truck leaves the *Société Algérienne d'Éclairage et de Force* behind and heads back up those damn ramps into Algiers. The climb's steep—a first-gear project all the way. Vendors with pushcarts loaded with boiling oil are not only keeping up with them but cooking fritters along the way. Three-legged dogs run and fight underneath the actual drive train of the truck. Detachment 2702 is also dogged by coffee-can-wearing natives threatening to play guitars made of jerry cans, and by orange vendors and snake charmers, and a few blue-eyed burnoose wearers holding up lumps of unwrapped and unlabelled dark stuff. Like hailstones, these may be classified by analogy to fruits and sporting goods. Typically they range from grape to baseball. At one point, the chaplain impulsively trades a Hershey bar for a golf ball of the stuff.

"What is that? Chocolate?" Bobby Shaftoe asks.

"If it was chocolate," Root says, "that guy wouldn't have taken a Hershey bar for it."

Shaftoe shrugs. "Unless it's shitty chocolate."

"Or shit!" blurts Private Nathan, provoking incredible hilarity.

"You heard of Mary Jane?" Root asks.

Shaftoe—role model, leader of men—stifles the impulse to say, *Heard of her? I've* fucked *her!*

"This is the concentrated essence," says Enoch Root.

"How would you know, Rev?" says Private Daniels.

The Rev is not rattled. "I'm the God guy here, right? I know the religious angle?"

"Yes, sir!"

"Well, at one time, there was a group of Muslims called the *hashishin* who would eat this stuff and then go out and kill people. They were so good at it, they became famous or infamous. Over time the pronunciation of the name has changed—we know them as assassins."

There is an appropriately respectful silence. Finally, Sergeant Shaftoe says, "What the hell are we waiting for?"

They eat some. Shaftoe, being the highest-ranking enlisted man present, eats more than the others. Nothing happens. "Only person I feel like assassinating is that guy who sold it to us," he says.

The airfield, eleven miles out of town, is busier than it was ever intended to be. This is nice grape- and olive-growing land, but stony mountains are visible farther inland, and beyond 'em is a patch of sand the size of the United States—most of which seems to be airborne and headed their way. Countless airplanes—predominantly Dakota transports, a.k.a. Gooney Birds—stir up vast, tongue-coating, booger-nucleating dust clouds. It doesn't occur to Shaftoe for quite some time that his dry eyes and mouth may not be entirely the result of dust in the air. His saliva has the consistency of tile adhesive.

The detachment is so damn secret that no one at the airfield even knows that they exist. There are a lot of Brits here, and in the desert, Brits wear shorts, which makes Shaftoe want to punch them in the nose. He controls the urge. But his obvious hostility towards men in short pants, combined with the fact that he is demanding to be pointed in the direction of a unit that is so secret that he cannot specify it by name or even vaguely describe it, leads to a lot of bafflement, a lot of incredulity, and generally gets the Anglo-American alliance off on the wrong foot.

Sergeant Shaftoe, however, now understands that anything to do with this detachment is liable to be way off to one side, shrouded in black

tarps and awnings. Like any other military unit, Detachment 2702 is rich
in some supplies and poor in others, but they do appear to control about
fifty percent of last year's total U.S. tarpage production. When Shaftoe
mentions this fact, and goes on about it to his comrades at great length,
some of the men look at him a little funny. It's left to Enoch Root to
say, "Between the giant lizards and the black tarps some people might
think you were acting a little paranoid."

"Let me tell you about paranoid," Shaftoe says, and he does, not
forgetting to mention Lieutenant Ethridge and his wastebaskets. By the
time he's had his say, the whole detachment has assembled on the far
side of those tarps, and everyone is nice and tense except for their newest
recruit, who, as Shaftoe notes approvingly, is beginning to relax. Lying
on the bed of the truck in his wetsuit, he *adjusts,* rather than bounces,
when they go over bumps.

Even so, he is still stiff enough to simplify the problem of getting him
out of the truck and into their assigned Gooney Bird: a bare-knuckled
variant of the DC-3, militarized and (to Shaftoe's skeptical eye) rendered
somewhat less than airworthy by a pair of immense cargo doors gouged
into one side, nearly cutting the airframe in half. This particular Dakota
has been flying around in the fucking desert so long that all the paint's
been sand-blasted off its propeller blades, the engine cowling, and the
leading edges of the wings, leaving burnished metal that will make an
inviting silver gleam for any Luftwaffe pilots within three hundred miles.
Worse: diverse antennas sprout from the skin of the fuselage, mostly
around the cockpit. Not just whip antennas but great big damn barbecue
grills that make Shaftoe wish he had a hacksaw. They are eerily like the
ones that Shaftoe humped down the stairway from Station Alpha in
Shanghai—a memory that has somehow gotten all mangled together,
now, with the other images in his head. When he tries to recollect it,
all he can see is a bloodied Jesus carrying a high-frequency dual-band
dipole down a stone staircase in Manila, and he knows that can't be right.

Though they are on the precincts of a busy airfield, Ethridge refuses
to let this operation go forward when there is as much as a single airplane
in the sky. Finally he says, "Okay, NOW!" In the truck, they lift the
body up, just in time to hear Ethridge shout, "No, WAIT!" at which
point they put him down again. Long after it has stopped being grimly
amusing, they put a tarp on Gerald Hott and get him carried on board,
and shortly thereafter are airborne. Detachment 2072 is headed for a
rendezvous with Rommel.

CYCLES

✝ IT IS EARLY IN NOVEMBER OF 1942 AND A SIMPLY UNBELIEVABLE amount of shit is going on, all at once, everywhere. Zeus himself would not be able to sort it all out, not even if he mobilized the caryatids—tell them never mind what we told you, just drop those loads. Temples collapsing everywhere, like spyglasses, he'd send those caryatids—and any naiads and dryads he could scare up—to library school, issue them green visors, dress them in the prim asexual uniforms of the OPAMS, the Olympian Perspective Archive Management Service, put them to work filling out three-by-five cards round the clock. Get them to use some of that vaunted caryatid steadfastness to tend Hollerith machines and ETC card readers. Even then, Zeus would probably still lack a handle on the situation. He'd be so pissed off he would hardly know which hubristical mortals to fling his thunderbolts at, nor which pinup girls and buck privates to molest.

Lawrence Pritchard Waterhouse is as Olympian as anyone right now. Roosevelt and Churchill and the few others on the Ultra Mega list have the same access, but they have other cares and distractions. They can't wander around the data flow capital of the planet, snooping over translators' shoulders and reading the decrypts as they come, *chunkity-chunkity-whirr,* out of the Typex machines. They cannot trace individual threads of the global narrative at their whim, running from hut to hut patching connections together, even as the WRENs in Hut 11 string patch cables from one bombe socket to another, fashioning a web to catch Hitler's messages as they speed through the ether.

Here are some of the things Waterhouse knows: the Battle of El Alamein is won, and Montgomery is chasing Rommel westwards across Cyrenaica at what looks like a breakneck pace, driving him back toward the distant Axis stronghold of Tunis. But it's not the rout it appears to be. If Monty would only grasp the significance of the intelligence coming through the Ultra channel, he would be able to move decisively, to surround and capture large pockets of Germans and Italians. But he never does, and so Rommel stages an orderly retreat, preparing to fight another day, and plodding Monty is roundly cursed in the watch rooms of Bletchley Park for his failure to exploit their priceless but perishable gems of intelligence.

The largest sealift in history just piled into Northwest Africa. It is called Operation Torch, and it's going to take Rommel from behind, serving as anvil to Montgomery's hammer, or, if Monty doesn't pick up the pace a bit, maybe the other way around. It looks brilliantly organized but it's not really; this is the first time America has punched across the Atlantic in any serious way and so a whole grab bag of stuff is included on those ships—including any number of signals intelligence geeks who are storming theatrically onto the beaches as if they were Marines. Also included in the landing is the American contingent of Detachment 2702—a hand-picked wrecking crew of combat-hardened leathernecks.

Some of these Marines learned what they know on Guadalcanal, a basically useless island in the Southwest Pacific where the Empire of Nippon and the United States of America are disputing—with rifles— each other's right to build a military airbase. Early returns suggest that the Nipponese Army, during its extended tour of East Asia, has lost its edge. It would appear that raping the entire female population of Nanjing, and bayoneting helpless Filipino villagers, does not translate into actual military competence. The Nipponese Army is still trying to work out some way to kill, say, a hundred American Marines without losing, say, five hundred of its own soldiers.

The Japanese Navy is a different story—they know what they are doing. They have Yamamoto. They have torpedoes that actually explode when they strike their targets, in stark contrast to the American models which do nothing but scratch the paint of the Japanese ships and then sink apologetically. Yamamoto just made another attempt to wipe out the American fleet off the Santa Cruz Islands, sank *Hornet* and blew a nice hole in *Enterprise*. But he lost a third of his planes. Watching the Japanese rack up losses, Waterhouse wonders if anyone in Tokyo has bothered to break out the abacus and run the numbers on this Second World War thing.

The Allies are doing some math of their own, and they are scared shitless. There are 100 German U-boats in the Atlantic now, operating mostly from Lorient and Bordeaux, and they are slaughtering convoys in the North Atlantic with such efficiency that it's not even *combat,* just a Lusitanian-level murder spree. They are on a pace to sink something like a million tons of shipping this month, which Waterhouse cannot really comprehend. He tries to think of a ton as being roughly equivalent to a car, and then tries to imagine America and Canada going out into the middle of the Atlantic and simply dropping a million cars into the ocean—just in November. Sheesh!

The problem is Shark.

The Germans call it Triton. It is a new cypher system, used exclusively by their Navy. It is an Enigma machine, but not the usual three-wheel

Enigma. The Poles learned how to break that old thing a couple of years ago, and Bletchley Park industrialized the process. But more than a year ago, a German U-boat was beached intact on the south coast of Iceland and gone over pretty thoroughly by men from Bletchley. They discovered an Enigma box with niches for *four*—not three—wheels.

When the four-wheel Enigma had gone into service on February 1st, the entire Atlantic had gone black. Alan and the others have been going after the problem very hard ever since. The problem is that they don't know how the fourth wheel is wired up.

But a few days ago, another U-boat was captured, more or less intact, in the Eastern Mediterranean. Colonel Chattan, who happened to be in the neighborhood, went there with sickening haste, along with some other Bletchleyites. They recovered a four-wheel Enigma machine, and though this doesn't break the code, it gives them the data they need to break it.

Hitler must be feeling cocky, anyway, because he's on tour at the moment, preparatory to a working vacation at his alpine retreat. That didn't prevent him from taking over what was left of France—apparently something about Operation Torch really got his goat, so he occupied Vichy France in its entirety, and then dispatched upwards of a hundred thousand fresh troops, and a correspondingly stupendous amount of supplies, across the Mediterranean to Tunisia. Waterhouse imagines that you must be able to cross from Sicily to Tunisia these days simply by hopping from the deck of one German transport ship to another.

Of course, if that were true, Waterhouse's job would be a lot easier. The Allies could sink as many of those ships as they wanted to without raising a single blond Teutonic eyebrow on the information-theory front. But the fact is that the convoys are few and far between. Just exactly how few and how far between are parameters that go into the equations that he and Alan Mathison Turing spend all night scribbling on chalkboards.

After a good eight or twelve hours of that, when the sun has finally come up again, there's nothing like a brisk bicycle ride in the Buckinghamshire countryside.

Spread out before them as they pump over the crest of the rise is a woods that has turned all of the colors of flame. The hemispherical crowns of the maples even contribute a realistic billowing effect. Lawrence feels a funny compulsion to take his hands off the handlebars and clamp them over his ears. As they coast into the trees, however, the air remains delightfully cool, the blue sky above unsmudged by pillars of black smoke, and the calm and quiet of the place could not be more different from what Lawrence is remembering.

"Talk, talk, talk!" says Alan Turing, imitating the squawk of furious hens. The strange noise is made stranger by the fact that he is wearing a gas mask, until he becomes impatient and pulls it up onto his forehead. "They love to hear themselves talk." He is referring to Winston Churchill and Franklin Roosevelt. "And they don't mind hearing each other talk—up to a point, at least. But voice is a terribly redundant channel of information, compared to printed text. If you take text and run it through an Enigma—which is really not all that complicated—the familiar patterns in the text, such as the preponderance of the letter E, become nearly undetectable." Then he pulls the gas mask back over his face in order to emphasize the following point: "But you can warp and permute voice in the most fiendish ways imaginable and it will still be perfectly intelligible to a listener." Alan then suffers a sneezing fit that threatens to burst the khaki straps around his head.

"Our ears know how to find the familiar patterns," Lawrence suggests. He is not wearing a gas mask because (a) there is no Nazi gas attack in progress, and (b) unlike Alan, he does not suffer from hay fever.

"Excuse me." Alan suddenly brakes and jumps off his bicycle. He lifts the rear wheel from the pavement, gives it a spin with his free hand, then reaches down and gives the chain a momentary sideways tug. He is watching the mechanism intently, interrupted by a few aftersneezes.

The chain of Turing's bicycle has one weak link. The rear wheel has one bent spoke. When the link and the spoke come into contact with each other, the chain will part and fall onto the road. This does not happen at every revolution of the wheel—otherwise the bicycle would be completely useless. It only happens when the chain and the wheel are in a certain position with respect to each other.

Based upon reasonable assumptions about the velocity that can be maintained by Dr. Turing, an energetic bicyclist (let us say 25 km/hr) and the radius of his bicycle's rear wheel (a third of a meter), if the clain's weak link hit the bent spoke on every revolution, the chain would fall off every one-third of a second.

In fact, the chain doesn't fall off unless the bent spoke and the weak link happen to coincide. Now, suppose that you describe the position of the rear wheel by the traditional θ. Just for the sake of simplicity, say that when the wheel starts in the position where the bent spoke is capable of hitting the weak link (albeit only if the weak link happens to be there to be hit) then $\theta = 0$. If you're using degrees as your unit, then, during a single revolution of the wheel, θ will climb all the way up to 359 degrees before cycling back around to 0, at which point the bent spoke will be back in position to knock the chain off. And now suppose that you describe the position of the chain with the variable C, in the following very simple way: you assign a number to each link on the chain. The weak link is numbered 0, the next is 1, and so on, up to $l - 1$ where l is the total number of links in the chain. And again, for simplicity's sake, say that when the chain is in the position where its weak link is capable of being hit by the bent spoke (albeit only if the bent spoke happens to be there to hit it) then $C = 0$.

For purposes of figuring out when the chain is going to fall off of Dr. Turing's bicycle, then, everything we need to know about the bicycle is contained in the values of θ and of C. That pair of numbers defines the bicycle's state. The bicycle has as many possible states as there can be different values of (θ, C) but only one of those states, namely (0, 0), is the one that will cause the chain to fall off onto the road.

Suppose we start off in that state; i.e., with $(\theta = 0, C = 0)$, but that the chain has not fallen off because Dr. Turing (knowing full well his bicycle's state at any given time) has paused in the middle of road (nearly precipitating a collision with his friend and colleague Lawrence Pritchard Waterhouse, because his gas mask blocks his peripheral vision). Dr. Turing has tugged sideways on the chain while moving it forward slightly, preventing it from being hit by the bent spoke. Now he gets on the bicycle again and begins to pedal forward. The circumference of his rear wheel is about two meters, and so when he has moved a distance of two meters down the road, the wheel has performed a complete revolution and reached the position $\theta = 0$ again—that being the position, remember, when its bent spoke is in position to hit the weak link.

What of the chain? Its position, defined by C, begins at 0 and reaches 1 when its next link moves forward to the fatal position, then 2 and so on. The chain must move in synch with the teeth on the sprocket at the center of the rear wheel, and that sprocket has n teeth, and so after a complete revolution of the rear wheel, when $\theta = 0$ again, $C = n$. After a second complete revolution of the rear wheel, once again $\theta = 0$ but now $C = 2n$. The next time it's $C = 3n$ and so on. But remember that the chain is not an infinite linear thing, but a loop having only l positions; at $C = l$ it loops back around to $C = 0$ and repeats the cycle. So when calculating the value of C it is necessary to do modular arithmetic—that is, if the chain has a hundred links ($l = 100$) and the total number of links that have moved by is 135, then the value of C is not 135 but 35. Whenever you get a number greater than or equal to l you just repeatedly subtract l until you get a number less than l. This operation is written, by mathematicians, as mod l. So the successive values of C, each time the rear wheel spins around to $\theta = 0$, are

$$C_i = n \bmod l,\ 2n \bmod l,\ 3n \bmod l,\ \ldots,\ in \bmod l$$

where $i = (1, 2, 3, \ldots \infty)$

more or less, depending on how close to infinitely long Turing wants to keep riding his bicycle. After a while, it seems infinitely long to Waterhouse.

Turing's chain will fall off when his bicycle reaches the state ($\theta = 0$, $C = 0$) and in light of what is written above, this will happen when i (which is just a counter telling how many times the rear wheel has revolved) reaches some hypothetical value such that $in \bmod l = 0$, or, to put it in plain language, it will happen if there is some multiple of n (such as, oh, $2n$, $3n$, $395n$ or $109{,}948{,}368{,}443n$) that just happens to be an exact multiple of l too. Actually there might be several of these so-called common multiples, but from a practical standpoint the only one that matters is the first one—the least common multiple, or LCM— because that's the one that will be reached first and that will cause the chain to fall off.

If, say, the sprocket has twenty teeth ($n = 20$) and the chain has a hundred teeth ($l = 100$) then after one turn of the wheel we'll have $C = 20$, after two turns $C = 40$, then 60, then 80, then 100. But since we are doing the arithmetic modulo 100, that value has to be changed to zero. So after five revolutions of the rear wheel, we have reached the state ($\theta = 0$, $C = 0$) and Turing's chain falls off. Five revolutions of the rear wheel only gets him ten meters down the road, and so with these values of l and n the bicycle is very nearly worthless. Of course, this is only true if Turing is stupid enough to begin pedaling with his bicycle in the chain-falling-off state. If, at the time he begins pedaling, it is in the state ($\theta = 0$, $C = 1$) instead, then the successive values will be $C = 21, 41, 61, 81, 1, 21, \ldots$ and so on forever—the chain will never fall off. But this is a degenerate case, where "degenerate," to a mathematician, means "annoyingly boring." In theory, as long as Turing put his bicycle into the right state before parking it outside a building, no one would be able to steal it—the chain would fall off after they had ridden for no more than ten meters.

But if Turing's chain has a hundred and one links ($l = 101$) then after five revolutions we have $C = 100$, and after six we have $C = 19$, then

$$C = 39, 59, 79, 99, 18, 38, 58, 78, 98, 17, 37, 57, 77, 97, 16, 36, 56, 76, 96, 15,$$
$$35, 55, 75, 95, 14, 34, 54, 74, 94, 13, 33, 53, 73, 93, 12, 32, 52, 72, 92, 11,$$
$$31, 51, 71, 91, 10, 30, 50, 70, 90, 9, 29, 49, 69, 89, 8, 28, 48, 68, 88, 7, 27,$$
$$47, 67, 87, 6, 26, 46, 66, 86, 5, 25, 45, 65, 85, 4, 24, 44, 64, 84, 3, 23, 43,$$
$$63, 83, 2, 22, 42, 62, 82, 1, 21, 41, 61, 81, 0$$

So not until the 101st revolution of the rear wheel does the bicycle return to the state ($\theta = 0$, $C = 0$) where the chain falls off. During these hundred and one revolutions, Turing's bicycle has proceeded for a distance of a fifth of a kilometer down the road, which is not too bad. So the bicycle is usable. However, unlike in the degenerate case, it is *not* possible for this bicycle to be placed in a state where the chain never falls off at all. This can be proved by going through the above list of values of C, and noticing that every possible value of C—every single number from 0 to 100—is on the list. What this means is that no matter what value C has when Turing begins to pedal, sooner or later it will work its way round to the fatal $C = 0$ and the chain will fall off. So Turing can leave his bicycle anywhere and be confident that, if stolen, it won't go more than a fifth of a kilometer before the chain falls off.

The difference between the degenerate and nondegenerate cases has to do with the properties of the numbers involved. The combination of ($n = 20$, $l = 100$) has radically different properties from ($n = 20$, $l = 101$). The key difference is that 20 and 101 are "relatively prime" meaning that they have no factors in common. This means that their least common multiple, their LCM, is a large number—it is, in fact, equal to $l \times n = 20 \times 101 = 2020$. Whereas the LCM of 20 and 100 is only 100. The $l = 101$ bicycle has a long *period*—it passes through many different states before returning back to the beginning—whereas the $l = 100$ bicycle has a period of only a few states.

Suppose that Turing's bicycle were a cipher machine that worked by alphabetic substitution, which is to say that it would replace each of the 26 letters of the alphabet with some other letter. An A in the plaintext might become a T in the ciphertext, B might become F, C might become M, and so on all the way through to Z. In and of itself this would be an absurdly easy cipher to break—kids-in-treehouses stuff. But suppose that the substitution scheme *changed* from one letter to the next. That is, suppose that after the first letter of the plaintext was enciphered using one particular substitution alphabet, the second letter of plaintext was enciphered using a completely different substitution alphabet, and the third letter a different one yet, and so on. This is called a polyalphabetic cipher.

Suppose that Turing's bicycle were capable of generating a different alphabet for each one of its different states. So the state ($\theta = 0$, $C = 0$) would correspond to, say, this substitution alphabet:

A B C D E F G H I J K L M N O P Q R S T U V W X Y Z
Q G U W B I Y T F K V N D O H E P X L Z R C A S J M

but the state (θ = 180, C = 15) would correspond to this (different) one:

A B C D E F G H I J K L M N O P Q R S T U V W X Y Z
B O R I X V G Y P F J M T C Q N H A Z U K L D S E W

No two letters would be enciphered using the same substitution alphabet—*until*, that is, the bicycle worked its way back around to the initial state (θ = 0, C = 0) and began to repeat the cycle. This means that it is a *periodic* polyalphabetic system. Now, if this machine had a short period, it would repeat itself frequently, and would therefore be useful, as an encryption system, only against kids in treehouses. The longer its period (the more relative primeness is built into it) the less frequently it cycles back to the same substitution alphabet, and the more secure it is.

The three-wheel Enigma is just that type of system (i.e., periodic polyalphabetic). Its wheels, like the drive train of Turing's bicycle, embody cycles within cycles. Its period is 17,576, which means that the substitution alphabet that enciphers the first letter of a message will not be used again until the 17577th letter is reached. But with Shark the Germans have added a fourth wheel, bumping the period up to 456,976. The wheels are set in a different, randomly chosen starting position at the beginning of each message. Since the Germans' messages are never as long as 450,000 characters, the Enigma never reuses the same substitution alphabet in the course of a given message, which is why the Germans think it's so good.

A flight of transport planes goes over them, probably headed for the aerodrome at Bedford. The planes make a weirdly musical diatonic hum, like bagpipes playing two drones at once. This reminds Lawrence of yet another phenomenon related to the bicycle wheel and the Enigma machine. "Do you know why airplanes sound the way they do?" he says.

"No, come to think of it." Turing pulls his gas mask off again. His jaw has gone a bit slack and his eyes are darting from side to side. Lawrence has caught him out.

"I noticed it at Pearl. Airplane engines are rotary," Lawrence says. "Consequently they must have an odd number of cylinders."

"How does that follow?"

"If the number were even, the cylinders would be directly opposed, a hundred and eighty degrees apart, and it wouldn't work out mechanically."

"Why not?"

"I forgot. It just wouldn't work out."

Alan raises his eyebrows, clearly not convinced.

"Something to do with cranks," Waterhouse ventures, feeling a little defensive.

"I don't know that I agree," Alan says.

"Just stipulate it—think of it as a boundary condition," Waterhouse says. But Alan is already hard at work, he suspects, mentally designing a rotary aircraft engine with an even number of cylinders.

"Anyway, if you look at them, they all have an odd number of cylinders," Lawrence continues. "So the exhaust noise combines with the propeller noise to produce that two-tone sound."

Alan climbs back onto his bicycle and they ride into the woods for some distance without any more talking. Actually, they have not been talking so much as mentioning certain ideas and then leaving the other to work through the implications. This is a highly efficient way to communicate; it eliminates much of the redundancy that Alan was complaining about in the case of FDR and Churchill.

Waterhouse is thinking about cycles within cycles. He's already made up his mind that human society is one of these cycles-within-cycles things* and now he's trying to figure out whether it is like Turing's bicycle (works fine for a while, then suddenly the chain falls off; hence the occasional world war) or like an Enigma machine (grinds away incomprehensibly for a long time, then suddenly the wheels line up like a slot machine and everything is made plain in some sort of global epiphany or, if you prefer, apocalypse) or just like a rotary airplane engine (runs and runs and runs; nothing special happens; it just makes a lot of noise).

"It's somewhere around . . . here!" Alan says, and violently brakes to a stop, just to chaff Lawrence, who has to turn his bicycle around, a chancy trick on such a narrow lane, and loop back.

They lean their bicycles against trees and remove pieces of equipment from the baskets: dry cells, electronic breadboards, poles, a trenching tool, loops of wire. Alan looks about somewhat uncertainly and then strikes off into the woods.

"I'm off to America soon, to work on this voice encryption problem at Bell Labs," Alan says.

Lawrence laughs ruefully. "We're ships passing in the night, you and I."

"We are *passengers* on ships passing in the night," Alan corrects him. "It is no accident. They need you precisely because I am leaving. I've been doing all of the 2701 work to this point."

"It's Detachment 2702 now," Lawrence says.

"Oh," Alan says, crestfallen. "You noticed."

---

*He has no hard data to back this up; it just seems like a cool idea.

"It was reckless of you, Alan."

"On the contrary!" Alan says. "What will Rudy think if he notices that, of all the units and divisions and detachments in the Allied order of battle, there is not a single one whose number happens to be the product of two primes?"

"Well, that depends upon how common such numbers are compared to all of the other numbers, and on how many other numbers in the range are going unused . . ." Lawrence says, and begins to work out the first half of the problem. "Riemann Zeta function again. That thing pops up everywhere."

"That's the spirit!" Alan says. "Simply take a rational and common-sense approach. *They* are really quite pathetic."

"Who?"

"Here," Alan says, slowing to a stop and looking around at the trees, which to Lawrence look like all the other trees. "This looks familiar." He sits down on the bole of a windfall and begins to unpack electrical gear from his bag. Lawrence squats nearby and does the same. Lawrence does not know how the device works—it is Alan's invention—and so he acts in the role of surgical assistant, handing tools and supplies to the doctor as he puts the device together. The doctor is talking the entire time, and so he requests tools by staring at them fixedly and furrowing his brow.

"*They* are—well, who do you suppose? The fools who use all of the information that comes from Bletchley Park!"

"Alan!"

"Well, it is foolish! Like this Midway thing. That's a perfect example, isn't it?"

"Well, I was happy that we won the battle," Lawrence says guardedly.

"Don't you think it's a bit *odd*, a bit *striking,* a bit *noticeable,* that after all of Yamamoto's brilliant feints and deceptions and ruses, this Nimitz fellow knew *exactly* where to go looking for him? Out of the *entire* Pacific Ocean?"

"All right," Lawrence says, "I was appalled. I wrote a paper about it. Probably the paper that got me into this mess with you."

"Well, it's no better with us Brits," Alan says.

"Really?"

"You would be horrified at what we've been up to in the Mediterranean. It is a scandal. A crime."

"What have we been up to?" Lawrence asks. "I say 'we' rather than 'you' because we are allies now."

"Yes, yes," Alan says impatiently. "So they claim." He paused for a moment, tracing an electrical circuit with his finger, calculating inductances in his head. Finally, he continues: "Well, we've been sinking convoys, that's what. German convoys. We've been sinking them right and left."

"Rommel's?"

"Yes, exactly. The Germans put fuel and tanks and ammunition on ships in Naples and send them south. We go out and sink them. We sink nearly all of them, because we have broken the Italian C38m cipher and we know when they are leaving Naples. And lately we've been sinking *just* the *very ones* that are most crucial to Rommel's efforts, because we have *also* broken his Chaffinch cipher and we know which ones he is complaining loudest about not having."

Turing snaps a toggle switch on his invention and a weird, looping squeal comes from a dusty black paper cone lashed onto the breadboard with twine. The cone is a speaker, apparently scavenged from a radio. There is a broomstick with a loop of stiff wire dangling from the end, and a wire running from that loop up the stick to the breadboard. He swings the broomstick around until the loop is dangling, like a lasso, in front of Lawrence's midsection. The speaker yelps.

"Good. It's picking up your belt buckle," Alan says.

He sets the contraption down in the leaves, gropes in several pockets, and finally pulls out a scrap of paper on which several lines of text have been written in block letters. Lawrence would recognize it anywhere: it is a decrypt worksheet. "What's that, Alan?"

"I wrote out complete instructions and enciphered them, then hid them under a bridge in a benzedrine container," Alan says. "Last week I went and recovered the container and decyphered the instructions." He waves the paper in the air.

"What encryption scheme did you use?"

"One of my own devising. You are welcome to take a crack at it, if you like."

"What made you decide it was time to dig this stuff up?"

"It was nothing more than a hedge against invasion," Alan says. "Clearly, we're not going to be invaded now, not with you chaps in the war."

"How much did you bury?"

"Two silver bars, Lawrence, each with a value of some hundred and twenty-five pounds. One of them should be very close to us." Alan stands up, pulls a compass out of his pocket, turns to face magnetic north, and squares his shoulders. Then he rotates a few degrees. "Can't remember whether I allowed for declination," he mumbles. "Right! In any case. One hundred paces north." And he strides off into the woods, followed by Lawrence, who has been given the job of carrying the metal detector.

Just as Dr. Alan Turing can ride a bicycle and carry on a conversation while mentally counting the revolutions of the pedals, he can count paces and talk at the same time too. Unless he has lost count entirely, which seems just as possible.

"If what you are saying is true," Lawrence says, "the jig must be up already. Rudy must have figured out that we've broken their codes."

"An informal system has been in place, which might be thought of as a precursor to Detachment 2701, or 2702 or whatever we are calling it," Alan says. "When we want to sink a convoy, we send out an observation plane first. It is *ostensibly* an observation plane. Of course, to observe is not its *real* duty—we already know exactly where the convoy is. Its *real* duty is *to be observed*—that is, to fly close enough to the convoy that it will be noticed by the lookouts on the ships. The ships will then send out a radio message to the effect that they have been sighted by an Allied observation plane. Then, when we come round and sink them, the Germans will not find it suspicious—at least, not quite so monstrously suspicious that we knew exactly where to go."

Alan stops, consults his compass, turns ninety degrees, and begins pacing westwards.

"That strikes me as being a very ad hoc arrangement," Lawrence says. "What is the likelihood that Allied observation planes, sent out purportedly at random, will just happen to notice every single Axis convoy?"

"I've already calculated that probability, and I'll bet you one of my silver bars that Rudy has done it too," Turing says. "It is a very small probability."

"So I was right," Lawrence says, "we have to assume that the jig is up."

"Perhaps not just yet," Alan says. "It has been touch and go. Last week, we sank a convoy in the fog."

"In the fog?"

"It was foggy the whole way. The convoy could not possibly have been observed. The imbeciles sank it anyway. Kesselring became suspicious, as would anyone. So we ginned up a fake message—in a cypher that we know the Nazis have broken—addressed to a fictitious agent in Naples. It congratulated him on betraying that convoy to us. Ever since, the Gestapo have been running rampant on the Naples waterfront, looking for the fellow."

"We dodged a bullet there, I'd say."

"Indeed." Alan stops abruptly, takes the metal detector from Lawrence, and turns it on. He begins to walk slowly across a clearing, sweeping the wire loop back and forth just above the ground. It keeps snagging on branches and getting bent out of shape, necessitating frequent repairs, but remains stubbornly silent the whole time, except when Alan, concerned that it is no longer working, tests it on Lawrence's belt buckle.

"The whole business is delicate," Alan muses. "Some of our SLUs in North Africa—"

"SLUs?"

"Special Liaison Units. The intelligence officers who receive the Ultra information from us, pass it on to field officers, and then make sure it is destroyed. Some of them learned, from Ultra, that there was to be a German air raid during lunch, so they took their helmets to the mess hall. When the air raid came off as scheduled, everyone wanted to know why those SLUs had known to bring their helmets."

"The entire business seems hopeless," Lawrence says. "How can the Germans not realize?"

"It seems that way to us because we know everything and our channels of communication are free from noise," Alan says. "The Germans have fewer, and much noisier, channels. Unless we continue to do stunningly idiotic things like sinking convoys in the fog, they will never receive any clear and unmistakable indications that we have broken Enigma."

"It's funny you should mention Enigma," Lawrence says, "since that is an extremely noisy channel from which we manage to extract vast amounts of useful information."

"Precisely. Precisely why I am worried."

"Well, I'll do my best to spoof Rudy," Waterhouse says.

"You'll do fine. I'm worried about the men who are carrying out the operations."

"Colonel Chattan seems pretty dependable," Waterhouse says, though there's probably no point in continuing to reassure Alan. He's just in a fretting mood. Once every two or three years, Waterhouse does something that is socially deft, and now's the time: he changes the subject: "And meanwhile, you'll be working it out so that Churchill and Roosevelt can have secret telephone conversations?"

"In theory. I rather doubt that it's practical. Bell Labs has a system that works by breaking the waveform down into several bands . . ." and then Alan is off on the subject of telephone companies. He delivers a complete dissertation on the subject of information theory as applied to the human voice, and how that governs the way telephone systems work. It is a good thing that Turing has such a large subject on which to expound, for the woods are large, and it has become increasingly obvious to Lawrence that his friend has no idea where the silver bars are buried.

Unburdened by any silver, the two friends ride home in darkness, which comes surprisingly early this far north. They do not talk very much, for Lawrence is still absorbing and digesting everything that Alan has disgorged to him about Detachment 2702 and the convoys and Bell Labs and voice signal redundancy. Every few minutes, a motorcycle whips past them, saddlebags stuffed with encrypted message slips.

ALOFT

ANY WAY THAT LIVESTOCK CAN TRAVEL, BOBBY SHAFTOE HAS too: boxcars, open trucks, forced cross-country marches. Military has now invented the airborne equivalent of these in the form of the Plane of a Thousand Names: DC-3, Skytrain, C-47, Dakota Transport, Gooney Bird. He'll survive. The exposed aluminum ribs of the fuselage are trying to beat him to death, but as long as he stays awake, he can fend them off.

The enlisted men are jammed into the other plane. Lieutenants Ethridge and Root are in this one, along with PFC Gerald Hott and Sergeant Bobby Shaftoe. Lieutenant Ethridge got dibs on all of the soft objects in the plane and arranged them into a nest, up forward near the cockpit, and strapped himself down. For a while he pretended to do paperwork. Then he tried looking out the windows. Now he has fallen asleep and is snoring so loudly that he is, no fooling, drowning out the engines.

Enoch Root has wedged himself into the back of the fuselage, where it gets narrow, and is perusing two books at once. It strikes Shaftoe as typical—he supposes that the books say completely different things and that the chaplain is deriving great pleasure from pitting them against each other, like those guys who have a chessboard on a turntable so that they can play against themselves. He supposes that when you live in a shack on a mountain with a bunch of natives who don't speak any of your half-dozen or so languages, you have to learn to have arguments with yourself.

There's a row of small square windows on each side of the plane. Shaftoe looks out to the right and sees mountains covered with *snow* and gets scared shitless for a moment thinking maybe they've strayed into the Alps. But off to the left, it still looks like the Mediterranean, and eventually it gives way to Devil's Tower type outcroppings rising up out of stony scrubland, and then after that it is just rocks and sand, or sand without the rocks. Sand puckered here and there, for no particular reason, by clutches of dunes. Damn it, they are still in Africa! You ought to be able to see lions and giraffes and rhinos! Shaftoe goes forward to lodge a complaint with the pilot and copilot. Maybe he can get a card game together. Maybe the view out the *front* of the plane is something to write home about.

He is, on all counts, thrown back in stinging defeat. He sees immediately that the project of finding a better view is doomed. There are only three things in the whole universe: sand, sea, and sky. As a Marine, he knows how boring the sea is. The other two are little better. There is a line of clouds far ahead of them—a front of some description. That's all there is.

He gets a general notion of their flight plan before the chart is snatched away and stashed out of his view. They seem to be attempting to fly across Tunisia, which is kind of funny, because last time Shaftoe checked, Tunisia was Nazi territory—the anchor, in fact, of the Axis presence on the African continent. Today's general flight plan seems to be that they'll cut across the straits between Bizerta and Sicily, then head east to Malta.

All of Rommel's supplies and reinforcements come across those very straits from Italy, and land at Tunis or Bizerta. From there, Rommel can strike out east towards Egypt or west towards Morocco. In the several weeks since the British Eighth Army kicked the crap out of him at El Alamein (which is way, way over there in Egypt) he has been retreating westwards back towards Tunis. In the few weeks since the Americans landed in Northwest Africa, he's been fighting on a second front to his west. And Rommel has been doing a damn good job of it, as far as Shaftoe can tell from listening between the stentorian lines of the Movietone newsreels, so laden with sinister cheer, whence the above facts were gleaned.

All this means that down below them, vast forces ought to be spread out across the Sahara in readiness for combat. Perhaps there is even a battle going on right now. But Shaftoe sees nothing. Just the occasional line of yellow dust thrown up by a convoy, a dynamite fuse sputtering across the desert.

So he talks to those flyboys. It's not until he notices them giving each other looks that he realizes he's going on at great length. Those Assassins must've killed their victims by talking them to death.

The card game, he realizes, is completely out of the question. These flyboys don't want to talk. He practically has to dive in and grab the control yoke to get them to say anything. And when they do, they sound funny, and he realizes that these guys are not guys nor fellas. They are blokes. Chaps. Mates. They are Brits.

The only other thing he notices about them, before he gives up and slinks back into the cargo hold, is that they are fucking armed to the teeth. Like they were expecting to have to kill twenty or thirty people on their way from the airplane to the latrine and back. Bobby Shaftoe has met a few of these paranoid types during his tour, and he doesn't like them very much. That whole mindset reminds him too much of Guadalcanal.

He finds a place on the floor next to the body of PFC Gerald Hott and stretches out. The teeny revolver in his waistband makes it impossible for him to lie on his back, so he takes it out and pockets it. This only transfers the center of discomfort to the Marine Raider stiletto holstered invisibly between his shoulder blades. He realizes that he is going to have to curl up on his side, which doesn't work because on one side he has a standard-issue Colt semiautomatic, which he doesn't trust, and on the other, his own six-shooter from home, which he does. So he has to find places to stash those, along with the various ammo clips, speed loaders, and maintenance supplies that go with them. The V-44 "Gung Ho" jungle-clearing, coconut-splitting, and Nip-decapitating knife, strapped to the outside of his lower leg, also has to be removed, as does the derringer that he keeps on the other leg for balance. The only thing that stays with him are the grenades in his front pockets, since he doesn't plan to lie down on his stomach.

They make their way around the headland just in time to avoid being washed out to sea by the implacable tide. In front of them is a muddy tidal flat, forming the floor of a box-shaped cove. The walls of the box are formed by the headland they've just gone round, another, depressingly similar headland a few hundred yards along the shore, and a cliff rising straight up out of the mudflats. Even if it were not covered with relentlessly hostile tropical jungle, this cliff would seal off access to the interior of Guadalcanal just because of its steepness. The Marines are trapped in this little cove until the tide goes back out.

Which is more than enough time for the Nip machine gunner to kill them all.

They all know the sound of the weapon by now and so they throw themselves down to the mud instantly. Shaftoe takes a quick look around. Marines lying on their backs or sides are probably dead, those on their stomachs are probably alive. Most of them are on their stomachs. The sergeant is conspicuously dead; the gunner aimed for him first.

The Nip or Nips have only one gun, but they seem to have all the ammunition in the world—the fruits of the Tokyo Express, which has been coming down the Slot with impunity ever since Shaftoe and the rest of the Marines landed early in August. The gunner rakes the mudflats leisurely, zeroing in quickly on any Marine who tries to move.

Shaftoe gets up and runs towards the base of the cliff.

Finally, he can see the muzzle flashes from the Nip gun. This tells him which way it's pointed. When the flashes are elongated it's pointed at someone else, and it's safe to get up and run. When they become foreshortened, it is swinging around to bear on Bobby Shaftoe—

He cuts it too close. There is very bad pain in his lower right abdomen. His scream is muffled by mud and silt as the weight of his web and helmet drive him face-first into the ground.

He loses consciousness for a while, perhaps. But it can't have been that long. The firing continues, implying that the Marines are not all dead yet. Shaftoe raises his head with difficulty, fighting the weight of the helmet, and sees a log between him and the machine gun—a piece of wave-burnished driftwood flung far up the beach by a storm.

He can run for it or not. He decides to run. It's only a few steps. He realizes, halfway there, that he's going to make it. The adrenaline is finally flowing; he lunges forward mightily and collapses in the shelter of the big log. Half a dozen bullets thunk into the other side of it, and wet, fibrous splinters shower down over him. The log is rotten.

Shaftoe has gotten himself into a bit of a hole, and cannot see forward or back without exposing himself. He cannot see his fellow Marines, only hear some of them screaming.

He risks a peek at the machine gun nest. It is well concealed by jungle vegetation, but it is evidently built into a cave a good twenty feet above the mudflat. He's not that far from the base of the cliff—he might just reach it with another sprint. But climbing up there is going to be murder. The machine gun probably can't depress far enough to shoot down at him, but they can roll grenades at him until the cows come home, or just pick him off with small arms as he gropes for handholds.

It is, in other words, grenade launcher time. Shaftoe rolls onto his back, extracts a flanged metal tube from his web gear, fits it onto the muzzle of his ought-three. He tries to clamp it down, but his fingers slip on the bloody wing nut. Who's the pencil-neck that decided to use a fucking *wing-nut* in this context? No point griping about it here and now. There is actually blood all over the place, but he is not in pain. He drags his fingers through the sand, gets them all gritty, tightens that wing nut down.

Out of its handy pouch comes one Mark II fragmentation grenade, a.k.a. pineapple, and with a bit more groping he's got the Grenade Projection Adapter, M1. He engages the former into the latter, yanks out the safety pin, drops it, then slips the fully prepped and armed Grenade Projection Adapter, M1, with its fruity payload, over the tube of the grenade launcher. Finally: he opens up one specially marked cartridge case, fumbles through bent and ruptured Lucky Strikes, finds one brass cylinder, a round of ammunition sans payload, crimped at the end but not endowed with an actual bullet. Loads same into the Springfield's firing chamber.

He creeps along the log so that he can pop up and fire from an unexpected location and perhaps not get his head chewed off by the machine gun. Finally raises this Rube Goldberg device that his Springfield has become, jams the butt into the sand (in grenade-launcher mode the recoil will break your collarbone), points it toward the foe, pulls the trigger. Grenade Projection Adapter, M1 is *gone* with a terrible *pow*, trailing a damn hardware store of now-superfluous parts, like a soul discarding its corpse. The pineapple is now soaring heavenward, even its pin and safety lever gone, its chemical fuse aflame so that it even has a, whattayoucallit, an inner light. Shaftoe's aim is true, and the grenade is heading where intended. He thinks he's pretty damn smart—until the grenade bounces back, tumbles down the cliff, and blows up another rotten log. The Nips have anticipated Bobby Shaftoe's little plan, and put up nets or chicken wire or something.

He lies on his back in the mud, looking up at the sky, saying the word "fuck" over and over. The entire log throbs, and something akin to peat moss showers down into his face as the bullets chew up the rotten wood. Bobby Shaftoe says a prayer to the Almighty and prepares to mount a banzai charge.

Then the maddening sound of the machine gun stops, and is replaced by the sound of a man screaming. His voice sounds unfamiliar. Shaftoe levers himself up on his elbow and realizes that the screaming is coming from the direction of the cave.

He looks up into the big, sky-blue eyes of Enoch Root.

The chaplain has moved from his nook at the back of the plane and is squatting next to one of the little windows, holding onto whatever he can. Bobby Shaftoe, who has rolled uncomfortably onto his stomach, looks out a window on the opposite side of the plane. He ought to see the sky, but instead he sees a sand dune wheeling past. The sight makes him instantly nauseated. He does not even consider sitting up.

Brilliant spots of light are streaking wildly around the inside of the plane, like ball lightning, but—and this is far from obvious at first—they are actually projected against the wall of the plane, like flashlight beams. He back-traces the beams, taking advantage of a light haze of vaporized hydraulic fluid that has begun to accumulate in the air, and finds that they originate in a series of small circular holes that some asshole has punched through the skin of the plane while he was sleeping. The sun is shining through these holes, always in the same direction of course; but the plane is going every which way.

He realizes that he has actually been lying on the ceiling of the airplane ever since he woke up, which explains why he was on his stomach. When this dawns on him, he vomits.

The bright spots all vanish. Very, very reluctantly, Shaftoe risks a glance out the window and sees only greyness.

He thinks he is on the floor now. He is next to the corpse, at any rate, and the corpse was strapped down.

He lies there for several minutes, just breathing and thinking. Air whistles through the holes in the fuselage, loud enough to split his head.

Someone—some madman—is up on his feet, moving about the plane. It is not Root, who is in his little nook dealing with a number of facial lacerations that he picked up during the aerobatics. Shaftoe looks up and sees that the moving man is one of the British flyboys.

The Brit has yanked off his headgear to expose black hair and green eyes. He's in his mid-thirties, an old man. He has a knobby, utilitarian face in which all of the various lumps, knobs and orifices seem to be there for a reason, a face engineered by the same fellows who design grenade launchers. It is a simple and reliable face, by no means handsome. He is kneeling next to the corpse of Gerald Hott and is examining it minutely with a flashlight. He is the very picture of concern; his bedside manner is flawless.

Finally he slumps back against the ribbed wall of the fuselage. "Thank god," he says, "he wasn't hit."

"Who wasn't?" Shaftoe says.

"This chap," the flyboy says, slapping the corpse.

"Aren't you going to check me?"

"No need to."

"Why not? I'm *still alive.*"

"You weren't hit," the flyboy says confidently. "If you'd been hit, you'd look like Lieutenant Ethridge."

For the first time, Shaftoe hazards movement. He props himself up on one elbow, and finds that the floor of the plane is slick and wet with red fluid.

He had noticed a pink mist in the cabin, and supposed that it was produced by a hydraulic fluid leak. But the hydraulic system now seems hunky-dory, and the stuff on the floor of the plane is not a petroleum product. It is the same red fluid that figured so prominently in Shaftoe's nightmare. It is streaming downhill from the direction of Lieutenant Ethridge's cozy nest, and the Lieutenant is no longer snoring.

Shaftoe looks at what is left of Ethridge, which bears a striking resemblance to what was lying around that butcher shop earlier today. He does not wish to lose his composure in the presence of the British pilot, and indeed, feels strangely calm. Maybe it's the clouds; cloudy days have always had a calming effect on him.

"Holy cow," he finally says, "that Kraut twenty-millimeter is something else."

"Right," the flyboy says, "we've got to get spotted by a convoy and then we'll proceed with the delivery."

Cryptic as it is, this is the most informative statement Bobby's ever heard about the intentions of Detachment 2702. He gets up and follows the pilot back to the cockpit, both of them stepping delicately around several quivering giblets that were presumably flung out of Ethridge.

"You mean, by an *allied* convoy, right?" Shaftoe asks.

"An *allied* convoy?" the pilot asks mockingly. "Where the hell are we going to find an *allied* convoy? This is *Tunisia*."

"Well, then, what do you mean, we've got to *get* spotted *by* a convoy? You mean we have to *spot* a convoy, right?"

"Very sorry," the flyboy says, "I'm busy."

When he turns back, he finds Lieutenant Enoch Root kneeling by a relatively large piece of Ethridge, going through Ethridge's attache case. Shaftoe cops a look of exaggerated moral outrage and points the finger of blame.

"Look, Shaftoe," Root shouts, "I'm just following orders. Taking over for him."

He pulls out a small bundle, all wrapped in thick, yellowish plastic sheeting. He checks it over, then glances up reprovingly, one more time, at Shaftoe.

"It was a fucking joke!" Shaftoe says. "Remember? When I thought those guys were looting the corpses? On the beach?"

Root doesn't laugh. Either he's pissed off that Shaftoe successfully bullshitted him, or he doesn't enjoy corpse-looting humor. Root carries the wrapped bundle back to that *other* body, the one in the wetsuit. He stuffs the bundle inside the suit.

Then he squats by the body and ponders. He ponders for a long time. Shaftoe kind of gets a kick out of watching Enoch ponder, which is like watching an exotic dancer shake her tits.

The light changes again as they descend from the clouds. The sun is setting, shining redly through the Saharan haze. Shaftoe looks out a window and is startled to see that they are over the sea now. Below them is a convoy of ships each making a neat white V in the dark water, each lit up on one side by the red sun.

The airplane banks and makes a slow loop around the convoy. Shaftoe hears distant pocking noises. Black flowers bloom and fade in the sky around them. He realizes that the ships are trying to hit them with ack-

ack. Then the plane ascends once more into the shelter of the clouds, and it gets nearly dark.

He looks at Enoch Root for the first time in a while. Root is sitting back in his little nook, reading by flashlight. A bundle of papers is open on his lap. It is the plastic-wrapped bundle that Root took out of Ethridge's attache case and shoved into Gerald Hott's wetsuit. Shaftoe figures that the encounter with convoy and ack-ack finally pushed Root over the edge, and that he yanked the bundle right back out again to have a look at it.

Root glances up and locks eyes with Shaftoe. He does not seem nervous or guilty. It is a strikingly calm and cool look.

Shaftoe holds his gaze for a long moment. If there were the slightest trace of guilt or nervousness there, he would turn the chaplain in as a German spy. But there isn't—Enoch Root ain't working for the Germans. He ain't working for the Allies either. He's working for a Higher Power. Shaftoe nods imperceptibly, and Root's gaze softens.

"They're all dead, Bobby," he shouts.

"Who?"

"Those islanders. The ones you saw on the beach on Guadalcanal."

So *that* explains why Root is so touchy about corpse-looting jokes. "Sorry," Shaftoe says, moving aft so they don't have to scream at each other. "How'd it happen?"

"After we got you back to my cabin, I transmitted a message to my handlers in Brisbane," Root says. "Enciphered it using a special code. Told them I'd picked up one Marine Raider, who looked like he might actually live, and would someone please come round and collect him."

Shaftoe nods. He remembers that he'd heard lots of dots and dashes, but he had been out of whack with fevers and morphine and whatever home remedies Root had pulled out of his cigar box.

"Well, they responded," Root went on, "and said 'We can't go there, but would you please take him to such-and-such place and rendezvous with some other Marine Raiders.' Which, as you'll recall, is what we did."

"Yeah," Shaftoe says.

"So far so good. But when I got back to the cabin after handing you over, the Nipponese had been through. Killed every islander they could find. Burned the cabin. Burned everything. Set booby traps around the place that nearly killed me. I just barely got out of the damn place alive."

Shaftoe nods, as only a guy who's seen the Nips in action can nod.

"Well they evacuated me to Brisbane where I started making a stink about codes. That's the only way they could have found me—obviously our codes had been broken. And after I'd made enough of a stink, someone apparently said, 'You're British, you're a priest, you're a medical doctor, you can handle a rifle, you know Morse code, and most importantly of all, you're a fucking pain in the ass—so off you go!" And next thing I know, I'm in that meat locker in Algiers."

Shaftoe glances away and nods. Root seems to get the message, which is that Shaftoe doesn't know anything more than he does.

Eventually, Enoch Root wraps the bundle up again, just like it was before. But he doesn't put it back in the attache case. He stuffs it into Gerald Hott's wetsuit.

Later they emerge from the clouds again, close to a moonlit port, and dip down very close to the ocean, going so slow that even Shaftoe, who knows nothing about planes, senses they are about to stall. They open the side door of the Dakota and, one-two-three-NOW, throw the body of PFC Gerald Hott out into the ocean. He makes what would be a big splash in the Oconomowoc town pool, but in the ocean it doesn't come to much.

An hour or so later they land the same Gooney Bird on an airstrip in the midst of a stunning aerial bombardment. They abandon the Skytrain at the end of the airstrip, next to the other C-47, and run through darkness, following the lead of the British pilots. Then they go down a stairway and are underground—in a bomb shelter, to be precise. They can feel the bombs now but can't hear them.

"Welcome to Malta," someone says. Shaftoe looks around and sees that he is surrounded by men in British and American uniforms. The Americans are familiar—it's the Marine Raider squad from Algiers, flown in on that other Dakota. The Brits are unfamiliar, and Shaftoe pegs them as the SAS men that those fellows in Washington were telling him about. The only thing they all have in common is that each man, somewhere on his uniform, is wearing the number 2702.

NON-DISCLOSURE

AVI SHOWS UP ON TIME, IDLING HIS FAIRLY GOOD, BUT NOT DIS-gustingly ostentatious, Nipponese sports car gingerly up the steep road, which has crazed into a loose mosaic of asphalt flagstones. Randy watches from the second-floor deck, staring fifty feet almost straight down through the sunroof. Avi is clad in the trousers of a good tropical-weight business suit, a tailored white Sea Island cotton shirt, dark ski goggles, and a wide-brimmed canvas hat.

The house is a tall, isolated structure rising out of the middle of a California grassland that slopes up from the Pacific, a few kilometers away. Chilly air climbs up the slope, rising and falling in slow surges, like surf on a beach. When Avi gets out of his car the first thing he does is pull on his suit-jacket.

He hauls two oversized laptop cases out of the tiny luggage compartment in the car's nose, walks into the house without knocking (he has not been to this particular house before, but he has been to others run along similar principles), finds Randy and Eb waiting in one of its many rooms, and hauls about fifteen thousand dollars worth of portable computer gear out of the bags. He sets them up on a table. Avi hits the start button on two laptops and, as they crawl through the boot process, plugs them into the wall so that the batteries won't drain. A power conduit, with grounded three-prong outlets spaced every eighteen inches, has been screwed down remorselessly along every inch of every wall, spanning drywall; holes in the drywall; primeval op-art contact paper; fake wood-grain paneling; faded Grateful Dead posters; and even the odd doorway.

One of the laptops is connected to a tiny portable printer, which Avi loads with a few sheets of paper. The other laptop starts up a few lines of text running across the screen, then beeps and stops. Randy ambles over and looks at it curiously. It is displaying a prompt:

FILO.

Which Randy knows is short for Finux Loader, a program that allows you to choose which operating system you want to run.

"Finux," Avi mumbles, answering Randy's unspoken question.

Randy types "Finux" and hits the return key. "How many operating systems you have on this thing?"

"Windows 95, for games and when I need to let some lamer borrow my computer temporarily," Avi says. "Windows NT for office type stuff. BeOS for hacking, and screwing around with media. Finux for industrial-strength typesetting."

"Which one do you want now?"

"BeOS. Going to display some JPEGs. I assume there's an overhead projector in this place?"

Randy looks over at Eb, the only person in the room who actually lives here. Eb seems bigger than he is, and maybe it's because of his detonating hair: two feet long, blond with a faint reddish glow, thick and wavy and tending to congeal into ropy strands. No ponytail holder can contain it, so when he bothers to tie it back, he uses a piece of string. Eb is doodling on one of those little computers that uses a stylus so that you can write on the screen. In general, hackers don't use them, but Eb (or rather, one of Eb's defunct corporations) wrote the software for this model and so he has a lot of them lying around. He seems to be absorbed in whatever he's doing, but after Randy has been looking in his direction for two seconds, he senses it, and looks up. He has pale green eyes and wears a luxuriant red beard, except when he's in one of his shaving phases, which usually coincide with serious romantic involvements. Right now his beard is about half an inch long, indicating a recent breakup, and implying a willingness to take new risks.

"Overhead projector?" Randy says.

Eb closes his eyes, which is what he does during memory access, then gets up and walks out of the room.

The tiny printer begins to eke paper. The first line of text, centered at the top of the page, is: NONDISCLOSURE AGREEMENT. More lines follow. Randy has seen them, or ones like them, so many times that his eyes glaze over and he turns away. The only thing that ever changes is the name of the company: in this case: EPIPHYTE(2) CORP.

"Nice goggles."

"If you think these are weird, you should see what I'm going to put on when the sun goes down," Avi says. He rummages in a bag and pulls out a contraption that looks like a pair of glasses without lenses, with a dollhouse-scale light fixture mounted above each eye. A wire runs down to a battery pack with belt loops. He slides a tiny switch on the battery pack and the lights come on: expensive-looking blue-white halogen.

Randy raises his eyebrows.

"It's all jet-lag avoidance," Avi explains. "I'm adjusted to Asian time. I'm going back there in two days. I don't want my body to get back on Left Coast time while I'm here."

"So the hat and goggles . . ."

"Simulate night. This thing simulates daylight. See, your body takes its cues from the light, adjusts its clock accordingly. Speaking of which, would you mind closing the blinds?"

The room has west-facing windows, affording a view down the grassy slope to Half Moon Bay. It is late afternoon and the sun is pouring through. Randy savors the view for a moment, then drops the blinds.

Eb stalks back into the room with an overhead projector dangling from one hand, looking for a moment like Beowulf brandishing a monster's severed arm. He puts it on the table and aims it at the wall. There is no need for a screen, because above the ubiquitous power strips, every wall in the house is covered with whiteboards. Many of the whiteboards are, in turn, covered with cryptical incantations, written in primary colors. Some of them are enclosed in irregular borders and labeled DO NOT ERASE! or simply DNE or NO! In front of where Eb has put the overhead projector, there is a grocery list, a half-erased fragment of a flowchart, a fax number in Russia, a couple of dotted quads—Internet addresses—and a few words in German, which were presumably written by Eb himself. Dr. Eberhard Föhr scans all of this, finds that none of it is enclosed in a DNE border, and wipes it away with an eraser.

Two more men come into the room, deeply involved in a conversation about some exasperating company in Burlingame. One of them is dark and lean and looks like a gunfighter; he even wears a black cowboy hat. The other is tubby and blond and looks like he just got out of a Rotary Club meeting. They have one detail in common: each is wearing a bright silver bracelet on his wrist.

Randy takes the NDAs out of the printers and passes them out, two copies each, each pair preprinted with a name: Randy Waterhouse, Eberhard Föhr, John Cantrell (the guy in the black cowboy hat) and Tom Howard (the fair-haired Middle American). As John and Tom reach for the pages, the silver bracelets intercept stray beams of light sneaking through the blinds. Each is printed with a red caduceus and several lines of text.

"Those look new," Randy says. "Did they change the wording again?"

"Yeah!" John Cantrell says. "This is version 6.0—just out last week."

Anywhere else, the bracelets would mean that John and Tom were suffering from some sort of life-threatening condition, such as an allergy to common antibiotics. A medic hauling them out of a wrecked car would see the bracelet and follow the instructions. But this is Silicon Valley and different rules apply. The bracelets say, on one side:

> IN CASE OF DEATH SEE REVERSE
> FOR BIOSTASIS PROTOCOL
> FOLLOW INSTRUCTIONS COLLECT
> REWARD $100,000

and on the other:

> CALL NOW FOR INSTRUCTIONS
> 1-800-NNN-NNNN
> PUSH 50,000 U HEPARIN IV
> AND DO CPR WHILE COOLING
> WITH ICE TO 10C.KEEP PH 7.5
> NO AUTOPSY OR EMBALMING

It is a recipe for freezing a dead, or nearly dead, person. People who wear this bracelet believe that, if this recipe is followed, the brain and other delicate tissues can be iced without destroying them. A few decades down the line, when nanotechnology has made it possible to be immortal, they hope to be thawed out. John Cantrell and Tom Howard believe that there is a reasonable chance that they will still be having conversations with each other a million years from now.

The room gets quiet as all of the men scan the forms, their eyes picking out certain familiar clauses. They have probably signed a hundred NDA forms between them. Around here, it is like offering someone a cup of coffee.

A woman comes into the room, burdened with tote bags, and beams an apology for being late. Beryl Hagen looks like a Norman Rockwell aunt, an apron-wearing, apple-pie-toting type. In twenty years, she's been the chief financial officer of twelve different small high-tech companies. Ten of them have gone out of business. Except in the case of the second one, this was through no fault of Beryl's. The sixth was Randy's Second Business Foray. One was absorbed by Microsoft, one became a successful, independent company in its own right. Beryl made enough money from the latter two to retire. She consults and writes while she looks for something interesting enough to draw her back into action, and her presence in this room suggests that Epiphyte(2) Corp. must not be completely bogus. Or maybe she's just being polite to Avi. Randy gives her a bearhug, lifting her off the floor, and then hands her two copies of the NDA with her name on them.

Avi has detached the screen from his big laptop and laid it flat on the surface of the overhead projector, which shines light through the liquid-crystal display and projects a color image on the whiteboard. It is a typical desktop: a couple of terminal windows and some icons. Avi goes around and picks up the signed NDAs, scans them all, hands one copy back to each person, files the rest in the outer pocket of a laptop bag. He begins to type on the laptop's keyboard, and letters spill across one of the windows. "Just so you know," Avi mumbles, "Epiphyte Corp., which I'll call Epiphyte(1) for clarity, is a Delaware corporation, one and one half years old. The shareholders are myself, Randy, and Springboard Capital. We're in the telecoms business in the Philippines. I can give you details later if you want. Our work there has positioned us to be aware of some new opportunities in that part of the world. Epiphyte(2) is a California corporation, three weeks old. If things go the way we are hoping they will go, Epiphyte(1) will be folded into it according to some kind of stock transfer scheme the details of which are too boring to talk about now."

Avi hits the return key. A new window opens on the desktop. It is a color map scanned in from an atlas, tall and narrow. Most of it is oceanic blue. A rugged coastline juts in through the top border, with a few cities labeled: Nagasaki, Tokyo. Shanghai is in the upper left corner. The Philippine archipelago is dead center. Taiwan is directly north of it, and to the south is a chain of islands forming a porous barrier between Asia and a big land mass labeled with English words like Darwin and Great Sandy Desert.

"This probably looks weird to most of you," Avi says. "Usually these presentations begin with a diagram of a computer network, or a flowchart or something. We don't normally deal with maps. We're all so used to working in a purely abstract realm that it seems almost bizarre to go out into the real world and physically do something.

"But I like maps. I've got maps all over my house. I'm going to suggest to you that the skills and knowledge we have all been developing in our work—especially pertaining to the Internet—have applications out here." He taps the whiteboard. "In the real world. You know, the big round wet ball where billions of people live."

There is a bit of polite snickering as Avi skims his hand over his computer's trackball, whacks a button with his thumb. A new image appears: the same map, with bright color lines running across the ocean, looping from one city to the next, roughly following the coastlines.

"Existing undersea cables. The fatter the line, the bigger the pipe," Avi says. "Now, what is wrong with this picture?"

There are several fat lines running east from places like Tokyo, Hong Kong, and Australia, presumably connecting them with the United States. Across the South China Sea, which lies between the Philippines and Vietnam, another fat line angles roughly north–south, but it doesn't connect either of those two countries: it goes straight to Hong Kong, then continues up the China coast to Shanghai, Korea, and Tokyo.

"Since the Philippines are in the center of the map," John Cantrell says, "I predict that you are going to point out that hardly any fat lines go to the Philippines."

"Hardly any fat lines go to the Philippines!" Avi announces briskly. He points out the one exception, which runs from Taiwan south to northern Luzon, then skips down the coast to Corregidor. "Except for this one, which Epiphyte(1) is involved with. But it's not just that. There is a general paucity of fat lines in a north–south direction, connecting Australia with Asia. A lot of data packets going from Sydney to Tokyo have to be routed through California. There's a market opportunity."

Beryl breaks in. "Avi, before you get started on this," she says, sounding cautious and regretful, "I have to say that laying long-distance, deep-sea cables is a difficult business to break into."

"Beryl is right!" Avi says. "The only people who have the wherewithal to lay those cables are AT&T, Cable & Wireless, and Kokusai Denshin Denwa. It's tricky. It's expensive. It requires massive NRE."

The abbreviation stands for "non-recoverable expenses," meaning engineering work to complete a feasibility study that would be money down the toilet if the idea didn't fly.

"So what are you thinking?" Beryl says.

Avi clicks up another map. This one is the same as the previous, except that new lines have been drawn in: a whole series of short island-to-island links. A bewilderingly numerous chain of short hops down the length of the Philippine archipelago.

"You want to wire the Philippines and patch them into the Net via your existing link to Taiwan," says Tom Howard, in a heroic bid to short-circuit what he senses will be a lengthy part of Avi's presentation.

"The Philippines are going to be hot shit informationally speaking," Avi says. "The government has its flaws, but basically it's a democracy modeled after Western institutions. Unlike most Asians, they do ASCII. Most of them speak English. Longstanding ties to the United States. These guys are going to be big players, sooner or later, in the information economy."

Randy breaks in. "We've already established a foothold there. We know the local business environment. And we have cash flow."

Avi clicks up another map. This one's harder to make out. It looks like a relief map of a vast region of high mountains interrupted by occasional plateaus. Its appearance in the middle of this presentation without any labels or explanation from Avi makes it an implicit challenge to the mental acumen of the other people in the room. None of them is going to ask for help anytime soon. Randy watches them squint and tilt their heads from side to side. Eberhard Föhr, who is good at odd puzzles, gets it first.

"Southeast Asia with the oceans drained," he says. "That high ridge on the right is New Guinea. Those bumps are the volcanoes of Borneo."

"Pretty cool, huh?" Avi says. "It's a radar map. U.S. military satellites gathered all this data. You can get it for next to nothing."

On this map the Philippines can be understood, not as a chain of separate islands, but as the highest regions of a huge oblong plateau surrounded by deep gashes in the earth's crust. To get from Luzon up to Taiwan by going across the ocean floor you would have to plunge into a deep trench, flanked by parallel mountain ranges, and follow it northwards for about three hundred miles. But south of Luzon, in the region where Avi is proposing to lay a network of inter-island cables, it's all shallow and flat.

Avi clicks again, superimposing transparent blue over the parts that are below sea level, green on the islands. Then he zooms in on an area in the center of the map, where the Philippine plateau extends two arms southwest toward northern Borneo, embracing, and nearly enclosing, a diamond-shaped body of water, three hundred and fifty miles across. "The Sulu Sea," he announces. "No relation to the token Asian on *Star Trek*."

No one laughs. They are not really here to be entertained—they are concentrating on the map. All of the different archipelagos and seas are confusing, even for smart people with good spatial relations. The Philippines form the upper right boundary of the Sulu Sea, north Borneo (part of Malaysia) the lower left, the Sulu Archipelago (part of the Philippines) the lower right, and the upper left boundary is one extremely long skinny Philippine island called Palawan.

"This reminds us that national boundaries are artificial and silly," Avi says. "The Sulu Sea is a basin in the middle of a larger plateau shared by the Philippines and Borneo. So if you're wiring up the Philippines, you can just as easily wire Borneo up to that network at the same time, just by outlining the Sulu Sea with shallow, short-hop cables. Like this."

Avi clicks again and the computer draws in more colored lines.

"Avi, why are we here?" Eberhard asks.

"That is a very profound question," Avi says.

"We know the economics of these startups," Eb says. "We begin with nothing but the idea. That's what the NDA is for—to protect your idea. We work on the idea together—put our brainpower into it—and get stock in return. The result of this work is software. The software is copyrightable, trademarkable, perhaps patentable. It is intellectual property. It is worth some money. We all own it in common, through our shares. Then we sell some more shares to an investor. We use the money to hire more people and turn it into a product, to market it, and so on. That's how the system works, but I'm beginning to think you don't understand it."

"Why do you say that?"

Eb looks confused. "How can we contribute to this? How can we turn our brainpower into equity that an investor will want to own a part of?"

Everyone looks at Beryl. Beryl's nodding agreement with Eb. Tom Howard says, "Avi. Look. I can engineer big computer installations. John wrote Ordo—he knows everything about crypto. Randy does Internet, Eb does weird stuff, Beryl does money. But as far as I know, none of us knows diddly about undersea cable engineering. What good will our resumes do you when you go up in front of some venture capitalists?"

Avi's nodding. "Everything you say is true," he concedes smoothly.

"We would have to be crazy to get involved in running cables through the Philippines. That is a job for FiliTel, with whom Epiphyte(1) has been joint-venturing."

"Even if we were crazy," Beryl says, "we wouldn't have the opportunity, because no one would give us the money."

"Fortunately we don't need to worry about that," Avi says, "because it's being done for us." He turns to the whiteboard, picks up a red magic marker, and draws a fat line between Taiwan and Luzon, his hands picking up a leprous, mottled look from the shaded relief of the ocean floor that is being projected against his skin. "KDD, which is anticipating major growth in the Philippines, is already laying another big cable here." He moves down and begins to draw smaller, shorter links between islands in the archipelago. "And FiliTel, which is funded by AVCLA—Asia Venture Capital Los Angeles—is wiring the Philippines."

"What does Epiphyte(1) have to do with that?" Tom Howard asks.

"To the extent they want to use that network for Internet Protocol traffic, they need routers and network savvy," Randy explains.

"So, to repeat my question: why are we here?" Eberhard says, patiently but firmly.

Avi works with his pen for a while. He circles an island at one corner of the Sulu Sea, centered in the gap between North Borneo and the long skinny Philippine island called Palawan. He labels it in block letters: SULTANATE OF KINAKUTA.

"Kinakuta was run by white sultans for a while. It's a long story. Then it was a German colony," Avi says. "Back then, Borneo was part of the Dutch East Indies, and Palawan—like the rest of the Philippines—was first Spanish and then American. So this was the Germans' foothold in the area."

"Germans always ended up holding the shittiest colonies," Eb says ruefully.

"After the First World War, they handed it over to the Japanese, along with a lot of other islands much farther to the east. All of these islands, collectively, were called the Mandates because Japan controlled them under a League of Nations Mandate. During the Second World War the Japanese used Kinakuta as a base for attacks on the Dutch East Indies and the Philippines. They retained a naval base and airfield there. After the war, Kinakuta became independent, as it had been before the Germans. The population is Muslim or ethnic Chinese around the edges, animist in the center, and it's always been ruled by a sultan—even while occupied by the Germans and the Japanese, who both co-opted the sultans but kept them in place as figureheads. Kinakuta had oil reserves, but they were unreachable until the technology got better and prices went up, around the time of the Arab oil embargo, which was also when the current sultan came into power. That sultan is now a very rich man—not as rich as the Sultan of Brunei, who happens to be his second cousin, but rich."

"The sultan is backing your company?" Beryl asks.

"Not in the way you mean," Avi says.

"What way do you mean?" Tom Howard asks, impatient.

"Let me put it this way," Avi says. "Kinakuta is a member of the United Nations. It is every bit as much an independent country and member of the community of nations as France or England. As a matter of fact, it is exceptionally independent because of its oil wealth. It is basically a monarchy—the sultan makes the laws, but only after extensive consultation with his ministers, who set policy and draft legislation. And I've been spending a lot of time, recently, with the Minister of Posts and Telecommunications. I have been helping the minister draft a new law that will govern all telecommunications passing through Kinakutan territory."

"Oh, my god!" John Cantrell says. He is awestruck.

"One free share of stock to the man in the black hat!" Avi says. "John has figured out Avi's secret plan. John, would you like to explain to the other contestants?"

John takes his hat off and runs his hand back through his long hair. He puts his hat back on and heaves a sigh. "Avi is proposing to start a data haven," he says.

A little murmur of admiration runs through the room. Avi waits for it to subside and says, "Slight correction: the sultan's starting the data haven. I'm proposing to make money off it."

ULTRA

LAWRENCE PRITCHARD WATERHOUSE GOES INTO BATTLE ARMED with one-third of a sheet of British typing paper on which has been typed some words that identify it as a PASS to Bletchley Park. His name and some other things have been scribbled on it in some upper-class officer's Mont Blanc blue-black, the words ALL SECTIONS circled, and a stamp smashed across it, blurred into a red whore's kiss, with sheer carelessness conveying greater Authority and Power than the specious clarity of a forger.

He finds his way round the mansion to the narrow lane that runs between it and its row of red-brick garages (or stables, as his grandparents would be likely to peg them). He finds it a very pleasant place for a cigarette. The lane is lined with trees, a densely planted hedge of them. The sun is just setting now. It is still high enough to snipe through any small defects that it finds in the defensive perimeter of the horizon, so narrow red beams strike him surprisingly in the eye as he ambles back and forth. He knows one is shining invisibly through the clear air several feet above him, because it is betraying an aerial: a strand of copper wire stretched from the wall of the mansion to a nearby cypress. It catches the light in precisely the same way as the strand of the spiderweb that Waterhouse was playing with earlier.

The sun will be down soon; it is already down in Berlin, as in most of the hellish empire that Hitler has built from Calais to the Volga. Time for the radio operators to begin their work. Radio does not, in general, go around corners. This can be a real pain when you are conquering the world, which is inconveniently round, placing all of your most active military units over the horizon. But if you use shortwave, then you can bounce the information off the ionosphere. This works a good deal better when the sun is not in the sky, sluicing the atmosphere with wideband noise. So radio telegraphers, and the people who eavesdrop on them (what the Brits call the Y Service) are, alike, nocturnal beings.

As Waterhouse has just observed, the mansion has an aerial or two. But Bletchley Park is a huge and ravenous spider that requires a web the size of a nation to feed it. He has seen enough evidence, from the black cables climbing the mansion's walls and the smell and hiss of the massed teletypes, to know that the web is at least partly made of copper wires. Another piece of the web is made of rude stuff like concrete and asphalt.

The gate swings open and a man on a green motorcycle banks steeply into the lane, the two cylinders of his machine blatting away, the noise stinging Waterhouse's nose as he rides by. Waterhouse strides after him for some distance, but loses his trail after a hundred yards or so. That is acceptable; more of them will be along soon, as the Wehrmacht's nervous system awakens and its signals are picked up by the Y Service.

The motorcyclist went through a quaint little gate that joins two old buildings. The gate is topped by a tiny cupola with a weathervane and a clock. Waterhouse goes through it and finds himself in a little square that evidently dates back to when Bletchley Park was a precious Buckinghamshire farmstead. To the left, the line of stables continues. Small gables have been set into the roof, which is stained with bird shit. The building is quivering with pigeons. Directly in front of him is a nice little red-brick Tudor farmhouse, the only thing he has seen so far that is not architecturally offensive. Off to his right is a one-story building. Strange information is coming out of this building: the hot-oil smell of teletypes, but no typing noises, just a high mechanical whine.

A door opens on the stable building and a man emerges carrying a large but evidently lightweight box with a handle on the top. Cooing noises come from the box and Waterhouse realizes that it contains pigeons. Those birds living up in the gables are not feral; they are homing pigeons. Carriers of information, strands of Bletchley Park's web.

He homes in on the building that smells of hot oil and gazes into a window. As evening falls, light has begun to leak out of it, betraying information to black German reconnaissance planes, so a porter is strutting about the courtyard slamming the black shutters closed.

Some information comes into Waterhouse's eyes at least: on the other side of that window, men are gathered around a machine. Most of them are wearing civilian clothes, and they have been too busy, for too long, to trifle much with combs and razors and shoe polish. The men are intensely focused upon their work, which all has to do with this large machine. The machine consists of a large framework of square steel tubing, like a bedstead set up on one end. Metal drums with the diameter of dinner plates, an inch or so thick, are mounted at several locations on this framework. Paper tape has been threaded in a bewilderingly loopy trajectory from drum to drum. It looks as if a dozen yards of tape are required to thread the machine.

One of the men has been working on a rubber drive belt that goes around one of the drums. He steps back from it and makes a gesture with his hand. Another man flips a switch and the drums all begin to spin at once. The tape begins to fly through the system. Holes punched in the tape carry data; it all blurs into a grey streak now, the speed creating an illusion in which the tape appears to dissolve into a ribbon of smoke.

No, it is not an illusion. Real smoke is curling up from the spinning drums. The tape is running through the machine so fast that it is catching fire before the eyes of Waterhouse and the men inside, who watch it calmly, as if it were smoking in an entirely new and interesting way.

If there is a machine in the world capable of reading data from a tape that fast, Waterhouse has never heard of it.

The black shutter slams home. Just as it does, Waterhouse gets one fragmentary glimpse of another object standing in the corner of the room: a steel rack in which a large number of grey cylindrical objects are stored in neat rows.

Two motorcyclists come through the courtyard at once, running in the darkness with their headlights off. Waterhouse jogs after them for a bit, leaving the picturesque old courtyard behind and entering into the world of the huts, the new structures thrown up in the last year or two. "Hut" makes him think of a tiny thing, but these huts, taken together, are more like that new Pentagon thing that the War Department has been putting up across the river from D.C. They embody a blunt need for space unfiltered through any aesthetic or even human considerations.

Waterhouse walks to an intersection of roads where he thought he heard the motorcycles making a turn, and stops, hemmed in by blast walls. On an impulse, he clambers to the top of a wall and takes a seat. The view from here is no better. He knows that thousands of people are at work all around him in these huts, but he sees none of them, there are no signposts.

He is still trying to work out that business that he saw through the window.

The tape was running so fast that it *smoked*. There is no point of driving it that fast unless the machine can read the information that fast— transforming the pattern of holes in the tape into electrical impulses.

But why bother, if those impulses had nowhere to go? No human mind could deal with a stream of characters coming in at that speed. No teletype that Waterhouse knew of could even print them out.

It only makes sense if they are constructing a machine. A mechanical calculator of some sort that can absorb the data and then do something with it—perform some calculation—presumably a cipher-breaking type of calculation.

Then he remembers the rack he glimpsed in the corner, its many rows of identical grey cylinders. Viewed end-on, they looked like some kind of ammunition. But they are too smooth and glossy for that. Those cylinders, Waterhouse realizes, are made of blown glass.

They are vacuum tubes. Hundreds of them. More tubes in one place than Waterhouse has ever seen.

Those men in that room are building a Turing machine!

———————

It is no wonder, then, that the men in the room accept the burning of the tape so calmly. That strip of paper, a technology as old as the pyramids, is merely a vessel for a stream of information. When it passes through the machine, the information is abstracted from it, transfigured into a pattern of pure binary data. That the mere vessel burns is of no consequence. Ashes to ashes, dust to dust—the data has passed out of the physical plane and into the mathematical, a higher and purer universe where different laws apply. Laws, a few of which are dimly and imperfectly known to Dr. Alan Mathison Turing and Dr. John von Neumann and Dr. Rudolf von Hacklheber and a few other people Waterhouse used to hang around with in Princeton. Laws about which Waterhouse himself knows a thing or two.

Once you have transfigured the data into the realm of pure information, all that is required is a tool. Carpenters work with wood and carry a box of technology for measuring it, cutting it, smoothing it, joining it. Mathematicians work with information and need a tool of their own.

They have been building these tools, one at a time, for years. There is, just to name one example, a cash register and typewriter company called the Electrical Till Corporation that makes a dandy punched-card machine for tabulating large quantities of data. Waterhouse's professor in Iowa was tired of solving differential equations one at a time and invented a machine to solve them automatically by storing the information on a capacitor-covered drum and cranking through a certain algorithm. Given enough time and enough vacuum tubes, a tool might be invented to sum a column of numbers, and another one to keep track of inventories, and another one to alphabetize lists of words. A well-equipped business would have one of each: gleaming cast-iron monsters with heat waves rising out of their grilles, emblazoned with logos like ETC and Siemens and Hollerith, each carrying out its own specialized task. Just as a carpenter had a miter box and a dovetail jig and a clawhammer in his box.

Turing figured out something entirely different, something unspeakably strange and radical.

He figured out that mathematicians, unlike carpenters, only needed to have one tool in their toolbox, if it were the right sort of tool. Turing realized that it should be possible to build a meta-machine that could be reconfigured in such a way that it would do any task you could conceivably do with information. It would be a protean device that could turn into any tool you could ever need. Like a pipe organ changing into a different instrument every time you hit a preset button.

The details were a bit hazy. This was not a blueprint for an actual machine, rather a thought experiment that Turing had dreamed up in order to resolve an abstract riddle from the completely impractical world of pure logic. Waterhouse knows this perfectly well. But he cannot get one thing out of his mind as he sits there atop the blast walls at the dark intersection in Bletchley Park: the Turing machine, if one really existed, would rely upon having a tape. The tape would pass through the machine. It would carry the information that the machine needed to do its work.

Waterhouse sits there staring off into the darkness and reconstructs Turing's machine in his mind. More of the details are coming back to him. The tape, he now recollects, would not move through the Turing machine in one direction; it would change direction frequently. And the Turing machine would not just read the tape; it would be able to erase marks or make new ones.

Clearly you cannot erase holes in a paper tape. And just as clearly the tape only moves through this Bletchley Park machine in one direction. So, much as Waterhouse hates to admit this fact to himself, the rack of tubes he just spied is not a Turing machine. It is some lesser device—a special-purpose tool like a punched-card reader or Atanasoff's differential equation solver.

It is still bigger and more fiendishly terrific than anything Waterhouse has ever seen.

A night train from Birmingham blows through, carrying bullets to the sea. As its sound dies away to the south, a motorcycle approaches the park's main gate. Its engine idles as the rider's papers are checked, then Waterhouse hears a Bronx cheer as it surges forward and cuts the sharp turn into the lane. Waterhouse climbs to his feet at the intersection of the walls, and watches carefully as the bike sputters past him and homes in on a "hut" a couple of blocks away. Light suddenly leaks from an open door as the cargo changes hands. Then the light is snuffed and the bike stretches a long loud raspberry down the road to the park's exit.

Waterhouse lets himself down to earth and gropes his way down the road through the moonless night. He stops before the entrance to the hut and listens to it teem for a minute. Then, working up his courage, he steps forward and pushes the wooden door open.

It is unpleasantly hot in here, and the atmosphere is a nauseating distillation of human and machine odors, held in and concentrated by the coffin doors slabbed down over all the windows. Many people are in here, mostly women working at gargantuan electrically powered type-writers. He can see even through his squint that the place is a running sluice for scraps of paper, maybe four by six inches each, evidently brought in by the motorcyclists. Near the door, they have been sorted and stacked up in wire baskets. Thence they go to the women at their giant typewriters.

One of the few men in the place has risen to his feet and is homing in on Waterhouse. He is about Waterhouse's age, that is, in his early twenties. He is wearing a British Army uniform. He has the air of a host at a wedding reception who wants to make sure that even the most long-lost, far-flung members of the family are properly greeted. Obviously he is no more a real military man than is Waterhouse himself. No wonder this place is surrounded by so much barbed wire and RAF men with machine guns.

"Good evening, sir. Can I help you?"

"Evening. Lawrence Waterhouse."

"Harry Packard. Pleased to meet you." But he has no idea who Waterhouse is; he is privy to Ultra, but not to Ultra Mega.

"Pleasure's mine. I imagine you'll want to have a look at this." Waterhouse hands him the magic pass. Packard's pale eyes travel over it carefully, then jump around to focus on a few sites of particular interest: the signature at the bottom, the smeared stamp. The war has turned Harry Packard into a machine for scanning and processing slips of paper and he goes about his work calmly and without fuss in this case. He excuses himself, works the crank on a telephone, and speaks to someone; his posture and facial expression suggest it is someone important. Waterhouse cannot hear the words above the clicking and thrumming of the massed typewriters, but he sees interest and bemusement on Packard's young, open, pink face. Packard gives Waterhouse a sidelong glance or two while he is listening to the person at the other end of the line. Then he says something respectful and reassuring into the phone and rings off.

"Right. Well, what would you like to see?"

"I'm trying to get an overall sense of how the information flows."

"Well, we are close to the beginning of it here—these are the headwaters. Our wellsprings are the Y Service—military and amateur radio operators who listen in on Jerry's radio transmissions, and provide us with these." Packard takes a slip from a motorcyclist's pannier and hands it to Waterhouse.

It is a form with various boxes at the top in which someone has written in a date (today's) and time (a couple of hours ago) and a few other data such as a radio frequency. The body of the form is mostly occupied by a large open space in which the following has been printed in hasty block letters:

A Y W B P R O J H K D H A O B Q T M D L T U S H I
Y P I J S L L E N J O P S K Y V Z P D L E M A O U
T A M O G T M O A H E C

the whole thing preceded by two groups of three letters each:

YUH ABG

"This one came in from one of our stations in Kent," Packard says. "It is a Chaffinch message."

"So—one of Rommel's?"

"Yes. This intercept came in from Cairo. Chaffinch gets top priority, which is why this message is on the top of the pile."

Packard leads Waterhouse down the central aisle of the hut, between the rows of typists. He picks out one girl who is just finishing up with a message, and hands her the slip. She sets it up next to her machine and commences typing it in.

At first glance, Waterhouse had thought that the machines represented some British concept of how to build an electric typewriter—as big as a dinner table, wrapped up in two hundred pounds of cast-iron, a ten-horse motor turning over under the hood, surrounded by tall fences and armed guards. But now that he is closer he sees that it is something much more complicated. Instead of a platen, it has a large flat reel on it carrying a roll of narrow paper tape. This is not the same kind of tape he saw earlier, smoking through the big machine. This is narrower, and when it emerges from the machine, it does not have holes punched through it for a machine to read. Instead, every time the girl slams down one of the keys on the keyboard—copying the text printed on the slip— a new letter is printed on the tape. But not the same letter that she typed.

It does not take her long to type in all of the letters. Then she tears the tape from her machine. It has a sticky backing which she uses to paste it directly onto the original intercept slip. She hands it to Packard, giving him a demure smile. He responds with something between a nod and a smart little bow, the kind of thing no American male could ever get away with. He glances at it and hands it to Waterhouse.

The letters on the tape say

EINUNDZWANZIGSTPANZERDIVISIONBERICHTET
KEINEBESONDEREEREIGNISSE

"In order to obtain those settings, you have to break the code—which changes every day?"

Packard smiles in agreement. "At midnight. If you stay here—" he checks his watch "—for another four hours, you will see fresh intercepts coming in from the Y Service that will produce utter gibberish when we run them through the Typex, because the Jerries will have changed all their codes on the stroke of midnight. Rather like Cinderella's magic carriage turning back into a pumpkin. We must then analyze the new intercepts using the bombes, and figure out the day's new codes."

"How long does that take?"

"Sometimes we are lucky and have broken the day's codes by two or three o'clock in the morning. Typically it does not happen until afternoon or evening. Sometimes we do not succeed at all."

"Okay, this is a stupid question, but I want to be clear. These Typex machines—which merely do a mechanical deciphering operation—are a completely different thing from the bombes, which actually break the codes."

"The bombes, compared to these, are of a completely different, enormously higher order of sophistication," Packard agrees. "They are almost like mechanical thinking machines."

"Where are they located?"

"Hut 11. But they won't be running just now."

"Right," Waterhouse says, "not until after midnight when the carriage turns back into a pumpkin, and you need to break tomorrow's Enigma settings."

"Precisely."

Packard steps over to a small wooden hatch set low into one of the hut's exterior walls. Next to it sits an office tray with a cup hook screwed into each end, and a string tied to each cup hook. One of the strings is piled up loose on the floor. The wall hatch has been slid shut on the other string. Packard puts the message slip on top of a pile of similar ones that has accumulated in the tray, then slides the hatch open, revealing a narrow tunnel leading away from the hut.

"Okay, your pull!" he shouts.

"Okay, my pull!" comes an answering voice a moment later. The string goes taught and the tray slides into the tunnel and disappears.

"On its way to Hut 3," Packard explains.

"Then so am I," Waterhouse says.

Hut 3 is only a few yards away, on the other side of the inevitable blast wall. GERMAN MILITARY SECTION has been scrawled on the door in cursive; Waterhouse presumes that this is as opposed to "NAVAL" which is in Hut 4. The ratio of men to women seems higher here. During wartime it is startling to see so many hale young men in one room together. Some are in Army or RAF uniforms, some in civvies, and there is even one Naval officer.

A large horseshoe-shaped table dominates the center of the building, with a rectangular table off to the side. Each chair at each table is occupied by intent workers. The intercept slips are pulled into the hut on the wooden tray and then move from chair to chair according to some highly organized scheme that Waterhouse can only vaguely grasp at this point. Someone explains to him that the bombes just broke the day's codes around sundown, and so the entire day's load of intercepts has just come down the tunnel from Hut 6 during the last couple of hours.

He decides to think of the hut as a mathematical black box for the time being—that is, he'll concentrate only on its inputs and outputs of information and ignore the internal details. Bletchley Park, taken in its entirety, is a black box of sorts: random letters stream into it, strategic intelligence streams out, and the internal particulars are of no interest to most of the people on the Ultra distribution list. The question that Waterhouse is here to figure out is: is there another vector of information coming out of this place, hidden subliminally in the teletype signals and the behaviors of the Allied commanders? And does it point to Rudolf von Hacklheber, Ph.D.?

KINAKUTA

WHOEVER LAID OUT THE FLIGHT PATHS INTO THE SULTAN'S NEW airport must have been in cahoots with the Kinakuta Chamber of Commerce. If you're lucky enough to be in a window seat on the left side of the plane, as Randy Waterhouse is, the view during the final approach looks like a propaganda flyby.

Kinakuta's matted green slopes surge out of a mostly calm blue sea, and eventually soar high enough to be dusted with snow at the summits, even though the island is only seven degrees north of the equator. Randy sees right away what Avi meant when he said that the place was Muslim around the edges and animist in the middle. The only places you could hope to build anything like a modern city are along the coast, where there's an intermittent fringe of nearly flat land—a beige rind clinging to a giant emerald. The biggest and best flat place is on the northeastern corner of the island, where the main river, several miles inland, bottoms out into a flood plain that broadens to an alluvial delta that reaches out into the Sulu Sea for a mile or two.

Randy gives up counting the oil rigs ten minutes before Kinakuta City even comes into sight. From high above they look like flaming tank traps scattered in the surf to deter incoming Marines. As the plane sheds altitude they begin to look more like factories on stilts, topped with high stacks where troublesome natural gas is flamed off. This gets more alarming as the plane gets closer to the water, and it begins to seem as if the pilot is threading his way between pillars of fire that would roast the 777 like a pigeon on the wing.

Kinakuta City looks more modern than anything in the States. He has been trying to read about the place but has found precious little: a couple of encyclopedia entries, a few fleeting mentions in World War II histories, some puckish but basically glowing articles in the *Economist*. Putting his rusty interlibrary loan skills to work, he paid the Library of Congress to make him a photocopy of the one book he could find specifically about Kinakuta: one of about a million out-of-print World War II memoirs that must have been penned by G.I.s during the late forties and fifties. So far, he hasn't had time to read it, and so the two-inch stack of pages is just dead weight in his luggage.

In any case, none of the maps he has seen tallies with the reality of the modern Kinakuta City. Anything that was there during the war has been torn down and replaced with new. The river has been dredged into a new channel. An inconvenient mountain called Eliza Peak has been dynamited, and the rubble shoved into the ocean to make several new square miles of real estate, most of which has been gobbled by the new airport. The dynamitings were so loud that they prompted complaints from the governments of the Philippines and of Borneo, hundreds of miles away. They also brought down the wrath of Greenpeace, which was afraid that the sultan was scaring whales in the central Pacific. So Randy expects half of Kinakuta City to be a smoking crater, but of course it's not. The stump of Eliza Peak has been neatly paved over and used as the foundation of the sultan's new Technology City. All of the glass-walled skyscrapers there, and in the rest of the city, have pointy tops, recalling a traditional architecture that has long since been bulldozed and used to fill in the harbor. The only building Randy can see that looks to be more than ten years old is the sultan's palace, which is ancient. Surrounded by miles of blue glass skyscrapers, it's like a reddish-beige mote frozen in a tray of ice.

Once Randy fixes on that, everything snaps into its proper orientation. He bends forward, risks the censure of the cabin crew by pulling his bag out from under the seat ahead of him, and pulls out his photocopied G.I. memoir. One of its first pages is a map of Kinakuta City as it appeared in 1945, and dead center is the Sultan's Palace. Randy rotates it before his face in the way of a panicky driver with a steering wheel, and gets it to line up with his view. There's the river. There's Eliza Peak, where the Nipponese used to have a signals intelligence detachment and a radar station, all built with slave labor. There's the former site of the Japanese Naval Air Force field, which became the Kinakuta Airport until the new one was built. Now it is a flock of yellow cranes above a blue nebula of rebar, lit from within by a constellation of flickering white stars—arc-welders at work.

Next to it is something that doesn't belong: a patch of emerald green, maybe a couple of city blocks, surrounded by a stone wall. Inside, there's a placid pond toward one end—the 777 is now so low that Randy can count the lily pads—a tiny Shinto temple hewn from black stone, and a little bamboo teahouse. Randy presses his face to the window and keeps turning his head to follow it, until suddenly his view is blocked by a high-rise apartment building just off the wingtip. Through an open kitchen window, he gets a microsecond's glimpse of a slender lady swinging a hatchet towards a coconut.

That garden looked like it belonged a thousand miles farther north—in Nippon. When Randy finally realizes what it was, the hairs stand up on the back of his neck.

Randy got on this plane a couple of hours ago at Ninoy Aquino International Airport in Manila. The flight was delayed and so he had plenty of time to look at the other passengers: three Westerners including himself, a couple of dozen Malay types (either Kinakutan or Filipino), and everyone else Nipponese. Some of the latter looked like businessmen, traveling on their own or in twos and threes, but most belonged to some kind of an organized tour group that marched into the boarding lounge precisely forty-five minutes before scheduled takeoff, queued behind a young woman in a navy blue skirt suit holding up a neat little logo on a stick. Retirees.

Their destination is not the Technology City, or any of the peculiar pointy-topped skyscrapers in the financial district. They are all going to that walled Nipponese garden, which is built on top of a mass grave containing the bodies of three and a half thousand Nipponese soldiers, who all died on August 23, 1945.

QWGHLM HOUSE

 WATERHOUSE SERRIES UP AND DOWN THE QUIET SIDE STREET, squinting at brass plaques on sturdy white row houses:

SOCIETY FOR THE UNIFICATION OF HINDUISM AND ISLAM

ANGLO-LAPP SOLIDARITY SOCIETY

FULMINANTS ASSOCIATION

CHIANG TZSE MUTUAL BENEVOLENT SOCIETY

ROYAL COMMITTEE ON MITIGATION OF MARINE CRANKSHAFT WEAR

BOLGER DAMSELFLY PROPAGATION FOUNDATION

ANTI-WELCH LEAGUE

COMITY FOR ΘE REFORMASHUN OF ENGLISH ORΘOGRAFY

SOCIETY FOR THE PREVENTION OF CRUELTY TO VERMIN

CHURCH OF VEDANTIC ETHICAL QUANTUM CONSCIOUSNESS

IMPERIAL MICA BOARD

At first he mistakes Qwghlm House for the world's tiniest and most poorly located department store. It has a bow window that looms over the sidewalk like the thrusting ram of a trireme, embarnacled with Victorian foofawfery, and housing a humble display: a headless mannequin dressed in something that appears to have been spun from steel wool (perhaps a tribute to wartime austerity?); a heap of sallow dirt with a shovel in it; and another mannequin (a recent addition shoehorned into one corner) dressed in a Royal Navy uniform and holding a wooden cutout of a rifle.

Waterhouse found a worm-eaten copy of the *Encyclopedia Qwghlmiana* in a bookshop near the British Museum a week ago and has been carrying it around in his attache case since then, imbibing a page or two at a time, like doses of strong medicine. The overriding Themes of the Encyclopedia are three, and they dominate its every paragraph as totally as the Three Sgrhs dominate the landscape of Outer Qwghlm. Two of these themes are wool and guano, though the Qwghlmians have other names for them, in their ancient, *sui generis* tongue. In fact, the same linguistic hyperspecialization occurs here that supposedly does with the Eskimos and snow or Arabs and sand, and the *Encyclopedia Qwghlmiana* never uses the English words "wool" and "guano" except to slander the inferior versions of these products that are exported by places like Scotland in a perfidious effort to confuse the naive buyers who apparently dominate the world's commodity markets. Waterhouse had to read the encyclopedia almost cover-to-cover and use all his cryptanalytic skills to figure out, by inference, what these products actually were.

Having learned so much about them, he is fascinated to find them proudly displayed in the heart of the cosmopolitan city: a mound of guano and a woman dressed in wool.* The woman's outfit is entirely grey, in keeping with Qwghlmian tradition, which scorns pigmentation as a loathsome and whorish innovation of the Scots. The top part of the ensemble is a sweater which appears, at a glance, to be made of felt. A closer look reveals that it is knit like any other sweater. Qwghlmian sheep are the evolutionary product of thousands of years' massive weather-related die-offs. Their wool is famous for its density, its corkscrewlike fibers, and its immunity to all known chemical straightening processes. It creates a matted effect which the *Encyclopedia* describes as being supremely desirable and for which there is an extensive descriptive vocabulary.

---

*He has made up his mind that he will use the English words rather than making a spectacle of himself by trying to pronounce the Qwghlmian ones.

The third theme of the *Encyclopedia Qwghlmiana* is hinted at by the mannequin with the gun.

Propped up against the stonework next to the building's entrance is a gaffer dressed in an antique variant of the Home Guard uniform, involving knickerbockers. His lower legs are encased in formidable socks made of one of the variants of Qwghlmian wool, and lashed in place, just below the knee, with tourniquets fashioned from thick cords woven together in a vaguely Celtic interlace pattern (on almost every page, the *Encyclopedia* restates that the Qwghlmians are not Celts, but that they did invent the best features of Celtic culture). These garters are the traditional ornament of true Qwghlmians; gentlemen wear them hidden underneath the trousers of their suits. They were traditionally made from the long, slender tails of the Skrrgh, which is the predominant mammal native to the islands, and which the *Encyclopedia* defines as "a small mammal of the order Rodentia and the order Muridae, common in the islands, subsisting primarily on the eggs of sea birds, capable of multiplying with great rapidity when that or any other food is made available to it, admired and even emulated by Qwghlmians for its hardiness and adaptability."

After Waterhouse has been standing there for a few moments, enjoying a cigarette and examining those garters, this mannequin moves slightly. Waterhouse thinks that it is falling over in a gust of wind, but then he realizes that it is alive, and not exactly falling over, but just shifting its weight from foot to foot.

The gaffer takes note of him, smiles blackly, and utters some word of greeting in his language, which, as has already become plain, is even less suited than English to transcription into the Roman alphabet.

"Howdy," Waterhouse says.

The gaffer says something longer and more complicated. After a while, Waterhouse (now wearing his cryptanalyst hat, searching for meaning midst apparent randomness, his neural circuits exploiting the redundancies in the signal) realizes that the man is speaking heavily accented English. He concludes that his interlocutor was saying, "What part of the States are you from, then?"

"My family's done a lot of traveling around," Waterhouse says. "Let's say South Dakota."

"Ahh," the gaffer says ambiguously whilst flinging himself against the slab of door. After a while it begins to move inwards, hand-hammered iron hinges grinding ominously as they pivot round inch-thick tholes. Finally the door collides with some kind of formidable Stop. The gaffer remains leaning against it, his entire body at a forty-five degree angle to prevent its swinging back and crushing Waterhouse, who scurries past. Inside, a tiny anteroom is dominated by a sculpture: two nymphets in diaphanous veils kicking the crap out of a scurrying hag, entitled *Fortitude and Adaptability Driving Out Adversity*.

This operation is repeated a few times with doors that are successively lighter but more richly decorated. The first room, it becomes clear, was actually a preäntepenultimate room, so it is a while before they can be said to be definitely inside Qwghlm House. By that time they seem to be deep in the center of the block, and Waterhouse half expects to see an Underground train screech by. Instead he finds himself in a windowless paneled room with a crystal chandelier that is painfully bright but does not seem to actually illuminate anything. His feet sink so deeply into the gaudy carpet that he nearly blows out a ligament. The far end of the room is guarded by a staunch Desk with a stout Lady behind it. Here and there are large ebony Windsor chairs, with the spindly but dangerous look of aboriginal game snares.

On the walls, diverse oil paintings. At a first glance Waterhouse sorts them into ones that are higher than they are wide, and others. The former category is portraits of gentlemen, all of whom seem to share a grievous genetic flaw that informs the geometry of the skull. The latter category is landscapes or, just as often, seascapes, all in the bleak and rugged category. These Qwghlmian painters are so fond of the locally produced blue-green-grey paint* that they apply it as if with the back of a shovel.

Waterhouse fights through the miring shag of the Carpet until he nears the Desk, where he is greeted by the Lady, who shakes his hand and pinches her face together in a sort of allusion to a smile. There is a long exchange of polite, perfunctory speech of which all Waterhouse remembers is: "Lord Woadmire will see you shortly," and: "Tea?"

Waterhouse says yes to the tea because he suspects that this lady (he has forgotten her name) is not really earning her keep. Clearly disgruntled, she ejects herself from her chair and loses herself in deeper and narrower parts of the building. The gaffer has already gone back to his post out front.

A photograph of the king hangs on the wall behind the desk. Waterhouse hadn't known, until Colonel Chattan discreetly reminded him, that His Majesty's full title was not simply By the Grace Of God of England King, but B.T.G.O.G. of the United Kingdom of Great Britain and Northern Ireland, the Isle of Man, Guernsey, Jersey, Outer Qwghlm, and Inner Qwghlm King.

Next to it is a smaller photograph of the man he is about to meet. This fellow and his family are covered rather sketchily by the *Encyclopedia*,

---

*According to the *E.Q.*, derived from lichen.

which is decades old, and so Waterhouse has had to do some additional background research. The man is related to the Windsors in a way so convoluted that it can only be expressed using advanced genealogical vocabulary.

He was born Graf Heinrich Karl Wilhelm Otto Friedrich von Übersetzenseehafenstadt, but changed his name to Nigel St. John Gloamthorpby, a.k.a. Lord Woadmire, in 1914. In his photograph, he looks every inch a von Übersetzenseehafenstadt, and he is entirely free of the cranial geometry problem so evident in the older portraits. Lord Woadmire is not related to the original ducal line of Qwghlm, the Moore family (Anglicized from the Qwghlmian clan name Mnyhrrgh) which had been terminated in 1888 by a spectacularly improbable combination of schistosomiasis, suicide, long-festering Crimean war wounds, ball lightning, flawed cannon, falls from horses, improperly canned oysters, and rogue waves.

The tea takes some time in coming and Lord Woadmire does not seem to be in any particular hurry to win the war either, so Waterhouse makes a circuit of the room, pretending to care about the paintings. The biggest one depicts a number of bruised and lacerated Romans dragging their sorry asses up onto a rocky and unwelcoming shore as splinters of their invasion fleet wash up around them. Front and center is a particular Roman who looks no less noble for wear and tear. He is seated wearily on a high rock, a broken sword dangling from one enervated hand, gazing longingly across several miles of rough water towards a shining, paradisiacal island. This isle is richly endowed with tall trees and flowering meadows and green pastures, but even so it can be identified as Outer Qwghlm by the Three Sghrs towering above it. The isle is guarded by a forbidding castle or two; its pale, almost Caribbean beaches are lined with the colorful banners of a defending host which (one can only assume) has just given the Roman invaders a bit of rough handling which they will not soon forget. Waterhouse does not bother to bend down and squint at the plaque; he knows that the subject of the painting is Julius Cæsar's failed and probably apocryphal attempt to add the Qwghlm Archipelago to the Roman Empire, the farthest from Rome he ever got and the least good idea he ever had. To say that the Qwghlmians have not forgotten the event is like saying that Germans can sometimes be a little prickly.

"Where Caesar failed, what hope has Hitler?"

Waterhouse turns towards the voice and discovers Nigel St. John Gloamthorpby a.k.a. Lord Woadmire, a.k.a. the Duke of Qwghlm. He is not a tall man. Waterhouse goose-steps through the carpet to shake his hand. Though Colonel Chattan briefed him on proper forms of address when meeting a duke, Waterhouse can no more remember this than he can diagram the duke's family tree, so he decides to structure all of his utterances so as to avoid referring to the duke by name or pronoun. This will be a fun game and make the time go faster.

"It is quite a painting," Waterhouse says, "a heck of a deal."

"You will find the islands themselves no less extraordinary, and for the same reasons," the duke says obliquely.

The next time Waterhouse is really aware of what's going on, he is sitting in the duke's office. He thinks that there has been some routine polite conversation along the way, but there is never any point in actually monitoring that kind of thing. Tea is offered to him, and is accepted, for the second or third time, but fails to materialize.

"Colonel Chattan is in the Mediterranean, and I have been sent in his place," Waterhouse explains, "not to waste time covering logistical details, but to convey our enormous gratitude for the most generous offer made in regards to the castle." There! No pronouns, no gaffe.

"Not at all!" The duke is taking the whole thing as an affront to his generosity. He speaks in the unhurried, dignified cadences of a man who is mentally thumbing through a German–English dictionary. "Even setting aside my own . . . patriotic obligations . . . cheerfully accepted, of course . . . it has almost become almost . . . terribly fashionable to have a whole . . . crew . . . of . . . uniformed fellows and whatnot running around in one's . . . pantry."

"Many of the great houses of Britain are doing their bit for the War," Waterhouse agrees.

"Well . . . by all means, then . . . use it!" the duke says. "Don't be . . . reticent! Use it . . . thoroughly! Give it a good . . . working over! It has . . . survived . . . a thousand Qwghlm winters and it will . . . survive your worst."

"We hope to have a small detachment in place very soon," Waterhouse says agreeably.

"May I . . . know . . . to satisfy my own . . . curiosity . . . what sort of . . . ?" the duke says, and trails off.

Waterhouse is ready for this. He is so ready that he has to hold back for a moment and try to make a show of discretion. "Huffduff."

"Huffduff!?"

"HFDF. High-Frequency Direction Finding. A technique for locating distant radio transmitters by triangulating from several points."

"I should have . . . thought you knew where all the . . . German . . . transmitters were."

"We do, except for the ones that move."

"Move!?" The duke furrows his brow tremendously, imagining a giant radio transmitter—building, tower and all—mounted on four parallel rail-road tracks like Big Bertha, creeping across a steppe, drawn by harnessed Ukrainians.

"Think U-boats," Waterhouse says delicately.

"Ah!" the duke says explosively. "Ah!" He leans back in his creaky leather chair, examining a whole new picture with his mind's eye. "They . . . pop up, do they, and send out . . . wireless?"

"They do."

"And you . . . eavesdrop."

"If only we could!" Waterhouse says. "No, the Germans have used all of that world–famous mathematical brilliance of theirs to invent ciphers that are totally unbreakable. We don't have the first idea what they are saying. But, by using huffduff, we can figure out where they are saying it *from,* and route our convoys accordingly."

"Ah."

"So what we propose to do is mount big rotating antennas, or aerials as you call them here, on the castle, and staff the place with huffduff boffins."

The duke frowns. "There will be proper . . . safeguards for lightning?"

"Naturally."

"And you are aware that you may . . . anticipate . . . ice storms . . . as late in the year as August?"

"The Royal Qwghlm Meteorological Station's reports, as a body of work, don't leave a heck of a lot to the imagination."

"Fine, then!" the duke blusters, warming to the concept. "Use the castle, then! And give them . . . give them hell!"

ELECTRICAL TILL CORPORATION

✠ As evidence of the Allies' slowly developing plan to kill the Axis by smothering them under a mountain of manufactured goods, there's this one pier in Sydney Harbor that is piled high with wooden crates and steel barrels: stuff that has been disgorged from the holds of ships from America, Britain, India and just left to sit there because Australia doesn't know how to digest it yet. It is not the only pier in Sydney that is choked with stuff. But because this pier isn't good for much else, it is mounded higher and the stuff is older, rustier, more infested with rats, more rimed with salt, more thickly frosted and flagrantly streaked with gull shit.

A man is picking his way over the pile, trying not to get any more of that gull shit on his khakis. He is wearing the uniform of a major in the United States Army and is badly encumbered by a briefcase. His name is Comstock.

Inside the briefcase are various identity papers, credentials, and an impressive letter from the office of The General in Brisbane. Comstock has had occasion to show all of the above to the doddering and yet queerly formidable Australian guards who, with their doughboy helmets and rifles, infest the waterfront. These men do not speak any dialect of the English language that the major can recognize and vice versa, but they can all read what is on those papers.

The sun is going down and the rats are waking up. The major has been clambering over docks all day long. He has seen enough of war and the military to know that what he is looking for will be found on the last pier that he searches, which happens to be this one. If he begins searching that pier at the near end, what he is looking for will be at the far end, and vice versa. All the more reason to stay sharp as he works his way along. After casting an eye around to make sure there are no leaking stacks of drums of aviation fuel nearby, he lights up a cigarette. War is hell, but smoking cigarettes makes it all worthwhile.

Sydney Harbor is beautiful at sunset, but he's been looking at it all day and can't really see it anymore. For lack of anything better to do, he opens up his briefcase. There's a paperback novel in there, which he's already read. And there is a clipboard which contains, in yellowed, crackling, sedimentary layers, a fossil record that only an archaeologist could unravel. It is the story of how The General, just after he got out of Corregidor and reached Australia in April, sent out a request for some stuff. How that request got forwarded to America and bounced pinball-like through the cluttered infinitude of America's military and civilian bureaucracies; how the stuff in question was duly manufactured, procured, trucked hither and yon, and caused to be placed on a ship; and finally, some evidence to the effect that said ship was in Sydney Harbor several months ago. There's no evidence that this ship ever unloaded the stuff in question, but unloading stuff is what ships always do when they reach port and so Comstock is going with that assumption for a while.

After Major Comstock finishes his cigarette, he resumes his search. Some of the papers on his clipboard specify certain magic numbers that ought to be stenciled on the outside of the crates in question; at least, that's what he's been assuming since he started this search at daybreak, and if he's wrong, he'll have to go back and search every crate in Sydney Harbor again. Actually getting a look at each crates' numbers means squeezing his body through narrow channels between crate piles and rubbing away the grease and grime that obscures the crucial data. The major is now as filthy as any combat grunt.

When he gets close to the end of the pier, his eye picks out one cluster of crates that appear to be all of the same vintage insofar as their salt encrustations are of similar thickness. Down low where the rain pools, their rough-sawn wood has rotted. Up where it is roasted by the sun, it has warped and split. Somewhere these crates must have numbers stenciled onto them, but something else has caught his eye, something that stirs Comstock's heart, just as the sight of the Stars and Stripes fluttering in the morning sun might do for a beleaguered infantryman. Those crates are proudly marked with the initials of the company that Major Comstock (and most of his comrades-in-arms up in Brisbane) worked for, before they were shunted, en masse, into the Army's Signal Intelligence Service. The letters are faded and grimy, but he would recognize them anywhere in the world: they form the logo, the corporate identity, the masthead, of ETC—the Electrical Till Corporation.

CRYPT

THE TERMINAL IS SUPPOSED TO ECHO THE LINES OF A ROW OF Malay longhouses jammed together side by side. A freshly painted jetway gropes out like a giant lamprey and slaps its neoprene lips onto the side of the plane. The elderly Nipponese tour group makes no effort to leave the plane, respectfully leaving the aisles clear for the businessmen: *You go ahead, the people we're going to visit won't mind waiting.*

On his march up the jetway, humidity and jet fuel condense onto Randy's skin in equal measure, and he begins to sweat. Then he's in the terminal, which notwithstanding the Malay longhouses allusion has been engineered specifically to look like any other brand-new airport terminal in the world. The air-conditioning hits like a spike through the head. He puts his bags down on the floor and stands there for a moment, collecting his wits beneath a Leroy Neiman painting the dimensions of a volleyball court, depicting the sultan in action on a polo pony. Trapped in a window seat during a short and choppy flight, he had never made it out to the lavatory, so he goes to one now and pees so hard that the urinal emits a sort of yodeling noise.

As he steps back, perfectly satisfied, he becomes conscious of a man backing away from an adjacent urinal—one of the Nipponese businessmen who just got off the plane. A couple of months ago, the presence of this man would have ruled out Randy's taking a leak at all. Today, he didn't even notice that the guy was there. As a longtime bashful kidney sufferer, Randy is delighted to have stumbled upon the magic remedy: not to convince yourself that you are a dominating Alpha Male, but rather to be too lost in your thoughts to notice other people around you. Bashful kidney is your body's way of telling you that you're thinking too hard, that you need to get off the campus and go get a fucking job.

"You were looking at the Ministry of Information site?" the business-man says. He is in a perfect charcoal-grey pinstripe suit, which he wears just as easily and comfortably as Randy does his souvenir t-shirt from the fifth Hackers Conference, surfer's jams, and Teva sandals.

"Oh!" Randy blurts, annoyed with himself. "I completely forgot to look for it." Both men laugh. The Nipponese man produces a business card with some deft sleight-of-hand. Randy has to rip open his nylon-and-velcro wallet and delve for his. They exchange cards in the tradi-tional Asian two-handed style, which Avi has forced Randy to practice until he gets it nearly right. They bow at each other, triggering howls from the nearest couple of computerized self-flushing urinals. The bath-room door swings open and an aged Nip wanders in, a precursor of the silver horde.

Nip is the word used by Sergeant Sean Daniel McGee, U.S. Army, Retired, to refer to Nipponese people in his war memoir about Kinakuta, a photocopy of which document Randy is carrying in his bag. It is a terrible racist slur. On the other hand, people call British people Brits, and Yankees Yanks, all the time. Calling a Nipponese person a Nip is just the same thing, isn't it? Or is it tantamount to calling a Chinese person a Chink? During the hundreds of hours of meetings, and mega-bytes of encrypted e-mail messages, that Randy, Avi, John Cantrell, Tom Howard, Eberhard Föhr, and Beryl have exchanged, getting Epiphyte(2) off the ground, each of them has occasionally, inadvertently, used the word Jap as shorthand for Japanese—in the same way as they used RAM to mean Random Access Memory. But of course Jap is a horrible racist slur too. Randy figures it all has to do with your state of mind at the time you utter the word. If you're just trying to abbreviate, it's not a slur. But if you are fomenting racist hatreds, as Sean Daniel McGee occasionally seems to be not above doing, that's different.

This particular Nipponese individual is identified, on his car, as GOTO Furudenendu ("Ferdinand Goto"). Randy, who has spent a lot of time recently puzzling over organizational charts of certain important Nip-ponese corporations, knows already that he is a vice president for special projects (whatever that means) at Goto Engineering. He also knows that organizational charts of Nipponese companies are horseshit and that job titles mean absolutely nothing. That he has the same surname as the guy who founded the company is presumably worth taking note of.

Randy's card says that he is Randall L. WATERHOUSE ("Randy") and that he is vice president for network technology development at Epiphyte Corporation.

Goto and Waterhouse stroll out of the washroom and start to follow the baggage-claim icons that are strung across the terminal like breadcrumbs. "You have jet lag now?" Goto asks brightly—following (Randy assumes) a script from an English textbook. He's a handsome guy with a winning smile. He's probably in his forties, though Nipponese people seem to have a whole different aging algorithm so this might be way off.

"No," Randy answers. Being a nerd, he answers such questions badly, succinctly, and truthfully. He knows that Goto essentially does not care whether Randy has jet lag or not. He is vaguely conscious that Avi, if he were here, would use Goto's question as it was intended—as an opening for cheery social batter. Until he reached thirty, Randy felt bad about the fact that he was not socially deft. Now he doesn't give a damn. Pretty soon he'll probably start being proud of it. In the meantime, just for the sake of the common enterprise, he tries his best. "I've actually been in Manila for several days, so I've had plenty of time to adjust."

"Ah! Did your activities in Manila go well?" Goto fires back.

"Yes, very well, thank you," Randy lies, now that his social skills, such as they are, have had a moment to get unlimbered. "Did you come directly from Tokyo?"

Goto's smile freezes in place for a moment, and he hesitates before saying, "Yes."

This is, at root, a patronizing reply. Goto Engineering is headquartered in Kobe and they would not fly out of the Tokyo airport. Goto said yes anyway, because, during that moment of hesitation, he realized that he was just dealing with a Yank, who, when he said "Tokyo," really meant "the Nipponese home islands" or "wherever the hell you come from."

"Excuse me," Randy says, "I meant to say Osaka."

Goto grins brilliantly and seems to execute a tiny suggestion of a bow. "Yes! I came from Osaka today."

Goto and Waterhouse drift apart from each other at the luggage claim, exchange grins as they breeze through immigration, and run into each other at the ground transportation section. Kinakutan men in brilliant white quasinaval uniforms with gold braid and white gloves are buttonholing passengers, proffering transportation to the local hotels.

"You are staying at the Foote Mansion also?" Goto says. That being *the* luxury hotel in Kinakuta. But he knows the answer already—tomorrow's meeting has been planned as exhaustively as a space shuttle launch.

Randy hesitates. The largest Mercedes-Benz he's ever seen has just pulled up to the curb, condensed moisture not merely fogging its windows but running down them in literal streamlines. A driver in Foote Mansion livery has erupted from it to divest Mr. Goto of his luggage. Randy knows that he need only make a subtle move toward that car and he will be whisked to a luxury hotel where he can take a shower, watch TV naked while drinking a hundred-dollar bottle of French wine, go swimming, get a massage.

Which is precisely the problem. He can already feel himself wilting in the equatorial heat. It's too early to go soft. He's only been awake for six or seven hours. There's work to be done. He forces himself to stand up at attention, and the effort makes him break a sweat so palpably that he almost expects to moisten everything within a radius of several meters. "I would enjoy sharing a ride to the hotel with you," he says, "but I have one or two errands to run first."

Goto understands. "Perhaps drinks this evening."

"Leave me a message," Randy says. Then Goto's waving at him through the smoked glass of the Mercedes as it pulls seven gees away from the curb. Randy does a one-eighty, goes back inside to the halal Dunkin' Donuts, which accepts eight currencies, and sates himself. Then he reemerges and turns imperceptibly toward a line of taxis. A driver hurls himself bodily towards Randy and tears his garment bag loose from his shoulder. "Ministry of Information," Randy says.

In the long run, it may, or may not, be a good idea for the Sultanate of Kinakuta to have a gigantic earthquake-, volcano-, tsunami-, and thermonuclear-weapon-proof Ministry of Information with a cavernous sub-sub-basement crammed with high-powered computers and data switches. But the sultan has decided that it would be sort of cool. He has hired some alarming Germans to design it, and Goto Engineering to build it. No one, of course, is more familiar with staggering natural disasters than the Nipponese, with the possible exception of some peoples who are now extinct and therefore unable to bid on jobs like this. They also know a thing or two about having the shit bombed out of them, as do the Germans.

There are subcontractors, of course, and a plethora of consultants. Through some miraculous feat of fast talking, Avi managed to land one of the biggest consulting contracts: Epiphyte(2) Corporation is doing "systems integration" work, which means plugging together a bunch of junk made by other people, and overseeing the installation of all the computers, switches, and data lines.

The drive to the site is surprisingly short. Kinakuta City isn't that big, hemmed in as it is by steep mountain ranges, and the sultan has endowed it with plenty of eight-lane superhighways. The taxi blasts across the plain of reclaimed land on which the airport is built, swings wide around the stump of Eliza Peak, ignoring two exits for Technology City, then turns off at an unmarked exit. Suddenly they are stuck in a queue of empty dump trucks—Nipponese behemoths emblazoned with the word GOTO in fat macho block letters. Coming towards them is a stream of other trucks that are identical except that these are fully laden with stony rubble. The taxi driver pulls onto the right shoulder and zooms past trucks for about half a mile. They're heading up—Randy's ears pop once. This road is built on the floor of a ravine that climbs up into one of the mountain ranges. Soon they are hemmed in by vertiginous walls of green, which act like a sponge, trapping an eternal cloud of mist, through which sparks of brilliant color are sometimes visible. Randy can't tell whether they are birds or flowers. The contrast between the cloud forest's lush vegetation and the dirt road, battered by the house-sized tires of the heavy trucks, is disorienting.

The taxi stops. The driver turns and looks at him expectantly. Randy thinks for a moment that the driver has gotten lost and is looking to Randy for instructions. The road terminates here, in a parking lot mysteriously placed in the middle of the cloud forest. Randy sees half a dozen big air-conditioned trailers bearing the logos of various Nipponese, German, and American firms; a couple of dozen cars; as many buses. All the accoutrements of a major construction site are here, plus a few extras, like two monkeys with giant stiff penises fighting over some booty from a Dumpster, but there is no construction site. Just a wall of green at the end of the road, green so dark it's almost black.

The empty trucks are disappearing into that darkness. Full ones come out, their headlights emerging from the mist and gloom first, followed by the colorful displays that the drivers have built onto the radiator grilles, followed by the highlights on their chrome and glass, and finally the trucks themselves. Randy's eyes adjust, and he can see now that he is staring into a cavern, lit up by mercury-vapor lamps.

"You want me to wait?" the driver asks.

Randy glances at the meter, does a quick conversion, and figures out that the ride to this point has cost him a dime. "Yes," he says, and gets out of the taxi. Satisfied, the driver kicks back and lights up a cigarette.

Randy stands there and gapes into the cavern for a minute, partly because it's a hell of a thing to look at and partly because a river of cool air is draining out of it, which feels good. Then he trudges across the lot and goes to the trailer marked "Epiphyte."

It is staffed by three tiny Kinakutan women who know exactly who he is, though they've never met him before, and who give every indication of being delighted to see him. They wear long, loose wraps of brilliantly colored fabric on top of Eddie Bauer turtlenecks to ward off the nordic chill of the air conditioners. They are all fearsomely efficient and poised. Everywhere Randy goes in Southeast Asia he runs into women who ought to be running General Motors or something. Before long they have sent out word of his arrival via walkie-talkie and cell-phone, and presented him with a pair of thick knee-high boots, a hard hat, and a cellular phone, all carefully labeled with his name. After a couple of minutes, a young Kinakutan man in hard hat and muddy boots opens the trailer's door, introduces himself as "Steve," and leads Randy into the entrance of the cavern. They follow a narrow pedestrian board-walk illuminated by a string of caged lightbulbs.

For the first hundred meters or so, the cave is just a straight passage barely wide enough to admit two Goto trucks and the pedestrian lane. Randy trails his hand along the wall. The stone is rough and dusty, not smooth like the surface of a natural cavern, and he can see fresh gouges wrought by jackhammers and drills.

He can tell by the echo that something's about to change. Steve leads him out into the cavern proper. It is, well, *cavernous*. Big enough for a dozen of the huge trucks to pull around in a circle to be laden with rock and muck. Randy looks up, trying to find the ceiling, but all he sees is a pattern of bluish-white high-intensity lights, like the ones in gymnasiums, perhaps ten meters above. Beyond that it's darkness and mist.

Steve goes off in search of something and leaves Randy alone for a few minutes, which is useful since it takes a long time for him to get his bearings.

Some of the cavern wall is smooth and natural; the rest of it is rough, marking the enlargements conceived by the engineers and executed by the contractor. Likewise, some of the floor is smooth, and not quite level. Some places it has been drilled and blasted to bring it down, others it has been filled in to bring it up.

This, the main chamber, looks to be about finished. The offices of the Ministry of Information will be here. There are two other, smaller chambers, deeper inside the mountain, still being enlarged. One will contain the engineering plant (power generators and so forth) and the other will be the systems unit.

A burly blond man in a white hard hat emerges from a hole in the chamber wall: Tom Howard, Epiphyte Corporation's vice president for systems technology. He takes his hard hat off and waves to Randy, then beckons him over.

The passageway that leads to the systems chamber is big enough that you could drive a delivery van down it, but it's not as straight or as level as the main entryway. It is mostly occupied by a conveyor system of terrifying power and speed, which is carrying tons of dripping grey muck out towards the main chamber to be dumped into the Goto trucks. In terms of apparent cost and sophistication, it bears the same relationship to a normal conveyor belt as an F-15 does to a Sopwith Camel. It is possible to speak but impossible to be heard when you are near it, and so Tom and Randy and the Kinakutan who calls himself Steve trudge silently down the passage for another hundred or so meters until they reach the next cavern.

This one is only large enough to contain a modest one-story house. The conveyor passes right through the middle of it and disappears down another hole; the muck is coming from deeper yet in the mountain. It's still too loud in here to talk. The floor has been leveled by pouring in concrete, and conduits rise from it every few meters with orange cables dangling from their open tops: optical fiber lines.

Tom walks towards another opening in the wall. It appears that several subsidiary caverns branch away from this one. Tom leads Randy through the opening, then turns to put a hand on his arm and steady him: they are at the top of a steep wooden staircase that has been built down a nearly vertical shaft that descends a good five meters or so.

"What you just saw is the main switch room," Tom says. "That'll be the largest router in the world when it's finished. We're using some of these other chambers to install computers and mass storage systems. The world's largest RAID, basically, buffered with a big, big RAM cache."

RAID means Redundant Array of Inexpensive Disks; it is a way to store vast quantities of information cheaply and reliably, and exactly the kind of thing you would want to have in a data haven.

"So we're still cleaning out some of these other chambers," Tom continues. "We discovered something, down here, that I thought you'd find interesting." He turns around and begins to descend the staircase. "Did you know that these caves were used as an air raid shelter by the Japanese, during the war?"

Randy has been carrying the map page from his photocopied book around in his pocket. He unfolds it and holds it up near a lightbulb. Sure enough, it includes a site, up in the mountains, labeled ENTRANCE TO AIR RAID SHELTER & COMMAND POST.

"And a command post?" Randy says.

"Yeah. How'd you know that?"

"Interlibrary loan," Randy says.

"We didn't know it until we got here and found all of these old cables and electrical shit strung around the place. We had to tear it out so we could string in our own."

Randy begins to descend the steps.

"This shaft was full of rocks," Tom says, "but we could see wires going down into it, so we knew something had to be down here."

Randy looks nervously at the ceiling. "Why was it full of rocks? Was there a cave-in?"

"No," Tom says, "the Japanese soldiers did it. They threw rocks down the shaft until it was full. It took a dozen of our laborers two weeks to pull all the rocks out by hand."

"So, what did the wires lead to?"

"Lightbulbs," Tom says, "they were just electrical wires—no communications."

"Then what was it they were trying to hide down here?" Randy asks. He has almost reached the bottom of the staircase, and he can see that there is a room-sized cavity.

"See for yourself," Tom says, and flicks a light switch.

The cavity is about the size of a one-car garage, with a nice level floor. There is a wooden desk, chair, and filing cabinet, fuzzy with fifty years' growth of grey-green fungus. And there is a metal footlocker, painted olive-drab, stenciled with Nipponese characters.

"I forced the lock on this thing," Tom says. He steps over to the footlocker and flips the lid open. It is filled with books.

"You were expecting maybe gold bars?" Tom says, laughing at the expression on Randy's face.

Randy sits down on the floor and grabs his ankles. He's staring open-mouthed at the books in the chest.

"You okay?" Tom asks.

"Heavy, heavy deja vu," Randy says.

"From this?"

"Yeah," Randy says, "I've seen this before."

"Where?"

"In my grandmother's attic."

———————

Randy finds his way up out of the network of caverns and into the parking lot. The warm air feels good on his skin, but by the time he has reached the Epiphyte Corp. trailer to turn in his hard hat and boots, he has begun to sweat again. He bids good-bye to the three women who work there, and once again is struck by their attentiveness, their solicitousness. Then he remembers that he is not just some interloper.

He is a shareholder, and an important officer, in the corporation that employs them—he is paying them or oppressing them, take your pick.

He trudges across the parking lot, moving very slowly, trying not to get that metabolic furnace het up. A second taxi has pulled alongside the one that is waiting for Randy, and the drivers are leaning out of their windows shooting the breeze.

As Randy approaches his taxi, he happens to glance back towards the entrance of the cavern. Framed in its dark maw, and dwarfed by the mountainous shapes of the Goto dump trucks, is a solitary man, silver-haired, stooped, but trim and almost athletic-looking in a warmup suit and sneakers. He is standing with his back to Randy, facing the cavern, holding a long spray of flowers. He seems rooted in the mud, perfectly motionless.

The front door of the Goto Engineering trailer flies open. A young Nipponese man in a white shirt, striped tie, and orange hard hat descends the stairs and moves briskly towards the old man with the flowers. When he is still some distance away, he stops, puts his feet together, and exe-cutes a bow. Randy hasn't spent enough time around Nipponese to understand the minutiae, but this looks to him like an extraordinarily major bow. He approaches the old man with a bright smile and holds one beckoning hand out towards the Goto trailer. The old man seems disoriented—maybe the cavern doesn't look like it used to—but after a few moments he returns a perfunctory bow and allows the young engi-neer to lead him out of the stream of traffic.

Randy gets in his taxi and says, "Foote Mansion," to the driver.

He has been harboring an illusion that he will read Sean Daniel McGee's war memoir slowly and thoroughly, from beginning to end, but this has now gone the way of all illusions. He hauls the photocopied stack out of his bag during the drive to the hotel and begins ruthless triage. Most of it has nothing to do with Kinakuta at all—it's about McGee's experiences fighting in New Guinea and the Philippines. McGee is no Churchill, but he does have a distant blarney-tinged narra-tive talent, which makes even banal anecdotes readable. His skills as raconteur must have made him a big hit around the bar at the NCOs' Club; a hundred tipsy sergeants must have urged him to write some of this shit down if he ever made it back to South Boston alive.

He did make it back, but unlike most of the other GIs who were in the Philippines on V-J day, he didn't go straight back home. He took a little detour to the Sultanate of Kinakuta, which was still home to almost four thousand Nipponese troops. This explains an oddity about his book. In most war memoirs, V-E Day or V-J Day happens on the last page, or at least in the last chapter, and then our narrator goes home and buys a Buick. But V-J day happens about two-thirds of the way through Sean Daniel McGee's book. When Randy sets aside the pre-August 1945 material, an ominously thick stack of pages remains. Clearly, Sergeant McGee has something to get off his chest.

The Nipponese garrison on Kinakuta had long since been bypassed by the war, and like the other bypassed garrisons, had turned what energies they had left to vegetable farming, and waiting for the extremely sporadic arrivals of submarines, which, towards the close of the war, the Nipponese used to haul the most extremely vital cargo and to ferry certain desperately needed specialists, like airplane mechanics, from one place to another. When they got Hirohito's broadcast from Tokyo, ordering them to lay down their arms, they did so dutifully but (one has to suspect) gladly.

The only hard part was finding someone to surrender to. The Allies had concentrated on planning the invasion of the Nipponese home islands, and it took them a while to get troops out to the bypassed garrisons like Kinakuta. McGee's account of the confusion in Manila is mordant— at this point in the book McGee starts to lose his patience, and his charm. He starts to rail. Twenty pages later, he's sloshing ashore at Kinakuta City. He stands at attention while his company captain accepts the surrender of the Nipponese garrison. He posts a guard around the entrance to the cavern, where a few diehard Nips have refused to surrender. He organizes the systematic disarming of the Nipponese soldiers, who are terribly emaciated, and sees to it that their rifles and ammunition are dumped into the ocean even as food and medical supplies are brought ashore. He helps a small contingent of engineers string barbed wire around the airfield, turning it into an internment camp.

Randy flips through all of this during the drive to the hotel. Then, words like "impaled" and "screams" and "hideous" catch his eye, so he flips back a few pages and begins to read more carefully.

The upshot is that the Nipponese had, since 1940, marched thousands of tribesmen out of the cool, clean interior of the island to its hot, pestilential edge, and put them to work. These slaves had enlarged the big cavern where the Nipponese built their air raid shelter and command post; improved the road to the top of Eliza Peak, where the radar and direction-finding stations were perched; built another runway at the airfield; filled in more of the harbor; and died by thousands of malaria, scrub typhus, dysentery, starvation, and overwork. These same tribesmen, or their bereaved brothers, had then watched, from their redoubts high in the mountains, as Sean Daniel McGee and his comrades came and stripped the Nipponese of their armaments and concentrated them all in the airfield, guarded by a few dozen exhausted GIs who were frequently drunk or asleep. Those tribesmen worked around the clock, up there in the jungle, making spears, until the next full moon illuminated the sleeping Nipponese like a searchlight. Then they poured out of the forest in what Sean Daniel McGee describes as "a horde," "a plague of wasps," "a howling army," "a black legion unleashed from the gates of Hell," "a screaming mass," and in other ways he could never get away with now. They flattened and disarmed the GI's, but did not hurt them. They flung tree limbs over the barbed wire until the fence had become a highway, and then swarmed into the airfield with their spears at the ready. McGee's account goes on for about twenty pages, and, as much as anything else, is the story of the night that one affable sergeant from South Boston became permanently unhinged.

"Sir?"

Randy is startled to realize that the taxi's door is open. He looks around and finds that he's under the awning of the Hotel Foote Mansion. The door is being held open for him by a wiry young bellhop with a different look than most of the Kinakutans Randy has encountered so far. This kid perfectly matches Sean Daniel McGee's description of a tribesman from the interior.

"Thank you," Randy says, and makes a point of tipping the fellow generously.

His room is all done up in furniture designed in Scandinavia but assembled locally from various endangered hardwoods. The view is towards the interior mountains, but if he goes onto his tiny balcony he can see a bit of water, a containership being unloaded, and most of the memorial garden built by the Nipponese on the site of the massacre.

Several messages and faxes await him: mostly the other members of Epiphyte Corp., notifying him that they have arrived, and letting him know in which room they can be found. Randy unpacks his bags, takes a shower, and sends his shirts down to the laundry for tomorrow. Then he makes himself comfortable at his little table, boots his laptop, and pulls up the Epiphyte (2) Corporation Business Plan.

BOBBY SHAFTOE AND HIS BUDDIES ARE JUST OUT FOR A NICE LITtle morning drive through the countryside.

In Italy.

Italy! He cannot fucking believe it. What gives?

Not his job to know. His job has been very clearly described to him. It has to be clearly described, because it makes no sense.

In the good old days, back on Guadalcanal, his commanding officer would say something like "Shaftoe, eradicate that pillbox!" and from there on out, Bobby Shaftoe was a free agent. He could walk, run, swim or crawl. He could sneak up and lob in a satchel charge, or he could stand off at a distance and hose the objective down with a flame thrower. Didn't matter as long as he accomplished the goal.

The goal of this little mission is completely beyond Shaftoe's comprehension. They awaken him; Lieutenant Enoch Root; three of the other Marines, including the radio man; and several of the SAS blokes in the middle of the night, and hustle them down to one of the few docks in Malta that hasn't been blasted away by the Luftwaffe. A submarine waits. They climb aboard and play cards for about twenty-four hours. Most of the time they are on the surface, where submarines can go a hell of a lot faster, but from time to time they dive, evidently for the best of reasons.

When next they are allowed up on the flat top of the submarine, it is the middle of the night again. They are in a little cove in a parched, rugged coastline; Shaftoe can see that much by the moonlight. Two trucks are waiting for them. They open hatches in the sub's deck and begin to take stuff out: into one of the trucks, the U.S. Marines load a bunch of cloth sacks bulging with what appears to be all kinds of trash. Meanwhile, the British Special Air Service are at work with wrenches, rags, grease and much profanity in the back of the other truck, assembling something from crates that they have brought up from another part of the submarine. This is covered up by a tarp before Shaftoe can get a good look, but he recognizes it as something you'd rather have pointed away from you.

There are a couple of dark men with mustachioes hanging around the dock smoking and arguing with the skipper of the submarine. After all of the stuff is unloaded, the skipper appears to pay them with more crates from the submarine. The men pry a couple of them open for inspection, and appear to be satisfied.

At this point Shaftoe still doesn't even know what continent they are on. When he first saw the landscape he figured Northern Africa. When he saw the men, he figured Turkey or something.

It is not until the sun comes up on their little convoy, and (lying in the back of the truck on top of the sacks of trash, peeking out from under the tarp) he is able to see road signs and Christian churches, that he realizes it has to be Italy or Spain. Finally he sees a sign pointing the way to ROMA and figures it's Italy. The sign points away from the midmorning sun, so they must be somewhere south or southeast of Rome. They are also south of some burg called Napoli.

But he doesn't spend a lot of time looking. It is not encouraged. The truck is being driven by some fellow who speaks the language, and who stops from time to time to converse with the natives. Some of the time this sounds like friendly banter. Sometimes it sounds like arguments over highway etiquette. Sometimes it is quieter, more guarded. Shaftoe figures out, slowly, that during these exchanges the truck driver is bribing someone to let them go through.

He finds it shocking that in a country actively embroiled in the middle of the greatest war in history—in a country run by belligerent Fascists for God's sake—two truckloads of heavily armed enemy soldiers can just drive around freely, protected by nothing except a couple of five-dollar tarps. Criminy! What kind of a sorry operation is this? He feels like leaping to his feet, casting the tarp aside, and giving these Eyties a good dressing-down. The whole place needs a good scrubbing with tooth-brushes anyway. It's like these people aren't even trying. Now, the Nips, think of them what you will, at least when those guys declare war on you they mean it.

He resists the temptation to upbraid the Italians. He thinks it goes against the orders he had thoroughly memorized before the shock of figuring out that he was driving around in an Axis country jangled every-thing loose from his brain. And if they hadn't come from the lips of Colonel Chattan himself—the chap or bloke who's the commanding officer of Detachment 2702—he wouldn't have believed them anyway.

They are going to be putting in some bivouac time. They are going to play a lot of cards for a while. During this time, the radio man is going to be very busy. This phase of the operation might last as long as a week. At some point, it is likely that strenuous, concerted efforts to kill them will be made by a whole lot of Germans and, if they happen to be feeling impetuous that day, Italians. When this happens, they are to send out a radio message, torch the joint, drive to a certain field that passes for an airstrip, and be picked up by those jaunty SAS flyboys.

Shaftoe didn't believe a word of it at first. He pegged it as some kind of British humor thing, some kind of practical joke/hazing ritual. In general he doesn't know what to make of the Brits because they appear (in his personal observation) to be the only other people on the face of the earth, besides Americans, who possess a sense of humor. He has heard rumors that some Eastern Europeans can do it, but he hasn't met any of them, and they don't have much to yuk it up about at the moment. In any case, he can never quite make out when these Brits are joking.

Any thought that this was just a joke evaporated when he saw the quantity of armaments they were being issued. Shaftoe has found that, for an organization devoted to shooting and blowing up people on a large scale, the military is infuriatingly reticent about passing out weapons. And most of the weapons they do pass out are for shit. It is for this reason that Marines have long found it necessary to buy their own tommy guns from home: the Corps wants them to kill people, but they just won't give them the stuff they need!

But this Detachment 2702 thing is a whole different outfit. Even the grunts are carrying trench brooms! And if that didn't get their attention, the cyanide capsules sure did. And the lecture from Chattan on the correct way to blow your own head off ("you would be astonished at how many otherwise competent chaps botch this apparently simple procedure").

Now, Shaftoe realizes that there is an unspoken codicil to Chattan's orders: oh, yeah, and if any of the Italians, who actually *live* in Italy, and who *run* the place, and who are *Fascists* and who are at *war* with us—if any of them *notice* you and, for some reason, *object* to your little plan, whatever the *fuck* it is, then by all means kill them. And if that doesn't work, please, by all means, kill yourself, because you'll probably do a neater job of it than the Fascists will. Don't forget suntan lotion!

Actually, Shaftoe doesn't mind this mission. It is certainly no worse than Guadalcanal. What bothers him (he decides, making himself comfortable on the sacks of mysterious trash, staring up at a crack in the tarp) is not understanding the purpose of it all.

The rest of the platoon may or may not be dead; he thinks he can still hear some of them crying out, but it's hard to tell between the pounding of the incoming surf and the relentless patter of the machine gun. Then he realizes that some of them must be alive or else the Nips would not continue to fire their gun.

Shaftoe knows that he is closer to the gun than any of his buddies. He is the only one who has a chance.

It is at this point that Shaftoe makes his Big Decision. It is surprisingly easy—but then, really stupid decisions are always the easiest.

He crawls along the log to the point that is closest to the machine gun. Then he draws a few deep breaths in a row, rises to a crouch, and vaults over the log! He has a clear view of the cave entrance now, the comet-shaped muzzle flash of the machine gun tesselated by the black grid of the net that they put up to reject incoming grenades. It is all remarkably clear. He looks back over the beach and sees motionless corpses.

Suddenly he realizes they are still firing the gun, not because any of his buddies are alive, but to use up all of their excess ammunition so that they will not have to pack it out. Shaftoe is a grunt, and understands.

Then the muzzle swings abruptly towards him—he has been sighted. He is in the clear, totally exposed. He can dive into the jungle foliage, but they will sweep it with fire until he is dead. Bobby Shaftoe plants his feet, aims his .45 into the cave, and begins pulling the trigger. The barrel of the machine gun is pointing at him now.

But it does not fire.

His .45 clicks. It's empty. Everything is silent except for the surf, and for the screaming. Shaftoe holsters his .45 and pulls out his revolver.

The voice that is doing the screaming is unfamiliar. It's not one of Shaftoe's buddies.

A Nipponese Imperial Marine bolts from the mouth of the cave, up above the level of Shaftoe's head. The pupil of Shaftoe's right eye, the sights of his revolver, and this Nip are all arranged briefly along the same line for a moment, during which Shaftoe pulls the trigger a couple of times and almost certainly scores a hit.

The Imperial Marine gets caught in the netting and plunges to the ground in front of him.

A second Nip dives out of the cave a moment later, grunting incoherently, apparently speechless with horror. He lands wrong and breaks one of his leg bones; Shaftoe can hear it snap. He begins running towards the surf anyway, hobbling grotesquely on the bad leg. He completely ignores Shaftoe. There is terrible bleeding from his neck and shoulder, and loose chunks of flesh flopping around as he runs.

Bobby Shaftoe holsters his revolver. He ought to shoulder his rifle and plug the guy, but he is too confused to do anything for the moment.

Something red flickers in the mouth of the cave. He glances up that way and sees nothing clear enough to register against the deafening visual noise of the jungle.

Then he sees the flash of red again, and it disappears again. It was shaped like a sharpened Y. It was shaped like the forked tongue of a reptile.

Then a moving slab of living jungle explodes from the mouth of the cave and crashes into the foliage below. The tops of the plants shake and topple as it moves.

It is out, free and clear, on the beach. It is low to the ground, moving on all fours. It pauses for a moment and flicks its tongue towards the Imperial Marine who is now hobbling into the Pacific Ocean some fifty feet distant.

Sand erupts into the air, like smoke from the burning tires of a drag racer, and the lizard is rocketing across the beach. It covers the distance to the Imperial Marine in one, two, three seconds, takes him in the backs of the knees, takes him down hard into the surf. Then the lizard is dragging the dead Nip back up onto the land. It stretches him out there among the dead Americans, walks around him a couple of times, flicking its tongue, and finally starts to eat him.

"Sarge! We're here!" says Private Flanagan. Before he even wakes up, Bobby Shaftoe notices that Flanagan is speaking in a normal voice and does not sound scared or excited. Wherever "here" is, it's not someplace dangerous. They are not under attack.

Shaftoe opens his eyes just as the tarp is being peeled back from the open top of the truck. He stares straight up into a blue Italian sky torn around the edges by the scrabbling branches of desperate trees. "Shit!" he says.

"What's wrong, Sarge?"

"I just always say that when I wake up," Shaftoe says.

———————

Their new home turns out to be an old stone farm building in an olive farm, plantation, orchard or whatever the fuck you call a place where olives are grown. If this building were in Wisconsin, any cheesehead who passed by would peg it as abandoned. Here, Shaftoe is not so sure. The roof has partly collapsed into the building under the killing weight of its red clay tiles, and the windows and doorways yawn, open to the elements. It's a big structure, big enough that after several hours of sledgehammer work they are able to drive one of the trucks inside and conceal it from airborne snoops. They unload the sacks of trash from the other truck. Then the Italian guy drives it away and never comes back.

Corporal Benjamin, the radio man, gets busy clambering up olive trees and stringing copper wires around the place. The blokes of the SAS go out and reconnoiter while the guys of the Marine Corps open the sacks of trash and start spreading them around. There are several months' worth of Italian newspapers. All of them have been opened, rearranged, haphazardly refolded. Articles have been torn out, other articles circled or annotated in pencil. Chattan's orders are beginning to filter back into Shaftoe's brain; he heaps these newspapers in the corners of the barn, oldest ones first, newer ones on top.

There is a whole sack filled with cigarette butts, carefully smoked to the nub. They are of a Continental brand unfamiliar to Shaftoe. Like a farmer broadcasting seeds, he carries this sack around the premises tossing handfuls onto the ground, concentrating mostly on places where people will actually work: Corporal Benjamin's table and another makeshift table they have set up for eating and playing poker. Likewise with a salad of wine corks and beer caps. An equal number of wine and beer bottles are flung, one by one, into a dark and unused corner of the barn. Bobby Shaftoe can see that this is the most satisfying work he will ever get, so he takes it over, and flings those bottles like a Green Bay Packer quarterback firing spiral passes into the sure hands of his plucky tight ends.

The blokes come back from reconnoitering and there is a swappage of roles; the Marines now go out to familiarize themselves with the territory while the SAS continue unloading garbage. In an hour's worth of wandering around, Sergeant Shaftoe and Privates Flanagan and Kuehl determine that this olive ranch is on a long skinny shelf of land that runs roughly north–south. To the west, the territory rises up steeply toward a conical peak that looks suspiciously like a volcano. To the east, it drops, after a few miles, down towards the sea. To the north, the plateau deadends in some nasty, impassable scrubland, and to the south it opens up on more farming territory.

Chattan wanted him to find a vantage point on the bay, as convenient as possible to the barn. Toward sunset, Shaftoe finds it: a rocky outcropping on the slopes of the volcano, half an hour's walk northeast of the barn and maybe five hundred feet above it in altitude.

He and his Marines almost don't find their way back to the barn because it has been so well hidden by this point. The SAS have put up blackout shades over every opening, even the small chinks in the collapsed roof. On the inside, they have settled in comfortably to the pockets of usable space. With all of the litter (now enhanced with chicken feathers and bones, tonsorial trimmings and orange peels) it looks like they've been living there for a year, which, Shaftoe guesses, is the whole point.

Corporal Benjamin has about a third of the place to himself. The SAS blokes keep calling him a lucky sod. He has his transmitter set up now, the tubes glowing warmly, and he has an unbelievable amount of paperwork. Most of it's old and fake, just like the cigarette butts. But after dinner, when the sun is down not only here but in London, he begins tapping out the Morse code.

Shaftoe knows Morse code, like everyone else in the place. As the guys and the blokes sit around the table, anteing up for what promises to be an all-night Hearts marathon, they keep one ear cocked towards Corporal Benjamin's keying. What they hear is gibberish. Shaftoe goes and looks over Benjamin's shoulder at one point, just to verify that he isn't crazy, and sees he's right:

XYHEL ANAOG GFQPL TWPKI AOEUT

and so on and so forth, for pages and pages.

The next morning they dig a latrine and then proceed to fill it halfway with a couple of barrels of genuine U.S. Mil. Spec. General Issue 100% pure certified Shit. As per Chattan's instructions, they pour the shit in a dollop at a time, throwing in handfuls of crumpled Italian newspapers after each dollop to make it look like it got there naturally. With the possible exception of being interviewed by Lieutenant Reagan, this is the worst nonviolent job Shaftoe has ever had to do in the service of his country. He gives everyone the rest of the day off, except for Corporal Benjamin, who stays up until two in the morning banging out random gibberish.

The next day they make the observation post look good. They take turns marching up there and back, up and back, up and back, wearing a trail into the ground, and they scatter some cigarette butts and beverage containers up there along with some general issue shit and general issue piss. Flanagan and Kuehl hump a footlocker up there and hide it in the lee of a volcanic rock. The locker contains books of silhouettes of various Italian and German naval and merchant ships, and similar spotter's guides for airplanes, as well as some binoculars, telescopes, and camera equipment, empty notepads, and pencils.

Even though Sergeant Bobby Shaftoe is for the most part running this show, he finds it uncannily difficult to arrange a moment alone with Lieutenant Enoch Root. Root has been avoiding him ever since their eventful flight on the Dakota. Finally, on about the fifth day, Shaftoe tricks him; he and a small contingent leave Root alone at the observation point, then Shaftoe doubles back and traps him there.

Root is startled to see Shaftoe come back, but he doesn't get particularly upset. He lights up an Italian cigarette and offers Shaftoe one. Shaftoe finds, irritatingly enough, that he is the nervous one. Root's as cool as always.

"Okay," Shaftoe says, "what did you see? When you looked through the papers we planted on the dead butcher—what did you see?"

"They were all written in German," Root says.

"Shit!"

"Fortunately," Root continues, "I am somewhat familiar with the language."

"Oh, yeah—your mom was a Kraut, right?"

"Yes, a medical missionary," Root says, "in case that helps dispel any of your preconceptions about Germans."

"And your Dad was Dutch."

"That is correct."

"And they both ended up on Guadalcanal why?"

"To help those who were in need."

"Oh, yeah."

"I also learned some Italian along the way. There's a lot of it going around in the Church."

"Fuck me," Shaftoe exclaims.

"But my Italian is heavily informed by the Latin that my father insisted that I learn. So I would probably sound rather old-fashioned to the locals. In fact, I would probably sound like a seventeenth-century alchemist or something."

"Could you sound like a priest? They'd eat that up."

"If worse comes to worst," Root allows, "I will try hitting them with some God talk and we'll see what happens."

They both puff on their cigarettes and look out across the large body of water before them, which Shaftoe has learned is called the Bay of Naples. "Well anyway," Shaftoe says, "what did it say on those papers?"

"A lot of detailed information about military convoys between Palermo and Tunis. Evidently stolen from classified German sources," Root says.

"Old convoys, or . . ."

"Convoys that were still in the future," Root says calmly.

Shaftoe finishes his cigarette, and does not speak for a while. Finally he says, "Fuckin' weird." He stands up and begins walking back towards the barn.

THE CASTLE

JUST AS LAWRENCE PRITCHARD WATERHOUSE DETRAINS, SOME rakehell hits him full in the face with a turn of brackish ice water. The barrage continues as he walks a gauntlet of bucket-slinging ne'er-do-wells. But then he realizes no one's there. This is just an intrinsic quality of the local atmosphere, like fog in London.

The staircase that leads over the tracks to Utter Maurby Terminal is enclosed with roof and walls, forming a gigantic organ pipe that resonates with an infrasonic throb as it is pummeled by wind and water. As he walks into the lower end of the staircase, the storm is suddenly peeled away from his face and he is able to stand there for a moment and give this phenom the full appreciation it deserves.

Wind and water have been whipped into an essentially random froth by the storm. A microphone held up in the air would register only white noise—a complete absence of information. But when that noise strikes the long tube of the staircase, it drives a physical resonance that manifests itself in Waterhouse's brain as a low hum. The physics of the tube extract a coherent pattern from meaningless noise! If only Alan were here!

Waterhouse experiments by singing the harmonics of this low fundamental tone: octave, fifth, fourth, major third, and so on. Each one resonates in the staircase to a greater or lesser degree. It is the same series of notes made by a brass instrument. By hopping from one note to another, Waterhouse is able to play some passable bugle calls on the staircase. He does a pretty decent reveille.

"How lovely!"

He spins around. A woman is standing behind him, lugging a portmanteau the size of a hay bale. She is perhaps fifty years old, with the physique of a stove, and she had a nice new big-city permanent until a few seconds ago when she stepped out of the train. Salt water is running down her face and neck and disappearing beneath her sturdy frock of grey Qwghlm wool.

"Ma'am," Waterhouse says. Then he busies himself with hauling her portmanteau up to the top of the stairs. This puts the two of them, and all of their luggage, on a narrow covered bridge that leads across the tracks and into the terminal building. The bridge has windows in it, and Waterhouse suffers a nauseating attack of vertigo as he looks through them, and through the half inch of rain and saltwater that is streaming down them at any given moment, towards the North Atlantic Ocean. This major body of water is only a stone's throw away and is trying vigorously to get much closer. This must be an optical illusion, but the tops of the waves appear to be level with the plane on which they're standing despite the fact that it's at least twenty feet off the ground. Each one of those waves must weigh as much as all of the freight trains in Great Britain combined, and they are rolling towards them relentlessly, simply hammering the living daylights out of the rocks. It all makes Waterhouse want to pitch a fit, fall down, and throw up. He plugs his ears.

"Are you a bandsman, then, I take it?" the lady enquires.

Waterhouse turns to look at her. Her gaze is darting back and forth around the front of his uniform, checking the insignia. Then she looks up into his face and gives him a grandmotherly smile.

Waterhouse realizes, in that instant, that this woman is a German spy. Holy cow!

"Only in peacetime, ma'am," he says. "The Navy has other uses, now, for men with good ears."

"Oh!" she exclaims, "you listen to things, do you?"

Waterhouse smiles. "Ping! Ping!" he says, mimicking sonar.

"Ah!" she says. "I am Harriett Qrtt." She holds out her hand.

"Hugh Hughes," Waterhouse says, and shakes.

"Pleasure."

"All mine."

"You'll be needing a place to stay, I suppose." She blushes ostentatiously. "Forgive me. I just assume you are bound for Outer." That's Outer, as in Outer Qwghlm. Right now, they are on Inner Qwghlm.

"Quite right, actually," Waterhouse says.

Like every other place name in the British Isles, Inner and Outer Qwghlm represent a gross misnomer with ancient and probably comical origins. Inner Qwghlm is hardly even an island; it is joined to the mainland by a sandbar that used to come and go with the tides, but that has been beefed up with a causeway that carries a road and the railway line. Outer Qwghlm is twenty miles away.

"My husband and I operate a small bed and breakfast," Mrs. Qrtt says. "We should be honored to have an Asdic man stay with us." Asdic is simply the British acronym for what Yanks refer to as sonar, but every time the word is mentioned in the presence of Alan, he gets a naughty look on his face and goes on an unstoppable punning tear.

So he ends up at the Qrtt residence. Waterhouse and Mr. and Mrs. Qrtt spend the evening huddled round the only source of heat: a coal-burning toaster that has been bricked into the socket of an old fireplace. Every so often Mr. Qrtt opens the door and pelts the ashes with a mote of coal. Mrs. Qrtt ferries out the chow and spies on Waterhouse. She notices his slightly asymmetrical walk and manages to ferret out that he had a spot of polio at one point. He plays the organ—they have a pedal-powered harmonium in the parlor—and she remarks on that.

Waterhouse first sees Outer Qwghlm through a scupper. He doesn't even know what a scupper is, except a modality of vomiting. The ferry crew gave him and the other half-dozen passengers detailed vomiting instructions before they fought past the Utter Maurby breakwater, the salient point being that if you leaned over the rail, you would almost certainly be swept overboard. Much better to get down on all fours and aim at a scupper. But half the time when Waterhouse peers down one of these, he sees not water but some distant point on the horizon, or seagulls chasing the ferry, or the distinctive three-pronged silhouette of Outer Qwghlm.

The prongs, called Sghrs, are basaltic columns. This being the middle of the Second World War, and Outer Qwghlm being the part of the British Isles closest to the action of the Battle of the Atlantic, they are now flecked with little white radio shacks and hairy with antennas. There is a fourth sghr, much lower than the others and easily mistaken for a mere hillock, that rises above Outer Qwghlm's only harbor (and, indeed, only settlement, not counting the naval base on the other side). On top of this fourth sghr is the castle that is the nominal home of Nigel St. John Gloamthorpby-Woadmire and that is to be the new headquarters of Detachment 2702.

Five minutes' walk encompasses the whole town. A furious rooster chases a feeble sheep down the main street. There is snow at the higher elevations, but just grey slush down here, which is indistinguishable from the grey cobblestones until you step on it and fall down on your ass. The *Encyclopedia Qwghlmiana* had made much use of the definite pronoun—the Town, the Castle, the Hotel, the Pub, the Pier. Waterhouse stops in at the Shithouse to deal with some aftershocks of the sea voyage, and then walks up the Street. The Automobile pulls up alongside and offers him a ride; it turns out to be the Taxi, too. It takes him round the Park where he notices the Statue (ancient Qwghlmians thrashing hapless Vikings); this gesture that does not go unnoted by the Taxi Driver, who veers into the Park to give him a better look.

The Statue is the sort that has a great deal to say and covers a correspondingly large expanse of real estate. Its pedestal is a slab of native basalt, covered on at least one side with what Waterhouse recognizes, from the *Encyclopedia,* as Qwghlmian runes. To an ignorant philistine, these might look like an endless, random series of sans-serif Xs, Is, Vs hyphens, asterisks, and upside-down Vs. But it is an enduring source of pride to—

"We didn't care for those Romans and that Julius Caesar fellow," observes the taxi driver, "and we weren't too taken with their alphabet either."

Indeed the *Encyclopedia Qwghlmiana* features a lengthy article about the local system of runes. The author of this article has such a chip on his shoulder that the thing is almost physically painful to read. *The Qwghlmian practice of eschewing the use of curves and loops, forming all glyphs out of straight lines, far from being crude—as some English scholars have asserted—gives the script a limpid austerity. It is an admirably functional style of writing in a place where (after all the trees were cut down by the English) most of the literate intellectual class suffered from chronic bilateral frostbite.*

Waterhouse has rolled down the window so that he can get a clearer view; apparently someone has lost the Squeegee. The chill breeze washing over his face finally begins to clear away his seasickness, to the point where he begins to wonder how he should go about making contact with the Whore.

Then he realizes, with some disappointment, that if the Whore has half a brain in her head, she's across the island at the naval base.

"Who's the wretch?" Waterhouse asks. He points to a corner of the statue, where a scrawny, downtrodden loser, with an iron collar welded around his neck and a chain dangling from that, quivers and quails at the carnage being meted out by the strapping Qwghlmian he-men. Waterhouse already knows the answer, but he can't resist asking.

"Hakh!" blurts the taxi driver, as if he is working up a loogie. "He is from Inner Qwghlm, I can only suppose."

"Of course."

This exchange seems to have put the driver into a foul and vengeful mood that can only be assuaged with some fast driving. There are a dozen or more switchbacks in the road up to the Castle, each one glazed with black ice and fraught with mortal danger. Waterhouse is glad he's not walking it, but the switchbacks and the skating motion of the taxi revive his motion sickness.

"Hakh!" the driver says, when they are about three-quarters of the way up, and nothing has been said for several minutes. "They practically laid out the welcome mat for the Romans. They spread their legs for the Vikings. There are probably Germans over there now!"

"Speaking of bile," Waterhouse says, "I need you to pull over. I'll walk from here."

The driver is startled and miffed, but he relents when Waterhouse explains that the alternative is a lengthy cleanup job. He even drives Duffel up to the top of the sghr and drops it off.

Detachment 2702 arrives at the Castle some fifteen minutes later in the person of Lawrence Pritchard Waterhouse USN, who is serving as the advance party. The walk gives him time to get his story straight, to get himself into character. Chattan has warned him that there will be servants, and that they will notice things, and that they will gossip. It would be much more convenient if the servants could simply be packed off to the mainland for the duration, but this would be a discourtesy to the duke. "You will," Chattan said, "have to work out a *modus vivendi*." Once Waterhouse had looked this term up, he agreed heartily.

The castle is a mound of rubble about the size of the Pentagon. The lee corner has been fitted out with a functional roof, electrical wiring, and a few other frills such as doors and windows. In this area, which is all Waterhouse gets to see for that first afternoon and evening, you can forget you are on Outer Qwghlm and pretend that you are in some greener and balmier place such as the Scottish Highlands.

The next morning, accompanied by the butler, Ghnxh, he strikes out into other parts of the building and is delighted to find that you can't even reach them without going outside; the internal connecting passages have been mortared shut to stanch the seasonal migrations of skrrghs (pronounced something like "skerries"), the frisky, bright-eyed, long-tailed mammals that are the mascot of the islands. This compartmentalization, while inconvenient, will be good for security.

Both Waterhouse and Ghnxh are encased in planklike wrappings of genuine Qwghlm wool, and the latter carries the GALVANICK LUCIPHER. The Galvanick Lucipher is of antique design. Ghnxh, who is about a hundred years old, can only smile in condescension at Waterhouse's U.S. Navy flashlight. In the *sotto voce* tones one might use to correct an enormous social gaffe, he explains that the galvanick lucipher is of such a superior design as to make any further reference to the Navy model a grating embarrassment for everyone concerned. He leads Waterhouse back to a special room behind the room behind the room behind the room behind the pantry, a room that exists solely for maintenance of the galvanick lucipher and the storage of its parts and supplies. The heart of the device is a hand-blown spherical glass jar comparable in volume to a gallon jug. Ghnxh, who suffers from a pretty advanced case of either hypothermia or Parkinson's, maneuvers a glass funnel into the neck of the jar. Then he wrestles a glass carboy from a shelf. The carboy, labeled AQUA REGIA, is filled with a fulminant orange liquid. He removes its glass stopper, hugs it, and heaves it over so that the orange fluid begins to glug out into the funnel and thence into the jar. Where it splashes out onto the tabletop, something very much like smoke curls up as it eats holes just like the thousands of other holes already there. The fumes get into Waterhouse's lungs; they are astoundingly corrosive. He staggers out of the room for a while.

When he ventures back, he finds Ghnxh whittling an electrode from an ingot of pure carbon. The jar of aqua regia has been capped off now, and a variety of anodes, cathodes, and other working substances are suspended in it, held in place by clamps of hammered gold. Thick wires, in insulating sheaths of hand-knit asbestos, twist out of the jar and into the business end of the galvanick lucipher: a copper salad bowl whose mouth is closed off by a Fresnel lens like the ones on a lighthouse. When Ghnxh gets his carbon whittled to just the right size and shape, he fits it into a little hatch in the side of this bowl, and casually throws a Frankensteinian blade switch. A spark pops across the contacts like a firecracker.

For a moment, Waterhouse thinks that one wall of the building has collapsed, exposing them to the direct light of the sun. But Ghnxh has simply turned on the galvanick lucipher, which soon becomes about ten times brighter, as Ghnxh adjusts a bronze thumbscrew. Crushed with shame, Waterhouse puts his Navy flashlight back into its prissy little belt holster, and precedes Ghnxh out of the room, the galvanick lucipher casting palpable warmth on the back of his neck. "We've got about two hours before she goes dead on us," Ghnxh says significantly.

They work out a *modus vivendi,* all right: Waterhouse kicks an old door open and then Ghnxh strides into the room that is on the other side and sweeps the beam of the lantern around as if it were a flame-thrower, driving back dozens or hundreds of squealing skerries. Waterhouse clambers cautiously into the room, typically making his way over the collapsed remnants of whatever roof or story used to be overhead. He gives the place a quick inspection, trying to gauge how much effort would be required to make it liveable for any more advanced organism.

Half of the castle has, at one point or another, been burned down by a combination of Barbary corsairs, lightning bolts, Napoleon, and smoking in bed. The Barbary corsairs did the best job of it (probably just trying to stay warm), or maybe it's just that the elements have had longer to decompose what little was left behind by the flames. In any case, in that section of the castle, Waterhouse finds a place where there's not too much rubble to shovel out, and where they can quickly enclose an adequate space with a combination of tarps and planks. It is diametrically opposed to the part of the castle that is still inhabited, which exposes it to winter storms but protects it from the prying eyes of the staff. Waterhouse paces off some rough measurements, then goes to his room, leaving Ghnxh to see to the decommissioning of the galvanick lucipher.

Waterhouse sketches out some plans for the upcoming work, at long last putting his hitherto misspent engineering skills to some use. He draws up a bill of required materials, naturally involving a good many numbers: 100 8' 2 x 4s is a typical entry. He writes out the list a second time, in words not numbers: ONE HUNDRED EIGHT FOOT TWO BY FOURS. This wording is potentially confusing, so he changes it to TWO BY FOUR BOARDS ONE HUNDRED COUNT LENGTH EIGHT FEET.

Next he pulls a sheet of what looks like ledger paper, divided vertically into groups of five columns. Into these columns he transcribes the message, ignoring spaces:

T W O B Y F O U R B O A R D S O N E H U N D R E D
C O U N T L E N G T H E I G H T F E E T

and so on. Wherever he encounters a letter J he writes I in its stead, so that JOIST comes out as IOIST. He only uses every third line of the page.

Ever since he left Bletchley Park, he has been carrying several sheets of onionskin paper around in his breast pocket; when he sleeps, he puts them under his pillow. Now he takes them out and selects one page, which has a serial number typed across the top and is otherwise covered with neatly typed letters like this:

A T H O P C O G N Q D L T U I C A P R H M U L E P

and so on, all the way down to the bottom of the page.

These sheets were typed up by a Mrs. Tenney, an aged vicar's wife who works at Bletchley Park. Mrs. Tenney has a peculiar job which consists of the following: she takes two sheets of onionskin paper and puts a sheet of carbon paper between them and rolls them into a typewriter. She types a serial number at the top. Then she turns the crank on a device used in bingo parlors, consisting of a spherical cage containing twenty-five wooden balls, each with a letter printed on it (the letter J is not used). After spinning the cage the exact number of times specified in the procedure manual, she closes her eyes, reaches through a hatch in the cage, and removes a ball at random. She reads the letter off the ball and types it, then replaces the ball, closes the hatch, and repeats the process. From time to time, serious-looking men come into the room, exchange pleasantries with her, and take away the sheets that she has produced. These sheets end up in the possession of men like Waterhouse, and men in infinitely more desperate and dangerous circumstances, all over the world. They are called one-time pads.

He copies the letters from the one-time pad into the empty lines beneath his message:

T W O B Y F O U R B O A R D S O N E H U N D R E D
A T H O P C O G N Q D L T U I C A P R H M U L E P

When he is finished, two out of every three lines are occupied.

Finally, he returns to the top of the page one last time and begins to consider the letters two at a time. The first letter in the message is T. The first letter from the one-time pad, directly below it in the same column, is A.

A is the first letter in the alphabet and so Waterhouse, who has been doing this cipher stuff for much too long, thinks of it as being synonymous with the number 1. In the same way, T is equivalent to 19 if you are working in a J-less alphabet. Add 1 to 19 and you get 20, which is the letter U. So, in the first column beneath T and A, Waterhouse writes a U.

The next vertical pair is W and T, or 22 and 19, which in normal arithmetic add up to 41, which has no letter equivalent; it's too large. But it has been many years since Waterhouse did normal arithmetic. He has retrained his mind to work in modular arithmetic—specifically, modulo 25, which means that you divide everything by 25 and consider only the remainder. 41 divided by 25 is 1 with a remainder of 16. Throw away the 1 and the 16 translates into the letter Q, which is what Waterhouse writes in the second column. In the third column, O and H give 14 + 8 = 22 which is W. In the fourth, B and O give 14 + 2 = 16 which is Q. And in the fifth, Y and P give 24 + 15 which is 39. 39 divided by 25 is 1 with a remainder of 14. Or, as Waterhouse would phrase it, 39 modulo 25 equals 14. The letter for 14 is O. So the first code group looks like

T W O B Y
A T H O P
U Q W Q O

By adding the random sequence ATHOP onto the meaningful sequence TWOBY, Waterhouse has produced undecipherable gibberish. When he has enciphered the entire message in this way, he takes out a new page and copies out only the ciphertext—UQWQO and so on.

The duke has a cast-iron telephone which he has put at Waterhouse's disposal. Waterhouse heaves it out of its cradle, rings the operator, places a call across the island to the naval station, and gets through to a radio man. He reads the ciphertext message to him letter by letter. The radio man copies it down and informs Waterhouse that it will be transmitted forthwith.

Very soon, Colonel Chattan, down in Bletchley Park, will receive a message that begins with UQWQO and goes on in that vein. Chattan possesses the other copy of Mrs. Tenney's one-time pad. He will write out the ciphertext first, using every third line. Beneath the ciphertext he will copy in the text from the one-time pad:

U Q W Q O

A T H O P

He will then perform a subtraction where Waterhouse performed an addition. U minus A means 20 minus 1 which equals 19 which gives the letter T. Q minus T means 16 minus 19 which equals -3, giving us 22 which is W. And so on. Having deciphered the whole message, he'll get to work, and eventually two by fours one hundred count will show up at the Pier.

WHY

EPIPHYTE CORP.'S BUSINESS PLAN IS ABOUT AN INCH THICK, NEI-ther fat nor skinny as these things go. The interior pages are slickly and groovily desktop-published out of Avi's laptop. The covers are rugged hand-laid paper of rice chaff, bamboo tailings, free-range hemp, and crystalline glacial meltwater made by wizened artisans operating out of a mist-shrouded temple hewn from living volcanic rock on some island known only to aerobically gifted, Spandex-sheathed Left Coast travel bores. An impressionistic map of the South China Sea has been dashed across these covers by molecularly reconstructed Ming Dynasty calligraphers using brushes of combed unicorn mane dipped into ink made of grinding down charcoal slabs fashioned by blind stylite monks from hand-charred fragments of the True Cross.

The actual content of the business plan hews to a logical structure straight out of the *Principia Mathematica*. Lesser entrepreneurs purchase business-plan-writing software: packages of boilerplate text and spread-sheets, craftily linked together so that you need only go through and fill in a few blanks. Avi and Beryl have written enough business plans between the two of them that they can smash them out from brute memory. Avi's business plans tend to go something like this:

MISSION: At [name of company] it is our conviction that [to do the stuff we want to do] and to increase shareholder value are not merely complementary activities—they are inextricably linked.

PURPOSE: To increase shareholder value by [doing stuff]

EXTREMELY SERIOUS WARNING (printed on a separate page,

in red letters on a yellow background): Unless you are as smart as Johann Karl Friedrich Gauss, savvy as a half-blind Calcutta bootblack, tough as General William Tecumseh Sherman, rich as the Queen of England, emotionally resilient as a Red Sox fan, and as generally able to take care of yourself as the average nuclear missile submarine commander, you should never have been allowed near this document. Please dispose of it as you would any piece of high-level radioactive waste and then arrange with a qualified surgeon to amputate your arms at the elbows and gouge your eyes from their sockets. This warning is necessary because once, a hundred years ago, a little old lady in Kentucky put a hundred dollars into a dry goods company which went belly-up and only returned her ninety-nine dollars. Ever since then the government has been on our asses. If you ignore this warning, read on at your peril—you are dead certain to lose everything you've got and live out your final decades beating back waves of termites in a Mississippi Delta leper colony.

Still reading? Great. Now that we've scared off the lightweights, let's get down to business.

EXECUTIVE SUMMARY: We will raise [some money], then [do some stuff] and increase shareholder value. Want details? Read on.

INTRODUCTION: [This trend], which everyone knows about, and [that trend], which is so incredibly arcane that you probably didn't know about it until just now, and [this other trend over here] which might seem, at first blush, to be completely unrelated, when all taken together, lead us to the (proprietary, secret, heavily patented, trademarked, and NDAed) insight that we could increase shareholder value by [doing stuff]. We will need $ [a large number] and after [not too long] we will be able to realize an increase in value to $ [an even larger number], unless [hell freezes over in midsummer].

DETAILS:

Phase 1: After taking vows of celibacy and abstinence and foregoing all of our material possessions for homespun robes, we (viz. appended resumes) will move into a modest complex of scavenged refrigerator boxes in the central Gobi Desert, where real estate is so cheap that we are actually being paid to occupy it, thereby enhancing shareholder value even before we have actually done anything. On a daily ration consisting of a handful of uncooked rice and a ladleful of water, we will [begin to do stuff].

Phase 2, 3, 4, . . . , n − 1: We will [do more stuff, steadily enhancing shareholder value in the process] unless [the earth is struck by an asteroid a thousand miles in diameter, in which case certain assumptions will have to be readjusted; refer to Spreadsheets 397–413].

Phase n: before the ink on our Nobel Prize certificates is dry, we will confiscate the property of our competitors, including anyone foolish enough to have invested in their pathetic companies. We will sell all of these people into slavery. All proceeds will be redistributed among our shareholders, who will hardly notice, since Spreadsheet 265 demonstrates that, by this time, the company will be larger than the British Empire at its zenith.

SPREADSHEETS: [Pages and pages of numbers in tiny print, conveniently summarized by graphs that all seem to be exponential curves screaming heavenward, albeit with enough pseudo-random noise in them to lend plausibility].

RESUMES: Just recall the opening reel of *The Magnificent Seven* and you won't have to bother with this part; you should crawl to us on hands and knees and beg us for the privilege of paying our salaries.

To Randy and the others, the business plan functions as Torah, master calendar, motivational text, philosophical treatise. It is a dynamic, living document. Its spreadsheets are palimpsests, linked to the company's bank accounts and financial records so that they automatically adjust whenever money flows in or out. Beryl handles that stuff. Avi handles the words—the underlying, abstract plan, and the concrete details, that inform those spreadsheets—interpreting the numbers. Avi's part of the plan mutates too, from week to week, as he gets new input from articles in the *Asian Wall Street Journal,* conversations with government officials in flyblown Shenzhen karaoke bars, remote-sensing data pouring in from satellites, and obscure technical journals analyzing the latest advances in optical fiber technology. Avi's brain also digests the ideas of Randy and the other members of the group and incorporates them into the plan. Every quarter, they take a snapshot of the business plan in its current state, trowel some Maybelline onto it, and ship out new copies to investors.

Plan Number Five is about to be mailed simultaneous with the company's first anniversary. An early draft had been sent to each of them a couple of weeks ago in an encrypted e-mail message, which Randy hadn't bothered to read, assuming he knew its contents. But little cues that he's picked up in the last few days tell him that he'd better find out what the damn thing actually says.

He fires up his laptop, plugs it into a telephone jack, opens up his communications software, and dials a number in California. This last turns out to be easy, because this is a modern hotel and Kinakuta has a modern phone system. If it hadn't been easy, it probably would have been impossible.

In a small, stuffy, perpetually dark, hot-plastic-scented wiring closet, in a cubicled office suite leased by Novus Ordo Seclorum Systems Incorporated, sandwiched between an escrow company and a discount travel agent in the most banal imaginable disco-era office building in Los Altos, California, a modem wakes up and spews noise down a wire. The noise eventually travels under the Pacific as a pattern of scintillations in a filament of glass so transparent that if the ocean itself were made out of the same stuff, you'd be able to see Hawaii from California. Eventually the information reaches Randy's computer, which spews noise back. The modem in Los Altos is one of half a dozen that are all connected to the back of the same computer, an entirely typical looking tower PC of a generic brand, which has been running, night and day, for about eight months now. They turned its monitor off about seven months ago because it was just wasting electricity. Then John Cantrell (who is on the board of Novus Ordo Seclorum Systems Inc., and made arrangements to put it in the company's closet) borrowed the monitor because one of the coders who was working on the latest upgrade of Ordo needed a second screen. Later, Randy disconnected the keyboard and mouse because, without a monitor, only bad information could be fed into the system. Now it is just a faintly hissing off-white obelisk with no human interface other than a cyclopean green LED staring out over a dark landscape of empty pizza boxes.

But there is a thick coaxial cable connecting it to the Internet. Randy's computer talks to it for a few moments, negotiating the terms of a Point-to-Point Protocol, or PPP connection, and then Randy's little laptop is part of the Internet, too; he can send data to Los Altos, and the lonely computer there, which is named Tombstone, will route it in the general direction of any of several tens of millions of other Internet machines.

Tombstone, or tombstone.epiphyte.com as it is known to the Internet, has an inglorious existence as a mail drop and a cache for files. It does nothing that a thousand online services couldn't do for them more easily and cheaply. But Avi, with his genius for imagining the most horrific conceivable worst-case scenarios, demanded that they have their own machine, and that Randy and the others go through its kernel code one line at a time to verify that there were no security holes. In every bookstore window in the Bay Area, piled in heaps, were thousands of copies of three different books about how a famous cracker had established total control over a couple of well-known online services. Consequently, Epiphyte Corp. could not possibly use such an online service for its secret files while with a straight face saying that it was exerting due diligence on its shareholders' behalf. Thus tombstone.epiphyte.com.

Randy logs on and checks his mail: forty-seven messages, including one that came two days ago from Avi (avi@epiphyte.com) that is labeled:

epiphyteBizPlan.5.4.ordo. Epiphyte Business Plan, 5th edition, 4th draft, in a file format that can only be read by [Novus] Ordo [Seclorum], which is wholly owned by the company of the same name, but whose hard parts were written, as it happens, by John Cantrell.

He tells the computer to begin downloading that file—it's going to take a while. In the meantime, he scrolls through the list of other messages, checking the names of their senders, subject headings, and sizes, trying to figure out, first of all, how many of these can simply be thrown away unread.

Two messages jump out because they are from an address that ends with aol.com, the cyberspace neighborhood of parents and children but never of students, hackers, or people who actually work in high-tech. Both of these are from Randy's lawyer, who is trying to get Randy's financial affairs disentangled from Charlene's with as little rancor as possible. Randy feels his blood pressure spiking, millions of capillaries in the brain bulging ominously. But they are very short files, and the subject headings seem innocuous, so he calms down and decides not to worry about them now.

Five messages originate from computers with extremely familiar names—systems that are part of the campus computer network he used to run. The messages come from system administrators who took over the reins when Randy left, guys who long ago asked him all the easy questions, such as *What's the best place to order pizza?* and *Where did you hide the staples?* and have now gotten to the point of e-mailing him chunks of arcane code that he wrote years ago with questions like, *Was this an error, or something incredibly clever I haven't figured out yet?* Randy declines to answer those messages just now.

There are about a dozen message from friends, some of them just passing along Net humor that he's already seen a hundred times. Another dozen from other members of Epiphyte Corp., mostly concerning the details of their itineraries as they all converge on Kinakuta for tomorrow's meeting.

That leaves a dozen or so other messages which belong in a special category that did not exist until a week ago, when a new issue of *TURING Magazine* came out, containing an article about the Kinakuta data haven project, and a cover photo of Randy on a boat in the Philippines. Avi had gone to some lengths to plant this article so that he would have something to wave in the faces of the other participants in tomorrow's meeting. *TURING* is such a visual magazine that it cannot be viewed without the protection of welding goggles, and so they insisted on a picture. A photographer was dispatched to the Crypt, which was found visually wanting. A tizzy ensued. The photographer was diverted to Manila Bay where he captured Randy standing on a boat deck next to a big reel of orange cable, a volcano rising from the smog in the background. The magazine won't even be on newsstands for another month, but the article is on the Web as of a week ago, where it instantly became a subject of discussion on the Secret Admirers mailing list, which is where all of the cool guys like John Cantrell hang out to discuss the very latest hashing algorithms and pseudo-random-number generators. Because Randy happened to be in the picture, they have mistakenly fastened upon him as being more of a prime mover than he really is. This has spawned a new category of messages in Randy's mailbox: unsolicited advice and criticism from crypto freaks worldwide. At the moment there are fourteen such messages in his in-box, eight of them from a person, or persons, identifying himself, or themselves, as Admiral Isoroku Yamamoto.

It would be tempting to ignore these, but the problem is that a solid majority of people on the Secret Admirers mailing list are about ten times as smart as Randy. You can check the list anytime you want and find a mathematics professor in Russia slugging it out with another mathematics professor in India, kilobyte for kilobyte, over some stupefyingly arcane detail in prime number theory, while an eighteen-year-old, tube-fed math prodigy in Cambridge jumps in every few days with an even more stupefying explanation of why they are both wrong.

So when people like this send him mail, Randy tries to at least skim it. He is a little leery of the ones who identify themselves as Admiral Isoroku Yamamoto, or with the number 56 (which is a code meaning Yamamoto). But just because they are political-verging-on-flaky doesn't mean they don't know their math.

```
To: randy@tombstone.epiphyte.com
From: 56@laundry.org
Subject: data haven
Do you have public key somewhere posted? I would like to
exchange mail with you but I don't want Paul Comstock to
read it:) My public key if you care to respond is
 —BEGIN ORDO PUBLIC KEY BLOCK—
 (lines and lines of gibberish)
 —END ORDO PUBLIC KEY BLOCK—
Your concept of data haven is good but has important lim-
its. What if Philippine government shuts down your cable?
Or if the good Sultan changes his mind, decides to nation-
alize your computers, read all the disks? What is needed
is not ONE data haven but a NETWORK of data havens—more
```

```
robust, just like Internet is more robust than single
machine.
  Signed,
  The Admiral Isoroku Yamamoto who signs his messages
thus:
  —BEGIN ORDO SIGNATURE BLOCK—
  (lines and lines of gibberish)
  —END ORDO SIGNATURE BLOCK—
```

Randy closes that one without responding. Avi doesn't want them talking to Secret Admirers for fear that they will later be accused of stealing someone's ideas, so the reply to all of these e-mails is a form letter that Avi paid some intellectual property lawyer about ten thousand dollars to draft.

He reads another message simply because of the return address:

```
From: root@pallas.eruditorum.org
```

On a UNIX machine, "root" is the name of the most godlike of all users, the one who can read, erase, or edit any file, who can run any program, who can sign up new users and terminate existing ones. So receiving a message from someone who has the account name "root" is like getting a letter from someone who has the title "President" or "General" on his letterhead. Randy's been root on a few different systems, some of which were worth tens of millions of dollars, and professional courtesy demands he at least read this message.

```
I read about your project.
Why are you doing it?
```

followed by an Ordo signature block.

One has to assume this is an attempt to launch some sort of philosophical debate. Arguing with anonymous strangers on the Internet is a sucker's game because they almost always turn out to be—or to be indistinguishable from—self-righteous sixteen-year-olds possessing infinite amounts of free time. And yet the "root" address either means that this person is in charge of a large computer installation, or (much more likely) has a Finux box on his desk at home. Even a home Finux user has got to be several cuts above your average Internet-surfing dilettante.

Randy opens up a terminal window and types

```
whois eruditorum.org
```

and a second later gets back a block of text from the InterNIC:

```
eruditorum.org (Societas Eruditorum)
```

followed by a mailing address: a P.O. Box in Leipzig, Germany.

After that a few contact numbers are listed. All of them have the Seattle area code. But the three-digit exchanges, after the area code, look familiar to Randy, and he recognizes them as gateways into a forwarding service, popular among the highly mobile, that will bounce your voice mail, faxes, etc. to wherever you happen to be at the moment. Avi, for example, uses it all the time.

Scrolling down, Randy finds:

```
Record last updated on 18-Nov-98.
Record created on 1-Mar-90.
```

The "90" jumps out. That's a prehistoric date by Internet standards. It means that Societas Eruditorum was way ahead of the game. Especially for a group based in Leipzig, which was part of East Germany until about then.

```
Domain servers in listed order:
NS.SF.LAUNDRY.ORG
```

. . . followed by the dotted quad for laundry.org, which is a packet anonymizer used by many Secret Admirers to render their communications untraceable.

It all adds up to nothing, yet Randy can't get away with assuming that this message came from a bored sixteen-year-old. He should probably make some token response. But he's afraid that it'll turn out to be a come-on for some kind of business proposition: probably some mangy high-tech company that's looking for capital.

In the latest version of the business plan, there is probably some explanation of why Epiphyte(2) is building the Crypt. Randy can simply cut and paste it into an e-mail reply to root@pallas.eruditorum.org. It'll be something vaporous and shareholder-pleasing, and therefore kind of alienating. With any luck it will discourage this person from pestering him anymore. Randy double-clicks on Ordo's eyeball/pyramid icon, and it opens up a little text window on the screen, where he is invited to type commands. Ordo's also got a lovely graphical user interface, but Randy scorns it. No menus or buttons for him. He types

```
>decrypt epiphyteBizPlan.5.4.ordo
```

The computer responds

```
verify your identity: enter the pass phrase or ''bio'' to
opt for biometric verification.
```

Before Ordo will decrypt the file, it needs to have the private key: all 4096 bits of it. The key is stored on Randy's hard disk. But bad guys can break into hotel rooms and read the contents of hard disks, so the key itself has been encrypted. In order to decrypt it, Ordo needs the key to the key, which (in Cantrell's one concession to user-friendliness) is a pass phrase: a string of words, easier to remember than 4096 binary digits. But it has to be a long phrase or else it's too easy to break.

The last time Randy changed his pass phrase, he was reading another World War II memoir. He types:

```
>with hoarse shouts of ''banzai!'' the drunken Nips
swarmed out of their trenches, their swords and bayonets
flashing in the beams of our searchlights
```

and hits the "return" key. Ordo responds:

```
incorrect pass phrase
reenter the pass phrase or ''bio'' to use biometric
verification.
```

Randy curses and tries it a few more times, with slight changes in punctuation. Nothing works.

In desperation and out of curiosity, he tries:

```
bio
```

and the software responds:

```
unable to locate biometric configuration file. Talk to Can-
trell :-/
```

Which is of course not a normal part of the software. Ordo does not come with biometric verification, nor do its error messages refer to John Cantrell, or anyone else, by name. Cantrell has apparently written a plug-in module, a little add-on, and distributed it to his friends in Epiphyte(2).

"Fine," Randy says, picks up his phone, and dials John Cantrell's room number. This being a brand-new, modern hotel, he gets a voice mail box in which John has actually bothered to record an informative greeting.

"This is John Cantrell of Novus Ordo Seclorum and Epiphyte Corporations. For those of you who have reached me using my universal phone number and consequently have no idea where I am: I am in the Hotel Foote Mansion in the Sultanate of Kinakuta—please consult a quality atlas. It is four o'clock in the afternoon, Thursday March twenty-first. I'm probably down in the Bomb and Grapnel."

The Bomb and Grapnel is the pirate-themed hotel bar, which is not as cheesy as it sounds. It is decorated with (among other museum-grade memorabilia) several brass cannon that seem authentic. John Cantrell is seated at a corner table, looking as at home here as a man in a black cowboy hat possibly can. His laptop is open on the table next to a rum drink that has been served up in a soup tureen. A two-foot-long straw connects it to Cantrell's mouth. He sucks and types. Watching incredulously is a cadre of tough-looking Chinese businessmen sitting at the bar; when they see Randy coming in, carrying his own laptop, they buzz up. *Now there's two of them!*

Cantrell looks up and grins—something he cannot do without looking fiendish. He and Randy shake hands triumphantly. Even though they've only been riding around on 747s, they feel like Stanley and Livingstone.

"Nice tan," Cantrell says puckishly, all but twirling his mustache. Randy's caught off guard, starts and stops talking twice, finally shakes his head in defeat. Both men laugh.

"I got the tan on boats," Randy says, "not by the hotel pool. The last couple of weeks, I've been putting out fires all over the place."

"Nothing that'll impact shareholder value, I hope," Cantrell deadpans.

Randy says, "You're looking encouragingly pale."

"Everything's fine on my end," Cantrell says. "It's like I predicted—lots of Secret Admirers want to work on a real data haven."

Randy orders a Guinness and says, "You also predicted that a lot of those people would turn out to be squirrelly and undisciplined."

"Didn't hire those," Cantrell says. "And with Eb to handle the weird stuff, we've been able to roll right over the few speed bumps we've encountered."

"Have you seen the Crypt?"

Cantrell raises an eyebrow and shoots him a flawless imitation of a paranoid glance. "It's like that NORAD command bunker in Colorado Springs," he says.

"Yeah!" Randy laughs. "Cheyenne Mountain."

"It's too big," Cantrell announces. He knows Randy is thinking the same thing.

So Randy decides to play devil's advocate. "But the sultan does everything big. There are big paintings of him in the big airport."

Cantrell shakes his head. "The Information Ministry is a serious project. The sultan didn't just make it up. His technocrats conceived it."

"I'm told Avi did a little bit of deft turkey-baster work . . ."

"Whatever. But the people behind it, like Mohammed Pragasu, are all Stanford B-School types. Oxford and Sorbonne graduates. It's been engineered to the doorstops by Germans. That cave is not a monument to the sultan."

"No, it's not a vanity project," Randy agrees, thinking of the chilly machine room that Tom Howard is building a thousand feet below the cloud forest.

"So there must be some *rational* explanation for how big it is."

"Maybe it's in the business plan?" ventures Randy.

Cantrell shrugs; he hasn't read it either. "The last one I read cover-to-cover was Plan One. A year ago," admits Randy.

"That was a good business plan," Cantrell says.*

Randy changes the subject. "I forgot my pass phrase. Need to do that biometric thing with you."

"It's too noisy here," Cantrell says, "it works by listening to your voice, doing Fourier shit, remembering a few key numbers. We'll do it in my room later."

Feeling some need to explain why he hasn't been keeping up with his e-mail, Randy says, "I have been totally obsessed, interfacing with these AVCLA people in Manila."

"Yup. How's that going?"

"Look. My job's pretty simple," Randy says. "There's that big Nipponese cable from Taiwan down to Luzon. A router at each end. Then there's the network of short-run, interisland cables that the AVCLA people are laying in the Philippines. Each cable segment begins and ends at a router, as you know. My job is to program the routers, make sure the data will always have a clear path from Taiwan to Kinakuta."

Cantrell glances away, worried that he's about to get bored. Randy practically lunges across the table, because he knows it's not boring. "John! You are a major credit card company!"

"Okay." Cantrell meets his gaze, slightly unnerved.

"You are storing your data in the Kinakuta data haven. You need to download a terabyte of crucial data. You begin the process—your encrypted bytes are screaming up through the Philippines at a gigabyte per second, to Taiwan, from there across to the States." Randy pauses and swigs Guinness, building the drama. "Then a ferry capsizes off Cebu."

"So?"

"So, in the space of ten minutes, a hundred thousand Filipinos all pick up their telephones simultaneously."

Cantrell actually whacks his forehead. "Oh, my god!"

"Now, you understand! I've been configuring this network so that no matter what happens, the data continues to flow to that credit-card company. Maybe at a reduced speed—but it flows."

"Well, I can see how that would keep you busy."

---

*Cantrell alludes to the fact that Plan One brought them a couple of million dollars in seed money from a venture capital outfit in San Mateo called the Springboard Group.

"And that's why all I'm really up to speed on is these routers. And incidentally they're good routers, but they just don't have enough capacity to feed a Crypt of that size, or justify it economically."

"The gist of Avi and Beryl's explanation," Cantrell says, "is that Epiphyte is no longer the sole carrier into the Crypt."

"But we're laying the cable here from Palawan—"

"The sultan's minions have been out drumming up business," Cantrell says. "Avi and Beryl are being vague, but from comparing notes with Tom, and reading tea leaves, methinks there's one, maybe two other cables coming into Kinakuta."

"Wow!" Randy says. It's all he can think of. "Wow!" He drinks about half of his Guinness. "It makes sense. If they're doing it once with us, they can do it again, with other carriers."

"They used us as leverage to bring in others," Cantrell says.

"Well . . . the question is, then, is the cable through the Philippines still needed? Or wanted?"

"Yup," Cantrell says.

"It is?"

"No. I mean, yup, that's the question, all right."

Randy considers it. "Actually, this could be good news for *your* phase of the operation. More pipes into the Crypt means more business in the long run."

Cantrell raises his eyebrows, a little worried about Randy's feelings. Randy leans back in his chair and says, "We've had debates before about whether it makes sense for Epiphyte to be screwing around with cables and routers in the Philippines."

Cantrell says, "The business plan has always maintained that it would make economic sense to be running a cable through the Philippines even if there weren't a Crypt at the end of it."

"The business plan has to say the Intra-Philippines network could be spun off as an independent business, and still survive," Randy says, "to justify our doing it."

Neither one of them needs to say any more. They've been concentrating on each other pretty intensely for a while, shutting out the rest of the bar with their postures, and now, spontaneously, both of them lean back, stretch, and begin looking around. The timing's fortuitous, because Goto Furudenendu has just come in with a posse of what Randy guesses are civil engineers: healthy-looking, clean-cut Nipponese men in their thirties. Randy invites him over with a smile, then flags down their waiter and orders a few of those great big bottles of bitterly cold Nipponese beer.

"This reminds me—the Secret Admirers are really on my case," Randy says.

Cantrell grins, showing some affection for those crazy Secret Admirers. "Smart, rabidly paranoid people are the backbone of cryptology," he says, "but they don't always understand business."

"Maybe they understand it too well," Randy says. He is left with some residual annoyance that he came down to the Bomb and Grapnel party in order to answer the question posed by root@eruditorum.org ("Why are you doing it?") and he still doesn't know. As a matter of fact, he knows less now than he did before.

Then the men from Goto join them, and it just happens that Eberhard Föhr and Tom Howard show up at just the same time. There is a combinatorial explosion of name-card exchanges and introductions. It seems like protocol demands a lot of serious social drinking—now Randy's had inadvertently challenged these guys' politeness by ordering them beer, and they have to demonstrate that they will not be bested in any such contest. Tables get pushed together and everything gets just unbelievably jovial. Eb has to order some beer for everyone too. Pretty soon things have degenerated into karaoke. Randy gets up and sings "Me and You and a Dog Named Boo." It's a good choice because it's a mellow, laid-back song that doesn't demand lots of emoting. Or singing ability, for that matter.

At some point Tom Howard puts his beefy arm up on the back of Cantrell's chair, the better to shout into his ear. Their matched Eutropian bracelets, engraved with "Hello Doctor, please freeze me as follows" messages, are glittery and conspicuous, and Randy's nervous that the Nipponese guys are going to notice this and ask questions that will be exceedingly difficult to answer. Tom is reminding Cantrell of something (for some reason they always refer to Cantrell in this way; some people are just made to be called by last names). Cantrell nods and shoots Randy a quick and somewhat furtive look. When Randy looks back at him, Cantrell glances down apologetically and takes to chivvying his beer bottle nervously between his hands. Tom just keeps looking at Randy kind of interestedly. All of this motivated glancing finally brings Randy and Tom and Cantrell together at the farthest end of the bar from the karaoke speakers.

"So, you know Andrew Loeb," Cantrell says. It's clear he's basically dismayed by this and yet sort of impressed too, as if he'd just learned that Randy had once beaten a man to death with his bare hands and then just never bothered to mention it.

"It's true," Randy says. "As well as anyone can know a guy like that."

Cantrell is paying undue diligence to the project of picking the label off of his beer bottle and so Tom picks up the thread now. "You were in business together?"

"Not really. Can I ask how you guys are aware of this? I mean, how do you even know that Andrew Loeb exists in the first place? Because of the Digibomber thing?"

"Oh, no—it was after that. Andy became a figure of note in some of the circles where Tom and I both hang out," Cantrell says.

"The only circles I can imagine that Andy'd be a part of would be primitive survivalists, and people who believe they've been Satanically ritually abused."

Randy says this mindlessly, as if his mouth is a mechanical teletype hammering out a weather forecast. It kind of hangs there.

"That helps fill in a few gaps," Tom finally says.

"What did you think when the FBI searched his cabin?" Cantrell asks, his grin returned.

"I didn't know what to think," Randy says. "I remember watching the videotape on the news—the agents coming out of that shack with boxes of evidence, and thinking my name must be on papers in them. That somehow I'd get mixed up in the case as a result."

"Did the FBI ever contact you?" Tom asks.

"No. I think that once they searched through all of his stuff, they figured out pretty quickly that he wasn't the Digibomber, and crossed him off the list."

"Well, not long after that happened, Andy Loeb showed up on the Net," Cantrell says.

"I find that impossible to believe."

"So did we. I mean, we'd all received copies of his manifestoes—printed on this grey recycled paper that was like the sheets of fuzz that you peel off a clothes dryer's lint trap."

"He used some kind of organic, water-based ink that flaked off like black dandruff," Tom says.

"We used to joke about having Andy-grit all over our desks," Cantrell says. "So when this guy called Andy Loeb showed up on the Secret Admirers mailing list, and the Eutropia newsgroup, posting all of these long rants, we refused to believe it was him."

"We thought that someone had just written really brilliant parodies of his prose style," Cantrell says.

"But when they kept coming, day after day, and he started getting into these long dialogs with people, it became obvious that it really was him," Tom grumbles.

"How did he square that with being a Luddite?"

Cantrell: "He said that he'd always thought of computers as a force that alienated and atomized society."

Tom: "But as the result of being the number one Digibomber suspect for a while, he'd been forcibly made aware of the Internet, which changed computers by connecting them."

"Oh, my god!" Randy says.

"And he'd been mulling over the Internet while he was doing whatever Andrew Loeb does," Tom continues.

Randy: "Squatting naked in icy mountain streams strangling muskrats with his bare hands."

Tom: "And he'd realized computers could be a tool to unite society."

Randy: "And I'll bet he was just the guy to unite it."

Cantrell: "Well, that's actually not far away from what he said."

Randy: "So, are you about to tell me that he became a Eutropian?"

Cantrell: "Well, no. It's more like he discovered a schism in the Eutropian movement we didn't know was there, and created his own splinter group."

Randy: "I think of the Eutropians as being totally hard-core individuals, pure libertarians."

"Well, yeah!" Cantrell says. "But the basic premise of Eutropianism is that technology has made us post-human. That Homo sapiens plus technology is effectively a whole new species: immortal, omnipresent because of the Net, and headed towards omnipotence. Now, the first people to talk that way were libertarians."

Tom says, "But the idea has attracted all kinds of people—including Andy Loeb. He showed up one day and started yammering about hive minds."

"And of course he was flamed to a crisp by most of the Eutropians, because that concept was anathema to them," Cantrell says.

Tom: "But he kept at it, and after a while, some people started agreeing with him. Turned out there was really a pretty substantial faction within the Eutropians who *didn't* especially care for libertarianism and who found the idea of a hive mind attractive."

"So, now Andy's the leader of that faction?" Randy asks.

"I would suppose so," Cantrell says. "They split away and formed their own newsgroup. We haven't heard much from them in the last six months or so."

"So how did you become aware of a connection between Andy and me?"

"He stills pops into the Secret Admirers newsgroup from time to time," Tom says. "And there's been a lot of discussion there about the Crypt lately."

Cantrell says, "When he found out that you and Avi were involved, he posted this vast rant—twenty or thirty K of run-on sentences. Not very complimentary."

"Well, Jesus. What's his beef? He won the case. Completely bankrupted me. You'd think he'd have something better to do than beat this dead horse," Randy says, thumping himself on the chest. "Doesn't he have a day job?"

"He's some kind of a lawyer now," Cantrell says.

"Ha! Figures."

"He's been denouncing us," Tom says. "Capitalist roader. Atomizing society. Making the world safe for drug traffickers and Third-World kleptocrats."

"Well, at least he got something right," Randy says. He's delighted to have an answer, finally, to the question of why they're building the Crypt.

RETROGRADE MANEUVER

SIO IS A MUD CEMETERY. THOSE WHO HAVE ALREADY GIVEN their lives for the emperor compete for mire space with those who intend to. Bizarre forktailed American planes dive out of the sun every day to murder them with terrible glowing rains of cannon fire and the mind-crushing detonations of bombs, so they sleep in open-topped graves and only come out at night. But their pits are full of reeking water that churns with hostile life, and when the sun goes down, rain beats them, carrying into their bones the deadly chill of high altitudes. Every man in the 20th Division knows that he will not leave New Guinea alive, so it remains only to choose the method of death: surrender to be tortured, then massacred by the Australians? Put grenades to their heads? Remain where they are to be killed by the airplanes all day, and all night by malaria, dysentery, scrub typhus, starvation, and hypothermia? Or walk two hundred miles over mountains and flooding rivers to Madang, which is tantamount to suicide even when it is peacetime and you have food and medicine . . . ?

But that is what they are ordered to do. General Adachi flies to Sio— it is the first friendly plane they have seen in weeks—and lands on the rutted septic field that they call an airstrip, and orders the evacuation. They are to move inland in four detachments. Regiment by regiment, they bury their dead, pack up what is left of their equipment, hoard what little food is left, wait for dark, and trudge towards the mountains. The later echelons can find their path by smell, following the reek of dysentery and of the corpses dropped behind the pathfinder groups like breadcrumbs.

The top commanders stay to the end, and the radio platoon stays with them; without a powerful radio transmitter, and the cryptographic paraphernalia that goes with it, a general is not a general, a division is not a division. Finally they go off the air, and begin breaking the transmitter down into the smallest pieces they can, which unfortunately are not all that small; a divisional radio transmitter is a powerful beast, made for lighting up the ionosphere. It has an electrical generator, transformers, and other components that cannot be made light. The men of the radio platoon, who would find it difficult to move even the weight of their own skeletons over the mountains and across the surging rivers, will carry the additional burdens of engine blocks, fuel tanks, and transformers.

And the big steel trunk with all of the Army codebooks. These books were heavy as death when they were bone dry; now they are sodden. To carry them out is beyond imagining. The rules dictate that they must therefore be burned.

The men of the 20th Division's radio platoon are not much inclined to humor of any kind at the moment, not even the grim sardonic humor universal among soldiers. If anything in the world is capable of making them laugh at this moment, it is the concept of trying to construct a bonfire out of saturated codebooks in a swamp during a rainstorm. They might be able to burn them if they used a lot of aviation fuel—more than they actually have. Then the fire would produce a towering column of smoke that would draw P-38s as the scent of human flesh draws mosquitoes.

Burning them can't be necessary. New Guinea is a howling maelstrom of decay and destruction; the only things that endure are rocks and wasps. They rip off the covers to bring home as proof that they have been destroyed, then pack the books into their trunk and bury it in the bank of an especially vindictive river.

It's not a very good idea. But they have been getting bombed a lot. Even if the shrapnel misses you, the bomb's shock wave is like a stone wall moving at seven hundred miles an hour. Unlike a stone wall, it passes through your body, like a burst of light through a glass figurine. On its way through your flesh, it rearranges every part of you down to the mitochondrial level, disrupting every process in every cell, including whatever enables your brain to keep track of time and experience the world. A few of these detonations are enough to break the thread of consciousness into a snarl of tangled and chopped filaments. These men are not as human as they were when they left home; they cannot be expected to think clearly or to do things for good reasons. They throw mud on the trunk not as a sane procedure for getting rid of it but as a kind of ritual, just to demonstrate the proper respect for its lode of strange information.

Then they shoulder their burdens of iron and rice and begin to strain up into the mountains. Their comrades have left a trampled path that is already growing back into jungle. The mileposts are bodies—by now just stinking battlegrounds—disputed by frenzied mobs of microbes, bugs, beasts, and birds never catalogued by scientists.

HUFFDUFF

THE HUFFDUFF MAST IS PLANTED BEFORE THEY EVEN HAVE A roof on the new headquarters of Detachment 2702, and the huff-duff antenna is raised before there is any electricity to run it. Waterhouse does his best to pretend as if he cares. He lets the workers know: vast tank armadas clashing in the African desert might be dashing and romantic, but the real battle of this war (ignoring, as always, the Eastern Front) is the Battle of the Atlantic. We can't win the Battle of the Atlantic without sinking some U-boats, and we can't sink them until we find them, and we need a way of finding them other than the tried-and-true approach of letting our convoys steam through them and get blown to bits. That way, men, is to get this antenna in action as soon as humanly possible.

Waterhouse is no actor, but when the second ice storm of the week blows through and inflicts grievous damage on the antenna, and he has to stay up all night repairing it by the light of the Galvanick Lucifer, he is pretty sure that he has them hooked. The castle staff work late shifts to keep him supplied with hot tea and brandy, and the builders give him some zesty hip-hip-hoorays the next morning when the patched antenna is winched back up to the top of the mast. They are all so sure that they are saving lives in the North Atlantic that they would probably lynch him if they knew the truth.

This huffduff story is ridiculously plausible. It is so plausible that if Waterhouse were working for the Germans, he'd be suspicious. The antenna is a highly directional model. It receives a strong signal when pointed towards the source and a weak signal otherwise. The operator waits for a U-boat to begin transmitting and then swings the antenna back and forth until it gives the maximum reading; the direction of the antenna then gives the azimuth to the source. Two or more such readings, supplied by different huffduff stations can be used to triangulate the origin of the signal.

In order to keep up appearances, the station needs to be manned 24 hours a day which almost kills Waterhouse during the first weeks of 1943. The rest of Detachment 2702 has not shown up on schedule, so it is up to Waterhouse to preserve the illusion in the meantime.

Everyone within ten miles—basically, the entire civilian population of Qwghlm, or, to put it another way, the entire Qwghlmian race—can see the new huffduff antenna rising from the mast on the castle. They are not stupid people and some of them, at least, must understand that the damn thing doesn't do any good if it is always pointed in the same direction. If it's not moving, it's not working. And if it's not working, then just what the hell is going on up there in the castle anyway?

So Waterhouse has to move it. He lives in the chapel, sleeping—when he sleeps—in a hammock strung at a perilous altitude above the floor ("skerries" are excellent jumpers, he has found).

If he sleeps during the daytime, even casual observers in the town will notice that the antenna does not move. That's no good. But he can't sleep at night, when the Germans bounce their transmissions off the ionosphere between the U-boats in the North Atlantic and their bases in Bordeaux and Lorient because a really close observer—say an insomniacal castle worker, or a German spy up in the rocks with a pair of binoculars—will suspect that the immobile huffduff antenna is just a cover story. So Waterhouse tries to split the difference by sleeping for a few hours around dusk and another few hours around dawn—a plan that does not go over well with his body. And when he gets up, he has absolutely nothing to look forward to besides sitting at the huffduff console for eight or twelve hours at a stretch, watching the breath come out of his mouth, twiddling the antenna, listening to—nothing!

He freely stipulates that he is a selfish bastard for feeling sorry for himself when other men are being blown to bits.

Having gotten that out of the way, what is he going to do to stay sane? He has got his routine down pat: leave the antenna pointed generally westwards for a while, then swing it back and forth in diminishing arcs, pretending to zero in on a U-boat, then leave it sit for a while and do jumping jacks to warm back up. He has ditched his uniform for raiments of warm Qwghlmian wool. Every once in a while, at totally unpredictable intervals, members of the castle staff will burst in on him with an urn of soup or tea service or simply to see how he is doing and tell him what a fine chap he is. Once a day, he writes down a bunch of gibberish—his purported results—and dispatches it over to the naval base.

He divides his time between thinking about sex and thinking about mathematics. The former keeps intruding upon the latter. It gets worse when the stout fiftyish cook named Blanche, who has been bringing him his meals, comes down with dropsy or ague or gout or colic or some other Shakespearian ailment and is replaced by Margaret, who is about twenty and quite fetching.

Margaret really messes up his head. When it gets really intolerable, he goes to the latrine (so that the staff will not break in on him at an inopportune moment) and executes a Manual Override. But one thing he learned in Hawaii was that a Manual Override is unfortunately not the same as the real thing. The effect wears off too soon.

While he's waiting for it to wear off, he gets a lot of solid math done. Alan provided him with some notes on redundancy and entropy, relating to the voice encryption work he is currently doing in New York City. Waterhouse works through that stuff and comes up with some nice lemmas which he lamentably cannot send to Alan without violating both common sense and any number of security procedures. This done, he turns his attention to cryptology, pure and raw. He spent enough time at Bletchley Park to realize just how little of this art he really understood.

The U-boats talk on the radio way too much and everyone in the German Navy knows it. Their security experts have been nagging their brass to tighten up their security, and they finally did it by introducing the four-rotor version of the Enigma machine, which has knocked Bletchley Park on its ass for about a year . . .

Margaret has to walk round the castle out of doors to bring Waterhouse his meals, and by the time she gets here, her cheeks have turned rosy red. The steam coming from her mouth floats around her face like a silken veil—

Stop that, Lawrence! The subject of today's lecture is the German Naval four-wheel Enigma, known to them as Triton and to the Allies as Shark. Introduced on 2 February of last year (1942), it wasn't until the recovery of the beached German U-boat U-559 on 30 October that Bletchley Park got the material they needed to break the code. A couple of weeks ago, on 13 December, Bletchley Park finally busted Shark, and the internal communications of the German Navy became an open book to the Allies once more.

The first thing they have learned, as a result, is that the Germans have broken our merchant shipping codes wide open, and that all year long they have known exactly where to find the convoys.

All of this information has been provided to Lawrence Pritchard Waterhouse within the last few days, via the totally secure one-time pad channel. Bletchley is telling him this stuff because it raises a question of information theory, which is *his* department and *his* problem. The question is: how quickly can we replace our busted merchant shipping codes without tipping the Germans off to the fact that we have broken Shark?

Waterhouse does not have to think about this one for very long before he concludes that it is far too tricky to play games with. The only way to handle the situation is to concoct an incident of some sort that will explain to the Germans why we have totally lost faith in our own merchant shipping codes and are changing them. He writes up a message to this effect, and begins to encrypt it using the one-time pad that he shares with Chattan.

"Is everything quite all right?"

Waterhouse stands and whirls around, heart thrashing.

It is Margaret, standing there veiled in the steam of her own breath, a grey wool overcoat thrown over her maid's uniform, supporting a tray of tea and scones with grey wool mittens. The only parts of her not encased in wool are her ankles and her face. The former are well turned; Margaret is not above wearing heels. The latter has never been exposed to the direct rays of the sun and brings to mind rose petals strewn over Devonshire clotted cream.

"Oh! Let me take it!" Waterhouse blurts, and lunges forward with a jerkiness born of passion blended with hypothermia. While taking the tray from her hands, he inadvertently pulls off one of her mittens, which falls to the floor. "Sorry!" he says, realizing he has never seen her hands before. She has red polish on the nails of the offended hand, which she cups over her mouth and blows on. Her large green eyes are looking at him, full of placid expectation.

"Beg pardon?" Waterhouse says.

"Is everything quite all right?" she repeats.

"Yes! Why shouldn't it be?"

"The antenna," Margaret says. "It hasn't moved in over an hour."

Waterhouse is so flummoxed he can barely remain standing.

Margaret is still breathing through her lacquered fingertips, so that Waterhouse can only see her green eyes, which now angle and twinkle mischievously. She glances towards his hammock. "Been napping on the job, have we?"

Waterhouse's first impulse is to deny it and to explain the truth, which is that he was thinking about sex and crypto and forgot to move the antenna. But then he realizes that Margaret has supplied him with a better excuse. "Guilty as charged," he says. "Was up late last night."

"That tea will keep you alert," Margaret says. Then her eyes return to the hammock. She pulls her mitten back on. "What is it like?"

"What is what like?"

"Sleeping in one of those. Is it comfortable?"

"Very comfortable."

"Can I just see what it's like?"

"Ah. Well, it's very difficult to get in—at that height."

"You manage it, though, don't you?" she says chidingly. Waterhouse feels himself blushing. Margaret walks over to the hammock and kicks off her heels. Waterhouse winces to see her bare feet on the stone floor, which has not been warm since the Barbary Corsairs burned the place down. Her toenails are also painted red. "I don't mind it," Margaret says, "I'm a farmer's daughter. Come on, give me a leg up!"

Waterhouse has completely lost whatever control he might ever have had over the situation and himself. His tongue seems to be made of erectile tissue. So he lumbers over, bends down, and makes a stirrup of his hands. She puts her foot into it and launches herself into the hammock, disappearing with a whoop and a giggle into his bulky nest of grey wool blankets. The hammock swings back and forth across the center of the chapel, like a censer dispersing a faint lavender scent. It swings once, twice. It swings five times, ten times, twenty. Margaret is silent and motionless. Waterhouse stands as if his feet were planted in mortar. For the first time in weeks he does not know exactly what is going to happen next, and the loss of control leaves him stunned and helpless.

"It's dreamy," she says. Dreamily. Then, finally, she shifts. Waterhouse sees her little face peeking out over the edge, shrouded in the grey cowl of a blanket. "Ooh!" she screams, and flips flat on her back again. The sudden movement puts an eccentric jiggle into the rhythmic motion of the hammock.

"What's wrong?" Waterhouse says hopelessly.

"I'm afraid of heights!" she exclaims. "I'm so sorry, Lawrence, I should have warned you. Is it all right if I call you Lawrence?" She sounds as if she would be terribly hurt if he said no. And how can Lawrence wound the feelings of a pretty, barefoot, acrophobic girl, helpless in a hammock?

"Please. By all means," he says. But he knows perfectly well that the ball is still in his court. "Can I be of any assistance?"

"I should be so obliged," Margaret says.

"Well, would you like to climb down onto my shoulders, or something?" Waterhouse essays.

"I'm really far too terrified," she says.

There is only one way out. "Well. Would you take it the wrong way if I came up there to help?"

"It would be so heroic of you!" she says. "I should be unspeakably grateful."

"Well, then . . ."

"But I insist that you continue with your duties first!"

"Beg pardon?"

"Lawrence," Margaret says, "when I get down from this hammock I shall go to the kitchen and mop the floor—which is already quite clean enough, thank you. You, on the other hand, have important work to do—work that might save the lives of hundreds of men on some Atlantic convoy! And I know that you have been very naughty in sleeping on the job. I refuse to allow you up here until you have made amends."

"Very well," Waterhouse says, "you leave me no alternative. Duty calls." He squares his shoulders, spins on his heel, and marches back to his desk. Skerries have already made off with all of Margaret's scones, but he pours himself some tea. Then he resumes encrypting his instructions to Chattan: ONLY BRUTE FORCE APPROACH WILL BE SAFE PUT CODE BOOK ON SHIP INSERT SHIP IN MURMANSK CONVOY WAIT FOR FOG RAM NORWAY.

The one-time pad encryption takes a while. Lawrence can do mod 25 arithmetic in his sleep, but doing it with an erection is a different matter. "Lawrence? What are you doing?" Margaret asks from her nest in the hammock, which, Lawrence imagines, is getting warmer and cozier by the minute. He glances surreptitiously at her discarded high heels.

"Preparing my report," Lawrence says. "Doesn't do me any good to make observations if I don't send them out."

"Quite right," Margaret says thoughtfully.

This is an excellent time to stoke the chapel's pathetic iron stove. He puts in a few scoops of precious coal, his worksheet, and the page from the one-time pad that he has just used to do the encryption. "Should warm up now," he says.

"Oh, lovely," Margaret says, "I'm all shivery."

Lawrence recognizes this as his cue to initiate a rescue operation. About fifteen seconds later, he is up there in the hammock with Margaret. To the great surprise of neither one of them, the quarters are awkward and tight. There is some flopping around which ends with Lawrence on his back and Margaret on top of him, her thigh between his.

She is shocked to discover that he has an erection. Ashamed, apparently, that she did not anticipate his need. "You poor dear!" she exclaims. "Of course! How could I have been so dense! You must have been so lonely here." She kisses his cheek, which is nice since he is too stunned to move. "A brave warrior deserves all the support we civilians can possibly give him," she says, reaching down with one hand to open his fly.

Then she pulls the grey wool over her head and burrows to a new position. Lawrence Pritchard Waterhouse is stunned by what happens next. He gazes up at the ceiling of the chapel through half-closed eyes and thanks God for having sent him what is obviously a German spy and an angel of mercy rolled into one adorable package.

When it's finished, he opens his eyes again and takes a deep breath of cold Atlantic air. He is seeing everything around him with newfound clarity. Clearly, Margaret is going to do wonders for his productivity on the cryptological front—if he can only keep her coming back.

PAGES

IT HAS BEEN A LONG TIME SINCE HORSES RAN AT THE ASCOT Racetrack in Brisbane. The infield's a commotion of stretched khaki. The grass has died from lack of sun and from the trampling feet of enlisted men. The field has been punctured with latrines, mess tents have been pitched. Three shifts a day, the residents trudge across the track, round back of the silent and empty stables. In the field where the horses used to stretch their legs, two dozen quonset huts that have popped up like mushrooms. The men work in those huts, sitting before radios or typewriters or card files all day long, shirtless in the January heat.

It has been just as long since whores sunned themselves on the long veranda of the house on Henry Street, and passing gentlemen, on their way to or from the Ascot Racetrack, peered at their charms through the white railing, faltered, checked their wallets, forgot their scruples, turned on their heels, and climbed up the house's front stairs. Now the place is full of male officers and math freaks: mostly Australians on the ground floor, mostly Americans upstairs, and a sprinkling of lucky Brits who were spirited out of Singapore before General Yamashita, the Tiger of Malaya and the conqueror of that city, was able to capture them and mine their heads for crucial data.

Today the old bordello has been turned upside down; everyone with Ultra clearance is out in the garage, which thrums and roars with the sound of fans, and virtually glows with contained heat. In that garage is a rusted steel trunk, still spattered with riverbank mud that partially obscures the Nipponese characters stenciled on its sides. Had a Nipponese spy glimpsed the trunk during its feverish passage from the port to the whorehouse's garage, he would have recognized it as belonging to the radio platoon of the 20th Division, which is currently lost in the jungles of New Guinea.

The rumor, shouted over the sound of the fans, is that a digger— an Australian grunt—found it. His unit was sweeping the abandoned headquarters of the 20th Division for booby traps when his metal detector went nuts along the banks of a river.

The codebooks are stacked inside as neatly as gold bars. They are wet and mildewed and their front covers are all missing, but this is mint condition by the standards of wartime. Stripped to the waist and stream- ing with sweat, the men raise the books out one by one, like nurses lifting newborn infants from the bassinette, and carry them to tables where they slice away the rotten bindings and peel the sodden pages off the stacks one by one, hanging them from improvised clotheslines strung overhead. The stench and damp of New Guinea saturate the air as the river water trapped in those pages is lifted out by the rushing air; it all vents to the outside eventually, and half a mile downwind, pedestrians wrinkle their noses. The whorehouse's closets—still redolent of French perfume, powder, hairspray and jism, but now packed to the ceiling with office supplies—are raided for more string. The web of clotheslines grows, new layers crisscrossing above and below the old ones, every inch of string claimed by a wet page as soon as it is stretched. Each page is a grid, a table with hiragana or katakana or kanji in one box, a group of digits or Romanji in another box, and the pages all cross-referenced to other pages in a scheme only a cryptographer could love.

The photographer comes in, trailed by assistants who are burdened with miles of film. All he knows is that each page must be photographed perfectly. The malarial reek practically flattens him the moment he walks in the door, but when he recovers, his eyes scan the garage. All he can see, stretching as if to infinity, are pages dripping and curling, turning white as they dry, casting their grids of information into sharp relief, like the reticules of so many bomb sights, the graven crosshairs of so many periscopes, plunging through cloud and fog to focus, distinctly on the abdomens of Nipponese troopships, pregnant with North Borneo fuel, alive with burning steam.

"Sir! Would you mind telling me where we are going, sir!"

Lieutenant Monkberg heaves a deep, quivering sigh, his ribcage shuddering like a tin shack in a cyclone. He executes a none too snappy pushup. His hands are planted on the rim, and so this action extricates his head from the bowl, of a toilet—or "head," as it is referred to in this context: an alarmingly rundown freighter. He jerks down a strip of abrasive Euro-bumwad and wipes his mouth before looking up at Sergeant Robert Shaftoe, who has braced himself in the hatchway.

And Shaftoe does need some serious bracing, because he is carrying close to his own weight in gear. All of it was issued to him thoughtfully prepacked.

He could have left it that way. But this is not how an Eagle Scout operates. Bobby Shaftoe has gone through and unpacked all of it, spread it out on the deck, examined it, and repacked it.

This allowed Shaftoe to do some serious inferring. To be specific, he infers that the men of Detachment 2702 are expected to spend most of the next three weeks trying as hard as they can not to freeze to death. This will be punctuated by trying to kill a lot of well-armed sons of bitches. German, most likely.

"N-N-N-Norway," Lieutenant Monkberg says. He looks so pathetic that Shaftoe considers offering him some m-m-m-morphine, which induces a mild nausea of its own but holds back the greater nausea of seasickness. Then he comes to his senses, remembers that Lieutenant Monkberg is an officer whose duty it is to send him off to die, and decides that he can just go fuck himself sideways.

"Sir! What is the nature of our mission in Norway, sir?"

Monkberg unloads a rattling belch. "Ram and run," he says.

"Sir! Ram what, sir?"

"Norway."

"Sir! Run where, sir?"

"Sweden."

Shaftoe likes the sound of this. The perilous sea voyage through U-boat-infested waters, the collision with Norway, the desperate run across frozen Nazi-occupied territory, all seem trivial compared with the shining goal of dipping into the world's largest and purest reservoir of authentic Swedish poontang.

"Shaftoe! Wake up!"

"Sir! Yes, sir!"

"You have noticed the way we are dressed." Monkberg refers to the fact that they have discarded their dog tags and are all wearing civilian or merchant-marine clothing.

"Sir! Yes, sir!"

"We don't want the Huns, or anyone else, to know what we really are."

"Sir! Yes, sir!"

"Now, you might ask yourself, if we're supposed to look like civilians, then why the hell are we carrying tommy guns, grenades, demolition charges, et cetera."

"Sir! That was going to be my next question, sir!"

"Well, we have a cover story all worked out for that. Come with me."

Monkberg looks enthusiastic all of a sudden. He clambers to his feet and leads Shaftoe down various passageways and stairs to the freighter's cargo hold. "You know those other ships?"

Shaftoe looks blank.

"Those other ships around us? We are in the middle of a convoy, you know."

"Sir, yes sir!" Shaftoe says, a little less certainly. None of the men has been abovedecks very much in the hours since they were delivered, via submarine, to this wallowing wreck. Even if they had gone up for a look around they would have seen nothing but darkness and fog.

"A Murmansk convoy," Monkberg continues. "All of these ships are delivering weapons and supplies to the Soviet Union. See?"

They have reached a cargo hold. Monkberg turns on an overhead light, revealing—crates. Lots and lots and lots of crates.

"Full of weapons," Monkberg says, "including tommy guns, grenades, demolition charges, et cetera. Get my drift?"

"Sir, no sir! I do not get the lieutenant's drift!"

Monkberg comes one step closer to him. Unsettlingly close. He speaks, now, in a conspiratorial tone. "See, we're all just crew members on this merchant ship, making the run to Murmansk. It gets foggy. We get separated from our convoy. Then, boom! We slam into fucking Norway. We are stuck on Nazi-held territory. We have to make a break for Sweden! But wait a second, we say to ourselves. What about all those Germans between us and the Swedish border? Well, we had better be armed to the teeth, is what. And who is in a better position to arm themselves to the teeth than the crew of this merchant ship that is jam-

packed with armaments? So we run down into the cargo hold and hastily
pry open a few crates and arm ourselves."

Shaftoe looks at the crates. None of them have been pried open.

"Then," Monkberg continues, "we abandon ship and head for
Sweden."

There is a long silence. Shaftoe finally rouses himself to say, "Sir!
Yes, sir!"

"So get prying."

"Sir! Yes, sir!"

"And make it look hasty! Hasty! C'mon! Shake a leg!"

"Sir! Yes, sir!"

Shaftoe tries to get into the spirit of the thing. What's he going to
use to pry a crate open? No crowbars in sight. He exits the cargo hold
and strides down a passageway. Monkberg following him closely, hovering, urging him to be hastier: "You're in a hurry! The Nazis are
coming! You have to arm yourself! Think of your wife and kids back
in Glasgow or Lubbock or wherever the fuck you're from!"

"Oconomowoc, Wisconsin, sir!" Shaftoe says indignantly.

"No, no! Not in real life! In your pretend role as this stranded merchant son of a bitch! Look, Shaftoe! Look! Salvation is at hand!"

Shaftoe turns around to see Monkberg pointing at a cabinet marked
FIRE.

Shaftoe pulls the door open to find, among other implements, one of
those giant axes that firemen are always carrying in and out of burning
structures.

Thirty seconds later, he's down in the cargo hold, Paul Bunyaning a
crate of .45-caliber ammunition. "Faster! More haphazard!" Monkberg
shouts. "This isn't a precise operation, Shaftoe! You are in a blind panic!"
Then he says, "Goddamn it!" and runs forward and seizes the ax from
Shaftoe's hands.

Monkberg swings wildly, missing the crate entirely as he adjusts to the
tremendous weight and length of the implement. Shaftoe hits the deck
and rolls to safety. Monkberg finally gets his range and azimuth worked
out, and actually makes contact with the crate. Splinters and chips skitter
across the deck.

"See!" Monkberg says, looking over his shoulder at Shaftoe, "I want
splinteriness! I want chaos!" He is swinging the ax at the same time as
he's talking and looking at Shaftoe, and he's moving his feet too because
the ship is rocking, and consequently the blade of the weapon misses the
crate entirely, overshoots, and comes down right on Monkberg's ankle.

"Gadzooks!" Lieutenant Monkberg says, in a quiet, conversational tone. He is looking down at his ankle in fascination. Shaftoe comes over to see what's so interesting.

A good chunk of Monkberg's lower left leg has been neatly cross-sectioned. In the beam of Shaftoe's flashlight, it is possible to see severed blood vessels and ligaments sticking out of opposite sides of the meaty wound, like sabotaged bridges and pipelines dangling from the sides of a gorge.

"Sir! You are wounded, sir!" Shaftoe says. "Let me summon Lieutenant Root!"

"No! You stay here and work!" Monkberg says. "I can find Root myself." He reaches down with both hands and squeezes his leg above the wound, causing blood to gush out onto the deck. "This is perfect!" he says meditatively. "This adds so much realism."

After several repetitions of this order, Shaftoe reluctantly goes back to crate-hacking. Monkberg hobbles and staggers around the hold for a few minutes, bleeding on everything, then drags himself off in search of Enoch Root. The last thing he says is, "Remember! We are aiming for a ransacked effect!"

But the bit with the leg wound gets the idea across to Shaftoe more than Monkberg's words ever could. The sight of the blood brings up memories of Guadalcanal and more recent adventures. His last dose of morphine is wearing off, which makes him sharper. And he's starting to get really seasick, which makes him want to fight it by doing some hard work.

So he more or less goes berserk with that ax. He loses track of what is going on.

He wishes that Detachment 2702 could have stayed on dry land—preferably dry warm land such as that place they stayed, for two sunny weeks, in Italy.

The first part of that mission had been hard work, what with humping those barrels of shit around. But the remainder of it (except for the last few hours) had been just like shore leave, except that there weren't any women. Every day they'd taken turns at the observation site, looking out over the Bay of Naples with their telescopes and binoculars. Every night, Corporal Benjamin sat down and radioed more gibberish in Morse code.

One night, Benjamin received a message and spent some time deciphering it. He announced the news to Shaftoe: "The Germans know we're here."

"What do you mean, they know we're here?"

"They know that for at least six months we have had an observation post overlooking the Bay of Naples," Benjamin said.

"We've been here less than two weeks."

"They're going to begin searching this area tomorrow."

"Well, then let's get the fuck out of here," Shaftoe said.

"Colonel Chattan orders you to wait," Benjamin said, "until you know that the Germans know that we are here."

"But I do know that the Germans know that we are here," Shaftoe said, "you just told me."

"No, no no no no," Benjamin said, "wait until you *would* know that the Germans knew even if you *didn't* know from being told by Colonel Chattan over the radio."

"Are you fucking with me?"

"Orders," Benjamin said, and handed Shaftoe the deciphered message as proof.

As soon as the sun came up they could hear the observation planes crisscrossing the sky. Shaftoe was ready to execute their escape plan, and he made sure that the men were too. He sent some of those SAS blokes down to reconnoiter the choke points along their exit route. Shaftoe himself just laid down on his back and stared up at the sky, watching those planes.

Did he know that the Germans knew now?

Ever since he'd woken up, a couple of SAS blokes had been following him around, staring at him. Shaftoe finally looked in their direction and nodded. They ran away. A moment later he heard wrenches crashing against the insides of toolboxes.

The Germans had observation planes all over the fucking sky. That was pretty strong circumstantial evidence that the Germans knew. And those planes were clearly visible to Shaftoe, so he could, arguably, know that they knew. But Colonel Chattan had ordered him to stay put "until positively sighted by Germans," whatever that meant.

One of those planes, in particular, was coming closer and closer. It was searching very close to the ground, cutting only a narrow swath on each pass. Waiting for it to pass over their position, Shaftoe wanted to scream. This was too stupid to be real. He wanted to send up a flare and get this over with.

Finally, in midafternoon, Shaftoe, lying on his back in the shade of a tree, looked straight up into the air and counted the rivets on the belly of that German airplane: a Henschel Hs 126* with a single swept-back wing mounted above the fuselage, so as not to block the view down-

---

*Shaftoe had had nothing to do for the last couple of weeks except play Hearts using KNOW YOUR ENEMY cards, so he could now peg model numbers of obscure Kraut observation planes.

wards, and with ladders and struts and giant awkward splay-footed landing gear sticking out all over. One German encased in a glass shroud
and flying the plane, another out in the open, peering down through
goggles and fiddling with a swivel-mounted machine gun. This one did
all but look Shaftoe in the eye, then tapped the pilot on the shoulder
and pointed down.

The Henschel altered its normal search pattern, cutting the pass short
to swing round and fly over their position again.

"That's it," Shaftoe said to himself. He stood up and began walking
towards the dilapidated barn. "That's it!" he shouted. "Execute!"

The SAS guys were in the back of the truck, under a tarp, working
with their wrenches. Shaftoe glanced in their direction and saw gleaming
parts from the Vickers laid out on clean white fabric. Where the hell
had these guys gotten clean white fabric? They'd probably been saving
it for today. Why couldn't they have got the Vickers in good working
order before? Because they'd had orders to assemble it hastily, at the last
possible minute.

Corporal Benjamin hesitated, one hand poised above his radio key.
"Sarge, are you sure they know we're here?"

Everyone turned to see how Shaftoe would respond to this mild challenge. He had been slowly gathering a reputation as a man who
needed watching.

Shaftoe turned on his heel and strolled out into the middle of a clearing
a few yards away. Behind him, he could hear the other men of Detachment 2702 jockeying for position in the doorway, trying to get a clear
view of him.

The Henschel was coming back for another pass, now so close to the
ground that you could probably throw a rock through its windshield.

Shaftoe unslung his tommy gun, pulled back the bolt, cradled it, swung
it up and around, and opened fire.

Now some might complain that the trench broom lacked penetrating
power, but he was positive he could see pieces of crap flying out of the
Henschel's motor. The Henschel went out of control almost immediately. It banked until its wings were vertical, veered, banked some more
until it was upside down, shed what little altitude it had to begin with,
and made an upside-down pancake landing in the olive trees no more
than a hundred yards distant. It did not immediately burst into flame:
something of a letdown there.

There was perfect silence from the other men. The only sound was
the beepity-beep of Corporal Benjamin, his question now answered,
sending out his little message. Shaftoe was able to follow the Morse code

for once—this message was going out plaintext. "WE ARE DISCOV-
ERED STOP EXECUTING PLAN TORUS."

As *their* first contribution to Plan Torus, the other men climbed onto
the truck, which pulled out from its hidey-hole in the barn and idled in
the trees nearby. When Benjamin was finished, he abandoned his radio
and joined them.

As *his* first task of Plan Torus, Shaftoe walked around the premises in
a neat crisscross pattern echoing that of the searching reconnaissance
planes. He was carrying an upside-down gasoline can with no lid on it.

He left the can about one-third full, standing upright in the middle
of the barn. He pulled the pin from a grenade, dropped it into the
gasoline, and ran out of the building. The truck was already pulling away
when he caught up with it and dove into the waiting arms of his unit,
who pulled him on board. He got himself situated in the back of the
truck just in time to see the building go up in a satisfying fireball.

"Okay," Shaftoe said to the men. "We got a few hours to kill."

All the men in the truck—except for the SAS blokes working on the
Vickers—looked at each other like *did he really just say that?*

"Uh, Sarge," one of them finally said, "could you explain that part
about killing some time?"

"The airplane's not going to be here for a while. Orders."

"Was there a problem or—"

"Nope. Everything's going fine. Orders."

Beyond that the men didn't want to gripe, but a lot more looks were
exchanged across the bed of the truck. Finally, Enoch Root spoke up,
"You men are probably wondering why we couldn't kill time for a few
hours *first,* before alerting the Germans to our presence, and rendezvous
with the plane just in the nick of time."

"Yeah!" said a whole bunch of guys and blokes, vigorously nodding.

"That's a good question," said Enoch Root. He said it like he already
knew the answer, which made everyone in the truck want to slug him.

The Germans had deployed some ground units to secure the area's
road intersections. When Detachment 2702 arrived at the first crossroads,
all of the Germans were freshly dead, and all they had to do was to slow
down momentarily so that some Marine Raiders could run out of hiding
and jump on board.

The Germans at the second intersection had no idea what was going
on. This was obviously the result of some kind of internal Wehrmacht
communications fuckup, clearly recognizable as such even across cultural
and linguistic boundaries. Detachment 2702 were able to simply open
fire from underneath the tarp and tear them to pieces, or at least drive
them into hiding.

The next Germans they ran into weren't having any of it; they had formed a roadblock out of a truck and two cars, and were lined up on the other side of it, pointing weapons at them. All of their weapons looked to be small arms. But by this time the Vickers had finally been put together, calibrated, fine-tuned, inspected, and loaded. The tarp came off. Private Mikulski, a surly, brooding two-hundred-and-fifty-pound Polish–British SAS man, commenced operations with the Vickers at about the same time that the Germans did with their rifles.

Now when Bobby Shaftoe had gone through high school, he'd been slotted into a vocational track and ended up taking a lot of shop classes. A certain amount of his time was therefore, naturally, devoted to sawing large pieces of wood or metal into smaller pieces. Numerous saws were available in the shop for that purpose, some better than others. A sawing job that would be just ridiculously hard and lengthy using a hand saw would be accomplished with a power saw. Likewise, certain cuts and materials would cause the smaller power saws to overheat or seize up altogether and therefore called for larger power saws. But even with the biggest power saw in the shop, Bobby Shaftoe always got the sense that he was imposing some kind of stress on the machine. It would slow down when the blade contacted the material, it would vibrate, it would heat up, and if you pushed the material through too fast it would threaten to jam. But then one summer he worked in a mill where they had a bandsaw. The bandsaw, its supply of blades, its spare parts, maintenance supplies, special tools and manuals occupied a whole room. It was the only tool he had ever seen with *infrastructure*. It was the size of a car. The two wheels that drove the blade were giant eight-spoked things that looked to have been salvaged from steam locomotives. Its blades had to be manufactured from long rolls of blade-stuff by unreeling about half a mile of toothed ribbon, cutting it off, and carefully welding the cut ends together into a loop. When you hit the power switch, nothing would happen for a little while except that a subsonic vibration would slowly rise up out of the earth, as if a freight train were approaching from far away, and finally the blade would begin to move, building speed slowly but inexorably until the teeth disappeared and it became a bolt of pure hellish energy stretched taut between the table and the machinery above it. Anecdotes about accidents involving the bandsaw were told in hushed voices and not usually commingled with other industrial-accident anecdotes. Anyway, the most noteworthy thing about the bandsaw was that you could cut anything with it and not only did it do the job quickly and coolly but it didn't seem to notice that it was doing anything. It wasn't even aware that a human being was sliding a great big chunk of stuff through it. It never slowed down. Never heated up.

In Shaftoe's post–high-school experience he had found that guns had much in common with saws. Guns could fire bullets all right, but they kicked back and heated up, got dirty, and jammed eventually. They could fire bullets in other words, but it was a big deal for them, it placed a certain amount of stress on them, and they could not take that stress forever. But the Vickers in the back of this truck was to other guns as the bandsaw was to other saws. The Vickers was *water-cooled*. It actually had a fucking *radiator* on it. It had *infrastructure,* just like the bandsaw, and a whole crew of technicians to fuss over it. But once the damn thing was up and running, it could fire continuously for *days* as long as people kept scurrying up to it with more belts of ammunition. After Private Mikulski opened fire with the Vickers, some of the other Detachment 2702 men, eager to pitch in and do their bit, took potshots at those Germans with their rifles, but doing so made them feel so small and pathetic that they soon gave up and just took cover in the ditch and lit up cigarettes and watched the slow progress of the Vickers' bullet-stream across the roadblock. Mikulski hosed down all of the German vehicles for a while, yawing the Vickers back and forth like a man playing a fire extinguisher against the base of a fire. Then he picked out a few bits of the roadblock that he suspected people might be standing behind and concentrated on them for a while, boring tunnels through the wreckage of the vehicles until he could see what was on the other side, sawing through their frames and breaking them in half. He cut down half a dozen or so roadside trees behind which he suspected Germans were hiding, and then mowed about half an acre of grass.

By this time it had become evident that some Germans had retreated behind a gentle swell in the earth just off to one side of the road and were taking potshots from there, so Mikulski swung the muzzle of the Vickers up into the air at a steep angle and shot the bullet-stream into the sky so that the bullets plunged down like mortar shells on the other side of the rise. It took him a while to get the angle just right, but then he patiently distributed bullets over the entire field, like a man watering his lawn. One of the SAS blokes actually did some calculations on his knee, figuring out how long Mikulski should keep doing this to make sure that bullets were distributed over the ground in question at the right density—say, one per square foot. When the territory had been properly sown with lead slugs, Mikulski turned back to the roadblock and made sure that the truck pulled across the pavement was in small enough pieces that it could be shoved out of the way by hand.

Then he ceased firing at last. Shaftoe felt like he should make an entry in a log book, the way ships' captains do when they pull a man-of-war into port. When they drove past the wreckage, they slowed down for a bit to gawk. The brittle grey iron of the German vehicles' engine blocks had shattered like glass and you could look into the engines all neatly cross-sectioned and see the gleaming pistons and crankshafts exposed to the sun, bleeding oil and coolant.

They passed through what was left of the roadblock and drove onwards into a sparsely populated inland area that made excellent strafing territory for the Luftwaffe. The first two fighters that came around were torn apart in midair by Mikulski and his Vickers. The next pair managed to destroy the truck, the big gun, and Private Mikulski in one pass. No one else was hurt; they were all in the ditch, watching as Mikulski sat placidly behind the controls of his weapon, playing chicken with two Messerschmidts and eventually losing.

By now it was getting dark. The detachment began to make its way cross-country on foot, carrying Mikulski's remains on a stretcher. They ran into a German patrol and fought it out with them; two of the SAS men were wounded, and one of these had to be carried the rest of the way. Finally they reached their rendezvous point, a wheat field where they laid down road flares to outline a landing strip for a U.S. Army DC-3, which executed a deft landing, took them all on board, and flew them to Malta without further incident.

And that was where they were introduced to Lieutenant Monkberg for the first time.

No sooner had they been debriefed than they were on another submarine, bound for parts unknown or at least unspecified. But when they turned in their warm-weather gear for ten-pound oiled-wool sweaters, they started to get an idea. A few claustrophobic days later, they had been transferred onto this freighter.

The vessel itself is such a pathetic heap that they have been amusing themselves by substituting the word "shit" for "ship" in various nautical expressions, e.g.: let's get this cabin shit-shape! Where in hell does the shit's master think he's taking us? And so on.

Now, in the shit's hold, an impassioned Bobby Shaftoe is doing his best to create a ransacked effect. He strews rifles and tommy guns around the deck. He opens boxes of .45 cartridges and flings them all over the place. He finds some skis, too—they'll be needing skis, right? He plants mines here and there, just to throw a scare into whatever German happens along to investigate this shitwreck. He opens crates of grenades. These do not look very ransacked, sitting there full, so he pulls out dozens of them, carries them abovedecks, and throws them overboard. He tosses out some skis also—maybe they will wash up on shore somewhere and contribute to the overall sense of chaos that is so important to Lieutenant Monkberg.

He is on his way across the upper deck, carrying an armload of skis, when something catches his eye out there in the fog. He flinches, of course. Many strafings have turned Bobby Shaftoe into a big flincher. He flinches so hard that he drops all of those skis on the deck and comes this close to throwing himself down among them. But he holds his ground long enough to focus in on this thing in the fog. It is directly in front of them, and somewhat higher than the bridge of the freighter, and (unlike plunging Zeros or Messerschmidts) it is not moving fast— just hanging there. Like a cloud in the sky. As if the fog had coagulated into a dense clump, like his mother's mashed potatoes. It gets brighter and brighter as he stands there watching it, and the edges get more and more sharply defined, and he starts to see other stuff around it.

The other stuff is green.

Hey, wait a minute! He is looking at a green mountainside with a big white snowfield in the middle of it.

"Heads up!" he screams, and throws himself down on the deck.

He is hoping to be surprised by the gradualness, the gentleness of their collision with the earth's crust. He has in mind the kind of deal where you run a little motorboat at a sandy beach, cut the motor and tilt it out of the water at the last minute, and glide up gently onto the cushioning sand.

This turns out to be a very poor analogy for what happens next. The freighter is actually going a lot faster than your typical putt-putt fishing boat. And instead of gliding up onto a sandy beach, they have a nearly head-on collision with a vertical granite wall. There is a really impressive noise, the prow of the vessel actually bends upwards, and suddenly, Bobby Shaftoe finds that he is sliding on his belly across the ice-glazed deck at a high speed.

He is terrified, for a moment, that he's going to slide right off the deck and go flying into the drink, but he manages to steer himself into an anchor chain, which proves an effective stopper. Down below, he can hear approximately ten thousand other small and large objects finding their own obstacles to slam into.

There follows a brief and almost peaceful interlude of near-total silence. Then a hue and cry rises up from the extremely sparse crew of the freighter: "ABANDON SHIT! ABANDON SHIT!"

The men of Detachment 2702 head for the lifeboats. Shaftoe knows that they can take care of themselves, so he heads for the bridge, looking for the few oddballs who always find a way to make things interesting: Lieutenants Root and Monkberg, and Corporal Benjamin.

The first person he sees is the skipper, slumped in a chair, pouring himself a drink and looking like a guy who just bled to death. This poor son of a bitch is a Navy lifer who got detached from his regular unit solely for the purpose of doing what he just did. It clearly does not sit well with him.

"Nice job, sir!" Shaftoe says, not knowing what else to say. Then he follows the sound of an argument into the signals cabin.

The dramatis personae are Corporal Benjamin, holding up a large Book, in a pose that recalls an exasperated preacher sarcastically acquainting his wayward parishioners with the unfamiliar sight of the Bible; Lieutenant Monkberg, semireclined in a chair, his damaged Limb up on a table; and Lieutenant Root, doing some needle-and-thread work on same.

"It is my sworn duty—" Benjamin begins.

Monkberg interrupts him. "It is your sworn duty, Corporal, to follow my orders!"

Root's medical supplies are scattered all over the deck because of the collision. Shaftoe begins to pick them up and sort them out, keeping an especially sharp eye out for any small bottles that may have gone astray.

Benjamin is very excited. Clearly, he is not getting through to Monkberg, and so he opens up the hefty Book at random and holds it up above his head. It contains line after line, column after column, of random letters. "This," Benjamin says, "is the Allied MERCHANT SHIPPING CODE! A copy of THIS BOOK is on EVERY SHIP of EVERY CONVOY in the North Atlantic! It is used by those ships to BROADCAST THEIR POSITIONS! Do you UNDERSTAND what is going to HAPPEN if THIS BOOK falls into the hands of THE GERMANS?!"

"I have given you my order," Lieutenant Monkberg says.

They go on in this vein for a couple of minutes as Shaftoe scours the deck for medical debris. Finally he sees what he's looking for: it has rolled beneath a storage cabinet and appears to be miraculously unscathed.

"Sergeant Shaftoe!" says Root peremptorily. It is the closest he has ever come to sounding like a military officer. Shaftoe straightens up reflexively.

"Sir! Yes, sir!"

"Lieutenant Monkberg's dose of morphine may wear off pretty soon. I need you to find my morphine bottle and bring it to me right away."

"Sir! Yes, sir!" Shaftoe is a Marine, which means he's really good at following orders even when his body is telling him not to. Even so, his fingers do not want to release their grip on the little bottle, and Root almost has to pry it loose.

Benjamin and Monkberg, locked in their dispute, are oblivious to this little exchange. "Lieutenant Root!" Benjamin says, his voice now high and trembly.

"Yes, Corporal," Root says absent-mindedly.

"I have reason to believe that Lieutenant Monkberg is a German spy and that he should be relieved of his command of this mission and placed under arrest!"

"You son of a bitch!" Monkberg shouts. As well he might, since Benjamin has just accused him of treason, for which he could face a firing squad. But Root has Monkberg's leg clamped in place up there on the table, and he can't move.

Root is completely unruffled. He seems to welcome this unbelievably serious accusation. It is an opportunity to talk about something with more substance than, for example, finding ways to substitute the word "shit" for "ship" in nautical expressions.

"I'll see you court-martialed for this, you bastard!" Monkberg hollers.

"Corporal Benjamin, what grounds do you have for this accusation?" says Enoch Root in a lullaby voice.

"The lieutenant has refused to allow me to destroy the codebooks, which it is my sworn duty to do!" Benjamin shouts. He has completely lost his temper.

"I am under very specific and clear orders from Colonel Chattan!" Monkberg says, addressing Root. Shaftoe is startled by this. Monkberg seems to be recognizing Root's authority in the matter. Or maybe he's scared, and looking for an ally. The officers closing ranks against the enlisted men. As usual.

"Do you have a written copy of those orders I could examine?" Root says.

"I don't think it's appropriate for us to be having this discussion here and now," Monkberg says, still pleading and defensive.

"How would you suggest that we handle it?" Root says, drawing a length of silk through Monkberg's numbed flesh. "We are aground. The Germans will be here soon. We either leave the code books or we don't. We have to decide now."

Monkberg goes limp and passive in his chair.

"Can you show me written orders?" Root asks.

"No. They were given verbally," Monkberg says.

"And did these orders specifically mention the code books?" Root asks.

"They did," Monkberg says, as if he's a witness in a courtroom.

"And did these orders state that the code books were to be allowed to fall into the hands of the Germans?"

"They did."

There is silence for a moment as Root ties off a suture and begins another one. Then he says, "A skeptic, such as Corporal Benjamin, might think that this business of the code books is an invention of yours."

"If I falsified my own orders," Monkberg says, "I could be shot."

"Only if you, and some witnesses to the event, all made their way back to friendly territory, and compared notes with Colonel Chattan," says Enoch Root, coolly and patiently.

"What the fuck is going on!?" says one of the SAS blokes, bursting in through a hatch down below and charging up the gangway. "We're all waiting in the fucking lifeboats!" He bursts into the room, his face red with cold and anxiety, and looks around wildly.

"Fuck off," Shaftoe says.

The SAS bloke pulls up short. "Okay, Sarge!"

"Go down and tell the men in the boats to fuck off too," Shaftoe says.

"Right away, Sarge!" the SAS man says, and makes himself scarce.

"As those anxious men in the lifeboats will attest," Enoch Root continues, "the likelihood of you and several witnesses making it back to friendly territory is diminishing by the minute. And the fact that you *just happened* to suffer a grievous *self-inflected* leg wound, just a few minutes ago, complicates our escape tremendously. Either we will all be captured together, or else you will volunteer to be left behind and captured. Either way, you are saved—assuming that you are a German spy—from the court-martial and the firing squad."

Monkberg can't believe his ears. "But—but it was an accident, Lieutenant Root! I hit myself in the leg with a fucking ax—you don't think I did that deliberately!?"

"It is very difficult for us to know," Root says regretfully.

"Why don't we just destroy the code books? It's the safest thing to do," Benjamin says. "I'd just be following a standing order—nothing wrong with that. No court-martial there."

"But that would ruin the mission!" Monkberg says.

Root thinks this one over for a moment. "Has anyone ever died," he says, "because the enemy stole one of our secret codes and read our messages?"

"Absolutely," Shaftoe says.

"Has anyone on our side ever died," Root continues, "because the enemy *didn't* have one of our secret codes?"

This is quite a poser. Corporate Benjamin makes his mind up soonest, but even he has to think about it. "Of course not!" he says.

"Sergeant Shaftoe? Do you have an opinion?" Root asks, fixing Shaftoe with a sober and serious gaze.

Shaftoe says, "This code business is some tricky shit."

Monkberg's turn. "I . . . I think . . . I believe I could come up with a hypothetical situation in which someone could die, yes."

"How about you, Lieutenant Root?" Shaftoe asks.

Root does not say anything for a long time now. He just works with his silk and his needles. It seems like several minutes go by. Perhaps it's not that long. Everyone is nervous about the Germans.

"Lieutenant Monkberg asks me to believe that it will prevent Allied soldiers from dying if we turn over the Allied merchant shipping code books to the Germans today," Root finally says. Everyone jumps nervously at the sound of his voice. "Actually, since we must use a sort of calculus of death in these situations, the real question is, will this somehow save *more* lives than it will lose?"

"You lost me there, padre," says Shaftoe. "I didn't even make it through algebra."

"Then let's start with what we know: turning over the codes will lose lives because it will enable the Germans to figure out where our convoys are, and sink them. Right?"

"Right!" Corporal Benjamin says. Root seems to be leaning his way.

"That will be true," Root continues, "until such time as the Allies change the code systems—which they will probably do as soon as possible. So, on the negative side of the calculus of death, we have some convoy sinkings in the short term. What about the positive side?" Root asks, raising his eyebrows in contemplation even as he stares down into Monkberg's wound. "How might turning over the codes save some lives? Well, that is an imponderable."

"A what?" Shaftoe says.

"Suppose, for example, that there is a secret convoy about to cross over from New York, and it contains thousands of troops, and some new weapon that will turn the tide in the war and save thousands of lives. And suppose that it is using a different code system, so that even after the Germans get our code books today they will not know about it. The Germans will focus their energies on sinking the convoys that they do know about—killing, perhaps, a few hundred crew members. But while their attention is on those convoys, the secret convoy will slip through and deliver its precious cargo and save thousands of lives."

Another long silence. They can hear the rest of Detachment 2702 shouting now, down in the lifeboats, probably having a detailed discussion of their own: if we leave all of the fucking officers behind on a grounded ship, does it qualify as mutiny?

"That's just hypothetical," Root says. "But it demonstrates that it is at least theoretically possible that there might be a positive side to the calculus of death. And now that I think about it, there might not even be a negative side."

"What do you mean?" Benjamin says. "Of course there's a negative side!"

"You are assuming that the Germans have not already broken that code," Root says, pointing a bloody and accusing finger at Benjamin's big tome of gibberish. "But maybe they have. They've been sinking our convoys left and right, you know. If that's the case, then there is no negative in letting it fall into their hands."

"But that contradicts your theory about the secret convoy!" Benjamin says.

"The secret convoy was just a *Gedankenexperiment*," Root says.

Corporal Benjamin rolls his eyes; apparently, he actually knows what that means. "If they've already broken it, then why are we going to all of this trouble, and risking our lives to GIVE IT TO THEM!?"

Root ponders that one for a while. "I don't know."

"Well, what do you think, Lieutenant Root?" Bobby Shaftoe asks a few excruciatingly silent minutes later.

"I think that in spite of my *Gedankenexperiment*, that Corporal Benjamin's explanation—i.e., that Lieutenant Monkberg is a German spy—is more plausible."

Benjamin lets out a sigh of relief. Monkberg stares up into Root's face, paralyzed with horror.

"But implausible things happen all the time," Root continues.

"Oh, for pete's sake!" Benjamin shouts, and slams his hand down on the book.

"Lieutenant Root?" Shaftoe says.

"Yes, Sergeant Shaftoe?"

"Lieutenant Monkberg's injury was an accident. I seen it happen."

Root looks up into Shaftoe's eyes. He finds this interesting. "Really?"

"Yes, sir. It was an accident all the way."

Root breaks open a package of sterile gauze and begins to wind it around Monkberg's leg; the blood soaks through immediately, faster than he can wind new layers around it. But gradually, Root starts to get the better of it, and the gauze stays white and clean. "Guess it's time to make a command decision," he says. "I say we leave the code books behind, just like Lieutenant Monkberg says."

"But if he's a German spy—" Benjamin begins.

"Then his ass is grass when we get back on friendly soil," Root says.

"But you said yourself the chances of that were slim."

"I shouldn't have said that," Enoch Root says apologetically. "It was not a wise or a thoughtful comment. It did not reflect the true spirit of

Detachment 2702. I am convinced that we will prevail in the face of our little problem here. I am convinced that we will make it to Sweden and that we will bring Lieutenant Monkberg along with us."

"That's the spirit!" Monkberg says.

"If at any point, Lieutenant Monkberg shows signs of malingering, or volunteers to be left behind, or in any way behaves so as to increase our risk of capture by the Germans, then we can all safely assume that he is a German spy."

Monkberg seems completely unfazed. "Well, let's get the fuck out of here, then!" he blurts, and gets to his feet, somewhat unsteady from blood loss.

"Wait!" Sergeant Shaftoe says.

"What is it now, Shaftoe?" Monkberg shouts, back in command again.

"How are we going to know if he's increasing our risk of capture?"

"What do you mean, Sergeant Shaftoe?" Root says.

"Maybe it won't be obvious," Shaftoe says. "Maybe there's a German detachment waiting to capture us at a certain location in the woods. And maybe Lieutenant Monkberg is going to lead us directly to the trap."

"Atta boy, Sarge!" Corporal Benjamin says.

"Lieutenant Monkberg," says Enoch Root, "as the closest thing we have to a ship's doctor, I am relieving you of your command on medical grounds."

"What medical grounds!?" Monkberg shouts, horrified.

"You are short on blood, and what blood you do have is tainted with morphine," says Lieutenant Enoch Root. "So the second-in-command will have to take over for you and make all decisions as to which direction we will take."

"But you're the only other officer!" Shaftoe says. "Except for the skipper, and *he* can't be a skipper without a boat."

"Sergeant Shaftoe!" Root barks, doing such an effective impersonation of a Marine that Shaftoe and Benjamin both stiffen to attention.

"Sir! Yes sir!" Shaftoe returns.

"This is the first and last order I am going to give you, so listen carefully!" Root insists.

"Sir! Yes sir!"

"Sergeant Shaftoe, take me and the rest of this unit to Sweden!"

"Sir! Yes sir!" Shaftoe hollers, and marches out of the cabin, practically knocking Monkberg aside. The others soon follow, leaving the code books behind.

After about half an hour of screwing around with lifeboats, Detachment 2702 finds itself on the ground again, in Norway. The snowline is about fifty feet above sea level; it is fortunate that Bobby Shaftoe knows what to do with a pair of skis. The SAS blokes also know this particular drill, and they even know how to rig up a sort of sled arrangement that they can use to pull Lieutenant Monkberg. Within a few hours, they are deep in the woods, headed east, not having seen a single human being, German or Norwegian, since they ran aground. Snow begins to fall, filling in their tracks. Monkberg is behaving himself—not demanding to be left behind, not sending up flares. Shaftoe begins to think that making it out to Sweden might be one of Detachment 2702's easier missions. The only hard part, as usual, is understanding what the fuck is going on.

DILIGENCE

MAPS OF SOUTHEAST ASIA ARE UP ON THE WALLS, AND EVEN covering the windows, lending a bunkerlike ambience to Avi's hotel room. Epiphyte Corp. has assembled for its first full-on shareholder's meeting in two months. Avi Halaby, Randy Waterhouse, Tom Howard, Eberhard Föhr, John Cantrell, and Beryl Hagen crowd into the room and pillage the minibar for snacks and soft drinks. Some of them sit on the bed. Eberhard sits barefoot and crosslegged on the floor with his laptop up on a footstool. Avi remains standing. He crosses his arms and leans back, eyes closed, against the endangered-mahogany doors of his entertainment center. He is wearing a brilliantly laundered white shirt, so freshly and heavily starched that it still cracks when he moves. Until fifteen minutes ago he was wearing a t-shirt he hadn't taken off his body for forty-eight hours.

Randy thinks for a minute that Avi may have fallen asleep in the unorthodox standing position. But "Look at that map," Avi says suddenly, in a quiet voice. He opens his eyes and swivels them in their sockets towards same, not wasting precious energy by turning his head. "Singapore, the southern tip of Taiwan, and the northernmost point of Australia form a triangle."

"Avi," says Eb solemnly, "any three points form a triangle." Generally they don't look to Eberhard to leaven the proceedings with humor, but a chuckle passes around the room, and Avi grins—not so much because it's funny as because it's evidence of good morale.

"What's in the middle of the triangle?"

Everyone looks again. The correct answer is *a point in the middle of the Sulu Sea,* but it's clear what Avi is getting at. "We are," Randy says.

"That's correct," Avi says. "Kinakuta is ideally situated to act as an electronic crossroads. The perfect place to put big routers."

"You're talking shareholderese," Randy warns.

Avi ignores him. "Really it makes a lot more sense this way."

"What way?" Eb asks sharply.

"I've become aware that there are other cable people here. There is a group from Singapore and a consortium from Australia and New Zealand. In other words: we used to be the sole carriers into the Crypt. As of later today, I suspect we will be one of three."

Tom Howard grins triumphantly: he works in the Crypt, he probably knew before anyone. Randy and John Cantrell exchange a look.

Eb sits up stiffly. "How long have you known about this?" he asks.

Randy sees a look of annoyance flash across Beryl's face. She does not like being probed.

"Would the rest of you excuse Eb and me for a minute?" Randy says, getting to his feet.

Dr. Eberhard Föhr looks startled, then gets up and follows Randy out of the room. "Where are we going?"

"Leave your laptop," Randy says, escorting him out into the hallway. "We're just going here."

"Why?"

"It's like this," Randy says, pulling the door closed but not letting it lock. "People like Avi and Beryl, who have been in business a lot, have this noticeable preference for two-person conversations—like the one you and I are having right now. Not only that, they rarely write things down."

"Explain."

"It's kind of an information theory thing. See, if worse comes to worst, and there is some kind of legal action—"

"Legal action? What are you talking about?"

Eb came from a small city near the border with Denmark. His father was a high school mathematics teacher, his mother an English teacher. His appearance would probably make him an outcast in his home town, but like many of the people who still live there, he believes that things should be done in a plain, open, and logical fashion.

"I don't mean to alarm you," Randy says, "I'm not implying that any such thing is happening, or about to. But America being the way it is right now, you'd be amazed how often business ventures lead to lawsuits. When that happens, any and all documents are disclosable. So people like Avi and Beryl never write anything down that they wouldn't want to see in open court. Furthermore, anyone can be asked, under oath, to testify about what happened. That's why two-person conversations, like this one, are best."

"One person's word against another. I understand this."

"I know you do."

"We should anyway have been discreetly told."

"The reason that Avi and Beryl didn't tell us about this until now was that they wanted to work out the problem face-to-face, in two-person conversations. In other words, they did it to protect us—not to hide anything from us. Now they are formally presenting us with the news."

Eberhard is no longer suspicious. Now he is irked, which is worse. Like a lot of techies, he can become obstreperous when he decides that others are not being logical. Randy holds up his hands, palms out, in surrender.

"I stipulate that this does not make sense," Randy says.

Eb glares into the distance, not mollified.

"Will you agree with me that the world is full of irrational people, and crazy situations?"

"*Jaaaa—*" Eb says guardedly.

"If you and I are going to hack and get paid for it, people have to hire us, right?"

Eb considers it carefully. Yes."

"That means dealing with those people, at some level, unpleasant as it may be. And accepting a whole lot of other nonsense, like lawyers and PR people and marketroids. And if you or I tried to deal with them, we would go out of our minds. True?"

"Most likely, yes."

"It is good, then, that people like Avi and Beryl have come into existence, because they are our interface." An image from the Cold War comes into Randy's head. He reaches out with both hands and gropes in the air. "Like those glove boxes that they use to handle plutonium. See?"

Eberhard nods. An encouraging sign.

"But that doesn't mean that it's going to be like programming computers. They can only filter and soften the irrational nature of the world beyond, so Avi and Beryl may still do things that seem a little crazy."

Eb has been getting a more and more faraway look in his eyes. "It would be interesting to approach this as a problem in information theory," he announces. "How can data flow back and forth between nodes in an internal network"—Randy knows that by this Eb means *people in a small corporation*—"but not exist to a person outside?"

"What do you mean, not exist?"

"How could a court subpoena a document if, from their reference frame, it had never existed?"

"Are you talking about encrypting it?"

Eb looks slightly pained by Randy's simple-mindedness. "We are already doing that. But someone could still prove that a document, of a certain size, had been sent out at a certain time, to a certain mailbox."

"Traffic analysis."

"Yes. But what if one jams it? Why couldn't I fill my hard drive with random bytes, so that individual files would not be discernible? Their very existence would be hidden in the noise, like a striped tiger in tall grass. And we could continually stream random noise back and forth to each other."

"That would be expensive."

Eberhard waves his hand dismissively. "Bandwidth is cheap."

"That is more an article of faith than a statement of fact," Randy says, "but it might be true in the future."

"But the rest of our lives will happen in the future, Randy, so we might as well get with the program now."

"Well," Randy says, "could we continue this discussion later?"

"Of course."

They go back into the room. Tom, who has spent the most time here, is saying: "The five-footers with yellowish-brown spots on an aqua background are harmless and makes great pets. The six-footers with brownish-yellow spots on a turquoise background kill you with a single bite, in ten minutes, unless you commit suicide in the meantime to escape the intolerable pain."

This is all a way of letting Randy and Eb know that the others have not been discussing business while they were out of the room.

"Okay," Avi says, "the upshot is that the Crypt is going to be potentially much bigger than we thought at first, so this is good news. But there is one thing that we have to deal with." Avi has known Randy forever, and knows that Randy won't really be bothered by what is to come.

All eyes turn towards Randy, and Beryl picks up the thread. She has arrogated to herself the role of worrying about people's feelings, since the other people in the company are so manifestly unqualified, and she speaks regretfully. "The work Randy's been doing in the Philippines, which is very fine work, is no longer a critical part of this corporation's activities."

"I accept that," Randy says. "Hey, at least I got my first tan in ten years."

Everyone seems immediately relieved that Randy is not pissed off.

Tom, typically, gets right to brass tacks: "Can we pull out of our relationship with the Dentist? Just make a clean break?"

The rhythm of the conversation is abruptly lost. It's like a power
failure in a discotheque.

"Unknown," Avi finally says. "We looked at the contracts. But they
were written by the Dentist's lawyers."

"Aren't some of his partners lawyers?" Cantrell asks.

Avi shrugs impatiently, as if that's not the half of it. "His partners. His
investors. His neighbors, friends, golfing buddies. His *plumber* is probably
a lawyer."

"The point being that he is famously litigious," Randy says.

"The other potential problem," Beryl says, "is that, if we did find a
way to extract ourselves from the deal with AVCLA, we would then
lose the short-term cash flow that we were counting on from the Philippines network. The ramifications of that turn out to be uglier than we
had expected."

"Damn!" Randy says, "I was afraid of that."

"What are the ramifications?" Tom says, hewing as ever to the bottom line.

"We would have to raise some more money to cover the shortfall,"
Avi says. "Diluting our stock."

"Diluting it how much?" John asks.

"Below fifty percent."

This magic figure touches off an epidemic of sighing, groaning and
shifting around among the officers of Epiphyte Corp., who collectively
hold over fifty percent of the company's stock. As they work through
the ramifications in their heads, they begin to look significantly at Randy.

Finally Randy stands, and holds out his hands as if warding them off.
"Okay, okay, okay," he says. "Where does this take us? The business
plan states, over and over, that the Philippines network makes sense in
and of itself—that it could be spun off into an independent business at
any time and still make money. As far as we know, that's still true, right?"

Avi thinks this over before issuing the carefully engineered statement:
"It is as true as it ever was."

This elicits a titter, and a bit of sarcastic applause, from the others.
Clever Avi! Where would we be without him?

"Okay," Randy says. "So if we stick with the Dentist—even though
his project is now irrelevant to us—we hopefully make enough money
that we don't need to sell any more stock. We can retain control over
the company. On the other hand, if we break our relationship with
AVCLA, the Dentist's partners start to hammer us with lawsuits—which
they can do at virtually no cost, or risk. We get mired in court in L.A.

We have to fly back there and testify and give depositions. We spend a
ton of money on lawyers."

"And we might even lose," Avi says.

Everyone laughs.

"So we have to stay in," Randy concludes. "We have to work with
the Dentist whether we want to or not."

No one says anything.

It's not that they disagree with Randy; on the contrary. It's just that
Randy is the guy who's been doing the Philippines stuff, and who is
going to end up handling this unfortunate situation. Randy's going to
take all the force of this blow personally. It is better that he volunteer
than that it be forced on him. He is volunteering now, loudly and
publicly, putting on a performance. The other actors in the ensemble
are Avi, Beryl, Tom, John, and Eb. The audience consists of Epiphyte
Corp.'s minority shareholders, the Dentist, and various yet-to-be-empan-
eled juries. It is a performance that will never come to light unless
someone files a lawsuit against them and brings them all to the witness
box to recount it under oath.

John decides to trowel it on a little thicker. "AVCLA's financing the
Philippines on spec, right?"

"Correct," Avi says authoritatively, playing directly to the hypothetical
juries-of-the-future. "In the old days, cable-layers would sell capacity
first to raise capital. AVCLA's building it with their own capital. When
it's finished, they'll own it outright, and they'll sell the capacity to the
highest bidder."

"It's not all AVCLA's money—they're not that rich," Beryl says.
"They got a big wad from NOHGI."

"Which is?" Eb asks.

"Niigata Overseas Holding Group Inc.," three people say in unison.
Eb looks baffled.

"NOHGI laid the deep-sea cable from Taiwan to Luzon," Randy says.

"Anyway," John says, "my point is that since the Dentist is wiring
the Philippines on spec, he is highly exposed. Anything that delays the
completion of that system is going to cause him enormous problems. It
behooves us to honor our obligations."

John is saying to the hypothetical jury in Dentist v. Epiphyte Corp.:
we carefully observed the terms of our contract with AVCLA.

But this is not necessarily going to look so good to the hypothetical
jury in the *other* hypothetical minority shareholder lawsuit, Springboard
Group v. Epiphyte Corp. So Avi hastens to add, "As I think we've
established, through a careful discussion of the issues, honoring our obli-

gations to the Dentist is part and parcel of our obligation to our own shareholders. These two goals dovetail."

Beryl rolls her eyes and heaves a deep sigh of relief.

"Let us therefore go forth and wire the Philippines," Randy says.

Avi addresses him in formal tones, as if his hand were resting, even now, on a Gideon Bible. "Randy, do you feel that the resources allotted to you are sufficient for you to meet our contractual obligations to the Dentist?"

"We need to have a meeting about that," Randy says.

"Can it wait until after tomorrow?" Avi says.

"Of course. Why shouldn't it?"

"I have to use the bathroom," Avi says.

This is a signal that Avi and Randy have used many times in the past. Avi gets up and goes into the bathroom. A moment later, Randy says, "Come to think of it . . ." and follows him in there.

He is startled to find that Avi is actually pissing. On the spur of the moment, Randy unzips and starts pissing right along with him. It doesn't occur to him how remarkable this is until he's well into it.

"What's up?" Randy asks.

"I went down to the lobby to change money this morning," Avi says, "and guess who came stalking into the hotel, fresh from the airport?"

"Oh, shit," Randy says.

"The Dentist himself."

"No yacht?"

"The yacht's following him."

"Did he have anyone with him?"

"No, but he might later."

"Why is he here?"

"He must have heard."

"God. He's the last guy I want to run into tomorrow."

"Why? Is there a problem?"

"Nothing I can put my finger on," Randy says. "Nothing dramatic."

"Nothing that, if it came to light later, would make you look negligent?"

"I don't think so," Randy says. "It's just that this Philippines thing is complicated and we need to talk about it."

"Well, for God's sake," Avi says, "if you run into the Dentist tomorrow, don't say anything about your work. Keep it social."

"Got it," Randy says, and zips up. But what he's really thinking is: why did I waste all those years in academia when I could have been doing great shit like this?

Which then reminds him of something: "Oh, yeah. Got a weird e-mail."

Avi immediately says "From Andy?"

"How'd you guess?"

"You said it was *weird*. Did you really get e-mail from him?"

"I don't really know who it was from. Probably not Andy. It wasn't weird in *that* way."

"Did you respond to it?"

"No. But dwarf@siblings.net did."

"Who's that? Siblings.net is the system you used to administer, right?"

"Yeah. I still have some privileges there. I created a new account there, name of dwarf, which can't be traced to me. Sent anonymous e-mail back to this guy telling him that until he proves otherwise, I'm assuming he is an old enemy of mine."

"Or a new one."

SPEARHEAD

THE YOUNG LAWRENCE PRITCHARD WATERHOUSE, VISITING HIS grandparents in Dakota, follows a plow across a field. The diving blades of the plow heave the black soil up out of the furrows and pile it into ridges, rough and jumbled when seen up close but mathematically clean and straight, like the grooves of a phonograph record, when viewed from a distance. A tiny surfboard-shaped object projects from the crest of one of those earthen waves. Young Waterhouse bends down and plucks it out. It is an Indian spearhead neatly chipped out of flint.

U-553 is a black steel spear point thrusting into the air about ten miles north of Qwghlm. The grey rollers pick it up and slam it down, but other than that, it does not move; it is grounded on a submerged outcropping known to the locals as Caesar's Reef, or Viking's Grief, or the Dutch-Hammer.

On the prairie, those flint arrowheads can be found lodged in every sort of natural matrix: soil, sod, the mud of a riverbank, the heartwood of a tree. Waterhouse has a talent for finding them. How can he walk across a field salted, by the retreat of the last glacier, with countless stones, and pick out the arrowheads? Why can the human eye detect a tiny artificial form lost in nature's torn and turbulent cosmos, a needle of data in a haystack of noise? It is a sudden, sparking connection between minds, he supposes. The arrowheads are human things broken loose from humanity, their organic parts perished, their mineral forms enduring—crystals of intention. It is not the form but the lethal intent that demands the attention of a selfish mind. It worked for young Waterhouse, hunting for arrowheads. It worked for the pilots of the airplanes that hounded U-553 this morning. It works for the listeners of the *Beobachtung Dienst,* who have trained their ears to hear what is being said by Churchill and FDR on what are supposed to be scrambled telephones. But it doesn't work very well with crypto. That is too bad for everyone except the British and the Americans, who have devised mathematical systems for picking out arrowheads amid pebbles.

Caesar's Reef gashed the underside of U-553's bow section open while shoving the entire boat up and partly out of the water. Momentum almost carried her over the hump, but she got hung up in the middle, stranded, a wave-battered teeter-totter. Her bows have mostly filled with water now, and so it is the sharp stern that projects up above the crests of the seas. She has been abandoned by her crew, which means that according to the traditions of maritime law, she is up for grabs. The Royal Navy has called dibs. A screen of destroyers patrols the area, lest some sister U-boat slip in and torpedo the wreck.

Waterhouse had been collected from the castle in unseemly haste. Dusk is now falling like a lead curtain, and wolf packs hunt at night. He is on the bridge of a corvette, a tiny escort ship that, in any kind of chop, has the exact hydrodynamics of an empty oil drum. If he stays down below he'll never stop vomiting, and so he stands abovedecks, feet braced wide, knees bent, holding onto a rail with both hands, watching the wreck come closer. The number 553 is painted on her conning tower, beneath a cartoon of a polar bear hoisting a beer stein.

"Interesting," he says to Colonel Chattan. "Five-five-three is the product of two prime numbers—seven and seventy-nine."

Chattan manages an appreciative smile, but Waterhouse can tell that it's nothing more than a spectacular display of breeding.

The remainder of Detachment 2702 is, meanwhile, finally arriving. Having just finished with the successful Norway-ramming mission, they were on their way to their new base of operations on Qwghlm when they received word of U-553's grounding. They rendezvoused with Waterhouse right here on this boat—haven't even had a chance to sit down yet, much less unpack. Waterhouse has told them several times how much they are going to like Qwghlm and has run out of other things to say—the crew of this corvette lacks Ultra Mega clearance, and there is nothing that Waterhouse could conceivably talk about with Chattan and the others that is not classified at the Ultra Mega level. So he's trying gamely with prime number chitchat.

Some of the detachment—the Marine lieutenant and most of the enlisted men—were dropped off in Qwghlm so that they could settle into their new quarters. Only Colonel Chattan and a noncom named Sergeant Robert Shaftoe have accompanied Waterhouse to the U-boat.

Shaftoe has a wiry build, bulging Alley Oop forearms and hands, and blond hair in a buzz cut that makes his big blue eyes look bigger. He has a big nose and a big Adam's apple and big acne scars and some other scars around the orbits of his eyes. The large features in the trim body give him an intense presence; it is hard not to keep looking over in his direction. He seems like a man with powerful emotions but an even more powerful discipline that keeps them under control. He stares directly and unblinkingly into the eyes of whomever is talking. When no one is talking, he stares at the horizon and thinks. When he is thinking, he twiddles his fingers incessantly. Everyone else is using their fingers to hold on to something, but Shaftoe is planted on the deck like a fat geezer waiting in line for a movie. He, like Waterhouse, but unlike Chattan, is dressed in heavy foul weather gear that they have borrowed from the stores of this torpedo boat.

It is known, and word has gone out to all present, that the U-boat's skipper—the last man to abandon ship—had the presence of mind to bring the boat's Enigma machine with him. The RAF planes, still circling overhead, watched the skipper rise to a precarious kneel in his life raft and fling the wheels of the machine in different directions, into the steep pitches of hill-sized waves. Then the machine itself went overboard.

The Germans know that the machine will never be recovered. What they do not know is that they will never even be looked for, because there is a place called Bletchley Park that already knows all that there is to know about the four-wheel naval Enigma. The Brits will make a show of looking anyway, in case anyone is watching.

Waterhouse is not looking for Enigma machines. He is looking for stray arrowheads.

The corvette first approaches the U-boat head-on, thinks better of it and swings far around astern of the wreck, then beats upwind towards it. That way, Waterhouse reckons, the wind will tend to blow them away from the reef. Seen from underneath, the U-boat is actually kind of fat-cheeked. The part that's supposed to be above water, when it's surfaced, is neutral grey, and it's as skinny as a knife. The part that's supposed to be below, when it hasn't just crashed into a great big rock, is wide and black. She has been boarded by adventuresome Royal Navy men who have cheekily raised a White Ensign from her conning tower.

They have apparently reached her in a shallow-draft whaler that is tied up alongside, loosely bound to her by a sparse web of lines, kept away by bald tires slung over the rail. The corvette carrying the members of Detachment 2702 edges towards the U-boat cautiously; each rolling wave nearly slams the boats together.

"We're definitely in a non-Euclidean spatial geometry now!" Waterhouse says puckishly. Chattan bends towards him and cups a hand to his ear. "Not only that but it's *real* time dependent, *definitely* something that has to be tackled in four dimensions not three!"

"I beg your pardon?"

Any closer and they'll be grounded on the reef themselves. The sailors launch an actual rocket that carries a line between the vessels, and devote some time to rigging up a ship-to-ship transfer system. Waterhouse is afraid they're going to put him on it. Actually he's more resentful than afraid, because he was under the impression that he wouldn't be put in any more danger for the rest of the war. He tries to kill time looking at the underside of the U-boat and watching the sailors. They've formed a sort of bucket brigade to haul books and papers up out of the wreck to the conning tower and from there down into the whaler. The conning tower has a complicated spidery look with gun barrels and periscopes and antennas sticking out all over the place.

Waterhouse and Shaftoe are indeed sent over to U-553 on a sort of trolley contraption that rolls along a stretched cable. The sailors put life jackets on them first, as a sort of hilarious token gesture, so that if they avoid being smashed to bits they can die of hypothermia instead of drowning.

When Waterhouse is halfway across, the trough of a wave passes beneath him, and he looks down into the sucking cavity and sees the top of Caesar's Reef, momentarily exposed, covered with an indigo fur of mussels. You could go down there and stand on it. For an instant. Then thousands of tons of really cold water slams into the cavity and rises up and punches him in the ass.

He looks up at U-553, entirely too much of which is above him. His basic impression is that it's hollow, more colander than warship. The hull is perforated with rows of oblong slots arranged in swirling patterns like streamlines tattooed onto the metal. It seems impossibly flimsy. Then he peers through the slots—light is shining all the way through from more slots in the deck—and perceives the silhouette of the pressure hull nested inside, curved and much more solid-looking than the outer hull. She's got two triple-bladed brass propellers, maybe a yard across, dinged here and there from contact with who knows what. Right now they are thrust up into the air, and looking at them Waterhouse feels the same absurd embarrassment he felt looking at dead guys in Pearl Harbor whose private parts were showing. Diving planes and rudders stick out of the hull downstream of the propellers, and aft of those, near the apex of the stern, are two crude hatchlike slabs of metal which, Waterhouse realizes, must be where the torpedoes come out.

He slides the last twenty feet at terrifying speed and is caught and held, in various places, by eight strong hands who lift him to what passes for safety: the deck of the U-boat, just aft of the conning tower, sort of nestled underneath an antiaircraft gun. Way up at the boat's stern, there's a big T-shaped stanchion with cables coming out of the ends of the crossbar and stretched tight all the way to the conning-tower railing, near to hand. Following the example of a Royal Navy officer who appears to be his appointed guardian, Waterhouse climbs uphill—i.e. towards the stern—using one of those cables as a sort of banister, and follows him down a hatch in the afterdeck and into the interior of the boat. Shaftoe follows a few moments later.

It is the worst place Waterhouse has ever been. Like the corvette he has just left, it rises smoothly on each roller, but unlike the corvette it comes down with a crash on the rocks, nearly throwing him to the deck. It is like being sealed up in a garbage can that is being beaten with a sledgehammer. U-553 is about half full of a rich brew of cheap wine, diesel fuel, battery acid, and raw sewage. Because of the way she is pitched, this soup quickly gets deeper as you go forward, but it rolls aft in a drenching tsunami every time her midsection slams down on the rocks. Fortunately, Waterhouse is now far beyond nausea, in some kind of transcendent state where his mind has become even more divorced from his body than usual.

The officer in charge waits for the noise to subside and then says, in a startlingly quiet voice, "Is there anything in particular you'd like to inspect, sir?"

Waterhouse is still trying to get some idea of where he is by shining his flashlight beam around the place, which is kind of like peering through a soda straw. He can't get any synoptic view of his surroundings, just narrow glimpses of pipes and wires. Finally he tries holding his head still and sort of scribbling the flashlight beam around really fast. A picture emerges: they are in a narrow crawl space, obviously designed by and for engineers, intended to give access to a few thousand linear miles of pipes and wires that have been forced through some kind of bottleneck.

"We are looking for the skipper's papers," Waterhouse says. The boat goes into free fall again; he leans against something slippery, claps his hands over his ears, closes his eyes and mouth, and exhales through his nose so that none of the soup will force its way into his body. The thing he's leaning against is really hard and cold and round. It's greasy. He shines his light on it; it's made of brass. The light-scribbling trick produces the image of a brass spaceship of some sort, nestled underneath (unless he's mistaken) a bunk. He's just on the verge of making a total ass of himself by asking what it is, when he identifies it as a torpedo.

In the next quiet interlude, he asks, "Is there anything like a private cabin where he might have . . ."

"It's forward," the officer says. Forward is not an encouraging view.

"Fuck!" Sergeant Shaftoe says. It's the first thing he has said in about half an hour. He begins to slosh forward, and the British officer has to hurry to catch up. The deck falls out from beneath their feet again and they stop and turn around so that the wave of sewage will hit them in the backs.

They travel downhill. Every step's a pitched battle vs. prudence and sound judgment, and they take a lot of steps. What Waterhouse had pegged as a bottleneck goes on and on—all the way, apparently, to the bow. Eventually they find something that gives them an excuse to stop: a cabin, or maybe (at about four by six feet) a corner of a cabin. There's a bed, a little fold-out table, and cabinets made of actual wood. These in combination with the photographs of family and friends give it a cozy, domestic flavor which is, however, completely ruined by the framed picture of Adolf Hitler on the wall. Waterhouse finds this to be in shockingly poor taste until he remembers it's a German boat. The mean high-tide level of the sewage angles across the cabin and cuts it approximately in half. Papers and other bureaucratic detritus are floating everywhere, written in the occult Gothic script that Waterhouse associates with Rudy.

"Take it all," Waterhouse says, but Shaftoe and the officer are already sweeping their arms through the brew and bringing them up wrapped in dripping papier-mâché. They stuff it all into a canvas sack.

The skipper's bunk is on the aft or uphill end of the cabin. Shaftoe strips it, looks under the pillow and under the mattress, finds nothing.

The fold-out table is on the totally submerged end. Waterhouse wades into it carefully, trying not to lose his footing. He finds the desk with his feet, reaches down into the murk with his hands, explores as a blind man would. He finds a few drawers which he is able to pull out of the desk entirely and hand off to Shaftoe, who dumps their contents into the sack. Within a short time he is pretty sure that there's nothing left in the desk.

The boat rises and slams down. As the sewage rolls forward, it exposes, for just a moment, something in the corner of the cabin, something attached to the forward bulkhead. Waterhouse wades over to identify it.

"It's a safe!" he says. He spins the dial. It's heavy. A good safe. German. Shaftoe and the British officer look at each other.

A British sailor appears in the open hatchway. "Sir!" he announces. "Another U-boat has been sighted in the area."

"I'd love to have a stethoscope," Waterhouse hints. "This thing have a sickbay?"

"No," says the British officer. "Just a box of medical gear. Should be floating around somewhere."

"Sir! Yes sir!" Shaftoe says, and vanishes from the room. A minute later he's back holding a German stethoscope up above his head to keep it clean. He tosses it across the cabin to Waterhouse, who snares it in the air, sockets it into his ears, and thrusts the business end down through the sewage to the front of the safe.

He has done a little of this before, as an exercise. Kids who are obsessed with locks frequently turn into adults who are obsessed with crypto. The manager of the grocery store in Moorhead, Minnesota, used to let the young Waterhouse play with his safe. He broke the combination, to the manager's great surprise, and wrote a report about the experience for school.

This safe is a lot better than that one was. Since he can't see the dial anyway, he closes his eyes.

He is vaguely conscious that the other fellows on the submarine have been shouting and carrying on about something for a while, as if some sensational news has just come in. Perhaps the war is over. Then the head of the stethoscope is wrenched loose from his grasp. He opens his eyes to see Sergeant Shaftoe lifting it to his mouth as if it were a microphone. Shaftoe stares at him coolly and speaks into the stethoscope: "Sir, torpedoes in the water, sir." Then Shaftoe turns and leaves Waterhouse alone in the cabin.

Waterhouse is about halfway up the conning tower ladder, looking up at a disk of greyish-black sky, when the whole vessel jerks and booms. A piston of sewage rises up beneath him and propels him upwards, vomiting him out onto the top deck of the boat, where his comrades grab him and very considerately prevent him from rolling off into the ocean.

The movement of the U-553 with the waves has changed. She's moving a lot more now, as if she's about to break free from the reef.

It takes Waterhouse a minute to get his bearings. He is starting to think he may have suffered some damage during all of that. Something is definitely wrong with his left arm, which is the one he landed on.

Powerful light sweeps over them: a searchlight from the British corvette that brought them here. The British sailors curse. Waterhouse levers himself up on his good elbow and sights down the hull of the U-boat,

following the beam of the searchlight to a bizarre sight. The boat has
been blown open just beneath the waterline, shards of her hull peeled
back from the wound and projecting jaggedly into the air. The foul
contents of the hull are draining out, staining the Atlantic black.

"Fuck!" Sergeant Shaftoe says. He shrugs loose from a small but heavy-
looking knapsack that he's been carrying around, pulls it open. His sudden activity draws the attention of the Royal Navy men who help out
by pointing their flashlights at his furious hands.

Waterhouse, who may be in some kind of delirium by this point,
can't quite believe what he sees: Shaftoe has pulled out a bundle of neat
brownish-yellow cylinders, as thick as a finger and maybe six inches long.
He also takes out some small items, including a coil of thick, stiff red
cord. He jumps to his feet so decisively that he nearly knocks someone
down, and runs to the conning tower and disappears down the ladder.

"Jesus," an officer says, "he's going to do some blasting." The officer
thinks about this for a very small amount of time; the ship moves terrifyingly with the waves and makes scraping noises which might indicate it's
sliding off the reef. "Abandon ship!" he hollers.

Most of them get into the whaler. Waterhouse is bundled back onto
the trolley contraption. He is about halfway across to the torpedo boat
when he feels, but scarcely hears, a sharp shock.

For the rest of the way over he can't really see diddly, and even after
he's back on the torpedo boat, all is confusion, and someone named
Enoch Root insists on taking him below and working on his arm and
his head. Waterhouse did not know until now that his head was damaged, which stands to reason, in that your head is where you know
things, and if it's damaged, how can you know it? "You'll get at least a
Purple Heart for this," Enoch Root says. He says it with a marked lack
of enthusiasm, as if he couldn't care less about Purple Hearts, but is
condescending to suppose that it will be a big thrill for Waterhouse.
"And Sergeant Shaftoe probably has another major decoration coming
too, damn him."

MORPHIUM

SHAFTOE STILL SEES THE WORD EVERY TIME HE CLOSES HIS EYES.
It would be a lot better if he were paying attention to the
work at hand: packing demolition charges around the gussets that
join the safe to the U-boat.

MORPHIUM. It is printed thus on a yellowed paper label. The label is glued to a small glass bottle. The color of the glass is the same deep purple that you see when your eyes have been dazzled by a powerful light.

Harvey, the sailor who has volunteered to help him, keeps shining his flashlight into Shaftoe's eyes. It is unavoidable; Shaftoe is wedged into a surpassingly awkward position beneath the safe, working with the charges, trying to set the primers with slimy fingers drained of warmth and strength. This would not even be possible if the boat hadn't been torpedoed; before, this cabin was half full of sewage and the safe was immersed in it. Now it has been conveniently drained.

Harvey is not wedged into anything; he is being flung around by the paroxysms of the U-boat, which like a beached shark, is trying stupidly but violently to thrash its way loose from the reef. The beam of his flashlight keeps sweeping across Shaftoe's eyes. Shaftoe blinks, and sees a cosmos of purple: tiny purple bottles labeled MORPHIUM.

"God damn it!" he hollers.

"Is everything all right, Sergeant?" Harvey says.

Harvey doesn't get it. Harvey thinks that Shaftoe is cursing at some problem with the explosives.

The explosives are just fucking *great*. There's no problem with the *explosives*. The problem is with Bobby Shaftoe's brain.

He was *right there*. Waterhouse sent him to find a stethoscope, and Shaftoe went chambering through the U-boat until he found a wooden box. He opened it up and saw right away it was full of medic stuff. He pawed through it, looking for what Waterhouse wanted, and there was the bottle, plain as day, right in front of his face. His hand brushed against it, for god's sake. He saw the label as the beam of his flashlight swept across it:

MORPHIUM.

But he didn't grab it. If it had said MORPHINE he would have grabbed it in a second. But it said MORPHIUM. And it wasn't until about thirty seconds later that he realized that this was a fucking German boat and of course the words would all be different and there was about a 99 percent chance that MORPHIUM was, in fact, exactly the same stuff as MORPHINE. When he realized that he planted his feet in the passageway of the darkened U-boat and let out a deep long scream from way down in his gut. With the noise of the waves, no one heard him. Then he continued onwards and carried out his duty, handing over the stethoscope to Waterhouse. He carried out his duty because he is a Marine.

Blowing this fucking safe off the wall is not his duty. It's just an idea that popped into his head. They've been training him how to use these explosives; why not put it into practice? He's blowing this safe up, not because he is a Marine, but because he is Bobby Shaftoe. And also because it's a great excuse to go back for that morphium.

The U-boat bucks and sends Harvey sprawling to the deck. Shaftoe waits for the motion to subside, then flails for handholds and pulls himself out from under the safe. His weight is mostly on his feet now, but it wouldn't be correct to say he's standing up. In this place, the best you can hope for is to scramble for balance somewhat faster than you are falling on your kiester. Harvey has just lost that race and Shaftoe is winning it for the moment.

"Fire in the hole!" Shaftoe hollers. Harvey finds his feet! Shaftoe gives him a helpful shove out into the passageway. Harvey turns left and heads uphill for the coming tower and the exit. Shaftoe turns right. He heads downhill. Towards the bow. Towards Davy Jones's Locker. Towards the box with the MORPHIUM.

Where the fuck is that box? When he found it before, it was bobbing in the soup. Maybe—horrible thought—maybe it just drained out of the hole made by the torpedo. He passes through a couple of bulkheads. The boat's angle is getting steeper all the time and he ends up walking backwards, like he's descending a ladder, making handholds out of pipes, electrical cables, and the chains that suspend the submarines' bunks. This boat is so damn *long*.

It seems like a strange way to kill people. Shaftoe's not sure if he approves of everything that is implied by this U-boat. Shaftoe has killed Chinese bandits on the banks of the Yangtze by stabbing them in the chest with a bayonet. He thinks he killed one, once, just by hitting him pretty hard in the head. On Guadalcanal he killed Nips by shooting at them with several different kinds of arms, by rolling rocks down on them, by constructing large bonfires at the entrances to caves where they were holed up, by sneaking up on them in the jungle and cutting their throats, by firing mortars into their positions, even by picking one up and throwing him off a cliff into the pounding surf. Of course he has known for a long time that this face-to-face style of killing the bad guys is kind of old-fashioned, but it's not like he's spent a lot of time *thinking* about it. The demonstration of the Vickers machine gun that he witnessed in Italy *did* sort of get him thinking, and now here he is, inside one of the most famous killing machines in the whole war, and what does he see? He sees valves. Or rather the cast-iron wheels that are used for opening and closing valves. Entire bulkheads are covered with iron wheels, ranging from a couple of inches to over a foot in diameter, packed in as densely as barnacles on a rock, in what looks like a completely random and irregular fashion. They are painted either red or black, and they are polished to a gleam from the friction of men's hands.

And where it's not valves it's switches, huge Frankenstein-movie ones. There is one big rotary switch, half green and half red, that's a good two feet in diameter. And it's not like this boat has a lot of windows in it. It's got no windows at all. Just a periscope that can only be used by one guy at a time. And so for these guys, the war comes down to being sealed up in an airtight drum full of shit and turning valve-wheels and throwing switches on command, and from time to time maybe some officer comes back and tells them that they just killed a bunch of guys.

There's that box—it ended up on a bunk. Shaftoe yanks it closer and hauls it open. The contents are all jumbled up, and there's more than one purple bottle in there, and he panics for a moment, thinking he'll have to read all of the labels in their creepy Germanic script, but in a few seconds he finds the MORPHIUM, grabs it, pockets it.

He's on his way back up towards the conning tower when a big roller slams into the outside of the boat and knocks him off balance. He tumbles downhill for a long, long ways, doing backward somersaults straight down the middle of the boat, before he gets himself under control. Everything has gone black; he's lost his flashlight.

He comes very close to panicking now. It's not that he's a panicky guy, just that it's been a while since he had morphine, and when he gets this way, his body reacts badly to things. He's half-blinded by a powerful flash of blue light that is gone before his eyes have time to blink. There's a sizzling noise down below. He moves his left hand and feels a tug on his wrist: the flashlight's lanyard, which he had the presence of mind to wrap around himself. The light scrapes and clanks against the steel grating on which Shaftoe is now spreadeagled, like a saint on the gridiron. There's another flash of blue light, reticulated by black lines, accompanied by a sizzling noise. Shaftoe smells electricity. He raps the flashlight against the grating a couple of times and it comes on again, flickeringly.

The grid's woven from pencil-thick rods spaced a couple of inches apart. He's facedown on it, looking into a hold that, if this U-boat were level, would be below him. The hold is a disaster, its neatly stacked and crated contents now Osterized into a slumgullion of shattered glass, splintered wood, foodstuffs, high explosives, and strategic minerals, all mingled with seawater so that it sloshes back and forth with the rocking of the dead U-boat. A perfect, quivering globe of silver falls through the grating right near his head and descends through his flashlight beam and explodes against a piece of debris. Then another. He looks uphill and sees a rain of silver globules bouncing and rolling down the deckplates toward him: the mercury columns that they use to measure pressure must have been ruptured. There's another blinding blue flash: an electrical spark with a lot of power behind it. Shaftoe looks down through the grid again and perceives that the hold is filled with huge metal cabinets with giant bolts sticking out of them. Every so often a piece of wet debris will bridge the gap between a couple of those bolts and a spark will light the place up: the cabinets are batteries, they are what enable the U-boat to run underwater.

As Sergeant Robert Shaftoe lies there with his face pressed against that chilly grid, taking a few deep breaths and trying to regain his nerve, a big wave rocks the boat back so hard that he's afraid he's going to fall backwards and plummet all the way to the submerged bow. The swill in the battery hold rolls downhill, gathering power and velocity as it falls, and batters the forward bulkhead of the hold with terrifying power; he can hear rivets giving way under the impact. As this happens, most of the battery hold is exposed to the beam of Bobby Shaftoe's flashlight, all the way down to the bottom. And that is when he sees the splintered crates down there—very small crates, such as might be used to contain very heavy supplies. They have been busted open. Through the gaps in the wreckage, Shaftoe can see yellow bricks, once neatly stacked, now scattered. They look exactly like he would imagine gold bars. The only thing wrong with that theory is that there are way too many of them down there for them to be gold bars. It is like when he turned over rotten logs in Wisconsin and found thousands of identical insect eggs sown on the dark earth, glowing with promise.

For a moment, he's tempted. The amount of money down there is beyond calculation. If he could get his hands on just one of those bars—

The explosives must have detonated, because Bobby Shaftoe has just gone deaf. That's his cue to get the fuck out of here. He forgets about the gold—morphine's good enough plunder for one day. He half scrambles and half climbs up the grid, up the passageway, up the skipper's cabin, smoke pouring out of its hatch, its bulkheads now weirdly ballooned by the blast wave.

The safe has broken loose! And the cable that he and Harvey attached to it, though it's damaged, is still intact. Someone must be hauling away on it up abovedecks because it is stubbornly and annoying taut. Right now the safe is caught up on jagged obstructions. Shaftoe has to pry it loose. The safe jerks onward and upward, drawn by the taut cable, until it gets caught in something else. Shaftoe follows the safe out of the cabin, up the passageway, up the conning tower ladder, and finally levers himself up out of the submarine and into the teeth of the storm, to a hearty cheer from the waiting sailors.

No more than five minutes later, the U-boat goes away. Shaftoe imagines it tumbling end-over-end down the side of the reef, headed for an undersea canyon, scattering gold bars and mercury globules into the black water like fairy dust. Shaftoe's back on the corvette and everyone is pounding him on the back and toasting him. He just wants to find a private place to open up that purple bottle.

SUIT

RANDY'S POSTURE IS RIGHTEOUS AND ALERT: IT IS ALL BECAUSE of his suit.

It is trite to observe that hackers don't like fancy clothes. Avi has learned that good clothes can actually be comfortable—the slacks that go with a business suit, for example, are really much more comfortable than blue jeans. And he has spent enough time with hackers to obtain the insight that is it not *wearing* suits that they object to, so much as *getting them on*. Which includes not only the donning process per se but also picking them out, maintaining them, and worrying whether they are still in style—this last being especially difficult for men who wear suits once every five years.

So it's like this: Avi has a spreadsheet on one of his computers, listing the necks, inseams, and other vital measurements of every man in his employ. A couple of weeks before an important meeting, he will simply fax it to his tailor in Shanghai. Then, in a classic demonstration of the Asian just-in-time delivery system as pioneered by Toyota, the suits will arrive via Federal Express, twenty-four hours ahead of time so that they can be automatically piped to the hotel's laundry room. This morning, just as Randy emerged from the shower, he heard a knock at his door, and swung it open to reveal a valet carrying a freshly cleaned and pressed business suit, complete with shirt and tie. He put it all on (a tenth-generation photocopy of a bad diagram of the half-Windsor knot was thoughtfully provided). It fit perfectly. Now he stands in a lobby of the Foote Mansion, watching electric numbers above an elevator count down, occasionally sneaking a glance at himself in a big mirror. Randy's head protruding from a suit is a sight gag that will be good for grins at least through lunchtime.

He is pondering the morning's e-mail.

To: dwarf@siblings.net
From: root@eruditorum.org
Subject: Re: Why?
Dear Randy,
I hope you don't mind if I address you as Randy, since it's

quite obvious that you are you, despite your use of an anonymous front. This is a good idea, by the way. I applaud your
prudence.

Concerning the possibility that I am ''an old enemy'' of
yours, I'm dismayed that one so young can already have old
enemies. Or perhaps you are referring to a recently acquired
enemy of advanced years? Several candidates come to mind.
But I suspect you are referring to Andrew Loeb. I am not he.
This would be obvious to you if you had visited his website
recently.

Why are you building the Crypt?
Signed,
—BEGIN ORDO SIGNATURE BLOCK—
(etc., etc.)
—END ORDO SIGNATURE BLOCK—

It is not at all interesting to watch the numbers over the elevators and try to predict which one will arrive first, but it is more interesting than just standing there. One of them has been stuck on the floor above Randy's for at least a minute; he can hear it buzzing angrily. In Asia many business-men—especially some of the overseas Chinese—would think nothing of commandeering one of the hotel's elevators around the clock for their own personal use, stationing minions in it, in eight-hour shifts, to hold their thumbs on the DOOR OPEN button, ignoring its self-righteous alarm buzzer.

Ding. Randy spins around on the balls of his feet (just try *that* little maneuver in a pair of sneakers!). Once again he has backed the wrong horse: the winner is an elevator that was on the very top floor of the hotel last time he scanned it. This is an elevator with purpose, a fast-track lift. He walks towards the green light. The doors part. Randy stares squarely into the face of Dr. Hubert (the Dentist) Kepler, D.D.S.

Or perhaps you are referring to a recently acquired enemy of advanced years?

"Good morning, Mr. Waterhouse! When you stand with your mouth open like that, you remind me of one of my patients."

"Good morning, Dr. Kepler." Randy hears his words from the other end of a mile-long bumwad tube, and immediately reviews them in his own mind to make sure he has not revealed any proprietary corporate information or given Dr. Kepler any reason to file a lawsuit.

The doors start to close and Randy has to whack them open with his laptop case.

"Careful! That's an expensive piece of equipment, I'd wager," says the Dentist.

Randy is about to say *I go through laptops like a transvestite goes through nylons* though maybe *like a high-speed drill through a necrotic molar* would be more thematically apropos, but instead he clams up and says nothing at all, finding himself in dangerous territory: he is carrying proprietary AVCLA information on this thing, and if the Dentist gets the impression that Randy's being cavalier with it, he might spew out a barrage of torts, like Linda Blair and the pea soup.

"It's, uh, a pleasant surprise to see you in Kinakuta," Randy stammers.

Dr. Kepler wears eyeglasses the size of a 1959 Cadillac's windshield. They are special dentist eyeglasses, as polished as the Palomar mirror, coated with ultrareflective material so that you can always see the reflection of your own yawning maw in them, impaled on a shaft of hot light. The Dentist's own eyes merely haunt the background, like a childhood memory. They are squinty grey-blue eyes, turned down at the edges as if he is tired of the world, with Stygian pupils. A trace of a smile always seems to be playing around his withered lips. It is the smile of a man who is worrying about how to meet his next malpractice insurance payment while patiently maneuvering the point of his surgical-steel crowbar under the edge of your dead bicuspid, but who has read in a professional magazine that patients are more likely to come back, and less likely to sue you, if you smile at them. "Say," he says, "I wonder if I could have a quick huddle with you sometime later."

Spit, please.

Saved by the bell! They have reached the ground floor. The elevator doors open to reveal the endangered-marble lobby of the Foote Mansion. Bellhops, disguised as wedding cakes, glide to and fro as if mounted on casters. Not ten feet away is Avi, and with him are two beautiful suits from which protrude the heads of Eb and John. All three heads turn towards them. Seeing the Dentist, Eb and John adopt the facial expressions of B-movie actors whose characters have just taken small-caliber bullets to the center of the forehead. Avi, by contrast, stiffens up like a man who stepped on a rusty nail a week ago and has just felt the first stirrings of the tetanus infection that will eventually break his spine.

"We've got a busy day ahead of us," Randy says. "I guess my answer is yes, subject to availability."

"Good. I'll hold you to it," says Dr. Kepler, and steps out of the elevator. "Good morning, Mr. Halaby. Good morning, Dr. Föhr. Good morning, Mr. Cantrell. Nice to see you all looking so very much like gentlemen."

Nice to see you acting like one.

"The pleasure is ours," Avi says. "I take it we'll be seeing you later?"

"Oh, yes," says the Dentist, "you'll be seeing me all day." *This procedure will be a lengthy one, I'm afraid.* He turns his back on them and walks across the lobby without further pleasantries. He is headed for a cluster of leather chairs nearly obscured by an explosion of bizarre tropical flowers. The occupants of those chairs are mostly young, and all smartly dressed. They snap to attention as their boss glides towards them. Randy counts three women and two men. One of the men is obviously a gorilla, but the women—inevitably referred to as Fates, Furies, Graces, Norns, or Harpies—are rumored to have bodyguard training, and to carry weapons, too.

"Who are those?" John Cantrell asks. "His hygienists?"

"Don't laugh," Avi says. "Back when he was in practice, he got used to having a staff of women do the pick-and-floss work for him. It shaped his paradigm."

"Are you shitting me?" Randy asks.

"You know how it works," Avi says. "When you go to the dentist, you never actually see the dentist, right? Someone else makes the appointment. Then there's always this elite coterie of highly efficient women who scrape the plaque out of the way, so that the dentist doesn't have to deal with it, and take your X-rays. The dentist himself sits in the back somewhere and looks at the X-rays—he deals with you as this abstract greyscale image on a little piece of film. If he sees holes, he goes into action. If not, he comes in and exchanges small talk with you for a minute and then you go home."

"So, why is he here?" demands Eberhard Föhr.

"Exactly!" Avi says. "When he walks into the room, you never know why he's here—to drill a hole in your skull, or just talk about his vacation in Maui."

All eyes turn to Randy. "What went on in that elevator?"

"I—nothing!" Randy blurts.

"Did you discuss the Philippines project at all?"

"He just said he wanted to talk to me about it."

"Well, shit." Avi says. "That means *we* have to talk about it first."

"I know that," Randy says, "so I told him that I might talk to him if I had a free moment."

"Well, we'd best make damn sure you have no free moments today," Avi says. He thinks for a moment and continues, "Did he have a hand in his pocket at any time?"

"Why? You expecting him to pull out a weapon?"

"No," Avi says, "but someone told me, once, that the Dentist is wired."

"You mean, like a police informant?" John asks incredulously.

"Yeah," Avi says, like it's no big deal. "He makes a habit of carrying a tiny digital recorder the size of a matchbook around in his pocket. Perhaps with a wire running up inside his shirt to a tiny microphone somewhere. Perhaps not. Anyway, you never know when he's recording you."

"Isn't that illegal or something?" Randy asks.

"I'm not a lawyer," Avi says. "More to the point, I'm not a Kinakutan lawyer. But it wouldn't matter in a civil suit—if he slapped us with a tort, he could introduce any kind of evidence he wanted."

They all look across the lobby. The Dentist is standing flatfooted on the marble, arms folded over his chest, chin pointed at the floor as he absorbs input from his aides.

"He might have put his hand in his pocket. I don't remember," Randy says. "It doesn't matter. We kept it extremely general. And brief."

"He could still subject the recording to a voice-stress analysis, to figure out if you were lying," John points out. He relishes the sheer unbridled paranoia of this. He's in his element.

"Not to worry," Randy says, "I jammed it."

"Jammed it? How?" Eb asks, not catching the irony in Randy's voice. Eb looks surprised and interested. It is clear from the look on his face that Eb longs to get into a conversation about something arcane and technical.

"I was joking," Randy explains. "If the Dentist analyzes the recording, he'll find nothing but stress in my voice."

Avi and John laugh sympathetically. But Eb is crestfallen. "Oh," Eb says. "I was thinking that we could absolutely jam his device if we so wanted."

"A tape recorder doesn't use radio," John says. "How could we jam it?"

"Van Eck phreaking," Eb says.

At this point, Tom Howard emerges from the cafe with a thoroughly ravished copy of the *South China Morning Post* under his arm, and Beryl emerges from an elevator, prepped for combat in a dress and makeup. The men avert their eyes shyly and pretend not to notice. Greetings and small talk ensue. Then Avi looks at his watch and says, "Let's head over to the sultan's palace," as if he were proposing they go grab some french fries at Mickey Ds.

CRACKER

WATERHOUSE HAS TO KEEP AN EYE ON THAT SAFE; SHAFTOE IS itching to blow it open with high explosives, and Chattan (who firmly overrules Shaftoe) intends to ship it back to London so that it can be opened by experts at the Broadway Buildings. Waterhouse only wants to have another crack at opening it himself, just to see if he can do it.

Chattan's position is the correct one. Detachment 2702 has a very clear and specialized mission which most certainly does not include opening safes from U-boats. For that matter, it does not include going onto abandoned U-boats to recover safes, or other crypto data, in the first place. The only reason they did that was because they happened to be the only people with Ultra clearance who were in the neighborhood, and U–553's precarious position did not give Bletchley Park time to send out its own experts.

But Waterhouse's desire to open the safe himself has nothing to do with Detachment 2702's mission, or his own personal duties, or even, particularly, with winning the war. It is something that Lawrence Pritchard Waterhouse is driven to do. His is not to reason why. Even as he was reeling down that stretched line from U–553 to the torpedo boat, battered by waves and wind and rain, with a busted arm and a busted head, not knowing from one moment to the next whether he would make it back to the boat or plunge into the Atlantic, he was remembering the infinitesimal tremors picked up by the half-frozen neurons in his fingertips as he twiddled the safe's submerged dial. Even as Enoch Root patched him up on board the boat, Waterhouse was constructing a crude mental model of how the safe's tumblers might be constructed, visualizing the thing in his mind's eye. And even as the rest of Detachment 2702 collapses into their cots and hammocks and sleeping bags around the chapel of Qwghlm Castle, the splinted and bandaged Waterhouse stalks the polished corridors of that building's better corner, looking for a couple of used razor blades and a hunk of carbon.

The razors he finds in a rubbish bin and the carbon he steals from the closet where Ghnxh keeps the Galvanick Lucipher. He brings them, plus a brick-sized crystal of hard glue and a blowtorch, back to the chapel, where everyone else is sleeping. Enlisted men are in the nave, as befits Marines who are basically a naval organization. Officers are in the transept: Chattan has the south arm of it all to himself, Waterhouse and Root and the SAS and USMC lieutenants have bunk beds in the north. A small moiety of Detachment 2702's astounding tarp supply has, then, been hung up across the eastern end of the place, partitioning off the chancel, Holy of Holies, where once the Body and Blood of Christ were housed. Now it contains a Hallicrafters Model S-27 15-tube superheterodyne radio receiver using state-of-the-art acorn tubes in its front end, capable of tuning VHF from 27 to 143 Megahertz and of receiving AM, FM, and CW, and including a signal strength meter which would come in handy if they were really operating a huffduff station here, which they aren't.

The lights are burning behind those tarps and one of the Marines is snoring away in a chair in front of the altar. Waterhouse wakes him up and sends him to bed. The Marine is ashamed; he knows he was supposed to be awake, twiddling that antenna convincingly.

The radio itself has hardly been used—they only turn it on when someone comes to visit who is not in on the Secret. It sits there on the altar, pristine, as if it had just come from the Hallicrafters factory in Chicago, Illinois. All of the altar's fancy bits (if it ever had them) have long since succumbed to fire, rot, plunder, or the gnawing tusks of nest-building skerries. What remains is a rectangular monolith of basalt, featureless except for some marks from the tools that were used to quarry and shape it. It is a perfect foundation for tonight's experiment.

Waterhouse gets the safe up there at some cost to the disks and ligaments in his lower back. It is tubular in shape, like an excerpt of naval gun barrel. He stands it up on its back end so that its round door, with the round dial in the center, is staring up at the ceiling like a blind eye, the radial lines on the dial looking very much like the striations of an iris.

Behind that dial is a bunch of mechanical stuff that has gotten Waterhouse completely pissed off, driven him into a frantic state. By manipulating this dial in some way, he should be able to tease that mechanical stuff into some configuration that allows the door to be opened. That's all there is to it. That this door remains locked is an outrage. Why should the tiny volume inside this safe—much less than a single cubic foot—be so different from the space that Waterhouse moves through at will? What the hell is inside there?

The glue looks like bad amber, flawed and bubbled but still beautiful. He fires up the little blowtorch and plays the flame over one end of it. The glue softens, melts, and drips onto the door of the safe, next to the dial, forming a little puddle about the size of a silver dollar.

Working quickly, Waterhouse sets two single-edged razor blades into it, the blades dangerously upward-facing, parallel and somewhat less than an inch apart. He holds them in place for a few moments while the frigid metal of the safe sucks the heat out of that glue and makes it hard again. He has employed a pair of toothpicks as spacers to make sure that the blunt backs of the blades do not actually touch the door of the safe; he does not want an electrical connection between them.

He solders a wire onto each of the razor blades and runs the wires across the altar toward the radio. Then he takes a little chunk of carbon and lays it across the two blades, forming a bridge between them.

He tears open the back of the radio and does a bit of rewiring. Most of the rig is already set up the way he needs it; basically he's looking for something that will convert electrical impulses into sound and pump that sound into the headphones, which is what a radio does. But the source of the signal is no longer a transmitter on a U-boat but rather the current flowing up one of Waterhouse's wires, into the left razor blade, across the carbon bridge, into the right razor blade, and back down the other wire.

Getting this hooked up the way he wants it takes some doing. When he blunders down a blind alley and gets frustrated, he will go over and twiddle the antenna for a while, pretending to zero in on a U-boat. Then an idea will occur to him and he will go back to work.

Sometime around dawn, he hears a squeal from the headphones: a pair of Bakelite cups bridged by a contraption that looks like a primitive surgical device, hooked up to the radio by a twisted pair of black and red wires. He turns the volume down and claps the phones over his head.

He reaches out and lays one fingertip on the safe, and hears a painful thud in his ears. He slides the fingertip over the surface of the cold metal and hears a rasping sound. Any vibrations cause the bridge of carbon to tremble on the razor blades, making and breaking the electrical connection, modulating the electrical current. The blades and the carbon are a microphone, and the microphone works—almost too well.

He takes his hand off the safe and just sits there and listens for a while. He can hear the footfalls of skerries going through the detachment's rations. He can hear the impact of waves on the shore, miles away, and the thump of the Taxi's bald tires on chuckholes out on the Road. Sounds like the Taxi has a little alignment problem! He can hear the scrub, scrub of Margaret cleaning the floor of the kitchen, and some minor arrhythmias in the heartbeats of the enlisted men, and the boom of glaciers calving on the coast of Iceland, and the squirrely drone of hastily machined propellers on approaching convoy ships. Lawrence Pritchard Waterhouse is plugged into the Universe in a way that exceeds even what Bletchley Park has to offer.

The center of that particular universe is the Safe from U-553, and its axis passes up through the center of the Dial, and now Waterhouse has his hand on it. He turns the volume way down before he touches anything so that he won't blow his eardrums out. The Dial spins heavily but easily, as if mounted on gas bearings. Still, there is mechanical friction in there which is not perceptible to Waterhouse's admittedly frozen fingers but which comes through in his earphones like a rockslide.

When the tumblers move, it sounds like Waterhouse is shooting the main bolt on the Gate of Hell. It takes him a little while, and a few more false starts, to get his bearings; he doesn't know how many numbers are in the combination, or which way he should turn the dial to begin with. But with experimentation, some patterns begin to show through, and eventually he works out the following combination:

23 right—37 left—7 right—31 left—13 right

and then there's a really meaty click and he knows in his marrow that he can take off the headphones. He spins a little wheel that is mounted on the front of the safe adjacent to the dial. This withdraws the radial dogs that have been holding the door shut. He hauls the door up, careful not to slash his hand on the twin razors, and looks into the safe.

His feeling of disappointment that accompanies this action has nothing to do with the contents of the safe. He is disappointed because he has solved the problem, and has gone back to the baseline state of boredom and low-level irritation that always comes over him when he's not doing something that inherently needs to be done, like picking a lock or breaking a code.

He sticks his arm all the way down to the bottom of the safe and finds a metal object about the size of a hot dog bun. He knew it would be there because, like children investigating wrapped presents in the days before Christmas, they have been tilting the safe this way and that, and when they did, they heard something sliding from one end to the other— going *tink, tonk, tink, tonk*—and wondered what it was.

This object is so cold, and sucks the heat out of his hands so efficiently, that it hurts to touch it. He shakes his hand to bring circulation back, then grasps the thing, yanks it out briskly, and throws it down on the altar. It bounces once, twice in a seesawing motion, and rings piercingly as it does—the closest thing to a musical sound that has shaken the air of this chapel in many centuries. It shines gaudily under the electric lights they have set up around the chancel. The glittering light catches the eye of Waterhouse, who has been living on grey and cloudy Qwghlm for weeks, wearing and sleeping in things that are black or khaki or olive drab. He is mesmerized by this thing, simply because of its brightness and beauty against the dull and rude basalt, even before his mind identifies it as a bar of solid gold.

It makes a heck of a paperweight, which is a good thing, because the chapel is nothing if not drafty, and the important contents of the safe consist of onionskin pages that fly away in the tiniest breeze. The pages are ruled with faint horizontal and vertical lines, dividing each one into a grid, and the grids are filled in with hand-printed letters in groups of five.

"Well, look what you found!" says a quiet voice. Waterhouse looks up into the unsettlingly calm and placid gaze of Enoch Root.

"Yes. Encrypted messages," Waterhouse says. "Non-Enigma."

"No," Root says. "I was referring to the Root of All Evil, here." He tries to pick up the gold bar, but his fingers merely slip off of it. He gets a firmer grip and hefts it up off the altar. Something about it catches his eye, and he turns to bring it under one of the electric lights, frowning at it with the critical intensity of a diamond cutter.

"It's got Hanzi characters stamped on it," Root says.

"Beg pardon?"

"Chinese or Japanese. No, Chinese—there's the chop of a bank in Shanghai. And here are some figures—the fineness and the serial number." Showing unexpected familiarity with such matters for a missionary priest.

Until this point, the gold bar has signified nothing to Waterhouse—it's just a bulk sample of a chemical element, like a lead weight or a flask of mercury. But the fact that it might convey information is quite interesting. He absolutely has to stand up and go look at it. Root is correct: the bar has been neatly marked with small Oriental characters, applied with a stamp. The tiny facets of the ideograms glitter under the light, sparks jumping the gap between the two halves of the Axis.

Root sets the gold bar down on the altar. He saunters over to a table where they keep stationery, and pulls out a sheet of onionskin and a fresh pencil. Returning to the altar, he lays the frail page over the top of the gold bar, then rubs the side of the pencil lead back and forth over it, turning it all black except for where the stamped numbers and characters are underneath. Within a few moments he has a perfect little rubbing, showing the inscription in full detail. He folds the page up and pockets it, then returns the pencil to the table.

Waterhouse has long since gone back to his examination of the pages from the safe. The numbers are all written in the same hand. Now, since they dredged all manner of other paperwork out of the sewage sloshing through the U-boat skipper's cabin, Waterhouse can recognize the captain's hand easily enough; these sheets were written by someone else.

The format of the messages makes it clear that they were not encrypted with an Enigma machine. Enigma messages always begin with two groups of three letters each, which tell the receiving clerk how to set the wheels on his machine. Those groups are missing on all of these sheets, so some other cipher system must have been used. Like every other modern nation, the Germans have a plethora of different cipher systems, some based on books and some on machines. Bletchley Park has broken most of them.

Still, it looks like an interesting exercise. Now that the rest of Detachment 2702 has arrived, making further trysts with Margaret impractical, Waterhouse has nothing to look forward to. Trying to crack the code used on these sheets will be a perfect puzzle to fill the gaping void that opened up as soon as Waterhouse broke the combination of the safe. He steals some paper of his own, sits down at the desk, and busies himself for an hour or two copying out the ciphertext from the skipper's pages, double- and triple-checking each code group to make sure he's got an accurate copy.

On the one hand, this is a pain in the ass. On the other, it gives him a chance to go through the ciphertext by hand, at the very lowest level, which might be useful later. The ineffable talent for finding patterns in chaos cannot do its thing unless he immerses himself in the chaos first. If they do contain patterns, he does not see them just now, in any rational way. But there may be some subrational part of his mind that can go to work, now that the letters have passed before his eyes and through his pencil, and that may suddenly present him with a gift-wrapped clue—or even a full solution—a few weeks from now while he is shaving or antenna-twiddling.

He has been dimly aware, for a while, that Chattan and the others are awake now. Enlisted men are not allowed into the chancel, but the officers get to gather round and admire the gold bar.

"Breaking the code, Waterhouse?" Chattan says, ambling over to the desk, warming his hands with a mug of coffee.

"Making a clean copy," Waterhouse says, and then, because he is not without a certain cunning, adds: "in case the originals are destroyed in transit."

"Very prudent," Chattan nods. "Say, you didn't hide a second gold bar anywhere, did you?"

Waterhouse has been in the military long enough that he does not rise to the bait. "The pattern of sounds made when we tilted the safe back and forth indicated that there was only a single heavy object inside, sir."

Chattan chuckles and takes a sip of his coffee. "I shall be interested to see whether you can break that cipher, Lieutenant Waterhouse. I am tempted to put money on it."

"I sure appreciate that, but it would be a lousy bet, sir," Waterhouse replied. "The chances are very good that Bletchley Park has already broken this cipher, whatever it may be."

"What makes you say that?" Chattan asks absently.

The question is so silly, coming from a man in Chattan's position, that it leaves Waterhouse disoriented. "Sir, Bletchley Park has broken nearly all of the German military and governmental codes."

Chattan makes a face of mock disappointment. "Waterhouse! How unscientific. You are making assumptions."

Waterhouse thinks back and tries to work out the meaning of this. "You think that this cipher might not be German? Or that it might not be military or governmental?"

"I am merely cautioning you against making assumptions," Chattan says.

Waterhouse is still thinking this one over as they are approached by Lieutenant Robson, the commanding officer of the SAS squad. "Sir," he says, "for the benefit of the fellows down in London, we would like to know the combination."

"The combination?" Waterhouse asks blankly. This word, devoid of context, could mean almost anything.

"Yes, sir," Robson says precisely. "To the safe."

"Oh!" Waterhouse says. He is faintly irritated that they would ask him this question. There seems little point in writing down the combination when the equipment needed to break into the safe is sitting right there. It is much more important to have a safe-breaking algorithm than to have one particular solution to a safe-breaking problem. "I don't know," he says. "I forgot."

"You forgot?" Chattan says. He says it on behalf of Robson who appears to be violently biting his tongue. "Did you perhaps write it down before you forgot it?"

"No," Waterhouse says. "But I remember that it consists entirely of prime numbers."

"Well! That narrows it down!" Chattan says cheerfully. Robson does not seem mollified, though.

"And there are five numbers in all, which is interesting since—"

"Since five is itself a prime number!" Chattan says. Once again, Waterhouse is pleased to see his commanding officer displaying signs of a tasteful and expensive education.

"Very well," Robson announces through clenched teeth. "I shall inform the recipients."

SULTAN

THE GRAND WAZIR OF KINAKUTA LEADS THEM INTO THE OFFICES of his boss, the sultan, and leaves them alone for a few minutes at one corner of the conference table, to build which a whole species of tropical hardwoods had to be extinguished. After that, it is a race among the founders of Epiphyte Corp. to see who can blurt out the first witticism about the size of the sultan's home office deduction. They are in the New Palace, three arms of which wrap around the exotic gardens of the ancient and magnificent Old Palace. This meeting

room has a ten-meter-high ceiling. The walls facing onto the garden are
made entirely of glass, so the effect is like looking into a terrarium that
contains a model of a sultan's palace. Randy has never known much
about architecture, and his vocabulary fails him abjectly. The best he
could say is that it's sort of like a cross between the Taj Mahal and
Angkor Wat.

To get here, they had to drive down a long boulevard of palm trees,
enter a huge vaulted marble entrance hall, submit to metal-detection and
frisking, sit in an anteroom for a while sipping tea, take their shoes off,
have warm rose water poured over their hands by a turbaned servant
wielding an ornate ewer, and then walk across about half a mile of
polished marble and oriental carpets. As soon as the door wafts shut
behind the grand wazir's ass, Avi says, "I smell a con job."

"A con job?" Randy scoffs. "What, you think this is a rear-screen
projection? You think this table is made of Formica?"

"It's all real," Avi admits sourly. "But whenever someone gives you
the treatment like this, it's because they're trying to impress you."

"I'm impressed," Randy says. "I admit it. I'm impressed."

"That's just a euphemism for, 'I'm about to do something moronic,' "
Avi says.

"What are we going to *do*? This isn't the kind of meeting where
anything actually gets *done,* is it?"

"If you mean, are we going to sign contracts, is money going to
change hands, then no, nothing is going to get done. But plenty is going
to happen."

The door opens again and the grand wazir leads a group of Nipponese
men into the room. Avi lowers his voice. "Just remember that, at the
end of the day, we're back in the hotel, and the sultan is still here, and
all of this is just a memory to us. The fact that the sultan has a big
garden has no relevance to anything."

Randy starts to get irked: this is so obvious it's insulting to mention
it. But part of the reason he's irked is because he knows Avi saw right
through him. Avi's always telling him not to be romantic. But he
wouldn't be here, doing this, if not for the romance.

Which leads to the question: why is *Avi* doing it? Maybe he has some
romantic delusions of his own, carefully concealed. Maybe that's why he
can see through Randy so damn well. Maybe Avi is cautioning himself
as much as he is the other members of Epiphyte Corp.

Actually this new group is not Nipponese, but Chinese—probably
from Taiwan. The grand wazir shows them their assigned seats, which
are far enough away that they could exchange sporadic gunfire with
Epiphyte Corp. but not converse without the aid of bullhorns. They

spend a minute or so pretending to give a shit about the gardens and the Old Palace. Then, a compact, powerfully built man in his fifties pivots towards Epiphyte Corp. and strides over to them, dragging out a skein of aides. Randy's reminded of a computer simulation he saw once of a black hole passing through a galaxy, entraining a retinue of stars. Randy recognizes the man's face vaguely: it has been printed in business journals more than once, but not often enough for Randy to remember his name.

If Randy were something other than a hacker, he'd have to step forward now and deal with protocol issues. He'd be stressed out and hating it. But, thank god, all that shit devolves automatically on Avi, who steps up to meet this Taiwanese guy. They shake hands and go through the rote exchange of business cards. But the Chinese guy is looking straight through Avi, checking out the other Epiphyte people. Finding Randy wanting, he moves on to Eberhard Föhr. "Which one is Cantrell?" he says.

John's leaning against the window, probably trying to figure out what parametric equation generated the petals on that eight-foot-tall, carnivorous plant. He turns around to be introduced. "John Cantrell."

"Harvard Li. Didn't you get my e-mail?"

Harvard Li! Now Randy is starting to remember this guy. Founder of Harvard Computer Company, a medium-sized PC clone manufacturer in Taiwan.

John grins. "I received about twenty e-mail messages from an unknown person claiming to be Harvard Li."

"Those were from me! I do not understand what you mean that I am an unknown person." Harvard Li is extremely brisk, but not exactly pissed off. He is, Randy realizes, not the kind of man who has to coach himself not to be romantic before a meeting.

"I hate e-mail," John says.

Harvard Li stares him in the eye for a while. "What do you mean?"

"The concept is good. The execution is poor. People don't observe any security precautions. A message arrives claiming to be from Harvard Li, they believe it's really from Harvard Li. But this message is just a pattern of magnetized spots on a spinning disk somewhere. Anyone could forge it."

"Ah. You use digital signature algorithm."

John considers this carefully. "I do not respond to any e-mail that is not digitally signed. Digital signature algorithm refers to one technique for signing them. It is a good technique, but it could be better."

Harvard Li begins nodding about halfway through this, acknowledging the point. "Is there a structural problem? Or are you concerned by the five-hundred-and-twelve-bit key length? Would it be acceptable with a one-thousand-twenty-four-bit key?"

About three sentences later, the conversation between Cantrell and Li soars over the horizon of Randy's cryptographic knowledge, and his brain shuts down. Harvard Li is a crypto maniac! He has been studying this shit personally—not just paying minions to read the books and send him notes, but personally going over the equations, doing the math.

Tom Howard is grinning broadly. Eberhard is looking about as amused as he ever gets, and Beryl's biting back a grin. Randy is trying desperately to get the joke. Avi notes the confusion on Randy's face, turns his back to the Taiwanese, and rubs his thumb and fingers together: *money*.

Oh, yeah. It had to be something to do with that.

Harvard Li cranked out a few million PC clones in the early nineties and loaded them all with Windows, Word, and Excel—but somehow forgot to write any checks to Microsoft. About a year ago, Microsoft kicked his ass in court and won a huge judgement. Harvard claimed bankruptcy: he doesn't have a penny to his name. Microsoft has been trying to prove he still has the odd billion or two salted away.

Harvard Li has clearly been thinking very hard about how to put money where guys like Microsoft can't get it. There are many time-honored ways: the Swiss bank account, the false-front corporation, the big real estate project in deepest, darkest China, bars of gold in a vault somewhere. Those tricks might work with the average government, but Microsoft is ten times smarter, a hundred times more aggressive, and bound by no particular rules. It gives Randy a little frisson just to imagine Harvard Li's situation: being chased across the planet by Microsoft's state-of-the-art hellhounds.

Harvard Li needs electronic cash. Not the lame stuff that people use to buy t-shirts on the Web without giving away their credit card numbers. He needs the full-on badass kind, based on hard crypto, rooted in an offshore data haven, and he needs it bad. So nothing's more logical than that he is sending lots of e-mail to John Cantrell.

Tom Howard sidles up to him. "The question is, is it just Harvard Li, or does he think he's discovered a new market?"

"Probably both," Randy guesses. "He probably knows a few other people who'd like to have a private bank."

"The missiles," Tom says.

"Yeah." China's been taking potshots at Taiwan with ballistic missiles lately, sort of like a Wild West villain shooting at the good guy's feet to make him dance. "There have been bank runs in Taipei."

"In a way," Tom says, "these guys are tons smarter than us, because they've never had a currency they could depend on." He and Randy look over at John Cantrell, who has crossed his arms over his chest and is unloading a disquisition on the Euler totient function while Harvard Li nods intently and his nerd-de-camp frantically scrawls notes on a legal pad. Avi stands far to one side, staring at the Old Palace, as in his mind the ramifications of this bloom and sprawl and twine about each other like a tropical garden run riot.

Other delegations file into the room behind the grand wazir and stake out chunks of the conference table's coastline. The Dentist comes in with his Norns or Furies or Hygienists or whatever the hell they are. There's a group of white guys talking in Down Underish accents. Other than that, they are all Asians. Some of them talk amongst themselves and some pull on their chins and watch the conversation between Harvard Li and John Cantrell. Randy watches them in turn: Bad Suit Asians and Good Suit Asians. The former have grizzled buzz cuts and nicotine-tanned skin and look like killers. They are wearing bad suits, not because they can't afford good ones, but because they don't give a shit. They are from China. The Good Suit Asians have high-maintenance haircuts, eyeglasses from Paris, clear skin, ready smiles. They are mostly from Nippon.

"I want to exchange keys, right now, so we can e-mail," Li says, and gestures to an aide, who scurries to the edge of the table and unfolds a laptop. "Something something Ordo," Li says in Cantonese. The aide points and clicks.

Cantrell is gazing at the table expressionlessly. He squats down to look under it. He strolls over and feels under the edge with his hand.

Randy bends and looks too. It's one of these high-tech conference tables with embedded power and communications lines, so that visitors can plug in their laptops without having to string unsightly cables around and fight over power outlets. The slab must be riddled with conduits. No visible wires connect it to the world. The connections must run down hollow legs and into a hollow floor. John grins, turns to Li, and shakes his head. "Normally I'd say fine," he says, "but for a client with your level of security needs, this is not an acceptable place to exchange keys."

"I'm not planning on using the phone," Li says, "we can exchange them on floppies."

John knocks on wood. "Doesn't matter. Have one of your staff look into the subject of Van Eck phreaking. That's with a 'p-h,' not an 'f,' " he says to the aide who's writing it down. Then, sensing Li's need for an executive summary, he says, "They can read the internal state of your computer by listening to the faint radio emissions coming out of the chips."

"Ahhhhh," Li says, and exchanges hugely significant looks with his technical aides, as if this explains something that has been puzzling the shit out of them.

Someone begins hollering wildly at the far end of the room—not the end by which the guests entered, but the other one. It is a chap in a getup similar to, but not quite as ornate as, the grand wazir's. At some point he switches to English—the same dialect of English spoken by flight attendants for foreign airlines, who have told passengers to insert the metal tongue into the buckle so many times that it rushes out in one phlegmy garble. Small Kinakutan men in good suits begin filing into the room. They take seats across the head end of the table, which is wide enough for a Last Supper tableau. In the Jesus position is a really big chair. It is the kind of thing you'd get if you went to a Finnish designer with a shaved head, rimless glasses, and twin Ph.D.s in semiotics and civil engineering, wrote him a blank check, and asked him to design a throne. Behind is a separate table for minions. All of it is backed up by tons of priceless artwork: an eroded frieze, amputated from a jungle ruin somewhere.

All the guests gravitate instinctively towards their positions around the table, and remain standing. The grand wazir glares at each one in turn. A small man slips into the room, staring vacantly at the floor in front of him, seemingly unaware that other people are present. His hair is lacquered down to his skull, his appearance of portliness minimized by Savile Row legerdemain. He eases into the big chair, which seems like a shocking violation of etiquette until Randy realizes that this is the sultan.

Suddenly everyone is sitting down. Randy pulls his chair back and falls into it. The leathery depths swallow his ass like a catcher's mitt accepting a baseball. He's about to pull his laptop out of its bag, but in this setting, both the nylon bag and the plastic computer have a strip-mall tawdriness. Besides, he has to resist this sophomoric tendency to take notes all the time. Avi himself said that nothing was going to happen at this meeting; all the important stuff is going to be subtextual. Besides, there is the matter of Van Eck phreaking, which Cantrell probably mentioned just to make Harvard Li paranoid, but which has Randy a bit rattled too. He opts for a pad of graph paper—the engineer's answer to the legal pad—and a fine-point disposable pen.

The sultan has an Oxford English accent with traces of garlic and red pepper still wedged in its teeth. He speaks for about fifteen minutes.

The room contains a few dozen living human bodies, each one a big sack of guts and fluids so highly compressed that it will squirt for a few yards when pierced. Each one is built around an armature of 206 bones connected to each other by notoriously fault-prone joints that are given to obnoxious creaking, grinding, and popping noises when they are in other than pristine condition. This structure is draped with throbbing steak, inflated with clenching air sacks, and pierced by a Gordian sewer filled with burbling acid and compressed gas and asquirt with vile enzymes and solvents produced by the many dark, gamy nuggets of genetically programmed meat strung along its length. Slugs of dissolving food are forced down this sloppy labyrinth by serialized convulsions, decaying into gas, liquid, and solid matter which must all be regularly vented to the outside world lest the owner go toxic and drop dead. Spherical, gel-packed cameras swivel in mucus-greased ball joints. Infinite phalanxes of cilia beat back invading particles, encapsulate them in goo for later disposal. In each body a centrally located muscle flails away at an eternal, circulating torrent of pressurized gravy. And yet, despite all of this, not one of these bodies makes a single sound at any time during the sultan's speech. It is a marvel that can only be explained by the power of brain over body, and, in turn, by the power of cultural conditioning over the brain.

Their host is trying to be appropriately sultanic: providing vision and direction without getting sucked down into the quicksand of management. The basic vision (or so it seems at first) is that Kinakuta has always been a crossroads, a meeting-place of cultures: the original Malays. Foote and his dynasty of White Sultans. Filipinos with their Spanish, American and Nipponese governors to the east. Muslims to the east. Anglos to the south. Numerous Southeast Asian cultures to the north. Chinese everywhere as usual. Nipponese whenever they are in one of their adventurous moods, and (for what it's worth) the neolithic tribesmen who inhabit the interior of the island.

Hence nothing is more natural than that the present-day Kinakutans should run big fat optical fiber cables in every direction, patch into every major national telco within reach, and become a sort of digital bazaar.

All of the guests nod soberly at the sultan's insight, his masterful ability to meld the ancient ways of his country with modern technology.

But this is nothing more than a superficial analogy, the sultan confesses.

Everyone nods somewhat more vigorously than they did before: indeed, everything that the sultan was just saying was, in fact, horseshit. Several people jot down notes, lest they lose the Sultan's thread.

After all, the sultan says, physical location no longer matters in a digitized, networked world. Cyberspace knows no boundaries.

Everyone nods vigorously except for, on the one hand, John Cantrell, and, on the other, the grizzled Chinese guys.

But hey, the sultan continues, that's just dizzy-headed cybercheerleading! What bullshit! Of course locations and boundaries matter!

At this point the room is plunged into dimness as the light pouring in through the window-wall is throttled by some kind of invisible mechanism built into the glass: liquid-crystal shutters or something. Screens descend from slots cunningly hidden in the room's ceiling. This diversion saves the cervical vertebrae of many guests, who are about to whiplash themselves by nodding even more vigorously at the sultan's latest hairpin turn. Goddamn it, does location matter in cyberspace or doesn't it? What's the bottom line here? This isn't some Oxford debating society! Get to the point!

The sultan is whipping some graphics on them: a map of the world in one of those politically correct projections that makes America and Europe look like icebound reefs in the high Arctic. A pattern of straight lines is superimposed on the map, each joining two major cities. The web of lines gets denser and denser as the sultan talks, nearly obscuring the land masses, and the oceans as well.

This, the sultan explains, is the conventional understanding of the Internet: a decentralized web connecting each place with all the other places, with no bottlenecks or, if you will, choke-points.

But it's more bullshit! A new graphic comes up: same map, different pattern of lines. Now we have webs within countries, sometimes within continents. But between countries, and especially between continents, there are only a few lines. It's not weblike at all.

Randy looks at Cantrell, who's nodding slyly.

"Many Net partisans are convinced that the Net is robust because its lines of communication are spread evenly across the planet. In fact, as you can see from this graphic, nearly all intercontinental Web traffic passes through a small number of choke-points. Typically these choke-points are controlled and monitored by local governments. Clearly, then, any Internet application that wants to stand free of governmental interference is undermined, from the very beginning, by a fundamental structure problem."

. . . *free of governmental interference.* Randy can't believe he's hearing this. If the sultan was a scruffy hacker talking to a room full of crypto-anarchists, that'd be one thing. But the sultan *is* a government, for god's sake, and the room is full of card-carrying Establishment types.

Like those Chinese buzz-cuts! Who the hell are they? Don't try to tell Randy those guys aren't part of the Chinese government, in some sense.

"Bottlenecks are only one of the structural barriers to the creation of a free, sovereign, location-independent cyberspace," the sultan continues blithely.

Sovereign!?

"Another is the heterogeneous patchwork of laws, and indeed of legal systems, that address privacy, free speech, and telecoms policy."

Another map graphic appears. Each country is colored, shaded, and patterned according to a scheme of intimidating complexity. A half-assed stab at explaining it is made by a complex legend underneath. Instant migraine. That, of course, is the whole point.

"The policy of any given legal system toward privacy issues is typically the result of incremental changes made over centuries by courts and legislative bodies," the sultan says. "With all due respect, very little of it is relevant to modern privacy issues."

The lights come back on, sun waxes through the windows, the screens disappear silently into the ceiling, and everyone's mildly surprised to see that the sultan is on his feet. He is approaching a large and (of course) ornate and expensive-looking Go board covered with a complex pattern of black and white stones. "Perhaps I can make an analogy to Go—though chess would work just as well. Because of our history, we Kinakutans are well-versed in both games. At the beginning of the game, the pieces are arranged in a pattern that is simple and easy to understand. But the game evolves. The players make small decisions, one turn at a time, each decision fairly simple in and of itself, and made for reasons that can be easily understood, even by a novice. But over the course of many such turns, the pattern develops such great complexity that only the finest minds—or the finest computers—can comprehend it." The sultan is gazing down thoughtfully at the Go board as he says this. He looks up and starts making eye contact around the room. "The analogy is clear. Our policies concerning free speech, telecommunications and cryptography have evolved from a series of simple, rational decisions. But they are today so complex that no one can understand them, even in one single country, to say nothing of all countries taken together."

The sultan pauses and walks broodingly around the Go board. The guests have mostly given up on the obsequious nodding and jotting by this point. No one is being tactical now, they are all listening with genuine interest, wondering what he's going to say next.

But he says nothing. Instead he lays one arm across the board and, with a sudden violent motion, sweeps all the stones aside. They rain down into the carpet, skitter across polished stone, clatter onto the tabletop.

There is a silence of at least fifteen seconds. The sultan looks stony. Then, suddenly, he brightens up.

"Time to start over," he says. "A very difficult thing to do in a large country, where laws are written by legislative bodies, interpreted by judges, bound by ancient precedents. But this is the Sultanate of Kinakuta and I am the sultan and I say that the law here is to be very simple: total freedom of information. I hereby abdicate all government power over the flow of data across and within my borders. Under no circumstances will any part of this government snoop on information flows, or use its power to in any way restrict such flows. That is the new law of Kinakuta. I invite you gentlemen to make the most of it. Thank you."

The sultan turns and leaves the room to a dignified ovation. Those are the ground rules, boys. Now run along and play.

Dr. Mohammed Pragasu, Kinakutan Minister of Information, now rises from his chair (which is to the right hand of the sultan's throne, naturally) and takes the conn. His accent is almost as American as the sultan's is British; he did his undergrad work at Berkeley and got his doctorate at Stanford. Randy knows several people who worked and studied with him during those years. According to them, Pragasu rarely showed up for work in anything other than a t-shirt and jeans, and showed just as strong an appetite for beer and sausage pizza as any non-Mohammedan. No one had a clue that he was a sultan's second cousin, and worth a few hundred million in his own right.

But that was ten years ago. More recently, in his dealings with Epiphyte Corp., he's been better dressed, better behaved, but studiously informal: first names only, please. Dr. Pragasu likes to be addressed as Prag. All of their meetings have started with an uninhibited exchange of the latest jokes. Then Prag inquires about his old school buddies, most of whom are working in Silicon Valley now. He delves for tips on the latest and hottest high-tech stocks, reminisces for a few minute about the wild times he enjoyed back in California, and then gets down to business.

None of them has ever seen Prag in his true element until now. It's a bit hard to keep a straight face—as if some old school chum of theirs had rented a suit, forged an ID card, and was now staging a prank at a stuffy business meeting. But there is a solemnity about Dr. Pragasu's bearing today that is impressive, verging on oppressive.

Those Chinese guys across the table look like the Maoist Mt. Rushmore; it is impossible to imagine that any of them has ever smiled in his life. They are getting a live translation of the proceedings through earpieces, connected through the mysterious table to a boiler room full of interpreters.

Randy's attention wanders. Prag's talk is dull because it is covering technical ground with which Randy is already painfully familiar, couched in simple analogies designed to make some kind of sense even after being translated with Mandarin, Cantonese, Nipponese, or what-have-you. Randy begins looking around the table.

There is a delegation of Filipinos. One of them, a fat man in his fifties, looks awfully familiar. As usual, Randy cannot remember his name. And there's another guy who shows up late, all by himself, and is ushered to a solitary chair down at the far end: he might be a Filipino with lots of Spanish blood, but he's more likely Latin American or Southern European or just an American whose forebears came from those places. In any case, he has scarcely settled into his seat before he's pulled out a cellphone and punched in a very long phone number and begun a hushed, tense conversation. He keeps sneaking glances up the table, checking out each delegation in turn, then blurting capsule descriptions into his cellphone. He seems startled to be here. No one who sees him can avoid noticing his furtiveness. No one who notices it can avoid speculating on how he acquired it. But at the same time, the man has a sullen glowering air about him that Randy doesn't notice until his black eyes turn to stare into Randy's like the twin barrels of a derringer. Randy stares back, too startled and stupid to avert his gaze, and some kind of strange information passes from the cellphone man to him, down the twin shafts of black light coming out of the man's eyes.

Randy realizes that he and the rest of Epiphyte(2) Corp. have fallen in among thieves.

SKIPPING

IT'S A HOT CLOUDY DAY IN THE BISMARCK SEA WHEN GOTO Dengo loses the war. The American bombers come in low and level. Goto Dengo happens to be abovedecks on a fresh-air-and-calisthenics drill. To breathe air that does not smell of shit and vomit makes him feel euphoric and invulnerable. Everyone else must be feeling the same way, because he watches the airplanes for a long time before he begins to hear warning klaxons.

The emperor's soldiers are supposed to feel euphoric and invulnerable all the time, because their indomitable spirit makes them so. That Goto Dengo only feels that way when abovedecks, breathing clean air, makes him ashamed. The other soldiers never doubt, or at least never show it. He wonders where he went astray. Perhaps it was his time in Shanghai, where he was polluted with foreign ideas. Or maybe he was polluted from the very beginning—the ancient family curse.

The troop transports are slow—there is no pretence that they are anything other than boxes of air. They have only the most pathetic armaments. The destroyers escorting them are sounding general quarters.

Goto Dengo stands at the rail and watches the crews of the destroyers scrambling to their positions. Black smoke and blue light sputter from the barrels of their weapons, and much later he hears them opening fire.

The American bombers must be in some kind of distress. He speculates that they are low on fuel, or desperately lost, or have been chased down below the cloud cover by Zeros. Whatever the reason, he knows they have not come here to attack the convoy because American bombers attack by flying overhead at a great altitude, raining down bombs. The bombs always miss because the Americans' bombsights are so poor and the crews so inept. No, the arrival of American planes here is just one of those bizarre accidents of war; the convoy has been shielded under heavy clouds since early yesterday.

The troops all around Goto Dengo are cheering. What good fortune that these lost Americans have blundered straight into the gunsights of their destroyer escort! And it is a good omen for the village of Kulu too, because half of the town's young men just happen to be abovedecks to enjoy the spectacle. They grew up together, went to school together, at the age of twenty took the military physical together, joined the army together and trained together. Now they are on their way to New Guinea together. Together they were mustered up onto the deck of the transport only five minutes ago. Together they will enjoy the sight of the American planes softening into cartwheels of flame.

Goto Dengo, at twenty-six, is one of the old hands here—he came back from Shanghai to be a leader and an example to them—and he watches their faces, these faces he has known since he was a child, never happier than at this moment, glowing like cherry petals in the grey world of cloud, ocean, and painted steel.

Fresh delight ripples across their faces. He turns to look. One of the bombers has apparently decided to lighten its load by dropping a bomb straight into the ocean. The boys of Kulu break into a jeering chant. The American plane, having shed half a ton of useless explosives, peels sharply upward, self-neutered, good for nothing but target practice. The Kulu boys howl at its pilot in contempt. A Nipponese pilot would have crashed his plane into that destroyer at the very least!

Goto Dengo, for some reason, watches the bomb instead of the airplane. It does not tumble from the plane's belly but traces a smooth flat parabola above the waves, like an aerial torpedo. He catches his breath for a moment, afraid that it will never drop into the ocean, that it will skim across the water until it hits the destroyer that stands directly across its path. But once again the fortunes of war smile upon the emperor's forces; the bomb loses its struggle with gravity and splashes into the water. Goto Dengo looks away.

Then he looks back again, chasing a phantom that haunts the edge of his vision. The wings of foam that were thrown up by the bomb are still collapsing into the water, but beyond them, a black mote is speeding away—perhaps it was a second bomb dropped by the same airplane. This time Goto Dengo watches it carefully. It seems to be rising, rather than falling—a mirage perhaps. No, no, he's wrong, it is losing altitude slowly now, and it plows into the water and throws up another pair of wings all right.

And then the bomb rises up out of the water again. Goto Dengo, a student of engineering, implores the laws of physics to take hold of this thing and make it fall and sink, which is what big dumb pieces of metal are supposed to do. Eventually it does fall again—but then it rises up again.

It is skipping across the water like the flat rocks that the boys of Kulu used to throw across the fish pond near the village. Goto Dengo watches it skip several more times, utterly fascinated. Once again, the fortunes of war have provided a bizarre spectacle, seemingly for no other reason than to entertain him. He savors it as if it were a cigarette discovered in the bottom of a pocket. Skip, skip, skip.

Right into the flank of one of the escorting destroyers. A gun turret flies straight up into the air, tumbling over and over. Just as it slows to its apogee, it is completely enveloped in a geyser of flame spurting out of the ship's engine room.

The Kulu boys are still chanting, refusing to accept the evidence of their own eyes. Something flashes in Goto Dengo's peripheral vision; he turns to watch another destroyer being snapped in half like a dry twig as its magazines detonate. Tiny black things are skip, skip, skipping all over the ocean now, like fleas across the rumpled bedsheets of a Shanghai whorehouse. The chant falters. Everyone watches silently.

The Americans have invented a totally new bombing tactic in the middle of a war and implemented it flawlessly. His mind staggers like a drunk in the aisle of a careening train. They saw that they were wrong, they admitted their mistake, they came up with a new idea. The new idea was accepted and embraced all the way up the chain of command. Now they are using it to kill their enemies.

No warrior with any concept of honor would have been so craven. So *flexible*. What a loss of face it must have been for the officers who had trained their men to bomb from high altitudes. What has become of those men? They must have all killed themselves, or perhaps been thrown into prison.

The American Marines in Shanghai weren't proper warriors either. Constantly changing their ways. Like Shaftoe. Shaftoe tried to fight Nipponese soldiers in the street and failed. Having failed, he decided to learn new tactics—from Goto Dengo. "The Americans are not warriors," everyone kept saying. "Businessmen perhaps. Not warriors."

Belowdecks, the soldiers are cheering and chanting. They have not the faintest idea what is really going on. For just a moment, Goto Dengo tears his eyes away from the sea full of exploding and sinking destroyers. He gets a bearing on a locker full of life preservers.

The airplanes all seem to be gone now. He scans the convoy and finds no destroyers in working order.

"Put on the life jackets!" he shouts. None of the men seem to hear him and so he makes for the locker. "Hey! Put on the life jackets!" He pulls one out and holds it up, in case they can't hear him.

They can hear him just fine. They look at him as if what he's doing is more shocking than anything they've witnessed in the last five minutes. What possible use are life jackets?

"Just in case!" he shouts. "So we can fight for the emperor another day." He says this last part weakly.

One of the men, a boy who lived a few doors away from him when they were children, walks up to him, tears the life jacket out of his hands, and throws it into the ocean. He looks Goto up and down, contemptuously, then turns around and walks away.

Another man shouts and points: the second wave of planes is coming in. Goto Dengo goes to the rail to stand among his comrades, but they sidle away. The American planes charge in unopposed and veer away, leaving behind nothing but more skipping bombs.

Goto Dengo watches a bomb come directly toward him for a few bounces, until he can make out the message painted on its nose: BEND OVER, TOJO!

"This way!" he shouts. He turns his back to the bomb and walks back across the deck to the locker full of life preservers. This time a few of the men follow him. The ones who don't—perhaps five percent of the population of the village of Kulu—are catapulted into the ocean when the bomb explodes beneath their feet. The wooden deck buckles upwards. One of the Kulu boys falls with a four-foot-long splinter driven straight up through his viscera. Goto Dengo and perhaps a dozen others make it to the locker on hands and knees and grab life preservers.

He would not be doing this if he had not already lost the war in his soul. A warrior would stand his ground and die. His men are only following him because he has told them to do it.

Two more bombs burst while they are getting the life preserves on and struggling to the rail. Most of the men below must be dead now. Goto Dengo nearly doesn't make it to the railing because it is rising sharply into the air; he ends up doing a chin-up on it and throwing one leg over the side, which is now nearly horizontal. The ship is rolling over! Four others get a grip on the rail, the rest slide helplessly down the deck and vanish into a pit of smoke. Goto Dengo ignores what his eyes are telling him and tries to listen to his inner ear. He is standing up on the side of the ship now, and looking toward the stern he can see one of the propellers spinning uselessly in the air. He begins running uphill. The four others follow him. An American fighter plane comes over. He doesn't even realize they are being strafed until he turns around and sees that the bullets have essentially cut one man in half and crippled another by exploding his knee, so that the lower leg and foot dangle by a few shreds of gristle. Goto Dengo throws the man over his shoulders like a sack of rice and turns to resume the uphill race, but finds that there is no more uphill to race towards.

He and the other two are standing on the summit of the ship now, a steel bulge that rises for no more than a man's height out of the water. He turns around once, then twice, looking for a place to run and sees nothing but water all around. The water bloops and fizzes angrily as air and smoke jet from the interior of the wrecked hull. Sea rushes in towards them. Goto Dengo looks down at the steel bubble supporting his feet and realizes that he is still, just for a moment, perfectly dry. Then the Bismarck Sea converges on his feet from all directions at once and begins to climb up his legs. A moment later the steel plate, which has been pressing so solidly against the soles of his boots, drops away. The weight of the wounded man on his shoulders shoves him straight down into the ocean. He gulps fuel oil into his sinuses, struggles out from beneath the wounded man, and comes to the surface screaming. His nose, and the cavities of his skull, are filled with oil. He swallows some of it and goes into convulsions as his body tries to eject it from every orifice at once: sneezing, vomiting, hawking it up out of his lungs. Reaching up to his face with one hand he feels the oil coating his skin thickly and knows that he dare not open his eyes. He tries to wipe the oil from his face with his sleeve, but the fabric is saturated with it.

He has to get down in the water and wipe himself clean so that he can see again, but the oil in his clothing makes him float. His lungs are finally clear now and he begins to gasp in air. It smells of oil but at least it's breathable. But the volatile chemicals in the oil have gotten into his blood now and he feels them spread through his body like fire. It feels as though a hot spatula is being shoved between his scalp and his skull. The other men are howling and he realizes that he is too. Some of the Chinese workers in Shanghai used to breathe gasoline to get high, and this was the noise that they made.

One of the men near him screams. He hears a noise approaching, like a sheet being torn in half to make bandages. Radiant heat strikes him in the face like a hot frying pan, just before Goto Dengo dives and kicks downwards. The motion exposes a band of flesh around his calf, between his boot and his trouser leg, and in the moment that it's poking straight up out of the water, it gets seared to a crisp.

He swims blind through an ocean of fuel oil. Then there is a change in the temperature and the viscosity of the fluid streaming over his face. Suddenly the life preserver begins to tug him upwards; he must be in water now. He swims for a few more kicks and begins to wipe at his eyes. The pressure on his ears tells him he's not that deep, maybe a couple of meters beneath the surface. Finally he risks opening his eyes. Ghostly, flickering light is illuminating his hands, making them glow a bright green; the sun must have come out. He rolls over on his back and looks straight up. Above him is a lake of rolling fire.

He rips the life preserver off over his head and lets it go. It shoots straight up and bursts out of the surface, burning like a comet. His oil-soaked clothing is tugging him relentlessly upwards, so he rips his shirt off and lets it tumble up towards the surface. His boots pull down, his oily pants push up, and he reaches some sort of equilibrium.

He grew up in the mines.

Kulu is near the north coast of Hokkaido, on the shore of a freshwater lake where rivers converge from the inland hills and commingle their waters before draining to the Sea of Okhotsk. The hills rise sharply from one end of that lake, looming over a cold silver creek that rushes down out of forest inhabited only by apes and demons. There are small islands in that part of the lake. If you dig down into the islands, or the hills, you will find veins of copper ore, and sometimes you will find zinc and lead and even silver. That is what the men of Kulu have done for many generations. Their monument is a maze of tunnels that snake through the hills, not following straight lines but tracking the richest veins.

Sometimes the tunnels dip below the level of the lake. When the mines were working these tunnels were pumped out, but now that they are exhausted, the water has been allowed to seek its level and has formed sumps. There are cavities and tunnels back in the hills that can only be reached by boys who are brave enough to dive into the cold black water and swim through the darkness for ten, twenty, thirty meters.

Goto Dengo went to all of those places when he was a boy. He even discovered some of them. Big, fat and buoyant, he was a pretty good swimmer. He was not the best swimmer, or the best at holding his breath. He was not even the bravest (the bravest did not put on life preservers, and went to their deaths like warriors).

He went where the others wouldn't because he, alone among all the boys of Kulu, was not afraid of the demons. When he was a boy, his father, a mining engineer, would take him hiking up into the places in the mountains where demons were said to live. They would sleep out under the stars and wake up to find their blankets covered with frost, and sometimes their food stolen by bears. But no demons.

The other boys believed that demons lived in some of those underwater tunnels, and that this explained why some of the boys who swam back there never returned. But Goto Dengo did not fear the demons and so he went back there fearing only the cold and the dark and the water. Which was plenty to fear.

Now he need only pretend that the fire is a stone ceiling. He swims some more. But he did not breathe properly before diving, and he is close to panic now. He looks up again and sees that the water is burning only in patches.

He is quite deep, he realizes, and he can't swim well in trousers and boots. He fumbles at his bootlaces, but they are tied in double knots. He pulls a knife from his belt and slashes through the laces, kicks the boots off, sheds his pants and drawers too. Naked, he forces himself to be calm for ten more seconds, brings his knees to his chest and hugs them. His body's natural buoyancy takes over. He knows that he must be rising slowly toward the surface now, like a bubble. The light is growing brighter. He need only wait. He lets go of the knife, which is only slowing him down.

His back feels cold. He explodes out of the fetal position and thrusts his head up into the air, gasping for breath. A patch of burning oil is almost close enough for him to touch, and the oil is trickling across the top of the ocean as if it were a solid surface. Nearly invisible blue flames seep from it, then turn yellow and boil off curling black smoke. He backstrokes away from a reaching tendril.

A glowing silver apparition passes over him, so close he can feel the warmth of its exhaust and read the English warning labels on its belly. The tips of its wing guns are sparkling, flinging out red streaks.

They are strafing the survivors. Some try to dive, but the oil in their uniforms pops them right back to the surface, legs flailing uselessly in the air. Goto Dengo first makes sure he is nowhere near any burning oil, then treads water, spinning slowly in the water like a radar dish, looking for planes. A P-38 comes in low, gunning for him. He sucks in a breath and dives. It is nice and quiet under the water, and the bullets striking its surface sound like the ticking of a big sewing machine. He sees a few rounds plunging into the water around him, leaving trails of bubbles as the water cavitates in their wake, slowing virtually to a stop in just a meter or two, then turning downwards and sinking like bombs. He swims after one of them and plucks it out of the water. It is still hot from its passage. He would keep it as a souvenir, but his pockets are gone with his clothes and he needs his hands. He stares at the bullet for a moment, greenish-silver in the underwater light, fresh from some factory in America.

How did this bullet come from America to my hand?

We have lost. The war is over.

I must go home and tell everyone.

I must be like my father, a rational man, explaining the facts of the world to the people at home, who are crippled by superstitions.

He lets the bullet go again, watches it drop towards the bottom of the sea, where the ships, and all of the young men of Kulu, are bound.

MUGS

HEY, IT'S AN IMMATURE MARKET.
The rationalizations have not actually begun yet—Randy's still sitting in the sultan's big conference room, and the meeting's just getting up to speed.

Naturally the early adopters are not going to be your regular joes.

Tom Howard has taken the floor to explain his work. Randy doesn't have much to do, so he's imagining tonight's conversation in the Bomb and Grapnel.

It's like the Wild West—a little unruly at first, then in a few years it settles down and you've got Fresno.

Most of the delegations have brought hired guns: engineers and security experts who'll get a bounty if they can find a flaw in Tom's system. One by one, these guys stand up to take their shots.

Ten years from now, widows and paperboys will be banking in cyberspace.

Magnificent isn't the word you would normally use to describe Tom Howard; he's burly and surly, completely lacking in social graces, and doesn't apologize for it. Most of the time he sits silently, wearing an expression of sphinxlike boredom, and so it's easy to forget how good he is.

But during this particular half hour of Tom Howard's life, it is of the essence that he be magnificent. He is going blade-to-blade with the

Seven Samurai here: the nerdiest high-octane Ph.D.s and the scariest private-security dicks that Asia can produce. One-by-one they come after him and he cuts their heads off and stacks them on the table like cannon-balls. Several times he has to stop and think for sixty seconds before delivering the deathblow. Once he has to ask Eberhard Föhr to make some calculations on his laptop. Occasionally he has to call on the crypto-graphic expertise of John Cantrell, or to look over at Randy for a nod or shake of the head. But eventually, he shuts the hecklers up. Beryl wears a not very convincing smile throughout the entire thing. Avi just grips the arms of his chair, his knuckles going from blue to white to pink to a normal healthy glow over the course of the final five minutes, when it's clear that the Samurai are withdrawing in disarray. It makes Randy want to empty a six-shooter into the ceiling and holler, "Yeee-haaw!" at the top of his lungs.

Instead he listens, just in case Tom gets tripped up in the briar patch of plesiosynchronous protocol arcana, whence only Randy can drag him out. This gives him some more time to survey the faces of the other people in the room. But the meeting is a couple of hours old now, and they are all as familiar to him as siblings.

Tom wipes his sword on his pantleg and thwacks his big ass resound-ingly into his leather chair. Minions scurry into the room bringing tea and coffee and sugar/fat pods. Dr. Pragasu stands up and introduces John Cantrell.

Sheesh! So far, the agenda is revolving entirely around Epiphyte Corp. What gives?

Dr. Pragasu, having developed a friendly relationship with these Cali-fornia hackers, is pimping them to his big money contacts. That's what gives.

This is very interesting from a business standpoint. But Randy finds it a bit irksome and threatening, this one-way flow of information. By the time they go home, this assemblage of shady gmokes is going to know everything about Epiphyte Corp., but Epiphyte will still be in the dark. No doubt that's exactly how they want it.

It occurs to Randy to look over at the Dentist. Dr. Hubert Kepler is sitting on the same side of the table as he is, and so it's hard to read his face. But it's clear he's not listening to John Cantrell. He's covering his mouth with one hand and staring into space. His Valkyries are furiously passing notes back and forth, like naughty cheerleaders.

Kepler's just as surprised as Randy. He doesn't seem like the kind of guy who delights in surprises.

What can Randy do right now to enhance shareholder value? Intrigue is not his specialty; he'll leave that to Avi. Instead, he tunes out the meeting, opens up his laptop, and begins to hack.

Hacking is an overly glorious word for this. Everyone in Epiphyte Corp. has a laptop with a tiny built-in video camera, so that they can do long-distance videoconferencing. Avi insisted on it. The camera is almost invisible: just an orifice a couple of millimeters across, mounted in the top center of the frame that surrounds the screen. It doesn't have a lens as such—it's a camera in the oldest sense, a camera obscura. One wall contains the pinhole and the opposite wall is a silicon retina.

Randy has the source code—the original program—for the videoconferencing software. It is reasonably clever in its use of bandwidth. It looks at the stream of frames (individual still images) coming from the pinhole camera and notices that, although the total amount of data in those frames is rather large, the difference from one frame to the next is tiny. It would be altogether different if Frame 1 were a talking head and Frame 2, a fraction of a second later, were a postcard shot of a Hawaiian beach and Frame 3 a diagram of a printed circuit and Frame 4 a closeup of a dragonfly's head. But in fact, each frame is a talking head—the same person's head, with minor changes in position and expression. The software can save on precious bandwidth by mathematically subtracting each new frame from the previous one (since, to the computer, each image is just a long number) and then transmitting only the difference.

What it all means is that this software has a lot of built-in capabilities for comparing one image with another, and gauging the magnitude of the difference from one frame to the next. Randy doesn't have to write that stuff. He just has to familiarize himself with these already-existing routines, learn their names and how to use them, which takes about fifteen minutes of clicking around.

Then he writes a little program called Mugshot that will take a snapshot from the pinhole camera every five seconds or so, and compare it to the previous snapshot, and, if the difference is large enough, save it to a file. An encrypted file with a meaningless, random name. Mugshot opens no windows and produces no output of its own, so the only way you can tell it's running is by typing the UNIX command

ps

and hitting the return key. Then the system will spew out a long list of running processes, and Mugshot will show up somewhere in that list.

Just in case someone thinks of this, Randy gives the program a fake name: VirusScanner. He starts it running, then checks its directory and verifies that it has just saved an image file: one mug shot of Randy. As long as he sits fairly still, it won't save any more mug shots; the pattern of light that represents Randy's face striking the far wall of the camera obscura won't change very much.

In the technology world, no meeting is complete without a demo. Cantrell and Föhr have developed a prototype of the electronic cash system, just to demonstrate the user interface and the built-in security features. "A year from now, instead of going to the bank and talking to a human being, you will simply launch this piece of software from any-where in the world," Cantrell says, "and communicate with the Crypt." He blushes as this word seeps through the translators and into the ears of the others. "Which is what we're calling the system that Tom Howard has been putting together."

Avi's on his feet, coolly managing the crisis. *"Mi fu,"* he says, speaking directly to the Chinese guys, "is a better translation."

The Chinese guys look relieved, and a couple of them actually crack smiles when they hear Avi speaking Mandarin. Avi holds up a sheet of paper bearing the Chinese characters:*

秘 符

Painfully aware that he has just dodged a bullet, John Cantrell contin-ues with a thick tongue. "We thought you might want to see the soft-ware in action. I'm going to demo it on the screen now, and during the lunch break you should feel free to come around and try it out yourselves."

Randy fires up the software. He's got his laptop plugged into a video jack on the underside of the table so that the sultan's lurking media geeks can project a duplicate of what Randy's seeing onto a large projection screen at the end of the room. It is running the front end to the cash demo, but his mug shot program is still running in the background. Randy slides the computer over to John, who runs through the demo (there should be a mug shot of John Cantrell stored on the hard disk now).

"I can write the best cryptographic code possible, but it's all worthless unless there is a good system for verifying the user's identify," John begins, regaining some poise now. "How does the computer know that

---

*The first one, *mì,* meaning "secret" and the second one, *fú,* having a dual connotation meaning, on the one hand, a symbol or mark, and on the other hand, Taoist magic.

you are you? Passwords are too easy to guess, steal, or forget. The computer needs to know something about you that is as unique to you as
your fingerprint. Basically it has to look at some part of your body, such
as the blood vessels in your retina or the distinctive sound of your voice,
and compare it against known values stored in its memory. This kind of
technology is called biometrics. Epiphyte Corp. boasts one of the top
biometrics experts in the world: Dr. Eberhard Föhr, who wrote what's
considered to be the best handwriting-recognition system in the world."
John rushes through this encomium. Eb and everyone else in the room
look bored by it—they've all seen Eb's resume. "Right now we're going
with voice recognition, but the code is entirely modular, so we could
swap in some other system, such as a hand geometry reader. That's up
to the customer."

John runs the demo, and unlike most demos, it actually works and
does not crash. He even tries to fake it out by recording his own voice
on a pretty good portable digital tape recorder and then playing it back.
But the software is not fooled. This actually makes an impression on the
Chinese guys, who, up to the point, have looked like the contents of
Madame Tussaud's Dumpster after an exhibit on the Cultural
Revolution.

Not everyone is such a tough sell. Harvard Li is a committed Cantrell
supporter, and the Filipino heavyweight looks like he can hardly wait to
deposit his cash reserves in the Crypt.

Lunchtime! Doors are hauled open to reveal a dining room with a buffet
along the far wall, redolent of curry, garlic, cayenne, and bergamot.
The Dentist makes a point of sitting at the same table with Epiphyte
Corp., but doesn't say very much—just sits there with a dreadfully cho-
leric expression on his face, staring and chewing and thinking. When
Avi finally asks him what he thinks, Kepler says, levelly: "It's been
informative."

The Three Graces cringe epileptically. Informative is evidently an extremely bad word in the Dentist's lexicon. It means that Kepler has
learned something at this meeting, which means that he did not know
absolutely everything going into it, which would certainly rate as an
unforgivable intelligence failure on his scale of values.

There is an agonizing silence. Then Kepler says, "But not devoid
of interest."

Deep sighs of relief ventilate the blindingly white, plaque-free dentition of the Hygienists. Randy tries to imagine which is worse: that Kepler
suspects that the wool was pulled over his eyes, or that he sees a new
opportunity here. Which is more terrible, the paranoia or the avarice of
the Dentist? They are about to find out. Randy, with his sappy, romantic

instinct for ingratiation, almost says something like, *"It's been informative for us, too!"* but he holds back, noticing that Avi has *not* said it. Saying it would not enhance shareholder value. Best to play one's cards close to the vest, let Kepler wonder whether Epiphyte Corp. knew the real agenda.

Randy has chosen his seat tactically, so that he can look straight through the door into the conference room and keep an eye on his laptop. One by one, members of the other delegations excuse themselves, go into the room, and run the demo, imprinting their own voices into the computer's memory and then letting it recognize them. Some of the nerds even type commands on Randy's keyboard; probably that ps command, snooping. Despite the fact that Randy's got it set up so it can't be meddled with too much, it bothers him at a deep level to see the fingertips of these strangers prodding away at *his* keyboard.

It gnaws at him all through the afternoon session, which is all about the communications links joining Kinakuta to the wide world. Randy ought to be paying attention to this, since it impinges massively on the Philippines project. But he doesn't. He broods over his keyboard, contaminated by a foreign touch, and then he broods about the fact that he brooding about it, which demonstrates his unfitness for Biz. It's technically Epiphyte's keyboard—not even his—and if it enhances shareholder value for sinister Eastern nerds to poke around his files, he should be happy to let them do it.

They adjourn. Epiphyte and the Nipponese dine together, but Randy's bored and distracted. Finally, about nine P.M., he excuses himself and goes to his room. He's mentally composing a response to root@eruditorum.org, along the lines of *because there seems to be a hell of a market for this kind of thing, and it's better that I fill the niche, than someone frankly and overly evil.* But before his laptop has even had time to boot up, the Dentist, clad in a white terrycloth robe and smelling like vodka and hotel soap, knocks on Randy's door and invites himself in. He invades Randy (no; the shareholders') bathroom and helps himself to a glass of water. He stands at the shareholders' window and glowers down at the Nipponese cemetery for several minutes before speaking.

"Do you realize who those people were?" he says. His voice, if subjected to biometric analysis, would reflect disbelief, bewilderment, maybe a trace of amusement.

Or maybe he's just faking it, trying to get Randy to let down his guard. Maybe *he* is root@eruditorum.org.

"Yeah," Randy lies.

When Randy revealed the existence of Mugshot, after the meeting, Avi gave him a commendation for deviousness, printed up the mugshots in his hotel room, and Federal Expressed them to a private dick in Hong Kong.

Kepler turns around and gives Randy a searching look. "Either I had bad information about you guys," he says, "or else you are in way over your heads."

If this were the First Business Foray, Randy would piss his pants at this point. If it were the Second, he would resign and fly back to California tomorrow. But it's the third, and so he manages to maintain composure. The light is behind him, so perhaps Kepler's momentarily dazzled and can't read his face very well. Randy takes a swallow of water and breathes deeply, asking, "In light of today's events," he says, "what's in store for our relationship?"

"It is no longer about providing cheap long-distance service to the Philippines—if, indeed, it ever was in the first place!" Kepler says darkly. "The data flowing through the Philippines network now takes on entirely new significance. It's a superb opportunity. At the same time, we're competing against heavy hitters: those Aussies and the Singapore group. *Can* we compete against them, Randy?"

It is a simple and direct question, the most dangerous kind. "We wouldn't be risking our shareholders' money if we didn't think so."

"That's a predictable answer," Kepler snorts. "Are we going to have a real conversation here, Randy, or should we invite our PR people into the room and exchange press releases?"

During an earlier business foray, Randy would have buckled at this point. Instead he says, "I'm not prepared to have a real conversation with you, here and now."

"Sooner and later we have to have one," says the Dentist. *Those wisdom teeth will have to come out someday.*

"Naturally."

"In the meantime, here is what you should be thinking about," Kepler says, getting ready to leave. "What the hell can we offer, in the way of telecommunications services, that stacks up competitively against the Aussies and those Singapore boys? Because we can't beat 'em on price."

This being Randy's Third Business Foray, he doesn't blurt out the answer: redundancy. "That question will certainly be on all of our minds," Randy says instead.

"Spoken like a flack," says Kepler, his shoulders sagging. He goes out into the hallway and turns around, saying, "See you tomorrow at the Crypt." Then he winks. "Or the Vault, or Cornucopia of Infinite Prosperity, or whatever the Chinese word for it is." Having knocked Randy off balance with this startling display of humanity, he walks away.

✝ TOJO AND HIS CLAQUE OF IMPERIAL ARMY BONEHEADS SAID TO
him, in effect: Why don't you go out and secure the Pacific
Ocean for us, because we'll need a convenient shipping lane,
say, oh, about ten thousand miles wide, in order to carry out our little
plan to conquer South America, Alaska, and all of North America west
of the Rockies. In the meantime we'll finish mopping up China. Please
attend to this ASAP.

By then they were running the country. They had assassinated anyone
in their way, they had the emperor's ear, and it was hard to tell them
that their plan was full of shit and that the Americans were just going
to get really pissed off and annihilate them. So, Admiral Isoroku Yamamoto, a dutiful servant of the emperor, put a bit of thought into the
problem, sketched out a little plan, sent out one or two boats on a small
jaunt halfway across the fucking planet, and blew Pearl Harbor off the
map. He timed it perfectly, right after the formal declaration of war. It
was not half bad. He did his job.

One of his aides later crawled into his office—in the nauseatingly
craven posture that minions adopt when they are about to make you
really, really unhappy—and told him that there had been a mix-up in
the embassy in Washington and that the diplomats there had not gotten
around to delivering the declaration of war until well after the American
Pacific Fleet had gone to the bottom.

To those Army fuckheads, this is nothing—just a typo, happens all the
time. Isoroku Yamamoto has given up on trying to make them understand that the Americans are grudge-holders on a level that is inconceiv-
able to the Nipponese, who learn to swallow their pride before they
learn to swallow solid food. Even if he could get Tojo and his mob of
shabby, ignorant thugs to comprehend how pissed off the Americans are,
they'd laugh it off. What're they going to do about it? Throw a pie in
your face, like the Three Stooges? Ha, ha, ha! Pass the sake and bring
me another comfort girl!

Isoroku Yamamoto spent a lot of time playing poker with Yanks
during his years in the States, smoking like a chimney to deaden the
scent of their appalling aftershave. The Yanks are laughably rude and
uncultured, of course; this hardly constitutes a sharp observation. Yamamoto, by contrast, attained some genuine insight as a side-effect of being

robbed blind by Yanks at the poker table, realizing that the big freckled louts could be dreadfully cunning. Crude and stupid would be okay—perfectly understandable, in fact.

But crude and clever is intolerable; this is what makes those red-headed ape-men extra double super loathsome. Yamamoto is still trying to drill the notion into the heads of his partners in the big Nipponese scheme to conquer everything between Karachi and Denver. He wishes that they would get the message. A lot of the Navy men have been around the world a few times and seen it for themselves, but those Army guys have spent their careers mowing down Chinamen and raping their women and they honestly believe that the Americans are just the same except taller and smellier. *Come on guys,* Yamamoto keeps telling them, *the world is not just a big Nanjing.* But they don't get it. If Yamamoto were running things, he'd make a rule: each Army officer would have to take some time out from bayoneting Neolithic savages in the jungle, go out on the wide Pacific in a ship, and swap 16-inch shells with an American task force for a while. Then maybe, they'd understand they're in a real scrap here.

This is what Yamamoto thinks about, shortly before sunrise, as he clambers onto his Mitsubishi G4M bomber in Rabaul, the scabbard of his sword whacking against the frame of the narrow door. The Yanks call this type of plane "Betty," an effeminatizing gesture that really irks him. Then again, the Yanks name even their *own* planes after women, and paint naked ladies on their sacred instruments of war! If they had samurai swords, Americans would probably decorate the blades with nail polish.

Because the plane's a bomber, the pilot and copilot are crammed into a cockpit above the main tube of the fuselage. The nose of the plane, then, is a blunt dome of curving struts, like the meridians and parallels of a globe, the trapezoids between them filled with sturdy panes of glass. The plane has been parked pointing east, so the glass nose is radiant with streaky dawn, the unreal hues of chemicals igniting in a lab. In Nippon nothing happens by accident, so he has to assume that this is a deliberate morale-building tip o' the helmet to the Rising Sun. Making his way up to the greenhouse, he straps himself in where he can stare out the windows as this Betty, and Admiral Ugaki's, take off.

In one direction is Simpson's Harbor, one of the best anchorages in the Pacific, an asymmetrical U wrapped in a neat grid of streets, conspicuously blighted by a fucking British cricket oval! In the other direction, over the ridge, lies the Bismarck Sea. Somewhere down there, the corpses of a few thousand Nipponese troops lie pickled in the wrinkled hulls of their transport ships. A few thousand more escaped to life rafts, but all of their weapons and supplies went to the bottom, so the men are just useless mouths now.

It's been like this for almost a year, ever since Midway, when the Americans refused to bite on Yamamoto's carefully designed feints and ruses up Alaska way, and just happened to send all of their surviving carriers directly into the path of his Midway invasion force. Shit. Shit Shit. Shit. Shit. Shit. Shit. Yamamoto's chewing on a thumbnail, right through his glove.

Now those clumsy, reeking, farmhands are sinking every transport ship that the Army sends to New Guinea. Double shit! Their observation planes are everywhere—always showing up in the right place at the right time—tally-hoing the emperor's furtive convoys in the sawing twang of bloody-gummed Confederates. Their coast-watchers infest the mountains of all these godforsaken islands, despite the Army's efforts to hunt them down and flush them out. All of their movements are known.

The two planes fly southeastwards across the tip of New Ireland and enter the Solomon Sea. The Solomon Islands spread out before them, fuzzy jade humps rising from a steaming ocean, 6500 feet below. A couple of small humps and then a much bigger one, today's destination: Bougainville.

Have to show the flag, go out on these inspection tours, give the frontline troops a glimpse of glory, build morale. Yamamoto frankly has better things to do with his time, so he tries to pack as many of these obligatory junkets into a single day as possible. He left his naval citadel at Truk and flew to Rabaul last week so that he could supervise his latest big operation: a wave of massed air attacks on American bases from New Guinea to Guadalcanal.

The air raids were purportedly successful; kind of. The surviving pilots reported vast numbers of sinkings, whole fleets of American aircraft destroyed on their mucky airstrips. Yamamoto knows perfectly well that these reports will turn out to be wildly exaggerated. More than half of his planes never came back—the Americans, and their almost equally offensive cousins, the Australians, were ready for them. But the Army and the Navy alike are full of ambitious men who will do everything they can to channel good news the emperor's way, even if it's not exactly the truth. Accordingly, Yamamoto has received a personal telegram of congratulations from none other than the sovereign himself. It is his duty, now, to fly round to his various outposts, hop out of his Betty, wave the sacred telegram in the air, and pass on the blessings of the emperor.

Yamamoto's feet hurt like hell. Like everyone else within a thousand miles, he has a tropical disease; in his case, beriberi. It is the scourge of the Nipponese and especially of the Navy, because they eat too much polished rice, not enough fish and vegetables. His long nerves have been corroded by lactic acid, so his hands quiver. His failing heart can't shove fluid through his extremities, so his feet swell. He needs to change his shoes several times a day, but he doesn't have room here; he is encumbered not only by the curvature of the plane's greenhouse, but also by his sword.

They are approaching the Imperial Navy airbase at Bougainville, right on schedule, at 9:35. A shadow passes overhead and Yamamoto glances up to see the silhouette of an escort, way out of position, dangerously close to them. Who is that idiot? Then the green island and the blue ocean rotate into view as his pilot puts the Betty into a power dive. Another plane flashes overhead with a roar that cuts through the noise of the Betty's engines, and although it is nothing more than a black flash, its odd forktailed silhouette registers in his mind. It was a P-38 Lightning, and the last time Admiral Yamamoto checked, the Nipponese Air Force wasn't flying any of those.

The voice of Admiral Ugaki comes through on the radio from the other Betty, right behind Yamamoto's, ordering Yamamoto's pilot to stay in formation. Yamamoto cannot see anything in front of them except for the surf washing ashore on Bougainville, and the wall of trees, seeming to grow higher and higher, as the plane descends—the tropical canopy now actually above them. He is Navy, not an Air Force man, but even he knows that when you can't see any planes in front of you in a dogfight, you have problems. Red streaks flash past from behind, burying themselves in the steaming jungle ahead, and the Betty begins to shake violently. Then yellow light fills the corners of both of his eyes: the engines are on fire. The pilot is heading directly for the jungle now; either the plane is out of control, or the pilot is already dead, or it is a move of atavistic desperation: run, run into the trees!

They enter the jungle in level flight, and Yamamoto is astonished how far they go before hitting anything big. Then the plane is bludgeoned wide open by mahogany trunks, like baseball bats striking a wounded sparrow, and he knows it's over. The greenhouse disintegrates around him, the meridians and parallels crumpling and rending which isn't quite as bad as it sounds since the body of the plane is suddenly filled with flames. As his seat tears loose from the broken dome and launches into space, he grips his sword, unwilling to disgrace himself by dropping his sacred weapon, blessed by the emperor, even in this last instant of his life. His clothes and hair are on fire as he tumbles like a meteor through the jungle, clenching his ancestral blade.

He realizes something: The Americans must have done the impossible: broken all of their codes. That explains Midway, it explains the Bismarck

Sea, Hollandia, everything. It especially explains why Yamamoto—who ought to be sipping green tea and practicing calligraphy in a misty garden—is, in point of fact, on fire and hurtling through the jungle at a hundred miles per hour in a chair, closely pursued by tons of flaming junk. He must get word out! The codes must all be changed! This is what he is thinking when he flies head-on into a hundred-foot-tall *Octomelis sumatrana*.

ANTAEUS

WHEN LAWRENCE PRITCHARD WATERHOUSE SETS FOOT ON THE Sceptered Isle for the first time in several months, at the ferry terminal in Utter Maurby, he is startled to find allusions to springtime all over the place. The locals have installed flower boxes around the pier, and all of them are abloom with some sort of pre-Cambrian decorative cabbage. The effect is not exactly cheerful, but it does give the place a haunted Druidical look, as if Waterhouse is looking at the northwesternmost fringe of some cultural tradition from which a sharp anthropologist might infer the existence of actual trees and meadows several hundred miles farther south. For now, lichens will do—they have gotten into the spirit and turned greyish purple and greyish green.

He and Duffel, their old companionship renewed, tussle their way over to the terminal and fight each other for a seat aboard the disconcertingly quaint two-car Manchester-bound whistle-stop. It will sit there for another couple of hours raising steam before leaving, giving him plenty of time to take stock.

He's been working on some information-theoretical problems occasioned by the Royal and U.S. Navies' recent* propensity to litter the floor of the Atlantic with bombed and torpedoed milchcows. These fat German submarines, laden with fuel, food, and ammunition, loiter in the Atlantic Ocean, using radio rarely and staying well away from the sea-lanes, and serve as covert floating supply bases so that the U-boats don't have to go all the way back to the European mainland to refuel and rearm. Sinking lots of 'em is great for the convoys, but must seem conspicuously improbable to the likes of a Rudolf von Hacklheber.

Usually, just for the sake of form, the Allies send out a search plane beforehand to pretend to stumble upon the milchcow. But, setting aside

---

*Ever since the four-wheel Enigma was broken.

some of their blind spots in the political realm, the Germans are bright chaps, and cannot be expected to fall for that ruse forever. If we are going to keep sending their milchcows to the bottom, we need to come up with a respectable excuse for the fact that we always know exactly where they are!

Waterhouse has been coming up with excuses as fast as he can for most of the late winter and early spring, and frankly he is tired of it. It has to be done by a mathematician if it's to be done correctly, but it's not exactly mathematics. Thank god he had the presence of mind to copy down the crypto worksheets that he discovered in the U-boat's safe, which give him something to live for.

In a sense he is wasting his time; the originals have long since gone off to Bletchley Park where they were probably deciphered within hours. But he's not doing it for the war effort per se, just trying to keep his mind sharp and maybe add a few leaves to the next edition of the *Cryptonomicon*. When he arrives at Bletchley, which is his destination of the moment, he will have to ask around and find out what those messages actually said.

Usually, he is above such cheating. But the messages from U-553 have him completely baffled. They were not produced on an Enigma machine, but they are at least that difficult to decrypt. He does not even know, yet, what kind of cipher he is dealing with. Normally, one begins by figuring out, based on certain patterns in the ciphertext, whether it is, for example, a substitution or a transposition system, and then further classifying it into, say, an aperiodic transposition cipher in which keying units of constant length encipher plaintext groups of variable length, or vice versa. Once you have classified the algorithm, you know how to go about breaking the code.

Waterhouse hasn't even gotten that far. He now strongly suspects that the messages were produced using a one-time pad. If so, not even Bletchley Park will be able to break them, unless they have somehow obtained a copy of the pad. He is half-hoping that they will tell him that this is the case so that he can stop ramming his head against this particular stone wall.

In a way, this would raise even more questions than it would answer. The Triton four-wheel naval Enigma was supposedly considered by the Germans to be perfectly impregnable to cryptanalysis. If that was the case, then why was the skipper of U-553 employing his own private system for certain messages?

The locomotive starts hissing and sputtering like the House of Lords as Inner Qwghlmians emerge from the terminal building and take their seats on the train. A gaffer comes through the car, selling yesterday's newspapers, cigarettes, candy, and Waterhouse purchases some of each. The train is just beginning to jerk forward when Waterhouse's eye falls on the lead headline of yesterday's newspaper: YAMAMOTO'S PLANE SHOT DOWN IN PACIFIC—ARCHITECT OF PEARL HARBOR THOUGHT TO BE DEAD.

"Malaria, here I come," Waterhouse mumbles to himself. Then, before reading any further, he sets the newspaper down and opens up his pack of cigarettes. This is going to take a lot of cigarettes.

———————

One day, and a whole lot of tar and nicotine later, Waterhouse climbs off the train and walks out the front door of Bletchley Depot into a dazzling spring day. The flowers in front of the station are blooming, a warm southern breeze is blowing, and Waterhouse almost cannot bear to cross the road and enter some windowless hut in the belly of Bletchley Park. He does it anyway and is informed that he has no duties at the moment.

After visiting a few other huts on other business, he turns north and walks three miles to the hamlet of Shenley Brook End and goes into the Crown Inn, where the proprietress, Mrs. Ramshaw, has, during these last three and a half years, made a tidy business out of looking after stray, homeless Cambridge mathematicians.

Dr. Alan Mathison Turing is seated at a table by a window, sprawled across two or three chairs in what looks like a very awkward pose but which Waterhouse feels sure is eminently practical. A full pint of something reddish brown is on the table next to him; Alan is too busy to drink it. The smoke from Alan's cigarette reveals a prism of sunlight coming through the window, centered in which is a mighty Book. Alan is holding the book with one hand. The palm of his other hand is pressed against his forehead, as if he could get the data from book to brain through some kind of direct transference. His fingers curl up into the air and a cigarette projects from between them, ashes dangling perilously over his dark hair. His eyes are frozen in place, not scanning the page, and their focus point is somewhere in the remote distance.

"Designing another Machine, Dr. Turing?"

The eyes finally begin to move, and swivel around towards the sound of the visitor's voice. "Lawrence," Alan says once, quietly, identifying the face. Then, once more warmly: "Lawrence!" He scrambles to his feet, as energetic as ever, and steps forward to shake hands. "Delighted to see you!"

"Good to see you, Alan," Waterhouse says. "Welcome back." He is, as always, pleasantly surprised by Alan's keenness, the intensity and purity of his reactions to things.

He is also touched by Alan's frank and sincere affection for him. Alan did not give this easily or lightly, but when he decided to make Waterhouse his friend, he did so in a way that is unfettered by either American or heterosexual concepts of manly bearing. "Did you walk the entire distance from Bletchley? Mrs. Ramshaw, refreshment!"

"Heck, it's only three miles," Waterhouse says.

"Please come and join me," Alan says. Then he stops, frowns, and looks at him quizzically. "How on earth did you guess I was designing another machine? Simply a guess based on prior observations?"

"Your choice of reading material," Waterhouse says, and points to Alan's book: *RCA Radio Tube Manual*.

Alan gets a wild look. "This has been my constant companion," he says. "You must learn about these valves, Lawrence! Or tubes as you would call them. Your education is incomplete otherwise. I cannot believe the number of years I wasted on *sprockets*! God!"

"Your zeta-function machine? I thought it was beautiful," Lawrence says.

"So are many things that belong in a *museum*," Lawrence says.

"That was six years ago. You had to work with the available technology," Lawrence says.

"Oh, Lawrence! I'm surprised at you! If it will take *ten* years to make the machine with *available* technology, and only *five* years to make it with a *new* technology, and it will only take *two* years to *invent* the new technology, then you can do it in *seven* years by inventing the new technology first!"

"Touché."

"This is the new technology," Alan says, holding up the *RCA Radio Tube Manual* like Moses brandishing a Tablet of the Law. "If I had only had the presence of mind to use these, I could have built the zeta-function machine much sooner, and others besides."

"What sort of a machine are you designing now?" Lawrence asks.

"I've been playing chess with a fellow named Donald Michie—a classicist," Alan says. "I am wretched at it. But man has always constructed tools to extend his powers—why not a machine that will help me play chess?"

"Does Donald Michie get to have one, too?"

"He can design his own machine!" Alan says indignantly.

Lawrence looks carefully around the pub. They are the only customers, and he cannot bring himself to believe that Mrs. Ramshaw is a spy. "I thought it might have something to do with—" he says, and nods in the direction of Bletchley Park.

They are building—I have helped them build—a machine called Colossus."

"I thought I saw your hand in it."

"It is built from old ideas—ideas we talked about in New Jersey, years ago," Alan says. Brisk and dismissive is his tone, gloomy is his face. He is hugging the *RCA Radio Tube Manual* to himself with one arm, doodling in a notebook with the other. Waterhouse thinks that really the *RCA Radio Tube Manual* is like a ball and chain holding Alan back. If he would just work with pure ideas like a proper mathematician he could go as fast as thought. As it happens, Alan has become fascinated by the incarnations of pure ideas in the physical world. The underlying math of the universe is like the light streaming in through the window. Alan is not satisfied with merely knowing that it streams in. He blows smoke into the air to make the light visible. He sits in meadows gazing at pine cones and flowers, tracing the mathematical patterns in their structure, and he dreams about electron winds blowing over the glowing filaments and screens of radio tubes, and, in their surges and eddies, capturing something of what is going on in his own brain. Turing is neither a mortal nor a god. He is Antaeus. That he bridges the mathematical and physical worlds is his strength and his weakness.

"Why are you so glum?" Alan says. "What have you been working on?"

"Same stuff, different context," Waterhouse says. With these four words he conveys, in full, everything that he has been doing on behalf of the war effort. "Fortunately, I came upon something that is actually rather interesting."

Alan looks delighted and fascinated to hear this news, as if the world had been completely devoid of interesting things for the last ten years or so, and Waterhouse had stumbled upon a rare find. "Tell me about it," he insists.

"It's a cryptanalysis problem," Waterhouse says. "Non-Enigma." He goes on to tell the story about the messages from U-553. "When I got to Bletchley Park this morning," he concludes, "I asked around. They said that they had been butting their heads against the problem as long as I had, without any success."

Suddenly, Alan looks disappointed and bored. "It must be a one-time pad," he says. He sounds reproachful.

"It can't be. The ciphertext is not devoid of patterns," Waterhouse says.

"Ah," replies Alan, perking up again.

"I looked for patterns with the usual *Cryptonomicon* techniques. Found nothing clear—just some traces. Finally, in complete frustration, I decided to start from a clean slate, trying to think like Alan Turing. Typically your approach is to reduce a problem to numbers and then bring the full power of mathematical analysis to bear on it. So I began by converting the messages into numbers. Normally, this would be an arbitrary process. You convert each letter into a number, usually between one and twenty-five, and then dream up some sort of arbitrary algorithm to convert this series of small numbers into one big number. But this message was different—it used thirty-two characters—a power of two—meaning that each character had a unique binary representation, five binary digits long."

"As in Baudot code," Alan says.* He looks guardedly interested again.

"So I converted each letter into a number between one and thirty-two, using the Baudot code. That gave me a long series of small numbers. But I wanted some way to convert all of the numbers in the series into one large number, just to see if it would contain any interesting patterns. But this was easy as pie! If the first letter is R, and its Baudot code is 01011, and the second letter is F, and its code is 10111, then I can simply combine the two into a ten-digit binary number, 0101110111. And then I can take the next letter's code and stick that onto the end and get a fifteen-digit number. And so on. The letters come in groups of five—that's twenty-five binary digits per group. With six groups on each line of the page, that's a hundred and fifty binary digits per line. And with twenty lines on the page, that's three thousand binary digits. So each page of the message could be thought of not as a series of six hundred letters, but as an encoded representation of a single number with a magnitude of around two raised to the three thousandth power, which works out to around ten to the nine hundredth power."

"All right," Alan says, "I agree that the use of thirty-two-letter alphabet suggests a binary coding scheme. And I agree that the binary coding scheme, in turn, lends itself to a sort of treatment in which individual groups of five binary digits are mooshed together to make larger numbers, and that you could even take it to the point of mooshing together all of the data on a whole page that way, to make one extremely large number. But what does that accomplish?"

---

*Baudot code is what teletypes use. Each of the 32 characters in the teletype alphabet has a unique number assigned to it. This number can be represented as a five-digit binary number, that is, five ones or zeroes, or (more useful) five holes, or absences of holes, across a strip of paper tape. Such numbers can also be represented as patterns of electrical voltages, which can be sent down a wire, or over the radio waves, and printed out at the other end. Lately, the Germans have been using encrypted Baudot-code messages for communications between high-level command posts; e.g., between Berlin and the various Army group headquarters. At Bletchley Park, this category of encryption schemes is called Fish, and the Colossus machine is being built specifically to break it.

"I don't really know," Waterhouse admits. "I just have an intuition that what we are dealing with here is a new encryption scheme based upon a purely mathematical algorithm. Otherwise, there would be no point in using the thirty-two-letter alphabet! If you think about it, Alan, thirty-two letters are all well and good—as a matter of fact, they are essential—for a teletype scheme, because you have to have special characters like line feed and carriage return."

"You're right," Alan says, "it is extremely odd that they would use thirty-two letters in a scheme that is apparently worked out using pencil and paper."

"I've been over it a thousand times," Waterhouse says, "and the only explanation I can think of is that they are converting their messages into large binary numbers and then combining them with other large binary numbers—one-time pads, most likely—to produce the ciphertext."

"In which case your project is doomed," Alan says, "because you can't break a one-time pad."

"That is only true," Waterhouse says, "if the one-time pad is truly random. If you built up that three-thousand digit number by flipping a coin three thousand times and writing down a one for heads and a zero for tails, then it would be truly random and unbreakable. But I do not think that this is the case here."

"Why not? You think there were patterns in their one-time pads?"

"Maybe. Just traces."

"Then what makes you think it is other than random?"

"Otherwise it makes no sense to develop a new scheme," Waterhouse says. "Everyone in the world has been using one-time pads forever. There are established procedures for doing it. There's no reason to switch over to this new, extremely odd system right now, in the middle of a war."

"So what do you suppose is the rationale for this new scheme?" asks Alan, clearly enjoying himself a great deal.

"The problem with one-time pads is that you have to make two copies of each pad and get them to the sender and the recipient. I mean, suppose you're in Berlin and you want to send a message to someone in the Far East! This U-boat that we found had cargo on board—gold and other stuff—from Japan! Can you imagine how cumbersome this must be for the Axis?"

"Ahh," Alan says. He gets it now. But Waterhouse finishes the explanation anyway:

"Suppose that you came up with a mathematical algorithm for generating very large numbers that were random, or at least random-looking."

"Pseudo-random."

"Yeah. You'd have to keep the algorithm secret, of course. But if you could get it—the algorithm, that is—around the world to your intended recipient, then they could, from that day forward, do the calculation themselves and figure out the one-time pad for that particular day, or whatever."

A shadow passes over Alan's otherwise beaming countenance. "But the Germans already have Enigma machines all over the place," he says. "Why should they bother to come up with a new scheme?"

"Maybe," Waterhouse says, "maybe there are some Germans who don't want the entire German Navy to be able to decipher their messages."

"Ah," Alan says. This seems to eliminate his last objection. Suddenly he is all determination. "Show me the messages!"

Waterhouse opens up his attache case, splotched and streaked with salt from his voyages to and from Qwghlm, and draws out two manila envelopes. "These are the copies I made before I sent the originals down to Bletchley Park," he says, patting one of them. "They are much more legible than the originals—" he pats the other envelope "—which they were kind enough to lend me this morning, so that I could study them again."

"Show the originals!" Alan says. Waterhouse slides the second envelope, encrusted with TOP SECRET stamps, across the table.

Alan opens the envelope so hastily that he tears it, and jerks out the pages. He spreads them out on the table. His mouth drops open in purest astonishment.

For a moment, Waterhouse is fooled; the expression on Alan's face makes him think that his friend has, in some Olympian burst of genius, deciphered the messages in an instant, just by looking at them.

But that's not it at all. Thunderstruck, he finally says, "I recognize this handwriting."

"You do?" Waterhouse says.

"Yes. I've seen it a thousand times. These pages were written out by our old bicycling friend. Rudolf von Hacklheber. Rudy wrote those pages."

Waterhouse spends much of the next week commuting to London for meetings at the Broadway Buildings. Whenever civilian authorities are going to be present at a meeting—especially civilians with expensive-sounding accents—Colonel Chattan always shows up, and before the meeting starts, always finds some frightfully cheerful and oblique way to tell Waterhouse to keep his trap shut unless someone asks a math question. Waterhouse is not offended. He prefers it, actually, because it leaves his mind free to work on important things. During their last meeting at the Broadway Buildings, Waterhouse proved a theorem.

It takes Waterhouse about three days to figure that the meetings themselves make no sense—he reckons that there is no imaginable goal that could be furthered by what they are discussing. He even makes a few stabs at proving that this is so, using formal logic, but he is weak in this area and doesn't know enough of the underlying axioms to reach a Q.E.D.

By the end of the week, though, he has figured out that these meetings are just one ramification of the Yamamoto assassination. Winston Spencer Churchill is very fond indeed of Bletchley Park and all its works, and he places the highest priority on preserving its secrecy, but the interception of Yamamoto's airplane has blown a gaping hole in the screen of deception. The Americans responsible for this appalling gaffe are now trying to cover their asses by spreading a story that native islander spies caught wind of Yamamoto's trip and radioed the news to Guadalcanal, whence the fatal P-38s were dispatched. But the P-38s were operating at the extreme limit of their fuel range and would have had to be sent out at precisely the correct time in order to make it back to Guadalcanal, so the Japanese would have to have their heads several feet up their asses to fall for that. Winston Churchill is pissed off in the extreme, and these meetings represent a prolonged bureaucratic hissy fit intended to produce some meaningful and enduring policy shift.

Every evening after the meetings, Waterhouse takes the tube to Euston and the train to Bletchley, and sits up late working on Rudy's numbers. Alan has been working on them during the daytime, so the two of them, combining their efforts, can almost pound away on it round the clock.

Not all of the riddles are mathematical. For example, why the hell do the Germans have Rudy copying out big long numbers by hand? If the letters do indeed represent big numbers that would indicate that Dr. Rudolf von Hacklheber had been assigned to a job as a mere cipher clerk. This would not be the stupidest move ever made by a bureaucracy, but it seems unlikely. And what little intelligence they've been able to gather from Germany suggests that Rudy has in fact been given a rather important job—important enough to keep extremely secret.

Alan's hypothesis is that Waterhouse has been making an understandable but totally wrong assumption. The numbers are *not* ciphertext. They are, rather, one-time pads that the skipper of U-553 was supposed to have used to encrypt certain messages too sensitive to go out over the regular Enigma channel. These one-time pads were, for some reason, drawn up personally by Rudy himself.

Usually, making one-time pads is just as lowly a job as enciphering messages—a job for clerks, who use decks of cards or bingo machines to choose letters at random. But Alan and Waterhouse are now operating on the assumption that this encryption scheme is a radical new invention—presumably, an invention of Rudy's—in which the pads are generated not at random but by using some mathematical algorithm.

In other words, there is some calculation, some equation that Rudy has dreamed up. You give it a value—probably the date, and possibly some other information as well, such as an arbitrary key phrase or number. You crank through the steps of the calculation, and the result is a number, some nine hundred digits long, which is three thousand binary digits, which gives you six hundred letters (enough to cover one sheet of paper) when you convert it using the Baudot code. The nine-hundred-digit decimal number, the three-thousand-digit binary number, and the six hundred letters are all the same abstract, pure number, encoded differently.

Meanwhile, your counterpart, probably on the other side of the world, is going through the same calculation and coming up with the same one-time pad. When you send him a message encrypted using the day's pad, he can decipher it.

If Turing and Waterhouse can figure out how the calculation works, they can read all of these messages too.

PHREAKING

THE DENTIST IS GONE, THE DOOR LOCKED, THE PHONE UN-plugged. Randall Lawrence Waterhouse lies naked on the starched, turned-down sheets of his king-sized bed. His head is propped up on a pillow so that he can peer through the vee of his feet at a BBC World Service newscast on the television. A ten-dollar minibar beer is near at hand. It's six in the morning in America and so rather than a pro basketball game, he has to settle for this BBC newscast, which is strongly geared to South Asian happenings. A long and very sober story about a plague of locusts on the India/Pakistan border, follows a piece on a typhoon about to nail Hong Kong. The king of Thailand is calling in some of his government's more corrupt officials to literally prostrate themselves before him. Asian news always has this edge of the fantastic to it, but it's all dead serious, no nods or winks anywhere. Now he's watching a story about a nervous system disease that people in New

Guinea come down with as a consequence of eating other people's brains. Just your basic cannibal story. No wonder so many Americans come here on business and never really go home again—it's like stepping into the pages of *Classics Comics*.

Someone is knocking on his door. Randy gets up and puts on his plush white hotel bathrobe. He peers through the peephole, half expecting to see a pygmy standing there with a blowpipe, though he wouldn't mind a seductive Oriental courtesan. But it's just Cantrell. Randy opens the door. Cantrell is already holding up his hands, palms out, in a cheerful "shut up already" gesture. "Don't worry," Cantrell says, "I'm not here to talk about Biz."

"In that case I won't break this beer bottle over your head," Randy says. Cantrell must feel exactly the same way Randy does, which is that so much wild shit happened today that the only way to deal with it is not to talk about it at all. Most of the brain's work is done while the brain's owner is ostensibly thinking about something else, so sometimes you have to *deliberately* find something else to think and talk about.

"Come to my room," Cantrell says. "Pekka is here."

"The Finn who got blown up?"

"The same."

"Why is he here?"

"Because there's no reason not to be. After he got blown up he adopted a technomadic lifestyle."

"So it's just a coincidence, or—"

"Nah," Cantrell says. "He's helping me win a bet."

"What kind of bet?"

"I was telling Tom Howard about Van Eck phreaking a few weeks ago. Tom said it sounded like bullshit. He bet me ten shares of Epiphyte stock that I couldn't make it actually work outside of a laboratory."

"Is Pekka good at that kind of thing?"

By way of saying yes, Cantrell adopts a serious look and says, "Pekka is writing a whole chapter about it for the *Cryptonomicon*. Pekka feels that only by mastering the technologies that might be used against us can we defend ourselves."

This sounds almost like a call to arms. Randy would have to be some kind of loser to retreat to his bed after that, so he backs into the room and steps into his trousers, which are standing there telescoped into the floor where he dropped them upon his return from the sultan's palace. *The sultan's palace!* The television is now broadcasting a news story about pirates plying the waters of the South China Sea, making freighter crews walk the plank. "This whole continent is like fucking Disneyland without the safety precautions," Randy observes. "Am I the only person who finds it surreal?"

Cantrell grins, but says, "If we begin talking about surreal, we'll end up talking about today."

"You got that right," Randy says. "Let's go."

Before Pekka became known around Silicon Valley as the Finn Who Got Blown Up, he was known as Cello Guy, because he had a nearly autistic devotion to his cello and took it with him everywhere, always trying to stuff it into overhead luggage racks. Not coincidentally, he was an analog kind of guy from way back whose specialty was radio.

When packet radio started to get big as an alternative to sending data down wires, Pekka moved to Menlo Park and joined a startup. His company bought their equipment at used-computer stores, and Pekka ended up scoring a pretty nice nineteen-inch high-res multisync monitor perfectly adequate for his adaptable twenty-four-year-old eyes. He hooked it up to a slightly used Pentium box jammed full of RAM.

He also installed Finux, a free UNIX operating system created by Finns, almost as a way of proclaiming to the rest of the world "this is how weird we are," and distributed throughout the world on the Net. Of course Finux was fantastically powerful and flexible and enabled you, among other things, to control the machine's video circuitry to the Nth degree and choose many different scanning frequencies and pixel clocks, if you were into that kind of thing. Pekka most definitely was into it, and so like a lot of Finux maniacs he set his machine up so that it could display, if he chose, a whole lot of tiny little pixels (which displayed a lot of information but was hard on the eyes) or, alternatively, fewer and larger pixels (which he tended to use after he had been hacking for twenty-four hours straight and lost ocular muscle tone), or various settings in-between. Every time he changed from one setting to another, the monitor screen would go black for a second and there would be an audible clunk from inside of it as the resonating crystals inside locked in on a different range of frequencies.

One night at three A.M., Pekka caused this to happen, and immediately after the screen went black and made that clunking noise, it exploded in his face. The front of the picture tube was made of heavy glass (it had to be, to withstand the internal vacuum) which fragmented and sped into Pekka's face, neck, and upper body. The very same phosphors that had been glowing beneath the sweeping electron beam, moments before, conveying information into Pekka's eyes, were now physically embedded in his flesh. A hunk of glass took one of his eyes and almost went through into his brain. Another one gouged out his voicebox, another zinged past the side of his head and bit a neat triangular hunk out of his left ear.

Pekka, in other words, was the first victim of the Digibomber. He almost bled to death on the spot, and his fellow Eutropians hovered around his hospital bed for a few days with tanks of Freon, ready to jump into action in case he died. But he didn't, and he got even more press because his startup company lacked health insurance. After a lot of hand-wringing in local newspapers about how this poor innocent from the land of socialized medicine had not had the presence of mind to buy health insurance, some rich high-tech guys donated money to pay his medical bills and to equip him with a computer voicebox like Stephen Hawking's.

And now here is Pekka, sitting in Cantrell's hotel room. His cello stands in the corner, dusty around the bridge from powdered rosin. He is facing a blank wall to which he has duct-taped a bunch of wires in precise loops and whorls. These lead to some home-brewed circuit boards which are in turn hooked up to his laptop.

"Hello Randy congratulations on your success," says a computer-generated voice as soon as the door is shut behind Randy and Cantrell. This is a little greeting that Pekka has obviously typed in ahead of time, anticipating his arrival. None of the foregoing seems particularly odd to Randy except for the fact that Pekka seems to think that Epiphyte has already achieved some kind of success.

"How are we doing?" Cantrell asks.

Pekka types in a response. Then he cups one hand to his mutilated ear while using his other hand to cue the voice generator: "He showers." Indeed, it's possible now to hear the pipes hissing in the wall. "His laptop radiates."

"Oh," Randy says, "Tom Howard's room is right next door?"

"Just on the other side of that wall," Cantrell says. "I specifically requested it, so that I could win this bet. See, his room is a mirror image of this one, so his computer is only a few inches away, just on the other side of this wall. Perfect conditions for Van Eck phreaking."

"Pekka, are you receiving signals from his computer right now?" Randy asks.

Pekka nods, types, and fires back, "I tune. I calibrate." The input device for his voice generator is a one-handed chord-board strapped to his thigh. He puts his right hand on it and makes flopping and groping motions. Moments later speech emerges, "I require Cantrell."

"Excuse me," Cantrell says, and goes to Pekka's side. Randy watches over their shoulders for a bit, understanding vaguely what they're doing.

If you lay a sheet of white paper on an old gravestone, and sweep the tip of a pencil across it, you get one horizontal line, dark in some places and faint in others, and not very meaningful. If you move downwards on the page by a small distance, a single pencil-line-width, and repeat, an image begins to emerge. The process of working your way down the page in a series of horizontal sweeps is what a nerd would call raster-scanning, or just rastering. With a conventional video monitor—a cathode-ray tube—the electron beam physically rasters down the glass something like sixty to eighty times a second. In the case of a laptop screen like Randy's, there is no physical scanning; the individual pixels are turned on or off directly. But still a scanning process is taking place; what's being scanned and made manifest on the screen is a region of the computer's memory called the screen buffer. The contents of the screen buffer have to be slapped up onto the screen sixty to eighty times every second or else (1) the screen flickers and (2) the images move jerkily.

The way that the computer talks to you is not by controlling the screen directly but rather by manipulating the bits contained in that buffer, secure in the knowledge that other subsystems inside the machine handle the drudge work of pipelining that information onto the actual, physical screen. Sixty to eighty times a second, the video system says shit! time to refresh the screen again, and goes to the beginning of the screen buffer—which is just a particular hunk of memory, remember—and it reads the first few bytes, which dictate what color the pixel in the upper left-hand corner of the screen is supposed to be. This information is sent on down the line to whatever is actually refreshing the screen, whether it's a scanning electron beam or some laptop-style system for directly controlling the pixels. Then the next few bytes are read, typically for the pixel just to the right of that first one, and so on all the way to the right edge of the screen. That draws the first line of the grave-rubbing.

Since the right edge of the screen has now been reached, there are no more pixels off in that direction. It is implicit that the next bytes read from memory will be for the leftmost pixel in the second raster-line down from the top. If this is a cathode-ray tube type of screen, we have a little timing problem here in that the electron beam is currently at the right edge of the screen and now it's being asked to draw a pixel at the left edge. It has to move back. This takes a little while—not long, but much longer than the interval of time between drawing two pixels that are cheek-by-jowl. This pause is called the *horizontal retrace interval*. Another one will occur at the end of every other line until the rastering has proceeded to the last pixel at the bottom right-hand corner of the screen and completed a single grave-rubbing. But then it's time to begin the process all over again, and so the electron beam (if there is one) has to jump diagonally all the way up to the upper left-hand pixel. This also takes a little while and is called the *vertical retrace interval*.

These issues all stem from inherent physical limitations of sweeping electron beams through space in a cathode-ray tube, and basically disappear in the case of a laptop screen like the one Tom Howard has set up a few inches in front of Pekka, on the other side of that wall. But the video timing of a laptop screen is still patterned after that of a cathode-ray tube screen anyway. (This is simply because the old technology is universally understood by those who need to understand it, and it works well, and all kinds of electronic and software technology has been built and tested to work within that framework, and why mess with success, especially when your profit margins are so small that they can only be detected by using techniques from quantum mechanics, and any glitches vis-à-vis compatibility with old stuff will send your company straight into the toilet.)

On Tom's laptop, each second of time is divided into seventy-five perfectly regular slices, during which a full grave-rubbing is performed followed by a vertical retrace interval. Randy can follow Pekka and Cantrell's conversation well enough to gather that they have already figured out, from analyzing the signals coming through the wall, that Tom Howard has his screen set up to give him 768 lines, and 1024 pixels on each line. For every pixel, four bytes will be read from the video buffer and sent on down the line to the screen. (Tom is using the highest possible level of color definition on his screen, which means that one byte apiece is needed to represent the intensity of blue, green, and red and another is basically left over, but kept in there anyway because computers like powers of two, and computers are so ridiculously fast and powerful now that, even though all of this is happening on a timetable that would strike a human being as rather aggressive, the extra bytes just don't make any difference.) Each byte is eight binary digits or bits and so, 1024 times a line, $4 \times 8 = 32$ bits are being read from the screen buffer.

Unbeknownst to Tom, his computer happens to be sitting right next to an antenna. The wires Pekka taped to the wall can read the electromagnetic waves that are radiating out of the computer's circuitry at all times.

Tom's laptop is sold as a computer, not as a radio station, and so it might seem odd that it should be radiating anything at all. It is all a byproduct of the fact that computers are binary critters, which means that all chip-to-chip, subsystem-to-subsystem communication taking place inside the machine—everything moving down those flat ribbons of wire, and the little metallic traces on the circuit boards—consists of transitions from zero to one and back again. The way that you represent bits in a computer is by switching the wire's voltage back and forth between zero and five volts. In computer textbooks these transitions are always graphed as if they were perfect square waves, meaning that you have this perfectly flat line at $V = 0$, representing a binary zero, and then it makes a perfect right-angle turn and jumps vertically to V = 5 and then executes another perfect right-angle turn and remains at five volts until it's time to go back to zero again, and so on.

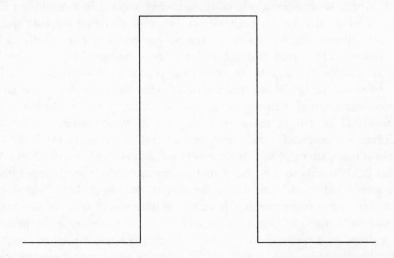

This is the Platonic ideal of how computer circuitry is supposed to operate, but engineers have to build actual circuits in the grimy analog world. The hunks of metal and silicon can't manifest the Platonic behavior shown in those textbooks. Circuits can jump between zero and five volts really, really abruptly but if you monitor them on an oscilloscope, you can see that it's not a perfectly square wave. Instead you get something that looks like this:

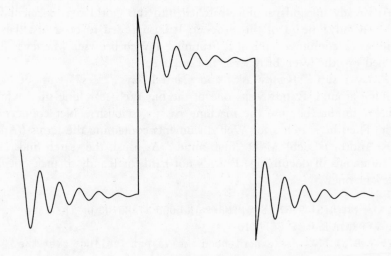

The little waves are called ringing; these transitions among binary digits hit the circuitry like a clapper striking a bell. The voltage jumps, but after it jumps it oscillates back and forth around the new value for a little while. Whenever you have an oscillating voltage in a conductor like this, it means that electromagnetic waves are propagating out into space.

Consequently each wire in a running computer is like a little radio transmitter. The signals that it broadcasts are completely dependent upon the details of what's going on inside the machine. Since there are a lot of wires in there, and the particulars of what they are doing are fairly unpredictable, it is difficult for anyone monitoring the transmissions to make head or tail of them. A great deal of what comes out of the machine is completely irrelevant from a surveillance point of view. But there is one pattern of signals that is (1) totally predictable and (2) exactly what Pekka wants to see, and that is the stream of bytes being read from the screen buffer and sent down the wire to the screen hardware. Amid all the random noise coming from the machine, the ticks of the horizontal and vertical retrace intervals will stand out as clearly as the beating of a drum in a teeming jungle. Now that Pekka has zeroed in on that beat, he should be able to pick up the radiation emanating from the wire that connects screen buffer to video hardware, and translate it back into a sequence of ones and zeroes that can be dumped out onto their own screen. They will be able to see exactly what Tom Howard sees, through the kind of surveillance called Van Eck phreaking.

That's what Randy knows. When it comes to the details, Cantrell and Pekka are way out of his league, so after a few minutes he feels himself losing interest. He sits down on Cantrell's bed, which is the only place left *to* sit, and discovers a little palmtop computer on the bedside table. It is already up and running, patched into the world over a telephone wire. Randy's heard of this product. It is supposed to be a first stab at a network computer, and so it's running a Web browser whenever it is turned on; the Web browser *is* the interface.

"May I surf?" Randy asks, and Cantrell says, "Yes," without even turning around. Randy visits one of the big Web-searching sites, which takes a minute because the machine has to establish a Net connection first. Then he searches for Web documents containing the terms ((Andy OR Andrew) Loeb) AND "hive mind." As usual, the search finds tens of thousands of documents. But it's not hard for Randy to pick out the relevant ones.

WHY RIST 9303 IS A MEMBER IN GOOD STANDING OF THE CALI-
FORNIA BAR ASSOCIATION
RIST 11A4 has experienced ambivalent feelings over the

fact that RIST 9E03 (insofar as s/he is construed, by atomized society, as an individual organism) is a lawyer.
No doubt the conflicted feelings of RIST 11A4 are quite
normal and natural. Part of RIST 11A4 abhors lawyers, and
the legal system in general, as symptoms of the end-stage
terminal disease of atomized society. Another part understands that disease can improve the health of the meme
pool if it slays an organism that is old and unfit for ongoing propagation of its **memotype**. Make no mistake about it:
the legal system in its current form is the worst imaginable system for society to resolve its disputes. It is appallingly expensive in terms of money and in terms of the
intellectual talent that goes to waste pursuing it as a
career. But part of RIST 11A4 feels that the goals of RIST
11A4 may actually be served by turning the legal system's
most toxic features against the rotten body politic of atomized society and in so doing hasten its downfall.

Randy clicks on **RIST 9E03** and gets

RIST 9E03 is the RIST that RIST 11A4 denotes by the arbitrarily chosen bit-pattern that, construed as an integer,
is 9E03 (in **hexadecimal notation**). Click **here** for more
about the system of bit-pattern designators used by RIST
11A4 to replace the obsolescent nomenclature systems of
''natural languages.'' Click **here** if you would like the
designator RIST 9E03 to be automatically replaced by a
conventional designator (name) as you browse this web
site.

Click.

From now on, the expression RIST 9E03 will be replaced
by the expression **Andrew Loeb.** Warning: we consider such
nomenclature fundamentally invalid, and do not recommend
its use, but have provided it as a service to first-time
visitors to this Web site who are not accustomed to thinking in terms of RISTs.

Click.

You have clicked on **Andrew Loeb** which is a designator
assigned by atomized society to the **memome** of RIST
9E03 . . .

Click.

. . . **memome** is the set of all memes that define the physical reality of a carbon-based **RIST**. Memes can be divided into two broad categories: genetic and semantic. Genetic memes are simply genes (DNA) and are propagated through normal biological reproduction. Semantic memes are ideas (ideologies, religions, fads, etc.) and are propagated by communications.

Click.

The genetic part of the **memome** of **Andrew Loeb** shares 99% of its contents with the data set produced by the **Human Genome Project.** This should not be construed as endorsing the concept of speciation (i.e. that the continuum of carbon-based life forms can or should be arbitrarily partitioned into paradigmatic species) in general, or the theory that there is a species called ''Homo sapiens'' in particular.

The semantic part of the **memome** of **Andrew Loeb** is still unavoidably contaminated with many primitive viral memes, but these are being gradually and steadily supplanted by new semantic memes generated *ab initio* by rational processes.

Click.

RIST stands for Relatively Independent Sub-Totality. It can be used to refer to any entity that, from one point of view, seems to possess a clear boundary separating it from the world (as do cells in a body) but that, in a deeper sense, is inextricably linked with a larger totality (as are cells in a body). For example, the biological entities traditionally known as ''human beings'' are nothing more than Relatively Independent Sub-Totalities of the social organism in which they are embedded.

A dissertation written under the name **Andrew Loeb,** who is now designated **RIST 9E03,** indicates that even in those parts of **RIST 0577** having temperate climates and abundant food and water, the life of an organism such as the type designated, in old meme-systems, as ''Homo sapiens,'' would have been primarily occupied with attempting to eat other RISTS. This narrow focus would inhibit the formation of advanced semantic meme systems (viz. civilization as that word is traditionally construed). RISTs of this type can only attain higher levels of functioning insofar as they are embedded in a larger society, the most logical evolutionary end-point of which is a **hive mind.**

Click.

A hive mind is a social organization of **RISTs** that are capable of processing semantic memes ("thinking"). These could be either carbon-based or silicon-based. **RISTs** who enter a hive mind surrender their independent identities (which are mere illusions anyway). For purposes of convenience, the constituents of the hive mind are assigned **bit-pattern designators.**

Click.

A bit-pattern designator is a random series of bits used to uniquely identify a **RIST.** For example, the organism traditionally designed as Earth (Terra, Gaia) has been assigned the designator 0577. This Web site is maintained by 11A4 which is a hive mind. **RIST 11A4** assigns bit-pattern designators with a pseudo-random number generator. This departs from the practice used by that *soi-disant* "hive mind" known to itself as the East Bay Area Hive Mind Project but designated (in the system of RIST 11A4) as RIST E772. This "hive mind" resulted from the division of "Hive Mind One" (designated in the system of RIST 11A4 as RIST 4032) into several smaller "hive minds" (the East Bay Area Hive Mind Project, the San Francisco Hive Mind, Hive Mind 1A, the Reorganized San Francisco Hive Mind, and the Universal Hive Mind) as the result of an irreconcilable contradiction between several different semantic memes that competed for mind-share. One of these semantic memes asserted that bit-pattern designators should be assigned in numerical order, so that (for example) Hive Mind One would be designated RIST 0001 and so on. Another meme asserted that numbers should be organized in order of importance, so that (for example) the RIST conventionally known as the planet Earth would be RIST 0001. Another semantic meme agreed with this one but disagreed as to whether the counting should begin with 0000 or 0001. Within both the 0000 and

0001 camps, there was disagreement about what RIST should
be assigned the first number: some asserted that Earth was
the first and most important RIST, others that some larger
system (the solar system, the Universe, God) was in some
sense more inclusive and fundamental.

This machine has an e-mail interface. Randy uses it.

To: root@eruditorum.org
From: dwarf@siblings.net
Subject: Re(2) Why?
Saw the website. Am willing to stipulate that you are
not RIST 9E03. Suspect that you are the Dentist, who
yearns for honest exchange of views. Anonymous, digitally
signed e-mail is the only safe vehicle for same.
If you want me to believe you are not the Dentist, pro-
vide plausible explanation for your question regarding
why we are building the Crypt.
Your truly,
—BEGIN ORDO SIGNATURE BLOCK—
(etc.)
—END ORDO SIGNATURE BLOCK—

"We've got bits," Cantrell says. "Are you in the middle of
something?"

"Nothing I'm not eager to get out of," Randy says, putting the palmtop down. He gets off the bed and stands behind Pekka. The screen of
Pekka's computer has a number of windows on it, of which the biggest
and frontmost is the image of another computer's screen. Nested within
that are various other windows and icons: a desktop. It happens to be a
Windows NT desktop, which is noteworthy and (to Randy) bizarre
because Pekka's computer isn't running Windows NT, it's running
Finux. A cursor is moving around on that Windows NT desktop, pulling
down menus and clicking on things. But Pekka's hand is not moving.
The cursor zooms over to a Microsoft Word icon, which changes color
and expands to form a large window.

This copy of Microsoft Word is registered to THOMAS
HOWARD.

"You did it!" Randy says.
"We see what Tom sees," Pekka says.
A new document window opens up, and words begin to spill across it.

Note to myself: let's see ''Letters to Penthouse''
print *this*!

I don't suppose that graduate students of either gender
are exactly sought out by sexual connoisseurs for their
great fucking skills. We think about it too much. Everything has to be verbalized. A person who believes that
fucking is a sexual discourse is simply never going to be
any good in the sack.

I have a thing about stockings. They have to be sheer
black stockings, preferably with seams up the back. When
I was thirteen years old I actually shoplifted some black
pantyhose from a grocery store just so that I could play
with them. Walking out of that store with those L'eggs in
my backpack, my heart was pounding, but the excitement of
the crime was nothing compared to opening up the package
and pulling them out, rubbing them against my fuzzy, adolescent cheeks. I even tried pulling them on, but this
just looked grotesque—what with my hairy legs—and did absolutely nothing for me. I didn't want to wear them. I
wanted someone else to. I masturbated four times that day.

It disturbed the shit out of me when I thought about it.
I was a smart boy. Smart boys are supposed to be rational.
So, when I was in college I figured out a rationalization
for this. There wasn't that many women who wore sheer
black stockings in college, but sometimes I would go into
the city and see the well-dressed office workers walking
down the street on their lunch breaks and make scientific
observations of their legs. I noticed that where the
stocking stretched itself thin to go over a wide part of
the leg, such as the muscle of the calf, it became paler,
just as a colored balloon becomes paler when it is inflated. Conversely, it was darker in narrow regions such
as the ankle. This made the calf look more shapely and the
ankle look more slender. The legs, as a whole, looked
healthier, implying that just above the place where they
joined together, a higher class of DNA was to be found.

Q.E.D. My thing about black stockings was a highly rational adaptation. It merely proved how smart I was, how
rational even the most irrational parts of my brain were.
Sex held no power over me, it was nothing to fear.

This was quintessentially sophomoric thinking, but
nowadays most educated people hold quintessentially

sophomoric opinions well into their thirties and so this stuck with me for a long time. My wife Virginia probably had some equally self-serving rationalization for her own sexual needs—of which I was not to become aware for many years. So it's no surprise that our premarital sex life was mediocre. Neither one of us *admitted* it was mediocre, of course. If I *had* admitted it, I would have had to admit that it was mediocre because Virginia didn't like to wear stockings, and at the time I was too concerned with being a Sensitive New Age Guy to admit such heresy. I loved Virginia for her mind. How could I be so shallow, so insensitive, so *perverse* as to spurn her because she didn't like to pull filmy tubes of nylon over her legs? As a pudgy nerd, I was lucky to have her.

Five years into our marriage, I attended the Comdex convention as president of a small new high-tech company. I was a little less pudgy and a little less nerdy. I met a marketing girl for a big software distribution chain. She was wearing sheer black stockings. We ended up fucking in my hotel room. It was the best sex I'd ever had. I went home baffled and ashamed. After that, my sex life with Virginia was pretty miserable. We had sex maybe a dozen times over the next couple of years.

Virginia's grandmother died and we went back to upstate New York for the funeral. Virginia had to wear a dress, which meant she had to shave her legs and wear stockings— something she'd done on only a handful of occasions since our marriage. I practically fell over when I saw her, and suffered through the funeral with a big, scratchy erection, trying to figure out how I could get her alone.

Now, Granny had lived by herself in a big old house on a hill until a couple of months earlier when she had fallen down and broken her hip, and been moved into a nursing home. All of her children, grandchildren, and great-grandchildren came together for the funeral, and that house became the central gathering-place. It was a nice place full of good old furniture, but in her declining years Granny had become something of a compulsive pack rat and so there were heaps of newspapers and accumulated mail squirreled away everywhere. In the end we had to haul away several truckloads of junk.

In some other ways, Granny had been pretty well-

organized and had left behind a very specific last will and
testament. Each one of her descendants knew exactly which
pieces of furniture, dishes, rugs, and curios they were
going to take home. She had a lot of possessions, but she
also had a lot of descendants, and so the loot had to be
sliced pretty thin. Virginia ended up with a black walnut
dresser which was stored in an unused bedroom. We went up
there to have a look at it, and I ended up fucking her
there. I stood up with the flimsy trousers of my dark suit
collapsed around my ankles while she sat on top of that
dresser with her legs wrapped around me and her stocking-
clad heels digging into my butt-cheeks. It was the best
fuck we'd ever had, bar none. Fortunately there were a lot
of people eating, drinking, and talking downstairs or
they would have heard her moaning and hollering.

I finally came clean to her about the stockings. It felt
good. I'd been reading a lot about how the brain develops
and had finally come to accept my stocking kink. It seems
that when you are a certain age, somewhere between about
two and five years, your mind just gels. The part of it
that's responsible for sex becomes set into a pattern that
you'll carry with you for the rest of your life. All of the
gay people I've ever discussed it with have told me that
they knew they were gay, or at least different, years before they even began thinking about sex, and all of them
agree that gayness cannot be converted into straightness,
or vice versa, no matter how hard you might try.

The part of your brain that handles sex frequently gets
cross-wired into other, seemingly irrelevant areas at
this age. This is when people pick up an orientation towards sexual dominance or submission, or when a lot of
guys pick up highly specific kinks—say, rubber, feathers,
or shoes. Some of them are unfortunate enough to get
turned on by little kids, and those guys are essentially
doomed from that point onwards—there is nothing to do except castrate them or lock them up. No therapy will unkink
the brain once it has kinked.

So, all things considered, being turned on by black
stockings wasn't such a bad sexual card to have been
dealt. I laid this all out to Virginia during the trip
home. I was surprised by how calmly she accepted it. I was

too big of a jerk to realize that she was thinking about how it all applied to her.

After we got back home, she gamely went out and bought some stockings and tried to wear them on occasion. This was not easy. Stockings imply a whole lifestyle. They look stupid with jeans and sneakers. A woman in stockings has to wear a dress or a skirt, and not just a blue denim skirt but something nicer, more formal. She also has to wear the type of shoes that Virginia didn't own and didn't like to wear. Stockings are not really compatible with riding a bicycle to work. They were not even really compatible with our house. During our frugal grad-student days we had accumulated a lot of furniture from Goodwill, or I had hammered it together myself out of two-by-fours. This furniture turned out to be riddled with hidden snags that a person in bluejeans would never notice but that would destroy a pair of stockings in a moment. Likewise, our half-finished house and our old junker cars had many small sharp edges that were death to stockings. On the other hand, when we went away for an anniversary trip to London, getting around in black taxis, staying in a nice hotel, and eating in good restaurants, we spent a whole week moving in a world that was perfectly adapted to stockings. It just went to show us how radically we would have to change our circumstances in order for her to dress that way routinely.

So, much money was spent on stockings in a fit of good intentions. Some good sex was had, though I seemed to enjoy it much more than Virginia did. She never achieved the shocking, animal intensity she had shown at Granny's house after the funeral. Attrition reduced her supply of stockings very quickly, sheer inconvenience prevented her from renewing it, and within a year after the funeral we were back to square one.

Other things were changing, though. I made a lot of money by cashing in some stock options, and we bought a new house up in the hills. We hired some movers to come pick up all of our junky furniture and move it into that house, where it looked much shabbier. Virginia's new job forced her to commute in a car. I didn't think our old junker was safe, and so I bought her a nice little Lexus with leather seats and wool carpet, all of it nicely snag-free. Soon, kids came along and I traded in my old beater pickup truck for a minivan.

Still, I couldn't bring myself to begin spending money on furniture until my back started going bad on me, and I realized it was because of the slack, twenty-year-old Goodwill mattress that Virginia and I were sleeping on. We had to buy a new bed. Since it was my back at stake, I went out and did the shopping.

I'd rather stub out cigarettes on my tongue than go shopping. The idea of hitting every big furniture store in the area, comparing beds, made me want to die. All I wanted was to go to one place and buy a bed and have done with it. But I didn't want a shitty bed that I'd be sick of in a year, or a cheap mattress that would mess up my back again in five years.

So I went straight down to my local Gomer Bolstrood Home Gallery. I had heard people talk about Gomer Bolstrood furniture. Women, in particular, seemed to speak of it in hushed, religious tones. Their factory was said to be up in some New England town where they had been based for the last three hundred years. It was said that loose curls of walnut and oak from Gomer Bolstrood's block plane had been used as tinder beneath the pyres of convicted witches. Gomer Bolstrood was the answer to a question I'd been ruminating over ever since Granny's funeral, namely: where does all of this high-quality grandma furniture come from? In every family, young people go to grandma's house for Thanksgiving, or other obligatory visits, and lust over the nice antique furniture, wondering which pieces they will take home when the old lady kicks the bucket. Some people lose patience and go to estate sales or antique stores and buy the stuff.

But if the supply of old, high-grade, heirloom-quality furniture is fixed, then where will the grannys of the future come from? I could see a situation, half a century in the future, when Virginia's and my descendants would all be squabbling over that one black walnut dresser, while bringing in Ryder trucks to haul the rest of our stuff straight to the dump. As the population grows, and the supply of old furniture remains constant, this kind of thing is inevitable. There must be a source for new granny-grade furniture, or else the Americans of tomorrow

will all end up sitting in vinyl beanbag chairs, leaking
little foam beads all over the floor.

The answer is Gomer Bolstrood, and the price is high.
Each Gomer Bolstrood chair and table really ought to come
in a little felt-lined box, like a piece of jewelry. But
at the time, I was rich and impatient. So I drove to Gomer
Bolstrood and stormed through the door, only to be brought
up short by a *receptionist*. I felt tacky in my white tennis
shoes and jeans. She had probably seen a lot of high-tech
millionaires come through those doors, and took it pretty
calmly. Before I knew it a middle-aged woman had emerged
from the back of the store and appointed herself my personal design consultant. Her name was Margaret. ''Where
are the beds?'' I asked. She stiffened and informed me
that this not the kind of place where you could walk into
a Bed Room and see a row of beds lined up like pig's feet
at a butcher shop. A Gomer Bolstrood Home Design Gallery
consists of a series of exquisitely decorated rooms, some
of which happen to be bedrooms and to contain beds. Once
we had that all straightened out, Margaret showed me the
bedrooms. As she led me from one room to the next, I
couldn't help noticing that she was wearing black stockings with seams up the back—perfectly straight seams.

My erotic feelings for Margaret made me uncomfortable.
For a while, I had to restrain the impulse to say ''just
sell me the biggest, most expensive bed you have.'' Margaret showed me beds in different styles. The names of the
styles meant nothing to me. Some looked modern and some
looked old-fashioned. I pointed to a very large, high
four-poster that looked like granny furniture and said,
''I'll take one of those.''

There was a three-month delay while the bed was hand-
carved by New England craftsmen working at the same wage
as plumbers or psychotherapists. Then it showed up at our
house and was assembled by technicians in white cover-
alls, like the guys who work in semiconductor chip fabri-
cation plants. Virginia came home from work. She was
wearing a denim skirt, heavy wool socks, and Birk-
enstocks. The kids were still at school. We had sex on the
bed. I performed dutifully enough, I suppose. I could not
really sustain an erection and ended up with my head stuck
between her bristly thighs. Even with my ears blocked by

her quadriceps, I could hear her moaning and screaming. She went into erotic convulsions near the end, and almost snapped my neck. Her climax must have lasted for two or three full minutes. This was the moment when I first came to terms with the fact that Virginia could not achieve orgasm unless she was in close proximity to—preferably on top of— a piece of heirloom-grade furniture that she owned.

The window containing the image of Tom Howard's desktop vanishes. Pekka has clicked it into oblivion.

"I could not stand it any more," he says, in his electronically generated deadpan.

"I predict a *ménage à trois*—Tom, his wife, and Margaret doing it on a bed at the furniture store, after hours," Cantrell says ruminatively.

"Is it Tom? Or a fictional character of Tom's?" Pekka asks.

"Does this mean you win the bet?" Randy asks.

"If only I can figure out how to collect on it," Cantrell says.

AFLOAT

A BROWN MIASMA HAS SETTLED ACROSS THE BISMARCK SEA, smelling of oil and barbecue. American torpedo boats hurtle out of this reeking fog, their fat hulls barely touching the water, their giant motors curving white scars into the sea as they line up their targets: the few remaining ships in Goto Dengo's troop convoy, whose decks are now covered with a dark mat of soldiers, like moss on an old rock. The torpedos spring into the air like crossbow bolts, driven by compressed gas from tubes on the boats' decks. They belly-flop into the water, settle to a comfortable depth where the water is always calm, and draw bubble trails across the sea, heading directly for the ships. The crowds on the ships' decks fluidize and gush over the edges. Goto Dengo turns away and hears but doesn't see the explosions. Hardly any of the Nipponese troops know how to swim.

Later, the airplanes come back to strafe them some more. Swimmers who have the wit and the ability to dive are invulnerable. Those who don't are dead very soon. The airplanes leave. Goto Dengo strips a life preserver off a shattered corpse. He has the worst sunburn of his life and it is only midafternoon, so he pilfers a uniform blouse, too, and ties it around his head like a burnoose.

The ones who are still alive, and who can swim, try to converge on each other. They are in a complicated strait between New Guinea and New Britain, and tidal currents rushing through it tend to pull them apart. Some men drift slowly away, calling out to their comrades. Goto Dengo ends up on the fringes of a dissolving archipelago of maybe a hundred swimmers. Many of them clutch life preservers or bits of wood to stay afloat. The seas are considerably higher than their heads and so they can't see very far.

Before sunset, the haze lifts for an hour. Goto Dengo can clearly fix the sun's position, so for the first time all day he knows west from east, north from south. Better, he can see peaks rising above the southern horizon, slathered with blue-white glaciers.

"I will swim to New Guinea," he shouts, and begins doing it. There is no point in trying to discuss it with the others. The ones who are inclined to follow him, do: maybe a few dozen in all. The timing is right—the sea has become miraculously calm. Goto Dengo settles into a slow, easy sidestroke. Most of the others are moving in an improvised dogpaddle. If they are making any progress at all it is totally imperceptible. As the stars begin to come out, he rolls over into a backstroke and gets a fix on Polaris. As long as he swims away from that, it is physically impossible for him to miss New Guinea.

Darkness falls. Dim light is shed by the stars and by a half-moon. The men call to one another, trying to stay bunched together. Some of them get lost; they can be heard but not seen, and those in the main group can do nothing but listen to their pleadings dwindle.

It must be around midnight when the sharks come. The first victim is a man who had lacerated his forehead on a hatch frame when scrambling out of a sinking ship, and who has been bleeding ever since, drawing a thin pink line across the sea, leading the sharks straight to them. The sharks do not know yet what they are dealing with, and so they kill him slowly, worrying him to death in small bites. When he turns out to be easy prey, they explode into some kind of berserk rage that is all the more fantastic for being hidden beneath the black water. Men's voices are cut off in mid-cry as they are jerked straight down. Sometimes a leg or head will suddenly burst free from the surface. The water splashing into Goto Dengo's mouth begins to taste of iron.

The attack goes on for several hours. It appears that the noise and smell have attracted some rival shark packs, because sometimes there is a lull followed by renewed ferocity. A severed shark tail bumps up against Goto Dengo's face; he hangs onto it. The sharks are eating them; why shouldn't he retaliate? In Tokyo restaurants charge a lot of money for shark sashimi. The skin of the shark tail is tough, but hunks of muscle are hanging out of the torn edge. He buries his face in the meat and feasts on it.

When Goto Dengo was young, his father had owned a fedora with English writing on its ivory silk liner, and a briar pipe, and tobacco that he bought through the mail from America. He would sit on a rock up in the hills and snug his fedora down to keep the chilly air from the bald spot on top of his head and smoke his pipe and just look at the world. "What are you doing?" Dengo would ask him.

"Observing," father would say.

"But how long can you observe the same thing?"

"Forever. Look over there." Father pointed with the stem of his pipe. A thread of white smoke piped out of the mouthpiece, like a silk thread being unwound from a cocoon. "That band of dark rock is mineral-bearing. We could get copper out of there, probably some zinc and lead too. We would run a cog railway up the valley to that flat spot there, then sink an angle shaft parallel to the face of the deposit . . . " Then Dengo would get into the act and decide where the workers would live, where the school would be built for their children, where the playing field would be. By the time they were finished they would have populated the whole valley with an imaginary city.

Goto Dengo has plenty of time to make observations this night. He observes that severed body parts almost never get attacked. The men who swim most violently are always the first to get it. So, when the sharks come in, he tries to float on his back and not move a muscle, even when the jagged ends of someone's ribs poke him in the face.

Dawn arrives, one or two hundred hours after the previous sunset. He has never stayed awake all night long before, and finds it shocking to see something as big as the sun go down on one side of the planet and come up on the opposite. He is a virus, a germ living on the surface of unfathomably giant bodies in violent motion. And, amazingly enough, he is still not alone: three other men have survived the night of the sharks. They converge on one another and turn to face the ice-covered mountains of New Guinea, salmon-colored in the dawn light.

"They have not gotten any closer," one of the men says.

"They are deep in the interior," Goto Dengo says. "We are not swimming to the mountains—only to the shore—much closer. Let's go before we die of dehydration!" And he plunges forward into a sidestroke.

One of the others, a boy who speaks with an Okinawan accent, is an excellent swimmer. He and Goto Dengo can easily outdistance the others. For most of the day, they try to stay together with the other two anyway. The waves come up and make it difficult even for good swimmers to move.

One of the slower swimmers has been fighting diarrhea since long before his ship was sunk out from under him and was probably dehydrated to begin with. Around midday, when the sun is coming straight down on top of them like a flamethrower, he goes into convulsions, gets some water into his lungs, and disappears.

The other slow swimmer is from Tokyo. He's in much better physical condition—he simply doesn't know how to swim. "There is no better time or place to learn," Goto Dengo says. He and the Okinawan spend an hour or so teaching him the sidestroke and backstroke, and then they resume swimming southwards.

Around sunset, Goto Dengo catches the Okinawan gulping down mouthful after mouthful of seawater. It is painful to watch, mostly because he himself has been wanting to do it. "No! It will make you sick!" he says. His voice is weak. The effort of filling his lungs, expanding his ribcage against the relentless pressure of the water, is ruining him; every muscle in his torso is rigid and tender.

The Okinawan has already started retching by the time Goto Dengo reaches him. With the help of the Tokyo boy, he sticks his fingers down the Okinawan's throat and gets him to vomit it all up.

He is very sick anyway, and until late at night cannot do anything except float on his back and mumble deliriously. But just as Goto Dengo is about to abandon him, he becomes lucid, asking "Where is Polaris?"

"It is cloudy tonight," Goto Dengo says. "But there is a bright spot in the clouds that might be the moon."

Based on the position of that bright spot, they guess the position of New Guinea and resume swimming. Their arms and legs are like sacks of clay, and all of them are hallucinating.

The sun seems to be coming up. They are in a nebula of vapor, radiant with peach-colored light, as if hurtling through a distant part of the galaxy.

"I smell something rotten," says one of them. Goto Dengo cannot tell which.

"Gangrene?" guesses the other.

Goto Dengo fills his nostrils, an act that consumes about half of his remaining energy reserves. "It is not rotten flesh," he says. "It is vegetation."

None of them can swim anymore. If they could, they wouldn't know which direction to choose, because the mist glows uniformly. If they picked a direction, it wouldn't matter, because the current is taking them where it will.

Goto Dengo sleeps for a while, or maybe he doesn't.

Something bumps his leg. Thank god; the sharks have come to finish them.

The waves have grown aggressive. He feels another bump. The burned flesh on his leg screams. It is something very hard, rough, and sharp.

Something is projecting out of the water just ahead, something bumpy and white. A coral head.

A wave breaks behind them, picks them up, and flings them forward across the coral, half-flaying them. Goto Dengo breaks a finger and counts himself lucky. The next breaker takes what little skin he has left and flings him into a lagoon. Something forces his feet upwards, and because his body is just a limp sack of shit at this point, doubles him over head-first into the water. His face strikes a bed of sharp coral sand. Then his hands are in it too. His limbs have forgotten how to do anything except swim, and so it takes him a while to plant them in the bottom and lift his head out of the water. Then he begins to crawl on his hands and knees. The odor of rotten vegetation is overpowering now, as if a whole division's food supplies had been left out in the sun for a week.

He finds some sand that is not covered with water, turns around, and sits down on it. The Okinawan is right behind him, also on hands and knees, and the Tokyo boy has actually clambered to his feet and is wading ashore, being knocked this way and that by incoming waves. He is laughing.

The Okinawan boy collapses on the sand next to Goto Dengo, not even trying to sit up.

A wave knocks the Tokyo boy off-balance. Laughing, he collapses sideways into the surf, throwing out one hand to break his fall.

He stops laughing and jerks back sharply. Something is dangling from his forearm: a wriggling snake. He snaps it like a whip and it flies off into the water.

Scared and sober, he splashes the last half-dozen steps up onto the beach and then falls flat on his face. By the time Goto Dengo reaches him, he is stone dead.

Goto Dengo gathers his forces for some period of time that is difficult to measure. He may have fallen asleep sitting up. The Okinawan boy is still lying on the sand, raving. Goto Dengo gets his feet underneath himself and staggers off in search of fresh water.

This is not a proper beach, merely a sandbar maybe ten meters long and three wide, with some tall grassy stuff sprouting out of the top. On the other side of it is a brackish lagoon that meanders between banks, not of earth, but of living things all tangled together. That tangle is obviously too thick to penetrate. So, notwithstanding what just happened to the Tokyo boy, Goto Dengo wades into the lagoon, hoping that it will lead inland to a freshwater stream.

He wanders for what seems like an hour, but the lagoon takes him back to the edge of the sea again. He gives up and drinks the water he's wading in, hoping it will be a little less salty. This leads to a great deal of vomiting but makes him feel slightly better somehow. Again he wades into the swamp, trying to keep the sound of the surf behind him, and after an hour or so he finds a rivulet of water that is actually fresh. When he has finished drinking from that, he feels strong enough to go back and carry the Okinawan boy here, if need be.

He gets back to the beach in midafternoon and finds that the Okinawan is gone. But the sand is all churned up by footprints. The sand is dry and so the footprints are too indistinct to read. They must have made contact with a patrol! Surely their comrades must have heard about the attack on the convoy and are combing beaches for survivors. There must be a bivouac in the jungle not far away!

Goto Dengo follows the trail into the jungle. After he's proceeded a mile or so, the track crosses a small, open mud flat where he gets a good look at the footprints, all made by bare feet with enormous, bizarrely splayed toes. Footprints of people who have never worn shoes in their lives.

He proceeds more cautiously for another few hundred meters. He can hear voices now. The Army taught him all about jungle infiltration tactics, how to creep through the enemy's lines in the middle of the night without making a sound. Of course, when they practiced it in Nippon they weren't being eaten alive by ants and mosquitoes the whole time. But it hardly matters to him now. An hour of patient work gets him to a vantage point from which he can see into a flat clearing with a stagnant creek wandering through it. Several long dark houses are built on tree-trunk stilts to keep them up out of the ooze, and roofed with bushy heaps of palm fronds.

Before he finds the Okinawan, Goto Dengo needs to get some food. In the middle of the clearing, white porridge is steaming in a pot over an open fire, but it's being tended by several tough-looking women, naked except for short fringes of fibrous stuff tied round their waists and just barely concealing their genitals.

Smoke is rising from some of the long buildings too. But to get inside one of them, he would have to clamber up its heavy, slanting ladder and then worm through what looks like a rather small doorway. A child, standing inside one of those doorways with a stick, could prevent an intruder from coming in. Hanging outside some of the doorways are sacks, improvised from lengths of fabric (so at least they have textiles!)

and filled with big round lumps: coconuts, possibly or some kind of preserved food set up to keep it away from the ants.

Perhaps seventy people are gathered around something of interest in the middle of the clearing. As they move around, Goto Dengo gets occasional momentary glimpses of someone, possibly Nipponese, who is sitting at the base of a palm tree with his hands behind his back. There's a lot of blood on his face and he's not moving. Most of these people are men, and they tend to carry spears. They have those fringes of hairy stuff (sometimes dyed red or green) concealing their private parts, and some of the bigger and older ones have decorated themselves by tying strips of fabric around their arms. Some have painted designs on their skin in pale mud. They have shoved various objects, some of them quite large, sideways through their nasal septums.

The bloodied man seems to have captured everyone's attention, and Goto Dengo reckons that this will be his only chance to steal some food. He picks the longhouse farthest away from where the villagers have gathered, clambers up its ladder, and reaches for the bulging sack that hangs by the entrance. But the fabric is very old and it has rotted from the damp of the swamp, and maybe from the attacks of the hundreds of flies that buzz around it, and so when he grasps it has fingers go right through. A long swath of it tears away and the contents tumble out around Goto Dengo's feet. They are dark and sort of hairy, like coconuts, but their shape is more complicated, and he knows intuitively that something is wrong even before he recognizes them as human skulls. Maybe half a dozen of them. Scalp and skin still stuck on. Some of them are dark-skinned with bushy hair, like the natives, and others look distinctly Nipponese.

Sometime later, he is able to think coherently again. He realizes that he does not know how long he might have spent up here, in full view of the villagers, gazing on the skulls. He turns around to look, but all attention is still focused on the wounded man seated at the base of the tree.

From this vantage point Goto Dengo is able to see that it is indeed the Okinawan, and that his arms have been tied together behind the tree trunk. A boy of maybe twelve is standing over him, holding a spear. He steps forward cautiously and suddenly pokes it into the midsection of the Okinawan, who comes awake and thrashes from side to side. The boy's obviously startled by this, and jumps back. Then an older man, his head decorated with a fringe of cowrie shells, takes a stance behind and beside the boy, showing him how to hold the spear, guiding him forward again. He adds his own strength to the youngster's and they shove the spear straight into the Okinawan's heart.

Goto Dengo falls off the house.

The men become very excited and pick the boy up on their shoulders and parade him around the clearing hollering and leaping and twirling, jabbing their spears defiantly into the air. They are pursued by all but the very youngest children. Goto Dengo, bruised but not damaged by the fall onto the mucky ground, belly-crawls into the jungle and looks for a place of concealment. The women of the village carry pots and knives towards the Okinawan's body and begin to cut it up with the conspicuous skill of a sushi chef dismantling a tuna.

One of them is concentrating entirely on his head. Suddenly she jumps into the air and begins to dance around the clearing, waving something bright and glittery. *"Ulab! Ulab! Ulab!"* she cries ecstatically. Some women and children begin following her around, trying to get a look at whatever it is she's holding. Finally she stops and centers her hand in a rare shaft of sunlight coming down through the trees. Resting in the palm of her hand is a gold tooth.

"Ulab!" say the women and children. One of the kids tries to snatch it out of her hand and she knocks him flat on his ass. Then one of the big spear-carrying men runs up and she hands the booty over to him.

Several of the men now gather round to marvel at the find.

The women go back to working over the Okinawan boy, and soon his body parts are stewing in pots over an open fire.

SHINOLA

✠ Men who believe that they are accomplishing *something* by speaking speak in a different way from men who believe that speaking is a *waste of time*. Bobby Shaftoe has learned most of his practical knowledge—how to fix a car, butcher a deer, throw a spiral, talk to a lady, kill a Nip—from the latter type of man. For them, trying to do anything by talking is like trying to pound in a nail with a screwdriver. Sometimes you can even see the desperation spread over such a man's face as he listens to himself speak.

Men of the other type—the ones who use speech as a tool of their work, who are confident and fluent—aren't necessarily more intelligent, or even more educated. It took Shaftoe a long time to figure that out.

Anyway, everything was neat and tidy in Bobby Shaftoe's mind until he met two of the men in Detachment 2702: Enoch Root and Lawrence Pritchard Waterhouse. He can't put his finger on what bugs him about

those two. During the weeks they spent together on Qwghlm, he spent
a lot of time listening to them yammer at each other, and began to
suspect that there might be a third category of man, a kind so rare that
Shaftoe never met any of them until now.

Officers are discouraged from fraternizing with enlisted men and noncoms, which has made it more difficult for Shaftoe to pursue his research
into the matter. Sometimes, though, circumstances jumble all of the ranks
together willy-nilly. A prime example would be this Trinidadian tramp
steamer.

Where do they get this stuff? wonders Shaftoe. Does the U.S. government
keep a bunch of Trinidadian tramp steamers riding at anchor at a naval
yard somewhere, just in case one is needed?

He thinks not. This one shows signs of a very recent and hasty change
of ownership. It is a mother lode of yellowed, ragged, multiethnic pornography, some of it very run-of-the-mill and some so exotic that he
mistook it for medical literature at first. There is a lot of stray paperwork
on the bridge and in certain cabins, most of which Shaftoe only sees out
of the corner of his eye as these areas tend to be the domain of officers.
The heads are still littered with their predecessors' curly black pubic
hairs, and the storage lockers are sparsely stocked with exotic Caribbean
foodstuffs, much of them rapidly going bad. The cargo hold is filled with
bales and bales of coarse brown fibrous material—raw material for life
preservers or bran muffins, he supposes.

None of them much cares, because Detachment 2702 has been freezing its ass off in the Far North ever since they left Italy a few months
ago, and now they are running around shirtless, of all things. One little
airplane ride, that's all it took, and they were in the balmy Azores. They
did not get any R and R there—they went straight from the airfield to
the Trinidadian ship, in the dead of night, huddled under tarps in a
covered truck. But even the warm air that streamed in underneath the
tarp felt like an exotic massage in a tropical whorehouse. And once they
steamed out of sight of port, they were allowed to come up abovedecks
and take in some sun.

This gives Bobby Shaftoe the opportunity to strike up a few conversations with Enoch Root, partly just for the hell of it and partly so that
he can try to figure out this whole business about the third category of
men. Progress comes slowly.

"I don't like the word 'addict' because it has terrible connotations,"
Root says one day, as they are sunning themselves on the afterdeck.
"Instead of slapping a label on you, the Germans would describe you as
'*Morphiumsüchtig.*' The verb *suchen* means to seek. So that might be trans-
lated, loosely, as 'morphine seeky' or even more loosely as 'morphine-

seeking.' I prefer 'seeky' because it means that you have an inclination to seek morphine."

"What the fuck are you talking about?" Shaftoe says.

"Well, suppose you have a roof with a hole in it. That means it is a leaky roof. It's leaky all the time—even if it's not raining at the moment. But it's only leak*ing* when it happens to be raining. In the same way, morphine-seeky means that you always have this tendency to look for morphine, even if you are not looking for it at the moment. But I prefer both of them to 'addict,' because they are adjectives modifying Bobby Shaftoe instead of a noun that obliterates Bobby Shaftoe."

"So what's the point?" Shaftoe asks. He asks this because he is expecting Root to give him an order, which is usually what men of the talkative sort end up doing after jabbering on for a while. But no order seems to be forthcoming, because that's not Root's agenda. Root just felt like talking about words. The SAS blokes refer to this kind of activity as wanking.

Shaftoe has had little direct contact with that Waterhouse fellow during their stay on Qwghlm, but he has noticed that men who have just finished talking to Waterhouse tend to walk away shaking their heads—and not in the slow way of a man saying "no," but in the sudden convulsive way of a dog who has a horsefly in his middle ear. Waterhouse never gives direct orders, so men of the first category don't know what to make of him. But apparently men of the second category fare no better; such men usually talk like they have an agenda in their heads and they are checking off boxes as they go, but Waterhouse's conversation doesn't go anywhere in particular. He speaks, not as a way of telling you a bunch of stuff he's already figured out, but as a way of making up a bunch of new shit as he goes along. And he always seems to be hoping that you'll join in. Which no one ever does, except for Enoch Root.

After they've been out to sea for a day, the captain (Commander Eden—the same poor son of a bitch who got the job of ramming his previous command into Norway) staggers out of his cabin, making use of every railing or other handhold that comes within flailing distance. He announces in a slurred voice that from here on out, according to orders from On High, anyone going abovedecks must wear black turtlenecks, black gloves, and black ski masks *underneath* their other clothes. These articles are duly issued to the men. Shaftoe gets the skipper really pissed off by asking him three times whether he's sure he has the order worded correctly. One of the reasons Shaftoe is so highly regarded by the enlisted men is that he knows how to ask these kinds of questions without technically violating the rules of military etiquette. The skipper, to his credit, doesn't just pull rank and yell at him. He takes Shaftoe back to his cabin and shows him a khaki-covered Army manual, printed in black block letters:

TACTICAL NEGRO IMPERSONATION
VOLUME III: NEGROES OF THE CARIBBEAN

It is a pretty interesting order, even by Detachment 2702 standards. Commander Eden's drunkenness is also kind of disturbing—not the fact that he is drunk, but the particular *type* of drunk—the sort of drunk of say, a Civil War soldier who knows that the surgeon is about to remove his femur with a bucksaw.

After Shaftoe has finished getting the turtlenecks, gloves, and ski masks passed out to the men, and told them to simmer down and do the lifeboat drills again, Shaftoe finds Root in what passes for the sickbay. Because he figures it is time to have one of those open-ended conversations in which you try to figure out a bunch of shit, Root is his man.

"I know you're expecting me to ask for morphine, but I'm not gonna," Shaftoe says. "I just want to talk."

"Oh," Root says. "Should I put on my chaplain hat, then?"

"I'm a fucking Protestant. I can talk to God myself whenever I goddamn well feel like it."

Root is startled and bewildered by Shaftoe's burst of hostility. "Well, what do you want to talk about, Sergeant?"

"This mission."

"Oh. I don't know anything about the mission."

"Well, let's try to figure it out, then," Shaftoe says.

"I thought you were just supposed to follow orders," Root says.

"I'll follow 'em, all right."

"I know you will."

"But in the meantime I got a lot of time to kill, so I might as well use that time to figure out what the fuck is going on. Now, the skipper says to wear this stuff if we are abovedecks, where we might be seen. But who the hell is going to see us, out here?"

"An observation plane?"

"Germans don't have no observation planes, not out there."

"Another ship?" Root asks rhetorically, getting into the spirit of the thing.

"We'll see them at the same time they see us, and that'll give us plenty of time to put that shit on."

"It would have to be a U-boat that the skipper is worried about, then."

"Bingo," Shaftoe says, "because a U-boat could look at us through its periscope, and we'd never know we were being looked at."

But that day, they don't get much further in their attempt to figure out the deeper question of why their commanding officers want them to make themselves look like Negroes in the eyes of German U-boat captains.

The next day, the skipper plants himself on the bridge, where he evidently means to keep a close eye on things. He seems less drunk but no happier. He is wearing a colorful short-sleeved madras shirt over a long-sleeved black turtleneck, and rope sandals over black socks. Every so often he puts on his black gloves and ski mask and goes out to scan the horizon with binoculars.

The ship continues westwards for a few hours after sunrise, then turns north for a short time, then heads east for an hour, then goes north again, then turns back to the west. They are running a search pattern, and Commander Eden does not appear to be looking forward to finding whatever it is that they are searching for. Shaftoe runs another lifeboat drill, then checks the lifeboats himself, making sure that they are lavishly stocked.

Around noon, a lookout hollers. The ship changes course, headed roughly northeast. The skipper emerges from the bridge and, with an air of sepulchral finality, presents Bobby Shaftoe with a crate of dark brown shoe polish and a sealed envelope containing detailed orders.

Minutes later, the men of Detachment 2702, under orders from Sergeant Shaftoe, strip to their briefs and begin coating themselves with shoe polish. They already own black Shinola, which they are ordered to massage into their hair if it's not already black. Just another example of how the military screws the little man—Shinola ain't free.

"Do I look like a Negro yet?" Shaftoe asks Root.

"I have traveled a bit," Root says, "and you don't look like a Negro to me. But to a German who has never seen the genuine article, and who's looking through a periscope—what the heck?" Then: "I take it you've figured out the mission?"

"I read the fucking orders," Shaftoe says guardedly.

They are headed towards a ship. As they get closer, Shaftoe checks it out with a borrowed spyglass, and is startled, but not really surprised, to see that it's not one ship but two ships side by side. Both of these ships have the long fatal lines of U-boats, but one of them is fatter, and he figures it's a milchcow.

Beneath his feet, he feels the engines throttling back to a dim idle.

The sudden quiet, and the palpable loss of momentum and power, are not reassuring. He gets the usual sick, electric, nauseous, hyperactive feeling that always makes combat such a stimulatin' experience.

The beat-up Trinidadian steamer has plied the waters of the Atlantic without incident throughout the war to date, running back and forth between African and Caribbean ports, and occasionally venturing as far north as the Azores. Perhaps it has been sighted, from time to time, by a patrolling U-boat, and judged to be not worth spending a torpedo on. But today its luck has changed—for the worse. They have, by random chance, blundered across a milchcow—a supply U-boat of the Kriegsmarine of the Third Reich. The steamer's normally jaunty crew of shoe-brown Negroes has gathered at the rails to peer across the ocean at this peculiar sight—two ships tied together in the middle of the ocean, going nowhere. But as they draw closer, they realize that one of those ships is a killer, and that the other is flying the battle flag of the Kriegsmarine. Too late, they cut their engines.

There is wild confusion for a minute or so—this might be an interesting spectacle to the lowly, deck-swabbing Negroes, but the smart Negroes up on the bridge know they're in trouble—they've seen something they shouldn't have. They swing her around to the south and make a run for it! For an hour they dash desperately across the seas. But they are trailed implacably by a U-boat, cutting through the waves like a Bowie knife. The U-boat has its whip aerial up, is monitoring the usual frequencies, and hears the Trinidadian steamer fire up her radio and send out an SOS. In a short stream of dits and dahs, the steamer broadcasts her location—and that of the milchcow, and in so doing taps out her own death warrant.

Pesky *untermenschen!* They've really gone and done it now! It won't be twenty-four hours before the milchcow is located and sunk by the Allies. There is a good chance that a few U-boats will be hounded to their deaths as part of the bargain. That is not a good way to die—being chased across the ocean for several days, suffering the death of a thousand cuts from strafings and bombings. Stuff like this really drives home, to the common ordinary Obertorpedomaat, the wisdom of the Führer's plan to go out and find all of the people who aren't Germans and kill them.

Meanwhile, our basic Kapitänleutnant has got to be asking himself: what the hell are the chances that a tramp Trinidadian steamer is going to just happen upon us and our milchcow, out in the vastness of the Atlantic Ocean?

You could probably work it out, given the right data:

N_n =number of Negroes per square kilometer
N_m =number of milchcows
A_A =Area of the Atlantic Ocean

. . . and so on. But wait a sec, neither Negroes nor milchcows are randomly distributed, so the calculation becomes immensely more complicated. Far too complicated for a Kapitänleutnant to mess around with, especially when he's busy trying to effect a dramatic reduction in N_n.

The Trinidadian steamer is brought up short by a shell fired across her bows from the U-boat's deck gun. The Negroes gather on the decks, but they hesitate, just for a moment, to launch the lifeboats. Perhaps the Germans are going to give them a break.

Typical, sloppy, sentimental *untermenschen* thinking. The Germans brought them up short so they would hold still to be torpedoed. As soon as they realize this, the Negroes stage an impressive lifeboat drill. It's remarkable that they even have enough lifeboats to go around, but the calm, practiced skill with which they launch and board them is truly phenomenal. It's enough to make a German naval officer reconsider, just for a moment, his opinions about the shortcomings of darkies.

It is a textbook torpedoing! The torpedo is set to run nice and deep, and as it passes underneath the ship, the detonation circuit senses a change in the magnetic field and triggers the explosive, neatly snapping the ship's keel, breaking its back, and sending it down with incredible speed. For the next five or ten minutes, bales of brown stuff erupt from the water, released from the cargo holds as the ship plummets towards the bottom. It gives the whole scene an unexpectedly festive air.

Some U-boat skippers would not be above machine-gunning the survivors, at this point, just to let off a little steam.

But the commander, Kapitänleutnant Günter Bischoff, is not yet a card-carrying member of the Nazi Party and probably never will be.

On the other hand, Bischoff is wrapped in a straightjacket and blasted half out of his mind on drugs.

Acting commander of the U-boat is Oberleutnant zur See Karl Beck. He *is* a card-carrying National Socialist, and, in other circumstances, he might be game for a bit of punitive machine-gunning, but at the moment he's exhausted and pretty badly shook up. He is intensely conscious of the fact that he's probably not going to live very long now that their location has been reported.

So he doesn't. The Negroes are jumping out of the lifeboats, swimming to the bales, and clinging to them with just their heads out of the water, realizing it would take forever to hunt them all down. OL Beck knows the Liberators and the Catalinas are already airborne and vectored towards him, so he has to get the hell out of there. Since he has plenty of fuel, he decides to head south for a while, planning to double back north in a day or two, when the coast might be a bit clearer. It is the kind of thing that KL Bischoff would do if he had not gone crazy, and everyone on the boat has unlimited respect for the old man.

They run on the surface, as they always do when they are not making a positive effort to sink a convoy, so they can send and receive radio messages. Beck gives one to Oberfunkmaat Huffer, explaining what has just happened, and Huffer gives it to one of his Funkmaats, who sits down in front of U-691's Enigma machine and encrypts it using the key for the day, then taps it out on the radio.

An hour later, they get a message back, straight from U-boat Command at Wilhelmshaven, and when the Funkmaat runs it through the Enigma, what he comes up with is: CAPTURE SURVIVING OFFICERS.

It's a classic example of military commandsmanship: if the order had come in a more timely fashion it would have been easy to obey, but now that they are an hour away it will be extremely difficult and dangerous. The order doesn't make any sense, and no effort is made to clarify it.

Given the time lag, Beck figures he can get away with giving this one a half-assed try. He really should swing round and approach the wreck on the surface, which would get him there faster, but which would be nearly suicidal. So instead, he closes the hatches and descends to periscope depth as he draws closer. This cuts the U-boat's speed to a crawling seven knots, so it takes them about three hours to get back to the atoll of bobbing brown bales that marks the site.

A damn good thing, too, because another fucking submarine is there, picking up survivors. It is a Royal Navy submarine.

This is so weird it makes the hairs on the back of Beck's neck stand up—and there's a lot of hair there, because like most submariners, Beck hasn't shaved in weeks. There's nothing weird, though, that can't be settled with a single well-placed torpedo. Seconds later the submarine explodes like a bomb; the torpedo must have touched off her munitions. Her crew, and most of the rescued Negroes, are trapped within, and don't have a chance of getting out even if they survived the explosions. The submarine drops off the surface of the ocean like the wreckage of the Hindenburg tumbling down on New Jersey.

"*Gott in Himmel,*" Beck mumbles, watching this all through the periscope. He'd been pleased by the success, until he'd remembered that he had specific orders, and that killing everyone in sight was not one of them. Will there be any survivors for him to pick up?

He takes the U-boat up onto the surface, and climbs up on the conning tower with his officers. First thing they do is scan the skies for

Catalinas. Finding none, they post lookouts, then begin to nose the U-boat through the sea of bales, which by now has spread out to cover at least a square kilometer. It is getting dark, and they have to bring up searchlights.

All looks rather dismal until one searchlight picks out a survivor—just a head, shoulders, and a pair of arms reaching up clenching a rope around a bale. The survivor does not move or respond as they approach, and not until a wave rolls the bale over is it revealed that everything below the man's solar plexus has been bitten off by sharks. The sight sets even this hardened crew of murderers to gagging. In the quiet that ensues, they hear low voices echoing across the calm water. With a bit more searching, they find two men, evidently talkative sorts, sharing a bale.

When the searchlight picks them out, one of the Negroes lets go of the bale and dives beneath the surface. The other just stares calmly and expectantly into the light. This Negro's eyes are pale, almost colorless, and he has a skin condition: parts of him are turning white.

As they draw closer, the pale eyed Negro speaks to them in perfect German. "My comrade attempts to drown himself," he explains.

"Is that even possible?" asks Kapitänleutnant Beck.

"He and I were just discussing that very question."

Beck checks his wristwatch. "He must want to kill himself very badly," he says.

"Sergeant Shaftoe takes his duty very seriously. It's kind of ironic. His cyanide capsule dissolved in the seawater."

"I am afraid that all irony has become tedious and depressing to me," Beck says, as a body breaks the surface nearby. It is Shaftoe, and he seems to be unconscious.

"You are?" Beck asks.

"Lieutenant Enoch Root."

"I'm only supposed to take officers," Beck says, casting a cold eye in the direction of Sergeant Shaftoe's back.

"Sergeant Shaftoe has exceptionally broad responsibilities," says Lieutenant Root calmly, "in some respects exceeding those of a junior officer."

"Get them both. Fetch the medicine box. Revive the sergeant," Beck says. "I will talk to you later, Lieutenant Root." And then he turns his back on the prisoners, and heads for the nearest hatch. He is going to spend the next week trying very hard to stay alive, in spite of the best efforts of the Royal and United States Navies. It's going to be quite an interesting challenge. He should be thinking about his strategy. But he can't get the image of Sergeant Shaftoe's back out of his mind. His fucking head was still underneath the water! If they weren't about to fish him out of the ocean, he would have succeeded in drowning himself. So it was possible. At least for one person.

HOSTILITIES

As the vans, taxis, and limousines pull into the parking lot at the Ministry of Information site, the members of Epiphyte Corp. are greeted by smiling and bowing Nipponese virgins wearing, and bearing, gleaming white Goto Engineering helmets. The time is about eight in the morning, and up here on the mountain the temperature is still tolerable, though humid. Everyone mills around before the cavern's maw, carrying their hardhats in their hands, as no one wants to be the first to put his on and look stupid. Some of the younger Nipponese executives are mugging hilariously with theirs. Dr. Mohammed Pragasu circulates. He has an authentically used and battered hardhat which he whirls absentmindedly around one finger as he strolls from group to group.

"Has anyone simply asked Prag what the fuck is going on?" says Eb. He rarely uses English profanity, so when he does, it's funny.

The only member of Epiphyte Corp. who does not at least crack a smile is John Cantrell, who has been looking distant and tense ever since yesterday. ("It's one thing to write a dissertation about mathematical techniques in cryptography," he said, on the way up here, when someone asked him what was bothering him. "And another to gamble billions of dollars' worth of Other People's Money on it."

"We need a new category," Randy said. "Other, Bad People's Money."

"Speaking of which—" Tom began, but Avi cut him off by glaring significantly at the back of the driver's head.)

    To: dwarf@siblings.net
    From: root@eruditorum.org
    Subject: Re(3) Why?
    Randy,
    You ask me to justify my interest in why you are building
    the Crypt.
    My interest is a mark of my occupation. This is, in a
    sense, what I do for a living.

You continue to assume that I am someone you know. Today you think I'm the Dentist, yesterday you thought I was Andrew Loeb. This guessing game will rapidly become tedious for both of us, so please believe me when I tell you that we have never met.

—BEGIN ORDO SIGNATURE BLOCK—

(etc.)

—END ORDO SIGNATURE BLOCK—

To: root@eruditorum.org

From: dwarf@siblings.net

Subject: Re(4) Why?

Damn, after you said you did it for a living, I was going to guess that you were Geb, or another one of my ex-girlfriend's crowd.

Why don't you tell me your name?

—BEGIN ORDO SIGNATURE BLOCK—

(etc.)

—END ORDO SIGNATURE BLOCK—

To: dwarf@siblings.net

From: root@eruditorum.org

Subject: Re(5) Why?

Randy,

I've already told you my name, and it meant nothing to you. Or rather, it meant the wrong thing. Names are tricky that way. The best way to know someone is to have a conversation with them.

Interesting that you assume I'm an academic.

—BEGIN ORDO SIGNATURE BLOCK—

(etc.)

—END ORDO SIGNATURE BLOCK—

To: root@eruditorum.org

From: dwarf@siblings.net

Subject: Re(6) Why?

Gotcha!

I didn't specify who Geb was. And yet you knew that he and my ex-girlfriend were academics. If (as you claim) I don't know you, then how do you know these things about me?

—BEGIN ORDO SIGNATURE BLOCK—

(etc.)

—END ORDO SIGNATURE BLOCK—

Everyone now turns to look towards Prag, who seems to be having trouble with his peripheral vision today. "Prag is avoiding us," Avi snaps.

"Which means it will be completely impossible for us to reach him until after this is all over."

Tom steps towards Avi, drawing the corporate circle in closer. "The investigator in Hong Kong?"

"Got some IDs, struck out on others," Avi says. "Basically, the heavyset Filipino gentleman is Marcos's bagman. Responsible for keeping the famous billions out of the hands of the Philippine government. The Taiwanese guy—not Harvard Li but the other one—is a lawyer whose family has deep connections to Japan, dating back to when Taiwan was part of their empire. He has held down half a dozen government positions at various times, mostly in finance and commerce—now he's sort of a fixer who does jobs of all sorts for high-ranking Taiwanese officials."

"What about the scary Chinese guy?"

Avi raises his eyebrows and heaves a little sigh before answering. "He's a general in the People's Liberation Army. Equivalent to a four-star rank. He's been working their investment arm for the last fifteen years."

"Investment arm? The Army!?" Cantrell blurts. He's been getting uneasier by the minute, and now looks mildly nauseated.

"The People's Liberation Army is a titanic business empire," Beryl says. "They control the biggest pharmaceutical company in China. The biggest hotel chain. A lot of the communications infrastructure. Railways. Refineries. And, obviously, armaments."

"What about Mr. Cellphone?" Randy asks.

"Still working on him. My man in Hong Kong is sending his mug shot to a colleague in Panama."

"I think that after what we saw in the lobby, we can make some assumptions," Beryl says.*

> To: dwarf@siblings.net
> From: root@eruditorum.org
> Subject: Re(7) Why?
> Randy,
> You ask how I know these things about you. There are many
> things I could say, but the basic answer is surveillance.

---

*Half an hour ago, as Epiphyte Corp. was gathering in the lobby, a big black Mercedes came in, fresh from the airport. 747s come into Kinakuta four times a day, and from the time that a person presents himself at the registration desk of his luxury hotel, you can figure out which city he flew in from. These guys came in from Los Angeles. Three Latino men: a middle-aged fellow of great importance, a somewhat younger assistant, and a palooka. They were met in the lobby by the solitary fellow who showed up late yesterday with the cellphone.

```
—BEGIN ORDO SIGNATURE BLOCK—
(etc.)
—END ORDO SIGNATURE BLOCK—
```

Randy figures there's no better time to ask this question. And because he's known Avi longer than anyone else, he's the only one who can get away with asking it. "Do we really want to be involved with these people?" he says. "Is this what Epiphyte Corp. is for? Is this what we are for?"

Avi heaves a big sigh and thinks about it for a while. Beryl looks at him searchingly; Eb and John and Tom study their shoes, or search the triple-canopy jungle for exotic avians, while listening intently.

"You know, back in the forty-niner days, every gold mining town in California had a nerd with a scale," Avi says. "The assayer. He sat in an office all day. Scary-looking rednecks came in with pouches of gold dust. The nerd weighed them, checked them for purity, told them what the stuff was worth. Basically, the assayer's scale was the exchange point—the place where this mineral, this dirt from the ground, became money that would be recognized as such in any bank or marketplace in the world, from San Francisco to London to Beijing. Because of the nerd's special knowledge, he could put his imprimatur on dirt and make it money. Just like we have the power to turn bits into money.

"Now, a lot of the people the nerd dealt with were incredibly bad guys. Peg house habitues. Escaped convicts from all over the world. Psychotic gunslingers. People who owned slaves and massacred Indians. I'll bet that the first day, or week, or month, or year, that the nerd moved to the gold-mining town and hung out his shingle, he was probably scared shitless. He probably had moral qualms too—very legitimate ones, perhaps," Avi adds, giving Randy a sidelong glance. "Some of those pioneering nerds probably gave up and went back East. But y'know what? In a surprisingly short period of time, everything became pretty damn civilized, and the towns filled up with churches and schools and universities, and the sort of howling maniacs who got there first were all assimilated or driven out or thrown into prison, and the nerds had boulevards and opera houses named after them. Now, is the analogy clear?"

"The analogy is clear," Tom Howard says. He is less troubled by this than any of them, with the possible exception of Avi. But then, his hobby is collecting and shooting rare automatic weapons.

No one else will say anything; it is Randy's job to be troublesome. "Uh, how many of those assayers got gunned down in the street after they pissed off some psychotic gold miner?" he asks.

"I don't have any figures on that," Avi says.

"Well, I am not fully convinced that I really need this," Randy says.

"We all need to decide that question for ourselves," says Avi.

"And then vote, as a corporation whether to stay in or pull out—right?" Randy says.

Avi and Beryl look meaningfully at each other.

"Getting out, at this point, would be, uh, complicated," Beryl says. Then, seeing a look on Randy's face, she hastens to add: "not for individuals who might want to leave Epiphyte. That's easy. No problem. But for Epiphyte to get out of this, uh . . ."

"Situation," Cantrell offers.

"Dilemma," Randy says.

Eb mumbles a word in German.

"Opportunity," Avi counters.

". . . would be all but impossible," Beryl says.

"Look," Avi says, "I don't want anyone to feel compelled to stay in a situation where they have moral qualms."

"Or fear imminent summary execution," Randy adds helpfully.

"Right. Now, we've all put a ton of work into this thing, and that work ought to be worth something. To be totally above-board and explicit, let me reiterate what is already in the bylaws, which is that anyone can pull out; we'll buy back your stock. After what's happened here the last couple of days, I'm pretty confident that we could raise enough money to do so. You'd make at least as much as if you had stayed home doing a regular salaried job."

Younger, less experienced high-tech entrepreneurs would have scoffed bitterly at this. But everyone on this crew actually finds it impressive that Avi can put a company together and keep it alive long enough to make it worth the work they've put into it.

The black Mercedes cruises up. Dr. Mohammed Pragasu strides over to meet it, greets the South Americans in fairly decent Spanish, makes a couple of introductions. The scattered clumps of businessmen, begin to draw closer together, converging on the cavern's entrance. Prag is making a head count, taking attendance. Someone's missing.

One of the Dentist's aides is maneuvering towards Prag in lavender pumps, a cellphone clamped to her head. Randy breaks away from Epiphyte and sets a collision course, reaching Prag's vicinity just in time to hear the woman tell him, "Dr. Kepler will be joining us late—some important business in California. He sends his apologies."

Dr. Pragasu nods brightly, somehow avoids eye contact with Randy, who is now close enough to floss Prag's teeth, and turns, clamping his

hardhat down on top of his glossy hair. "Please follow me, everyone,"
he announces, "the tour begins."

It is a dull tour, even for those who have never been inside the place.
Whenever Prag leads them to a new spot, everyone looks around and
gets their bearings; conversation lulls for ten or fifteen seconds, then picks
up again; the high-ranking executives stare unseeingly at the hewn stone
walls and mutter to each other while their engineering consultants converge on the Goto engineers and ask them learned questions.

All of the construction engineers work for Goto and are, of course,
Nipponese. There is another who stands apart. "Who's the heavyset
blond guy?" Randy asks Tom Howard.

"German civil engineer on loan to Goto. He seems to specialize in
military issues."

"*Are* there any military issues?"

"At some point, about halfway into this project, Prag suddenly decided
he wanted the whole thing bombproof."

"Oh. Is that Bomb with a capital B, by any chance?"

"I think he's just about to talk about that," Tom says, leading
Randy closer.

Someone has just asked the German engineer whether this place is
nuclear-hardened.

"Nuclear-hardened is not the issue," he says dismissively. "Nuclear-
hardened is easy—it just means that the structure can support a brief
overpressure of so many megapascals. You see, half of Saddam's bunkers
were, technically, nuclear-hardened. But this does no good against preci-
sion-guided, penetrating munitions—as the Americans proved. And it is
far more likely this structure will be attacked in that way than that it
would ever be nuked—we do not anticipate that the sultan will get
involved in a nuclear war."

This is the funniest thing that anyone has said all day, and it gets
a laugh.

"Fortunately," the German continues, "this rock above us is far more
effective than reinforced concrete. We are not aware of any earth-
penetrating munitions currently in existence that could break through."

"What about the R and D the Americans have done on the Libyan
facility?" Randy asks.

"Ah, you are talking about the gas plant in Libya, buried under a
mountain," the German says, a bit uneasily, and Randy nods.

"That rock in Libya is so brittle," says the German, "you can shatter
it with a hammer. We are working with a different kind of rock here,
in many layers."

Randy exchanges a look with Avi, who looks as if he is about to bestow another commendation for deviousness. At the same time Randy grins, he senses someone's stare. He turns and locks eyes with Prag, who is looking inscrutable, verging on pissed off. A great many people in this part of the world would cringe and wither under the glare of Dr. Mohammed Pragasu, but all Randy sees is his old friend, the pizza-eating hacker.

So Randy stares right back into Prag's black eyes, and grins.

Prag prepares for the staredown. *You asshole, you tricked my German— for this you shall die!* But he can't sustain it. He breaks eye contact, turns away, and raises one hand to his mouth, pretending to stroke his goatee. The virus of irony is as widespread in California as herpes, and once you're infected with it, it lives in your brain forever. A man like Prag can come home, throw away his Nikes, and pray to Mecca five times a day, but he can never eradicate it from his system.

The tour lasts for a couple of hours. When they emerge, the temperature has doubled. Two dozen cellphones and beepers sing out as they exit the radio silence of the cavern. Avi has a brief and clipped conversation with someone, then hangs up and herds Epiphyte Corp. towards their car. "Small change of plans," he says. "We need to break away for a little meeting." He utters an unfamiliar name to the driver.

Twenty minutes later, they are filing into the Nipponese cemetery, sandwiched between two busloads of elderly mourners.

"Interesting place for a meeting," says Eberhard Föhr.

"Given the people we're dealing with, we have to assume that all of our rooms, our car, the hotel restaurant, are bugged," Avi snaps. No one speaks for a minute, as Avi leads them down a gravel path towards a secluded corner of the garden.

They end up in the corner of two high stone walls. A stand of bamboo shields them from the rest of the garden, and rustles soothingly in a sea breeze that does little to cool their sweaty faces. Beryl's fanning herself with a Kinakuta street map.

"Just got a call from Annie-in-San-Francisco," he says.

Annie-in-San-Francisco is their lawyer.

"It's, uh . . . seven P.M. there right now. Seems that just before the close of business, a courier walked into her office, fresh off the plane from LA, and handed her a letter from the Dentist's office."

"He's suing us for something," Beryl says.

"He's this far away from suing us."

"For what!?" Tom Howard shouts.

Avi sighs. "In a way, Tom, that is beside the point. When Kepler thinks it's in his best interests to file a tactical lawsuit, he'll find a pretext.

We must never forget that this is not about legitimate legal issues, it is about tactics."

"Breach of contract, right?" Randy says.

Everyone looks at Randy. "Do you know something we should know?" asks John Cantrell.

"Just an educated guess," Randy says, shaking his head. "Our contract with him states that we are to keep him informed of any changes in conditions that may materially alter the business climate."

"That's an awfully vague clause," Beryl says reproachfully.

"I'm paraphrasing."

"Randy's right," Avi says. "The gist of this letter is that we should have told the Dentist what was going on in Kinakuta."

"But we did not know," says Eb.

"Doesn't matter—remember, this is a tactical lawsuit."

"What does he want?"

"To scare us," Avi says. "To rattle us. Tomorrow or the next day, he'll bring in a different lawyer to play good cop—to make us an offer."

"What kind of offer?" Tom asks.

"We don't know, of course," Avi says, "but I'm guessing that Kepler wants a piece of us. He wants to own part of the company."

Light dawns on the face of everyone except Avi himself, who maintains his almost perpetual mask of cool control. "So it's bad news, good news, bad news. Bad news number one: Anne's phone call. Good news: because of what has happened here in the last two days, Epiphyte Corp. is suddenly so desirable that Kepler is ready to play hardball to get his hands on some of our stock."

"What's the second bit of bad news?" Randy asks.

"It's very simple." Avi turns away from them for a moment, strolls away for a couple of paces until he is blocked by a stone bench, then turns to face them again. "This morning I told you that Epiphyte was worth enough, now, that we could buy people out at a reasonable rate. You probably interpreted that as a good thing. In a way, it was. But a small and valuable company in the business world is like a bright and beautiful bird sitting on a branch in a jungle, singing a happy song that can be heard from a mile away. It attracts pythons." Avi pauses for a moment. "Usually, the grace period is longer. You get valuable, but then you have some time—weeks or months—to establish a defensive position, before the python manages to slither up the trunk. This time, we happened to get valuable while we were perched virtually on top of the python. Now we're not valuable any more."

"What do you mean?" Eb says. "We're just as valuable as we were this morning."

"A small company that's being sued for a ton of money by the Dentist is most certainly *not* valuable. It probably has an enormous *negative* value. The only way to give it positive value again is to make the lawsuit go away. See, Kepler holds all the cards. After Tom's incredible performance yesterday, all of the other guys in that conference room probably wanted a piece of us just as badly as Kepler did. But Kepler had one advantage: he was already in business with us. Which gave him a pretext for filing the lawsuit.

"So I hope you enjoyed our morning in the sun, even though we spent it in a cave," Avi concludes. He looks at Randy, and lowers his voice regretfully. "And if any of you were thinking of cashing out, let this be a lesson to you: be like the Dentist. Make up your mind and act fast."

FUNKSPIEL

✝ COLONEL CHATTAN'S AIDE SHAKES HIM AWAKE. THE FIRST THING Waterhouse notices is that the guy is breathing fast and steady, the way Alan does when he comes in from a cross-country run. "Colonel Chattan requests your presence in the Mansion most urgently."

Waterhouse's billet is in the vast, makeshift camp five minutes' walk from Bletchley Park's Mansion. Striding briskly whilst buttoning up his shirt, he covers the distance in four. Then, twenty feet from the goal, he is nearly run over by a pack of Rolls-Royces, gliding through the night as dark and silent as U-boats. One comes so close that he can feel the heat of its engine; its muggy exhaust blows through his trouser leg and condenses on his skin.

The old farts from the Broadway Buildings climb out of those Rolls-Royces and precede Waterhouse into the Mansion. In the library, the men cluster obsequiously round a telephone, which rings frequently and, when picked up, makes distant, tinny, shouting noises that can be heard, but not understood, from across the room. Waterhouse estimates that the Rolls-Royces must have driven up from London at an average speed of about nine thousand miles per hour.

Long tables are being looted from other rooms and chivvied into the library by glossy-haired young men in uniform, knocking flecks of paint off the doorframes. Waterhouse takes an arbitrary chair at an arbitrary table. Another aide wheels in a cart of wire baskets piled with file folders, still smoking from the friction of being jerked out of Bletchley Park's infinite archives. If this were a proper meeting, mimeographs might have been made up ahead of time and individually served. But this is sheer panic, and Waterhouse knows instinctively that he'd better take advantage of his early arrival if he wants to know anything. So he goes over to the cart and grabs the folder on the bottom of the stack, guessing that they'd have pulled the most important one first. It is labeled: U-691.

The first few pages are just a form: a U-boat data sheet consisting of many boxes. Half of them are empty. The other half have been filled in by different hands using different writing implements at different times, with many erasures and cross-outs and marginal notes written by bet-hedging analysts.

Then there is a log containing everything U-691 is ever known to have done, in chronological order. The first entry is its launch, at Wilhelmshaven on September 19, 1940, followed by a long list of the ships it has murdered. There's one odd notation from a few months ago: REFITTED WITH EXPERIMENTAL DEVICE (SCHNORKEL?). Since then, U-691 has been tearing up and down like mad, sinking ships in the Chesapeake Bay, Maracaibo, the approaches to the Panama Canal, and a bunch of other places that Waterhouse, until now, has thought of only as winter resorts for rich people.

Two more people come into the room and take seats: Colonel Chattan, and a young man in a disheveled tuxedo, who (according to a rumor that makes its way around the room) is a symphonic percussionist. This latter has clearly made some effort to wipe the lipstick off his face, but has missed some in the crevices of his left ear. Such are the exigencies of war.

Yet another aide rushes in with a wire basket filled with ULTRA message decrypt slips. This looks like much hotter stuff; Waterhouse puts the file folder back and begins leafing through the slips.

Each one begins with a block of data identifying the Y station that intercepted it, the time, the frequency, and other minutiae. The heap of slips boils down to a conversation, spread out over the last several weeks, between two transmitters.

One of these is in a part of Berlin called Charlottenburg, on the roof of a hotel at Steinplatz: the temporary site of U-boat Command, recently moved there from Paris. Most of these messages are signed by Grand Admiral Karl Dönitz. Waterhouse knows that Dönitz has recently become the Supreme Commander-in-Chief of the entire German Navy, but he has elected to hold onto his previous title of Commander-in-Chief of U-boats as well. Dönitz has a soft spot for U-boats and the men who inhabit them.

The other transmitter belongs to none other than U-691. These messages are signed by her skipper, Kapitänleutnant Günter Bischoff.

Bischoff: Sank another merchantman. This newfangled radar shit is everywhere.

Dönitz: Acknowledged. Well done.

Bischoff: Bagged another tanker. These bastards seem to know exactly where I am. Thank god for the schnorkel.

Dönitz: Acknowledged. Nice work as usual.

Bischoff: Sank another merchantman. Airplanes were waiting for me. I shot one of them down; it landed on me in a fireball and incinerated three of my men. Are you sure this Enigma thing really works?

Dönitz: Nice work, Bischoff! You get another medal! Don't worry about the Enigma, it's fantastic.

Bischoff: I attacked a convoy and sank three merchantmen, a tanker, and a destroyer.

Dönitz: Superb! Another medal for you!

Bischoff: Just for the hell of it, I doubled back and finished off what was left of that convoy. Then another destroyer showed up and dropped depth charges on us for three days. We are all half dead, steeped in our own waste, like rats who have fallen into a latrine and are slowly drowning. Our brains are gangrenous from breathing our own carbon dioxide.

Dönitz: You are a hero of the Reich and the Führer himself has been informed of your brilliant success! Would you mind heading south and attacking the convoy at such-and-such coordinates? P.S. please limit the length of your messages.

Bischoff: Actually, I could use a vacation, but sure, what the heck.

Bischoff (a week later): Nailed about half of that convoy for you. Had to surface and engage a pesky destroyer with the deck gun. This was so utterly suicidal, they didn't expect it. As a consequence we blew them to bits. Time for a nice vacation now.

Dönitz: You are now officially the greatest U-boat commander of all time. Return to Lorient for that well-deserved R & R.

Bischoff: Actually I had in mind a Caribbean vacation. Lorient is cold and bleak at this time of year.

Dönitz: We have not heard from you in two days. Please report.

Bischoff: Found a nice secluded harbor with a white sand beach. Would rather not specify coordinates as I no longer trust security of Enigma. Fishing is great. Am working on my tan. Feeling somewhat better. Crew is most grateful.

Dönitz: Günter, I am willing to overlook much from you, but even the Supreme Commander-in-Chief must answer to his superiors. Please end this nonsense and return home.

U-691: This is Oberleutnant zur See Karl Beck, second-in-command of U-691. Regret to inform you that KL Bischoff is in poor health. Request orders. P.S. He does not know I am sending this message.

Dönitz: Assume command. Return, not to Lorient, but to Wilhelms-haven. Take care of Günter.

Beck: KL Bischoff refuses to relinquish command.

Dönitz: Sedate him and get him back here, he will not be punished.

Beck: Thank you on behalf of me and the crew. We are underway, but short of fuel.

Dönitz: Rendezvous with U-413 [a milchcow] at such-and-such coordinates.

Now more people come into the room: a wizened rabbi; Dr. Alan Mathison Turing; a big man in a herringbone tweed suit whom Water-house remembers vaguely as an Oxford don; and some of the Naval intelligence fellows who are always hanging around Hut 4. Chattan calls the meeting to order and introduces one of the younger men, who stands up and gives a situation report.

"U-691, a Type IXD/42 U-boat under the nominal command of Kapitänleutnant Günter Bischoff, and the acting command of Oberleut-nant zur See Karl Beck, transmitted an Enigma message to U-boat Com-mand at 2000 hours Greenwich time. The message states that, three hours after sinking a Trinidadian merchantman, U-691 torpedoed and sank a Royal Navy submarine that was picking up survivors. Beck has captured two of our men: Marine Sergeant Robert Shaftoe, an American, and Lieutenant Enoch Root, ANZAC."

"How much do these men know?" demands the don, who is making a stirringly visible effort to sober up.

Chattan fields the question: "If Root and Shaftoe divulged everything that they know, the Germans could infer that we were making strenuous efforts to conceal the existence of an extremely valuable and comprehen-sive intelligence source."

"Oh, bloody hell," the don mumbles.

An extremely tall, lanky, blond civilian, the crossword puzzle editor of one of the London newspapers currently on loan to Bletchley Park, hustles into the room and apologizes for being late. More than half of the people on the Ultra Mega list are now in this room.

The young naval analyst continues. "At 2110, Wilhelmshaven replied with a message instructing OL Beck to interrogate the prisoners immedi-ately. At 0150, Beck replied with a message stating that in his opinion the prisoners belonged to some sort of special naval intelligence unit."

As he speaks, carbon copies of the fresh message decrypts are being passed round to all the tables. The crossword puzzle editor studies his with a tremendously furrowed brow. "Perhaps you covered this before I arrived, in which case I apologize," he says. "but where does the Trinidadian merchantman come in to all of this?"

Chattan silences Waterhouse with a look, and answers: "I'm not going to tell you." There is appreciative laughter all around, as if he had just uttered a *bon mot* at a dinner party. "But Admiral Dönitz, reading these same messages, must be just as confused as you are. We should like to keep him that way."

"Datum 1: He knows a merchantman was sunk," pipes up Turing, ticking off points on his fingers. "Datum 2: He knows a Royal Navy submarine was on the scene a few hours later, and was also sunk. Datum 3: He knows two of our men were pulled out of the water, and that they are probably in the intelligence business, which is a rather broad categorization as far as I am concerned. But he cannot necessarily draw any inferences, based upon these extremely terse messages, about which vessel—the merchantman or the submarine—our two men came from."

"Well, that's obvious, isn't it?" says Crossword Puzzle. "They came from the submarine."

Chattan responds only with a Cheshire grin.

"Oh!" says Crossword Puzzle. Eyebrows go up all around the room.

"As Beck continues to send messages to Admiral Dönitz, the likelihood increases that Dönitz will learn something we don't want him to know," Chattan says. "That likelihood becomes a virtual certainty when U-691 reaches Wilhelmshaven intact."

"Correction!" hollers the rabbi. Everyone is quite startled and there is a long silence while the man grips the edge of the table with quivering hands, and rises precariously to his feet. "The important thing is not whether Beck transmits messages! It is whether Dönitz *believes* those messages!"

"Hear, hear! Very astute!" Turing says.

"Quite right! Thank you for that clarification, Herr Kahn," Chattan says.

"Pardon me for just a moment," says the don, "but why on earth *wouldn't* he believe them?"

This leads to a long silence. The don has scored a telling point, and brought everyone very much back to cold hard reality. The rabbi begins to mumble something that sounds rather defensive, but is interrupted by a thunderous voice from the doorway: "FUNKSPIEL!"

Everyone turns to look at a fellow who has just come in the door. He is a trim man in his fifties with prematurely white hair, extremely thick glasses that magnify his eyes, and a howling blizzard of dandruff covering his navy blue blazer.

"Good morning, Elmer!" Chattan says with the forced cheerfulness of a psychiatrist entering a locked ward.

Elmer comes into the room and turns to face the crowd. "FUNKSPIEL!" he shouts again, in an inappropriately loud voice, and Waterhouse wonders whether the man is drunk or deaf or both. Elmer turns his back to them and stares at a bookcase for a while, then turns round to face them again, a look of astonishment on his face. "Ah was expectin' a chalkboard t'be there," he says in a Texarkana accent. "What kind of a classroom is this?" There is nervous laughter around the room as everyone tries to figure out whether Elmer is cutting loose with some deadpan humor, or completely out of his mind.

"It means 'radio games,' " says Rabbi Kahn.

"Thank, you, sir!" Elmer responds quickly, sounding pissed off. "Radio games. The Germans have been playing them all through the war. Now it's our turn."

Just moments ago, Waterhouse was thinking about how very British this whole scene was, feeling very far from home, and wishing that one or two Americans could be present. Now that his wish has come true, he just wants to crawl out of the Mansion on his hands and knees.

"How does one play these games, Mr., uh . . ." says Crossword Puzzle.

"You can call me Elmer!" Elmer shouts. Everyone scoots back from him.

"Elmer!" Waterhouse says, "would you please stop shouting?"

Elmer turns and blinks twice in Waterhouse's direction. "The game is simple," he says in a more normal, conversational voice. Then he gets excited again and begins to crescendo. "All you need is a radio and a couple of players with good ears, and good hands!" Now he's hollering. He waves at the corner where the albino woman with the headset and the percussionist with lipstick on his ear have been huddled together. "You want to explain fists, Mr. Shales?"

The percussionist stands up. "Every radio operator has a distinctive style of keying—we call it his fist. With a bit of practice, our Y Service people can recognize different German operators by their fists—we can tell when one of them has been transferred to a different unit, for example." He nods in the direction of the albino woman. "Miss Lord has intercepted numerous messages from U-691, and is familiar with the fist of that boat's radio operator. Furthermore, we now have a wire recording of U-691's most recent transmission, which she and I have been studying intensively." The percussionist draws a deep breath and screws his courage up before saying, "We are confident that I can forge U-691's fist."

Turing chimes in. "And since we have broken Enigma, we can compose any message we want, and encrypt it just as U-691 would have."

"Splendid. Splendid!" says one of the Broadway Buildings guys.

"We cannot prevent U-691 from sending out her own, legitimate messages," Chattan cautions, "short of sinking her. Which we are making every effort to do. But we can muddy the waters considerably. Rabbi?"

Once again, the rabbi rises to his feet, drawing everyone's attention as they wait for him to fall down. But he doesn't. "I have composed a message in German naval jargon. Translated into English, it says, roughly, 'Interrogation of prisoners proceeding slowly request permission to use torture' and then there are several Xs in a row and then is added the words WARNING AMBUSH U-691 HAS BEEN CAPTURED BY BRITISH COMMANDOS.' "

Sharp intakes of breath all around the room.

"Is contemporary German naval jargon a normal part of Talmudic studies?" asks the don.

"Mr. Kahn has spent a year and a half analyzing naval decrypts in Hut 4," Chattan says. "He has the lingo down pat." He goes on: "we have encrypted Mr. Kahn's message using today's naval Enigma key, and passed it on to Mr. Shales, who has been practicing."

Miss Lord rises to her feet, like a child reciting her lessons in a Victorian school, and says, "I am satisfied that Mr. Shales's rendition is indistinguishable from U-691's."

All eyes turn towards Chattan, who turns towards the old farts from the Broadway Buildings, who even now are on the phone relaying all this to someone of whom they are clearly terrified.

"Don't the Jerrys have huffduff?" asks the Don, as if probing a flaw in a student's dissertation.

"Their huffduff network is not nearly so well developed as ours," responds one of the young analysts. "It is most unlikely that they would bother to triangulate a transmission that appeared to come from one of their own U-boats, so they probably won't figure out the message originated in Buckinghamshire, rather than the Atlantic."

"However, we have anticipated your objection," Chattan says, "and made arrangements for several of our own ships, as well as various aeroplanes and ground units, to flood the air with transmissions. Their huffduff network will have its hands full at the time of our fake U-691 transmission."

"Very well," mutters the don.

Everyone sits there in churchly silence while the most senior of the Broadway Buildings contingent winds up his conversation with Whom Is at the Other End. After hanging up the phone, he intones solemnly, "You are directed to proceed."

Chattan nods at some of the younger men, who dash across the room, pick up telephones, and begin to talk in calm, clinical voices about cricket scores. Chattan looks at his watch. "It will take a few minutes for the huffduff smokescreen to develop. Miss Lord, you will notify us when the traffic has risen to a suitably feverish pitch?"

Miss Lord makes a little curtsey and sits down at her radio.

"FUNKSPIEL!" shouts Elmer, scaring everyone half out of their skins. "We already done sent out some other messages. Made 'em look like Royal Navy traffic. Used a code the Krauts just broke a few weeks ago. These messages have to do with an operation—a fictitious operation, y'know—in which a German U-boat was supposedly boarded and seized by our commandos."

There is a whole lot of tinny shouting from the telephone. The gentleman who has the bad luck to be holding it translates into what is probably more polite English: "What if Mr. Shales's performance is not convincing to the radio operators at Charlottenburg? What if they do not succeed in decrypting Mr. Elmer's false messages?"

Chattan fields that one. He steps over to a map that has been set up on an easel at the end of the room. The map depicts a swath of the Central Atlantic bordered on the east by France and Spain. "U-691's last reported position was here," he says, pointing to a pin stuck in the lower left corner of the map. "She has been ordered back to Wilhelmshaven with her prisoners. She will go this way," he says, indicating a length of red yarn stretched in a north-northeasterly direction, "assuming she avoids the Straits of Dover.*

"There happens to be another milchcow here," Chattan continues, indicating another pin. "One of our own submarines should be able to reach it within twenty-four hours, at which point it will approach at periscope depth and engage it with torpedoes. Chances are excellent that the milchcow will be destroyed immediately. If she has time to send out any transmissions, she will merely state that she is being attacked by a submarine. Once we have destroyed this milchcow, we will call once again upon the skills of Mr. Shales, who will transmit a fake distress call that will appear to originate from the milchcow, stating that they have come under attack from none other than U-691."

"Splendid!" someone proclaims.

"By the time the sun rises tomorrow," Chattan concludes, "we will have one of our very best submarine-hunting task forces on the scene. A light carrier with several antisubmarine planes, will comb the ocean night and day, using radar, visual reconnaissance, huffduff, and Leigh lights to hunt for U-691. The chances are excellent that she will be

---

*This is dry humor, and is received as such by everyone in the room; at this point in the war, a U-boat could no more run up the English Channel than it could travel up the Mississippi, sink a few barges in Dubuque, and make its escape.

found and sunk long before she can approach the Continent. But should she find her way past this formidable barrier, she will find the German Kriegsmarine no less eager to hunt her down and destroy her. Any information she may transmit to Admiral Dönitz in the meantime will be regarded with the most profound suspicion."

"So," Waterhouse says, "the plan, in a nutshell, is to render all information from U-691 unbelievable, and subsequently to destroy her, and everyone on her, before she can reach Germany."

"Yes," Chattan says, "and the former task will be greatly simplified by the fact that U-691's skipper is already known to be mentally unstable."

"So it seems likely that our guys, Shaftoe and Root, will not survive," Waterhouse says slowly.

There is a long, frozen silence, as if Waterhouse had interrupted high tea by making farting sounds with his armpit.

Chattan responds in a precise, arch tone that indicates he's really pissed off. "There is the possibility that when U-691 is engaged by our forces, she will be forced to the surface and will surrender."

Waterhouse studies the grain of the tabletop. His face is hot and his chest is burning.

Miss Lord rises to her feet and speaks. Several important heads turn toward Mr. Shales, who excuses himself and goes to a table in the corner of the room. He fiddles with the controls on a radio transmitter for a few moments, spreads the encrypted message out in front of himself, and takes a deep breath, as though preparing for a big solo. Finally he reaches out, rests one hand lightly on the radio key, and begins to tap out the message, rocking from side to side and cocking his head this way and that. Mrs. Lord listens with her eyes closed, concentrating intensely.

Mr. Shales stops. "Finished," he announces in a quiet voice, and looks nervously at Mrs. Lord, who smiles. Then there is polite applause around the library, as if they had just finished listening to a harpsichord concerto. Lawrence Pritchard Waterhouse keeps his hands folded in his lap. He has just heard the death warrant of Enoch Root and Bobby Shaftoe.

HEAP

To: root@eruditorum.org
From: dwarf@siblings.net
Subject: Re(8) Why?
Let me just take stock of what I know so far: you say that asking ''why?'' is part of what you do for a living; you're

not an academic; and you are in the surveillance business.
I am having trouble forming a clear picture.

—BEGIN ORDO SIGNATURE BLOCK—

(etc.)

—END ORDO SIGNATURE BLOCK—

To: dwarf@siblings.net

From: root@eruditorum.org

Subject: Re(9) Why?

Randy,

I never said that I, myself, am in the surveillance business. But I know people who are. Formerly public- and now private-sector. We stay in touch. The grapevine and all that. Nowadays, my involvement in such things is limited to noodling around with novel cryptosystems, as a sort of hobby.

Now, to get back to what I would consider to be the main thread of our conversation. You guessed that I was an academic. Were you being sincere, or was this purely an attempt to ''gotcha'' me?

The reason I ask is that I am, in fact, a man of the cloth, so naturally I consider it my job to ask ''why?'' I assumed this would be fairly obvious to you. But I should have taken into account that you are not the churchy type. This is my fault.

It is conventional now to think of clerics simply as presiders over funerals and weddings. Even people who routinely go to church (or synagogue or whatever) sleep through the sermons. That is because the arts of rhetoric and oratory have fallen on hard times, and so the sermons tend not to be very interesting.

But there was a time when places like Oxford and Cambridge existed almost solely to train ministers, and their job was not just to preside over weddings and funerals but also to say something thought-provoking to large numbers of people several times a week. They were the retail outlets of the profession of philosophy.

I still think of this as the priest's highest calling—or at least the most interesting part of the job—hence my question to you, which I cannot fail to notice, remains unanswered.

—BEGIN ORDO SIGNATURE BLOCK—

(etc.)

—END ORDO SIGNATURE BLOCK—

"Randy, what is the worst thing that ever happened?"

This is never a difficult question to answer when you are hanging around with Avi. "The Holocaust," Randy says dutifully.

Even if he didn't know Avi, their surroundings would give him a hint. The rest of Epiphyte Corp. have gone back to the Foote Mansion to prepare for hostilities with the Dentist. Randy and Avi are sitting on a black obsidian bench planted atop the mass grave of thousands of Nipponese in downtown Kinakuta, watching the tour buses come and go.

Avi pulls a small GPS receiver out of his attache case, turns it on, and sets it out on a boulder in front of them where it will have a clear view of the sky. "Correct! And what is the highest and best purpose to which we can devote our allotted lifespans?"

"Uh . . . enhancing shareholder value?"

"Very funny." Avi is annoyed. He is baring his soul, which he does rarely. Also, he's in the midst of cataloging another small-h holocaust site, adding it to his archives. It is clear he would appreciate some fucking solemnity here. "I visited Mexico a few weeks ago," Avi continues.

"Looking for a site where the Spanish killed a bunch of Aztecs?" Randy asks.

"This is *exactly* the kind of thing I'm fighting," Avi says, even more irritated. "No, I was *not* looking for a place where a bunch of Aztecs were massacred. The Aztecs can go *fuck* themselves, Randy! Repeat after me: the Aztecs can go fuck themselves."

"The Aztecs can go fuck themselves," Randy says cheerfully, drawing a baffled look from an approaching Nipponese tour guide.

"To begin with, I was hundreds of miles from Mexico City, the former Aztec capital. I was on the outer fringes of the territory that the Aztecs controlled." Avi scoops his GPS off the boulder and begins to punch keys on its pad, telling it to store the latitude and longitude in its memory. "I was looking," Avi continues, "for the site of a Nahuatl city that was raided by the Aztecs hundreds of years before the Spanish even showed up. You know what those fucking Aztecs did, Randy?"

Randy uses his hands to squeegee away sweat from his face. "Something unspeakable?"

"I hate that word 'unspeakable.' We *must* speak of it."

"Speak then."

"The Aztecs took twenty-five thousand Nahuatl captives, brought them back to Tenochtitlan, and killed them all in a couple of days."

"Why?"

"Some kind of festival. Super Bowl weekend or something. I don't know. The point is, they did that kind of shit all the time. But *now,*

Randy, when I talk about Holocaust-type stuff happening in Mexico, you give me this shit about the mean nasty old Spaniards! Why? Because history has been distorted, that's why."

"Don't tell me you're about to come down on the side of the Spaniards."

"As the descendant of people who were expelled from Spain by the Inquisition, I have no illusions about them," Avi says, "but, at their worst, the Spaniards were a million times better than the Aztecs. I mean, it really says something about how bad the *Aztecs* were that, when the *Spaniards,* showed up and raped the place, things actually got a lot *better* around there."

"Avi?"

"Yes."

"We are sitting here in the Sultanate of Kinakuta, trying to build a data haven while fending off an oral surgeon-turned-hostile-take-over-maven. I have pressing responsibilities in the Philippines. Why are we discussing the Aztecs?"

"I'm giving you a pep talk," Avi says. "You are bored. Dangerously so. The Pinoy-gram thing was cool for a while, but now it's up and running, there's no new technology there."

"True."

"But the Crypt is amazingly cool. Tom and John and Eb are going nuts, and every Secret Admirer in the world is spamming me with re-sumes. The Crypt is exactly what you would like to be doing right now."

"Again, true."

"Even if you were working on the Crypt, though, philosophical issues would be gnawing at you—issues based on the types of people who you see getting involved, who may be our first customers."

"I cannot deny that I have philosophical issues," Randy says. Suddenly he has come up with a new hypothesis: *Avi* is actually root@eruditorum.org.

"Instead, you are laying cable in the Philippines. This is a job that—because of changes we just became aware of yesterday—is basically irrele-vant to our corporate mission. But it's a lingering contractual obligation, and if we put anyone less important than you on it, the Dentist will be able to prove to the most half-witted jury of tofu-brained Californians that we are malingering."

"Well, thank you for making it so clear why I should be miserable," Randy says forbearingly.

"So," Avi continues, "I wanted to let you know that you aren't necessarily just making license plates here. And furthermore that the

Crypt is not a morally bankrupt endeavor. Actually, you are playing a big role in the most important thing in the world."

Randy says, "You asked me earlier what is the highest and best purpose to which we could dedicate our lives. And the obvious answer is 'to prevent future Holocausts.' "

Avi laughs darkly. "I'm glad it's obvious to *you,* my friend. I was beginning to think I was the only one."

"What!? Get over yourself, Avi. People are commemorating the Holocaust all the time."

"Commemorating the Holocaust is *not,* not not not not *not,* the same thing as fighting to prevent future holocausts. Most of the commemorationists are just whiners. They think that if everyone feels bad about past holocausts, human nature will magically transform, and no one will want to commit genocide in the future."

"I take it you do not share this view, Avi?"

"Look at Bosnia!" Avi scoffs. "Human nature doesn't change, Randy. Education is hopeless. The most educated people in the world can turn into Aztecs or Nazis just like that." He snaps his fingers.

"So what hope is there?"

"Instead of trying to educate the potential *perpetrators* of holocausts, we try to educate the potential *victims. They* will at least pay some fucking *attention.*"

"Educate them in what way?"

Avi closes his eyes and shakes his head. "Oh, shit, Randy, I could go on for hours—I have drawn up a whole curriculum."

"Okay, we'll get into that later."

"Definitely later. For now, the key point is that the Crypt is all-important. I can take all of my ideas and put them into a single pod of information, but almost every government in the world would prevent distribution to its citizens. It is essential to build the Crypt so that the HEAP can be freely distributed throughout the world."

"HEAP?"

"Holocaust Education and Avoidance Pod."

"Oh, Jesus Christ!"

"*This* is the true meaning of what you are working on," Avi says, "and so I urge you not to lose heart. Whenever you are about to get bored stamping out those license plates in the Philippines, think of the HEAP. Think of what those Nahuatl villagers could have done to those fucking Aztecs if they'd had a holocaust prevention manual—a handbook on guerilla warfare tactics."

Randy sits and ponders for a while. "We have to go and buy some water," he finally says. "I've sweated away a few liters just sitting here."

"We can just go back to the hotel," Avi says, "I'm basically finished."

"You're finished. I haven't even started," Randy says.

"Started what?"

"Telling you why there's no chance I'm going to be bored in the Philippines."

Avi blinks. "You met a girl?"

"No!" Randy says testily, meaning *Yes,* of course. "Come on, let's go."

They go to a nearby 24 Jam and purchase bluish plastic bottles of water the size of cinderblocks. Then they wander around through streets crowded with unbearably savory-smelling food carts, guzzling the water.

"I got e-mail from Doug Shaftoe a few days ago," Randy says. "From his boat, via satellite phone."

"In the clear?"

"Yeah. I keep bothering him to get Ordo and encrypt his e-mail, but he won't."

"That is really unprofessional," Avi grumbles. "He needs to be more paranoid."

"He's so paranoid that he doesn't even trust Ordo."

Avi's scowl eases. "Oh. That's okay then."

"His e-mail contained a stupid joke about Imelda Marcos."

"You took me on this walk to tell me a joke?"

"No, no, no," Randy says. "The joke was a prearranged signal. Doug told me that he would send me e-mail containing an Imelda joke if a certain thing happened."

"What certain thing?"

Randy takes a big swig of water, draws a deep breath, and composes himself. "More than a year ago, I had a conversation with Doug Shaftoe during that big party that the Dentist threw on board the *Rui Faleiro*. He wanted us to hire his company, Semper Marine Services, to do the survey work on all future cable lays. In return he offered to cut us in on any sunken treasure he found while performing the survey."

Avi skids to a stop and clutches his water bottle in both hands as if he's afraid he might drop it. "Sunken treasure, like, yo-ho-ho and a bottle of rum? Pieces of six? That kind of thing?"

"Pieces of *eight*. Same basic idea," Randy says. "The Shaftoes are treasure hunters. Doug is obsessed with the idea that there are vast hoards of treasure in and around the Philippines."

"From where? Those Spanish galleons?"

"No. Well, *yes*, actually. But that's not what Doug's after." He and Avi have begun walking again. "Most of it is either much older than that—pottery from sunken Chinese junks—or much more recent—Japanese war gold."

As Randy had expected, the mention of Japanese war gold makes a huge impact on Avi. Randy keeps talking. "Rumor has it that the Nipponese left a lot of gold in the area. Supposedly, Marcos recovered a big stash buried in a tunnel somewhere—that's where he got all his money. Most people think Marcos was worth something like five, six billion dollars, but a lot of people in the Philippines think he recovered more like sixty billion."

"Sixty billion!" Avi's spine stiffens. "Impossible."

"Look, you can believe the rumors or not, I don't care," Randy says. "But since it looks like one of Marcos's bag men is going to be a founding depositor in the Crypt, it is the kind of thing you should know."

"Keep talking," Avi says, suddenly ravenous for data.

"Okay. So people have been running all over the Philippines ever since the war, digging holes and dredging the seafloor, trying to find the legendary Nipponese war gold. Doug Shaftoe is one of those people. Problem is, making a thorough sidescan sonar survey of the whole area is quite expensive—you can't just go out and do it on spec. He saw an opportunity when we came along."

"I see. Very smart," Avi says approvingly. "He would do the survey work that we needed anyway, in order to lay the cables."

"Perhaps a bit more than was strictly necessary, as long as he was out there."

"Right. Now I remember some angry mail from the Dentist's due diligence harpies because the survey was costing too much and taking too long. They felt we could have hired a different company and gotten the same results quicker and cheaper."

"They were probably right," Randy admits. "Anyway, Doug wanted to cut a deal that gave us ten percent of whatever he found. More, if we wanted to underwrite recovery operations."

All of a sudden Avi's eyes go wide and he swallows a big gulp of air. "Oh, shit, he says. "He wanted to keep the whole thing a secret from the Dentist."

"Exactly. Because the Dentist would end up taking all of it. And because of the Dentist's peculiar domestic situation, that means that the Bolobolos would know everything about it too. These guys would happily kill to get their hands on gold."

"Wow!" Avi says, shaking his head. "Y'know, I don't want to seem like one of those hackneyed Jews that you see in heartwarming movies. But at times like this, all I can say is 'Oy, gevalt!' "

"I never told you about this deal, Avi, for two reasons. One of them is just our general policy of not blabbing about things. The other reason is that we decided to hire Semper Marine Services anyway—just on their own merits—so Doug Shaftoe's proposition was irrelevant."

Avi thinks this one over. "Correction. It was irrelevant, *as long as Doug Shaftoe didn't find any sunken treasure.*"

"Right. And I assumed that he wouldn't."

"You assumed wrong."

"I assumed wrong," Randy admits. "Shaftoe has found the remains of an old Nipponese submarine."

"How do you know that?"

"If he found a Chinese junk he was going to send me a joke about Ferdinand Marcos. If he found World War II stuff, it was going to be Imelda. If it was a surface ship, it was going to be about Imelda's shoes. If it was a submarine, her sexual habits. He sent me a joke about Imelda's sexual habits."

"Now, did you ever formally respond to Doug Shaftoe's proposition?" Avi says.

"No. Like I said, it wasn't relevant, we were going to hire him anyway. But then, after the contracts were all signed and we were drawing up the survey schedule, he told me about this code involving the Marcos jokes. I realized then he believed that by hiring him, we had implicitly said yes to his proposition."

"It's a funny way to do business," Avi says, wrinkling his nose. "You'd think he would have been more explicit."

"He is the kind of guy who does deals on a handshake. On personal honor," Randy says. "Once he had made the proposition, he would never withdraw it."

"The problem with those honorable men," Avi says, "is that they expect everyone else to be honorable in the same way."

"It is true."

"So he believes, now, that we are accomplices in this plan to hide the existence of this sunken treasure from the Dentist and the Bolobolos," Avi says.

"Unless we come clean to them right away."

"In which case we are betraying Doug Shaftoe," Avi says.

"Cravenly backstabbing the ex-SEAL who served six years of combat duty in Vietnam, and who has scary and well-connected friends all over the world," Randy adds.

"Damn, Randy! I thought I was going to freak you out by telling you about the HEAP."

"You did."

"And then you spring this on me!"

"Life's rich pageant. And all that," Randy says.

Avi thinks for a minute. "Well, I guess it comes down to whom would we rather have on our side in a bar fight."

"The answer can only be Douglas MacArthur Shaftoe," Randy says. "But that doesn't mean we'll make it out of the bar alive."

SEEKY

THEY HAVE STUFFED HIM INTO THE NARROW GAP BETWEEN THE U-boat's slotted outer hull and the pressure hull within, so that bitterly cold, black water streams through with the bludgeoning force of a firehose and wracks him with malarial chills: bones cracking, joints freezing, muscles knotting. He is wedged in tightly between uneven surfaces of hard rough steel, bending him in ways he's not supposed to bend, and punishing him when he tries to move. Barnacles are beginning to grow on him: sort of like lice but bigger and capable of burrowing deeper into the flesh. Somehow he is able to fight for breath anyway, just enough to stay alive and really savor just how unpleasant the situation is. He's been breathing cold seawater for a long time, it has made his windpipe raw, and he suspects that plankton or something are eating his lungs from the inside out. He pounds on the pressure hull but the impact makes no noise. He can sense the warmth and heat inside, and he would like to get in and enjoy both of them. Finally some kind of dream-logic thing happens and he finds a hatch. The current sweeps Shaftoe out, leaving him suspended alone in the watery cosmos, and the U-boat hisses away and abandons him. Shaftoe is lost now. He cannot tell up from down. Something bashes him on the head. He sees a few black drumlike things moving inexorably through the water with parallel comet-trails of bubbles behind them. Depth charges.

Then Shaftoe comes awake and knows that this was all just his body desiring morphine. He is certain for a moment that he is back in Oakland and that Lieutenant Reagan is looming over him, preparing for Phase 2 of the interview.

"Good afternoon, Sergeant Shaftoe," Reagan says. He has adopted a heavy German accent for some reason. A joke. These actors! Shaftoe smells meat, and other things not so inviting. Something heavy, but not especially hard, thuds into his face. Then it draws back. Then it hits him again.

———————

"Your companion is morphium-seeky?" says Beck.

Enoch Root is a bit taken aback; they've only been on the boat for eight hours. "Is he already making a nuisance of himself?"

"He is semiconscious," Beck says, "and has a great deal to say about giant lizards—among other subjects."

"Oh, that's normal for him," Root says, relieved. "What makes you think he is morphium-seeky?"

"The morphium bottle and hypodermic syringe that were in his pocket," Beck says with that deadpan Teutonic irony, "and the needle marks in his arms."

Root observes that the U-boat is like a tunnel bored out of the sea and lined with hardware. This cabin (if that's not too grand a word for it) is by far the largest open space Root has seen, meaning that he can almost stretch his arms out without hitting someone or inadvertently tripping a switch or a valve. It even sports some wooden cabinetry, and has been sealed off from the corridor by a leather curtain. When they first brought Root in here, he thought it was a storage closet. But as he looks around the place, he begins to realize that it's the nicest place on the whole boat: the captain's private cabin. This is confirmed when Beck unlocks a desk drawer and produces a bottle of Armagnac.

"Conquering France hath its privileges," Beck says.

"Yeah," Root says, "you blokes really know how to sack a place."

———————

Lieutenant Reagan is back again, molesting Bobby Shaftoe with a stethoscope that appears to have been kept in a bath of liquid nitrogen until ready for use. "Cough, cough, cough!" he keeps saying. Finally he takes the instrument away.

Something is fucking with Shaftoe's ankles. He tries to get up on his elbows to look, and smashes his face into a blistering hot pipe. When he's recovered from that, he peeks carefully down the length of his body and sees a goddamn hardware store down there. The bastards have put him in leg irons!

He lies back down and gets slugged in the face by a dangling ham. Above him is a firmament of pipes and cables. Where has he seen this before? On the Dutch-Hammer, that's where. Except the lights are on in this U-boat, and it doesn't appear to be sinking, and it's full of Germans. The Germans are calm and relaxed. None of them is bleeding or screaming. Damn! The boat rocks sideways, and a giant Blutwurst socks him in the belly.

He begins looking around, trying to get his bearings. There's not much else to see except hanging meat. This cabin is a six-foot-long slice of U-boat, with a narrow gangway down the center, hemmed in by bunks. Or maybe they are bunks. The one directly across from him is occupied by a dirty canvas sack.

Fuck that. Where is the box with the purple bottles?

"It is amusing to read my communications from Charlottenburg," Beck says to Root, changing the subject to the message decrypts on his table. "They were perhaps written by that Jew Kafka."

"How so?"

"It seems that they do not expect that we will ever make it home alive."

"What makes you say that?" Root says, trying not to savor the Armagnac too much. When he brings it up to his nose and inhales, its perfume nearly obliterates the reek of urine, vomit, rotten food, and diesel that suffuses everything on the U-boat down to the atomic level.

"They are pressing us for information about our prisoners. They are very interested in you guys," Beck says.

"In other words," Root says carefully, "they want you to question us now."

"Precisely."

"And send the results in by radio?"

"Yes," Beck says. "But I really should be concentrating on how to keep us alive—the sun will be up soon, and then we are in for some very bad trouble. You'll remember that your ship radioed our coordinates before I sunk it. Every allied plane and ship is now out looking for us."

"So, if I cooperate," Root says, "you can get back to the business of keeping us all alive."

Beck tries to control a smile. His little tactic was crude and obvious to begin with, and Root has already seen through it. Beck is, if anything, more uncomfortable than Root with this whole interrogation business.

"Suppose I tell you everything I know," Root says. "If you send it all back to Charlottenburg, you'll be running your radio, on the surface, for hours. Huffduff will pick you out in a few seconds and then every destroyer and bomber within a thousand miles will jump on you."

"On us," Beck corrects him.

"Yes. So if I really want to stay alive, it's best if I shut up," Root says.

"Are you looking for this?" says the German with the stethoscope, who (Shaftoe has learned) is not a real doctor—just the guy who happens to be in charge of the box of medical stuff. Anyway, he is holding up just the thing. The very thing.

"Gimme that!" Shaftoe says, making a weak grab for it. "That's mine!"

"Actually, it's mine," the medic says. "Yours is with the captain. I might share some of mine with you, if you are cooperative."

"Fuck you," Shaftoe says.

"Very well then," the medic says, "I will by-leave it." He puts the syringe full of morphine on the bunk opposite and one level below Shaftoe's, so that Shaftoe, by peering between a couple of Knockwursts, can see it. But he can't reach it. Then the medic leaves.

"Why was Sergeant Shaftoe carrying a German morphine bottle and a German syringe?" says Beck quizzically, doing his best to make it sound conversational and not interrogational. But the effort is too much for him and that smile tries to seize control of his lips again. It is the smile of a whipped dog. Root finds this somewhat alarming, since Beck's the guy in charge of keeping everyone on the boat alive.

"That's news to me," Root says.

"Morphine is closely regulated," Beck says. "Each bottle has a number. We have already radioed the number on Sergeant Shaftoe's bottle to Charlottenburg, and soon they'll know where it came from. Even though they may not tell us."

"Good work. That should keep them busy for a while. Why don't you go back to running the ship?" Root suggests.

"We are in the calm before the storm," Beck says, "and I have not so much to do. So I try to satisfy my own curiosity about you."

"We're fucked, aren't we!?" says a German voice.

"Huh?" Shaftoe says.

"I said, we're fucked! You guys broke the Enigma!"

"What's the Enigma?"

"Don't play stupid," says the German.

Shaftoe feel prickly on the back of his neck. That sounds exactly like the kind of thing a German would say before commencing torture.

Shaftoe composes his face into the cool, heavy-lidded, dopey expression that he always uses when he's trying to irritate an officer. As best he can when his legs are bolted down, he rolls over on his side, towards the sound of the voice. He is expecting to see an aquiline SS officer in a black uniform, jackboots, death's-head insignia, and riding crop, perhaps twiddling a pair of thumbscrews in his black leather gloves.

Instead he sees no one at all. Shit! Hallucinations again!

Then the dirty canvas sail bag in the bunk opposite him begins to move around. Shaftoe blinks and resolves a head sticking out of one end: straw-blond but prematurely half bald, contrasting black beard, catlike pale green eyes. The man's canvas garment is not exactly a bag, but a voluminous overcoat. He has his arms crossed over his body.

"Oh, well," the German mutters, "I was just trying to make conversation." He turns his head and scratches his nose by nuzzling his pillow for a while. "You can tell me any secret you want," he says. "See, I've already notified Dönitz that the Enigma is shit. And it made no difference. Except he ordered me a new overcoat." The man rolls over, exposing his back to Shaftoe The sleeves of the garment are sewn shut at the ends and tied together behind his back. "It is more comfortable than you would think, for the first day or two."

———

A mate pulls the leather curtain aside, nods apologetically, and hands Beck a fresh message decrypt. Beck reads it, raises his eyebrows, and blinks tiredly. He sets it down on the table and stares at the wall for fifteen seconds. Then he picks it up and reads it again, carefully.

"It says that I am not to ask you any more questions."

"What!?"

"Under no circumstances," Beck says, "am I to extract any more information from you."

"What the hell does that mean?"

"Probably that you know something I am not authorized to know," Beck says.

———

It has been about two hundred years, now, since Bobby Shaftoe had a trace of morphine in his system. Without it, he cannot know pleasure or even comfort.

The syringe gleams like a cold star on the shelf underneath the crazy German in the straitjacket. He'd rather that they just tore his fingernails out or something.

He knows he's going to crack. He tries to think of a way to crack that won't kill any Marines.

"I could bring you the syringe in my teeth," suggests the man, who has introduced himself as Bischoff.

Shaftoe mulls it over. "In exchange for?"

"You tell me whether the Enigma has been decrypted."

"Oh." Shaftoe's relieved; he was afraid maybe Bischoff was going to demand a blow job. "That's the code machine thingamajig you were telling me about?" He and Bischoff have had a lot of time to shoot the breeze.

"Yeah."

Shaftoe's desperate. But he's also highly irritable, which serves him well now. "You expect me to believe that you are just a crazy guy who is curious about Enigma, and not a German naval officer who's dressed up in a straitjacket to trick me?"

Bischoff is exasperated. "I already said that I've told Dönitz that Enigma is crap! So if you tell me it's crap, that doesn't make any difference!"

"Let me ask you a question, then," Root says.

"Yes?" Beck says, making a visible effort to raise his eyebrows and look like he cares.

"What have you told Charlottenburg about us?"

"Names, ranks, serial numbers, circumstances of capture."

"But you told them that yesterday."

"Correct."

"What have you told them recently?"

"Nothing. Except for the serial number on the morphium bottle."

"And how long after you told them that did they send you the message to stop extracting information from us?"

"About forty-five minutes," Beck says. "So, yes, I would very much like to ask you where that bottle came from. But it is against orders."

"I might consider answering your question about Enigma," Shaftoe says, "if you tell me whether this pipe bomb is carrying any gold."

Bischoff's brow furrows; he's having translation problems. "You mean money? *Geld?*"

"No. Gold. The expensive yellow metal."

"A little, maybe," Bischoff says.

"Not petty cash," Shaftoe says. "Tons and tons."

"No. U-boats don't carry tons of gold," Bischoff says flatly.

"I'm sorry you said that, Bischcoff. Because I thought you and I were starting a good relationship. Then you went and lied to me—you fuck!"

To Shaftoe's surprise and mounting irritation, Bischoff thinks that it's absolutely hilarious to be called a fuck. "Why the hell should I lie to you? For god's sake, Shaftoe! Since you bastards broke Enigma and put radar on everything that moves, virtually every U-boat that's put to sea has been sunk! Why would the Kriegsmarine load tons of gold onto a ship that they know is doomed!?"

"Why don't you ask the guys who loaded it on board U-553?"

"Ha! This only proves you are full of shit!" Bischoff says. "U-553 was sunk a year ago, during a convoy attack."

"Not so. I was on board it just a couple of months ago," Shaftoe says, "off Qwghlm. It was full of gold."

"Bullshit," Bischoff says. "What was painted on its conning tower?"

"A polar bear holding a beer stein."

Long silence.

"You want to know more? I went into the captain's cabin," Shaftoe said, "and there was a photo of him with some other guys, and now that I think of it, one of them looked like you."

"What were we doing?"

"You were all in swimming trunks. You all had whores on your laps!" Shaftoe shouts. "Unless those were your wives—in which case I'm sorry your wife is a whore!"

"Oh, ho ho ho ho ho!" Bischoff says. He rolls onto his back and stares up into the plumbing for a while, considering this, and then continues. "Ho ho ho ho ho ho ho!"

"What, did I just say something secret? Fuck you and your mother if I did," Shaftoe says.

"Beck!" Bischoff screams. *"Achtung!"*

"What're you doing?" Shaftoe asks.

"Getting you your morphine."

"Oh. Thank you."

Half an hour later, the skipper's there. Pretty punctual by officer standards. He and Bischoff talk for a while in German. Shaftoe hears the word *morphium* several times. Finally, the skipper summons the medic, who pokes the needle into Shaftoe's arm and injects about half of it.

"You have something to say?" the skipper asks Shaftoe. Seems like a nice enough guy. They all seem like pretty nice guys, now.

First, Shaftoe addresses Bischoff. "Sir! I'm sorry I used harsh language on you, sir!"

"It's okay," Bischoff replied, "she was a whore, like you said."

The skipper clears his throat impatiently.

"Yeah. I was just wondering," Shaftoe says turning to the skipper, "you have any gold on this U-boat?"

"The yellow metal?"

"Yeah. Bars of it."

The captain is still nonplussed. Shaftoe is beginning to feel a certain mischievous satisfaction. Playing with officers' minds isn't as good as having a brain saturated with highly refined opiates, but it will do in a pinch. "I thought all these U-boats carried it," he says.

Beck dismisses the medic. Then he and Bischoff talk about Shaftoe for a while in German. In the middle of this conversation, Beck drops some kind of a bomb on Bischoff. Bischoff is stunned, and refuses to believe it for a while, and Beck keeps telling him it's true. Then Bischoff goes back into that strange ho-ho-ho thing.

"He can't ask you questions," Bischoff says. "Orders from Berlin. Ho, ho! But I can."

"Shoot," Shaftoe says.

"Tell us more about gold."

"Give me more morphine."

Beck summons the medic again, and the medic gives him the rest of the syringe. Shaftoe's never felt better. What a fucking deal! He's getting morphine out of the Germans in exchange for telling them *German* military secrets.

Bischoff starts interrogating Shaftoe in depth, while Beck watches. Shaftoe tells the whole story of U-553 about three times over. Bischoff is fascinated, Beck looks sad and scared.

When Shaftoe mentions that the gold bars had Chinese characters stamped on them, both Beck and Bischoff are floored. Their faces come aglow, as if lit up by the scanning beam of a Leigh light on a moonless night. Beck begins to sniffle, as if he's caught a cold, and Shaftoe's startled to realize that he's actually crying. He is crying tears of shame. But Bischoff is still fascinated and focused.

Then a mate bursts in and hands Beck a message. The mate is clearly shocked and scared out of his wits. He keeps looking, not at Beck, but at Bischoff.

Beck gets a grip on himself and reads the message. Bischoff lunges out of his bunk, hooks his chin over Beck's shoulder, and reads it at the same time. They look like a two-headed circus geek who hasn't bathed since the Hoover Administration. Neither speaks for at least a minute. Bischoff is silent because his mental wheels are spinning like the gyroscope of a torpedo. Beck is silent because he's on the verge of blacking out. Outside the cabin, Shaftoe can hear the news, whatever it is, traveling up and down the length of the U-boat with the speed of sound.

Some of the men are shouting in rage, some sobbing, some laughing hysterically. Shaftoe figures a big battle must have been won, or lost. Maybe Hitler's been assassinated. Maybe Berlin's been sacked.

Beck is now visibly terrified.

The medic enters. He has adopted an erect military posture—the first time Shaftoe's seen such formality on the U-boat. He addresses Beck briefly in German. Beck nods continuously while the medic is talking. Then he helps the doctor get Bischoff out of his straitjacket.

Bischoff's a bit stiff, a bit unsteady, but he limbers up fast. He's shorter than average, with a strong frame and a trim waist, and as he pounces from bunk to deck, he reminds Shaftoe of a jaguar deploying itself from a tree. He shakes hands heartily with the medic, and with the miserable Beck. Then he opens the hatch that leads towards the control room. Half the crew is jammed into the gangway, watching that door, and when they see Bischoff, ecstasy floods over their faces and they erupt into wild cheering. Bischoff accepts handshakes from all of them, making his way towards his duty station like a politician through an adoring crowd. Beck slinks out the other hatch and loses himself among the hammering diesels.

Shaftoe has no idea what the fuck's going on until Root shows up a quarter of an hour later. Root picks the message up off the deck and reads it. His perpetually bemused affect, normally so annoying, serves him well at times like this. "This is a broadcast to all ships at sea from German supreme naval command, Tirpitzufer, Berlin. It says that U-691—which is this boat we're on, Bobby—has been boarded and captured by Allied commandos, and has already attacked and sunk a milch-cow in the Atlantic. Now it appears to be on its way towards continental Europe where it will presumably try to infiltrate German naval bases and sink more ships. All German naval and air forces are ordered to be on the lookout for U-691 and to destroy it on sight."

"Shit," Shaftoe says.

"We are on the wrong boat at the wrong time," Root says.

"What's the deal with that Bischoff character?"

"He was relieved of command earlier. Now he's back."

"That maniac's running the boat?"

"He is the *captain*," Root says.

"Well, where's he going to take us?"

"I'm not sure if even *he* knows that."

Bischoff goes to his cabin and pours himself a slug of that Armagnac. Then he goes to the chart room, which he's always preferred to his cabin. The chart room is the only civilized place on the whole boat. It's got a beautiful sextant in a polished wooden box, for example. Speaking tubes converge here from all over the boat, and even though no one is speaking into them directly, he can hear snatches of conversation from them, the distant clamor of the diesels, the zap of a deck of cards being shuffled, the hiss of fresh eggs hitting the griddle. Fresh eggs! Thank god they managed to rendezvous with the milchcow before she was sunk.

He unrolls a small-scale chart that encompasses the whole Northeast Atlantic, divided into numbered and lettered grid-squares for convoy-hunting. He should be looking at the southern part of the chart, which is where they are now. But eyes are drawn, again and again, north-wards—to the Qwghlm Archipelago.

Put it at the center of a clock. Then Great Britain is at five and six o'clock, and Ireland is at seven o'clock. Norway is due east, at three o'clock. Denmark is just south of Norway, at four o'clock, and at the base of Denmark, where it plugs into Germany, is Wilhelmshaven. France, home to so many U-boats, is far, far to the south—completely out of the picture.

A U-boat that was headed from the open sea towards a safe port on Fortress Europe would just go to the French ports on the Bay of Biscay—Lorient, most likely. Getting to Germany's North Sea and Baltic ports would be a far longer and more complicated and dangerous trip. The U-boat would have to get around Great Britain somehow. To the south, it would have to make a dash up the Channel, which (setting aside that it's a bottleneck, crackling with British radar) has been turned into a maze of sunken block-ships and minefields by those Royal Navy spoil-sports. There is a lot more room up north.

Assuming Shaftoe's story is true—and there must be *some* truth in it, or else where would he have gotten the morphine bottle—then it should have been a reasonably simple matter for U-553 to get around Great Britain via the northern route. But U-boats almost always had mechanical problems to *some* degree, especially after they had been at sea for a while. This might cause a skipper to hug the coast rather than taking to the open seas, where there would be no hope of survival if the engines shut down entirely. During the last couple of years, stricken U-boats had been abandoned on the coasts of Ireland and Iceland.

But supposing that an ailing, coast-hugging U-boat happened to pass near the Royal Navy base at Qwghlm at just the time some other U-boat was staging a raid there, as Shaftoe claimed. Then the dragnet of destroyers and airplanes that was sent out to capture the raiders could quite easily capture U-553, especially if her ability to maneuver were impaired to begin with.

There are two implausibilities in Shaftoe's story. One, that a U-boat would be carrying a trove of solid gold. Two, that a U-boat would be headed for German ports instead of one of the French ports.

But these two together are more plausible than either one of them by itself. A U-boat carrying that much gold might have very good reasons for going straight to the Fatherland. Some highly placed person wanted to keep this gold secret. Not just secret from the enemy, but secret from other Germans as well.

Why are the Japanese giving gold to Germans? The Germans must be giving them something they need in return: strategic materials, plans for new weapons, advisors, something like that.

He writes out a message:

Dönitz!

It is Bischoff. I am back in command. Thank you for the pleasant vacation. Now I am refreshed.

How uncivilized for you to order that we should be sunk. There must be a misunderstanding. Can we not discuss it face to face?

A drunken polar bear told me some fascinating things. Perhaps I will broadcast this information in an hour or so. Since I do not trust the Enigma anyway, I will not bother to encrypt it.

Yours respectfully.

Bischoff

A flock of white Vs migrates north from Gibraltar across a sunlit sea. At the apex of each V is a nitlike mote. The motes are ships, hauling megatons of war crap, and thousands of soldiers from North Africa (where their services are no longer needed) to Great Britain. That's how it looks to the pilots of the airplanes over the Bay of Biscay. All of those pilots and all of those planes are English or American—the Allies own Biscay now and have turned it into a crucible for U-boat crews.

Most of the Vs track straight parallel courses northwards, but a few of them curl and twist incessantly: these are destroyers, literally running circles around the plodding transports, pinging. Those tin cans will protect the convoys; the pilots of the airplanes who are trying to find U-691 can therefore search elsewhere.

The powerful sun casts a deep shadow in front of each ship; the eyes of the lookouts, irised down to pinpoints and squinting against the maritime glare, can no more penetrate that shade than they could see through plywood. If they could, they might notice that one of the big transports in the front rank has got some kind of unusual attachment: a pipe sticking vertically out of the water just in front and to one side of its bow.

Actually it is a cluster of pipes, one sucking in air, another spewing diesel exhaust, another carrying a stream of information in the form of prismatically reflected light. Follow that data stream a few yards down into the water and you will enter the optic nerve of one Kapitänleutnant Gunter Bischoff. This in turn leads to his brain, which is highly active.

In the age of sonar, Bischoff's U-boat was a rat in a dark, cluttered, infinite cellar, hiding from a man who had neither torch nor lantern: only two rocks that would spark when banged together. Bischoff sank a lot of ships in those days.

One day, while he was on the surface, trying to make some time across the Caribbean, a Catalina appeared out of nowhere. It came from a clear blue sky and so Bischoff had plenty of time to dive. The Catalina dropped a few depth charges and then went away; it must have been at the end of its range.

Two days later, a front moved in, the sky became mostly cloudy, and Bischoff made the mistake of relaxing. Another Catalina found them: this one used the clouds to conceal his approach, waited until U-691 was crossing a patch of sunlit water, and then dove, centering his own shadow on the U-boat's bridge. Fortunately, Bischoff had double sun sector air lookouts. This was a jargonic way of saying that at any given moment, two shirtless, stinking, unshaven, sunburned men were standing on the deck, casting shadows over their eyes with their outstretched hands. One of these men said something in a quizzical tone of voice, which alerted Bischoff. Then both lookouts were torn apart by a rocket. Five more of Bischoff's men were wounded by canon fire and rockets before Bischoff could get the boat under the surface.

The next day, the front had covered the sky with low blue-grey clouds from horizon to horizon. U-691 was far out of sight of land. Even so, Bischoff had Holz, his chief engineer, take her up to periscope depth first. Bischoff scanned the horizon meticulously. Satisfied that they were perfectly alone, he had Holz bring her to the surface. They fired up the diesels and pointed the boat east. Their mission was finished, their boat was damaged, it was time to go home.

Two hours later a flying boat bellied down through the cloud layer and dropped a skinny black egg on them. Bischoff was up on the bridge, enjoying some fresh air, and had the presence of mind to scream something about evasive action into the speaking tube. Metzger, the helmsman, instantly took it hard to starboard. The bomb plunged into the water exactly where the deck of U-691 would have been.

It continued in that vein until they got far away from land. When they finally limped back to their base at Lorient, Bischoff told this story to his superiors in tones of superstitious awe, when they finally broke the news to him that the enemy had this new thing called radar.

Bischoff studied it and read the intelligence reports: the Allies were even putting the shit on airplanes now! It could see your periscope!

His U-boat is no longer a rat in a dark cellar. Now it is a wingless horsefly dragging itself across an immaculate tablecloth in the streaming light of the afternoon sun.

Dönitz, bless him, is trying to build new U-boats that can stay submerged all the time. But he has to beg for every ton of steel and for the services of every engineer. In the meantime there is this stopgap measure, the Schnorkel, which is just plumbing: a pipe that sticks up out of the water and enables you to run on diesel power, just beneath the surface. Even the Schnorkel will show up on radar, but less brilliantly. Every time U-691 surfaces for more than an hour, Holz is up there working on the Schnorkel, welding new bits on, grinding old bits off, wrapping it in rubber or some other stuff that he hopes will absorb the radar. The engineers who installed the Schnorkel in Lorient six months ago wouldn't recognize it now because it has evolved, like shrews evolving into tigers. If Bischoff can just get U-691 back to a safe port, others can learn from Holz's innovations, and the few U-boats that haven't been sunk can derive some benefit from the experiment.

He snaps out of it. This must be how officers die, and get their men killed: they spend more time reviewing the past than planning for the future. It is nothing short of masturbation for Bischoff to be thinking about all of this. He must concentrate.

He doesn't have to worry so much about being sunk by Germans. As soon as he sent Dönitz the message threatening to broadcast the information about the gold, Dönitz retracted his general order to sink U-691. But there is the possibility that some ship might have received the first order but missed the second one, so he still has to watch himself.

Big deal. There is hardly any German Navy left to sink him anyway. He can worry about being sunk by the Allies instead. They will be intently irritated when they figure out that he has been shadowing this convoy for two whole days. Bischoff is pretty irritated himself; it is a fast convoy that protects itself by zigzagging, and if U-691 does not zigzag in perfect unison with the ship above it, it will either be crushed by her, or blunder out of her shadow and be noticed. This has put quite a strain on skipper and crew, and quite a drain on the boat's supply of benzedrine. But they've covered five hundred miles! Soon, fatal Biscay will be behind them, Brittany will be off to starboard, and Bischoff will have a choice: hang a right into the English Channel, which would be suicidal;

head north between Britain and Ireland, which would be suicidal; or veer to the west around Ireland, which would be suicidal.

Of course there's always France, which is friendly territory, but it is a siren whose allure must be sternly resisted. It's not enough for Bischoff just to run the U-boat aground on a godforsaken beach somewhere; he wants to get the thing back to a proper base. But the skies above the proper bases are infested with Catalinas, illuminating the sea with the satanic light of their radars. It is much cleverer to make them think that he's headed for France, and then head for a German port instead.

Or at least it seemed that way two days ago. Now the complexities of the plan are weighing on him.

The shadow of the ship above them suddenly seems much longer and deeper. This means either that the earth's rotation has just sped up tremendously, moving the sun around to a different angle, or that the ship has veered towards them. "Hard to starboard," Bischoff says quietly. His voice travels down a pipe to the man who controls the rudder. "Anything on the radio?"

"Nothing," says the Funkmaat. That's weird; usually when the ships are zigzagging, they coordinate it on the radio. Bischoff spins the periscope around and gets a load of the transport, still trying to shoulder its way into them. He checks his course; the bitch has veered a full ninety degrees!

"They've seen us," Bischoff says. "We'll dive in just a moment." But before he loses his ability to use the periscope, he does one more three-sixty, just to verify that his mental map of the convoy is accurate. It is, more or less; why, there's a destroyer, right there where he thought it was. He steadies the 'scope, calls out target bearings. The Torpedomaat echoes the digits while dialing them into the targeting computer: the very latest fully analog technology. The computer grinds through some calculations and sets the gyroscopes on a couple of torpedoes. Bischoff says: *fire, fire, dive*. It happens, almost that fast. The diesels' anvil chorus, which has been subtly driving them all insane for a couple of days, is replaced by a startling silence. They are running on batteries now.

As has always been the case, and as will continue to be the case for at least another half century, batteries suck. The convoy seems to bolt forward as U-691's speed drops to a pathetic wallow. The destroyers can go about five times as fast as they can now. Bischoff hates this part.

"The destroyer is taking evasive action," says the sound man.

"Did we have time to get the weather forecast?" he asks.

"Storm front moving in this evening. Foul weather tomorrow."

"Let's see if we can stay alive until the storm hits," Bischoff says. "Then we'll run this bucket of shit straight up the middle of the English

Channel, right up Winston Churchill's fat ass, and if we die, we'll die
like men."

A terrible clamor radiates through the water and pierces the hull. The
men cheer sullenly; they have just sunk another ship. Whoopdy-doo!

"I think it was the destroyer," says the sound man, as if he can hardly
believe their luck.

"Those homing torpedoes are bastards," Bischoff says, "when they
don't turn round and home in on *you*."

One destroyer down, three to go. If they can sink another one, they
have a chance of escaping the remaining two. But it's nearly impossible
to escape from three destroyers.

"There's no time like the present," he says. "Periscope depth! Let's
see what the fuck is going on, while we've got them rattled."

It is like this: one of the destroyers is sinking and another is heading
towards it to render assistance. The other two are converging on where
U-691 was about thirty seconds ago, but they are hindered by having
to make their way through the middle of the convoy. Almost immediately, they begin to fire their guns. Bischoff looses a spread of torpedoes
towards the assisting destroyer. Water is spouting up all around them
now as they are straddled by shells from the other two. He does another
three-sixty, fixing the image of the convoy in his mind's eye.

"Dive!" he says.

Then he has a better idea. "Belay that! Surface and go to flank speed,"

Any other U-boat crew would cut his throat at this moment, then
surrender. But these guys don't even hesitate; either they really do love
him, or they've all decided they're going to die anyway.

Twenty seconds of raw terror ensue. U-691 is screaming across the
surface, banking like a Messerschmidt as shells pound into the water all
around her. Crewmen are spilling out of her hatches, looking like prison
camp inmates in the bright sun, trying not to side off the deck as it tilts
this way and that, diving to snap the carabiners of their safety lines onto
cables before they are blown out of their shoes by the waterspouts from
the exploding shells. They are manning the guns.

Then there's a big transport ship between them and the two destroyers.
They're safe now, for a minute. Bischoff's up on the conning tower. He
turns aft and gets a load of the other destroyer, spiraling crazily in an
effort to shake off those homing torpedoes.

When they come out from behind the shelter of the big transport,
Bischoff sees that his mental map of the convoy was more or less accurate.
He speaks more orders to the rudder and the engines. Before the two
attacking destroyers have a chance to open up with their guns again,
Bischoff has got himself positioned between them and a troop transport:

a decrepit ocean liner covered with a hasty coat of wartime camo. They
can't shoot at him now without blowing hundreds of their own troops
to shreds. But he can shoot at them. When Bischoff's men see the liner
above them, and gaze across the water at the impotent destroyers, they
actually break out into song: a congratulatory beer hall ditty.

U-691 is topheavy with weaponry, armed to the teeth because of the
aircraft threat. Bischoff's crew opens fire on the destroyers with all of
the small and medium-sized stuff, to give the deck gun crew a chance
to line up its shot. At this range, the danger is that the shell will pass all
the way through the destroyer's hull, and out the other side, without
detonating. You have to be patient, take your time, aim for the engines.
Bischoff's crew knows this.

A skull-cracking explosion sounds from the barrel of the deck gun;
the shell skims the water, hits the closest destroyer right in the boilers.
The destroyer doesn't blow up, but it does go dead in the water. They
take a few more shots at the other destroyer and manage to knock out
one of its guns and one of its depth charge launchers. Then the lookouts
see airplanes headed their way, and it's time to dive. Bischoff does one
final periscope scan before they go under, and is surprised to see that
the destroyer that was trying to evade the torpedoes managed to do so;
apparently two of them curved back and hit transport ships instead.

They go straight down to a hundred and sixty meters. Destroyers drop
depth charges on them for eight hours. Bischoff takes a nap. When he
wakes up, depth charges are booming all over the place and everything
is fine. It should be dark and stormy up there now: bad weather for
Catalinas. He evades the destroyers by (in a nutshell) doing clever things
he has learned the hard way. The U-boat is as thin as a knitting needle,
and when you turn it directly toward or away from the source of a ping,
it makes almost no reflection. All that's required is a clear mental map
of where you are with respect to the destroyers.

After another hour, the destroyers give up and leave. Bischoff takes
U-691 up to schnorkel depth and points her straight up the middle of
the English Channel, as advertised. He also uses the periscope to verify
that the weather is, also as advertised, awful.

Those bastards have a big fat red pin on the map marking his position
as last reported by those destroyers. Around that pin, as the hours go by,
they will draw circles of steadily increasing radius, widening gyres enclosing the set of all points in the ocean where U-691 could possibly be at
the moment, based on their assumptions about her speed. The square
mileage that must be searched will increase as the square of that radius.

Going up the Channel, *while submerged*, just isn't going to work—
they'll run into one of the block ships that the Brits sank there to prevent

U-boats from doing just that. The surface is the only way, and it's a hell of a lot faster too. This raises the airplane issue. Airplanes search not for the boat itself, which is tiny and dark, but for its wake, which is white and spreads for miles on calm water. There will be no wake behind U-691 tonight—or rather, there will be, but it will be lost in random noise of much higher amplitude. Bischoff decides that covering distance is more important than being subtle at the moment, and so he brings her up to the surface and then pins the throttle. This will burn fuel insanely, but U-691 has a range of eleven thousand miles.

Sometime around noon the next day, U-691, battering its way through a murderous storm, lances the Straits of Dover and breaks through into the North Sea. She must be lighting up every radar screen in Europe, but airplanes can't do much in this weather.

"The prisoner Shaftoe wishes to speak to you," says Beck, who has gone back to being his second-in-command, as if nothing had ever been different. War gives men good ignoring skills. Bischoff nods.

Shaftoe enters the control room, accompanied by Root, who will apparently serve as translator, spiritual guide, and/or wry observer. "I know a place where we can go," Shaftoe says.

Bischoff is floored. He hasn't thought about where they were actually *going* in days. The concept of having a coherent goal is almost beyond his comprehension.

"It is—" Bischoff gropes "—*touching* that you have taken an interest."

Shaftoe shrugs. "I heard you were in deep shit with Dönitz."

"Not as bad as I was," Bischoff says, immediately perceiving the folksy wisdom of this American barnyard metaphor. "The depth is the same, but now I am head up instead of head down."

Shaftoe chuckles delightedly. They are all buddies now. "You have any charts of Sweden?"

This strikes Bischoff as a good but half-witted idea. Seeking temporary refuge in a neutral country: fine. But much more likely is that they run the boat aground on a rock.

"There's a bay there, by this little town," Shaftoe says. "We know the depths."

"How could that be?"

"Because we charted the fucking thing ourselves, a couple of months ago, with a rock on a string."

"Was this before or after you boarded the mysterious U-boat full of gold?" Bischoff asks.

"Just before."

"Would it be out of line for me to inquire what an American Marine

Raider and an ANZAC chaplain were doing in Sweden, a neutral country, performing bathymetric surveys?"

Shaftoe doesn't seem to think it's out of line at all. He's in such a good mood from the morphine. He tells another yarn. This one begins on the coast of Norway (he is deliberately vague about how he got there) and is all about how Shaftoe led Enoch Root and a dozen or so men, including one who had a serious ax wound to the leg (Bischoff raises his eyebrows) all the way across Norway on skis, slaying pursuing Germans right and left, and into Sweden. The story then bogs down for a while because there are no more Germans to kill, and Shaftoe, sensing that Bischoff's attention is beginning to wander, tries to inject some lurid thrills into the narrative by describing the progress of the gangrene up the leg of the officer who ran afoul of the ax (who, as far as Bischoff can make out, was under suspicion as a possible German spy). Shaftoe keeps encouraging Root to jump in and tell the story of how Root performed several consecutive amputations of the officer's leg, all the way up to the pelvis. Just as Bischoff is finally starting to actually care about this poor bastard with the gangrenous leg, the story takes another zigzag: they reach a little fishing town on the Gulf of Bothnia. The gangrenous officer is delivered into the hands of the town doctor. Shaftoe and his comrades hole up in the woods and strike up what sounds like an edgy relationship with a Finnish smuggler and his lissome daughter. And now it's clear that Shaftoe has reached his favorite part of the story, which is this Finnish girl. And indeed, up to this point his story-telling style has been as rude and blunt and functional as the inside of a U-boat. But now he relaxes, begins to smile, and becomes damn near poetic—to the point where a few members of Bischoff's crew, who speak a little bit of English, start to loiter within earshot. Essentially the story goes totally off the rails at this point, and while it's entertaining material, it appears to be headed exactly nowhere. Bischoff finally interrupts with "What about the guy with the bad leg?" Shaftoe frowns and bites his lip. "Oh, yeah," he finally says, "he died."

"The rock on the string," prompts Enoch Root. "Remember? That's why you were telling the story."

"Oh, yeah," Shaftoe says, "they came and picked us up with a little submarine. That's how we got to Qwghlm and saw the U-boat with the gold. But before they could enter the harbor, they had to have a chart. So Lieutenant Root and I went out on a fucking rowboat with a rock on a string and charted it."

"And you still have a copy of this chart with you?" Bischoff asks skeptically.

"Nah," Shaftoe says, with a flip coolness that in a less charismatic man would be infuriating. "But the lieutenant remembers it. He's really good at remembering numbers. Aren't you, sir?"

Enoch shrugs modestly. "Where I grew up, memorizing the digits of pi was the closest thing we had to entertainment."

CANNIBALS

GOTO DENGO FLEES THROUGH THE SWAMP. HE IS FAIRLY CERtain that he is being chased by the cannibals who just cooked up the friend with whom he had washed ashore. He climbs up a tangle of vines and hides himself several meters above the ground; men with spears search the general area, but they do not find him.

He passes out. When he wakes up, it's dark, and some small animal is moving in the branches nearby. He is so desperate for food that he grabs at it blindly. The creature has a body the size of a house cat, but long leathery arms: some kind of huge bat. It bites him several times on the hands before he crushes it to death. Then he eats it raw.

The next day he goes forth into the swamp, trying to put more distance between himself and the cannibals. Around midday he finds a stream—the first one he's seen. For the most part the water just seeps out of New Guinea through marshes, but here is an actual river of cold, fresh water, just narrow enough to jump across.

A few hours later he finds another village that is similar to the first one, but only about half as big. The number of dangling heads is much smaller; maybe these headhunters are not quite as fearsome as the first group. Again there is a central fire where white stuff is being cooked in a pot: in this case, it appears to be a wok, which they must have gotten through trade. The people of this village don't know a starving Nipponese soldier is lurking in the vicinity, so they are not very vigilant. Around twilight, when the mosquitoes come out of the swamps in a humming fog, they all retire into their longhouses. Goto Dengo runs out into the middle of the compound, grabs the wok, and makes off with it. He forces himself not to take any of the food until he is far away, hidden in a tree again, and then he gorges himself. The food is a rubbery gel of what would appear to be pure starch. Even to a ravenous man, it has no flavor at all. Nevertheless he licks the wok clean. While he is doing so, an idea comes to him.

The next morning, when the sun's bubble bursts out of the sea, Goto Dengo is kneeling in the bed of the river, scooping sand up into the wok and swirling it around, hypnotized by the maelstrom of dirt and foam, which slowly develops a glittering center.

The next morning Dengo is standing on the edge of the village bright and early, shouting: *"Ulab! Ulab! Ulab!"* which is what the people in the first village called gold.

The villagers wriggle out of their tiny front doors, bewildered at first, but when they see his face and the wok dangling from one hand, rage flashes over them like the sun burning out from behind a cloud. A man charges with a spear, sprinting straight across the clearing. Goto Dengo dances back and takes half-shelter behind a coconut tree, holding the wok up over his chest like a shield. *"Ulab! Ulab!"* he cries again. The warrior falters. Goto Dengo holds out his fist, swings it to and fro until it finds a warm shaft of sunlight, and then loosens it slightly. A tiny cascade of glittering flakes trickles out, catching the sun, then plunges into shadow, hissing as it strikes the leaves below.

It gets their attention. The man with the spear stops. Someone behind him says something about *patah*.

Goto Dengo levels the wok, resting it on his forearm, and sprinkles the entire handful of gold dust into it. The village watches, transfixed. There is a great deal more whispering about *patah*. He steps forward into the clearing, holding the wok out before him as an offering to the warrior, letting them see his nakedness and his pitiful condition. Finally he collapses to his knees, bows his head very low, and sets the wok on the ground at the warrior's feet. He remains there, head bowed, letting them know that they can kill him now if they want to.

If they want to choke off their newly discovered gold supply, that is.

The matter will require some discussion. They tie his elbows together behind his back with vines, put a noose around his neck, and tie that to a tree. All of the kids in the village stand around him and stare. They have purple skin and frizzy hair. Flies swarm around their heads.

The wok is taken into a hut that is decorated with more human heads than any of the other huts. All of the men go in there. Furious discussion ensues.

A mud-daubed woman with long skinny breasts brings Goto Dengo half a shell of coconut milk and a handful of white, knuckle-sized grubs wrapped up in leaves. Her skin is a tangle of overlapping ringworm scars and she is wearing a necklace that consists of a single human finger strung on a piece of twine. The grubs squirt when Goto Dengo bites down on them.

The children abandon him to watch a pair of American P-38s fly by, out over the ocean. Bored with airplanes, Goto Dengo squats on his haunches and observes the menagerie of arthropods that have converged on him in hopes of sucking his blood, taking a bite of his flesh, eating his eyeballs out of his skull, or impregnating him with their eggs. The haunch position is a good one because every five seconds or so he has to bash his face against one knee, then the other, in order to keep the bugs out of his eyes and nostrils. A bird drops out of a tree, lands clumsily on his head, pecks something out of his hair, and flies away. Blood jets out of his anus and pools hotly under the arches of his feet. Creatures with many legs gather at the edge of the pool and begin to feast. Goto Dengo moves away, and leaving them to it, gets a few minutes' respite.

The men in the hut arrive at some sort of agreement. The tension is broken. There is laughter, even. He wonder what counts as funny to these guys.

The guy who wanted to impale him earlier comes across the clearing, takes his leash, and tugs Goto Dengo to a standing position. *"Patah,"* he says.

He looks at the sky. It is getting late, but he does not relish trying to explain to them that they should simply wait until tomorrow. He stumbles across the clearing to the cooking fire and nods at a pan full of brain stew. "Wok," he says.

It doesn't work. They think he wants to trade gold for the wok.

There follows about eighteen hours of misunderstandings and failed attempts to communicate. Goto Dengo almost dies; at least he feels like he might. Now that he is not on the move, the last few days are really catching up with him. But finally, in the middle of the next morning, he gets to show his magic. Squatting in the nearby stream, his elbows unbound, the wok in his hands, surrounded by skeptical village fathers still keeping a tight grip on his rustic noose, he begins to pan for gold. Within a few minutes he has managed to summon a few flakes of the stuff out of the riverbed, demonstrating the basic concept.

They want to learn it themselves. He was expecting this. He tries to show one of them how it's done, but (as Goto Dengo himself learned long ago) it is one of those harder-than-it-looks deals.

Back to the village. He actually gets a place to sleep this night: they stuff him into a long skinny sack of woven grass and tie it shut above his head—this is how they keep themselves from being eaten alive by insects while they are asleep. Malaria hits him now: alternating waves of chill and heat swamping his body with the force of riptides.

Time goes out of whack for a while. Later, he realizes he has been here for a while now, because his broken forefinger is now solid and gnarled, and the abrasions that he got from the coral head are now a field of fine, parallel scars, like the grain in a piece of wood. His skin is covered with mud and he smells of coconut oil and of the smoke that they fill their huts with to chase away the bugs. His life is simple: when malaria has him teetering on the brink of death, he sits in front of a felled palm tree and chips away at it mindlessly for hours, slowly creating a heap of fibrous white stuff that the women use to make starch. When he is feeling stronger, he drags himself over to the river and pans for gold. In return they do what they can to keep New Guinea from killing him. He's so weak they do not even bother to send a chaperone with him when he goes out.

It would be an idyllic tropical paradise if not for the malaria, the insects, the constant diarrhea and resulting hemorrhoids, and the fact that the people are dirty and smell bad and eat each other and use human heads for decoration. The one thing that Goto Dengo thinks about, when he's capable of thinking, is that there is a boy in this village who looks to be about twelve years old. He remembers the twelve-year-old who was initiated by driving a spear through his companion's heart, and wonders who's going to be used for this boy's initiation rite.

From time to time the village elders pound on a hollow log for a while, then stand around listening to other hollow logs being pounded in other villages. One day there is an especially long episode of pounding, and it would seem that the villagers are pleased by what they have heard. The next day, they have visitors: four men and a child who speak a completely different language; their word for gold is *gabitisa*. The child whom they have brought with them is about six years old, and obviously retarded. There is a negotiation. Some of the gold that Goto Dengo has panned out of the stream is exchanged for the retarded child. The four visitors disappear into the jungle with their *gabitisa*. Within a few hours, the retarded child has been tied to a tree and the twelve-year-old boy has stabbed it to death and become a man. After some parading around and dancing, the older men sit on top of the younger man and cut long complicated gashes into his skin and pack dirt into them so that they will heal as decorative welts.

Goto Dengo cannot do very much except gape in numb astonishment. Every time he begins to think beyond the next fifteen minutes, tries to formulate a plan of action, the malaria comes back, flattens him for a week or two, scrambles his brain and forces him to start again from scratch. Despite all of this he manages to extract a few hundred grams of gold dust from that stream. From time to time the village is visited by relatively light-skinned traders who move up and down the coast in outrigger canoes and who speak yet another different language. These traders begin to come more frequently, as the village elders start trading the gold dust for betel nuts, which they chew because it makes them feel good, and for the occasional bottle of rum.

One day, Goto Dengo is on his way back from the river, carrying a teaspoon of gold dust in the wok, when he hears voices from the village—voices speaking in a cadence that used to be familiar.

All of the men of the village, some twenty in all, are standing up with their backs to coconut trees, their arms secured behind the trees with ropes. Several of these men are dead, with their intestines spilling down onto the ground, already black with flies. The ones who are not dead yet are being used for bayonet practice by a few dozen gaunt, raving Nipponese soldiers. The women ought to be standing around screaming, but he doesn't see them. They must be inside the huts.

A man in a lieutenant's uniform swaggers out of a hut, smiling broadly, wiping blood off of his penis with a rag, and almost trips over a dead child.

Goto Dengo drops the wok and puts his hands up in the air. "I am Nipponese!" he shouts, even though all he wants to say at this moment is *I am not Nipponese.*

The soldiers are startled, and several of them try to swing their rifles around in his direction. But the Nipponese rifle is an awful thing, nearly as long as the average soldier is tall, too heavy to maneuver even when its owner is in perfect health. Luckily all of these men are clearly starving to death and half-crippled by malaria and bloody flux, and their minds work quicker than their bodies. The lieutenant bellows, "Hold your fire!" before anyone can get off a shot in the direction of Goto Dengo.

There follows a long interrogation in one of the huts. The lieutenant has many questions, and asks most of them more than once. When he repeats a question for the fifth or thirteenth time, he adopts a grand magnanimity, as if giving Goto Dengo the opportunity to retract his earlier lies. Goto Dengo tries to ignore the screams of the bayoneted men and the raped women, and concentrate on giving the same answer each time without variation.

"You surrendered to these savages?"

"I was incapacitated and helpless. They found me in this condition."

"What efforts did you make to escape?"

"I have been building my strength and learning from them how to survive in the jungle—what foods I can eat."

"For six months?"

"Pardon me, sir?" He hasn't heard this question before.

"Your convoy was sunk six months ago."

"Impossible."

The lieutenant steps forward and slaps him across the face. Goto

Dengo feels nothing but tries to cringe anyway, so as not to humiliate the man.

"Your convoy was coming to reinforce our division!" bellows the lieutenant. "You dare to question me?"

"I humbly apologize, sir!"

"Your failure to arrive forced us to make a retrograde maneuver!* We are marching overland to rendezvous with our forces at Wewak!"

"So, you are—the advance guard for the division?" Goto Dengo has seen perhaps two dozen men, a couple of squads at most.

"We are the division," the lieutenant says matter-of-factly. "So, again, you surrendered to these savages?"

––––––––––

When they march out the following morning, no one remains alive in the village; all of them have been used for bayonet practice or shot while trying to run away.

He is a prisoner. The lieutenant had decided to execute him for the crime of having surrendered to the enemy, and was in the act of drawing his sword when one of the sergeants prevailed upon him to wait for a while. Impossible as it might seem, Goto Dengo is in far better physical condition than any of the others and therefore useful as a pack animal. He can always be properly executed in front of a large audience when they reach a larger outpost. So he marches in the middle of the group now, unfettered, the jungle serving the purpose of chains and bars. They have loaded him down with the one remaining Nambu light machine gun, which is too heavy for anyone else to carry, and too powerful for them to fire; any man who pulled the trigger on this thing would be shaken to pieces by it, the jungle-rotted flesh scattering from jittering bones.

After a few days have gone by, Goto Dengo requests permission to learn how to operate the Nambu. The lieutenant's reply is to beat him up—though he does not have the strength to beat anyone up properly—so Goto Dengo has to help him, crying out and doubling over when the lieutenant thinks he has landed a telling blow.

Every couple of days, when the sun comes up in the morning, this or that soldier is found to have more bugs on him than any of the others. This means that he is dead. Lacking shovels or the strength to dig, they leave him where he lies and march onward. Sometimes they get lost, march back over the same territory, and find these corpses all swollen and black; when they begin to smell rotting human flesh, they know

––––––––––

*Nipponese Army-speak for "retreat."

that they have just wasted a day's effort. But in general they are gaining altitude now, and it is cooler. Ahead of them, their route is blocked by a ridge of snow-capped peaks that runs directly to the sea. According to the lieutenant's maps, they will have to climb up one side of it and down the other in order to reach Nipponese-controlled territory.

The birds and plants are different up here. One day, while the lieutenant is urinating against a tree, the foliage shakes and an enormous bird runs out. It looks vaguely like an ostrich, but more compact and more colorful. It has a red neck, and a cobalt-blue head with a giant helmetlike bone sticking out of the top of its skull, like the nose of an artillery shell. It prances straight up to the lieutenant and kicks him a couple of times, knocking him flat on his ass, then bends his long neck down, shrieks in his face, and runs back into the jungle, using its head-bone as a kind of battering-ram to clear a path through the brush.

Even if the men were not dying on their feet, they would be too startled to raise their weapons and take a shot at it. They laugh giddily. Goto Dengo laughs until he cries. The bird must have delivered a powerful kick, though, because the lieutenant lies there for a long time, clutching his stomach.

Finally one of the sergeants regains his composure and walks over to help the poor man. As he draws closer, he suddenly turns around to face the rest of the group. His face has gone slack.

Blood is fountaining out of a couple of deep stab wounds in the lieutenant's belly, and his body is already going limp when the rest of the group gathers around him. They sit and watch until they are pretty sure he is dead, and then they march onwards. That evening, the sergeant shows Goto Dengo how to disassemble and clean the Nambu light machine gun.

They are down to nineteen. But it seems as though all of the men who were susceptible to dying in this place have now died, because they go for two, three, five, seven days without losing any more. This is in spite of, or maybe because of, the fact that they are climbing up into the mountains. It is brutal work, especially for the heavily laden Goto Dengo. But the cold air seems to clear up their jungle rot and quench the ravenous internal fires of malaria.

One day they break their march early at the edge of a snowfield, and the sergeant orders double rations for everyone. Black stone peaks rise above them, with an icy saddle in between. They sleep huddled together, which does not prevent some of them waking up with frostbitten toes. They eat most of what remains of their food supply and then set out towards the pass.

The pass turns out to be almost disappointingly easy; the slope is so gentle that they're not really aware that they've reached the summit until they notice that the snow is sloping downwards beneath their feet. They are above the clouds, and the clouds cover the world.

The gentle slope stops abruptly at the edge of a cliff that drops almost vertically at least a thousand feet down—then it passes through the cloud layer, so there's no way of knowing its true height. They find the memory of a trail traversing the slope. It seems to head down more frequently than it heads up and so they follow it. It is new and exciting at first, but then it grows just as brutally monotonous as every other landscape where soldiers have ever marched. As the hours go by, the snow gets patchier, the clouds get closer. One of the men falls asleep on his feet, stumbles, and tumbles end-over-end down the slope, occasionally bounding into free fall for several seconds. By the time he vanishes through the cloud layer, he's too far away to see.

Finally the eighteen descend into a clammy mist. Each sees the one in front of him only when very close, and then only as a grey, blurred form, like an ice demon in a childhood nightmare. The landscape has become jagged and dangerous and the lead man has to grope along practically on hands and knees.

They are working their way around a protruding rib of fog-slicked stone when the lead man suddenly cries out: "Enemy!"

Some of the eighteen actually laugh, thinking it is a joke.

Goto Dengo distinctly hears a man speaking English, with an Australian accent. The man says, "Fuck 'em."

Then a noise starts up that seems powerful enough to split the mountain in half. He actually thinks it is a rock avalanche for awhile until his ears adjust, and he realizes that it is a weapon: something big, and fully automatic. The Australians are firing at them.

They try to retreat, but they can only move a few steps every minute. Meanwhile, thick lead slugs are hurtling through the fog all around them, splintering against the rock, sending stone shards into their necks and faces. "The Nambu!" someone shouts. "Get the Nambu!" But Goto Dengo can't fire the Nambu until he finds a decent place to stand.

Finally he gets to a ledge about the size of a large book, and unslings the weapons. But all he can see is fog.

There is a lull of a few minutes. Goto Dengo calls out the names of his comrades. The three behind him are accounted for. The others do not seem to answer his calls. Finally, one man struggles back along the path. "The others are all dead," he says, "you may fire at will."

So he begins to fire the Nambu into the fog. The recoil almost knocks him off the mountain, so he learns to brace it against an outcropping.

Then he sweeps it back and forth. He can tell when he's hitting the rock because it makes a different sound from hitting fog. He aims for the rock.

He spends several clips without getting any results. Then he begins walking forward along the path again.

The wind gusts, the fog swirls and parts for a moment. He sees a blood-covered path leading directly to a tall Australian man with a red mustache, carrying a tommy gun. Their eyes meet. Goto Dengo is in a better position and fires first. The man with the tommy gun falls off the cliff.

Two other Australians, concealed on the other side of the rock rib, see this happen, and begin cursing.

One of Goto Dengo's comrades scampers down the path, shouts, "Banzai!" and disappears around the corner, carrying a fixed bayonet. There is a shotgun blast and two men scream in unison. Then there is the now-familiar sound of bodies tumbling down the rock face. "Goddamn it!" hollers the one remaining Aussie. "Fucking Nips."

Goto Dengo has only one honorable way out of this. He follows his comrade around the corner and opens up with the Nambu, pouring it into the fog, sweeping the rock face with lead. He stops when the magazine is empty. Nothing happens after that. Either the Aussie retreated down the path or else Goto Dengo shot him off the cliff.

By nightfall, Goto Dengo and his three surviving comrades are back down in the jungle again.

WRECK

....

To: root@eruditorum.org
From: randy@epiphyte.com
Subject: answer
That you are a retail-level philosopher who just happens to have buddies who are in the surveillance business is simply too big a coincidence for me to accept.
So I'm not going to tell you why.
But in case you are worried, let me assure you that we have our reasons for building the Crypt. And it's not just to make money—though it will be very good for our share-

holders. Did you think we were just a bunch of nerds who stumbled into this and got in over our heads? We aren't.

P.S. What do you mean when you say that you ''noodle around with novel cryptosystems?'' Give me an example.

Randall Lawrence Waterhouse
Current meatspace coordinates, hot from the GPS re-ceiver card in my laptop:
8 degrees, 52.33 minutes N latitude 117 degrees, 42.75 minutes E longitude
Nearest geographical feature: Palawan, the Philippines

To: randy@epiphyte.com
From: root@eruditorum.org
Subject: Re: answer
Randy,
Thank you for your oddly defensive note. Very pleased you have a good reason. Never thought otherwise. Of course you should not feel obligated to share it with me.

My having friends in the world of electronic intelli-gence-gathering is not the big coincidence you make it out to be.

How did you come to be a founder of the Crypt?
By being good at science and math.
How did you come to be good at science and math?
By standing on the shoulders of the ones who came be-fore you.
Who were those people?
We used to call them natural philosophers.
Likewise, my friends in the surveillance business owe their skills to the practical application of philosophy. They have the wit to understand this, and to give credit where credit is due.

P.S. You forgot to use the ''dwarf@siblings.net'' front address. I assume this was deliberate?

P.P.S. You say you want an example of a novel cryptosys-tem that I am working on. This sounds like a test. You and I both know, Randy, that the history of crypto is strewn with the wreckage of cryptosystems invented by arrogant dilettantes and soon demolished by clever codebreakers. You probably suspect that I don't know this—that I'm just another arrogant dilettante. Quite cleverly, you ask me

```
to stick my neck out, so that you and Cantrell and his
like-minded friends can cut it off. You are testing me—
trying to find my level.
  Very well. I'll send you another message in a few days.
I'd love to have the Secret Admirers take a crack at my
scheme anyway.
```

In a narrow-hulled double-outrigger boat in the South China Sea, America Shaftoe stands astride a thwart, her body pointing straight up at the sun, despite the rollers, as if she is gyroscopically stabilized. She is wearing a sleeveless diving vest that reveals strong, deeply tanned shoulders, the walnut-brown skin etched with a couple of black tattoos and brilliantly jeweled with beads of water. The handle of a big knife projects from a shoulder holster. The blade is that of a regular diving knife but the handle is that of a kris, an ornate traditional weapon of Palawan. A tourist can buy a kris at the duty-free shop at NAIA, but this one appears to be less flashy but better made than the tourist-shop jobs, and worn from use. She has a gold chain around her neck with a gnarled black pearl dangling from it. She has just emerged from the water holding a tiny jeweler's screwdriver between her teeth. Her mouth is open to breathe, displaying crooked, bright white teeth with no fillings. For this brief moment she is in her element, completely absorbed in what she is doing, totally unself-conscious. At this moment Randy thinks he understands her: why she spends most of her time living here, why she didn't bother with going to college, why she left behind her mother's family, who raised her, lovingly, in Chicago, to be in business with her father, the wayward veteran who walked out of the household when America was nine years old.

Then she turns to scan the approaching launch, and sees Randy on it staring at her. She rolls her eyes, and the mask falls down over her face again. She says something to the Filipino men who are squatting in the boat around her and two of them go into action, scampering down the outrigger poles, like balance-beam artists, to stand on the outrigger pontoon. They hold their arms out as shock absorbers to ease the contact between the launch—which Doug Shaftoe has cheerfully christened. *Mekong Memory*—and the much longer, much narrower pamboat.

One of the other Filipinos plants his bare foot against the top of a small Honda portable generator and pulls on the ripcord, the tendons and wiry muscles popping out of his arm and back for a moment like so many ripcords themselves. The generator starts instantly, with a nearly inaudible purr. It is good stuff, part of the capital improvements that

Semper Marine made as part of its contract with Epiphyte and Filitel. Now they are using it, effectively, to defraud the Dentist.

"She lies one hundred and fifty-four meters below that buoy," says Doug Shaftoe, pointing to a gallon plastic milk jug bobbing on the swells. "She was lucky, in a way."

"Lucky?" Randy clambers off the launch and rests his weight on the outrigger, shoving it down so that the warm water comes up to his knees. Holding out his arms like a tightrope walker, he makes his way down an arm toward the canoe hull in the center.

"Lucky for us," Shaftoe corrects himself. "We're on the flank of a seamount. The Palawan Trough is nearby." He's following Randy, but without all of the teetering and arm-waving. "If she had sunk in that, she'd have gone down so deep that she'd be hard to reach, and the pressure down there would've crushed her. But at two hundred meters, there wouldn't've been such an implosion." Reaching the boat's hull, he makes dramatic crushing motions with his hands.

"Do we care?" Randy asks. "Gold and silver don't implode."

"If her hull is intact, getting the goods out is a hell of a lot easier," says Doug Shaftoe.

Amy has vanished beneath the pamboat's canopy. Randy and Doug follow her into its shade, and find her sitting crosslegged on a fiberglass equipment case that is encrusted with airport baggage stickers. Her face is socketed into the top of a black rubber pyramid whose base is the screen of a ruggedized cathode-ray tube. "How's the cable business?" she mutters. Months ago, she gave up even trying to hide her scorn for the dull work of cable-laying. Pretenses are shabby things that, like papier-mâché houses, must be energetically maintained or they will dissolve. Another case in point: some time ago, Randy gave up pretending that he was not completely fascinated with Amy Shaftoe. This is not exactly the same thing as being in love with her, but it has quite a few things in common with that. He has always had a weird, sick fascination with women who smoked and drank a lot. Amy does neither, but her complete disregard of modern skin-cancer precautions puts her in the same category: people too busy leading their lives to worry about extending their life expectancy.

In any case, he has a desperate craving to know what Amy's dream is. For a while he thought it was treasure-hunting in the South China Sea. This she definitely enjoys, but he is not sure if it gives her satisfaction entire.

"Been adjusting the trim on those dive planes again," she explains. "I don't think those pushrod things were engineered very well." She pulls her head out of the black rubber cowl and gives Randy a quick sidelong look, holding him responsible for the shortcomings of all engineers. "I hope it'll run now without corkscrewing all over the place."

"Are you ready?" her father asks.

"Whenever you are," she answers, slamming the ball back into his court.

Doug rises to a crouch and duck-walks out from under the low canopy. Randy follows him, wanting to see the ROV for himself.

It rests in the water alongside the pamboat's center hull: a stubby yellow torpedo with a glass dome for a nose, held in place by a Filipino crewman who leans over the gunwale to grip it with both hands. Pairs of stunted wings are mounted at the nose and at the tail, each wing supporting a miniature propeller mounted in a cowl. Randy is reminded of a dirigible with its outlying engine gondolas.

Noting Randy's interest, Doug Shaftoe squats alongside it to point out the features. "It's neutrally buoyant, so when we have it alongside like this, we have it in this foam cradle, which we will now take off." He begins jerking loose some quick-release bungee cords, and molded segments of foam peel away from the ROV's hull. It drops lower in the water, nearly pulling the crewman over the side with it, and he lets go, keeping his arms extended so he can prevent it from bumping into them with each swell. "You'll notice there's no umbilical," Doug says. "Normally that is mandatory for an ROV. You need the umbilical for three reasons."

Randy grins, because he knows that Doug Shaftoe is about to enumerate the three reasons. Randy has spent almost no time around military people, but he is finding that he gets along with them surprisingly well. His favorite thing about them is their compulsive need to educate everyone around them, all the time. Randy does not need to know anything about the ROV, but Doug Shaftoe is going to give him a short course anyway. Randy supposes that when you are in a war, practical knowledge is a good thing to spread around.

"One," says Douglas MacArthur Shaftoe, "to provide power to the ROV. But this ROV carries its own power source—an oxygen/natural gas swash-plate motor, adapted from torpedo technology, and *part of our peace dividend*" (that is the other thing Randy likes about military people—their mastery of deadpan humor) "that generates enough electricity to run all of the thrusters. Two, for communications and control. But this unit uses blue-green lasers to communicate with the control console which Amy is manning. Three, for emergency recovery in the event of total systems failure. But if this unit fails, it is smart enough, supposedly, to inflate a bladder and float up to the surface where it will activate a strobe light so that we can go recover it."

"Jeez," Randy says, "isn't this thing incredibly expensive?"

"It is *incredibly* expensive," Douglas MacArthur Shaftoe says, "but the guy who runs the company that makes it is an old buddy of mine—we were at the Naval Academy together—he loans it to me sometimes, when I have a pressing need."

"Does your friend know what the pressing need is in this case?"

"He does not know specifically," says Doug Shaftoe, mildly offended, "but I suppose he is not a stupid man either."

"Clear!" shouts Amy Shaftoe, sounding rather impatient.

Her father takes a good look at each of the thrusters in turn. "Clear," he responds. A moment later, something begins to thrum inside the ROV, and a stream of bubbles spurts from an orifice on its tail, and then the thrusters begin to spin around. They swivel on the ends of their stubby wings until they are facing downwards, throwing fountains into the air, and the ROV sinks rapidly. The fountains diminish and become slight upwellings in the sea. Seen through the water's rough surface, the ROV is a yellow splatter. It shortens as the vehicle's nose pitches down, then rapidly disappears as the thrusters drive it straight down. "Always kinda takes my breath away to see something that costs so much going off to who knows where," Doug Shaftoe says meditatively.

The water around the boat has begun to emit a kind of dreadful, sickly light, like radiation in a low-budget horror film. "Jeez! The laser?" Randy says.

"Mounted to the bottom of the hull, in a little dome," Doug says. "Punches through even turbid water with ease."

"What kind of bandwidth can you transmit on it?"

"Amy is seeing decent monochrome video on her little screen right now, if that is what you mean. It is all digital. All packetized. So if some of the data doesn't make it through, the image gets a little choppy, but we do not lose visuals altogether."

"Cool."

"Yes, it is cool," Doug Shaftoe allows. "Let us go and watch TV."

They crouch beneath the canopy. Doug turns on a small Sony portable television, a ruggedized waterproof model encased in yellow plastic, and patches its input cable into a spare output jack on the back of Amy's rig. He turns it on and they begin to see a bit of what Amy is seeing. They do not have the benefit of the dark cowl that Amy is using, and so the glare of the sun washes out everything but a straight white line emerging from the dark center of the picture and expanding towards the edge. It is moving.

"I am following the buoy line down," she explains. "Kind of boring."

Randy's calculator watch beeps twice. He checks the time; it is three in the afternoon.

"Randy?" Amy says, in a velvet voice.

"Yes?"

"Could you give me the square root of three thousand eight hundred twenty-three on that thing?"

"Why do you want that?"

"Just do it."

Randy holds his wrist up so that he can see the watch's digital display, takes a pencil out of his pocket, and begins using its eraser to press the tiny little buttons. He hears a metallic snicking noise, but pays it no mind.

Something cool and smooth glides along the underside of his wrist. "Hold still," Amy says. She bites her lip and pulls. The watch falls off, and comes away in her left hand, its vinyl band neatly severed. She's holding the kris in her right, the edge of its blade still decorated with a few of Randy's arm hairs. "Huh. Sixty-one point eight three oh four. I would've guessed higher." She tosses the watch over her shoulder and it disappears into the South China Sea. "Square roots are tricky that way."

"Amy, you're losing the rope!" says her father impatiently, focused entirely on the screen of the TV.

Amy jams the kris back into its sheath, smiles sweetly at Randy, and plugs her face back into the rig. Randy is speechless for a while.

The question of whether or not she is a lesbian is rapidly becoming more than purely academic. He performs a quick mental review of all of the lesbians he has known. Usually they are mid-level, nine-to-five city dwellers with sensible haircuts. In other words, they are just like most of the other people Randy knows. Amy is too flagrantly exotic, too much like a horny film director's idea of what a lesbian would be. So maybe there is some hope here.

"If you're gonna stare at my daughter that way," Doug Shaftoe says, "you'd better start boning up on your ballroom dancing."

"Is he starin' at me? I can never tell when I have my face stuck in this thing," Amy says.

"He was in love with his watch. Now he has no object for his affections," Doug says. "So, hold on to your hats!"

Randy can tell when someone is trying to rattle him. "What is it that offended you so much about my watch? The alarm?"

"The whole package was pretty annoying," Amy says, "but the alarm is what made me psychotic."

"You should have said something. Being a true geek, I actually know how to turn that alarm off."

"Then why didn't you?"

"I don't want to lose track of time."

"Why? Got a cake in the oven?"

"The Dentist's due diligence people will be all over me."

Doug shifts position and screws up his face curiously. "You mentioned that before. What is due diligence?"

"It's like this. Alfred has some money that he wants to invest."

"Who's Alfred?"

"A hypothetical person whose name begins with A."

"I don't understand."

"In the crypto world, when you are explaining a cryptographic protocol, you use hypothetical people. Alice, Bob, Carol, Dave, Evan, Fred, Greg, and so on."

"Okay."

"Alfred invests his money in a company that is run by Barney. When I say 'run by' what I mean is that Barney has ultimate responsibility for what that company does. So, perhaps Barney is the chairman of the board of directors in this case. He's been chosen, by Alfred, Alice, Agnes, Andrew, and the other investors, to look after the company. He and the other directors hire corporate officers—such as Chuck, who is the president. Chuck and the other officers hire Drew to run one of the company's divisions. Drew hires Edgar, the engineer, and so on and so forth. So, in military terms, there is a whole chain of command that extends down to the guys in the trenches, like Edgar."

"And Barney's the man at the top of the chain of the command," Doug says.

"Right. So, just like a general, he is ultimately responsible for everything that is done below him. Alfred has personally entrusted Barney with that money. Barney is legally required to exercise due diligence in seeing that the money is spent responsibly. If Barney fails to show due diligence, he is in major legal trouble."

"Ah."

"Yeah. That gets Barney's attention. Alfred's lawyers might show up at any moment and demand proof that due diligence is being exercised. Barney needs to stay on his toes, make sure that his ass is covered at all times."

"Barney in this case is the Dentist?"

"Yeah. Alfred, Agnes, and the others are all of the people in his investment club—half of the orthodontists in Orange County."

"And you are Edgar the Engineer."

"No, you are Edgar the Engineer. I am a corporate officer of Epiphyte. I am more like Chuck or Drew."

Amy breaks in. "But what does the Dentist have over you? You don't work for him."

"I'm sorry to tell you that is no longer the case, as of yesterday."

This gets the Shaftoes' attention.

"The Dentist now owns ten percent of Epiphyte."

"How did that come about? Last I was informed of anything," Doug says accusingly, "the son of a bitch was suing you."

"He was suing us," Randy says, "because he wanted in. None of our stock was for sale, and we were not planning to go public anytime soon, so the only way he could get in was by essentially blackmailing us with a lawsuit."

"You said it was a bogus lawsuit!" Amy exclaims, the only person here who is bothering to show, or feel, any moral outrage.

"It was. But it would have cost so much to litigate it that it would have bankrupted us. On the other hand, when we offered to sell the Dentist some stock, he dropped the suit. We got our hands on some of his money, which is always useful."

"But now you are beholden to his due diligence people."

"Yeah. They are on the cable ship even as we speak—they came out on a tender this morning."

"What do they think you are doing?"

"I told them that the sidescan sonar revealed some fresh anchor scars near the cable route, which needed to be assessed."

"Very routine."

"Yeah. Due diligence people are easy to manipulate. You just have to act really diligent. They eat it up."

"We're there," Amy says, and hauls back on a joystick, twisting her body to put a little English on the maneuver.

Doug and Randy look at the TV screen. It is completely dark. Digits along the bottom state that the pitch is five degrees and the roll is eight, which means that the ROV is nearly level. The yaw number is spinning around rapidly, meaning that the ROV is rotating around its vertical axis like a fishtailing car. "Should come into view at around fifty degrees," Amy mutters.

The yaw numbers slow down, dropping through a hundred degrees, ninety, eighty. At around seventy degrees, something rotates into view at the edge of the screen. It looks like a rugged, particolored sugarloaf rising from the seafloor. Amy gooses the controls a couple of times and the rotation drops to a crawl. The surgarloaf glides into the center of the screen and then stops. "Locking in the gyros," Amy says, whacking a button. "All forward." The sugarloaf slowly begins to get bigger. The

ROV is moving towards it, its direction automatically stabilized by its built-in gyroscropes.

"Swing wide around it to starboard," Doug says. "I want a different angle on this." He pays some attention to a VCR that's supposed to be recording this feed.

Amy lets the joystick come back to neutral, then executes a series of moves that causes them to lose the image of the wreck for a minute. All they can see are coral formations passing beneath the ROV's cameras. Then she yaws it around to the left and there it is again: the same streamlined projectile shape. But from this angle, they can see it's actually projecting from the seafloor at a forty-five degree angle.

"It looks like the nose of an airplane. A bomber," Randy says. "Like a B-29."

Doug shakes his head. "Bombers had to have a circular cross-section because they were pressurized. This thing does not have a circular cross-section. It is more eliptical."

"But I don't see all of the railings and guns and, and—"

"*Crap* that a classic German U-boat would have hanging off of it. This is a more modern streamlined shape," Doug says. He shouts something in Tagalog at one of his crew, over on *Glory IV*.

"Looks pretty crusty," Randy says.

"There will be plenty of crap growing on her," Doug says, "but she's still recognizable. There was not a catastrophic implosion."

A crew member runs onto the pamboat carrying an old picture book from *Glory IV*'s small but idiosyncratic library: a pictorial history of German U-boats. Doug flips past the first three-quarters of the book and stops at a photograph of a sub whose lines are strikingly familiar.

"God, that looks just like the Beatles' Yellow Submarine," Randy says. Amy pulls her head out of the viewer and crowds him out of the way to look.

"Except it's not yellow," Doug says. "This was the new generation. Hitler could've won the war if he'd made a few dozen of these." He flips forward a few pages. There are pictures of more U-boats with similar lines, but much larger.

A cross-sectional diagram shows a thin-walled, elliptical outer hull enclosing a thick-walled, perfectly circular inner hull. "The circle is the pressure hull. Always kept at one atmosphere and full of air, for the crew. Outside of it, an outer hull, smooth and streamlined, with room for fuel and hydrogen peroxide tanks—"

"It carried its own oxidizer? Like a rocket?"

"Sure—for running submerged. Any interstices in this outer hull would have been filled with seawater, pressurized to match the external pressure of the ocean, to keep it from collapsing."

Doug holds the book up beneath the television monitor and rotates it, comparing the lines of a U-boat to the shape on the screen. The latter is rugged and furry with coral and other growths, but the similarity is obvious.

"Why isn't it lying flat on the bottom, I wonder?" Randy says.

Doug grabs a plastic water bottle, which is still mostly full, and tosses it overboard. It floats upside-down.

"Why isn't it lying flat, Randy?"

"Because there's an air bubble trapped in one end," Randy says sheepishly.

"She suffered damage at the stern. The bow pitched up. There was a partial collapse. Seawater, rushing into the breach at the stern, forced all of the air into the bow. The depth is a hundred and fifty-four meters, Randy. That's fifteen atmospheres of pressure. What does Boyle's Law tell you?"

"That the volume of the air must have been reduced by a factor of fifteen."

"Bingo. Suddenly, fourteen-fifteenths of the boat is full of water, and the other fifteenth is a pocket of compressed air, capable of supporting life briefly. Most of her crew dead, she fell fast and settled hard onto the bottom, breaking her back and leaving the bow section pointing upwards, as you see her. If anyone was still alive in the bubble, they died a long, slow death. May God have mercy on their souls."

In other circumstances, the religious reference would make Randy uncomfortable, but here it seems like the only appropriate thing to say. Think what you will about religious people, they always have something to say at times like this. What would an atheist come up with? *Yes, the organisms inhabiting that submarine must have lost their higher neural functions over a prolonged period of time and eventually turned into pieces of rotten meat. So what?*

"Closing in on what passes for the conning tower," Amy says. According to the book, this U-boat isn't going to have the traditional high vertical tower rising out of its back: just a low streamlined bulge. Amy has piloted the ROV very close to the U-boat now, and once again she brings it to a stop and yaws it around. The hull pans into the screen, a variegated mountain of coral growths, completely unrecognizable as a manmade object—until something dark enters the screen. It turns into a perfectly circular hole. An eel comes snaking out of it and snaps angrily at the camera for a moment, its teeth and gullet filling the screen. When it swims away, they can see a dome-shaped hatch cover hanging from its hinges next to the hole.

"Someone opened the hatch," Amy says.

"My god," says Douglas MacArthur Shaftoe. "My god." He leans away from the TV as if he can't handle the image any more. He crawls out from under the canopy and stands up, staring out across the South China Sea. "Someone got out of that U-boat."

Amy is still fascinated, and one with her joysticks, like a thirteen-year-old boy in a video arcade. Randy rubs the strange empty place on his wrist and stares at the screen, but he is not seeing anything now except that perfect round hole.

After a minute or so, he goes out to join Doug, who is ritualistically lighting up a cigar. "This is a good time to smoke," he mumbles. "Want one?"

"Sure. Thanks." Randy pulls out a folding multipurpose tool and cuts the end from the cigar, a pretty impressive-looking Cuban number. "Why do you say it's a good time to smoke?"

"To fix it in your memory. To mark it." Doug tears his gaze from the horizon and looks at Randy searchingly, almost beseeching him to understand. "This is one of the most important moments in your life. Nothing will ever be the same. We might get rich. We might get killed. We might just have an adventure, or learn something. But we have been changed. We are standing close to the Heraclitean fire, feeling its heat on our faces." He produces a flaring safety match from his cupped palms like a magician, and holds it up before Randy's eyes, and Randy puffs the cigar alive, staring into the flame.

"Well, here's to it," Randy says.

"And here's to whoever got out," replies Doug.

SANTA MONICA

THE UNITED STATES MILITARY (WATERHOUSE HAS DECIDED) IS first and foremost an unfathomable network of typists and file clerks, secondarily a stupendous mechanism for moving stuff from one part of the world to another, and last and least a fighting organization. For the last couple of weeks he has been owned by the second group. They put him on a luxury liner too swift to be caught by U-boats—though this is a moot point since, as Waterhouse and a few other people know, Dönitz has declared defeat in the Battle of the Atlantic, and pulled his U-boats off the map until he can build the new generation, which will run on rocket fuel and need never come to the surface. In this way Waterhouse got to New York. From Penn Station he took trains to the Midwest, where he spent a week with his family and reassured them for the ten thousandth time that, because of what he knew, he could never be sent into actual combat.

Then it was trains again to Los Angeles, and now he waits for what sounds like it will be a killing series of airplane flights halfway round the world to Brisbane. He is one of about a million young men and women in uniform and on leave, wandering around Los Angeles looking for some entertainment.

Now, they say that this city is the entertainment capital and so entertainment shouldn't be hard to find. Indeed you can hardly walk down a city block without bumping into half a dozen prostitutes and passing an equal number of night spots, movie theaters, and pool halls. Waterhouse samples all of these during his four-day layover, and is distressed to find that he is no longer entertained by any of them. Not even the whores!

Maybe this is why he is walking along the bluff north of the Santa Monica Pier, looking for a way down to the beach, which is completely empty—the only thing in Los Angeles that isn't generating commissions and residuals for someone. The beach lures but does not pander. The plants up here, standing watch over the Pacific, are like something from another planet. No, they do not even look like real plants from any conceivable planet. They are too geometric and perfect. They are schematic diagrams for plants sketched out by some impossibly modern designer with a strong eye for geometry but who has never been out in a woods and seen a real plant. They don't even grow out of any recognizable organic matrix, they are embedded in the sterile ochre dust that passes for soil in this part of the country. Waterhouse knows that this is just the beginning, that it will only get weirder from here on out. He heard enough from Bobby Shaftoe to know that the other side of the Pacific is going to be indescribably strange.

The sun is preparing to go down and the pier, down the beach to his left, is alight, a gaudy galaxy; the zoot suits of the carnival barkers stand out from a mile away, like emergency flares. But Waterhouse is in no hurry to reach it. He can see ignorant armies of soldiers, sailors, marines milling around, distinguishable by the hues of their uniforms.

The last time he was in California, before Pearl Harbor, he was no different from all of those guys on the pier—just a little smarter, with a knack for numbers and music. But now he understands the war in a way that they never will. He is still wearing the same uniform, but only as a disguise. He believes now that the war, as those guys understand it, is every bit as fictional as the war movies being turned out across town in Hollywood.

They say that Patton and MacArthur are daring generals; the world watches in anticipation of their next intrepid sortie behind enemy lines. Waterhouse knows that Patton and MacArthur, more than anything else, are intelligent consumers of Ultra/Magic. They use it to figure out where the enemy has concentrated his forces, then loop around them and strike where he is weakest. That's all.

They say that Montgomery is a steady hand, cagey and insightful. Waterhouse has no use for Monty; Monty's an idiot; Monty doesn't read his Ultra; he ignores it, in fact, to the detriment of his men and of the war effort.

They say that Yamamoto was killed by a lucky accident when some roving P-38s just happened across an anonymous flight of Nipponese planes and shot them down. Waterhouse knows that Yamamoto's death warrant was hammered out by an Electrical Till Corporation line printer in a Hawaiian cryptanalysis factory, and that the admiral was the victim of a straightforward political assassination.

Even his concept of geography has changed. When he was home, he sat down with his grandparents and they looked at the globe, spinning it around until all they saw was blue, tracing his route across the Pacific, from one lonely volcano to the next godforsaken atoll. Waterhouse knows that those little islands, before the war, had only one economic function: information processing. The dots and dashes traveling along the undersea cable are swallowed up by the earth currents after a few thousand miles, like ripples in heavy surf. The European powers colonized those islands at about the same time as the long cables were being laid, and constructed power stations where the dots and dashes coming down the line were picked up, amplified, and sent on to the next chain of islands.

Some of those cables must plunge into the deep not far from this beach. Waterhouse is about to follow the dots and dashes over the western horizon, where the world ends.

He finds a ramp that leads down to the beach and lets gravity draw him towards sea level, gazing to the south and west. The water is pacific and colorless beneath a hazy sky, the horizon line is barely discernable.

The fine dry sand plumps under his feet in fat circular waves that crest around his ankles, so he has to stop and unlace his hard leather shoes. Sand has become trapped in the matrix of his black socks and he pulls them off too and stuffs them in his pockets. He walks towards the water carrying one shoe in each hand. He sees others who have tied their shoes together through belt loops, leaving their hands free. But the asymmetry of this offends him, so he carries his shoes as if preparing to invert himself and wade on his hands with his head dangling into the water.

The low sun shines flatly across the sand, grazing the chaos and creating a knife-sharp terminator at the crest of each dunelet. The curves flirt and osculate with one another in some pattern that is, Waterhouse guesses, deeply fascinating and significant but too challenging for his tired mind to attack. Some areas have been stomped level by seagulls.

The sand at the surf line has been washed flat. A small child's footprints wander across it, splaying like gardenia blossoms on thin shafts. The sand looks like a geometric plane until a sheet of ocean grazes it. Then small imperfections are betrayed by swirls in the water. Those swirls in turn carve the sand. The ocean is a Turing machine, the sand is its tape; the water reads the marks in the sand and sometimes erases them and sometimes carves new ones with tiny currents that are themselves a response to the marks. Plodding through the surf, Waterhouse strikes deep craters in the wet sand that are read by the ocean. Eventually the ocean erases them, but in the process its state has been changed, the pattern of its swirls has been altered. Waterhouse imagines that the disturbance might somehow propagate across the Pacific and into some super-secret Nipponese surveillance device made of bamboo tubes and chrysanthemum leaves; Nip listeners would know that Waterhouse had walked that way. In turn, the water swirling around Waterhouse's feet carries information about Nip propeller design and the deployment of their fleets—if only he had the wit to read it. The chaos of the waves, gravid with encrypted data, mocks him.

The land war is over for Waterhouse. Now he is gone, gone to the sea. This is the first time he's taken a good look at it—the sea, that is— since he reached Los Angeles. It looks big to him. Before, when he was at Pearl, it was just a blank, a nothing. Now it looks like an active participant and a vector of information. Fighting a war out on that thing could turn you into some kind of a maniac, make you deranged. What must it be like to be the General? To live for years among volcanoes and alien trees, to forget about oaks and cornfields and snowstorms and football games? To fight the terrible Nipponese in the jungle, burning them out of caves, driving them off cliffs into the sea? To be an oriental potentate—the supreme authority over millions of square miles, hundreds of millions of people. Your only tether to the real world a slender copper fiber rambling across the ocean floor, a faint bleating of dots and dashes in the night? What kind of man would this make you?

OUTPOST

✛ WHEN THEIR SERGEANT WAS AEROSOLIZED BY THE AUSTRALIAN with the tommy gun, Goto Dengo and his surviving comrades were left mapless, and mapless in the jungles of New Guinea during a war is bad, bad, bad.

In another country, they might have been able to keep walking downhill until they reached the ocean, and then follow the coastline to their destination. But travel along the coast is even more nearly impossible than travel in the interior, because the coast is a chain of pestilential headhunter-infested marshes.

In the end, they find a Nipponese outpost by simply following the sound of the explosions. They may not have maps, but the American Fifth Air Force does.

The relentless bombing is reassuring, in a way, to Goto Dengo. After their encounter with the Australians, he entertains an idea that he dare not voice: that by the time they reach their destination, it might already have been overrun by the enemy. That he can even conceive of such a possibility proves beyond all doubt that he is no longer fit to be a soldier of the emperor.

In any case, the drone of the bombers' engines, the tympanic thuds of the explosions, the flashes on the night horizon give them plenty of helpful hints as to where the Nipponese people are located. One of Goto Dengo's comrades is a farmboy from Kyushu who seems to be capable of substituting enthusiasm for food, water, sleep, medicine, and any other bodily needs. As they trudge onwards through the jungle, this boy keeps his spirits up by looking forward to the day when they draw close enough to hear the sound of the antiaircraft batteries and see the American planes, torn open by shellfire, spiraling into the sea.

That day never arrives. As they get closer, though, they can find the outpost with their eyes closed, simply by following the reek of dysentery and decaying flesh. Just as the stench draws close enough to be overpowering, the enthusiastic boy makes an odd grunting sound. Goto Dengo turns to see a peculiar, small, oval-shaped entrance wound in the center of the boy's forehead. The boy falls down and lies on the ground quivering.

"We are Nipponese!" Goto Dengo says.

The tendency of bombs to fall out of the sky and blow up among them whenever the sun is up dictates that bunkers and foxholes be dug. Unfortunately ground coincides with water table. Footprints fill up with water before the foot has even been worried loose from the clutching mud. Bomb craters are neat, circular ponds. Slit trenches are zigzagging canals. There are no wheeled vehicles and no beasts of burden, no livestock, no buildings. Those pieces of charred aluminum must have been parts of airplanes once. There are a few heavy weapons, but their barrels are cracked and warped from explosions, and pocked with small craters. Palm trees are squat stumps crowned with a few jagged splinters radiating away from the site of the most recent explosion. The expanse of red mud is flecked with random clutches of gulls tearing at bits of food; Goto Dengo suspects already what they're eating, and confirms this when he cuts his bare foot on an excerpt of a human jawbone. The sheer volume of high explosive that has detonated here has suffused every molecule of the air, water, and earth with the chemical smell of TNT residue. This smell reminds Goto Dengo of home; the same stuff is good for pulverizing any rock that is standing between you and a vein of ore.

A corporal escorts Goto Dengo and his one surviving comrade from the perimeter to a tent that has been pitched out on the mud, its ropes tied not to stakes but to jagged segments of tree trunks, or heavy fragments of ruined weapons. Inside, the mud is paved with the lids of wooden crates. A shirtless man of perhaps fifty sits crosslegged on top of an empty ammunition box. His eyelids are so heavy and swollen that it is difficult to tell whether he is awake. He breathes erratically. When he inhales, his skin retracts into the interstices between ribs, producing the illusion that his skeleton is trying to burst free from his doomed body. He has not shaved in a long time, but doesn't have enough whiskers to muster a real beard. He is mumbling to a clerk, who squats on his haunches atop a crate lid stenciled MANILA and copies down his words.

Goto Dengo and his comrade stand there for perhaps half an hour, desperately trying to master their disappointment. He expected to be lying in a hospital bed drinking miso soup by now. But these people are in worse shape than he is; he is afraid that *they* might ask *him* for help.

Still, it is good just to be under canvas, and standing in the presence of someone who has authority, who is taking charge. Clerks enter the tent carrying message decrypts, which means that somewhere around here is a functioning radio station, and a staff with codebooks. They are not totally cut off.

"What do you know how to do?" says the officer, when Goto Dengo is finally granted the opportunity to introduce himself.

"I am an engineer," says Goto Dengo.

"Ah. You know how to build bridges? Airstrips?"

The officer is engaging in a bit of whimsy here; bridges and airstrips are as far beyond their grasp as intergalactic starships. All of his teeth have fallen out and so he gums his words, and sometimes must pause to draw breath two or three times in the course of a sentence.

"I will build such things if it is my commander's wish, though for such things, others have skill far better than mine. My specialty is underground works."

"Bunkers?"

A wasp stings him on the back of the neck and he inhales sharply. "I will build bunkers if it is my commander's wish. My specialty is tunnels, in earth or in rock, but especially in rock."

The officer stares at Goto Dengo fixedly for a few moments, then directs a glance at his clerk, who nods a little bow and takes it down. "Your skills are useless here," he says offhandedly, as if this is true of just about everyone.

"Sir! Also, I am proficient with the Nambu light machine gun."

"The Nambu is a poor weapon. Not as good as what the Americans and Australians have. Still, useful in jungle defense."

"Sir! I will defend our perimeter to my last breath—"

"Unfortunately they will not attack us from the jungle. They bomb us. But the Nambu cannot hit a plane. When they come, they will come from the ocean. The Nambu is useless against an amphibious assault."

"Sir! I have lived in the jungle for six months."

"Oh?" For the first time, the officer seems interested. "What have you been eating?"

"Grubs and bats, sir!"

"Go and find me some."

"At once, sir!"

———————

He untwists some old rope to make twine, and knots the twine into nets, and hangs the nets in trees. Once that is done, his life is simple: every morning he climbs up into the trees to collect bats from the nets. Then he spends the afternoon digging grubs out of rotten logs with a bayonet. The sun goes down and he stands in a foxhole full of sewage until it comes up again. When bombs go off nearby, the concussion puts him into a state of shock so profound as to separate mind from body entirely; for several hours afterwards, his body goes around doing things without his telling it to. Stripped of its connections to the physical world, his mind runs in circles like an engine that has sheared its driveshaft and is screaming along at full throttle, doing no useful work while burning itself up. He usually does not emerge from this state until someone speaks to him. Then more bombs fall.

One night he notices that there is sand beneath his feet. Strange.

The air smells clean and fresh. Unheard of.

Others are walking on the sand with him.

They are being escorted by a couple of shambling privates, and a corporal bent under the weight of a Nambu. The corporal is peering into Goto Dengo's face strangely. "Hiroshima," he says.

"Did you say something to me?"

"Hiroshima."

"But what did you say before you said 'Hiroshima'?"

"in"

"In?"

"In Hiroshima."

"What did you say before you said 'in Hiroshima'?"

"Aunt."

"You were talking to me about your aunt in Hiroshima?"

"Yes. Her too."

"What do you mean, her too?"

"The same message."

"What message?"

"The message that you memorized for me. Give her the same message."

"Oh," Goto Dengo says.

"You remember the whole list?"

"The list of people I'm supposed to give the message to?"

"Yes. Recite the list again."

The corporal has an accent from Yamaguchi, which is where most of the soldiers posted here came from. He seems more rural than urban. "Uh, your mother and father back on the farm in Yamaguchi."

"Yes!"

"And your brother, who is—in the Navy?"

"Yes!"

"And your sister, who is—"

"A schoolteacher in Hiroshima, very good!"

"As well as your aunt who is also in Hiroshima."

"And don't forget my uncle in Kure."

"Oh, yeah. Sorry."

"That's okay! Now tell me the message again, just to make sure you won't forget it."

"Okay," says Goto Dengo, and draws a deep breath. He is really starting to come around now. They are trudging down to the sea: he and half a dozen others, all unarmed and carrying small bundles, accompanied by the corporal and privates. Below, in the gentle surf, a rubber boat awaits them.

"We're almost there! Tell me the message! Tell it back to me!"

"My beloved family," Goto Dengo begins.

"Very good—perfect so far!" says the corporal.

"My thoughts are with you as always," Goto Dengo guesses.

The corporal looks a bit crestfallen. "Close enough—keep going."

They have reached the boat. The crew shoves it out into the surf a few paces. Goto Dengo stops talking for a few moments as he watches the others wade out to it and climb in. Then the corporal prods him in the back. Goto Dengo staggers out into the ocean. No one has started yelling at him yet—in fact they reach for him, pulling him in. He tumbles into the bottom of the boat and clambers up to a kneeling position as the crew begin to row it out into the surf. He locks eyes with the corporal, back on the beach.

"This is the last message you will receive from me, for by now I have long since gone to my rest on the sacred soil of the Yasukuni Shrine."

"No! No! That's totally wrong!" hollers the corporal.

"I know that you will visit me there and remember me fondly, as I remember you."

The corporal splashes into the surf, trying to chase the boat, and the privates plunge in after him and grab him by the arms. The corporal shouts, "Soon we will deal the Americans a smashing defeat and then I will march home through the streets of Hiroshima in triumph along with my comrades!" He recites it like a schoolboy doing his lessons.

"Know that I died bravely, in a magnificent battle, and never for one moment shirked my duty!" Goto Dengo shouts back.

"Please send me some strong thread so that I can mend my boots!" the corporal cries.

"The Army has looked after us well, and we have lived the last months of our lives in such comfort and cleanliness that you would hardly guess we had ever left the Home Islands!" Goto Dengo shouts, knowing that he must be difficult to hear now above the surf. "When the final battle came, it came quickly, and we went to our deaths in the full flower of our youth, like the cherry blossoms spoken of in the emperor's rescript, which we all carry against our breasts! Our departure from this world is a small price to pay for the peace and prosperity that we have brought to the people of New Guinea!"

"No, that's totally wrong!" wails the corporal. But his comrades are dragging him up the beach now, back towards the jungle, where his voice is lost in an eternal cacophony of hoots, screeches, twitters and eerie cries.

Goto Dengo smells diesel and stale sewage. He turns around. The stars behind them are blocked out by something long and black and shaped kind of like a submarine.

"Your message is much better," someone mumbles. It is a young fellow carrying a toolbox: an airplane mechanic who has not seen a Nipponese airplane in half a year.

"Yes," says another man—also a mechanic, apparently. "His family will find your message much more comforting."

"Thank you," Goto Dengo says. "Unfortunately I have no idea what the kid's name is."

"Then go to Yamaguchi," says the first mechanic, "and pick some old couple at random."

METEOR

"YOU SURE DON'T *FUCK* LIKE A SMART GIRL," SAYS BOBBY Shaftoe, his voice suffused with awe.

The wood stove glows in the corner, even though it's only September for crissakes, in Sweden, where Shaftoe has spent the last six months.

Julieta is dark and lanky. She reaches one long arm far across the bed, gropes on the nightstand for a cigarette.

"Could you reach that jiz rag?" Shaftoe says, eyeing a neatly folded United States Marine Corps handkerchief next to the cigarettes. His arm is too short.

"Why?" Julieta speaks great English like all the other Finns.

Shaftoe sighs in exasperation and buries his face in her black hair. The Gulf of Bothnia whooshes and foams down below them, like a badly tuned radio pulling in strange information.

Julieta is given to asking big questions.

"I just don't want there to be a big mess when I execute my withdrawal, ma'am," he says.

He hears the flint of Julieta's lighter itching once, twice, thrice behind his ear. Then her chest pushes him up as her lungs fill with smoke.

"Take your time," she purrs, her vocal cords syrupy with condensed tar. "What are you going to do, go for a swim? Invade Russia?"

Somewhere out there, across the Gulf, is Finland. There are Russians there, and Germans.

"See, even when you mention going for a swim, my dick gets smaller," Shaftoe says. "So it's going to come out. Inevitably." He thinks he pronounces this last word correctly.

"Then what will happen?" Julieta says.

"We'll get a wet spot."

"So? It's natural. People have been sleeping on wet spots as long as beds have existed."

"God damn it," Shaftoe says, and lunges heroically for the Semper Fi handkerchief. Julieta digs her fingernails into one of the sensitive spots that she has located during her exhaustive cartographic survey of his body. He squirms to no avail; all the Finns are great athletes. He pops out. Too late! He knocks his wallet onto the floor while grabbing the hanky, then rolls off Julieta and wraps it around himself, a flag on a broken pole, the only flag of surrender Bobby Shaftoe will ever wave.

Then he just lies there for a while, listening to the surf, and the popping of the wood in the stove. Julieta rolls away from him and lies curled up on her side, avoiding the wet spot, even though it is natural, and enjoying her cigarette, even though it isn't.

Julieta smells like coffee. Shaftoe likes to nuzzle and smell her coffee-scented flesh.

"The weather is not too bad. Uncle Otto should be back before night," she says. She is lazily regarding a map of Scandinavia. Sweden dangles like a flaccid, circumcised phallus. Finland bulges scrotally underneath. Its eastern border, with Russia, no longer bears any resemblance to reality. This illusive frontier is furiously crosshatched with pencil marks, the axes of Stalin's repeated efforts to castrate Scandinavia, obsessively recorded and annotated by Julieta's uncle, who like all Finns is an expert skier, crack shot, and indomitable warrior.

Still they despise themselves. Shaftoe thinks it's because they eventually farmed out the defense of their country to the Germans. Finns excelled at an old-fashioned, personalized, retail style of Russian-killing, but when they started to run low on Finns, they had to call in the Germans, who are more numerous and who have perfected a wholesale Russian-slaughtering operation.

Julieta scoffs at this simple-minded theory: the Finns are a million times more complex than Bobby Shaftoe can ever understand. Even if the war had never happened, there would be an infinity of reasons for them to be depressed all the time. There is no point even in trying to explain it all. She can only provide him with the haziest glimpses into Finnish psychology by fucking his brains out once every couple of weeks.

He has been lying there for too long. Soon the left-over jism in his tract will harden like epoxy. This peril spurs him to action. He slides out of bed, cringes from the chill, hops across cold planks to the rug, scurries instinctively toward the warmth of the stove.

Julieta rolls over onto her back to watch this. She looks at him appraisingly. "Be a man," she says. "Make me some coffee."

Shaftoe snatches the cabin's cast-iron kettle, which could double as a ship anchor if need arose. He throws a blanket over his shoulders and runs outside. He stops at the brink of the seawall, knowing that the splintery pier will not be kind to his bare feet, and pisses down onto the beach. The yellow arc is veiled in steam, redolent of coffee. He squints across the gulf and sees a tug pulling a boom of logs down the coast, and a couple of sails, but not Uncle Otto's.

Behind the cabin is a standpipe that is fed from a spring in the hills. Shaftoe fills the kettle, snatches a couple of hunks of firewood and scampers back inside, maneuvering between stacked bricks of foil-packed java and crates of Suomi machine pistol ammunition. He sets the kettle on the iron stove and then stokes it up with the wood.

"You use too much wood," Julieta says, "Uncle Otto will be noticing."

"I'll chop more," Shaftoe says. "This whole fucking country is full of nothing but wood."

"You'll be chopping wood all day if Uncle Otto gets angry at you."

"So it's okay for me to sleep with Otto's niece, but burning a couple of sticks of wood to make her coffee is grounds for dismissal?"

"Grounds," Julieta says. "Coffee grounds."

The entire country of Finland (to hear Otto tell it) has been plunged into an endless night of existential despair and suicidal depression. The usual antidotes have been exhausted: self-flagellation with steeped birch twigs, mordant humor, week-long drinking bouts. The only thing to save Finland now is coffee. Unfortunately the government of that country has been short-sighted enough to raise taxes and customs duties through the roof. Supposedly it is to pay for killing Russians, and for resettling the hundreds of thousands of Finns who have to pull up stakes and move whenever Stalin, in a drunken lunge, or Hitler, in a psychotic fit, attacks a map with a red Crayola. It just has the effect of making coffee harder to obtain. According to Otto, Finland is a nation of unproductive zombies, except in areas that have been penetrated by the distribution networks of coffee smugglers. Finns are generally strangers to the entire concept of good fortune, however they *are* lucky enough to live right across the Gulf of Bothnia from a neutral, reasonably prosperous country famous for its coffee.

With this background, the existence of a small Finnish colony in Norrsbruck becomes pretty much self-explanatory. The only thing that is missing is muscle to load the coffee onto the boat, and to unload whatever swag Otto brings back. Needed: one muscular lunkhead willing to be paid off the record in whatever specie Otto comes up with.

Sergeant Bobby Shaftoe, USMC, pours some beans into the grinder and starts to belabor the crank. A black flurry begins to accumulate in the coffeepot below. He has learned to make this stuff the Swedish way, using an egg to settle the grounds.

Chopping wood, fucking Julieta, grinding coffee, fucking Julieta, pissing on the beach, fucking Julieta, loading and unloading Otto's ketch. This has been pretty much it for Bobby Shaftoe during the last half year. In Sweden he has found the calm, grey-green eye of the blood hurricane that is the world.

Julieta Kivistik is the central mystery. They do not have a love affair; they have a series of love affairs. At the beginning of each affair, they are not even speaking to each other, they do not even know each other, Shaftoe is just a drifter who loads for her uncle. At the end of each affair they are in bed fucking. In between, there is anywhere from one to three weeks of tactical maneuver, false starts, and arduous cut-and-thrust flirtation.

Other than that, each affair is completely different, like a whole new relationship between two entirely different people. It is crazy. Probably because Julieta is crazy—much crazier than Bobby Shaftoe. But there's no reason for Shaftoe not to be crazy, here and now.

He boils the coffee, does the trick with the egg, pours her a mug. This is nothing more than a courtesy: their affair just ended and the new one hasn't started yet.

When he brings her the mug, she is sitting up in bed, smoking another cigarette, and (just like a woman) cleaning out his wallet, which is something that he has not done since—well, since he first made it, ten years ago, in Oconomowoc, in fulfillment of the requirements for the Leatherworking merit badge. Julieta has pulled the stuffing out of the thing and is going through it as if it were a paperback book. Much of the stuff in there has been ruined by seawater. But she is looking, analytically, at a snapshot of Glory.

"Gimme that!" he says, and snatches it from her.

If she were his lover, she would try to play keep-away with him, there would be silliness and, perhaps, more sex at the end of it. But she is a stranger now and she lets him have the wallet.

She watches him set down the coffee, as if he's a waiter in a cafe.

"You have a girlfriend—where? In Mexico?"

"Manila," Bobby Shaftoe says, "if she's even still alive."

Julieta nods, completely impassive. She is neither jealous of Glory, nor worried about Glory's fate at the hands of the Nips. What's happening in the Philippines can't be any worse than what she's seen in Finland. And why should she care, anyway, about the past romantic entanglements of her uncle's stevedore, young what's-his-name?

Shaftoe pulls on boxers, wool pants, a shirt and a sweater. "I'm going into town," he says. "Tell Otto I'll be back to unload the boat."

Julieta says nothing.

As a last, polite gesture, Shaftoe stops at the door, reaches behind a stack of crates, hauls out the Suomi machine pistol* and checks it: clean, loaded, ready for action, just like it was about an hour ago, the last time he checked it. He puts it back in its place, turns around, locks eyes with Julieta for a moment. Then he goes out and pulls the door shut. Behind him, he can hear her naked feet on the cold floor, and the satisfying sound of the door's bolts being rammed home.

He steps into a pair of tall rubber boots and then begins to trudge south along the beach. The boots are Otto's and are a couple of sizes too big for his feet. They make him feel like a little boy, splashing through puddles in Wisconsin. This is what a boy of his age ought to be doing: working, hard and honest, at a simple job. Kissing girls. Walking into town to buy some smokes and maybe have a beer. The idea of flying around on heavily armed warplanes and using modern weapons systems to kill hundreds of foreign homicidal maniacs now strikes him as dated and inappropriate.

He slows down every few hundred yards to look at a steel drum, or other war debris, cast up by the waves, half-buried in sand, stenciled cryptically in Cyrillic or Finnish or German. They remind him of the Nipponese drums on that Guadalcanal beach.

---

*It goes without saying that the Finns have to have their own *sui generis* brand of automatic weapon.

Moon lifts sea, but not
the ones who sleep on the beach
Each wave a shovel

A lot of stuff gets wasted in a war—not just stuff that comes in crates and drums. It frequently happens, for example, that men are called upon to die willingly that others may live. Shaftoe learned on Guadalcanal that you can never tell when circumstances will make you into that guy. You can go into battle with the clearest, simplest, smartest plan ever devised, worked out by Annapolis-trained, battle-hardened Marine officers, and based upon tons of intelligence. But ten seconds after the first trigger has been pulled, shit is happening all over the place, people are running around like maniacs. The battle plan that was genius a minute ago suddenly looks as sweetly naive as the inscriptions in your high school yearbook. Guys are dying. Some of them are dying because a shell happens to fall on them, but surprisingly often, they are dying because they are ordered to.

It was like that with U-691. That whole thing with the Trinidadian steamer was probably a brilliant plan (Waterhouse's, he suspects) at some point. But then it all went wrong, and some Allied commander gave the order that Shaftoe and Root, along with the crew of U-691, were to die.

He should have died on the beach on Guadalcanal, along with his buddies, and he didn't. Everything between then and U-691 was just sort of an extra bonus life. He got a chance to go home and see his family, sort of like Jesus after the Resurrection.

Now Bobby Shaftoe is dead for sure. This is why he walks so slowly down the beach, and takes such a brotherly interest in these items, because Bobby Shaftoe is, too, a corpse washed up on the beach in Sweden.

He is thinking about this when he sees the Heavenly Apparition.

The sky here is like a freshly galvanized bucket that has been inverted over the world to block out inconvenient sunlight; if someone lights up a cigarette half a mile away, it blazes like a nova. By those standards, the Heavenly Apparition looks like a whole galaxy falling out of orbit to graze the surface of the world. You could almost mistake it for an airplane, except that it does not make the requisite chesty, droning thrum. This thing emits a screaming whine—and a long trail of fire. Besides, it goes too fast for an airplane. It comes streaking in from the Gulf of Bothnia and crosses the shoreline a couple of miles north of Otto's cabin, gradually losing altitude and slowing down. But as it slows down, the flames burgeon, and claw their way forward up the thing's black body, which resembles the crumpled, curling wick at the root of a candle flame.

It disappears behind trees. Around here, everything disappears behind trees sooner or later. A ball of fire erupts from those trees, and Bobby Shaftoe says, "One thousand one, one thousand two, one thousand three, one thousand four, one thousand five, one thousand six, one thousand seven" and then stops, hearing the explosion. Then he turns around and walks into Norrsbruck, going faster now.

LAVENDER ROSE

RANDY WANTS TO GO DOWN AND LOOK AT THE U-BOAT IN PERson. Doug says evenly that Randy is welcome to do so, but he needs to draw up a valid dive plan first, and reminds him that the depth of the wreck is one hundred and fifty-four meters. Randy nods as if he had, of course, expected to draw up a dive plan.

He wants everything to be like driving cars, where you just hop in and go. He knows a couple of guys who fly airplanes, and he can still remember how he felt when he learned that you can't just get in a plane (even a small one) and take off—you have to have a flight plan, and it takes a whole briefcase full of books and tables and specialized calculators, and access to weather forecasts above and beyond the normal consumer-grade weather forecasts, to come up with even a *bad, wrong* flight plan that will surely kill you. Once Randy had gotten used to this idea, he grudgingly admitted it made sense.

Now Doug Shaftoe's telling him he needs a plan just to strap some tanks on his back and swim a hundred and fifty-four meters (straight down, admittedly) and back. So Randy yanks a couple of diving books off the bungeed shelves of *Glory IV* and tries to come up with even a vague idea of what Doug's talking about. Randy has never gone scuba diving in his life, but he's seen them doing it on Jacques Cousteau and it seems straightforward enough.

The first three books he consults contain more than enough detail to perfectly reproduce the crestfallenness that Randy experienced when he learned about *flight* plans. Before he'd opened the books Randy had gotten out his mechanical pencil and his graph paper in preparation for making marks on the page; half an hour later he's still trying to get a handle on the contents of the tables, and he hasn't made any marks at all. He notes that the depths in these tables only go down as far as a hundred and thirty, and at that level they only talk in terms of staying down there five or ten minutes. And yet he knows that Amy, and the

Shaftoe's colorful and ever-enlarging cast of polyethnic scuba divers, are spending much longer at this depth, and are in fact beginning to come up to the surface with artifacts from the wreck. There is, for example, an aluminum briefcase wherein Doug hopes to find clues as to who was on this U-boat and why it was on the wrong side of the planet.

Randy begins to fear that the entire wreck is going to be stripped bare before he even makes any marks on his piece of graph paper. The divers show up, one or two each day, on speedboats or outrigger canoes from Palawan. Blond surf boys, taciturn galoots, cigarette-smoking Frenchmen, Nintendo-playing Asians, beer-can-crumpling ex-Navy guys, blue-collar hillbillies. *They* all have diving plans. Why doesn't Randy have a diving plan?

He starts sketching one out based on the depth of one hundred and thirty, which seems reasonably close to one hundred and fifty-four. After working on it for about an hour (long enough to imagine all sorts of specious details) he happens to notice that the table he's been using is in *feet*, not *meters*, which means that all of these divers have been going down to a depth that is way more than three times as deep as the maximum that is even talked about on these tables.

Randy closes up all of the books and looks at them peevishly for a while. They are all nice new books with color photographs on the covers. He picked them off the shelf because (getting introspective here) he is a computer guy, and in the computer world any book printed more than two months ago is a campy nostalgia item. Investigating a little more, he finds that all three of these shiny new books have been personally autographed by the authors, with long personal inscriptions: two addressed to Doug, and one to Amy. The one to Amy has obviously been written by a man who is desperately in love with her. Reading it is like moisturizing with Tabasco.

He concludes that these are all consumer-grade diving books written for rum-drenched tourists, and furthermore that the publishers probably had teams of lawyers go over them one word at a time to make sure there would not be liability trouble. That the contents of these books, therefore, probably represent about one percent of everything that the authors actually know about diving, but that the lawyers have made sure that the authors don't even *mention* that.

Okay, so divers have mastered a large body of occult knowledge. That explains their general resemblance to hackers, albeit physically fit hackers.

Doug Shaftoe is not going down to the wreck himself. As a matter of fact he looked surprised, bordering on contemptuous, when Randy asked him whether he *would* go down. Instead, he's going over the stuff that is brought up from the wreck by the younger divers. They began by doing a photographic survey, using digital cameras, and Doug's been printing out blowups of the inside of the U-boat on his laser printer and pasting them up around the walls of his personal wardroom on *Glory IV*.

Randy does a sorting procedure on the diving books now: he ignores anything that has color photographs, or that appears to have been published within the last twenty years, or that has any quotes on the back cover containing the words *stunning, superb, user-friendly,* or, worst of all, *easy-to-understand*. He looks for old, thick books with worn-out bindings and block-lettered titles like DIVE MANUAL. Anything with angry marginal notes written by Doug Shaftoe gets extra points.

```
To: randy@epiphyte.com
From: root@eruditorum.org
Subject: Pontifex
Randy,
For now, let's use ''Pontifex'' as the working title of
this cryptosystem. It is a post-war system. What I mean by
that is that, after seeing what Turing and company did to
Enigma, I came to the (now obvious) conclusion that any
modern system had better be resistant to machine crypt-
analysis. Pontifex uses a 54-element permutation as its
key—one key per message, mind you!—and it uses that permu-
tation (which we will denote as T) to generate a keystream
which is added, modulo 26, to the plaintext (P), as in a
one-time pad. The process of generating each character in
the keystream alters T in a reversible but more or less
''random'' fashion.
```

At this point, a diver comes up with a piece of actual gold, but it's not a bar: it's a sheet of hammered gold, maybe eight inches on a side and about a quarter of a millimeter thick, with a pattern of tiny neat holes punched through it, like a computer card. Randy spends a couple of days obsessing over this artifact. He learns that it came out of a crate stored in the hold of the U-boat, and that there are thousands more of them.

Now all of a sudden he's reading stuff by guys whose names are preceded by naval ranks and succeeded by M.D.s and Ph.D.s and they are going on for dozens of pages about the physics of nitrogen bubble formation in the knee, for example. There are photographs of cats strapped down in benchtop pressure chambers. Randy learns that the reason Doug Shaftoe doesn't dive to one hundred and fifty-four meters is that certain age-related changes in the joints tend to increase the likelihood of bubble formation during the decompression process. He comes to terms with the fact that the pressure at the depth of the wreck is going to be fifteen or sixteen atmospheres, meaning that as he ascends to the surface, any nitrogen bubbles that happen to be rattling around in his body are going to get fifteen or sixteen times as large as they were to begin with and that this is true whether those bubbles happen to be in his brain, his knee, the little blood vessels of the eyeball, or trapped underneath his fillings. He develops a sophisticated layman's understanding of dive medicine, which amounts to little because everyone's body is different—hence the need for each diver to have a completely different dive plan. Randy will need to figure out his body fat percentage before he can even begin marking up his sheet of graph paper.

It is also path-dependent. These divers' bodies get partly saturated with nitrogen every time they go down, and not all of it goes out of their bodies when they come back up—all of them, sitting around *Glory IV* playing cards, drinking beer, talking to their girlfriends on their GSM phones, are all *outgassing* all the time—nitrogen is seeping out of their bodies into the atmosphere, and each one of them knows more or less how much nitrogen's stuffed into his body at any given moment and understands, in a deep and nearly intuitive way, just exactly how that information propagates through any dive plan that he might be cooking up inside the powerful dive-planning supercomputer that each of these guys apparently carries around in his nitrogen-saturated brain.

One of the divers comes up with a plank from the crate that contained the stacks of gold sheets. It is in very bad shape, and it's still fizzing as gas comes out of it. Fizzing in a way that Randy has no trouble imagining his bones would do if he made any errors in working out his dive plan. There is some stenciled lettering just barely visible on the wood: NIZ-ARCH.

Glory IV has compressors for pumping air up to insanely high pressures to fill the scuba tanks. Randy develops an awareness that the pressure has to be insanely high or it won't even emerge from the tanks while these guys are down at depth. The divers are all being suffused with this pressurized gas; he half expects that one of these divers is going to bump into something and explode into a pink mushroom cloud.

```
To: randy@epiphyte.com
From: cantrell@epiphyte.com
Subject: Pontifex
R—
You forwarded me a message about a cryptosystem called
Pontifex. Was this invented by a friend of yours? In its
general outlines (viz. an n-element permutation that is
```

used to generate a keystream, and that slowly evolves) it
is similar to a commercial system called RC4, which enjoys
a complicated reputation among Secret Admirers—it seems
secure, and has not been broken, but it makes us nervous
because it is basically a single-rotor system, albeit a
rotor that evolves. Pontifex evolves in a much more complicated & asymmetrical way than RC4 and so *might* be more
secure.

Some things about Pontifex are slightly peculiar.

(1) He talks about generating ''characters'' in the keystream and then adding them, modulo 26, to the plaintext.
This is how people talked 50 years ago when ciphers were
worked out using pencil and paper. Today we talk in terms
of generating bytes and adding them modulo 256. Is your
friend pretty old?

(2) He speaks of T as a 54-element permutation. There is
nothing wrong with that—but Pontifex would work just as
well with 64 or 73 or 699 elements, so it makes more sense
to describe it as an n-element permutation where n could
be 54 or any other integer. I can't figure out why he settled on 54. Possibly because it is twice the number of letters in the alphabet—but this makes no particular sense.

Conclusion: the author of Pontifex is cryptologically
sophisticated but shows possible signs of being an elderly crank. I need more details in order to deliver a
verdict.

—Cantrell

"Randy?" says Doug Shaftoe, and beckons him into his wardroom.

The inside of the wardroom door is decorated with a big color photograph of a massive stone staircase in a dusty church. They stand in front of
it. "Are there a *lot* of Waterhouses?" Doug asks. "Is it a common name?"

"Uh, well, it's not a *rare* name."

"Is there anything you'd like to share with me about your family
history?"

Randy knows that as a possible suitor to Amy, he will be undergoing
thorough scrutiny at all times. The Shaftoes are doing due diligence on
him. "What kind of thing are you looking for? Something terrible? I
don't think there's anything worth hiding from you."

Doug stares at him distractedly for a while, then turns to face the now
open aluminum briefcase from the U-boat. Randy supposes that merely
opening it required coming up with a detailed plan. Doug has spread

out miscellaneous contents on a tabletop to be photographed and cata-
loged. Ex-Navy SEAL Douglas MacArthur Shaftoe has, at the peak of
his career, become a sort of librarian.

Randy sees a pair of gold-rimmed spectacles, a fountain pen, a few
rusty paper clips. But it looks as though a lot of sodden paper was taken
out of that briefcase too, and Doug Shaftoe has been carefully drying it
out and trying to read it. "Most wartime paper was crap," he says. "It
probably dissolved into mush within days of the sinking. The paper in
this briefcase was at least protected from marine critters, but most of it's
gone. However, the owner of this briefcase was apparently some sort of
aristocrat. Check out the glasses, the pen."

Randy checks them out. The divers have found teeth and fillings in
the wreck, but nothing that qualifies as a body. The places where people
died are marked by these trails of hard, inert remains, such as eyeglasses.
Like the debris footprint of an exploded airliner.

"So what I'm getting at is that he had a few scraps of good paper in
his briefcase," Doug continues. "Personal stationery. So we suspect his
name was Rudolf von Hacklheber. Does that name ring any bells with
you?"

"No. But I could do a web search . . ."

"I tried that," Doug says. "Turned up just a few hits. There was a
man by that name who wrote a couple of mathematics papers back in
the thirties. And there are some organizations in and around Leipzig,
Germany, that use the name: a hotel, a theater, a defunct reinsurance
company. That's about it."

"Well, if he was a mathematician, he might have had some connection
with my grandfather. Is that why you were asking about my family?"

"Check this out," Doug says, and pings one fingernail against a glass
tray full of a transparent liquid. An envelope, unglued and spreadeagled,
is floating in it. Randy bends over and peers at it. Something has been
written on the back in pencil, but it's impossible to read because the
flaps of the envelope have been spread apart. "May I?" he asks. Doug
nods and hands him a couple of latex surgical gloves. "I don't have to
file a diving plan for this, do I?" Randy asks, wiggling his fingers into
the gloves.

Doug is not amused. "It is deeper than it looks," he says.

Randy flips the envelope over, then folds the flapss back together,
reassembling the inscription. It says:

WATERHOUSE
LAVENDER ROSE.

BRISBANE

THROUGH A SMALL DUSTY WINDOW XED WITH MASKING TAPE, Lawrence Pritchard Waterhouse gazes out at downtown Brisbane. Bustling it ain't. A taxi limps down the street and pulls into the drive of the nearby Canberra Hotel, which is home to many mid-ranking officers. The taxi smokes and reeks—it is powered by a charcoal burner in the trunk. Marching feet can be heard through the window. It's not the tromp, tromp of combat boots, but the whack, whack of sensible shoes worn by sensible women: local volunteers. Waterhouse instinctively leans closer to the window to get a look at them, but he's wasting his time. You could march a regiment of pinup girls dressed in those uniforms through all the cabins and gangways of an active battleship and not draw a single wolf whistle, lewd suggestion, or butt-grab.

A delivery truck creeps out of a side street and backfires alarmingly as it tries to accelerate onto the main drag. Brisbane is still worried about attack from the air, and no one likes sudden loud noises. The truck looks like it is being attacked by an amoeba: on its back is a billowing rubberized-canvas balloon full of natural gas.

He's on the third floor of a commercial building so nondescript that the most interesting observation one can make about it is that it has four stories. There is a tobacconist on the ground floor. The rest of the place must have been empty until The General—beaten like a red-headed stepchild by those Nips—came to Brisbane from Corregidor, and made this city into the capital of the Southwest Pacific Theater. There must have been an incredible amount of surplus office space around here before The General showed up, because a lot of Brisbaners had fled south, expecting an invasion.

Waterhouse has had plenty of time to familiarize himself with Brisbane and its environs. He's been here for four weeks, and he's been given nothing to do. When he was in Britain, they couldn't shuffle him around fast enough. Whatever his job was at the moment, he did it feverishly—until he received top-secret, highest-priority orders to rush, by any available means of transportation, to his next assignment.

Then they brought him here. The Navy flew him across the Pacific, hopping from one island base to the next in an assortment of flying boats and transports. He crossed the equator and the international date line on the same day. But when he reached the boundary between Nimitz's Pacific Theater and The General's Southwest Pacific Theater, it was like he'd glided into a stone wall. It was all he could do to talk himself onboard a troop transport to New Zealand, and then to Fremantle. The transports were almost unbelievably hellish: steel ovens packed with men, baked by the sun, no one allowed to go abovedecks for fear they'd be sighted, and marked for slaughter, by a Nip submarine. Even at night they couldn't get a breeze through there, because all openings had to be covered with blackout curtains. Waterhouse couldn't really complain; some of the men had traveled this way all the way from the East Coast of the United States.

The important thing was that he made it to Brisbane, as per his orders, and reported to the right officer, who told him to await further orders. Which he's been doing until this morning, when he was told to show up at this office upstairs of the tobacconist. It is a room full of enlisted men typing up forms, trundling them around in wire baskets, and filing them. In Waterhouse's experience with the military, he has found that it's not a good sign when one is ordered to report to a place like this.

Finally he is allowed into the presence of an Army major who has several other conversations, and various pieces of important paperwork, going on at the same time. That is okay; Waterhouse doesn't need to be a cryptanalyst to get the message loud and clear, which is that he is not wanted here.

"Marshall sent you here because he thinks that The General is sloppy with Ultra," the major says.

Waterhouse flinches to hear this word spoken aloud, in an office where enlisted men and women volunteers are coming and going. It's almost as if the major wishes to make it clear that The General is, in fact, quite sloppy with Ultra, and rather likes it that way, thank you very much.

"Marshall's afraid that the Nips will get wise to us and change their codes. It's all because of Churchill." The major refers to General George C. Marshall and Sir Winston Churchill as if they were bullpen staff for a farm league baseball team. He pauses to light a cigarette. "Ultra is Churchill's baby. Oh yeah, Winnie just luuuuuves his Ultra. He thinks we're going to blow his secret and ruin it for him because he thinks we're idiots." The major takes a very deep lungful of smoke, sits back in his chair, and carefully puffs out a couple of smoke rings. It is a convincing display of insouciance. "So he's always nagging Marshall to tighten up security, and Marshall throws him a bone every so often, just to keep the Alliance on an even keel." For the first time, the major looks Waterhouse in the eye. "You happen to be the latest bone. That's all."

There is a long silence, as if Waterhouse is expected to say something.

He clears his throat. No one ever got court-martialed for following his orders. "My orders state that—"

"Fuck your orders, Captain Waterhouse," the major says.

There is a long silence. The major tends to one or two other distracting duties. Then he stares out the window for a few moments, trying to compose his thoughts. Finally he says, "Get this through your head. We are not idiots. The General is not an idiot. The General appreciates Ultra as much as Sir Winston Churchill. The General uses Ultra as well as any commander in this war."

"Ultra's no good if the Japanese learn about it."

"As you can appreciate, the General does not have time to meet with you personally. Neither does his staff. So you will not have an opportunity to instruct him on how to keep Ultra a secret," says the major. He glances down a couple of times at a sheet of paper on his blotter, and indeed he is now speaking like a man who is reading a prepared statement. "From time to time, since we learned that you were being sent to us, your existence has been brought to the General's attention. During the brief periods of time when he is not occupied with more pressing matters, he has occasionally voiced some pithy thoughts about you, your mission, and the masterminds who sent you here."

"No doubt," Waterhouse says.

"The general is of the opinion that persons not familiar with the unique features of the Southwest Pacific Theater may not be entirely competent to judge his strategy," says the major. "The General feels that the Nips will never learn about Ultra. Never. Why? Because they are incapable of comprehending what has happened to them. The General has speculated that he could go down to the radio station tomorrow and broadcast a speech announcing that we had broken all of the Nip codes and were reading all of their messages, and nothing would happen. The General's words were something to the effect that the Nips will never believe how totally we have fucked them, because when you get fucked that badly, it's your own goddamn fucking fault and it makes you look like a fucking shithead."

"I see," Waterhouse says.

"But The General said all of that at much greater length and without using a single word of profanity, because that is how The General expresses himself."

"Thank you for boiling it down," Waterhouse says.

"You know those white headbands that the Nips tie around their foreheads? With the meatball and the Nip characters printed on them?"

"I've seen pictures of them."

"I've seen them for real, tied around the heads of pilots of Nip fighter planes that were about fifty feet away firing machine guns at me and my men," says the major.

"Oh, yeah! Me too. At Pearl Harbor," Waterhouse says. "I forgot."

This appears to be the most irritating thing that Waterhouse has said all day. The major has to spend a moment composing himself. "That headband is called a *hachimaki*."

"Oh."

"Imagine this, Waterhouse. The emperor is meeting with his general staff. All of the top generals and admirals in Nippon parade into the room in full dress uniforms and bow down solemnly before the emperor. They have come to report on the progress of the war. Each of these generals and admirals is wearing a brand-new *hachimaki* around his forehead. These *hachimakis* are printed with phrases saying things like, 'I am a dipshit' and 'Through my personal incompetence I killed two hundred thousand of our own men' and 'I handed our Midway plans over to Nimitz on a silver platter.'"

The major now pauses and takes a phone call so that Waterhouse can savor this image for a while. Then he hangs up, lights another cigarette, and continues. "That's what it would look like for the Nips to admit at this point in the war that we have Ultra."

More smoke rings. Waterhouse has nothing to say. So the major continues. "See, we've gone over the watershed line of this war. We won Midway. We won North Africa. Stalingrad. The Battle of the Atlantic. Everything changes when you go over the watershed line. The rivers all flow a different direction. It's as if the force of gravity itself has changed and is now working in our favor. We've adjusted to that. Marshall and Churchill and all those others are still stuck in an obsolete mentality. They are defenders. But The General is not a defender. As a matter of fact, just between you and me, The General is lousy on defense, as he demonstrated in the Philippines. The General is a conqueror."

"Well," Waterhouse finally says, "what do you suggest I do with myself, seeing as how I'm here in Brisbane?"

"I'm tempted to say you should connect up with all of the other Ultra security experts Marshall sent out before you, and get a bridge group together," the major says.

"I don't care for bridge," Waterhouse says politely.

"You're supposed to be some expert codebreaker, right?"

"Right."

"Why don't you go to Central Bureau. The Nips have a zillion different codes and we haven't broken all of them yet."

"That's not my mission."

"You don't worry about your fucking mission," the major says. "I'll make sure that Marshall thinks you're doing your mission, because if Marshall doesn't think that, he'll give us no end of hassles. So you're clean with the higher-ups."

"Thank you."

"You can consider your mission accomplished," the major says. "Congratulations."

"Thank you."

"My mission is to beat the stuffing out of the fucking Nips, and that mission is *not* accomplished just yet, and so I have other matters to attend to," the major says significantly.

"Shall I just see myself out then?" Waterhouse asks.

DÖNITZ

ONCE, WHEN BOBBY SHAFTOE WAS EIGHT YEARS OLD, HE WENT to Tennessee to visit Grandma and Grandpa. One boring afternoon he began skimming a letter that the old lady had left lying on an end table. Grandma gave him a stern talking to and then recounted the incident to Grandpa, who recognized his cue and gave him forty whacks. That and a whole series of roughly parallel childhood experiences, plus several years in the Marine Corps, have made him into one polite fellow.

So he doesn't read others' mail. It be against the rules.

But here he is. The setting: a plank-paneled room above a pub in Norrsbruck, Sweden. The pub is a sailorly kind of place, catering to fishermen, which makes it congenial for Shaftoe's friend and drinking buddy: Kapitänleutnant Günter Bischoff, Kriegsmarine of the Third Reich (retired).

Bischoff gets a lot of interesting mail, and leaves it strewn all over the room. Some of the mail is from his family in Germany, and contains money. Consequently Bischoff, unlike Shaftoe, will not have to work even if this war continues, and he remains in Sweden cooling his boilers, for another ten years.

Some of the mail is from the crew of U-691, according to Bischoff. After Bischoff got them all here to Norrsbruck in one piece, his second-in-command, Oberleutnant-zur-See Karl Beck, cut a deal with the Kriegsmarine in which the crew were allowed to return to Germany, no hard feelings, no repercussions. All of them except for Bischoff climbed on board what was left of U-691 and steamed off in the direction of

Kiel. Only days later, the mail began to pour in. Every member of the crew, to a man, sent Bischoff a letter describing the heroes' welcome they had received: Dönitz himself met them at the pier and handed out hugs and kisses and medals and other tokens in embarrassing profusion. They can't stop talking about how much they want dear Günter to come back home.

Dear Günter isn't budging; he's been sitting in his little room for a couple of months now. His world consists of pen, ink, paper, candles, cups of coffee, bottles of aquavit, the soothing beat of the surf. Every crash of wave on shore, he says, reminds him that he is above sea level now, where men were meant to live. His mind is always back *there* a hundred feet below the surface of the gelid Atlantic, trapped like a rat in a sewer pipe, cringing from the explosions of the depths charges. He lived a hundred years that way, and spent every moment of those hundred years dreaming of the Surface. He vowed, ten thousand times, that if he ever made it back up to the world of air and light, he would enjoy every breath, revel in every moment.

That's pretty much what he's been doing, here in Norrsbruck. He has his personal journal, and he's been going through it, page by page, filling in all of the details that he didn't have time to jot down, before he forgets them. Someday, after the war, it'll make a book: one of a million war memoirs that will clog libraries from Novosibirsk to Gander to Sequim to Batavia.

The pace of incoming mail dropped dramatically after the first weeks. Several of his men still write to him faithfully. Shaftoe is used to seeing their letters scattered around the place when he comes to visit. Most of them are written on scraps of cheap, greyish paper.

Directionless silver light infiltrates the room through Bischoff's window, illuminating what looks like a rectangular pool of heavy cream on his tabletop. It is some kind of official Hun stationery, surmounted by a raptor clenching a swastika. The letter is handwritten, not typed. When Bischoff sets his wet glass down on it, the ink dissolves.

And when Bischoff goes to empty his bladder, Shaftoe can't keep his eyes away from it. He knows that this is bad manners, but the Second World War has led him into all sorts of uncouth behavior, and there don't seem to be any angry grandpas lurking in the trenches with doubled belts; no consequences at all for the wicked, in fact. Maybe that will change in a couple of years, if the Germans and the Nips lose the war. But that reckoning will be so great and terrible that Shaftoe's glance at Bischoff's letter will probably go unnoticed.

It came in an envelope. The first line of the address is very long, and consists of "Günter BISCHOFF" preceded by a string of ranks and titles, and followed by a series of letters. The return address has been savaged by Bischoff's letter opener, but it's somewhere in Berlin.

The letter itself is an impossible snarl of Germanic cursive. It is signed, hugely, with a single word. Shaftoe spends some time trying to make out that word; he whose John Huncock this is. Must have an ego that ranks right up there with the General's.

When Shaftoe figures out the signature belongs to Dönitz, he gets all tingly. That Dönitz is an important guy—Shaftoe's even seen him on a newsreel, congratulating a grimy U-boat crew, fresh from a salty spree.

Why's he writing love notes to Bischoff? Shaftoe can't read this stuff any better than he could Nipponese. But he can see a few figures. Dönitz is talking numbers. Perhaps tons of shipping sunk, or casualties on the Eastern Front. Perhaps money.

"Oh, yes!" Bischoff says, having somehow reappeared in the room without making any noise. When you're down in a U-boat, running silent, you learn how to walk quietly. "I have come up with a hypothesis on the gold."

"What gold?" Shaftoe says. He knows, of course, but having been caught in an act of flagrant naughtiness, his instinct is to play innocent.

"That you saw down in the batteries of U-553," Bischoff says. "You see, my friend, anyone else would say that you are simply a crazy jughead."

"The correct term is Jarhead."

"They would say, first of all, that U-553 sank many months before you claim to have seen it. Secondly, they would say that such a boat could not have been loaded with gold. But I believe that you saw it."

"So?"

Bischoff glances at the letter from Dönitz, looking mildly seasick. "I must tell you something about the Wehrmacht of which I am ashamed, first."

"What? That they invaded Poland and France?"

"No."

"That they invaded Russia and Norway?"

"No, not that."

"That they bombed England and . . ."

"No, no, no," Bischoff says, the very model of forbearance. "Something you did not know about."

"What?"

"It seems that, while I have been sneaking around the Atlantic, doing my duty—the Führer has come up with a little incentive program."

"What do you mean?"

"It seems that duty and loyalty are not enough for certain high-ranking officers. That they will not carry out their orders to the fullest unless they receive . . . special awards."

"You mean, like medals?"

Bischoff is smiling nervously. "Some generals on the Eastern Front have been given estates in Russia. Very, very large estates."

"Oh."

"But not everyone can be bribed with land. Some people require a more liquid form of compensation."

"Booze?"

"No, I mean liquid in the financial sense. Something you can carry with you, and that is accepted in any whorehouse on the planet."

"Gold," says Shaftoe, quietly.

"Gold would suffice," Bischoff says. It has been a long time since he looked Shaftoe in the eye. He's staring out the window instead. His green eyes might be a little moist. He takes a deep breath, blinks, and gets the bitter irony under control before continuing: "Since Stalingrad, it has not gone well on the Eastern Front. Let us say that Ukrainian real estate is no longer worth what it used to be, if the deed to the land happens to be written in German and issued in Berlin."

"It's getting harder to bribe a general by promising him a chunk of Russian land," Shaftoe translates. "So Hitler needs lots of gold."

"Yes. Now, the Japanese have lots of gold—consider that they sacked China. As well as many other places. But they are lacking in certain things. They need wolframite. Mercury. Uranium."

"What's uranium?"

"Who the hell knows? The Japanese want it, we provide it. We provide them technology too—blueprints for new turbines. Enigma machines." At this point Bischoff breaks off and laughs, painfully and darkly, for a long time. When he gets it under control, he continues: "So we have been shipping them these things, in U-boats."

"And the Nips pay you in gold."

"Yes. It is a dark economy, hidden beneath the ocean, trading small but valuable items over vast distances. You got a glimpse of it."

"You knew this was going on but you didn't know about U-553," Shaftoe points out.

"Ah, Bobby, there are many, many things going on in the Third Reich that a mere U-boat captain does not know about. You are a soldier, you know this is true."

"Yes," Shaftoe says, recalling the peculiarities of Detachment 2702. He looks down at the letter. "Why is Dönitz telling you all of this now?"

"He is not telling me anything," Bischoff says reprovingly. "I have figured this out myself." He gnaws on a lip for a while. "Dönitz is making me a proposition."

"I thought you'd retired."

Bischoff considers it. "I have retired from killing people. But the other day I sailed a little sloop around the inlet."

"So?"

"So it seems that I have not retired from going down to the sea in ships." Bischoff heaves a sigh. "Unfortunately, all of the really interesting ships are owned by major governments."

Bischoff is getting a little spooky, so Shaftoe opts for a little change in the subject. "Hey, speaking of really interesting things . . ." and he tells the story of the Heavenly Apparition that he saw while he was walking down here.

Bischoff is delighted by the story, which revives the hunger for excitement that he has kept pickled in salt and alcohol ever since reaching Norrsbruck. "You are sure it was manmade?" he asks.

"It whined. Chunks of shit were falling out of it. But I've never seen a meteor so I don't know."

"How far away?"

"It crashed seven kilometers from where I was standing. So, ten clicks from here."

"But ten kilometers is nothing for an Eagle Scout and a Hitler Youth!"

"You weren't a Hitler youth."

Bischoff broods over this for a moment. "Hitler—so embarrassing. I hoped that if I ignored him he would go away. Perhaps if I had joined the Hitler Youth, they would have given me a surface ship."

"Then you'd be dead."

"Right!" Bischoff's mood brightens considerably. "Ten kilometers is still nothing. Let's go!"

"It's already dark."

"We will follow the flames."

"They will have gone out."

"We will follow the trail of debris, like Hansel and Gretel."

"It didn't work for Hansel and Gretel. Didn't you even read the fucking story?"

"Don't be such a defeatist, Bobby," says Bischoff, diving into a hearty fisherman's sweater. "Normally you are not like this. What is troubling you?"

Glory.

It is October and the days are growing short. Shaftoe and Bischoff, both mired in the yet-to-be-discovered emotional dumps of Seasonal

Affective Disorder, are like two brothers trapped in the same pit of quicksand, each keeping a sharp eye on the other.

"Eh? *Was ist los,* buddy?"

"Guess I'm just feeling at loose ends."

"You need an adventure. Let's go!"

"I need an adventure like Hitler needs an ugly little toothbrush mustache," says Bobby Shaftoe. But he drags himself up out of his chair and follows Bischoff out the door.

Shaftoe and Bischoff are trudging through the dark Swedish woods like a pair of lost souls trying to find the side entrance to Limbo. They take turns carrying the kerosene lantern, which has an effective range about as long as a grown man's arm. Sometimes they go for a whole hour without talking, each man alone with his own struggle against suicidal depression. Then one of them (usually Bischoff) will perk up and say something, like:

"Haven't seen Enoch Root recently. What has he been up to since he finished curing you of your morphine addiction?" Bischoff asks.

"Don't know. He was such a fucking pain in the ass during that project that I never wanted to see him again. But I think he got a Russian radio transmitter from Otto and took it into that church basement where he lives; he's been messing around with it ever since."

"Yes. I remember. He was changing the frequencies. Did he ever get it to work?"

"Beats me," Shaftoe says, "but when big pieces of burning shit start falling out of the sky in my neighborhood, makes me wonder."

"Yes. Also he goes to the post office quite frequently," Bischoff says. "I chatted with him there once. He is carrying on a heavy correspondence with others around the world."

"Other *what?*"

"That is my question, too."

Eventually they find the wreck only by following the sound of a hacksaw, which reverberates through the pines like the shriek of some extraordinarily stupid and horny bird. This enables them to home in on it in a general way. Final coordinates are provided by a sudden, strobelike flashing light, devastating noise, and a sap-scented rain of amputated foliage. Shaftoe and Bischoff both hit the dirt and lie there listening to fat pistol slugs ricocheting from tree trunk to tree trunk. The hacksawing noise continues with no break in rhythm.

Bischoff starts talking Swedish, but Shaftoe shushes him. "That was a Suomi," he says. "Hey, Julieta! Knock it off! It's just me and Günter."

There is no answer. Then, Shaftoe remembers that he has recently fucked Julieta, and therefore needs to remember his manners. "Excuse me, ma'am," he says, "but I gather from the sound of your weapon that you are of the Finnish nation, for which I have unbounded admiration, and I wanted to let you know that I, former Sergeant Robert Shaftoe, and my friend, former Kapitänleutnant Günter Bischoff, mean you no harm."

Julieta, homing in on the sound of his voice in the darkness, responds with a controlled burst of fire that passes about a foot over Bobby Shaftoe's head. "Don't you belong in Manila?" she asks.

Shaftoe groans, and rolls over on his back as if he has been shot in the gut.

"What does she mean by this?" asks the bewildered Günter Bischoff. Seeing that his friend has been (emotionally) incapacitated, he tries: "This is Sweden, a peaceful and neutral country! Why are you trying to machine-gun us?"

"Go away!" Julieta must be with Otto, because they hear her talk to him before saying, "We do not want representatives of the American Marines and the Wehrmacht here. You are not welcome."

"Sounds like you are sawing away on something that is pretty damn heavy," Shaftoe finally retorts. "How you gonna haul it out of these woods?"

This leads to an animated conversation between Julieta and Otto. "You may approach," Julieta finally says.

They find the Kivistiks, Julieta and Otto, standing in a pool of lantern-light around the severed, charred wing of an airplane. Most Finns are hard to tell apart from Swedes, but Otto and Julieta both have black hair and black eyes, and could pass for Turks. The tip of the airplane wing is painted with the black-and-white cross of the Luftwaffe. An engine is mounted to that wing. If Otto's hacksaw has its way, it won't be for much longer. The engine has recently been set on fire and then used to knock down a large number of pine trees. But even so Shaftoe can see it's like no engine he has ever seen before. There is no propeller, but there are a lot of little fan blades.

"It looks like a turbine," says Bischoff, "but for air, rather than water."

Otto straightens up, squeezes his lower back theatrically, and hands Shaftoe the hacksaw. Then he hands him a bottle of benzedrine tablets for good measure. Shaftoe eats a few tablets, strips off his shirt to reveal splendid musculature, does a couple of USMC-approved stretching exercises, grabs the hacksaw, and sets to work. After a couple of minutes he looks up nonchalantly at Julieta, who is standing there holding the machine pistol and watching him with a look that is simultaneously frosty and smoldering, like baked Alaska. Bischoff stands off to the side, reveling in this.

Dawn is slapping her chapped and reddened fingers against a frostbitten sky, attempting to restore some circulation, when the remains of the turbine finally fall away from the wing. Pumped on benzedrine, Shaftoe has been operating the hacksaw for six hours; Otto has stepped in to change blades several times, a major capital investment on his part. Next, they devote half of the morning to dragging the engine through the woods and down a creek bed to the sea, where Otto's boat is waiting, and Otto and Julieta take their prize away. Bobby Shaftoe and Günter Bischoff trudge back up to the site of the wreck. They have not discussed this openly yet—it would be unnecessary—but they intend to find the part of the airplane that contains the body of the pilot, and see to it that he gets a proper burial.

"What is in Manila, Bobby?" Bischoff asks.

"Something that morphine made me forget," Shaftoe answers, "and that Enoch Root, that fucking bastard, made me remember."

Not fifteen minutes later they come to the gash in the woods that was carved by the plunging airplane, and hear a man's voice wailing and sobbing, completely out of his mind with grief. *"Angelo! Angelo! Angelo! Mein liebchen!"*

They cannot see the man who is crying out in this way, but they do see Enoch Root, standing there and brooding. He looks up alertly as they approach, and produces a semiautomatic from his leather jacket. Then he recognizes them, and relaxes.

"What the fuck is going on here?" Shaftoe says—never one to beat around in the bush. "Is that a fucking German you're with?"

"Yes, I am with a German," Root says, "as are you."

"Well, why is your German making such a fucking spectacle of himself?"

"Rudy is crying over the body of his lover," Root says, "who died in an attempt to reunite with him."

"A woman was flying that plane?" says the flabbergasted Shaftoe.

Root rolls his eyes and heaves a sigh. "You have forgotten to allow for the possibility that Rudy might be a homosexual."

It takes Shaftoe a long time to stretch his mind around this large, inconveniently shaped concept. Bischoff, in typical European fashion, seems completely unruffled. But he still has questions to ask. "Enoch, why are you . . . here?"

"Why has my spirit been incarnated into a physical body in this world *generally?* Or *specifically,* why am I here in a Swedish forest, standing on the wreck of a mysterious German rocket plane while a homosexual German sobs over the cremated remains of his Italian lover?

"Last rites," Root answers his own question. "Angelo was Catholic." Then, after a while, he notices that Bischoff is staring at him, looking completely unsatisfied. "Oh. I am here, in a larger sense, because Mrs. Tenney, the vicar's wife, has become sloppy, and forgotten to close her eyes when she takes the balls out of the bingo machine."

CRUNCH

THE CONDEMNED MAN SHOWERS, SHAVES, PUTS ON MOST OF A suit, and realizes that he is ahead of schedule. He turns on the television, gets a San Miguel out of the fridge to steady his nerves, and then goes to the closet to get the stuff of his last meal. The apartment only has one closet and when its door is open it appears to have been bricked shut, Cask of Amontillado-style, with very large flat red oblongs, each imprinted with the image of a venerable and yet oddly cheerful and yet somehow kind of hauntingly sad naval officer. The whole pallet load was shipped here several weeks ago by Avi, in an attempt to lift Randy's spirits. For all Randy knows more are still sitting on a Manila dockside ringed with armed guards and dictionary-sized rat traps straining against their triggers, each baited with a single golden nugget.

Randy selects one of the bricks from this wall, creating a gap in the formation, but there is another, identical one right behind it, another picture of that same naval officer. They seem to be marching from his closet in a peppy phalanx. "Part of this complete balanced breakfast," Randy says. Then he slams the door on them and walks with a measured, forcibly calm step to the living room where he does most of his dining, usually while facing his thirty-six-inch television. He sets up his San Miguel, an empty bowl, an exceptionally large soup spoon—so large that most European cultures would identify it as a serving spoon and most Asian ones as a horticultural implement. He obtains a stack of paper napkins, not the brown recycled ones that can't be moistened even by immersion in water, but the flagrantly environmentally unsound type, brilliant white and cotton-fluffy and desperately hygroscopic. He goes to the kitchen, opens the fridge, reaches deep into the back, and finds an unopened box-bag-pod-unit of UHT milk. UHT milk need not, techni-cally, be refrigerated, but it is pivotal, in what is to follow, that the milk be only a few microdegrees above the point of freezing. The fridge in Randy's apartment has louvers in the back where the cold air is blown in, straight from the freon coils. Randy always stores his milk-pods directly in front of those louvers. Not too close, or else the pods will block the flow of air, and not too far away either. The cold air becomes visible as it rushes in and condenses moisture, so it is a simple matter to sit there with the fridge door open and observe its flow characteristics, like an engineer testing an experimental minivan in a River Rouge wind tunnel. What Randy would like to see, ideally, is the whole milk-pod enveloped in an even, jacketlike flow to produce better heat exchange through the multilayered plastic-and-foil skin of the milk-pod. He would like the milk to be so cold that when he reaches in and grabs it, he feels the flexible, squishy pod stiffen between his fingers as ice crystals spring into existence, summoned out of nowhere simply by the disturbance of being squished.

Today the milk is almost, but not quite, that cold. Randy goes into his living room with it. He has to wrap it in a towel because it is so cold it hurts his fingers. He launches a videotape and then sits down. All is in readiness.

This is one of a series of videotapes that are shot in an empty basketball gym with a polished maple floor and a howling, remorseless ventilation system. They depict a young man and a young woman, both attractive, svelte, and dressed something like marquee players in the Ice Capades, performing simple ballroom dance steps to the accompaniment of strangled music from a ghetto blaster set up on the free-throw line. It is miserably clear that the video has been shot by a third conspirator who is burdened with a consumer-grade camcorder and reeling from some kind of inner-ear disease that he or she would like to share with others. The dancers stomp through the most simple steps with autistic determination. The camera operator begins in each case with a two-shot, then, like a desperado tormenting a milksop, aims his weapon at their feet and makes them dance, dance, dance. At one point the pager hooked to the man's elastic waistband goes off and a scene has to be cut short. No wonder: he is one of the most sought-after ballroom dance instructors in Manila. His partner would be too, if more men in this city were interested in learning to dance. As it is, she must scrape by earning maybe a tenth of what the male instructor pulls down, giving lessons to a small number of addled or henpecked stumblebums like Randy Waterhouse.

Randy takes the red box and holds it securely between his knees with the handy stay-closed tab pointing away from him. Using both hands in unison he carefully works his fingertips underneath the flap, trying to achieve equal pressure on each side, paying special attention to places where too much glue was laid down by the gluing-machine. For a few long, tense moments, nothing at all happens, and an ignorant or impatient observer might suppose that Randy is getting nowhere. But then the entire flap pops open in an instant as the entire glue-front gives way. Randy hates it when the box-top gets bent or, worst of all possible words, torn. The lower flap is merely tacked down with a couple of small glue-spots and Randy pulls it back to reveal a translucent, inflated sac. The halogen down-light recessed in the ceiling shines through the cloudy material of the sac to reveal gold—everywhere the glint of gold. Randy rotates the box ninety degrees and holds it between his knees so its long axis is pointed at the television set, then grips the top of the sac and carefully parts its heat-sealed seam, which purrs as it gives way. Removal of the somewhat milky plastic barrier causes the individual nuggets of Cap'n Crunch to resolve, under the halogen light, with a kind of preternatural crispness and definition that makes the roof of Randy's mouth glow and throb in trepidation.

On the TV, the dancing instructors have finished demonstrating the basic steps. It is almost painful to watch them doing the compulsories, because when they do, they must willfully forget everything they know about advanced ballroom dancing, and dance like persons who have suffered strokes, or major brain injuries, that have wiped out not only the parts of their brain responsible for fine motor skills but also blown every panel in the aesthetic-discretion module. They must, in other words, dance the way their beginning pupils like Randy dance.

The gold nuggets of Cap'n Crunch pelt the bottom of the bowl with a sound like glass rods being snapped in half. Tiny fragments spall away from their corners and ricochet around on the white porcelain surface. World-class cereal-eating is a dance of fine compromises. The giant heaping bowl of sodden cereal, awash in milk, is the mark of the novice. Ideally one wants the bone-dry cereal nuggets and the cryogenic milk to enter the mouth with minimal contact and for the entire reaction between them to take place in the mouth. Randy has worked out a set of mental blueprints for a special cereal-eating spoon that will have a tube running down the handle and a little pump for the milk, so that you can spoon dry cereal up out of a bowl, hit a button with your thumb, and squirt milk into the bowl of the spoon even as you are introducing it into your mouth. The next best thing is to work in small increments, putting only a small amount of Cap'n Crunch in your bowl at a time and eating it all up before it becomes a pit of loathsome slime, which, in the case of Cap'n Crunch, takes about thirty seconds.

At this point in the videotape he always wonders if he's inadvertently set his beer down on the fast-forward button, or something, because the dancers go straight from their vicious Randy parody into something that obviously qualifies as advanced dancing. Randy knows that the steps they are doing are nominally the same as the basic steps demonstrated earlier, but he's damned if he can tell which is which, once they go into their creative mode. There is no recognizable transition, and that is what pisses Randy off, and has always pissed him off, about dancing lessons. Any moron can learn to trudge through the basic steps. That takes all of half an hour. But when that half-hour is over, dancing instructors always expect you take flight and go through one of those miraculous time-lapse transitions that happen only in Broadway musicals and begin dancing brilliantly. Randy supposes that people who are lousy at math feel the same way: the instructor writes a few simple equations on the board, and ten minutes later he's deriving the speed of light in a vacuum.

He pours the milk with one hand while jamming the spoon in with the other, not wanting to waste a single moment of the magical, golden time when cold milk and Cap'n Crunch are together but have not yet begun to pollute each other's essential natures: two Platonic ideals separated by a boundary a molecule wide. Where the flume of milk splashes over the spoon-handle, the polished stainless steel fogs with condensation. Randy of course uses whole milk, because otherwise why bother? Anything less is indistinguishable from water, and besides he thinks that the fat in whole milk acts as some kind of a buffer that retards the dissolution-into-slime process. The giant spoon goes into his mouth before the milk in the bowl has even had time to seek its own level. A few drips come off the bottom and are caught by his freshly washed goatee (still trying to find the right balance between beardedness and vulnerability, Randy has allowed one of these to grow). Randy sets the milk-pod down, grabs a fluffy napkin, lifts it to his chin, and uses a pinching motion to sort of lift the drops of milk from his whiskers rather than smashing and smearing them down into the beard. Meanwhile all his concentration is fixed on the interior of his mouth, which naturally he cannot see, but which he can imagine in three dimensions as if zooming through it in a virtual reality display. Here is where a novice would lose his cool and simply chomp down. A few of the nuggets would explode between his molars, but then his jaw would snap shut and drive all of the unshattered nuggets straight up into his palate where their armor of razor-sharp dextrose crystals would inflict massive collateral damage, turning the rest of the meal into a sort of pain-hazed death march and rendering him Novocain-mute for three days. But Randy has, over time, worked out a really fiendish Cap'n Crunch eating strategy that revolves around playing the nuggets' most deadly features against each other. The nuggets themselves are pillow-shaped and vaguely striated to echo piratical treasure chests.

Now, with a flake-type of cereal, Randy's strategy would never work. But then, Cap'n Crunch in a flake form would be suicidal madness; it would last about as long, when immersed in milk, as snowflakes sifting down into a deep fryer. No, the cereal engineers at General Mills had to find a shape that would minimize surface area, and, as some sort of compromise between the sphere that is dictated by Euclidean geometry and whatever sunken-treasure-related shapes that the cereal-aestheticians were probably clamoring for, they came up with this hard-to-pin-down striated pillow formation. The important thing, for Randy's purposes, is that the individual pieces of Cap'n Crunch are, to a very rough approximation, shaped kind of like molars. The strategy, then, is to make the Cap'n Crunch chew itself by grinding the nuggets together in the center of the oral cavity, like stones in a lapidary tumbler. Like advanced ballroom dancing, verbal explanations (or for that matter watching videotapes) only goes so far and then your body just has to learn the moves.

By the time he has eaten a satisfactory amount of Cap'n Crunch (about a third of a 25-ounce box) and reached the bottom of his beer bottle, Randy has convinced himself that this whole dance thing is a practical joke. When he reaches the hotel, Amy and Doug Shaftoe will be waiting for him with mischievous smiles. They will tell him they were just teasing and then take him into the bar to talk him down.

Randy puts on the last few bits of his suit. Any delaying tactics are acceptable at this point, so he checks his e-mail.

To: randy@epiphyte.com
From: root@eruditorum.org
Subject: The Pontifex Transform, as requested
Randy,
You are right, of course—as the Germans learned the hard way, no new cryptosystem can be trusted until it has been published, so that people like your Secret Admirer friends can have a go at breaking it. I would be in your debt if you would do this with Pontifex.

The transform at the heart of Pontifex has various asymmetries and special cases that make it difficult to express in a few clean, elegant lines of math. It almost has to be written down as pseudo-code. But why settle for pseudo when you can have the real thing? What follows is Pontifex written as a Perl script. The variable $D contains the 54-element permutation. The subroutine e generates the next keystream value whilst evolving $D.

```
#!/usr/bin/perl -s
$f=$d?-1:1;$D=pack('C*',33..86);$p=shift;
$p=~y/a-z/A-Z/;$U='$D=~s/(.*)U$/U$1/;
$D=~s/U(.)/$1U/;';($V=$U)=~s/U/V/g;
$p=~s/[A-Z]/$k=ord($&)-64,&e/eg;$k=0;
while(<>){y/a-z/A-Z/;y/A-Z//dc;$o.=$_}$o.='X'
while length ($o)%5&&!$d;
$o=~s/./chr(($f*&e+ord($&)-13)%26+65)/eg;
$o=~s/X*$// if $d;$o=~s/.{5}/$& /g;
print"$o\n";sub v{$v=ord(substr($D,$_[0]))-32;
$v>53?53:$v}
sub w{$D=~s/(.{$_[0]})(.*)(.)/$2$1$3/}
sub e{eval"$U$V$V";$D=~s/(.*)([UV].*[UV])(.*)/$3$2$1/;
&w(&v(53));$k?(&w($k)):($c=&v(&v(0)),$c>52?&e:$c)}
```

There is also one message from his palimony lawyer in California, which he prints and puts into his breast pocket to savor while he is stuck in traffic. He takes the elevator downstairs and catches a taxi to the Manila Hotel. This (riding in a taxi through Manila) would be one of the more memorable experiences of his life if this were the first time he had ever done it, but is the millionth time and so nothing registers. For example, he sees two cars smashed together directly beneath a giant road sign that says NO SWERVING, but he doesn't really take note.

Dear Randy,

   The worst is over. Charlene and (more importantly) her lawyer seem to have accepted, finally, that you are not sitting on top of a huge pile of gold in the Philippines! Now that your imaginary millions are no longer confusing the picture, we can figure out how to dispose of the assets you actually have: primarily, your equity in the house. This would be much more complicated if Charlene wanted to remain there, however it now appears that she has landed that Yale job, which means that she is just as eager to liquidate the house as you are. The question, then, will be how the proceeds of the sale should be divided between you and her. Their position appears (not surprisingly) to be that the huge increase in the house's value since you bought it is a consequence of changes in the real estate market—never mind the quarter-million you spent shoring up the foundation, replacing the plumbing, etc., etc.

   I assume you kept all of the receipts, cancelled checks and other proof of how much money you spent on improve-

```
ments, because that's the kind of guy you are. It would
help me very much if I could pull these out and wave them
around during my next round of discussions with Char-
lene's lawyer. Can you produce them? I realize that this
will be something of an inconvenience for you. However,
since you have invested most of your net worth into that
house, the stakes are high.
```

Randy puts the page into his breast pocket and begins planning a trip to California.

Most of the ballroom dancing freaks in this town belong to the social class that can afford cars and drivers. The cars are lined up all the way down the hotel's drive and out into the street, waiting to discharge their passengers, whose bright gowns are visible even through tinted windows. Attendants blow whistles and gesture with their white gloves, vectoring cars into the parking lot, where they are sintered into a tight mosaic. Some of the drivers don't even bother getting out, and lean their seats back for a nap. Others gather beneath a tree at one end of the lot to smoke, joke, and shake their heads in dazed amusement at the world in the way that only your hardened future shocked Third Worlders can.

Since he has been dreading this so much, you'd think Randy might just sit back and savor the delay. But, like jerking a bandage off a hairy part of the body, it is a deed best done quickly and suddenly. As they pull to a stop at the back of the line of limos, he shoves money at his surprised driver, opens the door, and walks the last block to the hotel. He can feel the eyes of the gowned and perfumed Filipinas playing across his husky back like laser sights on commandos' rifles.

Aging Filipinas in prom dresses have come and gone across the lobby of the Manila Hotel for as long as Randy has known the place. He hardly noticed them during the early months when he was actually living there. The first time they appeared, he assumed that some function was underway in the grand ballroom: perhaps a wedding, perhaps a class-action suit being filed by aging beauty contest contestants against the synthetic fibers industry. That was about as far as he got before he stopped burning out his mental circuits trying to figure everything out. Pursuing an explanation for every strange thing you see in the Philippines is like trying to get every last bit of rainwater out of a discarded tire.

The Shaftoes are not waiting by the door to tell him it was all a joke, so Randy squares his shoulders and stomps doggedly across the vast lobby, all alone, like a Confederate infantryman in Pickett's Charge, the last man of his regiment. A photographer in a Ronald Reagan pompadour and a white tuxedo is planted before the door to the grand ballroom, shooting pictures of people on the way in, hoping that they will pay for copies on the way out. Randy shoots him such a fell look that the man's shutter finger cringes back from the button. Then it's through the big doors and into the ballroom, where, beneath swirling, colored lights, hundreds of Filipinas are dancing, mostly with much younger men, to the strains of a reprocessed Carpenters tune generated by a small orchestra in the corner. Randy shells out some pesos for a corsage of sampaguita flowers. Holding it at arm's length so that he will not be plunged into a diabetic coma by its fumes, he commences a Magallanian circumnavigation of the dance floor, which is surrounded by an atoll of round tables that are adorned with white linen tablecloths, candles, and glass ashtrays. A man with a thin mustache sits alone at one of those tables, back against the wall, a cellphone against his head, one side of his face illuminated fluoroscopically by the eerie green light of its keypad. A cigarette juts from his fist.

Grandma Waterhouse insisted that seven-year-old Randy take ballroom dance lessons because one day it would certainly come in handy. He begged to differ. Her Australian accent had turned lofty and English in the decades since she had come to America, or maybe that was his imagination. She sat there, bolt upright as always, on her floral-chintz Gomer Bolstrood settee, the sere hills of the Palouse visible through lace curtains behind her, sipping tea from a white china cup decorated with— was it lavender roses? When she tilted the cup back, seven-year-old Randy must have been able to read the name of the china pattern off the bottom. The information must be stored in his subconscious memory somewhere. Perhaps a hypnotist could extract it.

But seven-year-old Randy had other things on his mind: protesting, in the strongest possible terms, the assertion that ballroom dance skills could ever be of any use. At the same time, he was being patterned. Implausible, even ludicrous ideas were suffusing his brain, invisible and odorless as carbon monoxide gas: that the Palouse was a normal landscape. That the sky was this blue everywhere. That a house should look this way: with lace curtains, leaded-glass windows, and room after room full of Gomer Bolstrood furniture.

"I met your grandfather Lawrence at a dance, in Brisbane," Grandma announced. She was trying to tell him that he, Randall Lawrence Waterhouse, would not even exist had it not been for the practice of ballroom dancing. But Randy did not even know where babies came from yet and probably wouldn't have understood even if he did. Randy straightened up, remembering his posture, and asked her a question: did this encounter in Brisbane happen when she was seven years old, or, perhaps, a little later?

Perhaps if she had lived in a mobile home, the grown-up Randy would have sunk his money into a mutual fund, instead of paying ten thousand dollars to a *soi-disant* artisan from San Francisco to install leaded-glass windows around his front door, like at Grandma's house.

He provides tremendous, long-lasting amusement to the Shaftoes by walking right past their table without recognizing them. He looks right at Doug Shaftoe's date, a striking Filipina, probably in her forties, who is in the middle of making some forceful point. Without taking her eyes off Doug and Amy Shaftoe, she reaches out with one long graceful arm and snags Randy's wrist as he goes by, yanking him back like a dog on a meat leash. She then holds him there while she finishes her sentence, then looks up at him with a brilliant smile. Randy smiles back dutifully, but he does not give her the full attention she seems accustomed to, because he is a bit preoccupied by the spectacle of America Shaftoe in a dress.

Fortunately, Amy has not gone in for the prom queen look. She is wearing a form-fitting black number with long sleeves that hide her tattoos, and black tights, as opposed to stockings. Randy gives her the flowers, like a quarterback handing off the pigskin to a runner. She accepts them with a crooked expression, like a wounded soldier biting down on a bullet. Irony aside, she has a gleam in her eye that he has never seen before. Or maybe that is just light from the mirrored ball, reflecting off cigarette-smoke-induced tears. He senses in his gut that he did the right thing by showing up. As with all gut feelings, only time will tell whether this it is pathetic self-delusion. He was kind of afraid that she would go through some Hollywoodesque transfiguration into a radiant goddess, which would have the same effect on Randy as an ax to the base of the skull. The fact of the matter is that she looks quite good, but arguably, just as out of place as Randy is in his suit.

He is hoping that they can get the dancing over right away so that he can flee the building in Cinderellan obloquy, but they bid him sit down. The orchestra takes a break and the dancers return to their tables. Doug Shaftoe is comfortably sprawled back in his chair with the masculine confidence of a man who has not only killed people but who is, furthermore, escorting the most beautiful woman in the room. Her name is Aurora Taal, and she casts her flawlessly Lancomed gaze over the other Filipinas with the controlled amusement of one who has lived in Boston, Washington, and London, and seen it all, and come back to live in Manila anyway.

"So, did you learn anything more about this Rudolf von Hacklheber character?" Doug asks, after a few minutes of small talk. It follows that Aurora must be in on the whole secret. Doug mentioned, weeks ago,

that a small number of Filipinos knew about what they were doing, and
that they could be trusted.

"He was a mathematician. He was from a wealthy Leipzig family. He
was at Princeton before the war. His years there did, in fact, overlap
with my grandfather's."

"What kind of math did he do, Randy?"

"Before the war he did number theory. Which tells us nothing about
what he did during the war. It wouldn't be surprising if he'd ended up
working in the Third Reich's crypto apparatus."

"Which wouldn't explain how he ended up here."

Randy shrugs. "Maybe he did engineering work on the new generation of submarines. I don't know."

"So the Reich got him involved in some kind of classified work,
which killed him eventually," Doug says. "We could have guessed that
for ourselves, I suppose."

"Why did you mention crypto, then?" Amy asks. She has some kind
of emotional metal detector that screams whenever it comes near buried
assumptions and hastily stifled impulses.

"I guess I have crypto on the brain. And, if there was some kind of
connection between Von Hacklheber and my grandfather—"

"Was your grandfather a crypto guy, Randy?" Doug asks.

"He never said anything about what he did during the war."

"Classic."

"But he had this trunk up in the attic. A war souvenir. It actually
reminds me of a trunk full of Nipponese crypto materials that I recently
saw in a cave in Kinakuta." Doug and Amy stare at him. "It doesn't
amount to anything, probably," Randy concedes.

The orchestra starts in with a Sinatra tune. Doug and Aurora smile at
each other and rise to their feet. Amy rolls her eyes and looks the other
way, but it's put up or shut up time now, and Randy cannot conceive
of any way out. He stands up and extends his hand to the one he fears
and hopes for, and she, without looking, reaches out and puts her hand
into his.

Randy shuffles, which is no way to dance beautifully but does rule
out snapping his partner's metatarsals. Amy is essentially no better at this
than he is, but she has a better attitude. By the time they get to the end
of the first dance, Randy has at least reached the point where his face is
no longer burning, and has gone for some thirty seconds without having
to apologize for anything, and sixty without asking his partner whether
she will be needing medical attention. Then the song is over, and circumstances dictate that he has to dance with Aurora Taal. This is less intimidating; even though she is glamorous and a really good dancer, their

relationship is not one that allows for the possibility of grotesque pre-erotic fumbling. Also, Aurora smiles a lot, and she has a really spectacular smile, where Amy's face was intense and preoccupied. The next dance is announced as ladies' choice, and Randy is still trying to make eye contact with Amy when he finds this tiny middle-aged Filipina standing there asking Aurora if she would mind terribly. Aurora consigns him to the other lady like a pork belly futures contract on the commodity exchange, and suddenly Randy and the lady are dancing the Texas two-step to the strains of a pre-disco Bee Gees tune.

"So, have you found wealth in the Philippines yet?" asks the lady, whose name Randy did not quite catch. She acts as if she expects him to know her.

"Uh, my partners and I are exploring business opportunities," Randy says. "Maybe wealth will follow."

"I understand you are good with numbers," the lady says.

Randy is really racking his brain now. How does this woman know he's a numbers kind of guy? "I'm good with *math,*" he finally says.

"Isn't that what I said?"

"Nah, mathematicians stay away from actual, specific numbers as much as possible. We like to talk about numbers without actually exposing ourselves to them—that's what computers are for."

The lady will not be denied; she has a script and she's sticking to it. "I have a math problem for you," the lady says.

"Shoot."

"What is the value of the following information: fifteen degrees, seventeen minutes, forty-one point three two seconds north, and a hundred and twenty-one degrees, fifty-seven minutes, zero point five five seconds east?"

"Uh . . . I don't know. It sounds like a latitude and longitude. Northern Luzon, right?"

The lady nods.

"You want me to tell you the value of those numbers?"

"Yes."

"Depends on what's there, I guess."

"I suppose it does," the lady says. And that's all she says, for the rest of the dance. Other than complimenting Randy on his balletic skills, which is just as hard to interpret.

FLATS ARE HARDER AND HARDER TO FIND IN BRISBANE, WHICH has become a spy boomtown—Bletchley Park Down Under. There's Central Bureau, which has set up out at the Ascot Race-track, and another entity in a different part of town called Allied Intelligence Bureau. The people who work at Central Bureau tend to be pallid mathematics experts. The AIB people, on the other hand, remind Waterhouse very much of those Detachment 2702 fellows: tense, tanned, and taciturn.

Half a mile from the Ascot Racetrack, he sees one of the latter tripping lightly down the steps of a nice gingerbready rooming-house, carrying a five-hundred-pound duffel bag on his back. The man is dressed for a long trip. A grandmotherish lady in an apron is on the veranda, waving a tea towel at him. It is like a scene from a movie; you wouldn't even know that only a few hours' flight from here, men are turning black like photographic paper in a developer tray as their living flesh is converted into putrid gas by Clostridium bacteria.

Waterhouse does not stop to estimate the probability that he, who needs a place to live, should happen along at the exact moment that a room has become available. Cryptanalysts wait for lucky breaks, then exploit them. After the departing soldier has disappeared round the corner, he knocks on the door and introduces himself to the lady. Mrs. McTeague says (to the extent Waterhouse can penetrate her accent) that she likes his looks. She sounds distinctly astonished. It seems clear that the improbability of Waterhouse's having happened upon this vacant room is nothing compared to the improbability of having his looks liked by Mrs. McTeague. Thus, Lawrence Pritchard Waterhouse joins a small elite group of young men (four in all) whose looks Mrs. McTeague likes. They sleep, two to a room, in the bedrooms where Mrs. McTeague's offspring grew from the brightest and most beautiful children ever born into the finest adults who walk the earth except for the King of England, the General, and Lord Mountbatten.

Waterhouse's new roommate is out of town just now, but by glancing over his personal effects, Waterhouse estimates that he is paddling a black kayak from Australia to Yokosuka Naval Base, where he will slip on board a battleship and silently kill its entire crew with his bare hands before doing an Olympic-qualifying dive into the bay, punching out a few sharks, climbing back into his kayak and paddling back to Australia for a beer.

The next morning, at breakfast, he meets the fellows in the next room: a redheaded British naval officer who shows all the earmarks of working at Central Bureau, and a fellow named Hale, whose nationality cannot be pegged because he's not in uniform and he's too hung over to speak.

Having accomplished his mission (according to his understanding with the General's minions), found a place to live, and settled his other personal affairs, Waterhouse begins hanging around the Ascot Racetrack and the adjacent whorehouse, trying to find some way to make himself useful. Actually he would rather sit in his room all day and work on his new project, which is to design a high-speed Turing machine. But he has a duty to contribute to the war effort. Even if he didn't, he suspects that when his new roommate gets back from his mission, and finds him sitting indoors all day drawing circuit diagrams, he will thrash Waterhouse to the point where Mrs. McTeague will no longer like his looks.

To put it mildly, Central Bureau is not the kind of place where a stranger can just wander in, check the place out, introduce himself and find a job. Even the wandering-in part is potentially fatal. Fortunately, Waterhouse has Ultra Mega clearance, the highest clearance in the Entire World.

Unfortunately, this category of secrecy is itself so secret that its very existence is secret, and so he can't actually reveal it to anyone—unless he finds someone else with Ultra Mega clearance. There are only a dozen people with Ultra Mega clearance in all of Brisbane. Eight of them comprise the top of the General's command hierarchy, three work at Central Bureau, and one is Waterhouse.

Waterhouse sniffs out the nerve center in the old whorehouse. Superannuated Australian Territorial Guards in jaunty asymmetrical hats ring the place, clutching blunderbusses. Unlike Mrs. McTeague, they don't like his looks. On the other hand they are used to this kind of thing: smart boys from far away showing up at the gate with long and, in the end, boring stories about how the military screwed up their orders, put them in the wrong boat, sent them to the wrong place, gave them tropical diseases, threw their belongings overboard, left them to fend for themselves. They don't shoot him, but they don't let him in.

He hangs around and makes a nuisance of himself for a couple of days until he finally recognizes, and is recognized by, Abraham Sinkov. Sinkov is a top American cryptanalyst; he helped Schoen break Indigo. He and Waterhouse have crossed paths a few times, and though they aren't friends, per se, their minds work the same way. This makes them brothers in a weird family that has only a few hundred members, scattered about the world. In a way, it is a clearance that is rarer, harder to come by, and more mysterious than Ultra Mega. Sinkov writes him a new set of papers, giving him a clearance that is very high, but not so high that he can't reveal it.

Waterhouse gets a tour. Shirtless men sit in Quonset huts made stifling by the red-hot tubes of their radios. They pluck the Nipponese Army's messages out of the air and hand them off to legions of young Australian women who punch the intercepted messages onto ETC cards.

There is a cadre of American officers comprised entirely of a whole department of the Electrical Till Corporation. One day, early in 1942, they put their white shirts and blue suits into mothballs, donned Army uniforms, and climbed on ships to Brisbane. Their ringleader is a guy named Lieutenant Colonel Comstock, and he has gotten the whole code-breaking process totally automated. The cards punched by the Aussie girls come into the machine room stacked into ingots which are fed through the machines. Decrypts fly out of a line printer on the other end and are taken off to another hut where American nisei, and some white men trained in Nipponese, translate them.

A Waterhouse is the last thing these guys need. He's beginning to understand what the major said to him the other day: they have passed over the watershed line. The codes are broken.

Which reminds him of Turing. Ever since Alan got back from New York he's been distancing himself from Bletchley Park. He has moved up to another installation, a radio center called Hanslope in north Buckinghamshire, a place of reinforced concrete, wires, antennas, more military-formal in its atmosphere.

At the time, Waterhouse could not understand why Alan would want to move away from Bletchley. But now he knows how Alan must have felt after they turned decryption into a mechanical process, industrializing Bletchley Park. He must have felt that the battle was won, and with it the war. The rest might seem like glorious conquest to people like the General, but to Turing, and now to Waterhouse, it just looks like tedious mopping-up. It is exciting to discover electrons and figure out the equations that govern their movement; it is boring to use those principles to design electric can openers. From here on out, it's all can openers.

Sinkov provides Waterhouse with a desk in the whorehouse and begins to feed him the messages that Central Bureau hasn't been able to decrypt. There are still dozens of minor Nipponese codes that remain to be broken. Maybe, by breaking one or two, and teaching the ETC machines to read them, Waterhouse can shorten the war by a single day, or save a single life. This is a noble calling that he undertakes willingly, but in essence it is no different from being an Army butcher who saves lives by keeping his knives clean, or a lifeboat inspector in the Navy.

Waterhouse cracks those minor Nip codes one after the other. One month he even flies up to New Guinea, where Navy divers are salvaging code books from a sunken Nip submarine. He lives in the jungle for two weeks and tries not to die, comes back to Brisbane, and puts those recovered codebooks to good but dull use. Then one day the dullness of his work becomes irrelevant.

On that day, he returns to Mrs. McTeague's boardinghouse in the evening, goes to his room, and finds a large man snoring in the upper bunk. A lot of clothing and equipment is scattered about the place, emanating sulfurous reek.

The man sleeps for two days and then comes down late for breakfast one morning, peering around the room with Atabrine yellow eyes. He introduces himself as Smith. His oddly familiar accent is not made any easier to understand by the fact that his teeth are chattering violently. He doesn't seem especially bothered by this. He sits down and paws an Irish linen napkin into his lap with a hand that is stiff and raw. Mrs. McTeague fusses over him to the extent that all of the men at the table must resist the impulse to slug her. She pours him tea with plenty of milk and sugar. He takes a few sips, then excuses himself and goes to the WC, where he crisply and politely vomits. He comes back, eats a soft-boiled egg from a bone china egg cup, turns green, leans back in his chair, and closes his eyes for about ten minutes.

When Waterhouse returns from work that evening, he blunders into the parlor and interrupts Mrs. McTeague having tea with a young lady.

The young lady's name is Mary Smith; she is the cousin of Waterhouse's roommate, who is upstairs shivering and sweating in his bunk bed.

Mary stands up to be introduced, which is not technically necessary; but she is a girl from the outback and has no use for effete refinement. She is a petite girl dressed in a uniform.

She is the only woman Waterhouse has ever seen. She is the only other human being in the universe actually, and when she stands up to shake his hand, his peripheral vision shuts down as if he has been sucking on a tailpipe. Black curtains converge across a silver cyclorama, shuttering down his cosmos to a vertical shaft of carbon-arc glory, a pillar of light, a heavenly follow-spot targeted upon Her.

Mrs. McTeague, knowing the score, bids him sit down.

Mary is a tiny, white-skinned, red-headed person who is often seized by little fits of self-consciousness. When this happens she averts her eyes from his and swallows, and when she swallows there is a certain cord in her white neck, rounding the concavity from shoulder to ear, that stands out for a moment. It draws attention both to her vulnerability and to the white flesh of her neck, which is not white in a pallid sick way but in another way that Waterhouse could never have understood until recently: viz., from his little stint in New Guinea, where everything is either dead and decaying, or bright and threatening, or unobtrusive and invisible, Waterhouse knows that anything this tender and translucent is too vulnerable and tempting to hold its own in a world of violently competing destroyers, that it can only be sustained for a moment (let alone years) by the life force within. In the South Pacific where the forces of Death are so powerful, it leaves him vaguely intimidated. Her skin, as unmarked as clear water, is an extravagant display of vibrant animal power. He wants his tongue on it. The whole curve of her neck, from collarbone to earlobe, would make a perfect cradle for his face.

She sees him looking at her, and swallows again. The cord flexes, stretching the living skin of her neck out for just a moment, and then relaxes, leaving nothing but smoothness and calm. She may just as well have caved his head in with a stone and tied his penis round a hitching-rail. The effect must be calculated. But apparently she has not ever done it to anyone else, or there would be a band of gold round her pale left ring finger.

Mary Smith is beginning to get annoyed with him. She lifts the teacup to her lips. She has turned so that the light is grazing her neck in a new way, and this time when she swallows he can see her Adam's apple moving up. Then it comes down like a pile driver on what is left of his good judgment.

There is a thumping noise upstairs; her cousin has just regained consciousness. "Excuse me," she says, and she's gone, leaving only Mrs. McTeague's bone china as a reminder.

CONSPIRACY

DR. RUDOLF VON HACKLHEBER IS NOT MUCH OLDER THAN SERgeant Bobby Shaftoe, but even emotionally crushed, he has a certain bearing about him that men in Shaftoe's world don't acquire until they are in their forties, if then. His eyeglasses have tiny rimless lenses that look like they were scavenged from a sniper's telescopic sights. Behind them is a whole paintbox of vivid colors: blond lashes, blue eyes, red veins, lids swollen and purple from weeping. Even so, he has a perfect shave, and the silvery Nordic light coming in through the tiny windows of Enoch Root's church cellar glances from the planes of his face so as to highlight an interesting terrain of big pores, premature creases, and old dueling scars. He has tried to grease his hair back, but it misbehaves and keeps tumbling down over his brow. He is wearing a white dress shirt and a very long, heavy overcoat on top of that to ward off the cellar's chill. Shaftoe, who hiked back to Norrsbruck with him several days ago, knows that the long-legged von Hacklheber has the makings of a half-decent jock. But he can tell that rude sports like football would be out of the question; this Kraut would be a fencer or a mountain climber or a skier.

Shaftoe was only startled—not bothered—by von Hacklheber's homosexuality. Some of the China Marines in Shanghai had a lot more young Chinese boys hanging around their flats than they really needed to shine their boots—and Shanghai is far from the strangest or most far-flung place where Marines made themselves at home between the wars. You can worry about morality when you're off duty, but if you are always stewing and fretting over what the other guys are doing in the sack, then what the hell are you going to do when you're presented with an opportunity to hit a Nip squad with a flamethrower?

They buried the remains of Angelo, the pilot, two weeks ago, and only now is von Hacklheber feeling in any kind of shape to talk. He has rented a cottage outside of town, but he has come into Norrsbruck to meet with Root, Shaftoe, and Bischoff on this day, partly because he is convinced that German spies are watching it. Shaftoe shows up with a bottle of Finnish schnapps, Bischoff brings a loaf of bread, Root breaks out a tin of fish. Von Hacklheber brings information. Everyone brings cigarettes.

Shaftoe smokes early and often, trying to kill the mildewy smell of the cellar, which reminds him of being locked up there with Enoch Root, kicking his morphine habit. During that time, the pastor once had to come downstairs and ask him please to stop screaming for a while because they were trying to do a wedding upstairs. Shaftoe hadn't known he was screaming.

Rudolf von Hacklheber's English is, in some respects, better than Shaftoe's. He sounds unnervingly like Bobby's junior high school drafting teacher, Mr. Jaeger. "Before the war I worked under Dönitz for the Beobachtung Dienst of the Kriegsmarine. We broke some of the most secret codes of the British Admiralty even before the outbreak of hostilities. I was responsible for some advances in this field, involving the use of mechanical calculation. When war broke out there was much reorganization and I became like a bone that several dogs are fighting over. I was moved into *Referat* Iva of *Gruppe* IV, Analytical Cryptanalysis, which was part of *Hauptgruppe* B, Cryptanalysis, which reported ultimately to Major General Erich Fellgiebel, Chief of *Wehrmachtnachrichtungen-verbindungen.*"

Shaftoe looks around at the others, but none of them laughs, or even grins. They must not have heard it. "Come again?" Shaftoe asks, proddingly, like a man in a bar trying to get a shy friend to tell a sure-fire thigh-slapper.

"Wehrmachtnachrichtungenverbindungen," von Hacklheber says, very slowly, as if repeating nursery rhymes to a toddler. He blinks once, twice, three times at Shaftoe, then sits forward and says, brightly: "Perhaps I should explain the organization of the German intelligence hierarchy, since it will help you all to understand my story."

A BRIEF TRIP INTO HELL'S DEMO with HERR DOKTOR PROFESSOR RUDOLF VON HACKLHEBER ensues.

Shaftoe only hears the first couple of sentences. At about the point when von Hacklheber tears a sheet out of a notebook and begins to diagram the organizational tree of the Thousand-Year Reich, with "Der Führer" at the top, Shaftoe's eyes take on a heavy glaze, his body goes slack, he becomes deaf, and he accelerates up the throat of a nightmare, like the butt of a half-digested corn dog being reverse-peristalsed from the body of an addict. He has never been through this experience before, but he knows intuitively that this is how the trip to Hell works: no leisurely boat ride across the scenic Styx, no gradual descent into that trite tourist trap, Pluto's Cavern, no stops along the way to buy fishing licenses for the Lake of Fire.

Shaftoe is not (though he should be) dead, and so this is not hell. It is closely modeled after hell, though. It is like a mock-up slapped together from tar paper and canvas, like the fake towns where they practiced house-to-house warfare during boot camp. Shaftoe is gripped with a sort of giddy queasiness that, he knows, is the most pleasant thing he will feel here. "Morphine takes away the body's ability to experience pleasure," says the booming voice of Enoch Root, his wry, annoying Virgil, who for purposes of this nightmare has adopted the voice and physical shape of Moe, the mean, dark-haired Stooge. "It may be some time before you feel physically well."

The organizational tree of this nightmare begins, like von Hacklheber's, with Der Führer, but then branches out widely and crazily. There is an Asian branch, headed up by the General, and including, among other things, a Hauptgruppe of giant carnivorous lizards, a Referat of Chinese women holding up pale-eyed babies, and several Abteilungs of plastered Nips with swords. In the center of their domain is the city of

Manila, where, in a tableau that Shaftoe would identify as Boschian if he had not spent his high school art class out behind the school leg-fucking cheerleaders, a heavily pregnant Glory Altamira is being forced to do blow jobs on syphilitic Nipponese troops.

The voice of Mr. Jaeger, his drafting teacher—the most boring man Shaftoe had ever known, until perhaps today—fades in for a moment with the words, "but all of the organizational structures I have detailed to this point became obsolete at the outbreak of hostilities. The hierarchy was shuffled and several of the entities changed their names, as follows . . ." Shaftoe hears a new sheet of paper being torn from the notebook, but what he sees is Mr. Jaeger tearing up a diagram of a table leg bracket that the young Bobby Shaftoe had spent a week drafting. Everything has been reorganized, General MacArthur is still very high in the tree, walking a brace of giant lizards on steel leashes, but now the hierarchy is filled with grinning Arabs holding up lumps of hashish, frozen butchers, dead or doomed lieutenants, and that fucking weirdo, Lawrence Pritchard Waterhouse, dressed in a black, hooded robe, heading up a whole legion of pencil-necked Signals geeks, also in robes, holding bizarrely shaped antennas above their heads, wading through a blizzard of dollar bills printed on old Chinese newspapers. Their eyes glow, flashing on and off in Morse code.

"What are they saying?" Bobby says.

"Please, stop screaming," says Enoch Root. "Just for a little while."

Bobby's lying on a cot in a thatched hut in Guadalcanal. Swedish tribesmen run around in loincloths, gathering food: every so often, a ship gets blown up out in the Slot, and fish-shrapnel rains down and gets hung up in the branches, along with the occasional severed human arm or hunk of skull. The Swedes ignore the human bits and harvest the fish, taking it off to make lutefisk in black steel drums.

Enoch Root has an old cigar box on his lap. Golden light is shining out of the crack around its lid.

But he's not in the thatched hut anymore; he's inside a cold black metal phallus that has been probing around down below the surface of the nightmare: Bischoff's submarine. Depth charges are going off all over the place and it's filling up with sewage. Something clocks him on the side of the head: not a ham this time, but a human leg. The sub's lined with tubes that carry voices: in English, German, Arabic, Nipponese, Shanghainese, but confined and muffled in the plumbing so that they mingle together like the running of water. Then a pipe is ruptured by a near miss from a depth charge; from its jagged end issues a German voice:

"The foregoing may be taken as a rather coarse-grained treatment of the general organization of the Reich and particularly the military.

Responsibility for cryptanalysis and cryptography is distributed among a large number of small Amts and Diensts attached to various tendrils of this structure. These are continually being reorganized and rearranged, however I may be able to provide you with a reasonably accurate and detailed picture . . ."

Shaftoe, chained to a bunk in the submarine by fetters of gold, feels one of his small, concealed handguns pressing into the small of his back, and wonders whether it would be bad form to shoot himself in the mouth. He paws wildly at the broken tube and manages to slap it down into the rising sewage; bubbles come out, and von Hacklheber's words are trapped in them, like word balloons in a comic strip. When the bubbles reach the surface and burst, it sounds like screaming.

Root is sitting on the opposite bunk with the cigar box on his lap. He holds up his hand in a V for Victory, then levels it at Shaftoe's face and pokes him in the eyes. "I cannot help you with your inability to find physical comfort—it is a problem of body chemistry," he says. "It poses interesting theological questions. It reminds us that all the pleasures of the world are an illusion projected into our souls by our bodies."

A lot of the other speaking tubes have ruptured now, and screaming comes from most of them; Root has to lean close in order to shout into Bobby's ear. Shaftoe takes advantage of it to reach over and make a grab for the cigar box, which contains the stuff he wants: not morphine. Something better than morphine. Morphine is to the stuff in the cigar box what a Shanghai prostitute is to Glory.

The box flies open and blinding light comes out of it. Shaftoe covers his face. The salted and preserved body parts suspended from the ceiling tumble into his lap and begin to writhe, reaching out for other parts, assembling themselves into living bodies. Mikulski comes back to life, aims his Vickers at the ceiling of the U-boat, and cuts an escape hatch. Instead of black water, golden light rushes through.

"What was your position in all this, then?" asks Root, and Shaftoe nearly jumps out of his chair, startled by the sound of a voice other than von Hacklheber's. Given what happened the last time someone (Shaftoe) asked a question, this is heroic but risky. Starting with Hitler, von Hacklheber works his way down the chain of command.

Shaftoe doesn't care: he's on a rubber raft, along with various resurrected comrades from Guadalcanal and Detachment 2702. They are rowing across a still cove lit by giant flaming klieg lights in the sky. Standing behind the klieg lights is a man talking in a German accent: "My immediate supervisors, Wilhelm Fenner, from St. Petersburg, who headed all German military cryptanalysis from 1922 onwards, and his chief deputy, Professor Novopaschenny."

All of these names sound alike to Shaftoe, but Root says, "A Russian?"

Shaftoe is really coming around now, reemerging into the World. He sits up straight, and his body feels stiff, like it hasn't moved in a long time. He is about to apologize for the way he has been behaving, but since no one is looking at him funny, Shaftoe sees no reason to fill them in on what he's been doing these last few minutes.

"Professor Novopaschenny was a Czarist astronomer who knew Fenner from St. Petersburg. Under them, I was given broad authority to pursue researches into the theoretical limits of security. I used tools from pure mathematics as well as mechanical calculating devices of my own design. I looked at our own codes as well as those of our enemies, looking for weaknesses."

"What did you find?" Bischoff asks.

"I found weaknesses everywhere," von Hacklheber says. "Most codes were designed by dilettantes and amateurs with no grasp of the underlying mathematics. It is really quite pitiable."

"Including the Enigma?" Bischoff asks.

"Don't even talk to me of that shit," von Hacklheber says. "I dispensed with it almost immediately."

"What do you mean, dispensed with it?" Root asks.

"Proved that it was shit," von Hacklheber says.

"But the entire Wehrmacht still uses it," Bischoff says.

Von Hacklheber shrugs and looks at the burning tip of his cigarette. "You expect them to throw all those machines away because one mathematician writes a paper?" He stares at his cigarette a while longer, then puts it to his lips, draws on it tastefully, holds the smoke in his lungs, and finally exhales it slowly through his vocal cords whilst simultaneously causing them to emit the following sounds: "I knew that there must be people working for the enemy who would figure this out. Turing. Von Neumann. Waterhouse. Some of the Poles. I began to look for signs that they had broken the Enigma, or at least realized its weaknesses and begun trying to break it. I ran statistical analyses of convoy sinkings and U-boat attacks. I found some anomalies, some improbable events, but not enough to make a pattern. Many of the grossest anomalies were later accounted for by the discovery of espionage stations and the like.

"From this I drew no conclusion. Certainly if they were smart enough to break the Enigma they would be smart enough to conceal the fact from us at any cost. But there was one anomaly they could not cover up. I refer to human anomalies."

"Human anomalies?" Root asks. The phrase is classic Root-bait.

"I knew perfectly well that only a handful of people in the world had the acumen to break the Enigma and then to cover up the fact that they had broken it. By using our intelligence sources to ascertain where these men were, and what they were doing, I could make inferences." Von Hacklheber stubs out his cigarette, sits up straight, and drains a half-shot of schnapps, warming to the task. "This was a human intelligence problem—not signals intelligence. This is handled by a different branch of the service—" and he's off again talking about the structure of the German bureaucracy. Terrified, Shaftoe flees from the room, runs outside, and uses the outhouse. When he gets back, von Hacklheber is just winding up. "It all came down to a problem of sifting through large amounts of raw data—lengthy and tedious work."

Shaftoe cringes, wondering what something would have to be like in order to qualify as lengthy and tedious to this joker.

"After some time," von Hacklheber continues, "I learned, through some of our agents in the British Isles, that a man matching the general description of Lawrence Pritchard Waterhouse had been stationed to a castle in Outer Qwghlm. I was able to arrange for a young lady to place this man under the closest possible surveillance," he says dryly. "His security precautions were impeccable, and so we learned nothing directly. In fact, it is quite likely that he knew that the young woman in question was an agent, and so took added precautions. But we did learn that this man communicated through one-time pads. He would read his encrypted messages over the telephone to a nearby naval base whence they would be telegraphed to a station in Buckinghamshire, which would respond to him with messages encrypted using the same system of one-time pads. By going through the records of our various radio intercept stations we were able to accumulate a stack of messages that had been sent by this mysterious unit, using this series of one-time pads, over a period of time beginning in the middle of 1942 and continuing up to the present day. It was interesting to note that this unit operated in a variety of places: Malta, Alexandria, Morocco, Norway, and various ships at sea. Extremely unusual. I was very interested in this mysterious unit and so I began trying to break their special code."

"Isn't that impossible?" Bischoff asks. "There is no way to break a one-time pad, short of stealing a copy."

"That is true in theory," von Hacklheber says. "In practice, this is only true if the letters that make up the one-time pad are chosen perfectly randomly. But, as I discovered, this is not true of the one-time pads used by Detachment 2702—which is the mysterious unit that Waterhouse, Turing, and these two gentlemen all belong to."

"But how did you figure this out?" Bischoff asks.

"A few things helped me. There was a lot of depth—many messages to work with. There was consistency—the one-time pads were generated in the same way, always, and always exhibited the same patterns. I made some educated guesses which turned out to be correct. And I had a calculating machine to make the work go faster."

"Educated guesses?"

"I had a hypothesis that the one-time pads were being drawn up by a person who was rolling dice or shuffling a deck of cards to produce the letters. I began to consider psychological factors. An English speaker is accustomed to a certain frequency distribution of letters. He expects to see a great many e's, t's, and a's, and not so many z's and q's and x's. So if such a person were using some supposedly random algorithm to generate the letters, he would be subconsciously irritated every time a z or an x came up, and, conversely, soothed by the appearance of e or t. Over time, this might skew the frequency distribution."

"But Herr Doctor von Hacklheber, I find it unlikely that such a person would substitute their own letters for the ones that came up on the cards, or dice, or whatever."

"It is not very likely. But suppose that the algorithm gave the person some small amount of discretion." Von Hacklheber lights another cigarette, pours out more schnapps. "I set up an experiment. I got twenty volunteers—middle-aged women who wanted to do their part for the Reich. I set them to work drawing up one-time pads using an algorithm where they drew slips out of a box. Then I used my machinery to run statistical calculations on the results. I found that they were not random at all."

Root says, "The one-time pads for Detachment 2702 are being created by Mrs. Tenney, a vicar's wife. She uses a bingo machine, a cage filled with wooden balls with a letter stamped on each ball. She is supposed to close her eyes before reaching into the cage. But suppose she has become sloppy and no longer closes her eyes when she reaches into it."

"Or," von Hacklheber says, "suppose she looks at the cage, and sees how the balls are distributed inside of it, and *then* closes her eyes. She will subconsciously reach toward the E and avoid the Z. Or, if a certain letter has just come up recently, she will try to avoid choosing it again. Even if she cannot see the inside of the cage, she will learn to distinguish among the different balls by their feel—being made of wood, each ball will have a different weight, a different pattern in the grain."

Bischoff's not buying it. "But it will still be mostly random!"

"Mostly random is not good enough!" von Hacklheber snaps. "I was convinced that the one-time pads of Detachment 2702 would have a frequency distribution similar to that of the King James Version of the Bible, for example. And I strongly suspected that the content of those messages would include words such as Waterhouse, Turing, Enigma,

Qwghlm, Malta. By putting my machinery to work, I was able to break some of the one-time pads. Waterhouse was careful to burn his pads after using them once, but some other parts of the detachment were careless, and used the same pads again and again. I read many messages. It was obvious that Detachment 2702 was in the business of deceiving the Wehrmacht by concealing the fact that the Enigma had been broken."

Shaftoe knows what an Enigma is, if only because Bischoff won't shut up about them. When von Hacklheber explains this, everything that Detachment 2702 ever did suddenly makes sense.

"So, the secret is out then," Root says. "I assume you made your superiors aware of your discovery?"

"I made them aware of absolutely nothing," von Hacklheber snarls, "because by this time I had long since fallen into a snare of Reichsmarschall Hermann Göring. I had become his pawn, his slave, and had ceased to feel any loyalty whatsoever towards the Reich."

The knock on Rudolf von Hacklheber's door had come at four o'clock in the morning, a time exploited by the Gestapo for its psychological effect. Rudy is wide awake. Even if bombers had not been pounding Berlin all night long, he would have been awake, because he has neither seen nor heard from Angelo in three days. He throws a dressing gown over his pajamas, steps into slippers, and opens the door of his flat to reveal, predictably, a small, prematurely withered man backed up by a couple of classic Gestapo killers in long black leather coats.

"May I proffer an observation?" says Rudy von Hacklheber.

"But of course, Herr Doktor Professor. As long as it is not a state secret, of course."

"In the old days—the early days—when no one knew what the Gestapo was, and no one was afraid of it, this four in the morning business was clever. A fine way to exploit man's primal fear of the darkness. But now it is 1942, almost 1943, and everyone is afraid of the Gestapo. Everyone. More than they are of the dark. So, why don't you work during the daytime? You are stuck in a rut."

The bottom half of the withered man's face laughs. The top half doesn't change. "I will pass your suggestion up the chain of command," he says. "But, Herr Doktor, we are not here to instill fear. We have come at this inconvenient time because of the train schedules."

"Am I to understand that I am getting on a train?"

"You have a few minutes," the Gestapo man says, pulling back a cuff to divulge a hulking Swiss chronometer. Then he invites himself in and begins to pace up and down in front of Rudy's bookshelves, hands clasped behind back, bending at the waist to peer at the titles. He seems disappointed to find that they are all mathematical texts—not a single copy of the Declaration of Independence in evidence, though you can never tell when a copy of the Protocols of the Elders of Zion might be hidden between the pages of a mathematical journal. When Rudy emerges, dressed but still unshaven, he finds the man displaying a pained expression while trying to read Turing's dissertation on the Universal Machine. He looks like a lower primate trying to fly an aeroplane.

Half an hour later, they are at the train station. Rudy looks up at the departures board as they go in, and memorizes its contents, so that he will be able to deduce, from the track number, whether he's being taken in the direction of Leipzig or Konigsberg or Warsaw.

It is a clever thing to do, but it turns out to be a waste of effort, because the Gestapo men lead him to a track that is not listed on the board. A short train waits there. It does not contain any boxcars, a relief to Rudy, since he thinks that during the last few years he may have glimpsed boxcars that appeared to be crammed full of human beings. These glimpses were brief and surreal, and he cannot really sort out whether they really happened, or were merely fragments of nightmares that got filed in the wrong cranial drawer.

But all of the cars on this train have doors, guarded by men in unfamiliar uniforms, and windows, shrouded on the inside with shutters and heavy curtains. The Gestapo lead him to a coach door without breaking stride, and just like that, he is through. And he is alone. No one checks his papers, and the Gestapo do not enter behind him. The door is closed behind his back.

Doktor Rudolf von Hacklheber is standing in a long skinny car decorated like the anteroom of an upper-class whorehouse, with Persian runners on the polished hardwood floor, heavy furniture upholstered in maroon velvet, and curtains so thick that they look bulletproof. At one end of the coach, a French maid hovers over a table set with breakfast: hard rolls, slices of meat and cheese, and coffee. Rudy's nose tells him that it is real coffee, and the smell draws him down to the end of the car. The maid pours him a cup with trembling hands. She has plastered thick foundation beneath her eyes to conceal dark circles, and (he realizes, as she hands him the cup) she has also painted it onto her wrists.

Rudy savors the coffee, stirring cream into it with a golden spoon bearing the marque of a French family. He strolls up and down the length of the car, admiring the art on the walls: a series of Dürer engravings, and, unless his eyes deceive him, a couple of pages from a Leonardo da Vinci codex.

The door opens again and a man enters clumsily, as if thrown on board, and ends up sprawled over a velvet settee. By the time Rudy recognizes him, the train has already begun to pull out of the station.

"Angelo!" Rudy sets his coffee down on an end table and throws himself into the arms of his beloved.

Angelo returns the embrace weakly. He stinks, and he shudders uncontrollably. He is wearing a coarse, dirty, pajamalike garment, and is wrapped up in a grey wool blanket. His wrists are encircled by half-scabbed lacerations embedded in fields of yellow-green bruises.

"Don't worry about it, Rudy," Angelo says, clenching and opening his fists to prove that they still work. "They were not kind to me, but they took care with my hands."

"Thou canst still fly?"

"I can still fly. But that is not why they were so careful with my hands."

"Why, then?"

"Without hands, a man cannot sign a confession."

Rudy and Angelo gaze into each other's eyes. Angelo looks sad, exhausted, but still has some kind of serene confidence about him. Like a baptizing priest ready to receive the infant, he holds up his hands. He silently mouths the words: *But I can still fly!*

A suit of clothes is brought in by a valet. Angelo cleans up in one of the coach's lavatories. Rudy tries to peer out between the curtains, but heavy shutters have been pulled down over the windows. They breakfast together as the train maneuvers through the switching-yards of greater Berlin, perhaps working its way around some bombed-out sections of track, and finally accelerates into the open territory beyond.

Reichsmarschall Hermann Göring makes his way through the car, headed towards the rear of the train, where the most ornate coach is located. His body is about as big as the hull of a torpedo boat, draped in a circus-tent-sized Chinese silk robe, the sash of which drags on the floor behind him, like a leash trailing behind a dog. He has the largest belly of any man Rudy has ever seen, and it is covered with golden hair that deepens as the belly curves under, until it becomes a tawny thicket that completely conceals his genitals. He is not really expecting to see two men sitting here eating breakfast, but seems to consider Rudy and Angelo's presence here to be one of life's small anomalies, not really worth noticing. Given that Göring is the number-two man in the Third Reich—the designated successor to Hitler himself—Rudy and Angelo really should jump to attention and give him a "Heil Hitler!" But they are too stunned to move. Göring stumbles down the middle of the coach, paying them no mind. Halfway down, he begins talking, but he's talking to himself, and his words are slurred. He slams open the door at the end of the coach and proceeds into the next car.

Two hours later, a doctor in a white coat passes through, headed for Göring's coach, carrying a silver tray with a white linen cloth on it. Tastefully arrayed on this, like caviar and champagne, are a blue bottle and a glass hypodermic syringe.

Half an hour after that, an aide in a Luftwaffe uniform passes through carrying a sheaf of papers, and favors Rudy and Angelo with a crisp "Heil, Hitler!"

Another hour goes by, and then Rudy and Angelo are escorted back through the train by a servant. The coach at the rear of the train is darker and more gentlemanly than the florid parlor where they have been cooling their heels. It is paneled in darkly stained wood and contains an actual desk—a baronial monstrosity carved out of a ton of Bavarian oak. At the moment, its sole function is to support a single sheet of paper, hand-written, and signed at the bottom. Even from a distance, Rudy recognizes Angelo's handwriting.

They have to walk past the desk in order to reach Göring, who is spread across an equally massive couch at the end of the car, underneath a Matisse, and flanked between a couple of Roman busts on marble pedestals. He is dressed in red leather jodhpurs, red leather boots, a red leather uniform jacket, a red leather riding crop with a fat diamond set into the butt of the handle. Bracelet-sized gold rings, infected with big rubies, grip his pudgy fingers. A red leather officer's cap is perched on his head, with a gold death's head, with ruby eyes, centered above the bill. All of this is illuminated only by a few striations of dusty light that have forced their way in through tiny crevices between curtains and shutters; the sun is up now, but Göring's blue eyes, dilated to dime-sized pits by the morphine, cannot face it. He has his cherry-colored boots up on an ottoman; no doubt he has trouble with circulation in his legs. He is drinking tea from a thimble-sized porcelain cup, encrusted with gold leaf, looted from a chateau somewhere. Heavy cologne fails to mask his odor: bad teeth, intestinal trouble, and necrotizing hemorrhoids.

"Good morning, gentlemen," he says brightly. "Sorry to have kept you waiting. Heil Hitler! Would you like some tea?"

There is small talk. It goes on at length. Göring is fascinated with Angelo's work as a test pilot. Not only that, he has any number of peculiar ideas adapted from the Bavarian Illuminati, and is groping for some way to tie these in with higher mathematics. Rudy is afraid, for a while, that this task is about to be placed on his shoulders. But even Göring himself seems impatient with this phase of the conversation. Once or twice he reaches out with his riding crop to part a curtain slightly.

The outdoor light seems to cause him appalling pain and he quickly looks away.

But finally the train slows, maneuvers through more switches, and coasts to a gentle stop. They can see nothing, of course. Rudy strains his ears, and thinks he hears activity around them: many feet marching, and commands being shouted. Göring catches the eye of an aide and waves his riding crop towards the desk. The aide springs forward, snatches up the handwritten document, and bears it over to the Reichsmarschall, presenting it with a small, neat bow. Göring reads through it quickly. Then he looks up at Rudy and Angelo and makes tut-tut-tut noises, shaking his gigantic head from side to side. Various layers of jowls, folds, and wattles follow, always a few degrees out of phase. "Homosexuality," Göring says. "You must be aware of the Führer's policy regarding this sort of behavior." He holds up the sheet and shakes it. "Shame on you! Both of you. A test pilot who is a guest in our country, and an eminent mathematician working on great secrets. You must have known that the Sicherheitsdienst would get wind of this." He heaves an exhausted sigh. "How am I going to patch this up?"

When Göring says this, Rudy knows for the first time since the knock on his door that he is not going to die today. Göring has something else in mind.

But first his victims need to be properly terrified. "Do you know what could happen to you? Hmm? Do you?"

Neither Rudy nor Angelo answers. It is not the sort of question that really needs answering.

Göring answers it for them by reaching out with his riding crop and lifting up the curtain. Harsh blue light, reflected from snow, peals into the coach. Göring shuts his eyes and looks the other way.

They are in the middle of an open area, surrounded by tall barbed-wire fences, filled with long rows of dark barracks. In the center, a tall stack pours smoke into a white sky. SS troops in greatcoats and jackboots pace around, blowing into their hands. Just a few yards away from them, on an adjacent railway siding, a gang of wretches in striped clothing are at work in, and around, a boxcar, unloading pale cargo. A large number of naked human bodies have become all frozen together in a solid, tangled mass inside the boxcar, and the prisoners are at work with axes, bucksaws, and prybars, dismantling them and throwing the parts onto the ground. Because they are frozen solid, there is no blood, and so the entire operation is startlingly clean. The double-glazed windows of Göring's coach block sound so effectively that the impact of a big fire ax on a frozen abdomen comes through as a nearly imperceptible thud.

One of the prisoners turns towards them, carrying a thigh toward a wheelbarrow, and risks a direct look at the Reichsmarschall's train. This prisoner has a pink triangle sewn to the breast of his uniform. The prisoner's eyes are trying to probe through the window, past the curtain, trying to make a human connection with someone on the inside of the coach. Rudy stiffens in panic for a moment, thinking that the prisoner sees him. Then Göring withdraws the riding crop and the curtain falls. A few moments later, the train begins to move again.

Rudy looks at his lover. Angelo is sitting frozen, just like one of those corpses, with his hands over his face.

Göring flicks his crop dismissively. "Get out," he says.

"What?" ask Rudy and Angelo simultaneously.

Göring laughs heartily. "No, no! I don't mean get out of the train! I mean, Angelo, get out of this coach. I want to talk to Herr Doktor Professor von Hacklheber in private. You may wait in the parlor car."

Angelo leaves eagerly. Göring waves his crop at a couple of hovering aides, and they leave too. Göring and Rudy are alone together.

"I am sorry to show you these unpleasant things," Göring says. "I simply wanted to impress upon you the importance of keeping secrets."

"I can assure the Reichsmarschall that—"

Göring shushes him with a wave of the crop. "Don't be tedious. I know that you have sworn any number of great oaths, and been through all of the indoctrination concerning secrecy. I have no doubt of your sincerity. But it is all just words, and not good enough for the work that I wish you to begin doing for me. To work for me, you must see the thing I have shown you, so that you can really understand the stakes."

Rudy looks at the floor, takes a deep breath, and forces out the words: "It would be a great honor to work for you, Reichsmarschall. But since you have access to so many of the great museums and libraries of Europe, there is only one small favor I, as a scholar, might humbly request of you."

Back in the church basement in Norrsbruck, Sweden, Rudy yells, and drops a cigarette on the floor, having allowed it to burn down to his fingers, like a slow fuse, while relating this story. He puts his hand to his mouth, sucks on the finger briefly, then remembers his manners and composes himself. "Göring knew a surprising amount about cryptology, and was aware of my work on the Enigma. He didn't trust the machine. He told me that he wanted me to come up with the very best cryptosystem in the world, one that could never be broken—he wanted to communicate (he said) with U-boats at sea and with installations in Manila and Tokyo. And so, I came up with such a system."

"And you handed it over," Bischoff says.

"Yes," Rudy says, and here, for the first time all day, he allows himself a slight smile. "And it is a reasonably good system, despite the fact that I crippled it before giving it to Göring."

"Crippled it?" Root asks. "What do you mean?"

"Imagine a new engine for an aeroplane. Imagine it has sixteen cylinders. It is more powerful than any other engine in the world. Even so, a mechanic can do certain things—very simple things—to kill its performance. Such as pulling out half of the spark plug wires. Or tampering with the timing. This is an analogy to what I did with Göring's cryptosystem."

"So what went wrong?" Shaftoe asks. "They figured out that you had crippled it?"

Rudolf von Hacklheber laughs. "Not very likely. Maybe half a dozen people in the world could figure that out. No, what went wrong was that you fellows, you Allies, landed in Sicily, and then in Italy, and not long afterwards, Mussolini was overthrown, the Italians withdrew from the Axis, and Angelo, like all of the other hundreds of thousands of Italian nationals living and working in the Reich, fell under suspicion. His services were badly needed as a test pilot, but his situation was tenuous. He volunteered for the most dangerous work of all—flying the new Messerschmidt prototype, with the turbine-jet engine. This proved his loyalty in the eyes of some.

"Remember that, at the same time, I was decrypting the message traffic of Detachment 2702. I kept these results to myself, as I no longer felt any particular loyalty to the Third Reich. There had been a great burst of activity around the middle of April, and then no messages for a while—as if the detachment had ceased to exist. At exactly the same time, Göring's people were very active for a few days—they were afraid that Bischoff was going to broadcast the secret of U-553."

"So you know about that?" Bischoff asks.

"Natürlich. U-553 was Göring's treasure ship. Its existence was supposed to be a secret. When you, Sergeant Shaftoe, turned up on board Bischoff's U-boat, talking about this thing, Göring was very concerned for a few days. But then everything settled down, and there was no Detachment 2702 traffic through the late spring and early summer. Mussolini was overthrown in late June. Then the troubles began for me and Angelo. The Wehrmacht was defeated by the Russians at Kursk—absolute proof, for those who needed it, that the Eastern Front is lost. Since then Göring has redoubled his efforts to get his gold, jewels, and art out of the country." Rudy looks at Bischoff. "I am frankly surprised that he has not tried to recruit you."

"Dönitz has," Bischoff admits.

Rudy nods; it all fits.

"During all of this," Rudy continues, "I received only one message intercept in the Detachment 2702 code. It took my machinery several weeks to break it. It was a message from Enoch Root, stating that he and Sergeant Shaftoe were in Norrsbruck, Sweden, and requesting further instructions. I was aware that Kapitänleutnant Bischoff was also in the same town, and became interested. I decided that this would be a good place for me and Angelo to escape to."

"*Why!?*" Shaftoe says. "Of all the places—"

"Enoch and I had never met. But there are certain old family connections," Rudy says, "and certain shared interests."

Bischoff mutters something in German.

"The connections make a very long story. I would have to write a whole fucking book," Rudy says irritably.

Bischoff looks only slightly appeased, but Rudy goes on anyway. "It took us several weeks to make preparations. I packed up the Leibniz-Archiv—"

"Hold on—the what?"

"Certain materials I use in my research. They had been scattered among many libraries, all over Europe. Göring brought them all together for me—it makes men like him feel powerful, to do these little favors for their slaves. I departed from Berlin last week, on the pretext of going to Hannover, to do my Leibniz-research. Instead I made my way to Sweden through channels that were quite involved—"

"No shit! How'd you manage that little stunt?" Shaftoe asks.

Rudy looks at Enoch Root as if expecting him to answer the question. Root shakes his head minutely.

"It would be too tedious to explain here," Rudy says, sounding mildly annoyed. "I found Enoch. We got a message to Angelo saying that I was safe here. Angelo then tried to make his escape in the Messerschmidt prototype, with the results that we have all seen."

A long pause.

"And now, here we are!" says Bobby Shaftoe.

"Here we are," agrees Rudolf von Hacklheber.

"What do you think we should do?" asks Shaftoe.

"I think we should form a secret conspiracy," says Rudolf von Hacklheber offhandedly, as if proposing to go in together on a fifth of bourbon. "We should all make our way separately to Manila and, once we arrive, we should take some, if not all, of the gold that the Nazis and the Nipponese have been hoarding there."

"What do you want with a shitload of gold?" Bobby asks. "You're already rich."

"There are many deserving charities," Rudy says, looking significantly at Root. Root averts his eyes.

There is another long pause.

"I can provide secure lines of communication, which is the *sine qua non* of any secret conspiracy," says Rudolf von Hacklheber. "We will use the full-strength, uncrippled version of the same cryptosystem that I invented for Göring. Bischoff can be our man on the inside, since Dönitz wants him so badly. Sergeant Shaftoe can be—"

"Don't even say it, I already know," says Bobby Shaftoe.

He and Bischoff look at Root, who's sitting on his hands, staring at Rudy. Looking oddly nervous.

"Enoch the Red, your organization can get us to Manila," von Hacklheber says.

Shaftoe snorts. "Don't you think the Catholic Church has its hands sort of full right now?"

"I'm not talking about the Church," Rudy says. "I'm talking about *Societas Eruditorum*."

Root freezes.

"Congratulations there, Rudy!" Shaftoe says. "You surprised the padre. I didn't think it could be done. Now would you mind telling us what the fuck you're talking about?"

HOARD

LIKE A CLIENT OF ONE OF YOUR LESS REPUTABLE PUFFERFISH sushi chefs, Randy Waterhouse does not move from his assigned seat for a full ninety minutes after the jumbo leaves Ninoy Aquino International Airport. A can of beer is embedded in the core of his spiraled hand. His arm lies on the extra-wide Business Class armrest, a shank on a slab. He does not turn his head, or turret his eyeballs, even, to look out the window at northern Luzon. All that's out there is jungle, which has two sets of connotations going for it now. One is the spooky Tarzan/ Stanley & Livingstone/"The horror, the horror"/natives-are-restless/ Charlie's out there somewhere waiting for us kind. The second is the more modern and enlightened sort of Jacques Cousteauian teeming-repository-of-brilliant-and-endangered-species, lungs-of-the-planet kind. Neither really works for Randy anymore, which is why despite the state of hibernatory torpor he shunted into the moment his ass impacted on the navy blue leather of the seat, he feels a little spike of irritation every time one of the other passengers, peering out a window, pronounces the word "jungle." To him, it is just a shitload of trees now, trees going on for miles and miles, up the little hilly-willies and down the little hilly-willies. It is easy, now, for him to understand tropical denizens' shockingly frank and blunt craving to drive through this sort of territory in the largest and widest available bulldozers (the only parts of his body that move during the first hour and a half of the flight are certain facial muscles which pull the corners of his mouth back into an ironic rictus when he imagines what Charlene would think of this—it is just too perfect—Randy goes off on a Business Foray and comes back identifying with people who bulldoze rainforests). Randy wants to bulldoze the jungle, all of it. Actually, thermonuclear weapons, detonated at a suitable height, would do the job faster. He needs to rationalize this urge. He will do so, as soon as he solves the running-out-of-planetary-oxygen problem.

By the time it even occurs to him to lift the beer to his lips, the heat of his body has gone into it, and his hand has become as chilly and stiff as an uncooked rolled roast. For that matter, his whole body has adjourned into some kind of metabolic recess, and his brain is not exactly purring at high RPM's either. He feels kind of the way he does, sometimes, the day before he comes down with a total-body cold-and-flu scenario, one of those crushing viral Tet Offensives that, every few years, swats you out of the land of the fully living for a week or two. It is as if about three-quarters of his body's resources of nutrients and energy have been diverted to the task of manufacturing quintillions of viruses. At the currency exchange window of NAIA, Randy had stood behind a Chinese man who, just before he stepped back from the window with his money, unloaded a Sneeze of such titanic force that the rolling pressure wave turbulating outwards from his raw, flapping facial orifices caused the wall of bulletproof glass separating him from the moneychangers to flex slightly, so that the reflection of the Chinese man, Randy behind him, the lobby of NAIA and the sunlit passenger-dropoff lane outside underwent a subtle warpage. The viruses must have roiled back from the glass, reflected like light, and enveloped Randy. So maybe Randy is the personal vector of this year's version of the flu-named-after-some-city-in-East-Asia that annually tours the United States, just barely preceded by rush shipments of flu vaccine. Or maybe it's Ebola.

Actually, he feels fine. Other than the fact that his mitochondria have gone on strike, or that his thyroid seems to be failing (perhaps it was secretly removed by black-market organ transplanters? He makes a mental note to check for new scars in the next mirror) he is not experiencing any viral symptoms at all.

It is some kind of post-stress thing. This is the first time he has relaxed in a couple of weeks. Not once has he sat down in a bar with a beer, or put his feet up on a desk, or just collapsed like a decaying corpse in front of the television set. Now his body is telling him it's payback time. He does not sleep; he does not feel drowsy at all. Actually, he's been sleeping rather well. But his body refuses to move for an hour, and then most of another hour, and to the extent his brain is working at all it can only chase its tail.

But there is something that he could be doing. This is why laptops were invented, so that important business persons would not fritter away long flights relaxing. He can see it right there on the floor in front of him. He knows he should reach for it. But it would break the spell. He feels as if water condensed on his skin and froze into a carapace that will shatter as soon as he moves any part of his body. This is, he realizes, exactly how a laptop computer must feel when it drops into its power-saving mode.

Then a flight attendant is there holding a menu in front of his face and saying something that jolts him like a cattle prod. He nearly jumps out of his seat, spills his beer a little, gropes for the menu. Before he can drop back into his demi-coma, he continues the motion and reaches down for his laptop. The seat next to him is empty and he can put his dinner over there while he works on the computer.

People around him are watching CNN—live, from CNN Center in Atlanta—not a canned thing on tape. According to the plethora of pseudotechnical data cards jammed into the seatbacks, which Randy is the only person who ever reads, this plane has some kind of antenna that can keep a lock on a communications satellite as it flies across the Pacific. Furthermore, it's two-way, so you can even transmit e-mail. Randy spends a while familiarizing himself with the instructions, checks the rates, as if he really gives a shit how much it costs, then jacks the thing into the anus of his laptop. He opens up the laptop and checks his e-mail. Traffic is low because everyone in Epiphyte knows he's en route somewhere.

Nevertheless, there are three messages from Kia, Epiphyte's only actual employee, the administrative assistant for the whole company. Kia works in a totally alienated, abstracted office in the Springboard Capital corporate incubator complex in San Mateo. It is some sort of a federal regulation that nascent high-tech companies must not hire pudgy fifty-year-old support staff, the way big established companies do. They must hire topologically enhanced twenty-year-olds with names that sound like new models of cars. Since most hackers are white males, their companies are disaster areas when it comes to diversity, and it follows that all of the diversity must be concentrated in the one or two employees who are not hackers. In the part of a federal equal-opportunity form where Randy would simply check a box labeled CAUCASIAN, Kia would have to attach multiple sheets on which her family tree would be ramified backwards through time ten or twelve generations until reaching ancestors who could actually be pegged to one specific ethnic group without glossing anything over, and those ethnic groups would be intimidatingly hip ones—not Swedes, let's say, but Lapps, and not Chinese but Hakka, and not Spanish but Basque. Instead of doing this, on her job app for Epiphyte she simply checked "other" and then wrote in TRANS-ETHNIC. In fact, Kia is trans-just about every system of human categorization, and what she isn't trans-she is post-.

Anyway, Kia does a great job (it is part of the unspoken social contract with these people that they always do an absolutely fantastic job) and she has sent e-mail to Randy notifying him that she has recently fielded four trans-Pacific telephone calls from America Shaftoe, who wants to know Randy's whereabouts, plans, state of mind, and purity of spirit. Kia has informed Amy that Randy's on his way to California and has somehow insinuated, or Amy has somehow figured out, that the purpose of the visit is NOT BUSINESS. Randy senses a small pane of glass shattering over a neurological alarm button somewhere. He is in trouble. This is divine retribution for his having dared to sit still and not do anything for ninety whole minutes. He uses his word processor to whip out a note explaining to Amy that he needs to straighten out some paperwork in order to sever the last clinging tendrils of his dead, dead, dead relationship with Charlene (which was such a lousy idea to begin with that it causes him to lie awake at night questioning his own judgment and fitness to live), and that he has to be in California in order to do it. He faxes the note to Semper Marine in Manila, and also faxes it to *Glory IV* in case Amy's out on the water.

He then does something that probably means he's certifiably crazy. He gets up and strolls up and down the business-class aisle on pretext of using the bathroom, and checks out the people sitting nearby, paying special attention to their luggage, the stuff they've jammed into the overhead compartments, the bags under the seats in front of them. He is looking for anything that might contain a Van Eck phreaking type of antenna. It is a completely useless thing to do, because just about any type of luggage might contain such an antenna and he would never know it. Furthermore, any actual spy who had been planted on this plane to eavesdrop on his computer would not be sitting there holding up a big antenna and peering at an oscilloscope. But performing the check (like checking the rates for live data transmissions to the satellite) is sort of an empty ritual that makes him feel vaguely responsible and arguably non-stupid.

Returning to his seat, he fires up OrdoEmacs, which is a marvelously paranoid piece of software invented by John Cantrell. Emacs in its normal form is the hacker's word processor, a text editor that offers little in the way of fancy formatting capabilities but does the basic job of editing plain text very well. Your normally cryptographically paranoid hacker would create files using Emacs and then encrypt them with Ordo later. But if you forget to encrypt them, or if your laptop gets stolen before you get a chance to, or your plane crashes and you die but your laptop is sieved out of the muck by baffled-but-dogged crash investigators and falls into the hands of federal authorities, your files can be read. For that matter it is possible even to find ghostly traces of old bits on a hard drive's sectors even after the file has been overwritten with new data.

OrdoEmacs, on the other hand, works exactly like regular Emacs, except that it encrypts everything before writing it out to disk. At no time is plaintext ever laid down on a disk by OrdoEmacs—the only place it exists in its plain, readable form is in the pixels on the screen, and in the volatile RAM of the computer, whence it vanishes the moment power is shut down. Not only that, but it's coupled to a screensaver that uses the little built-in CCD camera in the laptop to check to see if you are actually there. It can't recognize your face, but it can tell whether or not a vaguely human-shaped form is sitting in front of it, and if that vaguely human-shaped form goes away, even for a fraction of a second, it will drop into a screen-saver that will blank the display and freeze the machine until such time as you type in a password, or biometrically verify your identity through voice recognition.

Randy opens up a document template that Epiphyte uses for internal memoranda and begins to lay out certain facts that will be fresh, and no doubt stimulating, to Avi, Beryl, John, Tom, and Eb.

```
MY TRIP TO THE JUNGLE
or
THE DRUMS OF THE HUKS
or
GET A LOAD OF THIS
or
HE SQUEEZED MY TESTICLES
or
THE WEIRD TURN PRO
```

a tale of adventure and discovery in the majestic rainforest of northern Luzon

by

Randall Lawrence Waterhouse

As I stepped on this unknown middle-aged Filipina's feet
during an ill-advised ballroom dancing foray, she leaned
close to me and uttered some latitude and longitude figures
with a conspicuously large number of significant digits of
precision, implying a maximum positional error on the
order of the size of a dinner plate. Gosh, was I ever curious! Subject provided these numbers as part of a conversational gambit/thought experiment concerning the inherent
value (as in monetary) of information, a subject (coincidentally?) of interest to us, the Management Team of Epi-
phyte(2) Corp. Examination of high-res maps of Luzon
indicated that the lat. and long. in question were in a
hilly (let's just go ahead and call it mountainous) region
some 250 km north of Manila. For those of you not familiar
with WW2 history, this area was within the final perimeter
controlled by General Yamashita, the Tiger of Malaya and
conqueror of Singapore, at the end of that war, when Gen.
MacArthur had driven him and his approx. 10^5 troops out of
the populated lowlands. And no, this is not just a fundamentally irrelevant historical note, as we shall see.

Relayed said data to one Douglas MacArthur Shaftoe
(refer to my exceptionally colorful and readable status
reports on cable survey for more anecdotal material concerning same) who asserted ''someone is trying to send you
a message'' (note: all cheesy dialog hereinafter is
DMS's) and offered his assistance with a vigor bordering
on scary aggressiveness. DMS is energetic and enterprising to a degree that from time to time leaves certain persons (e.g. those burdened with a petty fear of death or
torture) uneasy (see my prior speculation as to possibility DMS may have been born with a redundant Y chromosome).
Primary role of Yours Truly became as follows: source of
repetitious and evidently irritating counsels of caution, restraint, other virtues given a low priority by
DMS, who cites his longevity (which unavoidably exceeds
that of Yours Truly as he was born before me), network of
close personal relationships (murky, globe-spanning, re-
putedly puissant), financial prosperity (commodities,

e.g. precious metals, distributed among many locations DMS declines to reveal) and (as trump card) the corporeal perfection of his girlfriend (she must carry an umbrella while out of doors lest her face cause pilots of overflying commercial airliners to pitch forward, dumb and inert, onto their control yokes) all as proof that the ideas shared by Yours Truly vis-a-vis how to avoid death, dismemberment, etc. need not be given more than the most cursory attention. Yours Truly's only bargaining chips were, appropriately and ironically enough, information: namely the final few digits of the lat. and long. which were withheld from DMS lest he simply go there himself and check them out (note: DMS is honest to a fault, and so the concern is not that DMS might steal or appropriate anything but that situation would get out of hand, to the extent it ever was in hand to begin with).

Plans were made for a journey (''mission'' in DMS parlance) to said lat. and long. Extra batteries were purchased for the GPS receiver (see attached expense report). Drinking water, etc. laid in. A jeepney was retained. Concept of jeepney is impossible to convey fully here: a minibus, usually named after a pop star, Biblical figure, or abstract theological concept, whose engine & frame come from American, or Nipponese auto company but whose entire body, seats, upholstery, & encrustations of lurid decor are locally manufactured by high-spirited artisans. Jeepneys are normally made outside of Manila in towns or barangays (semiautonomous neighborhoods) that specialize in same; the design, materials, style, etc. of a jeepney reflect its provenance just as good wine allegedly betrays climate, soil, etc. of its terroir. Ours was (anomalously) a perfectly monochromatic jeepney mfged. out of pure stainless steel in the stainless-steel-fabrication-specialized bgy. of San Pablo, with (unlike normal jeepneys) no colored decorations at all---everything either stainless-steel-colored or (where use was made of electric lights) pure piercing halogen-white with bluish tinge nicely complementing hue of stainless steel. Seats in back were stainless-steel benches with surprisingly ergonomic lumbar support capabilities. Name of our jeepney was THE GRACE OF GOD. Readers of this memo will be disappointed to know that Bong-Bong Gad (sic), designer/

owner/driver/proprietor of the vehicle, anticipated the
inevitable ''there but for THE GRACE OF GOD go I'' witticism by unloading same on Yours Truly while we were still
shaking hands (Filipinos go in for long handshakes, and
the first party to initiate termination of a handshake---
usually the non-Filipino---is invariably left with a
nagging feeling that he is a shithead).

Yours Truly, in discreet one-on-one mode with DMS, ad-
verted to lack of windows in the rear (passenger) section
of THE GRACE OF GOD as prima facie evidence that it lacked
air-conditioning, a technology widely adopted in Philippine Islands. DMS evinced skepticism as to moral fiber of
Yours Truly, commenced with a series of probing questions
aimed at establishing my commitment to Mission, fiduciary
resp. to Epiphyte shareholders, level of physical & mental vigor, and overall level of ''serious''-ness (being
''serious'' is some kind of umbrella concept strongly
correlated with my fitness to live, to have the privilege
of knowing DMS, and to go on dates with his daughter. This
gives me an opening to mention what would normally be no
one's business but my own but which in these circumstances
it is ethically mandated that I disclose, namely, that I
am infatuated with daughter of DMS and that while not exactly reciprocating these feelings at full strength she
finds me sufficiently non-loathsome to have dinner with me
from time to time. It has only occurred to me at this very
moment that my pursuit of rel'nship w/the female in question, one America (sic) by name, would in context of modern U.S. society be classified as SEXUAL HARASSMENT and
that if desired culmination is achieved it might be classified as SEXUAL ABUSE or RAPE owing to ''power imbalance''
existing between me and her. Viz., Yours Truly is on Management Team of Corp that has retained Semper Marine for
large job & provided them with majority of their revenue
during last fiscal year. Anyone with thoughts of summoning
federal authorities to apprehend me upon arrival at SFO &
expose my misdeeds & subject me to public disgrace & compulsory consciousness-raising workshops is advised to
acquaint him or herself with the Shaftoes first & to at
least remain open to possibility that Dad's martial prow-
ess in combination with traditional feelings of psychotic
protectiveness toward his female offspring, combined

with Daughter's habit of carrying large Palawan stabbing
weapon known as a kris, and Daughter's overall psychic
fierceness & physical fitness & courage exceeding that of
Yours Truly, mitigate any perceived power imbalance, particularly given that most of our interactions take place
in settings which lend themselves admirably to discreet
homicide & corpse disposal. In other words, I make you
aware of this amor stuff not as confession of personal
misdeeds but to make full disclosure of situation that
could influence my judgment vis-a-vis Semper Marine and
conceivably negatively impact shareholder value, or,
much more plausibly, that could be SEEN as doing so by minority-shareholder lawyers who infest our industry like
guinea worms, and used as pretext for legal action).

Back to the question at hand, then. Yours Truly asserted
calmly (feeling that vigorous assertions would be perceived by DMS as defensiveness & hence a de facto confession of lack of ''serious''-ness) that (1) a couple of
days' travel in open AC-less vehicle through Philippine
hinterland would be a day at the beach, a picnic, a walk
in the park, & a sunday stroll all rolled into one, and (2)
furthermore that even if it were the most hideous torture
Yours Truly would gladly undergo it given that the stakes,
for all concerned (incl. Epiphyte shareholders) were so
high and generally Serious. In retrospect, (1) and (2) in
close succession seem to betray some kind of hedging
strategy on part of Yours Truly, however at the time DMS
was mollified, formally withdrew previous accusations as
to moral fiber, etc., and divulged that use of jeepney was
tactical masterstroke on his (DMS's) part in that, where
we were going, a Merc with smoked glass or fifty-thousand-
dollar Land Rover, or (by extension) any vehicle with ex-
travagances such as upholstered seats, windows with glass
in them, shock absorbers dating from post-Kennedy-assas-
sination era, etc., etc. would only draw undesired attention to Mission.

America Shaftoe remained in Manila to stay in touch with
Mission via radio & (I supposed) to call in napalm strikes
should we find selves embroiled. Bong-Bong Gad & his approx. 12-yr.-old son/business associate Fidel occupied
front seat. DMS & Yours Truly shared rear (passenger) section with three mysterious, precisely packed G.I. green

duffel bags; approx. 100 kilos of drinking water in plastic bottles; & two Asian gentlemen in their 30s or 40s who
exhibited   stereotypical   inscrutability/impassivity/
dignity, etc., etc. during the first four hours of the
journey, which were spent simply trying to drive from center of Manila to northern outskirts of same. Nationality
of these two was not immediately evident. Many Filipinos
are, racially, almost pure Chinese even though their families have been living here for centuries. Perhaps this
explained strongly Asian features of our traveling companions and (I now had to assume) business associates.

Proverbial ice was broken as one consequence of pig
truck incident which occurred on four-lane highway, nar-
rowed by construction to two, leading N from Manila. Casual obsvn. of Filipino swine suggests that their
ludicrous, pink, tabloid-sized ears function as heat exchangers, as do, e.g., the tongues of dogs. They are
transported in vehicles consisting of big cage constructed on bed of a straight (as opposed to semiarticu-
lated) truck. Construction of such vehicles appears to
tax local resources to the point where they are only eco-
nomical when maximum conceivable number of swine are
packed into confines at all times. Heat buildup ensues.
Pigs adapt by fighting their way to perimeter of cage &
hanging ear/heat exchangers out over the side to flap in
the wind of the truck's motion.

The appearance of such a vehicle when approached from
behind can be easily envisioned without further description. Readers who devote a few moments' consideration to
the subject of excreta need not be pounded over the head
vis-a-vis what flies, sprays, drips, etc. from such vehicles either. The Pig Truck Incident was a humorous demonstration of applied hydrodynamics, though since no actual
water was involved perhaps ''excretodynamics'' or ''sca-
todynamics'' might better fit. THE GRACE OF GOD had been
following a representative Pig Truck for some miles in the
hopes of passing it. The sheer quantity of excess body
heat radiating from its vast phased array of flapping pink
ears caused several of our drinking-water bottles to
achieve full rolling boil and explode. Bong-Bong Gad
maintained a respectful distance because of excreta hazards, which in no way simplified the problem of passing the

truck. Tension climbed to a palpable level & Bong-Bong was subjected to steadily increasing stream of good-natured heckling and unsolicited driving advice from passenger area, esp. from DMS who viewed lingering unwelcome presence of pig truck in our planned trajectory as personal affront & hence challenge to be overcome w/all due pluck, vigor, can-do spirit, & other qualities known to be possessed in abundance by DMS.

After some time Bong-Bong made his move, using one hand to manipulate steering wheel and other to time-share equally important responsibilities of shifting gears and depressing the horn button. As we drew alongside the Pig Truck (which was on my side of the jeepney) the Truck slalomed toward us as if perhaps swerving around some real or imagined roadside hazard. The primary horn of THE GRACE OF GOD was apparently going unheard, possibly because it was competing for audio bandwidth against large numbers of swine voicing their displeasure in same frequency range. With aplomb normally seen only among senescent English butlers, Bong-Bong reached up with his horn/gearshift hand and gripped a brilliant stainless-steel chain flailing from ceiling of cab with a stainless-steel crucifix on the end of it and jerked downwards, energizing the secondary, tertiary, and quaternary honking systems: a trio of tuba-sized stainless-steel horns mounted to the roof of THE GRACE OF GOD and collectively drawing so much power that our vehicle's speed dropped by (I would estimate) ten km/hr as its energies were diverted into decibel production. A demi-hyperbolic swath of agricultural crops twenty miles long was flattened to the ground by the blast, and, hundreds of miles north, the Taiwanese government, its collective ears still ringing, filed a diplomatic protest with the Philippine ambassador. Dead whales and dolphins washed ashore on the beaches of Luzon for days, and sonar operators in passing U.S. Navy submarines were sent into early retirement with blood streaming from their ears.

Terrified by this sound, all of the pigs (I would suppose) voided their bowels just as the driver of the Pig Truck swerved violently away from us. Certain first-year-physics conservation-of-momentum issues dictated that I be showered with former pig bowel contents in order to en-

hance shareholder value. This was evidently the funniest
thing that the two Asian-looking gentlemen had ever seen,
and rendered them helpless for several minutes. One of
them actually retched from laughing too hard (the first
time that our vehicle's lack of windows came in handy).
The other extended his hand and introduced himself as one
Jean Nguyen. This is the French male name ''zhohn'' and
not the Anglo female name ''jeen.'' Jean Nguyen looked at
me expectantly after telling me his name, as did DMS, as
if they were expecting me to get a fairly obvious joke.
Perhaps preoccupied with hygienic issues, I failed to get
it, and they pointed out to me that when ''Jean'' is pronounced like ''John'' and ''Nguyen'' is pronounced the
way a lot of Americans mangle it, the name sounds arguably
like ''John Wayne,'' which is how I was encouraged to address this Jean Nguyen from that point onwards. It seemed
in retrospect that I was being given an opportunity to
have a small chuckle at Jean Nguyen's expense and thereby
to even the scales, in some small but symbolically important sense, for the pig shit incident. My failure to exploit this opportunity left everyone feeling mildly
uneasy and like they still owed me one. The other gentleman was introduced as Jackie Woo. He spoke English with a
vaguely East Indian crackle which led me to peg him, spec-
ulatively, as a Malay Peninsula native of Chinese descent, e.g., from Singapore or Penang.

   First day's travel got us across the central Luzon plain
(rice and sugar cane) to the town of San Jose at the foot
of the southernmost extension of the Cordillera Central
(trees and bugs). By this point it was dark, and to my relief, neither DMS nor Bong-Bong was eager to brave twisty
Cordillera roads in darkness. We stayed in a guest house.
At this point, having devoted much time to detailed Pig
Truck description I will elide various details concerning
San Juan, its inhabitants (of various taxonomic phyla
some of which I had never encountered until that night),
the character-building nature of our lodgings and, in
particular, their fanciful plumbing system which was a
credit to the imagination, though not the hydrostatic
acumen, of its anonymous creator. It was the kind of hos-
tel that makes a traveler eager to get an early and explosively sudden start in the morning, which we did.

A note now about the physical properties of space, as
perceived by human beings imprisoned within bodies of
limited physical capabilities. I have long noticed that
space seems to be more compressed, more involuted, somehow psychically LARGER in some places than others. Covering a distance of three or four miles in the totally open
scrublands of central Washington State is a simple matter, and takes less than an hour on foot, and only a few
minutes if you have some kind of vehicle. Covering the
same distance in Manhattan takes much longer. It's not
just that the space in Manhattan is more physically ob-
structed (though it definitely is) but that there is some
kind of psychological impact that alters the way you perceive and experience distance. You cannot see as far, and
what you do see is full of people, buildings, goods, vehicles, and other stuff that it takes your brain some amount
of effort to sort through, to process. Even if you had some
kind of magic carpet that would glide past all of the physical obstructions the distance would seem much longer,
and would take longer to cover, simply because your mind
would have to deal with more stuff.

The same thing is true of a jungle type of environment
as opposed to the plains. Traversing the physical space is
basically an ongoing battle against hundreds of different
combatants each one of which is, to a traveler, an ob-
struction, a hazard, or both. I.e., no matter which one of
them predominates in a given ten-square-meter area, you
are still screwed, as far as getting across that ten
square meters is concerned. There are roads through the
jungle, but even when they are in good repair they seem
more like bottlenecks than vectors of motion, and they are
never in good repair---mudslides, fallen trees, huge
chuckholes, and the like block them every few hundred meters. Also the same perceptual thing is at work here---
you can't see more than a few meters in any direction, and
what you do see is dense with visual inputs, some of which,
like butterflies, are (okay, okay) beautiful. My reason
for mentioning this is that I know that everyone who reads
this probably has multiple maps of Luzon on their wall or
in their computer, which, when consulted, will cause it
to seem as if we are dealing with a triflingly small area,
and covering minuscule distances. But you must try not to

think this way and instead imagine that Luzon is effectively as large as, say, the United States west of the Mississippi. In terms of the time it takes to get around the
place, it is at least that big.

I mention this not out of some impulse to mewl and convince you all of how strenuously I have worked, but because until you grasp this central fact of the effectively
vast size of this part of the world, you will be completely
unable to believe the dumbfounding facts that I am slowly
getting around to revealing.

We went into the mountains. Around midday, we encountered our first military roadblock. Distance covered from
San Juan was pathetic from cartographic p.o.v., but in
terms of unexpected hassles creatively surmounted,
wrenchingly difficult decisions made, & pits of despair
climbed out of by the emotional fingernails, should be considered magnificent achievement on par with any given day
of the Lewis & Clark expedition, (excluding, of course,
anomalous days such as their first encounters with Ursus
horribilis & their epic, stocking-foot traversal of Bit-
terroot Range.) Roadblock was established in the low-key
Filipino style: one man in military uniform (U.S. Army
castoffs) standing by roadside smoking & beckoning. We
were at a rare wide spot in the road, a place where oncom-
ing Chicken-playing vehicles could pull aside abjectly.
Four members of Army (later pegged by insignia-savvy DMS
as a first lieutenant, a sergeant, and two privates) had
ensconced selves on parked Humvee type vehicle w/absurdly
long whip antenna clamped to bumper. The privates, armed
with M-16s, stiffly unfolded selves from repose & adopted
positions flanking THE GRACE OF GOD from behind, keeping
their weapons pointed vaguely at the ground, as if more
worried about entomological threats than our little band
of travelers. Sergeant was armed with what I first perceived as L-shaped nightstick fashioned from parts scavenged from plumbing aisle of home improvement store &
painted black, but on further examination proved to be a
submachine gun.

Said Sergeant approached Bong-Bong Gad's door & con-
versed with same in Tagalog. Lieutenant was armed only
with sidearm & supervised these operations from a shaded
area near the Humvee, seeming to espouse a hands-off, as

opposed to micromanaging, leadership style. This inspection was limited to the Sergeant peering in through TGOG's
glassless windows & exchanging hearty greetings with DMS
(evidently Jean Nguyen & Jackie Woo spoke even less Tagalog than Yours Truly). We were then allowed to proceed,
although I noticed that the lieutenant immediately commenced a radio transmission. ''The sergeant say there are
Nice People Around,'' Bong-Bong Gad explained to me,
using a coy local euphemism for NPA, or New People's Army,
a supposedly revolutionary, but evidently somewhat feck-
less guerilla organization descended in a direct line
from the Hukbalahaps, or Huks, the fighters who resisted
the Nipponese occupation (but not so desultorily) in WW2.

We then covered an amount of distance equivalent, in
terms of Fear, Uncertainty, and Doubt, to one more Lewis
And Clark Expedition Day, a convenient unit of distance,
danger, perspirational weight loss, poor sphincter control, wishing you were at home, exasperation, & emotional
toll which I will hereinafter abbreviate as LAC. So after
1 LAC we arrived at another roadblock similar to the first
except that here there was a troop truck in addition to
the Humvee, and some tents pitched, and a pit latrine,
whose odor & appearance suggested a long-standing military presence in this area. A luckless private was made to
crawl underneath THE GRACE OF GOD with a flashlight, inspecting its undercarriage. The three duffel bags were
removed and their contents spread out. I should mention
that upon my joining this expedition in Manila, DMS had
gone through my bag with a level of inquisitiveness
annoying at the time, refused to allow me to bring certain
items (such as pharmaceuticals) and transferred remaining items to clear plastic bags of Ziploc type which
were placed in the duffels. Merits of this highly modular
approach now became clear as inspection of our cargo was
wondrously facilitated: duffels were simply upended over
tarps spread on ground & contents inspected by sight
through transparent inner bags, sometimes by feel to
check for compositional inhomogeneities. Certain of
these bags contained cartons of American-brand tobacco
products which as expected did not make it back into the
duffels. Most of my DMS-mandated supply of alkaline AA
batteries, which I had thought radically out of propor-

tion to projected demand, also vanished at this time. We were sent on our way and after approx. 0.5 LAC (mostly occasioned by need to remove downed tree from roadway) arrived at a town that appeared seemingly out of nowhere in jungle valley, astride a river. Slept like a dead man in startlingly decent guesthouse that night. Woke up next morning & looked out window to observe large crowd of locals milling around in street below in their best meshback caps & American basketball t-shirts. Descended stairs to discover DMS in dining room, strategically flanked by Jean Nguyen & Jackie Woo, at other tables in corners of room, wearing climatically inappropriate jackets & generally projecting the image of concealed-weapon-equipped badass motherfuckers not to be trifled with.

Not wishing to interfere with this psychodrama, Yours Truly took innocuous position at yet another table, well away from projected gunfire corridors, accepted coffee from proprietor, declined local delicacies, negotiated (see expense report) for loan of bowl & spoon, breakfasted upon Cap'n Crunch & warm UHT milk from duffel bag (former had been packed into a Ziploc that when fully loaded adopted the distinctive pillow shape of an individual nugget of Cap'n Crunch, only much larger). Explosive crunching noises of nuggets caused Yours Truly to feel conspicuous and Western. Jean Nguyen & Jackie Woo had declined all refreshments except tea, the better to project image of hair-trigger alertness & potential for instantaneous violence. DMS was eating an omelette with approx. diameter of a Hula Hoop & engaging in one short conversation after another with locals, who were admitted through front door of building one at a time by proprietor and allowed to present their cases to DMS as if he were a traveling magistrate. Between two such interviews, DMS noted my presence in room & bade me join him. I moved my Cap'n Crunch infrastructure to corner of table not occupied by omelette & sat with him during the next couple of dozen interviews, which were conducted in mixture of English and Tagalog. Crowd in street dwindled gradually as they were interviewed and then dismissed by DMS.

Subject matter of interviews could be induced by Yours Truly only by recognizing occasional English words & adopting a basically intuitive pattern-recognition ap-

proach not amenable to rational explication here. Most
common keywords: Nippon, the Nipponese, the War, Gold,
Treasure, Excavations, Yamashita, Mass Executions. Emotional tenor of these conversations consisted of polite
but extreme skepticism on part of DMS, while confronted
by desperate need to be believed on part of interviewees.
In the end DMS did not believe any of them as far as I could
discern. They either became obstreperous & had to be shown
the door (glancing warily at Jean Nguyen & Jackie Woo) or
adopted a wounded & aggrieved stance. DMS was amused by
the former & disgusted by the latter. Yours Truly mused
silently upon inappropriateness of his own presence in
this setting & fondly remembered predictable comforts of
home, even of Manila. Upon completion of breakfast & of
interviews, DMS divulged, in response to my inquiries,
that he had been at it for two hours before I had arrived &
that formation of this milling crowd occurs spontaneously
before doors of any lodgings he takes in the Philippines
owing to his reputation as treasure-hunter. We had
avoided it in San Juan only because he goes there frequently and has already interviewed everyone in region
with Nipponese War Gold stories, found 99.9% of them lacking credibility, investigating the remaining .1% with occasionally lucrative results.

THE GRACE OF GOD had been washed and buffed by Fidel Gad
in magnificently insouciant gesture of defiance of jungle
elements. We proceeded across river. Racial variations
were conspicuous on faces, and in physiognomies, of
townspeople. Philippines were settled by countless overlapping waves of prehistoric migrants each racially &
linguistically incompatible with the last; this in combination with the spatial involution phenom. which I have, I
think sufficiently belabored by this point, makes for your
basic patchwork of different ethnic groups. The fork in
the river around which this town was nucleated was meet-
ing-point of unofficial turfs of three such different cultures. Lure of bright lights, or even dim, flickering ones,
has drawn thousands down from mountains in recent generations to establish several distinct barangays. This morning's interviewees were migrants from the mountains, or
their sons or grandsons, who claimed to have first-hand

knowledge of sites of Yamashita's hoards, or to have heard about same from late ancestors.

After covering about 1.5 LACs through jungle (roads, slopes, & conditions getting worse all the time) we encountered another military roadblock that had (somewhat incredibly to my mind) been established at a pass over a ridge, overlooking some rice terraces that had (even more incredibly) been hacked out of an essentially vertical south-facing slope thousands of years ago by the evidently fearsomely tenacious ancestors of the locals. Here we were thoroughly searched. My testicles were squeezed at some length by a sergeant with a pencil mustache, whose motives did not appear to be sexual, but who simultaneously looked me searchingly in the eye, awaiting a look of submission or hopelessness on the face of the squeezed. The others were subjected to the same treatment and probably endured it with more stoicism than Yours Truly. No lethal weapons were found attached to any of our scrota, but (surprise!) Jean (''John Wayne'') Nguyen and Jackie Woo were discovered to be armed to the teeth, and DMS somewhat less so. This is the part where Yours Truly expected to be shot in the nape of the neck whilst kneeling above a shallow grave, but ironically the authorities were far more interested in my cache of Cap'n Crunch than the weaponry sported by my comrades. Negotiations took place between DMS and the captain in charge of this outpost, in the privacy of a tent. DMS emerged with a thinner wallet and full clearance to proceed, on the conditions that (1) all supplies of Cap'n Crunch be donated to the officers' mess, and (2) a full inventory of weapons and ammo would be taken upon our return & compared with today's findings to make sure that we were not smuggling arms to the Nice People Around.

Three days' excruciatingly slow travel, comprising maybe another 10 LACs, awaited us. According to my map and GPS we were circumnavigating a cluster of active volcanoes that frequently spew out lahars (mud avalanches) which, when they impact upon ruts in the jungle that I'm here calling roads, cause logistical problems well into the realm of the absurd. We passed entire towns that had been buried and abandoned. Church steeples projected at angles from the grey mud, held up by the same flows that had

knocked them askew. Skulls of goats, dogs, etc. protruded
from mud that had hardened around living animals like concrete. We bedded down nightly at small settlements after
propitiating locals with gifts of penicillin (which Filipinos use like aspirin), batteries, disposable light-
ers, & whatever else had been left to us by the soldiers
at the roadblocks. We slept on benches, floor, roof, or
front seats of THE GRACE OF GOD, beneath mosquito nets.

Finally, when my GPS revealed that we were less than ten
km. from our mysterious destination, a local instructed
us to wait in a nearby village. We remained there for a
day & a night resting up and reading books (DMS is never
without a milk crate of techno-thrillers) until, at dawn,
we were approached by a trio of very young, short men, one
of whom carried an AK-47. He and his brethren climbed on
the roof of THE GRACE OF GOD and we proceeded into a jungle
track so narrow that I would not have pegged it even as a
footpath. A couple of km. into the jungle we reached a
point where we spent more time pushing the jeepney than
riding in it. Shortly thereafter we left Bong-Bong and
Fidel and one of the duffels behind, the four of us taking
turns humping the two other duffels. I consulted the GPS &
verified that, although we had for a time (alarmingly)
moved away from the Destination, we were now moving toward
it again. We were eight thousand m(eters) away and proceeding at a rate that varied between about five hundred
and a thousand m per hour, depending on whether we were
moving steeply uphill or steeply downhill. It was around
noon. Those of you with even rudimentary math skills will
have anticipated that when the sun went down we were still
a few thousand meters away.

The three Filipinos——our guides, guards, captors, or
whatever they were——wore the obligatory U.S. t-shirts
which make it so easy, nowadays, to underestimate cultural differences. They had not yet, however, attained
transethnicity. While in town they were shod in flip-flops,
but in the jungle they went barefoot (I have owned pairs
of shoes less durable than the calluses on their feet).
They spoke a language that apparently had zero in common
with the Tagalog I'd heard (''Tagalog'' is the old name;
the government is ragging on people to call it ''Pili-
pina,'' as if to imply that it is in some sense a common

language of the archipelago, which, as these guys demonstrated, is not the case). DMS had to converse with them
in English. At one point he gave one a throwaway plastic
ballpoint pen and their faces absolutely lit up. Then we
had to scrounge up two more pens for his companions. It
was like Christmas. Progress halted for several minutes
while they marveled at the pens' handy clicking mechanisms and doodled on the palms of their hands. The American t-shirts were, in other words, not worn as Americans
wear them but in the same spirit that the Queen of England
wore the exotic Koh-I-Noor Diamond on her crown. Not for
the first time I was overtaken by a strong not-exactly-in-
Kansas feeling.

   We slogged through the inevitable late-afternoon thun-
derstorm and kept moving into the night. DMS produced U.S.
Army MREs (Meals Ready to Eat) from the duffels, only a
couple of weeks past their stenciled expiration dates.
The Filipino men found these nearly as exciting as the
ballpoint pen, and saved the disposable foil trays for
later use as roofing material. We started slogging again.
The moon came out, which represented a bit of luck. I fell
down a couple of times and banged myself up on trees, which
ended up being a good thing because it put me into a state
of mild shock, dulling the pain and jacking me up on adrenaline. Our guides, at one point, seemed a little uncertain
as to which way they should go. I took a fix with the GPS
(using the screen's nightlight function) and established
that we were no more than fifty meters away from the destination, almost too small an error for my GPS to resolve. In
any event, it told us roughly which direction to proceed,
and we trudged through the trees for another few moments.
The guides became animated and very cheerful——finally
they had gotten their bearings, they knew where we were.
I bumped into something heavy, cold, and immovable that
nearly broke my knee. I reached down to touch it, expecting to find a rock outcropping, but instead felt something smooth and metallic. It seemed to be a stack of
smaller units, maybe comparable in size to loaves of
bread. ''Is this what we're looking for?'' I asked. DMS
turned on a battery-powered lantern and whipped the beam
around in my direction.

   I was instantly blinded by a thigh-high stack of gold

bars, about a meter and a half on a side, sitting out in the middle of the jungle, unmarked and unguarded.

DMS came over and sat down on top of it and lit a cigar. After a while, we counted the bars and measured them. They are trapezoidal in cross-section, about 10 cm wide and 10 high, and about 40 cm in length. This enabled us to estimate their mass at about 75 kg. each, which works out to 2400 troy ounces. Since gold is normally measured in troy ounces and not in kilograms (!) I'm going to make a wild guess that these bars were intended to weigh an even 2500 troy ounces apiece. At current rates ($400/troy oz.) this means each bar is worth a million dollars. There are 5 layers of bars in the stack, each layer consisting of 24 bars, and so the value of the stack is $120 million. Both the mass estimate and the value estimate presume that the bars are nearly pure gold. I took a rubbing of the stamp from one of the bars, which bears the mark of the Bank of Singapore. Each bar is marked with a unique serial number and I copied down as many of those as I could see.

Then we went back to Manila. All along the way, I tried to imagine the logistics of getting even a single one of those gold bars from the jungle out to the nearest bank where it could be turned into something useful, like cash.

Let me transition to a Q&A format here.

Q: Randy, I get the feeling that you are about to lay out in detail all of the hassles that would be involved in moving this gold overland, so let's just cut to the chase and talk about helicopters.

A: There is no place for a helicopter to land. Terrain is extremely rugged. The nearest sufficiently flat place is about one km. away. It would have to be cleared. In Vietnam this was accomplished using ''blockbuster'' bombs, but this is probably not an option here. Trees would have to be cut down, creating a gap in the jungles conspicuous from the air.

Q: Who cares if it's conspicuous? Who's going to see it?

A: As should be obvious from my anecdote, the people who control this gold have connections in Manila. We may assume that the area is overflown by the Philippine Air Force regularly, and kept under radar surveillance.

Q: What would be involved in getting the bars to the nearest decent road?

A: They would have to be carried over the jungle trails
I have described. Each bar weighs as much as a full-grown
man.

Q: Couldn't they be cut up into smaller pieces?

A: DMS rates it as unlikely that the current owners would
permit this.

Q: Is there any chance of smuggling the gold through the
military checkpoints?

A: Obviously not in the case of a mass shipment. The gold
weighs a total of around ten tons, and would require a
truck that could not negotiate most of the roads we saw.
Concealing ten tons of goods from the inspectors at these
checkpoints is not possible.

Q: How about smuggling the bars out one at a time?

A: Still very tricky. Might be possible to hike the bars
out to an intermediate point somewhere, melt or chop them
down, and somehow secrete them in the body of a jeepney or
other vehicle, then drive the vehicle to Manila and extract the gold. This operation would have to be repeated a
hundred times. Driving the same vehicle past one of these
checkpoints a hundred (or even two) times would strike
them as, to put it mildly, odd. Even if this were possible,
there is the payment issue.

Q: What is the payment issue?

A: Obviously the people who control the gold want to be
paid for it. Paying them in more gold, or in precious gems,
would be ludicrous. They do not have bank accounts. They
have to be paid in Philippine pesos. Anything bigger than
about a 500-peso note is useless in this area. A 500-peso
note is worth about $20, and so it would be necessary to
bring six million of them into the jungle to perform the
transaction. Based on some rudimentary calculations I
have made here using a mechanic's caliper and the contents
of my wallet, the stack of 500-peso notes would be about
(please wait while I switch my calculator over to the
''scientific notation'' mode) 25,000 inches high. Or, if
you prefer the metric system, something like two-thirds
of a kilometer. If you stacked the bills a meter high, you
would need six or seven hundred such stacks, which if
jammed close together would cover an area about three meters on a side. Basically we are talking about a large
Ryder box truck full of money. This would have to be trans-

ported into the middle of the jungle, and obviously, melting down cash and secreting it inside of a truck is not an option.

Q: Since the military seems to be the big obstacle here, why not simply cut a deal with them? Let them keep a big cut of the proceeds in exchange for not hassling us.

A: Because the money would go to the NPA which would use it to buy weapons for the purpose of killing people in the military.

Q: There must be some way to use the value of this gold to leverage some kind of extraction operation.

A: The gold is worthless to a bank until it has been assayed. Until then it is only a blurry Polaroid of a stack of yellow objects in what seems to be a jungle. In order to perform an assay you need to go into the jungle, find the gold, bore out a sample, and transport it safely back to a large city. But this proves nothing. Even if the potential backers believe that your assay really came from the jungle (i.e., that you did not switch samples along the way) all they know now is the purity of one end of one bar in the stack. Basically it is not possible to obtain full value for this gold until the entire stack has been extracted and taken to a vault where it can be systematically assayed.

Q: Could you maybe just get the gold to some local bank and then sell it at steep discount, so that the burden of transporting it would be on someone else's shoulders?

A: DMS relates the tale of one such transaction, in a provincial town in north Luzon, which was interrupted when local entrepreneurs literally blew one of the bank's walls off with dynamite, came in, and grabbed both the gold and the cash that was going to be used to pay for the gold. DMS asserts he would rather slit his own throat quietly than walk into a small-town bank with anything worth more than a few tens of thousands of dollars.

Q: Is the situation basically impossible then?

A: It is basically impossible.

Q: Then what was the point of the whole exercise?

A: To come full circle to the first thing DMS said. It was to send us a message.

Q: What is the message?

A: That money is not worth having if you can't spend it.

That certain people have a lot of money that they badly
want to spend. And that if we can give them a way to spend
it, through the Crypt, that these people will be very
happy, and conversely that if we screw up they will be very
sad, and that whether they are happy or sad they will be
eager to share these emotions with us, the shareholders
and management team of Epiphyte Corp.

And now I am going to e-mail this to all of you and then
summon the flight attendant and demand the array of alcoholic beverages I so richly deserve. Cheers.

—R

Randall Lawrence Waterhouse
Current meatspace coordinates, hot from the GPS receiver card in my laptop:
27 degrees, 14.95 minutes N latitude 143 degrees, 17.44
minutes E longitude
Nearest geographical feature: the Bonin Islands

ROCKET

JULIETA HAS RETREATED SOMEWHERE FAR UP BEYOND THE ARC-
tic Circle. Shaftoe has been pursuing her like a dogged Mountie,
slogging across the sexual tundra on frayed snowshoes and leaping
heroically from floe to floe. But she remains about as distant, and about
as reachable, as Polaris. She has spent more time lately with Enoch Root
than with him—and Root's a celibate priest or something. *Or is he?!*

On the few occasions Bobby Shaftoe has actually gotten Julieta to
crack a smile, she has immediately begun to ask difficult questions: Did
you have sex with Glory, Bobby? Did you use a condom? Is it possible
that she might have become pregnant? Can you absolutely rule out the
possibility that you have a child in the Philippines? How old would he
or she be right now? Let's see, you fucked her on Pearl Harbor Day, so
the child would have been born in early September of '42. Your child
would be fourteen, fifteen months old now—perhaps just learning to
walk! How precious!

It always gives Shaftoe the willies when tough girls like Julieta get all
fluttery and slip into baby talk. At first, he figures it's all a ruse to
keep him at arm's length. This smuggler's daughter, this atheist guerilla

intellectual—what does she care about some girl in Manila? Snap out of it, woman! There's a war on!

Then he comes up with a better explanation: Julieta's pregnant.

The day begins with the sound of a ship's horn in the harbor at Norrsbruck. The town is a jumble of neat, wide houses packed onto a spur of rock that sticks out into the Gulf of Bothnia, forming the southern shore of a slender but deep inlet lined with wharves. Half the town now turns out beneath an unsettling, turbulent peach-and-salmon dawn to see this quaint harbor being deflowered by an inexorable steel phallus. It comes complete with spirochetes: several score men in black dress uniforms stand on the top of the thing, lined up neat as stanchions. As the blast of the horn fades away, echoing back and forth between the stony ridges, it becomes possible to hear the spirochetes *singing:* belting out a bawdy German sea chanty which Bobby Shaftoe last heard during a convoy attack in the Bay of Biscay.

Two other people in Norrsbruck will recognize that tune. Shaftoe looks for Enoch Root in his church cellar, but he is not present, his bed and lamp are cold. Maybe the local chapter of *Societas Eruditorum* holds its meetings before dawn—or maybe he's found another welcoming bed. But trusty old Günter Bischoff can be seen, leaning out the window of his seaside garret, elbows in the air and his trusty Zeiss 735 binoculars clamped over his face, scanning the lines of the invading ship.

The Swedes stand with arms folded for a minute or so, regarding this apparition. Then they make some kind of collective decision that it does not exist, that nothing has happened here. They turn their backs, pad grumpily into their houses, begin to boil coffee. Being neutral is no less strange, no less fraught with awkward compromises, than being a belligerent. Unlike most of Europe, they can rest assured that the Germans are not here to invade them or sink their ships. On the other hand, the vessel's presence is a violation of their sovereign territory and they ought to run down there with pitchforks and flintlocks and fight the Huns off. On the third hand, this boat was probably made out of Swedish iron.

Shaftoe fails, at first, to recognize the German vessel as a U-boat because it is shaped all wrong. A regular U-boat is shaped like a surface vessel, except longer and skinnier. Which is to say it has a sort of V-shaped hull and a flat deck, studded with guns, from which rises a gigantic conning tower that is covered with junk: ack-ack guns, antennas, stanchions, safety lines, spray shields. The Krauts would put cuckoo clocks up there too if they had room. As a regular U-boat plunges through the waves, thick black smoke spews from its diesel engines.

This one is just a torpedo as long as a football field. Instead of a conning tower there's a streamlined bulge on the top, hardly noticeable.

No guns, no antennas, no cuckoo clocks; the whole thing's as smooth as a river rock. And it's not making smoke or noise, just venting a little bit of steam. The diesels don't rumble. The fucking thing doesn't even seem to *have* diesels. Instead there is a dim whine, like the sound that came out of Angelo's Messerschmidt.

Shaftoe intercepts Bischoff just as the latter is coming down the steps of the inn carrying a duffel bag the size of a dead sea lion. He's panting with exertion, or maybe excitement. "That's the one," he gasps. He sounds like he's talking to himself, but he's speaking English, so he must be addressing Shaftoe. "That's the rocket."

"Rocket?"

"Runs on rocket fuel—hydrogen peroxide, eighty-five percent. Never has to recharge its verdammt batteries! Clocks twenty-eight knots—*submerged!* That's my baby." He's as fluttery as Julieta.

"Can I help you carry anything?"

"Footlocker—upstairs," Bischoff says.

Shaftoe stomps up the narrow staircase to find Bischoff's room stripped to the bedsprings, and a pile of gold coins on the table, weighing down a thank-you note addressed to the owners. The black locker rests in the middle of the floor like a child's coffin. A wild hollering noise reaches his ears through the open window.

Bischoff is down there, heading for the pier beneath his duffel bag, and his men, up on the rocket, have caught sight of him. The U-boat has launched a dinghy, which is surging towards the pier like a racing scull.

Shaftoe heaves the locker up onto his shoulder and trudges down the stairs. It reminds him of shipping out, which is what Marines are supposed to do, and which he has not actually done in a long time. Vicarious excitement is not as good as the real thing, he finds.

He follows Bischoff's tracks through a film of snow, down the cobblestone street, and onto the pier. Three men in black scramble out of the launch, onto the ladder, up to the pier. They salute Bischoff and then two of them embrace him. Shaftoe's close enough and the salmon light is bright enough, that he can recognize these two: members of Bischoff's old crew. The third guy is taller, older, gaunter, grimmer, better-dressed, more highly decorated. All in all, more of a Nazi.

Shaftoe can't believe himself. When he picked up the locker he was just being considerate to his friend Günter—an ink-stained retiree with pacifist leanings. Now, all of a sudden, he's aiding and abetting the enemy! What would his fellow Marines think of him if they knew?

Oh, yeah. Almost forgot. He is actually participating in the conspiracy that he, Bischoff, Rudy von Hacklheber, and Enoch Root created in the basement of that church. He comes to a dead stop and slams the locker down right there, in the middle of the pier. The Nazi is startled by the noise and raises his blue eyes in the direction of Shaftoe, who prepares to stare him down.

Bischoff notices this. He turns towards Shaftoe and shouts something cheerful in Swedish. Shaftoe has the presence of mind to break eye contact with the chilly German. He grins and nods back. This conspiracy thing is going to be a real pain in the ass if it means backing down from casual fistfights.

A couple of sailors have come up the ladder now to handle Bischoff's luggage. One of them strides down the pier to get the footlocker. Shaftoe recognizes him, and he recognizes Shaftoe, at the same moment. Damn! The guy's surprised, but not unpleasantly so, to see Shaftoe here. Then something occurs to him and his face freezes up in horror and his eyes dart sideways, back toward the tall Nazi. Shit! Shaftoe turns his back on all of this, makes like he's strolling back into town.

"Jens! Jens!" Bischoff hollers, and then says something else in Swedish. He's running after Shaftoe. Shaftoe keeps his back prudently turned until Bischoff throws one arm around him with a final "JENS!" Then, sotto voce, in English: "You have my family's address. If I don't see you in Manila, let's get in touch after the war." He starts pounding Shaftoe on the back, pulls some paper money out of his pocket, stuffs it into Shaftoe's hand.

"Goddamn it, you'll see me there," Shaftoe says. "What is this shit for?"

"I am tipping the nice Swedish boy who carried my luggage," Bischoff says.

Shaftoe sucks his teeth and grimaces. He can tell he is not cut out for this cloak-and-dagger nonsense. Questions come to his mind, among them *How is that big torpedo full of rocket fuel safer than what you were riding around in before?* but he just says, "Good luck, I guess."

"Godspeed, my friend," Bischoff says. "This will remind you to check your mail." Then he punches Shaftoe in the shoulder hard enough to raise a three-day welt, turns around, and begins walking towards salt water. Shaftoe walks towards snow and trees, envying him. The next time he looks at the harbor, fifteen minutes later, the U-boat is gone. Suddenly this town feels just as cold, empty, and out in the middle of nowhere as it really is.

He's been getting his mail at the Norrsbruck post office, general delivery. When the place opens up a couple of hours later, Shaftoe's waiting by the door, venting steam from his nostrils, like he's rocket-fuel-powered. He receives a letter from his folks in Wisconsin, and one large envelope, posted yesterday from somewhere in Norrsbruck, Sweden, bearing no return address but inscribed in Günter Bischoff's hand.

It is full of notes and documents concerning the new U-boat, including one or two letters personally signed by John Huncock himself. Shaftoe's German is slightly better than it was before he went on his own U-boat ride, but he still can't follow most of it. He sees a lot of numbers there, a lot of technical-looking stuff.

It is your basic priceless naval intelligence. Shaftoe wraps the papers up carefully, sticks them in his pants, begins walking up the beach towards the Kivistik residence.

It is a long, cold, wet trudge. He has plenty of time to assess his situation: stuck in a neutral country on the other side of the world from where he wants to be. Alienated from the Corps. Lumped in with a vague conspiracy.

Technically speaking, he has been AWOL for several months now. But if he suddenly turns up at the American Embassy in Stockholm, carrying these documents, all will be forgiven. So this is his ticket home. And "home" is a very large country that includes places like Hawaii, which is closer to Manila than is Norrsbruck, Sweden.

Otto's boat is fresh in from Finland, bobbing on an incoming tide, tied up to his bird's nest of a jetty. The boat, he knows, is still loaded up with whatever Finns are exchanging for coffee and bullets at the moment. Otto himself is sitting in the cabin, drinking coffee naturally, red-eyed and plumb wrung out.

"Where's Julieta?" Shaftoe says. He's starting to worry that she moved back to Finland or something.

Otto turns a bit greyer every time he drives his tub across the Gulf of Bothnia. He looks especially grey today. "Did you see that monster?" he says, then shakes his head in a combination of wonderment, disgust, and world-weariness that can only be attained by hardened Finns. "Those German bastards!"

"I thought they were protecting you from the Russians."

This elicits a long thunder-roll of dark, chortling laughter from Otto. *"Zdrastuytchye, tovarishch!"* he finally says.

"Say what?"

"That means, 'Welcome, comrade' in Russian," Otto says. "I have been practicing it."

"You should be practicing the Pledge of Allegiance," Shaftoe says. "Soon as we get done taking down the Germans, I figure we'll just kick her into high gear and beat the Russkies all the way back to Siberia."

More laughter from Otto, who knows naïveté when he sees it, but is not above finding it charming. "I have buried the German air-turbine in Finland," he says. "I will sell it to the Russians or the Americans—whoever gets there first."

"Where's Julieta?" Shaftoe asks again. Speaking of naïveté.

"In town," Otto says. "Shopping."

"So you've got cash."

Otto looks seasick. Tomorrow is payday.

Then Shaftoe's going to be on a bus, headed for Stockholm.

Shaftoe sits down across from Otto and they drink coffee and talk about weather, smuggling, and the relative merits of various small fully automatic weapons for a while. Actually, what they are talking about is whether Shaftoe will get paid, and how much.

In the end, Otto issues a guarded promise to pay, provided that Julieta does not spend all of the money on her "shopping" trip, and provided that Shaftoe unloads the boat.

So Bobby Shaftoe spends the rest of the day carrying Soviet mortars, rusty tins of caviar, bricks of black tea from China, Lapp folk art, a couple of icons, cases of pine-flavored Finnish schnapps, coils of vile sausages, and bundles of pelts up out of the hold of Otto's boat, down the dock, into the cabin.

Meanwhile, Otto goes into town, and still has not come back long after night has fallen. Shaftoe sacks out in the cabin, tosses and turns for about four hours, sleeps for about ten minutes, and then is awakened by a knocking at the door.

He approaches the door on hands and knees, gets the Suomi machine pistol out of its hiding place, then crawsl to the far end of the cabin and exits silently through a trap door in the floor. There is ice on the rocks below, but his bare feet give him enough traction to clamber around and get a good view of whomever is standing there, pounding on the door.

It is Enoch Root himself, nowhere to be seen this last week or so.

"Yo!" Shaftoe says.

"Bobby," Root says, turning around, "I gather you heard."

"Heard what?"

"That we are in danger."

"Nah," Shaftoe says, "this is just how I always answer the door."

They go into the cabin. Root declines to turn on any lights and keeps looking out the windows like he's expecting someone. He smells faintly of Julieta's perfume, a distinctive scent that Otto has been smuggling into Finland by the fifty-five-gallon drum. Somehow, Shaftoe is not surprised by this. He proceeds to make coffee.

"A very complex situation has arisen," Root says.

"I can see that."

Root is startled by this, and looks up blankly at Shaftoe, his eyes glowing stupidly in the moonlight. You can be the smartest guy in the world, but when a woman comes into the picture, you're just like any other sap.

"Did you come all this way to tell me that you're fucking Julieta?"

"Oh, no, no, no!" Root says. He stops for a moment, furrows his brow. "I mean, I am. And I was going to tell you. But that's just the first part of a more complicated business." Root gets up, shoves hands in pockets, walks around the cabin again, looking out the windows. "You have any more of those Finnish guns?"

"In that crate to your left," Shaftoe says. "Why? We gonna have a shootout?"

"Maybe. Not between you and me! But other visitors may be coming."

"Cops?"

"Worse."

"Finns?" Because Otto has his rivals.

"Worse."

"Who then?" Shaftoe can't imagine worse.

"Germans. German."

"Oh, fuck!" Shaftoe hollers disgustedly. "How can you say they're worse than Finns?"

Root looks taken aback. "If you're going to tell me that Finns are worse, pound for pound, than Germans, then I agree with you. But the trouble with Germans is that they tend to be in communication with millions of other Germans."

"Okay," Shaftoe mutters.

Root hauls the lid off a crate, pulls out a machine pistol, checks the chamber, aims the barrel at the moon, peers through it like a telescope. "In any case, some Germans are coming to kill you."

"Why?"

"Because you know too much about certain things."

"What certain things? Günter and his new submarine?"

"Yes."

"And how, may I ask, do you know this? It has something to do with the fact that you're fucking Julieta, right?" Shaftoe continues. He's bored rather than pissed off. This whole Sweden thing is old and tired to him now. He belongs in the Philippines. Anything that doesn't get him closer to the Philippines just irritates him.

"Right." Root heaves a sigh. "She thinks highly of you, Bobby, but after she saw that picture of your girlfriend—"

"Snap out of it! She doesn't give a shit about you or me. She just wants to have all of the good parts of being a Finn without the bad parts."

"What are the bad parts?"

"Having to live in Finland," Shaftoe says. "So she has to marry someone with a good passport. Which nowadays means American or British. You might have noticed that she didn't fuck Günter."

Root looks a little queasy.

"Well, maybe she did then," Shaftoe says, heaving a sigh. "Shit!"

Root has rooted an ammo clip out of another crate and figured out how to affix it to the Suomi. He says, "You probably know that the Germans have a tacit arrangement with the Swedes."

"What does 'tacit' mean?"

"Let's just say they have an arrangement."

"The Swedes are neutral, but they let the Krauts push them around."

"Yes. Otto has to deal with Germans at each end of his smuggling route, in Sweden and in Finland, and he has to deal with their navy when he's out on the water."

"I'm aware that the fucking Germans are all over Europe."

"Well, to make a long story short, the local Germans have prevailed upon Otto to betray you," Root says.

"Did he?"

"Yes. He did betray you . . ."

"Okay. Keep talking, I'm listening to you," Shaftoe says. He begins to mount a ladder up into the attic.

". . . but then he thought better of it. I guess you could say he repented," Root says.

"Spoken like a true man of the cloth," Shaftoe mutters. He's into the attic now, crawling on hands and knees over the rafters. He stops and sparks up his Zippo. Most of its light is absorbed by a dark green slab: a crude wooden crate with Cryllic letters stenciled on it.

Root's voice is filtering up from below: "He came to, uh, the place where Julieta and I, uh, were."

Were fucking. "Get me the crowbar," Shaftoe shouts. "It's in Otto's toolbox, under the table."

A minute later, the crowbar rises up through the hatch, like the head of a cobra emerging from a basket. Shaftoe grabs it and begins assaulting the crate.

"Otto was torn. He had to do what he did, or the German could have shut down his livelihood. But he respects you. He couldn't bear it. He had to talk to someone. So he came to us, and told Julieta what he had done. Julieta understood."

"She understood!?"

"But she also was horrified at the same time."

"That is truly heartwarming."

"Um, at that point, the Kivistiks broke out the schnapps and began to discuss the situation. In Finnish."

"I understand," Shaftoe says. Give those Finns a grim, stark, bleak moral dilemma and a bottle of schnapps and you could pretty much forget about them for forty-eight hours. "Thanks for having the guts to come out here."

"Julieta will understand."

"That's not what I mean."

"Oh, I don't think Otto would hurt me."

"No, I mean—"

"Oh!" Root exclaims. "No, I had to tell you about Julieta sooner or later—"

"No, goddamn it, I mean the Germans."

"Oh. Well, I didn't even begin to think about them until I was almost here. It was not courage so much as a lack of foresight."

Shaftoe's pretty good at foresight. "Take this." He hands down a heavy steel tube of coffee-can diameter, a few feet long. "It's heavy," he adds, as Root's knees buckle.

"What is it?"

"A Soviet hundred-and-twenty-millimeter mortar," Shaftoe says.

"Oh." Root remains silent for a while, as he lays the mortar down on the table. When he speaks again, his voice sounds different. "I didn't realize Otto had this kind of stuff."

"The lethal radius of this bitch is a good sixty feet," Shaftoe says. He is hauling mortar bombs out of the crate and stacking them next to the hatch. "Or maybe it's meters, I can't remember." The bombs look like fat footballs with tailfins on one end.

"Feet, meters . . . the distinction is important," Root says.

"Maybe it's overkill. But we have to get back to Norrsbruck and take care of Julieta."

"What do you mean, take care of her?" Root says warily.

"Marry her."

"What?"

"One of us has to marry her, and fast. I don't know about you, but I kind of like her, and it'd be a shame if she spent the rest of her life sucking Russian dick at gunpoint," Shaftoe says. "Besides, she might be pregnant with one of our kids. Yours, mine, or Günter's."

"We, the conspiracy, have an obligation to look after our offspring," Root agrees. "We could establish a trust fund for them in London."

"There should be plenty of money for that," Shaftoe agrees. "But I can't marry her, because I have to be available to marry Glory when I get to Manila."

"Rudy can't do it," Root says.

"Because he's a fag?"

"No, they marry women all the time," Root says. "He can't do it because he's German, and what's she going to do with a German passport?"

"It would not be savvy exactly," Shaftoe agrees.

"That leaves me," Root says. "I'll marry her, and she'll have a British passport. Best in the world."

"Huh," Shaftoe says, "how does that square with your being a celibate monk or priest or whatever the fuck you supposedly are?"

Root says, "I'm supposed to be celibate—"

"But you're not," Shaftoe reminds him.

"But God's forgiveness is infinite," Root fires back, winning the point. "So, as I was saying, I'm supposed to be celibate—but that doesn't mean I can't get married. As long as I don't consummate the marriage."

"But if you don't consummate it, it doesn't count!"

"But the only person, besides me, who will know that we didn't consummate it, is Julieta."

"God will know," Shaftoe says.

"God doesn't issue passports," Root says.

"What about the church? They'll kick you out."

"Maybe I deserve to be kicked out."

"So let me get this straight," Shaftoe says, "when you really *were* fucking Julieta, you said you *weren't* and so you were able to remain a priest. Now you're going to marry her and *not* fuck her and say that you *are*."

"If you're trying to say that my relationship with the Church is very complicated, I already knew that, Bobby."

"Let's go, then," Shaftoe says.

Shaftoe and Root haul the mortar and a boxload of bombs down onto the beach, where they can take cover behind a stone retaining wall a good five feet high. But the surf makes it impossible to hear anything, so Root goes up and hides in the trees along the road, and leaves Shaftoe to fiddle with the Soviet mortar.

There turns out to be not much fiddling necessary. An unlettered tundra farmer with bilateral frostbite could get this thing up and running in ten minutes. If he'd stayed up late the night before—celebrating the fulfillment of the last five-year plan with a jug of wood alcohol—maybe fifteen minutes.

Shaftoe consults the instructions. It does not matter that these are printed in Russian, because they are made for illiterates anyway. A series of parabolas is plotted out, the mortar supporting one leg and exploding

Germans supporting the opposite. Ask a Soviet engineer to design a pair of shoes and he'll come up with something that looks like the boxes that the shoes came in; ask him to make something that will massacre Germans, and he turns into Thomas Fucking Edison. Shaftoe scans the terrain, picks out his killing zone, then climbs up and paces off the distance, assuming one meter per space.

He's back down on the beach, adjusting the tube's angle, when he's startled by a bulky form vaulting over the wall, so close it almost knocks him down. Root's breathing fast. "Germans," he says, "coming in from the main road."

"How do you know they're Germans? Maybe it's Otto."

"The engines sound like diesels. Huns love diesels."

"How many engines?"

"Probably two."

Root turns out to be right on the money. Two large black Mercedes issue from the forest, like bad ideas emerging from the dim mind of a green lieutenant. Their headlights are not illuminated. Each stops and then sits there for a moment, then the doors open quietly, Germans climb out and stand up. Several of them are wearing long black leather coats. Several are carrying those keen submachine guns that are the trademark of German infantry, and the envy of Yanks and Tommies, who must go burdened with primeval hunting rifles.

This is the moment, then. Nazis are right over there and it is the job of Bobby Shaftoe, and to a lesser degree Enoch Root, to kill them all. Not just a job but a moral requisite, because they are the living avatars of Satan, who publicly acknowledge being just as bad and vicious as they really are. It is a world, and a situation, to which Shaftoe and a lot of other people are perfectly adapted. He heaves a bomb up out of the box, introduces it to the muzzle of the fat tube, lets it go, and plugs his ears.

The mortar coughs like a kettledrum. The Germans look towards them. An officer's monocle glints in the moonlight. A total of eight Germans have gotten out of the cars. Three of them must be combat veterans because they are down on their stomachs in a microsecond. The trench-coated officers remain standing, as do a couple of civilian-clad goons, who immediately open fire in their general direction with their submachine guns. This makes a lot of noise but only impresses Shaftoe insofar as it is an impressive display of stupidity. The bullets sail far over their heads. Before they have had time to pepper the Gulf of Bothnia, the mortar bomb has exploded.

Shaftoe peeks over the top of the seawall. As he more or less expected, all of the people who were standing up are now draped over the nearest

Mercedes, having been bodily lifted off their feet and flung sideways by a moving curtain of shrapnel. But two of the survivors—the veterans— are belly-crawling towards Otto's cabin, whose thick log walls look extremely reassuring in these circumstances. The third survivor is blasting away with his submachine gun, but he has no idea where they are.

The ground is convex in a way that makes it hard to see those belly-crawling Germans. Shaftoe fires a couple more mortar rounds without much effect. He hears the two Germans kicking down the door to Otto's cabin.

Since it is only a one-room cabin, this would be a fine moment to be armed with grenades. But Shaftoe has none, and he doesn't really want to blow the place up anyway. "Why don't you kill the one German up there," he tells Root, and then heads down the beach, hugging the seawall in case the Germans are looking out the windows.

Indeed, when he's almost there the Germans smash the windows out and begin firing in the direction of Enoch Root. Shaftoe creeps underneath the cabin, opens the trap door, and emerges into the center of the room. The Germans are standing there with their backs to him. He fires his Suomi into their backs until they stop moving. Then he drags them over to the trapdoor and dumps them down onto the beach so they won't bleed all over the floor. The next high tide will carry them away, and with any luck they'll wash ashore on the Fatherland in a couple weeks.

It is silent now, the way it's supposed to be at an isolated cabin by the sea. But that doesn't mean anything. Shaftoe makes his way carefully up into the trees and circles around behind the action, surveying the killing zone from above. The one German is still crawling around on his elbows, trying to figure out what's going on. Shaftoe kills him. Then he makes his way down to the beach and finds Enoch Root bleeding into the sand. He has taken a bullet just under the collarbone and there is a lot of blood, both from the wound and from Root's mouth, whenever he exhales.

"I feel like I'm going to die," he says.

"Good," Shaftoe says, "that means you probably won't."

One of the Mercedes automobiles is still functional, though it has a number of shrapnel holes and a flat tire. Shaftoe jacks it up and swaps in a surviving tire from the other Mercedes, then drags Root over and gets him laid out in the backseat. He drives into Norrsbruck, fast. The Mercedes is a really great car and he wants to drive it all the way to Finland, Russia, Siberia, down through China—maybe stop for a little sushi in Shanghai—then on down through Siam and then Malaya, whence he could hop a sea-gypsy's boat to Manila, find Glory, and—

The ensuing erotic reverie is cut short by the voice of Enoch Root, bubbling through blood, or something. "Go to the church."

"Now padre, this is no time to be trying to convert me into a religious nut. You take it easy."

"No, go *now*. Take *me*."

"What, so you can make your peace with god? Hell, Rev, you ain't gonna *die*. I'll take you to the doctor's. You can go to church later."

Root drifts off into a coma, mumbling something about cigars.

Shaftoe ignores these ravings, burns rubber into Norrsbruck, and wakes up the doctor. Then he goes and finds Otto and Julieta and takes them over to the doctor's office. Finally, he goes round to the church and wakes up the minister.

When they get back to the clinic, Rudolf von Hacklheber's arguing with the doctor: Rudy (who's apparently speaking on behalf of Enoch, who can hardly even talk) wants Enoch's wedding to Julieta to happen now, in case Enoch dies on the table. Shaftoe is started by how bad the patient suddenly looks. But remembering what he and Enoch talked about earlier, he weighs in on Rudy's side, and insists that marriage must come before surgery.

Otto produces a diamond ring literally out of his asshole—he carries valuables around in a polished metal tube shoved up his rectum—and Shaftoe serves as best man, uneasily holding that ring, still hot from Otto. Root's too weak to thread it over Julieta's finger and so Rudy guides his hands. A nurse serves as bridesmaid. Julieta and Enoch are joined in holy matrimony. Root utters the words of the oath one at a time, pausing after each one to cough blood into a stainless-steel bowl. Shaftoe gets all choked up, and actually sniffles.

The doctor etherizes Root, opens his chest, and goes in to repair the damage. Combat surgery isn't his metier, and so he makes a few mistakes and generally does a great job of keeping the tension level high. Some major artery gives way, and it's necessary for Shaftoe and the minister to go out and yank Swedes off the streets and persuade them to donate blood. Rudy is nowhere to be found, and Shaftoe suspects for a few minutes that he has blown town. But then suddenly he shows up at Root's bedside holding an ancient Cuban cigar box, Spanish words all over it.

When Enoch Root dies, the only other people in the room are Rudolf von Hacklheber, Bobby Shaftoe, and the Swedish doctor.

The doctor checks his watch, then steps out of the room.

Rudy reaches out and closes Enoch's eyes, then stands there with his hand on the late padre's face, and looks at Shaftoe. "Go," he says, "and make sure that the doctor files the death certificate."

In war, it happens pretty frequently that one of your buddies dies, and you have to go right back into action, and save the waterworks for later. "Right," Shaftoe says, and leaves the room.

The doctor's sitting in his little office, umlaut-studded diplomas all over the walls, filling out the death certificate. A skeleton dangles in one corner. Bobby Shaftoe stands at attention on the opposite flank, he and the skeleton sort of triangulating on the doctor and watching him scrawl out the date and time of Enoch Root's demise.

When the doctor's finished, he leans back in his chair and rubs his eyes. "Can I buy you a cup of coffee?" asks Bobby Shaftoe.

"Thank you," says the doctor.

The young bride and her father are sprawled blearily in the doctor's waiting room. Shaftoe offers to buy them coffee too. They leave Rudy to keep watch over the body of their late friend and coconspirator, and walk down the high street of Norrsbruck. Swedish people are beginning to come out of their houses. They look *exactly* like American midwesterners, and Shaftoe's always startled when they fail to speak English.

The doctor stops in at the courthouse to drop off the death certificate. Otto and Julieta go on ahead to the cafe. Bobby Shaftoe loiters outside, staring back up the street. After a minute or two he sees Rudy poke his head out the door of the doctor's office and look one way, then the other. He pulls his head back inside for a moment. Then he and another man walk out of the office. The other man is wrapped in a blanket that covers even his head. They climb into the Mercedes, Blanket Man lies down in the back seat, and Rudy drives off in the direction of his cottage.

Bobby Shaftoe sits down in the cafe with the Finns.

"Later today I'm gonna get into that fucking Mercedes and drive into Stockholm like a fucking bat out of hell," Shaftoe says. Though the Finns will never appreciate it, he has chosen the "bat out of hell" phrase for a good reason. He understands, now, why he has thought of himself as a dead man ever since Guadalcanal. "Anyway. I hope y'all have a nice boat ride."

"Boat ride?" Otto says innocently.

"I gave you up to the Germans, just like you did to me," Shaftoe lies.

"You bastard!" Julieta begins. But Bobby cuts her off: "You got what you wanted and then some. A British passport and—" glancing out the window he sees the doctor emerging from the courthouse "—Enoch's survivor's benefits on top of it. And maybe more later. As for you, Otto, your career as a smuggler is over. I suggest you get the fuck out of here."

Otto's still too flabbergasted to be outraged, but he's sure enough gonna be outraged pretty soon. "And go where!? Have you bothered to look at a map?"

"Display some fucking adaptability," Shaftoe says. "You can figure out a way to get that tub of yours to England."

Say what you will about Otto, he likes a challenge. "I could traverse the Göta Canal from Stockholm to Göteborg—no Germans *there*—that would get me almost to Norway—but Norway's full of Germans! Even if I make it through the Skagerrak—you expect me to cross the North Sea? In winter? During a war?"

"If it makes you feel any better, after you get to England you have to sail to Manila."

"Manila!?"

"Makes England seem easy, huh?"

"You think I am a rich yachtsman, who sails around the world *for fun!?"*

"No, but Rudolf von Hacklheber is. He's got money, he's got connections. He's got a line on a good yacht that makes your ketch look like a dinghy," Shaftoe says. "C'mon, Otto. Stop whining, pull some more diamonds out of your asshole, and get it done. It beats being tortured to death by Germans." Shaftoe stands up and chucks Otto encouragingly on the shoulder, which Otto does not like at all. "See you in Manila."

The doctor's coming in the door. Bobby Shaftoe slaps some money down on the table. He looks Julieta in the eye. "Got some miles to cover now," he says, "Glory's waiting for me."

Julieta nods. So in the eyes of one Finnish girl, anyway, Shaftoe's not such a bad guy. He bends over and gives her a big succulent kiss, then straightens up, nods to the startled doctor, and walks out.

COURTING

WATERHOUSE HAS BEEN CHEWING HIS WAY THROUGH EXOTIC Nip code systems at the rate of about one a week, but after he sees Mary Smith in the parlor of Mrs. McTeague's boarding house, his production rate drops to near zero. Arguably, it goes negative, for sometimes when he reads the morning newspaper, its plaintext scrambles into gibberish before his eyes, and he is unable to extract any useful information.

Despite his and Turing's disagreements about whether the human brain is a Turing machine, he has to admit that Turing wouldn't have too much trouble writing a set of instructions to simulate the brain functions of Lawrence Pritchard Waterhouse.

Waterhouse seeks happiness. He achieves it by breaking Nip code systems and playing the pipe organ. But since pipe organs are in short supply, his happiness level ends up being totally dependent on breaking codes.

He cannot break codes (hence, cannot be happy) unless his mind is clear. Now suppose that mental clarity is designated by C_m, which is normalized, or calibrated, in such a way that it is always the case that

$$0 \leq C_m \leq 1$$

where $C_m = 0$ indicates a totally clouded mind and $C_m = 1$ is Godlike clarity—an unattainable divine state of infinite intelligence. If the number of messages Waterhouse decrypts, in a given day, is designated by $N_{decrypts}$, then it will be governed by C_m in roughly the following way:

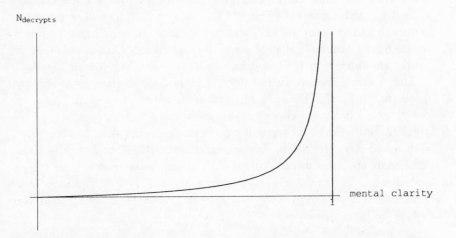

Clarity of mind (C_m) is affected by any number of factors, but by far the most important is horniness, which might be designated by σ, for obvious anatomical reasons that Waterhouse finds amusing at this stage of his emotional development.

Horniness begins at zero at time $t = t_0$ (immediately following ejaculation) and increases from there as a linear function of time:

$$\sigma \propto (t - t_0)$$

The only way to drop it back to zero is to arrange another ejaculation.

There is a critical threshold σ_c such that when $\sigma > \sigma_c$ it becomes impossible for Waterhouse to concentrate on anything, or, approximately,

$$C_m \propto \lim_{n \to \infty} \frac{1}{(\sigma - \sigma_c)^n}$$

which amounts to saying that the moment σ rises above the threshold σ_c it becomes totally impossible for Waterhouse to break Nipponese cryptographic systems. This makes it impossible for him to achieve happiness (unless there is a pipe organ handy, which there isn't).

Typically, it takes two to three days for σ to climb above σ_c after an ejaculation:

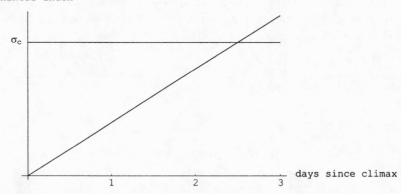

Critical, then, to the maintenance of Waterhouse's sanity is the ability to ejaculate every two to three days. As long as he can arrange this, σ exhibits a classic sawtooth-wave pattern, optimally with the peaks at or near σ_c [see p. 546 top] wherein the grey zones represent periods during which he is completely useless to the war effort.

So much for the basic theory. Now, when he was at Pearl Harbor, he discovered something that, in retrospect, should have been profoundly disquieting. Namely, that ejaculations obtained in a whorehouse (i.e., provided by the ministrations of an actual human female) seemed to drop σ below the level that Waterhouse could achieve through executing a Manual Override. In other words, the post-ejaculatory horniness level was not always equal to zero, as the naive theory propounded above assumes, but to some other quantity dependent upon whether the ejaculation was induced by Self or Other: $\sigma = \sigma_{self}$ after masturbation but $\sigma = \sigma_{other}$ upon leaving a whorehouse, where $\sigma_{self} > \sigma_{other}$, an inequality to which Waterhouse's notable successes in breaking certain Nip naval codes at Station Hypo were directly attributable, in that the many convenient whorehouses nearby made it possible for him to go somewhat longer between ejaculations.

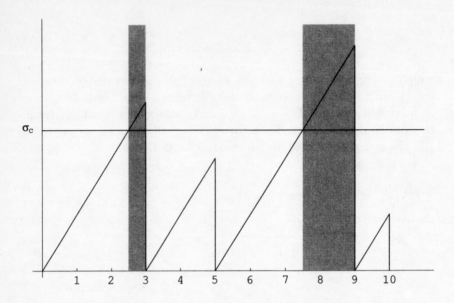

8May 1942: Prelude to Midway

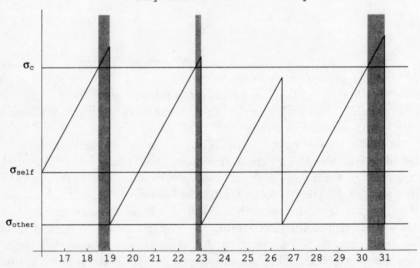

Note the twelve-day period [above], 19–30 May 1942, with only one brief interruption in productivity—during which Waterhouse (some might argue) personally won the Battle of Midway.

If he had thought about this, it would have bothered him, because $\sigma_{self} > \sigma_{other}$ has troubling implications—particularly if the values of these quantities w.r.t. the all-important σ_c are not fixed. If it weren't for this inequality, then Waterhouse could function as a totally self-contained and independent unit. But $\sigma_{self} > \sigma_{other}$ implies that he is, in the long run, dependent on other human beings for his mental clarity and, therefore, his happiness. What a pain in the ass!

Perhaps he has avoided thinking about this precisely because it is so troubling. The week after he meets Mary Smith, he realizes that he is going to have to think about it a lot more.

Something about the arrival of Mary Smith on the scene has completely fouled up the whole system of equations. Now, when he has an ejaculation, his clarity of mind does not take the upwards jump that it should. He goes right back to thinking about Mary. So much for winning the war!

He goes out in search of whorehouses, hoping that good old reliable σ_{other} will save his bacon. This is troublesome. When he was at Pearl, it was easy, and uncontroversial. But Mrs. McTeague's boardinghouse is in a residential neighborhood, which, if it contains whorehouses, at least bothers to hide them. So Waterhouse has to travel downtown, which is not that easy in a place where internal-combustion vehicles are fueled by barbecues in the trunk. Furthermore, Mrs. McTeague is keeping her eye on him. She knows his habits. If he starts coming back from work four hours late, or going out after dinner, he'll have some explaining to do. And it had better be convincing, because she appears to have taken Mary Smith under one quivering gelatinous wing and is in a position to poison the sweet girl's mind against Waterhouse. Not only that, he has to do much of his excuse-making in public, at the dinner table, which he shares with Mary's cousin (whose first name turns out to be Rod).

But hey, Doolittle bombed Tokyo, didn't he? Waterhouse should at least be able to sneak out to a whorehouse. It takes a week of preparations (during which he is completely unable to accomplish meaningful work because of the soaring σ level), but he manages it.

It helps a little, but only on the σ management level. Until recently, that was the only level and so it would have been fine. But now (as Waterhouse realizes through long contemplation during the hours when he should be breaking codes) a new factor has entered the system of equations that governs his behavior; he will have to write to Alan and tell him that some new instructions will have to be added to the Waterhouse-simulation Turing machine. This new factor is F_{MSp}, the Factor of Mary Smith Proximity.

In a simpler universe, F_{MSp}, would be orthogonal to σ, which is to say that the two factors would be entirely independent of each other. If it were thus, Waterhouse could continue the usual sawtooth-wave ejaculation management program with no changes. In addition, he would have to arrange to have frequent conversations with Mary Smith so that F_{MSp} would remain as high as possible.

Alas! The universe is not simple. Far from being orthogonal, F_{MSp} and σ are involved, as elaborately as the contrails of dogfighting airplanes. The old σ management scheme doesn't work anymore. And a platonic relationship will actually make F_{MSp} worse, not better. His life, which used to be a straightforward set of basically linear equations, has become a *differential* equation.

It is the visit to the whorehouse that makes him realize this. In the Navy, going to a whorehouse is about as controversial as pissing down the scuppers when you are on the high seas—the worst you can say about it is that, in other circumstances, it might seem uncouth. So Waterhouse has been doing it for years without feeling troubled in the slightest.

But he loathes himself during, and after, his first post-Mary-Smith whorehouse visit. He no longer sees himself through his own eyes but through hers—and, by extension, those of her cousin Rod and of Mrs. McTeague and of the whole society of decent God-fearing folk to whom he has never paid the slightest bit of attention until now.

It seems that the intrusion of F_{MSp} into his happiness equation is just the thin edge of a wedge which leaves Lawrence Pritchard Waterhouse at the mercy of a vast number of uncontrollable factors, and requiring him to cope with normal human society. Horrifyingly, he now finds himself getting ready to go to a dance.

The dance is being organized by an Australian volunteer organization—he doesn't know or care about the details. Mrs. McTeague evidently feels that the rent she collects from her boarders obligates her to find them wives as well as feeding and housing them, so she badgers all of them to go, and to bring dates if possible. Rod finally shuts her up by announcing that he will be attending with a large group, to include his country cousin Mary. Rod is about eight feet tall, and so it will be easy to pick him out across a crowded dance floor. With any luck, then, the diminutive Mary will be in his vicinity.

So Waterhouse goes to the dance, ransacking his mind for opening lines that he can use with Mary. He comes up with several possibilities:

"Do you realize that Nipponese industry is only capable of producing forty bulldozers per year?" To be followed up with: "No wonder they use slave labor to build their revetments!"

Or, "Because of antenna configuration limitations inherent in their design, Nipponese naval radar systems have a blind spot to the rear— you always want to come in from dead astern."

Or, "The Nip Army's minor, low-level codes are actually harder to break than the important high-level ones! Isn't that ironic?"

Or, "So, you're from the outback . . . do you can a lot of your own food? It might interest you to know that a close relative of the bacterium that makes canned soup go bad is responsible for gas gangrene."

Or, "Nip battleships have started to blow up spontaneously, because the high-explosive shells in their magazines become chemically unstable over time."

Or, "Dr. Turing of Cambridge says that the soul is an illusion and that all that defines us as human beings can be reduced to a series of mechanical operations."

And much more in this vein. So far he has not hit on anything that is absolutely guaranteed to sweep her off her feet. He doesn't, in fact, have the first idea what the fuck he's going to do. Which is how it's always been with Waterhouse and women, which is why he has never really had a girlfriend before.

But this is different. This is desperation.

What is there to say about the dance? Big room. Men in uniforms, mostly looking smarter than they have a right to. Mostly looking smarter, in fact, than Waterhouse. Women in dresses and hairdos. Lipstick, pearls, a big band, white gloves, fist fights, a little bit o' kissin' and a wee bit o' vomitin'. Waterhouse gets there late—that transportation thing again. All the gasoline is being used to hurl enormous bombers through the atmosphere so that high explosives can be showered on Nips. Moving the wad of flesh called Waterhouse across Brisbane so he can try to deflower a maiden is way down the priority list. He has to do a lot of walking in his stiff, shiny leather shoes, which become less shiny. By the time he gets there, he is pretty sure that they are functioning only as tourniquets preventing uncontrollable arterial bleeding from the wounds they've induced.

Rather late into the dance he finally picks out Rod on the dance floor and stalks him, over the course of several numbers (Rod having no shortage of dance partners), to a corner of the room where everyone seems to know each other, and all of them seem to be having a perfectly fine time without the intervention of a Waterhouse.

But finally he identifies Mary Smith's neck, which looks just as unspeakably erotic seen from behind through thirty yards of dense cigarette smoke as it did seen from the side in Mrs. McTeague's parlor. She is wearing a dress, and a string of pearls that adorn the neck's architecture quite nicely. Waterhouse sets his direction of march towards her and plods onward, like a Marine covering the last few yards to a Nip pillbox where he knows full well he's going to die. Can you get a posthumous decoration for being shot down in flames at a dance?

He's just a few paces away, still forging along woozily towards that white column of neck, when suddenly the tune comes to an end, and he can hear Mary's voice, and the voices of her friends. They are chattering away happily. But they are not speaking English.

Finally, Waterhouse places that accent. Not only that: he solves another mystery, having to do with some incoming mail he has seen at Mrs. McTeague's house, addressed to someone named cCmndhd.

It's like this: Rod and Mary are Qwghlmian! And their family name is not Smith—it just sounds vaguely like Smith. It's really cCmndhd. Rod grew up in Manchester—in some Qwghlmian ghetto, no doubt— and Mary's from a branch of the family that got into trouble (probably sedition) a couple of generations back and got Transported to the Great Sandy Desert.

Let's see Turing explain this one! Because what this proves, beyond all doubt, is that there is a God, and furthermore that He is a personal friend and supporter of Lawrence Pritchard Waterhouse. The opening line problem is solved, neat as a theorem. Q. E. D., baby. Waterhouse strides forward confidently, sacrificing another square centimeter of epidermis to his ravenous shoes. As he later reconstructs it, he has, without meaning to, interpolated himself between Mary cCmndhd and her date, and perhaps jostled the latter's elbow and forced him to spill his drink. It is a startling move that quiets the group. Waterhouse opens his mouth and says "Gxnn bhldh sqrd m!"

"Hey, friend!" says Mary's date. Waterhouse turns towards the sound of the voice. The sloppy grin draped across his face serves as a convenient bulls eye, and Mary's date's fist homes in on it unerringly. The bottom half of Waterhouse's head goes numb, his mouth fills with a warm fluid that tastes nutritious. The vast concrete floor somehow takes to the air, spins like a flipped coin, and bounces off the side of his head. All four of Waterhouse's limbs seem to be pinned against the floor by the weight of his torso.

Some sort of commotion is happening up on that remote plane of most people's heads, five to six feet above the floor, where social interaction traditionally takes place. Mary's date is being hustled off to the side by a large powerful fellow—it is hard to recognize faces from this angle, but a good candidate would be Rod. Rod is shouting in Qwghlmian.

Actually, everyone is shouting in Qwghlmain—even the ones who are speaking in English—because Waterhouse's speech-recognition centers have a bad case of jangly ganglia. Best to leave that fancy stuff for later, and concentrate on more basic phylogenesis: it would be nice, for example, to be a vertebrate again. After that quadrupedal locomotion might come in handy.

A perky Qwghlmian-Australian fellow in an RAAF uniform steps up and grabs his right anterior fin, jerking him up the evolutionary ladder before he's ready. He is not doing Waterhouse a favor so much as he is getting Waterhouse's face up where it can be better scrutinized. The RAAF fellow shouts at him (because the music has started again): "Where'd you learn to talk like that?"

Waterhouse doesn't know where to begin; god forbid he should offend these people again. But he doesn't have to. The RAAF guy screws up his face in disgust, as if he had just noticed a six-foot tapeworm trying to escape from Waterhouse's throat. "Outer Qwghlm?" he asks.

Waterhouse nods. The confused and shocked faces before him collapse into graven masks. Inner Qwghlmians! Of course! The inner islanders are perennially screwed, hence have the best music, the most entertaining personalities, but are constantly being shipped off to Barbados to chop sugar cane, or to Tasmania to chase sheep, or to—well, to the Southwest Pacific to be pursued through the jungle by starving Nips draped with live satchel charges.

The RAAF chap forces himself to smile, chucks Waterhouse gently on the shoulder. Someone in this group is going to have to take the unpleasant job of playing diplomat, smoothing it all over, and with the true Inner Qwghlmian's nose for a shit job, RAAF boy has just volunteered. "With us," he explains brightly, "what you just said isn't a polite greeting."

"Oh," Waterhouse says, "what did I say, then?"

"You said that while you were down at the mill to lodge a complaint about a sack with a weak seam that sprung loose on Thursday, you were led to understand, by the tone of the proprietor's voice, that Mary's great-aunt, a spinster who had a loose reputation as a younger woman, had contracted a fungal infection in her toenails."

There is a long silence. Then everyone speaks at once. Finally a woman's voice breaks through the cacophony: "No, no!" Waterhouse looks; it's Mary. "I understood him to say that it was at the pub, and that he was there to apply for a job catching rats, and that it was my neighbor's dog that had come down with rabies."

"He was at the basilica for confession—the priest—angina—" someone shouts from the back. Then everyone talks at once: "The dockside—

Mary's half-sister—leprosy—Wednesday—complaining about a loud party!"

There's a strong arm around Waterhouse's shoulders, turning him away from all for this. He cannot turn his head to see who owns this limb, because his vertebrae have again become unstacked. He figures out that it's Rod, nobly taking his poor addled Yank roommate under his wing. Rod pulls a clean hanky from his pocket and puts it up to Waterhouse's mouth, then takes his hand away. The hanky sticks to his lip, which is now shaped like a barrage balloon.

That's not the only decent thing he does. He even gets Waterhouse a drink, and finds him a chair. "You know about the Navajos?" Rod asks.

"Huh?"

"Your marines use Navajo Indians as radio operators—they can speak to each other in their own language and the Nips have no idea what the fuck they're saying."

"Oh. Yeah. Heard about that," Waterhouse says.

"Winnie Churchill heard about those Navajos. Liked the idea. Wanted His Majesty's forces to do likewise. We don't have Navajos. But—"

"You have Qwghlmians," Waterhouse says.

"There are two different programs underway," Rod says. "Royal Navy is using Outer Qwghlmians. Army and Air Force are using Inner."

"How's it working out?"

Rod shrugs. "So-so. Qwghlmain is a very pithy language. Bears no relationship to English or Celtic—its closest relatives are !Qnd, which is spoken by a tribe of pygmies in Madagascar, and Aleut. Anyway, the pithier, the better, right?"

"By all means," Waterhouse says. "Less redundancy—harder to break the code."

"Problem is, if it's not exactly a *dead* language, then it's lying on a litter with a priest standing over it making the sign of the cross. You know?"

Waterhouse nods.

"So everyone hears it a little differently. Like just now—they heard your Outer Qwghlmian accent, and assumed you were delivering an insult. But I could tell you were saying that you believed, based on a rumor you heard last Tuesday in the meat market, that Mary was convalescing normally and would be back on her feet within a week."

"I was trying to say that she looked beautiful," Waterhouse protests.

"Ah!" Rod says. "Then you should have said, 'Gxnn bhldh sqrd m!' "

"That's what I said!"

"No, you confused the mid-glottal with the frontal glottal," Rod says.

"Honestly," Waterhouse says, "can you tell them apart over a noisy radio?"

"No," Rod says. "On the radio, we stick to the basics: 'Get in there and take that pillbox or I'll fucking kill you.' And that sort of thing."

Before much longer, the band has finished its last set and the party's over. "Well," Waterhouse says, "would you tell Mary what I really did mean to say?"

"Oh, I'm sure there's no need," Rod says confidently. "Mary is a good judge of character. I'm sure she knows what you meant. Qwghlmians excel at nonverbal communication."

Waterhouse just barely restrains himself from saying *I guess you'd have to,* which would probably just earn him another slug in the face. Rod shakes his hand and departs. Waterhouse, marooned by his shoes, hobbles out.

INRI

GOTO DENGO LIES ON A COT OF WOVEN RUSHES FOR SIX WEEKS, under a white cone of mosquito netting that stirs in the breezes from the windows. When there is a typhoon, the nurses clasp mother-of-pearl shutters over the windows, but mostly they are left open day and night. Outside the window, an immense stairway has been hand-carved up the side of a green mountain. When the sun shines, the new rice on those terraces fluoresces; green light boils into the room like flames. He can see small gnarled people in colorful clothes transplanting rice seedlings and tinkering with the irrigation system. The wall of his room is plain, cream-colored plaster spanned with forking deltas of cracks, like the blood vessels on the surface of an eyeball. It is decorated only with a crucifix carved out of napa wood in maniacal detail. Jesus's eyes are smooth orbs without pupil or iris, as in Roman statues. He hangs askew on the crucifix, arms stretched out, the ligaments probably pulled loose from their moorings now, the crooked legs, broken by the butt of a Roman spear, unable to support the body. A pitted, rusty iron nail transfixes each palm, and a third suffices for both feet. Goto Dengo notices after a while that the sculptor has arranged the three nails in a perfect equilateral triangle. He and Jesus spend many hours and days staring at each other through the white veil that hangs around the bed; when it shifts in the mountain breezes, Jesus seems to writhe. An open scroll is fixed to the top of the crucifix; it says I.N.R.I. Goto Dengo spends a long time trying to fathom this. I Need Rapid something? Initiate Nail Removal Immediately?

The veil parts and a perfect young woman in a severe black-and-white habit is standing in the gap, radiant in the green light coming off the terraces, carrying a bowl of steaming water. She peels back his hospital gown and begins to sponge him off. Goto Dengo motions towards the crucifix and asks about it—perhaps the woman has learned a little Nipponese. If she hears him, she gives no sign. She is probably deaf or crazy or both; the Christians are notorious for the way they dote on defective persons. Her gaze is fixed on Goto Dengo's body, which she swabs gently but implacably, one postage-stamp-sized bit at a time. Goto Dengo's mind is still playing tricks with him, and looking down at his naked torso he gets all turned around for a moment and thinks that he is looking at the nailed wreck of Jesus. His ribs are sticking out and his skin is a cluttered map of sores and scars. He cannot possibly be good for anything now; why are they not sending him back to Nippon? Why haven't they simply killed him? "You speak English?" he says, and her huge brown eyes jump just a bit. She is the most beautiful woman he has ever seen. To her, he must be a loathsome thing, a specimen under a glass slide in a pathology lab. When she leaves the room she will probably go and wash herself meticulously and then do anything to flush the memory of Goto Dengo's body out of her clean, virginal mind.

He drifts away into a fever, and sees himself from the vantage point of a mosquito trying to find a way in through the netting: a haggard, wracked body splayed, like a slapped insect, on a wooden trestle. The only way you can tell he's Nipponese is by the strip of white cloth tied around his forehead, but instead of an orange sun painted on it is an inscription: I.N.R.I.

A man in a long black robe is sitting beside him, holding a string of red coral beads in his hand, a tiny crucifix dangling from that. He has the big head and heavy brow of those strange people working up on the rice terraces, but his receding hairline and swept-back silver-brown hair are very European, as are his intense eyes. "Iesus Nazarenus Rex Iudaeorum," he is saying. "It is Latin. Jesus of Nazareth, King of the Jews."

"Jew? I thought Jesus was Christian," said Goto Dengo.

The man in the black robe just stares at him. Goto Dengo tries again: "I didn't know Jews spoke Latin."

One day a wheeled chair is pushed into his room; he stares at it with dull curiosity. He has heard of these things—they are used behind high walls to transport shamefully imperfect persons from one room to another. Suddenly these tiny girls have picked him up and dropped him into it! One of them says something about fresh air and the next thing he knows he's being wheeled out the door and into a corridor! They have buckled him in so he doesn't fall out, and he twists uneasily in the chair, trying to hide his face. The girl rolls him out to a huge verandah that looks out over the mountains. Mist rises up from the leaves and birds scream. On the wall behind him is a large painting of I.N.R.I. chained naked to a post, shedding blood from hundreds of parallel whip-marks. A centurion stands above him with a scourge. His eyes look strangely Nipponese.

Three other Nipponese men are sitting on the verandah. One of them talks to himself unintelligibly and keeps picking at a sore on his arm that bleeds continuously into a towel on his lap. Another one has had his arms and face burned off, and peers out at the world through a single hole in a blank mask of scar tissue. The third has been tied into his chair with many wide strips of cloth because he flops around all the time like beached fish and makes unintelligible moaning noises.

Goto Dengo eyes the railing of the verandah, wondering if he can muster the effort to wheel himself over there and fling his body over the edge. Why has he not been allowed to die honorably?

The crew of the submarine treated him and the other evacuees with an unreadable combination of reverence and disgust.

When was he set apart from his race? It happened long before his evacuation from New Guinea. The lieutenant who rescued him from the headhunters treated him as a criminal and sentenced him to execution. Even before then, he was different. Why did the sharks not eat him? Does his flesh smell different? He should have died with his comrades in the Bismarck Sea. He lived, partly because he was lucky, partly because he could swim.

Why could he swim? Partly because his body was good at it—but partly because his father raised him not to believe in demons.

He laughs out loud. The other men on the verandah turn to look at him.

He was raised not to believe in demons, and now he is one.

Black-robe laughs out loud at Goto Dengo during his next visit. "I am not trying to convert you," he says. "Please do not tell your superiors about your suspicions. We have been strictly forbidden to proselytize, and there would be brutal repercussions."

"You aren't trying to convert me with words," Goto Dento admits, "but just by having me here." His English does not quite suffice.

Black-robe's name is Father Ferdinand. He is a Jesuit or something, with enough English to run rings around Goto Dengo. "In what way does merely having you in this place constitute proselytization?" Then, just to break Goto Dengo's legs out from under him, he says the same thing in half-decent Nipponese.

"I don't know. The art."

"If you don't like our art, close your eyes and think of the emperor."

"I can't keep my eyes closed all the time."

Father Ferdinand laughs snidely. "Really? Most of your countrymen seem to have no difficulty with keeping their eyes tightly shut from cradle to grave."

"Why don't you have happy art? Is this a hospital or a morgue?"

"La Pasyon is important here," says Father Ferdinand.

"La Pasyon?"

"Christ's suffering. It speaks deeply to the people of the Philippines. Especially now."

Goto Dengo has another complaint that he is not able to voice until he borrows Father Ferdinand's Japanese–English dictionary and spends some time working with it.

"Let me see if I understand you," Father Ferdinand says. "You believe that when we treat you with mercy and dignity, we are implicitly trying to convert you to Roman Catholicism."

"You bent my words again," says Goto Dengo.

"You spoke crooked words and I straightened them," snaps Father Ferdinand.

"You are trying to make me into—one of you."

"One of us? What do you mean by that?"

"A low person."

"Why would we want to do that?"

"Because you have a low-person religion. A loser religion. If you make me into a low person, it will make me want to follow that religion."

"And by treating you decently we are trying to make you into a low person?"

"In Nippon, a sick person would not be treated as well."

"You needn't explain that to us," Father Ferdinand says. "You are in the middle of a country full of women who have been raped by Nipponese soldiers."

Time to change the subject. "Ignoti et quasi occulti—Societas Eruditorum," says Goto Dengo, reading the inscription on a medallion that hangs from Father Ferdinand's neck. "More Latin? What does it mean?"

"It is an organization I belong to. It is ecumenical."

"What does that mean?"

"Anyone can join it. Even you, after you get better."

"I will get better," Goto Dengo says. "No one will know that I was sick."

"Except for us. Oh, I understand! You mean, no Nipponese people will know. That's true."

"But the others here will not get better."

"It is true. You have the best prognosis of any patient here."

"You are receiving those sick Nipponese men into your bosoms."

"Yes. This is more or less dictated by our religion."

"They are low people now. You want them to join your low-person religion."

"Only insofar as it is good for them," says Father Ferdinand. "It's not like those guys are going to run out and build us a new cathedral or something."

The next day, Goto Dengo is deemed to be cured. He does not feel cured at all, but he will do anything to get out of this rut: losing one staredown after another with the King of the Jews.

He expects that they will saddle him with a duffel bag and send him down to the bus terminal to fend for himself, but instead a car comes to get him. As if that's not good enough, the car takes him to an airfield, where a light plane picks him up. It is the first time he has ever flown in a plane, and the excitement revives him more than six weeks in the hospital. The plane takes off between two green mountains and heads south (judging from the sun's position) and for the first time he understands where he's been: in the center of Luzon Island, north of Manila.

Half an hour later, he's above the capital, banking over the Pasig River and then the bay, chockablock with military transports. The corniche is guarded by a picket line of coconut palms. Seen from overhead, their branches writhe in the sea breeze like colossal tarantulas impaled on spikes. Looking over the pilot's shoulder, he sees a pair of paved airstrips in the flat paddy-land just south of the city, crossing at an acute angle to form a narrow X. The light plane porpoises through gusts. It bounces down the airstrip like an overinflated soccer ball, taxiing past most of the hangars and finally fishtailing to a stop near an isolated guard hut where a man waits on a motorcycle with an empty sidecar. Goto Dengo is directed out of the plane and into the sidecar by means of gestures; no one will speak to him. He is dressed in an Army uniform devoid of rank and insignia.

A pair of goggles rests on the seat, and he puts them on to keep the bugs out of his eyes. He is a little nervous because he does not have papers and he does not have orders. But they are waved out of the airbase and onto the road without any checks.

The motorcycle driver is a young Filipino man who keeps grinning broadly, at the risk of getting insects stuck between his big white teeth. He seems to think that he has the best job in the whole world, and perhaps he does. He turns south onto a road that probably qualifies as a big highway around these parts, and commences weaving through traffic. Most of this is produce carts drawn by carabaos—big oxlike things with imposing crescent-moon-shaped horns. There are a few automobiles, and the occasional military truck.

For the first couple of hours the road is straight, and runs across damp table-land used for growing rice. Goto Dengo catches glimpses of a body of water off to the left, and isn't sure whether it is a big lake or part of the ocean. "Laguna de Bay," says the driver, when he catches Goto looking at it. "Very beautiful."

Then they turn away from the lake onto a road that climbs gently into sugar cane territory. Suddenly, Goto Dengo catches sight of a volcano: a symmetrical cone, black with vegetation, cloaked in mist as though protected by a mosquito net. The sheer density of the air makes it impossible to judge size and distance; it could be a little cinder cone just off the road, or a huge stratovolcano fifty miles away.

Banana trees, coconut palms, oil palms, date palms begin to appear, sparsely at first, transforming the landscape into a kind of moist savannah. The driver pulls into a shambolic roadside store to buy petrol. Goto Dengo unfolds his jangled body from the sidecar and sits down at a table beneath an umbrella. He wipes a crust of sweat and dirt from his forehead with the clean handkerchief that he found in his pocket this morning, and orders something to drink. They bring him a glass of ice water, a bowl of raw, locally-produced sugar, and a plate of pinball-sized calamansi limes. He squeezes the calamansis into the water, stirs in sugar, and drinks it convulsively.

The driver comes and joins him; he has cadged a free cup of water from the proprietors. He always wears a mischievous grin, as if he and Goto Dengo are sharing a little private joke. He raises an imaginary rifle to his face and makes a scratching motion with his trigger finger. "You soldier?"

Goto Dengo thinks it over. "No," he says, "I do not deserve to call myself a soldier."

The driver is astonished. "No soldier? I thought you were soldier. What are you?"

Goto Dengo thinks about claiming that he is a poet. But he does not deserve that title either. "I am a digger," he finally says, "I dig holes."

"Ahh," the driver says, as if he understands. "Hey, you want?" He takes two cigarettes out of his pocket.

Goto Dengo has to laugh at the smoothness of the gambit. "Over here," he says to the proprietor. "Cigarettes." The driver grins and puts his cigarettes back where they came from.

The owner comes over and hands Goto Dengo a pack of Lucky Strikes and a book of matches. "How much?" says Goto Dengo, and takes out an envelope of money that he found in his pocket this morning. He takes the bills out and looks at them: each is printed in English with the words THE JAPANESE GOVERNMENT and then some number of pesos. There is a picture of a fat obelisk in the middle, a monument to Jose P. Rizal that stands near the Manila Hotel.

The proprietor grimaces. "You have silver?"

"Silver? Silver metal?"

"Yes," the driver says.

"Is that what people use?"

The driver nods.

"This is no good?" Goto Dengo holds up the crisp, perfect bills.

The owner takes the envelope from Goto Dengo's hand and counts out a few of the largest denomination of bills, pockets them, and leaves.

Goto Dengo breaks the seal on the pack of Lucky Strikes, raps the pack on the tabletop a few times, and opens the lid. In addition to the cigarettes, there is a printed card in there. He can just see the top part of it: it is a drawing of a man in a military officer's cap. He pulls it out slowly, revealing an eagle insignia on the cap, a pair of aviator sunglasses, an enormous corncob pipe, a lapel bearing a line of four stars, and finally, in block letters, the words I SHALL RETURN.

The driver is looking purposefully nonchalant. Goto Dengo shows him the card and raises his eyebrows. "It is nothing," the driver says. "Japan very strong. Japanese people will be here forever. MacArthur good only for selling cigarettes."

When Goto Dengo opens the book of matches, he finds the same picture of MacArthur, and the same words, printed on the inside.

After a smoke, they are back on the road. More black cones coalesce, all around them now, and the road begins to ramble up over hills and down into valleys. The trees get closer and closer together until they are riding through a sort of cultivated and inhabited jungle: pineapples close to the ground, coffee and cocoa bushes in the middle, bananas and coco-nuts overheard. They pass through one village after another, each one a cluster of dilapidated huts huddled around a great white church, built squat and strong to survive earthquakes. They zigzag around heaps of fresh coconuts piled by the roadside, spilling out into the right-of-way. Finally they turn off of the main road and into a dirt track that winds through the trees. The track has been rutted by the tires of trucks that are much too big for it. Freshly snapped-off tree branches litter the ground.

They pass through a deserted village. Stray dogs flit in and out of huts whose front doors swing unlatched. Heaps of young green coconuts rot under snarls of black flies.

Another mile down the road, the cultivated forest gives way to the wild kind, and a military checkpoint bars the road. The smile vanishes from the driver's face.

Goto Dengo states his name to one of the guards. Not knowing why he is here, he can say nothing else. He is pretty sure now that this is a prison camp and that he is about to become an inmate. As his eyes adjust he can see a barrier of barbed wire strung from tree to tree, and a second barrier inside of that. Peering carefully into the undergrowth he can make out where they dug bunkers and established pillboxes, he can map out their interlocking fields of fire in his mind. He sees ropes dangling from the tops of tall trees where snipers can tie themselves into the branches if need be. It has all been done according to doctrine, but it has a perfection that is never seen on a real battlefield, only in training camps.

He is startled to realize that all of these fortifications are designed to keep people out, not keep them in.

A call comes through on the field telephone, the barrier is raised, and they are waved through. Half a mile into the jungle they come to a cluster of tents pitched on platforms made from the freshly hewn logs of the trees that were cut down to make this clearing. A lieutenant is standing in a shady patch, waiting for them.

"Lieutenant Goto, I am Lieutenant Mori."

"You have arrived in the Southern Resource Zone recently, Lieutenant Mori?"

"Yes. How did you know?"

"You are standing directly beneath a coconut tree."

Lieutenant Mori looks straight up in the air to see several wooly brown cannonballs dangling high over his head. "Ah, so!" he says, and moves out of the way. "Did you have any conversation with the driver on the way here?"

"Just a few words."

"What did you discuss with him?"

"Cigarettes. Silver."

"Silver?" Lieutenant Mori is very interested in this, so Goto Dengo recounts their whole conversation.

"You told him that you were a digger?"

"Something like that, yes."

Lieutenant Mori backs off a step, turning to an enlisted man who has been standing off to the side, and nods. The enlisted man picks the butt of his rifle up off the ground, wheels the weapon around to a horizontal position, and turns towards the driver. He covers the distance in about six steps, accelerating to a full sprint, and cuts loose with a throaty roar as he drives his bayonet into the driver's slim body. The victim is picked up off his feet, then sprawls on his back with a low gasp. The solider straddles him and thrusts the bayonet into his torso several more times, each stroke making a wet hissing sound as metal slides between walls of meat.

The driver ends up sprawled motionless on the ground, jetting blood in all directions.

"The indiscretion will not be held against you," says Lieutenant Mori brightly, "because you did not know the nature of your new assignment."

"Pardon me?"

"Digging. You are here to dig, Goto-san." He snaps to attention and bows deeply. "Let me be the first to congratulate you. Your assignment is a very important one."

Goto Dengo returns the bow, not sure how deep to make it. "So I'm not—" He gropes for words. In trouble? A pariah? Condemned to death? "I'm not a low person here?"

"You are a very high person here, Goto-san. Please come with me." Lieutenant Mori gestures towards one of the tents.

As Goto Dengo walks away, he hears the young motorcycle driver mumble something.

"What did he say?" Lieutenant Mori asks.

"He said, 'Father, into your hands I commend my spirit.' It's a religious thing," Goto Dengo explains.

CALIFORNIA

HALF OF THE PEOPLE WHO WORK AT SFO, SAN FRANCISCO International Airport, now seem to be Filipino, which certainly helps to ease the shock of reentry. Randy gets singled out, as he always does, for a thorough luggage search by the exclusively Anglo customs officials. Men traveling by themselves with practically no luggage seem to irritate the American authorities. It's not so much that they think you are a drug trafficker as that you fit, in the most schematic possible way, the profile of the most pathologically optimistic conceivable drug trafficker, and hence practically force them to investigate you. Irritated that you have forced their hand in this manner, they want to teach you a lesson: travel with a wife and four kids next time, or check a few giant trundling bags, or something, man! What were you thinking? Never mind that Randy is coming in from a place where DEATH TO DRUG TRAFFICKERS is posted all over the airport the way CAUTION: WET FLOOR is here.

The most Kafkaesque moment is, as always, when the customs official asks what he does for a living, and he has to devise an answer that will not sound like the frantic improvisations of a drug mule with a belly full of ominously swelling heroin-stuffed condoms. "I work for a private telecommunications provider" seems to be innocuous enough. "Oh, like a phone company?" says the customs official, as if she's having none of it. "The phone market isn't really that available to us," Randy says, "so we provide other communications services. Mostly data." "Does that involve a lot of *traveling around from place to place then?*" asks the customs official, paging through the luridly stamped back pages of Randy's passport. She makes eye contact with a more senior customs official who sidles over towards them. Randy now feels himself getting nervous, exactly the way your drug mule would, and fights the impulse to scrub his damp palms against his pant legs, which would probably guarantee him a trip through the magnetic tunnel of a CAT scanner, a triple dose of mint-flavored laxative, and several hours of straining over a stainless-steel evidence bucket. "Yes, it does," Randy says.

The senior customs official, trying to be unobtrusive and low key in a way that makes Randy stifle a sort of gasping, pained outburst of laughter, begins to flip through some appalling communications-industry magazine that Randy stuffed into his briefcase on his way out the door back in Manila. The word INTERNET appears at least five times on the front cover. Randy stares directly into the eyes of the female customs official and says, "The Internet." Totally factitious understanding dawns on the woman's face, and her eyes ping bosswards. The boss, still deeply absorbed in an article about the next generation of high-speed routers, shoves out his lower lip and nods, like every other nineties American male who senses that knowing this stuff is now as intrinsic to maleness as changing flat tires was to Dad. "I hear that's really exciting now," the woman says in a completely different tone of voice, and begins scooping Randy's stuff together into a big pile so that he can repack it. Suddenly the spell is broken, Randy is a member in good standing of American society again, having cheerfully endured this process of being ritually goosed by the Government. He feels a strong impulse to drive straight to the nearest gun store and spend about ten thousand dollars. Not that he wants to hurt anyone; it's just that any kind of government authority gives him the creeps now. He's probably been hanging out too much with the ridiculously heavily armed Tom Howard. First a hostility to rainforests, now a desire to own an automatic weapon; where is this all going?

Avi is waiting for him, a tall pale figure standing at the velvet rope surrounded by hundreds of Filipinas in a state of emotional riot, brandishing gladiola spears like medieval pikemen. Avi has his hands in the pockets of his floor-skimming coat, and keeps his head turned in Randy's direction but is sort of concentrating on a point about halfway between them, frowning in an owlish way. This is the same frown that Randy's grandmother used to wear when she was teasing apart a tangle of string from her junk drawer. Avi adopts it when he is doing basically the same thing to some new complex of information. He must have read Randy's e-mail message about the gold. It occurs to Randy that he missed a great opportunity for a practical joke: he could have loaded up his bag with a couple of lead bricks and then handed it to Avi and completely blown his mind. Too late. Avi rotates around his vertical axis as Randy comes abreast of him and then breaks into a stride that matches Randy's pace. There is some unarticulated protocol that dictates when Randy and Avi will shake hands, when they will hug, and when they will just act like they've only been separated for a few minutes. A recent exchange of e-mail seems to constitute a virtual reunion that obviates any hand-shaking or hugging. "You were right about the cheesy dialog," is the first thing Avi says. "You're spending too much time with Shaftoe, seeing things his way. This was not an attempt to send you a message, at least not in the way Shaftoe means."

"What's your interpretation, then?"

"How would you go about establishing a new currency?" Avi asks.

Randy frequently overhears snatches of business-related conversation from people he passes in airports, and it's always about how did the big presentation go, or who's on the short list to replace the departing CFO, or something. He prides himself on what he believes to be the much higher plane, or at least the much more bizarre subject matter, of his interchanges with Avi. They are walking together around the slow arc of SFO's inner ring. A whiff of soy sauce and ginger drifts out of a restaurant and fogs Randy's mind, making him unsure, for a moment, which hemisphere he's in.

"Uh, it's not something I have given much thought to," he says. "Is that what we are about now? Are we going to establish a new currency?"

"Well obviously *someone* needs to establish one that doesn't suck," Avi says.

"Is this some exercise in keeping a straight face?" Randy asks.

"Don't you ever read the newspapers?" Avi grabs Randy by the elbow and drags him over towards a newsstand. Several papers are running front-page stories about crashing Southeast Asian currencies, but this isn't all that new.

"I know currency fluctuations are important to Epiphyte," Randy says. "But my god, it's so tedious I just want to run away."

"Well, it's not tedious to *her,*" Avi says, yanking out three different newspapers that have all decided to run the same wire-service photograph: an adorable Thai moppet standing in a mile-long queue in front of a bank, holding up a single American dollar bill.

"I know it's a big deal for some of our customers," Randy says, "I just didn't really think of it as a business opportunity."

"No, think about it," Avi says. He counts out a few dollar bills of his own to pay for the newspapers, then swerves towards an exit. They enter a tunnel that leads to a parking garage. "The sultan feels that—"

"You've been just sort of hanging out with the sultan?"

"Mostly with Pragasu. Will you let me finish? We decided to set up the Crypt, right?"

"Right."

"What is the Crypt? Do you remember its original stated function?"

"Secure, anonymous, unregulated data storage. A data haven."

"Yeah. A bit bucket. And we envisioned many applications for this."

"Boy, did we ever," Randy says, remembering many long nights around kitchen tables and hotel rooms, writing versions of the business plan that are now as ancient and as lost as the holographs of the Four Gospels.

"One of these was electronic banking. Heck, we even predicted it might be one of the major applications. But whenever a business plan first makes contact with the actual market—the real world—suddenly all kinds of stuff becomes clear. You may have envisioned half a dozen potential markets for your product, but as soon as you open your doors, one just explodes from the pack and becomes so instantly important that good business sense dictates that you abandon the others and concentrate all your efforts."

"And that's what happened with the e-banking thing," Randy says.

"Yes. During our meetings at the Sultan's Palace," Avi says. "Before those meetings, we envisioned—well you know what we envisioned. What actually happened was that the room was packed with these guys who were exclusively interested in the e-banking thing. That was our first clue. Then, this!" He holds up his newspapers, whacks the dollar-brandishing moppet with the back of his hand. "So, that's the business we're in now."

"We are bankers," Randy says. He will have to keep saying this to himself for a while in order to believe it, like, "We are striving with all our might to uphold the goals of the 23rd Party Congress." *We are bankers. We are bankers.*

"Banks used to issue their own currencies. You can see these old banknotes in the Smithsonian. 'First National Bank of South Bumfuck will remit ten pork bellies to the bearer,' or whatever. That had to stop because commerce became nonlocal—you needed to be able to take your money with you when you went out West, or whatever."

"But if we're online, the whole world is local," Randy says.

"Yeah. So all we need is something to back the currency. Gold would be good."

"*Gold?* Are you *joking?* Isn't that kind of old-fashioned?"

"It was until all of the unbacked currencies in Southeast Asia went down the toilet."

"Avi, so far I am still kind of confused, frankly. You seem to be working your way around to telling me that my little trip to see the gold in the jungle was no coincidence. But how can we use that gold to back our currency?"

Avi shrugs as if it's such a minor detail he hasn't even bothered to think about it. "That's just a deal-making issue."

"Oh, god."

"These people who sent you a message want to get into business with us. Your trip to see the gold was a credit check."

They are walking through a tunnel toward the garage, stuck behind an extended clan of Southeast Asians in elaborate headdresses. Perhaps the entire remaining gene pool of some nearly extinct mountain dwelling minority group. Their belongings are in giant boxes wrapped in iridescent pink synthetic twine, balanced atop airport luggage carts.

"A credit check." Randy always hates it when he gets so far behind Avi that all he can do is lamely repeat phrases.

"You know how, when you and Charlene bought that house, the lender had to look at it first?"

"I bought it for cash."

"Okay, okay, but in general, before a bank will issue a mortgage on a house, they will inspect it. Not in great detail, necessarily. They'll just have some executive of the bank drive by the property to verify that it exists and is where the documents claim it is, and so on."

"So, that's what my journey to the jungle was about?"

"Yeah. Some of the potential, uh, participants in the project just wanted to make it clear to us that they were, in fact, in possession of this gold."

"I really have to wonder what 'possession' denotes in this case."

"Me too," Avi says. "I've been sort of puzzling over that one." Hence, Randy thinks, the frowny look in the airport.

"I just thought they wanted to sell it," Randy says.

"Why? Why sell it?"

"To liquidate it. So they could buy real estate. Or five thousand pairs of shoes. Or something."

Avi scrunches his face in disappointment. "Oh, Randy, that is really unworthy, alluding to the Marcoses. The gold you saw is pocket change compared to what Ferdinand Marcos dug up. The people who set up your trip to the jungle are satellites of satellites of him."

"Well. Consider it a cry for help," Randy says. "Words seem to be passing back and forth between us, but I understand less and less."

Avi opens his mouth to respond, but just then the animists trigger their car alarm. Unable to propitiate it, they form a circle around the car and grin at one another. Avi and Randy pick up their pace and get well away from it.

Avi stops and straightens, as if pulled up short. "Speaking of not understanding things," he says, "you need to communicate with that girl. Amy Shaftoe."

"Has she been communicating with you?"

"In the course of twenty minutes' phone conversation, she has deeply and eternally bonded with Kia," Avi says.

"I would believe that without hesitation."

"It wasn't even like they got to know each other. It was like they knew each other in a previous life and had just gotten back in touch."

"Yeah. So?"

"Kia now feels bound by duty and honor to present a united front with America Shaftoe."

"It all hangs together," Randy says.

"Acting sort of like Amy's emotional agent or lawyer, she has made it clear to me that we, Epiphyte Corporation, owe Amy our full attention and concern."

"And what does Amy want?"

"That was my question," Avi says, "and I was made to feel very bad for asking it. Whatever it is that we—that you—owe to Amy is something so obvious that merely manifesting a need to verbalize it is . . . just . . . really . . ."

"Shabby. Insensitive."

"Coarse. Brutish."

"A really transparent, toddler-level exercise in the cheapest kind of, of . . ."

"Of evasion of personal responsibility for one's own gross misdeeds."

"Kia was rolling her eyes, I imagine. Her lip was sort of curled."

"She drew breath as if to give me a good piece of her mind but then thought better of it."

"Not because you're her boss. But because you would never understand."

"This is just one of those evils that has to be sort of accepted and swallowed, by any mature woman who's been around the block."

"Who knows the harsh realities. Yeah," Randy says.

"Yup."

"Okay, you can tell Kia that her client's needs and demands have been communicated to the guilty party—"

"Have they?"

"Tell her that the fact that her client *has* needs and demands has been heavy-handedly insinuated to me and that it is understood that the ball is in my court."

"And we can stand down to some kind of detente while a response is prepared?"

"Certainly. Kia can return to her normal duties for the time being."

"Thank you, Randy."

Avi's Range Rover is parked in the most remote part of the roof of the parking ramp, in the center of about twenty-five empty parking spaces that form a sort of security buffer zone. When they have traversed about half of the glacis, the car's headlights flutter, and Randy hears the preparatory snap of a sound system being energized. "The Range Rover has picked us up on Doppler radar," Avi says hastily.

The Range Rover speaketh in a fearsome Oz-like voice cranked up to burning-bush decibel levels. "You are being tracked by Cerberus! Please alter your course immediately!"

"I can't believe you bought one of these things," Randy says.

"You have encroached on the Cerberus defensive perimeter! Move back. Move back," says the Range Rover. "An armed response team is being placed on standby."

"It is the only cryptographically sound car alarm system," Avi says, as if that settles the matter. He digs out a keychain attached to a black polycarbonate fob with the same dimensions, and number of buttons, as a television remote control. He enters a long series of digits and cuts off the voice in the middle of proclaiming that Randy and Avi are being recorded on a digital video camera that is sensitive into the near-infrared range.

"Normally it doesn't do that," Avi says. "I had it set to its maximum alert status."

"What's the worst that could happen? Someone would steal your car and the insurance company would buy you a new one?"

"I couldn't care less if it gets stolen. The worst that could happen would be a car bomb, or, not quite as bad, someone putting a bug in my car and listening to everything I say."

Avi drives Randy over the San Andreas Fault to his place in Pacifica, which is where Randy stores his car while he's overseas. Avi's wife Devorah is in at the doctor's for a routine prenatal and all the kids are either at school or being hustled around the neighborhood by their tag-team duo of tough Israeli nannies. Avi's nannies have the souls of war-hardened Soviet paratroopers in the bodies of nubile eighteen-year-old girls. The house has been utterly abandoned to kid-raising. The formal dining room has been converted to a nanny-barracks with bunk beds hammered together from unfinished two-by-fours, the parlor filled with cribs and changing-tables, and every square centimeter of cheap shag carpet in the place has been infused with a few dozen flakes of glitter, in various festive colors, which if they even cared about getting rid of it could only be removed through direct microsurgical extraction, one flake at a time. Avi plies Randy with a sandwich of turkey bologna and ketchup on generic Wonderoid bread. It is still too early in Manila for Randy to call Amy and make amends for whatever he did wrong. Down below them, in Avi's basement office, a fax machine shrieks and rustles like a bird in a coffee can. A laminated CIA map of Sierra Leone is spread out on the table, peeking out here and there through numerous overlying strata of dirty dishes, newspapers, coloring books, and drafts of the Epiphyte(2) Business Plan. Post-it notes are stuck to the map from place to place. Written on each note, in Avi's distinctive triple-ought Rapidograph drafting-pen hand, is a latitude and longitude with lots of significant digits, and some kind of precis of what happened there: "5 women, 2 men, 4 children, with machetes—photos:" and then serial numbers from Avi's database.

Randy was a little groggy on the drive over, and was irritable about the inappropriate daylight, but after the sandwich his metabolism tries to get into the spirit of things. He has learned to surf these mysterious endocrinological swells. "I'm going to get going," he says, and stands.

"Your overall plan, again?"

"First I go south," Randy says, superstitiously not even wanting to utter the name of the place where he used to live. "For no more than a day, I hope. Then jet lag will land on me like a plunging safe and I will hole up somewhere and watch basketball through the vee of my feet for maybe a day. Then I head north to the Palouse country."

Avi raises his eyebrows. "Home?"

"Yeah."

"Hey, before I forget—could you look for information on the Whitmans while you're up there?"

"You mean the missionaries?"

"Yeah. They came out to the Palouse to convert the Cayuse Indians, who were these magnificent horsemen. They had the best of intentions, but they accidentally gave them measles. Annihilated the whole tribe."

"Does that really land within the boundaries of your obsession? Inadvertent genocide?"

"Anomalous cases have heightened utility in that they help us delineate the boundaries of the field."

"I'll see what I can find about the Whitmans."

"May I inquire," Avi says, "why you are going up there? Family visit?"

"My grandmother is moving to a managed care facility. Her children are convening to divide up her furniture and so on, which I find a little ghoulish, but it's nobody's fault and it has to be done."

"And you are going to participate?"

"I am going to avoid it as much as I can, because it's probably going to be a catfight. Years from now, family members will still not be speaking to each other because they didn't get Mom's Gomer Bolstrood credenza."

"What is it with Anglo-Saxons and furniture? Could you explain that to me?"

"I am going because we found a piece of paper in a briefcase in a sunken Nazi submarine in the Palawan Passage that says, 'WATERHOUSE—LAVENDER ROSE.' "

Avi looks baffled now, in a way that Randy finds satisfying. He gets up and climbs into his car and starts driving south, down the coast, the slow and beautiful way.

ORGAN

✠ LAWRENCE WATERHOUSE'S LIBIDO IS SUPPRESSED FOR ABOUT A week by the pain and swelling in his jaw. Then the pain and swelling in his groin surges into the fore, and he begins searching his memories of the dance, wondering if he made any progress with Mary cCmndhd.

He wakes up suddenly at four o'clock one Sunday morning, clammily coated from his nipples to his knees. Rod is still sleeping soundly, thank god, and so if Waterhouse did any moaning or calling out of names during his dream, Rod's probably not aware of it. Waterhouse begins trying to clean himself off without making a lot of noise. He doesn't even want to think about how he's going to explain the condition of the sheets to Who Will Launder Them. "It was completely innocent, Mrs. McTeague. I dreamed that I came downstairs in my pajamas and that Mary was sitting in the parlor in her uniform, drinking tea, and she turned and looked me in the eye, and then I just couldn't control myself and aaaaAAAHHH! HUH! HUH! HUH! HUH! HUH! HUH! HUH! HUH! HUH! HUH! HUH! And then I woke up and just look at the mess."

Mrs. McTeague (and other old ladies like her all around the world) does the laundry only because it is her role in the giant Ejaculation Control Conspiracy which, as Waterhouse is belatedly realizing, controls the entire planet. No doubt she has a clipboard down in the cellar, next to her mangle, where she marks down the frequency and volume of the ejaculations of her four boarders. The data sheets are mailed into some Bletchley Park type of operation somewhere (Waterhouse guesses it's disguised as a large convent in upstate New York), where the numbers from all round the world are tabulated on Electrical Till Corporation machines and printouts piled up on carts that are wheeled into the offices of the high priestesses of the conspiracy, dressed in heavily starched white raiments, embroidered with the emblem of the conspiracy: a penis caught in a mangle. The priestesses review the data carefully. They observe that Hitler still isn't getting any, and debate whether letting him have some would calm him down a little bit or just give him license to run further out of control. It will take months for the name of Lawrence Pritchard Waterhouse to come to the top of the list, and months for orders to be sent out to Brisbane—and even then, the orders may condemn him to another year of waiting for Mary cCmndhd to show up in his dreams with a teacup.

Mrs. McTeague, and other ECC members (such as Mary cCmndhd and basically all of the other young women) are offended by easy girls, prostitutes, and whorehouses, not for religious reasons, but because they provide a refuge where men can have ejaculations that are not controlled, metered, or monitored in any way. Prostitutes are turncoats, collaborators.

All of this comes into Waterhouse's mind as he lies in his damp bed between four and six o'clock in the morning, considering his place in the world with the crystalline clarity that can only be obtained by getting a good night's sleep and then venting several weeks' jism production. He has reached a fork in the road.

Last night, before Rod turned in, he shined his shoes, explaining that tomorrow morning he had to be up bright and early for church. Now, Waterhouse knows what that means, having spent many a Sabbath on

Qwghlm, cringing and blushing under the glares of the locals, who were outraged that he appeared to be running the huffduff equipment on the day of rest. He has seen them shuffling into their morbid, thousand-year-old black-stone chapel on Sunday mornings for their three-hour services. Hell, Waterhouse even *lived* in a Qwghlmian chapel for several months. Its gloom suffused his whole being.

Going to church with Rod would mean giving in to the ECC, becoming their minion. The alternative is the whorehouse.

Even though he grew up in churches, raised by church people, Waterhouse (as must be obvious by this point) never really understood their attitudes about sex. Why did they get so hung up on that one issue, when there were others like murder, war, poverty, and pestilence?

Now, finally, he gets it: the churches are merely one branch of the ECC. And what they are doing, when they fulminate about sex, is trying to make sure that all the young people fall in line with the ECC's program.

So, what is the end result of the ECC's efforts? Waterhouse stares at the ceiling, which is starting to become fuzzily visible as the sun rises in the west, or the north, or wherever the hell it rises here in the Southern Hemisphere. He takes a quick inventory of the world and finds that basically the ECC is running the entire planet, good countries and bad countries alike. That all successful and respected men are minions of the ECC, or at least are so scared of it that they pretend to be. Non-ECC members live on the fringes of society, like prostitutes, or have been driven deep underground and must waste tremendous amounts of time and energy keeping up a false front. If you knuckle under and become a minion of the ECC, you get to have a career, a family, kids, wealth, house, pot roasts, clean laundry, and the respect of all the other ECC minions. You have to pay dues in the form of chronic nagging sexual irritation which can only be relieved by, and at the discretion and convenience of, one person, the person designated for this role by the ECC: your wife. On the other hand, if you reject the ECC and its works, you can't, by definition, have a family, and your career options are limited to pimp, gangster, and forty-year enlisted sailor.

Hell, it's not even that bad of a conspiracy. They build churches and universities, educate kids, install swingsets in parks. Sometimes they throw a war and kill ten or twenty million people, but it's a drop in the bucket compared to stuff like influenza—which the ECC campaigns against by nagging everyone to wash their hands and cover their mouth when sneezing.

The alarm clock. Rod rolls out of bed like it's a Nip air raid. Waterhouse stares at the ceiling for another few minutes, dithering. But he knows where he's going, and there's no point in wasting any more time. He's going to church, and not exactly because he has renounced Satan and all his works, but because he wants to fuck Mary. He almost can't help flinching when he says (to himself) this terrible-sounding thing. But the weird thing about church is that it provides a special context within which it is perfectly okay to want to fuck Mary. As long as he goes to church, he can want to fuck Mary as much as he wants, he can spend all of his time, in and out of church, thinking about fucking Mary. He can let her know that he wants to fuck her as long as he finds a more oblique way of phrasing it. And if he jumps through certain hoops (hoops of gold) he can even fuck Mary in actuality, and it will all be perfectly acceptable—at no time will he have to feel the slightest trace of shame or guilt.

He rolls out of bed, startling Rod, who (being some sort of jungle commando) is easily startled. "I'm going to fuck your cousin until the bed collapses into a pile of splinters," Waterhouse says.

Actually, what he says is "I'm going to church with you." But Waterhouse, the cryptologist, is engaging in a bit of secret code work here. He is using a newly invented code, which only he knows. It will be very dangerous if the code is ever broken, but this is impossible since there is only one copy, and it's in Waterhouse's head. Turing might be smart enough to break the code anyway, but he's in England, and he's on Waterhouse's side, so he'd never tell.

A few minutes later, Waterhouse and cCmndhd go downstairs, headed for "church," which in Waterhouse's secret code, means "headquarters of the Mary-fucking campaign of 1944."

As they step out into the cool morning air they can hear Mrs. McTeague bustling into their bedroom to strip their beds and inspect their sheets. Waterhouse smiles, thinking that he has just gotten away with something; the damning and overwhelming evidence found on his bed linens will be neatly cancelled out by the fact that he got up early and went to church.

He is expecting a prayer-group meeting in the basement of a dry-goods store, but it turns out that the Inner Qwghlmians got banished to Australia in droves. Many of them settled in Brisbane. In the downtown they managed to construct a United Ecclesiastical Church out of rough-hewn beige sandstone. It would look big, solid, and almost opulent if it were not directly across the street from the Universal Ecclesiastical Church, which is twice as big and made of smooth-faced limestone. Outer Qwghlmians, dressed in dour blacks and greys, and frequently in navy uniforms, shuffle up the wide, time-blackened steps of the Universal Ecclesiastical Church, occasionally turning their heads to throw disapproving looks across the street at the Inner Qwghlmians, who are actually dressed for the season (it is summer in Australia) or in Army uniforms. Waterhouse can see that what really pisses them off is the sound of the music that vents from the United Ecclesiastical Church whenever its red enameled front doors are hauled open. The choir is practicing and the organ is playing. But he can tell from half a block away that something's wrong with the instrument.

The look of the Inner Qwghlmian women in their pastel dresses and bright bonnets is reassuring. These do not look like people who engage in human sacrifice. Waterhouse tries to spring lightly up the steps as if he really wants to be here. Then he remembers that he *does* want to be here, because it is all part of his plan to fuck Mary.

The churchgoers are all talking in Qwghlmian, greeting each other and saying nice things to Rod, who is evidently well thought of. Waterhouse has no idea what they are saying, and finds it comforting to know that most of them don't either. He strolls into the central aisle of the church, stares down its vault to the altar, the choir behind it, singing beautifully; Mary is there, in the alto section, exercising those pipes of hers, which are framed attractively by the satin stole of her chorister's uniform. Above and behind the choir, a big old pipe organ spreads its tarnished wings, like a stuffed and mounted eagle that's been sitting in a damp attic for fifty years. It wheezes and hisses asthmatically, and emits bizarre, discordant drones when certain stops are used; this happens when a valve is stuck open, and it is called a cipher. Waterhouse knows all about ciphers.

Notwithstanding the pathetic organ, the choir is spectacular, and builds to a stirring six-part-harmony climax as Waterhouse ambles up the aisle, wondering whether his erection is visible. A shaft of light comes in through the stained-glass rosette above the organ pipes and pinions Waterhouse in its gaudy beam. Or maybe it just feels that way, because Waterhouse has it all figured out now.

Waterhouse is going to fix the church's organ. This project will be sure to have side benefits for his own organ, a single-pipe instrument that needs attention just as badly.

It turns out that, like all ethnic groups that have been consistently screwed for a long time, the Inner Qwghlmians have great music. Not only that, they actually have fun in church. The minister actually has a sense of humor. It's about as tolerable as church could ever be. Waterhouse hardly pays attention because he is doing a lot of staring: first at Mary, then at the organ (trying to figure out how it is engineered) then back to Mary for a while.

He is outraged and offended, after the service, when the powers that be are reluctant to let him, a total stranger and a Yank to boot, begin ripping off access panels and meddling with the inner workings of the organ. The minister is a good judge of character—a little too good to suit Waterhouse. The organist (and hence ultimate authority on all matters organic) looks to have been shipped over here with the very first load of convicts after having been convicted, in the Old Bailey, of talking too loud, bumping into things, not tying his shoelaces properly, and having dandruff so in excess of Society's unwritten standards as to offend the dignity of the Queen and of the Empire.

It all leads to an unbearably tense and complicated meeting in a Sunday school classroom near the offices of the minister, who is called the Rev. Dr. John Mnrh. He is a stout red-faced chap who clearly would prefer to have his head in a tun of ale but who is putting up with all of this because it's good for his immortal soul.

This meeting essentially becomes a venue within which the organist, Mr. Drkh, can vent his opinions on the sneakiness of the Japanese, why the invention of the well-tempered tuning system was a bad idea and how all music written since has been a shabby compromise, the sterling qualities of the General, the numerological significance of the lengths of various organ pipes, how the excessive libido of American troops might be controlled with certain dietary supplements, how the hauntingly beautiful modes of traditional Qwghlmian music are particularly ill-suited to the well-tempered tuning system, how the king's dodgy Germanic relatives are plotting to take over the Empire and turn it over to Hitler, and, first and foremost, that Johann Sebastian Bach was a bad musician, a worse composer, an evil man, a philanderer, and the figurehead of a worldwide conspiracy, headquartered in Germany, that has been slowly taking over the world for the last several hundred years, using the well-tempered tuning system as a sort of carrier frequency on which its ideas (which originate with the Bavarian illuminati) can be broadcast into the minds of everyone who listens to music—especially the music of Bach. And—by the way—how this conspiracy may best be fought off by playing and listening to traditional Qwghlmian music, which, in case Mr. Drkh didn't make this perfectly clear, is wholly incompatible with well-tempered tuning because of its haunting and beautiful, but numerologically perfect, scale.

"Your thoughts on numerology are most interesting," Waterhouse says loudly, running Mr. Drkh off the rhetorical road. "I myself studied with Drs. Turing and von Neumann at the Institute for Advanced Studies in Princeton."

Father John snaps awake, and Mr. Drkh looks as if he's just taken a fifty-caliber round in the small of his back. Clearly, Mr. Drkh has had a long career of being the weirdest person in any given room, but he's about to go down in flames.

In general, Waterhouse isn't good at just winging it, but he's tired and pissed off and horny, and this is a fucking war, and sometimes you *have* to. He mounts the podium, dives for a round of chalk, and starts hammering equations onto the blackboard like an ack-ack gun. He uses well-tempered tuning as a starting point, takes off from there into the deepest realms of advanced number theory, circles back all of a sudden to the Qwghlmian modal scale, just to keep them on their toes, and then goes screaming straight back into number theory again. In the process, he actually stumbles across some interesting material that he doesn't think has been covered in the literature yet, and so he diverts from strict bullshitting for a few minutes to explore this thing and actually prove something that he thinks could probably be published in a mathematical journal, if he just gets around to typing it up properly. It reminds him that he's not half bad at this stuff when he's recently ejaculated, and that in turn just fuels his resolve to get this Mary-fucking thing worked out.

Finally, he turns around, for the first time since he started. Father John and Mr. Drkh are both dumbfounded.

"Let me just demonstrate!" Waterhouse blurts, and strides out of the room and doesn't bother looking back. Back in the church, he goes to the console, blows the dandruff off the keys, hits the main power switch. The electric motors come on, somewhere back behind the screen, and the instrument begins to complain and whine. No matter—it can all be drowned out. He scans the rows of stops—he already knows what this organ's got, because he's listened and deconstructed. He starts yanking out knobs.

Now Waterhouse is going to demonstrate that Bach can sound good even played on Mr. Drkh's organ, if you choose the right key. Just as Father John and Mr. Drkh are about halfway up the aisle, Waterhouse slams into that old chestnut, Toccata and Fugue in D Minor, except that he's transposing it into C-sharp minor as he goes along, because (according to a very elegant calculation that just came into his head as he was running up the aisle of the church) it ought to sound good that way when played in Mr. Drkh's mangled tuning system.

The transposition is an awkward business at first and he hits a few wrong notes, but then it comes naturally and he transitions from the toccata into the fugue with tremendous verve and confidence. Gouts of dust and salvos of mouse droppings explode from the pipes as Waterhouse invokes whole ranks that have not been used in decades. Many of these are big bad loud reed stops that are difficult to tune. Waterhouse senses the pumping machinery straining to keep up with this unprecedented demand for power. The choir loft is suffused with a brilliant glow as the dust flung out of the choked pipes fills the air and catches the light coming through the rose window. Waterhouse muffs a pedal line, spitefully kicks off his terrible shoes and begins to tread the pedals the way he used to back in Virginia, with his bare feet, the trajectory of the bass line traced out across the wooden pedals in lines of blood from his exploded blisters. This baby has some nasty thirty-two-foot reed stops in the pedals, real earthshakers, probably put there specifically to irritate the Outer Qwghlmians across the street. None of the people who go to this church have ever heard these stops called into action, but Waterhouse puts them to good use now, firing off power chords like salvos from the mighty guns of the battleship *Iowa*.

All during the service, during the sermon and the scripture readings and the prayers, when he wasn't thinking about fucking Mary, he was thinking about how he was going to fix this organ. He was thinking back to the organ he worked on in Virginia, how the stops enabled the flow of air to the different ranks of pipes and how the keys on the keyboards activated all of the pipes that were enabled. He has this whole organ visualized in his head now, and while he is pounding through to the end of the figure, the top of his skull comes off, the filtered red light pours in, he sees the entire machine in his mind, as if in an exploded draftsman's view. Then it transforms itself into a slightly different machine—an organ that runs on electricity, with ranks of vacuum tubes here, and a grid of relays there. He has the answer, now, to Turing's question, the question of how to take a pattern of binary data and bury it into the circuitry of a thinking machine so that it can be later disinterred.

Waterhouse knows how to make electric memory. He must go write a letter to Alan instantly!

"Excuse me," he says, and runs from the church. On his way out, he brushes past a small young woman who has been standing there gaping at his performance. When he is several blocks away, he realizes two things: that he is walking down the street barefoot, and that the young woman was Mary cCmndhd. He will have to circle back later and get his shoes and maybe fuck her. But first things first!

HOME

RANDY OPENS HIS EYES FROM OUT OF A SLIDING NIGHTMARE. He was in his car, driving down the Pacific Coast Highway, when something went wrong with the steering. The car began to wander, first towards the vertical stone cliff on the left and then towards the sheer drop to huge jagged rocks projecting from thrashing waves on the right. Big rocks were rolling nonchalantly across the highway. He could not steer; the only way to stop moving is to open his eyes.

He is lying on a sleeping bag on a polished maple floor that is not level, and that is why he had the sliding dream. The eye/inner ear conflict makes his body spasm, he flails to plant both hands against the plane of the floor.

America Shaftoe sits, jeaned and barefoot, in the blue light of a window, bobby pins sprouting from chapped lips, looking at her face in an isosceles triangle of mirror whose scalpel-sharp edges depress but do not cut the pink skin of her fingertips. A web of lead ropes sags in the empty windowframe, a few lozenges of beveled glass still trapped in the interstices. Randy lifts his head slightly and looks downhill, into the corner of the room, and sees a great heap of swept shards. He rolls over, looks out the door and across the hallway and into what used to be Charlene's home office. Robin and Marcus Aurelius Shaftoe are sharing a double mattress in there, a shotgun and a rifle, a couple of big black cop flashlights, a Bible and a calculus textbook neatly arranged on the floor next to them.

The nightmare's feeling of panic, of needing to go somewhere and do something, subsides. Lying here in his ruined house listening to Amy's brush whistle through her hair, throwing off electrostatic snaps, is one of the calmer moments he's had.

"You just about ready to hit the road?" Amy says.

Across the hallway, one of the Shaftoe boys sits up without making any sound. The other opens his eyes, lifts his head, glances towards the weapons, lights, and Good Book, then relaxes again.

"I got a fire going out in the yard," Amy says, "and some water boiling. Didn't think it was safe to use the fireplace."

Everyone slept in their clothes last night. All they have to do is put their shoes on and piss out the windows. The Shaftoes move about the place faster than Randy does, not because they are more surefooted, but because they never saw this house when it was level and sound. But Randy lived here for years and years when it was, and his mind thinks it knows its way around the place. Going to bed last night, his biggest fear was that he would get up drowsily in the middle of the night and try to go downstairs. The house used to have a beautiful winding stairway which has now telescoped into the basement. Last night, by dint of pulling the U-Haul onto the front lawn and aiming its headlights directly in through windows (whose cracks and jags and facets refracted the light gorgeously), they were able to clamber into the basement and find a ten-foot aluminum extension ladder which they used to get into the upstairs. Once they had gotten up, they pulled the ladder up with them, like a drawbridge, so that even if looters did enter the downstairs, the Shaftoe boys would be able to sit at the top of what used to be the stairway and pick them off leisurely with the long guns (this scenario seemed plausible last night, in the dark, but now strikes Randy as a bumpkin's reverie).

Amy's turned some balusters from the veranda's railing into a nice bonfire in the front yard. She stomps a crushed saucepan back into shape with a small number of deftly aimed heel-strokes and cooks oatmeal. The Shaftoe boys throw whatever looks potentially useful into the back of the U-Haul, and check the oil in their hot rod.

All of Charlene's stuff is in New Haven now. In Dr. G. E. B. Kivistik's house, to be specific. He has generously offered to let her stay there while she looks for a house; Randy predicts she'll never leave. All of Randy's stuff is in Manila or in Avi's basement, and all of the disputed items are in a storage locker at the edge of town.

Randy spent most of yesterday evening cruising around town checking in on various old friends to see if they were all right. Amy went with him, taking a voyeuristic interest in this tour of his former life, and, from a social point of view, complicating things incalculably. In any case, they didn't make it back to the house until after dark, and so this is Randy's first chance to see the damage in full daylight. He orbits it again and again, amused, almost to the point of giggling, by how perfectly destroyed it is, taking pictures with a disposable camera he borrowed from Marcus Aurelius Shaftoe, trying to see if there is anything left that could conceivably be worth money.

The house's stone foundation rises three feet above grade. The wooden walls of the house were built on top of that, but not actually attached to it (a common practice in the old days, which, at the time he blew town, was on Randy's list of things to fix before the next earthquake). When the earth began to oscillate side-to-side at 2:16 in the afternoon yesterday, the foundation oscillated right along with it, but the house wanted to stay where it was. Eventually the foundation wall moved right out from underneath the house, one corner of which dropped three feet to the ground. Randy could probably estimate the amount of kinetic energy the house picked up during this fall, and convert it to an equivalent in pounds of dynamite or swings of a wrecking ball, but it would be a nerdy exercise, since he can see the effects for himself. Let's just say that when it smashed to earth the whole structure suffered a vicious shock. The parallel, upright joists in the floors all went horizontal, collapsing like dominoes. Every window and doorframe instantly became a parallelogram, so all of the glass broke, and in particular all of the leaded glass was rent asunder. The stairway fell into the basement. The chimney, which had been in need of tuck-pointing for some time, sprayed bricks all over the yard. Most of the plumbing was wrecked, which means that the heating system is history, since the house used radiators. The plaster fell from the lath everywhere, cumulative tons of old horse-hair plaster just exploding out of the walls and ceilings and mixing with the water from the busted plumbing to make a grey slurry that congealed in the downhill corners of the rooms. The hand-crafted Italian tiles that Charlene picked out for the bathrooms are seventy-five percent broken. The granite counters in the kitchen are now seamed tectonic systems. A few of the major appliances look repairable, but ownership of those was in dispute anyway.

"It's a tear-down, sir," says Robin Shaftoe. He has spent his whole life in some Tennessee mountain town, living in trailers and cabins, but even he has enough real estate acumen to sense this.

"Is there something you wanted to get out of the basement, sir?" says Marcus Aurelius Shaftoe.

Randy laughs. "There's a filing cabinet down there . . . wait!" he reaches out and puts a hand on Marcus's shoulder, to prevent him from sprinting into the house and diving like Tarzan into the stairway-pit. "The reason I wanted it was because it contains every single receipt for every penny I put into this house. See, it was a wreck when I bought it. Sort of like it is now. Maybe not as bad."

"You need those papers for your dee-vorce?"

Randy stops and clears his throat in mild exasperation. He has explained to them five times that he was never married to Charlene and so it's not a divorce. But this idea of living with a woman to whom one is not married is so embarrassing to the Tennessee branch of the Shaftoes that they simply cannot process it, and so they keep talking about "your ex-wahf" and "your dee-vorce."

Noting Randy's hesitation, Robin says, "Or for the IN-surance?"

Randy laughs with surprising heartiness.

"You did get IN-surance, didn't you sir?"

"Earthquake insurance, around here, is basically unobtainable," Randy says.

This is the first time it dawns on any of the Shaftoes that as of 2:16 P.M. yesterday afternoon, in an instant, Randy's net worth dropped by something like three hundred thousand dollars. They skulk away from him and leave him alone for a while, taking pictures to document the loss.

Amy comes over. "Oatmeal's ready," she says.

"Okay."

She stands close to him with her arms folded. The town is uncannily quiet: the power is off and few vehicles are on the streets. "I'm sorry I ran you off the road."

Randy looks at his Acura: the gouge, high on the left rear fender, where the bumper of Amy's U-Haul truck took him from behind, and the crumpled front right bumper where he was forced into a parked Ford Fiesta. "Don't worry about it."

"If I'd known—Jesus. The last thing you need is a body shop bill on top of everything else. I'll pay for it."

"Seriously. Don't worry about it."

"Well . . ."

"Amy, I know perfectly well you don't give a shit about my stupid car, and when you pretend otherwise, the strain shows."

"You're right. But I'm sorry I misapprehended the situation."

"It was my fault," Randy says, "I should have explained why I was coming here. Why the hell did you rent a U-Haul, anyway?"

"They were all out of regular cars at the San Francisco Airport. Some kind of big convention at the Moscone Center. So I displayed adaptability."*

"How the hell did you get here so fast? I thought I took the last flight out of Manila."

"I got to NAIA only a few minutes after you did, Randy. Your flight was full. I got on the next flight to Tokyo. I think my flight actually took off before yours did."

"Mine was delayed on the ground."

"Then from Narita I just grabbed the next flight to SFO. Landed a couple hours after you. So I was surprised that you and I pulled into town here at the same time."

"I stopped over at a friend's house. And I took the scenic route." Randy closes his eyes for a moment, remembering those loose boulders

———————————

*This phrase is a Douglas MacArthur Shaftoe parody.

on the Pacific Coast Highway, the roadway shaking beneath the tires of his Acura.

"See, when I saw your car, that's when I felt that God was with me, or something," Amy said. "Or with you."

"God was with me? How do you figure?"

"Well, first of all, I have to tell you that I left Manila not out of concern for you but out of burning rage, and a desire to just feed you your ass on a plate."

"I figured."

"It's not even clear to me that you and I constitute a potential couple. But you have started acting towards me in a way that indicates some interest in that direction, so you have certain obligations." Amy has now started to get pissed off and begun to move around the yard. The Shaftoe boys eye her warily from across their steaming oatmeal bowls, ready to spring into action and wrestle her to the ground if she should fly out of control. "It would be just . . . totally . . . unacceptable for you to make those kinds of representations to me and then jet off and cuddle with your California sweetheart without coming to me first and going through certain formalities, which would be awkward but which I would hope you would be man enough to endure. Right?"

"Absolutely right. Never felt otherwise."

"So you can imagine how it looked."

"I guess so. Assuming you have no faith in me whatsoever."

"Well, I'm sorry for that, but I will say that on the flight over I began to think that it wasn't your fault, that Charlene had somehow gotten to you."

"What do you mean, gotten to me?"

Amy looks at the ground. "I don't know, she must have some kind of hold over you."

"I think not." Randy sighs.

"Anyway, I thought that maybe you were just in the process of making a big, stupid mistake. So when I got on that plane in Tokyo I was just going to track you down and . . ." She draws a deep breath and mentally counts to ten. "But when I got off that plane I was *to boot* just obsessed with this disgusting image of you getting back together with this woman who obviously was no damn good for you. And I felt that would be an unfortunate outcome for you. And I thought I was too late to do anything about it. So, when I got into town, and pulled around the corner and saw your Acura in the lane right there in front of me, and you talking on your cellphone—"

"I was leaving a message on your answering machine in Manila," Randy says. "Explaining that I was just coming here to pick up some papers and there'd been an earthquake only minutes before and so I might be a while."

"Well, I didn't have *time* to check my messages, which were placed on my machine *too late* to accomplish any *useful purpose*," Amy says, "and so I had to go on an *imperfect knowledge* of these events since no one had bothered to *fill me in*."

"So . . ."

"I felt that cooler heads should prevail."

"And therefore you *ran me off the road?*"

Amy looks a little disappointed. She takes a patient, Montessori-pre-school-teacher tone of voice. "Now, Randy, think about priorities for just a minute. I could see the way you were driving."

"I was in a hurry to find out whether I was totally destitute, or merely bankrupt."

"But because of my *imperfect knowledge* of the situation I thought maybe you were rushing into your poor little Charlene's arms. In other words, that the emotional stress of the earthquake might induce you to—who knows what, relationship-wise."

Randy presses his lips together and takes a huge breath through his nose.

"Compared to that, a little bit of sheet metal just was not very important to me. Of course, I know that a lot of *guys* would just stand back and allow someone they cared about to do something extremely foolish and damaging, only so that everyone concerned could then drive off to a miserable and emotionally fucked-up future in perfect, shiny cars."

Randy can do nothing but roll his eyes. "Well," he says, "I am sorry that I blew up at you when I got out of the car."

"You are? Why, exactly? You *should* be pissed off when a truck driver runs you off the road."

"I didn't know who you were. I didn't recognize you in this context. It did not occur to me that you would do what you did with the airplanes."

Amy laughs in a goofy, mischievous way that doesn't seem right here. Randy feels quizzical and mildly irritated. She looks at him knowingly. "I'll bet you never blew up at Charlene."

"That's right," Randy says.

"You didn't? In all those years?"

"When we had issues, we talked them out."

Amy snorts. "I'll bet you had really boring—" She stops herself.

"Boring what?"

"Never mind."

"Look, I think that in a good relationship, you have to have ways for working out any issues that might come up." Randy says reasonably.

"And you don't consider ramming your car a good way, I'll bet."

"I can think of some problems with it."

"And you had ways of working out your problems with Charlene that were very sophisticated. No voices were ever raised. No angry words exchanged."

"No cars rammed."

"Yeah. And that worked, right?"

Randy sighs.

"How about that thing that Charlene wrote about beards?" Amy asks.

"How did you know about that?"

"Looked it up on the Internet. Was that an example of how you guys worked out your problems? By publishing totally oblique academic papers blasting the other person?"

"I feel like having some oatmeal."

"So don't apologize to me for blowing up at me."

"That oatmeal would really hit the spot."

"For having, and showing, emotion."

"Chow time!"

"Because that's what it's all about. That's the name of the game, Randy boy," she says, pulling abreast of him and whacking him between the shoulder blades in a gesture inherited from her dad. "Mmm, that oatmeal does smell good."

The caravan pulls out of town a little after noon: Randy leading the way in his damaged Acura, Amy sitting in the passenger seat with her bare, tanned feet up on the dashboard, spoked with white lines from the straps of her high-tech sandals, oblivious to the danger (alluded to by Randy) of her legs being snapped by an air bag deployment. The souped-up Impala is driven by its owner of record and chief engineer, Marcus Aurelius Shaftoe. Bringing up the rear, the almost totally empty U-Haul track, driven by Robin Shaftoe. Randy has that moving-through-syrup feeling he gets when enacting some emotionally huge transition in his life. He puts Samuel Barber's *Adagio for Strings* on the Acura's stereo and drives very slowly down the main street of the town, looking all around at the remains of the coffeehouses, bars, pizza places, and Thai restaurants where, for many years, he prosecuted his social life. He should have performed this little ceremony before he first left for Manila, a year and a half ago. But then he fled as if from the scene of a crime, or, at least, a grotesque personal embarrassment. He only had a day or two before he got on the plane, and he spent most of it on the floor of Avi's basement, dictating whole swathes of the business plan into a microcassette recorder, as opposed to typing them, because his hands had gone carpal.

He never even properly said good-bye to most of the people he knew here. He did not speak to them, and barely thought of them, until yesterday evening, when he pulled up in front of their skewed and occasionally smoking homes in his crumpled and U-Haul-orange-streaked car with this strange, wiry, tanned woman who, whatever strengths and shortcomings she might have, was not Charlene. So, taking everything into account, it was not precisely the way that Emily Post would have orchestrated a reunion with out-of-touch friends. The evening's tour is still a flurry of odd, emotionally charged images in his memory, but he's beginning to sort it out a little, to run the numbers as it were, and he would say that of the people he ran into yesterday—people he had exchanged dinner invitations with and loaned tools to, people whose personal computers he had debugged in exchange for six-packs of good beer, whom he had seen important movies with—that at least three-quarters of these people have really no interest whatsoever in seeing Randy's face again as long as they live, and were made to feel intensely awkward by his totally unexpected reappearance in their front yards, where they were throwing impromptu parties with salvaged beer and wine. This hostility was pretty strongly gender-linked, Randy is sad to conclude. Many of the females wouldn't talk to him it all, or would come near him only the better to fix him with frosty glares and appraise his presumed new girlfriend. This only stands to reason, since, before she left for Yale, Charlene had the better part of a year to popularize her version of events. She has been able to structure the discourse to her advantage, just like a dead white male. No doubt Randy has been classified as an abandoner, no better than the married man who up and walks out on his wife and children—never mind that he was the one who wanted to marry her and have kids with her. But his whining alert starts to buzz when he thinks about that, so he backs up and tries another path.

He embodies (he realizes) just about the worst nightmare, for many women, of what might happen in their lives. As for the men he saw last night, they were pretty strongly incented to back whatever stance their wives adopted. Some of them really did, apparently, feel similarly. Others eyed him with obvious curiosity. Some were openly friendly. Weirdly, the ones who adopted the sternest and most terrible Old Testament moral tone were the Modern Language Association types who believed that everything was relative and that, for example, polygamy was as valid as monogamy. The friendliest and most sincere welcome he'd gotten was from Scott, a chemistry professor, and Laura, a pediatrician, who, after knowing Randy and Charlene for many years, had one day divulged to Randy, in strict confidence, that, unbeknownst to the academic community at large, they had been spiriting their three children off to church every Sunday morning, and even had them all baptized.

Randy had gone into their house once to help Scott wrestle a freshly reconditioned clawfoot bathrub up the stairs, and had actually seen the word GOD written on actual pieces of paper stuck to the walls of their house—like on the refrigerator door, and the walls of the children's bedrooms, where juvenile art tends to be reposited. Little time-wasting projects they had done during Sunday school—pages torn from coloring books, showing a somewhat more multicultural Jesus than the one Randy had grown up with (curly hair, e.g.), talking to little biblical kids or assisting disoriented Holy Land livestock. The sight of this stuff around the house, commingled with normal (i.e., secular) kid-art-junk from elementary school, Batman posters, etc. made Randy feel grossly embarrassed. It was like going to the house of some supposedly sophisticated people and finding a neon-on-black-velvet Elvis painting hanging above their state-of-the-art Italian designer furniture. Definitely a social-class thing. And it wasn't like Scott and Laura were deadly earnest types, and neither were they glassy-eyed and foaming at the mouth. They had after all managed to pass themselves off as members in good standing of decent academic society for a number of years. They were a bit quieter than many others, they took up less space in the room, but then that was normal for people trying to raise three kids, and so they passed.

Randy and Amy had spent a full hour talking to Scott and Laura last night; they were the only people who made any effort to make Amy feel welcome. Randy hadn't the faintest idea what these people thought of him and what he had done, but he could sense right away that, essentially *that was not the issue* because even if they thought he had done something evil, they at least had a framework, a sort of procedure manual, for dealing with transgressions. To translate it into UNIX system administration terms (Randy's fundamental metaphor for just about everything), the post-modern, politically correct atheists were like people who had suddenly found themselves in charge of a big and unfathomably complex computer system (viz. society) with no documentation or instructions of any kind, and so whose only way to keep the thing running was to invent and enforce certain rules with a kind of neo-Puritanical rigor, because they were at a loss to deal with any deviations from what they saw as the norm. Whereas people who were wired into a church were like UNIX system administrators who, while they might not understand everything, at least had some documentation, some FAQs and How-tos and README files, providing some guidance on what to do when things got out of whack. They were, in other words, capable of displaying adaptability.

"Yo! Randy!" says America Shaftoe. "M.A. is honking at you."

"Why?" Randy asks. He looks in the rearview, sees a reflection of the ceiling of the Acura, and realizes he is slouched way down in his seat. He sits up straight, and spots the Impala.

"I think it's because you're driving ten miles an hour," Amy says, "and M.A. likes to go ninety."

"Okay," Randy says, and, just as simple as that, pushes down on the accelerator pedal and drives out of town forever.

BUNDOK

"THE NAME OF THIS PLACE IS BUNDOK," CAPTAIN NODA TELLS him confidently. "We have chosen it carefully." Goto Dengo and Lieutenant Mori are the only other persons present in the tent, but he speaks as if addressing a battalion drawn up on a parade ground.

Goto Dengo has been in the Philippines long enough to understand that in the local tongue *bundok* means any patch of rugged mountainous terrain, but he does not reckon that Captain Noda is the sort who would appreciate being brought up to speed by a subordinate. If Captain Noda says that this place is called Bundok, then Bundok it is, and forever will be.

Captain is not an especially high rank, but Noda carries himself as if he's a general. Somewhere, this man is important. He is pale-skinned, as if he's been spending the winter in Tokyo. His boots have not begun to rot on his feet yet.

A hard leather attache case rests on the table. He opens one end and draws out a large piece of folded white cloth. The two lieutenants scurry to assist him in unfolding this across the tabletop. Goto Dengo is startled by the feel of the linen. His fingertips are the only part of his body that will ever touch bedsheets as fine as these. THE MANILA HOTEL is printed along the selvedge.

A diagram has been sketched out on the bedsheet. Blue-black fountain-pen marks, punctuated with spreading blotches where the hand hesitated, reinforce an earlier stratum of graphite scratches. Someone terribly important (probably the last person to sleep on this bedsheet) has come in with a black grease pencil and reshaped the whole thing in his own image with fat thrusting strokes and hasty notations that look like unraveled braids in a woman's long hair. This work has been annotated politely by a fastidious engineer, probably Captain Noda himself, working with ink and a fine brush.

The heavy with the grease pencil has labeled the entire thing BUNDOK SITE.

Lieutenants Mori and Goto affix the sheet to the canvas of the tent with some small, rusty cotter pins that a private brings to them, triumphantly, in a cracked porcelain coffee cup. Captain Noda watches calmly, puffing on a cigarette. "Be careful," he jokes, "MacArthur slept on that sheet!"

Lieutenant Mori dutifully cracks up. Goto Dengo is standing on tiptoe, holding up the top edge of the sheet, examining the faint pencil marks underlying the whole diagram. He sees a couple of little crosses and, having spent too long in the Philippines, supposes at first that they are churches. In one place, three of them are clustered together and he imagines Calvary.

Nearby, diggings have been indicated. He thinks Golgotha: The Place of the Skull.

Lunatic! He needs to get his mind in order. Lieutenant Mori shoves pins through the linen with faint popping noises. Goto Dengo steps away, keeping his back to the Captain, closes his eyes, and gets his bearings. He is Nipponese. He is in the Southern Resource Zone of Greater Nippon. The cross-shaped marks represent summits. The diggings are some sort of excavation in which he is destined to play an important role.

The blue-black fountain-pen marks are rivers. Five of them sprawl from the triple summit of Bundok. Two of the south-going streams combine to make a larger river. A third stream roughly parallels this one. But the man with the black grease pencil has drawn a stout line across the stream with such force that loose curls of black grease can still be seen dangling from the linen. The fountain pen has been used to scratch out a bulge in the river just upstream of this mark. Apparently they want to dam the river and make a pool, or a pond, or a lake; it is difficult to get a sense of scale. It is labeled, LAKE YAMAMOTO.

Looking more closely, he sees that the larger river—the one formed by the confluence of the two tributaries—is also to be dammed, but much farther south. This has been dubbed TOJO RIVER. But there is no LAKE TOJO. It appears that this dam will thicken and deepen the Tojo River but not turn it into an actual lake. Goto Dengo infers from this that the valley of the Tojo River must be steep-sided.

The same basic pattern is repeated everywhere on the bedsheet. Grease pencil wants a complete perimeter security system. Grease pencil wants one and only one road leading to this place. Grease pencil wants two areas for barracks: one big area and one small area. The details have been worked out by smaller men with better penmanship.

"Worker housing," explains Captain Noda, pointing to the big area with his swagger stick. "Military barracks," he says, pointing to the small area. Bending closer, Goto Dengo can see that the larger, worker area is to be surrounded by an irregular polygon of barbed wire. Actually, two polygons, one nested within the other, a barren space in between. The vertices of this polygon are labeled with the names of weapons: Nambu, Nambu, Model 89 field mortar.

A road or trail, or something, leads from there up the bank of the Tojo River, past the dam, and terminates at the site of the proposed diggings.

Goto Dengo bends close and peers. The area including both Lake Yamamoto and the diggings has been surrounded by a tidy square, neatly crosshatched with Captain Noda's brush-and-ink, and labeled "special security zone."

He jerks back as Captain Noda shoves the end of his stick into the narrow space between his nose and the bedsheet, and whacks on the Special Security Zone a few times. Concentric ripples speed outwards, like shock waves from dynamite. "This area is your responsibility, Lieutenant Goto." He moves the pointer south and taps on the zone farther down the Tojo River, with the worker housing and the barracks. "This is Lieutenant Mori's." He circles the whole area, windmilling his arm to cover the entire security perimeter and the road that gives access to it. "The entirety is mine. I report to Manila. So, it is a very small chain of command for such a large area. Secrecy is of paramount importance. Your first and highest order is to preserve absolute secrecy at all costs."

Lieutenants Mori and Goto blurt "Hai!" and bow.

Addressing Mori, Captain Noda continues: "The housing area will appear to be a prison camp—for special prisoners. Its existence may be known to some on the outside—the local people will see trucks going in and out along the road and will guess as much." Turning to Goto Dengo, he says: "The existence of the Special Security Zone, however, will be totally unknown to the outside world. Your work will proceed under the cover of the jungle, which is extraordinarily dense here. It will be invisible to the enemy's observation planes."

Lieutenant Mori jerks back as if a bug has just flown into his eye. To him, the idea of enemy observation planes over Luzon is completely bizarre. MacArthur is nowhere near the Philippines.

Goto Dengo, on the other hand, has been to New Guinea. He knows what happens to Nipponese Army units who try to resist MacArthur in the jungles of the Southwest Pacific. He knows that MacArthur is coming, and obviously so does Captain Noda. More importantly, so do the men in Tokyo who sent Noda down to accomplish this mission—whatever it is.

They know. Everyone knows we are losing the war.

Everyone *important,* that is.

"Lieutenant Goto, you are not to discuss any details of your work with Lieutenant Mori except insofar as they pertain to pure logistics: road building, worker schedules, and so on." Noda is addressing this to both men; the clear implication is that if Goto gets loose-lipped, Mori is expected to turn him in. "Lieutenant Mori, you are dismissed!"

Mori grunts out another "Hai!" and makes himself scarce.

Lieutenant Goto bows. "Captain Noda, please permit me to say that I am honored to have been selected to construct these fortifications."

The stoic look on Noda's face dissolves for a moment. He turns away from Goto Dengo and paces across the floor of the tent for a moment, thinking, then turns to face him again. "It is not a fortification."

Goto Dengo is practically startled right out of his boots for a moment. Then he thinks, a gold mine! They must have discovered an immense gold deposit in this valley. Or diamonds?

"You must not think as if you were building a fortification," Noda says solemnly.

"A mine?" Goto Dengo says. But he says it weakly. He is already realizing that it does not make sense. It would be insane to put so much effort into mining gold or diamonds at this point in the war. Nippon needs steel, rubber, and petroleum, not jewelry.

Perhaps some new super-weapon? His heart nearly bursts from excitement. But Captain Noda's stare is as bleak as the fat muzzle of a tommy gun.

"It is a long-term storage facility for vital war-making materials," Captain Noda finally says.

He goes on to explain, in general terms, how the facility is to be built. It is to be a network of intersecting shafts bored through hard volcanic rock. Its dimensions are surprisingly small given the amount of effort that will be spent on building it. They won't be able to store much here: enough ammunition for a regiment to fight for a week, perhaps, assuming that they make minimal use of heavy weapons, and get their food off the land. But those supplies will be almost inconceivably well protected.

Goto Dengo sleeps that night in a hammock stretched between two trees, protected by mosquito netting. The jungle emits a fantastic din.

Captain Noda's sketches looked familiar, and he is trying to place them. Just as he's falling asleep, he remembers cutaway views of the Pyramids of Egypt that his father had shown him in a picture book, showing the design of the pharaoh's tombs.

A horrible thought comes to him then: he is building a tomb for the emperor. When Nippon falls to MacArthur, Hirohito will carry out the rite of seppuku. His body will be flown out of Nippon and brought to Bundok and buried in the chamber that Goto Dengo is building. He has a nightmare of being buried alive in a black chamber, the grey image of the emperor's face fading to black as the last brick is rammed home on its bed of mortar.

He sits in absolute darkness, knowing that Hirohito is there with him, afraid to move.

He is a little boy in an abandoned mine chamber, naked and soaked with icy water. His flashlight has died. Before it flickered out, he thought he saw the face of a demon. Now he hears only the drip, drip of ground-water into the sump. He can stay here and die, or he can dive into the water again and swim back.

When he wakes up, it's raining and the sun has climbed free of the horizon somewhere. He rolls out of his hammock and walks naked in the warm rain to wash himself. Goto Dengo has a job to do.

COMPUTER

✠ LIEUTENANT COLONEL EARL COMSTOCK OF THE ELECTRICAL Till Corporation and the United States Army, in that order, prepares for today's routine briefing from his subordinate, Lawrence Pritchard Waterhouse, much as a test pilot readies himself to be ripped into the stratosphere with a hot rocket engine under his ass. He turns in early the night before, wakes up late, talks to his aide and makes sure that (a) plenty of hot coffee is available and (b) none of it will be given to Waterhouse. He gets two wire recorders set up in the room, in case either goes on the fritz, and brings in a team of three crack stenographers with loads of technical savvy. He has a couple of fellows in his section—also ETC employees during peacetime—who are real math whizzes, so he brings them in too. He gives them a little pep talk: "I do not expect you fellows to understand what the fuck Waterhouse is talking about. I'm gonna be running after him as fast as I can. You just hug his legs and hold on for dear life so that I can sort of keep his backside in view as long as possible." Comstock is proud of this analogy, but the math whizzes seem baffled. Testily, he fills them in on the always-tricky literal vs. figurative dichotomy. Only twenty minutes remain before Waterhouse's arrival; right on schedule, Comstock's aide comes through the room with a tray of benzedrine tablets. Comstock takes two, attempting to lead by example. "Where's my darn chalkboard team?" he demands, as the powerful stimulant begins to rev up his pulse. Into the room come two privates equipped with blackboard erasers and damp chamois cloths, plus a three-man photography team. They set up a pair of cameras aimed at the chalkboard, plus a couple of strobe lights, and lay in a healthy stock of film rolls.

He checks his watch. They are running five minutes behind schedule. He looks out the window and sees that his jeep has returned; Waterhouse must be in the building. "Where is the extraction team?" he demands.

Sergeant Graves is there a few moments later. "Sir, we went to the church as directed, and located him, and, uh—" He coughs against the back of his hand.

"And what?"

"And who is more like it, sir," says Sergeant Graves, sotto voce. "He's in the lavatory right now, cleaning up, if you know what I mean." He winks.

"Ohhhh," says Earl Comstock, cottoning on to it.

"After all," Sergeant Graves says, "you can't *blow out* the *rusty pipes* of your *organ* unless you have a *nice little assistant* to get the job *properly done.*"

Comstock tenses. "Sergeant Graves—it is critically important for me to know—*did the job get properly done?*"

Graves furrows his brow, as if pained by the very question. "Oh, by all means sir. We wouldn't dream of interrupting such an operation. That's why we are late—begging your pardon."

"Don't mention it," Comstock stays, slapping Graves heartily on the shoulder. "That is why I try to give my men broad discretion. It has been my opinion for quite some time that Waterhouse is badly in need of some relaxation. He concentrates a little too hard on his work. Sometimes I frankly cannot tell whether he is saying something very brilliant, or just totally incoherent. And I think you have made a pivotal, Sergeant Graves, a pivotal contribution to today's meeting by having the good sense to stand off long enough for Waterhouse's affairs to be set in order." Comstock realizes that he is breathing very fast, and his heart is pounding madly. Perhaps he overdid the benzedrine?

Waterhouse drifts into the room ten minutes later on flaccid legs, as if he had inadvertently left his own skeleton behind in bed. He barely makes it to his designated seat and thuds into it like a sack of guts, popping a few strands of wicker out of its bottom. He is breathing raggedly through his mouth, blinking heavy eyelids frequently.

"Looks like today's going to be a milk run, men!" Comstock announces brightly. Everyone except Waterhouse snickers. Waterhouse has been in the building for a quarter of an hour, and it took at least that long for Sergeant Graves to drive him here from the church, and so it has been at least half an hour. And yet, to look at him, you'd think that it had happened five seconds ago.

"Someone pour that man a cup of coffee!" Comstock orders. Someone does. Being in the military is *amazing*; you give orders, and things happen. Waterhouse does not drink, or even touch, the coffee, but at least it gives his eyes something to focus on. Those orbs wander around under their rumpled lids for a while, like ack-ack guns trying to track a housefly, before finally fixing on the white coffee mug. Waterhouse clears his throat at some length, as if preparing to speak, and the room goes silent. It remains silent for about thirty seconds. Then Waterhouse mumbles something that sounds like "coy."

The stenographers take it down in unison.

"Beg pardon?" says Comstock.

One of the math whizzes says, "He might be talking about Coy Functions. I think I saw them when I was flipping through a graduate math textbook once."

"I thought he was saying 'quantum' something," says the other ETC man.

"Coffee," Waterhouse says, and heaves a deep sigh.

"Waterhouse," says Comstock, "how many fingers am I holding up?"

Waterhouse seems to realize that there are other people in the room now. He closes his mouth, and his nostrils flare as air begins to rush through them. He tries to move one of his hands, realizes that he is sitting on it, and shifts heavily to and fro until it flops loose. He gets his eyes all the way open, providing a really good, clear view of that coffee mug. He yawns, stretches, and farts.

"The Nipponese cryptosystem that we call Azure is the same thing as the German system that we call Pufferfish," he announces. "Both of them are also related somehow to another, newer cryptosystem I have dubbed Arethusa. All of these have something to do with gold. Probably gold mining operations of some sort. In the Philippines."

Whammo! The stenographers go into action. The photographer fires off his strobes, even though there's nothing to take pictures of—just nerves. Comstock glances beadily at his wire recorders, makes sure those reels are spinning. He is a little unnerved by how rapidly Waterhouse is coming up to speed. But one of the responsibilities of leadership is to mask one's own fears, to project confidence at all times. Comstock grins and says, "You sound awfully sure of yourself, Waterhouse! I wonder if you can get me to feel that same level of confidence."

Waterhouse frowns at the coffee mug. "Well, it's all math," he says. "If the math works, why then you *should* be sure of yourself. That's the whole point of math."

"So you have a mathematical basis for making this assertion?"

"Assertions," Waterhouse says. "Assertion number one is that Puff-erfish and Azure are different names for the same cryptosystem. Assertion number two is that Pufferfish/Azure is a cousin of Arethusa. Three: all of these cryptosystems are related to gold. Four: mining. Five: Philippines."

"Maybe you could just chalk those up on the blackboard as you go along," Comstock says edgily.

"Glad to," Waterhouse says. He stands up and turns toward the black-board, freezes for a couple of seconds, then turns back around, lunges for the coffee mug, and drains it before Comstock or any of his aides can rip it from his grasp. Tactical error! Then Waterhouse chalks up his assertions. The photographer records it. The privates massage their cham-ois cloths and glance nervously in Comstock's direction.

"Now, you have some sort of, er, mathematical proof for each one of these assertions?" Comstock asks. Math isn't his bag, but running meetings is, and what Waterhouse has just chalked up on that board looks, to him, like the rudiments of an agenda. And Comstock feels a lot better when he has an agenda. Without an agenda, he's like a grunt running around in the jungle without a map or a weapon.

"Well, sir, that's one way to look at it," Waterhouse says after some thought. "But it is much more elegant to view all of these as corollaries stemming from the same underlying theorem."

"Are you telling me that you have succeeded in breaking Azure? Because if so, congratulations are in order!" Comstock says.

"No. It is still unbroken. But I *can* extract information from it."

This is the moment where the joystick snaps off in Comstock's hand. Still, he can pound haplessly on the control panel. "Well, would you mind taking them one at a time, at least?"

"Well, let's just take, for example, Assertion Four, which is that Azure/ Pufferfish has something to do with mining." Waterhouse sketches out a freehand map of the Southwest Pacific theater of operations, from Burma to the Solomons, from Nippon to New Zealand. It takes him about sixty seconds. Just for grins, Comstock pulls a printed map out of his clipboard and compares it against Waterhouse's version. They are basically identical.

Waterhouse draws a circle with a letter A in it at the entrance to Manila Bay. "This is one of the stations that transmits Azure messages."

"You know that from huff-duff, correct?"

"That's right."

"Is that on Corregidor?"

"One of the smaller islands near Corregidor."

Waterhouse draws another circle-A in Manila itself, one in Tokyo, one in Rabaul, one in Penang, one in the Indian Ocean.

"What's that?" Comstock asks.

"We picked up an Azure transmission from a German U-boat here," Waterhouse says.

"How do you know it was a German U-boat?"

"Recognized the fist," Waterhouse says. "So, this is the spatial arrangement of Azure transmitters—not counting the stations in Europe that are making Pufferfish transmissions, and hence, according to Assertion One, are part of the same network. Anyway, now let us say that an Azure message originates from Tokyo on a certain date. We don't know what it says, because we haven't broken Azure yet. We just know that the message went out to these places." Waterhouse draws lines radiating downward from Tokyo to Manila, Rabaul, Penang. "Now, each one of these cities is a major military base. Consequently, each is the source of a steady stream of traffic, communicating with all of the Nipponese bases in its region." Waterhouse draws shorter lines radiating from Manila to various locations in the Philippines, and from Rabaul to New Guinea and the Solomons.

"Correction, Waterhouse," Comstock says. "We own New Guinea now."

"But I'm going back in time!" Waterhouse says. "Back to 1943, when there were Nip bases all along the north coast of New Guinea, and through the Solomons. So, let us say that within a brief window of time following this Azure message from Tokyo, a number of messages are transmitted from places like Rabaul and Manila to smaller bases in those areas. Some of them are in ciphers that we have learned how to break. Now, it is not unreasonable to suppose that some of these messages were sent out as a consequence of whatever orders were contained in that Azure message."

"But those places send out thousands of messages a day," Comstock protests. "What makes you think that you can pick out the messages that are a consequence of the Azure orders?"

"It's just a brute force statistics problem," Waterhouse says. "Suppose that Tokyo sent the Azure message to Rabaul on October 15th, 1943. Now, suppose I take all of the messages that were sent out from Rabaul on October 14th and I index them in various ways: what destinations they were transmitted to, how long they were, and, if we were able to decrypt them, what their subject matter was. Were they orders for troop movements? Supply shipments? Changes in tactics or procedures? Then, I take all of the messages that were sent out from Rabaul on October 16th—the day after the Azure message came in from Tokyo—and I run exactly the same statistical analysis on them."

Waterhouse steps back from the chalkboard and turns into a blinding fusillade of strobe lights. "You see, it is all about information flow. Information flows from Tokyo to Rabaul. We don't know what the information was. But it will, in some way, influence what Rabaul does afterwards. Rabaul is changed, irrevocably, by the arrival of that information, and by comparing Rabaul's observed behavior before and after that change, we can make inferences."

"Such as?" Comstock says warily.

Waterhouse shrugs. "The differences are very slight. They hardly stand out from the noise. Over the course of the war, thirty-one Azure messages have gone out from Tokyo, so I have that many data sets to work with. Any one data set by itself might not tell me anything. But when I combine all of the data sets together—giving me greater depth—then I can see some patterns. And one of the patterns that I most definitely see is that, on the day after an Azure message went out to, say, Rabaul, Rabaul was much more likely to transmit messages having to do with mining engineers. This has ramifications that can be traced all the way back until the loop is closed."

"Loop is closed?"

"Okay. Let's take it from the top. Azure message goes from Tokyo to Rabaul," Waterhouse says, drawing a heavy line down the chalkboard joining those two cities. "The next day, a message in some other crypto-system—one that we have broken—goes from Rabaul to a submarine operating out of a base here, in the Moluccas. The message states that the submarine is to proceed to an outpost on the north coast of New Guinea and pick up four passengers, who are identified by name. From our archives, we know who these men are: three aircraft mechanics and one mining engineer. A few days later, the submarine transmits from the Bismarck Sea stating that it has picked those men up. A few days after that, our waterfront spies in Manila inform us that the same submarine has showed up there. On the same day, another Azure message is transmitted from Manila back up to Tokyo," Waterhouse concludes, adding a final line to the polygon, "closing the loop."

"But that could all be a series of random, unconnected events," says one of Comstock's math whizzes, before Comstock can say it. "The

Nips are desperate for aircraft mechanics. There's nothing unusual about this kind of message traffic."

"But there is something unusual about the patterns," Waterhouse says. "If, a few months later, another submarine is sent, in the same way, to pick up some mining engineers and some surveyors who have been trapped in Rabaul, and, upon its arrival in Manila, another Azure message is sent from Manila up to Tokyo, it begins to look very suspicious."

"I don't know," Comstock stays, shaking his head. "I'm not sure if I can sell this to the General's staff. It's too much of a fishing expedition."

"Correction, sir, it *was* a fishing expedition. But now I'm *back* from the fishing expedition, and I've got the fish!" Waterhouse storms out of the room and down the hall toward his lab—half the fucking wing. Good thing Australia is a big continent, because Waterhouse is going to take all of it if he's not held sternly in check. Fifteen seconds later he's back with a stack of ETC cards a foot high, which he pounds down on the tabletop. "It's all right here."

Comstock has never fired a gun in his life, but he knows card-punching and -reading machinery like a jarhead knows his Springfield, and he's not impressed. "Waterhouse, that stack of cards carries about as much information as a letter home to Mom. Are you trying to tell me—"

"No, this is just the summary. The result of the statistical analysis."

"Why the hell did you punch it onto ETC cards? Why not just turn in a plain old typed report like everyone else?"

"I didn't punch it," Waterhouse says. "The machine punched it."

"The machine punched it," Comstock says very slowly.

"Yes. When it was done performing the analysis." Waterhouse suddenly breaks into his braying laugh. "You didn't think this was the raw inputs, did you?"

"Well, I—"

"The inputs filled several rooms. I had to run almost every message we have intercepted through the whole war through this analysis. Remember all those trucks I requisitioned a few weeks ago? Those trucks were just to carry the cards back and forth from storage."

"Jesus Christ!" Comstock says. He remembers the trucks now, their incessant comings and goings, fender-benders in the motor pool, exhaust fumes coming through his window, the enlisted men shoving heavy carts up and down the hallways, laden with boxes. Running over people's feet. Scaring the secretaries.

And the noise. The noise, the noise, from Waterhouse's goddamned machine. Flowerpots vibrating their way off file cabinets, standing waves in coffee cups.

"Wait a sec," says one of the ETC men, with the nasal skepticism of a man who has just realized he's being bullshitted. "I saw those trucks. I saw those cards. Are you trying to get us to believe that you were actually running a statistical analysis on each and every single one of those message decrypts?"

Waterhouse looks a little defensive. "Well, that was the only way to do it!"

Comstock's math whiz is homing in for the kill now. "I agree that the only way to accomplish the analysis that is implied by that"—he waves at the mandala of intersecting polygons on Waterhouse's map—"is to go through all of those truckloads of old decrypts one by one. That is clear. That is not what we are objecting to."

"What are you objecting to, then?"

The whiz laughs angrily. "I'm just worried about the *inconvenient fact* that there is no machine in the whole world that is capable of processing all of that data, that fast."

"Didn't you hear the noise?" Waterhouse asks.

"We all heard the goddamn noise," Comstock says. "What does that have to do with anything?"

"Oh," Waterhouse says, and rolls his eyes at his own stupidity. "That's right. Sorry. Maybe I should have explained that part first."

"What part?" Comstock asks.

"Dr. Turing, of Cambridge University, has pointed out that bobbadah bobbadah hoe daddy yanga langa furjeezama bing jingle oh yeah," Waterhouse says, or words to that effect. He pauses for breath, and turns fatefully towards the blackboard. "Do you mind if I erase this?" A private lunges forward with an eraser. Comstock sinks into a chair and grips its arms. A stenographer reaches for a benzedrine tablet. An ETC man chomps down on a number two lead pencil like a dog on a drumstick. Strobes flash. Waterhouse grabs a fresh stick of chalk, reaches up, and presses its tip to the immaculate slate. The crisp edge of the stick fractures with a slight pop, and a tiny spray of chalk particles drifts to the floor spreading into a narrow parabolic cloud. Waterhouse bows his head for a minute, like a priest getting ready to stride up the aisle, and then draws a deep breath.

The benzedrine wears off five hours later and Comstock finds himself sprawled across a table in a room filled with haggard, exhausted men. Waterhouse and the privates are pasty with chalk dust, giving them a ghoulish appearance. The stenographers are surrounded with used pads, and frequently stop writing to flap their limp hands in the air like white flags. The wire recorders are spinning uselessly, one reel full and one empty. Only the photographer is still going strong, hitting that strobe every time Waterhouse manages to fill the chalkboard.

Everything smells like underarm sweat. Comstock realizes that Waterhouse is looking at him expectantly. "See?" Waterhouse asks.

Comstock sits up and glances furtively at his own legal pad, where he hoped to draw up an agenda. He sees Waterhouse's four assertions, which he copied down during the first five minutes of the meeting, and then nothing except a tangled field of spiky doodles surrounding the words BURY and DISINTER.

It behooves Comstock to say *something*.

"This thing, the, uh, the burying procedure, that's the, uh—"

"The key feature!" Waterhouse says brightly. "See, these ETC card machines are great for input and output. We've got that covered. The logic elements are straightforward enough. What was needed was a way to give the machine memory, so that it could, to use Turing's terminology, bury data quickly, and just as quickly disinter it. So I made one of those. It is an electrical device, but its underlying principles would be familiar to any organ maker."

"Could I, uh, see it?" Comstock asks.

"Sure! It's down in my lab."

Going to see it is more complicated. First everyone has to use the toilet, then the cameras and strobes have to be moved down to the lab and set up. When they've all filed in, Waterhouse is standing next to a giant rack of pipes with thousands of wires hanging out of it.

"That's it?" Comstock says, when the group is finally assembled.

Pea-sized drops of mercury are scattered around the floor like ball bearings. The flat soles of Comstock's shoes explode them into bursts rolling in all directions.

"That's it."

"What did you call it again?"

"The RAM," Waterhouse says. "Random Access Memory. I was going to put a picture of a ram on it. Y'know, one of those sheeps with the big huge curly horns?"

"Yes."

"But I didn't have time, and I'm not that good at drawing pictures."

Each pipe is four inches in diameter and thirty-two feet long. There must be a hundred of them, at least—Comstock is trying to remember that requisition that he signed, months ago—Waterhouse had ordered enough drain pipe to plumb a whole goddamn military base.

The pipes are laid out horizontally, like a rank of organ pipes that has been knocked flat. Stuck into one end of each pipe is a little paper speaker ripped from an old radio.

"The speaker plays a signal—a note—that resonates in the pipe, and creates a standing wave," Waterhouse says. "That means that in some parts of the pipe, the air pressure is low, and in other parts it is high." He is backing down the length of one of the pipes, making chopping motions with his hand. "These U-tubes are full of mercury." He points to one of several U-shaped glass tubes that are plumbed into the bottom of the long pipe.

"I can see that very plainly, Waterhouse," Comstock says. "Could you keep backing up to the next one?" he requests, peering over the photographers' shoulder through the viewfinder. "You're blocking my view—that's better—farther—farther—" because he can still see Waterhouse's shadow. "That's good. Hit it!"

The photographer pulls the trigger, the strobe flares.

"If the air pressure in the organ pipe is high, it pushes the mercury down a little bit. If it's low, it sucks the mercury up. I put an electrical contact into each U-tube—just a couple of wires separated by an air gap. If those wires are high and dry (like because high air pressure in the organ pipe is shoving the mercury down away from them), no current flows. But if they are immersed in the mercury (because low air pressure in the organ pipe is sucking the mercury up to cover them), then current flows between them, because mercury conducts electricity! So the U-tubes produce a set of binary digits that is like a picture of the standing wave—a graph of the harmonics that make up the musical note that is being played on the speaker. We feed that vector back to the oscillator circuit that is driving the speaker, so that the vector of bits keeps refreshing itself forever, unless the machine decides to write a new pattern of bits into it."

"Oh, so the ETC machinery actually can control this thing?" Comstock asks.

Again with the laugh. "That's the whole point! This is where the logic boards bury and disinter the data!" Waterhouse says. "I'll show you!" And before Comstock can order him not to, Waterhouse has nodded to a corporal standing at the other end of the room, wearing the protective earmuffs that are generally issued to the men who fire the very largest artillery. That corporal nods and hits a switch. Waterhouse slams his hands over his ears and grins, showing a little too much gum for Comstock's taste, and then time stops, or something, as all of those pipes come alive playing variations on the same low C.

It's all Comstock can do not to drop to his knees; he has his hands over his ears, of course, but the sound's not really coming in through his ears, it is entering his torso directly, like X-rays. Hot sonic tongs are rummaging through his viscera, beads of sweat being vibrated loose from his scalp, his nuts are hopping around like Mexican jumping beans. The crescents of mercury in all those U-tubes are shifting up and down, opening and closing the contacts, but systematically: it is not turbulent sloshing around, but a coherent progression of discrete controlled shiftings, informed by some program.

Comstock would draw his sidearm and put a bullet through Waterhouse's head, but he'd have to take one hand off one ear. Finally it stops.

"The machine just calculated the first hundred numbers in the Fibonacci sequence," Waterhouse says.

"As I understand it, this RAM is just the part where you bury and disinter the data," Comstock says, trying to master the higher harmonics in his own voice, trying to sound and act as if he saw this kind of thing daily. "If you had to give a name to the whole apparatus, what would you call it?"

"Hmmm," Waterhouse says. "Well, its basic job is to perform mathematical calculations—like a computer."

Comstock snorts. "A computer is a human being."

"Well . . . this machine uses binary digits to do its computing. I suppose you could call it a digital computer."

Comstock writes it out in block letters on his legal pad: DIGITAL COMPUTER.

"Is this going to go into your report?" Waterhouse asks brightly.

Comstock almost blurts *report? This* is *my report!* Then a foggy memory comes back to him. Something about Azure. Something about gold mines. "Oh, yeah," he murmurs. *Oh, yeah, there's a war on.* He considers it. "Nah. Now that you mention it, this isn't even a footnote." He looks significantly at his pair of hand-picked math whizzes, who are gazing at the RAM like a couple of provincial Judean sheep-shearers getting their first look at the Ark of the Covenant. "We'll probably just keep these photos for the archives. You know how the military is with its archives."

Waterhouse goes into that dreadful laugh again.

"Do you have anything else to report before we adjourn?" Comstock says, desperate to silence him.

"Well, this work has given me some new ideas on information theory which you might find interesting—"

"Write them down. Send them to me."

"There's one other thing. I don't know if it is really germane here, but—"

"What is it, Waterhouse?"

"Uh, well . . . it seems that I'm engaged to be married!"

CARAVAN

RANDY HAS LOST ALL HE OWNED, BUT GAINED AN ENTOURAGE. Amy has decided that she might as well come north with him, as long as she happens to be on this side of the Pacific Ocean. This makes him happy. The Shaftoe boys, Robin and Marcus Aurelius, consider themselves invited along—like much else that in other families would be the subject of extended debate, this goes without saying, apparently.

This makes it imperative that they *drive* the thousand or so miles to Whitman, Washington, because the Shaftoe boys are not really the sort who are in position to simply drop the hot-rod off at the Park 'n' Ride, run into the airport, and demand tickets on the next flight to Spokane. Marcus Aurelius is a college sophomore on an ROTC scholarship and Robin's attending some kind of military prep school. But even if they did have that kind of money rattling around in their pockets, actually spending it would offend their native frugality. Or so Randy assumes, for the first couple of days. It's the obvious assumption to make, given that the Cash Flow Issue seems always to be on their mind. For example the boys made Herculean efforts to consume every spoonful of the gut-busting vat of oatmeal cooked by Amy the morning after the quake, and finding it beyond their endurance they carefully decanted the remainder into a Ziploc bag while fretting at length about the high cost of Ziploc bags and didn't Randy have any old glass jelly jars or something, somewhere in the basement, that might be unbroken and usable for this purpose.

Randy has had plenty of time to disabuse himself of this fallacy (namely that their airplane-avoidance is dictated by financial constraints) and to draw the real reason out of them after they have dropped Amy's U-Haul off near SFO and begun to caravan northwards in the Acura and the jacked-up, thundering Impala. People are rotated from car to car whenever they stop, according to some system that no one is divulging to Randy, but that always situates him alone in a car with either Robin or Marcus Aurelius. Both of them are too dignified to spill their guts on light pretexts, and too polite to assume that Randy gives a shit about anything they think, and perhaps too basically suspicious of Randy to share a whole lot with him. Some kind of bonding is required first. The ice doesn't start to break up until Day 2 of the drive, after they have all slept in an Interstate 5 rest area near Redding in the reclined seats of the vehicles (each of the Shaftoe boys solemnly and separately informs him that the chain of lodgings known as Motel 6 is one giant con game, that if those rooms ever did cost six dollars a night, which is doubtful, they certainly don't now, and many are the innocent young travelers who have been drawn in by the siren calls of those fraudulent signs rising above interstate cloverleaves; they try to sound impartial and wise about it, but the way their faces flush and their eyes glance aside and their voices rise makes Randy suspect he is actually listening to some thinly veiled personal and recent history). Again without anyone saying anything, it is taken to be obvious that Amy, as the female, will require her own car to sleep in, which puts Randy in the hot-rod with Robin and Marcus Aurelius. As the guest, Randy gets the reclining passenger seat, the best bed in the house, and M.A. curls up on the back seat while Robin, the youngest, sleeps behind the steering wheel. For about the first thirty seconds after the dome light has gone off and the Shaftoes have finished saying their prayers out loud, Randy lies there feeling the Impala rock on its suspension from the wake-blasts of passing long-haul semis and feels considerably more alienated than he did while trying to sleep in the jeepney in the jungle town in northern Luzon. Then he opens his eyes and it's morning, and Robin's out there doing one-handed pushups in the dust.

"When we get there," Robin pants, after he's finished, "do you s'pose you could show me that video-on-the-Internet thing you were telling me about?" He asks it with all due boyishness. Then suddenly he looks abashed and adds, "Unless it's like real expensive or something."

"It's free. I'll show it to you," Randy says. "Let's get some breakfast."

It goes without saying that McDonald's and their ilk charge scandalously more for, e.g., a disk of hash browns than one would pay for the equivalent mass of potatoes in raw form at (if you think money grows on trees) Safeway or (if you have any kind of decent regard for the value of a buck) farmer's markets situated at lonely interchanges in the boondocks. So for breakfast they must drive to a small town (grocery stores in big places like Redding being a ripoff) and find an actual grocery store (convenience stores being etc., etc., etc.) and purchase breakfast in the most elemental form conceivable (deeply discounted well-past-their prime bananas that are not even in a bunch but swept up from the floor, or something, and gathered together in a gaily printed paper sack, and generic Cheerio-knockoffs in a tubular bag, and a box of generic powdered milk) and eat it from tin military-surplus messkits that the Shaftoes produce with admirable coolness from the hot rod's trunk, a ferrous, oily chasm all a-bang with tire chains, battered ammo boxes, and, unless Randy's eyes are playing tricks on him, a pair of samurai swords.

Anyway, this is all done pretty nonchalantly, and not like they are trying to test Randy's mettle or anything, and so he doesn't imagine that it qualifies as a true bonding experience. If, hypothetically, the Impala throws a rod in the desert and they have to fix it with parts stolen from a nearby junkyard guarded by rabid dogs and shotgun-packing gypsies, that would be a bonding experience. But Randy's wrong. On Day 2 the Shaftoes (the male ones anyway) open up to him a bit.

It seems (and this is abstracted from many hours of conversation) that when you are an able-bodied young male Shaftoe and you are a stranger in a strange land with a car that you have, with plenty of advice and elbow grease from your extended family, fixed up pretty nicely, the idea of *parking it* in favor of some other mode of conveyance is, in addition to obvious financial folly, some kind of moral failure, pure and simple. That's why they are driving to Whitman, Washington. But why (one of them finally summons the boldness to inquire) why are they taking two cars? There is plenty of room in the Impala for four. Randy has gotten the sense all along that the Shaftoes are dismayed by Randy's insistence on taking the redundant and repulsively scarred Acura, and that only their formidable politeness has prevented them from pointing out the sheer madness of it. "I do not imagine that we will stay together beyond Whitman," Randy says (after being around these guys for a couple of days he has begun to fall out of the habit of using contractions—those tawdry shortcuts of the verbally lazy and pathologically rushed). "If we have two cars, we can split up at that point."

"The drive is not that far, Randall," says Robin, slapping the Impala's gas pedal against the floor to rip the transmission into passing gear, and careening around a gasoline tanker. From the initial "Sir" and "Mr. Waterhouse," Randy has been able to talk them down into addressing him by his first name, but they have agreed to it only on the condition (apparently) that they use the full "Randall" instead of "Randy." Early attempts to use "Randall Lawrence" as a compromise were vigorously denounced by Randy, and so "Randall" it is for now. "M.A. and I would be happy to drop you back off at the San Francisco Airport—or, uh, wherever you elected to park your Acura."

"Where else would I park it?" Randy says, not getting this last bit.

"Well, I mean that you could probably find a place where you could park it free of charge for a few days, if you did some looking around. Assuming you wanted to keep it." He adds encouragingly, "That Acura probably would have some decent resale value even considering all the body work it needs."

Only at this point does Randy figure out that the Shaftoes believe him to be utterly destitute, helpless, and adrift in the wide world. A total charity case. He recalls, now, seeing them discard a whole sack of

McDonald's wrappers when they arrived at his house. This whole austerity binge has been concocted to avoid putting financial pressure on
Randy.

Robin and M.A. have been observing him carefully, talking about
him, thinking about him. They happen to have made some faulty assumptions, and come to some wrong conclusions, but all the same, they
have shown more sophistication than Randy was giving them credit for.
This causes Randy to go back and review the conversations he has had
with them the last couple of days, just to get some idea of what *other*
interesting and complicated things might have been going on in their
heads. M.A. is a pretty straightforward by-the-book type, the kind who'll
get good grades and fit well into any kind of hierarchical organization.
Robin, on the other hand, is more of a wild card. He has the makings
of either a total loser or a successful entrepreneur, or maybe one of those
guys who will oscillate between those two poles. Randy realizes now,
in retrospect, that he has spilled a hell of a lot of information to Robin,
in just a couple of days, about the Internet and electronic money and
digital currency and the new global economy. Randy's mental state is
such that he is prone to babbling aimlessly for hours at a time. Robin
has hoovered it all up.

To Randy it's just been aimless ventilating. He hasn't even considered,
until now, what effect it has been exerting on the trajectory of Robin
Shaftoe's life. Randall Lawrence Waterhouse hates *Star Trek* and avoids
people who don't hate it, but even so he has seen just about every
episode of the damn thing, and he feels, at this moment, like the Federa-
tion scientist who beams down to a primitive planet and thoughtlessly
teaches an opportunistic pre-Enlightenment yahoo how to construct a
phaser cannon from commonly available materials.

Randy still has *some* money. He cannot begin to guess how he can
convey this fact to these guys without committing some grievous protocol error, so the next time they stop for gas, he asks Amy to convey it
to them. He thinks (based on his hazy understanding of the rotation
system) that it's his turn to be alone in a car with Amy, but if Amy is
going to convey this data about the money to one of the boys, she'll
need to spend the next leg with him, because it must be conveyed
indirectly, which will take a while, and because of that indirectness, time
will then need to be allotted for it to sink in. But three hours later, then,
at the gas stop after that, it naturally follows that M.A. and Robin must
be placed together in the same car, so that Robin (who now knows and
understands, and who gets out of the Impala with a big grin on his face
and punches Randy affably on the shoulder) can pass the message on to
M.A., whose recent conversational gambits vis-à-vis Randy made no

sense at all until Randy figured out that they thought of him as a beggar and that M.A. was trying in a really oblique way to find out if Randy needed to share any of M.A.'s personal toiletry items. At any rate, Randy and Amy get into the Acura and they head north into Oregon, trying to keep up with the hot rod.

"Well, it's nice to have a chance to spend some time with you," Randy says. His back is still a bit sore from where Amy struck him whilst asserting, the other morning, that expressing one's feelings was "the name of the game." So he figures he will express those aspects of his feelings least likely to get him in serious trouble.

"Ah figgered you 'n' ah'ud have plenny a tahm to chew the rag," Amy says, having reverted utterly to the tongue of her ancestors in the last couple of days. "But it has been ages and ages since I saw those two boys, and you've never seen 'em at all."

"Ages and ages? Really?"

"Yeah."

"How long?"

"Well, last time I saw Robin he was just starting kindergarten. And I saw M.A. more recently—he was probably eight or ten."

"And you are related to them how, one more time?"

"I think Robin is my second cousin. And I could explain M.A.'s relationship to me, but you'd start shifting around and heaving great big sighs before I got more'n halfway through it."

"So, to these guys, you are a shirttail relative they glimpsed once or twice when they were tiny little boys."

Amy shrugs. "Yeah."

"So, like what possessed them to come out here?"

Amy looks blank.

"I mean," Randy says, "from the general attitude they copped, when they fishtailed to a stop in the middle of my front yard and leapt out of their red-hot, bug-encrusted vehicle, fresh from Tennessee, obviously the number one mission objective was to ensure that the flower of Shaftoe womanhood was being treated with all of the respect, decency, worship-fulness, et cetera, properly owed it."

"Oh. That's not really the vibe that I got."

"Oh, it *wasn't*? Really?"

"No. Randy, my family sticks together. Just 'cause we haven't seen each other for a while doesn't mean our obligations have lapsed."

"Well, you are making an implied comparison to my family here which I'm not that crazy about and maybe we should talk about later. But as far as those family obligations go, I do *certainly* think that one of those obligations is to preserve your notional virginity."

"Who says it's notional?"

"It's *got* to be notional to *them* because they haven't seen you for most of your life. That's all I mean."

"I think you are blowing the perceived sexual aspect of this thing way out of proportion," Amy says. "Which is perfectly normal, for a guy, and I don't think less of you for it."

"Amy, Amy. Have you done the math on this thing?"

"Math?"

"Counting the trip through Manila traffic to NAIA, the check-in procedure, and formalities at SFO, my entire journey from Manila to San Francisco took me something like eighteen hours. Twenty for you. Another four hours to get down to my house. Then eight hours after we got to my house, in the middle of the night, Robin and Marcus Aurelius showed up. Now, if we assume that the Shaftoe family grapevine functions at the speed of light, it means that these guys, shooting hoops in front of their trailer in Tennessee, received a news flash that a female Shaftoe was in some kind of guy-related personal distress at about the time you jumped off of *Glory IV* and hopped in a taxi in Manila."

"I sent e-mail from *Glory*," Amy says.

"To whom?"

"The Shaftoe mailing list."

"God!" Randy says, slapping himself in the face. "What did this e-mail say?"

"Can't remember," Amy says. "That I was headed for California. I might have made some kind of backhanded remark about a young man I wanted to talk to. I was kinda upset at the time and I can't remember exactly what I have said."

"I think you said something like 'I am going to California where Randall Lawrence Waterhouse, who has AIDS, is going to forcibly sodomize me upon arrival.'"

"No, it was nothing of the kind."

"Well, I think that someone read it between the lines. So, anyway, Ma or Auntie Em or someone emerges from the side door, shaking flour out of her gingham apron—I'm imagining this."

"I can tell."

"And she says, 'Boys, your umpteenth cousin thrice removed America Shaftoe has sent us e-mail from Uncle Doug's boat in the South China Sea stating that she is having some kind of dispute with a young man and it's not out of the question that she might need someone around to lend her a hand. In California. Would you swing by and look in on her?' And they put away their basketball and say, 'Yes ma'am, what city and address?' and she says, 'Never you mind, just get on Interstate 40 and drive west not failing to maintain an average speed of between one hundred and a hundred and twenty percent of the legal speed limit and call me collect from a Texaco somewhere and I will supply you with specific target coordinates later,' and they say, 'Yes ma'am' and thirty seconds later they are laying a patch in the driveway as they pull five gees backing out of the garage and thirty hours subsequently they are in my front yard, shining their twenty-five-D-cell flashlights into my eyes and asking me a lot of pointed questions. Do you have any idea how far the drive is?"

"I have no idea."

"Well, according to M.A.'s Rand McNally Road Atlas, it is an even twenty-one hundred miles."

"So?"

"So that means that they maintained an average speed of seventy miles an hour for a day and a half."

"A day and a quarter," Amy says.

"Do you have any idea how difficult that is to do?"

"Randy, you push on the gas pedal and keep it between the lines. How hard is that?"

"I'm not saying it's an intellectual challenge. I'm saying that this will-ingness to, e.g., urinate into empty McDonald's cups rather than stop the car, suggests a kind of urgency. Passion, even. And being a guy, and having had the experience of being a guy of the age of M.A. and Robin, I can tell you that one of the few things that gets your blood boiling to that extent is this notion of some female you love being done wrong by a strange male."

"Well, what if they did?" Amy says. "Now they think you're okay."

"They do? Really?"

"Yeah. The financial disaster aspect makes you more human. More approachable. And it excuses a lot."

"Do I need an excuse for something?"

"Not in my book."

"But to the extent they thought I was a rapist, it kind of palliates my image problems."

A brief lull in the conversation ensues. Then Amy pipes up.

"So tell me about your family, Randy."

"In the next couple of days, you're going to learn a great deal more than I would like you to about my family. And so am I. So let's talk about something else."

"Okay. Let's talk about business."

"Okay. You go first."

"We got a German television producer coming out next week to have a look at the U-boat. They might do a documentary about it. We have already hosted several German print journalists."

"You have?"

"It has caused a sensation in Germany."

"Why?"

"Because no one can figure out how it got there. Now, your turn."

"We are going to launch our own currency." By saying this, Randy is divulging proprietary information to someone not authorized to hear it. But he does it anyway, because opening himself up to Amy in this way, making himself vulnerable to her, gives him a hard-on.

"How do you go about that? Don't you have to be a government?"

"No. You have to be a bank. Why do you think they're called bank-notes?" Randy is fully aware of the insanity of divulging secret business information to a woman solely for purposes of sexual self-titillation but it is in the nature of things, right now, that he doesn't especially care.

"Okay but still, usually it's done by *government* banks, right?"

"Only because people tend to *respect* the government banks. But government banks in Southeast Asia have a huge image problem right now. That image problem translates directly into crashing exchange rates."

"So, how do you do it?"

"Get a big pile of gold. Issue certificates saying 'this certificate can be redeemed for such-and-such an amount of gold.' That's all there is to it."

"What's wrong with dollars and yen and stuff?"

"The certificates—the banknotes—are printed on paper. We're going to issue electronic banknotes."

"No paper at all?"

"No paper at all."

"So you can only spend it on the Net."

"Correct."

"What if you want to buy a sack of bananas?"

"Find a banana merchant on the Net."

"Seems like paper money'd be just as good."

"Paper money is traceable and perishable and has other drawbacks. Electronic banknotes are fast and anonymous."

"What's an electronic banknote look like, Randy?"

"Like any other digital thing: a bunch of bits."

"Doesn't that make it kind of easy to counterfeit?"

"Not if you have good crypto," Randy says. "Which we do."

"How did you get it?"

"By hanging out with maniacs."

"What kind of maniacs?"

"Maniacs who think that having good crypto is of near-apocalyptic importance."

"How'd they get around to thinking any such thing?"

"By reading about people like Yamamoto who died because they had bad crypto, and then projecting that kind of thing into the future."

"Do you agree with them?" Amy asks. It might be one of those pivotal-moment-in-the-relationship questions.

"At two in the morning, when I'm lying awake in bed, I do," Randy says. "In the light of day, it all seems like paranoia." He glances over at Amy, who's looking at him appraisingly, because he hasn't actually answered the question yet. He's got to pick one thing or the other. "Better safe than sorry, I guess. Having good crypto can't hurt, and it might help."

"And it might make you a lot of money along the way," Amy reminds him.

Randy laughs. "At this point, it's not even about trying to make money," he says. "I just don't want to be totally humiliated."

Amy smiles cryptically.

"What?" Randy demands.

"You sounded just like a Shaftoe when you said that," Amy says.

Randy drives the car in silence for about half an hour after that. He was right, he suspects: it *was* a pivotal moment in the relationship. All he can do now is totally screw it up. So he shuts up and drives.

THE GENERAL

 FOR TWO MONTHS HE SLEEPS ON A BEACH ON NEW CALEDONIA, stretched out under a mosquito net, dreaming of worse places, polishing his line.

In Stockholm, someone from the British Embassy got him to a certain cafe. A gentleman he met in the cafe got him to a car. The car got him to a lake where a floatplane just happened to be sitting with its motors running and its lights off. The Special Air Service got him to London. Naval Intelligence got him back to D.C., drained his brain, and turned him over to the Marines with a big stamp on his papers saying that he must never again be sent into combat; he Knew Too Much to be taken prisoner. The Marines found that he Knew Too Little to serve as a Rear-Echelon Motherfucker, and gave him a choice: a one-way ticket home, or higher education. He opted for the ticket home, then talked a green officer into believing that his family had moved, and home was now San Francisco.

You could practically cross San Francisco Bay by jumping from one Navy ship to the next. The waterfront was lined with the Navy's piers, depots, hospitals, and prisons. All of them were guarded by Shaftoe's military brothers. Shaftoe's tattoos were obscured by civilian clothes and his haircut grown out. But he only had to look a Marine in the eye from a stone's throw, and that Marine would recognize him for a brother in need and open any gate for him, break any regulation, probably even lay down his life. Shaftoe stowed away on a ship bound for Hawaii so fast he didn't even have time to get drunk. From Pearl, it took him four days to get on a ship to Kwajalein. There, he was a legendary hero. His money was no good on Kwaj; he smoked, drank and ate for a week without being allowed to spend a dime, and finally his brothers got him on a plane that took him a couple of thousand miles due south to Noumea, in New Caledonia.

They did so with great reluctance. They would willingly have hit a beach with him, but this was different: they were sending him perilously close to SOWESPAC, the Southwest Pacific Theater, the domain of The General. Even now, a couple of years after The General had sent them into action, poorly armed and poorly supported, on Guadalcanal, Marines still spent approximately fifty percent of their waking hours talking about what a bad guy he was. He secretly owned half of Intramuros. He had become a billionaire from Spanish gold that his father had dug up when he'd been governor of the Philippines. Quezon had secretly named him postwar dictator of the archipelago. The General was running for president, and in order to win he was going to start throwing battles just to make F.D.R. look bad, and blaming it all on the Marines. And if that didn't work he'd come back to the States and stage a coup d'etat. Which would be beaten back, against enormous odds, by the United States Marine Corps. Semper Fi!

Anyway, his brothers got him to New Caledonia. Noumea's a neat French city of wide streets and tin-roofed buildings, fronting on a big harbor lined with mountainous dumps of nickel and chromium ore from gigantic mines up-island. The place is about one-third Free French (there's pictures of de Gaulle all over the place), one-third American servicemen, and one-third cannibals. Word on the street is that the cannibals have not eaten any white people in twenty-seven years, so Bobby Shaftoe, sleeping out on that beach, feels almost as safe as he did in Sweden.

But when he reached Noumea he slammed into a barrier more impervious than any brick wall: the imaginary line between the Pacific theater

(Nimitz's turf) and SOWESPAC. Brisbane, The General's headquarters, is just a short (by Pacific standards) hop almost due west. If he can just get there and deliver his line, everything's going to be fine.

During his first couple of weeks on the beach, he's stupidly optimistic. Then he's depressed for about a month, thinking he'll never get off this place. Finally he starts to come around, starts to display adaptability again. He's had no luck getting on board a ship. But the amont of air traffic is incredible. Seems that The General likes airplanes. Shaftoe starts tailing flyboys. The MPs won't give him the time of day, he can't get into an Army NCOs' Club to save his life.

But an NCOs' Club offers strictly limited entertainments. Customers in search of more profound satisfactions must leave the perimeter defined by hardassed MPs and enter the civilian economy. And when horny, well-paid American flyboys are dropped into a culture defined half by cannibals and half by Frenchmen, you get a hell of a civilian economy. Shaftoe finds a vantage point outside an airbase gate, plants himself there, his pockets loaded with cigarette packs (the Marines on Kwaj left him with a lifetime supply) and waits. Flyboys come out in twos and threes. Shaftoe picks out the sergeants, follows them to bars and whorehouses, sits down in their line of sight, begins to chain-smoke. Before long they've come over and started to bum cigarettes off him. This leads to conversations.

Once he gets this routine figured out, he learns a lot about the Fifth Air Force in a big hurry, makes a lot of friends. In a few weeks, he strikes the jackpot. He goes over the airfield fence at 1:00 A.M. of a moonless night, belly-crawls for about a mile along the shoulder of a runway, and just barely makes a rendezvous with the crew of the Tipsy Tootsie, a B-24 Liberator bound for Brisbane. In fairly short order, he finds himself stuffed into the glass sphere at the tail of the plane: the rear ball turret. Its purpose, of course, is to shoot down Zeroes, which tend to attack from behind. But Tipsy Tootsie's crew seems to think that they are about as likely to find Zeroes around here as they would be over central Missouri.

They warned him to wear something warm, but he didn't have anything of that nature. Tipsy Tootsie has barely left the runway when he begins to understand his mistake: the temperature drops like a five-hundred-pound bomb. It is physically impossible for him to get out of the turret. Even if he could, it would just lead to his getting arrested; he has been smuggled on board without the knowledge of the officers who are actually flying the plane. Calmly he decides to add prolonged hypothermia to his already extensive knowledge of suffering. After a couple of hours, he either loses consciousness or falls asleep, and this helps.

He is awakened by pink light that comes from every direction at once. The plane has lost altitude, the temperature has risen, his body has thawed out enough to bring him awareness. After a few minutes he's able to move his arms. He reaches into the pink glow and rubs condensation off the inside of the ball turret. He takes out a hanky, wipes the whole thing clean, and now he's looking straight down the throat of a Pacific dawn.

The sky is streaked and mottled by black clouds, like jets of squid ink in a Caribbean cove. For a while, it's as if he is under water with Bischoff.

Puckered scars mar the Pacific in loops and lines, and he is reminded of his own naked flesh. But the hard jagged pieces work their way out of the scar tissue like old shrapnel: coral reefs emerging from a shallowing sea. Warmer and warmer. He begins to shiver again.

Someone has dumped brown dust into the Pacific, made a great pile of it. On the edge of the pile is a city. The city swings around them, comes closer. Warmer and warmer. It's Brisbane. A runway streaks up and he thinks it's going to take his ass off, like the world's biggest belt sander. The plane stops. He smells gasoline.

The pilot discovers him, loses his temper, and makes ready to call the MPs. "I'm here to work for The General," Shaftoe mumbles through blue lips. It just makes the pilot want to slug him. But after Shaftoe has uttered these words, everything is different, the angry officers stand a pace or two farther away from him, tone down their language, knock off the threats. Shaftoe knows, from this, that The General does things differently.

He spends a day recovering in a flophouse, then rises, shaves, drinks a cup of coffee, and strikes out in search of brass.

To his extreme chagrin, he learns that The General has relocated his headquarters to Hollandia, in New Guinea. But his wife and son, and a bunch of his staff, are still staying at Lennon's Hotel. Shaftoe goes there and analyzes the traffic pattern: to pull into the hotel's horseshoe drive, the cars have to come around a particular corner, just up the street. Shaftoe finds a good loitering-place near that corner, and waits. Looking through the windows of the approaching cars, he can see the epaulets, count the stars and eagles.

Seeing two stars, he decides to make his move. Jogging down the block, he reaches the awning of the hotel just as this general's door is being hauled open by his driver.

" 'Scuse me, General, Bobby Shaftoe reporting for duty, sir!" he blurts, snapping out the perfectest salute in military history.

"And who the hell might you be, Bobby Shaftoe?" says this general, hardly batting an eye. He talks like Bischoff! This guy actually has a German accent!

"I've killed more Nips than seismic activity. I'm trained to jump out of airplanes. I speak a little Nip. I can survive in the jungle. I know Manila like the back of my hand. My wife and child are there. And I'm kinda at loose ends. Sir!"

In London, in D.C., he'd never have gotten this close, and if he had he'd have been shot or arrested.

But this is SOWESPAC, and so the next morning at dawn he's on a B-17 bound for Hollandia, wearing Army green, no rank.

New Guinea is a nasty-looking piece of work: a gangrenous dragon with a wicked, rocky spine, covered with ice. Just looking at it makes Shaftoe shiver from a queasy combination of hypothermia and incipient malaria. The whole thing belongs to The General now. Shaftoe can plainly see that such a country could only be conquered by a man who was completely fucking out of his mind. A month in Stalingrad would be preferable to twenty-four hours down there.

Hollandia is on the north shore of this beast, facing, naturally, towards the Philippines. It is well known throughout Marinedom that The General has caused a palace to be built for himself there. Some credulous fools actually believe the rumor that it is merely a complete 200%-scale replica of the Taj Mahal, built by enslaved Marines, but savvy jarheads know that it is actually a much vaster compound built out of construction materials stolen from Navy hospital ships, dotted with pleasure domes and fuck houses for his string of Asiatic concubines, with a soaring cupola so high that The General can go up there and see what the Nips are doing to his extensive real estate holdings in Manila, 1500 miles to the northwest.

Bobby Shaftoe sees no such thing out the windows of the B-17. He glimpses one large and nice-looking house up on a mountain above the sea. He supposes that it is a mere sentry post, marking the benighted perimeter of The General's domain. But almost immediately the B-17 bounces down on a runway. The cabin is invaded by an equatorial miasma. It's like breathing Cream O' Wheat direct from a blurping vat. Shaftoe feels his bowels loosening up already. Of course there are many Marines who feel that Army uniform trousers look best when feces-stained. Shaftoe must put such thoughts out of his head.

All the passengers (mostly colonels and better) move as to avoid working up a sweat, even though they are already drenched. Shaftoe wants to kick their fat, waffled butts downstairs—he's in a hurry to get to Manila.

Pretty soon he is hitching a ride on the rear bumper of a jeep full of brass. The airfield is still ringed with ack-ack guns, and shows signs of having been bombed and strafed not too long ago. Some of these signs are obvious physical evidence like shell holes, but Shaftoe gets most of his information from watching the men: their posture, their facial expressions as they stare into the sky, tell him exactly what the threat level is.

No wonder, he thinks, remembering the sight of that big white house up on the mountain. You can probably see that thing by moonlight, for crissakes! It must be visible from Tokyo! It's just begging to be strafed.

Then, as the jeep begins to trundle up the mountain in first gear, he figures it out: that thing's just a decoy. The General's real command post must be a network of deep tunnels hidden beneath the jungle floor, and *that* is where you would have to look for your Asiatic concubines, etc.

The trip up the mountain takes an eon. Shaftoe jumps off and soon outpaces the whining jeep, and the one in front of it. Then he's on his own, walking through the jungle. He'll just follow the tracks until they lead him straight to the cleverly camouflaged mineshaft that leads down to The General's HQ.

The walk gives him plenty of time to have a couple of smokes and savor the unrelieved nightmarishness of the New Guinea jungle, compared to which Guadalcanal, which he thought was the worst place on earth, seems like a dewy meadow strewn with bunnies and butterflies. Nothing is more satisfying than to consider that the Nips and the United States Army spent a couple of years beating the crap out of each other here. Pity the Aussies had to get mixed up in it, though.

The tracks take him straight to that big white clay pigeon of a house up on the mountainside. They've gone way overboard in trying to make the house look like someone's actually living there. Shaftoe can see furniture and everything. The walls are crisscrossed by bullet trails. They have even set up a mannequin on the balcony, in a *pink silk dressing gown,* corncob pipe, and aviator sunglasses, scanning the bay through binoculars! As reluctant as he is to approve of anything done by the Army, Shaftoe cannot keep himself from laughing out loud at this witticism. Military humor at its finest. He can't believe they got away with it. A couple of press photographers are standing down below, taking pictures of the scene.

Standing in the middle of the house's mud parking lot, he plants his feet wide and thrusts his middle finger up at that mannequin. Hey, asshole, this one's from the Marines on Kwajalein! Damn, this feels good.

The mannequin swivels and aims its binoculars directly at Bobby Shaftoe, who freezes solid in his bird-flipping posture as if caught in the gaze of a basilisk. Down below, air-raid sirens begin to weep and wail.

The binoculars come away from the sunglasses. A puff of smoke blurts out of the pipe. The General snaps out a sarcastic salute. Shaftoe remembers to put his finger away, then stands there, rooted like a dead mahogany.

The General reaches up and removes the pipe from his mouth so he can say, "Magandang gabi."

"You mean, *'magandang umaga,'* " Shaftoe says. "*Gabi* means *night* and *umaga* means *morning.*"

The drone of airplane engines is now getting quite noticeable. The press photographers decide to pack it in, and disappear into the house.

"When you're headed north from Manila towards Lingayen and you get to the fork in the road at Tarlac and you take the right fork, there, and head across the cane breaks towards Urdaneta, what's the first village you come to?"

"It's a trick question," Shaftoe says. "North of Tarlac there are no cane breaks, just rice paddies."

"Hmm. Very good," The General says grumpily. Down below, the antiaircraft guns open up with a fantastic clattering; from this distance it sounds as if the north coast of New Guinea is being jackhammered into the sea. The General ignores it. If he were only *pretending* to ignore it, he would at least *look* at the incoming the Zeroes, so that he could *stop* pretending to ignore them when it got too dangerous. But he doesn't even do so much as look. Shaftoe forces himself not to look either. The General asks him a big long question in Spanish. He has a beautiful voice. He sounds like he is standing in an anechoic sound booth in New York City or Hollywood, narrating a newsreel about how great he is.

"If you're trying to find out if I *hablo Español,* the answer is, *un poquito,*" Shaftoe says.

The General cups a hand to his ear irritably. He can't hear anything except for the pair of Zeroes converging on him and Shaftoe at three hundred odd miles per hour, liquefying tons of biomass with dense streams of 12.7-millimeter slugs. He keeps a sharp eye on Shaftoe as a trail of bullets thuds across the parking lot, spraying Shaftoe's trouser legs with mud. The same line of bullets makes a sudden upwards right-angle turn when it reaches the wall of the General's house, climbs straight up the wall, tears out a chunk of the balcony's railing about a foot away from where the General's hand is resting, beats up a bunch of furniture back inside the house, and then clears the roof of the house and vanishes.

Now that the planes have passed overhead, Shaftoe can look at them without having to worry that he is giving The General the idea that he is some kind of lily-livered pansy. The meatballs on their wings broaden and glower as they bank sharply, sharper than any American plane, and come round for a second try.

"I said—" The General begins. But then the atmosphere's riven by a series of bizarre whizzing noises. One of the house's windows is suddenly punched out of its frame. Shaftoe hears a thud from inside and some crockery breaking. For the first time, The General shows some awareness that a military action is taking place. "Warm up my jeep, Shaftoe," he says, "I have a bone to pick with my triple-A boys." Then he turns around and Shaftoe gets a look at the back of his pink silk dressing gown. It is embroidered, in black thread, with a giant lizard, rampant.

The General suddenly turns around. "Is that you screaming down there, Shaftoe?"

"Sir, no sir!"

"I distinctly heard you scream." MacArthur turns his back on Shaftoe again, giving him another look at the lizard (which on second thought might be some sort of Chinese dragon design) and goes inside the house, mumbling irritably to himself.

Shaftoe gets into the vehicle indicated and starts the engine.

The General emerges from the house and begins to plod across the lot cradling an unexploded antiaircraft shell in his arms. The wind makes his pink silk dressing gown billow all around him.

The Zeroes come back and strafe the parking lot again, cutting a truck nearly in half. Shaftoe feels as if his intestines have dissolved and are about to spurt from his body. He closes his eyes, puckers his anal sphincter, and clenches his teeth. The General takes a seat next to him. "Down the hill," he orders. "Drive towards the sound of the guns."

They have barely gotten onto the road when their progress is blocked by the two jeeps that had been carrying all the brass up from the airfield. They now sit empty on the road, their doors hanging open, engines still running. The General reaches across in front of Shaftoe and honks the horn.

Colonels and brigadier generals begin to emerge from the shadows of the jungle, like some especially bizarre native tribe, clutching their attache cases talismanically. They salute The General, who ignores them testily. "Move my vehicles!" he intones, jabbing at them with the stem of his pipe. "This is the *road*. The *parking lot* is *that* way."

The Zeroes come back for a third pass. Shaftoe now realizes (as perhaps The General has) that these pilots are not the best; it is late in the war and all the good pilots are dead. Consequently they do not line their trajectories up properly with the road; the strafing trails cut across it diagonally. Still, a bullet bores through the engine block of one of the jeeps. Hot oil and steam spray out of it.

"Come on, push it out of the way!" The General says. Shaftoe instinctively begins to climb out of the jeep, but The General yanks him back with a word: "Shaftoe! I need you to drive this vehicle."

Wielding his pipestem like a conductor's baton, The General gets his staff back out on the road and they begin shoving the ruined jeep into the jungle. Shaftoe makes the mistake of inhaling through his nose and gets a strong diarrheal whiff—at least one of these officers has shit his pants. Shaftoe's still trying hard not to do the same, and probably would have if he'd pushed the jeep. The Zeroes are trying to line up for another strafing run, but a few American fighter planes have now appeared on the scene, which complicates matters.

Shaftoe maneuvers them through a gap between the remaining jeep and a huge tree, then guns it down the road. The General hums to himself for a while, then says, "What's your wife's name?"

"Gory."

"What!?"

"I mean, Glory."

"Ah. Good. Good Filipina name. Filipinas are the most beautiful women in the world, don't you think?"

Experienced world traveler Bobby Shaftoe screws up his face and begins to review his experiences in a systematic way. Then he realizes that The General probably does not actually want his considered opinion.

Of course, The General's wife is American, so this could be tricky. "I guess the woman you love is always the most beautiful," Shaftoe finally says.

The General looks mildly pissed off. "Of course, but . . ."

"But if you don't really give a shit about them, the Filipinas are the most beautiful, sir!" Shaftoe says.

The General nods. "Now, your boy. What's his name, then?"

Shaftoe swallows hard and thinks fast. He doesn't even know if he *has* a kid—he fabricated that to make his line sound better—and even if he does, the chances are only fifty-fifty that it's a boy. But if he does have a boy, he knows already what the name will be. "His name—well, sir, his name—and I hope you don't mind this—but his name is Douglas."

The General grins delightedly and cackles, slapping the antiaircraft shell in his lap for emphasis. Shaftoe flinches.

When they arrive at the airfield, a full-fledged dogfight is in progress overhead. The place is deserted because everyone except them is hiding behind sandbags. The General has Shaftoe drive up and down the length of the field, stopping at each gun emplacement so that he can peer over the barrier.

"There's the fellow!" The General finally says, pointing his swagger stick at a gun on the opposite side of the runway. "I just saw him poking his head out, yammering on the telephone."

Shaftoe guns it across the runway. A flaming Zero, traveling at about half the speed of sound, impacts the runway a few hundred feet away and disintegrates into a howling cloud of burning spare parts that comes skittering and rolling and bounding across the runway in their general direction. Shaftoe falters. The General yells at him. Reckoning that he can't avoid what he can't see, Shaftoe turns into the storm. Having seen this kind of thing happen before, he knows that the first thing to come their way will be the engine block, a red-hot tombstone of fine Mitsubishi iron. And indeed there it is, one of its exhaust manifolds still dangling from it like a broken wing, spinning end-over-end and spading huge divots out of the runway with each bounce. Shaftoe swings wide around it. He identifies the fuselage and sees that it has plowed to a stop already. He looks for the wings; they broke up into a few large pieces that are slowing down rapidly, but the tires broke loose from the landing gear and are bounding along towards them, burning wheels of red fire. Shaftoe maneuvers the jeep between them, guns it across a small patch of flaming oil, then makes another hard turn and continues towards their objective.

The explosion of the Zero sent everyone back down behind their sandbags. The General has to climb out of the jeep and peer over the top of the barrier. He holds the antiaircraft shell up above his head. "Say, Captain," he says in his perfect radio-announcer voice, "this arrived on my end table with no return address, but I believe it came from your unit." The captain's helmeted head pops into view over the top of the sandbags as he jumps to attention. He is gaping at the shell. "Would you please look after it, and make sure that it has been properly defused?" The General tosses the shell at him sideways, like a watermelon, and the captain barely has the presence of mind to catch it. "Carry on," The General says, "let's see if we can actually shoot down some Nips next time." He waves disparagingly at the burning wreckage of the Zero and climbs into the jeep with Shaftoe. "All right, back up the hill, Shaftoe!"

"Yes, sir!"

"Now, I know that you hate me because you are a Marine."

Officers like it when you pretend to be straight with them. "Yes, sir, I do hate you, sir, but I do not feel that this need be an impediment to our killing some Nips together, sir!"

"We agree. But in the mission I have in mind for you, Shaftoe, killing Nips will not be the primary objective."

Shaftoe's a bit off balance now. "Sir, with all due respect, I believe that killing Nips is my strong point."

"I don't doubt it. And that is a fine skill for a Marine. Because in this war, a Marine is a first-rate fighting man under the command of admirals who don't know the first thing about ground warfare, and who think that the way to win an island is to hurl their men directly into the teeth of the Nips' prepared defenses."

The General pauses here, as if giving Shaftoe an opportunity to respond. But Shaftoe says nothing. He is remembering the stories that his brothers told him on Kwajalein, about all the battles they had fought on small Pacific islands, precisely as The General describes.

"Consequently, a Marine must be very good at killing Nips, as I have no doubt you are. But now, Shaftoe, you are in the Army, and in the Army we actually have certain wonderful innovations, such as strategy and tactics, which certain admirals would be well-advised to acquaint themselves with. And so your new job, Shaftoe, is not simply to kill Nips, but to use your head."

"Well, I know that you probably think I am a stupid jarhead, General, but I do think that I have a good head on my shoulders."

"And on your shoulders is exactly where I would like it to stay!" The General says, slapping him heartily on the back. "What we are trying to do now is to create a tactical situation that is favorable to us. Once that is accomplished, the actual killing of Nips can be handled by more efficient means such as aerial bombardment, mass starvation, and the like. It will not be necessary for you to personally cut the throat of every Nip you run into, as eminently qualified as you might be for such an operation."

"Thank you, General, sir."

"We have millions of Filipino guerillas, and hundreds of thousands of troops, to handle the essentially quotidian business of turning live Nips into dead, or at least captive, Nips. But in order to coordinate their activities, I need intelligence. That will be one of your missions. But the country is already crawling with my spies, and so it will be a secondary mission."

"And the primary mission, sir?"

"Those Filipinos need leadership. They need coordination. And perhaps most of all, they need fighting spirit."

"Fighting spirit, sir?"

"There are many reasons for the Filipinos to be down in the dumps. The Nips have not been kind to them. And although I have been very busy, here in New Guinea, preparing the springboard for my return, the Filipinos don't know about any of this, and many of them probably think I have forgotten about them entirely. Now it is time to let them know I'm coming. That I shall return—but soon!"

Shaftoe snickers, thinking that The General is engaging in some self-mocking humor here—yes, a bit of *irony*—but then he notes that The General does not seem especially amused. "Stop the vehicle!" he shouts.

Shaftoe parks the jeep at the apex of a switchback, where they can look northwest across the outermost reaches of the Philippine Sea. The General extends one arm toward Manila, hand slightly cupped, palm canted upward, gesturing like a Shakespearean actor in a posed photograph. "Go there, Bobby Shaftoe!" says The General. "Go there and tell them that I am coming."

Shaftoe knows his cue, and he knows his line. "Sir, yes sir!"

ORIGIN

FROM THE POINT OF VIEW OF ADMITTEDLY PRIVILEGED WHITE male technocrats such as Randy Waterhouse and his ancestors, the Palouse was like one big live-in laboratory for nonlinear aerodynamics and chaos theory. Not much was alive there, and so one's observations were not forever being clouded by trees, flowers, fauna, and the ploddingly linear and rational endeavors of humans. The Cascades blocked any of those warm, moist, refreshing Pacific breezes, harvesting their moisture to carpet ski areas for dewy-skinned Seattleites, and diverting what remained north to Vancouver or south to Portland. Consequently the Palouse had to get its air shipped down in bulk from the Yukon and British Columbia. It flowed across the blasted volcanic scab land of central Washington in (Randy supposed) a more or less continuous laminar sheet that, when it hit the rolling Palouse country, ramified into a vast system of floods, rivers and rivulets diverging around the bald swelling hills and recombining in the sere declivities. But it never recombined exactly the way it was before. The hills had thrown entropy into the system. Like a handful of nickels in a batch of bread dough this could be kneaded from place to place but never removed. The entropy manifested itself as swirls and violent gusts and ephemeral vortices. All of these things were clearly visible, because all summer the air was full of dust or smoke, and all winter it was full of windblown snow.

Whitman had dust devils (snow devils in the winter) in the way that medieval Guangzhou presumably had rats. Randy followed dust devils to school when he was a kid. Some were small enough that you could almost cup them in your hand, and some were like small tornadoes, fifty or a hundred feet high, that would appear on hilltops or atop shopping malls like biblical prophecies as filtered through the low-budget SFX technology and painfully literal-minded eye of a fifties epic film director. They at least scared the bejesus out of newcomers. When Randy got bored in school, he would look at the window and watch these things chase each other around the empty playground. Sometimes a roughly car-sized dust devil would glide across the four-square courts and between the swingsets and score a direct hit on the jungle gym, which was an old-fashioned, unpadded, child-paralyzing unit hammered together by some kind of Dark Ages ironmonger and planted in solid concrete, a real school-of-hard-knocks, survival-of-the-fittest one. The dust devil would seem to pause as it enveloped the jungle gym. It would completely lose its form and become a puff of dust that would begin to settle back down to the ground as all heavier-than-air things really ought to. But then suddenly the dust devil would reappear on the other side of the jungle gym and keep going. Or perhaps two dust devils would spin off in opposite directions.

Randy spent plenty of time chasing and carrying out impromptu experiments on dust devils while walking to and from school, to the point of getting bounced off the grille of a shrieking Buick once when he chased a roughly shopping-cart-sized one into the street in an attempt to climb into the center of it. He knew that they were both fragile and tenacious. You could stomp down on one of them and sometimes it would just dodge your foot, or swirl around it, and keep going. Other times, like if you tried to catch one in your hands, it would vanish— but then you'd look up and see another one just like it twenty feet away, running away from you. The whole concept of matter spontaneously organizing itself into grotesquely improbable and yet indisputably self-perpetuating and fairly robust systems sort of gave Randy the willies later on, when he began to learn about physics.

There was no room for dust devils in the laws of physics, as least in the rigid form in which they were usually taught. There is a kind of unspoken collusion going on in mainstream science education: you get your competent but bored, insecure and hence stodgy teacher talking to an audience divided between engineering students, who are going to be responsible for making bridges that won't fall down or airplanes that won't suddenly plunge vertically into the ground at six hundred miles an hour, and who by definition get sweaty palms and vindictive attitudes when their teacher suddenly veers off track and begins raving about wild and completely nonintuitive phenomena; and physics students, who derive much of their self-esteem from knowing that they are smarter and morally purer than the engineering students, and who by definition don't want to hear about anything that makes no fucking sense. This collusion results in the professor saying: (something along the lines of) dust is heavier than air, therefore it falls until it hits the ground. That's all there is to know about dust. The engineers love it because they like their issues dead and crucified like butterflies under glass. The physicists love it because they want to think they understand everything. No one asks difficult questions. And outside the windows, the dust devils continue to gambol across the campus.

Now that Randy's back in Whitman for the first time in several years, watching (because it's winter) ice devils zigzagging across the Christmas-empty streets, he is inclined to take a longer view of the matter, which goes a little something like this: these devils, these vortices, are a consequence of hills and valleys that are probably miles and miles upwind. Basically, Randy, who has blown in from out of town, is in a mobile frame of mind, and is seeing things from the wind's frame of reference— not the stationary frame of reference of the little boy, who rarely left town. From the wind's frame of reference, it (the wind) is stationary and the hills and valleys are moving things that crumple the horizon and then rush towards it and then interfere with it and go away, leaving the wind to sort out consequences later on down the line. And some of the consequences are dust or ice devils. If there was more stuff in the way, like expansive cities filled with buildings, or forests filled with leaves and branches, then that would be the end of the story; the wind would become completely deranged and cease to exist as a unitary thing, and all of the aerodynamic action would be at the incomprehensible scale of micro-vortices around pine needles and car antennas.

A case in point would be the parking lot of Waterhouse House, which is normally filled with cars and therefore a complete wind-killer. You aren't going to see dust devils at the downwind edge of a full parking lot, just a generalized seepage of dead and decayed wind. But it is Christmas break and there are all of three cars parked in this space, which doubles as football-overflow and hence is about the size of an artillery practice range. The asphalt is dead-monitor-screen grey. A volatile gas of ice swirls across it as freely as a sheen of fuel on warm water, except where it strikes the icy sarcophagi of these three abandoned vehicles, which have evidently been sitting in this otherwise empty lot for a couple of weeks now, since all of the other cars went away on Christmas break. Each car has become the first cause of a system of wakes and standing vortices that extends downstream for hundreds of yards. The wind here is a glinting abrasive thing, a perpetual, face-shredding, eyeball-poking tendency in the fabric of spacetime, inhabited by vast platinum-blond arcs of fire that are centered on the low winter sun. Crystalline water is suspended in it all the time, is why: shards of ice that are smaller than snowflakes—probably just individual legs of snowflakes that have been sheared off and borne into the air as the wind snapped and rattled over the crests of Canadian snow-dunes. Once airborne, they stay airborne unless they find themselves ducted into some pocket of dead air: the eye of a vortex or the still boundary layer of a dead car's parking-lot wake. And so over the weeks the vortices and standing waves have become visible, like three-dimensional virtual-reality renderings of themselves.

Waterhouse House rises above this tableau, a high-rise dorm that no person prominent enough to have a dorm named after him would want to have named after him. Out of its climatically inappropriate acreage of picture window shines the same embarrassing, greenish light radiated by algae-scummed domestic aquaria. Janitors are going through it with machines the size of hot dog carts, wrangling these mile-long coils of thumb-thick orange power cable, steaming beer vomit and artificial popcorn-butter lipids up out of the thin grey mats that, when Randy was there, seemed not so much like carpet as references to carpeting or carpet signifiers. When Randy now pulls into the main vehicle entrance, past the big tombstone that says WATERHOUSE HOUSE, he cannot but look straight out the windshield and through the dorm's front windows and straight at a large portrait of his grandfather, Lawrence Pritchard Waterhouse—one of a dozen or so figures, mostly departed now, who compete for the essentially bogus title of "inventor of the digital computer." The portrait is securely bolted to the cinderblock wall of the lobby and imprisoned under a half-inch-thick slab of Plexiglass that must be replaced every couple of years, as it fogs from repeated scrubbings and petty vandalizations. Seen through this milky cataract, Lawrence Pritchard Waterhouse is grimly resplendent in full doctoral robes. He has one foot up on something, his elbow planted on the elevated knee, and has tucked his robes back behind the other arm and planted his fist on his hip. It is meant to be a sort of dynamic leaning-into-the-winds-of-the-future posture, but to Randy, who at the age of five was present for its unveiling, it has a kind of incredulous what-the-hell-are-those-little-people-doing-down-there vibe about it.

Other than the three dead cars in their shells of hardened, dust-infused ice, there is nothing in the parking lot save about two dozen items of antique furniture and a few other treasures such as a complete sterling silver tea service and a dark, time-wracked trunk. As Randy pulls in with his Uncle Red and his Aunt Nina, he notes that the Shaftoe boys have discharged the responsibilities for which they will be drawing minimum wage plus twenty-five percent all day long: namely they have moved all of these items from where Uncle Geoff and Auntie Anne placed them back to the Origin.

In a gesture of companionship and/or unclesque bonhomie, Uncle Red, much to the evident resentment of Aunt Nina, has claimed the Acura's passenger seat, leaving Aunt Nina marooned in the back where she evidently feels much more psychically isolated than the situation would seem to warrant. She makes lateral sliding motions trying to center the eyes of first Randy, then Uncle Red, in the rearview mirror. Randy has taken to relying solely on the outside rearview mirrors during the ten-minute drive over from the hotel, because when he glances at the inside one he keeps seeing Aunt Nina's dilated pupils aimed down his throat like twin shotgun barrels. The blast of the heater/defroster forms a pocket of auditory isolation back there which on top of her already prominent feelings of near-animal rage and stress have left her volatile and obviously dangerous.

Randy heads straight for the Origin, as in the intersection of the X and Y axes, which is marked by a light pole with its very own multiton system of wind-deposited wakes and vortices.

"Look," says Uncle Red, "all we want to accomplish here is to make sure that your mother's legacy, if that is the correct term for the posses-sions of one who is not actually dead but merely moved into a long-term care facility, is equally divided among her five offspring. Am I right?"

This is not addressed to Randy, but he nods anyway, trying to show a united front. He has been grinding his teeth for two days straight; the places where his jaw-muscles anchor to his skull have become the foci of tremendous radiating systems of surging and pulsing pain.

"I think you'd agree that an equal division is all we want," Uncle Red continues. "Correct?"

After a worrisomely long pause, Aunt Nina nods. Randy manages to glimpse her face in the rearview as she makes another dramatic lateral move, and sees there a look of almost nauseous trepidation, as if this equal-division concept might be some Jesuitical snare.

"Now, here's the interesting part," says Uncle Red, who is the chair-man of the mathematics department at Okaley College in Macomb, Illi-nois. "How do we define 'equal'? This is what your brothers, and brothers-in-law, and Randy and I were debating so late into the night last night. If we were dividing up a stack of currency, it would be easy, because currency has a monetary value that is printed right on its face, and the bills are interchangeable—no one gets emotionally attached to a particular dollar bill."

"This is why we should have an objective appraiser—"

"But everyone's going to disagree with what the appraiser says, Nina, love," says Uncle Red. "Furthermore, the appraiser will totally miss out on the emotional dimension, which evidently looms very large here, or so it would seem, based on the, uh, let's say *melodramatic* character of the, uh, discussion, if discussion isn't too dignified a term for what some might perceive as more of a, well, catfight, that you and your sisters were conducting all day yesterday."

Randy nods almost imperceptibly. He pulls up and parks next to the furniture that is again clustered around the Origin. At the edge of the parking lot, near where the Y axis (here denoting perceived emotional value) meets a retaining wall, the Shaftoes' hot rod sits, all steamed up on the inside.

"The question reduces," Uncle Red says, "to a mathematical one: how do you divide up an inhomogeneous set of n objects among m people (or couples actually); i.e, how do you partition the set into m subsets $(S_1, S_2, \ldots, S_m)$ such that the value of each subset is as close as possible to being equal?"

"It doesn't seem that hard," Aunt Nina begins weakly. She is a professor of Qwghlmian linguistics.

"It is actually shockingly difficult," Randy says. "It is closely akin to the Knapsack Problem, which is so difficult to solve that it has been used as the basis for cryptographic systems."

"And that's not even taking into account that each of the couples would appraise the value of each of the n objects differently!" Uncle Red shouts. By this point, Randy has shut off the car, and the windows have begun to steam up. Uncle Red pulls off a mitten and begins to draw figures in the fog on the windshield, using it like a blackboard. "For each of the m people (or couples) there exists an n-element value vector, V, where V_1 is the value that that particular couple would place on item number 1 (according to some arbitrary numeration system) and V_2 is the value they would place on item number 2 and so on all the way up to item number n. These m vectors, taken together, form a value matrix. Now, we can impose the condition that each vector must total up to the same amount; i.e., we can just arbitrarily specify some notional value for the entire collection of furniture and other goods and impose the condition that

$$\sum_{i=1}^{n} V_i = \tau$$

where τ is a constant."

"But we might all have different opinions as to what the total value is, as well!" says Aunt Nina, gamely.

"That has no impact mathematically," Randy whispers.

"It is just an arbitrary scaling factor!" Uncle Red says witheringly. "This is why I ended up agreeing with your brother Tom, though I didn't at first, that we should take a cue from the way he and the other relativistic physicists do it, and just arbitrarily set $\tau = 1$. Which forces us to deal with fractional values, which I thought some of the ladies, present company excluded of course, might find confusing, but at least it emphasizes the arbitrary nature of the scaling factor and helps to eliminate *that* source of confusion." Uncle Tom tracks asteroids in Pasadena for the Jet Propulsion Laboratory.

"There's the Gomer Bolstrood console," Aunt Nina exclaims, rubbing a hole in the fog on her window, and then continuing to orbitally rub away with the sleeve of her coat as if she is going to abrade an escape route through the safety glass. "Just sitting out in the snow!"

"It's not actually precipitating," Uncle Red says, "this is just blowing snow. It is absolutely bone dry, and if you go out and look at the console or whatever you call it, you will find that the snow is not melting on it at all, because it has been sitting out in the U-Stor-It ever since your mother moved to the managed care facility and it has equilibrated to the ambient temperature which I think we can all testify is well below zero Celsius."

Randy crosses his arms over his abdomen, leans his head back, and closes his eyes. The tendons in his neck are as stiff as subzero Silly Putty and resist painfully.

"That console was in my bedroom from the time I was born until I left for college," Aunt Nina says. "By any decent standard of justice, that console is mine."

"Well, that brings me to the breakthrough that Randy and Tom and Geoff and I finally came up with at about two A.M., namely that the perceived economic value of each item, as complicated as that is in and of itself, viz the Knapsack Problem, is only one dimension of the issues that have got us all on such a jagged emotional edge. The other dimension—and here I really do mean dimension in a Euclidean geometry sense—is the emotional value of each item. That is, in theory we could come up with a division of the set of all pieces of furniture that would give you, Nina, an equal share. But such a division might leave you, love, just deeply, deeply unsatisfied because you didn't get that console, which, though it's obviously not as valuable as say the grand piano, has much greater emotional value to you."

"I don't think it's out of the question that I would commit physical violence in order to defend my rightful ownership of that console," Aunt Nina says, suddenly reverting to a kind of dead-voiced frigid calm.

"But that's not necessary, Nina, because we have created this whole setup here just so that you can give your feelings the full expression they deserve!"

"Okay. What do I do?" Aunt Nina says, bolting from the car. Randy and Uncle Red hastily gather up their gloves and mittens and hats and follow her out. She is now hovering over the console, watching the dust of ice swirl across the dark but limpid, virtually glowing surface of the console in the turbulent wake of her body, forming little Mandelbrotian epi-epi-epi-vortices.

"As Geoff and Anne did before us, and the others will do afterwards, we are going to move each of these items to a specific position, as in (x, y) coordinates, in the parking lots. The x axis runs this way," Uncle Red says, facing the Waterhouse House and holding his arms out in a cruciform attitude, "and the y axis this way." He toddles around ninety degrees so that one of his hands is now pointing at the Shaftoes' Impala. "Perceived financial value is measured by x. The farther in that direction it is, the more valuable you think it is. You might even assign something a negative x value is if you think it has negative value—e.g., that overstuffed chair over there—which might cost more to re-upholster than it is actually worth. Likewise, the y axis measures perceived emotional value. Now, we have established that the console has extreme emotional value to you and so I think that we can just go right ahead and move it down the line over to where the Impala is located."

"Can something have negative emotional value?" Aunt Nina says, sourly and probably rhetorically.

"If you hate it so much that just owning it would cancel out the emotional benefits of having something like the console, then yes," Uncle Red says.

Randy hoists the console onto his shoulder and begins to walk in a positive y direction. The Shaftoe boys are available to hump furniture at a moment's notice, but Randy needs to mark a bit of territory here, just to indicate that he is not without some masculine attributes himself, and so he ends up carrying more furniture than he probably needs to. Back at the Origin, he can hear Red and Nina going at it. "I have a problem with this," Nina says. "What's to prevent her from just putting everything down at the extreme y axis—claiming that everything is terribly emotionally important to her?" *Her* in this case can only mean Aunt Rachel, the wife of Tom. Rachel is a multiethnic East Coast urbanite who is not blessed or afflicted with the obligatory Waterhousian diffidence and so has always been regarded as a sort of living incarnation of rapacity, a sucking maw of need. The worst-case scenario here is that Rachel somehow goes home with *everything*—the grand piano, the silver, the china, the Gomer Bolstrood dining room set. Hence the need for elaborate rules and rituals, and a booty division system that is mathematically provable as fair.

"That's where τ_e and τ_s enter into it," Uncle Red says soothingly.

$$\sum_{i=1}^{n} V_i^e = \tau_e, \text{ and } \sum_{i=1}^{n} V_i^s = \tau_s$$

"All of our choices will be mathematically scaled so that they add up to the same total values on both the emotional and financial scales. So if someone clumped everything together in the extreme corner, then, after scaling, it'd be as if they never expressed any preferences at all."

Randy nears the steamed-up Impala. One of the doors makes a crackling noise as superannuated weatherstripping peels away from steel. Robin Shaftoe emerges, breathes into his cupped hands, and takes a parade-rest position, signifying that he is available to discharge any responsibilities out here on the Cartesian coordinate plane. Randy looks up over the Impala and the retaining wall and the ice-clogged xeriscape above that and into the lobby of Waterhouse House, where Amy Shaftoe has her feet up on a coffee table and is looking through some of the extremely sad Cayuse-related literature that Randy bought for Avi. She looks down and smiles at him and just barely, he thinks, restrains the impulse to reach up and twirl one finger around her ear.

"That's good, Randy!" shouts Uncle Red from the Origin, "now we need to give it some $x!$" Meaning that the console is not devoid of economic value either. Randy does a right-face and begins to walk into the $(+x, +y)$ quadrant, counting the yellow lines. "Give it about four parking spaces! That's good!" Randy plonks the console down, then pulls a pad of graph paper out of his coat, whips back the first sheet, which contains the (x,y) scatterplot of Uncle Geoff and Auntie Anne, and notes down the coordinates of the console. Sound carries in the Palouse, and from the Origin he can hear Aunt Nina saying to Uncle Red, "How much of our τ_e have we just spent on that console?"

"If we leave everything else down here at y equals zero, a hundred percent after scaling," Uncle Red says. "Otherwise it depends on how we distribute these things in the y dimension." Which is of course the correct answer, albeit totally useless.

If these days in Whitman don't make Amy flee from Randy in terror, nothing will, and so he's glad in a sick way that she is seeing this. The subject of his family has not really come up until now. Randy is not given to talking about his family because he feels there is nothing to report: small town, good education, shame and self-esteem doled out in roughly equal quantities and usually where warranted. Nothing spectacular along the lines of grotesque psychopathologies, sexual abuse, massive, shocking trauma, or Satanic rallies in the backyard. So normally when people are talking about their families, Randy just shuts up and listens, feeling that he has nothing to say. His familial anecdotes are so tame, so pedestrian, that it would be presumptuous even to relate them, especially after someone else has just divulged something really shocking or horrific.

But standing there and looking at these vortices he starts to wonder. Some people's insistence that "Today I: smoke/am overweight/have a shitty attitude/am depressed because: my mom died of cancer/my uncle put his thumb up my butt/my dad hit me with a razor strop" seems kind of overly deterministic to Randy; it seems to reflect a kind of lazy or half-witted surrender to bald teleology. Basically, if everyone has a vested interest in believing that they understand everything, or even that people are *capable in principle* of understanding it (either because believing this dampens their insecurities about the unpredictable world, or makes them feel more intelligent than others, or both) then you have an environment in which dopey, reductionist, simple-minded, pat, glib thinking can circulate, like wheelbarrows filled with inflated currency in the marketplaces of Jakarta.

But things like the ability of some student's dead car to spawn repeating patterns of thimble-sized vortices a hundred yards downwind would seem to argue in favor of a more cautious view of the world, an openness to the full and true weirdness of the Universe, an admission of our limited human faculties. And if you've gotten to this point, then you can argue that growing up in a family devoid of gigantic and obvious primal psychological forces, and living a life touched by many subtle and even forgotten influences rather than one or two biggies (e.g., active participation in the Church of Satan) can lead, far downwind, to consequences that are not entirely devoid of interest. Randy hopes, but very much doubts, that America Shaftoe, sitting up there in the algae-colored light reading about the inadvertent extermination of the Cayuse, sees it this way.

Randy rejoins his aunt at the Origin. Uncle Red has been explaining to her, somewhat condescendingly, that they must pay careful attention to the distribution of items on the economic scale, and for his troubles he has been sent on a long, lonely walk down the $+x$ axis carrying the complete silver tea service. "Why couldn't we just have stayed inside and worked this all out on paper?" Aunt Nina asks.

"It was felt that there was value in physically moving this stuff around, giving people a direct physical analog of the value-assertions that they were making," Randy says. "Also that it would be useful to appraise this stuff literally in the cold light of day." As opposed to ten or twelve emotionally fraught people clambering around a packed-to-the-ceiling U-Stor-It locker with flashlights, sniping at each other from behind the armoires.

"Once we've all made our choices, then what? You sit down and figure it out on a spreadsheet, or something?"

"It is much too computationally intensive to be solved that way. Probably a genetic algorithm is called for—certainly there won't be a mathematically exact solution. My father knows a researcher in Geneva who has done work on problems isomorphic to this one, and sent him e-mail last night. With any luck we will be able to ftp some suitable software and get it running on the Tera."

"The Terror?"

"Tera. As in Teraflops."

"That does me no good at all. When you say 'as in' you are supposed to give me something more familiar to relate it to."

"It is one of the ten fastest computers on the planet. Do you see that red brick building just to the right of the end of the $-y$ axis," Randy says, pointing down the hill, "just behind the new gym?"

"The one with all the antennas?"

"Yes. The Tera machine is in there. It was made by a company in Seattle."

"It must have been very expensive."

"My dad talked it out of them."

"Yes!" says Uncle Red cheerfully, returning from high-x-value territory. "The man is a legendary donation-raiser."

"He must have a persuasive side to him that I have not been perceptive enough to notice yet," Aunt Nina says, wandering curiously towards some large cardboard boxes.

"No," Randy says, "it's more like he just goes in and flops around on the conference table until they become so embarrassed for his sake that they agree to sign the check."

"You've seen him do this?" Aunt Nina says skeptically, sizing up a box labeled CONSTITUENTS OF UPSTAIRS LINEN CLOSET.

"Heard about it. High-tech is a small town," Randy says.

"He's been able to make great capital of his father's work," Uncle Red says. " 'If my father had patented even one of his computer inventions, Palouse College would be bigger than Harvard,' and so on."

Aunt Nina has got the box open now. It is almost completely filled by a single Qwlghmian blanket, in a dark greyish-brown on dark brownish-grey plaid. The blanket in question is about an inch thick, and, during wintertime family reunions, was infamous as a booby prize of sorts among the Waterhouse grandchildren. The smell of mothballs, mildew, and

heavily oiled wool causes Aunt Nina's nose to wrinkle, as it did Aunt
Annie's before her. Randy remembers bedding down beneath this blanket once at the age of about nine, and waking up at two in the morning
with bronchial spasms, hyperthermia, and vague memories of a nightmare
about being buried alive. Aunt Nina slams the box flaps shut, turns
around, and looks in the direction of the Impala. Robin Shaftoe is already
running towards them. Being not bad at math himself, he was quick to
pick up on this whole concept, and knows from experience that the
blanket box will have to be trundled deep out into $(-x,-y)$ territory.

"I guess I'm just worried," Aunt Nina says, "about having my preferences mediated by this supercomputer. I have tried to make it clear what
I want. But will the computer understand that?" She has paused by the
CERAMICS box in a way that is tantalizing Randy, who badly wants to
have a look inside, but doesn't want to arouse suspicions. He's the referee
and is sworn to objectivity. "Forget the china," she says, "too old-
ladyish."

Uncle Red wanders over and disappears behind one of the dead cars,
presumably to take a leak. Aunt Nina says, "How about you, Randy? As
the eldest son of the eldest son, you must have some feelings about this."

"No doubt when my parents' time comes, they will pass on some of
Grandma and Grandpa's legacy to me," Randy says.

"Oh, very circumspect. Well done," Aunt Nina says. "But as the only
grandchild who has any memories of your grandfather at all, there must
be something here that you might like to have."

"There'll probably be some odds and ends that nobody wants," Randy
says. Then like an almost perfect moron—like an organism genetically
engineered to be a total, stupid idiot—Randy glances directly at the
Trunk. Then he tries to hide it, which only makes it more conspicuous.
He guesses that his mostly beardless face must be an open book, and
wishes he had never shaved. A bullet of ice strikes him in the right
cornea with a nearly audible splot. The ballistic impact blinds him and
the thermal shock gives him an ice-cream headache. When he recovers
enough to see again, Aunt Nina is walking around the trunk, kind of
spiraling in towards it in a rapidly decaying orbit. "Hmm. What's in
here?" She grips the handle at one end and finds she can barely get it
off the ground.

"Old Japanese code books. Bundles of ETC cards."

"Marcus?"

"Yes, ma'am!" says Marcus Aurelius Shaftoe, returning from the dou-
ble-negative quadrant.

"What is the angle exactly in between the $+x$ and $+y$ axes?" Aunt

Nina asks. "I would ask the referee, here, but I'm beginning to have doubts about his objectivity."

M.A. glances at Randy and decides he had best interpret this last comment as good-natured familial horsing-around. "Would you like that in radians or degrees, ma'am?"

"Neither. Just demonstrate it for me. Take this great big trunk on that strong back of yours and just split the middle between $+x$ and $+y$ axes and keep walking until I say when."

"Yes, ma'am." M.A. hefts the trunk and starts walking, frequently looking back and forth to verify that he's exactly in the middle. Robin stands off at a safe distance watching with interest.

Uncle Red, returning from his piss-break, watches this in horror. "Nina! Love! That's not worth the cost of shipping it home! What on earth are you doing?"

"Making sure I get what I want," Nina says.

Randy gets a small part of what he wants two hours later, when his own mother breaks the seal on the CERAMICS box to verify that the china is in good condition. At the time, Randy and his father are standing next to the Trunk. It is rather late in his parent's value-plotting work and so pieces of fine furniture are now widely scattered across the parking lot, looking like the aftermath of one of those tornadoes that miraculously sets things down intact after whirling them through the skies for ten miles. Randy is trying to find a way to talk up the emotional value of this trunk without violating his oath of objectivity. The chances of anyone other than Nina ending up with this trunk are actually quite miserable, since she (to Red's horror) left almost everything clumped around the Origin except for it and the coveted Console. But if Dad would at least move the thing off dead center—which no one except Nina has done—then, if the Tera awards it to him tomorrow morning, Randy can plausibly argue that it's something other than a computer error. But Dad is taking most of his cues from Mom and is having none of it.

Mom has bitten her gloves off and is parting layer after layer of crumpled newsprint with magenta hands. "Oh, the gravy boat!" she exclaims, and hoists up something that is more of a heavy cruiser than a boat. Randy agrees with Aunt Nina that the design is old-ladyish in the extreme, but that's kind of tautological since he has only seen it in the house of his grandmother, who has been an old lady for as long as he has known her. Randy walks towards his mother with his hands in his pockets, still trying to play it cool for some reason. This obsession with secrecy may have gone a bit far. He has seen this gravy boat maybe twenty times in his life, always at family reunions, and seeing it now roils up a whole silt-cloud of long-settled emotions. He reaches out, and Mom remits it to his mittened hands. He pretends to admire it from the side, and then flips it over to read the words glazed on the bottom. ROYAL ALBERT—LAVENDER ROSE.

For a moment he is sweating under a vertical sun, swaying to keep his balance on a rocking boat, smelling the neoprene of hoses and flippers. Then he's back in the Palouse. He begins thinking about how to sabotage the computer program to ensure that Aunt Nina gets what she wants, so that she'll give him what is rightfully his.

GOLGOTHA

✝ LIEUTENANT NINOMIYA REACHES BUNDOK ABOUT TWO WEEKS after Goto Dengo, accompanied by several bashed and scraped wooden cases. "What is your specialty?" asks Goto Dengo, and Lieutenant Ninomiya responds by opening up one of the cases to reveal a surveyor's transit swaddled in clean, oiled linen. Another case contains an equally perfect sextant. Goto Dengo gawks. The gleaming perfection of the instruments is a marvel. But even more marvelous is that they sent him a surveyor only twelve days after he requested one. Ninomiya grins at the look on his new colleague's face, revealing that he has lost all of his front teeth except for one, which happens to be mostly gold.

Before any engineering can be done, all of this wilderness must be brought into the realm of the known. Detailed maps must be prepared, watersheds charted, soil sampled. For two weeks Goto Dengo has been going around with a pipe and a sledgehammer taking core samples of the dirt. He has identified rocks from the streambeds, estimated the flow rates of the Yamamoto and Tojo Rivers, counted and catalogued trees. He has trudged through the jungle and planted flags around the approximate boundaries of the Special Security Zone. The whole time, he's been worrying about having to perform the survey himself, using primitive, improvised tools. And all of a sudden, here is Lieutenant Ninomiya with his instruments.

The three Lieutenants, Goto, Mori and Ninomiya, spend a few days surveying the flat, semi-open land straddling the lower Tojo River. The year, 1944, is turning out to be dry so far, and Mori does not want to construct his military barracks on land that will turn into a marsh after the first big rain. He is not concerned about the comfort of the prisoners, but he would at least like to ensure that they won't get washed away. The lay of the land is also important in setting up the interlocking fields of fire that will be necessary to put down any riots or mass escape attempts. They put Bundok's few enlisted men to work gathering bamboo stakes, then drive these in to mark the locations of roads, barracks, barbed-wire fences, guard towers, and a few carefully sited mortar emplacements from which the guards will be able to fill the atmosphere in any chosen part of the camp with shrapnel.

When Lieutenant Goto takes Lieutenant Ninomiya up into the jungle, clambering up the steep valley of the Tojo, Lieutenant Mori must stay behind—in accordance with Captain Noda's orders. This is just as well, since Mori has his work cut out for him down below. The captain has granted Ninomiya a special dispensation to see the Special Security Zone.

"Elevations are of supreme importance in this project," Goto Dengo tells the surveyor on the way up. They are burdened with surveying equipment and fresh water, but Ninomiya clambers up the rocky gulch of the half-parched river just as ably as Goto Dengo himself. "We will begin by establishing the level of Lake Yamamoto—which does not exist yet—and then work downwards from there."

"I have also been ordered to obtain the precise latitude and longitude," says Ninomiya.

Goto Dengo grins. "That's hard—there is nowhere to see the sun."

"What about the three peaks?"

Goto Dengo turns to see if Ninomiya is joking. But the surveyor is looking intently up the valley.

"Your dedication sets a good example," Goto Dengo says.

"This place is paradise compared to Rabaul."

"Is that where you were sent from?"

"Yes."

"How did you escape? It is cut off, isn't it?"

"It has been cut off for some time," Ninomiya says curtly. Then, he adds: "They came and got me in a submarine." His voice is husky and faint.

Goto Dengo is silent for a while.

Ninomiya has a system all worked out in his head, which they put into effect the next week, after they have done a rough survey of the Special Security Zone. Early in the morning, they hoist an enlisted man into a tree with a canteen, a watch, and a mirror. There is nothing special about this tree except for a bamboo stake recently driven into the ground nearby, labeled MAIN DRIFT.

Then Lieutenants Ninomiya and Goto climb to the top of the mountain, which takes them about eight hours. It is dreadfully arduous, and Ninomiya is shocked that Goto volunteers to go with him. "'I want to see this place from the top of Calvary," Goto Dengo explains. "Only then will I have the insight to perform my duty well."

On the way up, they compare notes, New Guinea vs. New Britain. It seems that the latter's only saving grace is the settlement of Rabaul, a formerly British port complete with a cricket oval, now the linchpin of Nipponese forces in Southwest Asia. "For a long time it was a great place to be a surveyor," Ninomiya says, and describes the fortifications that they built there in preparation for MacArthur's invasion. He has a draftsman's enthusiasm for detail and at one point talks nonstop for an hour describing a particular system of bunkers and pillboxes down to the last booby trap and glory hole.

As the climb gets harder, the two vie with each other in belittling its difficulty. Goto Dengo tells the tale of climbing over the snow-covered mountain range in New Guinea.

"Nowadays, on New Britain we climb volcanoes all the time," Ninomiya says offhandedly.

"Why?"

"To collect sulfur."

"Sulfur? Why?"

"To make gunpowder."

After this they don't talk for a while.

Goto Dengo tries to dig them out of a conversational hole. "It'll be a bad day for MacArthur when he tries to take Rabaul!"

Ninomiya trudges along silently for a bit, trying to control himself, and fails. "You idiot," he says, "don't you see? MacArthur isn't coming. There's no need."

"But Rabaul is the cornerstone of the whole theater!"

"It is a cornerstone of soft, sweet wood in a universe of termites," Ninomiya snaps. "All he has to do is ignore us for another year, and then everyone will be dead of starvation or typhus."

The jungle thins out. The plants are wrestling for footholds on a loose slope of volcanic cinders, and only smaller ones endure. This puts Goto Dengo in the mind of writing a poem in which the small, tenacious Nipponese prevail over the big, lumbering Americans, but it has been a long time since he wrote a poem and he can't make the words go together.

Someday the plants will turn this cone of scoria and rubble into soil, but not yet. Now that Goto Dengo can finally see for more than a few yards he is beginning to understand the lay of the land. The numerical data that he and Ninomiya have compiled over the last week is being synthesized, within his mind, into a solid understanding of how this place works.

Calvary is an old cinder cone. It started as a fissure from which ash and scoria were ejected, one fragment at a time, for thousands of years, tumbling up and outwards in a family of mortar-shell-like parabolic curves, varying in height and distance depending on the size of each fragment and the direction of the wind. They landed in a wide ring centered on the fissure. As the ring grew in height it naturally spread out into a broad, truncated cone with a central pit gouged out of its top, with the spitting fissure in the bottom of that pit.

The winds here tend to come from a little bit east of due south, and so the ash tended to be pushed towards the north-by-northwest edge of the cone's rim. That is still the highest point of the cinder cone. But the fissure died out eons ago, or perhaps was plugged by its own emissions, and the whole structure has been much eroded since then. The southern rim of the cone is just a barrier of low hills perforated by the courses of the Yamamoto River and the two tributaries that come together to form the Tojo River. The central pit is a bowl of loathsome jungle, so saturated with chlorophyll that it looks black from above. Birds cruise above the canopy, looking like colored stars from up here.

The northern rim still rises a good five hundred meters above the bowl of jungle, but its formerly smooth arc has been dissected by erosion to form three distinct summits, each one a pile of red scoria half-concealed by a stubble of green vegetation. Without discussion, Ninomiya and Goto Dengo head for the one in the middle, which is the highest. They reach it at about two-thirty in the afternoon, and immediately wish they hadn't because the sun is beating almost straight down on top of them. But there is a cool breeze up here, and once they have protected their heads with makeshift burnooses, it's not so bad. Goto Dengo sets up the tripod and the transit while Ninomiya uses his sextant to shoot the sun. He has a pretty good German watch which he zeroed against the radio transmission from Manila this morning, and this enables him to reckon the longitude. He works the calculation out on a scrap of paper on his lap, then goes back and does it again to double-check the numbers, speaking them out loud. Goto Dengo copies them down in his notebook, just in case Ninomiya's notes get lost.

At three o'clock sharp, the enlisted man down in the tree begins to flash his mirror at them: a brilliant spark from a dark rug of jungle that is otherwise featureless. Ninomiya centers his transit on this signal and takes down more figures. In combination with various other data from maps, aerial photos and the like, this should enable him to make an estimate of the main shaft's latitude and longitude.

"I don't know how accurate this will be," he frets, as they trudge down the mountain. "I have the peak exactly—what did you call it? Cavalry?"

"Close enough."

"This means soldiers on horseback, correct?"

"Yes."

"But the site of the shaft I will not have very precisely unless I can use better techniques."

Goto Dengo considers telling him that this is perfectly all right, that the place was made to be lost and forgotten. But he keeps his mouth shut.

The survey work takes another couple of weeks. They figure out where the shore of Lake Yamamoto will be and calculate its volume. It will be more of a pond than a lake—less than a hundred meters across— but it will be deceptively deep, and it will hold a lot of water. They calculate the angle of the shaft that will connect the bottom of the lake to the main network of tunnels. They figure out where all of the horizontal tunnels will emerge from the walls of the Tojo River's gorge, and stake out the routes of roads and railways that will lead to those openings, so that debris can be removed and precious war material brought in for storage. They double- and triple-check all of it to make sure that no fragment of the works will be visible from the air.

Meanwhile, down below, Lieutenant Mori and a small work detail have planted some fenceposts and strung some barbed wire—just enough to contain a hundred or so prisoners, who arrive packed into a couple of military trucks. When these are put to work, the camp expands very rapidly; the military barracks go up in a few days and the double barbed-wire perimeter is completed. They never seem to lack for supplies here. Dynamite comes in by the truckload, as if it weren't desperately needed in places like Rabaul, and is carefully stored under the supervision of Goto Dengo. Prisoners carry it into a special shed that has been constructed for this purpose in the shade of the jungle. Goto Dengo has not been close to the prisoners before, and is startled to realize that they are all Chinese. And they are not speaking the dialect of Canton or of Formosa, but rather one that Goto Dengo heard frequently when he was posted in Shanghai. These prisoners are northern Chinese.

It is stranger and stranger all the time, this Bundok place.

The Filipinos, he knows, have been uniquely surly about their inclusion in the Greater East Asia Coprosperity Sphere. They are well-armed, and MacArthur has been egging them on. Many thousands of them have been taken prisoner. Within half a day's drive of Bundok there are more than enough Filipino prisoners to fill Lieutenant Mori's camp and accomplish Lieutenant Goto's project. And yet the powers that be have shipped hundreds of Chinese people all the way down from Shanghai to do this work.

At times like this he begins to doubt his own sanity. He feels an urge to discuss the matter with Lieutenant Ninomiya. But the surveyor, his friend and confidant, has made himself scarce since his work was completed. One day, Goto Dengo goes by Ninomiya's tent and finds it empty. Captain Noda explains that the surveyor was called away suddenly to perform important work elsewhere.

About a month later, when the road-building work in the Special Security Zone is well underway, some of the Chinese workers who are digging begin shouting excitedly. Goto Dengo understands what they are saying.

They have uncovered human remains. The jungle has done its work and practically nothing is left but bones, but the smell, and the legions of ants, tell him that the corpse is a fairly recent one. He grabs a shovel from one of the workers and pulls up a scoop of dirt and carries it over to the river, dripping tangles of ants. He lowers it carefully into the running water. The dirt dissolves into a brown trail in the river and the skull is soon revealed: the dome of the head, the eye sockets still not entirely empty, the nasal bone with some fragments of cartilage still attached, and finally the jaws, pocked with old abcesses and missing most of their teeth, except for one gold tooth in the middle. The current turns the skull over slowly, as if Lieutenant Ninomiya is hiding his face in shame, and Goto Dengo sees a neat hole punched through the base of the skull.

He looks up. A dozen Chinese are gathered above him on the riverbank, watching him impassively.

"Do not speak of this to any of the other Nipponese," Goto Dengo says. Their eyes go wide and their lips part in astonishment as they hear him speaking the precise dialect of Shanghai prostitutes.

One of the Chinese workers is nearly bald. He seems to be in his forties, though prisoners age rapidly and so it is always difficult to tell. He is not scared like the others. He is looking at Goto Dengo appraisingly.

"You," Goto Dengo says, "pick two other men and follow me. Bring shovels."

He leads them into the jungle, into a place where he knows there will be no further digging, and shows them where to put Lieutenant Ninomiya's new grave. The bald man is a good leader as well as a strong worker and he gets the grave dug quickly, then transfers the remains without squeamishness or complaint. If he has been through the China Incident and survived for this long as a prisoner of war, he has probably seen and done much worse.

Goto Dengo does his part by distracting Captain Noda for a couple of hours. They go up and tour the dam work on the Yamamoto River. Noda is anxious to create Lake Yamamoto as soon as possible, before MacArthur's air force makes detailed surveys of the area. The sudden appearance of a lake in the jungle would probably not go unnoticed.

The site of the lake is a natural rock bowl, covered by jungle, with the Yamamoto River running through the middle of it. Right next to the riverbank, men are already at work with rock drills, placing dynamite charges. "The inclined shaft will start here," Goto Dengo tells Captain Noda, "and runs straight—" turning his back on the river he makes one hand into a blade and thrusts it into the jungle "—straight down to Golgotha." *The Place of the Skull.*

"Gargotta?" Captain Noda says.

"It is a Tagalog word," Goto Dengo says authoritatively. "It means 'hidden glade.' "

"Hidden glade. I like it! Very good. Gargotta!" Captain Noda says. "Your work is proceeding very well, Lieutenant Goto."

"I am only striving to live up to the high standard that was set by Lieutenant Ninomiya," says Goto Dengo.

"He was an excellent worker," Noda says evenly.

"Perhaps when I am finished here, I can follow him to—wherever he was sent."

Noda grins. "Your work is only beginning. But I can say with confidence that when you are finished you will be reunited with your friend."

SEATTLE

LAWRENCE PRITCHARD WATERHOUSE'S WIDOW AND FIVE CHILdren agree that Dad did something in the war, and that's about all. Each of them seems to have a different 1950s B-movie, or 1940s Movietone newsreel, in his or her head, portraying a rather different set of events. There is not even agreement on whether he was in

the Army or the Navy, which seems like a pretty fundamental plot point
to Randy. Was he in Europe or Asia? Opinions differ. Grandma grew
up on an Outback sheep farm. One might therefore think that, at some
point in her life, she might have been an earthy cuss—the type of woman
who would not only remember which service her late husband had been
in but would be able to take down his rifle from the attic and field-strip
it blindfolded. But she had evidently spent something like seventy-five
percent of her waking hours in church (where she not only worshipped
but went to school and transacted essentially all of her social life), or in
transit thereto or therefrom, and her own parents quite explicitly did not
want her to wind up living on a farm, ramming her arm up livestock
vaginas and slapping raw steaks over the black eyes dished out by some
husband. Farming might have been an adequate sort of booby prize for
one or at most two of their sons, sort of a fallback for any offspring who
happened to suffer major head injuries or fall into chronic alcoholism.
But the real purpose of the cCmndh kids was to restore the past and
lost glories of the family, who allegedly had been major wool brokers
around the time of Shakespeare and well on their way to living in Ken-
sington and spelling their name Smith before some combination of
scrapie, long-term climatic change, nefandous conduct by jealous Outer
Qwghlmians, and a worldwide shift in fashions away from funny-smelling
thirty-pound sweaters with small arthropods living in them had driven
them all into honest poverty and then not-so-honest poverty and led to
their forcible transportation to Australia.

The point here being that Grandma was incarnated, indoctrinated, and
groomed by her Ma to wear stockings and lipstick and gloves in a big
city somewhere. The experiment had succeeded to the point where Mary
cCmndh could, at any point in her post-adolescent life, have prepared
and served high tea to the Queen of England on ten minutes' notice,
flawlessly, without having to even glance in a mirror, straighten up her
dwelling, polish any silver, or bone up on any etiquette. It had been a
standing joke among her male offspring that Mom could walk unescorted
into any biker bar in the world and simply by her bearing and appearance
cause all ongoing fistfights to be instantly suspended, all grubby elbows
to be removed from the bar, postures to straighten, salty language to be
choked off. The bikers would climb over one another's backs to take
her coat, pull her chair back, address her as ma'am, etc. Though it had
never been performed, this biker bar scene was like a whole sort of
virtual or notional comedy sketch that was a famous moment in entertainment for the Waterhouse family, like the Beatles on *Ed Sullivan* or
Belushi doing his samurai bit on *Saturday Night Live*. It was up there on

their mental videocassette shelves right next to their imaginary newsreels and B-movies of what the Patriarch had done in the war.

The bottom line was that the ability to run a house in the way Grandma was legendary or infamous for doing, to keep the personal grooming up to that standard, to send out a few hundred Christmas cards every year, each written in flawless fountain-pen longhand, etc., etc., that all of these things taken together took up as much space in her brain as, say mathematics might take up in a theoretical physicist's.

And so when it came to anything of a practical nature she was perfectly helpless, and probably always had been. Until she had gotten too old to drive, she had continued to tool around Whitman in the 1965 Lincoln Continental, which was the last vehicle her husband had purchased, from Whitman's Patterson Lincoln-Mercury, before his untimely death. The vehicle weighed something like six thousand pounds and had more moving parts than a silo full of Swiss watches. Whenever any of her offspring came to visit, someone would discreetly slip out to the garage to yank the dipstick, which would always be mysteriously topped up with clear amber-colored 10W40. It eventually turned out that her late husband had summoned the entire living male lineage of the Patterson family—four generations of them—into his hospital room and gathered them around his deathbed and wrought some kind of unspecified pact with them along the general lines of that, if at any point in the future, the tire pressure in the Lincoln dropped below spec or the maintenance in any other way lapsed, all of the Pattersons would not merely sacrifice their immortal souls, but literally be pulled out of meetings or lavatories and dragged off to hell on the spot, like Marlowe's Dr. Faustus. He knew that his wife had only the vaguest idea of what a tire was, other than something that from time to time a man would heroically jump out of the car and change while she sat inside the car admiring him. The world of physical objects seemed to have been made solely for the purpose of giving the men around Grandma something to do with their hands; and not, mind you, for any practical reason, but purely so that Grandma could twiddle those men's emotional knobs by reacting to how well or poorly they did it. Which was a fine setup as long as men were actually around, but not so good after Grandpa died. So guerilla mechanic teams had been surveilling Randy's grandmother ever since and occasionally swiping her Lincoln from the church parking lot on Sunday mornings and taking it down to Patterson's for sub rosa oil changes. The ability of the Lincoln to run flawlessly for a quarter of a century without maintenance—without even putting gasoline in the tank—had only confirmed Grandmother's opinions about the amusing superfluity of male pursuits.

In any event, what it all came down to was that Grandma, whose grasp of practical matters had only declined (if that was even possible) with advanced age, was not the sort of person you would go to for information about her late husband's war record. Defeating the Nazis was in the same category as changing a flat tire: an untidy business that men were expected to know how to do. And not just the men of yore, the supermen of her generation; Randy was expected to know about these things too. If the Axis reconstituted itself tomorrow, Grandma would expect Randy to be suited up behind the controls of a supersonic fighter plane the day after that. And Randy would sooner spiral into the ground at Mach 2 than bear her tidings that he wasn't up to the job.

Luckily for Randy, who has recently become intensely curious about Grandpa, an old suitcase has been unearthed. It's a rattan-and-leather thing, sort of a snappy Roaring Twenties number complete with some badly abraded hotel stickers plotting Lawrence Pritchard Waterhouse's migration from the Midwest to Princeton and back—which is completely filled with small black-and-white photographs. Randy's father dumps the contents out on a ping-pong table that inexplicably sits in the center of the rec room at Grandma's managed care facility, whose residents are about as likely to play ping-pong as they are to get their nipples pierced. The photos are messed out into several discrete piles which are in turn sorted through by Randy and his father and his aunts and uncles. Most of them are photos of the Waterhouse kids, so everyone's fascinated until they have found pictures of themselves at a couple of different ages. Then the pile of photos begins to look depressingly large. Lawrence Pritchard Waterhouse was evidently a shutterbug of sorts and now his offspring are paying the price.

Randy has a different set of motives, and so he stays there late, going through pictures by himself. Ninety-nine out of a hundred are snapshots of Waterhouse brats from the 1950s. But some are older. He finds a photo of Grandpa in a place with palm trees, in a military uniform, with a big white disk-shaped officer's cap on his head. Three hours later he comes across a picture of a very young Grandpa, really just a turkey-necked adolescent costumed in grownup clothes, standing in front of a gothic building with two other men: a grinning dark-haired chap who looks vaguely familiar, and an aquiline blond fellow in rimless glasses. All three men have bicycles; Grandpa is straddling his, and the other two, perhaps considering this to be not so dignified, are supporting theirs with their hands. Another hour goes by, and then there's Grandpa in a khaki uniform with more palm trees in the background.

The next morning he sits down next to his grandmother, after she has finished her daily hourlong getting-out-of-bed ritual. "Grandmother, I found these two old photographs." He deals them out on the table in front of her and gives her a few moments to switch contexts. Grandma doesn't turn on a dime conversationally, and besides, those stiff old-lady corneas take a little while to shift focus.

"Yes, these are both Lawrence when he was in the service." Grandmother has always had this knack for telling people the obvious in a way that is scrupulously polite but that makes the recipient feel like a butthead for having wasted her time. By this point she is obviously tired of IDing photographs, a tedious job with an obvious subtext of "you're going to die soon and we were curious—who is this lady standing next to the Buick?"

"Grandmother," Randy says brightly, trying to rouse her interest, "in this photo here, he is wearing a Navy uniform. And in this photo here, he is wearing an Army uniform."

Grandma Waterhouse raises her eyebrows and looks at him with the synthetic interest she would use if she were at a formal affair of some kind, and some man she'd just met tried to give her a tutorial on tire-changing.

"It is, uh, I think, kind of unusual," Randy says, "for a man to be in both the Army and the Navy during the same war. Usually it's one or the other."

"Lawrence had both an Army uniform and a Navy uniform," Grandmother says, in the same tone she'd used to say he had both a small intestine and a large intestine, "and he would wear whichever one was appropriate."

"Of course he would," Randy says.

The laminar wind is gliding over the highway like a crisp sheet being stripped from a bed, and Randy's finding it hard to keep the Acura on the pavement. The wind isn't strong enough to blow the car around, but it obscures the edges of the road; all he can see is this white, striated plane sliding laterally beneath him. His eye tells him to steer into it, which would be a bad idea since it would take him and Amy straight into the lava fields. He tries to focus on a distant point: the white diamond of Mount Rainier, a couple of hundred kilometers west.

"I don't even know when they got married," Randy says. "Isn't that horrible?"

"September of 1945," Amy says. "I dragged it out of her.'

"Wow."

"Girl talk."

"I didn't know you were even rigged for girl talk."

"We can all do it."

"Did you learn anything else about the wedding? Like—"

"The china pattern?"

"Yeah."

"It was in fact Lavender Rose," Amy says.

"So it fits. I mean, it fits *chronologically*. The submarine went down in May of 1945 off of Palawan—four months before the wedding. Knowing my grandmother, wedding preparations would have been well advanced by that point—they definitely would have settled on a china pattern."

"And you think you have a photo of your grandpa in Manila around that time?"

"It's definitely Manila. And Manila wasn't liberated until March of '45."

"So what do we have, then? Your grandpa must've had some kind of connection with someone on that U-boat, between March and May."

"A pair of eyeglasses was found on the U-boat." Randy pulls a photo out of his shirt pocket and hands it across to Amy. "I'd be interested to know if they match the specs on that guy. The tall blond."

"I can check it out when I go back. Is the geek on the left your grandpa?"

"Yeah."

"Who's the geek in the middle?"

"I think it's Turing."

"Turing, as in *TURING Magazine*?"

"They named the magazine after him because he did a lot of early work with computers," Randy says.

"Like your grandpa did."

"Yeah."

"How about this guy we're going to see in Seattle? He's a computer guy too? Ooh, you're getting this look on your face like 'Amy just said something so stupid it caused me physical pain.' Is this a common facial expression among the men of your family? Do you think it is the expression that your grandfather wore when your grandmother came home and announced that she had backed the Lincoln Continental into a fire hydrant?"

"I am sorry if I make you feel bad sometimes," Randy says. "The family is full of scientists. Mathematicians. The least intelligent of us become engineers. Which is sort of what I am."

"Excuse me, did you just say you were one of the least intelligent?"

"Least focused, maybe."

"Hmmmm."

"My point is that precision, and getting things right, in the mathematical sense, is the one thing we have going for us. Everyone has to have a way of getting ahead, right? Otherwise you end up working at McDonald's your whole life, or worse. Some are born rich. Some are born into a big family like yours. We make our way in the world by knowing that two plus two equals four, and sticking to our guns in a way that is kind of nerdy and that maybe hurts people's feelings sometimes. I'm sorry."

"Hurts whose feelings? People who think that two plus two equals five?"

"People who put a higher priority on social graces than on having every statement uttered in a conversation be literally true."

"Like, for example . . . female people?"

Randy grinds his teeth for about a mile, and then says, "If there is any generalization at all that you can draw about how men think versus how women think, I believe it is that men can narrow themselves down to this incredibly narrow laser-beam focus on one tiny little subject and think about nothing else."

"Whereas women can't?"

"I suppose women *can*. They rarely seem to *want* to. What I'm characterizing here, as the female approach, is essentially saner and healthier."

"Hmmmm."

"See, you are being a little paranoid here and focusing on the negative too much. It's not about how women are deficient. It's more about how men are deficient. Our social deficiencies, lack of perspective, or whatever you want to call it, is what enables us to study one species of dragonfly for twenty years, or sit in front of a computer for a hundred hours a week writing code. This is not the behavior of a well-balanced and healthy person, but it can obviously lead to great advances in synthetic fibers. Or whatever."

"But you said that you yourself were not very focused."

"Compared to other men in my family, that's true. So, I know a little about astronomy, a lot about computers, a little about business, and I have, if I may say so, a slightly higher level of social functioning than the others. Or maybe it's not even *functioning,* just an acute awareness of when I'm *not* functioning, so that I at least know when to feel embarrassed."

Amy laughs. "You're definitely good at that. It seems like you sort of lurch from one moment of feeling embarrassed to the next."

Randy gets embarrassed.

"It's fun to watch," Amy says encouragingly. "It speaks well of you."

"What I'm saying is that this does set me apart. One of the most frightening things about your true nerd, for many people, is not that he's socially inept—because everybody's been *there*—but rather his complete lack of embarrassment about it."

"Which is still kind of pathetic."

"It was pathetic when they were in high school," Randy says. "Now it's something else. Something very different from pathetic."

"What, then?"

"I don't know. There is no word for it. You'll see."

Driving over the Cascades produces a climatic transition that would normally require a four-hour airplane flight. Warm rain spatters the windshield and loosens the rinds of ice on the wipers. The gradual surprises of March and April are compressed into a terse executive summary. It is about as tantalizing as a strip-tease video played on fast-forward. The landscape turns wet, and so green it's almost blue, and bolts straight up out of the soil in the space of about a mile. The fast lanes of Interstate 90 are strewn with brown snow turds melted loose from homebound skiers' Broncos. Semis plummet past them in writhing conical shrouds of water and stream. Randy's startled to see new office buildings halfway up the foothills, sporting high-tech logos. Then he wonders why he's startled. Amy has never been here, and she takes her feet down from the airbag deployment panel and sits up straight to look, wishing out loud that Robin and Marcus Aurelius had come along, instead of turning back towards Tennessee. Randy remembers to glide over into the right lanes and slow down as they shed the last thousand feet of altitude into Issaquah, and sure enough the highway patrol is out there ticketing speeders. Amy's duly impressed by this display of acumen. They are still miles outside of the city core, in the half-forested suburbs of the East Side, where street and avenue numbers are up in the triple digits, when Randy pulls onto an exit ramp and drives them down a long commercial strip that turns out to be just the sphere of influence of a big mall. Several satellite malls have burst from the asphalt all around it, wiping out old landmarks and screwing up Randy's navigation. Everything is crowded because people are out returning their Christmas gifts. After a little bit of driving around and cursing, Randy finds the core mall, which looks a little shabby compared to its satellites. He parks in the far corner of the lot, explaining that it is more logical to do this and then walk for fifteen seconds than it is to spend fifteen minutes looking for a closer space.

Randy and Amy stand behind the Acura's open trunk for a minute peeling off layers of suddenly gratuitous Eastern Washington insulation. Amy frets about her cousins and wishes that she and Randy had donated all of their cold-weather gear to them; when last seen they were circling the Impala like a pair of carrier-based fighter aircraft orbiting their mother ship in preparation for landing, checking tire pressures and fluid levels with an intensity, an alertness, that made it seem as if they were about to do something much more exciting than settle their asses into bucket seats and drive east for a couple of days. They have a gallant style about them that must knock the girls dead back home. Amy hugged them both passionately, as if she'd never see them again, and they accepted her hugs with dignity and forbearance, and then they were gone; resisting the urge to lay a patch until they were a couple of blocks distant.

They go into the mall. Amy still wondering aloud why they are here, but game. Randy is a little bit turned around, but eventually homes in on a dimly heard electronic cacophony—digitized voices prophesying war—and emerges into the mall's food court. Navigating now partly by sound and partly by smell, he comes to the corner where a lot of males, ranging from perhaps ten to forty years old, are seated in small clusters, some extracting quivering chopstick-loads of Szechuan from little white boxes but most fixated on what, from a distance, looks like some kind of paperwork. As backdrop, the ultraviolet maw of a vast game arcade spews digitized and sound-lab-sweetened detonations, whooshes, sonic booms and Gatling farts. But the arcade seems nothing more than a defunct landmark around which has gathered this intense cult of paperwork-hobbyists. A wiry teenager in tight black jeans and a black t-shirt prowls among the tables with the provocative confidence of a pool hustler, a long skinny cardboard box slung over his shoulder like a rifle. "These are my ethnic group," Randy explains in response to the look on Amy's face. "Fantasy role-playing gamers. This is Avi and me ten years ago."

"They look like they're playing cards." Amy looks again, and wrinkles her nose. "Weird cards." Amy barges curiously into the middle of a four-nerd game. Almost anywhere else, the appearance of a female with discernible waist among these guys would cause some kind of a stir. Their eyes would at least travel rudely up and down her body. But these guys only think about one thing: the cards in their hands, each contained in a clear plastic sleeve to keep it mint condition, each decorated with a picture of a troll or wizard or some other leaf on the post-Tolkienian evolutionary tree, and printed on the back with elaborate rules. Mentally, these guys are not in a mall on the East Side of greater Seattle. They are on a mountain pass trying to kill each other with edged weapons and numinous fire.

The young hustler is sizing Randy up as a potential customer. His box is long enough to contain a few hundred cards, and it looks heavy. Randy would not be surprised to learn something depressing about this kid, like that he makes so much money from buying cards low and selling them high that he owns a brand-new Lexus he's too young to drive. Randy catches his eye and asks, "Chester?"

"Bathroom."

Randy sits down and watches Amy watching the nerds play their game. He thought he'd hit bottom in Whitman, out there on the parking lot, that surely she would get scared and flee. But this is potentially worse. A bunch of tubby guys who never go outside, working themselves into a frenzy over elaborate games in which nonexistent characters go out and do pretend things that mostly are not as interesting as what Amy, her father, and various other members of her family do all the time without making any fuss about it. It is almost like Randy is deliberately hammering away at Amy trying to find out when she'll break and run. But her lip hasn't started to writhe nauseously yet. She's watching the game impartially, peeking over the nerds' shoulders, following the action, occasionally squinting at some abstraction in the rules.

"Hey, Randy."

"Hey, Chester."

So Chester's back from the bathroom. He looks exactly like the Chester of old, except spread out over a somewhat larger volume, like the classic demo of the expanding-universe theory in which a face, or some other figure, is drawn on a partly inflated balloon which is then inflated some more. The pores have gotten larger, and the individual shafts of hair farther apart, which produces an illusion of impending baldness. It seems like even his eyes have gotten farther apart and the flecks of color in the irises grown into blotches. He is not necessarily fat—he has the same rumpled heftiness he used to. Since people do not literally grow after their late teens, this must be an illusion. Older people seem to take up a larger space in the room. Or maybe older people see more.

"How's Avid?"

"As avid as ever," Randy says, which is lame but obligatory. Chester is wearing a sort of photographer's vest with a gratuitous number of small pockets, each of which is stuffed with gaming cards. Maybe that's why he seems big. He has like twenty pounds of cards strapped to him. "I note that you have made the transition to card-based RPGs," Randy says.

"Oh, yeah! It is so much better than the old pencil-and-paper way. Or even computer-mediated RPGs, with all due respect to the fine work that you and Avi did. What are you working on now?"

"Something that might actually be relevant to this," Randy says. "I was just realizing that if you have a set of cryptographic protocols suitable for issuing an electronic currency that cannot be counterfeited—which oddly enough we do—you could adapt those same protocols to card games. Because each one of these cards is like a banknote. Some more valuable than others."

Chester nods all the way through this, but does not rudely interrupt Randy as a younger nerd would. Your younger nerd takes offense quickly when someone near him begins to utter declarative sentences, because he reads into it an assertion that he, the nerd, does not already know the information being imparted. But your older nerd has more self-confidence, and besides, understands that frequently people need to think out loud. And highly advanced nerds will furthermore understand that uttering declarative sentences whose contents are already known to all present is part of the social process of making conversation and therefore should not be construed as aggression under any circumstances. "It's already being done," Chester says, when Randy's finished. "In fact, that company you and Avi worked for in Minneapolis is one of the leaders—"

"I'd like you to meet my friend, Amy," Randy interrupts, even though Amy is a good distance away, and not paying attention. But Randy is afraid that Chester's about to tell him that stock in that Minneapolis company is now up to the point where its market capitalization exceeds that of General Dynamics, and that Randy should've held onto his shares. "Amy, this is my friend Chester," Randy says, leading Chester between tables. At this point some of the gamers actually do look up interestedly—not at Amy, but at Chester, who (Randy infers) has probably got some one-of-a-kind cards tucked away in that vest, like THE THERMONUCLEAR ARSENAL OF THE UNION OF SOVIET SOCIALIST REPUBLICS or YHWH. Chester exhibits a marked improvement in social skills, shaking Amy's hand with no trace of awkwardness and dropping smoothly into a pretty decent imitation of a mature and well-rounded individual engaging in polite small talk. Before Randy knows it, Chester has invited them over to his house.

"I heard it wasn't done yet," Randy says.

"You must've seen the article in *The Economist,*" Chester says.

"That's right."

"If you'd seen the article in *The New York Times*, you'd know that the article in *The Economist* was wrong. I am now living in the house."

"Well, it'd be fun to see it," Randy says.

"Notice how well-paved my street is?" Chester says sourly, half an hour later. Randy has parked his hammered and scraped Acura in the guest parking lot of Chester's house and Chester has parked his 1932 Dusenberg roadster in the garage, between a Lamborghini and some other vehicle that would appear to be literally an aircraft, built to hover on ducted fans.

"Uh, I can't say that I did," Randy says, trying not to gape at anything. Even the pavement under his feet is some kind of custom-made mosaic of Penrose tiles. "I sort of vaguely remember it as being broad and flat and not having any chuckholes. Well-paved, in other words."

"This," Chester says, head-faking towards his house, "was the first house to trigger the LOHO."

"LOHO?"

"The Ludicrously Oversized Home Ordinance. Some malcontents rammed it through the city council. You get these, like cardiovascular surgeons and trust-fund parasites who like to have big nice houses, but God forbid some dirty hacker should try to build a house of his own, and send a few cement trucks down their street occasionally."

"They made you repave the street?"

"They made me repave half the fucking town," Chester says. "I mean, some of the neighbors were griping that the house was an eyesore, but after we got off on the wrong foot my attitude was, to hell with 'em." Indeed, Chester's house does resemble nothing so much as a regional trucking hub with a roof made entirely of glass. He waves his arm down a patchily turfed slab of mud that slopes down into Lake Washington. "Obviously the landscaping hasn't even begun yet. So it looks like a science fair project on erosion."

"I was going to say the Battle of the Somme," Randy says.

"Not as good an analogy because there are no trenches," Chester says. He is still pointing down towards the lake. "But if you look near the waterline you can just make out some railroad ties, half-buried. That's where we laid the tracks."

"Tracks?" Amy says, the only word she's been able to get out of her mouth since Randy drove his Acura through the main gate. Randy told her, on the way over here, that if he, Randy, had a hundred thousand dollars for every order of magnitude by which Chester's net worth currently exceeds his, then he (Randy) would never have to work again. This turned out to be more clever than informative, and so Amy was not prepared for what they have found here and is still steepling her eyebrows.

"For the locomotive," Chester says. "There are no railway lines nearby, so we barged the locomotive in and then winched it up a short railway into the foyer."

Amy just scrunches up her face, silent.

"Amy hasn't seen the articles," Randy says.

"Oh! Sorry," Chester says, "I'm into obsolete technology. The house is a museum of dead tech. Stick your hand into these things."

Lined up before the front entrance are four waist-high pedestals, emblazoned with the Novus Ordo Seclorum eyeball/pyramid logo, with outlines of hands stenciled onto their lids, and knobs in the lagoons between the fingers. Randy fits his hand into place and feels the knobs slide in their grooves, reading and memorizing the geometry of his hand. "The house knows who you are now," Chester says, typing their names into a ruggedized, weatherproofed keyboard, "and I'm giving you a certain privilege constellation that I use for personal guests—now you can come in through the main gate and park your car and wander around the grounds whether or not I'm home. And you can enter the house if I'm home, but if I'm not home, it'll be locked to you. And you can wander freely in the house except for certain offices where I keep proprietary corporate documents."

"You have your own company or something?" Amy says weakly.

"No. After Randy and Avi left town, I dropped out of college and snagged a job with a local company, which I still have," Chester says.

The front door, a translucent crystal slab on a track, slides open. Randy and Amy follow Chester into his house. As advertised, there is a full-scale steam locomotive in the foyer.

"The house is patterned after flex-space," Chester says.

"What's that?" Amy asks. She is completely turned off by the locomotive.

"A lot of high-tech companies get started in flex-space, which just means a big warehouse with no internal walls or partitions—just a few pillars to hold up the ceiling. You can drag partitions around to divide it up into rooms."

"Like cubicles?"

"Same idea, but the partitions go up higher so you have a feeling of being in a real room. Of course, they don't go all the way up to the ceiling. Otherwise, there wouldn't be room for the TWA."

"The what?" Amy asks. Chester, who is leading them into the maze of partitions, answers the question by tilting his head back and looking straight up.

The roof of the house is made entirely of glass, held up by a trusswork of white painted steel tubes. It is maybe forty or fifty feet above the floor. The partitions rise to a height of maybe twelve feet. In the gap above the partitions and below the ceiling, a grid has been constructed, a scaffolding of red pipes, nearly as vast as the house itself. Thousands, millions, of aluminum shreds are trapped in that space grid, like torn tufts caught in a three-dimensional screen. It looks like an artillery shell the length of a football field that has exploded into shrapnel a microsecond ago and been frozen in place; light filters through the metal scraps, trickles down bundles of shredded wiring and glances flatly off the crusts of melted and hardened upholstery. It is so vast and so close that when Amy and Randy first look up at it they flinch, expecting it to fall on them. Randy already knows what it is. But Amy has to stare at it for a long time, and prowl from room to room, viewing it from different angles, before it takes shape in her mind, and becomes recognizable as something familiar: a 747.

"The FAA and NTSB were surprisingly cool about it," Chester muses. "Which makes sense. I mean, they've reconstructed this thing in a hangar, right? Dredged up all the pieces, figured out where they go, and hung them on this grid. They've gone over it and gathered all the forensic evidence they could find, hosed out all the human remains and disposed of them properly, sterilized the debris so that the crash investigation team doesn't have to worry about getting AIDS from touching a bloody flange or something. And they're done with it. And they're paying like rent on this hangar. They can't throw it away. They have to store it somewhere. So all I had to do was get the house certified as a federal warehouse, which was a pretty easy legal hack. And if there's a lawsuit, I have to let the lawyers in to go over it. But really it was not a problem to do this. The Boeing guys love it, they're over here all the time."

"It's like a resource to them," Randy guesses.

"Yeah."

"You like to play that role."

"Sure! I have defined a privilege constellation specifically for engineer types who can come here anytime they want to access the house as a museum of dead tech. That's what I mean by the flex space analogy. To me and my guests, it's a home. To these visitors . . . there's one right there." Chester waves his arm across the room (it is a central room maybe fifty meters on a side) at an engineer type who has set up a

Hasselblad on a huge tripod and is pointing it straight up at a bent landing gear strut ". . . to them it's exactly like a museum in that there are places they can go and other places that if they step over the line will set off alarms and get them in trouble."

"Is there a gift shop?" Amy jokes.

"The gift shop is roughed in, but not up and running—the LOHO throws up all kinds of impediments," Chester grumbles.

They end up in a relatively cozy glass-walled room with a view across the churned mud to the lake. Chester fires up an espresso machine that looks like a scale model of an oil refinery and generates a brace of lattes. This room happens to be underneath the TWA's left wing tip, which is relatively intact. Randy realizes, now, that the entire plane has been hung in a gentle banking attitude, like it's making an imperceptible course change, which is not really appropriate; a vertical dive would make more sense, but then the house would have to be fifty stories high to accommodate it. He can see a repeating pattern of tears in the wing's skin that seems to be an expression of the same underlying math that generates repeating vortices in a wake, or swirls in a Mandelbrot set. Charlene and his friends used to heckle him for being a Platonist, but everywhere he goes he sees the same few ideal forms shadowed in the physical world. Maybe he's just stupid or something.

The house lacks a woman's touch. Randy gathers, from hints dropped by Chester, that the TWA has not turned out to be the conversation starter that he had hoped it would be. He is considering building fake ceilings over some of the house's partitions so that they will feel more like rooms, which, he admits, might make "some people" feel more comfortable there and open the possibility of their committing themselves to "an extended stay." So evidently he is in early negotiations with some kind of female, which is good news.

"Chester, two years ago you sent me e-mail about a project you were launching to build replicas of early computers. You wanted information about my grandfather's work."

"Yeah," Chester says. "You want to see that stuff? It's been on the back burner, but—"

"I just inherited some of his notebooks," Randy says.

Chester's eyebrows go up. Amy glances out the window; her hair, skin, and clothes take on a pronounced reddish tinge from Doppler effect as she drops out of the conversation at relativistic velocity.

"I want to know if you have a functioning ETC card reader."

Chester snorts. "That's all?"

"That's all."

"You want a 1932 Mark III card reader? Or a 1938 Mark IV? Or a—"

"Does it make any difference? They all read the same cards, right?"

"Yeah, pretty much."

"I have some cards from circa 1945 that I would like to have read out onto a floppy disk that I can take home."

Chester picks up a cellphone the size of a gherkin and begins to prod it. "I'll call my card man," he says. "Retired ETC engineer. Lives on Mercer Island. Comes up here on his boat a couple times a week and tinkers with this stuff. He'll be really excited to meet you."

While Chester is conversing with his card man, Amy meets Randy's eyes and gives him a look that is almost perfectly unreadable. She seems a bit deflated. Worn down. Ready to go home. Her very unwillingness to show her feelings confirms this. Before this trip, Amy would have agreed that it takes all kinds to make a world. She'd still assent to it now. But Randy's been showing her some practical applications of that concept, in the last few days, that are going to take her a while to fit into her world-view. Or, more importantly, into her Randy-view. And sure enough, the moment Chester's off the phone, she's asking if she can use it to call the airlines. There is only a momentary upward flick of the eyes towards the TWA. And once Chester gets over his astonishment that anyone still uses voice technology to make airline reservations in this day and age, he takes her to the nearest computer (there is a fully outfitted UNIX machine in every room) and patches into the airline databases directly and begins searching for the optimal route back home. Randy goes and stares out the window at the chilly whitecaps slapping the mud shore and fights the urge to just stay here in Seattle, which is a town where he could be very happy. Behind him Chester and Amy keep saying "Manila," and it sounds ridiculously exotic and hard to reach. Randy thinks that he is marginally smarter than Chester and would be even richer if he'd only stayed here.

A fast white boat comes larruping around the point from the direction of Mercer Island and banks towards him. Randy sets down his cold coffee and goes out to his car and retrieves a certain trunk—a lovely gift from a delighted Aunt Nina. It is full of certain old treasures, like his grandfather's high school physics notebooks. He sets aside (for example) a box labeled HARVARD-WATERHOUSE PRIME FACTORING CHALLENGE '49-52 to reveal a stack of bricks, neatly wrapped in paper that has gone gold with age, each consisting of a short stack of ETC cards, and each labeled ARETHUSA INTERCEPTS with a date from 1944 or '45. They have been in suspended animation for more than fifty years, stored on a dead medium, and now Randy is going to breathe life into them again, and maybe send them out on the Net, a few strands of fossil DNA broken out of their amber shells and released in the world again.

Probably they will fail and die, but if they flourish, it should make Randy's life a little more interesting. Not that it's devoid of interest now, but it is easier to introduce new complications than to resolve the old ones.

ROCK

BUNDOK IS GOOD ROCK; WHOEVER PICKED IT MUST HAVE known this. That basalt is so strong that Goto Dengo can carve into it any system of tunnels that he desires. As long as he observes a few basic engineering principles, he need not worry about tunnels collapsing.

Of course, cutting holes into such rock is hard work. But Captain Noda and Lieutenant Mori have provided him with an unlimited supply of Chinese laborers. At first the chatter of their drills drowns out the sounds of the jungle. Later, as they burrow into the earth, it fades to a thick tamping beat, leaving only the buzzing drone of the air compressors. Even at night they work by the dim light of lanterns, which cannot penetrate the canopy overhead. Not that MacArthur is sending observation planes over Luzon in the middle of the night, but work lights shining up on the mountain would be noticed by the lowland Filipinos.

The inclined shaft connecting the bottom of Lake Yamamoto to Golgotha is by far the longest part of the complex, but it need not have a very great diameter: just big enough for a single worker to worm his way up to the end and operate his drill. Before the lake is created, Goto Dengo has a crew dig the extreme upper end of that shaft, tunneling out and down from the riverbank with a dip angle of some twenty degrees. This excavation continually fills up with water—it is effectively a well—and removing the waste rock is murder, because it all has to be hauled uphill. So when it has proceeded for some five meters, Goto Dengo has the opening sealed up with stones and mortar.

Then he has the latrines filled in, and the area around the lake cleared of workers. They can do nothing now but contaminate the place with evidence. Summer has arrived, the rainy season on Luzon, and he is worried that rain will find the ruts worn into the soil by the Chinese workers' feet and turn them into gullies, impossible to conceal. But the unusually dry weather holds, and vegetation rapidly takes root on the bare ground.

Goto Dengo is faced with a challenge that would seem familiar to the designer of a garden back home: he needs to create an artificial formation that seems natural. It needs to look as though a boulder rolled down the mountain after an earthquake and wedged itself in a bottleneck of the Yamamoto River. Other rocks, and the logs of dead trees, piled up against it, forming a natural dam that created the lake.

He finds the boulder he needs sitting in the middle of the riverbed about a kilometer upstream. Dynamite would only shatter it, and so he brings in a stout crew of workers with iron levers, and they get it rolling. It goes a few meters and stops.

This is discouraging, but the workers have the idea now. Their leader is Wing—the bald Chinese man who helped Goto Dengo bury the corpse of Lieutenant Ninomiya. He has the mysterious physical strength that seems to be common among bald men, and he has a kind of mesmerizing leadership power over the other Chinese. He somehow manages to get them excited about moving the boulder. Of course, they have to move it, because Goto Dengo has let it be known that he wants it moved, and if they don't, Lieutenant Mori's guards will shoot them on the spot. But above and beyond this, they seem to welcome the challenge. Certainly standing in cool running water beats working down in the mineshafts of Golgotha.

The boulder is in place three days later. The water divides around it. More boulders follow, and the river begins to pool. Trees do not naturally sprout from lakes, and so Goto Dengo has workers fell the ones that are standing here—not with axes, though. He shows them how to excavate the roots one at a time, like archaeologists digging up a skeleton, so that it looks as if the trees were uprooted during a typhoon. These are piled up against the boulders, and smaller stones and gravel follow. Suddenly the level of Lake Yamamoto begins to rise. The dam leaks, but the leaks peter out as more gravel and clay are dumped in behind it. Goto Dengo is not above plugging troublesome holes with sheets of tin, as long as it's down where no one will ever see it. When the lake has reached its desired level, the only sign it's manmade is a pair of wires trailing up onto its shore, rooted in demolition charges molded into the concrete plug on its bottom.

Golgotha is cut into a ridge of basalt that is flung out from the base of the mountain—like a buttress root from the trunk of a jungle tree— that separates the watersheds of the Yamamoto and Tojo Rivers. Moving southwards from the summit of Calvary, then, one would pass through the teeming bowl of its extinct crater first, over the remains of its southern rim, and then onto the gradual downward slope of a much larger mountain on which Calvary's cinder cone is just a blemish, like a wart on a nose. The small Yamamoto River runs generally parallel to the Tojo on the other side of the basalt ridge, but descends more gradually, so that its elevation gets higher and higher above that of the Tojo River as both work their way down the mountain. At the site of Lake Yama-moto, it is fifty meters above the Tojo. By drilling the connecting tunnel in a southeasterly direction rather than straight east underneath the ridge, one can bypass a chain of rapids and a waterfall on the Tojo which drop that river's elevation to almost a hundred meters beneath the bottom of the lake.

When The General comes to inspect the works, Goto Dengo aston-ishes him by taking him up the Tojo River in the same Mercedes he used to drive down from Manila. By this point, the workers have constructed a single-lane road that leads from the prison camp up the rocky bed of the river to Golgotha. "Fortune has smiled on our endeavor by giving us a dry summer," Goto Dengo explains. "With the water low, the riverbed makes an ideal roadway—the rise in altitude is gentle enough for the heavy trucks that we will be bringing in. When we are finished, we will create a low dam near the site that will conceal the most obvious signs of our work. When the river rises to its normal height, there will be no visible trace that men were ever here."

"It is a good idea," The General concedes, then mumbles something to his aide about using the same technique at the other sites. The aide nods and *hai*s and writes it down.

A kilometer into the jungle, the banks rise up into vertical walls of stone that climb higher and higher above the water's level until they actually overhang the river. There is a hollow in the stony channel where the river broadens out; just upstream is the waterfall. At this point the road makes a left turn directly into the rock wall, and stops. Everyone gets out of the Mercedes: Goto Dengo, The General, his aide, and Cap-tain Noda. The river runs over their feet, ankle-deep.

A mouse-hole has been dug into the rock here. It has a flat bottom and an arched ceiling. A six-year-old could stand upright in here, but anyone taller will have to stoop. A pair of iron rails runs into the opening. "The main drift," says Goto Dengo.

"This is it?"

"The opening is small so that we can conceal it later," Captain Noda explains, cringing, "but it gets wider inside."

The General looks pissed off and nods. Led by Goto Dengo, all four men squat and duck-walk into the tunnel, pushed by a steady current of air. "Notice the excellent ventilation," Captain Noda enthuses, and Goto Dengo grins proudly.

Ten meters in, they are able to stand up. Here, the drift has the same vaulted shape, but it's six feet high and six wide, buttressed by reinforced-concrete arches that they have poured in wooden forms on the floor. The iron rails run far away into blackness. A train of three mine cars sits on them—sheet metal boxes filled with shattered basalt. "We remove waste by hand tramming," Goto Dengo explains. "This drift, and the rails, are perfectly level, to keep the cars from running out of control."

The General grunts. Clearly he has no respect for the intricacies of mine engineering.

"Of course, we will use the same cars to move the, er, material into the vault when it arrives," Captain Noda says.

"Where did this waste come from?" The General demands. He is pissed off that they are still digging at this late stage.

"From our longest and most difficult tunnel—the inclined shaft to the bottom of Lake Yamamoto," says Goto Dengo. "Fortunately, we can continue to extend that shaft even while the material is being loaded into the vault. Outgoing cars will carry waste from the shaft work, incoming cars will carry the *materiél*."

He stops to thrust his finger into a drill hole in the ceiling. "As you can see, all of the holes are ready for the demolition charges. Not only will those charges bring down the ceiling, but they will leave the surrounding rock so rotten as to make horizontal excavation very difficult."

They walk down the main drift for fifty meters. "We are in the heart of the ridge now," Goto Dengo says, "halfway between the two rivers. The surface is a hundred meters straight up." In front of them, the string of electric lights terminates in blackness. Goto Dengo gropes for a wall switch.

"The vault," he says, and hits the switch.

The tunnel has abruptly broadened into a flat-bottomed chamber with an arched ceiling, shaped like a Quonset hut, lined with concrete, the concrete massively ribbed every couple of meters. The floor of the vault is perhaps the size of a tennis court. The only opening is a small vertical shaft rising up from the middle of the ceiling, just barely big enough to contain a ladder and a human body.

The General folds his arms and waits while the aide goes around with a tape measure, verifying the dimensions.

"We go up," says Goto Dengo, and, without waiting for The General to bristle, mounts the ladder up into the shaft. It only goes up for a few meters, and then they are in another drift with another narrow-gauge railway on the floor. This one's shored up with timbers hewn from the surrounding jungle.

"The haulage level, where we move rock around," Goto Dengo explains, when they have all convened at the top of the ladder. "You asked about the waste in those cars. Let me show you how it got there." He leads the group down the tracks for twenty or thirty meters, past a train of battered cars. "We are headed northwest, towards Lake Yamamoto."

They reach the end of the drift, where another narrow shaft pierces the ceiling. A fat reinforced hose runs up into it, compressed air keening out through tiny leaks. The sound of drills can be heard, from very far away. "I would not recommend that you look up this shaft, because stray rocks occasionally come down from where we are working," he warns. "But if you looked straight up, you would see that, about ten meters above us, this shaft comes up into the floor of a narrow inclined shaft that goes uphill that way—" he motions northwest "—towards the lake, and downhill that way—" He turns a hundred and eighty degrees, back towards the vault.

"Toward the fool's chamber," The General says, with relish.

"Hai!" answers Goto Dengo. "As we extend the shaft up toward the lake, we rake the broken rock downhill with an iron hoe drawn by a winch, and when it reaches the top of this vertical shaft that you see here, it falls down into waiting cars. From here we can drop it down into the main vault and from there hand-tram it to the exit."

"What are you doing with all the waste?" asks The General.

"Spreading some of it down the riverbed, using it to make the roadway that we drove up on. Some of it is stored above to backfill various ventilation shafts. Some is being crushed into sand for a trap which I will explain later." Goto Dengo leads them back in the direction of the main vault, but they pass by the ladder and turn into another drift, then another. Then the drifts become narrow and cramped again, like the one at the entrance. "Please forgive me for leading you into what seems like a three-dimensional maze," Goto Dengo says. "This part of Golgotha is intentionally confusing. If a thief ever manages to break into the fool's chamber from above, he will expect to find a drift through which the material was loaded into it. We have left one there for him to find—a false drift that seems to lead away toward the Tojo River. Actually, a whole complex of false drifts and shafts that will all be demolished by dynamite when we are finished. It will be so difficult, not to mention dangerous, for the thief to work his way through so much rotten rock, that he will probably be satisfied with what he finds in the fool's chamber."

He keeps pausing and looking back at The General, expecting him to tire of this, but clearly the general is getting a second wind. Captain Noda, taking up the rear, gestures him onwards impatiently.

The maze takes some time to negotiate and Goto Dengo, like a prestidigitator, tries to fill up the time with some convincing patter. "As I'm sure you understand, shafts and drifts must be engineered to counteract lithostatic forces."

"What?"

"They must be strong enough to support the rock overhead. Just as a building must be strong enough to hold up its own roof."

"Of course," says The General.

"If you have two parallel drifts, one above the other like storeys in a building, then the rock in between them—the floor or the ceiling, depending on which way you look at it—must be thick enough to support itself. In the structure we are walking through, the rock is just barely thick enough. But when the demolition charges have been set off, the rock will be shattered so that reconstructing these drifts will be a physical impossibility."

"Excellent!" says The General, and again tells his aide to make a note of it—apparently so that the other Goto Dengos in the other Golgothas can do the same.

At one point a drift has been plugged by a wall made of rubble stuck together with mortar. Goto Dengo shines his lantern on it, lets the General see the iron rails disappearing beneath the masonry. "To a thief coming down from the fool's chamber, this will look like the main drift," he explains. "But if he demolishes that wall, he dies."

"Why?"

"Because on the other side of that wall is a shaft that connects to the Lake Yamamoto pipe. One blow from a sledgehammer and that wall will explode from the water pressure that will be on the other side of it. Then Lake Yamamoto rushes forth from that hole like a tsunami."

The General and his aide spend some time cackling over this one.

Finally they waddle down a drift into a vault, half the dimensions of the main vault, that is illuminated from above by dim bluish sky-light. Goto Dengo turns on some electric lights as well. "The fool's vault," he announces. He points up the vertical shaft in the ceiling. "Our ventilation has been courtesy of this." The General peers upwards and sees, a hundred meters above them, a circle of radiant green-blue jungle quartered by the spinning swastika of a big electric fan. "Of course, we would not want thieves to find the fool's chamber too easily or it wouldn't fool anyone. So we have added some features, up there, to make it interesting."

"What sorts of features?" asks Captain Noda, stepping crisply into his role as straight man.

"Anyone who attacks Golgotha will attack from above—to gain horizontal access, the distance is too great. This means they will have to tunnel downwards, either through fresh rock or through the column of rubble with which this ventilation shaft will be filled. In either case, they will discover, when they are about halfway down, a stratum of sand, three to five meters in depth, spread across the whole area. I need hardly remind you that, in nature, pockets of sand are never found in the middle of igneous rock!"

Goto Dengo begins climbing up the ventilation shaft. Halfway to the surface, it comes up into a network of small, rounded, interconnected chambers, whittled out of the rock, with fat pillars left in place to hold up the ceiling. The pillars are so thick and numerous that it's not possible to see very far, but when the others have arrived, and Goto Dengo begins leading them from room to room, they learn that this system of chambers extends for a considerable distance.

He takes them to a place where an iron manhole is set into a hole in the rock wall, sealed in place with tar. "There are a dozen of these," he says. "Each one leads to the Lake Yamamoto shaft—so pressurized water will be behind it. The only thing holding them in place right now is tar—obviously not enough to hold back the pressure of the lake water. But when we have filled these rooms with sand, the sand will hold the manholes in place. But if a thief breaks in and removes the sand, the manhole explodes out of its seat and millions of gallons of water force their way into his excavation."

From there, another climb up the shaft takes them to the surface, where Captain Noda's men are waiting to move the ventilation fan out of their way, and his aide is waiting with bottles of water and a pot of green tea.

They sit at a folding table and refresh themselves. Captain Noda and The General talk about goings-on in Tokyo—evidently The General just flew down from there a few days ago. The general's aide performs calculations on his clipboard.

Finally, they hike up over the top of the ridge to take a look at Lake Yamamoto. The jungle is so thick that they almost have to fall into it before they can see it. The General pretends to be surprised that it is an artificial body of water. Goto Dengo takes this as a high commendation. They stand, as people often will, at the edge of the water, and say nothing for a few minutes. The General smokes a cigarette, squinting through the smoke across the lake, and then turns to the aide and nods. This seems to communicate much to the aide, who turns to face Captain

Noda and pipes up with a question: "What is the total number of workers?"

"Now? Five hundred."

"The tunnels were designed with this assumption?"

Captain Noda shoots an uneasy look at Goto Dengo. "I reviewed Lieutenant Goto's work and found that it was compatible with that assumption."

"The quality of the work is the highest we have seen," the aide continues.

"Thank you!"

"Or expect to see," The General adds.

"As a result, we may wish to increase the amount of material stored at this site."

"I see."

"Also . . . the schedule may have to be greatly accelerated."

Captain Noda looks startled.

"He has landed on Leyte with a very great force," The General says bluntly, as if this had been expected for years.

"Leyte!? But that is so close."

"Precisely."

"It is insane," Noda raves. "The Navy will crush him—it is what we have been waiting for all these years! The Decisive Battle!"

The General and the aide stand uncomfortably for a few long moments, seemingly unable to speak. Then The General fixes Noda with a long, frigid stare. "The Decisive Battle was yesterday."

Captain Noda whispers, "I see." He suddenly looks about ten years older, and he is not at a point in his life where he can spare ten years.

"So. We may accelerate the work. We may bring more workers for the final phase of the operation," says the aide in a soft voice.

"How many?"

"The total may reach a thousand."

Captain Noda stiffens, grunts out a *"Hai!"* and turns towards Goto Dengo. "We will need more ventilation shafts."

"But sir, with all due respect, the complex is very well ventilated."

"We will need more deep, wide ventilation shafts," Captain Noda says. "Enough for an additional five hundred workers."

"Oh."

"Begin the work immediately."

THE MOST CIGARETTES

To: randy@epiphyte.com
From: cantrell@epiphyte.com
Subject: Pontifex Transform: tentative verdict
Randy,

I forwarded the Pontifex transform to the Secret Admirers mailing list as soon as you forwarded it to me, so it
has been rattling around there for a couple of weeks now.
Several very smart people have analyzed it for weaknesses, and found no obvious flaws. Everyone agrees that
the specific steps involved in this transform are a little
bit peculiar, and wonders who came up with them and how—
but that is not uncommon with good cryptosystems.

So the verdict, for now, is that root@euditorum.org
knows what he's doing—notwithstanding his strange fixa-
tion on the number 54.

—Cantrell

"Andrew Loeb," Avi says.

He and Randy are enduring some kind of a forced march up the
beach in Pacifica; Randy's not sure why. Over and over again, Randy
is surprised by Avi's physical vigor. Avi looks like he is wasting away
from some vague disease invented as a plot device by a screenwriter. He
is kind of tall, but this just makes him seem more perilously drawn out.
His slender body is a tenuous link between huge feet and a huge head;
he has the profile of a lump of silly putty that has been drawn apart until
the middle part is just a tendril. But he can stomp up a beach like a
Marine. It is January, after all, and according to the Weather Channel
there is this flume of water vapor originating in a tropical storm about
halfway between Nippon and New Guinea and jetting directly across the
Pacific and taking a violent left turn just about here. The waves thrashing
the beach, not that far away, are so big that Randy has to look slightly
upwards to see their crests.

He has been telling Avi all about Chester, and Avi has (Randy thinks) used
this as a segue into reminiscing about the old days back in Seattle. It is somewhat
unusual for Avi to do this; he tends to be very disciplined about having any
given conversation be either business or personal, but never both at once. "I'll

never forget," Randy says, "going up to the roof of Andrew's building to talk to him about the software, thinking to myself 'gosh, this is kind of fun,' and watching him just slowly and gradually go berserk before my eyes. It could almost make you believe in demonic possession."

"Well, his dad apparently believed in it," Avi says. "It was his dad, right?"

"It's been a long time. Yeah, I think it was his mom who was the hippie, who had him in this commune, and then his dad was the one who extracted him from there, forcibly—he brought in these paramilitary guys from Northern Idaho to actually do the job—they literally took Andrew out in a bag—and then put him through all kinds of repressed-memory therapy to prove that he'd been Satanically ritually abused."

This tweaks Avi's interest. "Do you think his dad was into the militia thing?"

"I only met him once. During the lawsuit. He took my deposition. He was just this Orange County white-shoe lawyer, in a big practice with a bunch of Asians and Jews and Armenians. So I assumed he was just using the Aryan Nations guys because they were convenient, and for sale."

Avi nods, apparently finding that a satisfactory hypothesis. "So he was probably not a Nazi. Did he believe in the Satanic ritual abuse?"

"I doubt it," Randy says. "Though after spending some time with Andrew I found it highly plausible. Do we have to talk about this? Gives me the creeps," Randy says. "Depresses me."

"I recently learned what became of Andrew," Avi says.

"I saw his web site a while ago."

"I'm speaking of very recent developments."

"Let me guess. Suicide?"

"Nope."

"Serial killer?"

"Nope."

"Thrown into prison for stalking someone?"

"He is not dead or in prison," Avi says.

"Hmmm. Is this anything to do with his hive mind?"

"Nope. Are you aware that he went to law school?"

"Yeah. Is this something to do with his legal career?"

"It is."

"Well, if Andrew Loeb is practicing law, it must be some really annoying and socially nonconstructive form of it. Probably something to do with suing people on light pretexts."

"Excellent," Avi says. "You're getting warm now."

"Okay, don't tell me, let me think," Randy says. "Is he practicing in California?"

"Yes."

"Oh, well, I've got it, then."

"You do?"

"Yes. Andrew Loeb would be one of these guys who gins up minority-shareholder lawsuits against high-tech companies."

Avi smiles with his lips pressed tightly together, and nods.

"He'd be perfect," Randy continues, "because he would be a true believer. He wouldn't think that he was just out there being an asshole. He would really, truly, sincerely believe that he was representing this class of shareholders who had been Satanically ritually abused by the people running the company. He would work thirty-six hours at a stretch digging up dirt on them. Corporate memories that had been repressed. No trick would be too dirty, because he would be on the side of righteousness. He would only sleep or eat under medical orders."

"I can see that you got to know him incredibly well," Avi says.

"Wow! So, whom is he suing at the moment?"

"Us," Avi says.

There is now this five-minute stoppage in the conversation, and in the hike, and possibly in some of Randy's neurological processes. The color map of his vision goes out of whack: everything's in extremely washed-out shades of yellow and purple. Like someone's clammy fingers are around his neck, modulating the flow in his carotids to the bare minimum needed to sustain life. When Randy finally returns to full consciousness, the first thing he does is to look down at his shoes, because he is convinced for some reason that he has sunk into the wet sand to his knees. But his shoes are barely making an impression on the firmly packed sand.

A big wave collapses into a sheet of foam that skims up the beach and divides around his feet.

"Gollum," Randy says.

"Was that an utterance, or some kind of physiological transient?" Avi says.

"Gollum. Andrew is Gollum."

"Well, Gollum is suing us."

"Us, as in you and me?" he asks. It takes Randy about a full minute of time to get these words around his tongue. "He's suing us over the game company?"

Avi laughs.

"It's possible!" Randy says. "Chester told me that the game company is now like the size of Microsoft or something."

"Andrew Loeb has filed a minority-shareholder lawsuit against the board of directors of Epiphyte(2) Corporation," Avi says.

Randy's body has now finally had time to deploy a full-on fight-or-flight reaction—part of his genetic legacy as a stupendous badass. This must have been very useful when saber-toothed tigers tried to claw their way into his ancestors' caves but is doing him absolutely no good in these circumstances.

"On behalf of whom?"

"Oh, come on, Randy. There aren't that many candidates."

"Springboard Capital?"

"You told me yourself that Andrew's dad was a white-shoe Orange County lawyer. Now, archetypally, where would a guy like that put his retirement money?"

"Oh, shit."

"That's right. Bob Loeb, Andrew's dad, got in on AVCLA very early. He and the Dentist have been sending each other Christmas cards for like twenty years. And so when Bob Loeb's idiot son graduated from law school, Bob Loeb, knowing full well that the kid was too much of a head case to be employable anywhere else, paid a call on Dr. Hubert Kepler, and Andrew's been working for him ever since."

"Fuck. Fuck!" Randy says. "All these years. Treading water."

"How's that?"

"That time in Seattle—during the lawsuit—was a fucking nightmare. I came out of it dead broke, without a house, without anything except a girlfriend and a knowledge of UNIX."

"Well, that's something," Avi says. "Normally those two are mutually exclusive."

"Shut up," Randy says, "I'm trying to agonize."

"Well, I think that agonizing is so fundamentally pathetic that it borders on funny," Avi says. "But please go ahead."

"Now, after all those years—all that fucking work—I'm back where I started. A net worth of zero. Except this time I don't even have a girlfriend per se."

"Well," Avi says, "to begin with, I think it's better to aspire to having Amy than to actually have Charlene."

"Ouch! You are a cruel man."

"Sometimes wanting is better than having."

"Well, that's good news," Randy says brightly, "because—"

"Look at Chester. Would you rather be Chester, or you?"

"Okay, okay."

"Also, you have a substantial amount of stock in Epiphyte, which I'm quite convinced is worth something."

"Well, that all depends on the lawsuit, right?" Randy says. "Have you actually seen any of the documents?"

"Of course I have," Avi says, irked. "I'm the president and CEO of the fucking corporation."

"Well, what's his beef? What's the pretext for the lawsuit?"

"Apparently the Dentist is convinced that Semper Marine has stumbled upon some kind of vast hoard of sunken war gold, as a direct byproduct of the work they did for us."

"He knows this, or he suspects this?"

"Well," Avi says, "reading between the lines, I gather that he only suspects it. Why do you ask?"

"Never mind for now—but he's going after Semper Marine, too?"

"No! That would rule out the lawsuit he's filing against Epiphyte."

"What do you mean?"

"His point is that if Epiphyte had been competently managed—if we had exercised due diligence—then we would have drawn up a much more thorough contract with Semper Marine than we did."

"We've got a contract with Semper Marine."

"Yes," Avi says, "and Andrew Loeb is disparaging it as little better than a handshake agreement. He asserts that we should have turned negotiations over to a big-time law firm with expertise in maritime and salvage law. That such a law firm would have anticipated the possibility that the sidescan solar plots created by Semper Marine for the cable project would reveal something like a sunken wreck."

"Oh, Jesus Christ!"

Avi gets a look of forced patience. "Andrew has produced, as exhibits, actual copies of actual contracts that other companies made in similar circumstances, which all contain such language. He argues it's practically boilerplate stuff, Randy."

"I.e., that it's gross negligence to have failed to put it in our contract with Semper."

"Precisely. Now, Andrew's lawsuit can't go anywhere unless there are some damages. Can you guess what the damages are in this case?"

"If we'd made a better contract, then Epiphyte would own a share of what is salvaged from the submarine. As it is, we, and the shareholders, get nothing. Which constitutes obvious damages."

"Andrew Loeb himself could not have put it any better."

"Well, what do they expect us to do about it? It's not like the corporation has deep pockets. We can't give them a cash settlement."

"Oh, Randy, it's not about that. It's not like the Dentist needs our cigar box full of petty cash. It's a control thing."

"He wants a majority share in Epiphyte."

"Yes. Which is a good thing!"

Randy throws back his head and laughs.

"The Dentist can have any company he wants," says Avi, "but he wants Epiphyte. Why? Because we are badass, Randy. We have got the Crypt contract. We have got the talent. The prospect of running the world's first proper data haven, and creating the world's first proper digital currency, is fantastically exciting."

"Well, I can't tell you how excited I am."

"You should never forget what a fundamentally strong position we are in. We are like the sexiest girl in the world. And all of this bad behavior on the Dentist's part is just his way of showing that he wants to mate with us."

"And control us."

"Yes. I'm sure that Andrew has been ordered to produce an outcome in which we are found negligent, and liable for damage. And then upon looking into our books the court will find that the damages exceed our ability to pay. At which point the Dentist will magnanimously agree to take his payment in the form of Epiphyte stock."

"Which will strike everyone as poetic justice because it will also enable him to take control of the company and make sure it's managed competently."

Avi nods.

"So, that's why he's not going up against Semper Marine. Because if he recovers anything from them, it renders his beef against us null and void."

"Right. Although, that would not prevent him from suing them later, after he's gotten what he wanted from us."

"So—Jesus! This is perverse," Randy says. "Every valuable item that the Shaftoes pull up from that wreck actually gets us in deeper trouble."

"Every nickel that the Shaftoes make is a nickel of damages that we allegedly inflicted on the shareholders."

"I wonder if we can get the Shaftoes to suspend the salvage operation."

"Andrew Loeb has no case against us," Avi says, "unless he can prove that the contents of that wreck are worth something. If the Shaftoes keep bringing stuff up, that's easy. If they stop bringing stuff up, then Andrew will have to establish the value of the wreck in some other way."

Randy grins. "That's going to be really difficult for him to do, Avi. The Shaftoes don't even know what's down there. Andrew probably doesn't even have the coordinates of the wreck."

"There is a latitude and longitude specified in the lawsuit."

"Fuck! To how many decimal places?"

"I don't remember. The precision didn't reach out and poke me in the eye."

"How the hell did the Dentist learn about this wreck? Doug has been trying to keep it secret. And he knows a few things about operational secrecy."

"You yourself told me," Avi says, "that the Shaftoes have brought in a German television producer. That doesn't sound like secrecy to me."

"But it is. They flew this woman into Manila, put her on board *Glory IV*. Allowed her to take minimal baggage. Went through her stuff to verify she didn't have a GPS. Took her out into the South China Sea and ran in circles for a while so she couldn't even use dead reckoning. Then took her to the site."

"I've been on *Glory*. It's got GPS readouts all over the place."

"No, they didn't let her see any of that stuff. There's no way a guy like Doug Shaftoe would screw this up."

"Well," Avi says, "the Germans aren't the most plausible source for the leak anyway. Do you remember the Bolobolos?"

"Filipino syndicate that used to pimp for Victoria Vigo, the Dentist's wife. Probably set up the liaison between her and Kepler. Hence, presumably, still has influence over the Dentist."

"I would phrase it differently. I would say that they have a long-standing relationship with the Dentist that probably works both ways. And I'm thinking that they got wind of the salvage operation somehow. Maybe a high-ranking Bolobolo overheard something in the German television producer's hotel. Maybe a low-ranking one has been keeping an eye on the Shaftoes, taking note of the special equipment they've been shipping in."

Randy nods. "That works. Supposedly the Bolobolos have a big presence at NAIA. They would notice something like an underwater ROV being rush-shipped to Douglas MacArthur Shaftoe. So I'll buy that."

"Okay."

"But that wouldn't give them the latitude and longitude."

"I'll bet you half of my valuable stock in Epiphyte Corp. That they used SPOT for that."

"SPOT? Oh. Rings a bell. French photo-imaging satellite?"

"Yeah. You can buy time on SPOT for a very reasonable fee. And it's got enough resolution to distinguish *Glory IV* from, say, a container-ship or an oil tanker. So all they had to do was wait until their spies on the waterfront told them that *Glory* was out to sea, outfitted for salvage work, and then use SPOT to locate them."

"What kind of precision can SPOT provide in terms of latitude and longitude?" Randy asks.

"That's a very good question. I'll have someone look into it," Avi says.

"If it's to within a hundred meters, then Andrew can find the wreck by just sending some people there. If it's much more than that, he'll have to go out and do a survey of his own."

"Unless he subpoenas the information from us," Avi says.

"I'd like to see Andrew Loeb go up against the Philippine legal system."

"You aren't in the Philippines—remember?"

Randy swallows and it comes out sounding like *gollum* again.

"Do you have any information about that wreck on your laptop?"

"If I do, it's encrypted."

"So he'll just subpoena your encryption key."

"What if I forget my encryption key?"

"Then it's further evidence of how incompetent you are as a manager."

"Still, it's better than—"

"What about e-mail?" Avi asks. "Have you ever sent the location of the wreck in an e-mail message? Have you ever put it into a file?"

"Probably. But it's all encrypted."

This doesn't seem to ease the sudden tension on Avi's face.

"Why do you ask?" Randy says.

"Because," Avi says, pivoting to face in the general direction of downtown Los Altos. "All of a sudden I am thinking about Tombstone."

"Through which passeth all of our e-mail," Randy says.

"On whose hard drives all of our files are stored," Avi says.

"Which is located in the State of California, within easy subpoena range."

"Suppose you cc'd all of us on the same e-mail message," Avi says. "Cantrell's software, running on Tombstone, would have made multiple copies of that message and encrypted each one separately using the recipient's public key. These would have been mailed out to the recipients. Most of whom keep copies of their old e-mail messages on Tombstone."

Randy's nodding. "So if Andrew could subpoena Tombstone, he could find all of those copies and insist that you, Beryl, Tom, John, and Eb supply your decryption keys. And if all of you claimed you had forgotten your keys, then you are obviously lying through your teeth."

"Contempt of court for the whole gang," Avi says.

"The most cigarettes," Randy says. This is a contraction of the phrase, "We could end up in prison married to the guy with the most cigarettes," which Avi coined during their earlier Andrew-related legal troubles and had so many occasions to repeat that it was eventually reduced to this vestigial three words. Hearing it come out of his own mouth takes Randy back a few years, and fills him with a spirit of defiant nostalgia. Although he would feel considerably more defiant if they had actually won that case.

"I am just trying to figure out whether Andrew would know of Tombstone's existence," Avi says.

He and Randy begin following their own footprints back towards

Avi's house. Randy notices that his stride is longer now. "Why not? The Dentist's due diligence people have been lodged in our butt-cracks ever since we gave them those shares."

"I detect some resentment in your voice, Randy."

"Not at all."

"Perhaps you disagree with my decision to settle the earlier breach-of-contract lawsuit by giving the Dentist some Epiphyte shares."

"It was a sad day. But there was no other way out of the situation."

"Okay."

"If I'm going to resent you for that, Avi, then you should resent me for not having made a better contract with Semper Marine."

"Ah, but you did! Handshake deal. Ten percent. Right?"

"Right. Let's talk about Tombstone."

"Tombstone's in a closet that we are subletting from Novus Ordo Seclorum Systems," Avi says. "I can tell you the due diligence boys have never been to Ordo."

"We must be paying rent to Ordo, then. They'd see the rent checks."

"A trivial amount of money. For storage space."

"The computer's a Finux box. A donated piece of junk running free software. No paper trail there," Randy says. "What about the T1 line?"

"They would have to be aware of the T1 line," Avi says. "That is both more expensive and more interesting than renting some storage space. And it generates a paper trail a mile wide."

"But do they know where it goes?"

"They would only need to go to the telephone company and ask them where the line is terminated."

"Which would give them what? The street address of an office building in Los Altos," Randy says. "There are, what, five office suites in that building."

"But if they were smart—and I'm afraid that Andrew does have this particular kind of intelligence—they would notice that one of those suits is leased by Novus Ordo Seclorum Systems Inc.—a highly distinctive name that also appears on those rent checks."

"And a subpoena against Ordo would follow immediately," Randy says. "When did you first hear about this lawsuit, by the way?"

"I got the call first thing this morning. You were still sleeping. I can't believe you drove down from Seattle in one push. It's like a thousand miles."

"I was trying to emulate Amy's cousins."

"You described them as *teenagers*."

"But I don't think that teenagers are the way they are because of their age. It's because they have nothing to lose. They simultaneously have a lot of time on their hands and yet are very impatient to get on with their lives."

"And that's kind of where you are right now?"

"It's exactly where I am."

"Horniness too."

"Yeah. But there are ways to deal with that."

"Don't look at me that way," Avi says. "I don't masturbate."

"Never?"

"Never. Formally gave it up. Swore off it."

"Even when you're on the road for a month?"

"Even then."

"Why on earth would you do such a thing, Avi?"

"Enhances my devotion to Devorah. Makes our sex better. Gives me an incentive to get back home."

"Well, that's very touching," Randy says, "and it might even be a good idea."

"I'm quite certain that it is."

"But it's more masochism than I'm really willing to shoulder at this point in my life."

"Why? Are you afraid that it would push you into—"

"Irrational behavior? Definitely."

"And by that," Avi says, "you mean, actually committing to Amy in some way."

"I know you *think* that you just kicked me in the nuts rhetorically," Randy says, "but your premise is totally wrong. I'm ready to commit to her at any time. But for god's sake, I'm not even sure she's heterosexual. It'd be madness to put a lesbian in charge of my ejaculatory functions."

"If she were a lesbian—exclusively—she'd have had the basic decency to tell you by now," Avi says. "My feeling about Amy is that she steers by her gut feelings, and her gut feeling is that you just don't have the level of passion that a woman like her probably would like to see as a prequisite for getting involved."

"Whereas, if I stopped masturbating, I would become such a deranged maniac that she could trust me."

"Exactly. That's exactly how women think," Avi says.

"Don't you have some kind of rule against mixing business and personal conversations?"

"This is essentially a business conversation in that it is about your state of mind, and your current level of personal desperation, and what new options it may have opened up for you," Avi says.

They walk for five minutes without saying anything.

Randy says, "I have a feeling that we are about to get into a conversation about tampering with evidence."

"How interesting that you should bring that up. What's your feeling about it?"

"I'm against it," Randy says. "But to beat Andrew Loeb, I would do anything."

"The most cigarettes," Avi points out.

"First, we have to establish that it's necessary," Randy says. "If Andrew already knows where the wreck is, why bother?"

"Agreed. But if he has only a vague idea," Avi says, "then Tombstone becomes perhaps very important—if the information is stored on Tombstone."

"It almost certainly is," Randy says. "Because of my GPS signature. I know I sent at least one e-mail message from *Glory* while we were anchored directly over the wreck. The latitude and longitude will be right there."

"Well, if that's the case, then this could actually be kind of significant," Avi says. "Because if Andrew gets the exact coordinates of the wreck, he can send divers down and do an inventory and come up with some actual figures to use in the lawsuit. He can do this all very quickly. And if those figures exceed about half the value of Epiphyte, which frankly wouldn't be very difficult, then we become indentured servants of the Dentist."

"Avi, it's full of fucking gold bars," Randy says.

"It is?"

"Yes. Amy told me."

It is Avi's turn to come to a stop for a while and make swallowing noises.

"Sorry, I would have mentioned it earlier," Randy says, "but I didn't know it was relevant until now."

"How did Amy become aware of this?"

"Night before last, before she climbed on the plane at SeaTac, I helped her check her e-mail. Her father sent her a message saying that a certain number of intact Kriegsmarine dinner plates had been found on the submarine. This was a prearranged code for gold bars."

"You said 'full of fucking gold bars.' Could you translate that into an actual number, like in terms of dollars?"

"Avi, who gives a shit? I think we can agree that if the same thing is discovered by Andrew Loeb, we're finished."

"Wow!" Avi says. "So, in this, a hypothetical person who was not above tampering with evidence would certainly have a strong motive."

"It is make-or-break," Randy agrees.

They stop conversing for a while because they now have to dodge cars across the Pacific Coast Highway, and there is this unspoken agreement between them that not getting hit by speeding vehicles merits one's full attention. They end up running across the last couple of lanes in order to exploit a fortuitous break in the northbound traffic. Then neither of them especially feels like dropping back to a walk, so they run all the way across the parking lot of the neighborhood grocery store and into the wooded creek-valley where Avi has his house. They are back at the house directly, and then Avi points significantly at the ceiling, which is his way of saying that they had better assume the house is bugged now. Avi walks over to his answering machine, which is blinking, and ejects the incoming-message tape. He shoves it in his pocket and strides across the house's living room, ignoring frosty glares from one of his Israeli nannies, who doesn't like him to wear shoes inside the house. Avi scoops a brightly colored plastic box off the floor. It has a handle, and rounded corners, and big bright buttons, and a microphone trailing behind it on a coiled yellow cord. Avi continues through the patio doors without breaking stride, the microphone bouncing up and down behind him on its helical cord. Randy follows him outside, across a strip of dead grass, and into a grove of cypress trees. They keep walking until they have dropped into a little dell that shields them from view of the street. Then Avi squats down and ejects a Raffi tape from the little-kid tape recorder and shoves in his incoming-message tape, rewinds it, and plays it.

"Hi, Avi? This is Dave? Calling from Novus Ordo Seclorum Systems? I'm the, uh, president here, you might remember? You have this computer in our wiring closet? Well, we just, like, got some visitors here? Like, guys in suits? And they said that they wanted to see that computer? And, like, if we handed it over to them right away they would be totally cool about it? But if we didn't, they'd come back with a subpoena and with cops and turn the place inside-out and just take it? So, now we're playing stupid? Please call me."

"The machine said there were two messages," Avi says.

"Hi, Avi? This is Dave again? Playing stupid didn't work, and so now we told them to fuck off. The head suit is very mad at us. He called me out. We had a really tense discussion in the McDonald's across the street. He says that I am being stupid. That when they come and turn the place upside-down looking for Tombstone, that it will totally fuck up Ordo's corporate operations and inflict major losses on our shareholders. He said that this would probably be grounds for a minority-shareholder lawsuit against me and that he'd be happy to file that lawsuit. I haven't told him yet that Ordo has only five shareholders and that all of us work here. The manager of the McDonald's asked us to leave because we were disrupting some children's Happy Meals. I acted scared and told him that I would go in and look at Tombstone and see what would be involved in removing it. Instead, I am calling you. Hal and Rick and Carrie are uploading the entire contents of our own system to a remote location so that when these cops come and rip everything out nothing will be lost. Please call me. Good-bye."

"Gosh," Randy says, "I feel like shit for having inflicted all of this on Dave and his crew."

"It'll be great publicity for them," Avi says. "I'm sure Dave has half a dozen television crews poised in the McDonald's at this moment, stoking themselves to the rim of insanity on thirty-two-ounce coffees."

"Well . . . what do you think we should do?"

"It is only fitting and proper that I should go there," Avi says.

"You know, we could just 'fess up. Tell the Dentist about the ten-percent handshake deal."

"Randy, get this through your head. The Dentist doesn't give a shit about the submarine. The Dentist doesn't give a shit about the submarine."

"The Dentist doesn't give a shit about the submarine," Randy says.

"So, I am going to replace this cassette," Avi says, popping the tape out of the machine, "and start driving really really fast."

"Well, I'm going to do what my conscience tells me to do," Randy says.

"The most cigarettes," Avi says.

"I'm not going to do it from here," Randy says, "I'm going to do it from the Sultanate of Kinakuta."

CHRISTMAS 1944

GOTO DENGO HAS POINTED WING OUT TO LIEUTENANT MORI, and Mori's guard troops, and made it clear that they are not to run their bayonets through Wing's torso and wiggle the blades around in his vitals unless there is some exceptionally good reason, such as suppressing all-out rebellion. The same qualities that make Wing valuable to Goto Dengo make him the most likely leader of any organized breakout attempt.

As soon as the general and his aide have departed from Bundok, Goto Dengo goes and finds Wing, who is supervising the boring of the diagonal shaft towards Lake Yamamoto. He is one of those lead-by-example types and so he is way up at the rock face, working a drill, at the end of a few hundred meters of tunnel so narrow that it has to be negotiated on hands and knees. Goto Dengo has to present himself at the Golgotha end of the tunnel and send a messenger crawling up into it, wearing a rusty helmet to protect himself from the shattered stone that drizzles down from the rock face.

Wing appears fifteen minutes later, black from the rock dust that has condensed onto his sweaty skin, red where the skin has been abraded or slashed by stone. He devotes a few minutes to methodically hawking dust up out of his lungs. Every so often he rolls his tongue like a peashooter and fires a jet of phlegm against the wall and clinically observes it run down the stone. Goto Dengo stands by politely. These Chinese have an entire medical belief system centering on phlegm, and working in the mines gives them a lot to talk about.

"Ventilation not good?" Goto Dengo says. Whorehouse Shanghainese has not equipped him with certain technical terms like "ventilation," so Wing has taught him the vocabulary.

Wing grimaces. "I want to finish tunnel. I do not want to sink more ventilation shaft. Waste of time!"

The only way to keep the workers at the rock face from suffocating is by sinking vertical air shafts from the surface down to the diagonal shaft at intervals. They have devoted as much effort to these as they have to the diagonal itself, and were hoping they'd never have to dig another.

"How much farther?" Goto Dengo asks, as Wing finishes another paroxysm.

Wing looks thoughtfully at the ceiling. He has Golgotha mapped out in his head better than its designer does. "Fifty meter."

The designer cannot help grinning. "Is that all? Excellent."

"We go fast now," Wing says proudly, his teeth gleaming for a moment in the lamplight. Then he seems to remember that he is a slave laborer in a death camp and the teeth disappear. "We can go faster if we dig in straight line."

Wing is alluding to the fact that the diagonal to Lake Yamamoto:

is laid out in the blueprints like this. But Goto Dengo, without changing the blueprints, has ordered that it actually be dug like this:

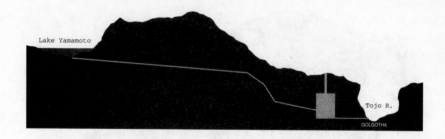

These bends increase the length of the tunnel by quite a bit. Furthermore the rubble tends to pile up in the flatter western section and must be raked along by hand. The only people who know about the existence of these bends are him, Wing, and Wing's crew. The only person who understands the true reason for their existence is Goto Dengo.

"Do not dig in a straight line. Keep digging as I said."

"Yes."

"Also, you will need a new ventilation shaft."

"*More* ventilation shaft! No . . ." Wing protests.

The ventilation shafts shown on the plans, awkward zig-zags and all, are bad enough.

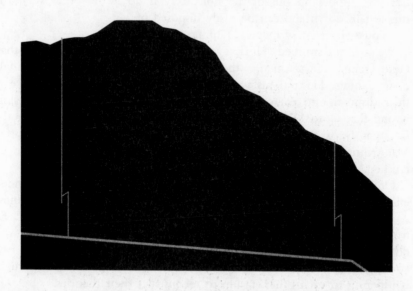

But Goto Dengo has several times told Wing and his crew to begin work on some additional "ventilation shafts," before changing his mind and telling them to abandon the work—with this result:

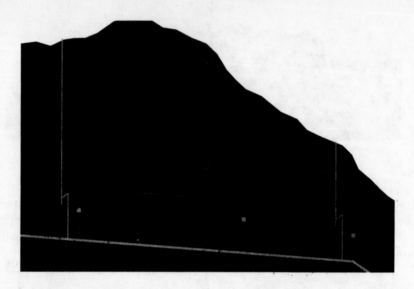

"These new ventilation shafts will be dug from the top down," says
Goto Dengo.

"No!" says Wing, still completely flabbergasted. This is utter madness
in that if you dig a vertical shaft from the top downwards, you have to
haul the rubble up out of the hole. If you do it the other way, the
rubble falls down and can be easily disposed of.

"You will get new helpers. Filipino workers."

Wing looks stunned. He is even more cut off from the world than
Goto Dengo. He must infer the progress of the war from maddeningly
oblique hints. He and his workers fit the crazily scattered evidence at
their disposal into elaborate theories. These theories are all so wildly
wrong that Goto Dengo would laugh out loud at them, if not for the
fact that he is sympathetic. Neither he nor Captain Noda knew that
MacArthur had landed on Leyte, or that the Imperial Navy had been
crushed, until the general told them.

One thing that Wing and his men have got right is that Bundok
employs imported labor in order to ensure secrecy. If any of the Chinese
workers do manage to escape, they will find themselves on an island, far
from home, among people who do not speak their language, and who
do not especially like them. The fact that Filipino workers will soon be
arriving gives them a lot to think about. They will be up all night
whispering to each other, trying to reconstruct their theories.

"We don't need new workers. We are almost done," Wing says, his
pride hurt again.

Goto Dengo taps himself on both shoulders with both index fingers,
suggesting epaulets. It takes Wing only an instant to realize that he's

talking about the general, and then a profoundly conspiratorial look comes over his face and he takes half a step closer. "Orders," Goto Dengo says. "We dig lots of ventilation shafts now."

Wing was not a miner when he arrived at Bundok, but he is now. He is baffled. As he should be. "Ventilation shafts? To where?"

"To nowhere," Goto Dengo says.

Wing's face is still blank. He thinks Goto Dengo's bad Shanghainese is preventing understanding. But Goto Dengo knows that Wing will figure it out soon, some night during the bad fretful moments that always come just before sleep.

And then he will lead the rebellion, and Lieutenant Mori's men will be ready for it; they will open fire with their mortars, they will detonate the mines, use the machine guns, sweeping across their carefully plotted interlocking fields of fire. None of them will survive.

Goto Dengo doesn't want that. So he reaches out and slaps Wing on the shoulder. "I will give you instructions. We will make a special shaft." Then he turns around and leaves; he has surveying to do. He knows that Wing will put it all together in time to save himself.

Filipino prisoners arrive, in columns that have degenerated into ragged skeins, shuffling on bare feet, leaving a wet red trail up the road. They are prodded onwards by the boots and bayonets of Nipponese Army troops, who look almost as wretched. When Goto Dengo sees them staggering into the camp, he realizes that they must have been on their feet continuously since the order was given by the general, two days ago. The general promised five hundred new workers; slightly fewer than three hundred actually arrive, and from the fact that none of them is being carried on stretchers—a statistical impossibility, given their average physical condition—Goto Dengo assumes that the other two hundred must have stumbled or passed out en route, and been executed where they hit the ground.

Bundok is eerily well stocked with fuel and rations, and he sees to it that the prisoners and the Army troops alike are well fed, and given a day of rest.

Then he puts them to work. Goto Dengo has been commanding men long enough, now, that he picks out the good ones right away. There is a toothless, pop-eyed, character named Rodolfo with iron-grey hair and a big cyst on his cheek, arms that are too long, hands like grappling hooks, and splay-toed feet that remind him of the natives he lived with on New Guinea. His eyes are no particular color—they seem to have been put together from shards of other people's eyes, scintillas of grey, blue, hazel, and black all sintered together. Rodolfo is self-conscious about his lack of teeth and always holds one of his sprawling, prehensile paws over his mouth when he speaks. Whenever Goto Dengo or another authority figure comes nearby, all of the young Filipino men avert their gaze and look significantly at Rodolfo, who steps forward, covers his mouth, and fixes his weird, alarming stare upon the visitor.

"Form your men into half a dozen squads and give each squad a name and a leader. Make sure each man knows the name of his squad and of his leader," Goto Dengo says rather loudly. At least some of the other Filipinos must speak English. Then he bends closer and says quietly, "Keep a few of the best and strongest men for yourself."

Rodolfo blinks, stiffens, steps back, removes his hand from his mouth and uses it to snap out a salute. His hand is like an awning that throws a shadow over his entire face and chest. It is obvious that he learned to salute from Americans. He turns on his heel.

"Rodolfo."

Rodolfo turns around again, looking so irritated that Goto Dengo must stifle a laugh.

"MacArthur is on Leyte."

Rodolfo's chest inflates like a weather balloon and he gains about three inches in height, but the expression on his face does not change.

The news ramifies through the Filipino camp like lightning seeking the ground. The tactic has the desired effect of giving the Filipinos a reason to live again; they suddenly display great energy and verve. A supply of badly worn drills and air compressors has arrived on carabao-drawn carts, evidently brought in from one of the other Bundok-like sites around Luzon. The Filipinos, experts at internal combustion, cannibalize some compressors to fix others. Meanwhile the drills are passed around to Rodolfo's squads, who drag them up onto the top of the ridge between the rivers and begin sinking the new "ventilation shafts" while Wing's Chinese men put the last touches on the Golgotha complex below.

The carts that brought in the equipment were simply grabbed off the roads by the Nipponese Army, along with their drivers—mostly farm-boys—and pressed into service on the spot. The farmboys can never leave Bundok, of course. The weaker carabaos are slaughtered for meat, the stronger ones put to work on Golgotha, and the drivers are assimilated into the workforce. One of these is a boy named Juan with a big round head and a distinctly Chinese cast to his features. He turns out to be trilingual in English, Tagalog, and Cantonese. He can communicate in a sort of pidgin with Wing and the other Chinese, frequently by using a finger to draw Chinese characters on the palm of his hand. Juan is small, healthy, and has a kind of wary agility that Goto Dengo thinks may be useful in what is to come, and so he becomes one of the special crew.

The submerged plumbing in Lake Yamamoto needs to be inspected. Goto Dengo has Rodolfo ask around and see if there are any men among them who have worked as pearl divers. He quickly finds one, a lithe, frail-looking fellow from Palawan, named Agustin. Agustin is weak from dysentery, but he seems to perk up around water, and after a couple of days' rest is diving down to the bottom of Lake Yamamoto with no trouble. He becomes another one of Rodolfo's picked men.

There are really too many Filipinos for the number of tools and holes that they have available, and so the work goes quickly at first as fresh men are quickly rotated through by the squad leaders. Then, one night at about two in the morning, an unfamiliar sound reverberates through the jungle, filtering up from the lowlands where the Tojo River meanders through cane fields and rice paddies.

It is the sound of vehicles. Masses of them. Since the Nipponese have been out of fuel for months, Goto Dengo's first thought is that it must be MacArthur.

He throws on a uniform and runs down to Bundok's main gate along with the other officers. Dozens of trucks, and a few automobiles, are queued up there, engines running, headlights off. When he hears a Nipponese voice coming from the lead car, his heart sinks. He long ago stopped feeling bad about wanting to be rescued by General Douglas MacArthur.

Many soldiers ride atop the trucks. When the sun rises, Goto Dengo savors the novel and curious sight of fresh, healthy, well-fed Nipponese men. They are armed with light and heavy machine guns. They look like Nipponese soldiers did way back in 1937, when they were rolling across northern China. It gives Goto Dengo a strange feeling of nostalgia to remember a day when a terrible defeat was not imminent, when they were not going to lose everything horribly. A lump actually gathers in his throat, and his nose begins to run.

Then he snaps out of it, realizing that the big day has finally arrived. The part of him that is still a loyal soldier of the emperor has a duty to see that the vital war materiel, which has just arrived, is stored away in the big vault of Golgotha. The part of him that isn't a loyal soldier anymore still has a lot to accomplish.

In war, no matter how much you plan and prepare and practice, when the big day actually arrives, you still can't find your ass with both hands. This day is no exception. But after a few hours of chaos, things get straightened out, people learn their roles. The heavier trucks cannot make it up the rough road that Goto Dengo has had built up the streambed of the Tojo River, but a couple of the small ones can, and these become the shuttles. So the big trucks pull, one by one, into a heavily fenced and guarded area—well sheltered from MacArthur's observation planes— that was built months ago. Filipinos swarm into these trucks and unload crates, which are small, but evidently quite heavy. Meanwhile the smaller trucks shuttle the crates up the Tojo River Road to the entrance of Golgotha, where they are unloaded onto hand cars and rolled into the tunnel to the main vault. As per the instructions handed down from on high, Goto Dengo sees to it that every twentieth crate is diverted to the fool's chamber.

The unloading proceeds automatically from there, and Goto Dengo devotes most of these days to supervising the final stages of the digging. The new ventilation shafts are proceeding on schedule, and he only needs to check them once a day. The diagonal is now only a few meters away from the bottom of Lake Yamamoto. Groundwater has begun to seep through small cracks in the bedrock and trickle down the diagonal into Golgotha, where it collects in a sump that drains into the Tojo. Another few meters of cutting and they will break through into the short stub tunnel that Wing and his men created many months ago, digging down-wards from what later became the bottom of the lake.

Wing himself is otherwise engaged these days. He and Rodolfo and their special crew are completing final preparations. Rodolfo and com-pany are digging down from the top of the ridge, cutting what looks like just another vertical ventilation shaft. Wing and company are directly below, engaged in a complicated subterranean plumbing project.

Goto Dengo has entirely lost track of what day it is. About four days after the trucks come, though, he gets a clue. The Filipinos spontaneously break into song over their evening rice bowls. Goto Dengo recognizes the tune vaguely; he occasionally heard the American Marines singing it in Shanghai.

> What child is this,
> Who laid to rest,
> On Mary's lap is sleeping?

The Filipinos sing that and other songs, in English and Spanish and Latin, all evening long. After they get their lungs unlimbered they sing astonishingly well, occasionally breaking into two- and three-part har-mony. At first, Lieutenant Mori's guards get itchy trigger fingers, thinking it's some kind of a signal for a mass breakout. Goto Dengo doesn't want to see his work cut short by a massacre, and so he explains to them that it is a religious thing, a peaceful celebration.

That night, another midnight truck convoy arrives and the workers are rousted to unload it. They work cheerfully, singing Christmas carols and making jokes about Santa Claus.

The whole camp stays up well past sunrise unloading trucks. Bundok has gradually become a nocturnal place anyway, to avoid the gaze of observation planes. Goto Dengo is just thinking of hitting the sack when a fusillade of sharp crackling noises breaks out up above the camp on the Tojo River. Ammunition being in short supply, hardly anyone actually fires guns anymore, and he almost doesn't recognize the sound of the Nambu.

Then he jumps onto the running board of a truck and tells the driver to head upstream. The shooting has died down as suddenly as it started. Beneath the bald tires of the truck, the river has turned opaque and bright red.

About two dozen corpses lie in the water before the entrance to Golgotha. Nipponese soldiers stand around them, up to their calves in the red water, their weapons slung from their shoulders. A sergeant is going around with a bayonet, stirring the guts of the Filipinos who are still moving.

"What is going on?" Goto Dengo says. No one answers. But no one shoots him, either; he will be allowed to figure it out himself.

The workers had clearly been unloading another small truck, which is still parked there at the head of the road. Resting beneath its tailgate is a wooden crate that was apparently dropped. Its heavy contents have exploded the crate and spilled across the uneven conglomerate of river rocks, poured concrete and mine tailings that make up the riverbed here.

Goto Dengo sloshes up to it and looks. He sees it clearly enough, but he can't somehow absorb the knowledge until he feels it in his hands. He bends down, wraps his fingers around a cold brick on the bottom of the river, and heaves it up out of the water. It is a glossy ingot of yellow metal, incredibly heavy, stamped with words in English: BANK OF SINGAPORE.

There is a scuffle behind him. The sergeant stands at the ready as two of his men jerk the Filipino driver out of the cab of his truck that Goto Dengo rode in on. Calmly—looking almost bored—the sergeant bayonets the driver. The men drop him in the red water and he disappears. "Merry Christmas" one of the soldiers cracks. Everyone laughs, except for Goto Dengo.

PULSE

As Avi walks back through his house, he utters something biblical-sounding in Hebrew that causes his kids to burst into tears, and his nannies to rise from the kid-mat and begin shoving stuff into bags. Devorah emerges from a back room where she's been sleeping off some morning sickness. She and Avi embrace tenderly in the hallway and Randy begins to feel like a fleck of debris lodged in someone's eye. So he heads straight for an exit, goes out to his car and starts driving. He winds through the hills over the San Andreas Fault to Skyline and then heads south. Ten minutes later, Avi's car howls past him in the left lane, doing ninety or a hundred. Randy barely has time to read the bumper sticker: MEAN PEOPLE SUCK.

Randy's looking for a totally anonymous location where he can patch into the Internet. A hotel doesn't work because a hotel keeps good records of outgoing telephone calls. What he should really do is use this packet radio interface he has for his laptop, but even that requires a place to sit down and work undisturbed for a while. Which gets him thinking in terms of a fast food joint, not to be found in the mid-peninsular wasteland. By the time he has reached the northern skirts of the Valley—Menlo Park and Palo Alto—he has decided fuck it, he'll just go to the scene of the action. Maybe he could be of some use there. So he gets off at the El Monte exit and heads into the business district of Los Altos, a pretty typical mid-twentieth-century American downtown gradually being metabolized by franchises.

A major street intersects, at something other than a ninety-degree angle, a smaller commercial street, defining two (smaller) acute-angle lots and two (larger) obtuse-angle lots. On one side of the major street, the obtuse-angle lot is occupied by a two-storey office building, home of Ordo's offices and Tombstone. The acute-angle lot is occupied by the McDonald's. On the opposite side of the major street, the acute-angle lot is occupied by, weirdly enough, a 24 Jam, the only one Randy has ever seen in the Western Hemisphere. The obtuse-angle lot is occupied by a Park 'n' Lock, where you can park for the old-fashioned purpose of wandering around the business district from store to store.

The parking lot of the McDonald's is full, and so Randy pulls through its drive-through window, chooses *n*, where *n* is a random number between one and six, and asks for Value Meal *n* with super-size fries. This having been secured, he guns the Acura directly across the big street into the Park 'n' Lock just in time to see its last available space being seized by a minivan bearing the logo of a San Jose television station. Randy is not planning to stray far from his car, so he just blocks in another car. But as he is setting the parking brake, he notices movement inside it, and with a bit of further attention realizes he is watching a man with long hair and a beard methodically ramming shells into a pump shotgun. The man catches sight of Randy in his rearview mirror and turns around with a scrupu- lously polite pardon-me-sir-but-you-seem-to-have-blocked-me-in look. Randy recognizes him as Mike or Mark, a graphics card hacker who farms ostriches in Gilroy (quirky hobbies being de rigueur in the high- tech world). He moves the Acura, blocking in what looks like an aban- doned van from the *Starsky and Hutch* epoch.

Randy climbs up on the roof of his car with his laptop and his Value Meal *n*. Until recently he would never have sat on top of his Acura because his considerable mass would dimple the sheet metal. But after Amy rammed it with the truck, Randy became much less anal, and now sees it as a tool to be used until it is just a moraine of rusted shards. He happens to have a twelve-volt adapter for the laptop, so he runs that down into his cigarette lighter socket. Finally, he's settled, and gets a chance to take a good look around.

The parking lot of Novus Ordo Seclorum's office building is filled with cop cars, and BMWs and Mercedes Benzes that Randy assumes belong to lawyers. Avi's Range Rover is parked jauntily on top of some landscaping, and a few TV camera crews have set up, as well. In front of the building's main entrance a lot of people are jammed into the smallest possible space screaming at each other. They are surrounded by ring after concentric ring of cops, media, and law-firm minions—collec- tively, what Tolkien would call Men—and a few non- or post-human creatures imbued with peculiar physiognomies and vaguely magical pow- ers: Dwarves (steady, productive, surly) and Elves (brilliant in a more ethereal way). Randy, a Dwarf, has begun to realize that his grandfather may have been an Elf. Avi is a Man with a strong Elvish glow about him. Somewhere in the center of this whole thing, presumably, is Gollum.

There is a little window on the screen of Randy's laptop showing a cheesy 1940s-newsreel-style animation of a radio tower, with zigzaggy conceptual radio waves radiating outwards from it over the whole earth, which is shown ludicrously not to scale in this rendering—the diameter of the earth is about equal to the height of the radio tower. That these Jovian info-bolts are visible and moving is a visual cue that his radio adapter has managed to patch itself into the packet radio network. Randy opens a terminal window and types

```
telnet laundry.org
```

and in a few seconds bang! he gets a login prompt. Randy now has another look at the animated window, and notes with approval that the info-bolts have been replaced with gouts of question marks. This means that his computer has recognized laundry.org as a S/WAN machine—running the Secure Wide Area Network protocol—which means that every packet going back and forth between Randy's laptop and laundry.org is encrypted. Definitely a good idea when you are about to do something illegal over the radio.

Mike or Mark gets out of his car, cutting a dramatic figure in a long black Western-style coat, a look rather spoiled by the t-shirt he's got on underneath it: black with a fat red question mark in the middle. He hitches the strap of his shotgun up onto his shoulder and leans into his back door to retrieve a large black cowboy hat, which he places on the roof of his car. He thrusts his elbows into the air and gathers his long hair back behind his ears, staring up at the sky, and then clamps the cowboy hat down on his head. Tied loosely around his neck is a black bandanna with a question-mark pattern, which he now pulls up over the bridge of his nose so that just an eye-slit shows between it and the cowboy hat. Randy would be really alarmed if it weren't for the fact that several of his friends, such as John Cantrell, often go around looking this way. Mike or Mark strides across the Park 'n' Lock, tracked carefully by a panning cameraman, and jogs across the street to the 24 Jam.

Randy logs onto laundry.org using ssh—"secure shell"—a way of further encrypting communications between two computers. Laundry.org is an anonymizing service; all packets routed through it to another computer are stripped of identifying information first, so that anyone down the line who intercepts one of those packets has no way of knowing where it originated. Once he's patched into the anonymizer, Randy types

```
telnet crypt.kk
```

and hits the return key and then actually, literally, prays. The Crypt is still going through its shakedown period (which, indeed, is the only reason that all of Tombstone's contents have not been moved onto it yet).

In the lot of the 24 Jam, Mike or Mark has joined three other elvish-looking sorts in black cowboy hats and bandannas, whom Randy can identify based on the length and color of their ponytails and beards. There's Stu, a Berkeley grad student who is somehow mixed up in Avi's HEAP project, and Phil, who invented a major programming language a couple of years ago and goes helicopter-skiing in his spare time, and Craig, who knows everything there is to know about encrypted credit-card transactions on the Net and is a devotee of traditional Nipponese archery. Some of these guys are wearing long coats and some aren't. There is a lot of Secret Admirers iconography: t-shirts bearing the number 56, which is a code for Yamamoto, or just pictures of Yamamoto himself, or big fat question marks. They are having an energetic and very happy conversation—though it looks a bit forced—because, to a man, they are carrying long weapons out in plain sight. One of them has a hunting rifle, and each of the others is slinging a rudimentary-looking gun with a banana clip sticking out of the side. Randy thinks, but is not sure, that these are HEAP guns.

This scene, not surprisingly, has caught the attention of the police, who have surrounded these four with squad cars, and who are standing at the ready with rifles and shotguns. It is an oddity of the law in many jurisdictions that, while carrying (say) a concealed one-shot .22 derringer requires a license, openly carrying (e.g.) a big game rifle is perfectly legal. Concealed weapons are outlawed or at least heavily regulated, and unconcealed ones are not. So a lot of Secret Admirers—who tend to be gun nuts—have taken to going around conspicuously armed as a way of pointing out the absurdity of those rules. Their point is this: who gives a shit about concealed weapons anyway, since they are only useful for defending oneself against assaults by petty criminals, which almost never happens? The real reason the Constitution provides for the right to bear arms is defending oneself against oppressive governments, and when it comes to that, your handgun is close to useless. So (according to these guys) if you are going to assert your right to keep and bear arms you should do it openly, by packing something really big.

A bunch of junk scrolls up Randy's screen. WELCOME TO THE CRYPT, it begins, and then there's a paragraph of information about what a great idea the Crypt is and how anyone who gives a damn about privacy should get an account here. Randy truncates the commercial message with the whack of a key, and logs in as Randy. Then he enters the command

```
telnet tombstone.epiphyte.com
```

and gets two gratifying messages in return: one saying that a connection has been established with Tombstone, and the next saying that a S/WAN link has been automatically negotiated. Finally he gets

```
tombstone login:
```

which means that he is now free to log on to the machine right across the street from him. And now Mr. Randy has a little decision to make.

So far, he's clean. The bits coming out of his laptop are encrypted; so even if someone is monitoring the local packet radio net, all they know is that some encrypted bits are flying around. They cannot trace any of those bits to Randy's machine without bringing in an elaborate radio direction-finding rig and zeroing in on him most conspicuously. Those encrypted bits are eventually finding their way to laundry.org up in Oakland, which is a big Internet host that probably has thousands of packets rushing in and out of it every second. If someone were tapping laundry.org's T3 line, which would require an enormous investment in computers and communications gear, they would detect a very small number of encrypted packets going out to crypt.kk in Kinakuta. But these packets would have been stripped of any identifying information before leaving laundry.org and so there would be no way to tell where they originated. Now, crypt.kk is also an anonymizer, and so an entity tapping its straggeringly enormous T5 line (a job on the order of eavesdropping on a small country's tele-communications system) might theoretically be able to detect a few packets going back and forth between crypt.kk and Tombstone. But again, these would be stripped of identifying information, and so it would be impossible to trace them even as far back as laundry.org, to say nothing of tracing them all the way back to Randy's laptop.

But in order for Randy to get into Tombstone and begin actually tampering with the evidence, he must now log on. If it were a poorly secured host of the type that used to be legion on the Internet, he could just exploit one of its numerous security holes and crack his way into it, so that if his activities on the machine were discovered, he could claim that it wasn't him—just some cracker who happened to break into the machine at the very moment it was being seized by the cops. But Randy has spent the last several years of his life making machines such as this one impregnable to crackers, and he knows it's impossible.

Furthermore, there's no point in logging on as just any old user—like using a guest account. Guests are not allowed to tamper with system files. In order to do any meaningful evidence-tampering here, Randy has to log on as the superuser. The name of the superuser account is, inconveniently, "randy" and you can't actually log in as "randy" without entering a password that only Randy would know. So after using the very latest in cryptographic technology and trans-oceanic packet-switching communications to conceal his identity, Randy now finds himself faced with the necessity of typing his name into the fucking machine.

A little scenario flashes up in his head in which he sends an anonymous broadcast message to all laundry.org users telling them that the password for the "randy" account on "tombstone.epiphyte.com" is such and such and urging them to spread this information all over the Internet as fast as possible. This might have been a decent idea if he had thought of it an hour ago. Now it is too late; any sentient prosecutor tracing the time-stamps on the messages would be able to prove that it was just a blind.

Besides, time is running low. The discussion across the street, which is just a shrill hubbub at this distance, is rising to some sort of climax.

Randy has meanwhile booted up his browser and gone to the ordo. net home page. Usually it's a pretty dull corporate home page, but today all of the blurbs and quotidian press releases have been obliterated by a window showing live color video of what is going on in front of the building (or rather, what was going on a couple of seconds ago; coming over his miserable low-bandwidth radio link, the video changes frames about once every three seconds). The video is originating from Ordo itself, where they've evidently aimed a camera out the window and are slamming the images straight out over their very own T3 line.

Randy glances up just in time to see the guy who invented the term "virtual reality" walking across the lot, deep in conversation with the executive editor of *TURING Magazine*. Not far behind them is Bruce, an operating systems engineer who, in his spare time, records Tierra del Fuegan folk music and makes it available for free over the Internet.

"Bruce!" Randy shouts.

Bruce falters and looks over in Randy's direction. "Randy," he says.

"Why are you here?"

"Word on the street is that the Feds were raiding Ordo," Bruce says.

"Interesting. . . . any particular Feds?"

"Comstock," Bruce says. Meaning Paul Comstock, who, by virtue of being Attorney General of the United States, runs the FBI. Randy does not believe this rumor, but in spite of himself he scans the area for people fitting the general profile of FBI agents. The FBI hates and fears strong crypto. Meanwhile another Secret Admirer type shouts, "I heard Secret Service!" Which is even creepier, in a way, because the Secret Service is part of the Treasury Department, and is charged with combating wire fraud and protecting the nation's currency.

Randy says, "Would you be open to the possibility that it's all a Net rumor? That what's really going on is that a piece of equipment inside Ordo's offices is being seized as part of a legal squabble?"

"Then why are all these cops here?" Bruce says.

"Maybe the masked men with assault rifles drew them."

"Well, why did the Secret Admirers show up in the first place if it wasn't a government raid?"

"I don't know. Maybe it's just some kind of spontaneous self-organizing phenomenon—like the origin of life in the primordial soup."

Bruce says, "Isn't it just as possible that the legal squabble is a pretext?"

"In other words that the squabble is sort of like a Trojan horse put together by Comstock?"

"Yeah."

"Knowing all of the parties involved, I'd rate it as unlikely," Randy says, "but let me think about it."

The noise and intensity of the argument in the Ordo parking lot spike upwards. Randy looks at the video window, which unfortunately has no sound track. The transactions between frames come as isolated blocks of new pixels slapped up one at a time over the old, like a large billboard being posted in sections. High-definition TV it ain't. But Randy definitely recognizes Avi, standing there tall, pale, and calm, flanked by one guy who's probably Dave the Ordo president, and another guy who's obviously a lawyer. They are literally standing in the doorway of the building and facing off against two cops and none other than Andrew Loeb, who is in rapid motion and hence poses an insurmountable bandwidth problem. The Internet video gear is smart enough not to mess with parts of an image that aren't changing very much, and so the planted cops get refreshed maybe a couple of times a minute, and then just in a few rectangular image-shards. But Andrew Loeb is waving his arms around, hopping up and down, lunging towards Avi from time to time, pulling back and taking calls on his cellphone, and waving documents in the air. The computers have identified him as a bunch of pixels that require a great deal of attention and bandwidth, and so somewhere some poor algorithm is churning through the high-pressure slurry of compressed pixels that is the image of Andrew Loeb, and doing its level best to freeze the most rapidly-moving parts into discrete frames and chop them up into checkerboard-squares that can be broadcast as packets over the Net. These packets arrive in Randy's computer as the radio network passes them along, i.e., sporadically and in the wrong order. So Andrew Loeb appears as a cubist digital-video artifact, a rectilinear amoeba of mostly trench-coat-beige pixels. From time to time his eyes or his mouth will suddenly appear, disembodied, in the center of an image-block, and remain frozen there for a few seconds, crystallized in a moment of howling rage.

This is weirdly mesmerizing until Randy's startled out of his reverie by a clunk. He looks over to see that the van he's blocked in wasn't abandoned after all; it was full of Dwarves, who have now thrown the back doors open to reveal a nest of cables and wires. A couple of the Dwarves are heaving a boxy apparatus up onto the roof of the van. Cables run out of it to another boxy apparatus down below. The apparatus is electrical in nature—and doesn't appear capable of firing projectiles—so Randy decides not to pay it much attention for the moment.

Voices well up across the street. Randy sees some cops climbing out of a cop-van carrying a battering ram.

Randy types:

    randy

and hits the return key. Tombstone answers:

    password:

and Randy types it in. Tombstone informs him that he's logged on, and that he has mail.

The fact that Randy has logged on has now been recorded by the system in several locations on the hard drive. He has, in other words, just slapped big greasy fingerprints all over a weapon that the police are moments away from seizing as evidence. If Tombstone is shut down and grabbed by the cops before Randy can erase those traces, they will know he has logged on at the very moment that Tombstone was confiscated, and will put him in prison for tampering with evidence. He very much wishes that Douglas MacArthur Shaftoe could somehow be made aware of what a ballsy thing he is doing here. But then Doug has probably done all kinds of ballsy things of which Randy will never be aware, and Randy respects him anyway because of his bearing. Maybe the way to get that kind of bearing is to go around doing ballsy things in secret that somehow percolate up to the surface of your personality.

Randy could just reformat the hard drive with a single command, but (1) it would take several minutes to execute and (2) it would not thoroughly erase the incriminating bits, which could be lifted from the hard drive by a motivated technician. Because he knows which files have recorded his log-on, he executes a command that finds those files on the hard drive. Then he types another command that causes random numbers to be written over those areas of the hard drive seven times in a row.

The cops are slamming the battering ram against the side door of the office building when Randy's right pinky slams the Enter key and executes that command. He is almost certainly safe from the tampering-with-evidence charge now. But he hasn't actually tampered yet, which is the whole point of this exercise. He needs to find all the copies of the e-mail message that specifies the latitude and longitude of the wreck, and do the same multiple-erase trick on them. If the damn things were not encrypted, he could search for the critical strings of digits. As it is, he will have to search for files that were created during a certain time period, around the time that Randy was out on *Glory,* anchored over the wreck. Randy knows roughly what day that was, and so he sets the limits of the search to give him any files created five days either side of that, just to be safe, and limits it to only those directories used for e-mail.

The search takes forever, or maybe it just seems that way because the cops have smashed the side door off its hinges now and are inside the building. The video window catches Randy's eye as it changes dramatically; he gets a veering montage of grainy frozen images of a room; a doorway; a hallway; a reception area; and finally a barricade. The Ordo guys have yanked their video camera out of the window and restationed it at their front desk, recording a barrier built of cheap modular office furniture piled against the glass entrance to the reception. The camera tilts up to show that one of the four glass door slabs has already been crystallized by (one supposes) the impact of the battering ram.

Randy's "find" command finally returns with a list of about a hundred files. The half-dozen or so critical ones are on the list somewhere, but Randy doesn't have time to go through the list figuring out which is which. He has the system generate a list of the disk blocks occupied by those files, so that he can go back later and do a super-erase. Once he's got that information, he does a "rm" or "remove" command on all of them. This is a paltry and miserable way to expunge secrets from a hard drive, but Randy's afraid he may not have time to do it more thoroughly. The "rm" only takes a few moments and then Randy goes back and has the system write random numbers on top of those disk blocks seven times in a row, just as he did earlier. By this time the barricade has been scattered all over Ordo's lobby and the cops are inside. They have weapons drawn and pointed at the ceiling and they don't look very happy.

There is one thing left to do. Actually it's a pretty big thing. The Epiphyte people use Tombstone for all kinds of purposes, and there's no way of telling whether other copies of that latitude and longitude exist on it somewhere. Most of Epiphyte is made up of inveterate computer users who would be just the sort to write little scripts to back up all of their old e-mail messages to an archive every week. So he whips up his own script that will just write random information to every sector on the entire hard drive, then go back and do it again, and again, and again, forever—or until the cops pull the plug. Just after he whacks the Enter key to send this command in to Tombstone, he hears an electrical buzzing noise from the van that makes his hair stand on end for a moment. He sees a cop in the video window, frozen. Then the screen of his computer goes blank.

Randy looks over toward the old van. The Dwarves are high-fiving each other.

There is a screeching of tires, and the sound of a low-speed collision, out on the street. About a dozen cars have rolled quietly to a stop, and some have been rear-ended by others that are still functioning. The McDonald's has gone dark. Television technicians are cursing inside their mobile units. Police officers and lawyers are pounding their walkie-talkies and cellphones against their hands.

"Pardon me," Randy says to the Dwarves, "but would you gentlemen like to share anything with me?"

"We just took out the whole building," says one of the Dwarves.

"Took it out, in what sense?"

"Nailed it with a big electromagnetic pulse. Fried every chip within range."

"So it's a scorched-earth kind of deal? Go ahead and confiscate that gear, you damn Feds, it's all worthless junk now?"

"Yeah."

"Well, it certainly worked on those cars," Randy says, "and it definitely worked on this piece of junk that used to be my computer."

"Don't worry—it has no effect on hard drives," the Dwarf says, "so all of your files are intact."

"I know you are expecting me to take that as good news," Randy says.

BUDDHA

A CAR IS COMING. THE ENGINE NOISE IS EXPENSIVELY MUFFLED, but it sounds like a diesel. Goto Dengo is awake, waiting for it, and so is the rest of the camp. No one stirs at Bundok during the day anymore, except for the radio men and those manning the anti-aircraft guns. They have not been told that MacArthur is on Luzon, but they all sense The General's presence. The American planes rip across the sky all day long, glittering and proud, like starships from a distant future that none of them will ever see, and the earth rings like a bell from the impacts of distant naval guns. The shipments have become smaller but more frequent: one or two broken-down lorries every night, their rear bumpers practically scraping the road under crippling burdens of gold.

Lieutenant Mori has placed anther machine gun at the front gate, concealed in the foliage, just in case some Americans happen to blunder up this road in a jeep. Somewhere out there in the dark, the barrel of that weapon is tracking this car as it jounces up the road. The men know every dip and rise in that road, and can tell where the vehicles are by listening for the scrape of their undercarriages against the hardpan, a signature pattern of metallic dots and dashes.

The car's headlamps are off, of course, and the guards at the gate dare not shine bright lights around. One of them risks opening up a kerosene lantern, and aims its beam at the visitor. A silver Mercedes-Benz hood ornament springs forth from the blackness, supported by a chrome-plated radiator grille. The beam of the lantern fondles the car's black fenders, its sweeping silver exhaust pipes, its running boards, clotted with the meat of young coconuts—it must have sideswiped a pile on its way up here. In the driver's side window is the face of a Nipponese man in his forties, so haggard and tired he looks as though he is about to burst into tears. But he is just a driver. Next to him is a sergeant with a sawed-off shotgun, Nipponese rifles being generally too long to wield in the front seat of a luxury car. Behind them, a drawn curtain conceals whatever, or whomever, is in the backseat.

"Open!" demands the guard, and the driver reaches up behind his head and parts the curtain. The lantern beam falls through the opening and bounces back sharply from a pale face in the back seat. Several of the soldiers shout. Goto Dengo steps back, rattled, then moves in for a better look.

The man in the backseat has a very large head. But the strange thing about him is that his skin is a rich yellow color—not the normal Asian yellow—and it glitters. He is wearing a peculiar, pointed hat, and he has a calm smile on his face—an expression the likes of which Goto Dengo has not seen since the war began.

More lantern beams come on, the ring of soldiers and officers closes in on the Mercedes. Someone pulls the rear door open and then jumps back as if he has burned his hand on it.

The passenger is sitting crosslegged on the backseat, which has been crushed into a broad V beneath his weight.

It is a solid gold Buddha, looted from somewhere else in the Greater East Asia Co-Prosperity Sphere, coming to meditate in serene darkness atop the hoard of Golgotha.

It turns out to be small enough to fit through the entrance, but too big to go in one of the little railway cars, and so the strongest Filipino men must spend the next hours shoving it down the tunnel one inch at a time.

The early shipments were neatly crated, and the crates were stenciled with labels identifying the contents as machine gun ammunition or mortar rounds or the like. The crates that come later don't have the stencils. At a certain point, the gold begins to arrive in cardboard boxes and rotten steamer trunks. They fall open all the time, and the workers patiently gather the gold up and carry it to the tunnel entrance in their arms and throw it into the hand cars. The bars tumble end over end and smash into the sheet-metal with a din that scares clouds of birds out of the overhanging trees. Goto Dengo cannot help looking at the bars. They come in different sizes, some of them so large that it takes two men to carry one. They are stamped with the names of central banks from a few places Goto Dengo has been and many he's only heard of: Singapore, Saigon, Batavia, Manila, Rangoon, Hong Kong, Shanghai,

Canton. There is French gold that was apparently shipped to Cambodia, and Dutch gold shipped to Jakarta, and British gold shipped to Singapore—all to keep it out of the hands of the Germans.

But some shipments consist entirely of gold from the Bank of Tokyo. They get five convoys in a row of the stuff. According to the tally that Gotto Dengo is keeping in his head, two-thirds of the tonnage stored in Golgotha ends up coming straight from Nippon's central reserves. All of it is cold to the touch, and stored in good but old crates. He concludes that it was shipped to the Philippines a long time ago and has been sitting in a cellar in Manila ever since, waiting for this moment. They must have shipped it here at about the same time that Goto Dengo was plucked off the beach in New Guinea, way back in late 1943.

They have known. They have known for that long that they were going to lose the war.

By the middle of January, Goto Dengo has begun to look back on the Christmas Day massacre with something almost like nostalgia, missing the atmosphere of naive innocence that made the killings necessary. Until that morning, even he had managed to convince himself that Golgotha was an arms cache that the emperor's soldiers would someday use to stage a glorious reconquest of Luzon. He knows that the workers believed it too. Now everyone knows about the gold, and the camp has changed. Everyone understands that there will be no exit.

At the beginning of January, the workers are made up of two types: those who are resigned to die here, and those who aren't. The latter group make various escape attempts of a desultory and hopeless nature and are shot by the guards. The era of hoarding ammunition seems to be over, or perhaps the guards are just too sick and hungry to climb down out of the watch towers and personally bayonet all of the people who present themselves to be killed. So it is all done with bullets, and the bodies left to balloon and blacken. Bundok is immanent with their stench.

Goto Dengo hardly notices, though, because the camp is suffused with the crazy, sick tension that always precedes a battle. Or so he supposes; he has seen a lot of excitement in this war, but he has never been in a proper battle. The same is automatically true of most of the Nipponese here, because essentially all of the Nipponese who go into battles wind up dead. In this army you are either a greenhorn or a corpse.

Sometimes, a briefcase arrives along with the gold shipment. The briefcase is always handcuffed to the wrist of a soldier who has grenades dangling all over his body so that he can blow himself and it to powder if the convoy should be assaulted by Huks. The briefcases go straight to the Bundok radio station and their contents are placed in a safe. Goto

Dengo knows that they must contain codes—not the usual books, but some kind of special codes that are changed every day—because every morning, after the sun has come up, the radio officer performs a ceremony of burning a single sheet of paper in front of the transmitter shack, and then rubbing the withered leaf of ash between his hands.

It is through that radio station that they will receive the final order. All is in readiness, and Goto Dengo goes through the complex once a day checking everything.

The diagonal tunnel finally reached the stub tunnel at the bottom of Lake Yamamoto a couple of weeks ago. The stub was filled with water that had seeped past the concrete plug during the months since it had been put into place, and so when the two tunnels were finally joined, several tons of water ran down the diagonal into Golgotha. This was expected and planned for; all of it went into a sump and drained from there into the Tojo River. Now it is possible to go all the way up the diagonal and look at the concrete plug from the underside. Lake Yamamoto is on the other side. Goto Dengo goes up there every couple of days, ostensibly to check the plug and its demolition charges, but really to check on the progress being made, unbeknownst to Captain Noda, by Wing's and Rodolfo's crews. They are mostly drilling upwards, making more of those short, vertical, dead-end shafts, and enlarging the chambers at their tops. The system (including the new "ventilation shafts" ordered by The General, and dug from the top down just to the east of the ridgeline) looks like this now:

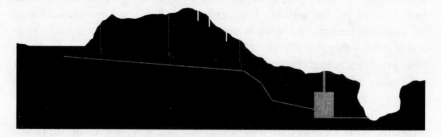

Inside the primary storage complex is a small room that Captain Noda has dubbed the Hall of Glory. It does not look very glorious right now. Most of it is filled with a snarl of wires which have been run into it from all parts of the Golgotha complex, and which dangle from the ceiling or trail on the floor with hand-lettered paper tags dangling from them, saying things like MAIN ENTRANCE DEMOLITION CHARGES. There are several crates of lead-acid batteries to supply power for the detonations, and to give Goto Dengo a few minutes of electric light by which to read those paper tags. Extra boxes of dynamite and blasting caps are stacked at one end of the Hall of Glory in case some tunnels need a little extra destruction, and coils of red fuse cord in case the electrical system fails completely.

But the demolition order hasn't yet come, so Goto Dengo does the things soldiers do while waiting to die. He writes letters to his family that will never be delivered or even mailed. He smokes. He plays cards. He goes and checks his equipment another time, and then another. A week goes by without any gold deliveries. Twenty prisoners try to escape together. The ones who don't get sprayed across the killing ground by mines get tangled in barbed wire and are each shot by a team of two guards, one aiming a flashlight and the other aiming a rifle. Captain Noda spends all night, every night, pacing back and forth in front of the main gate and smoking cigarettes, then drinks himself to sleep at dawn. The radio men sit in front of their rig watching the tubes glow, jerking like electrified frog legs whenever a feeble string of beeps comes in on their frequency. But the order does not come.

One night, then, the trucks come again, just as they did the first time. The convoy must contain all that's left of the Nipponese motor pool on Luzon. They all come together, making a rumble that can be heard half an hour before they actually reach the gate. When their cargo has been taken out and stacked on the ground, the soldiers guarding this convoy remain behind at Bundok. The only people who leave are the drivers.

It takes two days to move this last hoard into the tunnels. One of their shuttle trucks has broken down for good and been cannibalized to keep the other one going. It is running on half of its cylinders and is so feeble that it has to be pushed up the riverbed road by teams of workers and hauled over the rough patches on ropes. It has finally begun to rain, and the Tojo River is rising.

The main vault is nearly full of treasure, and so is the fool's vault. The new shipment has to be packed in wherever it will fit; they break it out of its crates and jam it into crannies. The crates are stenciled with double-headed eagles and swastikas, and the gold bars inside come from Berlin, Vienna, Warsaw, Prague, Paris, Amsterdam, Riga, Copenhagen, Budapest, Bucharest, Milan. There are also cardboard boxes filled with diamonds. Some of the crates are still damp, and smell of the sea. Seeing this, Goto Dengo knows that a big submarine must have arrived from Germany, filled with Nazi treasure. So that explains the two-week lull: they've been awaiting the arrival of this U-boat.

He works in the tunnels for two days, wearing a miner's headlamp, shoving jewels and gold bars into crevices. He goes into a sort of trance that is finally interrupted by a heavy thud reverberating through the rock.

Artillery, he thinks. Or a bomb from one of MacArthur's planes.

He comes up the main ventilation shaft to the top of the ridge, where it's broad daylight. He is crushed to discover that there is no battle underway. MacArthur isn't going to rescue him. Lieutenant Mori has brought almost all of the workers up here, and they are hauling on ropes, dragging Bundok's heavy equipment up and throwing it down into the recently dug "ventilation shafts." Both of the trucks are up here, and men with torches and sledgehammers are breaking them up into pieces small enough to drop down the shafts. Goto Dengo arrives just in time to see the engine block of the radio station's generator tumbling down a shaft into blackness. The rest of the radio gear follows it directly.

Somewhere nearby, concealed in the trees, someone is grunting heavily, doing some kind of hard physical labor. It is a practiced martial-arts type of grunt, from way down in the diaphragm.

"Lieutenant Goto!" says Captain Noda. He is daft with alcohol. "Your duties are below."

"What was that loud noise?"

Noda beckons him over to an outcropping from which they can see down into the valley of the Tojo River. Goto Dengo, unsteady for any number of reasons, suffers a spell of dizziness and nearly falls off. The problem is disorientation: he does not recognize the river. Until now, it has always been a few trickles of water braided down a rocky bed. Even before they ran a road up it, you could get up almost as far as the waterfall by hopping from one dry rock to the next.

Now, all of a sudden, the river is wide, deep, and murky. The tips of a few big rocks protrude from the surface here and there.

He remembers something he saw a hundred years ago, in a previous incarnation, on another planet: a bedsheet from the Manila Hotel with a crude map sketched on it. The Tojo River drawn in with a fat trail of blue fountain-pen ink.

"We dynamited the rockfall," Noda says, "according to the plan."

Long ago, they had poised rocks above a bottleneck in the river, ready to create a little dam. But setting off that dynamite was supposed to be almost the last thing they did before sealing themselves up inside.

"But we are not ready," Goto Dengo says.

Noda laughs. He seems quite high-spirited. "You have been telling me for a month that you are ready."

"Yes," Lieutenant Goto says, slowly and thickly, "you are right. We are ready."

Noda slaps him on the back. "You must get to the main entrance before it floods."

"My crew?"

"Your crew is waiting for you there."

Goto Dengo begins walking towards the trail that will take him down to the main entrance. Along the way, he passes the top of another ventilation shaft, Several dozen workers are queued up there, thumbs lashed together behind their backs with piano wire, guarded by soldiers with fixed bayonets. One by one, prisoners kneel at the lip of the shaft. Lieutenant Mori whips his officer's sword into the nape of each neck with a terrific grunt. Head and body tumble forward into the ventilation shaft and thud meatily into other bodies, far below, a couple of seconds later. Every leaf and pebble within a three-meter radius of the shaft opening is saturated with bright red blood, and so is Lieutenant Mori.

"Don't worry about that," Captain Noda says. "I will see to it that the tops of the shafts are backfilled with rubble, as we discussed. The jungle will grow over them long before the Americans ever find this place."

Goto Dengo averts his eyes and turns to leave.

"Lieutenant Goto!" says a voice. He turns around. It is Lieutenant Mori, pausing for a moment to catch his breath. A Filipino kneels before him, mumbling a prayer in Latin, fumbling with a rosary that dangles from his bound hands.

"Yes, Lieutenant Mori."

"According to my roster, six prisoners are signed out to you. I will need them."

"Those six prisoners are down below, helping to load in the last shipment."

"But all of the shipment is inside the tunnels now."

"Yes, but not well placed. The entire purpose of the fool's vault is ruined if we strew gold and diamonds around the place in such a way as to lead thieves deeper into the caverns. I need these men to continue that work."

"You take full responsibility for them?"

"I do," Goto Dengo says.

"If there are only six," Captain Noda says, "then your crew should be able to keep them under control."

"I will see you at Yasukuni, Goto Dengo," says Lieutenant Mori.

"I will look forward to it," Goto Dengo says. He does not add that Yasukuni must be a very crowded place by now, and they will probably have a terrible time finding each other.

"I envy you. The end will be longer and harder for those of us on the outside." Lieutenant Mori snaps his blade into the back of the Filipino's head, cutting him off between an Ave and a Maria.

"Your heroism will not go unrewarded," Goto Dengo says.

Lieutenant Mori's crew awaits him down below, in front of the mouse-hole that leads into Golgotha: four hand-picked soldiers. Each wears a thousand-stitch headband, and so each has an orange ball centered on his forehead, reminding Goto Dengo not of the Rising Sun but of an exit wound. The water is up to mid-thigh now, and the entrance tunnel is half full. When Goto Dengo arrives, followed closely by Captain Noda, the men all cheer him politely.

Goto Dengo squats in the opening. Only his head and shoulders are above the water. Before him the tunnel is black. It takes a powerful effort of will for him to enter. But it is no worse than what he used to do in the abandoned mines, back in Hokkaido.

Of course, the abandoned mines weren't going to be dynamited shut behind him.

Going forward is his chance to survive. If he hesitates, Noda will kill him on the spot, and all his crew, and others will be sent in to finish the job. Noda made sure that others were trained to do it.

"See you at Yasukuni," he says to Captain Noda, and without waiting for a response he sloshes forward into blackness.

PONTIFEX

BY THE TIME RANDY REACHES THE AIR KINAKUTA BOARDING lounge, he has already forgotten how he reached the airport. He honestly can't remember. Did he hail a taxi? Not likely in downtown Los Altos. Did he get a ride from some hacker? He couldn't have driven the Acura, because the Acura's electronics had been burned to a crisp by the electromagnetic pulse gun. He had pulled the title out of the glove compartment and signed it over to a Ford dealer three blocks away, in exchange for five thousand dollars in cash.

Oh, yeah. The Ford dealer gave him a ride to the airport.

He has always wanted to pull the stunt of walking up to the counter of an exotic foreign airline and saying, "Get me on the next plane to X." But now he's just done it and it wasn't cool and romantic as he had hoped. It was sort of bleak and stressful and expensive. He had to buy a first-class ticket, which consumed most of the five thousand dollars. But he doesn't feel like beating himself to death over how he is managing his assets just now, i.e., at a time when his net worth is a negative number that can only be expressed using scientific notation. The probability is high that he failed to wipe Tombstone's hard drive before the cops seized it, and that the Dentist's lawsuit will consequently succeed.

On his way down the concourse he stands and stares at a bank of telephones for a while. He very much wants to notify the Shaftoes of recent events. It would be a good thing if they could somehow strip the sunken sub clean of treasure as fast as possible, reducing its value and hence the damage that the Dentist can inflict on Epiphyte.

The math is pretty simple here. The Dentist has a way to claim damages from Epiphyte. The amount of those damages is x, where x is what the Dentist, as a minority shareholder, would have made in capital gains if Randy had been responsible enough to write a better contract with Semper Marine. If such a contract had specified a fifty-fifty split, then x would be equal to fifty percent of the cash value of the wreck times the one tenth of Epiphyte that the Dentist owns minus a few percent for taxes and other frictional effects of the real world. So if there's ten million dollars in the wreck, then x works out to around half a million bucks.

In order for the Dentist to gain control of Epiphyte, he has to acquire an additional forty percent of its stock. The price of that stock (if it were for sale) is simply 0.4 times the total value of Epiphyte. Call it y.

If $x > y$, the Dentist wins. Because then the judge is going to say, "You, Epiphyte, owe this poor aggrieved minority shareholder \$$x$. But as I look at the parlous state of the corporation's finances I see that there's no way for you to raise that kind of money. And so the only way to settle the debt is to give the plaintiff the one asset you have in abundance, which is your crappy stock. And since the value of the whole corporation is really, really close to being zero, you're going to have to give him almost all of it."

So how to make $x < y$? Either reduce the value of the wreck, by stripping it of its gold, or else increase the value of Epiphyte, by— what, exactly?

In better times they could maybe take the company public. But setting up an IPO takes months. And no investor's going to touch it when it's encumbered by a lawsuit from the Dentist.

Randy has this vision of driving through the jungle with an end-loader and scooping up that big pile of gold bars he found with Doug and taking it straight to a bank and depositing it in Epiphyte's account. That'd do it. The whole concept makes his body tingle as he stands there in the middle of the international concourse.

Off to the left, some kind of huddled or teeming mass, heavy on the women and children, passes, and Randy hears some familiar voices. His mind has wrapped itself like a starving squid around this gold-in-the-jungle concept, and in order to address reality for just a second, he has to peel the tentacles away, popping those suckers off of it one by one. He eventually focuses in on the scuttling group and identifies it as Avi's family: Devorah and a bunch of kids and the two nannies, clutching passports and tickets in El Al jackets. The kids are small and prone to sudden darting tactics, the adults are tense and not inclined to let them stray, so the group's movement down the concourse has the general aspect of a sack of beagles heading in the approximate direction of some fresh meat. Randy is probably personally responsible for this exodus and would much rather slink into the men's room and crawl down a toilet, but he has to say something. So he catches up with Devorah and startles her by offering to carry the child support bag that she has slung over her shoulder. This turns out to be shockingly heavy: several gallons of apple juice, he would estimate, plus complete asthma-attack management infrastructure, and maybe a few bricks of solid gold in case of some totalizing civil breakdown en route.

"So. Uh, going to Israel?"

"El Al doesn't fly to Acapulco." Pow! Devorah is in peak form.

"Did Avi give you any kind of rationale for this?"

"You're asking me? I kind of assumed you would know," Devorah says.

"Well, things have been, certainly, volatile," Randy says. "I don't know if fleeing the country is warranted."

"Then why are you in the airport with an Air Kinakuta ticket sticking out of your pocket?"

"Oh, you know . . . some business issues need resolving."

"You seem really depressed. Do you have a problem?" Devorah asks. Randy sighs. "That depends. Do you?"

"Do I what? Have a problem? Why should I have a problem?"

"Because you've been uprooted and sent packing on ten minutes' notice."

"We're going to Israel, Randy. That's not being uprooted. That's being rerooted." Or perhaps she is saying "rerouted." Without a transcript, there is no way for Randy to tell.

"Yeah, but it's still kind of a hassle—"

"Compared to what?"

"Compared to staying at home and living your life."

"This is my life, Randy." Devorah is definitely kicking out a prickly vibe here. Randy figures that she is incredibly pissed off, but under some kind of emotional nondisclosure agreement. This is probably better than the only other two alternatives Randy can think of, namely (1) dissolving into hysterical recriminations and (2) beatific serenity. It is an I'll-do-my-job, you-do-yours, why-are-you-in-my-face attitude. Randy feels like an idiot, all of a sudden, for having taken Devorah's bag. She is clearly just this side of aghast, wondering why the fuck Randy is toiling as a skycap at this critical moment. Like she and the nannies are not capable of humping a sack down a hallway. Has she, Devorah, offered to step in and help Randy write any code lately? And if Randy really has nothing better to do, why doesn't he be a man, and strap grenades all over his body and give the Dentist a big hug?

Randy says, "I assume you'll be in touch with Avi before you take off. Would you give him a message?"

"What's the message?"

"Zero."

"That's it?"

"That's it," Randy says.

Devorah is perhaps not familiar with Randy and Avi's practice of conserving precious bandwidth by communicating in binary code, one bit at a time, à la Paul Revere and the Old North Church. In this case, "zero" means that Randy did not succeed in wiping out all the data on Tombstone's hard drive.

Air Kinakuta's first-class lounge, with its free drinks and highly un-American concept of service, beckons. Randy avoids it because he knows he will sink straight into a coma if he goes there, and they would have to load him onto the 747 with a forklift. Instead he walks around the airport, clutching his hip spastically everytime he re-realizes that his laptop isn't dangling there. He is not adjusting very quickly to the fact that most of the laptop is stuffed into a wastebasket at the Ford dealership where he unloaded the Acura. While he was waiting for his man to scurry back from the bank with the five grand, he used the screwdriver attachments on his multipurpose pocket tool to extract the laptop's hard drive, and then threw away the rest.

Very large television sets hang from the ceilings in the departure lounge, showing the Airport Channel, which is a parade of news-bits even more punishingly flimsy than normal television news, mixed in with a great deal of weather and stock quotes. Randy is struck, but not precisely surprised, to see footage of black-hatted Secret Admirers exercising their Second Amendment rights in the streets of Los Altos, and of Ordo's barricade avalanching towards the camera, and the police storming over it weapons drawn. Paul Comstock is shown—pausing, as he climbs into a limousine to say something, looking hale and smug. The conventional wisdom about TV news is that the image is everything and if that is the case then this is a big win for Ordo, which looks like the victim of jackbooted thugs. Which gets Epiphyte nowhere, since Ordo is, or ought to be, nothing more than a bystander. This is supposed to be a private conflict between the Dentist and Epiphyte and now it's become a public one between Comstock and Ordo, and this makes Randy irritated and confused.

He goes and gets on his plane and starts eating caviar. Normally he doesn't partake, but caviar has a decadent fiddling-while-Rome-burns thing going for it that works for him just now.

As is his nerdly custom, Randy actually reads the informational cards that are stuffed in among the in-flight magazines and vomit-sacs. One of these extols the fact that Sultan-Class passengers (as first-class passengers are called) can not only make outgoing phone calls from their seats but can also receive incoming ones. So Randy dials the number for Douglas MacArthur Shaftoe's GSM telephone. It's an Australian phone number, but it'll ring anywhere on the planet. Right now it's something like six A.M. in the Philippines, but Doug is bound to be awake, and indeed he answers his phone on the second ring. Randy can tell from the sound of horns and diesels that he is stuck in Manila traffic, probably in the back of a taxi.

"It's Randy. On a plane," says Randy. "An Air Kinakuta plane."

"Randy! Well I've just been watching you on television," Doug says.

It takes a minute for that to sink in; Randy has used a couple of vodkas to cleanse his palate of the caviar.

"Yeah," Doug continues, "I turned on CNN when I woke up and glimpsed you sitting on top of a car typing. What's going on?"

"Nothing! Nothing at all," Randy says. He figures that this is a big stroke of luck. Now that Doug has seen him on CNN, he'll be more likely to effect superbly dramatic measures out of sheer paranoia. Randy slurps vodka and says, "Wow, this Sultan-Class service is great. Anyway, if you do a Web search on Ordo, you'll see this nonsense had absolutely nothing to do with us. Nothing."

"That's funny, because Comstock is denying that it's a crackdown on Ordo," Doug says. When speaking of official U.S. government denials, Vietnam combat veterans like Doug are capable of summoning up a drawling irony that is about as subtle as having automotive jumper cables connected directly to your fillings, but much funnier. Vodka climbs about halfway up Randy's nose before he controls it. "They say that it's just a little old civil suit," Doug says, now using a petal-soft, wounded-innocent tone.

"Ordo's status as purveyor of stuff that the government hates and fears is just coincidental," Randy guesses.

"That's right."

"Well then, I'm sure there's nothing to it other than our troubles with the Dentist," Randy says.

"What troubles are those, Randy?"

"Happened during the middle of the night, your time. I'm sure you will have some interesting faxes awaiting you this morning."

"Well, maybe I should look at those faxes, then," Doug Shaftoe says.

"Maybe I'll give you a buzz when I reach Kinakuta," Randy says.

"You have a good flight, Randall."

"Have a nice day, Douglas."

Randy puts the phone back in its armrest cradle and prepares to sink into a well-deserved plane-coma. But five minutes later the phone rings. It is so disorienting to have one's phone ring on an airplane that he doesn't know what to make of it for a while. When he finally realizes what's going on, he has to consult the instruction card to figure out how to answer it.

When he finally has the thing turned on and at his ear, a voice says, "You call that subtle? You think that you and Doug Shaftoe are the only two people in the world who know that Sultan-Class passengers can receive incoming phone calls?" Randy is certain he's never heard this voice before. It is the voice of an old man. Not a voice worn out or cracking with age, but a voice that's been slowly worn smooth, like the steps of a cathedral.

"Um, who's this?"

"Am I right in thinking that you want Mr. Shaftoe to go to a pay telephone somewhere and then call you back?"

"Who is this, please?"

"You think that's more secure than his GSM phone? It's not really." The speaker pauses frequently before, during, and after sentences, as if he's been spending a lot of time alone, and is having trouble hitting his conversational stride.

"Okay," Randy says, "you know who I am and whom I was calling. So obviously you are surveilling me. You're not working for the Dentist, I take it. That leaves—what? The United States Government? The NSA, right?"

The man laughs. "As a rule the Fort Meade boys don't bother to check in with the people whose lines they are tapping." The caller has an un-American crispness in his voice, vaguely Northern European. "In your case the NSA might make an exception, it's true—when I was there, they were all great admirers of your grandfather's work. In fact, they liked it so much they stole it."

"No higher flattery, I guess."

"You should be a billionaire, Randy. Thank god you're not."

"Why do you say that?"

"Oh, because then you'd be a highly intelligent man who never has to make difficult choices—who never has to exert his mind. It is a state much worse than being a moron."

"Did Grandpa work for you at the NSA?"

"He wasn't interested. Said he had a higher calling. So while he made better and better computers to solve the Harvard-Waterhouse Prime Factoring Challenge, my friends at the NSA watched him, and learned."

"And you did too."

"I? Oh, no, I have only modest skills with a soldering iron. I was there to watch the NSA watching your grandfather."

"On behalf of—whom? Don't tell me—eruditorum.org?"

"Well done, Randy."

"What should I call you—Root? Pontifex?"

"Pontifex is a nice word."

"It's true," Randy says. "I checked it out, looking for clues in the etymology—it's an old Latin word meaning 'priest.' "

"Catholics call the Pope 'Pontifex Maximus,' or pontiff for short," says Pontifex agreeably, "but the word was also used by pagans to denote their priests, and Jews their rabbis—it is ever so ecumenical."

"But the literal meaning of the word is 'bridge builder,' and so it's a good name for a cryptosystem," Randy says.

"Or, I hope, for me," Pontifex says drily. "I am glad you feel that way, Randy. Many people would think of a cryptosystem as a wall, rather than a bridge."

"Well, gosh. It's nice to telephonically meet you, Pontifex."

"The pleasure is mutual."

"You've been so quiet on the e-mail front recently."

"Didn't want to give you the creeps. I was afraid if I bothered you any more, you'd think I was proselytizing."

"Not at all. By the way—people in the know think your cryptosystem is weird, but good."

"It's not weird at all, once you understand it," Pontifex says politely.

"Well, uh, what occasions this phone call? Obviously your *friends* are still surveilling me on behalf of—whom, exactly?"

"I don't even know," Pontifex says. "But I do know that you're trying to crack Arethusa."

Randy cannot even remember ever uttering the word "Arethusa." It was printed on the wrappers on the bricks of ETC cards that he ran through Chester's card reader. Now Randy pictures a box inside Grandpa's old trunk labeled *Harvard-Waterhouse Prime Factoring Challenge* and dated in the early 1950s. So that at least gives him a date to peg on Pontifex. "You were at NSA during the late forties and early fifties," Randy says. "You must have worked on Harvest." Harvest was a legendary code-breaking supercomputer, three decades ahead of its time, built by ETC engineers working under an NSA contract.

"I told you," Pontifex says, "your grandfather's work came in handy."

"Chester's got this retired ETC engineer working on his card machinery," Randy says. "He helped me read the Arethusa cards. Saw the wrappers. He's a friend of yours. He called you."

Pontifex chuckles. "Among our little band there is hardly a word with more memories attached to it than Arethusa. He nearly hit the floor when he saw it. Called me from the cellphone on his boat, Randy."

"Why? Why was Arethusa such a big deal?"

"Because we spent ten years of our lives trying to break the damned code! And we failed!"

"It must have been really frustrating," Randy says, "you still sound angry."

"I'm angry at Comstock."

"Not the—"

"Not Attorney General Paul Comstock. His father. Earl Comstock."

"What!? The guy that Doug Shaftoe threw off the ski lift? The Vietnam guy?"

"No, no! I mean, yes. Earl Comstock *was* largely responsible for our Vietnam policy. And Doug Shaftoe did get his fifteen minutes of fame by throwing him off a ski lift in, I believe, 1979. But all of that Vietnam nonsense was just a coda to his real career."

"Which was?"

"Earl Comstock, to whom your grandfather reported in Brisbane during World War II, was one of the founders of the NSA. And he was my boss from 1949 through about 1960. He was obsessed with Arethusa."

"Why?"

"He was convinced it was a Communist cipher. That if we could break it, we could then exploit that break to get into some later Soviet codes that were giving us difficulty. Which was ridiculous. But he believed it—or claimed to—and so we battered our heads against Arethusa for years. Strong men had nervous breakdowns. Brilliant men concluded that they were stupid. In the end it turned out to be a joke."

"A joke? What do you mean by that?"

"We ran those intercepts through Harvest backwards and forwards. The lights dimmed in Washington and Baltimore, we used to say, when we were doing Arethusa work. I still have the opening groups memorized: AADAA FGTAA and so on. Those double As! People wrote dissertations about their significance. We concluded in the end that they were just flukes. We invented entire new systems of cryptanalysis to attack it—wrote new volumes of the *Cryptonomicon*. The data were very nearly random. Finding patterns in them was like trying to read a book that had been burned, and its ashes mixed with all the cement that went into the Hoover Dam. We never got anything that was worth a damn.

"After ten years or so, we began using it to haze incoming recruits. By that time the NSA was getting fantastically huge, we were hiring all of the most brilliant math prodigies in the United States, and when we got one who was especially cocky we'd put him on the Arethusa project just to give him the message that he wasn't as smart as he thought he was. We broke a lot of kids on that wheel. But then, around 1959, this one kid came in—the smartest kid we had seen yet—and he broke it."

"Well, I assume you didn't place this phone call just to keep me in suspense," Randy says. "What did he find?"

"He found that the Arethusa intercepts did not represent coded messages at all. They were simply the output of a particular mathematical function, a Riemann zeta function, which has many uses—one being that it is used in some cryptosystems as a random number generator. He proved that if you set up this function in a particular way, and then gave it, as input, a particular string of numbers, it would crank out the exact sequence that was on those intercepts. So that was all she wrote. And it almost ended Comstock's career."

"Why?"

"Partly because of the insane amount of money and manpower he had thrown into the Arethusa project. But mostly because the input string—the seed for the random number generator—was the boss's name. C-O-M-S-T-O-C-K."

"You're kidding."

"We had the proof right there. It was impeccable from a pure math standpoint. So, either Comstock had generated the Arethusa intercepts himself, and been stupid enough to use his own name as the seed—and believe me, he really was that kind of guy—or else someone had played an enormous practical joke on him."

"Which do you think it was?"

"Well, he never divulged where he had gotten these intercepts in the first place and so it was difficult to form a hypothesis. I am inclined toward the joke theory, because he was the sort of man who gives his subordinates a powerful urge to play practical jokes on him. But in the end it didn't matter. He was drummed out of the NSA at the age of forty-six. A classic grey man, a war veteran, a technocrat with a high security clearance and any number of high-powered connections. He went more or less straight to Kennedy's National Security Counsel from there, and the rest is history."

"Wow!" Randy says, kind of awed. "What a jerk!"

"No kidding," says Pontifex. "And now, his son—well, don't get me started on his son."

As Pontifex's voice trails off, Randy asks, "So, you are calling me now for what purpose?"

Pontifex doesn't answer for a few moments, as if he's wrestling with the question himself. But Randy doubts that's the case. *Someone is trying to send you a message.* "I suppose that I am just appalled by the very idea of more young bright men throwing themselves against Arethusa. Until I received that call from a boat on Lake Washington, I had thought it was dead and buried."

"But why should you care?"

"You've already been cheated out of a fortune in computer patents," Pontifex says. "It wouldn't be fair."

"So, it's pity, then."

"Furthermore—as I said—it is my friend's job to keep you under surveillance. He's going to hear almost every word you say for the next few months, or at least read transcripts. For you and Cantrell and those others to spend that entire time yammering about Arethusa would be more than he could bear. Hideous deja vu. Just intolerably Kafkaesque. So please, just let it go."

"Well, thanks for the tip."

"You're welcome, Randy. And may I give you a word of advice?"

"That's what Pontifex is supposed to do."

"First a disclaimer: I've been out of circulation for a while. Have not picked up the postmodern unwillingness to make value judgments."

"Okay, I am bracing myself."

"My advice: do try to build the best Crypt you possibly can. Your clients—some of them, anyway—are, for all practical purposes, aborigines. They will either make you rich or kill you, like something straight out of a Joseph Campbell footnote."

"So you're talking about your basic Colombian drug lord types, here?"

"Yes, I am, but I'm also referring to certain white men in suits. It only takes a single generation to revert to savagery."

"Well, we provide state-of-the-art cryptographic services to all of our clients—even the ones with bones in their noses."

"Excellent! And now—as much as I hate to sign off on a dark note— I must say good-bye."

Randy hangs up, and the phone rings again almost immediately.

"Who the fuck are you?" Doug Shaftoe says, "I call you on the airplane, and I get a busy signal."

"I have a funny story to tell you," Randy says, "about a guy you ran into once while skiing. But unfortunately it will have to wait."

BARE-CHESTED, CAMOUFLAGE-PAINTED, TRENCH KNIFE IN HAND, Colt .45 stuck in the waistband of his khaki trousers, Bobby Shaftoe moves like a cloud of mist through the jungle. He stops when he can get a clear view of the Nip Army truck, framed between the hairy, cluttered trunks of a couple of date palms. A skirmish line of ants crawls over the skin of his sandaled foot. He ignores them.

It has all the earmarks of a piss stop. Two Nipponese privates climb out of the truck and confer for a few moments. One of them wades into the jungle. The other leans against the truck's fender and lights up a cigarette. Its glowing tip echoes the light of the sunset behind him. The one in the jungle drops his trousers, squats, leans back against a tree to take a shit.

At this moment they are supremely vulnerable. The contrast between the brightness of the sunset and the dimness of the jungle renders them nearly blind. The shitter is helpless, and the smoker looks exhausted. Bobby Shaftoe sheds his sandals. He emerges from the jungle onto the road behind the truck, strides forward on ant-bitten feet, crouches behind the truck's bumper. The weapon comes out of his hip pocket silently. Without taking his eyes off the smoker's feet—visible beneath the truck's chassis—he peels away the backing and slaps the payload onto the truck's tailgate. Then, just to rub it in, he slaps up another one. Mission accomplished! Take that, Tojo!

Moments later, he's back in the jungle, watching as the Nip truck drives away, now sporting two red, white, and blue stickers reading: I SHALL RETURN! Bobby congratulates himself on another successful mission.

Long after dark, he reaches the Hukbalahap camp up on the volcano. He works his way in through the booby-trapped perimeter and makes plenty of noise as he approaches, so that the Huk sentries won't shoot at him in the darkness. But he needn't have bothered. Discipline has broken down, they are all drunk and getting drunker, because of something they heard on the radio: MacArthur has returned. The General has landed on Leyte.

Bobby Shaftoe's response is to boil up some powerful coffee and begin pouring it into their signal man, Pedro. While the caffeine works its magic, Shaftoe grabs a message pad and the stub of a pencil, and writes out his idea for the seventh time: OPPORTUNITY EXISTS TO CONTACT AND SUPPLY FILAMERICAN ELEMENTS IN CONCEPCION STOP I VOLUNTEER FOR SAME STOP AWAIT INSTRUCTIONS STOP SIGNED SHAFTOE.

He gets Pedro to encrypt it and send it off. After that, all he can do is wait and pray. This shit with the stickers has to stop.

He has been tempted, a thousand times, to desert, and to go into Concepcion himself. But just because he's out in the boondocks with a band of Huk irregulars doesn't mean he's beyond the reach of military discipline. Deserters can still get shot or hanged, and despite the fact that he was one in Sweden, Bobby Shaftoe believes that they deserve to be.

Concepcion is down in the lowlands north of Manila. From the high places of the Zambales Mountains you can actually see the town lying amid the green rice paddies. Those lowlands are still totally Nip-controlled. But when the General lands, he's probably going to land north of here at Lingayen Gulf, just like the Nips did when they invaded in '41, and then Concepcion is going to lie right in the middle of his route to Manila. He's going to need eyes there.

Sure enough, the order comes through a couple of days later: RENDEZVOUS TARPON POINT GREEN 5 NOVEMBER STOP CONVEY TRANSMITTER CONCEPCION STOP AWAIT FURTHER ORDERS STOP.

Tarpon is the submarine that has been bringing them ammunition, medical supplies, I SHALL RETURN stickers, cartons of American cigarettes with I SHALL RETURN inserts in each pack, I SHALL RETURN matchbooks, I SHALL RETURN coasters, and I SHALL RETURN condoms. Shaftoe has been stockpiling the condoms because he knows they won't go over well in a Catholic country. He figures that when he finds Glory he'll go through a long ton of condoms in about a week.

Three days later, he and a squad of Huks are on hand to meet Tarpon at "Point Green," which is their code name for a tiny cove on the west coast of Luzon, down beneath Mount Pinatubo, not all that far north of Subic Bay. The submarine glides in at around midnight, running on its electric motors so it won't make any sound, and the Huks pull up alongside in rubber boats and outrigger canoes and unload the cargo. Sure enough, the transmitter's there. And this time there's none of those goddamn stickers or matchbooks. The cargo is ammunition and a few fighting men: some Filamerican commandoes fresh from a debriefing with MacArthur's intelligence chief, and a couple of Americans—MacArthur's advance scouts.

Over the next several days, Shaftoe and a few hand-picked Huks carry the transmitter up one slope of the Zambales Mountains and down the other. They stop when the foothills finally give way to low-lying paddy land. The main north–south road, from Manila up towards Lingayen Gulf, lies directly across their path.

After a few days of scrambling and scrounging, they are able to load the transmitter on board a farm cart and bury it in manure. They harness the cart to a pathetic carabao, loaned by a loyal but poor farmer, and set out across Nip country, headed for Concepcion.

At this point they have to split up, though, because there's no way that blue-eyed Shaftoe can travel in the open. Two Huks, pretending to be farmboys, take the manure cart while Shaftoe begins making his way cross-country, traveling at night, sleeping in ditches or in the homes of trusted American sympathizers.

It takes him a week and a half to cover the fifty kilometers, but in time, with patience and perseverance, he reaches the town of Concepcion, and knocks on the door of their local contact around midnight. The contact is a prominent local citizen—the manager of the town's only bank. Mr. Calagua is astonished to see an American standing at his back door. This tells Shaftoe that something must have gone wrong— the boys with the transmitter should have arrived a week ago. But the manager tells him that no one has shown up—though rumor has it that the Nips recently caught some boys trying to smuggle contraband in a farm cart and executed them on the spot.

So Shaftoe is marooned in Concepcion with no way to get orders or to send messages. He feels bad for the boys who died, but in a way, this isn't such a bad situation for him. The only reason he wanted to be in Concepcion is that the Altamira family comes from here. Half of the local farmers are related to Glory in some way.

Shaftoe breaks into the Calaguas' stables and improvises a bed. They would put him up in a spare bedroom if he asked, but he tells them that the stables are safer—if he gets caught, the Calaguas can at least claim ignorance. He recuperates on a pile of straw for a day or two, then starts trying to learn something about the Altamiras. He can't go out nosing around by himself, but the Calaguas know everyone in town, and they have a good sense of who can be trusted. So inquiries go out, and within a couple of days, information has come back in.

Mr. Calagua explains it to him over glasses of bourbon in his study. Wracked by guilt over the fact that his honored guest is sleeping on a pile of hay in an outbuilding, he pushes bourbon at him all the time, which is fine with Bobby Shaftoe.

"Some of the information is reliable, some is—er—farfetched," Mr. Calagua says. "Here is the reliable part. First of all, your guess was correct. When the Japanese took over Manila, many members of the

Altamira family came back to this area to stay with relatives. They believed it would be safer."

"Are you telling me Glory is up here?"

"No," Mr. Calagua says sadly, "she is not up here. But she was definitely here on September 13th, 1942."

"How do you know?"

"Because she gave birth to a baby boy on that day—the birth certificate is on file at the town hall. Douglas MacArthur Shaftoe."

"Well, I'll be fucked sideways," Shaftoe says. He starts calculating dates in his head.

"Many of the Altamiras who fled here have since gone back to the city—supposedly to obtain work. But some of them are also serving as eyes and ears for the resistance."

"I knew they would do the right thing," Shaftoe says.

Mr. Calagua smiles cautiously. "Manila is full of people who claim to be the eyes and ears of the resistance. It is easy to be eyes and ears. It is harder to be fists and feet. But some of the Altamiras are fighting, too—they have gone into the mountains to join the Huks."

"Which mountains? I didn't run across any of them up in the Zambales."

"South of Manila and Laguna de Bay are many volcanoes and heavy jungle. This is where some of Glory's family are fighting."

"Is that where Glory is? And the baby? Or are they in the city?"

Mr. Calagua is nervous. "This is the part that may be far-fetched. It is said that Glory is a famous heroine of the fight against the Nips."

"Are you telling me she's dead? If she's dead, just tell me."

"No, I have no information that she is dead. But she is a heroine. This is for certain."

The next day, Bobby Shaftoe's malaria comes back and keeps him laid up for about a week. The Calaguas move him right into their house and bring in the town doctor to look after him. It's the same doctor who delivered Douglas MacArthur Shaftoe two years ago.

When he's feeling a little stronger, he lights out for the south. It takes him three weeks to reach the northern outskirts of Manila, hitching rides on trains and trucks, or sloshing through paddies in the middle of the night. He kills two Nipponese soldiers stealthily, and three of them in a firefight at an intersection. Each time, he has to go to ground for a few days to avoid capture. But get to Manila he does.

He can't go into the heart of the city—in addition to being really stupid, it would just slow him down. Instead he skirts it, taking advantage of the thriving resistance network. He is passed from one barangay to the next, all the way around the outskirts of Manila, until he has reached the coastal plain between Laguna de Bay and Manila Bay. At this point nothing is left to the south except for a few miles of rice paddies and then the volcanic mountains where Altamiras are making names for themselves as guerilla fighters. During his trip he has heard a thousand rumors about them. Most of them are patently false—people telling him what he obviously wants to hear. But several times he has heard what sounds like a genuine scrap of information about Glory.

They say that she has a healthy young son, living in the apartment in the Malate neighborhood of Manila, being cared for by the extended family while his mother serves in the war.

They say that she has put her nursing skills to work, acting as a sort of Florence Nightingale for the Huks.

They say that she is a messenger for the Fil-American forces, that no one surpasses her daring in crossing through Nipponese checkpoints carrying secret messages and other contraband.

The last part doesn't make much sense to Shaftoe. Which is she, a nurse or a messenger? Maybe they have her confused with someone else. Or maybe she's both—maybe she's smuggling medicine through the checkpoints.

The farther south he gets, the more information he hears. The same rumors and anecdotes pop up over and over again, differing only in their small details. He runs into half a dozen people who are dead certain that Glory is south of here, working as a messenger for a brigade of Huk guerillas in the mountains above Calamba.

He spends Christmas Day in a fisherman's hut on the shores of the big lake, Laguna de Bay. There are plenty of mosquitoes. Another bout of malaria strikes him then; he spends a couple of weeks wracked with fever dreams, having bizarre nightmares about Glory.

Finally he gets well enough to move again, and hitches a boat ride into the lakeside town of Calamba. The black volcanoes that loom above it are a welcome sight. They look nice and cool, and they remind him of the ancestral Shaftoe territory. According to their family lore, the first Shaftoes to come to America worked as indentured servants in tobacco and cotton fields, raising their eyes longingly towards those cool mountains as they stooped in sweltering fields. As soon as they could get away, they did, and headed uphill. The mountains of Luzon beckon Shaftoe in the same way—away from the malarial lowlands, up towards Glory. His journey's almost over.

But he gets stuck in Calamba, forced to hide in a boathouse, when the city's Nipponese Air Force troops begin gathering their forces for some kind of a move. Those Huks up on the mountain have been giving them a hard time, and the Nips are getting crazed and vicious.

The leader of the local Huks finally sends an emissary to get Shaftoe's story. The emissary goes away and several days pass. Finally a Fil-American lieutenant returns bearing two pieces of good news: the Americans have landed in force at Lingayen Gulf, and Glory is alive and working with the Huks only a few miles away.

"Help me get out of this town," Shaftoe pleads. "Take me out in a boat on the lake, drop me off in the countryside, then I can move."

"Move where?" says the lieutenant, playing stupid.

"To the high ground! To join those Huks!"

"You would be killed. The ground is booby-trapped. The Huks are extremely vigilant."

"But—"

"Why don't you go the other way?" the lieutenant asks. "Go to Manila."

"Why would I want to go there?"

"Your son is there. And that is where you are needed. Soon the big battle will be in Manila."

"Okay," Shaftoe says, "I'll go to Manila. But first I want to see Glory."

"Ah," the lieutenant says, as if light has finally dawned. "You say you want to see Glory."

"I'm not just saying it. I do want to see Glory."

The lieutenant exhales a cloud of cigarette smoke and shakes his head. "No you don't," he says flatly.

"What?"

"You don't want to see Glory."

"How can you say that? Are you fucking out of your mind?"

The lieutenant's face goes stony. "Very well," he says, "I will make inquiries. Perhaps Glory will come here and visit you."

"That's crazy. It's much too dangerous."

The lieutenant laughs. "No, *you* don't understand," he says. "You are a white man in a provincial city in the Philippines occupied by starving, beserk Nips. It is impossible for you to show your face outside. Impossible. Glory, on the other hand, is free to move."

"You said they're inspecting people almost every block."

"They will not bother Glory."

"Do the Nips ever—you know. Molest women?"

"Ah. You are worried about Glory being raped." The lieutenant takes another long draw on his cigarette. "I can assure you that this will not happen." He rises to his feet, tired of the conversation. "Wait here," he says. "Gather your strength for the Battle of Manila."

He walks out, leaving Shaftoe more frustrated than ever.

Two days later, the owner of the boathouse, who speaks very little English, shakes Shaftoe awake before sunrise. He beckons Shaftoe into a small boat and rows him out into the lake, then half a mile up the shore toward a sandbar. The dawn is just breaking over the other side of the big lake, illuminating planet-sized cumulus clouds. It's as if the biggest fuel dump in the whole world is being blown up in a sky diced into vast trapezoids by the linear contrails of American planes on dawn patrol.

Glory is strolling out on the sandbar. He can't see her face because she is wrapped in a silk scarf, but he would know the shape of her body anywhere. She walks back and forth along the shore, letting the warm water of the lake lap against her bare feet. She is really loving that sunrise—she keeps her back turned to Shaftoe so that she can enjoy it. What a flirt. Shaftoe gets as hard as an oar. He pats his back pocket, making sure he's well stocked with I SHALL RETURN condoms. It will be tricky, bedding down with Glory on a sandbar with this old codger here, but maybe he can pay the guy to go out and exercise his back for an hour.

The guy keeps looking over his shoulder to judge the distance to the sandbar. When they are about a stone's throw away, he sits up and ships the oars. They coast for a few yards and then come to a stop.

"What are you doing?" Shaftoe asks. Then he heaves a sigh. "You want money?" He rubs his thumb and fingertips together. "Huh? Like that?"

But the guy is just staring into his face, with an expression as tough and stony as anything that Shaftoe has seen on a hundred battlefields around the world. He waits for Shaftoe to shut up, then cocks his head and jerks it back in the direction of Glory.

Shaftoe looks up at Glory, just as she's turning around to face him. She reaches up with clublike hands, all wrapped up in long strips of cloth like a mummy's, and paws the scarf away from her face.

Or what used to be a face. Now it's just the front of her skull.

Bobby Shaftoe breathes in deep, and lets out a scream that can probably be heard in downtown Manila.

The boatman casts an anxious look toward the town, then stands up, blocking Shaftoe's view as he's drawing in another breath. One of the oars is in his hands. Shaftoe is just cutting loose with another scream when the oar clocks him in the side of the head.

THE SUN HAS MADE A LONG, SKIDDING CRASH-LANDING ALONG the Malay Peninsula a few hundred kilometers west, breaking open and spilling its thermonuclear fuel over about half of the horizon, trailing out a wall of salmon and magenta clouds that have blown a gash all the way through the shell of the atmosphere and erupted into space. The mountain containing the Crypt is just a charcoal shard against that backdrop. Randy is annoyed with the sunset for making it difficult to see the construction site. By now the scar in the cloud forest has mostly healed over, or, at least, some kind of green stuff has taken over the bare, lipstick-colored mud. A few GOTO ENGINEERING containers still glower in the color-distorting light of the mercury-vapor lamps around the entrance, but most of them have either moved inside the Crypt or gone back to Nippon. Randy can make out the headlights of one house-sized Goto truck winding down the road, probably filled with debris for another one of the sultan's land reclamation projects.

Seated up in the plane's nose, Randy can actually look forward out his window and see that they are landing on the new runway, built partly on such fill. The buildings of downtown are streaks of blue-green light on either side of the plane, tiny black human figures frozen in them: a man with a phone clamped between his ear and his shoulder, a woman in a skirt hugging a pile of books to her chest but thinking about something far away. The view turns empty and indigo as the plane's nose tilts up for the landing, and then Randy's looking out over the Sulu Sea at dusk, where the *badjaos'* kite-sailed boats are scuttling into port from a day's fishing, hung all about with gutted stingrays, flying fresh sharks' tails like flags. Not long ago it was ridiculously exotic to him, but now he feels more at home here then he did in California.

For Sultan-Class passengers, everything happens with cinematic, quick-cut speed. The plane lands, a beautiful woman hands you your jacket, and you get off. The planes used by Asian airlines must have special chutes in the tail where flight attendants are ejected into the stratosphere on their twenty-eighth birthdays.

Usually there's someone waiting for a Sultan-Class passenger. This evening it's John Cantrell, still ponytailed but now clean-shaven; eventually the heat has its way with everyone. He's even taken to shaving the back of his neck, a good trick for shedding a couple of extra BTUs. Cantrell greets Randy with an awkward simultaneous handshake and one-armed hug/body check maneuver.

"Good to see you, John," Randy says.

"You too, Randy," John says, and each man averts his eyes shyly.

"Who's where?"

"You and I are here in the airport. Avi checked into a hotel in downtown San Francisco for the duration."

"Good. I didn't think he was safe in that house by himself."

Cantrell looks provoked. "Any particular reason? Have there been threats?"

"None that I know of. But it's hard to ignore the high number of vaguely terrifying people wrapped up in this."

"No victim Avi. Beryl's flying back to S.F. from Amsterdam—actually she's probably there by now."

"I heard she was in Europe. Why?"

"Strange government shit is going on there. I'll tell you later."

"Where's Eb?"

"Eb has been holed up in the Crypt for a week with his team, doing this kind of incredible D-Day-like push to finalize the biometric identification system. We won't bother him. Tom's been drifting back and forth between his house and the Crypt, running various kinds of torture tests on the internal Crypt network systems. Probing the inner trust boundaries. That's where we're going now."

"To the inner trust boundaries?"

"No! Sorry. His house." Cantrell shakes his head. "It's . . . well. It's not the house I would build."

"I want to see it."

"His paranoia is getting just a little out of hand."

"Hey speaking of that . . ." Randy stops. He was about to tell Cantrell about Pontifex, but they are very close to the halal Dunkin' Donuts, and people are looking at them. There's no way of telling who might be listening. "I'll tell you later."

Cantrell looks momentarily baffled and then grins wickedly. "Good one."

"We have a car?"

"I borrowed Tom's car. His Humvee. Not one of those cushy civilian models. A real military one."

"Oh, that's great," Randy says. "Does it come complete with big machine gun on the back?"

"He looked into it—he could certainly get a license to own one in

Kinakuta—but his wife drew the line at having an actual heavy machine gun in their domicile."

"How about you? Where do you stand on this gun stuff?"

"I own them and know how to use them, as you are aware," Cantrell says.

They are winding their way down a gauntlet of duty-free shops, really more of a duty-free shopping mall. Randy cannot figure out who actually buys all of these large bottles of liquor and expensive belts. What kind of blandly orgiastic lifestyle demands this particular selection of goods?

In the time that's thus passed Cantrell has evidently decided that a more thorough answer to Randy's gun question is merited. "But the more I practiced with them the more scared I got. Or maybe depressed."

"What do you mean?" This is Randy in unaccustomed sounding-board mode, psychotherapeutically prompting Cantrell for his feelings. It must have been a weird day for John Cantrell, and no doubt there are some feelings that need to be addressed.

"Holding one of those things in your hands, cleaning the barrel and shoving the rounds into clips, really brings you face-to-face with what a desperate, last-ditch measure they really are. I mean, if it gets to the point where we are shooting at people and vice versa, then we have completely screwed up. So in the end, they only strengthened my interest in making sure we could do without them."

"And hence the Crypt?" Randy asks.

"My involvement in the Crypt is arguably a direct result of a few very bad dreams that I had about guns."

It is wonderfully healthy to be talking like this, but it is a portentous departure from their usual hard-core technical mode. They are wondering about whether it is even worth it for them to be mixed up in this stuff. Heedless certainty sure is easier.

"Well, what about those Secret Admirers who were hanging around outside Ordo?" Randy asks.

"What about them? You're asking me about their state of mind?"

"Yeah. That is what we are talking about. States of mind."

Cantrell shrugs. "I don't know specifically who they were. I'd guess there are one or two honest-to-god scary fanatics. Setting them aside, maybe a third of them are just too young and immature to understand what's going on. It was just a lark for them. The other two-thirds probably had very sweaty palms."

"They looked like they were trying awfully hard to keep up a cheerful front."

"They were probably happy to get out of there, and to go sit in a dark cool room and drink beer afterwards. Certainly a lot of them have been sending me e-mail about the Crypt since then."

"As an alternative to violent resistance to the United States Government, I assume and hope you mean."

"Exactly. Sure. I mean, that's what the Crypt is becoming. Right?"

The question sounds a little querulous to Randy. "Right," he says. He wonders why he feels so much more settled about this stuff than John Cantrell does, and then recalls that he has nothing left to lose.

Randy takes one last breath of dry, machine-cooled air and holds it refreshingly in his lungs as they step out into the heat of the evening. He has learned to relax into the climate; you can't fight it. There is a humming logjam of black Mercedes-Benzes waiting to pick up the Sultan- and Vizier-Class passengers. Very few Wallah-Class passengers get off at Kinakuta; most of them are in transit to India. Because this is the kind of place where everything works just perfectly, Randy and John are in the Humvee about twenty seconds later, and twenty seconds after that driving at a hundred and twenty kilometers per hour down a long horizontal shaft of ghastly blue-green freeway-light.

"We have been assuming that this Humvee is not bugged," Cantrell says, "so, if you were holding back on something, you can speak freely now."

Randy writes, *Let's stop assuming anything of the kind* on a notepad and holds it up. Cantrell raises his eyebrows one notch but of course does not seem especially surprised—he spends all of his time around people trying to outdo each other in paranoia. Randy writes *We have been under srv'nce by a former NSA hondo gone private.* Then he adds, *Prob. Working for 1 or more Crypt clients.*

How do you know? Cantrell mouths.

Randy sighs, then writes: *I was contacted by a Wizard.*

Then, as long as John's preoccupied with working his way around a left-lane fender bender, he adds, *Think of it as due diligence, underworld style.*

Cantrell says out loud, "Tom has been pretty scrupulous about making sure his house is bug-free. I mean, he built the thing, or had it built, from the ground up." He veers off onto an exit ramp and plunges into the jungle.

"Good. We can talk there," Randy says, then writes, *Remember the new U.S. Embassy in Moscow—bugs mixed into the concrete by KGB—had to be torn down.*

Cantrell grabs the pad and scribbles blind on the dashboard while maneuvering the Humvee up a curving mountain road into the cloud forest. *What do you want to talk about that is so secret? Arethusa? Give me agenda pls.*

Randy: *(1) Lawsuit & whether Epiphyte can continue to exist. (2) That NSA tapper, and Wizard, exist. (3) Maybe Arethusa.*

Cantrell grins and writes, *I have good news re: Tombstone's /.*

"/" in this context is UNIX for the root of the file system, which in the case of Tombstone is synonymous with the hard drive that Randy tried to wipe. Randy raises his eyebrows skeptically and Cantrell grins, nods, and draws his thumb across his throat.

Chez Howard is a flat-roofed concrete structure that from certain angles looks like a very large drainage culvert set vertically in a mound of grout on the top of a foothill. It becomes visible from one of those angles about ten minutes before they actually arrive, because the road must make several switchbacks across the broad slope of that foothill, which has been involuted and fractalized by relentless drainage. Even when it's not raining here, the mere condensation of moisture from the South Seas breezes gathers on leaves and rains from their drip-tips all the time. Between the rain and the plant life, erosion must be a violent and ravenous force here, which makes Randy a little uneasy about all of these mountains, because mountains could only exist in such an environment if the underlying tectonic forces were thrusting rock into the air at a rate that would make your ears pop standing still. But then again, having just lost a house to a temblor, he is naturally inclined to a conservative view.

Cantrell is now drawing an elaborate diagram, and has even slowed down, almost to a stop, the better to draw it. It begins with a tall rectangle. Set within that is a parallelogram, the same size, but skewed a little bit downwards, and with a little circle drawn in the middle of one edge. Randy realizes he's looking at a perspective view of a door-frame with its door hanging slightly ajar, the little circle being its knob. *STEEL FRAME,* Cantrell writes, *hollow metal channels.* Quick meandering scribbles suggest the matrix of wall surrounding it, and the floor underneath. Where the uprights of the doorframe are planted in the floor, Cantrell draws small, carefully foreshortened circles. *Holes in the floor.* Then he encircles the doorframe in a continuous hoop, beginning at one of those circles and climbing up one side of the doorframe, across the top, down the other side, through the other hole in the floor, and then horizontally beneath the door, then up through the first hole again, completing the loop. He draws one or two careful iterations of this and then numerous sloppy ones until the whole thing is surrounded in a vague, elongated tornado. *Many turns of fine wire.* Finally he draws two leads away from this huge door-sized coil and connects them to a sand-wich of alternating long and short horizontal lines, which Randy recog-nizes as the symbol for a battery. The diagram is completed with a huge arrow drawn vigorously through the center of the doorway, like an airborne battering ram, labeled B which means a magnetic field. *Ordo computer room door.*

"Wow," Randy says. Cantrell has drawn a classic elementary-school electromagnet, the kind of thing young Randy made by winding a wire around a nail and hooking it up to a lantern battery. Except that this one is wound around the outside of a doorframe and, Randy guesses, hidden inside the walls and beneath the floor so that no one would know it was there unless they tore the building apart. Magnetic fields are the styli of the modern world, they are what writes bits onto disks, or wipes them away. The read/write heads of Tombstone's hard drive are exactly the same thing, but a lot smaller. If they are fine-pointed draftsman's pens, then what Cantrell's drawn here is a firehose spraying India ink. It probably would have no effect on a disk drive that was a few meters away from it, but anything that was actually carried through that doorway would be wiped clean. Between the pulse-gun fired into the building from outside (destroying every chip within range) and this doorframe hack (losing every bit on every disk) the Ordo raid must have been purely a scrap-hauling run for whoever organized it—Andrew Loeb or (according to the Secret Admirers) Attorney General Comstock's sinister Fed forces who were using Andy as a cat's paw. The only thing that would have made it through that doorway intact would have been information stored on CD-ROM or other nonmagnetic media, and Tombstone had none of that.

Finally they have made it up to the top of the hill, which Tom Howard has shaved to the bedrock in a kind of monk's tonsure. Not because he hates living things, though he probably has no particular affection for them, but to hold at bay the forces of erosion and to create a defensive glacis across which the movements of incredibly poisonous snakes, squirrel-sized insects, opportunistic lower primates, and villainous upper primates will be visible on the array of video cameras he has built into fairly subtle recesses and crevices up on the walls. Seen up close, the house is surprisingly not as dour and fortresslike as it looked at first. It is not just a single large culvert but a bundle of them in different diameters and lengths, like a faggot of bamboo. There is a decent number of windows, particularly on the north side where there's a view, down the slope that John and Randy have just climbed, to a crescent-shaped beach. The windows are set deeply into the walls, partly to back them out of the nearly vertical rays of the sun and partly because each one has a retractable steel shutter, hidden in the wall, that can be dropped down in front of it. It is an okay house, and Randy wonders if Tom Howard would be willing to deed it over to the Dentist and hock his colossal suite of Gomer Bolstrood furniture and move his family into a crowded apartment building just in order to retain control of Epiphyte Corporation. But maybe that won't even be necessary.

John and Randy climb out of the Humvee to the sound of gunfire. Artificial light radiates upwards from a slot neatly dissected out of the jungle nearby. Humidity and clouds of insects make light a nearly solid and palpable thing here. John Cantrell leads Randy across the perfectly sterile parking-slab and into a screened and fenced tunnel that has been stabbed into the black vegetation. Underfoot is some kind of black plastic grid that keeps the nude soil from becoming a glue-trap. They walk down the tunnel, until twenty or thirty paces later it opens up into an extremely long, narrow clearing: the source of the light. At the far end of it, the ground rises abruptly in a sort of berm, partly natural, Randy thinks, and partly enhanced with fill dirt excavated from the house's foundation. Two large paper targets in the shape of human silhouettes are clipped to a rack there. At the near end, two men with ear protectors pulled down around their necks are examining a gun. One of these men is Tom Howard. Randy is struck but not really astonished by the fact that the other one is Douglas MacArthur Shaftoe, evidently fresh in from Manila. The gun looks like exactly the same model that some of the black-hatted and bandanna-masked posse were carrying yesterday in Los Altos: a long pipe with a sickle-shaped clip curving away from one side, and a very simple stock made of a few bare metal parts bolted together.

Doug is in the middle of saying something, and is not the type to interrupt his train of thought and fall all over himself being friendly just because Randy has recently traversed the Pacific Ocean. "I never knew my father," he says, "but my Filipino uncles used to tell me stories that he had told. When he was on Guadalcanal, they—the Marines—were still using their Springfields, the ought-three model, so four decades old— when finally the M-1 rifle began to show up. So they took one of each rifle and tossed it into the water and rolled it around in the sand for a while and did God knows what else to it—but nothing that would be unusual in a real combat situation, for a Marine—and then tried to operate them and found that the ought-three still worked and the M-1 didn't. So they stuck to their Springfields. And I would say that some testing along those lines would be in order if you think you are really designing an insurgency weapon, as you say. Good evening, Randy."

"Doug, how are you?"

"I am just fine, thank you!" Doug is one of these guys who always interprets "how are you" as a literal request for information, not just an empty formality, and always seems slightly touched that someone would care enough to ask. "Mr. Howard here says that when you were sitting on top of that car typing you were actually doing something clever. And dangerous. At least from a legal point of view."

"Were you monitoring that?" Randy asks Tom.

"I saw packets moving through the Crypt, and later saw you on television. I put two and two together," Tom says. "Nice job, Randy." He lumbers forward and shakes Randy's hand. This is an almost embarrassing outpouring of emotion by Tom Howard standards.

"What I did there probably failed," Randy says. "If Tombstone's disk was blanked, it was blanked by the doorframe coil, and not by what I did."

"Well, you deserve recognition anyway, which is what your friend is trying to give you," Doug says, mildly irked at Randy's obtuseness.

"I should offer you a drink, and a chance to relax, and all of that," Tom says, looking towards his house, "but on the other hand Doug says you were flying Sultan Class."

"Let's talk out here," Randy says. "But actually there is one thing you could get me."

"What's that?" Tom asks.

Randy pulls the little disembodied hard drive out of his pocket and holds it up in the light, the wire-ribbon adangle. "A laptop computer and a screwdriver."

"Done," Tom says, and disappears down the tunnel. Doug meanwhile begins dismantling the weapon, as if just to keep his hands busy. He takes the parts out one by one and regards them curiously.

"What do you think of the HEAP gun?" Cantrell asks.

"I don't think it's as crazy as when I first heard of it," Doug says, "but if your friend Avi thinks that people are going to be able to manufacture rifled gun barrels in their basements to protect themselves against ethnic cleansing, he's got another think coming."

"Rifled barrels are hard," Cantrell says. "There's no way around it. They'd have to be stockpiled and smuggled. But the idea is that anyone who downloaded the HEAP, and who had access to some basic machine tools, could build the rest of the weapon."

"I need to sit down with you sometime and explain everything else that's wrong with the idea," Doug says.

Randy changes the subject. "How's Amy?"

Doug looks up and eyes Randy carefully. "You want my opinion? I think she is lonely, and in need of reliable support and companionship."

Now that Doug has totally alienated both Randy and John, the gun range is completely silent for a while, which is probably how Doug likes it. Tom comes out with a laptop in one hand and, in the other, half a dozen blue plastic water bottles all shrink-wrapped together, already dribbling a trail of condensation.

"I have an agenda," Cantrell says, holding up the notepad.

"Wow! You guys are organized," Tom says.

"Item the first: Lawsuit and whether Epiphyte can continue to exist."

Randy lays the laptop out on the same table where Doug is working with the HEAP gun and begins to remove screws. "I assume you guys know of the lawsuit and have worked out the implications of it yourself," he says. "If the Dentist can prove that Doug discovered the wreck as a byproduct of work he did for us, and if the value of that wreck is high enough compared to the value of the company, then the Dentist owns us, and for all practical purposes owns the Crypt."

"Whoa! Wait a minute. The *Sultan* owns the Crypt," Tom says. "If the Dentist controls Epiphyte, all he gets out of it is a contract to provide certain technical services in the Crypt."

Randy senses everyone's looking at him. He twirls screws out of the computer, refusing to agree with this.

"Unless there's something here I'm not getting," Tom says.

"I guess I'm just being paranoid and sort of assuming that the Dentist is somehow collaborating with forces in the U.S. government that are anti-privacy and anti-crypto," Randy says.

"Attorney General Comstock's cabal, in other words," Tom says.

"Yeah. For which I have never actually seen any evidence at all. But in the wake of the Ordo raid everyone seems to be assuming it. If that is the case, and the Dentist ends up providing technical services to the Crypt, then the Crypt is compromised. We have to assume, in that case, that Comstock has a man on the inside."

"Not just Comstock," Cantrell says.

"Okay, the U.S. government."

"Not just the U.S. government," Cantrell says. "The Black Chamber."

"What the hell do you mean by that?" Doug asks.

"There was a high-level conference a couple of weeks ago in Brussels. Hastily organized we think. Chaired by Attorney General Comstock. Representatives of all the G7 countries and a few others. We know people from the NSA were there. People from Internal Revenue. Treasury people—Secret Service. Their counterparts in the other countries. And a lot of mathematicians known to have been co-opted by the government. The U.S. vice president was there. Basically we think that they are planning to form some kind of international body to clamp down on crypto and particularly on digital money."

"The International Data Transfer Regulatory Organization," Tom Howard says.

"The Black Chamber is a nickname for that?" Doug asks.

"That's what people on the Secret Admirers mailing list have started calling it," Cantrell says.

"Why form this organization now?" Randy wonders.

"Because the Crypt is about to go hot, and they know it," Cantrell says.

"They are scared shitless about their ability to collect taxes when everyone is using systems like the Crypt," Tom explains to Doug.

"This has been the talk of the Secret Admirers mailing list for the last week. And so when Ordo was raided, it really hit a raw nerve."

"Okay," Randy says, "I've been wondering why people showed up there almost immediately with guns and stranger things." He has got the laptop opened up now and disconnected its hard drive.

"You have wandered off the agenda," Doug says, pulling an oily rag down the barrel of the HEAP gun. "The question is, does the Dentist have you guys by the balls, or only by the short hairs? And that question basically revolves around yours truly. Right?"

"Right!" Randy says, a little too forcefully—he's feeling desperate for a change in subject. The whole Kepler/Epiphyte/Semper Marine thing is stressful enough all by itself, and the last thing he needs is to be hanging around with people who believe it is nothing more than a skirmish in a war to decide the fate of the Free World—a preliminary round of the Apocalypse. Avi's obsession with the Holocaust seemed fine to Randy as long as Holocausts were things that happened long ago or far away— being personally involved in one is something Randy can do without. He should have stayed in Seattle. But he didn't, and so the next best thing for him is to limit the conversation to straightforward things like bars of gold.

"In order for him to have a claim, the Dentist needs to prove that Semper Marine found that wreck when it was doing the cable survey. Right?" Doug asks.

"Right," Cantrell says, before Randy can step in and say that it's a bit more complicated than that.

"Well, I *have* been kicking around this part of the world for half of my life, and I can always testify that I found the wreck on an earlier survey. That son of a bitch can never prove that I'm lying," Doug says.

"Andrew Loeb—his lawyer—is smart enough to know that. He will not put you on the stand," Randy says, screwing his own hard drive into place.

"Fine. Then all he's got is circumstantial evidence. Namely, the proximity of the wreck to the cable survey corridor."

"Right. Which implies a correlation," Cantrell says.

"Well, it is not that damn close," Doug says. "I was cutting a very wide swath at the time."

"I have bad news," Randy says. "First of all, it is a civil case and so circumstantial evidence is all he needs to win. Secondly, I just heard from Avi, on the plane, that Andrew Loeb is filing a second suit, for breach of contract."

"What goddamn contract?" Doug demands.

"He has anticipated everything you just said," Randy says. "He still doesn't know where the wreck is. But if it turns out to be miles and miles away from the survey corridor, he will claim that by surveying such a wide swath you were basically risking the Dentist's money in order to go prospecting, and that thus the Dentist still deserves a share of the proceeds."

"Why does the Dentist want a beef with me?" Doug says.

"Because then he can pressure you into testifying against Epiphyte. You get to keep all the gold. That gold becomes damages which the Dentist leverages into control of Epiphyte."

"Jesus fuckin' Christ!" Doug exclaims. "He can kiss my ass."

"I know that," Randy says, "but if he gets wind of that attitude, he'll just come up with another tactic and file another suit."

Doug begins, "Well that's kind of defeatist—"

"Where I'm headed with this," Randy says, "is that we cannot fight the Dentist on his turf—which is the courtroom—any more than the Viet Cong could have fought a pitched battle in the open against the U.S. Army. So there are some really good reasons to get that gold out of the wreck surreptitiously, before the Dentist can prove it's there."

Doug looks outraged. "Randy, have you ever tried to swim while holding a gold bar in one hand?"

"There's got to be a way to do it. Little submarines or something."

Doug laughs out loud and mercifully decides not to debunk the concept of little submarines. "Supposing it was possible. What do I do with the gold then? If I deposit it in a bank account, or spend it on something, what's to keep this Andrew Loeb guy from taking that as circumstantial evidence that the wreck had a ton of money in it? You're saying I have to sit on this money for the rest of my life in order to protect you from this lawsuit."

"Doug. You can do this," Randy says. "You get the gold. You put it on a boat. My friends here can explain the rest." Randy fits the laptop's plastic case back together and begins maneuvering the little screws back into their recesses.

Cantrell says, "You bring the boat here."

Tom continues, "To that beach, right down the hill. I'll be waiting for you with the Humvee."

"And you and Tom can drive it downtown and deposit that bullion in the vaults of the Central Bank of Kinakuta." Cantrell concludes.

Someone has finally said something that actually knocked Doug Shaftoe off balance. "And get what in return?" he asks suspiciously.

"Electronic cash from the Crypt. Anonymous. Untraceable. And untaxable."

Doug's regained his composure now, and is back to belly laughs. "What'll that buy me? Pictures of naked girls on the World Wide Web?"

"Soon enough, it'll buy you anything that money *can* buy," Tom says.

"I would have to know a little more about it," Doug says. "But once again we are straying from the agenda. Let's leave it at this: you guys need me to strip that wreck bare, quickly and secretly."

"It's not just what *we* need. It might be in your best interests, too," Randy says, groping on the back of the laptop for the power switch.

"Item the second: A former NSA hondo is surveilling us—and something about a Wizard?" John says.

"Yeah."

Doug's giving Randy a queer look and so Randy launches into a brief summary of his classification system of Wizards, Elves, Dwarves, and Men—not to mention Gollums, which makes practically no sense to Doug, who hasn't read *Lord of the Rings*.

Randy goes on to tell them about his conversation with Pontifex on the airplane phone. John Cantrell and Tom Howard are interested in this, as Randy would expect them to be, but what surprises him is how intently Doug Shaftoe listens.

"Randy!" Doug almost shouts. "Didn't you at any point ask this guy why Old Man Comstock was so interested in the Arethusa messages?"

"Coincidentally, this is the third item on the agenda," Cantrell says.

"Why didn't you ask him on the ski lift?" Randy jokes.

"I was giving him a very closely reasoned explanation of why I was about to sever the linkage between his ugly and perfumed corporeal self and his eternally condemned soul," Doug says. "Seriously! You got the messages from your grandpa's old war souvenirs. Right?"

"Right."

"And your grandpa Waterhouse picked them up where?"

"Judging from the dates, he must have been in Manila."

"Well, what do you imagine could have happened in Manila around that time that would be so damned important to Earl Comstock?"

"I told you, Comstock thought it was a Communist code."

"But that's bullshit!" Doug says. "Jesus! Haven't you guys spent any time at all around people like Comstock? Can't you recognize bullshit? Don't you think it would be a useful item to add to your intellectual toolkits to be capable of saying, when a ton of wet steaming bullshit lands on your head, 'My goodness, this appears to be bullshit'? Now. What do you think is the real reason Comstock wanted to crack Arethusa?"

"I have no idea," Randy says.

"The reason is gold," Doug says.

Randy snorts. "You have got gold on the brain."

"Did I or did I not take you out into the jungle and show you something?" Doug demands.

"You did. Sorry."

"Gold is the only thing that could account for it. Because otherwise, the Philippines just were not that important during the fifties, to justify such an effort at the NSA."

"There was an ongoing Huk insurrection," Tom says. "But you're right. The real focus—around here anyway—was Vietnam."

"You know something?" fires back Doug. "During the Vietnam war—which was Old Man Comstock's brainchild—the American military presence in the Philippines was huge. That son of a bitch had soldiers and marines crawling over Luzon, supposedly on training missions. But I think they were looking for something. I think they were looking for the Primary."

"As in primary gold repository?"

"You got it."

"Is that what Marcos eventually found?"

"Opinions differ," Doug says. "A lot of people think that the Primary is still waiting to be discovered."

"Well, there isn't any information about the Primary, or anything else, in these messages," Randy says. The laptop has booted up now, in UNIX mode, with a torrent of error messages triggered by its inability to find various pieces of hardware that were present on Randy's laptop (which is in a Ford dealership's dumpster in Los Altos) but are not on Tom's. And yet the basic kernel works to the point that Randy can look at the file system and makes sure it's intact. The Arethusa directory is still there, with its long list of short files, each file the result of running a different stack of cards through Chester's card-reader. Randy opens up the first one and finds several lines of random capital letters.

"How do you know there's no information about the primary in those messages, Randy?" Doug asks.

"The NSA couldn't decrypt these messages in ten years," Randy says. "It all turned out to be a hoax. The output of a random number generator."

Randy jumps back out to the file listing and types

```
grep AADAA *
```

and hits the return key. It is a command to find the opening letter group in the ETC card messages, the famous one to which Pontifex had alluded. The machine answers back almost immediately with an empty prompt, meaning that the search failed.

"Ho-ly shit," Randy says.

"What?" everyone says at once.

Randy takes a long, deep breath. "These are not the same messages that Earl Comstock spent ten years attempting to break."

DELUGE

IT TAKES GOTO DENGO ABOUT HALF A MINUTE TO WADDLE UP the narrow entrance of the tunnel. He is trailing the fingers of one hand along the stone ceiling just above his head, feeling the scars of the drills. Behind him he can hear the four members of his crew making their way along, muttering to each other calmly.

His fingers slide over a lip and rise up into empty, dark space; he's into the main drift now. He stands up and wades forward. Perfect blackness is cozy and reassuring to him—in it, he can always pretend that he is still a boy, back on Hokkaido. He can make believe that the last few years of his life have never happened.

But in fact he is a grownup and he is trapped in a hole in the Philippines and surrounded by armies of demons. He opens the valves on an acetylene headlamp and sparks it into life. He is perfectly capable, by this point, of finding his way around Golgotha in the dark, but his crew is not, and he leaves them far behind. He stubs his toe brutally on a large gold bar that has carelessly been left lying across the iron railway, and curses.

"Is everything okay, Lieutenant?" says one of his crew, fifty meters behind him.

"Fine," Goto Dengo says, loudly and clearly. "You four be careful you do not break your toes on this bar."

So now, Wing and Rodolfo and their men, waiting up ahead, know the number of Nipponese soldiers they have to kill.

"Where are the last few workers?" one of the crew shouts.

"In the fool's vault."

It takes them several minutes to pick their way through the main vault, because it is packed with treasure. The starry core of a galaxy must look like this. They clamber up the shaft in its ceiling and make their way to the Hall of Glory. Goto Dengo finds the bare wires that lead to the electric light bulb and attaches them to the screw terminals on a battery. Running at the wrong voltage, the bulb looks like a tangerine floating in ink.

"Shut off your headlamps," Goto Dengo says, "to conserve fuel. I will leave mine burning in case there is an interruption in the power."

He pulls a fistful of white cotton from a sterile box. It is the cleanest whitest thing he has seen in several years. He pulls it apart into smaller wads, like Father Ferdinand breaking the bread of the mass, and passes them out to the men, who stuff it ritualistically into their ears. "There is no more time to waste," he hollers, "Captain Noda must be growing impatient out there."

"Sir!" one of the men says, standing at attention and handing him a pair of wires marked MAIN TUNNEL DEMOLITION.

"Very well," Goto Dengo says, and screws the wires down to a pair of terminals on a wooden switch box.

It seems as though he should say something ceremonious, but nothing comes to mind. Nipponese men are dying all over the Pacific without first getting to make speeches.

He clenches his teeth together, shuts his eyes, and twists the switch handle.

The shock wave comes through the floor first, whacking the soles of their feet like a flying plank. A moment later it comes through the air and strikes them like a moving wall of stone. The cotton in the ears seems to accomplish nothing. Goto Dengo feels his eyes bounce off the backs of their sockets. All of his teeth feel as though they have been crisply sheared off at the gumline with cold chisels. The wind is all forced out of his lungs. They are empty for the first time since the moment of his birth. Like newborn infants, he and the other men can only writhe and look around themselves in a panic until their bodies learn how to draw breath again.

One of the men brought a bottle of sake, which has shattered. They pass around the jagged bottom of the bottle, each man taking a gulp of what remains. Goto Dengo tries to pull the cotton out of his ears and finds that the shock wave drove it in so deep that it cannot be extracted. So he merely shouts: "Check your watches." They all do. "In two hours, Captain Noda will demolish the plug on the bottom of the lake and flood the water traps. In the meantime, we have work to do. You all know your jobs—get to work!"

They all *hai,* turn on their heels, and go their separate ways. It is the first time that Goto Dengo has actually sent men off to their deaths. But they are all dead men anyway, and so he doesn't know how to feel about it.

If he still believed in the emperor—still believed in the war—he would think nothing of it. But if he still believed, he wouldn't be doing what he is about to do.

It is important to keep up the appearance that this is a normal operation, and so he descends to the vault to perform his next scheduled duty: inspect what used to be the main drift. The vault is filled with a fog of rock dust around which his windpipe clenches like a fist grabbing a rope. His acetylene lamp only makes the dust glow, giving him a visibility of perhaps six inches. All he can see is the bullion right in front of his face, which still glimmers beneath a film of dust and smoke. The shock wave has deranged his formerly neat stacks of crates and bricks and turned the entire hoard into a rude mound that is still shedding avalanches, seeking its angle of repose. A 75-kilogram gold brick slides down the pile like a runaway boxcar, emerging suddenly from the cloud of dust, and he jumps out of its way. Bits of rock are still sifting down from the crazed ceiling and plinking against his helmet.

He scrambles carefully over the heap, breathing through a wad of cotton, until he can see what used to be the main drift. The dynamite has done the right thing: shattered the roof of the drift into billions of shards. Collapsed on the floor, they occupy a larger volume than the same mass of stone did when it was all in one piece. The drift is filled with tons of loose stone, all the way down to the entrance along the Tojo River, where Captain Noda's men are at work even now, concealing the tiny puncture wound behind river rocks.

He feels, rather than hears, a small explosion, and knows that something is going wrong. No one should be setting off explosions now.

Movement in this place is agonizingly slow, like a nightmare when you are trying to run away from a demon. It takes him so long to get back to the Hall of Glory that there is almost no point in doing it; whatever was happening is over when he arrives.

What he sees, when he arrives, is a group of three men waiting for him: Wing, Rodolfo, and the Filipino named Bong.

"The soldiers?"

"All dead," Rodolfo says flatly, irritated by the stupidity of the question.

"The others?"

"One soldier set off a grenade. Killed himself and my two men," Wing says.

"Another soldier heard the grenade and had a knife ready when Agustin came for him," Bong says. He shakes his head sorrowfully. "I think that Agustin was not ready to kill a man. He hesitated."

Goto Dengo stares at Bong, fascinated. "And you?"

Bong doesn't understand the question for a moment. Then light dawns. "Oh, no, I did not hesitate, Lieutenant Goto. A Nipponese soldier hurt my sister one time, in a very inappropriate way."

Goto Dengo stands there silently for a while, until he notices that the other men are all looking at him expectantly. Then he checks his watch. He is shocked to see that only half an hour has gone by since he set off the dynamite.

"We have an hour and a half before the water traps are flooded. If we are not in the Bubble by then, we will be sealed off, with no escape possible," says Goto Dengo.

"We go there and wait," Wing suggests, in Shanghainese.

"No. Captain Noda listens, outside, for more explosions," Goto Dengo says, also in Chinese; then, in English, tells the Filipinos, "We have to set off the demolition charges at certain times or Noda-san will grow suspicious."

"Whoever sets them off will be trapped forever in this chamber," Rodolfo says, gesturing around them at the Hall of Glory.

"We will not set them off from here," says Goto Dengo, pulling the lid from a crate. Inside are several long coils of two-stranded telephone wire. He hands the coils out to Rodolfo, Wing, and Bong. They understand, and begin to splice the new wires onto the ones that terminate here.

They retreat through Golgotha in stages, lugging battery packs with them and unrolling the wires as they go, dynamiting the tunnel sections behind them one by one. As they do this, certain oddities of the tunnel system finally become clear to Rodolfo, Wing, and Bong. It becomes fully evident to them, for the first time, that the entire complex was carefully designed by Goto Dengo to serve two entirely contradictory purposes. To a loyal Nipponese engineer like Captain Noda it looks like precisely what he was ordered to build: a vault laced with booby traps. But to the four men sealed inside, Golgotha has a second function. It is an escape machine. As the purposes of certain rooms, drifts, and other features suddenly become clear, they straighten up, blinking, and turn to look at Goto Dengo, with the same expressions as the soldiers wore, weeks ago, when they discovered the Buddha in the Mercedes.

Their destination is the Bubble, a niche that Goto Dengo had them carve out of the stone during the last couple of months. He claimed, to anyone who asked, that it was a water reservoir, put there to increase the deadliness of one of the traps. It is a wide vertical shaft, four meters in diameter, that begins in the ceiling of a peripheral drift and goes straight up for a few meters, then dead-ends. Ladders still cling to its walls, and by ascending, they can reach a rock ledge big enough to sit on. Canteens of water and boxes of biscuits have already been stocked here by Wing and his men.

By the time they reach their seats in the top of the Bubble, all of the others are in awe of Goto Dengo, and ready to do whatever he says. He senses this. It fills him with unutterable misery.

They have fifteen minutes to wait. The others spend it sipping water and nibbling biscuits. Goto Dengo fills it with self-recrimination. "I am a loathsome worm," he says, "a traitor, a filthy piece of dog shit, not worthy to clean out the latrines of true soldiers of Nippon. I am bereft—totally cut off from the nation I've betrayed. I am now part of a world of people who hate Nippon—and who therefore hate me—but at the same time I am hateful to my own kind. I will stay here and die."

"You are alive," Rodolfo says. "You have saved our lives. And you are rich."

"Rich?"

Wing and Rodolfo and Bong look at each other, confused. "Yes, of course!" Bong says.

Goto Dengo is still looking nonplussed. Reckoning that he has merely gone deaf or daft from the explosions, Bong reaches into his trousers and pulls out a hand-sewn pouch, teases it open, and displays a healthy double handful of diamonds. Wing and Rodolfo scarcely take note.

Goto Dengo looks away despondently. He himself has saved no treasure except these men's lives. But that's not why he feels so bad. He had hoped that being thus saved they would all be noble, and not think of the treasure. But maybe that was too much to hope for.

A distant thump lifts them slightly off the ledge, just for a moment. Goto Dengo feels a strange sensation in his head: the air pressure is beginning to rise. The column of air trapped in the diagonal is being compressed by a piston of water rushing down it from the lake. Captain Noda has dynamited the plug.

Goto Dengo is so excited that he forgets to die.

He is an engineer, trapped inside one of his own machines. The machine was designed to keep him alive, and he will never know whether it worked unless it works. After he has achieved that satisfaction, he supposes, he can always kill himself at leisure.

He pinches his nose shut, presses his lips together, and begins to blow air into his Eustachian tubes, equalizing the pressure. The others follow his lead.

All of Golgotha's traps are basically the same. All of them derive their killing power from the pressure of the water communicated down to this level from the bottom of Lake Yamamoto. In any number of places in the complex, false walls have been constructed, designed to be pierced by greedy thieves, or to collapse of their own accord when thieves dig out the sand that holds them up. Then the water will rush in with explosive force and probably crush them before they have a chance to drown.

At its Golgotha end, the diagonal tunnel forks again and again, like a river breaking up into distributaries. Goto Dengo explained it to inspecting officers by likening it to the plumbing inside a modern hotel, which is supplied by a single main that is pressurized by a distant water tower, but which divides into many different pipes that supply pressurized water to taps all over the structure.

Golgotha seethes, hisses, and moans as every pipe in its ramified system is pressurized by the deluge unleashed by Captain Noda's dynamite charge. The bubbles of air trapped at the ends of those pipes are seeking escape: some are leaking out through cracks in the walls and others are bubbling away into the diagonal. The surface of Lake Yamamoto must be boiling like a cauldron, and Captain Noda must be standing above it, watching the air flee Golgotha, grinning with satisfaction. In moments, the floors of the tunnels are obscured by whirling lagoons of dirty water, and the barrels and railcars that were left there have begun to rise, bobbing like corks and clanging together.

Most of the air trapped in the Golgotha does not, however, come bubbling up out of Lake Yamamoto. Most of it rises towards the Bubble, because that is how Goto Dengo planned it. He knows it's working because his ears begin to pop.

Eventually the water rises up into the Bubble itself, but it rises slowly, because the pressure of the air in here has become quite high already. As the water climbs, it further pressurizes the bubble of air in which Goto Dengo and the others are trapped. The pressure of the air rises steadily until it becomes equal to the pressure of the water. Then balance is achieved, and the water cannot rise any more. Another kind of balance is being reached within their bodies, as the compressed air floods into their chests, and the nitrogen in that air seeps through the membranes of their lungs and dissolves into their bloodstreams.

"Now we wait," says Goto Dengo, and shuts off his acetylene lamp, leaving them in darkness. "As long as we do not burn lamps, there is enough air in this chamber to keep us alive for several days. Captain Noda and his men will spend at least that long tidying up the Bundok site, erasing all traces of our work, and killing themselves. So we must wait, or else his men will only kill us when we appear on the shores of Lake Yamamoto. I would like to spend the time educating you on the subject of caisson disease, also known as the bends."

Two days later they set off one last, relatively small dynamite charge, blowing a hole through the wall of the Bubble that is large enough to admit a human being. On the other side, the diagonal to Lake Yama-moto begins.

Rodolfo is more terrified than anyone else, and so they send him first. Then goes Bong, and then Wing. Finally Goto Dengo leaves the foul, used-up air of the Bubble behind. Within a few moments they have found their way into the ascending diagonal tunnel. They begin to swim uphill through total darkness. All of them are trailing their hands against the tunnel ceiling, feeling for the opening of the first vertical shaft. Ro-dolfo is supposed to stop when he feels it, but the others must also be alert in case Rodolfo misses.

They thud into one another in the darkness like a loosely connected train bumping to a halt. Rodolfo has stopped—with any luck, he has found the first vertical shaft. Wing finally moves forward, and Goto Dengo follows straight up the vertical shaft and finally into a bulb at its top where a bubble of air has been trapped. The bulb is just barely wide enough to accommodate four men. They pause there, all jammed to-gether in a cluster of bodies, heaving as they exhale the nitrogen- and carbon-dioxide-tainted air that they've been living on for the last sixty seconds, and breathe in fresh lungfuls. Goto Dengo feels his ears popping as pressure is relieved.

They have covered only a small fraction of the four hundred and fifty meters that separate Golgotha from the lake *horizontally*. But half of the hundred-meter *vertical* distance has already been covered. That is, the pressure of the air they are breathing in this chamber is only half of what it was in the Bubble.

Goto Dengo is not a diver, and knows very little of diving medicine. But his father used to speak of how caissons were used to send workers deep underwater, to build things or to mine. That is how he learned about caisson disease, and how he learned the rule of thumb that most men will not suffer its symptoms if you have them decompress for a while at half the original air pressure. If they stop and breathe for a while, the nitrogen will come out of the tissues. Once this is done, the air pressure may be halved again.

In the Bubble, the air pressure was nine or ten atmospheres. Here in the first chamber, it's more like five. But there's not much air in this one—just enough to let them breathe for fifteen or twenty minutes, and bleed nitrogen out of their tissues, and get lungfuls of air for the next leg of the swim.

"Okay," Gogo Dengo says, "we go." He finds Rodolfo in the darkness and slaps him encouragingly on the shoulder. Rodolfo takes a series of deep breaths, getting ready, and Goto Dengo recites the numbers that they all know by heart: "Twenty-five strokes straight. Then the tunnel bends up. Forty strokes up a steep hill. Where the tunnel bends again, you go straight up to the next air chamber."

Rodolfo nods, crosses himself, and then does a somersault in the water and kicks himself downwards. Then goes Bong, then Wing, and finally Goto Dengo.

This leg is very long. The last fifteen meters is a vertical ascent into the air chamber. Goto Dengo had hoped that the natural buoyancy of their bodies would make this easy, even if they were on the verge of drowning. But as he is kicking up the narrow shaft, pushing frantically on the feet of Wing, who is above him and not going as fast as he would like, he feels a growing panic in his lungs. Finally he understands that he must fight the urge to hold his breath—that his lungs are filled with air at a much higher pressure than the water around him, and that if he doesn't let some of that air out, his chest will explode. So against his instinct to save that precious air, he lets it boil out of his mouth. He hopes that the bubbles will pass by the faces of the men above him and give them the idea too. But shortly after he does it, they all stop moving entirely.

For perhaps ten seconds Goto Dengo is trapped in total darkness in a water-filled vertical hole in the rock that is not much wider than his own body. Of all the things he has experienced in the war, this is the worst. But just as he gives up and prepares to die, they begin moving again. They are half dead when they get to the breathing chamber.

If Goto Dengo's calculations were right, then the pressure in here should be no more than two or three atmospheres. But he is beginning to doubt those calculations. When he has breathed in enough air to restore full consciousness, he's aware of sharp pains in his knees, and it's clear from the sounds that the others are making that they are suffering the same way.

"This time we wait as long as we can," he says.

The next leg is shorter, but it's made more difficult by the pain in their knees. Again Rodolfo goes first. But when Goto Dengo rises up into the next air chamber, about one and a half atmospheres above normal, only Bong and Wing are there.

"Rodolfo missed the opening," Bong says. "I think he went too far—up the ventilation shaft!"

Goto Dengo nods. Only a few meters beyond where they turned into this passage is a ventilation shaft that goes all the way to the surface. It has a sharp sideways jog in the middle that Goto put there so that when Captain Noda filled it up with rubble (which he has presumably done by now), the diagonal tunnel—their escape route—would not be blocked. If Rodolfo went up that shaft, he found a cul-de-sac, with no air bubble in the top.

Goto Dengo doesn't have to tell the others that Rodolfo is dead. Bong crosses himself and says a prayer. Then they stay for a while and take advantage of the air that Rodolfo should be sharing. The pain in Goto Dengo's knees becomes sharper, but after a while it plateaus.

"From here, only small changes in altitude, not much need to decompress. Mostly we swim for distance now," he says. They still have more than three hundred horizontal meters to cover, pierced with four more shafts for air. The last of these doubles as a legitimate ventilation shaft.

So from there on it is just swimming and resting, swimming and resting, until finally the walls of the tunnel peel away from them and they find themselves in Lake Yamamoto.

Goto Dengo breaks the surface and does nothing for a long time but tread water and breathe clean air. It is nighttime, and for the first time in a year, Bundok is quiet, except for the sound of Bong, kneeling on the shore of the lake, making the sign of the cross and mumbling prayers as fast as his lips can move.

Wing has already departed, without so much as a good-bye. This is shocking to Goto Dengo until he realizes what it means: he, too, is free to go. As far as the world knows, he is dead, all of his obligations discharged. For the first time in his life, he can do whatever he wants.

He swims to the shore, gets up on his feet, and starts walking. His knees hurt. He cannot believe that he has come through all of this, and his only problem is sore knees.

BUST

. . . .

"KOPI," RANDY SAYS TO THE FLIGHT ATTENDANT, THEN RECONSIDERS, remembering that he is in steerage this time, and getting to a toilet might not be so easy. It's just a little Malaysian Air 757. The flight attendant sees the indecision on his face and wavers. Her face is framed in a gaudy, vaguely Islamic scarf that is the most tokenistic nod to sexual modesty he has ever seen. "Kopi *nyahkafeina*," Randy says, and she beams and pours from the orange carafe. It is not that she doesn't speak English, just that Randy is starting to feel comfortable with the local pidgin. He realizes that this is the first step in a long process that will eventually turn him into one of these cheerful, burly, sunburned expats who infest the airport bars and Shangri-La hotels of the Rim.

Outside his window, the long slender isle of Palawan lies parallel to their flight path. A fogbound pilot could almost get from Kinakuta to Manila by following Palawan's beaches, but that is a moot point on a day like this. Those beaches slope gradually into the transparent waters of the South China Sea. When you're down there planted in the sand, looking at a glancing angle across the waves, it probably doesn't look like much, but from up here you can see straight down through the water for many fathoms, and so all of the islands, and even the coral heads, have skirts that start out dark brown or dun near the water and blend into yellow and finally into swimming-pool blue before eventually fading into the deep blue of the ocean. Every little coral head and sandbar looks like the iridescent eye on a peacock's plume.

After the conversation at Tom Howard's last night, Randy slept in his guest room and then spent most of the day in Kinakuta buying a new laptop, complete with a new hard drive, and transferring all of the data from the drive he salvaged in Los Altos onto the new one, encrypting everything in the process. Considering all of the completely boring and useless corporate documents he has subjected to state-of-the-art encryption, he can't believe he carried the Arethusa stuff around on his hard drive, unencrypted, for several days, and across a couple of national borders. Not to mention the original ETC punch-cards, which now reside in Tom Howard's basement safe. Of course that stuff is encrypted to begin with, but that was done in 1945, and so by modern standards it might as well have been enciphered with a cereal-box decoder ring. Or at least that is what Randy is kind of hoping. Another thing he did this morning was to download the current version of the *Cryptonomicon* from the ftp server where it lives in San Francisco. Randy's never looked at it in detail, but he has heard it contains samples of code, or at least algorithms, that he could use to attack Arethusa. With luck, the very latest public code-breaking techniques in the *Cryptonomicon* might match up to the classified technology that Pontifex and his colleagues were employing at the NSA thirty years ago. Those techniques didn't work against the Arethusa messages that they were trying to decrypt, but this was probably only because those messages were random numbers—not the real messages. Now that Randy has what he suspects are the real messages, he may be able to accomplish what Earl Comstock tried and failed to do during the fifties.

They are angling across the terminator—not the robotic assassin of moviedom, but the line between night and day through which our planet incessantly rotates. Looking east, Randy can see over the rim of the world to places where it is dusk, and the clouds catch only the reddest fraction of the sun's light, squatting in darkness but glowing with sullen contained fire like coals in their feathery ruffs of ash. The airplane is still in the daylight, and is assiduously tracked by mysterious bars of rainbow, little spectral doppelgangers—probably some new NSA surveillance technology. Some of the Palawan's rivers run blue and straight into the ocean and some carry enormous plumes of eroded silt that feather out into the ocean and are swept up the shore by currents. In Kinakuta there is less deforestation than there is here, but only because they have oil instead. All of these countries are burning resources at a fantastic rate to get their economies stoked up, gambling that they'll be able to make the jump into hyperspace—some kind of knowledge economy, presumably—before they run out of stuff to sell and turn into Haiti.

Randy is paging his way through the opening sections of the *Cryptonomicon,* but he can never concentrate when he's on an airplane. The opening sections are stolen pages from World War II-era military manuals. These used to be classified until ten years ago, when one of Cantrell's friends found copies just sitting in a library in Kentucky and drove there with a shitload of dimes and photocopied them. That got public, civilian cryptanalysis up to where the government was in the 1940s. The Xeroxes have been scanned and OCRed and converted to the HTML format used for Web pages so that people can put in links and marginal notes and annotations and corrections without messing with the original text, and this they have done enthusiastically, which is all very well but makes it hard to read. The original text is set in a deliberately crabbed, old-fashioned typeface to make it instantly distinguishable from the cyber-era annotations. The introduction to the *Cryptonomicon* was written, probably before Pearl Harbor, by a guy named William Friedman, and is filled with aphorisms probably intended to keep neophyte code-breakers from slapping grenades to their heads after a long week of wrestling with the latest Nipponese machine ciphers.

The fact that the scientific investigator works 50 percent of his time by nonrational means is, it seems, quite insufficiently recognized.

Intuition, like a flash of lightning, lasts only for a second. It generally comes when one is tormented by a difficult decipherment and when one reviews in his mind the fruitless experiments already tried. Suddenly the light breaks through and one finds after a few minutes what previous days of labor were unable to reveal.

And, Randy's favorite,
As to luck, there is the old miners' proverb: "Gold is where you find it."

So far so good, but then with a few whacks of the Page Down key Randy's looking at endless staggered grids of random letters (some kind of predigital method for solving ciphers) which the author would not have put into the document if they did not convey some kind of useful lesson to the reader. Randy is miserably aware that until he has learned to read through these grids he will not even be up to the level of competence of a World War II novice cryptanalyst. The sample messages used are like ONE PLANE REPORTED LOST AT SEA and TROOPS HAVING DIFFICULTY MAINTAINING CONNECTION WITH FORTY FIFTH INFANTRY STOP which Randy finds kind of hokey until he remembers that the book was written by people who probably didn't know what "hokey" meant, who lived in some radically different pre-hokiness era where planes really did get lost at sea and the people in those planes never came back to see their families and in which people who even raised the issue of hokeyness in conversation were likely to end up pitied or shunned or maybe even psychoanalyzed.

Randy feels like a little shit when he thinks about this stuff. He wonders about Chester. Is the shattered 747 hanging from Chester's ceiling just a monumental act of bad taste, or is Chester actually making a Statement with that thing? Could it be that nerdy Chester is actually some kind of deep thinker who has transcended the glibness and superficiality of his age? This very subject has been debated by serious people at some length, which is why learned articles about Chester's house keep showing up in unexpected places. Randy wonders if he's ever had a serious experience in his life, an experience that would be worth the time it would take to reduce it to a pithy STOP-punctuated message in capital letters and run it through a cryptosystem.

They must have flown right by the site of the wreck. In a few days Randy will turn right around and come halfway back to Kinakuta to make what meager contribution he can to the job of dragging gold bars out of it. He's only going to Manila to take care of some business there; some kind of urgent meeting demanded by one of Epiphyte's Filipino partners. The stuff that Randy came to Manila to do, a year and a half ago, mostly runs itself now, and when it actually requires his attention he finds it fantastically annoying.

He can see that the modern way of thinking about stuff, as applied to the *Cryptonomicon*, isn't going to help him very much in his goal of decrypting the Arethusa intercepts. The original writers of the *Cryptonom-icon* actually had to decrypt and read these goddamn messages in order to save the lives of their countrymen. But the modern annotators have no interest in reading other people's mail per se; the only reason they pay attention to this subject at all is that they aspire to make new crypto-systems that cannot be broken by the NSA, or now this new IDTRO thing. The Black Chamber. Crypto experts won't trust a cryptosystem until they have attacked it, and they can't attack it until they know the basic cryptanalytical techniques, and hence the demand for a document like this modern, annotated version of the *Cryptonomicon*. But their attacks gener-ally don't go any further than demonstrating a system's vulnerabilities in the abstract. All they want is to be able to say *in theory* this system could be attacked in the following way because from a formal number-theory stand-point it belongs to such-and-such class of problems, and those problems as a group take about so many processor cycles to attack. And this all fits very well with the modern way of thinking about stuff in which all you need to do, in order to attain a sense of personal accomplishment and earn the accolades of your peers, is to demonstrate an ability to slot new examples of things into the proper intellectual pigeon-holes.

But the gap between demonstrating the vulnerability of a cryptosystem in the abstract, and actually breaking a bunch of messages written in that cryptosystem, is as wide, and as profound, as the gap between being able to criticize a film (e.g., by slotting it into a particular genre or movement) and being able to go out into the world with a movie camera and a bunch of unexposed film and actually make one. Of these issues the *Cryptonomicon* has nothing to say until you tunnel down to its oldest and deepest strata. Some of which, Randy suspects, were written by his grandfather.

The head flight attendant comes in on the intercom and says something in various languages. Each transition to a new language is accompanied by a sort of frisson of confusion running through the whole passenger compartment: first the English-speaking passengers all ask each other what the English version of the announcement said and just as they are giving it up as a lost cause the Cantonese version winds down and the Chinese-speaking passengers ask each other what it said. The Malay version gets no reaction at all because no one actually speaks the Malay language, except maybe for Randy when he is asking for coffee. Presumably the message has something to do with the fact that the plane is about to land. Manila sprawls out below them in the dark, vast patches of it flickering on and off as different segments of the electrical power grid struggle with their own particular challenges vis-à-vis maintenance and overload. In his mind, Randy is already sitting in front of his TV tucking into a bowl of Cap'n Crunch. Maybe there is a place in NAIA where he can purchase a brick of ice-cold milk, so that he will not even have to stop at a 24 Jam on the way home.

The Malaysian Air flight attendants all have big smiles for him on the way out; as globe-trotting expat technocrats all know, hospitality-industry people think it is just adorable, or pretend to think so, when you try to use some language—any language—other than English, and they remember you for it. Soon he is inside good old NAIA, which is sort of, but not fully, air-conditioned. There is a whole group of girls in identical windbreakers gathered by his baggage carousel, chattering like an exaltation of larks under a DEATH TO DRUG TRAFFICKERS sign. The bags take a long time to arrive—Randy wouldn't have checked baggage at all except that he acquired a lot of books, and a few other souvenirs, on his trip—some salvaged from the ruined house and some inherited from his grandfather's trunk. And in Kinakuta he bought some new diving gear that he hopes he will put to use very soon. Finally he had to buy a big sort of duffel-bag-on-wheels to carry it all. Randy enjoys watching the girls, apparently some kind of high school or college field-hockey team on the road. For them, even waiting for the baggage carousel to start up is a big adventure, full of thrills and chills; e.g., when the carousel groans into action for a few moments and then shuts down again. But finally it starts up for real, and out comes a whole row of identical gym bags, color-coordinated to match the girls' uniforms, and in the middle of them is Randy's big duffel. He heaves it off the carousel and checks the tiny combination padlocks: one on the zipper for the main compartment and one on a smaller pocket at the end of the bag. There is one more tiny pocket on the top of the bag which has no practical function that Randy can think of; he didn't use it and so he didn't lock it.

He deploys the bag's telescoping handle, lifts it up onto its built-in wheels, and heads for customs. Along the way he gets mixed into the group of field-hockey players, who find this extremely titillating and hilarious, which is slightly embarrassing for him until they start finding their own hilarity hilarious. There are only a few customs lanes open, and there is a sort of traffic director waving people this way and that; he shoos the girls towards the green lane and then, inevitably, ducts Randy into a red one.

Looking through the lane, Randy can see the area on the other side where people wait to greet arriving passengers. There is a woman in a nice dress there. It's Amy. Randy comes to a complete stop the better to gape at her. She looks fantastic. He wonders if it's totally presumptuous of him to think that Amy put on a dress for no other reason than that she knew Randy would enjoy looking at her in it. Whether it's presumptuous or not, that's what he does think, and it almost makes him want to faint. He doesn't want to let his mind run completely out of control here, but maybe there is something better in store for him tonight than digging into a bowl of Cap'n Crunch.

Randy steps into the lane. He wants to just bolt through and head straight for Amy, but this would be a bad idea. But it's okay. Anticipation never killed anyone. Anticipation can actually be kind of enjoyable. What did Avi say? *Sometimes wanting is better than having.* Randy's pretty sure that having Amy would not disappoint, but wanting ain't such a bad thing either. He is holding his laptop bag out before him and drawing the big duffel behind, slowing gradually to a stop so that it won't roll forward under its own momentum and break his knees. There is the requisite long stainless-steel table and a bored fireplug-shaped gentleman behind it saying, "Nationality? Port of embarkation?" for the hundred thousandth time in his life. Randy hands over his documents and answers the questions while bending down to heft the duffel bag up onto the metal tabletop. "Remove the locks please?" the customs inspector says. Randy bends down and squints at the tiny brass wheels, trying to line them up into the right combination. While he's doing that, he hears the customs inspector working right next to his head, unzipping the tiny, empty pocket on the top of the duffel bag. There is a rustling noise. "What is this?" the inspector asks. "Sir? Sir?"

"Yes, what is it?" Randy says, straightening up and looking the inspector in the eye.

Like a model in an infomercial, the inspector holds up a small Ziploc bag right next to his head and points to it with the other hand. A door opens behind him and people come out. The Ziploc bag has been partly filled with sugar, or something—maybe confectioner's sugar—and rolled into a cigar-shaped slug.

"What is this, sir?" the inspector repeats.

Randy shrugs. "How should I know? Where did it come from?"

"It came from your bag, sir," the inspector says, and points to the little pocket.

"No, it didn't. That pocket was empty," Randy says.

"Is this your bag, sir?" the inspector says, reaching with one hand to look at the paper claim check dangling from its handle. Quite a crowd has gathered behind him, still indistinct to Randy who is understandably focusing on the inspector.

"I should hope so—I just opened the locks," Randy says. The inspector turns around and gestures to the people behind him, who en masse move forward into the light. They are wearing uniforms and most of them are carrying guns. Very soon, some of them are behind him. They are, as a matter of fact, surrounding him. Randy looks towards Amy, but sees only a pair of abandoned shoes: she is sprinting barefoot toward a line of pay telephones. He'll probably never see her in a dress again.

He wonders whether it would be a bad idea, from a narrowly tactical point of view, to ask for a lawyer this soon.

THE BATTLE OF MANILA

BOBBY SHAFTOE IS AWAKENED BY THE SMELL OF SMOKE. IT IS NOT the smoke of cookies left too long in the oven, piles of autumn leaves being burned, or Boy Scout campfires. It is a mixture of other kinds of smoke with which he has become quite familiar in the last couple of years: tires, fuel, and buildings, for example.

He props himself up on one elbow and realizes that he is lying in the bottom of a long skinny boat. Just above his head, a dirty canvas sail luffs in a treacherous and foul-smelling breeze. It is the middle of the night.

He turns his head to look upwind. His head doesn't like it. Fierce pain is trying to batter down the doors of his mind. But the pain is not getting in. He senses the muffled booms of the pain's hobnailed boots against his front door, but that's about it.

Ah! Someone has given him morphine. Shaftoe grins appreciatively. Life is good.

The world is dark—a matte black hemisphere inverted over the plane of the lake. But there is a horizontal crack around the edge, off to the boat's port side, where yellow light is leaking through. The light glimmers and sparkles like stars viewed through the heat waves above the hood of a black automobile.

He sits up, peers at it, gradually getting an idea of scale. The ragged trail of yellow light extends from the boat's eight o'clock, all the way around past the bow, to about one o'clock. Maybe it is some incredibly weird sunrise phenomenon.

"Myneela," says a voice behind him.

"Huh?"

"It is Manila," says another voice, closer to him, speaking the English version of the name.

"Why's it all lit up?" Bobby Shaftoe has not seen a city lit up at night since 1941, and has forgotten what it looks like.

"The Japanese have put it to the torch."

"The Pearl of the Orient!" someone says, farther back in the boat, and there is rueful laughter.

Shaftoe's head is clearing now. He rubs his eyes and takes a better look. A couple of miles off to port, a steel drum full of fuel takes off into the sky like a rocket, and disappears. He begins to make out the bony silhouettes of palm trees along the lake shore, standing out against the flames. The boat moves on across the warm water quietly, tiny waves chiming against its hull. Shaftoe feels as if he has just been born, a new person coming into a new world.

Anyone else would ask why they are traveling into the burning city, instead of running away from it. But Shaftoe doesn't ask, any more than a newborn infant would ask questions. This is the world he has been born into, and he looks at it wide-eyed.

The man who has been speaking to him is sitting on a gunwale next to Shaftoe, a pale face hovering above a black garment, a white rectangular notch in his collar. The light of the burning city refracts warmly in a string of amber beads from which depends, a heavy, swinging crucifix. Shaftoe lies back down in the hull of the boat and stares up at him for awhile.

"They gave me morphine."

"I gave you morphine. You were difficult to control."

"I apologize, sir," Shaftoe says with profound sincerity. He remembers those China Marines who went Asiatic on the trip down from Shanghai, and how they disgraced themselves.

"We could not tolerate noise. The Nipponese would have found us."

"I understand."

"Seeing Glory was a very bad shock for you."

"Level with me, padre," says Bobby Shaftoe. "My boy. My son. Is he a leper too?"

The black eyes close, and the pale face moves back and forth in a no. "Glory contracted the disease not long after the child was born, working in a camp in the mountains. The camp was not a very clean place."

Shaftoe snorts. "No shit, Sherlock!"

There is a long, uncomfortable silence. Then the padre says, "I have already taken confessions from the other men. Would you like me to take yours now?"

"Is that what Catholics do when they're about to die?"

"They do it all the time. But yes, it is advisable to confess immediately before death. It helps—what is the expression—grease the skids. In the afterlife."

"Padre, it looks to me like we're only an hour or two away from hitting the beach. If I start confessing my sins to you right now, I might get up to stealing cookies from the cookie jar when I was eight years old."

The padre laughs. Someone hands Shaftoe a cigarette, already lit. He takes a big suck on it.

"We wouldn't have time to get into any of the good stuff, like nailing Glory and killing a whole lot of Nips and Krauts." Shaftoe thinks about it for a minute, enjoying the cigarette. "But if this is one of those deals where we are all going to die—and it sure looks like one of those deals to me—there is one thing I gotta do. Is this boat going back to Calamba?"

"We hope that the owner can take some women and children back across the lake."

"Anyone got a pencil and paper?"

Someone passes up a pencil stub, but there is no paper to be found. Shaftoe searches his pockets and finds nothing but a skein of I SHALL RETURN condoms. He opens one of them, peeling the halves of the wrapper apart carefully, and tosses the rubber into the lake. Then he spreads the wrapper out on the top of an ordnance crate and begins to write: "I, Robert Shaftoe, being of sound mind and body, hereby leave all of my worldly goods, including my military death benefits, to my natural-born son, Douglas MacArthur Shaftoe."

He looks up into the burning city. He considers adding something like, "if he's still alive," but nobody likes a whiner. So he just signs the fucking thing. The padre adds his signature as witness. Just to add some extra credibility, Shaftoe pulls off his dog tags and wraps the will around them, then wraps the dog tags' chain around the whole thing. He passes it down to the stern of the boat, where the boatman pockets it and cheerfully agrees to do the right thing with it when he gets back to Calamba.

The boat isn't wide, but it's very long and has a dozen Huks crammed onto it. All of them are armed to the teeth with ordnance that has obviously come off an American submarine recently. The weight of men and weaponry keeps the boat so low in the water that waves occasionally splash over the gunwales. Shaftoe paws through crates in the dark. He can't see for shit, but his hands identify the components of a few Thompson submachine guns down in there.

"Parts for weapons," one of the Huks explains to him, "don't lose those!"

"Parts, nothing!" Shaftoe says, a few busy seconds later. He produces a fully assembled trench broom from the crate. The red coals of half a dozen I SHALL RETURN cigarettes leap upwards into the Huks' mouths as they free their hands for a light round of applause. Someone passes him a pie-shaped magazine, heavy with .45 caliber cartridges. "Y'know, they invented this kind of ammo just to knock down crazy Filipino bastards," Shaftoe announces.

"We know," one of the Huks says.

"It's overkill for Nips," Shaftoe continues, jacking the tommy gun and the magazine together. The Huks all laugh nastily. One of them is moving up from the stern, making the whole boat rock from side to side. He is a very young, slight fellow. He holds out his hand to Bobby Shaftoe. "Uncle Robert, do you remember me?"

Being called Uncle Robert is hardly the weirdest thing that has happened to Shaftoe in the last few years, so he lets it slide. He peers at the boy's face, which is dimly illuminated by the combustion of Manila. "You're one of the Altamira boys," he guesses.

The boy salutes him crisply, and grins.

Then, Shaftoe remembers. Three years ago, the Altamira family apartment, carrying the freshly impregnated Glory up the stairs as air raid sirens wailed all around the city. An apartment filled with Altamiras. A squad of boys with wooden swords and rifles, staring at Bobby Shaftoe in awe. Shaftoe throwing them a salute, then running out of the place.

"All of us fought the Nips," the boy says. Then his face falls, and he crosses himself. "Two are dead."

"Some of you were pretty damn young."

"The youngest ones are still in Manila," the boy says. He and Shaftoe silently stare across the water into the flames, which have merged into a wall now.

"In the apartment? In Malate?"

"I think so. My name is Fidel."

"Is my son in the same place?"

"I think so. Maybe not."

"We'll go find those kids, Fidel."

———

Half the population of Manila seems to be standing along the water's edge, or in the water, waiting for a boat like theirs to show up. MacArthur is coming down from the north, and the Nipponese Air Force troops are coming up from the south, so the isthmus between Manila Bay and Laguna de Bay is corked at both ends by great military forces waging total war. A ragged Dunkirk-style evacuation is in progress along the lake side of the isthmus, but the number of boats is not adequate. Some of the refugees are behaving like civilized human beings, but others are wading and swimming out towards them trying to get first dibs. A wet hand reaches up out of the water and grabs the boat's gunwale until

Shaftoe crushes it with the butt of his trench broom. The swimmer falls away, clutching his hand and screaming, and Shaftoe tells him he's ugly.

There is about half an hour's more ugliness as the boat cruises back and forth just out of swimming range and the padre handpicks an assortment of women carrying small children. They are pulled up into the boat one by one, and the Huks climb off the boat one by one, and when it's all finished the boat turns around and glides off into the darkness. Shaftoe and the Huks wade ashore, carrying crates of ammunition between them. By this point, Shaftoe has grenades dangling off his body all over the place, like teats on a pregnant sow, and most of the Huks are walking all slow and stiff-legged, trying not to collapse under the weight of the bandoliers in which they have practically mummified themselves. They stagger into the city, bucking a tide of smoky refugees.

This low land along the shore of the lake is not the city proper—it is a suburb of humble buildings made in the traditional style, of woven rattan screens with thatched roofs. They burn effortlessly, throwing up the red sheets of flame that they watched from the boat. Inland, and a few miles north, is the city proper, with many masonry buildings. The Nipponese have put it to the torch also, but it burns sporadically, as isolated towers of flame and smoke.

Shaftoe and his band had been expecting to hit the beach like Marines and get mowed down at the water's edge. Instead, they march for a good mile and a half inland before they actually lay eyes on the enemy.

Shaftoe's actually glad to see some real Nips; he has been getting nervous, because the lack of opposition has made the Huks giddy and overconfident. Then half a dozen Nip Air Force troops spill out of a store which they have evidently been looting—they are all carrying liquor bottles—and stop on the sidewalk to set fire to the place, fashioning Molotov cocktails from stolen bottles of firewater. Shaftoe pulls the pin on a grenade and underhands it down the sidewalk, watches it skitter for a while, and then ducks into a doorway. When he hears the explosion, and sees shrapnel crack the windshield of a car parked along the street, he jumps out onto the sidewalk, ready to open up with the tommy gun. But it's not necessary; all of the Nips are down, thrashing weakly in the gutter. Shaftoe and the other Huks all take cover and wait for more Nipponese troops to arrive, and help their injured comrades, but it doesn't happen.

The Huks are elated. Shaftoe stands in the street brooding while the padre administers last rites to the dead and dying Nipponese. Obviously, discipline has completely broken down. The Nips know they are trapped. They know MacArthur is about to run right over them, like a lawn-mower plowing through an anthill. They have become a mob. For

Shaftoe, it's going to be easier to fight mobs of drunken, deranged looters, but there's no telling what they might be doing to civilians farther
north.

"We're wasting our fucking time," Shaftoe says, "let's get to Malate
and avoid further engagements."

"You are not in command of this group," says one of the others.
"I am."

"Who's that?" Shaftoe asks, squinting against the light of the burning
liquor store.

It turns out to be a Fil-American lieutenant, who was sitting way back
in the boat, and who has been of no use at all to this point. Shaftoe
knows in his bones that this guy is not going to be a good combat leader.
He inhales deeply, trying to heave a sigh, then gags on smoke instead.

"Sir, yes sir!" he says, and salutes.

"I am Lieutenant Morales, and if you have any more suggestions, bring
them to me, or keep them to yourself."

"Sir, yes sir!" Shaftoe says. He doesn't bother to memorize the lieutenant's name.

They work their way north through narrow, clogged streets for a
couple of hours. The sun comes up. A small airplane flies over the city,
drawing ragged fire from exhausted, drunken Nipponese troops.

"It is a P-51 Mustang!" Lieutenant Morales exclaims.

"It's a fucking Piper Cub, goddamn it!" Shaftoe says. He has been
holding his tongue to this point, but he can't help it now. "It's an
artillery spotter plane."

"Then why is it flying over Manila?" Lieutenant Morales asks smugly.
He enjoys this rhetorical triumph for about thirty seconds. Then the first
artillery rounds begin to bore in from the north and blast the shit out
of various buildings.

They get into their first serious firefight about half an hour later,
against a platoon of Nipponese Air Force troops holed up in a stone
bank at the vee formed by a couple of intersecting avenues. Lieutenant
Morales comes up with an extremely complicated plan that involves
breaking up into three smaller groups. Morales takes three men forward
into the cover of a large fountain that sits in the middle of the square.
There, they are immediately trapped by heavy fire from the Nipponese.
They squat and huddle behind the shelter of the fountain for about a
quarter of an hour, at which point an artillery shell glides in from the
north, a black pellet easing downwards in a flawless parabolic trajectory,
and scores a direct hit on the fountain. It turns out to be a high-explosive
shell, which does not blow up until it hits something—the fountain, in
this case. The padre gives Lieutenant Morales and his men last rites from

a safe distance of a hundred yards or so, which is as good a place as any, since there is nothing left of their physical bodies.

Bobby Shaftoe is voted new squad leader by acclamation. He leads them around the square, giving the whole intersection a wide berth. Way up north somewhere, one of The General's batteries is doggedly trying to zero in on that fucking bank, blowing up half the neighborhood in the process. A Piper Cub banks overhead doing lazy figure-eights, offering suggestions over the radio: "Almost there—a little to the left— no, too far—now bring it in a little bit."

It takes Shaftoe's group a whole day to make another mile's progress towards Malate. They could get there in no time by simply running up the middle of major streets, but the artillery fire is coming in heavier and heavier as they head north. Worse, much of it consists of antiperson- nel rounds with radar proximity fuses that blow up while they're still several yards above the ground, the better to spray shrapnel all over the place. The air bursts look like the splayed foliage of burned coconut palms.

Shaftoe sees no point in getting them all killed. So they take it a block at a time, sprinting one by one from doorway to doorway, and scouting the buildings with great care in case there are any Nips lying in wait to shoot at them from the windows. When that happens, they have to hunker down, scout the place out, count windows and doors, make guesses about the building's floor plan, send men out to check various lines of sight. Usually, it is not really difficult to root the Nips out of these buildings, but it is time-consuming.

They hole up in a half-burned apartment building around sunset, and take turns getting a couple of hours' sleep. Then they push on through the night, when the artillery fire is less intense. Bobby Shaftoe gets the whole remaining squad, nine men including the padre, into Malate at about four in the morning. By the time dawn breaks, they have reached the street where the Altamiras live, or lived. They arrive just in time to see the entire apartment block being systematically blasted into rubble by round after high-explosive round.

No one runs out of it; no cries or screams can be heard in between the explosions. The place is empty.

They break down the barricaded door of a drugstore across the street and have a chat with the sole living occupants: a seventy-five-year-old woman and a six-year-old boy. The Nipponese came through the neigh- borhood a couple of days ago, she says, heading north, in the direction of Intramuros. They herded the women and children out of the buildings and marched them in one direction. They pulled out all of the men, and the boys over a certain age, and marched them off in another. She and her grandson escaped by hiding in a cupboard.

Shaftoe and his squad emerge from the drugstore onto the street, leaving the padre behind to grease some heavenly skids. Fifteen seconds later, two of them are killed by shrapnel from an antipersonnel round that detonates above the street nearby. The remainder of the squad backs right into a group of marauding Nipponese stragglers coming around the corner, and a completely insane close-quarters firefight ensues. They have the Nips heavily outgunned, but half of Shaftoe's men are too stunned to fight. They are accustomed to the jungle. Some of them have never been to the city before, even in peacetime, and they just stand there gaping. Shaftoe ducks into a doorway and begins to make a fantastic amount of noise with his trench broom. The Nips start throwing grenades around like firecrackers, doing as much damage to themselves as to the Huks. The engagement is ridiculously confused, and doesn't really end until another artillery round comes in, kills several of the Nips, and leaves the rest so stunned that Shaftoe is able to walk out in the open and dispatch them with shots from his Colt.

They drag two of their wounded into the drugstore and leave them there. One other man is dead. They are down to five fighting men and one increasingly busy padre. Their firefight has brought down another barrage of antipersonnel artillery, and so the best they can do for the rest of the day is find a basement to hide in, and try to get some sleep.

Shaftoe sleeps hardly at all, and so when night falls he takes a couple of benzedrine tablets, shoots a bit of morphine to take the edge off, and leads his squad out into the streets. The next neighborhood to the north is called Ermita. It has a lot of hotels. After Ermita is Rizal Park. The walls of Intramuros rise up from Rizal Park's northern edge. After Intramuros is the Pasig River, and MacArthur's on the far side of the Pasig. So if Shaftoe's son and the rest of the Altamiras are still alive, they have to be somewhere in the couple of miles between here and Fort Santiago on the near bank of the Pasig.

Shortly after they cross into the neighborhood of Ermita, they happen upon a stream of blood trickling out of a doorway, across the sidewalk, into the gutter. They kick down the door of the building and discover that its ground floor is filled with the corpses of Filipino men—several dozen in all. All of them have been bayoneted. One is still alive. Shaftoe and the Huks carry him out onto the sidewalk and begin looking for some place to put him while the padre circulates through the building, touching each corpse briefly and muttering something in Latin. When he comes out, he is bloody up to the knees.

"Any women? Children?" Shaftoe asks him. The padre shakes his head no.

They are only a few blocks from the Philippine General Hospital, so they carry the wounded man in that direction. Coming around the corner they see that the hospital's buildings have been half destroyed by MacArthur's artillery, and the grounds are covered with human beings laid out on sheets. Then they realize that the men circulating around the area, carrying rifles, are Nipponese troops. A couple of shots are fired in their direction. They have to duck into an alley and set the wounded man down. A few moments later, a trio of Nipponese soldiers appears in hot pursuit. Shaftoe has had enough time to think this one through, so he lets them get a good few paces into the alley. Then he and the Huks kill them silently, with blades. By the time reinforcements have been sent out after them, Shaftoe and his group have disappeared into the alleyways of Ermita, which in many places are running red with the blood of slaughtered Filipino men and boys.

CAPTIVITY

"SOMEONE IS TRYING TO SEND YOU A MESSAGE," ATTORNEY Alejandro says, scant minutes into his first interview with his new client.

Randy's ready for it. "Why does everyone here have these incredibly cumbersome ways of sending me messages? Don't you people have e-mail?"

The Philippines are one of those countries where "Attorney" is used as a title, like "Doctor." Attorney Alejandro has a backswept grey pompadour that gets a little curly down around the nape of his neck which, as he probably well knows, makes him look distinguished in a nineteenth-century-statesman kind of way. He smokes a lot, which bothers Randy hardly a bit since he has been in places, for a couple of days, where everyone smokes. You don't even need to bother with cigarettes and matches in a jail. Just breathe, and you get the equivalent of one or two packs a day worth of slightly pre-owned tar and nicotine.

Attorney Alejandro decides to act as if Randy has never made this last comment. He attends to a bit of business with his cigarette. If he wants that cigarette up and burning between his lips, he can make it happen without even moving his hands; suddenly it's just there, as if he had been hiding it, already lit, inside his mouth. But if he needs to introduce a caesura into the conversation, he can turn the selection, preparation, and ignition of a cigarette into something that in terms of solemn ritual is just this side of the *cha-no-yu*. It must knock 'em dead in the courtroom. Randy's feeling better already.

"What do you suppose the message is? That they are capable of killing me if they want to? Because I already know that. I mean, shit! How much does it cost to have a man killed in Manila?"

Attorney Alejandro frowns fiercely. He has taken this question the wrong way: as a suggestion that he is the kind of guy who would know such a thing. Of course, given that he was personally recommended by Douglas MacArthur Shaftoe, he probably is just precisely that kind of guy, but it is probably rude to aver this. "Your imagination is running wild," he says. "You have blown the death penalty aspect of this thing all out of proportion." As Attorney Alejandro probably expected, this display of blitheness renders Randy speechless long enough for him to execute another bit of patter with a cigarette and a stainless-steel lighter encrusted with military regalia. Attorney Alejandro has mentioned, twice, that he was a colonel in the Army and lived for years in the States. "We reinstated the death penalty in '95 after a hiatus of ten years approximately." The word approximately crackles and explodes from his mouth like a spark from a Tesla coil. Filipinos enunciate better than Americans and they know it.

Randy and Alejandro are meeting in a high, narrow room somewhere in between the jail and the courtroom in Makati. A prison guard loitered in the room with them for a few minutes, hunched over with sheepishness, leaving only when Attorney Alejandro went over and spoke to him in low, fatherly tones and pressed something into his hand. There is an open window, and the sound of honking horns comes through it from the street two stories below. Randy's half expecting Doug Shaftoe and his comrades to rappel down from the roof and enter suddenly in glittering and screaming cloaks of broken window-glass and extract Randy while Attorney Alejandro heaves his bulk against this half-ton nara table and uses it to block the door shut.

Coming up with fantasies like this one helps to break the tedium of being in jail, and probably does a lot to explain Randy's jailmates' taste in videos, which they cannot actually watch but which they talk about incessantly in a mixture of English and Tagalog that he now almost understands. The videos, or rather the lack of them, has given rise to some kind of retrograde media-evolution phenomenon: an oral storytelling rooted in videos that these guys once saw. A particularly affecting description of, for example, Stallone in *Rambo III* cauterizing his abdominal bullet wound by igniting a torn-open rifle cartridge and shooting gunpowder-flames through it will plunge all of the men into several moments of reverent awe. It is about the only quiet time Randy gets now, and he has consequently begun cooking up a new plan: he will exploit his Californian provenance by asserting that he has seen martial-arts films that have not yet been bootlegged to the streets of Manila, and narrate them in terms so eloquent that the entire jailhouse will for a few minutes become a place of monastic contemplation, like the idealized Third-World prison that Randy wishes he were in. Randy read *Papillon* cover-to-cover a couple of times when he was a kid and has always imagined Third-World prisons as places of supreme and noble isolation: steep tropical sunlight setting the humid and smoky air aglow as it slants in over iron bars close-set in thick masonry walls. Sweaty, shirtless steppenwolves prowling back and forth in their cells, brooding about where it all went wrong. Prison journals furtively scribbled on cigarette papers.

Instead, the jail where they've been keeping Randy is just a really crowded urban society where some of the people cannot actually leave. Everyone there is extremely young except for Randy and an ever-rotating population of drunks. It makes him feel old. If he sees one more video-addled boy strutting around in a bootleg "Hard Rock Cafe" t-shirt and fronting hand gestures from American gangsta rappers, he may actually have to become a murderer.

Attorney Alejandro says, rhetorically, "Why 'Death to Drug Smugglers'?" Randy hasn't asked why, but Attorney Alejandro wants to share something with him about why. "The Americans were very angry that some people in this part of the world persisted in selling them the drugs that they want so very badly."

"Sorry. What can I say? We suck. I know we suck."

"And so as a gesture of friendship between our peoples, we instituted the death penalty. The law specified two, and only two, methods of execution," Attorney Alejandro continues, "the gas chamber and the electric chair. As you can see, we took our lead—in this as in many other things, some wise and some foolish—from the Americans. Now, at the time, we did not have a gas chamber anywhere in the Philippines. A study was made. Plans were drawn up. Do you have any idea what is involved in constructing a proper gas chamber?" Attorney Alejandro now goes off on a fairly lengthy riff, but Randy finds it hard to concentrate until something in Attorney Alejandro's tone tells him that a coda is approaching. ". . . prison service said, 'How can you expect us to construct this space-age facility when we have not even the funds to purchase rat poison for the overcrowded prisons we already have?' As you can see they were just whining for more funding. You see?" Attor-

ney Alejandro raises his eyebrows significantly and sucks in his cheeks,
as he reduces a good two or three centimeters of a Marlboro to ash.
That he feels it necessary to explain the underlying motivations of the
prison service so baldly seems to imply that his estimate of Randy's
intelligence is none too favorable, which given the way he was arrested
at the airport might be fair enough. "So this left only the electric chair.
But do you know what happened to the electric chair?"

"I can't imagine," Randy says.

"It burned. Faulty wiring. So we had no way to kill people." All of
a sudden Attorney Alejandro, who has betrayed no amusement thus far,
remembers to laugh. It is perfunctory, and by the time Randy has be-
stirred himself to show a little polite amusement, it's over and Alejandro's
back to being serious. "But Filipinos are highly adaptable.

"Once again," Attorney Alejandro says, "we looked to America. Our
friend, our patron, our big brother. You are familiar with the expression
Ninong? Of course you are, I forget you have spent a whole lotta time
here." Randy is always impressed by the mixture of love, hate, hope,
disappointment, admiration, and derision that Filipinos express towards
America. Having actually been a part of the United States at one point,
they can take digs at it in a way that's usually reserved for lifelong U.S.
citizens. The failure of the United States to protect them from Nippon
after Pearl Harbor is still the most important thing that ever happened
to them. Probably just slightly more important than MacArthur's return
to the country a few years later. If that doesn't inculcate a love-hate
relationship . . .

"The Americans," Attorney Alejandro continues, "were also reeling
under the expense of executing people and having embarrassments with
their electric chairs. Maybe they should have jobbed it out."

"Pardon me?" Randy says. He gets the idea that Attorney Alejandro
is just checking to see if he's awake.

"Jobbed it out. To the Nipponese. Gone to Sony or Panasonic or
one of those guys and said (now reverting to a perfect American-yokel
accent), 'We just love the VCRs that y'all've been sellin' us—why don't
you make an electric chair that actually works?' Which the Nips would
have done—it is the kind of thing they would excel at—and then after
they sold Americans all of the electric chairs they needed, we could have
purchased some factory seconds at cut-rate." Whenever Filipinos slag
America in earshot of an American, they usually try to follow it up with
some really vile observations about the Nipponese, just to put everything
in perspective.

"Where are we going with this?" Randy says.

"Please forgive my digression. The Americans had gone over to executing prisoners by lethal injection. And so we have once again decided to take a cue from them. Why didn't we just hang people? We have plenty of rope—this is where rope comes from, you know—"

"Yes."

"—or shoot them? We have plenty of guns. But no, the congress wanted to be modern like Uncle Sam, and so lethal injection it was. But then we sent a delegation to see how the Americans lethally injected people, and you know what they reported when they came back?"

"It takes all kinds of special equipment."

"It takes all kinds of special equipment, and a special room. This room has not yet been constructed. So, you know how many people we have on death row now?"

"I can't imagine."

"More than two hundred and fifty. Even if the room were built tomorrow, most of them could not be executed, because it is illegal to carry out the execution until one year has passed since the final appeal."

"Well, wait a minute! If you've lost your final appeal, then why wait a whole year?"

Attorney Alejandro shrugs.

"In America, they usually do the final appeal while the prisoner is lying strapped to the table with the needle in his arm."

"Maybe they wait in case there is a miracle during that year. We are a very religious people—even some of the death row prisoners are very religious. But they are now begging to be executed. They cannot stand the wait any longer!" Attorney Alejandro laughs and slaps the table. "Now, Randy, all of these two hundred and fifty people are poor. All of them." He stops significantly.

"I hear you," Randy says. "Did you know that my net worth is less than zero, by the way?"

"Yes, but you are rich in friends and connections." Attorney Alejandro starts frisking himself. A picture of a fresh pack of Marlboros appears over his head in a little thought-balloon. "I recently received a telephone call from a friend of yours in Seattle."

"Chester?"

"Yes, he's the one. He has money."

"You could say that."

"Chester is seeking ways to put his financial resources to work on your behalf. He feels frustrated and unsure of himself because while his resources are quite significant, he does not know the fine points of how to wield them in the context of the Philippine judicial system."

"That's him all over. Is there any chance that you might be able to give him some pointers?"

"I'll talk to him."

"Let me ask you this," Randy says. "I understand that financial re-sources, wielded properly, could free me. But what if some rich person wanted to use his money to send me to death row?"

This one stops Attorney Alejandro dead for a minute. "There are more efficient ways for a wealthy person to kill someone. For the reasons I have described, a would-be assassin would first look somewhere outside of the Philippine capital-punishment apparatus. That is why, in my opin-ion as your lawyer, what is really going on here is that—"

"Someone is trying to send me a message."

"Exactly. You see, now you are beginning to understand."

"Well, I'm wondering if you could give me a ballpark estimate of how long I'm going to be locked up. I mean, do you want me to plead to a lesser charge and then serve a few years?"

Attorney Alejandro looks pained and scoffs. He doesn't deign to answer.

"I didn't think so," says Randy. "But at what point in these proceed-ings do you imagine I could get out? I mean, they refused to release me on bail."

"Of course! You are charged with a capital crime! Even though every-one knows it is a joke, proper respect must be shown."

"They pulled the planted drugs out of my bag—there are a million witnesses. It was a drug, right?"

"Malaysian heroin. Very pure," Attorney Alejandro says admiringly.

"So there are all of these people who can testify that a sack of heroin was found in my luggage. That would seem to complicate the job of getting me out of jail."

"We can probably get it dismissed before an actual trial is launched, by pointing out flaws in the evidence," Attorney Alejandro says. Some-thing in his tone of voice, and the way he's staring out the window, suggests this is the first time he's actually thought about how he's going to specifically attack this problem. "Perhaps a baggage handler at NAIA will step forward and testify that he saw a shadowy figure planting the drugs in your bag."

"A shadowy figure?"

"Yesss," says Attorney Alejandro irritably, anticipating sarcasm.

"Are there a lot of those hanging around backstage at NAIA?"

"We don't need a lot."

"How much time do you think might pass before this baggage han-dler's conscience finally gets the better of him and he decides to step forward?"

Attorney Alejandro shrugs. "A couple of weeks, perhaps. For it to be done properly. How are your accommodations?"

"They suck. But you know what? Nothing really bothers me anymore."

"There is concern among some of the officials of the prison service that when you get out, you may say harsh things about the conditions."

"Since when do they care?"

"You are a little famous in America. Not very famous. A little. Do you remember the American boy in Singapore, who was caned?"

"Of course."

"Very bad publicity for Singapore. So there are officials of the prison service who would be sympathetic to the idea of putting you in a private cell. Clean. Quiet."

Randy cops a questioning look, and holds up one hand and rubs his thumb and fingers together in the "money" gesture.

"It is done already."

"Chester?"

"No. Someone else."

"Avi?"

Attorney Alejandro shakes his head.

"The Shaftoes?"

"I cannot answer your question, Randy, because I do not know. I was not involved in this decision. But whoever did it was also listening to your request for some way to kill the time. You requested books?"

"Yeah. Do you have some?"

"No. But they will allow this." Attorney Alejandro now opens up his briefcase, reaches in with both hands, and pulls out—Randy's new laptop. It still has a police evidence sticker on it.

"Give me a fucking break!" Randy says.

"No! Take it!"

"Isn't it like evidence or something?"

"The police are finished. They have opened it up and looked for drugs inside. Dusted it for fingerprints—you can still see the dust. I hope that it did not damage the delicate machinery."

"Yeah, me too. So, are you telling me that I'm free to take this to my new, clean, quiet, private cell?"

"That is what I am telling you."

"And I can use it there? No restrictions?"

"They will give you an electrical socket. A plug-in," Attorney Alejandro says, and then adds significantly, "I asked them," which is clearly a little reminder that any fees eventually paid to him will have been richly earned.

Randy draws a nice deep breath, thinking, *Well, it is just fantastically generous—in fact, a little bit startling—that the powers that want to convict and*

*execute me are willing to go to such lengths to allow me to dick around on my
computer while I am awaiting my trial and death.* He exhales and says, "Thank
god, at least I'll be able to get some work done." Attorney Alejandro
nods approvingly.

"Your girlfriend is waiting to see you," he announced.

"She's not really my girlfriend. What does she want?" Randy demands.

"What do you mean, what does she want? She wants to see you. To
give you emotional support. To let you know that you are not all alone."

"Shit!" Randy mutters. "I don't want emotional support. I want to
get the fuck out of jail."

"That is my department," Attorney Alejandro says proudly.

"You know what this is? It's one of those men-are-from-Mars,
women-are-from-Venus things."

"I have not heard of this phrase but I understand immediately what
you are saying."

"It's one of those American books where once you've heard the title
you don't even need to read it," Randy says.

"Then I won't."

"You and I see just that someone is trying to fuck me over and that
I need to get out of jail. Very simple and clean. But to her, it is much
more than that—it is an opportunity to have a conversation!"

Attorney Alejandro just rolls his eyes and makes the universal "females
yammering" gesture: thumb and fingertips closing and opening like a
disembodied flapping jaw.

"To share deep feelings and emotionally bond," Randy continues,
closing his eyes.

"But this is not so bad," Attorney Alejandro says, radiating insincerity
like a mirrored ball in a disco.

"I'm doing okay in this jail. Surprisingly okay," Randy says, "but it's
all about keeping up a kind of emotionless front. Many barriers between
me and my surroundings. And so it just makes me crazy that she's picking
this particular moment to implicitly demand that I let my guard down."

"She knows you are weak," Attorney Alejandro says, and winks. "She
smells your vulnerability."

"That's not all she's going to smell. Is this new cell going to have
a shower?"

"Everything. Remember to put something heavy on the drain so that
rats do not climb up out of it during the night."

"Thanks. I'll just put my laptop there." Randy leans back in his chair
and wiggles his butt around. There is a problem now with an erection.
It has been at least a week for Randy. Three nights in the jail, the night
before that at Tom Howard's house, before that the airplane, before that

Avi's basement floor . . . actually it has probably been a lot more than a week. Randy needs badly to get into that private cell if for no other reason than it will give him an opportunity to vent that which is bearing down hard on his prostate gland and get his mind back on an even keel. He prays to god that he's only going to be seeing Amy through a thick glass partition.

Attorney Alejandro opens the door and says something to the waiting guard, who leads them down a hallway toward another room. This one's bigger, and has a number of long tables, with little familial clusters of Filipinos scattered about. If these tables were ever intended to serve as barriers against physical contact, it has long been forgotten; it would take something more like the Berlin Wall to prevent Filipinos from showing affection for each other. So Amy is there, already striding around the end of one of the tables as a couple of guards pointedly look the other way (though their eyes dart back to check out her ass after she has blown by them). No dress this time. Randy predicts it will be a few years before he sees Amy in a dress again. Last time he did, his dick got hard, his heart pounded, he literally salivated, and then suddenly armed men were putting handcuffs on him.

Right now, Amy's in old jeans ripped out at the knee, a tank-top undershirt and a black leather jacket, better to accommodate her concealed weapons. Knowing the Shaftoes, they've probably gone to some very high Defcon level, the one just short of all-out nuclear exchange. Doug Shaftoe probably showers with a SEAL knife clenched in his teeth now. Amy, who normally goes for a low, one-armed, sidelong type of hug, now throws both arms up as if signaling a touchdown and crooks both elbows behind the nape of Randy's neck and lets him feel everything. The flesh of his lower belly can count the stitch-marks in Amy's appendectomy scar. So that he has a boner is probably about as obvious to her as that he smells bad. He might as well have one of those long fluorescent orange bicycle flags lashed to the shaft of his phallus and sticking up out of his pants.

She steps back, looks down at it, then very deliberately looks him in the eye and says, "How do you feel?" which being as it is the obligatory question of females, is hard to read—deadpan/ironic or just sweetly naive?

"I miss you," he says, "and I apologize if my limbic system has misinterpreted your gesture of emotional support."

She takes this levelly, shrugs, and says, "No need to apologize. It's all a part of *you,* Randy. I don't have to get to know you in pieces, do I?"

Randy resists the impulse to check his watch, which would be pointless because it has been confiscated anyway. She has undoubtedly set some kind of world speed record here, in the male/female conversation category, for working the subject around to Randy's own failure to be emotionally available. To do it in this setting displays a certain chutzpah that he cannot help but admire.

"You've talked to Attorney Alejandro," she says.

"Yeah. I assume he's imparted to me whatever he was supposed to impart."

"I don't have much more for you," she says. Which on a pure tactical level means a lot. If the wreck had been found by the Dentist's minions, or their salvage work had been somehow interrupted, she'd say something. For her to say nothing means that they are probably hauling gold out of that submarine at this very moment.

So. She's busy working on the gold salvage operation, to which her contributions are no doubt vital. She has absolutely no specific information to impart to him about anything. So why has she made the long, alternately dull and dangerous trek to Manila? In order to do what exactly? It is one of these fiendish mind-reading exercises. She has her arms crossed over her bosom and is eyeing him coolly. *Someone is trying to send you a message.*

He suddenly gets the feeling that she's got him right where she wants him. Maybe she's the one who planted the heroin in his bag. It's a power thing, that's all.

A big slab of memory floats up to the surface of Randy's mind, like a floe calved off the polar icecap. He and Amy and the Shaftoe boys were in California, right after the earthquake, going through all the old crap in the basement looking for a few key boxes of papers. Randy heard Amy squealing with laughter and found her sitting in the corner on top of some old book boxes, reading a paperback novel by flashlight. She had uncovered a huge cache of paperback romance novels, none of which Randy had ever seen before. Bodice-rippers of the most incredibly cheesy sort. Randy assumed they'd been left behind by the house's previous owners until he flipped through a couple of them, checking the copyright dates: all from the years when he and Charlene were living together. Charlene must have been reading them at a rate of about one a week.

"Ooh baby," Amy said, and read him a passage about a rugged but sensitive but tough but loving but horny but smart hero having his way with a protesting but willing but struggling but yielding tempestuous female. "God!" She frisbeed the book into a puddle on the basement floor.

"I always got the sense she had furtive reading habits."

"Well, now you know what she wanted," Amy said. "Did you give her what she wanted, Randy?"

And Randy has been thinking about that ever since. And when he got over his surprise that Charlene was a bodice-ripper addict, he decided it wasn't necessarily a bad thing, though in her circle, reading books like that would be tantamount to wearing a tall pointy hat in the streets of Salem Village, Mass. circa 1692. She and Randy had tried, awfully hard, to have an egalitarian relationship. They had spent money on relationship counseling trying to keep the egalitarian relationship alive. But she had become more and more angry, without ever giving him a reason, and he had become more and more confused. Eventually he stopped being confused and just got irritated, and tired of her. After Amy discovered those books in the basement, Randy slowly put a whole new and different story together in his head: that Charlene's limbic system was simply hooked up in such a way that she liked dominant men. Again, not in a whips and chains sense, just in the sense that in most relationships someone's got to be active and someone's got to be passive, and there's no particular logic to that, but there's nothing bad about it either. In the end, the passive partner can have just as much power, and just as much freedom.

Intuition, like a flash of lightning, lasts only for a second. It generally comes when one is tormented by a difficult decipherment and when one reviews in his mind the fruitless experiments already tried. Suddenly the light breaks through and one finds after a few minutes what previous days of labor were unable to reveal.

Randy has this very strong feeling that Amy doesn't read bodice-ripper novels. She goes the other way. She can't tolerate surrendering to anyone. Which makes it hard for her to function in polite society; she could not have been happy sitting at home during her senior year of high school, waiting for a boy to invite her to the prom. This feature of her personality is extremely prone to misinterpretation, so she bailed out. She would rather be lonely, and true to herself, and in control, in an out-of-the-way part of the world, with her music-by-intelligent-female-singer-songwriters to keep her company, than misinterpreted and hassled in America.

"I love you," he says. Amy looks away and heaves a big sigh like, *At last we're getting somewhere.* Randy continues, "I've been infatuated with you ever since we met."

Now she's back to looking at him expectantly.

"And the reason I've been slow to, uh, to actually show it, or do anything about it, is first of all because I wasn't sure whether or not you were a lesbian."

Amy scoffs and rolls her eyes.

". . . and later just because of my own reticence. Which is unfortu-nately part of me too, just like this part." He glances down just for a microsecond.

She's shaking her head at him in amazement.

"The fact that the scientific investigator works fifty percent of his time by nonrational means is quite insufficiently recognized," Randy says.

Amy sits down on his side of the table, jacknifes, spins around neatly on her ass, and comes to light on the other side. "I'll think about what you said," she says. "Hang in there, sport."

"Smooth sailing, Amy."

Amy gives him a little smile over her shoulder, then walks straight to the exit, turning around once in the doorway to make sure he's still looking at her.

He is. Which, he feels quite confident, is the right answer.

GLAMOR

A COUPLE OF SQUADS OF NIPPONESE AIR FORCE SOLDIERS, armed with rifles and Nambus, pursue Bobby Shaftoe and his crew of Huks towards the Manila Bay seawall. If it comes to the point where they must stand and slug it out, they can probably kill a lot of Nips before they are overwhelmed. But they are here to find and assist the Altamiras, not to die heroically, and so they retreat through the neighborhood of Ermita. One of MacArthur's circling Piper Cubs catches sight of one of those Nip squads as it is clambering over the ruins of a collapsed building, and calls in a strike—artillery rounds spiral in from the north like long passes in a football game. Shaftoe and the Huks try to time the incoming rounds, guessing at how many tubes are firing on them, trying to run from one place of concealment to the next when they think there's going to be a few seconds' pause in the shrapnel. Maybe half of the Nips are killed or wounded by this barrage, but they are fighting at such close quarters that two of Shaftoe's Huks are hit as well. Shaftoe is trying to drag one of them out of danger when he looks down and sees that he is stomping across a mess of shattered white crockery that is marked with the name of a hotel—the same hotel where he slow-danced with Glory on the night that the war started.

The wounded Huks are still capable of moving and so the retreat continues. Shaftoe's calming down a bit, thinking about the situation with more clarity. The Huks find a good defensive position and stall the attackers for a few minutes while he gets his bearings, works out a plan. Fifteen minutes later, the Huks abandon their position and fall back in panic, or appear to. About half of the Nipponese squad rushes forward in pursuit and finds that they have been lured into a killing ground, a cul-de-sac created by the partial collapse of a building into an alley. One of the Huks opens up with a tommy gun while Shaftoe—who stayed behind, hiding in a burned-out car—heaves grenades at the other half of the squad, pinning them down and preventing them from coming to help their comrades who are being noisily slaughtered.

But these Nips are relentless. They regroup under a surviving officer and continue their pursuit. Shaftoe, now on his own, ends up being chased around the foundations of another hotel, a luxury place that rises up above the bay, near the American Embassy. He trips over the body of a young woman who apparently leaped, fell, or was thrown from one of the windows. Crouching behind some shrubbery for a breather, he hears a shrill keening drifting out of the hotel's windows. The place is full of women, he realizes, and all of them are either screaming or sobbing.

His pursuers seem to have lost track of him. The Huks have lost him, too. Shaftoe stays there for a while, listening to all of those women, wishing he could go inside and do something for them. But the place must be filled with Nip soldiers, or else the women wouldn't be screaming as they are.

He listens carefully for a while, trying to ignore the lamentations of the women. A fourteen-year-old girl in a bloody nightgown plummets down from the fifth floor of the hotel, thuds into the ground like a sack of cement, and bounces once. Shaftoe closes his eyes and listens until he is absolutely sure that he does not hear any children.

The picture's getting clearer now. The males are marched away and killed. The women are marched off in another direction. Young women without children are brought to this hotel. Women with children must have been taken somewhere else. Where?

He hears tommy gun fire on the other side of the hotel. It must be his buddies. He creeps around to a corner of the hotel and listens again, trying to figure out where they are—somewhere in Rizal Park, he thinks. But then MacArthur's artillery opens up hell-for-leather and the world begins to heave beneath him like a rug being shaken, and he can't hear trench brooms or screaming women or anything. He has a view east and south towards the parts of Ermita and Malate from which they have just come, and he can see big pieces of debris spinning up from the ground over there, and gouts of dust. He has seen enough of war to know what it means: the Americans are advancing from the south now *as well,* push-

ing towards Intramuros. Shaftoe and his band of Huks were operating
on their own, but it appears that they have inadvertently served as harbin-
gers of a big infantry thrust.

Terrified by the barrage, a bunch of Nip soldiers stagger out of a side
exit of the hotel, almost too drunk to stand, some of them still pulling
their trousers up. Shaftoe disgustedly throws a grenade at them and then
gets the hell out without bothering to examine the results. It is getting
to the point where killing Nips is no fun anymore. There is no sense of
accomplishment in it. It is a tedious and dangerous job that never seems
to end. When will these stupid bastards knock it off? They are embarrassing themselves in front of the whole world.

He finds his men in Rizal Park, beneath the shadow of Intramuros's
ancient Spanish wall, disputing possession of a baseball diamond with
what is left of the Nipponese squads that pursued them here. The timing
is both good and bad. Any earlier, and Nip reinforcements in the surrounding neighborhood would have heard the skirmish, flooded into the
park and wiped them out. Any later, and the American infantry would
be here. But Rizal Park is in the middle of a deranged urban battleground
right now, and nothing makes any kind of sense. They have to impose
their will on the situation, the kind of thing Bobby Shaftoe has gotten
fairly good at.

The one thing they have going for them is that the artillery is pointed
elsewhere for the time being. Shaftoe squats down behind a coconut tree
and tries to figure out how the hell he is going to reach that baseball
diamond, which is a couple of hundred yards away across totally flat,
open ground.

He knows the place; Uncle Jack took him to a baseball game there.
Wooden bleachers rise along the left and right field lines. Beneath each
one is a dugout. Shaftoe knows how battles work, and so he knows that
one of those dugouts is full of Nips and one is full of Huks and that
they are pinned down in them by each other's fire just like Great War
troops in their opposing trenches. There are a few buildings under the
bleachers, containing toilets and a refreshment stand. The Nips and the
Huks will be creeping through those buildings right now, trying to get
into a position from which they can shoot into the dugouts.

A Nipponese grenade flies towards him from the direction of the left
field bleachers, making a stripping noise as it passes through the fronds
of a palm tree. Shaftoe ducks his head behind another tree so that he
can't see the grenade. It explodes and tears the clothing, and a good deal
of the skin, from one of his arms and one of his legs. But like all Nip
grenades it is poorly made and miserably ineffectual. Shaftoe turns around
and uncorks a spume of .45-caliber rounds in the general direction the

grenade came from; this should give the thrower something to think about while Shaftoe gets his bearings.

This is actually a stupid idea, because he runs out of ammunition. He has a few rounds in his Colt, and that's it. He also has one grenade left. He considers throwing it towards the baseball diamond, but his throwing arm is in pretty bad shape now.

Besides—Jesus Christ! That baseball diamond is just too far away. Even in peak condition he could not throw a grenade from here to there.

Perhaps one of those corpses out in the grass, between here and there, isn't really a corpse. Shaftoe crawls towards them on his belly and establishes that they are most definitely dead people.

Giving the field a wide berth, he begins working his way around behind home plate toward the right field line, where his people are. He would love to sneak up on the Nips from behind, but that grenade thrower really threw a fright into him. Where the hell is he?

The firing from the dugouts has become sporadic. They have stalemated now and are trying to conserve ammunition. Shaftoe risks rising to a crouch. He runs for about three paces before he sees the door to the women's toilet swing open and a man jump out, winding up like Bob Feller getting ready to throw a fastball right down the middle of the plate. Shaftoe fires his .45 once, but the weapons' absurdly vicious recoil jerks it right out of his lamed hand. The grenade comes flying towards him, perfectly on target. Shaftoe dives to the ground and scrambles for his .45. The grenade actually bounces off his shoulder and falls spinning into the dust, making a fizzing noise. But it doesn't explode.

Shaftoe looks up. The Nip is standing framed in the women's room door. His shoulders slump miserably. Shaftoe recognizes him; there's only one Nip who could throw a grenade like that. He lies there for a few moments, counting syllables on his fingers, then stands up, cups his hands around his mouth, and hollers:

Pineapple fastball—
Guns of Manila applaud—
Hit by pitch—free base!

Goto Dengo and Bobby Shaftoe lock themselves inside the women's room and share a nip from a bottle of port that the former has looted from a store somewhere. They spend a few minutes catching up with each other in a general way. Goto Dengo is already somewhat drunk, which makes his grenade-throwing performance all the more impressive. "I'm hyped to the gills on benzedrine," Shaftoe says. "Keeps you going, but kind of screws up your aim."

"I noticed!" Goto Dengo says. He is so skinny and haggard he looks more like some hypothetical sick uncle of Goto Dengo's.

Shaftoe pretends to take offense at this and drops into a judo stance. Goto Dengo laughs uneasily and waves him off. "No more fighting," he says. A rifle bullet passes through the women's room wall and digs a crater into a porcelain sink.

"We gotta come up with a plan," Shaftoe says.

"The plan: You live, I die," Goto Dengo says.

"Fuck that," Shaftoe says. "Hey, don't you idiots know you're surrounded?"

"We know," Goto Dengo says wearily. "We know for a long time."

"So give up, you fucking morons! Wave a white flag and you can all go home."

"It is not Nipponese way."

"So come up with another fucking way! Show some fucking adaptability!"

"Why are you here?" Goto Dengo asks, changing the subject. "What is your mission?"

Shaftoe explains that he's looking for his kid. Goto Dengo tells him where all of the women and children are: in the Church of St. Agustin, in Intramuros.

"Hey," Shaftoe says, "if we surrender to you, you'll kill us. Right?"

"Yes."

"If you guys surrender to us, we won't kill you. Promise. Scout's honor."

"For us, living or dying is not the important thing," Goto Dengo says.

"Hey! Tell me something I didn't fucking already know!" Shaftoe says. "Even winning battles isn't important to you. Is it?"

Goto Dengo looks the other way, shamefaced.

"Haven't you guys figured out yet that banzai charges DON'T FUCKING WORK?"

"All of the people who learned that were killed in banzai charges," Goto Dengo says.

As if on cue, the Nips in the left field dugout begin screaming "Banzai!" and charge, as one, out onto the field. Shaftoe puts his eye up to a bullet hole in the wall and watches them stumbling across the infield with fixed bayonets. Their leader clambers up the pitcher's mound as if he's going to plant a flag there, and takes a slug in the middle of his face. His men are being dismantled all around him by thoughtfully placed rifle slugs from the Huks' dugout. Urban warfare is not the metier of the Hukbalahaps, but calmly slaughtering banzai-charging Nipponese is old hat. One of the Nips actually manages to crawl all the way to the first base coach's box. Then a few pounds of meat come flying out of his back and he relaxes.

Shaftoe turns to see that Goto Dengo is aiming a revolver at him. He chooses to ignore this for a moment. "See what I mean?"

"I have seen it many times before."

"Then why aren't you dead?" Shaftoe asks the question with all due flippancy, but it has a terrible effect on Goto Dengo. His face scrunches up and he begins to cry. "Aw, shit. You pull a gun on me and start bawling at the same time? How unfair can you get? Why don't you kick some fucking dirt in my eyes while you're at it?"

Goto Dengo lifts the revolver to his own temple. But Shaftoe sees that one coming a mile away. He knows Nips well enough, by this point, to figure out when they are about to go hari-kari on you. Shaftoe jumps forward as soon as the barrel of the revolver begins to move. By the time it is against Goto Dengo's skull, Shaftoe has his finger stuck into the gap between the hammer and the firing pin.

Goto Dengo collapses to the floor sobbing piteously. It just makes Shaftoe want to kick him. "Knock it off!" he says. "What the fuck is eating at you?"

"I came to Manila to redeem myself—to get back my lost honor!" Goto Dengo says. "I could have done it here. I could be dead on that field right now, and my spirit going to Yasukuni. But then—you came! You ruined my concentration!"

"Concentrate on this, dumbshit!" Shaftoe says. "My son is in a church right over on the far side of that wall, with a bunch of other helpless women and chidlren. If you want to redeem yourself, why not help me get 'em out alive?"

Goto Dengo seems to have gone into a trance now. His face, which was blubbering just a minute ago, has solidified into a mask. "I wish I could believe what you believe," he says. "I have died, Bobby. I was buried in a rock tomb. If I were a Christian, I could be born again now, and be a new man. Instead, I must go on living, and accept my karma."

"Well, shit! There's a padre right out there in the dugout. He can Christianize your ass in about ten seconds flat." Bobby Shaftoe strides across the bathroom and swings the door open.

He is startled to see a man standing just a few paces away. The man is dressed in an old but clean khaki uniform, devoid of insignia except for a pentagon of stars on the collar. He has jammed a wooden match down into the bowl of a corncob pipe and is puffing away futilely. But it's as if all of the oxygen has been sucked out of the air by the burning of the city. He throws the match away in disgust, then looks up into the face of Bobby Shaftoe—staring at him through a pair of dark aviator sunglasses that give his gaunt face the appearance of a skull. His mouth forms into an O for a moment. Then his jaw sets. "Shaftoe . . . Shaftoe! SHAFTOE!" he says.

Bobby Shaftoe feels his body stiffening to attention. Even if he had been dead for a few hours, his body would do this out of some kind of dumb ingrained reflex. "Sir, yes sir!" he says wearily.

The General composes his thoughts for half a second, and then says: "You were supposed to be in Concepcion. You failed to be there. Your superiors did not know what to think. They have been worried sick about you. And the Department of the Navy has been positively insufferable ever since they became aware that you were working for me. They assert, in the most high-handed way, that you know important secrets, and should never have been placed in danger of capture. In short, your whereabouts and your status have been the subject of the most intense, nay, feverish speculation for the last several weeks. Many supposed that you were dead, or, worse, captured. This distraction has been most unwelcome to me, inasmuch as the planning and execution of the reconquest of the Philippine Islands have left me little time to devote to such nagging distractions." An artillery shell rips through the air and detonates in the bleachers, sending jagged fragments of planks, about the size of canoe paddles, whirling through the air all around them. One of them embeds itself like a javelin in the dirt between The General and Bobby Shaftoe.

The General takes advantage of this to draw breath, and then continues, as if he were reading this from a script. "And now, when I least expect it, I encounter you, here, many leagues distant from your assigned post, out of uniform, in a disheveled condition, accompanied by a Nipponese officer, violating the sanctity of a ladies' powder room! Shaftoe, have you no sense whatsoever of military honor? Do you not respect decorum? Do you not believe that a representative of the United States military should comport himself with more dignity?"

Shaftoe's kneecaps are joggling up and down uncontrollably. His guts have become molten, and he feels strange bubbling processes going on in his rectum. His molars are chattering together like a teletype machine. He senses Goto Dengo behind him, and wonders what the poor bastard can possibly be thinking.

"Begging your pardon, General, not to change the subject or anything, but are you here all by yourself?"

The General juts his chin towards the men's room. "My aides are in there relieving themselves. They were in a great hurry to do so, and it is good that we came upon this place. But none of them considered invading the powder room," he says severely.

"I apologize for that, sir," Bobby Shaftoe says hastily, "and for all of those other things that you mentioned. But I still think of myself as a Marine, and Marines do not make excuses, so I will not even try."

"That is not satisfactory! I need an explanation for where you've been."

"I have been out in the world," Bobby Shaftoe says, "getting butt-fucked by Fortune."

The door of the men's room opens and one of The General's aides walks out, woozy and bowlegged. The General ignores him; he is gazing right past Shaftoe now.

"Pardon my manners, sir," Shaftoe says, turning sideways. "Sir, my friend Goto Dengo. Goto-san, say hi to General of the Army Douglas MacArthur."

Goto Dengo has been standing there like a pillar of salt this whole time, utterly dumbfounded, but now he snaps out of it, and bows very low. MacArthur nods crisply. His aide is staring darkly at Goto Dengo and has already drawn his Colt.

"Pleasure," The General said airily. "Pray tell, what sort of business were you two gentlemen prosecuting in the ladies'?"

Bobby Shaftoe knows how to lunge for an opening. "Uh, it is very funny you should ask that question, sir," he says offhandedly, "but Goto-san, just now, saw the light, and converted to Christianity."

Some Nips on top of the wall open up on them with a machine gun. The flimsy, tumbling rounds crack through the air and thump into the ground. General of the Army Douglas MacArthur stands motionless for a long time, lips pursed. His sniffles once. Then he removes his aviator glasses carefully and wipes his eyes on the immaculate sleeve of his uniform. He pulls out a neatly folded white hankie and wraps it around his hawklike nose and honks into it a few times. He folds it up carefully and puts it back in his pocket, squares his shoulders, and then walks right up to Goto Dengo and wraps him up in a big, manly bearhug. The remainder of The General's aides emerge from the shitter *en bloc* and view the scene with reticence and palpable tension all over their faces. Profoundly mortified, Bobby Shaftoe looks down at his feet, wiggles his toes, and caresses the linear scab running upside his head where the oar clocked him a few days ago. The machine-gun crew up on the wall are being picked off one by one by a sniper; they writhe and scream operatically. The Huks have come up from the dugout and stumbled into this little tableau; they all stand motionless with their jaws hanging down around their navels.

Finally MacArthur unhands the stiff body of Goto Dengo, steps back dramatically, and presents him to his staff. "Meet Goto-san," he announces. "You have all heard the expression, 'the only good Nip is a dead Nip'? Well, this young fellow is a counterexample, and as we learned in mathematics, it only takes one counterexample to disprove the theorem."

His staff observe cautious silence.

"It seems only fitting that we take this young fellow to the Church of St. Agustin, over yonder in Intramuros, to carry out the sacrament of baptism," The General says.

One of the aides steps forward, hunched over in that he's expecting to get a slug between the shoulder blades any minute. "Sir, it is my duty to remind you that Intramuros is still controlled by the enemy."

"Then it is high time we made our presence felt!" MacArthur says. "Shaftoe will get us there. Shaftoe and these fine Filipino gentlemen." The General throws one arm around Goto Dengo's neck in a highly affectionate, companionable way, and begins strolling with him towards the nearest gate. "I would like you to know, young man, that when I set up my headquarters in Tokyo—which, God willing, should be within a year—I want you there bright and early the first day!"

"Yes sir!" Goto Dengo says. All things considered, it is unlikely he would say anything else.

Shaftoe draws a deep breath, tilts his head back, and stares up into a smoky heaven. "God," he says, "usually I bow my head when I'm talking to You, but I figure this is a good time for us to have a face-to-face. You see and know all things and so I will not explain the situation to You. I would just like to submit a request for You. I know You are getting requests from lonely soldiers all over the fucking place at this time, but since this one has to do with a shitload of women and children, and General MacArthur too, maybe You can jump me to the top of the stack. You know what I want. Let's get it done."

He borrows a small, straight twenty-round tommy gun magazine from one of his comrades and they set out for Intramuros. The gates are sure to be guarded, so Shaftoe and the Huks run up the sloping walls instead, directly beneath that wiped-out machine-gun nest. They turn the gun around into Intramuros, and plant one of the wounded Huks there to operate it.

The first time Shaftoe gazes into the town, he nearly falls off the wall. Intramuros is gone. If he didn't know where he was, he would never recognize it. Essentially all of the buildings have been leveled. Manila Cathedral and the Church of St. Agustin still stand, both with heavy damage. A few of the fine old Spanish houses still exist as hasty, freehand sketches of their former selves, missing roofs, wings, or walls. But most of the blocks are just jumbles of masonry and shattered red roof tiles with smoke and steam seething out of them. There are dead bodies all over the place, sowed all over the neighborhood like timothy seed broadcast onto freshly plowed soil. The artillery has mostly stopped—there being nothing left to destroy—but small-arms and machine-gun fire sound on almost every block.

Shaftoe is thinking he'll have to assault one of the gates. But before he can even come up with a plan, MacArthur is up there with the rest of his group, having scrambled up the rampart behind them. This is evidently the first time that The General has gotten a good look at Intramuros, because he is stunned and, for once, speechless. He stands there for a long time with his mouth open, and begins to draw fire from a few Nips hidden in the wreckage below. The turned-around machine gun silences them.

It takes them several hours to make their way up the street and into the Church of St. Agustin. A bunch of Nips have barricaded themselves inside the place along with what sounds like every hungry infant and irritable two-year-old in Manila. The church is just one side of a large compound that includes a monastery and other buildings. Many of the structures have been torn open by artillery fire. The treasures hoarded in that place by the monks over the course of the last five hundred years have tumbled out into the street. Blown all over the neighborhood like shrapnel, and commingled with the bayoneted corpses of Filipino boys, are huge oil paintings of Christ being scourged, fantastic wooden sculptures of the Romans hammering the spikes through his wrists and ankles, marbles of Mary holding the dead and mangled Christ in her lap, tapestries of the whipping post and the cat o' nine tails in action, blood coursing out of Christ's back through hundreds of parallel gouges.

The Nips still inside the church defend its main doors with the suicidal determination that Shaftoe has begun to find so tedious, but thanks to The General's artillery, there are plenty of other ways, besides doors, to get into the place now. So it is that, even while a company of American infantry mount a frontal assault on the main entrance, Bobby Shaftoe and his Huks, Goto Dengo, The General, and his aides are already kneeling in a little chapel in what used to be part of the monastery. The padre leads them through a couple of extremely truncated prayers of thanksgiving and baptizes Goto Dengo with water from a font, with Bobby Shaftoe taking the role of beaming parent and General of the Army Douglas MacArthur serving as godfather. Shaftoe later remembers only one line of the ceremony.

"Do you reject the glamor of Evil, and refuse to be mastered by it?" says the padre.

"I do!" says MacArthur with tremendous authority even as Bobby

Shaftoe is muttering, "Fuck yes!" Goto Dengo, nods, gets wet, and becomes a Christian.

Bobby Shaftoe excuses himself and goes wandering through the compound. It seems as big and crazy as that Casbah in Algiers, all gloomy and dusty on the inside, and filled with still more La Pasyon art, made by artists who had obviously witnessed whippings firsthand, and who didn't need any priest spouting little homilies about the glamor of Evil. He goes up and down the great stairway once, for old time's sake, remembering the night Glory took him here.

There is a courtyard with a fountain in the center, surrounded by a long shaded gallery where Spanish friars could stroll in the shade and look out over the flowers and hear the birds singing. Right now the only things singing are shells passing overhead. But little Filipino kids are running races up and down the gallery, and their mothers and aunts and grannies are encamped in the courtyard, drawing water from the fountain and cooking rice over piles of burning chair legs.

A grey-eyed two-year-old with a makeshift bludgeon is chasing some bigger kids down a stone arcade. Some of his hairs are the color of Bobby's and some are the color of Glory's, and Bobby Shaftoe can see Glory-ness shining almost fluoroscopically out of his face. The boy has the same bone structure that he saw on the sandbar a few days ago, but this time it is clothed in chubby pink flesh. The flesh admittedly bears bruises and abrasions. No doubt honorably earned. Bobby squats down and looks the little Shaftoe in the eye, wondering how to begin to explain *everything*. But the boy says, "Bobby Shaftoe, you have boo-boos," and drops his club and walks up to examine the wounds on Bobby's arm. Little kids don't bother to say hello, they just start talking to you, and Shaftoe figures that's a good way to handle what would otherwise be pretty damn awkward. The Altamiras have probably been telling little Douglas M. Shaftoe, since the day he was born, that one day Bobby Shaftoe would come in glory from across the sea. That he has now done so is just as routine and yet just as much of a miracle as that the sun rises every day.

"I see that you and yours have displayed adaptability and that is good," says Bobby Shaftoe to his son, but sees immediately that he's not getting through to the kid at all. He feels a need to get something into the kid's head that is going to stick, and this need is stronger than the craving for morphine or sex ever was.

So he picks up the boy and carries him through the compound, down semicollapsed hallways and over settling rubble-heaps and between dead Nipponese boys to that big staircase, and shows him the giant slabs of granite, tells how they were laid, one on top of the next, year by year, as the galleons full of silver came from Acapulco. Doug M. Shaftoe has been playing with blocks, so he zeroes in on the basic concept right away. Dad carries son up and down the stairway a few times. They stand at the bottom and look up at it. The block analogy has struck deep. Without any prompting, Doug M. raises both arms over his head and hollers "Soooo big" and the sound echoes up and down the stairs. Bobby wants to explain to the boy that *this is how it's done,* you pile one thing on top of the next and you keep it up and keep it up—sometimes the galleon sinks in a typhoon, you don't get your slab of granite that year— but you stick with it and eventually you end up with something *sooo big.*

He wishes that he could also make some further point about Glory and how she's been hard at work building her own staircase. Maybe if he was a word man like Enoch Root he would be able to explain. But he knows that this is going way over the toddler's head, just as it went over Bobby's head when Glory first showed him the steps. The only thing that'll stick with Douglas MacArthur Shaftoe is the memory that his father brought him here and carried him up and down the staircase, and if he lives long enough and thinks hard enough maybe he'll come to understand it too, the way Bobby does. That is a good enough start.

Word has gotten around, among the women in the courtyard, that Bobby Shaftoe has arrived—better late than never!—and so he does not have time for meaningful speeches anyway. The Altamiras send him out on an errand: to find Carlos, an eleven-year-old boy who was rounded up a few days ago when the Nips swept through Malate. Shaftoe finds MacArthur and Goto Dengo first, and excuses himself. Those two are deeply involved in a discussion of Goto Dengo's tunnel-building acumen, and how it might be put to use during the rebuilding of Nippon, a project that The General is eager to launch as soon as he finishes reducing the entire Pacific Rim to rubble.

"You have sins to atone for, Shaftoe," The General says, "and you can't atone for them by getting down on your knees and saying Hail Marys."

"I understand that, sir," Shaftoe says.

"I have a little job that needs doing—precisely the kind of thing for which a Marine Raider with parachute training would be ideally suited."

"What's the Department of the Navy going to think of that, sir?"

"I have no intention of letting the swabbies know I've found you until you have carried out this mission. But when you are finished—all is forgiven."

"I'll be right back," Shaftoe says.

"Where are you going, Shaftoe?"

"Got some other people who need to forgive me first."

He heads in the direction of Fort Santiago with a reconstituted, re-armed and beefed-up squad of Huks. The old Spanish fort has been liberated, within the last couple of hours, by the Americans. They have thrown open the doors to the dungeons and the subterranean caverns along the Pasig River. Finding eleven-year-old Carlos Altamira is, then, a problem of sorting through several thousand corpses. Almost all of the Filipinos who were herded into this place by the Nips died, either through out-and-out execution, or by suffocating in the dungeons, or by drowning when the tide came up the river and flooded the cells. Bobby Shaftoe doesn't really know what Carlos looked like, and so the best he can do is cull out the young-looking corpses and present them to members of the Altamira family for inspection. The benzedrine he took a couple of days ago has worn off, and he feels half dead himself. He trudges through the Spanish dungeon with a kerosene lantern, shining the dim yellow light on the faces of the dead, muttering the words to himself like a prayer.

"Do you reject the glamor of Evil, and refuse to be mastered by it?"

WISDOM
....

A FEW YEARS AGO, WHEN RANDY BECAME TIRED OF THE CEASE-less pressure in his lower jaw, he went out onto the north-central Californian oral-surgery market looking for someone to extract his wisdom teeth. His health plan covered this, so price was not an obstacle. His dentist took one of those big cinemascopic wraparound X-rays of his entire lower head, the kind where they pack your mouth with half a roll of high-speed film and then clamp your head in a jig and the X-ray machine revolves around you spraying radiation through a slit, as the entire staff of the dentist's office hits the deck behind a lead wall, resulting in a printed image that is a none-too-appetizing distortion of his jaw into a single flat plane. Looking at it, Randy eschewed cruder analogies like "head of a man run over several times by steamroller while lying flat on his back" and tried to think of it as a mapping transformation—just one more in mankind's long history of ill-advisedly trying to represent three-D stuff on a flat plane. The corners of this coordinate plane were anchored by the wisdom teeth themselves, which even to the dentally unsophisticated Randy looked just a little disturbing in that each one was about the size of his thumb (though maybe this was just a distortion in the coordinate transform—like the famously swollen Greenland of Mercator) and they were pretty far away from any other teeth, which (logically) would seem to put them in parts of his body not normally considered to be within a dentist's purview, and they were at the wrong angle—not just a little crooked, but verging on upside down and backwards. At first he just chalked all of this up to the Greenland phenomenon. With his Jaw-map in hand, he hit the streets of Three Siblings-land looking for an oral surgeon. It was already beginning to work on him psychologically. Those were some big-ass teeth! Brought into being by the workings of relict DNA strands from the hunter-gatherer epoch. Designed for reducing tree bark and mammoth gristle to easily digestible paste. Now these boulders of living enamel were horrifyingly adrift in a gracile cro-magnon head that simply did not have room for them. Think of the sheer extra weight he had been carrying around. Think of the use that priceless head-real-estate could have been put to. When they were gone, what would fill up the four giant molar-shaped voids in his melon? It was moot until he could find someone to get rid of them. But one oral surgeon after another turned him down. They would put the X-ray up on their light boxes, stare into it and blanch. Maybe it was just the pale light coming out of the light-boxes but Randy could have sworn they were blanching. Disingenuously—as if wisdom teeth normally grew someplace completely different—they all pointed out that the wisdom teeth were buried deep, deep, deep in Randy's head. The lowers were so far back in his jaw that removing them would practically break the jawbone in twain structurally; from there, one false move would send a surgical-steel demolition pick into his middle ear. The uppers were so deep in his skull that the roots were twined around the parts of his brain responsible for perceiving the color blue (on one side) and being able to suspend one's disbelief in bad movies (on the other) and between these teeth and actual air, light and saliva lay many strata of skin, meat, cartilage, major nerve-cables, brain-feeding arteries, bulging caches of lymph nodes, girders and trusses of bone, rich marrow that was working just fine thank you, a few glands whose functions were unsettlingly poorly understood, and many of the other things that made Randy Randy, all of them definitely falling into the category of sleeping dogs.

Oral surgeons, it seemed, were not comfortable delving more than elbow-deep into a patient's head. They had been living in big houses and driving to work in Mercedes-Benz sedans long before Randy had dragged his sorry ass into their offices with his horrifying X-ray and they had absolutely nothing to gain by even attempting to remove these— not so much wisdom teeth in the normal sense as apocalyptic portents from the Book of Revelations. The best way to remove these teeth was with a guillotine. None of these oral surgeons would even consider undertaking the extraction until Randy had signed a legal disclaimer too thick to staple, something that almost had to come in a three-ring binder, the general import of which was that one of the normal consequences of the procedure was for the patient's head to end up floating in a jug of formaldehyde in a tourist trap just over the Mexican border. In this manner Randy wandered from one oral surgeon's office to another for a few weeks, like a teratomic outcast roving across a post-nuclear waste-land being driven out of one village after another by the brickbats of wretched, terrified peasants. Until one day when he walked into an office and the nurse at the front desk almost seemed to expect him, and led him back into an exam room for a private consult with the oral surgeon, who was busy doing something in one of his little rooms that involved putting a lot of bone dust into the air. The nurse bade him sit down, proffered coffee, then turned on the light box and took Randy's X-rays and stuck them up there. She took a step back, crossed her arms, and gazed at the pictures in wonder. "So," she murmured, "these are the *famous* wisdom teeth!"

That was the last oral surgeon Randy visited for a couple of years. He still had that relentless 24-Jam pressure in his head, but now his attitude had changed; instead of thinking of it as an anomalous condition easily remedied, it became his personal cross to bear, and really not all that bad compared to what some people had to suffer with. There, as in many other unexpected situations, his extensive fantasy-role-playing-game experience came in handy, as while spinning out various epic scenarios he had inhabited the minds, if not the bodies, of many characters who were missing limbs or had been burned over some algorithmically determined percentages of their bodies by dragon's breath or wizard's fireball, and it was part of the ethics of the game that you had to think pretty hard about what it would actually be like to live with such injuries and to play your character accordingly. By those standards, feeling all the time like you had an automotive jack embedded in your skull, ratcheting up the pressure one click every few months, was not even worth men-tioning. It was lost in the somatic noise.

So Randy lived that way for several years, as he and Charlene insensi-bly crept upwards on the socioeconomic scale and began finding them-selves at parties with people who had arrived in Mercedes-Benzes. It was at one of these parties where Randy overheard a dentist extolling some brilliant young oral surgeon who had just moved to the area. Randy had to bite his tongue not to start asking all kinds of questions about just what "brilliant" meant in an oral-surgery context—questions that were motivated solely by curiosity but that the dentist would be likely to take the wrong way. Among coders it was pretty obvious who was brilliant and who wasn't, but how could you tell a brilliant oral surgeon apart from a merely excellent one? It gets you into deep epistemological shit. Each set of wisdom teeth could only be extracted once. You couldn't have a hundred oral surgeons extract the same set of wisdom teeth and then compare the results scientifically. And yet it was obvious from watching the look on this dentist's face that this one particular oral surgeon, this new guy, was brilliant. So later Randy sidled up to this dentist and allowed as how he might have a challenge—he might personally *embody* a challenge—that would put this ineffable quality of oral-surgery brilliance to some good use, and could he have the guy's name please.

A few days later he was talking to this oral surgeon, who was indeed young and conspicuously bright and had more in common with other brilliant people Randy had known—mostly hackers—than he did with other oral surgeons. He drove a pickup truck and kept fresh copies of TURING magazine in his waiting room. He had a beard, and a staff of nurses and other female acolytes who were all permanently aflutter over his brilliantness and followed him around steering him away from large obstacles and reminding him to eat lunch. This guy did not blanch when he saw Randy's Mercato-roentgeno-gram on his light box. He actually lifted his chin up off his hand and stood a little straighter and spake not for several minutes. His head moved minutely every so often as he animadverted on a different corner of the coordinate plane, and admired the exquisitely grotesque situation of each tooth—its paleolithic heft and its long gnarled roots trailing off into parts of his head never charted by anatomists.

When he finally turned to face Randy, he had this priestlike aura about him, a kind of holy ecstasy, a feeling of cosmic symmetry revealed, as if Randy's jaw, and his brilliant oral-surgery brain, had been carved out by the architect of the Universe fifteen billion years ago specifically so that they could run into each other, here and now, in front of this light box. He did not say anything like, "Randy let me just show you how close the roots of this one tooth are to the bundle of nerves that distinguishes you from a marmoset," or "My schedule is incredibly full and I was thinking of going into the real estate business anyway," or "Just a second while I call my lawyer." He didn't even say anything like, "Wow, those suckers are really in deep." The young brilliant oral surgeon just said, "Okay," stood there awkwardly for a few moments, and then walked out of the room in a display of social ineptness that totally cemented Randy's faith in him. One of his minions eventually had Randy sign a legal disclaimer stipulating that it was perfectly all right if the oral surgeon decided to feed Randy's entire body into a log chipper, but this, for once, seemed like just a formality and not the opening round in an inevitable Bleak House-like litigational saga.

And so finally the big day came, and Randy took care to enjoy his breakfast because he knew that, considering the nerve damage he was about to incur, this might be the last time in his life that he would be able to taste food, or even chew it. The oral surgeon's minions all looked at Randy in awe when he actually walked in the door of their office, like *My god he actually showed up!* then flew reassuringly into action. Randy sat down in the chair and they gave him an injection and then the oral surgeon came in and asked him what, if anything, was the difference between Windows 95 and Windows NT. "This is one of these conversations the sole purpose of which is to make it obvious when I have lost consciousness, isn't it?" Randy said. "Actually, there is a secondary purpose, which is that I am considering making the jump and wanted to get some of your thoughts about that," the oral surgeon said.

"Well," said Randy, "I have a lot more experience with UNIX than with NT, but from what I've seen, it appears that NT is really a decent enough operating system, and certainly more of a serious effort than Windows." He paused to draw breath and then noticed that suddenly everything was different. The oral surgeon and his minions were still there and occupying roughly the same positions in his field of vision as they had been when he started to utter this sentence, but now the oral surgeon's glasses were askew and the lenses misted with blood, and his face was all sweaty, and his mask flecked with tiny bits of stuff that very much looked like it had come from pretty far down in Randy's body, and the air in the room was murky with aerosolized bone, and his nurses were limp and haggard and looked like they could use makeovers, face-lifts, and weeks at the beach. Randy's chest and lap, and the floor, were littered with bloody wads and hastily torn-open medical supply wrappers. The back of his head was sore from being battered against the head-rest by the recoil of the young brilliant oral surgeon's cranial jack-hammer. When he tried to finish his sentence ("so if you're willing to pay the premium I think the switch to NT would be very well advised") he noticed that his mouth was jammed full of something that prevented speech. The oral surgeon pulled his mask down off his face and scratched his sweat-soaked beard. He was staring not at Randy but at a point very far away. He heaved a big, slow sigh. His hands were shaking.

"What day is it?" Randy mumbled through cotton.

"As I told you before," the brilliant young oral surgeon said, "we charge for wisdom tooth extractions on a sliding scale, depending on the degree of difficulty." He paused for a moment, groping for words. "In your case I'm afraid that we will be charging you the maximum on all four." Then he got up and shambled out of the room, weighed down, Randy thought, not so much by the stress of his job as by the knowledge that no one was ever going to give him a Nobel prize for what he had just accomplished.

Randy went home and spent about a week lying on his couch in front of the TV eating oral narcotics like jellybeans and moaning with pain, and then he got better. The pressure in his skull was gone. Just totally gone. He cannot even remember now what it used to feel like.

Now as he rides in the police car to his new private jail cell, he remembers the whole wisdom-tooth-extraction saga because of its many points in common with what he just went through emotionally with young America Shaftoe. Randy's had a few girlfriends in his life—not many—but all of them were like oral surgeons who just couldn't cut the mustard. Amy's the only one who had the skill and the sheer balls to just look at him and say "okay" and then tunnel into his skull and come back with the goods. It was probably exhausting for her. She will extract a high price from him in exchange. And it will leave Randy lying around moaning with pain for a good long while. But he can tell already that the internal pressure has been relieved and he is glad, so glad, that she came into his life, and that he finally had the good sense and, arguably, guts to do this. He completely forgets, for a few hours, that he has been marked for death by the Philippine government.

From the fact that he's in a car, he infers that his new, private cell is in a different building. No one explains anything to him because he is, after all, a prisoner. Since the bust at NAIA he's been in a jail down south, a newish concrete-block number on the edge of Makati, but now they are taking him north into older parts of Manila, probably into some more stylish and gothic prewar facility. Fort Santiago, on the banks of the Pasig, had cells that were in the intertidal zone, so that prisoners locked into them at low tide would be dead by high. Now it's a historical site, so he knows they're not headed there.

The new jail cell is indeed in a big scary old building somewhere in the torus of major governmental institutions that surrounds the dead hole of Intramuros. It is not in, but it is right next to, a major court building. They drive through alleys among these big old stone buildings for a while and then present credentials at a guardhouse and wait for a big iron gate to be rolled aside, and then they drive across a paved courtyard that hasn't been swept out in a while and present more credentials and wait for an actual portcullis to be winched up, clearing an orifice that ramps them down beneath the building itself. Then the car stops and they are abruptly surrounded by men in uniforms.

The process is uncannily like pulling up to the main entrance of an

Asian business hotel, except that the men in the uniforms carry guns and
don't offer to tote Randy's laptop. He has a chain around his waist and
manacles attached to that chain in front, and leg chains that shorten his
stride. The chain between his ankles is supported in the middle by another chain that goes up to his waist so that it will not scrape the ground
as he walks. He has just enough manual dexterity to grip the laptop and
keep it pressed up against his lower abdomen. He's not just any chained
wretch, he is a digital chained wretch, Marley's Ghost on the Information
Superhighway. That a man in his situation is being allowed to have the
laptop is so grotesquely implausible that it causes him to doubt even his
own supremely cynical assessment of it, namely that Someone—presumably the same Someone who is Sending Him a Message—has already
discovered that everything on the hard drive is encrypted, and is now
trying to gull him into firing the machine up and using it so that—so
that what? Maybe they've rigged up a camera in his cell and will be
peering over his shoulder. But that would be easy for him to defeat; he
just has to not be completely stupid.

The guards lead Randy down a corridor and through some prisoner
check-in stuff that doesn't really apply to him since he has already filled
out the forms and turned over his personal effects at another jail. Then
the great big scary metal doors commence, and corridors that don't smell
so good, and he hears the generalized hubbub of a jail. But they take
him past the hubbub and into other corridors that seem to be older and
less used, and finally through an old-fashioned jailhouse door of iron bars
and into a long vaulted stone room containing a single row of maybe
half a dozen cells, with a guard's passageway running along past the doors
of the iron cages. Like a theme-park simulacrum of a jail. They take
him all the way down to the last cell and put him there. A single iron
bedstead awaits him, a thin cotton mattress with stained but clean sheets
and an army blanket folded and stacked on top of it. An old wooden
filing cabinet and folding chair have been moved into the cell and placed
in one corner, right against the stone wall that is the terminus of this
long room. The filing cabinet is evidently meant to serve as Randy's
work table. The drawers are locked shut. This cabinet has actually been
locked into place with a few turns of heavy chain and a padlock, so it's
very clear that he is expected to use the computer there, in that corner
of the cell, and nowhere else. As Attorney Alejandro promised, an extension cord has been plugged into a wall outlet near the cellblock entrance
and run down the passageway and securely knotted around a pipe out
of Randy's reach and the tail end of it allowed to trail across in the
direction of the filing cabinet. But it does not quite reach into Randy's
cell, so the only way to plug the computer in is to set it up on that

cabinet and stick the power cord into the back and then toss the other end out through the iron bars to a guard, who can mate it with the extension cord.

At first this appears to be just one of these maddening control-freak things, an exercise of power for the pure sadistic pleasure of it. But after Randy's been unchained, and locked in his cell, and left alone for a few minutes to run through it in his head, he thinks otherwise. Of course normally Randy could leave the computer on the card table while the batteries charged and then carry it over to his bed and use it there until the batteries ran down. But the batteries were removed from the machine before Attorney Alejandro gave it to him, and there don't seem to be any ThinkPad battery packs lying around his cell. So he will have to keep it plugged in all the time, and because of the way they have set up the filing cabinet and the extension cord, he is forced by certain immutable properties of three-dimensional Euclidean spacetime to use the machine in one and only one place: right there on top of that damn filing cabinet. He does not think this is an accident.

He sits down on that filing cabinet and scans the wall and ceiling for over-the-shoulder video cameras, but he doesn't look very hard and he doesn't really expect to see one. To make out text on a screen they would have to be very high-resolution cameras, which would imply big and obvious; subtle pinhole cameras wouldn't do it. There aren't any big cameras around here.

Randy becomes almost certain that if he could unlock that filing cabinet, he would find some electronic gear inside it. Directly underneath his laptop there is probably an antenna to pick up Van Eck signals emanating from the screen. Below that, there is some gear to translate those signals into a digital form and transmit the results to a listening station nearby, probably right on the other side of one of these walls. Down in the bottom are probably some batteries to make it all run. He rocks the cabinet back and forth as much as the chains will allow, and finds that it is indeed rather bottom-heavy, as if there's a car battery sitting in the bottom drawer. Or maybe it's just his imagination. Maybe they are letting him have his laptop just because they are nice guys.

So this is it then. This is the setup. This is the deal. It is all very clean and simple. Randy fires up the laptop just to prove that it still works. Then he makes his bed and goes and lies down on it, just because it feels really good to lie down. It is the first time he's had anything like privacy in at least a week. Notwithstanding Avi's bizarre admonition against self-abuse on the beach in Pacifica, it is high time that Randy took care of something. He needs to concentrate really hard now, and a certain distraction must be done away with. Replaying his last conversation with Amy is enough to give him a good erection. He reaches down into his pants and then abruptly falls asleep.

He wakes up to the sound of the cellblock door clanging open. A new prisoner is being led in. Randy tries to sit up and finds that his hand is still in his pants, having failed to accomplish its mission. He pulls it out of there reluctantly and sits up. He swings his feet down off the bed and onto the stone floor. Now he's got his back to the adjacent cell, which is a mirror image of his; i.e., the beds and the toilets of the two cells are right next to each other along their shared partition. He stands up and turns around and watches this other prisoner being led into the cell next to his. The new guy is a white man, probably in his sixties, maybe even seventies, though you could make a case for fifties or eighties. Quite vigorous, anyway. He's wearing a prison coverall just like Randy's, but accessorized differently: instead of a laptop, he's got a crucifix dangling from a rosary with great big fat amber beads, and some sort of medallion on a silver chain, and he's clutching several books to his belly: a Bible, and something big and in German, and a current bestselling novel.

The guards are treating him with extreme reverence; Randy assumes the guy is a priest. They are talking to him in Tagalog, asking him questions—being, Randy thinks, solicitous to his needs and desires—and the white man answers them in reassuring tones and even tells a joke. He makes a polite request; a guard scurries out and returns moments later with a deck of cards. Finally the guards back out of the cell, practically bowing and scraping, and lock him in with apologies that start to get a little monotonous. The white man says something, forgiving them wittily. They laugh nervously and leave. The white man stands there in the middle of his cell for a minute, staring at the floor contemplatively, maybe praying or something. Then he snaps out of it and starts looking around. Randy leans into the partition and sticks his hand through the bars. "Randy Waterhouse," he says.

The white man frisbees his books onto the bed, glides towards him, and shakes his hand. "Enoch Root," he says. "It's a pleasure to meet you in person, Randy." His voice is unmistakably that of Pontifex— root@eruditorum.org.

Randy freezes up for a long time, like a man who has just realized that a colossal practical joke is being played on him, but doesn't know just *how* colossal it is, or what to do about it. Enoch Root sees that Randy is paralyzed, and steps smoothly into the gap. He flexes the deck of cards in one hand and shoots them across to the other; the queue of airborne cards just hangs there between his hands for a moment, like an accordion. "Not as versatile as ETC cards, but surprisingly useful," he muses. "With any luck, Randy, you and I can *make* a *bridge*—as long as you are just standing there *pontificating* anyway."

"Make a bridge?" Randy echoes, feeling and probably sounding rather stupid.

"I'm sorry, my English is a bit rusty—I meant *bridge* as in a card game. Are you familiar with it?"

"Bridge? No. But I thought it took four people."

"I have come up with a version that is played by *two*. I only hope this deck is complete—the game requires fifty-four cards."

"Fifty-four," Randy muses. "Is your game anything like Pontifex?"

"One and the same."

"I think I have the rules for Pontifex squirreled away on my hard drive somewhere," Randy says.

"Then let's play," says Enoch Root.

FALL

SHAFTOE JUMPS OUT OF THE AIRPLANE. THE AIR IS BRACINGLY cold up here, and the wind chill factor is something else. It is the first time in a year that he has not been loathsomely hot and sweaty.

Something jerks mightily on his back: the static line, still attached to the airplane—God forbid that American fighting men should be entrusted to pull their own ripcords. He can just imagine the staff meeting where they dreamed up the concept of the static line: "For God's sake, General, they're just enlisted men! As soon as they jump out of the airplane they'll probably start daydreaming about their girlfriends, take a few hits from their pocket flasks, catch forty winks, and before you know it they'll all pile into the ground at a couple of hundred miles an hour!"

The drogue chute flutters out, catches air, and then eviscerates his main pack in one jerk. There's a bit of flopping and buffeting as Bobby Shaftoe's body pulls the disorganized cloud of silk downwards, then it thunks open and he is left hanging in space, his dark body forming a small perfect bullseye in the center of the off-white canopy for any Nipponese riflemen down below.

No wonder those paratroopers think they are gods among men: they get such a nice view of things, so much better than a poor Marine grunt stuck down on the beach, who is always looking uphill into courses of pillboxes. All of Luzon stretches out before him. He can see one or two hundred miles north, across a mat of vegetation as dense as felt, to the mountains in the far north where General Yamashita, the Lion of Malaya, is holed up with a hundred thousand troops, each of whom would like nothing better than to strap lots of explosives to his body, sneak through the lines at night, run into the middle of a large concentration of American soldiers, and blow himself up for his emperor. To Shaftoe's starboard is Manila Bay, and even from this distance, some thirty miles, he can see the jungle suddenly turn thin and brown as it nears the shore, like a severed leaf that is dying from the edge inwards—that would be what's left of the city of Manila. The fat twenty-mile-long tongue of land protruding towards him is Bata'an. Just off the tip of it is a rocky island shaped like a tadpole with a green head and a bony brown tail: Corregidor. Smoke jets from many vents on the island, which has been mostly reconquered by the Americans. Quite a few Nipponese blew themselves up in their underground bunkers rather than surrender. This heroic act has given someone in The General's chain of command a nifty idea.

A couple of miles from Corregidor, motionless on the water, is something that looks like an absurdly squat, asymmetrical battleship, except much bigger. It is encircled by American gunboats and amphibious landing forces. From a source on its lid, a long wisp of red smoke trickles downwind: a smoke bomb dropped out of Shaftoe's plane a few minutes ago, on a parachute. As Shaftoe descends, and the wind blows him directly towards it, he can see the grain of the reinforced concrete of which this prodigy is made. It used to be a dry rock in Manila Bay. The Spanish built a fort there, the Americans built a chain of gun emplacements on top of that, and when the Nips showed up they turned the entire thing into a solid reinforced-concrete fortress with walls thirty feet thick, and a couple of double-barreled fourteen-inch gun turrets on the top. Those guns have long since been silenced; Shaftoe can see long cracks in their barrels, and craters, like frozen splashes in the steel. Even though he is parachuting onto the roof of an impregnable Nipponese fortress chock-full of heavily armed men who are desperately looking for a picturesque way to die, Shaftoe is perfectly safe; every time a Nip pokes a rifle barrel or a pair of binoculars out of a gun slit, half a dozen American antiaircraft gunners open up on him at point-blank range from the nearby ships.

A tremendous racket ensues as a small power boat pops out of a little cave along the waterline of the island and heads directly towards an American landing craft. A hundred guns open fire on it simultaneously. Supersonic bits of metal crash into the water all around the little boat, ton after ton of them. Each bit makes a splash. All of the splashes combine into a jagged, volcanic eruption of white water centered on the little boat. Bobby Shaftoe puts his fingers in his ears. Two thousand pounds of high explosive packed into the little boat's nose detonate. The shock wave flashes across the surface of the water, a powdery white ring expanding with supernatural velocity. It hits Bobby Shaftoe like a baseball to the bridge of the nose. He neglects to steer his chute for a while, and trusts the winds to carry him to the right place.

The smoke bomb was dropped as proof of the concept that a man on a parachute might actually be able to land on the roof of this fortress. Bobby Shaftoe is, of course, the final and irrefutable test of this proposition. As he gets closer, and his head clears from the explosion, Shaftoe sees that the smoke bomb never actually reached the roof: its little chute got tangled up in the briar patch of antennas growing out of the top of the thing.

All kinds of fucking antennas! Even during his days in Shanghai, Shaftoe had a weird feeling around antennas. Those Station Alpha pencil-necks, in their little wooden roof-shack with all the antennas sprouting from it—those were not soldiers, sailors, or Marines in the normal sense. Corregidor was covered with antennas before the Nips came and took it. And everywhere that Shaftoe went during his Detachment 2702 stint, there were antennas.

He is going to spend the next few moments concentrating very hard on those antennas, and so he turns his head for a moment to get a bearing on the American LCM—the landing craft that the Nip suicide boat was hoping to destroy. It is exactly where it is supposed to be—halfway between the encircling force of naval ships and the sheer, forty-foot-high wall of the fortress. Even if Shaftoe didn't already know the plan, he would, at a glance, identify this vessel as a Landing Craft, Mechanized (Mark 3), a fifty-foot-long steel shoebox designed to cough a medium-sized tank up onto a beach. It has a couple of fifty-caliber machine guns on it which are pounding away dutifully at various targets on the wall of the fortress which Shaftoe cannot see. But from his vantage point On High he can see something that the Nipponese can't: the LCM is not carrying a tank, in the sense of a vehicle on caterpillar treads with a gun turret. It is carrying, rather, a tank in the sense of a large steel container with pipes and hoses and stuff attached to it.

The Nips in the fortress are taking potshots at the approaching LCM, but the only target at which they have to aim is its front door, a piece of metal that can flop down to become a ramp, and which was designed, incredibly enough, on the assumption that doomed Nips would spend a lot of time trying to blow holes in it with various projectile weapons. So the defenders are not getting anywhere. Antiaircraft gunners on other ships have begun raking the walls of the fortress insanely, making it hard for the Nipponese to poke their heads and their gun barrels out. Shaftoe notes fragments of antennas skittering and bouncing across the roof of the fortress, and occasional streaks of tracers, and hopes that the men on those ships have the presence of mind to hold their fire before he lands on the fucking thing, which will be in a few seconds.

Shaftoe realizes that his mental concept of what this mission was going to be like, as he reviewed it with the officers in the LCM, bears no relationship to the reality. This is only about the five thousandth time Shaftoe has experienced this phenomenon in the course of the Second World War; you'd think he would no longer be surprised by it. The antennas, which looked wispy and inconsequential on the reconnaissance photos, are in fact sizable engineering works. Or they were until they got de-engineered by the naval gunfire that silenced those big guns. Now they are just wreckage of a sort that is going to be peculiarly nasty to parachute down on top of. The antennas were, and the wreckage is, made of all kinds of different shit: spars of Philippine mahogany, sturdy columns of bamboo, welded steel trusses. The most common bits are the ones that catch a parachutist's eye: long metal poky things, and miles and miles of guy wire, snarled into a briarpatch, some of it taut enough to cut a plummeting Marine's head off and some of it all loose and tangly with sharp hovering ends.

It dawns on Shaftoe that this pile isn't just a gun emplacement; it's a Nip intelligence headquarters. "Waterhouse, you fucking son of a bitch!" Shaftoe hollers. As far as he knows, Waterhouse is still in Europe. But he realizes, as he's clapping his hands protectively over his eyes and falling into the nightmare, that Waterhouse must have something to do with this.

Bobby Shaftoe has landed. He tries to move and the wreckage moves with him; he is one with it.

He opens his eyes carefully. His head is wrapped up in a snarl of heavy wire—a guy wire that broke under tension and whipped around him. Peering between loops of wire, he sees three lengths of quarter-inch metal tubing projecting out of his torso. Another one has gone through his thigh, and yet another through his upper arm. He's pretty sure he has a broken leg too.

He lies there for a while, listening to the sound of the guns all around him.

There is work that needs to be done. All he can think of is the boy.

He gropes for the wire cutter with his free hand and begins to cut himself loose from the snarl.

The jaws of the wire cutter just barely fit over the metal tubing of the antenna. He reaches behind himself, finds the places where the tubes poke into his back, and cuts them off, snip, snip, snip. He cuts the tube that has impaled his arm. He leans forward and cuts the one that goes through his leg. Then he pulls the tubes out of his flesh and drops them on the concrete, plink, plink, plink, plink, plink. Lots of blood follows.

He doesn't even try to walk. He just begins to drag himself across the concrete roof of the fortress. The sun has warmed the concrete and it feels good. He cannot see the LCM, but he can see the few antennas that stick out of its top, and he knows it is in position now.

The rope should be there. Shaftoe props himself up on his elbows and looks. Sure enough, there it is, a manila rope (natch!) tied to a grapnel, one point of the grapnel lodged in a shell crater near the edge of the roof.

He gets to it eventually, and begins to pull on the rope. He closes his eyes, but tries not to fall asleep. He keeps pulling, and eventually feels something big and thick between his hands: the hose.

Almost finished. Lying on his back, hugging the end of the hose to his chest, he rolls his head from side to side until he can see the air vent that they picked out on the reconnaissance photos. It used to have a sheet-metal hood on the top of it, but that's long gone now, it's just a hole in the roof with a few jagged bits of metal at its edges. He crawls over to it and feeds in the end of the hose.

Someone must be watching him on one of the ships, because the hose stiffens, like a serpent coming alive, and between his hands Bobby Shaftoe can feel the fuel oil streaming through it. Ten thousand gallons of the stuff. Straight down into the fortress. He can hear the Nips down there, singing hoarse songs. By now they will have figured out what is about to happen. General MacArthur is giving them exactly what they've been praying for.

At this point, Bobby Shaftoe is supposed to abseil down a rope into the LCM, but he knows it isn't going to happen. No one can reach him now, no one can help him. When the fuel oil stops streaming through the hose, he summons all the concentration he has left. Pretends, one last time, that he actually gives a damn. Jerks the safety pin from a white phosphorus grenade, lets the handle fly off and tinkle merrily across the roof. He can feel it come alive in his hand, the thrumming animal fizz of its inner fuse. He drops it into the air shaft: a circular pipe straight down, a black disk centered on a field of dingy grey, like the ashes of a Nipponese flag.

Then, on an impulse, he dives in there after it.

Semper Fidelis
Dawn star flares on disk of night
I fall, sun rises

METIS

THE APPEARANCE OF ROOT@ERUDITORUM.ORG IN THE CELL right next to Randy's is like the crowning plot twist in this Punch-and-Judy show that has been performed for his benefit ever since his plane landed at NAIA. As with any puppet show, he knows that there must be a lot of people hidden just outside the range of his senses, in furious motion, trying to make it all happen. For all he knows, some significant fraction of the Philippine gross national product is being devoted to keeping up these pretenses for his benefit.

There is a meal waiting on the floor of Randy's cell, and a rat on top of the meal. Randy usually reacts pretty badly to the sight of rats; they rupture the containment system that his upbringing and his education built around the part of his mind where the collective-unconscious stuff dwells, and send him straight into Hieronymus Bosch territory. But in these circumstances it doesn't bother him any more than seeing one at the zoo would. The rat has a surprisingly attractive buckskin-colored pelt and a tail about a thick as a pencil that has evidently run afoul of a farmer's wife with a carving knife, and woggles stiffly in the air like the blunt antenna of a cellphone. Randy is hungry, but he doesn't want to eat anything that a rat has left footprints on, so he just watches it.

His body feels like it slept for a long time. He turns on his computer and types in a command called "date." The nails of his left hand look funny, as if they all got bruised. Focusing on them he sees a club drawn in blue ballpoint pen ink on the nail of the index finger, a diamond on the forefinger, a heart on the ring finger, a spade on the pinky. Enoch Root told him that in Pontifex, as in bridge, each card in the deck has a numerical value: clubs 1-13, diamonds 14-26, hearts 27-39, spades 40-52. Randy drew the symbols on his nails so he wouldn't forget.

Anyway, "date" tells him that he apparently slept all of yesterday afternoon and evening, all night, and about half of today. So this rat is actually eating his lunch.

Randy's computer runs Finux, so when it boots up it gives him a black screen with big fat white letters scrolling up it one line at a time, a real circa-1975 type of user interface. Also presumably the easiest possible thing to read through Van Eck phreaking. Randy types in "startx" and the screen goes black for a moment and then turns a particular shade of indigo that Randy happens to like, and beige windows appear on it with much smaller and crisper black letters. So now he is running the X Windows System, or X as people like Randy call it, which provides all of the graphical junk that people expect in a user interface: menus, buttons, scroll bars, and so on. As with anything else under UNIX (of which Finux is a variant), there are a million options that only young, lonely, or obsessed people have the time and patience to explore. Randy has been all three at various times of his life and knows a lot about these options. For example, the background of his screen happens to be a uniform indigo at the moment, but it could be an image. Theoretically you could use a movie, so that all of your windows and menus and so on would float around on top of, say, *Citizen Kane* running in an endless loop. You can, in fact, take any piece of software and make it into your screen background, and it will purr along happily, doing whatever it does, and not even known that it's being used as window-dressing. This has given Randy some ideas on how to approach the Van Eck thing.

In its current state, this computer is just as vulnerable to Van Eck phreaking as it was before Randy started up X. Before it was white letters on a black background. Now it's black on beige. The letters are a little smaller and they live in windows, but it makes no difference: the electronics inside his computer still have to make these transitions between zero and one, i.e. between high intensity (white or beige) and minimal (black) as they trace out these patterns of dots on the screen.

Randy fundamentally does not know what the fuck is going on in his life right now, and probably hasn't for a long time, even back in the days when he thought that he *did* know. But his working hypothesis is that the people who set this whole situation up (prime candidates: the Dentist and his cohorts in the Bolobolo syndicate) know that he has some cool information on his hard drive. How should they know this? Well, Pontifex—the Wizard—Enoch Root—whatever the fuck he's called—when he phoned Randy on the plane, knew that Randy had Arethusa, so God knows who else might know. Someone set up the fake drug bust at NAIA so that they could nab his laptop and yank the hard drive and make a copy of its contents. Then they found out that it was all doubly encrypted. That is, the Arethusa intercepts are encrypted to begin with in a pretty good World War II cryptosystem, which anyone should be able to break nowadays, but on top of that they are furthermore encrypted in a state-of-the-art modern system that no one can break. If they know what's good for them, they won't even try to break it. The only way for them to get the information is to get Randy to decrypt it for them, which he can do by biometrically identifying himself to his laptop (by talking to it) or by typing in a pass-phrase that only he knows. They are hoping that Randy will decrypt the Arethusa intercept files and, like a moron, display their contents on the screen. The moment that stuff appears on the screen, the game is over. The Dentist's (or whoever's) surveillance guys can feed the intercepts to some kind of a cryptanalytic supercomputer that will break them open in no time.

That doesn't mean that Randy dare not open those files—just that he daren't display them on the screen. This distinction is crucial. Ordo can read the encrypted files from the hard drive. It can write them into the computer's memory. It can decrypt them, and write the results into another region of the computer's memory, and leave that data there indefinitely, and the Van Eck phreakers will never be the wiser. But as soon as Randy tells the computer to show him that information in a window on the screen, the Arethusa intercepts will belong to the Van Eck phreakers; and whoever they are, they can probably break them faster than Randy can.

The fun and interesting thing is that Randy doesn't have to actually see those intercepts in order to work on them. As long as they are sitting in the computer's memory, he can subject them to every cryptanalystic technique in the whole *Cryptonomicon*.

He starts tapping out some lines in a language called Perl. Perl's a scripting language; useful for controlling your computer's functions and automating repetitive tasks. A UNIX machine like this one is rooted in a filesystem that contains tens of thousands of different files, mostly in straight ASCII text format. There are many different programs for opening these files, displaying them on the screen, and editing them. Randy intends to write a Perl script that will roam through the filesystem choosing files at random, opening each file in a randomly sized and located window, paging through it for a while, and then closing it again. If you run the script fast enough, the windows will pop open all over the place in a kind of rectangularized fireworks-burst that will go on forever. If this script is used as the screen background, in place of solid indigo, then this will go on underneath the one window on the screen where Randy's actually working. The people monitoring his work will go crazy trying to track all of this. Especially if Randy writes a script that will cause the real window to change its shape and location at random every few seconds.

It would be really stupid to open the Arethusa intercepts in a window—he's not going to do that. But he can use this technique to conceal whatever else he's doing in the way of decryption work. It occurs to him, however, when he gets a few lines into writing this Perl script, that if he pulls a stunt like that so early in his incarceration, the people surveilling him will know right away that he is on to them. And maybe it's better if he lets them believe, for a while, that he suspects nothing.

So he saves his Perl script and stops working on it for now. If he writes it in short bursts, opening it once or twice a day to type in a few lines and then closing it, it's unlikely that the surveillors will be able to follow what he is up to, even if they happen to be hackers. Just to be an asshole, he modifies his X Windows options in such a way that none of the windows on the screen will have a title bar at the top. That way the surveillance people won't be able to tell what file he is working on at any given moment, which will make it a lot harder for them to string a long series of observations together into a coherent picture of what's in his Perl script.

Too, he opens up the old message from root@eruditorum.org giving the Pontifex Transform, expressed as a few lines of Perl code. The steps that looked so unwieldy when carried out by a computer seem straight-forward—easy, even—now that he construes them as manipulations of a deck of cards.

"Randy."

"Hmmm?" Randy looks up from the screen and is startled to find that he is in a jail in the Philippines.

"Dinner is served."

It is Enoch Root, looking at him through the bars. He points at the floor of Randy's cell where a new tray of food has just been slid in. "Actually, it was served an hour ago—you might want to have at it before the rats come."

"Thank you," Randy says. Making sure all the windows on his screen have been closed, he goes over and lifts his dinner up from the spatter of old rat-turds on the floor. It is rice and lechon, a simple and traditional pork dish. Enoch Root finished eating a long time ago—he sits on his bed, next to Randy, and plays an unusual game of solitaire, pausing occasionally to mark down a letter. Randy watches the manipulation of the deck carefully, growingly certain that it is the same set of operations he was just reading about in the old e-mail message.

"So what are you in for?" Randy asks.

Enoch Root finishes counting through the deck, glances at a 7 of spades, closes his eyes for a few moments, and marks down a W on his napkin. Then he says, "Disorderly conduct. Trespassing. Incitement to riot. I'm probably guilty of the first two."

"Tell me about it."

"First tell me what you're in for."

"Heroin was found in my bag at the airport. I stand accused of being the world's stupidest drug smuggler."

"Is someone angry at you?"

"That would make for a much longer story," Randy says, "but I think you have the drift."

"Well, in my case, it's like this. I have been working at a mission hospital up in the mountain."

"You're a priest?"

"Not anymore. I'm a lay worker."

"Where's your hospital?"

"South of here. Out in the boondocks," Enoch Root says. "The people there cultivate pineapple, coffee, coconut, bananas, and a few other cash crops. But their land is being torn apart by treasure hunters."

Funny that Enoch Root should suddenly be on the subject of buried treasure. And yet he has been so tight-lipped. Randy guesses he's intended to play stupid. He takes a stab at it: "Is there supposed to be some treasure down there?"

"The old-timers say that many Nipponese trucks went down a particular road during the last few weeks before MacArthur's return. Past a certain point it was not possible to know where they went, because the road was blocked, and minefields set up to discourage the curious."

"Or kill them," Randy says.

Enoch Root takes this in stride. "That road gives way to a rather vast area in which gold might hypothetically have been hidden. Hundreds of square miles. Much of it is jungle. Much has difficult topography. Lots of volcanoes, some extinct, some vomiting up mudflows from time to time. But some is flat enough to grow tropical crops, and in those places, people have settled during the decades since the war, and put together the rudiments of an economy."

"Who owns the land?"

"You've gotten to know the Philippines well," Enoch Root says. "You go immediately to the central question."

"Around here, asking who owns the land is like complaining about the weather in the Midwest," Randy muses.

Enoch Root nods. "I could spend a long time answering your question. The answer is that patterns of ownership changed just after the war, and then changed again under Marcos, and yet again in the last few years. So we have several epochs, if you will. First epoch: before the war. Land owned by certain families."

"Of course."

"Of course. Second epoch: the war. A vast area sealed off by the Nipponese. Some of the families who owned the land prospered under the occupation. Others went bankrupt. Third epoch: postwar. The bankrupt families went away. The prosperous ones expanded their holdings. As did the church and the government."

"Why?"

"The government made part of the land—the jungle—into a national park. And after the eruptions, the church established the mission where I work."

"Eruptions?"

"In the early 1950s, just to make things interesting—you know, things are never interesting enough in the Philippines—the volcanoes acted up. A few lahars came through the area, wiped out some villages, redirected some rivers, displaced many people. The church set up the hospital to help those people."

"A hospital doesn't take up very much land," Randy observes.

"We also have farms. We are trying to help the locals become more self-reliant." Enoch Root acts like he basically does not want to talk about this. "At any rate, things then settled down into a pattern that more or less endured until the Marcos era, when various people were forced to sell some of their holdings to Ferdinand and Imelda and various of their cousins, nephews, cronies, and bootlicks."

"They were looking for Nipponese war gold."

"Certain of the locals have made a business of pretending to remember where the gold is," Enoch Root says. "Once it was understood just how remunerative this could be, it spread like a virus. Everyone claims to have hazy memories of the war now, or of tales that Dad or Granddad told them. The Marcos-era treasure-hunters did not display the cautious skepticism that might have been expected from people with more piercing intellects. Many holes were dug. No gold was found. Things settled down. Then, in the last few years, the Chinese came in."

"Filipinos of Chinese ancestry, or—"

"Chinese of Chinese ancestry," Enoch Root says. "Northern Chinese. Robust ones who like spicy food. Not the usual gracile Cantonese-speaking fish-eaters."

"These people are from where, then—Shanghai?"

Root nods. "Their company is one of these post-Maoist monstrosities. Headed up by an actual Long March veteran. Wily survivor of many purges. Name of Wing. Mr. Wing—or General Wing as he likes to be addressed when he is feeling nostalgic—handled the transition to capitalism rather deftly. Built hydroelectric projects with slave labor during the Great Leap Forward, parlayed that into control of a very large government ministry which has now become a sort of corporation. Mr. Wing has the ability to shut off the electricity to just about any home or factory or even military base in China, and by Chinese standards this makes him into a distinguished elder statesman."

"What does Mr. Wing want there?"

"Land. Land. More land."

"What sort of land?"

"Land in the jungle. Oddly enough."

"Maybe he wants to build a hydroelectric project."

"Yes, and maybe you're a heroin smuggler. Say, Randy, don't think I'm rude for saying so, but you have sauce in your beard." Enoch Root thrusts a hand through the bars, proffering a paper napkin. Randy takes it and, lifting it to his face, notes that the following letters are written on it: OSKJJ JGTMW. Randy pretends to daub sauce off his beard.

"Now I've gone and done it," says Enoch Root, "given you my whole supply of bumwad."

"Greater love hath no man," Randy says. "And I see you gave me your other deck of cards too—you are too generous."

"Not at all—I thought you might want to play solitaire, *just as I did*."

"Don't mind if I do," Randy says, setting his dinner tray aside and reaching for the deck.

The card on top is an eight of spades. Skimming it and a few more cards out of the way, he finds a joker, with small stars in the corners; according to hints that Enoch has already dropped, this is the A joker. It's the work of a moment to slip it beneath the card below, which happens to be a Jack of clubs. About two-thirds of the way down into the pack he finds a big-star joker, and B stands for Big, so he knows that is Joker B; he moves it down two cards, below the six of clubs and the nine of diamonds. Straightening up the pack and then smearing through it once more, he sticks various fingers in as he re-finds those jacks, and ends up with a good half of the pack—the full inter-Joker span, plus the two Jokers themselves—trapped between his index and forefingers. The thinner stacks above and below he pulls out and swaps with each other. Enoch watches all of this and seems to approve.

Randy pushes out the bottom-most card, now, and it turns out to be a jack of clubs. On second thought he pulls that jack out and leaves it on his knee for the time being, so he won't mess the next part up. According to the mnemonic symbols he's marked on his fingernails, the numerical value of this jack of clubs is simply 11. So, starting from the top of the deck, he counts down to the 11th card, cuts the deck below it, then swaps the two halves, and finally takes the jack of clubs off his knee and puts it on the bottom of the deck again.

The card on the top of the deck is now a joker. "What's the numerical value for a joker?" he asks, and Enoch Root says, "it's fifty-three, for either one of them." So Randy gets a free ride this time; he knows that if he begins counting down from the top of the deck, when he reaches 53 he'll be staring at the last card. And that card happens to be the

Jack of Clubs, with a value of 11. Eleven, then is the first number in the keystream.

Now, the first letter in the ciphertext that Enoch Root wrote on the napkin is O, and (setting the deck of cards down, now, so that he can count through the alphabet on his fingers) O is letter fifteen. If he subtracts eleven from that, he gets four, and he doesn't even have to count on his fingers to know that letter number four is D. He has one letter deciphered.

Randy remarks, "We still haven't gotten to your being arrested."

"Yes! Well, it's like this," says Enoch Root. "Mr. Wing has been digging some holes of his own up in the jungle lately. A lot of trucks have been going through. Ruining the roads. Running over stray dogs, which as you know are an important food source for these people. A boy was hit by one of these trucks and has been in our hospital ever since. The runoff from Mr. Wing's operations has been fouling the river that many people rely on for fresh water. And there are questions of ownership too—some feel that Mr. Wing is encroaching on land that is properly owned by the government. Which in some extremely attenuated sense, means it is owned by the people."

"Does he have a permit?"

"Ah! Once again your knowledge of local politics is evident. As you know, the normal procedure is for local officials to approach people who are digging large holes in the ground, or undertaking any kind of productive or destructive activity whatsoever, and demand that they obtain a permit, which simply means that they want a bribe or else they'll raise a stink about it. Mr. Wing's company has not obtained a permit."

"Has a stink been raised?"

"Yes. But Mr. Wing has forged a very strong relationship with certain Filipinos of Chinese ancestry who are well placed in the government, and so the stink has been unavailing."

The second time through, the joker-moving part went quickly since one of the jokers started out on top. The King of Hearts ends up on the bottom, and hence on Randy's knee. That son of a bitch has a numerical index of 39, and so Randy has to count most of the way through the deck to reach the card in the thirty-ninth position, which is a ten of diamonds. He splits and swaps the deck, then puts the King of Hearts back on the bottom. Top card is now a four of diamonds, which translates to an index of seventeen. Counting the seventeen top cards into his hand he stops and looks at the eighteenth, which is a four of hearts. That works out to a value of $26 + 4 = 30$. But everything here is modulo 26, so adding the 26 was a waste of time, because now he has to subtract it right off again. The result is four. The second letter in Enoch's ciphertext is S, which is the nineteenth letter in the alphabet, and subtracting four from that gives him O. So the plaintext, so far, is "DO."

"I get the picture."

"I was sure that you would, Randy."

Randy doesn't know what to make of the Wing business. It puts him in mind of Doug Shaftoe's yarns. Maybe Wing is looking for the Primary, and maybe Enoch Root is too, and maybe the Primary is what Old Man Comstock was trying to find by decrypting the Arethusa messages. Maybe, in other words, the location of the Primary is sitting on Randy's hard drive right now, and Root's worried that Randy, like an idiot, is going to give it away.

How'd he arrange to get into a cell next to Randy's? Presumably the Church's internal lines of communication are first-rate. Root could have known for a few days that Randy was in the clink. Time enough to hatch a plan.

"How'd you end up here, then?" Randy asks.

"We decided to raise a bit of a stink ourselves."

"We being the Church?"

"What do you mean by the Church? If you are asking me whether the Pontifex Maximus and the College of Cardinals put on their pointy bifurcated hats and sat down together in Rome and drew up plans for a stink, the answer is no. If by 'church' you mean the local community in my neighborhood, almost all of whom happen to be devout Catholics, then yes."

"So the community protested, or something, and you were the ringleader."

"I was an example."

"An example?"

"It frequently does not occur to these people to challenge the powers that be. When someone actually does, they always find it incredibly novel, and derive much entertainment from it. That was my role. I had been making a stink about Mr. Wing for quite some time."

Randy can almost guess what the next two letters are going to be, but he has to keep working through the algorithm or the deck will get out of whack. He generates a 23 and then a 47 which, modulo 26, is 21, and subtracting the 23 and the 21 from the next two ciphertext letters K and J (again, modulo 26) gives him N and O as expected. So he has "DONO" deciphered. And continuing to work through it, one letter at a time, the cards getting a little sweaty in his hands now, he eventually gets DONOTUSEP and finally loses his place while trying to generate the last keystream letter. So now the deck is out of whack and completely unrecoverable, reminding him that he'd better be careful next time. But he can guess that this message must be: DO NOT USE PC. Enoch is worried that Randy did not anticipate Van Eck phreaking.

"So. There was a demonstration. You blocked a road or something?"

"We blocked roads, we lay down in front of bulldozers. Some people slashed a few tires. The locals put their ingenuity to work, and things got a bit out of hand. Mr. Wing's dear friends in the government took offense and called out the Army. Seventeen people were arrested. Unreasonably high bail was set for them as a punitive measure—if these people can't get out of jail they can't make money and their families suffer terribly. I could get bailed out if I wanted to, but have elected to stay behind bars as a gesture of solidarity."

It all seems like a plausible enough cover story to Randy. "But I'm guessing that a lot of people in the government are appalled by the fact that they have thrown a saint into jail," he says, "and so they have moved you here, to the high-prestige luxury jail with private cells."

"Once again your understanding of the local culture is conspicuous," Enoch Root says. He shifts position on the bed and his crucifix swings back and forth ponderously. He also has a medallion around his neck with something startling written on it.

"Do you have some occult symbol there?" Randy asks, squinting.

"I beg your pardon?"

"I can make out the word 'occult' on your medallion there."

"It says *ignoti et quasi occulti,* which means 'unknown and partly hidden' or words to that effect," says Enoch Root. "It is the motto of a society to which I belong. You must know that the word 'occult' does not intrinsically have anything to do with Satanic rituals and drinking blood and all of that. It—"

"I was trained as an astronomer," Randy says. "So I learned all about occultation—the concealment of one body behind another, as during an eclipse."

"Oh. Well, then, I'll shut up."

"In fact, I know more than you might think about occultation," Randy says. It might seem like he's beating a dead horse, except that he catches the eye of Enoch Root while he's saying it, and gives a significant sidelong glance at his computer. Root processes this for a moment and then nods.

"Who's the lady in the middle? The Virgin Mary?" Randy asks.

Root fingers the medallion without looking at it, and says, "Reasonable guess. But wrong. It's Athena."

"The Greek goddess?"

"Yes."

"How do you square that with Christianity?"

"When I phoned you the other day, how did you know it was me?"

"I don't know. I just recognized you."

"Recognized me? What does that mean? You didn't recognize my *voice.*"

"Is this some roundabout way of answering my question about Athena worship v. Christianity?"

"Doesn't it strike you as remarkable that you can look at a stream of characters on the screen of your computer—e-mail from someone you've never seen—and later 'recognize' the same person on the phone? How does that work, Randy?"

"I haven't the faintest idea. The brain can do some weird—"

"Some complain that e-mail is impersonal—that your contact with me, during the e-mail phase of our relationship, was mediated by wires and screens and cables. Some would say that's not as good as conversing face-to-face. And yet our seeing of things is always mediated by corneas, retinas, optic nerves, and some neural machinery that takes the information from the optic nerve and propagates it into our minds. So, is looking at words on a screen so very much inferior? I think not; at least then you are conscious of the distortions. Whereas, when you see someone with your eyes, you forget about the distortions and imagine you are experiencing them purely and immediately."

"So what's your explanation of how I recognized you?"

"I would argue that inside your mind was some pattern of neurological activity that was not there before you exchanged e-mail with me. The Root Representation. It is not *me. I'm* this big slug of carbon and oxygen and some other stuff on this cot right next to you. The Root Rep, by contrast, is the thing that you'll carry around in your brain for the rest of your life, barring some kind of major neurological insult, that your mind uses to represent me. When you think about me, in other words, you're not thinking about me qua this big slug of carbon, you are thinking about the Root Rep. Indeed, some day you might get released from jail and run into someone who would say, 'You know, I was in the Philippines once, running around in the boondocks, and I ran into this old fart who started talking to me about Root Reps.' And by exchanging notes (as it were) with this fellow you would be able to establish beyond a reasonable doubt that the Root Rep in your brain and the Root Rep in his brain were generated by the same actual slug of carbon and oxygen and so on: me."

"And this has something to do, again, with Athena?"

"If you think of the Greek gods as real supernatural beings who lived on Mount Olympus, no. But if you think of them as being in the same class of entities as the Root Rep, which is to say, patterns of neurological activity that the mind uses to represent things that it sees, or thinks it sees, in the outside world, then yes. Suddenly, Greek gods can be just as interesting and relevant as real people. Why? Because, in the same way as you might one day encounter another person with his own Root Rep so, if you were to have a conversation with an ancient Greek person, and he started talking about Zeus, you might—once you got over your initial feelings of superiority—discover that you had some mental representations inside your own mind that, though you didn't name them Zeus and didn't think of them as a big hairy thunderbolt-hurling son of a Titan, nonetheless had been generated as a result of interactions with entities in the outside world that are the same as the ones that cause the Zeus Representation to appear in the Greek's mind. And here we could talk about the Plato's Cave thing for a while—the Veg-O-Matic of metaphors—it slices! it dices!"

"In which," Randy says, "the actual entities in the real world are the three-dimensional, real things that are casting the shadows, this Greek dude and I are the wretches chained up looking at the shadows of those things on the walls, and it's just that the shape of the wall in front of me is different from the shape of the wall in front of the Grecian—"

"—so that given a shadow projected on *your* wall is going to adopt a different shape from the same shadow projected on *his* wall, where the different wall-shapes here correspond to let's say your modern scientific worldview versus his ancient pagan worldview."

"Yeah. *That* Plato's Cave metaphor."

At this very moment some wag of a prison guard, out in the corridor, throws a switch and shuts off all of the lights. The only illumination now is from the screensaver on Randy's laptop, which is running animations of colliding galaxies.

"I think we can stipulate that the wall in front of you, Randy, is considerably flatter and smoother, i.e. it generally gives you a much more accurate shadow than his wall, and yet it's clear that he's still capable of seeing the same shadows and probably drawing some useful conclusions about the shapes of the things that cast them."

"Okay. So the Athena that you honor on your medallion isn't a super-natural being—"

"—who lives on a mountain in Greece, et cetera, but rather whatever entity, pattern, trend, or what-have-you that, when perceived by ancient Greek people, and filtered through their perceptual machinery and their pagan worldview, produced the internal mental representation that they dubbed Athena. The distinction being quite important because Athena-the-supernatural-chick-with-the-helmet is of course nonexistent, but

'Athena' the external-generator-of-the-internal-representation-dubbed-Athena-by-the-ancient-Greeks *must* have existed back then, or else the internal representation never would have been generated, and if she existed back then, the chances are excellent that she exists now, and if all that is the case, then whatever ideas the ancient Greeks (who, though utter shitheads in many ways, were terrifyingly intelligent people) had about her are probably still quite valid."

"Okay, but why Athena and not Demeter or someone?"

"Well, it's a truism that you can't understand a person without knowing something about her family background, and so we have to do kind of a quick Cliff's Notes number on the ancient Greek Theogony here. We start out with Chaos, which is where all theogonies start, and which I like to think of as a sea of white noise—totally random broadband static. And for reasons that we don't really understand, certain polarities begin to coalesce from this—Day, Night, Darkness, Light, Earth, Sea. Personally, I like to think of these as crystals—not in the hippy-dippy Californian sense, but in the hardass technical sense of resonators, that received certain channels buried in the static of Chaos. At some point, out of certain incestuous couplings among such entities, you get Titans. And it's arguably kind of interesting to note that the Titans provide really the full complement of basic gods—you've got the sun god, Hyperion, and an ocean god, Oceanus, and so on. But they all get overthrown in a power struggle called the Titanomachia and replaced with new gods like Apollo and Poseidon, who end up filling the same slots in the organizational chart, as it were. Which is kind of interesting in that it seems to tie in with what I was saying about the same entities or patterns persisting through time, but casting slightly different shaped shadows for different people. Anyway, so now we have the Gods of Olympus as we normally think of them: Zeus, Hera, and so on.

"A couple of basic observations about these: first, they all, with one exception I'll get to soon, were produced by some kind of sexual coupling, either Titan-Titaness or God-Goddess or God-Nymph or God-Woman or basically Zeus and whom- or whatever Zeus was fucking on any particular day. Which brings me to the second basic observation, which is that the Gods of Olympus are the most squalid and dysfunctional family imaginable. And yet there is something about the motley asymmetry of this pantheon that makes it more credible. Like the Periodic Table of the Elements or the family tree of the elementary particles, or just about any anatomical structure that you might pull up out of a cadaver, it has enough of a pattern to give our minds something to work on and yet an irregularity that indicates some kind of organic provenance—you have a sun god and a moon goddess, for example, which is all clean and symmetrical, and yet over here is Hera, who has no role whatsoever except to be a literal bitch goddess, and then there is Dionysus who isn't even fully a god—he's half human—but gets to be in the Pantheon anyway and sit on Olympus with the Gods, as if you went to the Supreme Court and found Bozo the Clown planted among the justices.

"Now what I'm getting to here is that Athena was exceptional in every way. To begin with she wasn't created through sexual reproduction in any kind of normal sense; she sprang fully-formed from the head of Zeus. According to some versions of the story, this happened after Zeus fucked Metis, about whom we'll hear more in due course. Then he was warned that Metis would later give birth to a son who would dethrone him, and so he ate her, and later Athena came out of his head. Whether you buy into the Metis story or not, I think we can still agree that something a little peculiar was going on with the nativity of Athena. She was also exceptional in that she did not participate in the moral squalor of Olympus; she was a virgin."

"Aha! I knew that was a picture of a virgin on your medallion."

"Yes, Randy, you do have a keen eye for virgins. Hephaestus leg-fucked her once but did not achieve penetration. She's quite important in the *Odyssey,* but there are really very few myths, in the usual sense of that term, that involve her. The one exception really proves the rule: the story of Arachne. Arachne was a superb weaver who became arrogant and began taking credit herself, instead of attributing her talent to the gods. Arachne went so far as to issue an open challenge to Athena, who was the goddess of weaving, among other things.

"Now keep in mind that the typical Greek myth goes something like this: innocent shepherd boy is minding his own business, an overflying god spies him and gets a hard-on, swoops down and rapes him silly; while the victim is still staggering around in a daze, that god's wife or lover, in a jealous rage, turns him—the *helpless, innocent victim,* that is—into let's say an immortal turtle and e.g. power-staples him to a sheet of plywood with a dish of turtle food just out of his reach and leaves him out in the sun forever to be repeatedly disemboweled by army ants and stung by hornets or something. So if Arachne had dissed anyone else in the Pantheon, she would have been just a smoking hole in the ground before she knew what hit her.

"But in this case, Athena appeared to her in the guise of an old woman and recommended that she display the proper humility. Arachne declined her advice. Finally Athena revealed herself as such and challenged Arachne to a weaving contest, which you'll have to admit was uncommonly fair-minded of her. And the interesting thing is that the contest turned out to be a draw—Arachne really was just as good as Athena! Only

problem was that her weaving depicted the gods of Olympus at their
shepherd-raping, interspecies-fucking worst. This weaving was simply a
literal and accurate illustration of all of those *other* myths, which makes
this into a sort of meta-myth. Athena flew off the handle and whacked
Arachne with her distaff, which might seem kind of like poor anger
management until you consider that during the struggle against the
Giants, she wasted Enceladus by dropping Sicily on him! The only effect
was to cause Arachne to recognize her own hubris, at which she became
so ashamed that she hanged herself. Athena then brought her back to
life in the form of a spider.

"So anyway, you probably learned in elementary school that Athena
wears a helmet, carries a shield called Aegis, and is the goddess of war
and of wisdom, as well as crafts—such as the aforementioned weaving.
Kind of an odd combination, to say the least! Especially since Ares was
supposed to be the god of war and Hestia the goddess of home economics—why the redundancy? But a lot's been screwed up in translation.
See, the kind of wisdom that we associate with old farts like yours truly,
and which I'm trying to impart to you here, Randy Waterhouse, was
called *dike* by the Greeks. That's *not* what Athena was the goddess of!
She was the goddess of *metis,* which means cunning or craftiness, and
which you'll recall was the name of her mother in one version of the
story. Interestingly Metis (the personage, not the attribute) provided
young Zeus with the potion that caused Cronus to vomit up all of the
baby gods he'd swallowed, setting the stage for the whole Titanomachia.
So now the connection to crafts becomes obvious—crafts are just the
practical application of *metis.*"

"I associate the word 'crafts' with making crappy belts and ashtrays in
summer camp," Randy says. "I mean, who wants to be the fucking
goddess of macrame?"

"It's all bad translation. The word that we use today, to mean the
same thing, is really *technology.*"

"Okay. Now we're getting somewhere."

"Instead of calling Athena the goddess of war, wisdom, and macrame,
then, we should say war and technology. And here again we have the
problem of an overlap with the jurisdiction of Ares, who's supposed to
be the god of war. And let's just say that Ares is a complete asshole. His
personal aides are Fear and Terror and sometimes Strife. He is constantly
at odds with Athena even though—maybe *because*—they are nominally
the god and goddess of the same thing—war. Heracles, who is one of
Athena's human proteges, physically wounds Ares on two occasions, and
even strips him of his weapons at one point! You see the fascinating
thing about Ares is that he's completely incompetent. He's chained up

by a couple of giants and imprisoned in a bronze vessel for thirteen months. He's wounded by one of Odysseus's drinking buddies during the *Iliad*. Athena knocks him out with a rock at one point. When he's not making a complete idiot of himself in battle, he's screwing every human female he can get his hands on, and—get this—his sons are all what we would today call serial killers. And so it seems very clear to me that Ares really was a god of war as such an entity would be recognized by people who were involved in wars all the time, and had a really clear idea of just how stupid and ugly wars are.

"Whereas Athena is famous for being the backer of Odysseus, who, let's not forget, is the guy who comes up with the idea for the Trojan Horse. Athena guides both Odysseus and Heracles through their struggles, and although both of these guys are excellent fighters, they win most of their battles through cunning or (less pejoratively) *metis*. And although both of them engage in violence pretty freely (Odysseus likes to call himself 'sacker of cities') it's clear that they are being held up in opposition to the kind of mindless, raging violence associated with Ares and his offspring—Heracles even personally rids the world of a few of Ares's psychopathic sons. I mean, the records aren't totally clear—it's not like you can go to the Thebes County Courthouse and look up the death certificates on these guys—but it appears that Heracles, backed up by Athena all the way, personally murders at least half of the Hannibal Lecterish offspring of Ares.

"So insofar as Athena is a goddess of war, what really do we mean by that? Note that her most famous weapon is not her sword but her shield Aegis, and Aegis has a gorgon's head on it, so that anyone who attacks her is in serious danger of being turned to stone. She's always described as being calm and majestic, neither of which adjectives anyone ever applied to Ares."

"I don't know, Enoch. Defensive versus offensive war, maybe?"

"The distinction is overrated. Remember when I said that Athena got leg-fucked by Hephaestus?"

"It generated a clear internal representation in my mind."

"As a myth should! Athena/Hephaestus is sort of an interesting coupling in that he is another technology god. Metals, metallurgy, and fire were his specialties—the old-fashioned Rust Belt stuff. So, no wonder Athena gave him a hard-on! After he ejaculated on Athena's thigh, she's all *eeeeeyew!* and she wipes it off and throws the rag on the ground, where it somehow combines with the earth and generates Erichthonius. You know who Erichthonius was?"

"No."

"One of the first kings of Athens. You know what he was famous for?"

"Tell me."

"Invented the chariot—*and introduced the use of silver as a currency.*"

"Oh, Jesus!" Randy clamps his head between his hands and makes moaning noises, only for a little while.

"Now in many other mythologies you can find gods that have parallels with Athena. The Sumerians had Enki, the Norse had Loki. Loki was an inventor-god, but psychologically he had more in common with Ares; he was not only the god of technology but the god of evil too, the closest thing they had to the Devil. Native Americans had tricksters— creatures full of cunning—like Coyote and Raven in their mythologies, but they didn't have technology yet, and so they hadn't coupled the Trickster with Crafts to generate this hybrid Technologist-god."

"Okay," Randy says, "so obviously where you're going with this is that there must be some universal pattern of events that when filtered through the sensory apparatus and the neural rigs of primitive, superstitious people always gives rise to internal mental representations that they identify as gods, heroes, etc."

"Yes. And these can be recognized across cultures, in the same way that two persons with Root Reps in their mind might 'recognize' me by comparing notes."

"So, Enoch, you want me to believe that these gods—which aren't really gods, but it's a nice concise word—all share certain things in common precisely because the external reality that generated them is consistent and universal across cultures."

"That is right. And in the case of Trickster gods the pattern is that cunning people tend to attain power that un-cunning people don't. And all cultures are fascinated by this. Some of them, like many Native Americans, basically admire it, but never couple it with technological development. Others, like the Norse, hate it and identify it with the Devil."

"Hence the strange love-hate relationship that Americans have with hackers."

"That's right."

"Hackers are always complaining that journalists cast them as bad guys. But you think that this ambivalence is deeper-seated."

"In *some* cultures. The Vikings—to judge from their mythology— would instinctively hate hackers. But something different happened with the Greeks. The Greeks liked their geeks. That's how we get Athena."

"I'll buy that—but where does the war-goddess thing come in?"

"Let's face it, Randy, we've all known guys like Ares. The pattern of human behavior that caused the internal mental representation known as

Ares to appear in the minds of the ancient Greeks is very much with us today, in the form of terrorists, serial killers, riots, pogroms, and aggressive tinhorn dictators who turn out to be military incompetents. And yet for all their stupidity and incompetence, people like that can conquer and control large chunks of the world if they are not resisted."

"You must meet my friend Avi."

"Who is going to fight them off, Randy?"

"I'm afraid you're going to say *we* are."

"Sometimes it might be other Ares-worshippers, as when Iran and Iraq went to war and no one cared who won. But if Ares-worshippers aren't going to end up running the whole world, someone needs to do violence to them. This isn't very nice, but it's a fact: civilization requires an Aegis. And the only way to fight the bastards off in the end is through intelligence. Cunning. *Metis.*"

"Tactical cunning, like Odysseus and the Trojan Horse, or—"

"Both that, and technological cunning. From time to time there is a battle that is out-and-out won by a new technology—like longbows at Crecy. For most of history those battles happen only every few centuries—you have the chariot, the compound bow, gunpowder, ironclad ships, and so on. But something happens around, say, the time that the *Monitor,* which the Northerners believe to be the only ironclad warship on earth, just happens to run into the *Merrimack,* of which the Southerners believe exactly the same thing, and they pound the hell out of each other for hours and hours. That's as good a point as any to identify as the moment when a spectacular rise in military technology takes off—it's the elbow in the exponential curve. Now it takes the world's essentially conservative military establishments a few decades to really comprehend what has happened, but by the time we're in the thick of the Second World War, it's accepted by everyone who doesn't have his head completely up his ass that the war's going to be won by whichever side has the best technology. So on the German side alone we've got rockets, jet aircraft, nerve gas, wire-guided missiles. And on the Allied side we've got three vast efforts that put basically every top-level hacker, nerd, and geek to work: the codebreaking thing, which as you know gave rise to the digital computer; the Manhattan Project, which gave us nuclear weapons; and the Radiation Lab, which gave us the modern electronics industry. Do you know why we won the Second World War, Randy?"

"I think you just told me."

"Because we built better stuff than the Germans?"

"Isn't that what you said?"

"But why did we build better stuff, Randy?"

"I guess I'm not competent to answer, Enoch, I haven't studied that period well enough."

"Well the short answer is that we won because the Germans worshipped Ares and we worshipped Athena."

"And am I supposed to gather that you, or your organization, had something to do with all that?"

"Oh, come now, Randy! Let's not allow this to degenerate into conspiracy theories."

"Sorry. I'm tired."

"So am I. Goodnight."

And then Enoch goes to sleep. Just like that.

Randy doesn't.

To the *Cryptonomicon!*

Randy is mounting a known-ciphertext attack: the hardest kind. He has the ciphertext (the Arethusa intercepts) and nothing else. He doesn't even know the algorithm that was used to encrypt them. In modern cryptanalysis, this is unusual; normally the algorithms are public knowledge. That is because algorithms that have been openly discussed and attacked within the academic community tend to be much stronger than ones that have been kept secret. People who rely on keeping their algorithms secret are ruined as soon as that secret gets out. But Arethusa dates from World War II, when people were much less canny about such things.

This would be a hell of a lot easier if Randy knew some of the plaintext that is encrypted within these messages. Of course, if he knew all of the plaintext, he wouldn't even need to decrypt them; breaking Arethusa in that case would be an academic exercise.

There is a compromise between the two extremes of, on the one hand, not knowing any of the plaintext at all, and, on the other, knowing all of it. In the *Cryptonomicon* that falls under the heading of *cribs*. A crib is an educated guess as to what words or phrases might be present in the message. For example if you were decrypting German messages from World War II, you might guess that the plaintext included the phrase "HEIL HITLER" or "SIEG HEIL." You might pick out a sequence of ten characters at random and say, "Let's assume that this represented HEIL HITLER. If that is the case, then what would it imply about the remainder of the message?"

Randy's not expecting to find any HEILHITLERs in the Arethusa messages, but there might be other predictable words. He's been making a list of cribs in his head: MANILA, certainly. WATERHOUSE, perhaps. And now he's thinking GOLD and BULLION. So, in the case of MANILA he could pick out any six-character string from the intercepts and say, "What if these characters are the encrypted form of MANILA?" and then work from there. If he were working with an intercept only six characters long, then there would be only one such six-character segment to choose from. A seven-character-long message would give him two possibilities: it could be the first six or the last six characters. The upshot is that for a message intercept that is n characters long, the number of six-character-long segments is equal to $(n - 5)$. In the case of a 105-character-long intercept, he will have 100 different possible locations for the word MANILA. Actually, a hundred and one: because it's of course possible—even likely—that MANILA is not in there at all. But each of these 100 guesses has its own set of ramifications vis-à-vis all of the other characters in the message. What those ramifications are, exactly, depends on what assumptions Randy is making about the underlying algorithm.

As far as that goes: the more he thinks about it, the more he believes he has some good stuff to go on—thanks to Enoch, who (in retrospect) has been feeding him some useful clues when not spamming him through the bars with theogonical analysis. Enoch mentioned that when the NSA started attacking what later turned out to be the fake Arethusa intercepts, they were going on the assumption that they were somehow related to another cryptosystem dubbed Azure. And sure enough, Randy learns from the *Cryptonomicon* that Azure was an oddball system used by both the Nipponese and the Germans that employed a mathematical algorithm to generate a different one-time pad every day. This is awfully vague, but it helps Randy rule out a lot. He knows for example that Arethusa isn't a rotor system like Enigma. And he knows that if he can find two messages that were sent on the same day, they will probably use the same one-time pad.

What kind of mathematical algorithm was used? The contents of Grandpa's trunk provides clues. He remembers the photograph of Grandpa with Turing and von Hacklheber at Princeton, where all three of them were evidently fooling around with zeta functions. And in the trunk were several monographs on the same subject. And the *Cryptonomicon* states that zeta functions are even today being used in cryptography, as sequence generators—which is to say, machines for spitting out series of pseudo-random numbers, which is exactly what a one-time pad is. Everything points to that Azure and Arethusa are siblings and that both are just implementations of zeta functions.

The big thing standing in his way right now is that he doesn't have any textbooks on zeta functions sitting around his jail cell. The contents of Grandpa's trunk would be an excellent resource—but they are currently stored in a room in Chester's house. But on the other hand, Chester's rich, and he wants to help.

Randy calls for a guard and demands to see Attorney Alejandro. Enoch Root goes very still for a few moments, and then shunts directly back into the loping, untroubled sleep of a man who is exactly where he wants to be.

SLAVES

✟ PEOPLE SMELL ALL KINDS OF WAYS BEFORE THEY HAVE BURNED, but only one way afterwards. As the Army boys lead Waterhouse down into the darkness, he sniffs cautiously, hoping he won't smell that smell.

Mostly it smells like oil, diesel, hot steel, the brimstony tang of burnt rubber and exploded munitions. These smells are overpoweringly strong. He draws in a lungful of reek, blows it out. And that, of course, is when he catches a whiff of barbecue and knows that this concrete-coated island is, among other things, a crematorium.

He is following the Army boys down black-smudged tunnels bored through a variegated matrix of concrete, masonry, and solid rock. The caves were there first, eaten into the stone by rain and waves, then enlarged and rationalized by Spaniards with chisels, jackhammers, blasting powder. Then along came the Americans with bricks, and finally the Nipponese with reinforced concrete.

As they work their way into the maze, they pass down some tunnels that apparently acted like blowtorches: the walls have been scoured clean as if a torrent had been running through it for a million years, silver pools lie on the floor where guns or filing cabinets melted into puddles. Stored heat still radiates from the walls, adding to the heat of the Philippine climate, making all of them sweat even more, if that is possible.

Other corridors, other rooms were nothing more than backwaters in the river of fire. Looking into doorways, Waterhouse can see books that were charred but not consumed, blackened papers spilling from burst cabinets—

"One moment," he says. His escort spins around just in time to see Waterhouse ducking through a low door into a tiny room, where something has caught his eye.

It's a heavy wooden cabinet, mostly transmuted into charcoal now, so it looks like the cabinet's gone but its shadow persists. Someone has already pulled one of its doors off its hinges, allowing black confetti to flood into the room. The cabinet was filled with slips of paper, mostly burned now, but thrusting his hand into the ash-heap (slowly! Most of this place is still hot) Waterhouse pulls out a bundle, nearly intact.

"What kind of money is that?" the Army guy asks.

Waterhouse pulls a bill from the top of the bundle. The top is printed in Japanese characters and bears an engraved picture of Tojo. He flips it over. The back is printed in English: TEN POUNDS.

"Australian currency," Waterhouse says.

"Don't look Australian to me," the Army guy says, glowering at Tojo.

"If the Nips had won . . ." Waterhouse says, and shrugs. He throws the stack of ten-pound notes onto the ash-heap of history and carries his single copy out into the corridor. A necklace of lightbulbs has been strung along the ceiling. The light glances off what looks like pools of quicksilver on the floor: the remains of guns, belt buckles, steel cabinets and doorknobs, melted down into puddles in the holocaust, now congealed.

The fine print on the bill says, IMPERIAL RESERVE BANK, MANILA.

"Sir! You okay?" the Army guy says. Waterhouse realizes he's been thinking for a while.

"Carry on," he says, and stuffs the bill in his pocket.

He was thinking about whether it was okay to take some of this money with him. It's okay to take souvenirs, but not to loot. So he can take the money if it's worthless, but not if it is real money.

Now, someone who was not so inclined to think and ponder everything to the nth degree would immediately see that the money was worthless, because, after all, the Japanese did not take Australia and never will. So that money's just a souvenir, right?

Probably right. The money is effectively worthless. But if Waterhouse were to find a real Australian ten-pound note and read the fine print, it would also probably bear the imprimatur of a reserve bank somewhere.

Two pieces of paper, each claiming to be worth ten pounds, each very official-looking, each bearing the name of a bank. One of them a worthless souvenir and one legal tender for all debts public and private. What gives?

What it comes down to is that people trust the claims printed on one of those pieces of paper but don't trust the other. They believe that you could take the real Australian note to a bank in Melbourne, slide it over the counter, and get silver or gold—or *something* at least—in exchange for it.

Trust goes a long way, but at some point, if you're going to sponsor a stable currency, you must put up or shut up. Somewhere, you have to actually have a shitload of gold in the basement. Around the time of the evacuation from Dunkirk, when the Brits were looking at an imminent invasion of their islands by the Germans, they took all of their gold reserves, loaded them on board some battleships and passenger liners, and squirted them across the Atlantic to banks in Toronto and Montreal. This would have enabled them to keep their currency afloat even if the Germans had overrun London.

But the Japanese have to play by the same rules as everyone else. Oh, sure, you can get a kind of submission from a conquered people by scaring the shit out of them, but it doesn't work very well to hold a knife to someone's throat and say, "I want you to believe that this piece of paper is worth ten pounds sterling." They might say that they believe it, but they won't really believe it. They won't *act* as if they believe it. And if they don't *act* that way, then there is no currency, workers don't get paid (you can enslave them, but you still have to pay the slavedrivers), the economy doesn't work, you can't extract the natural resources that prompted you to conquer the country in the first place. Basically, if you're going to run an economy you have to have a currency. When someone walks into a bank with one of your notes you have to be able to give them gold in exchange for it.

The Nipponese are maniacs for planning things out. Waterhouse knows this; he has been reading their decrypted messages twelve, eighteen hours a day for a couple of years now, he knows their minds. He knows, as surely as he knows how to play a D major scale, that the Nipponese must have given thought to this problem of backing their imperial currency—not just for Australia but New Zealand, New Guinea, the Philippines, Hong Kong, China, Indochina, Korea, Manchuria . . .

How much gold and silver would you need in order to convince that many human beings that your paper currency was actually worth something? Where would you put it?

The escort takes him down a couple of levels and finally to a surprisingly large room, deep down. If they are in the bowels of the island, then this must be the vermiform appendix or something. It is glob-shaped, walls smooth and ripply in most places, chisel-gnawed where men have seen fit to enlarge it. The walls are still cool and so is the air.

There are long tables in this room, and at least three dozen empty chairs—so Waterhouse nips in tiny whiffs of air at first, terrified that he will smell dead people. But he doesn't.

It figures. They're in the center of the rock. There's only one way into the room. No way to get a good draft through this place—no blowtorch effect—no burning at all, apparently. This room was bypassed. The air is as thick as cold gravy.

"Found forty dead in this room," the escort says.

"Dead of what?"

"Asphyxiation."

"Officers?"

"One Japanese captain. The rest were slaves."

Before the war started, the term "slave" was, to Lawrence Waterhouse, as obsolete as "cooper" or "chandler." Now that the Nazis and the Nipponese have revived the practice, he hears it all the time. War's weird.

His eyes have been adjusting to the dim light ever since they stepped into the chamber. There's a single 25-watt bulb for the whole cavern and the walls absorb nearly all of the light.

He can see squarish things on the tables, one in front of each chair. When he first came in he assumed that these were sheets of paper— indeed, some of them are. But as his vision gets better he can see that most of them are hollow frames, sprinkled with abstract patterns of round dots.

He fumbles for his flashlight and nails the switch. Mostly all it does is create a fuzzy yellow cone of oily smoke, swirling fatly and lazily in front of him. He steps forward shooing the smoke out of his away, and bends over the table.

It's an abacus, its beads still frozen in the middle of some calculation. Two feet down the table is another. Then another.

He turns to face the Army guy. "What's the plural of abacus?"

"Beg pardon, sir?"

"Shall we say abaci?"

"Whatever you say, sir."

"Were any of these abaci touched by any of your men?"

There is a flurry of discussion. The Army guy has to confer with several enlisted men, dispatch gofers to interview people, and make a couple of phone calls. This is a good sign; there are a lot of men who would just say "no, sir," or whatever they thought Waterhouse wanted to hear, and then he would never know whether they were telling the truth. This guy seems to understand that it's important for Waterhouse to get an honest answer.

Waterhouse walks up and down the rows of tables with his hands clasped carefully behind his back, looking at the abaci. Next to most of them is a sheet of paper, or a whole notebook, with a pencil handy. These are all covered with numbers. From place to place, he sees a Chinese character.

"Did any of you see the bodies of these slaves?" he says to an en- listed man.

"Yes, sir. I helped carry 'em out."

"Did they look like Filipinos?"

"No, sir. They looked like regular Asiatics."

"Chinese, Korean, something like that?"

"Yes, sir."

After a few minutes, the answer comes back: no one will admit to having touched an abacus. This chamber was the last part of the fortress to be reached by Americans. The bodies of the slaves were mostly found piled up near the door. The body of the Nipponese officer was on the bottom of the pile. The door had been locked from the inside. It is a metal door, and has a slight outward bulge, as the fire upstairs apparently sucked all the air out of the room in a big hurry.

"Okay," Waterhouse says, "I am going to go upstairs and report back to Brisbane. I am personally going to take this room apart like an archaeologist. Make sure that nothing is touched. Especially the abaci."

ARETHUSA

ATTORNEY ALEJANDRO COMES TO SEE RANDY THE NEXT DAY and they swap small talk about the weather and the Philippine Basketball Association whilst exchanging handwritten slips of paper across the table. Randy gives his lawyer a note saying, "Give this note to Chester" and then another note asking Chester to go through that trunk and find any old documents on the subject of zeta functions and get them to Randy somehow. Attorney Alejandro gives Randy a somewhat defensive and yet self-congratulatory note itemizing his recent efforts on Randy's behalf, which is probably meant to be encouraging but which Randy finds to be unsettlingly vague. He had rather expected some specific results by this point. He reads it and looks askance at Attorney Alejandro, who grimaces and taps himself on the jaw, which is code for "the Dentist" and which Randy interprets to mean that said billionaire is interfering with whatever Attorney Alejandro is trying to accomplish. Randy hands Attorney Alejandro another note saying, "Give this note to Avi" and then yet another note asking Avi to find out whether General Wing is one of the Crypt's clients.

Then nothing happens for a week. Since Randy lacks the information that he needs about zeta functions, he can't do any actual codebreaking work during this week. But he can lay the groundwork for the work he'll do later. The *Cryptonomicon* contains numerous hunks of C code intended to perform certain basic cryptanalytical operations, but a lot of it is folk code (poorly written) and anyway needs to be translated into the more modern C++ language. So Randy does that. The *Cryptonomicon* also describes various algorithms that will probably come in handy, and Randy implements those in C++ too. It is scut work, but he has nothing else to do, and one of the good things about this particular kind of scut work is that it acquaints you with every little detail of the mathematics; if you don't understand the math you can't write the code. As the days go by, his mind turns into some approximation of a cryptanalyst's. This transformation is indexed by the slow accretion of code in his code-breaking library.

He and Enoch Root get into the habit of having conversations during and after their meals. Both of them seem to have rather involved inner lives that require lots of maintenance and so the rest of the day they ignore each other. Anecdote by anecdote, Randy plots the trajectory of his life to date. Likewise Enoch speaks vaguely of some wartime events, then about what it was like to live in postwar England, and then in the U.S. in the fifties. Apparently he was a Catholic priest for a while but got kicked out of the Church for some reason; he doesn't say why, and Randy doesn't ask. After that all is vague. He mentions that he began spending large amounts of time in the Philippines during the Vietnam War, which fits in with Randy's general hypothesis: if it's true that Old Man Comstock had U.S. troops combing the Philippine boondocks for the Primary, then Enoch would have wanted to be around, to interfere or at least keep an eye on them. Enoch claims he's also been gadding about trying to bring Internet stuff to China, but to Randy this just sounds like a cover story for something else.

It is hard not to get the idea that Enoch Root and General Wing may have other reasons to be pissed off at each other.

"Like, if I can just play Pluto's advocate here, what do you mean exactly when you talk about defending civilization?"

"Oh, Randy, you know what I mean."

"Yeah, but China is civilized, right? Has been for a while."

"Yes."

"So maybe you and General Wing are actually on the same team."

"If the Chinese are so civilized, how come they never invent anything?"

"What—paper, gunpowder—"

"Anything in the last *millennium* I mean."

"Beats me. What do you think, Enoch?"

"It's like the Germans in the Second World War."

"I know that all the bright lights fled Germany in the thirties—Einstein, Born—"

"And Schrödinger, and von Neumann, and others—but do you know why they fled?"

"Well, because they didn't like the Nazis, of course!"

"But do you know specifically why the Nazis didn't like *them*?"

"A lot of them were Jews . . ."

"It goes deeper than mere anti-Semitism. Hilbert, Russell, Whitehead, Gödel, all of them were engaged in a monumental act of tearing mathematics down and beginning from scratch. But the Nazis believed that mathematics was a heroic science whose purpose was to reduce chaos to order—just as National Socialism was supposed to do in the political sphere."

"Okay," Randy says, "but what the Nazis didn't understand was that if you tore it down and rebuilt it, it was even more heroic than before."

"Indeed. It led to a renaissance," Root says, "like in the seventeenth century, when the Puritans tore everything to rubble and then slowly built it back up from scratch. Over and over again we see the pattern of the Titanomachia repeated—the old gods are thrown down, chaos returns, but out of the chaos, the same patterns reemerge."

"Okay. So—again—you were talking about civilization?"

"Ares always reemerges from the chaos. It will never go away. Athenian civilization defends itself from the forces of Ares with *metis,* or technology. Technology is built on science. Science is like the alchemists' uroburos, continually eating its own tail. The *process* of science doesn't work unless young scientists have the freedom to attack and tear down old dogmas, to engage in an ongoing Titanomachia. Science flourishes where art and free speech flourish."

"Sounds teleological, Enoch. Free countries get better science, hence superior military power, hence get to defend their freedoms. You're proclaiming a sort of Manifest Destiny here."

"Well, *someone's* got to do it."

"Aren't we beyond that sort of thing now?"

"I know you're just saying that to infuriate me. Sometimes, Randy, Ares gets chained up in a barrel for a few years, but he never goes away. The next time he emerges, Randy, the conflict is going to revolve around bio-, micro-, and nanotechnology. Who's going to win?"

"I don't know."

"Are you not just a bit unsettled by *not knowing*?"

"Look, Enoch, I'm trying my best here—I really am—but I'm broke, and I'm locked up in this fucking cage, all right?"

"Oh, stop whining."

"What about you? Suppose you go back to your yam farm, or whatever, and one day your shovel hits something that rings, and you suddenly dig up a few kilotons of gold? You'd invest it all in high-tech weapons?"

Root, not surprisingly, has an answer: the gold was stolen from all of Asia by the Nipponese, who intended to use it as backing for a currency that would become the legal tender of the Greater East Asia Co-Prosperity Sphere, and that while it goes without saying that those particular Nips were among the most egregious buttheads in planetary history, some aspects of their plan weren't such a shitty idea. That to the extent life still sucks for many Asians, things would get a lot better, for a lot of people, if the continent's economy could get jerked into the twenty-first, or at least the twentieth, century and hopefully *stay there* for a while instead of collapsing whenever some dictator's-nephew-in-charge-of-a-central-bank loses control of his sphincters and wipes out a major currency. So maybe stabilizing the currency situation would be a good thing to accomplish with a shitload of gold, and that's the only moral thing to do with it anyway considering whom it was stolen from—you can't just go out and *spend* it. Randy finds this answer appropriately sophisticated and Jesuitical and eerily in sync with what Avi has written into the latest edition of the Epiphyte(2) Business Plan.

After a decent number of days has gone by, Enoch Root comes right back and asks Randy what he'd do with a few kilotons of gold, and Randy mentions the Holocaust Education and Avoidance Pod. Turns out that Enoch Root already knows about the HEAP, has already downloaded various revisions of it over the gleaming new communications network that Randy and the Dentist strung through the islands, thinks it's right in line with his ideas vis-à-vis Athena, Aegis, etc., but has any number of difficult questions and trenchant criticisms.

Shortly thereafter, Avi himself comes in for a visit and says very little, but does let Randy know that, yes, General Wing is one of the Crypt's clients. The grizzled Chinese gentlemen who sat around the table with them in Kinakuta, and whose mugs were secretly captured by the pinhole camera on Randy's laptop, are among Wing's chief lieutenants. Avi also lets him know that the legal pressure has eased; the Dentist has suddenly reined in Andrew Loeb and allowed any number of legal deadlines to be extended. The fact that Avi says nothing at all about the sunken submarine would seem to imply that the salvage operation is going well, or at least going.

Randy's still processing these pieces of news when he receives a visit from none other than the Dentist himself.

"I assume that you think I had you framed," says Dr. Hubert Kepler.

He and Randy are alone in a room together, but Randy is conscious of many aides, bodyguards, lawyers, and Furies or Harpies or whatever just on the other side of the nearest door. The Dentist seems ever so slightly amused, but Randy gradually collects that he is actually quite serious. The Dentist's upper lip is permanently arched, or shorter than it ought to be, or both, with the result that his glacier-white incisors are always slightly exposed, and depending on how the light is hitting his face he looks either vaguely beaverish or else as if he's none too effectively fighting back a sneering grin. Even a gentle soul like Randy cannot gaze upon such a face without thinking how much better it would look with the application of some knuckles. From the perfection of Hubert Kepler's dentition it is possible to infer that he had a sheltered upbringing (full-time bodyguards from the time his adult teeth erupted from the gumline) or that his choice of careers was motivated by a very personal interest in reconstructive oral surgery. "And I know that you're probably not going to believe me. But I'm here to say that I had nothing to do with what happened at the airport."

The Dentist now stops and gazes at Randy for a while, by no means one of those guys who feels any need to nervously fill in gaps in conversation. And so it is during the ensuing, lengthy pause that Randy figures out that the Dentist isn't grinning at all, that his face is simply in its state of natural repose. Randy shudders a bit just to think of what it must be like to never be able to lose this alternatively beaverish and sneering look. For your lover to gaze on you while you're sleeping and see this. Of course, if the stories are to be believed, Victoria Vigo has her own ways of exacting retribution, and so maybe Hubert Kepler really is suffering the abuse and humiliation that his face seems to be asking for. Randy heaves a little sigh when he thinks of this, sensing some trace of cosmic symmetry revealed.

Kepler is certainly correct in saying that Randy is not inclined to believe a single word he says. The only way for Kepler to gain any credibility is for him to show up in person at this jail and utter the words face-to-face, which given all of the other things that he could be doing, for fun or profit or both, at this moment, gives a lot of weight to what he's saying. It is implicit that if the Dentist wanted to lie, badly and baldly, to Randy, he could send his lawyers around to do it for him, or just send him a fucking telegram, for that matter. So either he's telling the truth, or else he's lying but it's very important to him that Randy should believe in his lies. Randy cannot work out why on earth the Dentist should give a flying fuck whether Randy believes in his lies or not, which pushes him in the direction of thinking that maybe he really is telling the truth.

"Who framed me, then?" Randy asks, kind of rhetorically. He was just in the middle of doing some pretty cool C++ coding when he got yanked out of his cell to have this surprise encounter with the Dentist, and is surprising himself with just how bored and irritated he is. He has reverted, in other words, back into a pure balls-to-the-wall nerdism rivaled only by his early game-coding days back in Seattle. The sheer depth and involution of the current nerdism binge would be hard to convey to anyone. Intellectually, he is juggling a dozen lit torches, Ming vases, live puppies, and running chainsaws. In this frame of mind he cannot bring himself to give a shit about the fact that this incredibly powerful billionaire has gone to a lot of trouble to come and F2F with him. And so he asks the above question as nothing more than a perfunctory gesture, the subtext being *I wish you'd go away but minimal standards of social decency dictate that I should say something*. The Dentist, no slouch himself in the social ineptness department, comes right back as if it were an actual request for information. "I can only assume that you have somehow gotten embroiled with someone who has a lot of influence in this country. It appears that someone is trying to send you a—"

"No! Just stop," Randy says. "Don't say it." Hubert Kepler is now looking at him quizzically, so Randy continues. "The message theory doesn't hold up."

Kepler looks genuinely baffled for a few moments, then actually does grin a little bit. "Well, it certainly isn't an attempt to do away with you, because—"

"Obviously," Randy says.

"Yes. Obviously."

There is another one of those long pauses; Kepler seems unsure of himself. Randy arches his back and stretches. "The chair in my cell is not what you call ergonomic," he says. He holds his arms out and wiggles the fingers. "My carpals are going to start acting up again. I can tell."

Randy is looking at Kepler pretty carefully when he says this, and there's no doubt that genuine astonishment is now spreading across the Dentist's face. The Dentist only has one facial expression (already described) but it changes in intensity; it gets more so and less so depending on his emotions. The Dentist's expression proves he had no idea, until now, that Randy's been allowed to have a computer in his cell. In the trying-to-figure-out-what-the-fuck-is-going-on department, the computer is the single most important datum, and Kepler didn't even know about it until just now. So to whatever extent the Dentist actually gives a shit, he has a lot of thinking to do. He excuses himself pretty soon after.

Not half an hour later, some twenty-five-year-old American guy with a ponytail shows up and has a brief audience with Randy. It turns out that he works for Chester in Seattle and has just now flown across the Pacific on Chester's personal jet and came here straight from the airport. He is completely jazzed, totally in bat-out-of-hell mode, and cannot shut up. The sheer amazingness of his sudden flight across the ocean on a rich guy's private jet has made a really, really deep impression on him and he obviously needs someone to share it with. He has brought a "care package" consisting of some junk food, a few trashy novels, the largest bottle of Pepto-Bismol Randy's ever seen, a CD Walkman, and a cubical stack of CDs. This guy can't get over the battery thing; he was told to bring a lot of extra batteries, and so he did, and sure enough, between the luggage guys at the airport and the customs inspectors, all of the batteries disappeared en route except for one package that he's got in the pocket of his long baggy Seattle-grunge-boy shorts. Seattle's full of guys like this who flipped a coin when they graduated from college (heads Prague, tails Seattle) and just showed up with this expectation that because they were young and smart they'd find a job and begin making money, and then appallingly enough did exactly that. Randy can't figure out what the world must look like to a guy like this. He has a hard time getting rid of the guy, who shares the common assumption (increasingly annoying) that just because Randy's in jail, he doesn't have a life, has nothing better to do than interface with visitors.

When Randy gets back to his cell, he sits crosslegged on his bed with the Walkman and begins dealing out the CDs like cards in a solitaire game. The selection is pretty reasonable: a two-disc set of the Brandenburg Concertos, a collection of Bach organ fugues (nerds have a thing about Bach), some Louis Armstrong, some Wynton Marsalis, and then various selections from Hammerdown Systems, which is a Seattle-based record label in which Chester is a major investor. It is a second-generation Seattle-scene record label; all of its artists are young people who came to Seattle after they graduated from college in search of the legendary Seattle music scene and discovered that it didn't really exist—it was just a couple of dozen guys who sat around playing guitar in one another's basements—and so who were basically forced to choose between going home in ignominy or fabricating the Seattle music scene of their imagination from whole cloth. This led to the establishment of any number of small clubs, and the foundation of many bands, that were not rooted in any kind of authentic reality whatsoever but merely reflected the dreams and aspiration of pan-global young adults who had all flocked to Seattle on the same chimera hunt. This second wave scene came in for a lot of abuse from those of the original two dozen people who had not yet died of drug overdose or suicide. There was something of a backlash; and yet, about thirty-six hours after the backlash reached its maximum intensity, there was an antibacklash backlash from young immigrants who asserted their right to some kind of unique cultural identity as people who had naively come to Seattle and discovered that there was no there there and that they would have to create it themselves. Fueled by that conviction, and by their own youthful libidinous energy, and by a few cultural commentators who found this whole scenario fetchingly post-modern, they started a whole lot of second-generation bands and even a couple of record labels, of which Hammerdown Systems is the only one that didn't either go out of business or get turned into a wholly-owned subsidiary of an L.A. or New York-based major label inside of six months.

And so Chester has decided to favor Randy with those recent Hammerdown selections of which he is most proud. Perversely, almost all of these are from bands that are not even in Seattle at all but in small, prohibitively hip college towns in North Carolina and the Upper Peninsula of Michigan. But Randy does find one from an evidently Seattle-based band called Shekondar. *Evidently,* that is, because on the back of the CD is a blurry photograph of several band members drinking sixteen-ounce lattes in cups bearing the logo of a chain of coffee bars that as far as Randy knows has not yet burst free from the city limits of Seattle to crush everything in its path worldwide in the now wearisomely predictable manner of Seattle-based companies. Now, Shekondar happens to have been the name of an especially foul underworld deity who played an important role in some of the game scenarios that Randy played with Avi and Chester and the gang back in the old days. Randy opens up the case of the CD and notes immediately that the disc has the golden hue of a master, not the traditional silver of a mere copy. Randy puts that golden master into his Walkman and hits the Play button and is treated to some passable post-Cobain-mortem material, genetically engineered to have nothing in common with what is traditionally thought of as the Seattle sound and in that sense absolutely typical of Seattle du jour. He jumps forward through a couple more tracks and then rips the earphones off his head, cursing, as the Walkman attempts to translate a stream of pure digital information, representing something other than music, into sound. This feels a bit like needles of dry ice jabbed into his eardrums.

Randy moves the golden disc to the CD-ROM drive that is built into his laptop, and checks it out. Indeed it does sport a couple of audio tracks (as he's discovered) but almost all of the disc's capacity is given over to computer files. There are several directories, or folders, each named after one of the documents that was in grandfather's trunk. Within each of these directories is a long list of files named PAGE.001.jpeg,

PAGE.002.jpeg, and so on. Randy starts opening them up, using the same net-browser software that he uses to read the *Cryptonomicon*, and discovers that they are all scanned image files. Evidently Chester had a bunch of minions de-staple those documents and feed them page by page through a scanner. At the same time he must have had graphic artists, presumably people he knows through Hammerdown Systems, hastily whipping up this fake Shekondar album cover. It's even got a package insert, photographs of Shekondar in concert. What it really is is a parody of the post-Seattle Scene Seattle scene that aligns perfectly with the faulty notions of same that could be expected in the imagination of a Philippine airport customs inspector, who like everyone else is fantasizing about moving to Seattle. The lead guitarist looks kind of like Chester in a wig.

All of this sneaky stuff is probably gratuitous. It probably would have been okay for Chester to just Fedex the fucking documents straight to the jail. But Chester, sitting in his house by Lake Washington, is working on a set of assumptions about Manila just as faulty as what half of the world believes about Seattle. At least Randy gets a laugh out of it before diving into zeta functions.

A word about libido: it's been something like three weeks for Randy now. He was just beginning to address this situation when a highly intelligent and perceptive Catholic ex-priest was suddenly introduced into the cell next to his and began sleeping six inches away from him. Since then, masturbation per se has been pretty much out of the question. To the extent Randy believes in any god at all, he's been praying for a nocturnal emission. His prostate gland now has the size and consistency of a croquet ball. He feels it all the time, and has begun to think of it as his Hunk of Burning Love. Randy had a spot of prostate trouble once when he was chronically drinking too much coffee, and it made everything between his nipples and his knees hurt. The urologist explained that Little Man 'tate is neurologically wired into just about every other part of your body, and he didn't have to exert any rhetorical skill, or marshall any detailed arguments, in order to make Randy believe that. Randy has believed, ever since, that the ability of men to become moronically obsessed with copulation is in some way a reflection of this wiring diagram; when you are ready to give the external world the benefit of your genetic material, i.e. when the 'tate is fully loaded, even your pinkies and eyelids know about it.

And so it might be expected that Randy would be thinking all the time about America Shaftoe, his sexual target of choice, who (just to make things a lot worse) has probably been spending a lot of time in wetsuits lately. And indeed that is where his thoughts were directed at the moment Enoch Root was dragged in. But since then it has become evident that he needs to exercise some kind of iron mental discipline here and not think about Amy at all. Whilst juggling all of those chainsaws and puppies, he is also walking a sort of intellectual tightrope, with decryption of the Arethusa intercepts at the end of that tightrope, and as long as he keeps his eyes fixed on that goal and just keeps putting one foot in front of the other, he'll get there. Amy-in-a-wetsuit is down below somewhere, no doubt trying to be emotionally supportive, but if he even glances in her direction he's a goner.

What he's reading here is a set of academic papers, dating to the 1930s and early forties, that have been heavily marked up by his grandfather, who went through them none-too-subtly gleaning anything that could be useful on the cryptographic front. That it's none too subtle is a good thing for Randy, whose grasp of pure number theory is just barely adequate here. Chester's minions had to scan not only the fronts of these pages but the backs too, which were originally blank but on which Grandpa wrote many notes. For example there is a paper written by Alan Turing in 1937 in which Lawrence Pritchard Waterhouse has found some kind of error, or at least, something that Turing didn't go into in sufficient detail, forcing him to cover several pages with annotations. Randy's blood absolutely runs cold at the very idea that he is being so presumptuous as to participate in such a colloquy. When he realizes just how deep over his head he is intellectually, he turns off his computer and goes to bed and sleeps the bootless sleep of the depressed for ten hours. Eventually he convinces himself that most of the junk in these papers probably has no direct relevance to Arethusa and that he just needs to calm down and filter the material carefully.

Two weeks pass. His prayers vis-à-vis the Hunk of Burning Love are answered, giving him at least a couple of days of relief during which he can admit the concept of Amy Shaftoe into his awareness, but only in a really austere and passionless way. Attorney Alejandro shows up occasionally to tell Randy that things are not going very well. Surprising obstacles have arisen. All of the people he was planning to bribe have been preemptively counter-bribed by Someone. These meetings are tedious for Randy, who thinks he has figured everything out. To begin with it's Wing, and not the Dentist, who has caused all of this, and so Attorney Alejandro's working on faulty assumptions.

Enoch, when he called Randy on the plane, said his old NSA buddy was working for one of the Crypt's clients. It seems clear now that this client is Wing. Consequently Wing knows that Randy has Arethusa. Wing believes that the Arethusa intercepts contain information about the location of the Primary. He wants Randy to decrypt those messages so that he'll know where to dig. Hence the whole setup with the laptop.

All of Attorney Alejandro's efforts to spring Randy loose will be unavailing until Wing has the information that he wants—or thinks he does.
Then, all of a sudden, the ice will break, and Randy will unexpectedly
be cut loose on a technicality. Randy's so sure of this that he finds
Attorney Alejandro's visits annoying. He would like to explain all of this
so that Attorney Alejandro could knock it off with the wild goose chase,
and his increasingly bleak and dull situation reports on same. But then
Wing, who presumably surveils these attorney/client conferences, would
know that Randy had figured out the whole game, and Randy doesn't
want Wing to know that. So he nods through these meetings with his
lawyer and then, for good measure, goes back and tries to sound convincingly bewildered and depressed as he gives Enoch Root the update.

He gets to the point, conceptually, where his grandfather was when
he commenced breaking the Arethusa messages. That is, he has a theory
in mind now of how Arethusa worked. If he doesn't know the exact
algorithm, he knows what family of algorithms it belongs to, and that
gives him a search space with many fewer dimensions than he had before.
Certainly few enough for a modern computer to explore. He goes on a
forty-eight-hour hacking binge. The nerve damage in his wrists has
mounted to the point where he practically has sparks shooting out of his
fingertips. His doctor told him never again to work on these nonergo-
nomic keyboards. His eyes start to go out on him too, and he has to
invert the screen colors and work with white letters on a black background, gradually increasing the size of the letters as he loses the ability
to focus. But at last he gets something that he thinks is going to work,
and he fires it up and sets it to running on the Arethusa intercepts, which
live inside the computer's memory but have never yet been displayed
upon its screen. He falls asleep. When he wakes up, the computer is
informing him that he's got a probable break into one of the messages.
Actually, three of them, all intercepted on 4 April 1945 and hence all
encrypted using the same keystream.

Unlike human codebreakers, computers can't read English. They can't
even recognize it. They can crank out possible decrypts of a message at
tremendous speed but given two character strings like

SEND HELP IMMEDIATELY
and
XUEBP TOAFF NMQPT

they have no inherent ability to recognize the first as a successful decryption of a message and the second as a failure. But they can do a
frequency count on the letters. If the computer finds that E is the most
common, followed by T, and so on and so forth, then it's a pretty strong
indication that the text is some natural human language and not just

random gibberish. By using this and other slightly more sophisticated tests, Randy's come up with a routine that should be pretty good at recognizing success. And it's telling him this morning that 4 April 1945 is broken. Randy dare not display the decrypted messages onscreen for fear that they contain the information that Wing's looking for, and so he cannot actually read these messages, as desperately as he'd like to. But by using a command called *grep*, which searches through text files without opening them, he can at least verify that the word MANILA occurs in two places.

Based on this break, with several more days' work Randy solves Arethusa entirely. He comes up, in other words, with $A(x) = K$, such that for any given date x he can figure out what K, the keystream for that day would be; and just to prove it, he has the computer crank out K for every day in 1944 and 1945 and then use them to decrypt the Arethusa intercepts that came in on those days (without displaying them) and does the frequency count on them and verifies that it worked in each case.

So now he has decrypted all of the messages. But he cannot actually read them without transmitting their contents to Wing. And so now, the subliminal channel comes into play.

In cryptospeak, a subliminal channel is a trick whereby secret information is subtly embedded in a stream of other stuff. Usually it means something like manipulating the least significant bits of an image file to convey a text message. Randy's drawn inspiration from the concept in his labors here in jail. Yes, he has been working on decrypting Arethusa, and that has involved screwing around with a tremendous number of files and writing a lot of code. The number of separate files he's read, created, and edited in the last few weeks is probably in the thousands. None of them have had title bars on their windows, and so the Van Eck phreakers surveilling him have presumably had a terrible time keeping track of which is which. Randy can open a file by typing its title in a window and hitting the return key, all of which happens so fast that the surveillance people probably don't have time to read or understand what he has typed before it disappears. This, he thinks, may have given him just a bit of leeway. He has kept a subliminal channel going in the background: working on a few other bits of code that have nothing to do with breaking Arethusa.

He got the idea for one of these when he was paging through the *Cryptonomicon* and discovered an appendix that contained a listing of the Morse code. Randy knew Morse code when he was a Boy Scout, and learned it again a few years ago when he was studying for a ham radio license, and it doesn't take him long to refresh his memory. And neither does it take him very long to write a little bit of code that turns his computer's space bar into a Morse code key, so that he can talk to the machine by whacking out dots and dashes with his thumb. This might look a little conspicuous, if not for the fact that Randy spends half of his time reading text files in little windows on the screen, and the way you page through a text file in most UNIX systems is by whacking the space bar. All he has to do is whack it in a particular rhythm, a detail he's relying on the surveillance guys to miss. The results all go into a buffer that is never displayed on the screen, and get written out to files with completely meaningless names. So, for example, Randy can whack out the following rhythm on his spacebar while pretending to read a lengthy section of the *Cryptonomicon*:

dash dot dot dot (pause) dot dot dash (pause) dash dot (pause) dash dot dot (pause) dash dash dash (pause) dash dot dash

which ought to spell out BUNDOK. He doesn't want to open the resulting file on screen, but later, while he's in the middle of a long series of other cryptic commands he can type

```
grep ndo (meaningless file name) > (another meaningless
file name)
```

and grep will search through the first-named file to see if it contains the string "ndo" and put the results into the second-named file, which he can then check quite a bit later. He can also do "grep bun" and "grep dok" and if the results of all of these greps are true then he can be pretty confident that he has successfully coded the sequence "BUNDOK" into that one file. In the same way he can code "COORDINATES" into some other file and "LATITUDE" into another, and various numbers into others, and finally by using another command called "cat" he can slowly combine these one-word files into longer ones. All of these demands the same ridiculous patience as, say, tunneling out of a prison with a teaspoon, or sawing through iron bars with a nail file. But there comes a point, after he's spent about a month in jail, when suddenly he's able to make a window appear on the screen that contains the following message:

```
COORDINATES OF PRIMARY STORAGE LOCATIONS
SITE BUNDOK: LATITUDE NORTH FOURTEEN DEGREES THIRTY-TWO
MINUTES... LONGITUDE EAST ONE TWO ZERO DEGREES FIFTY-
SIX MINUTES...
SITE MAKATI: (etc.)
SITE ELDORADO: (etc.)
```

All of which is total bullshit that he just made up. The coordinates given for the Makati site are those of a luxury hotel in Manila, sited at a major intersection that used to be the site of a Nipponese military airbase. Randy happens to have these numbers in his computer because he took them down during his very early days in Manila, when he was doing the GPS survey work for siting Epiphyte's antennas. The coordinates given for SITE ELDORADO are simply the location of the pile of gold bars that he and Doug Shaftoe went to examine, plus a small random error factor. And those given for SITE BUNDOK are the real coordinates of Golgotha plus a couple of random error factors that should have Wing digging a deep hole in the ground about twenty kilometers away from the real site.

How does Randy know that there is a site called Golgotha, and how does he know its real coordinates? His computer told him using Morse code. Computer keyboards have LEDs on them that are essentially kind of useless: one to tell you when NUM LOCK is on, one for CAPS LOCK, and a third one whose purpose Randy can't even remember. And for no reason other than the general belief that every aspect of a computer should be under the control of hackers, someone, some-where, wrote some library routines called XLEDS that make it possible for programmers to turn these things on and off at will. And for a month, Randy's been writing a little program that makes use of these routines to output the contents of a text file in Morse code, by flashing one of those LEDs. And while all kinds of useless crap has been scrolling across the screen of his computer as camouflage, Randy's been hunched over gazing into the subliminal channel of that blinking LED, reading the contents of the decrypted Arethusa intercepts. One of which says:

THE PRIMARY IS CODE NAMED GOLGOTHA. COORDINATES OF THE MAIN DRIFT ARE AS FOLLOWS: LATTITUDE NORTH (etc.)

THE BASEMENT

AT THIS POINT IN HISTORY (APRIL OF 1945) THE WORD THAT denotes a person who sits and performs arithmetical calculations is "computer." Waterhouse has just found a whole room full of dead computers. Anyone in his right mind—anyone other than Water-house and some of his odd Bletchley Park friends, like Turing—would have taken one look at these computers and assumed that they were the accounting department, or something, and that each slave in the room was independently toting up figures. Waterhouse really *ought* to remain open to this idea, because it is so obvious. But from the very beginning he has had a hypothesis of his own, much more interesting and peculiar. It is that the slaves were functioning, collectively, as cogs in a larger computation machine, each performing a small portion of a complex calculation: receiving numbers from one computer, doing some arithmetic, producing new numbers, passing them on to another computer.

Central Bureau is able to trace the identities of five of the dead slaves. They came from places like Saigon, Singapore, Manila, and Java, but they had in common that they were ethnic Chinese and they were shopkeepers. Apparently the Nipponese had cast a wide net for expert abacus users and brought them together, from all over the Co-Prosperity Sphere, to this island in Manila Bay.

Lawrence Waterhouse tracks down a computer of his own in the ruins of Manila, a Mr. Gu, whose small import/export business was destroyed by the war (it is hard to run such a business when you are on an island, and every ship that leaves or approaches the island gets sunk by Americans). Waterhouse shows Mr. Gu photos of the abaci as they were left by the dead computers. Mr. Gu tells him what numbers are encoded in those bead positions, as well as giving Waterhouse a couple of days' tutorial on basic abacus technique. The important thing learned from this is not really abacus skills but rather the remarkable speed and precision with which a computer like Mr. Gu can churn out calculations.

At this point, Waterhouse has reduced the problem to pure data. About half of it's in his memory and the other half scattered around on his desk. The data includes all of the scratch paper left behind by the computers. To match up the numbers on the scratch paper with the numbers left on the abaci, and thus to compile a flash-frozen image of the calculations that were underway in that room when the apocalypse struck, is not that difficult—at least, by the standards of difficulty that apply during wartime, when, for example, landing several thousand men and tons of equipment on a remote island and taking it from heavily armed, suicidal Japanese troops with the loss of only a few dozen lives is considered to be easy.

From this it is possible (though it approaches being difficult) to generalize, and to figure out the underlying mathematical algorithm that generated the numbers on the abaci. Waterhouse becomes familiar with some of the computers' handwriting, and develops evidence that slips of scratch paper were being handed from one computer to another and then to yet another. Some of the computers had logarithm tables at their stations, which is a really important clue as to what they were doing. In this way he is able to draw up a map of the room, with each computer's station identified by number, and a web of arrows interconnecting the stations, depicting the flow of paper, and of data. This helps him visualize the collective calculation as a whole, and to reconstruct what was going on in that subterranean chamber.

For weeks it comes in bits and pieces, and then one evening, some switch turns on in Lawrence Waterhouse's mind, and he knows, in some preconscious way, that he's about to get it. He works for twenty-four hours. By that point he has come up with a lot of evidence to support, and none to contradict, the hypothesis that this calculation is a variant of a zeta function. He naps for six hours, gets up, and works for another thirty. By that point he's figured out that it definitely is some kind of zeta function, and he's managed to figure out several of its constants and terms. He almost has it now. He sleeps for twelve hours, gets up and walks around Manila to clear his head, goes back to work, and hammers away at it for thirty-six hours. This is the fun part, when big slabs of the puzzle, painstakingly assembled from fragments, suddenly begin to lock together, and the whole thing begins to make sense.

It all comes down to an equation written down on one sheet of paper. Just looking at it makes him feel weirdly nostalgic, because it's the same type of equation he used to work with back at Princeton with Alan and Rudy.

Another pause for sleep, then, because he has to be alert to do the final thing.

The final thing is as follows: he goes into the basement of a building in Manila. The building has been turned into a signals intelligence head-quarters by the United States Army. He is one of some half-dozen people on the face of the planet who are allowed to enter this particular room. The room amounts to a bit more than a quarter of the basement's total square footage, and in fact shares the basement with several other rooms, some of which are larger than it is, and some of which are serving as offices for men with higher rank than Waterhouse wears on his uniform. But there are a few oddities connected with Waterhouse's room:

(1) At any given moment, no fewer than three United States Marines are loitering directly in front of the door of this room, carrying pump shotguns and other weapons optimized for close-range indoor flesh-shredding.

(2) Lots of power cables go into this room; it has its own fuse-panel, separate from the rest of the building's electrical system.

(3) The room emits muffled, yet deafening quasimusical noises.

(4) The room is referred to as the Basement, even though it's only part of the basement. When "the Basement" is written down, it is capitalized. When someone (let's say Lieutenant Colonel Earl Comstock) is going to verbalize this, he will come to a complete stop in mid-sentence,

so that all of the preceding words kind of pile into each other like cars in a colliding train. He will, in fact, bracket "the Basement" between a pair of full one-second-long caesuras. During the first of these, he will raise his eyebrows and purse his lips simultaneously, altering the entire aspect ratio of his face so that it becomes strikingly elongated in the vertical dimension, and his eyes will dart sideways in case any Nipponese spies somehow managed to escape the recent apocalypse and found a place to lurk around the fringes of his peripheral vision. Then he will say "the" and then he will say "Basement," drawing out the *s* and primly articulating the *t*. And then will come another caesura during which he will incline his head towards the listener and fix him with a sober, appraising look, seeming to demand some kind of verbal or gestural acknowledgment from the listener that something appallingly significant has just passed between them. And then he will continue with whatever he was saying.

Waterhouse nods to the Marines, one of whom hauls the door open for him. A really funny thing happened shortly after the Basement was established, when it was still just a bunch of wooden crates and a stack of 32-foot-long-sewer pipe segments, and the electricians were still running in the power lines: Lieutenant Colonel Earl Comstock tried to enter the Basement to inspect it. But owing to a clerical error, Lieutenant Colonel Earl Comstock's name was not on the list, and so a difference of opinion ensued that culminated with one of the Marines drawing his Colt .45 and taking the safety off and chambering a round, pressing the barrel of the weapon directly into the center of Comstock's right thigh, and then reminiscing about some of the spectacular femur-bursting wounds he had personally witnessed on places like Tarawa and in general trying to help Comstock visualize just what his life would be like, both short- and long-term, if a large piece of lead were to pass through the middle of said major bone. To everyone's surprise, Comstock was delighted with this encounter, almost enchanted, and hasn't stopped talking about it since. Of course, now his name's on the list.

The Basement is filled with ETC card machines and with several racks of equipment devoid of corporate logos, inasmuch as they were designed and largely built by Lawrence Pritchard Waterhouse in Brisbane. When all of these things are hooked together in just the right way, they constitute a Digital Computer. Like a pipe organ, a Digital Computer is not so much a machine as a meta-machine that can be made into any of a number of different machines by changing its internal configuration. At the moment, Lawrence Pritchard Waterhouse is the only guy in the world who understands the Digital Computer well enough to actually do this, though he's training a couple of Comstock's ETC men to do it themselves. On the day in question, he is turning the Digital Computer into a machine for calculating the zeta function that he thinks is at the core of the cryptosystem called Azure or Pufferfish.

The function requires a number of inputs. One of these is a date. Azure is a system for generating one-time pads that change every day, and circumstantial evidence from the room of the dead abacus slaves tells him that, at the moment of their death, they were working on the one-time pad for 6 August 1945, which is four months in the future. Waterhouse writes it down in the European style (day of the month first, then month) as 06081945, then lops off the leading zero to get 6,081,945—a pure quantity, an integer, unmarred by decimal point, rounding error, or any of the other compromises so abhorrent to number theorists. He uses this as one of the inputs to the zeta function. The zeta function requires a few other inputs too, which the person who designed this cryptosystem (presumably Rudy) was at liberty to choose. Surmising which inputs Rudy used has occupied much of Waterhouse's thoughts in the last week. He puts in the numbers he has guessed, anyway, which is a matter of converting them to binary notation and then physically incarnating those ones and zeros on a neat row of stainless-steel toggle switches: down for zero, up for one.

Finally he puts on his artilleryman's ear protectors and lets the Digital Computer howl through the calculation. The room gets much hotter. A vacuum tube burns out, and then another one. Waterhouse replaces them. That's easy because Lieutenant Colonel Comstock has made a basically infinite supply of tubes available to him—quite a remarkable feat during wartime. The filaments of all those massed tubes glow redly and shine palpable radiant heat across the room. The smell of hot oil rises from the louvers on the ETC card machines. The stack of blank cards in the input hopper shortens mysteriously as they vanish into the machine. Cards skitter into the output bin. Waterhouse pulls them out and looks at them. His heart is pounding very hard.

It's quiet again. The cards have numbers on them, nothing more. They just happen to be exactly the same numbers that were frozen on certain abaci down in the room of the computer slaves.

Lawrence Pritchard Waterhouse has just demolished another enemy cryptosystem: Azure/Pufferfish may now be mounted like a stuffed head on the wall of the Basement. And indeed, looking at those numbers he feels the same kind of letdown that a big game hunter must feel when he's stalked some legendary beast halfway across Africa and finally brought it down with a slug through the heart, walked up to the corpse, and discovered that after all it's just a big, messy, pile of meat. It's dirty and it's got flies on it. Is that all there is to it? Why didn't he solve this thing a long time ago? All of the old Azure/Pufferfish intercepts can be decrypted now. He'll have to read them, and they will turn out to be the usual numb mutterings of giant bureaucracies trying to take over the world. He doesn't, frankly, care anymore. He just wants to get the hell out of here and get married, play the organ, and program his Digital Computer, and hopefully get someone to pay him a salary to do one or the other. But Mary's in Brisbane and the war's not over yet—we haven't even gotten around to invading Nippon, for crissakes, and conquering the place is going to take *forever,* with all those plucky Nipponese women and children drilling on soccer fields with pointed bamboo staves—and it's probably going to be something like 1955 before he can even get discharged from the military. The war is not over yet, and as long as it goes on they will need him to stay down here in the Basement doing more of what he just did.

Arethusa. He still hasn't broken Arethusa. Now *that's* a cryptosystem! He's too tired. He can't break Arethusa just now.

What he really needs is someone to talk to. Not about anything in particular. Just to talk. But there's only half a dozen people on the planet he can really talk to, and none of them is in the Philippines. Fortunately, there are long copper wires running underneath the oceans which made geographical location irrelevant, as long as you have the right clearance. Waterhouse does. He gets up and leaves the Basement and goes to have a chat with his friend Alan.

AKIHABARA

As Randy's plane banks into Narita, a low stratum of cloud screens the countryside like a silk veil. It must be Nippon: the only two colors are the orange of the earth-moving equipment and the green of the earth that has not yet been moved. Other than that, everything is greyscale: grey parking lots divided into rectangles by white lines, the rectangles occupied with black, white, or grey cars, fading off into silvery fog beneath a sky the color of aviation alloy. Nippon is soothing, a good destination for a man who has just been rousted from his jail cell, hauled up before a judge, tongue-lashed, driven to the airport, and expelled from the Philippines.

The Nipponese look more American than Americans. Middle-class prosperity is lapidary; the flow of cash rounds and smooths a person like water does riverbed stones. The goal of all such persons seems to be to make themselves cuddly and nonthreatening. The girls in particular are unbearably precious, although perhaps Randy just thinks so because of that troublesome neurological hookup between his brain and Little Man 'tate. The old folks, instead of looking weathered and formidable, tend to wear sneakers and baseball caps. Black leather, studs, and handcuffs-as-accessories are the marks of the powerless lower classes, the people who tend to end up in the pokey in Manila, and not of the persons who actually dominate the world and crush everything in their path.

"The doors are about to close." "The bus is leaving in five minutes." Nothing happens in Nippon without a perky, breathy woman's voice giving you a chance to brace yourself. It is safe to say that this is not true of the Philippines. Randy thinks about taking a bus into Tokyo until he comes to his senses and remembers that he's carrying around in his head the precise coordinates of a mine that probably contains not less than a thousand tons of gold. He hails a taxi. On the way into town, he passes by a road accident: a tanker truck has crossed the white line and flipped over on the shoulder. But in Nippon, even traffic accidents have the grave precision of ancient Shinto rituals. White-gloved cops direct traffic, moon-suited rescue workers descend from spotless emergency vans. The taxi passes beneath Tokyo Bay through a tunnel that was built, three decades ago, by Goto Engineering.

Randy ends up in a big old hotel, "old" meaning that the physical structure was constructed during the fifties, when Americans competed with Soviets to build the most brutalistic space-age buildings out of the most depressing industrial materials. And indeed one can easily imagine Ike and Mamie pulling up to the front door in a five-ton Lincoln Continental. Of course the interior has been gutted and redone more frequently than many hotels steam-clean their carpets, and so everything is perfect. Randy has a strong impulse to lie in bed like a sack of shit, but he is tired of being confined. And there are many people he could talk to on the phone, but he is supremely paranoid about telephone conversations now. Any talking that he might do would have to be censored. Talking openly and freely is a pleasure, talking carefully is work, and Randy doesn't feel like work. He calls his parents to tell them everything's fine, calls Chester to thank him.

Then he takes his laptop downstairs and sits in the middle of the hotel's lobby, which is ostentatiously vast by Tokyo standards; the value of the land beneath the lobby alone probably exceeds that of Cape Cod. No one can even get near him with a Van Eck antenna here, and even if they do there will be plenty of interference from the nearby computers of the concierge desk. He starts ordering drinks, alternating between brutally cold pale Nipponese beer and hot tea, and writes a memo explaining more or less what he has spent the last month accomplishing. He writes it very slowly because his hands are practically immobilized now by carpal tunnel syndrome, and any motion that even faintly resembles typing causes him a lot of pain. He ends up cadging a pencil from the concierge and then using its eraser to punch the keys one at a time. The memo begins with the word "carpal" which is a little code that they have developed to explain why the following text seems unnaturally terse and devoid of capital letters. He's barely got that tapped out when he's approached by a devastatingly cute and fluttery young thing in a kimono who tells him that there is a staff of typists on call in the Business Center to help him with this should he desire it. Randy declines as politely as he knows how, which is probably not politely enough. Kimono Girl backs away in tiny steps, bowing and uttering truncated subvocal *hais*. Randy goes back to work with the pencil eraser. He explains, as briefly and clearly as he can, what he's been doing, and what he thinks is going on with General Wing and Enoch Root. He leaves the subject of what the fuck's going on with the Dentist open for speculation.

When he's done, he encrypts it and then goes up to his room to e-mail it. He can't get over the cleanliness of his lodgings. The sheets appear to have been tightened around the mattress with turnbuckles, then dipped in starch. This is the first time in over a month that he hasn't had the warm wet reek of sewer gas climbing up his nostrils and the ammoniacal tang of evaporating urine stinging his eyes. Somewhere in Nippon, a man in a clean white coverall stands in a room with a fat hose-fed gun vomiting freshly chopped glass fibers slathered with polyester resin onto a curvaceous form; peeled off the form, the result is bathrooms like this one: a single topological surface pierced in at most two or three places by drains and nozzles. While Randy's e-mailing his memo he lets hot water run into the largest and smoothest depression in the bathroom-surface. Then he takes off his clothes and climbs into it. He never takes baths, but between the foulness that seems infused into his flesh now, and the throbbing of his Hunk of Burning Love, there was never a better time.

The last few days were the worst. When Randy finished his project, and displayed the bogus results on the screen, he expected that the cell door would swing open immediately. That he'd walk out onto the streets of Manila and that, just for extra bonus points, Amy might even be waiting for him. But nothing at all happened for a whole day, and then Attorney Alejandro came to tell him that a deal might be possible but that it would take some work. And then it turned out that the deal was actually a pretty bad one: Randy was not going to be exonerated as such. He was going to be deported from the country under orders not to come back. Attorney Alejandro never claimed that this was a particularly good deal, but something in his manner made it clear that there was no point griping about it; The Decision Had Been Made at levels that were not accessible.

He could very easily take care of the Hunk of Burning Love problem now that he has privacy, but astonishes himself by electing not to. This may be perverse; he's not sure. The last month and a half of total celibacy, relieved only by nocturnal emissions at roughly two-week intervals, has definitely got him in a mental space he has never been to before, or come near, or even heard about. When he was in jail he had to develop a fierce mental discipline in order not to be distracted by thoughts of sex. He got alarmingly good at it after a while. It's a highly unnatural approach to the mind/body problem, pretty much the antithesis of every sixties and seventies-tinged philosophy that he ever imbibed from his Baby Boomer elders. It is the kind of thing he associates with scary hardasses: Spartans, Victorians, and mid-twentieth-century American military heroes. It has turned Randy into something of a hardass in his approach to hacking, and meanwhile, he suspects, it has got him into a much more intense and passionate head space than he's ever known when it comes to matters of the heart. He won't really know that until he comes face to face with Amy, which looks like it's going to be a while, since he's just been kicked out of the country where she lives and works. Just as an experiment, he decides he's going to keep his hands off of himself for now. If it makes him a little tense and volatile compared to his pathologically mellow West Coast self, then so be it. One nice thing about being in Asia is that tense, volatile people blend right in. It's not like anyone ever died from being horny.

So he arises from the bath unsullied and wraps himself in a vestal white robe. His cell in Manila did not have a mirror. He knew he was probably losing weight, but not until he climbs out of the bath and gives himself a look in the mirror does he realize just how much. For the first time since he was an adolescent, he has a waist, which makes a white bathrobe into a quasi-practical garment.

He's scarcely recognizable. Before the beginning of this the Third Business Foray he kind of assumed that, going into his mid-thirties, he had figured out who he was, and that he'd keep being the way he was forever, except with a gradually decaying body and gradually increasing net worth. He didn't imagine it was possible to change so much, and he wonders where it's going to end. But this is nothing more than an anomalous moment of reflection. He shakes it off and gets back to his life.

The Nipponese have, and have always had, a marvelous skill with graphic images—this is clear in their manga and their anime, but reaches

its fullest expressive flower in safety ideograms. Licking red flames, buildings splitting and falling as the jagged earth parts beneath them, a fleeing
figure silhouetted in a doorway, suspended in the stroboscopic flash of a
detonation. The written materials accompanying these images are, of
course, not understandable to Randy, and so there is nothing for his
rational mind to work on; the terrifying ideograms blaze, fragmentary
nightmare images popping up on walls, and in the drawers of his room's
desk, whenever he lets his guard down for a moment. What he can read
is not exactly soothing. Trying to sleep, he lies in bed, mentally checking
the locations of his bedside emergency flashlight and the pair of freebie
slippers (much too small) thoughtfully left there so that he can sprint out
of the burning and collapsing hotel without cutting his feet to sashimi
when the next magnitude 8.0 tremblor shivers the windows out of their
frames. He stares up at the ceiling, which is fraught with safety equipment
whose LEDs form a glowering red constellation, a crouching figure
known to the ancient Greeks as Ganymede, the Anally Receptive Cup-
bearer, and to the Nipponese, as Hideo, the Plucky Disaster Relief
Worker, bending over to probe a pile of jagged concrete slabs for anything that's squishy. All of this leaves him in a state of free-floating terror.
He gets up at five in the morning, grabs two capsules of Japanese Snack
from his minibar, and leaves the hotel, following one of the two emergency exit routes that he has memorized. He starts wandering, thinking
it would be fun to get lost. Getting lost happens in about thirty seconds.
He should have brought his GPS, and marked the latitude and longitude
of the hotel.

The latitude and longitude of Golgotha are expressed, in the Arethusa
intercept, in degrees, minutes, seconds, and tenths of a second of latitude
and longitude. A minute is a nautical mile, a second is about a hundred
feet. In the seconds figure, the Golgotha numbers have one digit after
the decimal point, which implies a precision of ten feet. GPS receivers
can give you that kind of precision. Randy's not so sure about the
sextants that the Nipponese surveyors presumably used during the war.
Before he left, he wrote the numbers down on a scrap of paper, but he
rounded off the seconds part and just expressed it in the form of "XX
degrees and twenty and a half minutes" implying a precision of a couple
of thousand feet. Then he invented three other locations in the same
general vicinity, but miles away, and put them all into a list, with the
real location being number two on the list. Above it he wrote "Who
owns these parcels of land?" or, in crypto-speak, WHOOW NSTHE
SEPAR etc. and then spent an almost unbelievably tedious evening syn-
chronizing the two decks of cards and encrypting the entire message
with the Solitaire algorithm. He gave the ciphertext and the unused deck

to Enoch Root, then swiped the plaintext through some of the leftover grease in his dinner tray and left it by the open drain. Within the hour, a rat had come around and eaten it.

He wanders all day. At first it is just bleak and depressing and he thinks he's going to give up very soon, but then he gets into the spirit of it, and learns how to eat: you approach gentlemen on streetcorners selling little fried-octopus balls and make neolithic grunting noises and proffer yen until you discover food in your hands and then you eat it.

Through some kind of nerdish homing instinct he finds Akihabara, the electronics district, and spends a while wandering through stores looking at all of the consumer electronics that will go on sale in the States a year from now. That's where he is when his GSM telephone rings.

"Hello?"

"It's me. I'm standing behind a fat yellow line."

"Which airport?"

"Narita."

"Delighted to hear it. Tell your driver to take you to the Mr. Donut in Akihabara."

Randy's there an hour later, flipping through a phone-book-sized manga epic, when Avi walks in. The unspoken Randy/Avi greeting protocol dictates that they hug each other at this point, so they do, somewhat to the astonishment of their fellow donut-eaters who usually make do with bowing. The Mr. Donut is a three-level affair jammed into a sliver of real estate with approximately the same footprint as a spiral staircase and is quite crowded with people who took compulsory English in their excellent and highly competitive schools. Besides, Randy broadcast the time and location of the meeting over a radio an hour ago. So as long as they are there, Randy and Avi talk about relatively innocuous things. Then they go out for a stroll. Avi knows his way around this neighborhood. He leads Randy through a doorway and into nerdvana.

"Many people," Avi explains, "do not know that the word normally spelled and pronounced 'nirvana' can be more accurately transliterated 'nirdvana' or, arguably, 'nerdvana.' This is nerdvana. The nucleus around which Akihabara accreted. This is where the *pasocon otaku* go to get the stuff they need."

"*Pasocon otaku?*"

"Personal computer nerds," Avi says. "But as in so many other things, the Nipponese take it to an extreme that we barely imagine."

The place is laid out precisely like an Asian food market: it is a maze of narrow aisles winding among tiny stalls, barely larger than phone booths, where merchants have their wares laid out for inspection. The first thing they see is a wire stall: at least a hundred reels of different types and gauges of wire in gaily hued plastic insulation. "How apropos!" Avi says, admiring the display, "we need to talk about wires." It need not be stated that this place is a great venue for a conversation: the paths between the stalls are so narrow that they have to walk in single file. No one can follow them, or get close to them, here, without being ridiculously blatant. An array of soldering irons bristles wickedly, giving one stall the look of a martial arts store. Coffee-can-sized potentiometers are stacked in pyramids. "Tell me about wires," Randy says.

"I don't need to tell you how dependent we are on submarine cables," Avi says.

" 'We' meaning the Crypt, or society in general?"

"Both. Obviously the Crypt can't even function without communications linkages to the outside world. But the Internet and everything else are just as dependent on cables."

A *pasocon otaku* in a trench coat, holding a plastic bowl as shopping cart, hunches over a display of gleaming copper toroidal coils that look to have been hand-polished by the owner. Finger-sized halogen spotlights mounted on an overhead rack emphasize their geometric perfection.

"So?"

"So, cables are vulnerable."

They wander past a stall that specializes in banana plugs, with a sideline in alligator clips, arranged in colorful rosettes around disks of cardboard.

"Those cables used to be owned by PTAs. Which were basically just branches of governments. Hence they pretty much did what governments told them to. But the new cables going in today are owned and controlled by corporations beholden to no one except their investors. Puts certain governments in a position they don't like very much."

"Okay," Randy says, "they used to have ultimate control over how information flowed between countries in that they ran the PTTs that ran the cables."

"Yes."

"Now they don't."

"That's right. There's been this big transfer of power that has taken place under their noses, without their having foreseen it." Avi stops in front of a stall that sells LEDs in all manner of bubble-gum colors, packed into tiny boxes like ripe tropical fruits in crates, and standing up from cubes of foam like psychedelic mushrooms. He is making big transfer-of-power gestures with his hands, but to Randy's increasingly warped mind this looks like a man moving heavy gold bars from one pile to another. Across the aisle, they are being stared at by the dead eyes of a hundred miniature video cameras. Avi continues, "And as we've talked about many times, there are many reasons why different governments might want to control the flow of information. China might want to institute political censorship, whereas the U.S. might want to regulate electronic cash transfers so that they can keep collecting taxes. In the old days they could ultimately do this insofar as they owned the cables."

"But now they can't," Randy says.

"Now they can't, and this change happened very fast, or at least it looked fast to government with its retarded intellectual metabolism, and now they are way behind the curve, and scared and pissed off, and starting to lash out."

"They are?"

"They are."

"In what way are they lashing out?"

A toggle switch merchant snaps a rag over rows and columns of stainless steel merchandise. The tip of the rag breaks the sound barrier and generates a tiny sonic pop that blasts a dust mote from the top of a switch. Everyone is politely ignoring them. "Do you have any idea what down time on a state-of-the-art cable costs nowadays?"

"Of course I do," Randy says. "It can be hundreds of thousands of dollars a minute."

"That's right. And it takes at least a couple of days to repair a broken cable. A couple of days. A single break in a cable can cost the companies that own it tens or even hundreds of millions of dollars in lost revenue."

"But that hasn't been that much of an issue," Randy says. "The cables are plowed in so deeply now. They're only exposed in the deep ocean."

"Yes—where only an entity with the naval resources of a major government could sever them."

"Oh, shit!"

"This is the new balance of power, Randy."

"You can't seriously be telling me that governments are threatening to—"

"The Chinese have already done it. They cut an older cable—first-generation optical fiber—joining Korea to Nippon. The cable wasn't that important—they only did it as a warning shot. And what's the rule of thumb about governments cutting submarine cables?"

"That it's like nuclear war," Randy says. "Easy to start. Devastating in its results. So no one does it."

"But if the Chinese have cut a cable, then other governments with a vested interest in throttling information flow can say, 'Hey, the Chinese did it, we need to show that we can retaliate in kind.' "

"Is that actually happening?"

"No, no, no!" Avi says. They've stopped in front of the largest display of needlenose pliers Randy has ever seen. "It's all posturing. It's not aimed at other governments so much as at the entrepreneurs who own and operate the new cables."

Light dawns in Randy's mind. "Such as the Dentist."

"The Dentist has put more money into privately financed submarine cables than just about anyone. He has a minority stake in that cable that the Chinese cut between Korea and Nippon. So he's trapped like a rat. He has no choice—no choice at all—other than to do as he's told."

"And who's giving the orders?"

"I'm sure that the Chinese are very big in this—they don't have any internal checks and balances in their government, so they are more prone to do something that is grossly irregular like this."

"And they obviously have the most to lose from unfettered information flow."

"Yeah. But I'm just cynical enough to suspect that a whole lot of other governments are right behind them."

"If that's true," Randy says, "then everything is completely fucked. Sooner or later a cable-cutting war is going to break out. All the cables will get chopped through. End of story."

"The world doesn't work that way anymore, Randy. Governments get together and negotiate. Like they did in Brussels just after Christmas. They come up with agreements. War does not break out. Usually."

"So—there's an agreement in place?"

Avi shrugs. "As best as I can make out. A balance of power has been struck between the people who own navies—i.e., the people who have the ability to cut cables with impunity—and the people who own and operate cables. Each side is afraid of what the other can do to it. So they have come to a genteel understanding. The bureaucratic incarnation of it is IDTRO."

"And the Dentist is in on it."

"Precisely."

"So maybe the Ordo siege really was ultimately directed by the government."

"I very much doubt that Comstock ordered it," Avi says. "I think it was the Dentist demonstrating his loyalty."

"How about the Crypt? Is the sultan party to this understanding?"

Avi shrugs. "Pragasu isn't saying much. I told him what I have just told you. I laid out my theory of what is going on. He looked tolerantly amused. He did not confirm or deny. But he did give me cause to believe that the Crypt is still going to be up and running on schedule."

"See, I find that hard to believe," Randy says. "It seems like the Crypt is their worst nightmare."

"Whose worst nightmare?"

"Any government that needs to collect taxes."

"Randy, governments will always find ways to collect taxes. If worse comes to worst, the IRS can just base everything on property taxes— you can't hide real estate in cyberspace. But keep in mind that the U.S. government is only a part of this thing—the Chinese are very big in it, too."

"Wing!" Randy blurts. He and Avi cringe and look around them. The *pasocon otaku* don't care. A man selling rainbow-colored wire ribbons eyes them with polite curiosity, then looks away. They move out of the bazaar and onto the sidewalk. It has started to rain. A dozen nearly identical young women in miniskirts and high heels march in wedge formation down the center of the street sporting huge umbrellas blazoned with the face of a video game character.

"Wing's digging for gold in Bundok," Randy says. "He thinks he knows where Golgotha is. If he finds it, he'll need a really special kind of bank."

"He's not the only guy in the world who needs a special bank," Avi says. "Over the years, Switzerland has done a hell of a lot of business with governments, or people connected with governments. Why didn't Hitler invade Switzerland? Because the Nazis couldn't have done without it. So the Crypt definitely fills a niche."

"Okay," Randy says, "so the Crypt will be allowed to remain in existence."

"It has to. The world needs it," Avi says. "And we'll need it, when we dig up Golgotha."

Suddenly Avi's got an impish look on his face; he looks to have shed about ten years of age. This gets a belly-laugh out of Randy, the first time he's really laughed in a couple of months. His mood has gone through some seismic shift all of a sudden, the whole world looks different to him. "It's not enough to know where it is. Enoch Root says that these hoards were buried deep in mines, down in the hard rock. So we're not going to get that gold out without launching a pretty major engineering project."

"Why do you think I'm in Tokyo?" Avi says. "C'mon, let's get back to the hotel."

While Avi's checking in, Randy collects his messages from the front desk, and finds a FedEx envelope waiting for him. If it was tampered with en route, the tamperers did a good job of covering their traces. It contains a hand-enciphered message from Enoch Root, who evidently has figured out some way to get himself sprung from the clink with his scruples intact. It is several lines of seemingly random block letters, in groups of five. Randy has been carrying around a deck of cards ever since he got sprung from jail: the prearranged key that will decipher this message. The prospect of several hours of solitaire seems a lot less inviting in Tokyo than it did in prison—and he knows it will take that long to decipher a message as long as this one. But he's already programmed his laptop to play Solitaire according to Enoch's rules, and he's already punched in the key that is embodied in the deck that Enoch gave him and stored it on a floppy disk that he keeps rubber-banded to the deck in his pocket. So he and Avi go up to Avi's room, pausing along the way to collect Randy's laptop, and while Avi sorts through his messages, Randy types in the ciphertext and gets it deciphered. "Enoch's message says that the land above Golgotha is owned by the Church," Randy mutters, "but in order to reach it we have to travel across land owned by Wing, and by some Filipinos."

Avi doesn't appear to hear him. He's fixated on a message slip.

"What's up?" Randy asks.

"A little change of plans for tonight. I hope you have a really good suit with you."

"I didn't know we had plans for tonight."

"We were going to meet with Goto Furundenendu," Avi says. "I sort of figured that they were the right guys to approach about digging a big hole in the ground."

"I'm with you," Randy says. "What's the change in plan?"

"The old man is coming down from his retreat in Hokkaido. He wants to buy us dinner."

"What old man?"

"The founder of the company, Goto Furudenendu's father," Avi says. "Protegé of Douglas MacArthur. Multi-multi-multi-millionaire. Golf partner and confidant of prime ministers. An old guy by the name of Goto Dengo."

PROJECT X

IT IS EARLY IN APRIL OF THE YEAR 1945. A MIDDLE-AGED Nipponese widow feels the earth turning over, and scurries out of
her paper house, fearing a tremblor. Her house is on the island of Kyushu, near the sea. She gazes out over the ocean and sees a black ship on the horizon, steaming out of a rising sun of its own making: for when its guns go off the entire vessel is shrouded in red fire for a

moment. She hopes that the *Yamato*, the world's greatest battleship, which steamed away over that horizon a few days ago, has returned victorious, and is firing its guns in celebration. But this is an American battleship and it is dropping shells into the port that the *Yamato* just left, making the earth's bowels heave as if it were preparing to throw up.

Until this moment, the Nipponese woman has been convinced that the armed forces of her nation were crushing the Americans, the British, the Dutch, and the Chinese at every turn. This apparition must be some kind of bizarre suicide raid. But the black ship stays there all day long, heaving ton after ton of dynamite into sacred soil. No airplanes come out to bomb it, no ships to shell it, not even a submarine to torpedo it.

In a shocking display of bad form, Patton has lunged across the Rhine ahead of schedule, to the irritation of Montgomery who has been making laborious plans and preparations to do it first.

The German submarine U-234 is in the North Atlantic, headed for the Cape of Good Hope, carrying ten containers holding twelve hundred pounds of uranium oxide. The uranium is bound for Tokyo where it will be used in some experiments, still in a preliminary phase, towards the construction of a new and extremely powerful explosive device.

General Curtis LeMay's Air Force has spent much of the last month flying dangerously low over Nipponese cities showering them with incendiary devices. A quarter of Tokyo has been leveled; 83,000 people died there, and this does not count the similar raids on Nagoya, Osaka, and Kobe.

The night after the Osaka raid, some Marines raised a flag on Iwo Jima and they put a picture of it in all the papers.

Within the last few days, the Red Army, now the most terrible force on earth, has taken Vienna and the oil fields of Hungary, and the Soviets have declared that their Neutrality Pact with Nippon will be allowed to expire rather than being renewed.

Okinawa has just been invaded. The fighting is the worst ever. The invasion is supported by a vast fleet against which the Nipponese have launched everything they have. The *Yamato* came after them, her eighteen-inch guns at the ready, carrying only enough fuel for a one-way voyage. But the cryptanalysts of the U.S. Navy intercepted and decrypted her orders and the great ship was sent to the bottom with 2500 men. The Nipponese have launched the first of their Floating Chrysanthemum assaults against the invasion fleet: clouds of kamikaze planes, human bombs, human torpedoes, speedboats packed with explosives.

To the irritation and bafflement of the German High Command, the Nipponese government has sent a message to them, requesting that, in the event that all of Germany's European naval bases are lost, the Kriegsmarine should be given orders to continue operating with the Nipponese in the Far East. The message is encrypted in Indigo. It is duly intercepted and read by the Allies.

In the United Kingdom, Dr. Alan Mathison Turing, considering the war to be effectively finished, has long since turned his attentions away from the problem of voice encryption and into the creation of thinking machines. For about ten months—ever since the finished Colossus Mark II was delivered to Bletchley Park—he has had the opportunity to work with a truly programmable computing machine. Alan invented these machines long before one was ever built, and has never needed hands-on experience in order to think about them, but his experiences with Colossus Mark II have helped him to solidify some ideas of how the next machine ought to be designed. He thinks of it as a postwar machine, but that's only because he's in Europe and hasn't been concerned with the problem of conquering Nippon as much as Waterhouse has.

"I've been working on BURY and DISINTER," says a voice, coming out of small holes in a Bakelite headset clamped over Waterhouse's head. The voice is oddly distorted, nearly obscured by white noise and a maddening buzz.

"Please say it again?" Lawrence says, pressing the phones against his ear.

"BURY and DISINTER," says the voice. "They are, er, sets of instructions for the machine to execute, to carry out certain algorithms. They are programmes."

"Right! Sorry, I just wasn't able to hear you the first time. Yes, I've been working on them too," Waterhouse says.

"The next machine will have a memory storage system, Lawrence, in the form of sound waves traveling down a cylinder filled with mercury— we stole the idea from John Wilkins, founder of the Royal Society, who came up with it three hundred years ago, except he was going to use air instead of quicksilver. I—excuse me, Lawrence, did you say you had been working on them?"

"I did the same thing with tubes. Valves, as you would call them."

"Well that's all well and good for you Yanks," Alan says, "I suppose if you are infinitely rich you could make a BURY/DISINTER system out of steam locomotives, or something, and retain a staff of thousands to run around squirting oil on the squeaky bits."

"The mercury line is a good idea," Waterhouse admits. "Very resourceful."

"Have you actually gotten BURY and DISINTER to work with *valves?*"

"Yes. My DISINTER works better than our shovel expeditions," Lawrence says. "Did you ever find those silver bars you buried?"

"No," Alan says absently. "They are lost. Lost in the noise of the world."

"You know, that was a Turing test I just gave you," Lawrence says.

"Beg pardon?"

"This damned machine screws up your voice so bad I can't tell you from Winston Churchill," Lawrence says. "So the only way I can verify it's you is by getting you to say things that only Alan Turing could say."

He hears Alan's sharp, high-pitched laugh at the other end of the line. It's him all right.

"This Project X thing really is appalling," Alan says. "Delilah is infinitely superior. I wish you could see it for yourself. Or hear it."

Alan is in London, in a command bunker somewhere. Lawrence is in Manila Bay, on the Rock, the island of Corregidor. They are joined by a thread of copper that goes all the way around the world. There are many such threads traversing the floors of the world's oceans now, but only a few special ones go to rooms like this. The rooms are in Washington, London, Melbourne, and now, Corregidor.

Lawrence looks through a thick glass window into the engineer's booth, where a phonograph record is playing on the world's most precise and expensive turntable. This is, likewise, the most valuable record ever turned out: it is filled with what is intended to be perfectly random white noise. The noise is electronically combined with the sound of Lawrence's voice before it is sent down the wire. Once it gets to London, the noise (which is being read off an identical phonograph record there) is subtracted from his voice, and the result sent into Alan Turing's headphones. It all depends on the two phonographs being perfectly synchronized. The only way to synchronize them is to transmit that maddening buzzing noise, a carrier wave, along with the voice signal. If all goes well, the opposite phonograph player can lock onto the buzz and spin its wax in lockstep.

The phonograph record is, in other words, a one-time pad. Somewhere in New York, in the bowels of Bell Labs, behind a locked and guarded door stenciled PROJECT X, technicians are turning out more of these things, the very latest chart-topping white noise. They stamp out a few copies, dispatch them by courier to the Project X sites around the globe, then destroy the originals.

They would not be having this conversation at all, except that a couple of years ago Alan went to Greenwich Village and worked at Bell Labs for a few months, while Lawrence was on Qwghlm. H.M. Government sent him there to evaluate this Project X thing and let them know whether it was truly secure. Alan decided that it was—then went back home and began working on a much better one, called Delilah.

What the hell does this have to do with dead Chinese abacus slaves? To Lawrence, staring through the window at the spinning white-noise disk, the connection could hardly be clearer. He says, "Last I spoke to you, you were working on generating random noise for Delilah."

"Yes," Alan says absently. That was a long time ago, and that whole project has been BURIED in his memory storage system; it will take him a minute or two to DISINTER it.

"What sorts of algorithms did you consider to create that noise?"

There is another five-second pause, then Alan launches into a disquisition about mathematical functions for generating pseudorandom number sequences. Alan had a good British boarding-school education, and his utterances tend to be well-structured, with outline form, topic sentences, the whole bit:

PSEUDO-RANDOM NUMBERS

I.   Caveat: they aren't really random, of course, they just look that way, and that's why the pseudo-
II. Overview of the Problem
   A. It seems as if it should be easy
   B. Actually it turns out to be really hard
   C. Consequences of failure: Germans decrypt our secret messages, millions die, humanity is enslaved, world plunged into an eternal Dark Age
   D. How can you tell if a series of numbers is random
      1, 2, 3, . . . (A list of different statistical tests for randomness, the advantages and disadvantages of each)
III. A bunch of stuff that I, Alan Turing, tried
      A, B, C, . . . (A list of different mathematical functions that Alan used to generate random numbers; how almost all of them failed abjectly; Alan's initial confidence is replaced by surprise, then exasperation, then despair, and finally by guarded confidence as he at last finds some techniques that work)
IV. Conclusions
   A. It's harder than it looks
   B. It's not for the unwary
   C. It can be done if you keep your wits about you
   D. In retrospect a surprisingly interesting mathematical problem deserving of further research

When Alan finishes with this perfectly structured whirlwind tour of the Surprising World of Pseudo-Randomness, Lawrence says, "How about zeta functions?"

"Didn't even consider those," Alan says.

Lawrence's mouth drops open. He can see his own semitransparent reflection in the window, superimposed on the spinning phonograph, and he sees that he has got a sort of mildly outraged look on his face. There must be something conspicuously nonrandom about the output of the zeta function, something so obvious to Alan that he dismissed it out of hand. But Lawrence has never seen any such thing. He knows that Alan is smarter than he is, but he's not used to being so desperately far behind him.

"Why . . . why not?" he finally stammers.

"Because of Rudy!" Alan thunders. "You and I and Rudy all worked on that damn machine at Princeton! Rudy knows that you and I have the knowledge to build such a device. So it is the first thing that he would assume we would use."

"Ah." Lawrence sighs. "But leaving that aside, the zeta function might still be a good way of doing it."

"It might," Alan says guardedly, "but I have not investigated it. You're not thinking of using it, are you?"

Lawrence tells Alan about the abaci. Even through the noise and the buzz, he can tell that Alan is thunderstruck. There is a pause while the technicians at each end flip over their phonograph records. When the connection is reestablished, Alan's still very excited. "Let me tell you something more," Lawrence says.

"Yes, go ahead."

"You know that the Nipponese use a plethora of different codes, and we still have only broken some of them."

"Yes."

"There is an unbroken cipher system that Central Bureau calls Arethusa. It's incredibly rare. Only thirty-some Arethusa messages have ever been intercepted."

"Some company code?" Alan asks. This is a good guess; each major Nipponese corporation had its own code system before the war, and much effort has gone into stealing code books for, and otherwise breaking, the Mitsubishi code, to name one example.

"We can't figure out the sources and destinations of Arethusa messages," Lawrence continues, "because they use a unique site code system. We can only guess at their origins by using huffduff. And huffduff tells us that most of the Arethusa messages have originated from submarines. Possibly just a single submarine, plying the route between Europe and Southeast Asia. We have also seen them from Sweden, from London, Buenos Aires, and Manila."

"Buenos Aires? Sweden?"

"Yes. And so, Alan, I took an interest in Arethusa."

"Well, I don't blame you!"

"The message format matches that of Azure/Pufferfish."

"Rudy's system?"

"Yes."

"Nice work on that, by the way."

"Thank you, Alan. As you must have heard by now, it is based on zeta functions. Which you did not even consider using for Delilah because you were afraid Rudy would think of it. And this raises the question of whether Rudy intended us to break Azure/Pufferfish all along."

"Yes, it does. But why would he want us to?"

"I have no idea. The old Azure/Pufferfish messages may contain some clues. I am having my Digital Computer generate retroactive one-time pads so that I can decrypt those messages and read them."

"Well, then, I shall have Colossus do the same. It is busy just now," Alan says, "working on Fish decrypts. But I don't think Hitler has much longer to go. When he is finished, I can probably get down to Bletchley and decrypt those messages."

"I'm also working on Arethusa," Lawrence says. "I'm guessing it all has something to do with gold."

"Why do you say that?" Alan says. But at this point the tone arm of the phonograph reaches the end of its spiral groove and lifts off the record. Time's up. Bell Labs, and the might of the Allied governments, did not install the Project X network so that mathematicians could indulge in endless chitchat about obscure functions.

LANDFALL

THE SAILING SHIP GERTRUDE WHEEZES INTO THE COVE SHORTLY after sunrise, and Bischoff cannot help but laugh. Barnacles have grown so thick around her hull that the hull itself (he supposes) could be removed entirely, and the shell of barnacles could be outfitted with a mast and canvas, and sailed to Tahiti. A hundred-yard-long skein of seaweed, rooted in those barnacles, trails behind her, making a long greasy disturbance in her wake. Her mast has evidently been snapped off at least once. It has been replaced by a rude jury-rigged thing, a tree trunk that has received some attention from a drawknife but still has bark adhering to it in places, and long dribbles of golden sap like wax trails on a candle, themselves streaked with sea salt. Her sails are nearly black with dirt and mildew, and rudely patched, here and there, with fat black stitches, like the flesh of Frankenstein's monster.

The men on board are scarcely in better shape. They do not even bother to drop anchor—they just run *Gertrude* aground on a coral head at the entrance to the cove, and call it a day. Most of Bischoff's crew has gathered on the top of *V-Million,* the rocket-submarine, they think it's the most hilarious thing they've ever seen. But when the men on *Gertrude* climb into a dinghy and begin rowing towards them, Bischoff's men remember their manners, and stand at attention, and salute.

Bischoff tries to recognize them as they row closer. It takes a while. There are five in all. Otto has lost his pot-belly and gone much greyer. Rudy is a completely different man: he has long flowing hair ponytailed down his back, and a surprisingly thick, Viking-like beard, and he appears to have lost his left eye somewhere along the way, because he's got an actual black patch over it!

"My god," Bischoff says, "pirates!"

The other three men he has never seen before: a Negro with dreadlocks; a brown-skinned, Indian-looking fellow; and a red-headed European.

Rudy is watching a stingray furling and unfurling its meaty wings ten meters straight down.

"The clarity of the water is exquisite," he remarks.

"When the Catalinas come for us, Rudy, then you will long for the old northern murk," Bischoff says.

Rudolf von Hacklheber swings his one eye around to bear on Bischoff, and allows just a trace of amusement to show on his face. "Permission to come aboard, Captain?" Rudy asks.

"Granted with pleasure," Bischoff says. The dinghy has come alongside the round hull of the submarine, and Bischoff's crew unrolls a rope ladder to them. "Welcome to the *V-Million!*"

"I have heard of the V-1 and the V-2, but . . ."

"We could not guess how many other V-weapons Hitler might have invented, and so we chose a very, very large number," Bischoff says proudly.

"But Günter, you know what the V stands for?"

"*Vergeltungswaffen,*" Bischoff says. "You're not thinking about it hard enough, Rudy."

Otto's puzzled, and being puzzled makes him angry. "*Vergeltung* means revenge, doesn't it?"

"But it can also mean to pay someone back, to compensate them, to reward them," says Rudy, "even to *bless* them. I like it very much, Günter."

"Admiral Bischoff to you," Günter returns.

"You are the supreme commander of the *V-Million*—there is no one above you?"

Bischoff clicks his heels together sharply and holds out his right arm. "Heil Dönitz!" he shouts.

"What the hell are you talking about?" asks Otto.

"Haven't you been reading the papers? Hitler killed himself yesterday. In Berlin. The new Führer is my personal friend Karl Dönitz."

"Is *he* part of the conspiracy too?" Otto mutters.

"I thought my dear mentor and protector Hermann Göring was going to be Hitler's successor," Rudy says, sounding almost crestfallen.

"He is down in the south somewhere," Bischoff says, "on a diet. Just before Hitler took cyanide, he ordered the SS to arrest that fat bastard."

"But in all seriousness, Günter—when you boarded this U-boat in Sweden, it was called something else, and there were some Nazis on board, yes?" asks Rudy.

"I had completely forgotten about them." Bischoff cups his hands around his mouth and shouts down the hatch in the top of the sleek rounded-off conning tower. "Has anyone seen our Nazis?"

The command echoes down the length of the U-boat from sailor to sailor: *Nazis? Nazis? Nazis?* but somewhere it turns into *Nein! Nein! Nein!* and echoes back up the conning tower and out the hatch.

Rudy climbs up *V-Million*'s smooth hull on bare feet. "Do you have any citrus fruit?" He smiles, showing magenta craters in his gums where teeth might be expected.

"Get the calamansis," Bischoff says to one of his mates. "Rudy, for you we have the Filipino miniature limes, great piles of them, with more vitamin C than you could ever want."

"I doubt that," Rudy says.

Otto just looks at Bischoff reproachfully, holding him personally responsible for having been thrown together with these four other men for all of 1944 and the first four months of 1945. Finally he speaks: "Is that son of a bitch Shaftoe here?"

"That son of a bitch Shaftoe is dead," Bischoff says.

Otto averts his glare and nods his head.

"I take it you received my letter from Buenos Aires?" asks Rudy von Hacklheber.

"Mr. G. Bishop, General Delivery, Manila, the Philippines," Bischoff recites. "Of course I did, my friend, or else we would not have known where to meet you. I picked it up when I went into town to renew my acquaintance with Enoch Root."

"He made it?"

"He made it."

"How did Shaftoe die?"

"Gloriously, of course," Bischoff says. "And there is other news from Julieta: the conspiracy has a son! Congratulations, Otto, you are a grand-uncle."

This actually elicits a smile, albeit black and gappy, from Otto. "What's his name?"

"Günter Enoch Bobby Kivistik. Eight pounds, three ounces—superb for a wartime baby."

There is hand-shaking all around. Rudy, ever debonair, produces some Honduran cigars to mark the occasion. He and Otto stand in the sun and smoke cigars and drink calamansi juice.

"We have been waiting here for three weeks," Bischoff says. "What kept you?"

Otto spits out something that is pretty bad-looking. "I am sorry that you have had to spend three weeks tanning yourselves on the beach while we have been sailing this tub of shit across the Pacific!"

"We were dismasted, and lost three men, and my left eye, and two of Otto's fingers, and a few other items, going around Cape Horn," Rudy says apologetically. "Our cigars got a little wet. It played havoc with our schedule."

"No matter," Bischoff says. "The gold isn't going anywhere."

"Do we know where it is?"

"Not exactly. But we have found one who does."

"Clearly, we have much to discuss," Rudy says, "but I have to die first. Preferably on a soft bed."

"Fine," Bischoff says. "Is there anything that needs to be removed from *Gertrude* before we cut her throat, and let her barnacles pull her to the bottom?"

"Sink the bitch now, please," Otto says. "I will even stay up here and watch."

"First you must remove five crates marked *Property of the Reichsmarschall*," Rudy says. "They are down in the bilge. We used them as ballast."

Otto looks startled, and scratches his beard in wonderment. "I forgot those were down there." The year-and-a-half-old memory is slowly resolving in his mind's eye. "It took a whole day to load them in. I wanted to kill you. My back still aches from it."

Bischoff says, "Rudy—you made off with Göring's pornography collection?"

"I wouldn't like *his* kind of pornography," Rudy answers evenly. "These are cultural treasures. Loot."

"They will have been ruined by bilge water!"

"It's all gold. Sheets of gold foil with holes in it. Impervious."

"Rudy, we are supposed to be *exporting* gold from the Philippines, not *importing* it."

"Don't worry. I shall export it again one day."

"By that time, we'll have money to hire stevedores, so poor Otto won't have to put his back out again."

"We won't need stevedores," Rudy says. "When I export what is on those sheets, I'll do it on wires."

They all stand there on the deck of *V-Million* in the tropical cove watching the sun set and the flying fish leap and hearing birds and insects cry and buzz from the flowering jungle all around. Bischoff's trying to imagine wires strung from here to Los Angeles, and sheets of gold foil sliding down them. It doesn't really work. "Come below, Rudy," he says, "we need to get some vitamin C into you."

GOTO-SAMA

AVI MEETS RANDY IN THE HOTEL LOBBY. HE HAS BURDENED HIM-self with a square, old-fashioned briefcase that pulls his slender frame to one side, giving him the asymptotic curve of a sapling in a steady wind. He and Randy take a taxi to Some Other Part of Tokyo—Randy cannot begin to fathom how the city is laid out—enter the lobby of a skyscraper, and take an elevator up far enough that Randy's ears pop. When the doors slide open, a maître d' is standing right there anticipating them with a radiant smile and a bow. He leads them into a foyer where four men wait: a couple of younger minions; Goto Furude-nendu; and an elderly gentleman. Randy was expecting one of these gracile, translucent Nipponese seniors, but Goto Dengo is a blocky fellow with a white buzz-cut, somewhat hunched and collapsed with age, which only goes to make him seem more compact and solid. At first blush he seems more like a retired village blacksmith, or perhaps a master sergeant in a daimyo's army, than a business executive, and yet within five or ten seconds this impression is swallowed up by a good suit, good manners, and Randy's knowledge of who he really is. He's the only guy in the place who isn't grinning from ear to ear: apparently when you reach a certain age you are allowed to get away with staring tunnels through other people's skulls. In the manner of many old people, he looks vaguely startled that they have actually shown up.

Still, he levers himself up on a big, gnarled cane and shakes their hands firmly. His son Furudenendu proffers a hand to help him to his feet and he shrugs it off with glare of mock outrage—this transaction looks pretty well-practiced. There's a brief exchange of small talk that goes right over Randy's head. Then the two minions peel off, like a fighter escort no longer needed, and the maître d' leads Randy, Avi, and Goto *père et fils* across a totally empty restaurant—twenty or thirty tables set with white linen and crystal—to a corner table, where waiters stand at attention to pull their chairs back. This building is of the sheer-walls-of-solid glass school of architecture and so the windows go floor-to-ceiling, providing, through a bead curtain of raindrops, a view of nighttime Tokyo that stretches over the horizon. Menus are handed out, printed in French only. Randy and Avi get the girl menus, with no prices. Goto Dengo gets the wine list, and pores over it for a good ten minutes before grudgingly selecting a white from California and a red from Burgundy. Meanwhile, Furudenendu is leading them in exceedingly pleasant small talk about the Crypt.

Randy can't stop looking at Tokyo on the one hand and the empty restaurant on the other. It's like this setting was picked specifically to remind them that the Nipponese economy has been on the skids for the last several years—a situation that the Asian currency crisis has only worsened. He half expects to see executives dropping past the window.

Avi ventures to ask about various tunnels and other stupefyingly vast engineering projects that he happens to have noticed around Tokyo and whether Goto Engineering had anything to do with them. This at least gets the patriarch to glance up momentarily from his wine list, but the son handles the inquiries, allowing as how, yes, their company did play a small part in those endeavors. Randy figures that it's not the easiest thing in the world to engage a personal friend of the late General of the Army Douglas MacArthur in polite chitchat; it's not like you can ask him if he caught the latest episode of *Star Trek: More Time-Space Anomalies*. All they can really do is cling to Furudenendu and let him take the lead. Goto Dengo clears his throat like the engine of a major piece of earth-moving equipment rumbling to life, and recommends the Kobe beef. The sommelier comes around with the wines and Goto Dengo interrogates him in a mixture of Nipponese and French for a while, until a film of sweat has broken out on the sommelier's brow. He samples the wines very carefully. The tension is explosive as he swirls them around in his mouth, staring off into the distance. The sommelier seems genuinely startled, not to mention relieved, when he accepts both of them. The subtext here would seem to be that hosting a really first-class dinner is a not insignificant management challenge, and that Goto Dengo should not be bothered with social chatter while he is coping with these responsibilities.

At this point Randy's paranoia finally kicks in: is it possible that Goto-sama bought the whole restaurant out for the evening, just to get a little privacy? Were the two minions just aides with unusually bulky briefcases, or were they security, sweeping the place for surveillance devices? Again, subtext-wise, the message seems to be that Randy and Avi are not to worry their pretty, young little heads about these things. Goto Dengo is seated underneath a can light in the ceiling. His hair stands perpendicularly out from his head, a bristling stand of normal vectors, radiating halogenically. He has a formidable number of scars on his face and his hands, and Randy suddenly realizes that he must have been in the war. Which should've been perfectly obvious considering his age.

Goto Dengo inquires about how Randy and Avi got into their current lines of work, and how they formed their partnership. This is a reasonable question, but it forces them to explain the entire concept of fantasy role-playing games. If Randy had known this would happen, he would have thrown himself bodily through a window instead of taking a seat. But Goto Dengo takes it pretty calmly and instantly cross-correlates it to late-breaking developments in the Nipponese game industry, which has been doing this gradual paradigm shift from arcade to role-playing games with actual narratives; by the time he's finished he makes them feel not like lightweight nerds but like visionary geniuses who were ten years ahead of their time. This more or less obligates Avi (who is taking conversational point) to ask Goto Dengo how he got into *his* line of work. Both of the Gotos try to laugh it off, as if how could a couple of young American visionary Dungeons and Dragons pioneers possibly be interested in something as trivial as how Goto Dengo singlehandedly rebuilt postwar Nippon, but after Avi displays a bit of persistence, the patriarch finally shrugs and says something about how his pop was in the mining racket and so he's always had a certain knack for digging holes in the ground. His English started out minimal and is getting better and better as the evening proceeds, as if he is slowly dusting off substantial banks of memory and processing power, nursing them on-line like tube amplifiers.

Dinner arrives; and so everyone has to eat for a bit, and to thank Goto-sama for his excellent recommendation. Avi gets a bit reckless and asks the old man if he might regale them with some reminiscences about Douglas MacArthur. He grins, as if some secret has been ferreted out of him, and says, "I met the General in the Philippines." Just like that, he's jujitsued the topic of conversation around to what everyone actually wants to talk about. Randy's pulse and respiration ratchet up by a good twenty-five percent and all of his senses become more acute, almost as if his ears have popped again, and he loses his appetite. Everyone else seems to be sitting up a bit straighter too, shifting in their chairs slightly. "Did you spend much time in that country?" Avi asks.

"Oh, yes. Much time. A hundred years," says Goto Dengo, with a rather frosty grin. He pauses, giving everyone a chance to get good and uneasy, and then continues, "My son tells me that you want to dig a grave there."

"A hole," Randy ventures, after much uncomfortableness.

"Excuse me. My English is rusty," says Goto Dengo, none too convincingly.

Avi says, "What we have in mind would be a major excavation by our standards. But probably not by yours."

Goto Dengo chuckles. "That all depends on the circumstances. Permits. Transportation issues. The Crypt was a big excavation, but it was easy, because the sultan was supporting it."

"I must emphasize that the work we are considering is still in a very early planning phase," Avi says. "I regret to say I can't give you good information about the logistical issues."

Goto Dengo comes this close to rolling his eyes. "I understand," he says with a dismissive wave of the hand. "We will not talk about these things this evening."

This produces a really awkward pause, while Randy and Avi ask themselves *what the hell are we going to talk about then?* "Very well," Avi says, sort of weakly lobbing the ball back in Goto Dengo's general direction.

Furudenendo steps in. "There are many people who dig holes in the Philippines," he explains with a big knowing wink.

"Ah!" Randy says. "I have met some of the people you are talking about!" This produces a general outburst of laughter around the table, which is none the less sincere for being tense.

"You understand, then," says Furudenendo, "that we would have to study a joint venture very carefully." Even Randy easily translates this to: *we will participate in your loony-tunes treasure hunt when hell freezes over.*

"Please!" Randy says, "Goto Engineering is a distinguished company. Top of the line. You have much better things to do than to gamble on joint ventures. We would never propose such a thing. We would be able to pay for your services up front."

"Ah!" The Gotos look at each other significantly. "You have a new investor?" *We know you are broke.*

Avi grins. "We have new resources." This leaves the Gotos nonplussed. "If I may," Avi says. He heaves his briefcase up off the floor and onto his lap, flips the latches open, and reaches into it with both hands. Then he performs a maneuver that, in a bodybuilding gym, would be called a barbell curl, and lifts a brick of solid gold into the light.

The faces of Goto Dengo and Goto Furudenendo are transmuted to stone. Avi holds the bar up for a few moments, then lowers it back into his briefcase.

Eventually, Furudenendo scoots his chair back a couple of centimeters and rotates it slightly toward his father, basically excusing himself from the conversation. Goto Dengo eats dinner and drinks wine calmly, and silently, for a very, very long fifteen or twenty minutes. Finally, he looks across the table at Randy and says, "Where do you want to dig?"

"The site is in mountains south of Laguna de Bay—"

"Yes, you already told my son that. But that is a large area of boondocks. Many holes have been dug there. All worthless."

"We have better information."

"Some old Filipino has sold you his memories?"

"Better than that," Randy says. "We have a latitude and longitude."

"To what degree of precision?"

"Tenths of a second."

This occasions another pause. Furudenendo tries to say something in Nipponese, but his father cuts him off gruffly. Goto Dengo finishes his dinner and crosses his fork and knife on the plate. A waiter's there five seconds later to clear the table. Goto Dengo says something to him that sends him fleeing back into the kitchen. They have essentially a whole floor of the skyscraper to themselves now. Goto Dengo utters something to his son, who produces a fountain pen and two business cards. Furudenendo hands the pen, and one card, to his father, and the other card to Randy. "Let's play a little game," Goto Dengo says. "You have a pen?"

"Yes," Randy says.

"I am going to write down a latitude and longitude," Goto Dengo says, "but only the seconds portion. No degrees and no minutes. Only the seconds part. You understand?"

"Yes."

"The information is useless by itself. You agree?"

"Yes."

"Then there is no risk for you to write down the same."

"It's true."

"Then we will exchange cards. Agreed?"

"I agree."

"Very well." Goto Dengo starts writing. Randy takes a pen from his pocket and jots down the seconds and tenths of a second: latitude 35.2, longitude 59.0. When he's done, Goto Dengo's looking at him expectantly. Randy holds out his card, numbers facing down, and Goto Dengo holds out his. They exchange them with the small bow that is obligatory around here. Randy cups Goto-sama's card in his palm and turns it into the light. It says

35.2/59.0

No one says anything for ten minutes. It's a measure of how stunned Randy is that he doesn't realize, for a long time, that Goto Dengo is just as stunned as he is. Avi and Furudenendu are the only people at the table whose minds are still functioning, and they spend the whole time looking at each other uncertainly, neither one really understanding what's going on.

Finally Avi says something that Randy doesn't hear. He nudges Randy firmly and says it again: "I'm going to the lavatory."

Randy watches him go, counts to ten, and says, "Excuse me." He follows Avi to the men's washroom: black polished stone, thick white towels, Avi standing there with his arms crossed. "He knows," Randy says.

"I don't believe it."

Randy shrugs. "What can I say? He knows."

"If he knows, everyone knows. Our security broke down somewhere along the line."

"Everyone doesn't know," Randy says. "If everyone knew, all hell would be breaking loose down there, and Enoch would have gotten word to us."

"Then how can he know?"

"Avi," Randy says, "*he must be the one who buried it.*"

Avi looks outraged. "Are you shitting me?"

"You have a better theory?"

"I thought all the people who buried the stuff were killed."

"It's fair to say that he's a survivor. Wouldn't you agree?"

Ten minutes later they return to the table. Goto Dengo has allowed the restaurant staff back into the room, and dessert menus have been brought out. Weirdly, the old man has gone back into polite chitchat mode, and Randy gradually figures out that he's trying to work out how the hell Randy knows what he knows. Randy mentions, offhandedly, that his grandfather was a cryptanalyst in Manila in 1945. Goto Dengo sighs, visibly, with relief and cheers up somewhat. Then it's more completely meaningless chatter until postprandial coffee has been served, at which point the patriarch leans forward to make a point. "Before you sip—look!"

Randy and Avi look into their cups. A weirdly glittering layer of scum is floating atop their coffee.

"It is gold," Furudenendu explains. Both of the Gotos laugh. "During the eighties, when Nippon had so much money, this was the fashion: coffee with gold dust. Now it is out of fashion. Too ostentatious. But you go ahead and drink."

Randy and Avi do—a bit nervously. The gold dust coats their tongues, then washes away down their throats.

"Tell me what you think," Goto Dengo demands.

"It's stupid," Randy says.

"Yes." Goto Dengo nods solemnly. "It is stupid. So tell me, then: why do you want to dig up more of it?"

"We're businessmen," Avi says. "We make money. Gold is worth money."

"Gold is the corpse of value," says Goto Dengo.

"I don't understand."

"If you want to understand, look out the window!" says the patriarch, and sweeps his cane around in an arc that encompasses half of Tokyo. "Fifty years ago, it was flames. Now it is lights! Do you understand? The leaders of Nippon were stupid. They took all of the gold out of Tokyo and buried it in holes in the ground in the Philippines! Because they thought that The General would march into Tokyo and steal it. But The General didn't care about the gold. He understood that the real gold is here—" he points to his head "—in the intelligence of the people, and here—" he holds out his hands "—in the work that they do. Getting rid of our gold was the best thing that ever happened to Nippon. It made us rich. Receiving that gold was the worst thing that happened to the Philippines. It made them poor."

"Then let's get it out of the Philippines," Avi says, "so that they too can have the opportunity to become rich."

"Ah! Now you are making sense," says Goto Dengo. "You are going to take the gold out and dump it into the ocean, then?"

"No," Avi says, with a nervous chuckle.

Goto Dengo raises his eyebrows. "Oh. So, you wish to become rich as part of the bargain?"

At this point Avi does something that Randy's never seen him do, or even come close to doing, before: he gets pissed off. He doesn't flip the table over, or raise his voice. But his face turns red, the muscles of his head bulge as he clenches his teeth together, and he breathes heavily through his nose for a while. The Gotos both seem to be rather impressed by this, and so no one says anything for a long time, giving Avi a chance to regain his cool. It seems as though Avi can't bring words forth, and so finally he takes his wallet out of his pocket and flips through it until he's found a black-and-white photograph, which he pulls from its trans-

parent sleeve and hands across to Goto Dengo. It's a family portrait:
father, mother, four kids, all with a mid-twentieth century, Middle-
European look about them. "My great-uncle," Avi says, "and his family.
Warsaw, 1937. His teeth are down in that hole. You buried my uncle's teeth!"

Goto Dengo looks up into Avi's eyes, neither angry nor defensive.
Just sad. And this seems to have an effect on Avi, who softens, exhales
finally, breaks eye contact.

"I know you probably had no choice," Avi says. "But that's what
you did. I never knew him, or any of my other relatives who died in
the Shoah. But I would gladly dump every ounce of that gold into the
ocean, just to give them a decent burial. That's what I'll do if you make
it a condition. But what I was really planning on doing was using it to
make sure that nothing of the kind ever happens again."

Goto Dengo ponders this for a while, looking stonefaced out over the
lights of Tokyo. Then he unhooks his cane from the edge of the table,
jams it into the floor, and shoves himself to his feet. He turns towards
Avi, straightens his posture, and then bows. It's the deepest bow Randy's
ever seen. Eventually he straightens up and retakes his seat.

The tension has been broken. Everyone's relaxed, not to say exhausted.

"General Wing is very close to finding Golgotha," Randy says, after
a decent interval has ticked by. "It's him or us."

"It's us, then," says Goto Dengo.

R.I.P.

THE CLAMOR OF THE MARINES' RIFLES ECHOES THROUGH THE
cemetery, the sharp reports pinging from tombstone to tombstone like pachinko balls. Goto Dengo bends down and thrusts
his hand into a pile of loose dirt. It feels good. He scoops up a handful
of the stuff; it trickles out from between his fingers and trails down the
legs of his crisp new United States Army uniform, getting caught in the
trouser cuffs. He steps to the sharp brink of the grave and pours the
earth from his hand onto the General Issue coffin containing Bobby
Shaftoe. He crosses himself, staring at the coffin lid stained with dirt, and
then, with some effort, lifts his head up again, towards the sunlit world
of things that live. Other than a few blades of grass and some mosquitoes,
the first living thing that he sees is a pair of feet in sandals made from

old jeep tires, supporting a white man wrapped in a shapeless brown garment of rough fabric with a large hood on the top. Staring out from the shade of that hood is the supernaturally weird-looking (in that he has a red beard and grey hair) head of Enoch Root—a character who keeps bumping into Goto Dengo as he goes around Manila trying to carry out his duties. Goto Dengo is seized and paralyzed by his wild stare.

They stroll together across the burgeoning cemetery.

"You have something you would like to tell me?" Enoch says.

Goto Dengo turns his head to look into Root's eyes. "I was told that the confessional was a place of perfect secrets."

"It is," Enoch says.

"Then, how did you know?"

"Know what?"

"I think your Church brothers told you something that you should not know."

"Put this idea out of your mind. The secrecy of the confessional has not been violated. I did not talk to the priest who took your first confession, and if I did, he would tell me nothing."

"Then how do you know?" Goto Dengo asks.

"I have several ways of knowing things. One thing I know is that you are a digger. A man who engineers big holes in the ground. Your friend and mine, Father Ferdinand, told me that."

"Yes."

"The Nipponese went to much trouble to bring you here. They would not have done this unless they wanted you to dig an important hole."

"There are many reasons they might have done this."

"Yes," Enoch Root says, "but only a few that make sense."

They stroll silently for a while. Root's feet kick the hem of his robe out with each step. "I know other things," he continues. "South of here, a man brought diamonds to a priest. This man said he had attacked a traveler on the road, and taken from him a small fortune in diamonds. The victim died of his injuries. The murderer gave the diamonds to the Church as penance."

"Was the victim Filipino or Chinese?" asks Goto Dengo.

Enoch Root stares at him coolly. "A Chinese man knows of this?"

More strolling. Root will gladly walk from one end of Luzon to the other if that's how long it takes for the words to come out of Goto Dengo.

"I have information from Europe too," Root says. "I know that the Germans have been hiding treasure. It is widely known that General

Yamashita is burying more war gold in the northern mountains even as we speak."

"What do you want from me?" Goto Dengo asks. There's no preliminary moistening of the eyeballs, the tears leap out of him and run down his face. "I came to the Church because of some words."

"Words?"

"*This is Jesus Christ who taketh away the sins of the world,*" Goto Dengo says. "Enoch Root, no one knows the sins of the world better than me. I have swum in those sins, drowned in them, burned in them, dug in them. I was like a man swimming down a long cave filled with black cold water. Looking up, I saw a light above me, and swam towards it. I only wanted to find the surface, to breathe air again. Still immersed in the sins of the world, at least I could breathe. This is what I am now."

Root nods and waits.

"I had to confess. The things that I saw—the things I did—were so terrible. I had to purify myself. That is what I did, in my first confession." Goto Dengo heaves a deep, shuddering sigh. "It was a very, very long confession. But it is finished. Jesus has taken away my sins, or so the priest said."

"Good. I'm glad it helped you."

"Now, you want me to speak of these things again?"

"There are others," says Enoch Root. He stops in his tracks, and turns, and nods. Silhouetted on the top of a rise, on the other side of several thousand white tombstones, are two men in civilian clothes. They look Western, but that is all Goto Dengo can tell from here.

"Who are they?"

"Men who have been to hell and come back, as you did. Men who know about the gold."

"What do they want?"

"To dig up the gold."

Nausea wraps around Goto Dengo like a wet bedsheet. "They would have to tunnel down through a thousand fresh corpses. It is a grave."

"The whole world is a grave," says Enoch Root. "Graves can be moved, corpses reinterred. Decently."

"And then? If they got the gold?"

"The world is bleeding. It needs medicine and bandages. These cost money."

"But before this war, all of this gold was out here, in the sunlight. In the world. Yet look what happened." Goto Dengo shudders. "Wealth that is stored up in gold is dead. It rots and stinks. True wealth is made every day by men getting up out of bed and going to work. By schoolchildren doing their lessons, improving their minds. Tell those men that if they want wealth, they should come to Nippon with me after the war. We will start businesses and build buildings."

"Spoken like a true Nipponese," Enoch says bitterly. "You never change."

"Please make me understand what you are saying."

"What of the man who cannot get out of bed and work, because he has no legs? What of the widow who has no husband to work, no children to support her? What of children who cannot improve their minds because they lack books and schoolhouses?"

"You can shower gold on them," Goto Dengo says. "Soon enough, it will all be gone."

"Yes. But some of it will be gone into books and bandages."

Goto Dengo does not have a rejoinder for this. He is not outsmarted so much as sad and tired. "What do you want? You think I should give the gold to the Church?"

Enoch Root looks mildly taken aback, as if the idea hadn't really occurred to him before. "You could do worse, I suppose. The Church has two thousand years of experience in using its resources to help the poor. It has not always been perfect. But is has built its share of hospitals and schools."

Goto Dengo shakes his head. "I have only been in your Church for a few weeks and already I have many doubts about it. It has been a good thing for me. But to give it so much gold—I am not sure if this is a good idea."

"Don't look at me as if you expect me to defend the Church's imperfections," says Enoch Root. "They have kicked me out of the priesthood."

"Then what shall I do?"

"Perhaps give it to the Church with conditions."

"What?"

"You can stipulate that it only be used to educate children, if you choose."

Goto Dengo says, "Educated men created this cemetery."

"Then choose some other condition."

"My condition is that if that gold ever comes out of the ground, it should be used so that we do not have any more wars like this one."

"And how should we accomplish such a thing, Goto Dengo?"

Goto Dengo sighs. "You put a big weight on my shoulders!"

"No. I did not put the weight on your shoulders. It has always been there." Enoch Root stares mercilessly into Goto Dengo's tormented face. "Jesus takes away the sins of the world, but the world remains: a physical reality on which we are doomed to live until death takes us away from it. You have confessed, and you have been forgiven, and so the greater part of your burden has been taken away by grace. But the gold is still there, in a hole in the ground. Did you think that the gold all turned into dirt when you swallowed the bread and the wine? That is not what we mean by transubstantiation." Enoch Root turns his back and walks away, leaving Goto Dengo alone in the bright avenues of the city of the dead.

RETURN

"I SHALL RETURN" WROTE RANDY IN HIS FIRST E-MAIL MESSAGE to Amy after he got to Tokyo. Returning to the Philippines is not a very good idea at all, and probably not the kind of thing that the old mellow Randy would have even considered. But here he is on a beach in the Sultanate of Kinakuta, down below Tom Howard's personal citadel, dipped in sunblock and Dramamined to the gills, getting ready to return. Reckoning that the goatee would make him easy to identify, he has shaved it off, and reckoning that hair is useless where he's headed (the jungle, jail, and Davy Jones's Locker being the three most likely possibilities), has run a buzzer over his head and shorn himself down to about an eighth of an inch all around. This in turn has necessitated finding a hat, to prevent radiation burns of the skull, and the only hat in Tom Howard's house that fits Randy is an outback number that some cephalomegalic Aussie contractor left behind there, evidently because its fragrance had begun to attract nocturnal rodents with a proclivity for aimless gnawing.

A pamboat is drawn up on the beach, and a couple of families' worth of badjao kids are tear-assing around, exactly like kids at a rest area on the interstate who know that in ten minutes they have to get back into the Winnebago. The boat's main hull is carved from a single rainforest tree, fifty feet long if it's an inch, narrow enough at its widest point that Randy could sit in the middle and touch both gunwales with out-stretched hands. Most of the hull's shaded under a thatched roof of palm fronds, almost all grey-brown from age and salt-spray, though in one place an older woman is patching it with fresh greens and plastic twine. On each side a narrow bamboo outrigger is connected to the hull by bamboo poles. There's a sort of bridge that sticks way out over the bow, painted with bright red and green and yellow curlicues, like chains of vortices thrown off in the wake of a boat and reflecting the colors of a tropical sunset.

Speaking of which, the sun's going down right now, and they are making preparations to bring the final load of gold up out of the hull of the pamboat. The land drops so precipitously towards the water that there's no road access to the beach, which is probably a good thing since they want this to be as private as possible. But Tom Howard had a lot of heavy stuff shipped in here when he was constructing his house, and so he already has a short section of narrow-gauge railway in place. This sounds more impressive than it is: a pair of steel I-beams, already rusting, bracketed to half-buried concrete ties, running fifty yards straight up a forty-five-degree slope to a small plateau that's accessible via private road. There he's got a diesel-powered winch that he can use to drag stuff up the rails. It is more than adequate for this evening's job, which is to move a couple of hundred kilograms of bullion—the last of the gold from the sunken submarine—up from the beach and into the vault in his house. Tomorrow, he and the others can truck it into downtown Kinakuta at their leisure, and turn it into strings of bits representing very large numbers with noteworthy cryptological properties.

The badjaos share the same maddening refusal to be exotic that Randy has found everywhere on his travels: the guy who's running the show insists that his name is Leon, and the kids on the beach are forever copping stereotyped martial-arts poses and hollering "hi-yaaa!" which Randy knows is a Power Rangers thing, because Avi's kids did exactly the same thing until their father banned all Power Ranger emulation inside the house. When the first milk crate full of gold bars is dropped off the high bridge of the pamboat by Leon, and half-buries itself in the floury damp sand below, Avi stands over it and tries to utter some kind of solemn prayer for the dead in Hebrew, and gets maybe half a dozen phonemes into it before two of the badjao kids, having pegged him as a permanent stationary object, decide to use him as tactical cover, and take up positions on either side of him madly hi-yaaaing each other. Avi's not so full of himself that he can't see the humor in this, and yet not so sentimental that he doesn't obviously want to strangle them.

John Wayne is patrolling the surf with a cigarette and a pump shotgun. Douglas MacArthur Shaftoe rates the probability of frogman attack rather low because the gold in the pamboat is only worth two and half million dollars, an amount that hardly rates anything as elaborate, and expensive, as a seaborne assault. John Wayne needs to be there in case someone gets the mistaken impression that they've somehow managed to pack ten or twenty times that much gold into the pamboat. This seems improbable from a hydrodynamics standpoint. But Doug says that overestimating the intelligence of the enemy is, if anything, more dangerous than underestimating it. He, Tom Howard, and Jackie Woo are up the hill guarding the roadhead with assault rifles. Tom's been positively strutting. All of his fantasies are coming true in this little tableau.

A large plastic box thuds into the sand, breaks open, and spills out a mess of shattered coral. Randy strolls over to it and sees leaves of gold inside the coral carapace, tiny holes punched into them. To him the holes are more interesting than the gold.

But everyone's reacting differently. Doug Shaftoe's always conspicuously cool and sort of pensive in the presence of a very large amount of gold, like he's always known that it was there, but touching it makes him think about where it came from and what was done to get it there. The sight of a single brick almost made Goto Dengo vomit up his Kobe beef. For Eberhard Föhr, who is out in the cove doing a lazy backstroke, it is the physical incarnation of monetary value, which for him, and the rest of Epiphyte, has mostly been a mathematical abstraction—a practical application of one particular sub-sub-sub-branch of number theory. So it has the same kind of purely intellectual attraction to him as a moon rock or a dinosaur tooth. Tom Howard sees it in the embodiment of some political principles that are almost as pure, and as divorced from human reality, as number theory. Mixed in with that is some sense of personal vindication. For Leon the Sea Gypsy, it's just a cargo to be hauled from point A to point B, for which he'll be compensated with something more useful. For Avi it's an inextricable mixture of the sacred and the satanic. For Randy—and if anyone knew about this, he would be dreadfully embarrassed, and would freely admit to its cloyingness—it is the closest thing he's got right now to a physical link with his beloved, in that she was pulling these bars out of the wreck of the submarine just a few days ago. And that is really the only sense in which he gives a damn about it, any more. In fact, in the few days since he decided to hire Leon to smuggle him up the Sulu Sea and into southern Luzon, he has had to remind himself over and over again that the nominal purpose of the trip is to open up Golgotha.

After the gold has been unloaded, and Leon has taken on some supplies, Tom Howard produces a bottle of single-malt scotch, finally answering Randy's question of who patronizes all of those duty-free stores in airports. Everyone gathers on the beach for a toast. Randy's a little edgy when he joins this circle, because he's not sure what he's going to propose a toast *to* if the responsibility falls to him. Unearthing Golgotha? He can't really drink to that. The meeting of minds between Avi and Goto Dengo was a spark jumping across an air gap—sudden, dazzling, and a little scary—and it hinged around their common understanding that all of this gold is blood money, that Golgotha is a grave they're preparing to desecrate. So that's not exactly toast material. How about a toast to abstract lofty principles, then?

Here Randy's got another hangup, something that's been slowly dawning on him as he stands on the beach beneath Tom Howard's concrete house: the perfect freedom that Tom's found in Kinakuta is a cut flower in a crystal vase. It's lovely, but it's dead, and the reason it's dead is that it has been alienated from its germinal soil. And what is that soil exactly? To a first approximation you could just say "America," but it's a little more complicated than that; America's just the hardest-to-ignore instantiation of a cultural and philosophical system that can be seen in a few other places. Not many. Certainly not in Kinakuta. The closest outpost is really not that far away: the Filipinos, for all of their shortcomings in the human rights department, have imbibed the whole Western freedom thing deeply, in a way that has arguably made them economic laggards compared to Asian countries where no one gives a shit about human rights.

In the end it's a moot point; Douglas MacArthur Shaftoe purposes a toast to smooth sailing. Two years ago Randy would have found this to be banal and simple-minded. Now he understands it as Doug's implicit nod to the world's moral ambiguity, and a pretty deft preemptive strike against any more inflated rhetoric. Randy downs his Scotch in a gulp and then says, "let's do it," which is also pretty stunningly banal, but this gathering-in-a-circle-on-the-beach thing really makes him nervous; he signed on to participate in a business opportunity, not to join a cabal.

Four days on the pamboat ensue. It putts along at a steady ten kilometers per hour day and night, and it sticks to shallow coastal waters along the periphery of the Sulu Sea. They are lucky with the weather. They stop twice on Palawan and once on Mindoro to take on diesel fuel and to barter for unspecified commodities. Cargo goes down in the hull, people go above it on the deck, which is just a few loose planks thrown crosswise over the gunwales. Randy feels more out-and-out lonely than he has since he was a teenaged geek, but he's not sad about it. He sleeps a lot, perspires, drinks water, reads a couple of books, and dicks around with his new GPS receiver. Its most salient feature is a mushroom-shaped external antenna that can pick up weak signals, which ought to be useful in triple-canopy jungle. Randy has punched Golgotha's latitude and longitude into its memory, so that by hitting a couple of buttons he can instantly see how far away it is, along what heading. From Tom Howard's beach it's almost exactly a thousand kilometers. When the pamboat finally noses up on a tidal mudflat in southern Luzon, and Randy sloshes ashore in full MacArthurian style, the distance is only about forty clicks.

But tumbledown volcanoes rise before him, black and mist-shrouded, and he knows from experience that forty kilometers in boondocks will be much rougher going than the first nine hundred and sixty.

The bell tower of an old Spanish church rises up above the coconut palms not far away, carved from blocks of volcanic tuff that are beginning to glow in the lambency of another damn mind-blowing tropical sunset. After he's snagged some extra bottles of water and said his good-byes to Leon and the family, Randy walks towards it. As he goes, he erases the memory of Golgotha's location from his GPS, just in case it gets confiscated or ripped off.

The next thought he has says something about his general frame of mind: that nuts are the genitalia of trees is never more obvious than when you are looking at a cluster of swelling young coconuts nestled in the hairy dark groin of a palm tree. It's surprising that the Spanish missionaries didn't have the whole species eradicated. Anyway, by the time he's reached the church, he's picked up a retinue of little bare-chested Filipino kids who apparently aren't used to seeing white men materialize out of nowhere. Randy's not crazy about this, but he'll settle for no one summoning the police.

A Nipponese sport-utility vehicle of the adorably styled, alarmingly high-center-of-gravity school is parked in front of the church, ringed by impressed villagers. Randy wonders if they could have done this any more conspicuously. A fiftyish driver leans against the front bumper smoking a cigarette and shooting the breeze with some local dignitaries: a priest and, for god's sake, a cop with a fucking bolt-action rifle. Just about everyone in sight is smoking Marlboros, which have apparently been distributed as a goodwill gesture. Randy's got to get himself back into a Philippine frame of mind: the way to sneak into the country is not to mount some cloak-and-dagger operation, crawling up onto an isolated beach in a matte black wetsuit in the middle of the night, but simply to waltz in and make friends with all of the people who see you. Because it's not like they're stupid; they are going to see you.

Randy smokes a cigarette. He had never done this in his life until a few months ago, when he finally got it through his head that it was a social thing, that some people take it as an insult when you turn down an offered cigarette, and that a few smokes weren't going to kill him in any case. None of these people, except for the driver and the priest, speaks a word of English, and so this is the only way he can communicate with them. Anyway, given all the other changes he's gone through, why the hell shouldn't he become a cigarette smoker while he's at it? Maybe next week he'll be shooting heroin. For something disgusting and lethal, cigarettes are amazingly enjoyable.

The driver is named Matthew, and he really turns out to be not so much a driver as a charismatic fixer/negotiator, a smoother of the way, a human road grader. Randy just stands there passively while Matthew charmingly and hilariously extricates them from this impromptu village meeting, a job that would probably be next to impossible if the priest were not so clearly complicit. The cop looks to the priest for cues as to what he should do, and the priest tells him something complicated with a series of looks and gestures, and in that way, somehow, Randy finds his way into the sport-utility vehicle's passenger seat and Matthew gets behind the wheel. Well after sunset they trundle out of the village along its execrable one-lane road, trailed by kids who run alongside keeping one hand on the car, like Secret Service agents in a motorcade. They are able to do this for quite a while because they've gone a few kilometers before the road gets good enough for Matthew to shift out of first gear.

This is not a part of the world where it makes any sense at all to drive at night, but clearly Matthew wasn't interested in an overnight stay at that village. Randy has a pretty good idea of what's going to happen now: many hours of driving very slowly on circuitous roads, half-blocked by piles of freshly harvested young coconuts, impeded by hunks of lumber thrown across the right-of-way as speed bumps to prevent kids and dogs from being run over. He leans his seat back.

Bright light is streaming into the car and he thinks: roadblock, cops, spotlights. The light's blocked by a silhouette. There's a rapping noise on the window. Randy looks over and sees the driver's seat empty, no keys in the ignition. The car's cool and dormant. He sits up and rubs his face, partly because it needs to be rubbed and partly because it's probably smart to keep one's hands in plain sight. More rapping on the windshield, growingly impatient. The windows are fogged and he can only see shapes. The light's reddish. He's got a completely inappropriate erection. Randy gropes for a window control, but the car's got power windows and they don't work when it's not running. He gropes around on the door until he's figured out how to unlock it, and almost instantly it flies open and someone's coming inside to join him.

She ends up on Randy's lap, lying sideways on top of him, her head on his chest. "Close the door," Amy says, and Randy does. Then she squirms around until she's face to face with him, her pelvic center of gravity grinding mercilessly against the huge generalized region between navel and thigh that has, in recent months, become one big sex organ for him. She brackets his neck between her forearms and grabs the carotid supports of the whiplash arrestor. He's busted. The obvious thing now would be a kiss, and she feints in that direction, but then reconsiders, as it seems like some serious looking is in order at this time. So they look at each other for probably a good minute. It's not a moony kind of look that they share, not a starry-eyed thing by any means, more like a *what the fuck have we gotten ourselves into* thing. As if it's really important to both of them that they mutually appreciate how serious everything is. Emotionally, yes, but also from a legal and, for lack of a better term, military standpoint. But once Amy is satisfied that her boy does indeed get it, on all of these fronts, she permits herself a vaguely incredulous-looking sneer that blossoms into a real grin, and then a chuckle that in a less heavily armed woman might be characterized as a giggle, and then, just to shut herself up, she pulls hard on the stainless steel goalposts of the whiplash arrestor and nuzzles her face up to Randy's and, after ten heartbeats' worth of exploratory sniffling and nuzzling, kisses him. It's a chaste kiss that takes a long time to open up, which is totally consistent with Amy's cautious, sardonic approach to everything, as well as with the hypothesis, alluded to once while they were driving to Whitman, that she is in fact a virgin.

Randy's life is essentially complete at the moment. He has come to understand during all of this that the light shining in through the windows is in fact the light of dawn, and he tries to fight back the thought that *it's a good day to die* because it's clear to him that although he might go on from this point to make a lot of money, become famous, or whatever, nothing's ever going to top this. Amy knows it too, and she makes the kiss last for a very long time before finally breaking away with a little gasp for air, and bowing her head so that her brow is supported on Randy's breastbone, the curve of her head following that of his throat, like the coastlines of South America and Africa. Randy almost can't take the pressure of her on his groin. He braces his feet against the floorboards of the sport-utility vehicle and squirms.

She moves suddenly and decisively, grabbing the hem of the left leg of his baggy shorts and yanking it almost up to his navel, taking his boxer shorts along with. Randy pops free and takes aim at her, straining upwards, bobbing slightly with each beat of his heart, glowing healthily (he thinks modestly) in the dawn light. Amy's in a sort of light wrap-around skirt, which she suddenly flings over him, producing a momentary tent-pole effect. But she's on the move, reaching up beneath to pull her underwear out of the way, and then before he can even believe it's happening she sits down on him, hard, producing a nearly electrical shock. Then she stops moving—daring him.

Randy's toe knuckles pop audibly. He lifts himself and Amy into the air, experiences some kind of synaesthetic hallucination very much like the famous "jump into hyperspace" scene from *Star Wars*. Or perhaps the air bag has accidentally detonated? Then he pumps something like

an Imperial pint of semen—it's a seemingly open-ended series of ejaculations, each coupled to the next by nothing more than a leap of faith that
another one is coming—and in the end, like all schemes built on faith
and hope, it lapses, and then Randy sits utterly still until his body realizes
it has not drawn breath in quite a while. He fills his lungs all the way,
stretching them out, which feels almost as good as the orgasm, and then
he opens his eyes—she's staring down at him in bemusement, but (thank
god!) not horror or disgust. He settles back into the bucket seat, which
squeezes his butt in a not-unpleasant gesture of light harassment. Between
that, and Amy's thighs, and other penetrations, he is not going anywhere
for a while, and he's moderately afraid of what Amy's going to say—she
has a lengthy menu of possible responses to all of this, most of them at
Randy's expense. She plants a knee, levers herself up, grabs the tail of
his Hawaiian shirt and cleans herself off a bit. Then she shoves the door
open, pats him twice on his whiskery cheek, says "Shave," and exits
stage left. Randy can now see that the air bag has not, in fact, deployed.
And yet he has the same feeling of a major sudden life change that one
might get after surviving a car crash.

He is a mess. Fortunately his bag's in the backseat, with another shirt.

A few minutes later he finally emerges from the fogged-up car and
gets a look at his surroundings. He's in a community built on a canted
plateau with a few widely spaced, very high coconut palms scattered
about. Downslope, which appears to be roughly south, there is a pattern
of vegetation that Randy recognizes as a tri-leveled cash-crop thing:
pineapples down on the ground, cacao and coffee at about head level,
coconuts and bananas above that. The yellowish green leaves of the
banana trees are especially appealing, seemingly big enough to stretch
out and sunbathe on. To the north, and uphill, a jungle is attempting to
tear down a mountain.

This compound that he's in is obviously a recent thing, laid out by
actual surveyors, designed by people with educations, subsidized by someone who can afford brand-new sheets of corrugated tin, ABS drainpipe,
and proper electrical wiring. It has something in common with a normal
Philippine town in that it's built around a church. In this case the church
is small—Enoch called it a chapel—but that it was designed by Finnish
architecture students would be obvious to Randy even if Root hadn't
divulged it. It has a bit of that Bucky Fuller tensegrity thing going for
it—lots of exposed, tensioned cables radiating from the ends of tubular
struts, all collaborating to support a roof that's not a single surface but a
system of curved shards. It looks awfully well designed to Randy, who
now judges buildings on the sole criterion of their ability to resist earthquakes. Root told him it was built by the brothers of a missionary order,

and by local volunteers, with materials contributed by a Nipponese foundation that is still trying to make amends for the war.

Music is coming out of the church. Randy checks his watch and discovers that it's Sunday morning. He avoids participating in the Mass, on the excuse that it's already underway and he doesn't want to interrupt it, and ambles toward a nearby pavilion—a corrugated roof sheltering a concrete floor slab with some plastic tables—where breakfast is being laid out. He arouses violent controversy among a loose flock of chickens that is straggling across his path, none of whom can seem to figure out how to get out of his way; they're scared of him, but not mentally organized enough to translate that fear into a coherent plan of action. Several miles away, a helicopter is flying in from the sea, shedding altitude as it homes in on a pad somewhere up in the jungle. It is a big and gratuitously loud cargo-carrying chopper with unfamiliar lines, and Randy vaguely suspects that it was built in Russia for Chinese customers and that it is part of Wing's operations.

He recognizes Jackie Woo lounging at one of the tables, drinking tea and reading a bright magazine. Amy's in the adjacent kitchen, embroiled in Tagalog girl-talk with a couple of middle-aged ladies who are handling the preparations for the meal. This place seems pretty safe, and so Randy stops in the open, punches in the digits that only he and Goto Dengo know, and takes a GPS reading. According to the machine, they are no more than 4500 meters away from the main drift of Golgotha. Randy checks the heading and determines that it is uphill from here. Although the jungle blurs the underlying shape of the earth, he thinks that it's going to be up in the valley of a nearby river.

Forty-five hundred meters seems impossibly close, and he's still standing there trying to convince himself that his memory is sound when the ragged voices of the worshippers suddenly spill out across the compound as the chapel's door is pushed open. Enoch Root emerges, wearing (inevitably) what Randy would describe as a wizard's robe. But as he walks across the compound he shucks it off to reveal sensible khakis underneath, and hands the robe to a young Filipino acolyte who scurries back inside with it. The singing trails off and then Douglas MacArthur Shaftoe emerges from the church, followed by John Wayne and several people who appear to be locals. Everyone drifts towards the pavilion. The alertness that comes with being in a new place, combined with the neurological aftermath of that shockingly big and long orgasm, has left Randy's senses sharper, and his mind clearer, than they've ever been, and he's impatient to get going. But he can't dispute the wisdom of getting a good breakfast, so he shakes hands all around and sits down with the others. There is a bit of small talk about how his pamboat voyage went.

"Your friends should have come into the country that way," says Doug Shaftoe, and then goes on to explain that Avi and both of the Gotos were supposed to be here yesterday, but they were detained at the airport for some hours and eventually had to fly back to Tokyo while some mysterious immigration hassles were ironed out. "Why didn't they go to Taipei or Hong Kong?" Randy wonders aloud since both those cities are much closer to Manila. Doug stares at him blankly and observes that both of those are Chinese cities, and reminds him that their presumed adversary now is General Wing, who has a lot of pull in places like that.

Several backpacks have already been prepared, laden mostly with bottled water. After everyone's had a chance to digest breakfast, Douglas MacArthur Shaftoe, Jackie Woo, John Wayne, Enoch Root, America Shaftoe, and Randall Lawrence Waterhouse all don packs. They begin to stroll uphill, passing out of the compound and into a transitional zone of big-leaved traveler trees and giant clusters of bamboo: ten-centimeter-thick trunks spraying out and up from central roots, like frozen shell-bursts, to heights of at least ten meters, the poles striped green and brown where the husky leaves are peeling away. The canopy of the jungle looms higher and higher, accentuated by the fact that it's uphill from here, and emits a fantastic whistling noise, like a phaser on overload. As they enter the shade of the canopy the racket of crickets is added to that whistling noise. It sounds as though there must be millions of crickets and millions of whatever's making the whistling noise, but from time to time the sound will suddenly stop and then start up again, so if there are a lot of them, they are all following the same score.

The place is filled with plants that in America are only seen in pots, but that grow to the size of oak trees here, so big that Randy's mind can't recognize them as, for example, the same kind of Diefenbachia that Grandmother Waterhouse used to have growing on the counter in her downstairs bathroom. There is an incredible variety of butterflies, for whom the wind-free environment seems to be congenial, and they weave in and out among huge spiderwebs that call to mind the design of Enoch Root's chapel. But it is clear that the place is ultimately ruled by ants; in fact it makes the most sense to think of the jungle as a living tissue of ants with minor infestations of trees, birds, and humans. Some of them are so small that they are, to other ants, as those ants are to people; they prosecute their ant activities in the same physical space but without interfering, like many signals on different frequencies sharing the same medium. But there are a fair number of ants carrying other ants, and Randy assumed that they are not doing it for altruistic reasons.

Where the jungle's dense it is impassable, but there are a fair number of places where the trees are spaced a few meters apart and the undergrowth is only knee-high, and light shines through. By moving from one such place to another they make slow progress in the general direction indicated by Randy's GPS. Jackie Woo and John Nguyen have disappeared, and appear to be moving parallel to them but much more quietly. The jungle is a nice place to visit, but you wouldn't want to live, or even stop moving, there. Just as the beggars in Intramuros see you as a bipedal automatic teller machine, the insects here see you as a big slab of animated but not very well defended food. The ability to move, far from being a deterrent, serves as an unforgeable guarantee of freshness. The canopy's tentpoles are huge trees—"Octomelis sumatrana," says Enoch Root—with narrow buttress roots splayed out explosively in every direction, as thin and sharp as machetes sunk into the earth. Some of them are almost completely obscured by colossal philodendrons winding up their trunks.

They crest a broad, gentle ridgeline; Randy had forgotten that they were moving uphill. The air suddenly becomes cooler and moisture condenses on their skins. When the whistlers and the crickets pause, it becomes possible to hear the murmur of a stream down below them. The next hour is devoted to slowly working their way down the slope towards it. They cover a total of a hundred meters; at this rate, Randy thinks, it should take them two days, hiking around the clock, to reach Golgotha. But he keeps this observation to himself. As they move downhill he starts to become aware of, and to be taken aback by, the sheer amount of biomass that happens to be above them—forty or fifty meters above them in many cases. He feels as though he's at the bottom of the food chain.

They enter a sunnier zone that consequently is snarled by much heavier undergrowth, and are forced to break out the machetes and hack their way through to the river. Enoch Root explains that this is a place where a small lahar, which had been funneled between the steep walls of the river's gorge farther upstream, spread out and mowed down a few hectares of ancient trees, clearing the path for smaller, opportunistic vegetation. This is fascinating for about ten seconds and then it's back to the machete work. Eventually they reach the edge of the river, all of them sticky and greenish and itching from the sap and juice and pulp of the vegetation they have assaulted in order to get here. The river's bed is shallow and rocky here, with no discernible bank. They sit down and drink water for a while. "What is the point of all this?" asks Enoch Root suddenly. "I don't mean to sound discouraged by these physical barriers, because I'm not. But I'm wondering whether you have worked out the goal of it in your own mind."

"This is fact-finding. Nothing more," Randy says.

"But there's no point in just aimlessly finding facts unless you're a pure scientist, or a historian. You are representing a business concern here. Correct?"

"Yes."

"And so if I were a shareholder in your company I could demand an explanation of why you are sitting here on the edge of this river right now instead of actually doing whatever it is that your company does."

"Assuming you were an intelligent shareholder, yes, that's what you'd be doing."

"And what would your explanation be, Randy?"

"Well—"

"I know where we are going, Randy." And Enoch quotes a string of digits.

"How did you know that?" Randy asks kind of hotly.

"I've known it for fifty years," Enoch says. "Goto Dengo told me."

All Randy can do for a while is fume. Doug Shaftoe's laughing. Amy just looks distracted. Enoch broods for a few moments, and finally says: "Originally the plan was to buy this land with a smaller cache of gold that was dug up and loaded aboard a certain submarine. We would then wait for the right moment and then dig up the rest. But the submarine sank, and the gold sank with it. I sat on the knowledge for many years. But then people started buying up land around here—people who were obviously hoping to find the Primary. If I'd had the money, I would have bought this land myself. But I didn't. So I saw to it that the Church bought it."

Doug Shaftoe says, "You haven't answered Enoch's question yet, Randy: what good are you doing your shareholders here?"

A red dragonfly hovers above a backwater of the stream, its wings moving so fast that the eye sees not wings in movement but a probability distribution of where the wings might be, like electron orbitals: a quantum-mechanical effect that maybe explains why the insect can apparently teleport from one place to another, disappearing from one point and reappearing a couple of meters away, without seeming to pass through the space in between. There sure is a lot of bright stuff in the jungle. Randy figures that, in the natural world, anything that is colored so brightly must be some kind of serious evolutionary badass.

"We took the gold that you recovered from the submarine and turned into electronic cash, right?" Randy says.

"So you claimed. I haven't actually *spent* any of that electronic cash yet," says Doug.

"We want to do the same thing for the Church—or Wing—or whoever ends up in possession of the gold. We want to deposit it in the Crypt, and make it usable as electronic currency."

Amy asks, "Do you understand that, in order to move the gold out of here, it'll be necessary to travel across land controlled by Wing?"

"Who says we have to move it?"

Silence for a minute, or what passes for silence in a jungle.

Doug Shaftoe says, "You're right. If the stories are even half true, this facility is far more secure than any bank vault."

"The stories are all true—and then some," Randy says. "The man who designed and built Golgotha is Goto Dengo himself."

"Shit!"

"He drew plans of it for us. And the larger issue of local and national security is not a problem here," Randy adds. "Of course the government has sometimes been unstable. But any invader who wants to physically seize possession of the gold will have to fight his way across this jungle with tens of millions of heavily armed Filipinos barring his path."

"Everyone knows what the Huks did against the Nips," Doug says, nodding vigorously. "Or the VC against us, for that matter. No one would be stupid enough to try it."

"Especially if we put you in charge, Doug."

Amy's been woolgathering through most of the conversation, but at this she turns and grins at her father.

"I accept," Doug says.

Randy's slowly becoming aware that most of the birds and bugs who live here move so fast that you can't even turn your head fast enough to center them in your vision. They exist only as slicing movements in your peripheral vision. The only exception would seem to be a species of gnat that has evolved into the specific niche of plunging into the left eyeballs of human beings at something just under the speed of sound. Randy has taken about four hits in the left eye, none in the right. He takes another one now, and as he's recovering from it, the earth jumps underneath them. It is a little like an earthquake in its psychological effect: a feeling of disbelief, and then betrayal, that the solid ground is having the temerity to move around. But it's all over by the time the sensation has moved up their spines to their brains. The river's still running, and the dragonfly is still hunting.

"That felt exactly like high explosive going off," says Doug Shaftoe, "but I didn't hear anything. Did anyone hear anything?"

No one heard anything.

"What that means," Doug continues, "is that someone is setting off explosives deep underground."

They start working their way up the riverbed. Randy's GPS indicates

that Golgotha is less than two thousand meters upstream. The river begins
to develop proper banks that get steadily higher and steeper. John Wayne
clambers up onto the left bank and Jackie Woo onto the right, so that
the high ground on either side will be guarded, or at least reconnoitered.
They pass back into the shade of the canopy. The ground here is some
kind of sedimentary rock with granite boulders embedded in it from
place to place, like mixed nuts in half-melted chocolate. It must be
nothing more than a scab of congealed ash and sediment on top of an
underlying monolith of hard rock. Those who are down in the streambed
move very slowly now. Part of the time they are down in the river,
struggling upstream against a powerful current, and part of the time they
are picking their way from boulder to boulder, or sidestepping along
crumbling ledges of harder rock that protrude from the banks here and
there. Every few minutes, Doug looks up and makes visual contact with
Jackie Woo and John Wayne—who must be contending with challenges
of their own, because sometimes they fall behind the main group. The
trees only seem to get higher as they work their way up into the mountains, and now their height is accentuated by the fact that they are rooted
in the top of a bank that rises above the stream two, five, ten, then
twenty and thirty meters. The bank actually overhangs them now: the
river's gorge is a tube mostly buried in the earth, open to the sky only
through a narrow slot in the top. But it's close to midday and the sun
is shining nearly straight down through it, illuminating all of the stuff
that makes its way down from the heights. The corpse of a murdered
insect drifts down from the upper canopy like winter's first snowflake.
Water seeping from the rims of the overhanging bank forms a drip curtain, each drop glittering like a diamond and making it nearly impossible
to see the dark cavity behind. Yellow butterflies weave among those
falling drops but never get hit.

They come around a gentle bend in the river and are confronted by
a waterfall some twenty meters high. At the base of the falls there's a
still and relatively shallow pool, filling the bottom of a broad melon-
shaped cavity formed by the concave, overhanging banks. The vertical
sun beams straight down on the cloud of white foam at the base of the
falls, which radiates the light back at blinding power, forming a sort of
natural light fixture that illuminates the whole inside of the cavity. The
stone walls, sweating and dripping and running with groundwater, glisten
in its light. The undersides of the ferns and big-leaved plants—epi-
phytes—sprouting from invisible footholds in the walls flicker and dapple
in the weirdly bluish foam-glow.

Most of the cavity's walls are hidden behind vegetation: fragile, cascad-
ing veils of moss growing from the rock, and vines depending from the

branches of the trees hundreds of feet above them and dangling halfway down into the gorge, where they have become entangled with protruding tree roots and formed a natural trellis for a finer network of creepers that is itself the warp and woof of a matted carpet of moss saturated with flowing ground water. The gorge is alive with butterflies burning with colors of radioactive purity, and down closer to the rustling water are damselflies, mostly black with aqua bodies that flash in the sun—their wings revealing glimpses of salmon and coral-red on the underside as they orbit around each other. But mostly the air is filled with this continual slow progress of things that didn't survive, making their way down through the column of air and into the water, which flushes them away: dead leaves and the exoskeletons of insects, sucked dry and eviscerated in some silent combat hundreds of feet above their heads.

Randy's keeping an eye on the display of his GPS, which has been having a hard time locking onto any satellites down in this gorge. But finally some numbers come up. He has it calculate the distance from here to Golgotha, and the answer comes up immediately: a long row of zeroes with a few insignificant digits trailing off the end.

Randy says, "This is it." But most of what he says is obscured by a sharp explosion from high above them on the bank. A few seconds later, a man begins to scream.

"No one move," says Doug Shaftoe, "we are in a minefield."

CRIBS

 ON A GRASSY KNOLL, A MAN CROUCHES BEHIND A TOMBSTONE, peering through a telescope on a tripod, and tracking the steady pace of a robed and hooded figure across the grass.

FUNERAL. That's the crib that broke these guys.

The Nipponese man in the American uniform, whom Enoch Root is leaving behind, must be that Goto Dengo fella. Lawrence Pritchard Waterhouse has seen that name punched on so many ETC cards that he no longer even has to read the printed letters at the top of the card: he can identify a "Goto Dengo" from arm's length simply by glancing at the pattern of punched-out rectangles. The same is true of some two dozen other Nipponese mining engineers and surveyors who were brought to Luzon in '43 and '44, in response to Azure/Pufferfish messages emanating from Tokyo. But, as far as Waterhouse can tell, all of the others are dead. Either that, or they retreated north with Yamashita.

Only one of them is alive, well, and living in what is left of Manila, and that's Goto Dengo. Waterhouse was going to rat him out to Army Intelligence, but that doesn't seem like such a good idea now that the unkillable Nip engineer has become a personal protegé of The General.

Root is heading in the direction of those two mysterious white men who attended Bobby Shaftoe's funeral. Waterhouse peers at them through the scope, but mediocre optics, combined with the heat waves rising from the grass, complicate this. One of them seems oddly familiar. Odd because Waterhouse doesn't know that many bearded men with long swept-back blond hairdoes and black eyepatches.

An idea springs out of his forehead fully formed, with no warning. This is how all the best ideas arrive. Ideas that he patiently cultivates from tiny seeds always fail to germinate or else grow up into monstrosities. Good ideas are just there all of a sudden, like angels in the Bible. You cannot ignore them just because they are ridiculous. Waterhouse stifles a giggle and tries not to get overly excited. The dull, tedious, bureaucratic part of his mind is feeling testy, and wants a few shreds of supporting evidence.

This is quickly supplied. Waterhouse knows, and has proved to Earl Comstock, that strange information is in the air, dotting and dashing furtively from a small number of feeble transmitters scattered around Luzon and the surrounding waters, encrypted using the Arethusa system. Lawrence and Alan have known for two years now that Rudy invented it, and from the decrypts chattering out of digital computers in Bletchley Park and Manila, they now know other things. They know that Rudy flew the coop late in 1943 and probably went to Sweden. They know that one Günter Bischoff, captain of the U-boat that plucked Shaftoe and Root out of the water, also ended up in Sweden, and that Dönitz persuaded him to take over the gold-running work that had been performed by U-553 until it ran aground off Qwlghm. The Naval Intelligence boys are fascinated by Bischoff, and so he had already been the subject of much research. Waterhouse has seen photos of him from his student days. The shorter of the two men he is peering at now could easily be the same fellow, now middle-aged. And the taller one, the one with the eyepatch, could most definitely be Rudy von Hacklheber himself.

It is, then, a conspiracy.

They have secure communications. If Rudy is the architect of Arethusa, then it will be essentially impossible to break, except for rare lapses such as this FUNERAL business.

They have a submarine. It cannot be found or sunk, because it is one of Hitler's new rocket-fuel-powered babies, and because Günter Bischoff, the greatest U-boat commander in history, is its skipper.

They have, at some level, the backing of the odd brotherhood that Root belongs too, the *ignoti et quasi occulti* guys.

And now they are trying to enlist Goto Dengo. The man who, it is safe to assume, buried the gold.

Three days ago, the intercept boys in Waterhouse's section picked up a brief flurry of Arethusa messages, exchanged between a hidden transmitter somewhere in Manila and a mobile one in the South China Sea. Catalinas were vectored toward the latter, and picked up diminishing radar echoes at first, but found nothing when they arrived on the scene. A team of journeyman codebreakers jumped on those messages and started trying to tear them apart by brute force. Lawrence Pritchard Waterhouse, the old hand, went for a stroll along the Manila Bay seawall. A breeze suddenly rose from the bay. He stopped to let it cool his face. A coconut fell from the top of a tree and smashed into the ground ten feet away. Waterhouse turned on his heel and went back to the office.

Just before the flurry of Arethusa messages began, Waterhouse had been sitting in his office listening to Armed Forces Radio. They had broadcast an announcement that, three days from now, at such-and-such a time, the funeral for the hero, Bobby Shaftoe, was going to be held at the big new cemetery down in Makati.

Sitting down in his office with the fresh Arethusa intercepts, he went to work, using FUNERAL as a crib: if this group of seven letters decrypts to FUNERAL, then what does the rest of the message look like? Gibberish? Okay, how about *this* group of seven letters?

Even with this gift thrown into his lap, it took him two and a half days of nonstop work to decrypt the message. The first one, transmitted from Manila, went: OUR FRIEND'S FUNERAL SATURDAY TEN THIRTY AM US MILITARY CEMETERY MAKATI.

The response from the submarine: WILL BE THERE SUGGEST YOU INFORM GD.

He aims the spyglass at Goto Dengo again. The Nipponese engineer is standing with his head bowed and his eyes tightly shut. Perhaps his shoulders are heaving, perhaps it's just the heat waves that make it seem so.

But then Goto Dengo straightens up and takes a step in the direction of the conspirators. He stops. Then he takes another step. Then another. His posture is straightening up miraculously. He seems to feel better with every stride. He walks faster and faster, until he is almost running.

Lawrence Pritchard Waterhouse is hardly a mind-reader, but he can easily enough tell what Goto Dengo is thinking: I have a burden on my shoulders, and it has been crushing me. And now I'm going to hand that burden over to someone else. Hot damn! Bischoff and Rudy von Hacklheber step forward to meet him, holding out their right hands enthusiastically. Bischoff, Rudy, Enoch, and Goto Dengo join into a knot, practically on top of Bobby Shaftoe's grave.

It is a shame. Waterhouse knew Bobby Shaftoe, and would have liked to attend his funeral standing up—not skulking around like this. But Enoch Root and Rudy would both recognize him. Waterhouse is their enemy.

Or is he? In a decade full of Hitlers and Stalins, it's hard to worry about a conspiracy that seemingly includes a priest, and that risks its very existence in order to attend a member's funeral. Waterhouse rolls over and lies on his back on some dead guy's grave and ponders it. If Mary were here, he would lay out the dilemma for her and she would tell him what to do. But Mary's in Brisbane, picking out bridesmaids' dresses and china patterns.

The next time he sees any of these fellows is one month later, in a clearing in the jungle a couple of hours south of Manila. Waterhouse gets there before they do, and spends a sweaty night under a mosquito net. In the morning, about half of Bischoff's submarine crew arrives, grumpy from an all-night march. As Waterhouse expected, they are quite nervous about being ambushed by the local Huk commander known as the Crocodile, and so they post a number of sentries in the jungle. That is why Waterhouse took pains to get here before they did: so that he would not have to infiltrate their picket line.

The Germans who aren't standing guard go to work with shovels, digging a hole in the ground next to a big piece of red pumice shaped vaguely like the continent of Africa. Waterhouse squats no more than twenty feet away, trying to figure out how he can make his presence known without being gunned down by a nervous white man.

He almost gets close enough to tap Rudy on the shoulder. Then he slips on a slimy rock. Rudy hears him, turns, and sees nothing except for a swatch of undergrowth being torn down by Waterhouse's falling body.

"Is that you, Lawrence?"

Waterhouse stands up cautiously, keeping his hands in plain sight. "Very good! How did you know?"

"Don't be stupid. There aren't that many people who could have found us."

They shake hands. Then they think better of it, and embrace. Rudy gives him a cigarette. The German sailors look on incredulously. There are some others: a Negro and an Indian, and a grizzled, dark man who looks like he wants to kill Waterhouse on the spot.

"You must be the famous Otto!" Waterhouse exclaims. But Otto does not seem eager to make new friends, or even acquaintances, at this juncture in his life, and turns away sourly. "Where's Bischoff?" Waterhouse asks.

"Minding the submarine. It is risky, lurking in the shallows. How did you find us, Lawrence?" He answers his own question before Waterhouse can. "By decrypting the long message, obviously."

"Yes."

"But how did you do that? Did I miss something? Is there a back door?"

"No. It wasn't easy. I broke one of your messages, a while back."

"The FUNERAL one?"

"Yes!" Waterhouse laughs.

"I could have killed Enoch for sending out a message with such an obvious crib." Rudy shrugs. "It is hard to teach crypto security, even to intelligent men. *Especially* to them."

"Maybe he wanted me to decrypt it," Waterhouse muses.

"It is possible," Rudy admits. "Perhaps he wanted me to break Detachment 2702's one-time pad, so that I would come and join him."

"I guess he figures if you're smart enough to break hard codes, you're automatically going to be on his side," Waterhouse says.

"I'm not sure that I agree . . . it is naive."

"It's a leap of faith," Waterhouse says.

"How did you break Arethusa? I am naturally curious," Rudy says.

"Because Azure/Pufferfish employs a different key every day, I assumed that Arethusa did the same."

"I call them by different names. But yes, continue."

"The difference is that the daily key for Azure/Pufferfish is simply the numerical date. Very easy to exploit, once you have figured it out."

"Yes. I intended it that way," Rudy says. He lights up another cigarette, taking extravagant pleasure in it.

"Whereas the daily key for Arethusa is something I haven't been able to put my finger on yet. Perhaps a pseudo-random function of the date, perhaps random numbers you are taking from a one-time pad. In any case it is not predictable, which makes Arethusa harder to break."

"But you did break the long message. Would you explain how?"

"Well, your meeting at the cemetery was brief. I guess you had to get out of there pretty fast."

"It did not seem a good place to linger."

"So, you and Bischoff went away—back to the submarine, I figured.

Goto Dengo went back to his post at The General's headquarters. I knew that he couldn't have told you anything substantive at the cemetery. That would have to come later, and it would have to be in the form of an Arethusa-encrypted message. You are justifiably proud of Arethusa."

"Thank you," Rudy says briskly.

"But the drawback of Arethusa, as with Azure/Pufferfish, is that it requires a great deal of computation. This is fine if you happen to have a computing machine, or a room full of trained abacus operators. I assume you have a machine on board the submarine?"

"That we do," Rudy says diffidently, "nothing very special. It still requires a great deal of manual calculation."

"But Enoch Root in Manila, and Goto Dengo, could not have had such a thing. They would have to encrypt the message by hand—doing all of the calculations on sheets of scratch paper. Enoch already knew the *algorithm,* and could tell it to Goto Dengo, but you would have to agree on a *key* to put into that algorithm. The only time you could have decided on the key was while you were all together at the cemetery. And during your conversation there, I saw you pointing at Shaftoe's headstone. So I figured that you were using that as a key—maybe his name, maybe his dates of birth and death, maybe his military serial number. It turned out to be the serial number."

"But still you did not know the algorithm."

"Yes, but I had some idea that it was related to the Azure/Pufferfish algorithm, which in turn is related to the zeta functions that we studied at Princeton. So I just sat down and said to myself, if Rudy were going to build the ultimate cryptosystem on this basis, and if Azure/Pufferfish is a simplified version of that system, then what is Arethusa? That gave me a handful of possibilities."

"And out of that handful you were able to pick the right one."

"No," Waterhouse says, "it was too hard. So I went to the church where Enoch was working, and looked through his wastebasket. Nothing. I went to Goto Dengo's office and did the same. Nothing. Both of them were burning their scratch paper as they went along."

Rudy's face suddenly relaxes. "Oh, good. I was afraid they were doing something incredibly stupid."

"Not at all. So, you know what I did?"

"What did you do, Lawrence?"

"I went and had an interview with Goto Dengo."

"Yes. He told us that much."

"I told him about the research I had been doing into Azure/Pufferfish, but I didn't tell him I had broken it. I got him talking, in a very general way, about what he was doing on Luzon during the last year. He told me the same story that he has stuck to all along, which is that he was building some minor fortifications somewhere, and that after escaping from that area he wandered lost in the jungle for several days before emerging near San Pablo and joining up with some Air Force troops who were heading north towards Manila.

" 'It's a good thing you got out of there,' I told him, 'because ever since then, the Hukbalahap leader who calls himself the Crocodile has been ransacking the jungle—he's convinced that you Nipponese buried a fortune in gold there.' "

As soon as the word "crocodile" emerges from Waterhouse's mouth, Rudy's face screws up in disgust and he turns away.

"So when the long message was finally transmitted last week, from the transmitter that Enoch has hidden on the top of that church's bell tower, I had two cribs. First of all, I suspected that the key was a number from the tombstone of Bobby Shaftoe. Secondly, I was confident that the words 'Hukbalahap,' 'crocodile,' and probably 'gold' or 'treasure' would appear somewhere in the message. I also looked for obvious candidates like 'latitude' and 'longitude.' With all of that to go on, breaking the message wasn't that hard."

Rudy von Hacklheber heaves a big sigh. "So. You win," he says. "Where is the cavalry?"

"Cavalry, or calvary?" Waterhouse jokes.

Rudy smiles tolerantly. "I know where Calvary is. Not far from Golgotha."

"Why do you think the cavalry is coming?"

"I know they are coming," Rudy says. "Your efforts to break the long message must have required a whole room full of computers. They will talk. Surely the secret is out." Rudy stubs out his half-smoked cigarette, as if preparing to leave. "So, you have been sent to give us an offer—surrender in a civilized way and we will get good treatment. Something like that."

"Au contraire, Rudy. No one knows except me. I did leave a sealed envelope in my desk, to be opened if I should die mysteriously on this little trip to the jungle. That Otto character has a fearsome reputation."

"I don't believe you. It is impossible," Rudy says.

"You of all people. Don't you see? I have a machine, Rudy! The machine does the work for me. So I don't need a room full of computers—human ones, leastways. And as soon as I read the decrypted message, I burned all of the cards. So I am the only one who knows."

"Ah!" Rudy says, stepping back and looking into the sky, adjusting his mind to these new facts. "So, I gather that you have come here to join us? Otto will be troublesome about it, but you are quite welcome."

Lawrence Pritchard Waterhouse actually has to think about it. This surprises him a little.

"Most of it is going to help victims of the war, in one way or another," Rudy says, "but if we take a tenth of a percent as commission, and distribute it among the entire crew of the submarine, we are all among the richest men in the world."

Waterhouse tries to imagine himself one of the richest men in the world. It doesn't seem to fit.

"I've been exchanging letters with a college in Washington State," he says. "My fiancée put me on to them."

"Fiancée? Congratulations."

"She's Qwlghmian-Australian. It seems that there's a colony of Qwlghmians in the Palouse Hills as well, where Washington and Oregon and Idaho all come together. Sheepherders mostly. But there is this little college there, and they need a mathematics professor. I could be chairman of the department within a few years." Waterhouse stands there in the Philippine jungle smoking his cigarette and imagining this. Nothing sounds more exotic. "It sounds like a nice life!" he exclaims, as if this were the first time he had thought of such a thing. "It sounds perfectly all right to me."

The Palouse Hills seem very far away. He is impatient to begin covering the distance.

"That it does," says Rudy von Hacklheber.

"You don't sound very convincing, Rudy. I know it wouldn't be so great for you. But for me it's the cat's pajamas."

"So, are you telling me you don't want in?"

"I'll tell you this. You said most of the money was going to charity. Well, the college can always use a donation. If your plan works out, how about endowing a chair for me at this college? That's all I really want."

"I will do that," Rudy says, "and I'll endow one for Alan too, at Cambridge, and I'll provide both of you with laboratories full of electrical computers." Rudy's eyes wander back to the hole in the ground, where the Germans—having withdrawn most of their sentries—are making steady progress. "You know that this is nothing more than one of the outlying caches. Seed capital to finance the Golgotha work."

"Yes. Just as the Nips planned it."

"We'll dig it up soon enough. Sooner, now that we no longer have to worry about the Crocodile!" Rudy says, and laughs. It is an honest, genuine laugh, the first time Waterhouse has ever seen him drop his guard. "Then we will go to ground until the war is over. In the meantime, maybe there will be enough left over to give you and your Qwlghmian bride a nice wedding present."

"Our china pattern is Lavender Rose by Royal Albert," Waterhouse says.

Rudy takes an envelope out of his pocket and writes that down. "It was very good of you to come out and say hello," he mumbles around his cigarette.

"Those bicycle rides in New Jersey might as well have taken place on a different planet," Waterhouse says, shaking his head.

"They did," Rudy says. "And when Douglas MacArthur marches into Tokyo, it's going to be a different planet yet again. See you there, Lawrence."

"See you, Rudy. Godspeed."

They embrace one more time. Waterhouse backs away and watches the shovels biting into the red mud for a few moments, then turns his back on all of the money in the world and starts walking.

"Lawrence!" Rudy shouts.

"Yes?"

"Don't forget to destroy that sealed envelope you left in your office."

Waterhouse laughs. "Aw, I was just lying about that. In case someone wanted to kill me."

"That's a relief."

"You know how people are always saying 'I can keep a secret' and they are always wrong?"

"Yes."

"Well," Waterhouse says, "I can keep a secret."

CAYUSE

 ANOTHER SHOCK WAVE PASSES SILENTLY THROUGH THE ground, setting up a pattern of waves, and reflections of waves, in the water that laps around their knees.

"Things are going to happen very slowly now for a while. Get used to it," says Doug Shaftoe. "Everyone needs a probe—a long knife or a rod. Even a stick."

Doug's got a big knife, he being that kind of guy, and Amy has her kris. Randy pulls the lightweight aluminum frame of his backpack apart to produce a couple of tubes; this takes a while but, as Doug said, everything is happening slowly now. Randy tosses one of the tubes to Enoch Root, who snatches a basically poorly aimed throw out of the air. Now that everyone is equipped, Doug Shaftoe gives them a tutorial on how to probe one's way through a minefield. Like every other lesson Randy's ever imbibed, this one is sort of interesting, but only until Doug divulges the main point, which is that you can poke a mine from the side and it won't blow up; you just can't poke it vertically. "The water is bad because it makes it hard to see what the hell we're doing," he says. Indeed, the water has a milky look, probably from suspended volcanic ash; you can see clearly for a foot, hazily for another foot, and below that you can see vague, greenish shapes at best; everything is covered in a uniform brown jacket of silt. "On the other hand, it's good because if a mine gets detonated by something other than your foot, the water's going to absorb some of the blast by flashing into steam. Now: tactically our problem is that we are exposed to an ambush from above left: the west bank. Poor old Jackie Woo is down and he can't protect that flank anymore. You can bet that John Wayne is covering things on the right as best as he can. Since it is the left bank that's most vulnerable, we will now head for the bank on that side, and try to reach the protection of the overhang. We should not all converge on the same point; we spread out so that if one of us detonates a mine it won't hit anyone else."

Each one of them picks a destination on the west bank and tells everyone else what it is, so that they won't converge on the same place, and then each begins probing his or her way towards it. Randy tries to resist the temptation to look up. He says, after about fifteen minutes: "I know what's going on with the explosions. Wing's people are tunneling their way toward Golgotha. They're going to remove the gold through some kind of an underground conduit. It'll look like they are excavating it from their own property. But they'll actually be taking it from here."

Amy grins. "They're robbing the bank."

Randy nods, mildly annoyed that she's not taking it more seriously.

"Wing must have been too busy with the Long March and the Great Leap Forward to buy this real estate when it was available," Enoch says.

A few minutes later, Doug Shaftoe says, "To what extent do you give a shit, Randy?"

"What do you mean?"

"Would you be willing to die to prevent Wing from getting that gold?"

"Probably not."

"Would you be willing to kill?"

"Well," says Randy, a bit taken aback, "I said I wouldn't be willing to die. So—"

"Don't give me that golden rule shit," Doug says. "If someone broke into your house in the middle of the night and threatened your family, and you had a shotgun in your hands, would you use it?"

Randy involuntarily looks towards Amy. Because this is not only an ethical conundrum. It's also a test to determine whether Randy is fit to be Doug's daughter's husband, and the father of his grandchildren. "Well, I should hope so," Randy says. Amy's pretending not to listen.

The water all around them makes a spattering, searing noise. Everyone cringes. Then they realize that a handful of small pebbles was tossed into the water from above. They look up at the rim of the overhang, and see a tiny, reciprocating movement: Jackie Woo, standing on the top of the bank, waving his hand at them.

"My eyes are going," Doug says. "Does he look intact to you?"

"Yes!" Amy says. She beams—her pearlies are very white in the sun—and waves back.

Jackie's grinning. He's carrying a long, muddy rod in one hand: his mine probe. In the other, he's got a dirty canister about the size of a clay pigeon. He holds it up and waggles it in the air. "Nip mine!" he shouts gleefully.

"Well, put it the fuck down, you asshole!" Doug hollers, "after all these years it's going to be incredibly unstable." Then he gets a look of incredulous confusion. "Who the hell set off the other mine if it wasn't you? Someone was screaming up there."

"I haven't found him," Jackie Woo says. "He stopped screaming."

"Do you think he's dead?"

"No."

"Did you hear any other voices?"

"No."

"Jesus Christ," Doug says, "someone's been shadowing us the whole way." He turned around and looks up at the opposite bank, where John Wayne has now probed his way to the edge and is taking this all in. Some kind of hand gesture passes between them (they brought walkie-talkies, but Doug scorns them as a crutch for lightweights and wannabes). John Wayne settles down onto his belly and gets out a pair of binoculars with objective lenses as big as saucers and begins scanning Jackie Woo's side.

The group in the riverbed probes onwards in silence for a while. None of them can figure out what is going on, and so it's good that they have this mine-probing thing to keep their hands and minds busy. Randy's probe hits something flexible, buried a couple of inches deep in silt and gravel. He flinches so hard he almost topples back on his ass, and spends a minute or two trying to get his composure back. The silt gives everything the blank but suggestive look of sheet-covered corpses. Trying to identify the shapes makes his mind tired. He clears some gravel aside and runs his hand lightly over this thing. Dead leaves tumble through the water and tickle his forearms. "Got an old tire down here," he says. "Big. Truck-sized. And bald as an egg."

Every so often a colored bird will descend from the shade of the overhanging jungle and flash into the sun, never failing to scare the shit out of them. The sun is brutal. Randy was only a few yards away from the shade of the bank when all of this started, and now he's pretty sure that he's going to pass out from sunstroke before he gets there.

Enoch Root starts muttering in Latin at one point. Randy looks over at him and sees that he's holding up a dripping, muddy human skull.

An irridescent bright blue bird with a yellow scimitar beak mounted in a black-and-orange head shoots out of the jungle, seizes control of a nearby rock, and cocks its head at him. The earth shakes again; Randy flinches and a bead curtain of sweat falls out of his eyebrows.

"Down under the rocks and mud there's reinforced concrete," Doug says. "I can see the rebar sticking out."

Another bird or something flashes out of the shadows, headed nearly straight down toward the water at tremendous speed. Amy makes a funny grunting sound. Randy's just turning to look her way when a tremendous, hammering racket opens up from above. He looks up to see a blossom of flame strobing out of the slotted flash arrestor on the muzzle of John Wayne's assault rifle. Seems like he's shooting directly across the river. Jackie Woo gets off a few shots too. Randy, who's squatting, loses his balance from all of this head-turning and has to put out a hand to steady himself, which fortunately doesn't come down on top of a mine. He looks over at Amy; only her head and shoulders are showing out of the water, and she's staring at nothing in particular, with a look in her eyes that Randy doesn't like at all. He rises to his feet and takes a step towards her.

"Randy, don't do that," says Doug Shaftoe. Doug has already reached the shade, and is only a couple of paces from the curtain of vegetation that hangs over the riverbank.

There is a piece of debris riding on the surface of the river not far from Amy's face, but it is not being moved by the current. It moves when Amy moves. Randy takes another step towards her, putting his foot down on a big silt-covered boulder whose top he can make out through the milky water. He squats on that boulder like a bird and focuses again on Amy, who is maybe fifteen feet away from him. John Wayne fires a series of individual shots from his rifle. Randy realizes that the piece of debris is made of feathers, bound to the butt of a narrow stick.

"Amy's been shot with an arrow," Randy says.

"Well that's just fucking great," Doug mutters.

"Amy, where are you hit?" says Enoch Root.

Amy still can't seem to speak. She stands up awkwardly, doing all the work with her left leg, and as she rises the arrow emerges from the water and turns out to be lodged squarely in the middle of her right thigh. The wound is washed clean at first but then blood wells out from around the arrow's shaft and begins to patrol down her leg in bifurcating streams.

Doug's engaged in some furious exchange of hand signals with the men up above. "You know," he whispers, "I can tell that this is one of those classic deals where what was supposed to be a simple reconnaissance suddenly turns into the actual battle."

Amy grabs the shaft of the arrow with both hands and tries to snap it, but the wood is green, and won't break cleanly. "I dropped my knife somewhere," she says. Her voice sounds calm, putting some effort into making it that way. "I think I can deal with this level of pain for a little," she says. "But I don't like it at all."

Near Amy, Randy can see another silt-covered boulder near the surface, maybe six feet away. He gathers himself and leaps towards it. But it topples under the impact of his foot and sends him splashing full-length into the streambed. When he sits up and gets a look at it, the boulder turns out to be a squat cylindrical object about as big around as a dinner plate and several inches thick.

"Randy, what you're looking at is a Nip anti-tank mine," Doug says. "It is highly unstable with age, and it contains enough high explosive to essentially decapitate everyone in our little group here. So if you could just stop being a complete asshole for a little bit, I'm sure that we would all appreciate it very much."

Amy shows Randy the palm of one hand. "I'm not looking for you to prove anything," she says. "If you're trying to say you love me, send me a fucking valentine."

"I love you," Randy says. "I want you to be okay. I want you to marry me."

"Well, that's very romantic," Amy says, sarcastically, and then starts crying.

"Oh, Jesus Christ," Doug Shaftoe says. "You guys can do this later! Will you ease up? Whoever fired that arrow is long gone. The Huks are guerrillas. They know how to make themselves scarce."

"It wasn't fired by a Huk," Randy says. "Huks have guns. Even I know that."

"Who fired it, then?" Amy asks, working hard to get her composure back.

"It looks like a Cayuse arrow," Randy says.

"Cayuse? You think it was fired by a Cayuse?" Doug demands. Randy admires that Doug, while skeptical, is essentially open to the idea.

"No," Randy says, taking another step towards Amy, and straddling the antitank mine. "The Cayuse are extinct. Measles. So it was made by a white man who is an expert in the hunting practices of Northwest Indian tribes. What else do we know about him? That's he's really good at sneaking around in the jungle. And that he's so totally fucking crazy that even when he's been injured by a land mine, he's still crawling around in the undergrowth taking shots at people." Randy's probing the riverbed as he's talking, and now he takes another step. Only six feet away from Amy now. "Not just anyone—he took a shot at Amy. Why? Because he's been watching. He saw Amy sitting next to me when we took that break, resting her head on my shoulder. He knows that if he wants to hurt me, the best thing he could possibly do is take a shot at her."

"Why does he want to hurt you?" Enoch asks.

"Because he's evil."

Enoch looks tremendously impressed.

"Well, who the hell is it?" Amy hisses. She's irritated now, which he takes to be a good sign.

"His name is Andrew Loeb," Randy says. "And Jackie Woo and John Wayne are never going to find him."

"Jackie and John are very good," Doug demurs.

Another step. He can almost reach out and touch Amy. "That's the problem," Randy says. "They're way too smart to run around in a minefield without probing every step. But Andrew Loeb doesn't give a shit. Andrew's totally out of his fucking mind, Doug. He's going to run around up there at will. Or crawl, or hop, or whatever. I'd wager that Andy with one foot blown off, and not caring whether he lives or dies, can move through a minefield faster than Jackie, when Jackie does care."

Finally, Randy's there. He crouches down before Amy, who leans forward, places a hand on each of his shoulders, and rests her weight on him, which feels good. The end of her ponytail paints the back of his neck with warm river water. The arrow's practically in his face. Randy takes his multipurpose tool out and turns it into a saw and cuts through the shaft of the arrow while Amy holds it steady with one fist. Then Amy splays her hand out, winds up, screams in Randy's ear, and slams the butt of the shaft. It disappears into her leg. She collapses over Randy's back and sobs. Randy reaches around behind her leg, cuts his hand on the edge of the arrowhead, grabs the shaft and yanks it out.

"I don't see evidence of arterial bleeding," says Enoch Root, who has a good view of her from behind.

Randy rises to his feet, lifting Amy into the air, collapsed over his shoulder like a sack of rice. He's embarrassed that Amy's body is basically shielding his from any further arrow attacks now. But she's making it clear that she's in no mood for walking.

The shade is only four steps away: shade, and shelter from above. "A land mine just takes a leg or a foot, right?" Randy says. "If I step on one, it won't kill Amy."

"Not one of your better ideas, Randy!" Doug shouts, almost contemptuously. "Just calm down and take your time."

"I just want to know my options," Randy says. "I can't poke around for mines while I'm carrying her."

"Then I'll work my way over to you," says Enoch Root. "Oh, to hell with it!" Enoch stands up and just walks over to them in half a dozen strides.

"Fucking amateurs!" Doug bellows. Enoch Root ignores him, squats down at Randy's feet and begins probing.

Doug rises up out of the stream onto a few boulders strewn along the bank. "I'm going to ascend the wall here," he says, "and go up and reinforce Jackie. He and I'll *find* this Andrew Loeb together." It's clear that "find" here is a euphemism for probably a long list of unpleasant operations. The bank is made of soft eroded stone with lumps of hard black volcanic rock jutting out of it frequently, and by clambering from one outcropping to the next, Doug is able to make his way halfway up the bank in the time it takes Enoch Root to locate one safe place to plant their feet. Randy wouldn't want to be the guy who just shot an arrow into Doug Shaftoe's daughter. Doug is stymied for a moment by the overhang; but by traversing the bank a short distance he's able to reach a tangle of tree roots that's almost as good as a ladder to the top.

"She's shivering," Randy announces. "Amy's shivering."

"She's in shock. Keep her head low and her legs high," says Enoch Root. Randy shifts Amy around, nearly losing his grip on a blood-greased leg.

One of the things that Goto Dengo spoke of during their dinner in Tokyo was the Nipponese practice of tuning streams in gardens by moving rocks from place to place. The sound of a brook is made by patterns in the flow of water, and those patterns encode the presence of rocks on the streambed. Randy found in this an echo of the Palouse winds thing, and said so, and Goto Dengo either thought it was terribly insightful or else was being polite. In any case, several minutes later there is a change in the sound of the water that is flowing around them, and so Randy naturally looks upstream to see that a man is standing in the water about a dozen feet away from them. The man has a shaved head that is sunburned as red as a three-ball. He's wearing what used to be a decent enough business suit, which has practically become one with the jungle now: it is impregnated with red mud, which has made it so heavy that it pulls itself all out of shape as he totters to a standing position. He's got a great big pole, a wizard's staff. He has planted it in the riverbed and is sort of climbing up it hand-over-hand. When he gets fully upright, Randy can see that his right leg terminates just below the knee, although the bare tibia and fibula stick out for a few inches. The bones are scorched and splintered. Andrew Loeb has fashioned a tourniquet from sticks and a hundred-dollar silk necktie that Randy's pretty sure he has seen in the windows of airport duty-free shops. This has throttled back the flow of blood from the end of his leg to a rate comparable to what you would see coming out a Mr. Coffee during its brew cycle. Once Andy has gotten himself fully upright, he smiles brightly and begins to move towards Randy and Amy and Enoch, hopping on his intact leg and using the wizard's staff to keep from falling down. In his free hand he is carrying a great big knife: Bowie-sized, but with all of the extra spikes, saw blades, blood grooves, and other features that go into a really top-of-the-line fighting and survival knife.

Neither Enoch nor Amy sees Andrew. Randy has this insight now that Doug pointed him in the direction of earlier, namely that the ability to kill someone is basically a mental stance, and not a question of physical means; a serial killer armed with a couple of feet of clothesline is far more dangerous than a cheerleader with a bazooka. Randy feels certain, all of a sudden, that he's got the mental stance now. But he doesn't have the means.

And that is the problem right there in a nutshell. The bad guys tend to have the means.

Andy's looking him right in the eye and smiling at him, precisely the same smile you would see on the face of some old acquaintance you had just accidentally run into on an airport concourse. As he approaches, he's kind of shifting the big knife around in his hand, getting it into the right grip for whatever kind of attack he's about to make. It is this detail that finally breaks Randy out of his trance and causes him to shrug Amy off and drop her into the water behind him. Andrew Loeb takes another step forward and plants his wizard's staff, which suddenly flies into the air like a rocket, leaving a steaming crater behind in the water, which instantly fills in, of course. Now Andy's standing there like a stork, having miraculously kept his balance. He bends his one remaining knee and hops towards Randy, then does it again. Then he is dead and toppling backwards and Randy is deaf, or maybe it happens in some other order. Enoch Root has become a column of smoke with a barking, spitting white fire in the center. Andrew Loeb has become a red, comet-shaped disturbance in the stream, marked by a single arm thrust out of the water, a French cuff that is still uncannily white, a cuff link shaped like a little honey bee, and a spindly fist gripping the huge knife.

Randy turns around and looks at Amy. She's levered herself up on one arm. In her opposite hand she's got a sensible, handy sort of revolver which she is aiming in the direction of where Andrew Loeb fell.

Something's moving in the corner of Randy's eye. He turns his head quickly. A coherent, wraith-shaped cloud of smoke is drifting away from Enoch over the surface of the river, just coming into the sun where it is suddenly brilliant. Enoch is just standing there holding a great big old .45 and moving his lips in the unsettled cadences of some dead language.

Andrew's fingers loosen, the knife falls, and the arm relaxes, but does not disappear. An insect lands on his thumb and starts to eat it.

BLACK CHAMBER

"WELL," WATERHOUSE SAYS, "I KNOW A THING OR TWO ABOUT keeping secrets."

"I know that perfectly well," says Colonel Earl Comstock. "It is a fine quality. It is why we want you. After the war."

A formation of bombers flies over the building, rattling its shellshocked walls with a drone that penetrates into their sinuses. They take this opportunity to heave their massive Buffalo china coffee cups off their massive Buffalo china saucers and sip weak, greenish Army coffee.

"Don't let that kind of thing fool you," Comstock hollers over the noise, glancing up toward the bombers, which bank majestically to the north, going up to blast hell out of the incredibly tenacious Tiger of Malaya. "People in the know think that the Nips are on their last legs. It's not too early to think about what you will be doing after the war."

"I told you, sir. Getting married, and—"

"Yeah, teaching math at some little school out west." Comstock sips coffee and grimaces. The grimace is as tightly coupled to the sip as recoil is to the pull of a trigger. "Sounds delightful, Waterhouse, it really does. Oh, there's all kinds of fantasies that sound great to us, sitting here on the outskirts of what used to be Manila, breathing gasoline fumes and swatting mosquitoes. I've heard a hundred guys—mostly enlisted men—

rhapsodize about mowing the lawn. That's all those guys can talk about, is mowing the lawn. But when they get back home, will they want to mow the lawn?"

"No."

"Right. They only talk like that because mowing the lawn sounds great when you're sitting in a foxhole picking lice off your nuts."

One of the useful things about military service is that it gets you acclimatized to having loud, blustery men say rude things to you. Waterhouse shrugs it off. "Could be I'll hate it," he concedes.

At this point Comstock sheds a few decibels, scoots closer, and gets fatherly with him. "It's not just you," he says. "Your wife might not be crazy about it either."

"Oh, she loves the open countryside. Doesn't care for cities."

"You wouldn't have to *live* in a city. With the kind of salary we are talking about here, Waterhouse—" Comstock pauses for effect, sips, grimaces, and lowers his voice another notch "—you could buy a nice little Ford or a Chevy." He stops to let that sink in. "With a V-8 that would give you power to burn! You could live ten, twenty miles away, and drive in every morning at *a mile a minute!*"

"Ten or twenty miles away from where? I'm not clear, yet, on whether I would be working in New York for Electrical Till, or in Fort Meade for this, uh, this new thing—"

"We're thinking of calling it the National Security Agency," Comstock says. "Of course, even that name is secret."

"I understand."

"There was a similar thing, between the wars, called the Black Chamber. Which has a nice ring to it. But a bit old-fashioned."

"That was disbanded."

"Yes. Secretary of State Stimson did away with it, he said 'Gentlemen do not read one another's mail.' " Comstock laughs out loud at this. He laughs for a long time. "Ahh, the world has changed, hasn't it, Waterhouse? Without reading Hitler's and Tojo's mail, where would we be now?"

"We would be in a heck of a fix," Waterhouse concedes.

"You have seen Bletchley Park. You have seen Central Bureau in Brisbane. Those places are nothing less than factories. Mail-reading on an industrial scale." Comstock's eyes glitter at the idea, he is staring through the walls of the building now like Superman with his X-ray vision. "It is the way of the future, Lawrence. War will never be the same. Hitler is gone. The Third Reich is history. Nippon is soon to fall. But this only sets the stage for the struggle with Communism. To build a Bletchley Park big enough for that job, why, hell! We'd have to take over the whole state of Utah or something. That is, if we did it the old-fashioned way, with girls sitting in front of Typex machines."

For the first time, now, Waterhouse gets it. "The digital computer," he says.

"The digital computer," Comstock echoes. He sips and grimaces. "A few roomfuls of that equipment would replace an acre of girls sitting in front of Typex machines." Comstock now gets a naughty, conspiratorial grin on his face, and leans forward. A drop of sweat rolls off the point of his chin and plonks into Waterhouse's coffee. "It would also replace a lot of the stuff that Electrical Till manufactures. So, you see, there is a confluence of interests here." Comstock sets his cup down. Perhaps he is finally convinced that there is no deep stratum of good coffee concealed underneath the bad; perhaps coffee is a frivolous thing compared to the importance of what he is about to divulge. "I have been in constant touch with my higher-ups at Electrical Till, and there is intense interest in this digital computer business. *Intense* interest. The machinery has already been set in motion for a business deal—and, Waterhouse, I only tell you this because, as we have established, you are good at keeping secrets."

"I understand, sir."

"A business deal that would bring Electrical Till, the world's mightiest manufacturer of business machines, together with the government of the United States to construct a machine room of titanic proportions at Fort Meade, Maryland, under the aegis of this new Black Chamber: the National Security Agency. It is an installation that will be the Bletchley Park of our upcoming war against the Communist threat—a threat both internal and external."

"And you would like me to get mixed up in this somehow?"

Comstock blinks. He draws back. He is suddenly cool and remote. "To be absolutely frank, Waterhouse, this thing will go forward with or without you."

Waterhouse chuckles. "I figured that."

"All I'm doing is giving you a greased path, as it were. Because I respect your skills, and I have a certain, I don't know, fatherly affection for you as the result of our work together. I hope you don't mind my saying so."

"Not at all."

"Say! And speaking of that—" Comstock stands up, walking around behind his terrifyingly neat desk, and plucks a single piece of typing paper off the blotter. "How are you coming with Arethusa?"

"Still archiving the intercepts as they come in. Still haven't broken it."

"I have some interesting news about Arethusa."

"You do?"

"Yes. Something you're not aware of." Comstock scans the paper. "After we took Berlin, we scooped up all of Hitler's crypto people and flew thirty-five of them back to London. Our boys there have been interrogating them in detail. Filling in a lot of blanks for us. What do you know about this Rudolf von Hacklheber fellow?"

All traces of moisture have disappeared from Waterhouse's mouth. He sips and does not grimace. "Knew him a little at Princeton. Dr. Turing and I thought we saw his handiwork in Azure/Pufferfish."

"You were right," Comstock says, rattling the paper. "But did you know that he was very likely a Communist?"

"I had no knowledge of his political leanings."

"Well, he is a homo, for one thing, and Hitler hated homos, so that might have pushed him into the arms of the Reds. Also, he was working under a couple of Russians at Hauptgruppe B. Supposedly they were Czarists, and pro-Hitler, but you never know. Well, anyway, in the middle of the war, sometime in late '43, he apparently fled to Sweden. Isn't that funny?"

"Why's it funny?"

"If you have the wherewithal to escape from Germany, why not go to England, and fight for the good guys? No, he went to the east coast of Sweden—directly across the water," Comstock says portentously, "from Finland. Which borders on the Soviet Union." He slaps the page down on his desk. "Seems pretty clear-cut to me."

"So . . ."

"And now, we have these goddamn Arethusa messages bouncing around. Some of them emanating from right here in Manila! Some coming from a mysterious submarine. Not a Nip submarine, evidently. It seems very much like a secret espionage ring of some description. Wouldn't you say so?"

Waterhouse shrugs. "Interpretation isn't my department."

"It is mine," Comstock says, "and I say it's espionage. Probably directed from the Kremlin. Why? Because they are using a cryptosystem that, according to you, is based on Azure/Pufferfish, which was invented by the Communist homo Rudolf von Hacklheber. I hypothesize that von Hacklheber only stayed in Sweden long enough to get some shuteye and maybe cornhole some nice blond boy and then scooted right over to Finland and from there to the waiting arms of Lavrenti Beria."

"Well, gosh!" Waterhouse says, "what do you think we should do?"

"I have taken this Arethusa thing off the back burner. We have become lazy and complacent. More than once, our huffduff people observed Arethusa messages emanating from this general area." Comstock raises his index finger to a map of Luzon. Then he catches himself, realizing that this would be more dignified if he used a pointer. He bends down and grabs a long pointer. Then he realizes he is too close, and has to back up a couple of steps in order to get the business end of the pointer on the part of the map that his index finger was touching a moment earlier. Finally situated, he vigorously circles a coastal region south of Manila, along the strait that separates Luzon from Mindoro. "South of all these volcanoes, along the coast here. This is where that submarine has been skulking around. We haven't gotten a good fix on the bastards yet, because all of our huffduff stations have been way up north here." The pointer swoops up for a lightning raid on the Cordillera Central, where Yamashita has gone to ground. "But not anymore." Down swoops the pointer, vengefully. "I have ordered several huffduff units to set up in this area, and at the northern end of Mindoro. Next time that submarine transmits an Arethusa message, we'll have Catalinas overhead within fifteen minutes."

"Well," Waterhouse volunteers, "maybe I should get cracking on breaking that darn code, then."

"If you could accomplish that, Waterhouse, it would be brilliant. It would mean victory in this, our first cryptological skirmish with the Communists. It would be a splendid kick-off for your relationship with Electrical Till and the NSA. We could set your new bride up with a nice house in the horse country, a gas stove, and a Hoover that would make her forget all about the Palouse Hills."

"Sounds pretty darn inviting," Waterhouse says. "I just can't hold myself back!" And with that, he's out the door.

In a stone room in a half-ruined church, Enoch Root looks out of a busted window and grimaces. "I am not a mathematician," he says. "I only did the calculations that Dengo asked me to do. You will have to ask him to encrypt the message."

"Find another place for your transmitter," Waterhouse says, "and be ready to use it on short notice."

Goto Dengo is right where he said he would be, sitting on the bleachers above third base. The ballfield has been repaired, but no one is playing now. He and Waterhouse have the place to themselves, except for a couple of poor Filipino peasants, driven down to Manila by the war up north, scavenging for dropped popcorn.

"What you ask is very dangerous," he says.

"It will be totally secret," Waterhouse says.

"Think into the future," says Goto Dengo. "One day, these digital computers you speak of will break the Arethusa code. Is this not so?"

"It is so. Not for many years."

"Say ten years. Say twenty years. The code is broken. Then they will go back and find all of the old Arethusa messages—including the message that you want to send to your friends—and read them. So?"

"Yes. It is true."

"And then they will see this message that says, 'Warning, warning, Comstock has laid a trap, the huffduff stations are waiting for you, do not transmit.' Then they will know that there was a spy in Comstock's office. Certainly they will know it was you."

"You're right. You're right. I didn't think of that," Waterhouse says. Then he realizes something else. "They'll know about you too."

Goto Dengo blanches. "Please. I am so tired."

"One of the Arethusa messages spoke of a person named GD."

Goto Dengo puts his head in his hands and is perfectly motionless for a long time. He does not have to say it. He and Waterhouse are imagining the same thing: twenty years in the future, Nipponese police burst into the office of Goto Dengo, prosperous businessman, and arrest him for being a Communist spy.

"Only if they decrypt those old messages," Waterhouse says.

"But they will. You said that they will decrypt them."

"Only if they have them," Waterhouse says.

"But they do have them."

"They are in my office."

Goto Dengo is shocked, horrified. "You are not thinking to steal the messages?"

"That's exactly what I'm thinking."

"But this will be noticed."

"No! I will replace them with others."

The voice of Alan Mathison Turing shouts above the buzz of the Project X synchronization tone. The long-playing record, filled with noise, spins on its turntable. "You want the latest in random numbers?"

"Yeah. Some mathematical function that will give me nearly perfect randomness. I know you've been working on this."

"Oh yes," Turing says. "I can provide a much higher degree of randomness than what is on these idiotic phonograph records that you and I are staring at."

"How do you do it?"

"I have in mind a zeta function that is simple to understand, extremely tedious to calculate. I hope you have laid in a good stock of valves."

"Don't worry about that, Alan."

"Do you have a pencil?"

"Of course."

"Very well then," Turing says, and begins to call out the symbols of the function.

The Basement is suffocatingly hot because Waterhouse shares it with a coworker who generates thousands of watts of body heat. The coworker both eats and shits ETC cards. What it does in between is Waterhouse's business.

He spends about twenty-four hours sitting there, stripped to the waist, his undershirt wrapped around his head like a turban so he won't drop sweat into the works and cause short circuits, flicking switches on the digital computer's front panel, swapping patch cords on the back, replacing burned-out tubes and bulbs, probing malfunctioning circuits with an oscilloscope. In order to make the computer execute Alan's random number function, he even has to design a new circuit board on the fly, and solder it together. The entire time, he knows, Goto Dengo and Enoch Root are at work somewhere in Manila with scratch paper and pencils, encrypting the final Arethusa message.

He doesn't have to wonder whether they've transmitted it. He will be told.

Indeed, a lieutenant from the Intercept section comes in at about five in the evening, looking triumphant.

"You got an Arethusa message?"

"Two of them," the lieutenant says, holding up two separate sheets with grids of letters on them. "A collision!"

"A collision?"

"A transmitter opened up down south first."

"On land, or—?"

"At sea—off the northeast end of Palawan. They transmitted this." He waves one of the sheets. "Then, almost immediately, a transmitter in Manila came on the air, and sent this." He waves the other sheet.

"Does Colonel Comstock know about this?"

"Oh, yes sir! He was just leaving for the day when the messages came through. He's been on the horn to his huffduff people, the Air Force, the whole bit. He thinks we've got the bastards!"

"Well, before you get carried away celebrating, could you do me a favor?"

"Yes, sir!"

"What did you do with all of the original intercept sheets for the archived Arethusa messages?"

"They're filed, sir. Do you want to see them?"

"Yes. All of them. I need to check them against the versions on the ETC cards. If Arethusa works the way I think it does, then even a single mistranscribed letter could render all of my calculations useless."

"I'll go and fetch them, sir! I'm not going home anyway."

"You're not?"

"Why, no sir! I want to wait around and see how it all comes out with that darned submarine."

Waterhouse goes to the oven and takes out a brick of hot, blank ETC cards. He has learned that he has to keep the cards hot, or else they will soak up the tropical humidity and jam the machinery; so before he moved the digital computer into this room, he insisted that a whole bank of ovens be installed.

He drops the hot cards into the hopper of a card punching machine, sits down at the keyboard, and clips the first intercept sheet up in front of him. He begins to punch the letters into it, one by one. It is a short message; it fits onto three cards. Then he begins punching in the second message.

The lieutenant comes in carrying a cardboard box. "All of the original Arethusa intercept sheets."

"Thank you, Lieutenant."

The lieutenant looks over his shoulder. "Can I help you transcribing those messages?"

"No. The best way for you to help me would be to refill my water pitcher and then don't bother me for the rest of the night. I have a bee in my bonnet about this Arethusa business."

"Yes, sir!" says the lieutenant, insufferably cheerful about the fact that the mystery submarine is, even now, on the run from Catalina bombers.

Waterhouse finishes punching in the second message, though he already knows what it would say if it were decrypted: "TRAP REPEAT TRAP DO NOT TRANSMIT STOP HUFFDUFF UNITS NEARBY."

He takes those cards out of the puncher's output tray and places them neatly in the box along with the cards containing all of the previous Arethusa messages. He then takes the entire contents of this box—a brick of messages about a foot thick—and puts them into his attache case.

He unclips the two fresh intercept slips from the card puncher and puts them on top of the stack of older slips. The brick of cards in his attache case, and the pile of slips in his hand, contain exactly the same information. They are the only copies in all the world. He flips through them to make sure that they contain all of the critical intercepts—such as the long message giving the location of Golgotha, and the one that mentions Goto Dengo's initials. He puts the whole stack of slips on top of one of the ovens.

He dumps a foot-thick stack of hot blank cards into the input hopper of the card punch. He connects the punch's control cable up to the digital computer, so that the computer can control it.

Then he starts the program he has written, the one that generates random numbers according to Turing's function. Lights flash, and the card reader whirrs, as the program is loaded into the computer's RAM. Then it pauses, waiting for input: the function needs a seed. A stream of bits that will get it going. Any seed will do. Waterhouse thinks about it for a moment, and then types in COMSTOCK.

The card punch rumbles into action. The stack of blanks begins to get shorter. Punched cards skitter into the output tray. When it's finished, Waterhouse pulls one of them out, holds it up to the light, and looks at the pattern of tiny rectangular holes punched out of the manila. A constellation of doorways.

"It'll look like any other encrypted message," he explained to Goto Dengo, up on the bleachers, "but the, uh, the crypto boys" (he almost said the NSA) "can run their computers on them forever and never break the code—because there *is* no code."

He puts this stack of freshly punched cards into the box labeled ARE-THUSA INTERCEPTS, and puts it back in its place on the shelf.

Finally, before leaving the lab, he goes back over to that oven, and slides the corner of that stack of intercept sheets very close to a pilot light. It is reluctant to catch, so he gives it some help with a flick of his Zippo. He stands back and watches the pile burn for a while, until he's sure that all of the strange information on those sheets has been destroyed.

Then he goes out into the hallway in search of a fire extinguisher. Upstairs, he can hear Comstock's boys, gathered around the radio, baying like hounds.

PASSAGE

WHEN HE HAS PICKED HIMSELF UP OFF THE DECK, AND HIS EARS have stopped ringing, Bischoff says, "Take her down to seventy-five meters."

The dial that tells their depth says twenty. Somewhere, perhaps a hundred meters above them, crewmen of a circling bomber are setting their depth charges to explode when they have sunk to a depth of twenty, and so twenty is a bad place to be for a while.

The dial does not move, though, and Bischoff has to repeat the command. Everyone on the boat must be deaf.

Either that, or the *V-Million* has sustained damage to her dive planes. Bischoff presses his skull against a bulkhead, and even though his ears don't work so well anymore, he can feel the whine of the turbines. At least they have power. They can move.

But Catalinas can move faster.

Say what you want about those old, clanking diesel U-boats, they at least had guns on them. You could surface, and go out on the decks in the sun and the air, and fight back. But in the *V-Million,* this swimming rocket, the only weapon is secrecy. In the Baltic, fine. But this is the Mindoro Strait, which is an ocean of window-glass. *V-Million* might as well be suspended in midair from piano wires, searchlights crossing on it.

The needle on the dial is moving now, passing down through twenty-five meters. The deck twists under Bischoff's feet as she recoils from another depth charge. But he can tell from the way it twists that this one has detonated too high to deal serious damage. From habit he glances at the dial that tells their speed, and notes it down along with the time: 1746 hours. The sun must be lower and lower in the sky, its light glancing off the tops of the waves, forcing the pilots of the Catalinas to peer down through a screen of bright noise. Another hour and *V-Million* will be completely invisible. Then, if Bischoff has kept careful records of their speed and course, dead reckoning will tell them approximately where they are, and enable them to run down the Palawan Passage in the night, or to cut west across the South China Sea if that seems like a good idea. But really he is hoping to find some nice pirate cove on the north coast of Borneo, marry a nice orangutan, and raise a little family.

The face of the depth dial says *Tiefenmesser* in that old-fashioned Gothic lettering that the Nazis loved so much. *Messer* means a gauge or meter, but it also means knife. *Das Messer sitzt mir an der Kehle.* The knife is at my throat; I am face-to-face with doom. When the knife is at your throat, you don't want it to move the way the needle on the *Tiefenmesser* is moving now. Every tick on the dial's face is another meter of water between Bischoff and the sun and the air.

"I would like to be a Messerschmidt," Bischoff mutters. A man who smashes *Messers* with a hammer, but also a beautiful thing that flies.

"You will see light, and breathe fresh air again, Günter," says Rudolf von Hacklheber, a civilian mathematician who really has no place on the bridge of a U-boat during a fight to the death. But there's no *good* place for him to be, and so here he is.

Now this is a fine thing for Rudy to say, a lovely show of support for Günter. But saving the life of everyone on the U-boat, and getting its cargo of gold to safety, now depends on Günter's emotional stability, and especially on his confidence. Sometimes, if you want to live and breathe tomorrow, you have to dive into the black depths today, and that is a leap of faith—faith in your U-boat, and your crew—beside which the saints' religious epiphanies amount to nothing.

So Rudy's promise is soon forgotten—or at least it is forgotten by Bischoff. Bischoff derives *strength* from having heard it, and from similar things that members of his crew say to him, and from their grins and thumbs-up and slaps on the shoulder, and their displays of pluck and initiative, the clever repairs that they make to broken plumbing and overtaxed engines. Strength gives him faith, and faith makes him into a good U-boat skipper. Some would say the best who ever lived. But Bischoff knows many others, better than him, whose bodies are trapped in knuckles of imploded metal on the floor of the North Atlantic.

It comes together like this: the sun has gone down, as it can be relied on to do every day, even when you are a beleaguered U-boat. The *V-Million* has reamed a tunnel through the Palawan Passage, screaming along, for several hours, at the completely unreasonable speed of twenty-nine knots—four times as fast as U-boats are supposed to be capable of going.

The Americans will have drawn a small circle around the point in the ocean where the mysterious U-boat was last sighted. But the speed of the *V-Million* is four times as great as they think it is. The real circle is four times as wide as the one they've drawn. The Yanks won't expect them to surface where they are.

But they have to surface because the *V-Million* wasn't made to run at twenty-nine knots forever; she burns fuel, and hydrogen peroxide, at a ridiculous rate when both of her six-thousand-horsepower turbines are spinning. There is plenty of fuel remaining. But she runs out of hydrogen peroxide at about midnight. She has a few miserable batteries, and electric motors, that just barely suffice to get her up to the surface. But then she has to breathe air for a while, and run her diesels.

So the *V-Million*, and a few crew members, get to enjoy some fresh air. Bischoff doesn't, because he is dealing with new complexities that have arisen in the engine room. This probably saves his life, because he doesn't even know they're being strafed until he hears the cannon rounds drumming against the outer hull.

Then it is the same old drill, the crash dive, which was so exciting when he was a young man practicing it in the Baltic, and has become so tedious for him now. Looking up through a hatch he gets a moment's glimpse of a single star in the sky before the view is blocked by a mutilated crewman being fed down from above.

Only five minutes later the depth charge scores a direct hit on the stern of the *V-Million* and tears a hole through both the outer and the pressure hull. The deck angles beneath Bischoff's feet, and his ears begin to pop. On a submarine, both of these are bad omens. He can hear hatches clanging shut as the crew try to stem the advance of the water towards the bow; each one seals the fate of whomever happens to be aft of it. But they're all dead anyway, it is just a question of timing now. Those hatches are not meant to stem five, six, seven, eight, nine, ten atmospheres of pressure. They give way, the pressure spikes upwards as the bubble of air in the front of the *V-Million* suddenly halves its volume, then halves it again, and again. Each wave of pressure comes as sudden crushing pressure on Bischoff's thorax, driving all the air out of his lungs.

Because the bow is pointed straight up, like a needle on a meter, there's no deck to stand on, and every time a bulkhead yields, and the water level shoots up towards the bow, it leaves them suddenly submerged, with crushed and evacuated lungs, and they must swim up and find the air bubble again.

But finally the mangled stern of the boat spikes into the seafloor and the *V-Million* settles down, the forwardmost cabin rotating around them, tremendous rock-crushing noises all around as a coral reef is destroyed by the boat's falling hull. And then it's finished. Günter Bischoff and Rudolf von Hacklheber are together in a safe cozy bubble of compressed air, all of the air that used to be in the *V-Million* reduced to a pocket the size of a car. It's dark.

He hears Rudy undoing the latches on his aluminum briefcase.

"Don't strike a match," Bischoff says. "This air is compressed, it will burn like a flare."

"That would be *terrible*," Rudy says, and instead turns on a flashlight. The light comes on and immediately dims and goes brown and shrinks to a tiny red speck: the glowing remains of the filament in the bulb.

"Your light bulb has imploded," Bischoff explains. "But at least I got a little glimpse of you, with that silly look on your face."

"You too have looked better," Rudy says. Bischoff can hear him closing up the briefcase, snapping the latches into place. "Do you think my briefcase will float here forever?"

"Eventually the pressure hull above us will corrode. The air will escape from it in a thin line of bubbles that will grow into gyrating nebulas of foul air as they rush towards the surface. The water level will rise and press your briefcase up against what is left of the pressure hull's forward dome, and it will fill with water. But still there will be a little pocket of air in one corner of your briefcase, perhaps."

"I was thinking of leaving a note in it."

"If you do, better address it to the United States government."

"Department of the Navy, you think?"

"Department of Spying. What do they call it? The OSS."

"Why do you say this?"

"They knew where we were, Rudy. The Catalinas were waiting for us."

"Maybe they found us with radar."

"I allowed for radar. Those planes came even faster. You know what it means?"

"Tell me."

"It means that those who were hunting us knew how fast the *V-Million* could go."

"Ah . . . so that is why you think of spies."

"I gave Bobby the plans, Rudy."

"The plans for the *V-Million?*"

"Yes . . . so that he could buy forgiveness from the Americans."

"Well, in retrospect maybe you shouldn't have done that. But I do not blame you for it, Günter. It was a magnificent gesture."

"Now they will come down and find us."

"After we're dead, you mean."

"Yes. The whole plan is ruined. Ah well, it was a nice conspiracy while it lasted. Perhaps Enoch Root will display some adaptability."

"You really think spies will come down to go through this wreck?"

"Who knows?" Bischoff says. "Why are you worrying about it?"

"I have the coordinates of Golgotha here in my briefcase," Rudy says. "But I know for certain that they are not written down anywhere else in *V-Million*."

"You know that because you're the one who decrypted that message."

"Yes. Maybe I should burn the message now."

"It would kill us," Bischoff says, "but at least we would die with some warmth and some light."

"You are going to be on a sandy beach, sunning yourself, in a few hours, Günter," Rudy says.

"Stop it!"

"I made a promise which I intend to keep," Rudy says.

There is a movement in the water, the strangled splash of a kicking foot being drawn under the surface.

"Rudy? Rudy?" Bischoff says. But he is alone in a black dome of
silence.

A minute later a hand grips his ankle.

Rudy climbs up his body like a ladder and thrusts his head above the
surface and howls for air. But this air is the good stuff, sixteen times as
much oxygen in a single lungful. He feels better quickly. Bischoff holds
him while he calms down.

"The hatch is open," Rudy says. "I saw light through it. The sun is
up, Günter!"

"Let's go, then!"

"You go. I'll stay and burn the message." Rudy's opening his briefcase
again, feeling through papers with his hands, taking something out, closing the briefcase again.

Bischoff cannot move.

"I strike the match in thirty seconds," Rudy says.

Bischoff launches himself towards Rudy's voice and wraps his arms
around him in the dark.

"I'll find the others," Bischoff says. "I'll tell them that some fucking
American spy is onto us. And we'll get that gold first, and we'll keep it
out of their hands."

"Go!" Rudy cries. "I want everything to happen fast now."

Bischoff kisses him once on each cheek and then dives.

Ahead of him is faint blue-green light, coming from no particular
direction.

Rudy swam to the hatch, opened it, and swam back, and was almost
dead when he returned. Bischoff has to find that hatch and then swim
all the way to the surface. He knows that it will be impossible.

But then much brighter, warmer light floods the interior of the *V-
Million*. Bischoff looks back and up, and sees the forward end of the
pressure hull turned into a dome of orange fire, the silhouette of a man
centered in it, lines of welds and rivets spreading away from that center
like the meridians of a globe. It's bright as day. He turns around and
swims easily away down the gangway, into the control room, and finds
the hatch: a disk of cyan light.

A life-ring is pressed up against what is now the ceiling of this room.
He grabs it and wrestles it down into the middle of the cabin, then
shoves it before him through the hatch, and kicks his way through.

There's coral all around him, and it's beautiful. He'd love to stay and
sightsee, but he's got responsibilities above. He keeps a grip on the life
preserver, and although he doesn't feel himself moving, he sees the coral
dropping away below. There's a big grey thing lying on it, bubbling and

bleeding, and this gets smaller and smaller, like a rocket flying away into the sky.

He looks up into the water that is streaming over his face. Both of Bischoff's arms are above his head, gripping the rim of the life-ring, and he sees a disk of sunlight through it, getting brighter and redder as he ascends.

His knees begin to hurt.

LIQUIDITY

THE REST OF IT ALL SEEMS LIKE HISTORY TO RANDALL LAWRENCE Waterhouse. He knows that technically speaking it is the present, and all of the really important stuff is future. But what's important to him is finished and settled. He would like to get on with his life, now that he's got one.

They carry Amy back to the missionary compound and the doctor who is there does some work on her leg, but they can't get her out to the hospital in Manila because Wing has blockaded them in there. This ought to seem threatening, but actually just seems stupid and annoying to them after they've had a little while to get used to it. The people who are doing it are Chinese Communist geronto-apparatchiks backed up by a few bootlicking cronies within the local government, and none of them has the slightest appreciation of things like encrypted spread-spectrum packet radio, which makes it easy for people like Doug and Randy to communicate with the outside world and explain precisely what is going on. Randy's blood type is compatible with Amy's and so he lets the doctor suck him nearly dry. The lack of blood seemingly halves his IQ for a day or two, but even so, when he sees Douglas MacArthur Shaftoe drawing up the shopping list of men and gear that they need to dig up Golgotha, he has enough presence of mind to say: strike all of that stuff. Forget the trucks and jackhammers and dynamite, the end-loaders and excavators and tunnel-boring machines, and just give me a drill, a couple of pumps, and a few thousand gallons of fuel oil. Doug gets it right away, as indeed how could he not, since he basically gave Randy the idea by telling him old war legends about his father. They get the shopping list out to Avi and Goto Dengo with no trouble at all.

Wing keeps them blockaded in the compound for a week; the subterranean explosions continue to shake the earth; Amy's leg gets infected and the doctor comes this close to sawing it off to save her life. Enoch Root spends some time alone with her and suddenly her leg gets a lot better. He explains that he applied a local folk remedy, but Amy refuses to say anything about it.

Meanwhile the rest of them kill time by clearing mines from around Golgotha, and trying to localize those explosions. The verdict seems to be that Wing still has most of a kilometer of hard rock to tunnel through in order to get access to Golgotha, and he's only making a few dozen meters per day.

They know that all hell is breaking loose in the outside world because media and military helicopters keep flying over the place. One day a Goto Engineering chopper lands in the compound. It's got earth-imaging sonar gear, and more importantly it's got antibiotics, which have a nearly magical impact on the jungle bugs in Amy's leg, which have never even met penicillin, much less this state-of-the-art stuff that makes penicillin look like chicken noodle soup. Amy's fever breaks in a couple of hours and she's hobbling within a day. The road gets opened up again and then their problem becomes trying to keep people out—it is jammed with media, opportunistic gold-seekers, and nerds. All of them apparently think they are present at some kind of radical societal watershed, as if global society has gotten so screwed up that the only thing to do is shut down and reboot it.

Randy sees people holding up banners with his name on them, and tries not to think about what this implies. The truckloads of equipment almost cannot make it through this traffic jam, but they do, and there's another really frustrating and tedious week of hauling all of the shit through the jungle. Randy spends most of his time hanging around with the earth-imaging sonar crew; they have this very cool gear that Goto Engineering uses to do CAT scans of the earth that they are about to dig into. By the time all of the heavy equipment is in place, Randy's got the entirety of Golgotha imaged down to a resolution of about a meter; he could fly through it in virtual reality if he were into that kind of thing. As it is, all he needs is to decide where to drill his three holes: two from the top down into the main vault, and then one from the side, coming in almost horizontally from the riverbank, but at a gentle upward angle, until it enters what he thinks is the lowest sump in the main chamber. The drain hole.

Someone arrives from the outside world and convinces Randy he's on the cover of both *TIME* and *Newsweek*. Randy doesn't consider it to be good news. He knows that he's got a new life. He had a particular mental image of what that new life is: mostly, being married to Amy and minding his own business until he dies of old age. It did not enter his calculations that being on the cover of newsweeklies, and people standing in the jungle holding banners with his name on them, would in any way characterize his life. Now he never wants to leave the jungle.

The pumps are mighty, house-sized things; they have to be to fight the back-pressure that they are going to engender. Goto Dengo's young engineers see to it that they are mated into the two vertical holes on top: one to supply compressed air, the other pressurized fuel oil. Doug Shaftoe would like to be involved in this, but he knows it's over his head technically, and he's got other duties: securing the defensive perimeter against gold-seekers and whatever creepy-crawly individuals Wing might have sent out to harass and sabotage them. But Doug has put the Word out, and a whole lot of Doug's very interesting and well-traveled friends have converged on Golgotha from all over the world and are now camped out in foxholes in the jungle, guarding a defensive perimeter strung with monofilament tripwires and other stuff that Randy doesn't even want to know about. Doug just tells him to stay away from the perimeter, and he does. But Randy can sense Doug's interest in the central project here, and so when the big day comes, he lets Doug be the one to throw the switch.

There is a lot of praying first: Avi's brought in a rabbi from Israel, and Enoch Root has brought in the Archbishop of Manila, and Goto Dengo has flown in some Shinto priests, and various Southeast Asian countries have gotten in on the act too. All of them pray or chant for the memory of their departed, though the prayers are practically drowned out by the choppers overhead. A lot of people don't want them disturbing Golgotha at all, and Randy thinks they are basically right. But he's gone out and earth-imaged Wing's tunnel, this subterranean tentacle of air reaching towards the hoard, and released three-dimensional maps of everything to the media, and made the case—reasonably well, he thinks—that it's better to do something constructive than to let it get ripped off by the likes of Wing. Some people have come around to his side and some haven't, but none of the latter group is on the cover of *Time* and *Newsweek*.

Doug Shaftoe is the last guy to take the floor. He removes his mesh-back cap, puts it over his heart, and with tears streaming down his face says something about his father, whom he just barely remembers. He speaks of the Battle of Manila and of how he saw his father for the first time in the wreckage of the Church of San Agustin, and how his father carried him up and down the stairway there before going off to bring hellfire down upon the Nipponese. He speaks about forgiveness and certain other abstractions, and the words are all chopped up and blurred by the helicopters overhead, which only makes it more powerful as far as Randy's concerned, since it's basically all about a bunch of memories that are all chopped up and blurred in Doug's memory to begin with. Finally Doug works his way around to some kind of resolution that is very clear in his heart and mind but poorly articulated, and hits the switch.

The pumps take a few minutes to pressurize Golgotha with a highly combustible mixture of air and fuel oil, and then Doug hits another switch that sets off a small detonation down below. Then the world shudders and rumbles before settling down into a kind of suppressed throbbing howl. A jet of white-hot flame shoots out of the drain hole down below, digs itself into the river very close to where Andrew Loeb came to rest, and throws up a cloud of steam that forces all of the choppers to gain altitude. Randy crawls down under the cover of that steam-cloud, sensing it's the last privacy he'll ever have, and sits down by the edge of the river to watch. After half an hour the jet of hot gas is joined by a rivulet of incandescent fluid that sinks to the bottom of the stream as soon as it emerges, clothed in a fuzz of wildly boiling water. For a long time there is really nothing to be seen except steam; but after Golgotha's been burning for an hour or two, it becomes possible to see that underneath the shallow water, spreading down the valley floor, indeed right around the isolated boulder where Randy's perched, is a bright, thick river of gold.

APPENDIX:
THE SOLITAIRE
ENCRYPTION ALGORITHM

by Bruce Schneier
Author, *Applied Cryptography*
President, Counterpane Systems
http://www.counterpane.com

IN NEAL STEPHENSON'S NOVEL *CRYPTONOMICON*, THE CHARACTER Enoch Root describes a cryptosystem code-named "Pontifex" to another character named Randy Waterhouse, and later reveals that the steps of the algorithm are intended to be carried out using a deck of playing cards. These two characters go on to exchange several encrypted messages using this system. The system is called "Solitaire" (in the novel, "Pontifex" is a code name intended to temporarily conceal the fact that it employs a deck of cards) and I designed it to allow field agents to communicate securely without having to rely on electronics or having to carry incriminating tools. An agent might be in a situation where he just does not have access to a computer, or may be prosecuted if he has tools for secret communication. But a deck of cards . . . what harm is that?

Solitaire gets its security from the inherent randomness in a shuffled deck of cards. By manipulating this deck, a communicant can create a string of "random" letters that he then combines with his message. Of course Solitaire can be simulated on a computer, but it is designed to be implemented by hand.

Solitaire may be low-tech, but its security is intended to be high-tech. I designed Solitaire to be secure even against the most well-funded military adversaries with the biggest computers and the smartest cryptanalysts. Of course there is no guarantee that someone won't find a clever attack against Solitaire (watch my web page for updates), but the algorithm is certainly better than any other pencil and paper cipher I've ever seen.

It's not fast, though. It can take an evening to encrypt or decrypt a reasonably long message. In David Kahn's book *Kahn on Codes,* he describes a real pencil-and-paper cipher used by a Soviet spy. Both the Soviet algorithm and Solitaire take about the same amount of time to encrypt a message.

ENCRYPTING WITH SOLITAIRE

Solitaire is an output-feedback mode stream cipher. Sometimes this is called a key-generator (KG in U.S. military speak). The basic idea is that

Solitaire generates a stream, often called a "keystream," of numbers between 1 and 26. To encrypt, generate the same number of keystream letters as plaintext letters. Then add them modulo 26 to plaintext letters, one at a time, to create the ciphertext. To decrypt, generate the same keystream and subtract modulo 26 from the ciphertext to recover the plaintext.

For example, to encrypt the first Solitaire message mentioned in Stephenson's novel, "DO NOT USE PC":

1. Split the plaintext message into five character groups. (There is nothing magical about five-character groups; it's just tradition.) Use X's to fill in the last group. So if the message is "DO NOT USE PC" then the plaintext is:

   D O N O T U S E P C

2. Use Solitaire to generate ten keystream letters. (Details are below.) Assume they are:

   K D W U P O N O W T

3. Convert the plaintext message from letters into numbers: $A = 1$, $B = 2$, etc:

   4 15 14 15 20 21 19 5 16 3

4. Convert the keystream letters similarly:

   11 4 23 21 16 15 14 15 23 20

5. Add the plaintext number stream to the keystream numbers, modulo 26. (All this means is, if the sum is more than 26, subtract 26 from the result.) For example, $1 + 1 = 2$, $26 + 1 = 27$, and $27 - 26 = 1$ . . . so $26 + 1 = 1$.

   15 19 11 10 10 10 7 20 13 23

6. Convert the numbers back to letters.

   O S K J J J G T M W

If you are really good at this, you can learn to add letters in your head, and just add the letters from steps (1) and (2). It just takes practice. It's easy to remember that $A + A = B$; remembering that $T + Q = K$ is harder.

DECRYPTING WITH SOLITAIRE

The basic idea is that the receiver generates the same keystream, and then subtracts the keystream letters from the ciphertext letters.

1. Take the ciphertext message and put it in five character groups. (It should already be in this form.)

   O S K J J J G T M W

2. Use Solitaire to generate ten keystream letters. If the receiver uses the same key as the sender, the keystream letters will be the same:

   K D W U P O N O W T

3. Convert the ciphertext message from letters into numbers:

   15 19 11 10 10 10 7 20 13 23

4. Convert the keystream letters similarly:

11 4 23 21 16   15 14 15 23 20

5. Subtract the keystream numbers from the ciphertext numbers, modulo 26. For example, $22 - 1 = 20$, $1 - 22 = 5$. (It's easy. If the first number is less than the second number, add 26 to the first number before subtracting. So $1 - 22 = ?$ becomes $27 - 22 = 5$.)

4 15 14 15 20   21 19 5 16 3

6. Convert the numbers back to letters.

D O N O T   U S E P C

Decryption is the same as encryption, except that you subtract the keystream from the ciphertext message.

GENERATING THE KEYSTREAM LETTERS

This is the heart of Solitaire. The above descriptions of encryption and decryption work for any output-feedback mode stream cipher. This section explains how Solitaire works.

Solitaire generates a keystream using a deck of cards. You can think of a 54-card deck (remember the jokers) as a 54-element permutation. There are 54!, or about 2.31×10^{71}, possible different orderings of a deck. Even better, there are 52 cards in a deck (without the jokers), and 26 letters in the alphabet. That kind of coincidence is just too good to pass up.

To be used for Solitaire, a deck needs a full set of 52 cards and two jokers. The jokers must be different in some way. (This is common. The deck I'm looking at as I write this has stars on its jokers: one has a little star and the other has a big star.) Call one joker A and the other B. Generally, there is a graphical element on the jokers that is the same, but different size. Make the "B" joker the one that is "bigger." If it's easier, you can write a big "A" and "B" on the two jokers, but remember that you will have to explain that to the secret police if you ever get caught.

To initialize the deck, take the deck in your hand, face up. Then arrange the cards in the initial configuration that is the key. (I'll talk about the key later, but it's different than the keystream.) Now you're ready to produce a string of keystream letters.

This is Solitaire:

1. Find the A joker. Move it one card down. (That is, swap it with the card beneath it.) If the joker is the bottom card of the deck, move it just below the top card.

2. Find the B joker. Move it two cards down. If the joker is the bottom card of the deck, move it just below the second card. If the joker is one up from the bottom card, move it just below the top card. (Basically, assume the deck is a loop . . . you get the idea.)

It's important to do these two steps in order. It's tempting to get lazy and just move the jokers as you find them. This is okay, unless they are very close to each other.

So if the deck looks like this before step 1:

    3 A B 8 9

at the end of step 2 it should look like:

    3 A 8 B 9

If you have any doubt, remember to move the A joker before the B joker. And be careful when the jokers are at the bottom of the deck.

3. Perform a triple cut. That is, swap the cards above the first joker with the cards below the second joker. If the deck used to look like:

    2 4 6 B 4 8 7 1 A 3 9

then after the triple cut operation it will look like:

    3 9 B 4 8 7 1 A 2 4 6

"First" and "second" jokers refer to whatever joker is nearest to, and furthest from, the top of the deck. Ignore the "A" and "B" designations for this step.

Remember that the jokers and the cards between them don't move; the other cards move around them. This is easy to do in your hands. If there are no cards in one of the three sections (either the jokers are adjacent, or one is on top or the bottom), just treat that section as empty and move it anyway.

4. Perform a count cut. Look at the bottom card. Convert it into a number from 1 through 53. (Use the bridge order of suits: clubs, diamonds, hearts, and spades. If the card is a ♣, it is the value shown. If the card is a ♦, it is the value plus 13. If it is a ♥, it is the value plus 26. If it is a ♠, it is the value plus 39. Either joker is a 53.) Count down from the top card that number. (I generally count 1 through 13 again and again if I have to; it's easier than counting to high numbers sequentially.) Cut after the card that you counted down to, leaving the bottom card on the bottom. If the deck used to look like:

    7 . . . cards . . . 4 5 . . . cards . . . 8 9

and the ninth card was the 4, the cut would result in:

    5 . . . cards . . . 8 7 . . . cards . . . 4 9

The reason the last card is left in place is to make the step reversible. This is important for mathematical analysis of its security.

5. Find the output card. Look at the top card. Convert it into a number from 1 through 53, in the same manner as above. Count down that many cards. (Count the top card as number one.) Write the card after the one you counted to on a piece of paper. (If you hit a joker, don't write anything down and start over again with step 1.) This is the first output card. Note that this step does not modify the state of the deck.

6. Convert the card to a number. As before, use the bridge suits to order them. From lowest to highest, we have clubs, diamonds, hearts, and spades. Hence, *A♣* through *K♣* is 1 through 13, *A♦* through *K♦* is 14 through 26, *A♥* through *K♥* is 1 through 13, and *A♠* through *K♠* is 14 through 26.

That's Solitaire. You can use it create as many keystream numbers as you need.

I know that there are regional differences in decks of cards, depending on the country. In general, it does not matter what suit ordering you use, or how you convert cards to numbers. What matters is that the sender and the receiver agree on the rules. If you're not consistent you won't be able to communicate.

KEYING THE DECK

Solitaire is only as secure as the key. That is, the easiest way to break Solitaire is to figure out what key the communicants are using. If you don't have a good key, none of the rest of this matters. Here are some suggestions for exchanging a key.

1. Shuffle the deck. A random key is the best. One of the communicants can shuffle up a random deck and then create another, identical deck. One goes to the sender and the other to the receiver. Most people are not good shufflers, so shuffle the deck at least ten times, and try to use a deck that has been played with instead of a fresh deck out of the box. Remember to keep a spare deck in the keyed order, otherwise if you make a mistake you'll never be able to decrypt the message. Also remember that the key is at risk as long as it exists; the secret police could find the deck and copy down its order.

2. Use a bridge ordering. A description of a set of bridge hands that you might see in a newspaper or a bridge book is about a 95-bit key. If the communicants can agree on a way to convert that to a deck ordering and a way to set the jokers (perhaps after the first two cards that are mentioned in the discussion of the game), this can work. Be warned: the secret police can find your bridge column and copy down the order. You can try setting up some repeatable convention for which bridge column to use; for example, "use the bridge column in your home-town newspaper for the day on which you encrypt the message," or some-thing like that. Or use a list of keywords to search the *New York Times* website, and use the bridge column for the day of the article that comes up when you search on those words. If the keywords are found or inter-cepted, they look like a passphrase. And pick your own convention; re-member that the secret police read Neal Stephenson's books, too.

3. Use a passphrase to order the deck. This method uses the Solitaire

algorithm to create an initial deck ordering. Both the sender and receiver share a passphrase. (For example, "SECRET KEY.") Start with the deck in a fixed order; lowest card to highest card, in bridge suits. Perform the Solitaire operation, but instead of Step 5, do another count cut based on the first character of the passphrase (19, in this example). (Remember to put the top cards just above the bottom card in the deck, as before.) Do this once for each character. Use another two characters to set the positions of the jokers. Remember, though, that there are only about 1.4 bits of randomness per character in standard English. You're going to want at least an 80-character passphrase to make this secure; I recommend at least 120 characters. (Sorry, but you just can't get good security with a shorter key.)

Sample Output

Here's some sample data to practice your Solitaire skills with:

Sample 1: Start with an unkeyed deck: A♣ through K♣, A♥ through K♥, A♦ through K♦, A♠ through K♠, A joker, B joker (you can think of this as 1–52, A, B). The first ten outputs are:

    4 49 10 (53) 24 8 51 44 6 33

The 53 is skipped, of course. I just put it there for demonstration. If the plain text is:

    A A A A A   A A A A A

then the cipher text is:

    E X K Y I   Z S G E H

Sample 2: Using keying method 3 and the key "FOO," the first fifteen outputs are:

    8 19 7 25 20 (53) 9 8 22 32 43 5 26 17 (53) 38 48

If the plain text is all As, the cipher text is:

    I T H Z U   J I W G R   F A R M W

Sample 3: Using keying method 3 and the key "CRYPTONOMI-CON," the message "SOLITAIRE" encrypts to:

    K I R A K   S F J A N

Of course, you should use a longer key. These samples are for test purposes only. There are more samples on the website, and you can use the book's PERL script to create your own.

Security Through Obscurity

Solitaire is designed to be secure even if the enemy knows how the algorithm works. I have assumed that *Cryptonomicon* will be a best seller, and that copies will be available everywhere. I assume that the NSA and everyone else will study the algorithm and will watch for it. I assume that the only secret is the key.

That's why keeping the key secret is so important. If you have a deck of cards in a safe place, you should assume the enemy will at least entertain the thought that you are using Solitaire. If you have a bridge column in your safe deposit box, you should expect to raise a few eyebrows. If any group is known to be using the algorithm, expect the secret police to maintain a database of bridge columns to use in cracking attempts. Solitaire is strong even if the enemy knows you are using it, and a simple deck of playing cards is still much less incriminating than a software encryption program running on your laptop, but the algorithm is no substitute for street smarts.

OPERATIONAL NOTES

The first rule of an output-feedback mode stream cipher, any of them, is that you should never use the same key to encrypt two different messages. Repeat after me: NEVER USE THE SAME KEY TO EN-CRYPT TWO DIFFERENT MESSAGES. If you do, you completely break the security of the system. Here's why: if you have two ciphertext streams, $A + K$ and $B + K$, and you subtract one from the other, you get $(A + K) - (B + K) = A + K - B - K = A - B$. That's two plaintext streams combined with each other, and is very easy to break. Trust me on this one: you might not be able to recover A and B from $A - B$, but a professional cryptanalyst can. This is vitally important: never use the same key to encrypt two different messages.

Keep your messages short. This algorithm is designed to be used with small messages: a couple of thousand characters. If you have to encrypt a 100,000-word novel, use a computer algorithm. Use shorthand, abbre-viations, and slang in your messages. Don't be chatty.

For maximum security, try to do everything in your head. If the secret police starts breaking down your door, just calmly shuffle the deck. (Don't throw it up in the air; you'd be surprised how much of the deck ordering is maintained during the game of 52-Pickup.) Remember to shuffle the backup deck, if you have one.

SECURITY ANALYSIS

There's quite a lot of it, but it's far too complicated to reproduce here. See http://www.counterpane.com, or write to Counterpane Systems, 1711 North Ave #16, Oak Park, IL 60302.

LEARNING MORE

I recommend my own book, *Applied Cryptography* (John Wiley & Sons, 1996), as a good place to start. Then read *The Codebreakers*, by David

Kahn (Scribner, 1996). After that, there are several books on computer cryptography, and a few others on manual cryptography. You can subscribe to my free e-mail newsletter at *http://www.counterpane.com/crypto-gram.html* or by sending a blank e-mail message to *crypto-gram-subscribe@chaparraltree.com*. It's a fun field; good luck.